THE WORKS OF TOBIAS SMOLLETT

The History and Adventures of the Renowned Don Quixote

# THE WORKS OF TOBIAS SMOLLETT

Jerry C. Beasley, General Editor
University of Delaware

O M Brack, Jr., Textual Editor
Arizona State University

Jim Springer Borck, Technical Editor
Louisiana State University

*This edition includes all of the works by which Tobias Smollett was best known
in his own day and by which he most deserves to be remembered.
The edition conforms to the highest standards of textual and editorial scholarship.
Individual volumes provide carefully prepared texts together with biographical
and historical introductions and extensive explanatory notes.*

Tf.Hayman inv. et del.                                                    C.Grignion Sculp.

The Decay of Chivalry.

# The History and Adventures of the Renowned Don Quixote

Translated from the Spanish of

MIGUEL DE CERVANTES SAAVEDRA

By TOBIAS SMOLLETT

Introduction and Notes by

MARTIN C. BATTESTIN

The Text Edited by

O M BRACK, JR.

The University of Georgia Press
Athens and London

© 2003 by the University of Georgia Press
Athens, Georgia 30602
Set in Janson Text by Graphic Composition, Inc., Athens, Georgia
Printed and bound by Thomson-Shore, Inc.
The paper in this book meets the guidelines for permanence and
durability of the Committee on Production Guidelines for
Book Longevity of the Council on Library Resources.
Printed in the United States of America
07 06 05 04 03 C 5 4 3 2 1
Library of Congress Cataloging-in-Publication Data
Cervantes Saavedra, Miguel de, 1547–1616.
[Don Quixote. English]
The history and adventures of the renowned Don Quixote /
Tobias Smollett ; translated from the Spanish of Miguel de
Cervantes Saavedra by Tobias Smollett ; introduction and notes
by Martin C. Battestin ; the text edited by O M Brack, Jr.
p. cm. — (The works of Tobias Smollett)
Includes bibliographical references.
ISBN 0-8203-2430-2 (hardcover : alk. paper)
I. Smollett, Tobias George, 1721–1771.   II. Battestin, Martin C.
III. Brack, O M.   IV. Title.   V. Series: Smollett, Tobias George,
1721–1771. Works. 1988.
PQ6329.A2 2003
863'.3—dc21
2002012307
British Library Cataloging-in-Publication Data available

TO THE BENEFACTORS AND STAFF
OF THE BRITISH LIBRARY

# CONTENTS

## The History and Adventures
## of the Renowned Don Quixote

### Volume One

### PART I.

#### BOOK I.

##### I.
Of the quality and amusements of the renowned
DON QUIXOTE DE LA MANCHA.   27

##### II.
Of the sage DON QUIXOTE's first sally from his own habitation.   31

##### III.
The diverting expedient Don Quixote falls upon, in order to be knighted.   36

##### IV.
Of what befel our knight, when he sallied from the inn.   42

##### V.
In which the story of our knight's misfortune is continued.   46

# Contents

## Volume Two

## PART II.

### BOOK I.

## BOOK IV.

# ILLUSTRATIONS

For the first edition of Smollett's *Don Quixote* (1755), printed in two quarto volumes on royal paper, the distinguished artist Francis Hayman (1708–76) designed a frontispiece and twenty-seven further illustrations, for which he was paid the generous sum of five guineas per drawing.[1] Hayman's professional association with Smollett had begun with the second edition of *Roderick Random* (1748), to which he contributed frontispieces for both volumes; it would end with his illustrations for the quarto and octavo editions of Smollett's *Complete History of England* (1757–58, 1758–60). By 1748, when he contracted with the booksellers John Osborn and Andrew Millar to illustrate the translation of *Don Quixote*, Hayman was recognized as the preeminent English artist in this medium: he had already illustrated such works as Richardson's *Pamela* (1742), Sir Thomas Hanmer's edition of Shakespeare (1743–44), Edward Moore's *Fables for the Female Sex* (1744), a new edition of *The Spectator* (1747), and the Reverend Thomas Newton's edition of *Paradise Lost*, for which the designs were completed several years before publication in 1749. Hayman's designs for Smollett's *Don Quixote* rank among his finest achievements in book illustration—a medium, as Brian Allen remarks, that Hayman, together with his friend Gravelot, "elevated . . . from its crude beginnings in the early years of the century to a significant art-form."[2]

Hayman's original drawings for *Don Quixote* passed from Andrew Millar, the publisher, to Millar's widow, Jane, later Lady Grant; they were acquired by the British Museum in 1859 (Prints and Drawings: 201.b.4).[3] Five of these drawings, selected to illustrate the differences between Hayman's designs and the engraved prints, are reproduced in the appendix to the present volume. (One notable difference common to all the prints, with a single exception [appendix, plate 2], is that they are mirror images of the originals.) So well were these illustrations received that by the late 1760s Hayman returned to the subject in a grander medium, doing a set of six oil paintings of scenes from *Don Quixote*, several of them based on his designs for Smollett's translation.[4]

The success of the illustrations was also owing to the skills of the four artists employed to do the engraving—at a fee, again generous, of ten guineas a plate. Chief among these were Hayman's principal collaborators during the period, Charles Grignon (1716–1810) and Simon François Ravenet (1706–74), who cut twelve and eight of the plates, respectively. The German-born artist Johann Sebastian Müller (1715–after 1785), who had previously done work for Hayman, was responsible for only two of the plates, but the freedom he allowed himself in rendering one of the designs is remarkable (see appendix, plate 1). The remaining six plates were executed by Louis Gérard Scotin the younger (1690–after 1755), for whom this appears to represent his only collaboration with Hayman. It is, however, in the quarto edition of 1755 alone that readers of Smollett's *Don Quixote* would enjoy the work of these four artists; for the second and subsequent editions, in four volumes duodecimo, Hayman's designs were reengraved and reduced by G. V. Neist for the smaller format.

Reproduction of the illustrations to the 1755 first edition is by permission of the Department of Special Collections, University of Virginia Library.

## Notes

1. See the introduction, p. xxxviii, n. 33. In 1746 George Vertue noted that, for illustrating Thomas Newton's edition of *Paradise Lost*, Hayman received four guineas for each drawing and Ravenet eight guineas for engraving the plates (quoted in Allen, 155).
2. Allen, 10.
3. The British Museum also has Hayman's preliminary study for the plate entitled "The Barber Confounded by the Assurances of Don Quixote, Don Fernando and the Rest that His Basin is a Helmet" (see the reproduction below, p.325). (Prints and Drawings: 1962-7-14-39*.)
4. Allen, 118–19; Catalogue, item 44.

### LIST OF ILLUSTRATIONS

Captions to the illustrations are those accompanying the original drawings in the British Museum. The engraver's name is supplied in parentheses. An asterisk indicates that Hayman's drawing for the illustration is reproduced in the appendix.

# PREFACE

If books, as is sometimes said, have lives of their own, the life of Smollett's *Don Quixote* has until recently followed the classic curve of tragedy: the fall from fame to utter ignominy. From its first appearance in 1755—in a pair of splendid quarto volumes handsomely illustrated by Francis Hayman—Smollett's spirited translation remained for many years the most popular version of Cervantes' masterpiece in English. Soon after the turn of the nineteenth century, however, its reputation began to suffer from the charge that it was little more than a paraphrase of Charles Jarvis's literal translation (1742); by the 1860s it was, as a commodity in the trade, decidedly moribund. For nearly 130 years no publisher risked reprinting it. Latterly, forged letters were adduced to "prove" that Smollett never wrote it, while the author of an academic monograph denounced it as a "hoax."

The redemption of Smollett's translation from this ill-deserved neglect and disdain began in 1986, when, in his foreword to a new edition of the work, the distinguished Mexican novelist Carlos Fuentes declared it to be what it surely is: "the authentic vernacular version" of *Don Quixote* in English—"not necessarily the most lexicographically accurate, but . . . the one where the feeling and the tone both come through."

> Tobias Smollett's translation of Miguel de Cervantes [Fuentes concluded] is the homage of a novelist to a novelist. It is a novelist's translation. Its immediacy and force, its playfulness and its freshness, will show the modern English language reader why *Don Quixote* is the first modern novel, perhaps the most eternal novel ever written, and certainly the fountainhead of European and American (Anglo and Latin) fiction: here we have Gogol and Dostoevsky, Dickens and Nabokov, Borges and Bellow, Sterne and Diderot in their genetic nakedness.[1]

While English readers are indebted to Fuentes for thus declaring the true worth of Smollett's *Don Quixote*, the form in which the translation appears in the edition he introduced is seriously flawed, not only by the editorial decision to disregard Smollett's revisions and to omit more than two thirds of Hayman's illustrations, but by numerous printers' errors (in following the first edition, for example, the compositors repeatedly mistook the long *s* for an *f* ).

In contrast, the present edition is the first to offer the translation in a form that represents Smollett's own intentions as faithfully as possible, including all twenty-eight of Hayman's illustrations as engraved for the original edition. Also included of course are Smollett's explanatory notes and his prefatory "Life of Cervantes." The latter, though heavily indebted to Ozell's translation of Gregorio's pioneering Spanish biography, is animated throughout by Smollett's style and personality, a quality especially notable in those passages where one finds him identifying sympathetically with Cervantes' character and circumstances; it is also the first biography of Cervantes in any language to make use of the colorful account of his captivity in Algiers found in Joseph Morgan's history of that region.

The introduction is chiefly historical in nature, relating the circumstances of the

work's composition, publication, and reception. It also considers the vexed question of Smollett's originality and the extent of his dependence on previous translations and on other sources for his commentary on the text. The judgment that the translation, far from being the "hoax" of a plagiarist, is very much Smollett's own performance is based on evidence set forth in greater detail in my article, "The Authorship of Smollett's *Don Quixote*," *Studies in Bibliography* 50 (1997):295–321. The notes make no attempt to gloss Cervantes' novel or his allusions. They are meant instead to identify Smollett's sources in the "Life" and in his commentary, to provide cross-references to his other works, and to illustrate his originality or his dependence on previous translations. Since quotations from the Spanish preserve the forms found in the original seventeenth- and eighteenth-century sources Smollett consulted, orthography and accenting will not always conform to modern expectations. A separate glossary defines unusual or obsolete locutions.

# Note

1. Smollett, *Don Quixote*, introduction by Carlos Fuentes (London: Deutsch; and New York: Farrar, Strauss and Giroux, 1986), xiii.

# ACKNOWLEDGMENTS

I have dedicated this work to the benefactors and staff of the British Library for two reasons: first, because I wish, in a general way, to acknowledge a debt extending through the whole of my life as a scholar since 1960; second, because I could not easily—perhaps not even possibly—have conducted the necessary research for this edition without having had access to the BL's extraordinary collection of Cervantes, which includes virtually all the numerous editions of *Don Quixote* both in the original Spanish and in translation. In the many directions in which our research took us over the years, my wife and I never failed to benefit from the courteous cooperation of the staffs of the Reading Room, the Manuscripts Room, and the North Library—and many of these professional relationships have developed into friendships.

The British Museum itself made an important contribution to this edition, for in the department of Prints and Drawings I was able to examine all of Hayman's original designs for the translation. I am grateful to the trustees of the museum for permission to reproduce the selection of these drawings included in the appendix.

To the University of Virginia and the staff of the Alderman Library I am no less grateful. Research leaves and grants provided under the terms of the William R. Kenan, Jr., Professorship enabled me to complete the work. By acquiring copies of the first three editions of the translation to supplement its own holdings, the Special Collections Department of the library enabled the editors to have convenient access to all relevant forms of the text; for this we are grateful to Mildred Abraham in particular. Pauline Page of the Alderman Library Copy Center provided excellent photographic reproductions of the twenty-eight plates of the first edition, as well as the title pages of the two volumes.

To the work of tracing Smollett's sources, my wife, Ruthe Rootes Battestin, contributed in various important ways: the most notable of these was her discovery of the single source of Smollett's twenty-one notes on the customs of chivalry—M. de la Curne de Ste. Palaye's "Mémoires sur l'ancienne chevalerie." I was directed to another of Smollett's sources, Louis Moréri's *Grand dictionnaire historique*, by my friend and colleague in the Georgia edition, the late Robert Adams Day.

I am particularly grateful to my friend Jerry Beasley, the General Editor, whose experienced eye saw the work through from beginning to end, as well as to Byron Gassman and William Kupersmith for their careful and constructive reading of the manuscript.

Thanks are also due to Sue Anne Beyer for carefully vetting the explanatory annotations; to Jennifer Bradt for checking the passages in Spanish; to Arthur F. Stocker for his translation of a number of Latin phrases; to Pamela Williams, James E. May, and David L. Vander Meulen for their advice on various bibliographical matters; and to Julian Browning for providing me with a copy of a newly discovered letter by Smollett.

# ABBREVIATIONS

| | |
|---|---|
| *Adventures of an Atom* | Tobias Smollett, *The History and Adventures of an Atom*, ed. Robert Adams Day (Athens: University of Georgia Press, 1989). |
| Allen | Brian Allen, *Francis Hayman* (New Haven and London: Yale University Press, 1987). |
| Alonso | Martin Alonso, *Diccionario Medieval Español* (Salamanca, 1986). |
| Battestin | Martin C. Battestin, "The Authorship of Smollett's *Don Quixote*," *Studies in Bibliography* 50 (1997): 295–321. |
| BL | British Library |
| Blainville | Blainville, *Travels through Holland, Germany, Switzerland, and Other Parts of Europe*, trans. William Guthrie et al., 3 vols. (London, 1743–45). |
| Boucé | Paul-Gabriel Boucé, *The Novels of Tobias Smollett*, trans. Antonia White (London and New York: Longman, 1976). |
| Cadena | Mariano Velázquez de la Cadena, rev. Edward Gray and Juan L. Iribas, *A New Pronouncing Dictionary of the Spanish and English Languages* (New York and London, 1900). |
| *Complete History* | Tobias Smollett, *A Complete History of England*, 4 vols. (London, 1757–58). |
| *Continuation* | Tobias Smollett, *Continuation of the Complete History of England*, 5 vols. (London, 1760–65). |
| Félibien | André Félibien, *Entretiens sur les vies et sur les ouvrages des plus excellens peintres anciens et modernes*, 2d ed., 2 vols. (Paris, 1696). |
| *Ferdinand Count Fathom* | Tobias Smollett, *The Adventures of Ferdinand Count Fathom*, ed. Jerry C. Beasley (Athens: University of Georgia Press, 1988). |
| *Gil Blas* | Alain René Le Sage, *The Adventures of Gil Blas of Santillane*, trans. Smollett, 2d ed., 4 vols. (London, 1750). |
| Gregorio | Don Gregorio Mayáns y Siscár, *The Life of Michael de Cervantes Saavedra*, trans. John Ozell (London, 1738). |

| | |
|---|---|
| *Humphry Clinker* | Tobias Smollett, *The Expedition of Humphry Clinker*, ed. Thomas R. Preston (Athens: University of Georgia Press, 1990). |
| Jarvis | Cervantes, *The Life and Exploits of the ingenious gentleman Don Quixote de la Mancha*, trans. Charles Jarvis, 2 vols. (London, 1742). |
| Jarvis 1749 | Cervantes, *The Life and Exploits of the ingenious gentleman Don Quixote de la Mancha*, trans. Charles Jarvis, 2d ed., rev., 2 vols. (London, 1749). |
| Jones | *Dictionary of Foreign Phrases and Classical Quotations*, ed. Hugh P. Jones (Edinburgh: J. Grant, 1929). |
| Kelly | James Fitzmaurice Kelly, *Miguel de Cervantes Saavedra: A Memoir* (Oxford: Clarendon Press, 1913). |
| Kelly, ed. | Lionel Kelly, ed., *Tobias Smollett: The Critical Heritage* (London and New York: Routledge & Kegan Paul, 1987). |
| Knapp | Lewis M. Knapp, *Tobias Smollett: Doctor of Men and Manners* (Princeton: Princeton University Press, 1949). |
| *Letters* | *The Letters of Tobias Smollett*, ed. Lewis M. Knapp (Oxford: Clarendon Press, 1970). |
| Mariana | Juan de Mariana, *General History of Spain*, trans. John Stevens (London, 1699). |
| Moréri | Louis Moréri, *Le Grand dictionnaire historique*, 18th ed., 8 vols. (Amsterdam, 1740). |
| Morgan | J[oseph] Morgan, *A Complete History of Algiers*, 2 vols. (London, 1728–29). |
| Motteux | Cervantes, *The History of the Renowned Don Quixote de la Mancha*, trans. Peter Motteux et al., 3d ed., 2 vols. (London, 1712). |
| Motteux/Ozell | Cervantes, *The History of the Renowned Don Quixote de la Mancha*, trans. Peter Motteux et al., rev. John Ozell, 8th ed., 4 vols. (London, 1749). |
| *OED* | *Oxford English Dictionary*, 2d ed., eds. J. A. Simpson and E. S. C. Weiner (Oxford: Clarendon Press, 1989). |
| Original | Cervantes, *Vida y Hechos del Ingenioso Hidalgo Don Quixote de la Mancha*, 2 vols. (Antwerp, 1697). |
| Ormsby | Cervantes, *The Ingenious Gentleman Don Quixote of La Mancha*, trans. John Ormsby, 4 vols. (London, 1885). |

| | |
|---|---|
| Philips | Cervantes, *The History of the Renowned Don Quixote of Mancha: And his Trusty Squire Sancho Pancha*, trans. J[ohn] P[hilips] (London, 1687). |
| Pineda | Pedro Pineda, *Nuevo Dicionario, Español e Ingles e Ingles y Español* (London, 1740). |
| Pineda, ed. | Cervantes, *Vida y hechos del ingenioso hidalgo Don Quixote de la Mancha*, [ed. Pedro Pineda], 4 vols. (London, 1738). |
| Putnam | Cervantes, *The Ingenious Gentleman Don Quixote de la Mancha*, trans. Samuel Putnam, 2 vols. (New York: Viking Press, 1949). |
| *Remarks* | [William Windham], *Remarks on the Proposals lately published for a new translation of Don Quixote* (London, 1755). |
| *Roderick Random* | Tobias Smollett, *The Adventures of Roderick Random*, 2 vols. (London, 1748). |
| Royal Dictionary | *Diccionario de la Lengua Castellana . . . Por la Real Academia Española*, 6 vols. (Madrid, 1726–39). |
| Ste. Palaye | M. de la Curne de Ste. Palaye, "Mémoires sur l'ancienne chevalerie, considérée comme un établissement politique & militaire," in *Mémoires de littérature, tirés des registres de l'Académie Royale des Inscriptions et Belles-Lettres, depuis l'année M.DCCXLIV, jusques & compris l'année M.DCCXLVI*, vol. 20 (Paris, 1753), 597–847. |
| Shelton | Cervantes, *The History of Don-Quichote*, trans. Thomas Shelton, 2 vols. (London, 1620). |
| Shelton/Stevens | Cervantes, *The History of the most Ingenious Knight Don Quixote de la Mancha*, trans. Thomas Shelton, rev. John Stevens, 2d ed., 2 vols. (London, 1706). |
| *Sir Launcelot Greaves* | Tobias Smollett, *The Life and Adventures of Sir Launcelot Greaves*, *British Magazine* (January 1760–December 1761). |
| Stevens | John Stevens, *A New Dictionary, Spanish and English, and English and Spanish* (London, 1726). |
| *Travels* | Tobias Smollett, *Travels through France and Italy*, ed. Frank Felsenstein (Oxford: Oxford University Press, 1979). |
| Watts | Cervantes, *The Ingenious Gentleman Don Quixote of La Mancha*, trans. Henry Edward Watts, 5 vols. (London, 1888). |

# INTRODUCTION

Fielding and Smollett, who together in the decade of the 1740s began the great tra-
dition of the comic novel in English, looked for their models to the Continent, and
to two authors in particular. *Joseph Andrews* (1742), as the title page declares, was "Writ-
ten in Imitation of the Manner of Cervantes, Author of *Don Quixote.*" This, Fielding ex-
plained in the prefatory chapter to book 3, was a work that surpassed the productions of
conventional historians by offering its readers a timeless "History of the World in gen-
eral"—an achievement comparable in his view only to that of Alain René Le Sage, the
"inimitable" author of *Gil Blas.* In the preface to his own immensely successful first
novel, *Roderick Random* (1748), Smollett attributed the invention of the modern realist
novel to these same two authors. Indeed, Le Sage's picaresque novel served Smollett as
the express model for *Roderick Random;* and in his last two works of fiction, he kept his
eye on Cervantes: *Sir Launcelot Greaves* (1760–61) is a contemporary version of *Don
Quixote,* and in *Humphry Clinker* (1771) Lismahago, the antic Scots lieutenant who is
one of Smollett's most memorable characters, recalls Cervantes' hero not only in his
features but in a number of misadventures that befall him.[1] What is more, Smollett
would pay Le Sage and Cervantes the finest tribute an English novelist could pay them
by translating *Gil Blas* and *Don Quixote,* brilliantly, into his own language.

    *Roderick Random,* published in January 1748, was so successful that a second edition
was immediately called for.[2] Less than six months later, Smollett had made such
progress with his version of *Gil Blas* (published in October of the same year)[3] that he was
ready to commit himself to the even more arduous project of translating Cervantes'
masterpiece. He refers to these arrangements in a helpful letter of 7 June written to his
friend Alexander Carlyle from London—probably from the comfortable rooms in
Beaufort Buildings near the Strand which he, his wife Anne, and infant daughter Eliz-
abeth began occupying this year after the success of his novel,[4] on which Carlyle had
congratulated him: "After having been so tediously impertinent on the subject of Rod-
erick, I will proceed (like a true Author enamoured of the first Person) to inform you
that I have contracted with two Booksellers to translate Don Quixote from the Spanish
Language, which I have studied some time. This perhaps you will look upon as a very
Desperate Undertaking, there being no fewer than four Translations of the same Book
already extant, but I am fairly engaged and cannot recede."[5]

    The nameless booksellers in question were John Osborn the younger (d. 1777) and,
very likely, Andrew Millar (1706–68). Osborn, whose importance in launching Smol-
lett's literary career has not been appreciated, was Smollett's principal publisher during
the period 1747–51.[6] His name alone appears as publisher in the earliest advertisements
for the translation, published in the *General Advertiser* in November 1748.[7] The follow-
ing year, Millar, Smollett's countryman and the publisher of such other Scots authors as
James Thomson and David Hume, collaborated with Osborn in bringing out an edition
of Smollett's unstageable tragedy, *The Regicide;* and after Osborn retired from the trade

in November 1751, Millar remained at the head of the consortium of booksellers who eventually published Smollett's *Don Quixote* in 1755.

The letter to Carlyle also provides us with Smollett's own assurance that he considered himself competent to undertake the translation, having "studied" the Spanish language "some time." That an author who contracts to translate a difficult work from one language to another has an adequate understanding of both is an assumption we might normally grant—particularly in the case of Smollett, who, having mastered Latin at the Dumbarton grammar school, where the lessons were conducted strictly in that language, was also proficient in French, could read the Italian classics in the original,[8] and, more to the present point, would later apply for "the Consulship of Madrid for which," he informed John Home, "I thought myself in some respects qualified, as I understood the Spanish Language."[9]

In the extraordinary case of Smollett's *Don Quixote*, however, the obvious needs belaboring before we can safely continue the story of the book's composition and production. For Smollett has had to be absolved of the charge that, knowing no Spanish, he either plagiarized the translation from that of Charles Jarvis or hired others to do so for him—an accusation that in time has proved damaging enough to sway no less an authority than the *British Library Catalogue* (1975) to preface its entry on Smollett's translation with a caveat casting doubt on his authorship of the work. This aspersion was first cast on him by his enemy John Shebbeare in 1757;[10] it was in effect echoed by Lord Woodhouselee in his influential *Essay on the Principles of Translation* (1791);[11] it was reiterated by a trio of eminent Victorian Cervantists—Duffield, Ormsby, and Watts[12]— who published rival translations in the 1880s; and in the middle decades of our own century it was ostensibly settled beyond all question by the American academics Francesco Cordasco and Carmine Rocco Linsalata. In 1948 Cordasco published three new letters which "proved," one of them ostensibly by Smollett's own confession, not only that he knew little Spanish, but that the real author of the translation of *Don Quixote* was a certain Isaiah Pettigrew of Bone Street. The letters, however, were shown to be spurious: no trace has been found of the phantom Pettigrew, nor was there ever a Bone Street in London until the nineteenth century.[13] Meanwhile, in his doctoral dissertation of 1949,[14] the fruits of which were later published in the monograph *Smollett's Hoax* (1956),[15] Linsalata, having demonstrated Smollett's debt to Jarvis, went so far as to deny him any part at all in the translation, surmising that he had jobbed it out not to any single ghost, but to an entire "school" of them, all "hacks" in his employ.

The story of this curious conspiracy of scholars to abstract Smollett wholly from the translation of *Don Quixote* that bears his name has recently been told at length, and the charges against him have been refuted in detail.[16] We need not rehearse the story here. In itself, of course, Smollett's knowledge of Spanish, however competent he may have been in that language, would have been inadequate to the task of producing a literally exact translation of *Don Quixote*—a work whose linguistic range and variety are comparable in English only to the canon of Shakespeare, Cervantes' contemporary. In the letter to Alexander Carlyle quoted above, however, Smollett indicated his awareness of several earlier translations that would serve to guide him through the more difficult passages of the text. He alludes to "four" previous translations, but—discounting the

frivolous one by Milton's nephew John Philips (1687)—there were in fact five useful English versions of *Don Quixote* available to him. These were as follows: (1) Thomas Shelton's work of 1612–20, the first translation of the novel into any language and a version, for its time, remarkably faithful to the original; (2) John Stevens's revision of Shelton, published in 1700; (3) the version, also published in 1700, known as Peter Motteux's but represented on the title page as translated "by several Hands, and publish'd" by Motteux; (4) John Ozell's revision of Motteux, published in 1725—the version current today in the Modern Library reprint; and (5) the translation by Pope's friend, the painter Charles Jervas (spelled "Jarvis" on the title page), published posthumously in 1742.

Of these, Jarvis's translation was Smollett's principal guide—a lifeless performance but one, thanks in part to its own dependence on Shelton, closer than any of its predecessors to the literal sense of the original. Less consistently, Smollett also consulted Ozell's revision of Motteux (in either the seventh [1743] or eighth [1749] edition), as well as Stevens's revision of Shelton (in either the first [1700] or second [1706] edition). Another source, second in importance only to Jarvis, was Stevens's Spanish-English *Dictionary* (1706 and 1726). Without naming them, Smollett at the start of his narrative quotes all four of these sources in an elaborate footnote mocking the haplessness of "former translators" who struggled to find an English equivalent for "duelos y quebrantos" (Don Quixote's meal on Saturdays)—his own no less hapless solution being "gripes and grumblings" (see below, p. 27, n.). Smollett's indebtedness to these works will be made clear in the explanatory annotations to the present edition. It is also clear, however, that Smollett throughout had his eye on Cervantes' text as he found it in one of the best editions of the original available to him.[17]

But to produce the version of *Don Quixote* he aimed at, Smollett did not need total mastery of Cervantes' Castillian. He needed what he alone, among translators before and since, already possessed: a complete mastery of his own language in its full idiomatic range from the formal and solemn to the ironic and burlesque, and the gifts of a novelist whose comic genius and skill at characterization were comparable to Cervantes' own. Smollett would admirably achieve the goal he set himself in his prefatory note to the reader: "to retain the spirit and ideas, without servilely adhering to the literal expression, of the original" (see below, p. 20). In this he was accepting principles laid down by Dryden in a famous passage that defined the theory of translation for a hundred years:

> The Qualification of a Translator worth Reading [Dryden declared] must be a Mastery of the Language he Translates out of, and that he Translates into; but if a deficience be to be allow'd in either, it is in the Original, since if he be but Master enough of the Tongue of his Author, as to be Master of his Sense, it is possible for him to express that Sense, with Eloquence, in his own, if he have a through Command of that. But without the Latter, he can never Arive at the Useful and the Delightful; without which, Reading is a Penance and Fatigue.
>
> 'Tis true, that there will be a great many Beautys, which in every Tongue depend on the Diction, that will be lost in the Version of a Man, not skill'd in the Original Language of the Author: But then on the other side, First it is impossible to render all those little Ornaments of Speech in any two Languages; and if he have a Mastery in the Sense and Spirit of his Au-

thor, and in his own Language have a Stile and Happiness of Expression, he will easily supply all that is lost by that defect.

A Translator, that wou'd write with any Force or Spirit of an Original, must never dwell on the Words of his Author: He ought to possess himself entirely, and perfectly comprehend the Genius and Sense of his Author, the Nature of the Subject, and the Terms of the Art or Subject treated of; and then he will express himself as justly, and with as much Life, as if he wrote an Original: Whereas, he who copies Word for Word, loses all the Spirit in the tedious Transfusion.[18]

In 1748, as he began writing his translation of Cervantes' masterpiece, these principles informed Smollett's conception of the task he had undertaken. They would enable him to produce the most readable version of *Don Quixote* we have had in English.

Smollett began work on the translation in the midst of numerous other literary projects that required his attention. The facility and dispatch with which he executed even the most demanding works are indeed among his most remarkable qualities as a writer. In June 1748, when he informed Carlyle of the agreement concerning *Don Quixote*, he would have been deep into his translation of *Gil Blas:* that long work, in four elegant "pocket volumes" illustrated with thirty-three cuts, was through William Strahan's presses by September of this year and was published by John Osborn on 13 October.[19] In the same letter Smollett also informed Carlyle that he was planning a comedy, "which will be finished by next winter." His friend, he predicted, would find this piece of news surprising "after having perused the Revenge I have taken on the Playhouse Managers in Roderick Random"— revenge taken on David Garrick in particular, whom Smollett roasted in the novel for having declined to stage *The Regicide*, the uninspired tragedy he had been peddling in vain for ten years. He was confident now, however, that Garrick, chastened by the satire, was ready to "court my good Graces." But these expectations came to nothing: his comedy—*The Absent Man*, in which Osborn owned half the copy—was never acted, the manuscript remaining in Smollett's possession after his publisher retired from the trade three years later.[20]

Despite these distractions Smollett proceeded steadily with *Don Quixote*. In four months' time he appears to have been energetically engaged with the translation, and his publishers had contracted with the gifted artist Francis Hayman to illustrate the work. Smollett had expected that, given the number of translations already in print, his friend Carlyle would think his "a very Desperate Undertaking"; and news of it certainly amused the antiquarian Daniel Wray, who, in a joking but informative letter of 19 October 1748, wrote Philip Yorke details of Smollett's "Quixotism": "As if the Rage about publishing & criticising Shakespeare & Milton were not enough to make us laugh, a certain Quixotism is likewise got abroad; and Hayman is designing a new Set of Cuts & Smallet (the writer of R. Random) preparing a new Translation of the Don, after all the Prints and Versions we have already. The Bookseller whom I talked with[,] after condemning the foregoing attempts concluded by holding Motteuxes to be the most tolerable, & what has rather to be followd."[21] A month later Osborn was sufficiently optimistic about Smollett's rate of progress to run the following advertisement in the *General Advertiser* (19 and 21 November 1748): "*Preparing for the PRESS,* | *A* NEW TRANSLATION, *of* | THE Life and Atchievements of the | Ingenious Knight DON QUI-

XOTE DE LA MANCHA, | from the Original Spanish of *Miguel Cervantes de Saave-dra*. | *By the Author of* RODERICK RANDOM. | With a new Set of CUTS design'd by *Hayman*, and engraved by the | best Masters. | Printed for J. Osborn, at the Golden Ball in Pater-noster Row."

This advertisement may have been intended to discourage potential readers from spending their money on a rival work, namely, the second edition of Jarvis's translation, publication of which was announced in the same paper for 23 November. But there are good reasons to suppose that Smollett's own *Don Quixote* was well under way at this early date. In March 1754 he published proposals for printing the translation by subscription, assuring an impatient public that they would not have much longer to wait before the book was in their hands: "the Work was begun," he declared, "and the greatest Part actually finished four Years ago."[22] Smollett, then, if we are to take him at his word, had completed most of the translation before March 1750. This claim squares with the fact that in September 1749 Osborn again ran the above announcement in the *General Advertiser*, this time perhaps to remind readers who might be tempted to spend their money on the eighth edition of the Motteux/Ozell translation (just published) that Smollett's version was indeed "preparing for the press."[23] The same early period of intense work on *Don Quixote* may be inferred from Smollett's statement in December 1754, as the book at last made its way through the press, that he had been paid for the translation "five years ago"[24]—that is, some time late in 1749. How much he was paid for it is not known, but the value of the work in the judgment of the booksellers who bid for it at Osborn's sale in November 1751 exceeded that of any other of Smollett's writings on offer—substantially more than even *Roderick Random*.[25]

During this same period of 1749 to early 1750, Smollett spared time enough from *Don Quixote* to indulge his hopes for a career in the theater. For two years he pressed Garrick in vain to stage *The Absent Man* at Drury Lane; and though John Rich at Covent Garden gave him three hundred pounds for the copy of his next play, *Alceste*[26]—"a sort of Tragedy," as Smollett called it,[27] which was to have music by Handel and an elaborate set by Servandoni—Smollett's expectation of a magnificent production was never realized. By May 1749, when he published *The Regicide* by subscription, complaining bitterly in the dedication of "the Mortification I have suffered," he had abandoned hope of staging this new tragedy.

In the summer of the same year, Smollett traveled abroad in France, Flanders and Holland, returning home by October. November saw the printing of the third edition of *Roderick Random*. By this time his stock as a skillful translator had risen appreciably with Osborn. Though initially Smollett had considered *Gil Blas* a mere "Bookseller's Job," declining to put his name to it, the public in four months had bought up all but four hundred copies of the three thousand originally published.[28] Osborn ordered a second, revised edition of a thousand copies, this time in a larger and more agreeable format, and with the title page proclaiming the translation to be "by The Author of RODERICK RANDOM." This edition was through Strahan's press in February 1750, the same month in which he printed for Osborn another of Smollett's translations of his favorite Le Sage, a version of *Le Diable boiteux* entitled *The Devil upon Crutches*.[29]

A measure both of the reputation Cervantes' great work enjoyed in the period[30] and

of Osborn's confidence in the literary gifts of the author of *Roderick Random* and *Gil Blas*, Smollett's *Don Quixote* was from its inception no mere "Bookseller's Job." In format it would be modeled on the handsome pair of quarto volumes in which the Tonsons and Robert Dodsley had published Jarvis's translation in 1742, a work that included Gregorio's pioneering biography of Cervantes (as Englished by Ozell) and that featured sixty-six illustrations by John Vanderbanck. Smollett's translation would be no less handsome—printed in two quarto volumes on royal paper, prefaced by his own "Life of Cervantes," and embellished with twenty-eight splendid illustrations by Hayman.

In Francis Hayman, Smollett and Osborn had secured the talents of one of England's most distinguished artists, an artist credited with having first raised book illustration in the century "to a significant art-form."[31] Just when Smollett and Hayman became friends is not known. They were associated professionally before April 1748, when the second edition of *Roderick Random* was published with frontispieces by Hayman to both volumes. By October of that year, as Daniel Wray's letter to Philip Yorke reveals, Hayman had agreed to design the illustrations for *Don Quixote*. A friendship had certainly formed by the spring of 1750, when Smollett wrote to thank Hayman for a favor already done and to ask him for another: namely, to deliver to Garrick a revised version of *The Absent Man*.[32] By November 1751 Hayman—no doubt prudently emulating Smollett's own now slower pace in writing the translation—had finished only eleven of the twenty-four designs specified in the original agreement (he was to be paid five guineas for each drawing, the engravers twice that amount).[33] Considering the close relationship between the two men, it is likely that Smollett directed Hayman in his choice of subjects for the illustrations: this, at least, was how Hayman worked in the case of Sir Thomas Hanmer's edition of Shakespeare, for which, in preparing the illustrations, he based his designs on Hanmer's detailed written instructions.[34]

Having completed "the greatest Part" of the translation and been paid for it, Smollett in 1750 appears to have put it aside. In June of that year he attempted to establish himself more securely in his chosen profession by purchasing the M.D. from Marischal College, Aberdeen, the degree probably being conferred in absentia. At about the same time, he and his family moved from town to enjoy the fresh air of Chelsea, where they would reside for the next thirteen years. Chelsea was, as Smollett's biographer remarks, "an ideal place in which to combine his writing and his medical practice."[35] But before settling into that taxing rhythm of business, Smollett allowed himself a summer's holiday in Paris.

When he returned to Chelsea in September, he was well advanced in writing *The Adventures of Peregrine Pickle*, published in February 1751. Smollett's second novel is a work half again as long as *Roderick Random*, and as far as his reputation was concerned, it was far more reckless in its sweeping, indeed savage, satire of some of the most eminent figures of the day, chief among them George Lyttelton and the earl of Chesterfield, Garrick and the actor James Quin, Fielding and the poet Mark Akenside. *Peregrine Pickle* was a reckless work in another sense as well, for, as Thomas Birch later observed, it "ruin'd [Smollett's] Reputation among the Booksellers in general."[36] This was because he had chosen not to sell the copyright according to the usual practice but to publish the work himself. Except for the printing of the third edition of *Gil Blas* in June 1751, Smol-

lett's association with John Osborn was now over; and Millar, according to Birch, was so stung by his behavior that he continued for some time "refusing to have any more Concern with him." There are indeed signs in Smollett's correspondence that his relations with Millar were often strained, but their professional association continued despite this friction. Millar remained at the head of the partnership of booksellers who published *Don Quixote*. It is pleasant to find that in a single passage of the *Continuation* of his history of England, Smollett made amends not only to Millar by praising his benevolence, but to Fielding as well, who posthumously received from the translator of *Don Quixote* the finest compliment he could pay: "The genius of Cervantes [Smollett wrote] was transfused into the novels of Fielding, who painted the characters, and ridiculed the follies of life with equal strength, humour, and propriety."[37]

Although the high prices paid for Osborn's shares in *Don Quixote* are proof that the trade in November 1751 saw no reason to think Smollett had abandoned the translation, there is no other sign that he was actively engaged with the work during the four-year period stretching from the winter of 1749–50 to the spring of 1754, when he issued proposals for publishing it by subscription. Since he had been paid for the translation in advance, there was no urgent need to complete it, especially as he soon found himself sinking deeply into debt.

The number and variety of his writings during these years attest not only to Smollett's remarkable energy, but to financial anxieties that are a continuing theme of his correspondence with friends and creditors.[38] In 1751, for example, besides publishing *Peregrine Pickle*, he finished work on Dr. William Smellie's *Treatise on the Theory and Practice of Midwifery*, the first of three volumes by that eminent obstetrician that he had contracted to prepare for the press.[39] In January 1752, soon after Fielding's *Amelia* appeared, Smollett was very probably the author of an anonymous pamphlet ridiculing his rival under the name *Habbakuk Hilding*; in March, subscribing himself for the first time in print as "T. Smollett, M.D.," he published *An Essay on the External Use of Water*;[40] and by the year's end he not only had produced a translation of Voltaire's comic romance *Micromegas*,[41] but had written his third novel, *The Adventures of Ferdinand Count Fathom*, published in February 1753.[42] In May 1753 he contracted to compile a *Compendium* of voyages in seven volumes (published in 1756), while in a separate transaction agreeing for one hundred guineas to act as ghost for Alexander Drummond's *Travels through different Cities of Germany, Italy, Greece, and Several Parts of Asia* (published in 1754).[43] When winter came, besides producing Smellie's second volume, he translated from the *Journal Œconomique* a work he entitled *Select Essays on Commerce, Agriculture, Mines, Fisheries, and Other Useful Subjects*, while at the same time making progress on a "History of the German Empire" to be published later in the *Universal History*.

In closing a letter of 1 May 1754 to his friend John Moore, Smollett reveals the toll these literary labors had taken on him: "In short, dear John, I am so jaded that I now write with infinite Reluctance."[44] Among the long, dull bookseller's jobs that drained Smollett's energies at this time was, however, another work of a very different order—indeed, one of the liveliest and most entertaining books he ever wrote. For Smollett was now also deeply engaged once again with the translation of *Don Quixote*, which he was determined to complete by the year's end. In a letter of 1 March 1754 to Moore, he thus

assured his friend, "my Translation of Don Quixote . . . will be published next year." Writing that same day to Alexander Carlyle, he was more specific about the present state of the work and imagined with pleasure what a handsome book it would make: "The Proposals for my Translation of Don Quixote are now printed, and what with the new Cutts and the Paper, it will make a very grand Appearance."[45]

Smollett had arranged with the partnership of booksellers who owned the copy to publish the translation by subscription at two guineas—subscribers to pay half the price at the time of subscribing, the remainder on publication of the book in sheets. On 14 March 1754 the *Public Advertiser* announced that proposals for the work were ready for distribution—a thousand of them, according to Strahan's account with the partners.[46] "[A]nnexed to" the proposal was a specimen of the translation consisting of the first chapter of text, as may be inferred from the published criticisms of William Windham that were based on the specimen.[47] No copy of either the proposal or the specimen has survived, but the announcement, in full, reads as follows:

> *This Day is Published,* | PROPOSALS for Printing by SUBSCRIPTION, | A New Transla- tion of DON QUIXOTE, | from the Original Castillian of MIGUEL DE CERVANTES | SAAVEDRA. To which will be prefix'd, Some Account of the | LIFE of that celebrated AUTHOR. | By T. SMOLLET, M.D. | I. That the Book shall be printed in two Volumes Quarto, on a | Royal Paper, and on the same Paper and Type as used in the Speci- | men of the Translation annexed to the Proposals: and be ready to be | delivered to the Subscribers in January next, as the Work was begun | and the greatest Part actually finished four Years ago. | II. That it shall be adorned with Twenty-eight new Prints, design'd | by Mr. *Hayman,* which it is hoped will do Honour to the Artists of | this Country. | III. The Price to Sub- scribers will be Two Guineas; one to be paid | at subscribing, and the other at the Delivery of the Book in Sheets. | Such Noblemen and Gentlemen as intend to encourage this Work, | will be pleased to call for Receipts, signed by Dr. Smollet, of the | following Booksellers; A. Millar in the Strand; T. Osborn in Gray's | Inn; T. and T. Longman, C. Hitch and L. Hawes, in Pater-noster | Row; J. Hodges, London Bridge; J. and J. Rivington, in St. | Paul's Church- yard; where Proposals may be had, and the Impres- | sions of eighteen Plates already en- graved, may be seen.[48]

In the story of the evolution of Smollett's *Don Quixote* this notice is of special inter- est. It contains, for example, the earliest reference to Smollett's plan to preface the translation with a "Life" of Cervantes—an interesting essay and, despite its otherwise heavy dependence on Gregorio for facts, original in including for the first time in any biography an account of Cervantes' captivity in Algiers, which Smollett found in Joseph Morgan's *Complete History* of the region (1728–29). The notice also reveals that Hayman had agreed by this time to contribute four additional illustrations to the work, making a total of twenty-eight; eighteen of these splendid drawings had already been engraved, and the prints were available for viewing by prospective subscribers. Here, too, is the list of the partners engaged in publishing the work. Of the original pair of booksellers with whom Smollett in June 1748 contracted to prepare the translation, only Andrew Millar remained, presumably having retained half the copyright after John Osborn sold his half in November 1751. Eight others now had shares in the enterprise:[49] namely, Thomas Osborne the younger (who before publication would be joined by Joseph Ship-

ton, his former apprentice); Thomas Longman and his nephew of the same name, who this year became a partner in the firm; Charles Hitch and his partner Lacy Hawes, whose shop was the Red Lion in Paternoster Row; James Hodges of the Looking Glass, London Bridge; and the brothers James and John Rivington, whose partnership was dissolved in 1756.[50]

The rest of this year in which Smollett completed the translation appears to have been one continued course of disappointments in financial matters and of the drudgery of writing under pressure to meet his promised date of publication. His hopes of large remittances from his wife's plantation in Jamaica were not realized, and his frequent pleas for loans exhausted the patience of family and friends. "Never," he wrote in November to his long-suffering benefactor Dr. George Macaulay, "was I so much harrassed with Duns as now."[51] A month later he was in even more desperate straits. On the night of 10 December, while journeying to London, he was robbed of his watch and money by a highwayman.[52] The next day he was obliged to put off Macaulay again: "For my own part, I never was reduced to such a dilemma as I am now brought into; for I have promised to pay away tradesmens' bills, to a considerable amount, by Christmas; and my credit absolutely depends on my punctuality. Nay, I am put to very great straits for present subsistence as I have done nothing all the last summer but worked upon Don Quixotte, for which I was paid five years ago."[53]

What, one wonders, could there have been left to do on the translation that required Smollett's full attention throughout the summer? In the prefatory note to the work, he assures readers "he cannot charge himself with carelessness or precipitation" in the performance; for, having finished "the greatest part" of it some years ago, "he has been for some time employed in revising and correcting it for the press" (see below, p. 20). No doubt he left until last such ancillary features of the work as the "Life of Cervantes" and the explanatory annotations. It is certain, at least, that the most interesting of these annotations—namely, the twenty-one notes on the customs of chivalry—were written after the publication in 1753 of Smollett's source, Ste. Palaye's "Mémoires sur l'ancienne chevalerie." But Smollett, who wrote with great facility, would not have needed much time to write the biographical essay and to add the annotations, though these number more than two hundred. It is likely that much of the translation itself remained to be written when the proposals were announced in March.

Even so, Smollett very nearly kept his promise to subscribers that the book would be in their hands in January. By 1 January Strahan had printed four fifths of an edition of 750 copies on royal paper; the work was finished a month later.[54] On 15 February an announcement in the *Public Advertiser* proved too cautious in promising publication for the first of March. Smollett's *Don Quixote* was published slightly before then, on Thursday, 25 February 1755. At the bottom of the advertisement in the *Public Advertiser* a pointing finger directs readers to the following notice: "☞Such Noblemen and Gentlemen as have subscribed to the Author will be pleased to send their Receipts, and second Payments, to A. Millar in the Strand, who will deliver their Books."[55]

Regrettably, since no list of subscribers was published, it is impossible to tell which or how many readers were inclined to support Smollett's translation in this way. For that matter, since Smollett stated that he had been paid for the work five years in advance, the decision to publish by subscription, announced in March 1754, is in itself puzzling.

It is clear, however, that despite Smollett's reputation as a gifted novelist and translator, and despite the physical beauty of the two quarto volumes, the book did not immediately sell. More than a month after publication the partners were still trying to dispose of what remained of the original 750 copies by placing notices in the *Public Advertiser.*[56] Indeed, though in the same year of 1755 an unauthorized edition of the work was published in Dublin,[57] copies of the first edition were still for sale more than five years later—even as, after a delay of eighteen months or more, the second edition was at last published in the summer of 1761.[58]

This lack of immediate interest in Smollett's long-awaited work is curious, for it would become, over the last four decades of the century, by far the most popular version of *Don Quixote* in English. Some readers, like Lady Mary Wortley Montagu, may have prejudged the book. On 1 January 1755, while it was still in press, she wrote from Italy to her daughter, the countess of Bute, dismissing the whole enterprise: "I am sorry my Freind Smallet loses his time in Translations. He has certainly a Talent for Invention, thô I think it flags a little in his last work [*Ferdinand Count Fathom*]. Don Quixote is a difficult undertaking: I shall never desire to read any attempt to new dress him; thô I am a meer pidler in the Spanish Language, I had rather take pains to understand him in the Original than sleep over a stupid Translation."[59]

Nor was Smollett's cause helped by the appearance on 28 February, three days after publication, of Col. William Windham's anonymous pamphlet, *Remarks on the Proposals lately published for a new translation of Don Quixote.*[60] Windham, basing his criticisms solely on the evidence of the specimen Smollett had published a year earlier, condemned the translation categorically. He complained of Smollett's ignorance of the Spanish language and customs, as well as his negligence in ignoring the two principal "helps" available to him: the Royal "Madrid" dictionary and Jarvis's more exact translation. Windham's criticisms, as Smollett himself silently acknowledged in correcting the work for the second edition, are often just. And ironically, his last-mentioned complaint ought to have chastened those later critics who accused Smollett of plundering Jarvis shamelessly. Smollett, Windham sneered, had shown "consummate effrontery" by refusing to use Jarvis's translation as his guide: "I can scarcely suppose he ever could have seen it, otherwise that translation alone must have prevented his publishing such egregious absurdities; and his subscribers would have been infinitely better used, if he had literally followed it throughout" (pp. 16–17). Smollett of course did use Jarvis as his guide; but, as Windham's response demonstrates, the effect of their two versions on the reader is utterly different. It is also pleasant to think that, if he had read Smollett's "Life of Cervantes" instead of confining himslf to the specimen alone, Windham might have softened his condemnation in one respect at least; for Smollett had anticipated him in what Windham proudly trumpeted as his own discovery: the story of Cervantes' captivity as told in Morgan's *Complete History of Algiers*, a book, he remarked, that "is not very common" (pp. 29–37).

At the time of publication, and indeed for more than three decades thereafter, only one reader committed to print anything resembling a considered judgment of Smollett's achievement in the translation as a whole. This was Ralph Griffiths, editor of the *Monthly Review*, who in the issue for September 1755 compared Smollett's version fa-

vorably with those of his predecessors, particularly Jarvis and Motteux.[61] After quoting Smollett's statement of his aims in the translation, Griffiths remarked on the great difficulty of fulfilling them. "*Don Quixote*," he reminded his readers, "is perhaps the most difficult book in the world to translate; and for this reason, that it is the most difficult to be understood." After enumerating the qualifications of an author who would attempt to produce a perfect version of Cervantes' novel, Griffiths concludes: "But as all these advantages must be considered as unattainable; as the best translation we can look for must be expected from the hand of a person chiefly qualified by books; we fancy a better than Dr. *Smollet*'s, upon the whole, will not speedily appear. *Jarvis*'s may, in some respects, be thought a more exact version; but in our opinion, the doctor's genius (notwithstanding some things that appear to be rather inaccuracies than defects in judgment) comes nearest the great original." To prove his point, Griffiths became the first critic to offer a comparison of the two versions. Placing Smollett's and Jarvis's translations side by side for comparison with the original, he transcribed the episode (part 2, book 2, chapter 14) in which Sancho tells a story "to expose the mistaken politeness of his master, in the affair of table-precedency." Smollett's version is slightly longer, but far brisker, and the writing is more assured.

This would in time become the verdict of the reading public in general. From 1755 to 1799 Smollett's *Don Quixote* was published in various editions and reprints no fewer than nineteen times, whereas the versions of his chief rivals, Jarvis and Motteux, were reissued in the same period just four times each.[62] The change in attitude toward the translation from Lady Mary's indifference and Windham's disdain is apparent by the decade of the 1760s, when three authoritative editions were called for: the revised second edition of 1761 was followed by a third edition in 1765 and a fourth in 1770, the year before Smollett's death. In 1768 Jonathan Potter explained that for his revision of Edmund Gayton's *Festivous Notes* on *Don Quixote* he had based his texts on Smollett's translation, "that being not only the most modern, but the best."[63] By the mid-1770s, the anonymous author of the earliest biographical account of Smollett expressed the judgment of the generality of readers: Smollett, he declared, "translated *Gil Blas* and *Don Quixote* both so happily, that all the former translations of these excellent productions of genius are in a fair way of being superseded by his."[64] But it was the poet William Cowper in the next decade who best accounted for the success of the translation. Having read the work for the first time, Cowper, in a letter of 6 May 1788 to his cousin Lady Hesketh, wrote of the pleasure it had given him: "My DEAREST COUSIN—You ask me how I like Smollett's *Don Quixote*? I answer, well,—perhaps better than any body's; but having no skill in the original, some diffidence becomes me. That is to say, I do not know whether I *ought* to prefer it or not. Yet there is so little deviation from other versions of it which I have seen, that I do not much hesitate. It has made me laugh I know immoderately, and in such a case *ça suffit.*"[65]

Not long after the turn of the nineteenth century, however, the balance of opinion began shifting against Smollett, as the criticism first expressed by Lord Woodhouselee in 1791 took hold. With Smollett's genius as a comic novelist in mind, Woodhouselee acknowledged the essential point that readers from Griffiths to Cowper had recognized: that it is "hardly possible to conceive a writer more completely qualified to give

a perfect translation" of Cervantes' masterpiece (p. 178). But, he insisted, Smollett gave us "little else than an improved edition" (pp. 181–82) of Jarvis's dull but faithful translation. The reputation of Smollett's *Don Quixote* declined thereafter to the extent that, after 1858, it ceased to be reprinted for 130 years, until in 1986 Farrar, Straus and Giroux published a new (but very imperfect) edition with a foreword and introduction by Carlos Fuentes.[66] In the resurrection of his work by this distinguished novelist, Smollett would have found his own theory of translation vindicated. For Fuentes, too, the best translation "is not necessarily the most lexicographically accurate, but it is the one where the feeling and the tone both come through."[67] In preferring Smollett's *Don Quixote* over all other English versions, Fuentes, moreover, was not alone among modern readers whose native language is the language of Cervantes: before his death in 1943 Francisco Rodríguez Marín, perhaps the preeminent Cervantist of the last century, wrote Cordasco that he was of the same opinion.[68]

Smollett, in translating *Don Quixote*, achieved the aim he expressed in a prefatory note to the reader: the aim of fidelity to the spirit of his great original. At the same time, for the particular enjoyment of his English audience, he may be said to have translated the work in another sense, bringing it home to them from another time and another country and making it, as Dryden had recommended, "an Original" in its own right. As Pope in his *Iliad* adapted Homer to the expectations of readers in England's Augustan Age, so Smollett succeeded in making Cervantes his contemporary. His gruff Biscainer speaks the Somerset dialect of Fielding's Squire Western; and Cervantes' narrator not only writes Smollett's mid-Georgian prose but at times echoes the phrases of Shakespeare and Milton or recalls a song from *The Beggar's Opera*.[69] The narrative is colored by homely locutions that would make the plains of La Mancha seem a familiar place to an Englishman—and often more especially to readers of Smollett's native Scotland: Sancho stuffs his budget with good things to eat, and his stomach wambles; waits strike up tunes, and a skinker pours the wine; hare-hunters search in vain for a scut; desperadoes discharge their fusils; mariners worry about ships that steer athwart their hause.

Samuel Johnson, Mrs. Piozzi tells us, considered *Don Quixote* second only to the *Iliad* as "the greatest" work of entertainment ever written.[70] As Johnson credited Pope with having produced in his translation of the *Iliad* "the noblest version" of poetry the world had seen,[71] we may at least, with Carlos Fuentes and Rodríguez Marín, allow that Smollett in his translation of *Don Quixote* gave us the most entertaining version of Cervantes' masterpiece in our language.

# Notes

1. Boucé, chap. 3 ("Two sources of inspiration: *Don Quixote* and *Gil Blas*").
2. The first edition of *Roderick Random*, amounting to two thousand copies, must have been largely bought up before the date of publication, 21 January 1748 (the date announced in the *General Advertiser*, 15–16 January). No notice of publication appears in the newspapers for that date, and the ledgers of William Strahan indicate that a second edition of three thousand copies was printed that same month (BL: Add. MS 48800, f. 62ᵛ). Enough copies remained, however, for Osborn to delay publication of the second edition until April.

3. See the *General Advertiser*, 13–15 October 1748.

4. Knapp, 73.

5. *Letters*, 8.

6. John Osborn was the son of a bookseller of the same name whose business, located at the Golden Ball, Paternoster Row, he inherited on his father's death in December 1745 (see the elder Osborn's will [Public Record Office: PCC 1745]). The younger Osborn's association with Smollett began as early as the summer of 1747: about August of that year William Strahan charged Osborn for printing 750 copies of Smollett's *Advice and Reproof*—published, according to the title page, for W. Owen in 1748; that Osborn owned the property is clear from the trade sale of his "Entire Stock" in November 1751, when Millar purchased "the Whole [copyright], with 566 Books," for £1.5.0. Strahan subsequently charged Osborn for printing the first three editions of *Roderick Random* (January 1748 [first and second editions], November 1749), the first three editions of Smollett's *Gil Blas* (September 1748, February 1750, June 1751), and his translation of Le Sage's *The Devil upon Crutches* (February 1750), as well as two thousand proposals for the subscription edition of *The Regicide* (February 1749). The sale catalog of November 1751 discloses that Osborn at the time owned the entire copyright of *The Devil upon Crutches* (Lots LXV–LXVIII), one-half of *Roderick Random* (Lots LXIX–LXXII), one-half of Smollett's *Don Quixote* (Lots LXXIII–LXXVI), and the whole of *Gil Blas* (Lots LXXXI–LXXXVIII). (See Strahan's ledger [BL: Add. MS 48800, f. 62ᵛ] and the sale catalogs of Osborn's stock, 14 and 19 November 1751 [BL: C.170.aa.1.(55–56)].) Left unsold was Osborn's half of the rights to the "Copy" of Smollett's comedy *The Absent Man*, a lost work never acted or published; Smollett himself retained the manuscript. (See Lot VII, "Books and Copies left unsold at Mr. John Osborn's Sale," appended to the catalog of the trade sale of Thomas Woodward's stock, 12 March 1752 [BL: C.170.aa.1.(58)]; first noted by A. D. McKillop, "Smollett's First Comedy," *Modern Language Notes* 45 [1930]: 396–97.) For Smollett's association with Strahan, see the pioneering but often inaccurate article by Lewis M. Knapp, "Smollett's Works as Printed by William Strahan," *The Library*, n.s. 13 (1932): 282–91.

7. See the *General Advertiser* for 19 and 21 November 1748 and also for 7–8 September 1749.

8. On 27 November 1759 Smollett wrote his friend William Huggins, the translator of Ariosto and Dante, that he had read Berni's version of the *Orlando Innamorato* and Ariosto's *Orlando Furioso* "in the Italian from one end to the other" (*Letters*, 84).

9. Smollett to John Home, 27 December 1762 (*Letters*, 111).

10. In *The Occasional Critic: or, The Decrees of the Scotch Tribunal in the Critical Review Rejudged* (1757), Shebbeare accused Smollett of having "translated from Translations already made" (p. 42) and of being "entirely ignorant" of both Spanish and French (p. 63). It was Shebbeare who spread the story that Millar, replying to a fellow Scot who objected that Smollett "did not understand *Spanish*" at the time he contracted to translate *Don Quixote*, "assured him that the Author had been full six Weeks to study that Language amongst the native *Spaniards* at *Brussels*" (p. 61, n.).

11. See Alexander Fraser Tytler, Lord Woodhouselee, *Essay on the Principles of Translation* (1791), who objected that in his translation of *Don Quixote* Smollett was merely Jarvis's "copiest and improver" (p. 184).

12. See the translations by Alexander James Duffield (1881), 1:xlviii–xlix; John Ormsby (1885), 4:420; and Henry Edward Watts (1888), 1:12–13, 285.

13. See Cordasco, "Smollett and the Translation of the 'Don Quixote': Important Unpublished Letters," *Notes & Queries* 193 (21 August 1948): 363–64. In an otherwise useful article published a fortnight later, Cordasco repeated that the letters proved the case against Smollett's authorship (see "Smollett and the Translation of the 'Don Quixote'—A Critical Bibliography,"

Notes & Queries 193 [4 September 1948]: 383–84); and he subsequently included the letters, as well as other "finds" from the same trove, in his edition, Letters of Tobias George Smollett: A Supplement to the Noyes Collection (Madrid, 1950). Their authenticity was challenged by Lewis Knapp and Lillian de la Torre in their review of this work in Philological Quarterly 30 (1951): 289–91. Having examined the evidence, a committee of experts headed by Allen T. Hazen declared the letters to be spurious—a judgment accepted by Cordasco, who, however, disclaimed responsibility for the deception. For the report of the committee and Cordasco's response, see Philological Quarterly 31 (1952): 299–300; see also "Correspondence," Modern Language Notes 67 (1952): 69–71, 360; and Knapp and de la Torre, "Forged 'Smollett' Letter," Modern Language Quarterly 14 (1953): 228. De la Torre's unpublished account of this remarkable affair is in the files of Philological Quarterly.

14. See Carmine Rocco Linsalata, "Tobias Smollett and Charles Jarvis: Translators of Don Quijote" (Ph.D. diss., University of Texas, Austin, 1949).

15. Smollett's Hoax: Don Quixote in English (Stanford: Stanford University Press, 1956).

16. See Battestin, "The Authorship of Smollett's Don Quixote," Studies in Bibliography 50 (1997): 295–321.

17. Internal evidence indicates that Smollett used the edition of Don Quixote printed for Juan Mommarte at Brussels in 1662 and subsequently reissued by the Verdussens of Antwerp in 1673 and 1697. This text, though not equal in authority to that edited by Pedro Pineda (London: J. and R. Tonson, 1738), was judged by Ormsby to be superior to all other Spanish editions published from 1637 to 1771. (See Battestin, 312).

18. Dryden's "Life of Lucian," in The Works of John Dryden: Prose 1691–1698, ed. A. E. Wallace Maurer and George R. Guffey (Berkeley, Los Angeles, London: University of California Press, 1989), 20:226–27. On the influence of Dryden, see John W. Draper, "The Theory of Translation in the Eighteenth Century," Neophilologus 6 (1921): 241–54.

19. BL: Add. MS 48800, f. 62ᵛ; General Advertiser, 13–15 October 1748.

20. In the catalog (dated 12 March 1752) of "Books and Copies left unsold" at Osborn's sale of November 1751 (see above, n. 6), Lot VII reads: "The Absent Man, a Comedy, wrote by Mr. Smollet, half the Copy-Right, and Profits in the Acting. The Copy is in the Possession of Mr. Smollet, and the Purchaser is to run all Risk of its being ever acted, or printed."

21. BL: Add. MS 35401, f. 94ᵛ. A letter of Thomas Birch to Philip Yorke, written three days later on 22 October 1748, is also of interest: "Mr. Smollet, the Author of Roderick Random, has given us a new Translation of Gil Blas in 4 Volumes in 12mo. & is engag'd in a new Version of Don Quixote. He is like wise preparing a Comedy for the Stage, which was formerly refus'd; but since the Success of his Novel may probably find Admittance there" (BL: Add. MS 35397, f. 178ᵛ).

22. Public Advertiser, 14–16, 18–19 March 1754. In a note to the first edition of the translation, published nearly a year after the proposals, Smollett again stated that he had finished "the greatest part" of the work "four years ago" (see below, p. 20). Overlooking the earlier statement in the advertisement for the proposals, his biographer inferred that this busy early period of composition ended in 1751, not 1750 (Knapp, 166).

23. For Osborn's announcement, see the General Advertiser, 7–8 September 1749; for publication of the Motteux/Ozell eighth edition, see the General Advertiser, 6 September 1749.

24. Smollett to George Macaulay, 11 December 1754 (Letters, 41).

25. Osborn's four one-eighth shares of Don Quixote were sold in four lots, the bids increasing each time, as follows: Lot LXXIII to Longman for £26.10.0; Lot LXXIV to Rivington for £28.10.0; Lot LXXV to Hodges for £28.15.0; Lot LXXVI to Thomas Osborne for £30.5.0. In comparison, Roderick Random (Lots LXIX–LXXII) brought £13.0.0 (Millar), £16.16.0 (Baldwin), £16.16.0 (Hodges), and £17.10.0 (Rivington).

26. See *Letters*, 10 (n. 1).
27. Smollett to Alexander Carlyle, 14 February 1748/9 (*Letters*, 9).
28. Smollett to Carlyle, 14 February 1748/9 (*Letters*, 9).
29. See Strahan's ledger (BL: Add. MS 48800, f. 62ᵛ).
30. On this subject see Susan Staves, "Don Quixote in Eighteenth-Century England," *Comparative Literature* 24 (1972): 193–215.
31. Allen, 10. On Hayman, see above, headnote to the list of illustrations.
32. See Smollett to Hayman, Beaufort Buildings, 11 May 1750 (*Letters*, 13).
33. See the catalog of John Osborn's trade sale for 19 November 1751, the second day of the sale: "Lot LXXIII. Don Quixote, by Smollet, eighth, the Purchaser to pay the Designing and Engraving the Plates, and Paper and Print. There are Eleven Plates design'd, and to be Twenty-four in all, at Ten Guineas each Engraving, Five Guineas Drawing" (BL: C.170.aa.1.[56]).
34. See Marcia Allentuck, "Sir Thomas Hanmer Instructs Francis Hayman: An Editor's Notes to his Illustrator," *Shakespeare Quarterly* 27 (1976): 288–315.
35. Knapp, 109.
36. See Birch's letter to Philip Yorke, 14 October 1752 (BL: Add. MS 35398, f. 105).
37. *Continuation* (1761), 4:127.
38. See Smollett's letters to William Hunter (c. 1751–52), Richard Oswald (11 February 1752), George Macaulay (27 May 1753), Alexander Telfer (13 December 1753), and Macaulay (16 November and 11 December 1754); *Letters*, nos. 12–13, 17–18, 24–25. Also relevant is a letter recently found among the papers of the Craufurd family of Craufurdland Castle, Kilmarnock, and offered for sale by Julian Browning, London (see his *The Eighteenth Century, Catalogue 12* [1995], item 34); I am grateful to Mr. Browning for providing me with a copy of the letter, written from Chelsea on 23 December 1754 to thank "John Crawford Esqʳ.," for extending the date when payment on a note was due. The letter reads as follows:

> Dear Sir
>  I shall with great Pleasure comply with the Expedient you propose, & at our next meeting, write a new note payable in three Months, which you may indorse. I am with great Truth, Gratitude & affection
> 
> Dear Crawford Yours Tˢ. Smollett
> 
> Chelsea Decʳ. 23ᵈ. 1754.

For what seems to be Smollett's later, less grateful, representation of the circumstances of this affair, see his letter to George Macaulay, 10 September 1756 (*Letters*, 48–49).
39. Strahan's papers indicate the value of these works to Smollett. Sometime before publication in February 1751, Strahan paid him four hundred pounds for the copyright of *Peregrine Pickle*, though the entries in the account books differ as to whether this sum was for the "whole" or only half of the copy. On 4 July 1751 Strahan paid Smollett £157.10.0 for half the rights to the three volumes of Smellie's work. See Albert Smith, "The Printing and Publication of Smollett's *Peregrine Pickle*," *The Library*, 5th ser., 26 (1971): 39–52; and BL: Add. MSS 48804, f. 37ᵛ; 48805, f. 3.
40. For March 1752 Strahan's account book records the printing of five hundred copies of "Smollet on Warm Bathing," the charges shared by "Mr. Wilson [i.e., David Wilson, bookseller] and Self" (BL: Add. MS 48803A, f. 3).
41. On Smollett's authorship of this translation, published in November 1752, see Louis L. Martz, *The Later Career of Tobias Smollett* (New Haven: Yale University Press, 1942), 92; and Knapp, 151.
42. On the date and circumstances of publication of *Ferdinand Count Fathom*, see Beasley, xix and

n. 1, xxv and n. 26; and the textual commentary by O M Brack, Jr., 441 and n. 1. It appears from Strahan's account books, however, that the publisher William Johnston did not, as has been thought, own the entire copyright to the novel: on 8 November 1752 Strahan, in addition to purchasing one-third of the rights to the novel from Johnston for forty pounds, also purchased another one-third share at the same rate of forty pounds from Smollett himself (see BL: Add. MSS 48804, f. 14ᵛ; 48805, f. 3).

43. See Smollett's letter to George Macaulay, 27 May 1753 (*Letters*, 27 and n. 3); and Knapp, 160.

44. *Letters*, 32.

45. *Letters*, 35.

46. In February 1755, before listing his charges for printing the work itself, Strahan recorded £1.3.0 for printing one thousand "Proposals," and £0.7.6 for what would appear to be the same number of subscription "Receits . . . on Writing Paper" (BL: Add. MS 48803A, f. 9ᵛ).

47. See Windham's *Remarks on the Proposals lately published for a new translation of Don Quixote* (1755).

48. This notice appeared in the *Public Advertiser* for 14–16, 18–19 March 1754. My transcription is based on the corrected version of 18–19 March.

49. By the date of publication, nine booksellers (excluding Shipton, Thomas Osborne's partner, whose name appears only in the advertisement) are listed in the imprint. It appears from Strahan's accounts, however, that twelve shares were in some way divided among the partners. In February he charged the "Partners in Don Quixotte" as a whole £122.7.0 for all costs incurred in printing the work, and he was paid "in Notes" on 12 April 1755 (BL: Add. MS 48803A, f. 9ᵛ). On 14 February 1755 he charged one of the partners, Charles Hitch, £10.3.11 "For printing your Share of Don Quixotte as per Note (Nº. 6)" (BL: Add. MS 48800, f. 94ᵛ)—an amount equal to one-twelfth of the total.

50. For information on these booksellers, see H. R. Plomer, *A Dictionary of the Printers and Booksellers Who Were at Work in England, Scotland and Ireland from 1726–1775* (Oxford University Press, 1932 [for 1930]); and D. F. McKenzie, *Stationers' Company Apprentices 1701–1800* (Oxford: Oxford Bibliographical Society, 1978).

51. Smollett to Macaulay, 16 November 1754 (*Letters*, 40).

52. On this episode, which Smollett reported to Macaulay in his letter of 11 December 1754 (*Letters*, 41), see Frank Felsenstein, "'None of Your Knockers-Down': John Fielding and Smollett's Watch," *Etudes Anglaises* 26 (1973): 269–77.

53. *Letters*, 41.

54. In Strahan's work book in the Library of the American Philosophical Society, Philadelphia, the following entry occurs under "Work unfinished" as of 1 January 1755: "750. Don Quixote 92 Sheets @ 18ˢ £82:16:0" (BL: . MSS.M[icrofilm]. 530). Among Strahan's papers in the British Library the record of printing charges for February 1755 indicates that, when completed, the work comprised 114 sheets (BL: Add. MS 48803A, f. 9ᵛ).

55. Beginning on 25 February 1755, advertisements for the work ran daily in the *Public Advertiser* until the end of the month.

56. See the *Public Advertiser* for 22, 24–27, 31 March, 1–6 April.

57. This work, printed "by T. Henshall, No. 3, Bride-Street, near Werburgh Street," is in five volumes duodecimo and, in addition to engraved title pages for each volume, includes sixteen plates. I am grateful to Pamela Williams for providing these details of the unique extant copy in the collection of the Central Library, Birmingham, U.K.

58. In the *Public Advertiser* for 18 August 1761 it is clear from Millar's advertisement of "BOOKS of ENTERTAINMENT" that copies of the first edition were still available; this advertise-

ment also contains the only notice I have seen of an approximate date of publication for the second edition. The two editions are listed together as follows:

> Don Quixote. Translated by Dr. SMOLLET. 2 Vols. 4to. with a Set of fine new Cuts.
> ☞ Speedily will be published, an Edition in Twelves, 4 Volumes.

William Upcott's collection of copyright assignments in the British Library reveals that the second edition was projected as early as the spring of 1760: on 3 April of that year Thomas Lowndes, for £26.10.00, acquired James Rivington's one-twelfth share of both the first and second editions (BL: Add. MS 38730, f. 152). That the trade in 1761 considered Smollett's *Don Quixote* a less promising investment than they had originally expected—less promising, indeed, than his translation of *Gil Blas*—is apparent from other notices of the second edition. In the *Public Advertiser* for 21 and 26 November 1761 the trade went to the expense of separate advertisements to announce publication of the third edition of *Gil Blas* while relegating the second edition of *Don Quixote* to a place in an appended list of Smollett's other works.

59. *The Complete Letters of Lady Mary Wortley Montagu*, ed. Robert Halsband (Oxford: Clarendon Press, 1967), 3:78.

60. See the *Public Advertiser*, 28 February, 1, 3–4 March 1755.

61. *Monthly Review* 13 (September 1755): 196–202. The only other contemporary notice was the "Specimen of a new Translation of *Don Quixote*," *Gentleman's Magazine* 25 (1755): 100–102.

62. The *Eighteenth-Century Short Title Catalogue* (CD-ROM, 1992) cites the following editions and reprints of these translations. Smollett: 1755, 1755 (Dublin: Henshall), 1761 (2d ed.), 1765 (3d ed.), 1766 (Dublin: Ewing), 1770 (4th ed.), 1782 (5th ed.), 1782 (Harrison), 1783 (Dublin: Price et al.), 1784 (Harrison), 1786 (Longman et al.), 1792 (6th ed.), 1792 (Harrison), 1793 (York?: Law et al.), 1794? (Hogg), 1795, 1795? (Dublin: Henshall), 1796 (Dublin: Chambers), 1799?. Jarvis: 1756 (3d ed.), 1766 (4th ed.), 1788 (5th ed.). Motteux: 1757 (Glasgow: Foulis), 1766 (Edinburgh: Donaldson), 1771, 1771 (Glasgow: Foulis). The *National Union Catalogue Pre-1956 Imprints* (1970), 101:529, col. 3, lists an additional imprint for Jarvis, dated 1776.

63. See Edmund Gayton, *Festivous Notes on the History and Adventures of the Renowned Don Quixote. First Publish'd . . . In the Year 1654. Revised, with Corrections, Alterations, and Additions; and Adapted to the Modern Translations of that celebrated Work*, ed. J[onathan] P[otter] (1768), x.

64. From *The Westminster Magazine* 3 (1775): 225–28, in Kelly, ed., 228.

65. *The Correspondence of William Cowper*, ed. Thomas Wright (1904), 3:242, in Kelly, ed., 251.

66. For a sample of the numerous printer's errors in this edition, see Battestin, 297, n. 11.

67. See Fuentes' foreword to *The Adventures of Don Quixote de la Mancha*, trans. Smollett (New York: Farrar, Straus and Giroux, 1986), xiii.

68. According to Cordasco, Rodríguez Marín wrote that he "heartily approved" the view that Smollett's translation had "an original literary value of its own" and declared that "of all English translations, he entertained a particular fondness for that of Smollett" (Cordasco, *Modern Language Quarterly* 13 [1952]: 36, n. 60).

69. For the Biscainer's speech, see below, p. 62; for allusions to Shakespeare, Milton, and *The Beggar's Opera*, see, respectively, pp. 595, 607, 548, and 427.

70. Hester Lynch Piozzi, *Anecdotes of the late Samuel Johnson*, in *Johnsonian Miscellanies*, ed. G. B. Hill (Oxford: Clarendon Press, 1897), 1:332–33.

71. Johnson, "Pope," in *Lives of the English Poets*, ed. G. B. Hill (Oxford: Clarendon Press, 1905), 3:119.

# The History
# and Adventures
# of the Renowned
# Don Quixote

## VOLUME ONE

THE

# HISTORY and ADVENTURES

OF THE RENOWNED

# DON QUIXOTE.

Translated from the SPANISH of

## MIGUEL DE CERVANTES SAAVEDRA.

To which is prefixed,

Some ACCOUNT of the AUTHOR's LIFE.

By T. SMOLLETT, M.D.

Illuftrated with Twenty-eight new Copper-Plates, defigned by HAYMAN,
And engraved by the beft ARTISTS.

---

IN TWO VOLUMES.

---

VOL. I.

---

LONDON:

Printed for A. MILLAR, over againft Catherine-Street, in the Strand;
T. OSBORN, T. and T. LONGMAN, C. HITCH and L. HAWES, J. HODGES,
and J. and J. RIVINGTON.
MDCCLV.

Title Page of First Edition, Volume 1, 1755.

To his Excellency

Don RICARDO WALL,[1]

PRINCIPAL SECRETARY OF STATE TO HIS MOST
CATHOLIC MAJESTY,

LIEUTENANT GENERAL OF THE ARMIES OF SPAIN,

COMMENDARY OF PENAUZENDE IN THE
ORDER OF St. JAGO, &c. &c.

AND HERETOFORE

AMBASSADOR AND PLENIPOTENTIARY

AT THE COURT OF GREAT BRITAIN.

SIR,

The permission I obtained to inscribe the following translation of Don Quixote to
your Excellency, while you resided in this Capital, affords me a double pleasure; as
it not only gives me an opportunity of expressing that profound respect and veneration
with which I contemplate your Excellency's character; but also implies your approba-
tion, which cannot fail to influence the public in behalf of the performance. I have the
honor to be,

SIR,

Your Excellency's most obedient
Humble Servant,

London, Feb. 7, 1755.                                    T. SMOLLETT.

# THE
# LIFE
## OF
# CERVANTES.[1]

Miguel de Cervantes Saavedra was at once the glory and reproach of Spain; for, if his admirable genius and heroic spirit conduced to the honour of his country, the distress and obscurity which attended his old age, as effectually redounded to her disgrace. Had he lived amidst Gothic darkness and barbarity, where no records were used, and letters altogether unknown, we might have expected to derive from tradition, a number of particulars relating to the family and fortune of a man so remarkably admired even in his own time. But, one would imagine pains had been taken to throw a veil of oblivion over the personal concerns of this excellent author. No inquiry hath, as yet, been able to ascertain the place of this nativity; and, although in his works he has declared himself a gentleman by birth, no house has hitherto laid claim to such an illustrious descendant.

One * author says he was born at Esquivias; but, offers no argument in support of his assertion: and probably the conjecture was founded upon the encomiums which Cervantes himself bestows on that place, to which he gives the epithet of Renowned, in his preface to Persiles and Sigismunda. Others affirm he first drew breath in Lucena, grounding their opinion upon a vague tradition which there prevails: and a † third set take it for granted that he was a native of Seville, because there are families in that city known by the names of Cervantes and Saavedra; and our author mentions his having, in his early youth, seen plays acted by Lope Rueda, who was a Sevilian. These, indeed, are presumptions that deserve some regard, tho', far from implying certain information, they scarce even amount to probable conjecture: nay, these very circumstances seem to disprove the supposition; for, had he been actually descended from those families, they would, in all likelihood, have preserved some memorials of his birth, which Don Nicholas Antonio would have recorded, in speaking of his fellow-citizen. All these pretensions are now generally set aside in favour of Madrid, which claims the honour of having produced Cervantes, and builds her title on an expression ‡ in his Voyage to Parnassus, which, in my opinion, is altogether equivocal and inconclusive.

In the midst of such undecided contention, if I may be allowed to hazard a conjecture, I would suppose that there was something mysterious in his extraction, which he had no inclination to explain, and that his family had domestic reasons for maintaining the like reserve. Without admitting some such motive, we can hardly account for his si-

---

* Thomas Tamayo de Vargas.                                        † Don Nicholas Antonio.[2]
‡ He describes his departure from Madrid in these words: "Out of my country and myself I go!"[3]

lence on a subject that would have afforded him an opportunity to indulge that self-respect which he so honestly displays in the course of his writings. Unless we conclude that he was instigated to renounce all connexion with his kindred and allies, by some contemptuous flight, mortifying repulse, or real injury he had sustained; a supposition which, I own, is not at all improbable, considering the jealous sensibility of the Spaniards in general, and the warmth of resentment peculiar to our author, which glows through his productions, unrestrained by all the fears of poverty, and all the maxims of old age and experience.

Whatever may have been the place of his nativity, we gather from the preface to his novels, that he was born in the year 1549: and his writings declare that his education was by no means neglected; for, over and above a natural fund of humour and invention, he appears to have possessed a valuable stock of acquired knowledge: we find him intimately acquainted with the Latin classics, well read in the history of nations, versed in the philosophy, rhetoric, and divinity of the schools, tinctured with astrology and geography, conversant with the best Italian authors, and perfectly master of his own Castilian language. His genius, which was too delicate and volatile to engage in the severer studies, directed his attention to the productions of taste and polite literature, which, while they amused his fancy, enlarged, augmented, and improved his ideas, and taught him to set proper bounds to the excursions of his imagination.

Thus qualified, he could not fail to make pertinent observations in his commerce with mankind: the peculiarities of character could not escape his penetration; whatever he saw became familiar to his judgment and understanding; and every scene he exhibits, is a just well drawn characteristic picture of human life.

How he exercised these talents in his youth, and in what manner the first years of his manhood were employed, we are not able to explain, because history and tradition are altogether silent on the subject; unless we admit the authority of one * author, who says, he was secretary to the duke of Alva, without alledging any one fact or argument in support of his assertion. Had he actually enjoyed a post of such importance, we should not, in all probability, have wanted material to supply this chasm in his life; nor should we find him afterwards in the station of a common soldier.

Others imagine that he served as volunteer in Flanders, where he was raised to the rank of ensign in the company commanded by Don Diego de Urbina; grounding this belief on the supposition that the history of the Captive, related in the first part of Don Quixote, is a literal detail of his own adventures. But, this notion is rejected by those who consider that Cervantes would hardly have contented himself with the humble appellation of soldier, which, in speaking of himself, he constantly assumes, had he ever appeared in any superior station of a military character. In a word, we have very little information touching the transactions of his life but what he himself is pleased to give through the course of his writings; and from this we learn that he was chamberlain to cardinal Aquaviva in Rome, and followed the profession of a soldier for some years, in the army commanded by Marco Antonio Colona †, who was, by pope Pius V. appointed

---

* Nicholas Antonio, Biblioth. Hisp.[4]          † His dedication of Galatea.[5]

general of the ecclesiastical forces employed against the Turk, and received the conse-
crated standard from the hands of his holiness, in the church of St. Peter.

Under this celebrated captain, Cervantes embarked in the christian fleet commanded
by Don John of Austria, who obtained over the Turks the glorious victory of Lepanto,[6]
where our author lost his left hand by the shot of an arquebus. This mutilation, which
redounded so much to his honour, he has taken care to record on divers occasions: and,
indeed, it is very natural to suppose his imagination would dwell upon such an adven-
ture, as the favourite incident of his life. I wish he had told us what recompence he re-
ceived for his services, and what consolation he enjoyed for the loss of his limb, which
must have effectually disqualified him for the office of a common soldier, and reduced
him to the necessity of exercising some other employment.

Perhaps it was at this period he entered into the service of cardinal Aquaviva, to whose
protection he was entitled by his gallantry and misfortune; and now, in all likelihood, he
had leisure and opportunity to prosecute his favourite studies, to cultivate the muse, and
render himself conspicuous by the productions of his genius, which was known and ad-
mired by several authors of distinction even before his captivity; for, Louis Galvez de
Montalvo, in his poem prefixed to Galatea, says, the world lamented his misfortune in
tears, and the muse expressed a widow's grief at his absence. I will even venture to sup-
pose, that, in this interval, his situation was such as enabled him to raise an independent
fortune; for, we find him afterwards relieving the wants of his fellow-captives in Bar-
bary, with such liberality as denoted the affluence of his own circumstances; and, in his
voyage to Parnassus, which was published in his old age, Apollo upbraids him with want
of oeconomy, and reminds him of his having once made his own fortune, which in the
sequel he squandered away.

I make no doubt but this was the most fortunate period of Saavedra's life, during
which he reformed and improved the Spanish theatre, and ushered into the world a
number of dramatic performances which were acted with universal applause. He * tells
us that he had seen plays acted by the great Lope de Rueda, who was a native of Seville,
and originally a gold-beater: when this genius first appeared, the Spanish drama was in
its infancy: one large sack or bag contained all the furniture and dress of the theatre,
consisting of four sheepskin jackets with the wool on, trimmed with gilt leather; four
beards and periwigs, and the same number of pastoral crooks. The piece was no other
than a dialogue or eclogue between two or three swains and a shepherdess, seasoned
with comic interludes, or rather low buffoonery, exhibited in the characters of a black-
a-moor, a bravo, a fool, and a Biscayan. The stage itself was composed of a few boards,
raised about three feet from the ground, upon four benches or forms. There was no
other scenery than a blanket or horse-cloth stretched across, behind which the musi-
cians sung old ballads unaccompanied by any sort of instrument. Lope de Rueda not
only composed theatrical pieces, but also acted in every character with great reputation;
in which he was succeeded by Naharro, a Toledan, who improved and augmented the
decorations, brought the music from behind the blanket and placed it forwards to the
audience, deprived the actors of their counterfeit beards, without which no man's part

---

* In the preface to his plays.[7]

had been hitherto performed, invented machines, clouds, thunder and lightening, and introduced challenges and combats with incredible success: but, still the drama was rude, unpolished, and irregular; and the fable, tho' divided into five acts, was almost altogether destitute of manners, propriety, and invention.

From this uncultivated state of ignorance and barbarity, Cervantes raised the Spanish theatre to dignity and esteem, by enriching his dramatic productions with moral sentiments, regularity of plan, and propriety of character; together with the graces of poetry, and the beauties of imagination. He published thirty pieces, which were represented at Madrid with universal applause; so that he may be justly deemed the patriarch of the Spanish drama; and, in this particular, revered above Lope de Vega[8] himself, who did not appear until he had left off writing for the stage.

In the year 1574,[9] he was unfortunately taken by a Barbary corsair, and conveyed to Algiers, where he was sold to a Moor, and remained a slave for the space of five years and an half; during which he exhibited repeated proofs of the most enterprizing genius and heroic generosity. Though we know not on what occasion he fell into the hands of the Barbarians, he himself gives us to understand, in the story of the Captive, that he resided at Algiers in the reign of Hassan Aga,[10] a ruffian renegado, whose cruelty he describes in these terms: "He was every day hanging one, impaling another, maiming a third, upon such slight occasions, frequently without any cause assigned, that the Turks themselves owned he acted thus out of meer wantonness and barbarity, as being naturally of a savage disposition, and an inveterate enemy to the whole human race. The person who used the greatest freedom with him, was one Saavedra, a Spanish soldier,[11] who, tho' he did many things which those people will not soon forget, in attempting to regain his liberty, he never gave him one blow, nor ordered him once to be chastised, nor even chid him with one hasty word; and yet, the least of all his pranks was sufficient, as we thought, to bring him to the stake; nay, he himself was more than once afraid of being impaled alive. If time would permit, I could here recount some of that soldier's actions, which, perhaps, might entertain and surprize you more than the relation of my own story."

Thus, Cervantes ascertains the time of his own slavery, delineates, with great exactness, the character of that inhuman tyrant, who is recorded in history as a monster of cruelty and avarice; and proves to demonstration, that his own story was quite different from that which the Captive related of himself. Saavedra's adventures at Algiers were truly surprizing; and tho' we cannot favour the public with a substantial detail of every incident, we have found means to learn such particulars of his conduct, as cannot fail to reflect an additional lustre on a character which has been long the object of admiration.

We are informed by a respectable historian *, who was his fellow slave and an eye witness of the transaction, that Don Miguel de Cervantes, a gallant, enterprizing Spanish cavalier, who, tho' he never wanted money, could not obtain his release without paying an exorbitant ransom, contrived a scheme for setting himself free, together with fourteen unhappy gentlemen of his own country, who were all in the like circumstances of thraldom under different patrons. His first step was to redeem one Viana, a bold Ma-

---

* F. Diego de Haedo.[12]

yorcan mariner, in whom he could confide, and with whom he sent letters to the governor of that island, desiring, in the name of himself and the other gentlemen captives, that he would send over a brigantine, under the direction of Viana, who had undertaken, at an appointed time, to touch upon a certain part of the coast, where he should find them ready to embark. In consequence of this agreement, they withdrew themselves from their respective masters, and privately repaired to a garden near the sea-side, belonging to a renegado Greek, whose name was Al-Caid Hassan; where they were concealed in a cave, and carefully screened from the knowledge of the owner, by his gardener, who was a christian captive. Viana punctually performed his promise, and returned in a vessel, with which he was supplied by the governor of Mayorca; but, some Moors chancing to pass, just as he anchored at the appointed place, the coast was instantly alarmed, and he found himself obliged to relinquish the enterprize. Meanwhile, the captives, being ignorant of this accident, remained in the cavern, which they never quitted except in the night, and were maintained by the liberality of Cervantes, for the space of seven months, during which the necessaries of life were brought to them by a Spanish slave, known by the appellation of El Dorador or The Gilder. No wonder that their hope and patience began to fail, and their constitutions to be affected by the dampness of the place, and the grief of their disappointment, which Don Miguel endeavoured to alleviate by the exercise of his reason, good humour and humanity; 'till, at last, their purveyor turned traitor, and, allured by the hope of receiving a considerable reward, discovered the whole affair to Hassan Basha. This tyrant, transported with joy at the information, immediately ordered the guardian Basha, with a body of armed men, to follow the perfidious wretch, who conducted them to the cave, where they seized those unhappy fugitives, together with their faithful gardener, and forthwith carried the whole number to the public Bagnio, except Cervantes, touching whose person they had received particular directions from Hassan, who knew his character, and had been long desirous of possessing such a notable slave. At present, however, his intention was to persuade Don Miguel to accuse Oliver, one of the fathers of the redemption then at Algiers, as an accomplice in the scheme they had projected, that he might, on this pretence, extort from the frier, by way of composition, the greatest part of the money which had been collected for the ransom of christian slaves. Accordingly, he endeavoured to inveigle Saavedra with artful promises, and to intimidate him with dreadful threats and imprecations, into the confession or impeachment, on which he wanted to lay hold: but, that generous Spaniard, with a resolution peculiar to himself, rejected all his offers, and despising the terrors of his menaces, persisted in affirming that he had no associate in the plan of their escape, which was purely the result of his own reflection.

After having in vain tampered with his integrity, in repeated trials that lasted for several days, he restored him and his companions to their respective patrons, notwithstanding the remonstrances of Al-Caid Hassan, owner of the garden in which they had been apprehended, who, probably with a view to manifest his own innocence, strenuously exhorted the Basha to inflict the most exemplary punishment on the offenders, and actually put his own gardener to death. Cervantes had so often signalized his genius, courage, and activity, that Hassan resolved to make him his own, and purchased him from his master for five hundred ducats: then he was heard to say, "While I hold

that maimed Spaniard in safe custody, my vessels, slaves, and even my whole city are se-cure." For, he had not only concerted a number of schemes for the deliverance of his fel-low captives, but his designs had even aspired to the conquest of Algiers, and he was at four different times on the point of being impaled, hooked, or burned alive. Any single attempt of that kind would have been deemed a capital offence, under the mildest government that ever subsisted among the Moors; but, there was something in the character or personal deportment of Cervantes, which commanded respect from bar-barity itself; for, we find that Hassan Basha treated him with incredible lenity, and his redemption was afterwards effected by the intercession of a trinitarian father, for a thousand ducats *.

From this account of his behaviour in Barbary, it appears that he acted a far more im-portant part than that of a poor mutilated soldier: he is dignified with the appellation of Don Miguel de Cervantes, and represented as a cavalier whose affluent fortune enabled him to gratify the benevolence and liberality of his disposition. We must therefore take it for granted that he acquired this wealth after the battle of Lepanto, where he surely would not have fought as a private soldier, could he have commanded either money or interest to procure a more conspicuous station in the service. Be that as it will, his con-duct at Algiers reflects honour upon his country, and while we applaud him as an author, we ought to revere him as a man; nor will his modesty be less the object of our admira-tion, if we consider that he has, upon this occasion, neglected the fairest opportunity a man could possibly enjoy, of displaying his own character to the greatest advantage, and indulging that self-complacency which is so natural to the human heart.

As he returned to his own country, with those principles by which he had been dis-tinguished in his exile, and an heart entendered and exercised in sympathizing with his fellow creatures in distress; we may suppose he could not advert to the lessons of œcon-omy, which a warm imagination seldom or never retains; but, that his heart glowed with all the enthusiasm of friendship, and that his bounty extended to every object of com-passion which fell within his view.

Notwithstanding all the shafts of ridicule which he hath so successfully levelled against the absurdities of the Spanish romance, we can plainly perceive, from his own writings, that he himself had a turn for chivalry: his life was a chain of extraordinary ad-ventures, his temper was altogether heroic, and all his actions were, without doubt, influenced by the most romantic notions of honour.

Spain has produced a greater number of these characters, than we meet with upon record in any other nation; and whether such singularity be the effect of natural or

---

* To this adventure he, doubtless, alludes, in the story of the Captive;[13] who says, that when he and his fellow slaves were deliberating about ransoming one of their number, who should go to Valen-cia or Mayorca, and procure a vessel with which he might return and fetch off the rest, the rene-gado, who was of their council, opposed the scheme, observing, that those who are once delivered seldom think of performing the promises they have made in captivity: as a confirmation of the truth of what he alledged, he briefly recounted a case which had lately happened to some christian gentleman, attended with the strangest circumstances ever known, even in those parts, where the most uncommon and surprizing events occur almost every day.

moral causes, or of both combined, I shall not pretend to determine. Let us only affirm, that this disposition is not confined[14] to any particular people or period of time: even in our own country, and in these degenerate days, we sometimes find individuals whom nature seems to have intended for members of those ideal societies which never did, and perhaps never can exist but in imagination; and who remind us of the characters described by Homer and Plutarch, as patriots sacrificing their lives for their country, and heroes encountering danger, not with indifference and contempt, but, with all the rapture and impetuosity of a passionate admirer.

If we consider Cervantes as a man inspired by such sentiments, and actuated by such motives; and at the same time, from his known sensibility and natural complexion, suppose him to have been addicted to pleasure and the amusements of gallantry; we cannot be surprised to find his finances in a little time exhausted, and the face of his affairs totally reversed. It was probably in the decline of his fortune, that he resolved to re-appear in the character of an author, and stand candidate for the public favour, which would be a certain resource in the day of trouble: he therefore, composed his Galatea[15] in six books, which was published in the year 1584, dedicated to Ascanio Colonna, at that time abbot of St. Sophia; and afterwards cardinal of the holy cross of Jerusalem.

The rich vein of invention, the tenderness of passion, the delicacy of sentiment, the power and purity of diction, displayed in this performance, are celebrated by Don Louis de Vargas Manrique, in a commendatory sonnet, which is a very elegant and honourable testimony of our author's success. Nevertheless, the production has been censured for the irregularity of its stile, the incorrectness of its versification, and the multiplicity of its incidents, which encumber and perplex the principal narration; and, over and above these objections, the design is not brought to a conclusion, so that the plan appears meagre and defective. He himself pleads guilty to some part of the charge, in the sentence pronounced by the curate, in the first part of Don Quixote, who when the barber takes up the Galatea of Miguel de Cervantes; "That same Cervantes," says he, "has been an intimate friend of mine these many years, and is, to my certain knowledge, more conversant with misfortunes than with poetry. There is a good vein of invention in his book, which proposes something, tho' it concludes nothing. We must wait for the second part which he promises, and then, perhaps, his amendment may deserve a full pardon, which is now denied."

Whether the success of Galatea encouraged our author to oblige the world with some of those theatrical pieces, which we have already mentioned as the first regular productions of the Spanish drama, or the whole number of these was written and acted before his captivity, I have not been able to determine; but, in all probability, his first essays of that kind were exhibited in the interval between the battle of Lepanto and the commencement of his slavery, and the rest published after his redemption.

Unless we suppose him to have been employed at Madrid in this manner for his subsistence, we must pass over two and twenty years, which afford us no particular information touching the life of Saavedra; tho', in that period, he married Donna Catalina de Salazar,[16] dissipated the remains of his fortune, experienced the ingratitude of those he had befriended in his prosperity, and, after having sustained a series of mortifications and distress, was committed to prison in consequence of the debts he had contracted.

In this dismal situation, he composed that performance which is the delight and admiration of all Europe; I mean, the first part of Don Quixote,[17] which he wrote with a view to ridicule and discredit those absurd romances, filled with the most nauseous improbability and unnatural extravagance, which had debauched the taste of mankind, and were indeed a disgrace to common sense and reason. Not that Cervantes had any intention to combat the spirit of knight-errantry,[18] so prevalent among the Spaniards; on the contrary, I am persuaded he would have been the first man in the nation, to stand up for the honour and defence of chivalry, which when, restrained within due bounds, was an excellent institution, that inspired the most heroic sentiments of courage and patriotism, and on many occasions conduced to the peace and safety of the commonwealth. In the character of Don Quixote, he exhibits a good understanding, perverted by reading romantic stories, which had no foundation in nature or in fact. His intellects are not supposed to have been damaged by the perusal of authentic histories, which recount the exploits of knights and heroes who really existed; but, his madness seems to have flowed from his credulity and a certain wildness of imagination which was captivated by the marvelous representation of dwarfs, giants, negromancers, and other preternatural extravagance. From these legends he formed his whole plan of conduct; and tho' nothing can be more ridiculous than the terms upon which he is described to have commenced knight-errant, at a time when the regulations of society had rendered the profession unnecessary, and indeed illegal; the criterion of his frenzy consists in that strange faculty of mistaking and confounding the most familiar objects with the fantastical illusions which those romances had engendered in his fancy. So that our author did not enter the lists against the memory of the real substantial chivalry, which he held in veneration; but, with design to expel an hideous phantome that possessed the brains of the people, waging perpetual war with true genius and invention.

The success of this undertaking must have exceeded his most sanguine hopes. Don Quixote no sooner made his appearance, than the old romances vanished like mist before the sun. The ridicule was so striking, that even the warmest admirers of Amadis[19] and his posterity seemed to wake from a dream, and reflected with amazement upon their former infatuation. Every dispassionate reader was charmed with the humorous characters of the knight and squire, who straight became the favourites of his fancy; he was delighted with the variety of entertaining incidents, and considered the author's good sense and purity of stile with admiration and applause.

He informs us, by the mouth of the batchelor Sampson Carrasco,[20] that even before the publication of the second part, twelve thousand copies of the first were already in print, besides a new impression then working off at Antwerp. "The very children," says he, "handle it, boys read it, men understand, and old people applaud the performance. It is no sooner laid down by one, than another takes it up, some struggling, and some entreating for a sight of it: in fine, this history is the most delightful and least prejudicial entertainment that ever was seen; for, in the whole book, there is not the least shadow of a dishonourable word, nor one thought unworthy of a good catholic."

Nor was this applause confined to the kingdoms and territories of Spain. The fame of Don Quixote diffused itself through all the civilized countries of Europe; and the work was so much admired in France, that some gentlemen who attended the French

embassador to Madrid, in a conversation with the licentiate Marques Torres,[21] chaplain to the archbishop of Toledo, expressed their surprize that Cervantes was not maintained from the public treasury, as the honour and pride of the Spanish nation.——Nay, this work which was first published at Madrid in the year 1605, had the good fortune to extort the approbation of royalty itself: Philip III.[22] standing in a balcony of his palace and surveying the adjacent country, perceived a student on the bank of the Manzanares, reading a book, and every now and then striking his forehead and bursting out into loud fits of laughter. His majesty having observed his emotions for some time; "That student," said he, "is either mad, or reading Don Quixote." Some of the courtiers in attendance had the curiosity to go out and inquire, and actually found the scholar engaged in the adventures of our Manchegan.

As the book was dedicated to the duke de Bejar, we may naturally suppose that nobleman, either by his purse or interest, obtained the author's discharge from prison; for, he congratulates himself upon the protection of such a patron, in certain verses prefixed to the book, and supposed to be written by Urganda the unknown.[23] He afterwards attracted the notice of the count of Lemos, who seems to have been his chief and favourite benefactor; and even enjoyed a small share of the countenance of the cardinal archbishop of Toledo: so that we cannot, with any probability, espouse the opinion of those who believe his Don Quixote was intended as a satire upon the administration of that nobleman. Nor is there the least plausible reason for thinking his aim was to ridicule the conduct of Charles V.[24] whose name he never mentions without expressions of the utmost reverence and regard. Indeed, his own indigence was a more severe satire than any thing he could have invented against the ministry of Philip III. for, tho' their protection kept him from starving, it did not exempt him from the difficulties and mortifications of want; and no man of taste and humanity can reflect upon his character and circumstances, without being shocked at the barbarous indifference of his patrons. What he obtained was not the offering of liberality and taste, but the scanted alms of compassion: he was not respected as a genius, but relieved as a beggar.

One would hardly imagine that an author could languish in the shade of poverty and contempt, while his works afforded entertainment and delight to whole nations, and even sovereigns were found in the number of his admirers: but, Cervantes had the misfortune to write in the reign of a prince whose disposition was sordid, and whose talents, naturally mean, had received no manner of cultivation; so that his head was altogether untinctured with science, and his heart an utter stranger to the virtues of beneficence. Nor did the liberal arts derive the least encouragement from his ministry, which was ever weak and wavering. The duke de Lerma seems to have been a proud, irresolute, shallow-brained politician, whose whole attention was employed in preserving the good graces of his master; tho' notwithstanding all his efforts, he still fluctuated between favour and disgrace, and at last was fain to shelter himself under the hat of a cardinal. As for the count de Lemos,[25] who had some share in the administration, he affected to patronize men of genius, tho' he had hardly penetration enough to distinguish merit; and the little taste he possessed, was so much warped by vanity and self-conceit, that there was no other avenue to his friendship but the road of adulation and panegyric: we need not, therefore, wonder that his bounty was so sparingly bestowed upon Cer-

vantes, whose conscious worth and spirit would not suffer him to practise such servility of prostration.

Rather than stoop so far beneath the dignity of his own character, he resolved to endure the severest stings of fortune, and, for a series of years, wrestled with unconceivable vexation and distress. Even in this low situation, he was not exempted from the ill offices of those who envied his talents and his fame. The bad writers vilified his genius, and censured his morals; they construed Don Quixote into an impertinent libel, and endeavoured to depreciate his exemplary novels, which were published at Madrid, in the year 1613. This performance is such as might be expected from the invention and elegance of Cervantes, and was accordingly approved by the best judges of his time. Indeed, it must have been a great consolation to him, in the midst of his misfortunes, to see himself celebrated by the choicest wits of Spain; and, among the rest, by the renowned Lope de Vega, prince of the Spanish theatre, who, both during the life, and after the death of our author, mentioned him in the most respectful terms of * admiration.

But, of all the insults to which he was exposed from the malevolence of mankind, nothing provoked him so much, as the outrage he sustained, from the insolence and knavery of an author, who, while he was preparing the second part of Don Quixote for the press, in the year 1614, published a performance, intituled, The second Volume of the sage Hidalgo Don Quixote de la Mancha, containing his third sally. Composed by the licentiate Alonzo Fernandez de Avellaneda,[27] a native of Tordesillas; dedicated to the alcalde, regidors, and gentlemen of the noble town of Argamesilla, the happy country of Don Quixote de la Mancha. This impostor, not contented with having robbed Cervantes of his plan, and, as some people believe, of a good part of his copy, attacked him personally, in his preface, in the most virulent manner; accusing him of envy, malice, peevishness, and rancour; reproaching him with his poverty, and taxing him with having abused his cotemporary writers, particularly Lope de Vega, under the shade of whose reputation this spurious writer takes shelter, pretending to have been lashed, together with that great genius, in some of our author's critical reflexions.[28]

In spite of the disguise he assumed, Cervantes discovered him to be an Arragonian; and in all probability knew his real name, which, however, he did not think proper to transmit to posterity; and, his silence in this particular, was the result either of discretion, or contempt. If he was a person of consequence, as some people suppose, it was undoubtedly prudent in Cervantes to pretend ignorance of his true name and quality; because, under the shadow of that pretence, he could then more securely chastise him for his dulness, scurrility, and presumption: but, if he knew him to be a man of no character or estimation in life, he ought to have deemed him altogether unworthy of his resentment; for, his production was such as could not possibly prejudice our author's interest or reputation. It is altogether void of invention and propriety: the characters of Don Quixote and Sancho are flattened into the most insipid absurdity; the adventures are unentertaining and improbable; and the stile barbarous, swoln, and pedantic.

Howsoever Saavedra's fortune might have been affected by this fraudulent anticipation, I am persuaded, from the consideration of his magnanimity, that he would have

* Laurèl de Apollo Selva 8.[26]

looked upon the attempt with silent disdain, had the fictitious Avellaneda abstained from personal abuse; but finding himself so injuriously upbraided with crimes which his soul abhorred, he gave a loose to his indignation and ridicule, which appear through the preface and second part of Don Quixote, in a variety of animadversions equally witty and severe. Indeed, the genuine continuation, which was published in the year 1615, convinced the world that no other person could complete the plan of the original projector. It was received with universal joy and approbation; and, in a very little time translated into the languages of Italy, France, England, and other countries, where, tho' the knight appeared to disadvantage, he was treated as a noble stranger of superlative merit and distinction.

In the year after the publication of his novels, Cervantes ushered into the world a poem, called, A Voyage to Parnassus,[29] dedicated to Don Rodrigo de Tapia, knight of St. Jago. This performance is an ironical satire on the Spanish poets of his time, written in imitation of Caesar Caporali, who lashed his cotemporaries of Italy under the same title: tho' Saavedra seems to have had also another scope; namely to complain of the little regard that was payed to his own age and talents. Those who will not allow this piece to be an excellent poem, cannot help owning that it abounds with wit and manly satire; and that nothing could be a more keen reproach upon the taste and patronage of the times, than the dialogue that passes between him and Apollo; to whom, after having made a bold, yet just recapitulation of his own success in writing, he pathetically complains, that he was denied a seat among his brethren; and takes occasion to observe, that rewards were not bestowed according to merit, but in consequence of interest and favour.

He has, upon other occasions, made severe remarks upon the scarcity of patrons among the nobility of Spain, and even aimed the shafts of his satire at the throne itself. In his dedication of the second part of Don Quixote, to the count de Lemos,[30] he proceeds in this ironical strain: "But, no person expresses a greater desire of seeing my Don Quixote, than the mighty emperor of China, who, about a month ago sent me a letter by an express, desiring, or rather beseeching, me to supply him with a copy of that performance, as he intended to build and endow a college for teaching the Spanish language from my book, and was resolved to make me rector or principal teacher. I asked if his majesty had sent me any thing towards defraying the charges; and, when he answered in the negative, 'Why then, friend,' said I, 'you may return to China as soon as you please; for my own part, I am not in a state of health to undertake such a long journey; besides, I am not only weak in body, but still weaker in purse, and so I am the emperor's most humble servant.' In short, emperor for emperor, and monarch for monarch, to take one with the other, and set the hare's head against the goose giblets, there is the noble count de Lemos, at Naples, who, without any rectorships, supports, protects, and favours me to my heart's content."

This facetious paragraph certainly alludes to some unsubstantial promise he had received from the court. At the same time, I cannot help observing, that his gratitude and acknowledgment to the count de Lemos, seem to have greatly exceeded the obligation; for, at this very time, while he is extolling his generosity, he gives us to understand that his circumstances were extremely indigent.

At the very time of this dedication, the poverty of Cervantes had increased to such a degree of distress, that he was fain to sell eight plays, and as many interludes, to Juan Villaroel,[31] because he had neither means nor credit for printing them at his own expence. These theatrical pieces, which were published at Madrid in the year 1615, tho' counted inferior to many productions of Lope de Vega, have, nevertheless, merit enough to persuade the discerning reader that they would have succeeded in the representation; but, he was no favourite with the players, who have always arrogated to themselves the prerogative of judging and rejecting the productions of the drama; and, as they forbore to offer, he disdained to sollicit their acceptance. The truth is, he considered actors as the servants of the public, who, tho' intitled to a certain degree of favour and encouragement for the entertainment they afforded, ought ever to demean themselves with modesty and respect for their benefactors; and he had often professed himself an enemy to the self-sufficiency, insolence, and outrageous behaviour of the king's company, some of whom had been guilty of the most flagrant crimes, and even committed murder with impunity.[32]

It is sometimes in the power of the most inconsiderable wretch to mortify a character of the highest dignity. Cervantes, notwithstanding his contempt of such petty critics, could not help feeling the petulance of a puny player, who presumed to depretiate the talents of this venerable father of the stage. "Some years * ago," says he, "I had recourse again to my old amusement, and, on the supposition that the times were not altered since my name was in some estimation, I composed a few pieces for the stage; but, found no birds in last year's nests: my meaning is, I could find no player who would ask for my performances, tho' the whole company knew they were finished; so that I threw them aside and condemned them to perpetual silence. About this time, a certain bookseller told me he would have purchased my plays, had he not been prevented by an actor, who said that from my prose much might be expected; but, nothing from my verse. I confess, I was not a little chagrined at hearing this declaration; and said to myself, Either I am quite altered or the times are greatly improved, contrary to common observation, by which the past is always preferred to the present. I revised my comedies, together with some interludes which had lain some time in a corner, and I did not think them so wretched, but that they might appeal from the muddy brain of this player, to the clearer perception of other actors less scrupulous and more judicious.——Being quite out of humour, I parted with the copy to a bookseller, who offered me a tolerable price: I took his money, without giving myself any further trouble about the actors, and he printed them as you see. I could wish they were the best in the world, or, at least possessed of some merit. Gentle reader, thou wilt soon see how they are, and if thou canst find any thing to thy liking, and afterwards shouldst happen to meet with my back-biting actor, desire him, from me, to take care and mend himself; for, I offend no man: as for the plays, thou mayest tell him, they contain no glaring nonsense, no palpable absurdities."

The source of this indifference towards Cervantes, we can easily explain, by observing that Lope de Vega had, by this time, engrossed the theatre, and the favour of the public, to such a degree as ensured success to all his performances; so that the players

* In his preface to his plays.[33]

would not run any risque of miscarriage, in exhibiting the productions of an old ne-
glected veteran, who had neither inclination nor ability to support his theatrical pieces
by dint of interest and cabal. Far from being able to raise factions in his favour, he could
hardly subsist in the most parsimonious manner, and in all probability would have ac-
tually starved, had not the charity of the count de Lemos enabled him barely to breathe.

The last work he finished was a novel, intituled, The Troubles of Persiles and Sigis-
munda, which, however, he did not live to see in print. This child of his old age he men-
tions * in the warmest terms of paternal affection, preferring it to all the rest of his pro-
ductions; a compliment which every author pays to the youngest offspring of his genius;
for, whatever sentence the world may pronounce, every man thinks he daily improves
in experience and understanding; and that in refusing the pre-eminence to his last ef-
fort, he would fairly own the decay and degeneracy of his own talents.

We must not, however, impute the encomiums which Cervantes bestows upon his
last performance to this fond partiality alone; because the book has indubitable merit,
and, as he himself says, may presume to vie with the celebrated romance of He-
liodorus[35] † in elegance of diction, entertaining incidents, and fecundity of invention.
Before this novel saw the light, our author was seized with a dropsy, which gradually
conveyed him to his grave; and nothing could give a more advantageous idea of his char-
acter, than the fortitude and good humour which he appears to have maintained to the
last moment of his life, overwhelmed as he was with misery, old age, and an incurable
distemper. The preface and dedication of his Persiles and Sigismunda, contain a jour-
nal of his last stage, by which we are enabled to guess at the precise time of his decease.
"Loving reader," said he,[37] "as two of my friends and myself were coming from the fa-
mous town of Esquivias—famous, I say, on a thousand accounts; first, for its illustrious
families, and, secondly, for its more illustrious wines, &c. I heard somebody galloping
after us, with intent, as I imagined, to join our company; and, indeed, he soon justified
my conjecture, by calling out to us to ride more softly. We accordingly waited for this
stranger, who, riding up to us upon a she ass, appeared to be a grey student; for, he was
cloathed in grey, with country buskins such as peasants wear to defend their legs in har-
vest time, round toed shoes, a sword provided, as it happened, with a tolerable chape, a
starched band, and an even number of three thread breeds; for, the truth is, he had but
two; and, as his band would every now and then shift to one side, he took incredible
pains to adjust it again. 'Gentlemen,' said he, 'you are going, belike, to sollicit some post
or pension at court: his eminence of Toledo must be there, to be sure, or the king, at
least, by your making such haste. In good faith, I could hardly overtake you, tho' my ass
hath been more than once applauded for a tolerable ambler.' To this address one of my
companions replied, 'We were obliged to set on at a good rate, to keep up with that there
mettlesome nag, belonging to signor Miguel de Cervantes.' Scarce had the student
heard my name, when, springing from the back of his ass, while his pannel fell one way,
and his wallet another, he ran towards me, and, taking hold of my stirrup, 'Aye, aye,'
cried he, 'this is the sound cripple! the renowned, the merry writer; in a word, the dar-

* Preface to his novels. Dedication of the last part of Don Quixote.[34]
† The Loves of Theagenes and Chariclea.[36]

ling of the muses!' In order to make some return to these high compliments, I threw my arms about his neck, so as that he lost his band by the eagerness of my embraces, and told him he was mistaken, like many of my well-wishers. 'I am, indeed, Cervantes,' said I, 'but not the darling of the muses, or in any shape deserving of those encomiums you have bestowed: be pleased, therefore, good signor, to remount your beast, and let us travel together like friends the rest of the way.' The courteous student took my advice, and as we jogged on softly together, the conversation happening to turn on the subject of my illness, the stranger soon pronounced my doom, by assuring me that my distemper was a dropsy, which all the water of the ocean, although it were not salt, would never be able to quench. 'Therefore, signor Cervantes,' added the student, 'you must totally abstain from drink, but, do not forget to eat heartily: and this regimen will effect your recovery without physic.' 'I have received the same advice from other people,' answered I, 'but I cannot help drinking, as if I had been born to do nothing else but drink. My life is drawing to a period, and by the daily journal of my pulse, which, I find, will have finished its course by next sunday at farthest, I shall also have finished my career; so that you come in the very nick of time to be acquainted with me, though I shall have no opportunity of shewing how much I am obliged to you for your good will.' By this time we had reached the Toledo bridge, where finding we must part, I embraced my student once more, and he having returned the compliment with great cordiality, spurred up his beast, and left me as ill disposed on my horse, as he was ill mounted on his ass; although my pen itched to be writing some humorous description of his equipage: but, adieu my merry friends all; for, I am going to die, and I hope to meet you again in the other world, as happy as heart can wish."

After this adventure, which he so pleasantly relates, nay even in his last moments, he dictated a most affectionate dedication to his patron, the count de Lemos,[38] who was at that time president of the supreme council in Italy. He begins facetiously with a quotation from an old ballad, then proceeds to tell his excellency, that he had received extreme unction, and was on the brink of eternity; yet he wished he could live to see the count's return, and even to finish the Weeks of the garden, and the Second part of Galatea, in which he had made some progress.

This dedication was dated April 19, 1617, and in all probability the author died the very next day,[39] as the ceremony of the unction is never performed until the patient is supposed to be in extremity: certain it is, he did not long survive this period; for, in September, a license was granted to Donna Catalina de Salazar, widow of Miguel de Cervantes Saavedra, to print the Troubles of Persiles and Sigismunda, a northern history, which was accordingly published at Madrid, and afterwards translated into Italian.

Thus have I collected and related all the material circumstances mentioned by history or tradition, concerning the life of Cervantes, which I shall conclude with the portrait of his person, drawn by his own pen,[40] in the preface to his novels. His visage was sharp and aquiline, his hair of a chesnut colour, his forehead smooth and high, his nose hookish or hawkish, his eye brisk and chearful, his mouth little, his beard originally of a golden hue, his upper-lip furnished with large mustachios, his complexion fair, his stature of the middling size: and he tells us, moreover, that he was thick in the shoulders, and not very light of foot.

In a word, Cervantes, whether considered as a writer or a man, will be found worthy of universal approbation and esteem; as we cannot help applauding that fortitude and courage which no difficulty could disturb, and no danger dismay; while we admire that delightful stream of humour and invention, which flowed so plenteous and so pure, surmounting all the mounds of malice and adversity.

The Translator's aim, in this undertaking, was to maintain that ludicrous solemnity and self-importance by which the inimitable Cervantes has distinguished the character of Don Quixote, without raising him to the insipid rank of a dry philosopher, or debasing him to the melancholy circumstances and unentertaining caprice of an ordinary madman; and to preserve the native humour of Sancho Panza, from degenerating into mere proverbial phlegm, or affected buffoonry.

He has endeavoured to retain the spirit and ideas, without servilely adhering to the literal expression, of the original;[1] from which, however, he has not so far deviated, as to destroy that formality of idiom, so peculiar to the Spaniards, and so essential to the character of the work.

The satire and propriety of many allusions, which had been lost in the change of customs and lapse of time, will be restored in explanatory notes; and the whole conducted with that care and circumspection, which ought to be exerted by every author, who, in attempting to improve upon a task already performed, subjects himself to the most invidious comparison.

Whatever may be the fate of the performance, he cannot charge himself with carelessness or precipitation; for it was begun, and the greatest part of it actually finished, four years ago;[2] and he has been for some time employed in revising and correcting it for the press.

# PREFACE

## TO THE

# READER.

Idle reader, without an oath thou mayest believe, that I wish this book, as the child of my understanding, were the most beautiful, sprightly and discreet production that ever was conceived. But, it was not in my power to contravene the order of nature, in consequence of which, every creature procreates its own resemblance: what therefore could be engendered in my barren, ill-cultivated genius, but a dry, meagre offspring, wayward, capricious and full of whimsical notions peculiar to my own imagination, as if produced in a prison, which is the seat of inconvenience, and the habitation of every dismal * sound. Quiet, solitude, pleasant fields, serene weather, purling streams, and tranquillity of mind, contribute so much to the fecundity even of the most barren genius, that it will bring forth productions so fair as to awaken the admiration and delight of mankind.

A man who is so unfortunate as to have an ugly child, destitute of every grace and favourable endowment, may be so hood-winked by paternal tenderness, that he cannot perceive his defects; but, on the contrary, looks upon every blemish as a beauty, and recounts to his friends every instance of his folly as a sample of his wit: but I, who, tho' seemingly the parent, am no other than the step-father of Don Quixote, will not fail with the stream of custom, nor like some others, supplicate the gentle reader, with the tears in my eyes, to pardon or conceal the faults which thou mayest spy in this production. Thou art neither its father nor kinsman; hast thy own soul in thy own body, and a will as free as the finest; thou art in thy own house, of which I hold thee as absolute master as the king of his revenue; and thou knowest the common saying, Under my cloak the king is a joke. These considerations free and exempt thee from all manner of restraint and obligation; so that thou mayest fully and frankly declare thy opinion of this history, without fear of calumny for thy censure, and without hope of recompense for thy approbation.

I wished only to present thee with the performance, clean, neat and naked, without the ornament of a preface, and unincumbered with an innumerable catalogue of such sonnets, epigrams and commendatory verses, as are generally prefixed to the productions of the present age; for, I can assure thee, that although the composition of the book hath cost me some trouble, I have found more difficulty in writing this preface, which is now under thy inspection: divers and sundry times did I seize the pen, and as often laid it aside, for want of knowing what to say; and during this uneasy state of suspense, while I was one day ruminating on the subject, with the paper before me, the quill behind my ear, my elbow fixed on the table, and my cheek leaning on my hand; a friend of mine, who possesses a great fund of humour, and an excellent understanding, suddenly

---

* This is a strong presumption, that the first part of Don Quixote was actually written in a jail.[1]

entered the apartment, and finding me in this musing posture, asked the cause of my being so contemplative. As I had no occasion to conceal the nature of my perplexity, I told him I was studying a preface for the history of Don Quixote; a task which I found so difficult, that I was resolved to desist, and even suppress the adventures of such a noble cavalier: for, you may easily suppose how much I must be confounded at the animadversions of that antient lawgiver the vulgar, when it shall see me, after so many years that I have slept in silence and oblivion, produce, in my old age, a performance as dry as a rush, barren of invention, meagre in stile, beggarly in conceit, and utterly destitute of wit and erudition; without quotations in the margin, or annotations at the end; as we see in other books, let them be never so fabulous and profane: indeed they are generally so stuffed with apothegms from Aristotle, Plato, and the whole body of philosophers, that they excite the admiration of the readers, who look upon such authors as men of unbounded knowledge, eloquence and erudition. When they bring a citation from the holy scripture, one would take them for so many St. Thomas's, and other doctors of the church; herein observing such ingenious decorum, that in one line they will represent a frantic lover, and in the very next begin with a godly sermon, from which the christian readers, and even the hearers receive much comfort and edification. Now, my book must appear without all these advantages; for, I can neither quote in the margin, nor note in the end: nor do I know what authors I have imitated, that I may, like the rest of my brethren, prefix them to the work in alphabetical order, beginning with Aristotle, and ending in Xenophon, Zoilus or Zeuxis, though one was a back-biter, and the other a painter. My history must likewise be published without poems at the beginning, at least without sonnets written by dukes, marquisses, counts, bishops, ladies, and celebrated poets: although, should I make the demand, I know two or three good natured friends, who would oblige me with such verses as should not be equalled by the most famous poetry in Spain.

In a word, my good friend, said I, signor Don Quixote shall be buried in the archives of la Mancha, until heaven shall provide some person to adorn him with those decorations he seems to want; for, I find myself altogether unequal to the task, through insufficiency and want of learning; and because I am naturally too bashful and indolent, to go in quest of authors to say, what I myself can say as well without their assistance. Hence arose my thoughtfulness and meditation, which you will not wonder at, now that you have heard the cause. My friend having listened attentively to my remonstrance, slapped his forehead with the palm of his hand, and bursting into a loud laugh: "'Fore God! brother," said he, "I am now undeceived of an error, in which I have lived during the whole term of our acquaintance; for, I always looked upon you as a person of prudence and discretion; but now, I see, you are as far from that character, as heaven is distant from the earth. What! is it possible that such a trifling inconvenience, so easily remedied, should have power to mortify and perplex a genius like yours, brought to such maturity, and so well calculated to demolish and surmount much greater difficulties? in good faith this does not proceed from want of ability, but from excessive indolence, that impedes the exercise of reason. If you would be convinced of the truth of what I alledge, give me the hearing, and, in the twinkling of an eye, all your difficulties shall vanish, and a remedy be prescribed for all those defects which, you say, perplex

your understanding, and deter you from ushering to the light, your history of the renowned Don Quixote, the luminary and sole mirrour of knight-errantry." Hearing this declaration, I desired he would tell me in what manner he proposed to fill up the vacuity of my apprehension, to diffuse light, and reduce to order the chaos of my confusion; and he replied, "Your first objection, namely the want of sonnets, epigrams and commendatory verses from persons of rank and gravity, may be obviated by your taking the trouble to compose them yourself, and then you may christen them by any name you shall think proper to choose, fathering them upon Prester John of the Indies, or the emperor of Trebisond, who, I am well informed, were very famous poets; and even should this intelligence be untrue, and a few pedants and batchelors of arts should backbite and grumble at your conduct, you need not value them three farthings; for, although they convict you of a lie, they cannot cut off the hand that wrote it *.

"With regard to the practice of quoting, in the margin, such books and authors as have furnished you with sentences and sayings for the embellishment of your history, you have nothing to do, but, to season the work with some Latin maxims, which your own memory will suggest, or a little industry in searching, easily obtain: for example, in treating of freedom and captivity, you may say, 'Non bene pro toto libertas venditur auro';[3] and quote Horace, or whom you please, in the margin. If the power of death happens to be your subject, you have at hand, 'Pallida mors aequo pulsat pede pauperum tabernas regumque turres.'[4] And in expatiating upon that love and friendship which God commands us to entertain even for our enemies, you may have recourse to the holy scripture, though you should have never so little curiosity, and say, in the very words of God himself, 'Ego autem dico vobis, diligite inimicos vestros.'[5] In explaining the nature of malevolence, you may again extract from the Gospel, 'De corde exeunt cogitationes malæ.'[6] And the instability of friends may be aptly illustrated by this distich of Cato, 'Donec eris felix, multos numerabis amicos; tempora si fuerint nubila, solus eris.'[7] By these, and other such scraps of Latin, you may pass for an able grammarian; a character of no small honour and advantage in these days. And as to the annotations at the end of the book, you may safely furnish them in this manner: when you chance to write about giants, be sure to mention Goliah, and this name alone, which costs you nothing, will afford a grand annotation, couched in these words: 'The giant Golias, or Goliat, was a Philistine, whom the shepherd David slew with a stone from a sling, in the valley of Terebinthus, as it is written in such a chapter of the book of Kings.'

"If you have a mind to display your erudition and knowledge of cosmography, take an opportunity to introduce the river Tagus into your history, and this will supply you with another famous annotation, thus expressed: 'The river Tagus, so called from a king of Spain, takes its rise in such a place, and is lost in the sea, after having kissed the walls of the famous city of Lisbon; and is said to have golden sands, &c.' If you treat of robbers, I will relate the story of Cacus, which I have by rote. If of harlots, the bishop of Mondoneda will lend you a Lamia, a Lais, and a Flora, and such a note will greatly redound to your credit. When you write of cruelty, Ovid will surrender his Medea. When you mention wizzards and enchanters, you will find a Calypso in Homer, and a Circe in

---

* Alluding to the loss of his hand in the battle of Lepanto.[2]

Virgil. If you have occasion to speak of valiant captains, Julius Caesar stands ready drawn in his own Commentaries; and from Plutarch you may extract a thousand Alexanders. If your theme be love, and you have but two ounces of the Tuscan tongue, you will light upon Leon Hebreo, who will fill up the measure of your desire: and if you do not choose to travel into foreign countries, you have at home Fonseca's treatise, On the love of God, in which all that you, or the most ingenious critic, can desire, is fully decyphered and discussed. In a word, there is nothing more to be done, than to procure a number of these names, and hint at their particular stories in your text; and leave to me the task of making annotations and quotations, with which I'll engage, on pain of death, to fill up all the margins, besides four whole sheets at the end of the book. Let us now proceed to the citation of authors, so frequent in other books, and so little used in your performance: the remedy is obvious and easy: take the trouble to find a book that quotes the whole tribe alphabetically, as you observed, from Alpha to Omega, and transfer them into your book; and though the absurdity should appear never so glaring, as there is no necessity for using such names, it will signify nothing. Nay, perhaps, some reader will be weak enough to believe you have actually availed yourself of all those authors, in the simple and sincere history you have composed; and if such a large catalogue of writers should answer no other purpose, it may serve at first sight to give some authority to the production: nor will any person take the trouble to examine, whether you have or have not followed those originals, because he can reap no benefit from his labour. But, if I am not mistaken, your book needs none of those embellishments in which you say it is defective; for, it is one continued satire upon books of chivalry; a subject which Aristotle never investigated, St. Basil never mentioned, and Cicero never explained. The punctuality of truth, and the observations of astrology, fall not within the fabulous relation of our adventures; to the description of which, neither the proportions of geometry, nor the confirmation of rhetorical arguments, are of the least importance; nor hath it any connection with preaching, or mingling divine truths with human imagination; a mixture which no christian's fancy should conceive. It only seeks to avail itself of imitation, and the more perfect this is, the more entertaining the book will be: now, as your sole aim in writing, is to invalidate the authority, and ridicule the absurdity of those books of chivalry, which have, as it were, fascinated the eyes and judgment of the world, and in particular of the vulgar, you have no occasion to go a begging maxims from philosophers, exhortations from holy writ, fables from poets, speeches from orators, or miracles from saints; your business is, with plain, significant, well chosen and elegant words, to render your periods sonorous, and your stile entertaining; to give spirit and expression to all your descriptions, and communicate your ideas without obscurity and confusion. You must endeavour to write in such a manner as to convert melancholy into mirth, increase good humour, entertain the ignorant, excite the admiration of the learned, escape the contempt of gravity, and attract applause from persons of ingenuity and taste. Finally, let your aim be levelled against that ill-founded bulwark of idle books of chivalry, abhorred by many, but applauded by more, which if you can batter down, you will have atchieved no inconsiderable exploit."

I listened to my friend's advice in profound silence, and his remarks made such impression upon my mind, that I admitted them without hesitation or dispute, and re-

solved that they should appear instead of a preface. Thou wilt, therefore, gentle reader, perceive his discretion, and my good luck in finding such a counsellor in such an emergency; nor wilt thou be sorry to receive, thus genuine and undisguised, the history of the renowned Don Quixote de la Mancha, who, in the opinion of all the people that live in the district of Montiel, was the most virtuous and valiant knight who had appeared for many years in that neighbourhood. I shall not pretend to inhance the merit of having introduced thee to such a famous and honourable cavalier; but I expect thanks for having made thee acquainted with Sancho Panza, in whom I think are united all the squirish graces, which we find scattered through the whole tribe of vain books written on the subject of chivalry. So, praying that God will give thee health, without forgetting such an humble creature as me, I bid thee heartily farewell.

# THE

# LIFE and ATCHIEVEMENTS

## Of the Sage and Valiant

## DON QUIXOTE de la Mancha.

## PART I. BOOK I.

### CHAPTER I.

Of the quality and amusements of the renowned DON QUIXOTE
de la Mancha.

In a certain corner of la Mancha, the name of which I do not choose to remember, there lately lived one of those country gentlemen, who adorn their halls with a rusty lance and worm-eaten target, and ride forth on the skeleton of a horse, to course with a sort of a starved greyhound.

Three fourths of his income were scarce sufficient to afford a dish of hodge-podge, in which the mutton bore * no proportion to the beef, for dinner; a plate of salmagundy, commonly at supper †; gripes and grumblings ‡ on saturdays, lentils on fridays, and the addition of a pigeon or some such thing on the Lord's-day. The remaining part of his revenue was consumed in the purchase of a fine black suit, with velvet breeches and slippers of the same, for holy-days, and a coat of home-spun, which he wore in honour of his country, during the rest of the week.

He maintained a female house-keeper turned of forty, a niece of about half that age,

---

* Mutton in Spain is counted greatly preferable to beef.[1]

† *Salpicon*, which is the word in the original, is no other than cold beef sliced, and eaten with oil, vinegar and pepper.[2]

‡ Gripes and grumblings, in Spanish *Duelos y Quebrantos*: the true meaning of which, the former translators[3] have been at great pains to investigate, as the importance of the subject (no doubt) required. But their labours have, unhappily, ended in nothing else but conjectures, which, for the entertainment and instruction of our readers, we beg leave to repeat. One interprets the phrase into collops and eggs, "being," saith he, "a very sorry dish." In this decision, however, he is contradicted by another commentator, who affirms, "it is a mess too good to mortify withal"; neither can this virtuoso agree with a late editor, who translates the passage in question, into an amlet, but takes occasion to fall out with Boyer for his description of that dish, which he most sagaciously under-

and a trusty young fellow, fit for field and market, who could turn his hand to any thing, either to saddle the horse or handle the hough *.

Our squire, who bordered upon fifty, was of a tough constitution, extremely meagre and hard-featur'd, an early riser, and in point of exercise, another Nimrod †. He is said to have gone by the name of Quixada, or Quesada, (for in this particular, the authors who mention that circumstance, disagree) though, from the most probable conjectures, we may conclude, that he was called by the significant name of Quixada ‡; but this is of small importance to the history, in the course of which it will be sufficient if we swerve not a tittle from the truth.

Be it known, therefore, that this said honest gentleman, at his leisure hours, which engrossed the greatest part of the year, addicted himself to the reading of books of chivalry, which he perused with such rapture and application, that he not only forgot the pleasures of the chase, but also utterly neglected the management of his estate: nay to such a pass did his curiosity and madness, in this particular, drive him, that he sold many good acres of Terra firma, to purchase books of knight-errantry, with which he furnished his library to the utmost of his power; but, none of them pleased him so much as those that were written by the famous Feliciano de Sylva, whom he admired as the pearl of all authors, for the brilliancy of his prose, and the beautiful perplexity of his expression. How was he transported, when he read those amorous complaints, and doughty challenges, that so often occur in his works.

"The reason of the unreasonable usage my reason has met with, so unreasons my reason, that I have reason to complain of your beauty": and how did he enjoy the following flower of composition! "The high Heaven of your divinity, which with stars divinely fortifies your beauty, and renders you meritorious of that merit, which by your highness is merited!"

The poor gentleman lost his senses, in poring over, and attempting to discover the meaning of these and other such rhapsodies, which Aristotle himself would not be able to unravel, were he to rise from the dead for that purpose only. He could not comprehend the probability of those direful wounds given and received by Don Bellianis,

---

stands to be a "bacon froize," or "rather fryze, from its being fried, from *frit* in French"; and concludes with this judicious query, "after all these learned disquisitions, who knows but the author means a dish of nichils?" If this was his meaning indeed, surely we may venture to conclude, that fasting was very expensive in la Mancha; for the author mentions the *Duelos y Quebrantos*, among those articles that consumed three fourths of the knight's income.

Having considered this momentous affair with all the deliberation it deserves, we in our turn present the reader, with cucumbers, greens, or pease porridge, as the fruit of our industrious researches; being thereunto determined by the literal signification of the text, which is not "grumblings and groanings," as the last mentioned ingenious annotator seems to think; but rather pains and breakings; and evidently points at such eatables as generate and expel wind; qualities (as every body knows) eminently inherent in those vegetables we have mentioned as our hero's saturday's repast.

* *Podadera* literally signifies a pruning-hook.[4]

† In the original, a lover of hunting.[5]

‡ *Quixadas* signifies jaws, of which our knight had an extraordinary provision.[6]

whose face, and whole carcase, must have remained quite covered with marks and scars, even allowing him to have been cured by the most expert surgeons of the age in which he lived.

He, notwithstanding, bestowed great commendations on the author, who concludes his book with the promise of finishing that interminable adventure; and was more than once inclined to seize the quill, with a view of performing what was left undone; nay, he would have actually accomplished the affair, and published it accordingly, had not reflexions of greater moment employed his imagination, and diverted him from the execution of that design.

Divers and obstinate were the disputes he maintained against the parson of the parish, (a man of some learning, who had taken his degrees at Siguenza *) on that puzzling question, whether Palmerin of England, or Amadis de Gaul, was the most illustrious knight-errant: but master Nicholas, who acted as barber to the village, affirmed, that none of them equalled the Knight of the Sun, or indeed could be compared to him in any degree, except Don Galaor, brother of Amadis de Gaul; for his disposition was adapted to all emergencies; he was neither such a precise, nor such a puling coxcomb as his brother; and in point of valour, his equal at least.

So eager and entangled was our Hidalgo † in this kind of history, that he would often read from morning to night, and from night to morning again, without interruption; till at last, the moisture of his brain being quite exhausted with indefatigable watching and study, he fairly lost his wits: all that he had read of quarrels, enchantments, battles, challenges, wounds, tortures, amorous complaints, and other improbable conceits, took full possession of his fancy; and he believed all those romantic exploits so implicitly, that, in his opinion, the holy scripture was not more true. He observed that Cid Ruydias was an excellent knight; but not equal to the Lord of the Flaming-sword, who with one back-stroke had cut two fierce and monstrous giants through the middle. He had still a better opinion of Bernardo del Carpio, who, at the battle of Ronsevalles, put the enchanted Orlando [9]‡ to death, by the same means that Hercules used, when he strangled the earth-born Anteus. Neither was he silent in the praise of Morgante, who, though of that gigantic race which is noted for insolence and incivility, was perfectly affable and well-bred. But his chief favourite was Reynaldo of Montalvan, whom he hugely admired for his prowess, in sallying from his castle to rob travellers; and above all things, for his dexterity in stealing that idol of the impostor Mahomet, which, according to the history, was of solid gold. For an opportunity of pummelling the traitor § Galalon, he would willingly have given his housekeeper, body and soul, nay, and his

---

* Siguenza, a town situated on the banks of the Henarés, in New Castile; in which there is a small university.[7]

† *Hidalgo* has much the same application in Spain, as 'squire in England; though it literally signifies the son of something, in contradistinction to those who are the sons of nothing.[8]

‡ Orlando, the supposed nephew of Charlemagne, and poetical hero of Boiardo and Ariosto, is said to have been invulnerable in all parts of his body, except the soles of his feet, which he therefore took care to secure with double plates of armour.

§ Galalon is said to have betrayed Charlemagne's army at Roncevalles, where it was roughly handled by the Moors, in his retreat from Spain.[10]

niece into the bargain. In short, his understanding being quite perverted, he was seized with the strangest whim that ever entered the brain of a madman. This was no other, than a full persuasion, that it was highly expedient and necessary, not only for his own honour, but also for the good of the public, that he should profess knight-errantry, and ride through the world in arms, to seek adventures, and conform in all points to the practice of those itinerant heroes, whose exploits he had read; redressing all manner of grievances, and courting all occasions of exposing himself to such dangers, as in the event would entitle him to everlasting renown. This poor lunatic looked upon himself already as good as seated, by his own single valour, on the throne of Trebisond; and intoxicated with these agreeable vapours of his unaccountable folly, resolved to put his design in practice forthwith.

In the first place, he cleaned an old suit of armour, which had belonged to some of his ancestors, and which he found in his garret, where it had lain for several ages, quite covered over with mouldiness and rust: but having scoured and put it to rights, as well as he could, he perceived that, instead of a complete helmet, there was only a simple headpiece without a beaver. This unlucky defect, however, his industry supplied by a vizor, which he made of paste-board, and fixed so artificially to the morrion, that it looked like an intire helmet. True it is that, in order to try if it was strong enough to risk his jaws in, he unsheathed his sword, and bestowed upon it two hearty strokes, the first of which, in a twinkling, undid his whole week's labour: he did not at all approve of the facility with which he hewed it in pieces; and therefore, to secure himself from any such danger for the future, went to work anew. He faced it with a plate of iron, in such a manner, as that he remained satisfied of its strength, without putting it to a second trial, and looked upon it as a most finished piece of armour.

He next visited his horse, which (though he had more corners than a * rial, being as lean as Gonela's, that "tantum pellis et ossa fuit"[12]) nevertheless, in his eye, appeared infinitely preferable to Alexander's Bucephalus, or the Cid's Babieca. Four days he consumed, in inventing a name for this remarkable steed; suggesting to himself, what an impropriety it would be, if an horse of his qualities, belonging to such a renowned knight, should go without some sounding and significant appellation: he therefore resolved to accommodate him with one that should not only declare his past, but also his present capacity; for he thought it but reasonable, that since his master had altered his condition, he should also change his horse's name, and invest him with some sublime and sonorous epithet, suitable to the new order and employment he professed: accordingly, after having chosen, rejected, amended, tortured and revolved a world of names, in his imagination, he fixed upon Rozinante †, an appellation, in his opinion, lofty, sonorous and expressive, not only of his former, but likewise of his present situation, which intitled him to the preference over all other horses under the sun. Having thus denominated his horse, so much to his own satisfaction, he was desirous of doing him-

---

* This is a joke upon the knight's steed, which was so meagre, that his bones stuck out like the corner of a Spanish rial, a coin of a very irregular shape, not unlike the figure in geometry, called *Trapezium.*[11]

† *Rozinante* implies that which was formerly an ordinary horse, though the *ante* seems to have been intended by the knight as a badge of distinction, by which he was ranked before all other horses.[13]

self the like justice, and, after eight days study, actually assumed the title of Don Qui-
xote: from whence, as hath been observed, the authors of this authentic history, con-
cluded, that his former name must have been Quixada, and not Quesada, as others are
pleased to affirm. But recollecting, that the valiant Amadis, not satisfied with that simple
appellation, added to it that of his country, and, in order to dignify the place of his na-
tivity, called himself Amadis de Gaul; he resolved, like a worthy knight, to follow such
an illustrious example, and assume the name of Don Quixote de la Mancha; which, in
his opinion, fully expressed his generation, and, at the same time, reflected infinite ho-
nour on his fortunate country.

Accordingly his armour being scoured, his beaver fitted to his head-piece, his steed
accommodated with a name, and his own dignified with these additions, he reflected,
that nothing else was wanting but a lady to inspire him with love; for a knight-errant
without a mistress, would be like a tree destitute of leaves and fruit, or a body without a
soul. "If," said he, "for my sins, or rather for my honour, I should engage with some
giant, an adventure common in knight-errantry, and overthrow him in the field, by
cleaving him in twain, or in short, disarm and subdue him; will it not be highly proper,
that I should have a mistress, to whom I may send my conquered foe; who, coming into
the presence of the charming fair, will fall upon his knees, and say, in an humble and sub-
missive tone: 'Incomparable princess, I am the giant Carculiambro, lord of the island
Malindrania, who being vanquished in single combat by the invincible knight Don Qui-
xote de la Mancha, am commanded by him to present myself before your beauty, that I
may be disposed of, according to the pleasure of your highness?'" How did the heart of
our worthy knight dance with joy, when he uttered this address; and still more, when he
found a lady worthy of his affection! This they say, was an hale, buxom country wench,
called Aldonza Lorenço, who lived in the neighbourhood, and with whom he had for-
merly been in love; though, by all accounts, she never knew, nor gave herself the least
concern about the matter. Her he looked upon as one qualified, in all respects, to be the
queen of his inclinations; and putting his invention again to the rack, for a name that
should bear some affinity with her own, and at the same time become a princess or lady
of quality, he determined to call her Dulcinea del Toboso, she being a native of that
place, a name, in his opinion, musical, romantic and expressive, like the rest which he
had appropriated to himself and his concerns.

## CHAPTER II.

## Of the sage DON QUIXOTE's first sally from his own habitation.

These preparations being made, he could no longer resist the desire of executing his
design; reflecting with impatience on the injury his delay occasioned in the world,
where there was abundance of grievances to be redressed, wrongs to be rectified, errors
to be amended, abuses to be reformed, and doubts to be removed; he therefore, with-

out communicating his intention to any body, or being seen by a living soul, one morn-
ing before day, in the scorching month of July, put on his armour, mounted Rozinante,
buckled his ill-contrived helmet, braced his target, seized his lance, and, thro' the back-
door of his yard, sallied into the fields, in a rapture of joy, occasioned by this easy and
successful beginning of his admirable undertaking: but, scarce was he clear of the vil-
lage, when he was assaulted by such a terrible objection, as had well nigh induced our
hero to abandon his enterprize directly: for, he recollected that he had never been
knighted; and therefore, according to the laws of chivalry, he neither could nor ought to
enter the lists with any antagonist of that degree; nay, even granting he had received that
mark of distinction, it was his duty to wear white armour, like a new knight, without any
device on his shield, until such time as his valour should intitle him to that honour *.

These cogitations made him waver a little in his plan; but his madness prevailing over
every other consideration, suggested, that he might be dubbed by the first person he
should meet, after the example of many others who had fallen upon the same expedient;
as he had read in those mischievous books which had disordered his imagination †. With
respect to the white armour, he proposed, with the first opportunity, to scour his own,
until it should be fairer than ermine; and having satisfied his conscience in this manner,
he pursued his design, without following any other road than that which his horse was
pleased to chuse; being persuaded, that in so doing, he manifested the true spirit of
adventure. Thus proceeded our flaming adventurer, while he uttered the following
soliloquy.

"Doubtless, in future ages, when the true history of my famed exploits shall come to
light, the sage author, when he recounts my first and early sally, will express himself in
this manner: 'Scarce had ruddy Phoebus, o'er this wide and spacious earth, display'd the
golden threads of his refulgent hair; and scarce the little painted warblers with their
forky tongues, in soft mellifluous harmony, had hail'd the approach of rosy-wing'd Au-
rora, who stealing from her jealous husband's couch, thro' the balconies and aerial gates
of Mancha's bright horizon, stood confessed to wondering mortals; when lo! the illus-
trious knight Don Quixote de la Mancha, up-springing from the lazy down, bestrode
fam'd Rozinante his unrival'd steed! and thro' Montiel's ancient, well known field
(which was really the case) pursu'd his way.'" Then he added, "O fortunate age! O happy
times! in which shall be made public my incomparable atchievements, worthy to be in-
graved in brass, on marble sculptured, and in painting shewn, as great examples to fu-
turity! and O! thou sage enchanter, whosoever thou may'st be, doom'd to record the
wondrous story! forget not, I beseech thee, my trusty Rozinante, the firm companion
of my various fate!" Then making a sudden transition, he exclaimed, as if he had been
actually in love, "O Dulcinea! sovereign princess of this captive heart, what dire afflic-
tion hast thou made me suffer, thus banished from thy presence with reproach, and fet-
tered by thy rigorous command, not to appear again before thy beauteous face! Deign,

---

* According to the ancient rules of chivalry, no man was intituled to the rank and degree of knight-
hood, until he had been in actual battle, and taken a prisoner with his own hand.[1]
† It was common for one knight to dub another. Francis I. king of France was knighted, at his own
desire, by the chevalier Bayard, who was looked upon as the flower of chivalry.[2]

princess, to remember this thy faithful slave, who now endures such misery for love of thee!" These, and other such rhapsodies, he strung together; imitating, as much as in him lay, the stile of those ridiculous books which he had read; and jogged along, in spite of the sun which beam'd upon him so intensely hot, that surely his brains, if any had remained, would have been fry'd in his skull: that whole day did he travel, without encountring any thing worth mentioning: a circumstance that grieved him sorely, for he had expected to find some object on which he could try the prowess of his valiant arm *.

Some authors say his first adventure was that of the pass of Lapice, but others affirm, that the Windmills had the maidenhead of his valour: all that I can aver of the matter, in consequence of what I found recorded in the annals of la Mancha, is, that having travelled the whole day, his horse and he, about twilight, found themselves excessively wearied and half dead with hunger; and that, looking around for some castle or sheep cot, in which he might allay the cravings of nature, by repose and refreshment, he descried not far from the road, an inn, which he looked upon as the star that would guide him to the porch, if not the palace, of his redemption: in this hope, he put spurs to his horse, and just in the twilight reached the gate, where, at that time, there happened to be two ladies of the game, who being on their journey to Seville, with the carriers, had chanced to take up their night's lodging in this place.

As our hero's imagination converted whatsoever he saw, heard or considered, into something of which he had read in books of chivalry; he no sooner perceived the inn, than his fancy represented it as a stately castle with its four towers and pinnacles of shining silver, accommodated with a draw-bridge, deep moat, and all other conveniencies that are described as belonging to buildings of that kind.

When he was within a small distance of this inn, which to him seemed a castle, he drew bridle, and stopt Rozinante, in hope that some dwarf would appear upon the battlements, and signify his arrival by sound of trumpet: but, as this ceremony was not performed so soon as he expected, and his steed expressed great eagerness to be in the stable; he rode up to the gate, and observing the battered wenches before-mentioned, mistook them for two beautiful maidens, or agreeable ladies, enjoying the cool breeze at the castle-gate. At that instant, a swine-herd, who, in a field hard by, was tending a drove of hogs, (with leave be it spoken)[4] chanced to blow his horn, in order to collect his scattered subjects: immediately the knight's expectation was fulfilled, and concluding that now the dwarf had given the signal of his approach, he rode towards the inn with infinite satisfaction. The ladies no sooner perceived such a strange figure, armed with lance and target, than they were seized with consternation, and ran affrighted to the gate; but Don Quixote, guessing their terror by their flight, lifted up his paste-board vizor, and discovering his meagre lanthorn jaws besmeared with dust, addressed them thus, with gentle voice and courteous demeanour: "Fly me not, ladies, nor dread the least affront; for, it belongs not to the order of knighthood, which I profess, to injure any mortal, much less such high-born damsels as your appearance declares you to be."

---

* He might have imitated the young knight described in Perceforest, who having been dubbed by king Alexander, rode into a wood, and attacked the trees with such fury and address, that the king and his whole court were convinced of his prowess and dexterity.[3]

The wenches, who stared at him with all their curiosity, in order to discover his face, which the sorry beaver concealed, hearing themselves HIGH-BORN DAMSELS, an epithet so foreign to their profession, could contain themselves no longer, but burst out into such a fit of laughing, that Don Quixote being offended, rebuked them in these words; "Nothing is more commendable in beautiful women than modesty; and nothing more ridiculous than laughter proceeding from a slight cause: but this I mention not as a re-proach, by which I may incur your indignation; on the contrary, my intention is only to do you service."

This address, which was wholly unintelligible to the ladies, together with the ludi-crous appearance of him who pronounced it, increased their mirth, which kindled the knight's anger, and he began to wax wroth, when luckily the landlord interposed. This innkeeper, who, by reason of his unwieldy belly, was of a pacific disposition, no sooner beheld the preposterous figure of our hero, equipped with such ill-suited accoutrements as his bridle, lance, target and corslet composed, than he was seized with an inclination to join the nymphs in their unseasonable merriment; but, being justly afraid of incens-ing the owner of such unaccountable furniture, he resolved to behave civilly, and ac-cordingly accosted him in these words: "Sir knight, if your worship wants lodging, you may be accommodated in this inn with every thing in great abundance, except a bed; for at present we have not one unengaged." Don Quixote perceiving the humility of the governor of the castle, for such he supposed the landlord to be, answered, "For me, signor Castellano, any thing will suffice; my dress is armour, battles my repose, &c." Mine host imagining that he called him Castellano *, because be looked like a hypo-critical rogue; tho' indeed he was an Andalusian, born on the coast of St. Lucar, as great a thief as Cacus, and more mischievous than a collegian or a page, replied with a sneer, "If that be the case, I suppose your worship's couch is no other than the flinty rock, and your sleep perpetual waking; so that you may alight with the comfortable assurance, that you will find, in this mansion, continual opportunities of defying sleep, not only for one night, but for a whole year, if you please to try the experiment." With these words, he laid hold of the stirrup of Don Quixote, who dismounting with infinite pain and difficulty, occasioned by his having travelled all day long without any refreshment, bad the landlord take special care of his steed; for, he observed, a better piece of horse-flesh had never broke bread.

The innkeeper, tho' with all his penetration he could not discern any qualities in Roz-inante sufficient to justify one half of what was said in his praise, led him civilly into the stable, and having done the honours of the place, returned to receive the commands of his other guest, whom he found in the hands of the high-born damsels, who having by this time reconciled themselves to him, were busied in taking off his armour: they had already disincumbered him of his back and breast-plates, but could fall upon no method of disengaging his head and neck from his ill-contrived helmet and gorget, which were fast tied with green ribbons, the gordian knots of which no human hands could loose; and he would, by no means, allow them to be cut; so that he remained all night, armed

---

* *Sano de Castella*, signifies a crafty knave.[5]

from the throat upwards, and afforded as odd and comical a spectacle as ever was seen *. While these kind harridans, whom he supposed to be the constable's lady and daughter, were employed in this hospitable office, he said to them with a smile of inconceivable pleasure, "Never was knight so honoured by the service of ladies as Don Quixote when he first ushered himself into the world;[7] ladies ministred unto him, and princesses took charge of his Rozinante. O Rozinante! (for that, fair ladies, is the name of my steed, and Don Quixote de la Mancha the appellation of his master) not that I intended to have disclosed myself until the deeds atchieved in your service should have made me known; but, in order to accommodate my present situation to that venerable romance of Sir Lancelot, I am obliged to discover my name a little prematurely: yet, the time will come, when your highnesses shall command, and I will obey, and the valour of this arm testify the desire I feel of being your slave."

The charmers, whom nature never designed to expose to such extraordinary compliments, answered not a syllable, but asked if he chose to have any thing for supper? To which kind question Don Quixote replied, that from the information of his bowels, he believed nothing eatable could come amiss. As it was unluckily a meagre day, the inn afforded no other fare than some bundles of that fish which is called Abadexo in Castile, Baccalao in Andalusia, Curadillo in some parts of Spain, and Truchuela in others: for there was no other fish to be had. "A number of troutlings," answered the knight, "will please me as much as one trout: for, in my opinion, eight single rials are equivalent to one piece of eight; besides, those troutlings may be as much preferable to trouts, as veal is to beef, or lamb to mutton †: be that as it will, let the fish be immediately produced; for, the toil and burthen of arms are not to be borne without satisfying the cravings of the stomach." A table being therefore covered at the inn-door, for the benefit of the cool air, mine host brought out a cut of Baccalao, wretchedly watered, and villainously cooked, with a loaf as black and greasy as his guest's own armour: but, his manner of eating afforded infinite subject for mirth; for, his head being inclosed in his helmet, and the beaver lifted up, his own hands could be of no service in reaching the food to his mouth; and therefore, one of the ladies undertook to perform that office; but, they found it impossible to convey drink in the same manner; and our hero must have made an uncomfortable meal, if the landlord had not bored a cane, and putting one end of it in his mouth, poured some wine into the other; an operation he endured with patience, rather than suffer the ribbons of his helmet to be destroyed.

While they were thus employed, a sow-gelder happened to arrive at the inn, and winding three or four blasts with his horn, confirmed Don Quixote in his opinion, that

---

* This circumstance of the ladies disarming the knight, is exactly conformable to the practice of chivalry: tho' his refusing to lay aside his helmet is no great argument of his courtesy or attachment to the laws and customs of his profession; for, among knights, it was looked upon as an indispensable mark of respect, to appear without the helmet in church, and in presence of ladies, or respectable personages, and indeed, in those iron times, this was considered as a necessary mark and proof of peaceable intention; hence we derive the custom of uncovering the head in salutation.[6]
† In the original, or kid to he-goat.[8]

he sat in some stately castle, entertained with music, during his repast, which, consisting of delicate troutling and bread of the finest flour, was served up, not by a brace of harlots, and a thievish innkeeper, but by the fair hands of two beautiful ladies, and the courteous governor of the place. This conceit justified his undertaking, and rendered him very happy in the success of his first sally; but, he was mortified when he recollected that he was not as yet knighted; because he thought he could not lawfully atchieve any adventure without having been first invested with that honourable order.

## CHAPTER III.

### The diverting expedient Don Quixote falls upon, in order to be knighted.

Harrassed by this reflection, he abridged his sorry meal, and called for the landlord, with whom having shut himself up in the stable, he fell upon his knees, and addressed the supposed constable in these words: "Never will I rise from this suppliant posture, thrice valiant knight, until your courtesy shall grant the boon I mean to beg; a boon! that will not only redound to your particular praise, but also to the inestimable benefit of mankind in general *." The innkeeper hearing such discourse proceed from the mouth of his guest, who kneeled before him, was astonished; and gazed at our hero, without knowing what to say or do: at length, however, he intreated him to rise; but this request was absolutely refused, until he assured him that his boon should be granted. "Signor," said Don Quixote, "I could expect no less from the courtesy of your magnificence: I will now therefore tell you, that the boon which I have begged, and obtained from your generosity, is, that you will, to-morrow morning, vouchsafe to confer upon me the order of knighthood. This night will I watch my arms in the chapel of your castle; that the morning, as I said, may fulfil my eager desire, and enable me, as I ought, to traverse the four corners of the world, in search of adventures for the relief of the distressed, according to the duty and office of chivalry, and of those knights-errant, in imitation of whom, my genius is strongly addicted to such atchievements."

The landlord, who, as we have already observed, was a sort of a wag, and had from the beginning suspected that his lodger's brain was none of the soundest, having heard him to an end, no longer entertained any doubts about the matter, and, in order to regale himself and the rest of his guests with a dish of mirth, resolved to humour him in his extravagance. With this view, he told him, that nothing could be more just and reasonable than his request, his conceptions being extremely well suited, and natural to such a peerless knight as his commanding presence and gallant demeanour demonstrated him to

---

* This request was a little premature, inasmuch as the practice of chivalry did not authorise the suppliant to ask a boon of his godfather, until he was dubbed, and then he had a right to demand it.[1]

be: that he himself had, in his youth, exercised the honourable profession of errantry, strolling from place to place, in quest of adventures, in the course of which he did not fail to visit the suburbs of Malaga, the isles of Riaran, the booths of Seville, the market-place of Segovia, the olive-gardens of Valencia, the little tower of Grenada, the bay of St. Lucar, the spout of * Cordova, the public-houses of Toledo, and many other places, in which he had exercised the dexterity of his hands as well as the lightness of his heels, doing infinite mischief, courting widows without number, debauching damsels, ruining heirs, and in short, making himself known at the bar of every tribunal in Spain: that, at length, he had retired to this castle, where he lived on his own means, together with those of other people; accommodating knights-errant of every quality and degree, solely on account of the affection he bore to them, and to the coin which they parted with in return for his hospitality. He moreover informed him, that there was no chapel in the castle at present, where he could watch his armour, it having been demolished in order to be rebuilt; but that, in case of necessity, as he very well knew, he might choose any other place; that the court-yard of the castle would very well serve the purpose, where, when the knight should have watched all night, he, the host, would in the morning, with God's permission, perform all the other ceremonies required, and create him not only a knight, but such an one as should not have his fellow in the whole universe.

He then asked, if he carried any money about with him, and the knight replied, that he had not a souse; for he had never read in the history of knights-errant, that they had ever troubled themselves with any such incumbrance. The innkeeper assured him that he was very much mistaken; for, that though no such circumstance was to be found in those histories, the authors having thought it superfluous to mention things that were so plainly necessary as money and clean shirts, it was not to be supposed that their heroes travelled without supplies of both: he might, therefore, take it for granted and uncontrovertible, that all those knights, whose actions are so voluminously recorded, never rode without their purses well-lined in cases of emergency †; not forgetting to carry a stock of linnen, with a small box of ointment to cure the wounds they might receive in the course of their adventures; for, it was not to be imagined, that any other relief was to be had every time they should have occasion to fight, and be wounded in fields and desarts; unless they were befriended by some sage enchanter, who would assist them by transporting through the air, in a cloud, some damsel, or dwarf, with a cordial of such virtue, that one drop of it would instantly cure them of their bruises and wounds, and make them as sound as if no such mischance had happened: but, the knights of former ages, who had no such assistance to depend upon, laid it down as a constant maxim, to order their squires to provide themselves with money and other nec-

---

* Literally the colt of Cordova, because the water gushes out of a fountain, resembling an horse's mouth. These are places of resort frequented by thieves and sharpers.[2]

† Here the landlord was more selfish than observant of the customs of chivalry; for, knights were actually exempted from all expence whatever; except when damages were awarded against them in a court of justice, and in that case they paid for their rank. This they looked upon as a mark of their preheminence; in consequence of which, at the siege of *Dun le Roy*, in the year 1411, each knight was ordered to carry eight fascines, while the squire was quit for half the number.[3]

essaries, such as ointment and lint for immediate application: and when the knight happened to be without a squire, which was very seldom the case, he himself kept them in very small bags, that hung scarce perceptible at his horse's rump, as if it were a treasure of much greater importance. Though indeed, except upon such an occasion, that of carrying bags was not much for the honour of knight-errantry; for which reason, he advised Don Quixote, and now that he was on the brink of being his godson, he might command him, never thenceforward to travel without money, and those other indispensable necessaries, with which he should provide himself as soon as possible; and then he would, when he least thought of it, find his account in having made such provision.

The knight promised to follow his advice with all deference and punctuality; and thereupon, received orders to watch his armour in a large court on one side of the inn, where, having gathered the several pieces on a heap, he placed them in a cistern that belonged to the well; then bracing on his target and grasping his lance, he walked with courteous demeanour backward and forward before the cistern, beginning this knightly exercise as soon as it was dark *. The roguish landlord having informed every lodger in his house, of our hero's frenzy, the watching of his armour, and his expectation of being dubbed a knight; they were astonished at such a peculiar strain of madness, and going out to observe him at a distance, beheld him with silent gesture sometimes stalking along, sometimes leaning on his spear, with his eyes fixed upon his armour, for a considerable space of time. Though it was now night, the moon shone with such splendour as might even vie with the source from which she derived her brightness; so that every motion of our noviciate was distinctly perceived by all present. At this instant, a carrier who lodged in the inn, took it in his head to water his mules, and it being necessary for this purpose to clear the cistern, he went to lift off Don Quixote's armour; when a loud voice accosted in these words: "O thou! whosoever thou art, bold and insolent knight, who presumest to touch the armour of the most valiant errant that ever girded himself with cold iron, consider what thou art about to attempt, and touch it not, unless thou art desirous of yielding thy life as the price of thy temerity."

The carrier, far from regarding these threats, which had he regarded his own carcase he would not have despised, laid hold on the sacred deposit, and threw it piecemeal into the yard with all his might. Don Quixote no sooner beheld this profanation, than lifting up his eyes to heaven, and addressing himself, in all likelihood, to his mistress Dulcinea, he said: "Grant me thy assistance, dear lady of my heart! in this insult offered to thy lowly vassal, and let me not be deprived of thy favourable protection in this my first perilous atchievement." Having uttered this, and some other ejaculations, he quitted his target, and raising his lance with both hands, bestowed it with such good will upon the carrier's head, that he fell prostrate on the ground, so effectually mauled, that, had the blow been repeated, there would have been no occasion to call a surgeon. This exploit

---

* This custom of watching armour in church or chapel, was a religious duty imposed upon knights, who used to consume the whole night in prayer to some saint, whom they chose as their patron; and this exercise of devotion was performed on the night preceding the said saint's day. The same ceremony was observed by those who were sentenced to the combat-proof.[4]

being performed, he replaced his armour, and returned to his walk, which he continued with his former composure.

It was not long before another carrier, not knowing what had happened to his companion, who still lay without sense or motion, arrived with the same intention of watering his mules, and went straight up to the cistern, in order to remove the armour; when Don Quixote, without speaking a syllable, or asking leave of any living soul, once more quitted his target, and lifting up his lance, made another experiment of its hardness upon the pate of the second carrier, which failed in the application, giving way in four different places. At the noise of this encounter, every body in the house, innkeeper and all, came running to the field, at sight of whom Don Quixote, snatching up his target and drawing his sword, pronounced aloud, "O lady! of transcendent beauty, the force and vigour of my enfeebled heart; now, if ever, is the time for thee to turn thy princely eyes on this thy caitif knight, who is on the eve of so mighty an adventure." So saying, he seemed to have acquired such courage, that had he been assaulted by all the carriers in the universe, he would not have retreated one step.

The companions of the wounded, seeing how their friends had been handled, began, at a distance, to discharge a shower of stones upon the knight, who, as well as he could, sheltered himself under his shield, not daring to leave the cistern, lest some mischance should happen to his armour. The innkeeper called aloud, entreating them to leave off, for, as he had told them before, the man being mad, would be acquitted on account of his lunacy, even tho' he should put every soul of them to death. At the same time Don Quixote, in a voice louder still, upbraided them as cowardly traitors, and called the constable of the castle a worthless and base-born knight, for allowing his guest to be treated in such an inhospitable manner; swearing, that if he had received the honour of knighthood, he would make him repent his discourteous behaviour. "But, as for you," said he, "ye vile, ill-mannered scum, ye are beneath my notice. Discharge, approach, come forward, and annoy me as much as you can, you shall soon see what reward you will receive for your insolent extravagance." These words delivered in a bold and resolute tone, struck terror into the hearts of the assailants, who, partly for this menace, and partly on account of the landlord's persuasion, gave over their attack, while he, on his side, allowed the wounded to retire, and returned to his watch, with his former ease and tranquillity.

These pranks of the knight were not at all to the liking of the landlord, who resolved to abridge the ceremony, and bestow this unlucky order of knighthood immediately, before any other mischief should happen. Approaching him therefore, he disclaimed the insolence with which his guest had been treated by those saucy plebeians, without his knowledge or consent; and observed that they had been justly chastised for their impudence: that, as he had told him before, there was no chapel in the castle, nor indeed, for what was to be done, was it at all necessary; nothing of the ceremony now remaining unperformed, except the cuff on the neck, and the thwack on the shoulders, as they are prescribed in the ceremonial of the order; and that this part might be executed in the middle of a field: he assured him also, that he had punctually complied with every thing that regarded the watching of his armour, which might have been finished in two hours, tho'

he had already remained double the time on that duty. Don Quixote believing every syllable that he spoke, said, he was ready to obey him in all things, and besought him to conclude the matter as soon as possible; for, in case he should be attacked again, after having been knighted, he would not leave a soul alive in the castle, except those whom he should spare at his request.

The constable, alarmed at this declaration, immediately brought out his day-book, in which he kept an account of the barley and straw that was expended for the use of the carriers, and attended by a boy with a candle's end in his hand, together with the two ladies before mentioned, came to the place where Don Quixote stood: then ordering him to kneel before him, mumbled in his manual, as if he had been putting up some very devout petition; in the midst of which, he lifted up his hand, and gave him an hearty thump on the neck; then, with the flat of his own sword, bestowed an handsome application across his shoulders, muttering all the time between his teeth, as if he had been employed in some fervent ejaculation *. This article being fulfilled, he commanded one of the ladies to gird on his sword, an office she performed with great dexterity and discretion, of which there was no small need to restrain her laughter at each particular of this strange ceremony: but, the effects they had already seen of the knight's disposition, kept their mirth effectually under the rein.

When this good lady had girded on his sword, "Heaven preserve your worship! adventurous knight," said she, "and make you fortunate in all your encounters." Don Quixote then begged to know her name, that he might thenceforward understand to whom he was obliged for the favour he had received at her hands, and to whom he might ascribe some part of the honour he should acquire by the valour of his invincible arm. She answered with great humility, that her name was Tolosa, daughter of an honest botcher in Toledo, who lived in one of the stalls of Sancho Minaya; that she should always be at his service, and acknowledge him for her lord and master. The knight professed himself extremely obliged to her for her love; and begged she would, for the future, dignify her name by calling herself Donna Tolosa. This request she promised faithfully to comply with; and a dialogue of the same kind passed between him and the other lady who buckled on his spur; when he asked her name, she told him it was Mollinera; and that her father was an honourable miller of Antequera. Don Quixote entreated her also, to ennoble her name with the same title of Donna, loaded her with thanks, and made a tender of his service. These hitherto unseen ceremonies being dispatched, as it were, with post haste, Don Quixote, impatient to see himself on horseback, in quest of adventures, saddled and mounted Rozinante forthwith, and embracing his host, uttered such a strange rhapsody of thanks for his having dubbed him knight, that it is impossible to rehearse the compliment. The landlord, in order to get rid of him the sooner, answered in terms no less eloquent, tho' something more laconic, and let him march off in happy hour, without demanding one farthing for his lodging.

---

* The slap on the shoulders, and the box on the ear being bestowed, the godfather pronounced, "In the name of God, St. Michael and St. George, I dub thee knight; be worthy, bold and loyal."[5]

*F. Hayman inv. et del.*                                    *C. Grignion sculp.*

Don Quixote Knighted by the Innkeeper.

## CHAPTER IV.

### Of what befel our knight, when he sallied from the inn.

It was early in the morning, when Don Quixote sallied from the inn, so well satisfied, so sprightly and so glad to see himself invested with the order of knighthood, that the very girths of his horse vibrated with joy: but, remembring his landlord's advice with regard to the necessaries he ought to carry along with him, in particular, the money and clean shirts; he resolved to return to his own house, and furnish himself not only with these, but also with a squire. For this office he fixed, in his own mind, upon a poor ploughman who lived in his neighbourhood, maintaining a family of children by his labour; a person in all respects qualified for the lower services of chivalry. With this view, he steered his course homeward; and Rozinante, as if he had guessed the knight's intention, began to move with such alacrity and nimbleness, that his hoofs scarce seemed to touch the ground.

He had not travelled far, when from the thickest part of a wood that grew on his right hand, his ear was saluted with shrill repeated cries, which seemed to issue from the mouth of some creature in grievous distress. No sooner did our hero hear this lamentation, than he exclaimed, "Heaven be praised for the favour with which it now indulges me, in giving me an opportunity so soon of fulfilling the duties of my profession, and reaping the fruit of my laudable intention! These cries doubtless proceed from some miserable male, or female, who stands in need of my immediate aid and protection": Then turning Rozinante, he rode towards the place whence the complaint seemed to come, and having entered the wood a few paces, he found a mare tied to one oak, and a lad about fifteen naked from the waist upwards, made fast to another. This was he who screamed so piteously, and indeed not without reason, for, a sturdy peasant was employed in making applications to his carcase with a leathern strap, accompanying each stripe with a word of reproof and advice.[1] Above all things, laying upon him strong injunctions, to use his tongue less, and his eyes more: the young fellow replied, with great fervency, "I will never do so again, master, so help me God! I won't do so any more; but, for the future, take more care, and use more dispatch."

Don Quixote observing what passed, pronounced aloud, with great indignation: "Discourteous knight, it ill becomes thee to attack one who cannot defend himself: mount thy steed, couch thy lance, (for there was actually a lance leaning against the tree, to which the mare was tied) and I will make thee sensible of the cowardice of the action in which thou art now engaged." The peasant seeing this strange figure, buckled in armour, and brandishing a lance over his head, was mortally afraid, and with great humility replied: "Sir knight, this lad whom I am chastising, is my own servant, hired to keep a flock of sheep, which feed in these fields; but, he is so negligent, that every day I lose one of the number, and because I punish him for his carelessness, or knavery, he says that I scourge him out of avarice, rather than pay him his wages: tho', upon my conscience, and as I shall answer to God, he tells a lie." "How! a lie, before me, base caitif,"

cried Don Quixote; "by the sun that enlightens this globe, I have a good mind to thrust this lance thro' thy body! pay the young man his wages strait without reply, or by the power that rules us! I will finish and annihilate thee in an instant: unbind him, therefore, without hesitation."

The countryman hung his head, and without speaking a syllable, untyed his man; who, being asked by the knight, how much money was due to him, said his master owed him for three quarters, at the rate of six rials a month. His deliverer having cast it up, found that the whole amounted to sixty-three rials, and ordered the peasant to disburse them instantly, unless he had a-mind to perish under his hands. The affrighted farmer affirmed, by the grievous situation in which he was, and the oath he had already taken, tho', by the bye, he had taken no oath at all, that the sum did not amount to so much; for, that he was to discount and allow for three pair of shoes he had received, and a rial for two bleedings while he was sick. "Granting that to be true," replied Don Quixote, "the shoes and the bleeding shall stand for the stripes you have given him without cause; for, if he has wore out the leather of the shoes that you paid for, you have made as free with the leather of his carcase; and if the barber let out his blood when he was sick, you have blooded him when he was well; he therefore stands acquitted of these debts." "The misfortune, Sir knight," said the peasant, "is this: I have not coin about me; but, if Andrew will go home to my house, I will pay him honestly in ready money." "Go with you," cried the lad, "the devil fetch me, if I do! no, no, master, I must not think of that; were I to go home with him alone, he would flea me like another St. Bartholomew." "He won't do so," replied the knight, "but shew more regard to my commands; and if he will swear to me by the laws of that order of knighthood which he has received, that he will pay you your wages, I will set him free, and warrant the payment." "Lord how your worship talks!" said the boy; "this master of mine is no gentleman, nor has he received any order of knighthood, but is known by the name of rich John Haldudo, and lives in the neighbourhood of Quintanar." "No matter," replied Don Quixote, "there may be knights among the Haldudos, especially as every one is the son of his own works." "True," said Andrew; "but what works is my master the son of, since he refuses to pay me for my labour, and the sweat of my brows?" "I don't refuse, honest Andrew," answered the peasant; "thou wilt do me a pleasure in going home with me; and I swear by all the honours of knighthood in the universe, that I will pay thee thy wages, as I said before, in ready money; nay, you shall have it perfumed into the bargain." "Thank you for your perfumes," said the knight, "pay him in lawful coin, and I shall be satisfied; and be sure you fulfil the oath you have taken; for, by the same obligation, I swear, that in case you fail, I will return to chastise you, and ferret you out, even tho' you should be more concealed than a lizard. If you would understand, who it is that lays such commands upon you, that you may find yourself under a necessity of performing them with reverence and awe, know, that I am the valiant Don Quixote de la Mancha, the redresser of wrongs, and scourge of injustice: so farewell, remember not to belie your promise and oath, on pain of the penalty prescribed." With these words, he clapped spurs to Rozinante, and was out of sight in a moment.

The countryman followed him with his eyes, till he saw him quite clear of the wood; then turning to Andrew, said, "Come hither, child, I must pay what I owe you, accord-

ing to the orders of that redresser of wrongs." "And adad," said Andrew, "you had best not neglect these orders of that worthy knight, who (blessings on his heart) is equally valiant and upright; for odds-bobs, if you do not pay me, he will return, and be as good as his word." "In faith, I am of the same opinion," replied the peasant; "but, out of my infinite regard for you, I am desirous of increasing the debt, that the payment may be doubled." So saying, he laid hold of his arm, and tying him again to the tree, flogged him so severely, that he had like to have died on the spot. "Now is the time, Mr. Andrew," said the executioner, "to call upon the redresser of grievances, who will find it difficult to re-dress this, which by the bye I am loth to finish, being very much inclined to justify your fear of being flead alive." At length, however, he unbound, and left him at liberty to find out his judge, who was to execute the sentence he had pronounced. Andrew sneaked off, not extremely well satisfied; on the contrary, vowing to go in quest of the valiant Don Quixote de la Mancha, and inform him punctually of every thing that had happened, an account which would certainly induce him to pay the countryman sevenfold.

In spite of this consolation, however, he departed blubbering with pain, while his master remained weeping with laughter. And thus was the grievance redressed by the valiant Don Quixote, who transported with the success, and the happy and sublime be-ginning which he imagined his chivalry had been favoured with, jogged on towards his own village, with infinite self-satisfaction, pronouncing with a low voice; "O Dulcinea del Tobosa, fairest among the fair! well may'st thou be counted the most fortunate beauty upon earth, seeing it is thy fate, to keep in subjection, and wholly resigned to thy will and pleasure, such a daring and renowned knight as Don Quixote de la Man-cha now is, and always will remain. He who, as all the world knows, but yesterday re-ceived the honour of knighthood, and has this day redressed the greatest wrong and grievance that ever injustice hatched, and cruelty committed! To-day he wrested the lash from the hand of the merciless enemy, who so unjustly scourged the body of that tender infant!" Having uttered this exclamation, he found himself in a road that divided into four paths, and strait his imagination suggested those cross-ways that were wont to perplex knights-errant in their choice; in imitation of whom, he paused a little, and af-ter mature deliberation, threw the reins on Rozinante's neck, leaving the decision to him, who following his first intention, took the path that led directly to his own stable.

Having travelled about two miles farther, Don Quixote descried a number of people, who, as was afterwards known, were six merchants of Toledo going to buy silks at Mur-cia, and who travelled with umbrelloes, attended by four servants on horseback, and three mule-drivers on foot. Don Quixote no sooner perceived them at a distance, than he imagined them to be some new adventure, and, in order to imitate as much as in him lay, those scenes he had read in his books of chivalry, he thought this was an occasion ex-pressly ordained for him to execute his purposed atchievement.

He therefore, with gallant and resolute deportment, seated himself firmly in his stir-rups, grasped his lance, braced on his target, and posting himself in the middle of the road, waited the arrival of those knights-errant, for such he judged them to be. When they were near enough to hear him, he pronounced in a loud and arrogant tone; "Let the whole universe cease to move, if the whole universe refuses to confess, that there is

not in the whole universe a more beautiful damsel than the peerless Dulcinea del To-
boso, the high and mighty empress of La Mancha."

The merchants hearing this declaration, and seeing the strange figure from which it
proceeded, were alarmed at both, and halting immediately, at a distance reconnoitred
the madness of the author. Curious, however, to know the meaning of that confession
which he exacted, one of them, who was a sort of a wag, tho' at the same time a man of
prudence and discretion, accosted him thus: "Sir knight, as we have not the honour to
know who this worthy lady is, be so good as to produce her; and if we find her so beau-
tiful as you proclaim her to be, we will gladly, and without any sort of reward, confess
the truth, according to your desire." "If I produce her," replied Don Quixote, "what is
the mighty merit of your confessing such a notorious truth? The importance of my de-
mand consists on your believing, acknowledging, affirming upon oath, and defending
her beauty before you have seen it. And this ye shall do, ye insolent and uncivil race, or
engage with me in battle forthwith. Come on then, one by one, according to the laws of
chivalry, or all together, as the treacherous custom is among such wretches as you; here
I expect you with full hope and confidence in the justice of my cause." "Sir knight,"
replied the merchant, "I humbly beg, in the name of all these princes here present, that
your worship will not oblige us to burden our consciences, by giving testimony to a
thing that we have neither seen nor heard, especially as it tends to the prejudice of the
queens and princesses of Alcarria and Estremadura: but, if your worship will be pleased
to shew us any sort of a picture of this lady, tho' it be no bigger than a grain of wheat, so
as we can judge of the clue by the thread, we will be satisfied with this sample, and you
shall be obeyed to your heart's content: for, I believe we are already so prepossessed in
her favour, that tho' the portrait should represent her squinting with one eye, and dis-
tilling vermilion and brimstone with the other, we will, notwithstanding, in compliance
to your worship, say what you desire in her favour." "Her eyes, infamous wretch!"
replied Don Quixote in a rage, "distil not such productions, but teem with amber and
rich perfume: neither is there any defect in her sight, or in her body, which is more strait
than a Guadarrama-spindle: but, you shall suffer for the licentious blasphemy you have
uttered against the unparallelled beauty of my sovereign mistress." So saying, he
couched his lance, and attacked the spokesman with such rage and fury, that, had not
Rozinante luckily stumbled and fallen in the midst of his career, the merchant would
have had no cause to rejoice in his rashness; but when the unhappy steed fell to the
ground, the rider was thrown over his head, and pitched at a good distance upon the
field, where he found all his endeavours to get up again ineffectual, so much was he en-
cumbered with his lance, target, helmet and spurs, together with the weight of his an-
cient armour.

While he thus struggled, but in vain, to rise, he bellowed forth, "Fly not, ye cowardly
crew; tarry a little, ye base caitifs; not thro' any fault of my own, but of my horse, am I
thus discomfited." One of the mule-drivers, who seems not to have been of a very milky
disposition, could not bear this arrogant language of the poor overthrown knight, with-
out making a reply upon his ribs. Going up to him, therefore, he laid hold on his lance,
and breaking it, began to thresh him so severely, that, in spite of the resistance of his ar-

mour, he was almost beaten into mummy, and tho' the fellow's master called to him to forbear, he was so incensed, that he could not leave off the game, until he had exhausted the whole of his choler. Gathering the other pieces of the lance, he reduced them all to shivers, one after another, on the miserable carcase of the Don, who, notwithstanding this storm of blows which descended on him, never closed his mouth, but continued threatning heaven and earth, and those banditti, for such he took the merchants to be.

The driver was tired at length of his exercise, and his masters pursued their journey, carrying with them sufficient food for conversation about this poor battered knight, who no sooner found himself alone, than he made another effort to rise; but, if he found this design impracticable when he was safe and sound, much less could he accomplish it now that he was disabled, and as it were wrought into a paste. He did not, however, look upon himself as unhappy, because this misfortune was, in his opinion, peculiar to knights-errant, and that he was not able to rise on account of the innumerable bruises he had received, he ascribed entirely to the fault of his horse.

## CHAPTER V.

### In which the story of our knight's misfortune is continued.

Finding it therefore impossible to move, he was fain to have recourse to his usual remedy, which was to amuse his imagination with some passages of the books he had read; and his madness immediately recalled to his memory that of Valdovinos and the marquis of Mantua, when Carloto left him wounded on the mountain: a piece of history that every boy knows, that every young man is acquainted with, and which is celebrated, nay more, believed by old age itself, though it be as apocryphal as the miracles of Mahomet; nevertheless, it occurred to him, as an occasion expresly adapted to his present situation. Therefore, with marks of extreme affliction, he began to roll about upon the ground, and with a languid voice, exclaim, in the words of the wounded knight of the wood,

> "Where art thou, lady of my heart,
> Regardless of my misery?
> Thou little know'st thy lover's smart,
> Or faithless art, and false, pardie!"

In this manner he went on repeating the romance, until he came to these lines:

> "O noble prince of Mantuan plains,
> My carnal kinsman, and my lord!"

Before he could repeat the whole couplet, a peasant who was a neighbour of his own, and lived in the same village, chanced to pass, in his way from the mill where he had been

with a load of wheat. This honest countryman seeing a man lying stretched upon the ground, came up, and asked him who he was, and the reason of his lamenting so piteously? Don Quixote doubtless believed, that this was his uncle, the marquis of Mantua, and made no other reply but the continuation of his romance, in which he gave an account of his own misfortune, occasioned by the amour betwixt his wife and the emperor's son, exactly as it is related in the book. The peasant, astonished at such a rhapsody, took off his beaver, which had been beaten to pieces by the mule-driver, and wiping his face, which was covered with dust, immediately knew the unfortunate knight. "Signor Quixada," said he, (for so he was called before he had lost his senses, and was transformed from a sober country-gentleman into a knight-errant) "who has left your worship in such a woeful condition!" But he, without minding the question that was put to him, proceeded as before, with his romance; which the honest man perceiving, went to work, and took off his back and breast-plates, to see if he had received any wound, but, he could perceive neither blood, nor scar upon his body. He then raised him upon his legs, and with infinite difficulty mounted him upon his own beast, which appeared to him a safer carriage than the knight's steed.

Having gathered up his armour, even to the splinters of the lance, he tied them upon Rozinante, and taking hold of the reins, together with the halter of his own ass, jogged on towards the village, not a little concerned to hear the mad exclamations of Don Quixote, who did not find himself extremely easy, for, he was so battered and bruised, that he could not sit upright upon the beast; but, from time to time vented such dismal groans, as obliged the peasant to ask again what was the matter with him? Indeed one would have thought, that the devil had assisted his memory in supplying him with tales accommodated to the circumstances of his own situation. For at that instant, forgetting Valdovinos, he recollected the story of Abindar-raez, the Moor, whom Rodrigo de Narvaez, governor of Antequera, took prisoner, and carried into captivity to the place of his residence: so that, when the countryman repeated his desire of knowing where he had been, and what was the matter with him, he answered to the purpose; nay, indeed in the very words used by the captive Abencerraje to the said Rodrigo de Narvaez, as may be seen in the Diana of George Monte-major, which he had read; and so well adapted for his purpose, that the countryman, hearing such a composition of folly, wished them both at the devil.

It was then he discovered, that his neighbour was mad; and therefore made all the haste he could to the village, that he might be the sooner rid of his uneasiness at the unaccountable harangue of Don Quixote, who had no sooner finished this exclamation, than he accosted his conductor in these words: "Know then, valiant Don Rodrigo de Narvaez, that this same beautiful Xarifa, whom I have mentioned, is no other than the fair Dulcinea del Toboso, for whom I have performed, undertake, and will atchieve the most renowned exploits, that ever were, are, or will be seen on earth." To this address the countryman replied with great simplicity: "How your worship talks! As I am a sinner, I am neither Don Rodrigo de Narvaez, nor the marquis of Mantua, but Pedro Alonzo, your neighbour; nor is your worship either Valdovinos, or Abindarraez, but the worthy gentleman, signor Quixada." "I know very well, who I am," replied Don Quixote, "and that it is possible for me to be not only those whom I have mentioned, but also the whole twelve peers of France, and even the nine worthies, seeing that my

atchievements will excel, not only those of each of them singly, but even the exploits of them all joined together."

Discoursing in this manner, they arrived at the village about twilight; but the peasant staid till it was quite dark, that the poor rib-roasted knight might not be seen in such a woeful condition. Then he conducted Don Quixote to his own house, which was all in confusion. When he arrived, the curate, and the barber of the village, two of his best friends and companions, were present, and his housekeeper was just saying, with a woeful countenance; "Mr. Licentiate Pero Perez" (that was the curate's name,) "some misfortune must certainly have happened to my master *; for six days, both he and his horse, together with the target, lance, and armour, have been missing; as I am a sinner, it is just come into my head, and it is certainly as true as that every one is born to die, those hellish books of knight-errantry, which he used to read with so much pleasure, have turned his brain: for, now I remember to have heard him say to himself more than once, that he longed to be a knight-errant, and stroll about in quest of adventures. May the Devil and Barrabas lay hold of such legends, which have perverted one of the soundest understandings in all La Mancha."

To this remark the niece assented, saying, "Moreover, you must know, Mr. Nicolas," (this was the name of the barber,) "my uncle would frequently, after having been reading in these profane books of misadventures, for two whole days and nights together, start up, throw the book upon the ground, and, drawing his sword, fence with the walls, till he was quite fatigued; then affirm, that he had killed four giants as big as steeples; and swear that the sweat of his brows, occasioned by this violent exercise, was the blood of the wounds he had received in battle: then he would drink off a large pitcher of cold water, and remain quiet and refreshed, saying, that the water was a most precious beverage, with which he was supplied by the sage Isquise, a mighty enchanter and friend of his: but I take the whole blame to myself, for not having informed your worship of my dear uncle's extravagances, that some remedy might have been applied, before they had proceeded to such excess; and that you might have burnt all those excommunicated books, which deserve the fire as much as if they were crammed with heresy."

"I am of the same opinion," said the curate, "and assure you, before another day shall pass, they shall undergo a severe trial, and be condemned to the flames, that they may not induce other readers to follow the same path, which I am afraid, my good friend has taken." Every syllable of this conversation was overheard by Don Quixote and his guide, which last had now no longer any doubt about his neighbour's infirmity, and therefore pronounced with a loud voice, "Open your gates to the valiant Valdovinos, and the great marquis of Mantua, who comes home wounded from the field, together with the Moor Abindarraez, who drags in captivity the valiant Rodrigo de Narvaez, governor of Antequera."

Alarmed at these words, they came all to the door, and perceiving who it was, the barber and curate went to receive their friend, and the women ran to embrace their master and kinsman, who, though he had not as yet alighted, for indeed it was not in his power,

---

* The author seems to have committed a small oversight in this paragraph; for the knight had not been gone above two days and one night, which he spent in watching his armour.

Don Quixote Brought Home by a Countryman on His Ass.

proclaimed aloud, "Let the whole world take notice, that the wounds I have received were owing to the fault of my horse alone; carry me therefore to bed, and send, if possible, for the sage * Urganda, to search and cure them." "See now in an evil hour," cried the housekeeper, hearing these words, "if I did not truly foretel, of what leg my master was lame? Your worship shall understand in good time, that without the assistance of that same Urganda, we know how to cure the hurts you have received; and cursed, I say, nay, a hundred and a hundred times cursed be those books of chivalry, which have so disordered your honour's brain." Having carried him to his bed, they began to search for his wounds; but could find none: and he told them that his whole body was one continued bruise, occasioned by the fall of his horse Rozinante, during his engagement with ten of the most insolent and outrageous giants, that ever appeared upon the face of the earth. "Ah, hah!" cried the curate, "have we got giants too in the dance! Now, by the faith of my function, I will reduce them all to ashes before to-morrow night."

A thousand questions did they ask of the knight, who made no other answer, but desired them to bring him some food, and leave him to his repose, which indeed was what he had most occasion for. They complied with his request, and the curate informed himself at large, of the manner in which he had been found by the countryman, who gave him full satisfaction in that particular, and repeated all the nonsense he had uttered, when he first found him; as well as what he afterwards spoke in their way home. This information confirmed the licentiate in his resolution, which was executed next day, when he brought his friend master Nicolas the barber along with him, to Don Quixote's house.

## CHAPTER VI.

### Of the diverting and minute scrutiny performed by the curate and the barber, in the library of our sagacious hero.

While the knight was asleep, his friends came, and demanded of his niece the key of the closet in which those books, the authors of his misfortune, were kept, and she delivering it with great chearfulness, they went into it in a body, house-keeper and all, and found upwards of an hundred volumes, great and small, extremely well bound; which were no sooner perceived by the governante, than she ran out with great eager-

---

* The name of a good-natured enchantress in Amadis de Gaul. During the age of knight-errantry, it was usual for ladies to study the art of surgery, in order to dress the wounds of those knights who were their servants. One of the heroines of Perceforest says to Norgal, "Fair nephew, methinks your arm is not at ease." "In faith, dear lady," answered Norgal, "you are in the right, and I beseech you to take it under your care." Then she called her daughter Helen, who entertained her cousin with good chear, and afterwards reduced his arm which was dislocated.[1]

ness, and immediately returned with a porringer of holy water, and a sprig of hysop, saying: "Here, master licentiate, pray take and sprinkle the closet, lest some one of the many enchanters contained in these books, should exercise his art upon us, as a punishment for our burning, and banishing them from the face of the earth."

The licentiate, smiling at the old housekeeper's simplicity, desired the barber to hand him the books, one by one, that he might see of what subjects they treated, because they might possibly find some that did not deserve to be purged by fire. "There is not one of them," replied the niece, "which deserves the least mercy, for they are all full of mischief and deceit. You had better, therefore, throw them out of the window into the court-yard, and there set fire to them, in a heap: or, let them be carried into the back-yard, where the bonfire may be made, and the smoke will offend no body." The housekeeper assented to this proposal, so eager were they both to destroy those innocents; but, the curate would by no means encourage such barbarity, without reading first, if possible, the title-pages.

The first that master Nicolas delivered into his hand, were the four volumes of Amadis de Gaul. "There is," said the good man, "something mysterious in this circumstance; for, as I have heard, that was the first book of chivalry printed in Spain, from which all the rest have derived their origin and plan; and therefore, in my opinion, we ought to condemn him to the fire, without hesitation, as the law-giver of such a pernicious sect." "By no means," cried the barber, "for I have also heard, that this is the best book of the kind that was ever composed, and therefore ought to be pardoned, as an original and model in its way." "Right," said the curate, "and for that reason, he shall be spared for the present. Let us see that author, who stands next to him." "This," says the barber, "contains the atchievements of Esplandian, the lawful son of Amadis de Gaul." "Truly then," said the curate, "the virtues of the father shall not avail the son: here mistress housekeeper, open that window, and toss him into the yard, where he shall serve as a foundation for the bonfire, we intend to make."

This task the housekeeper performed with infinite satisfaction, and the worthy Esplandian took his flight into the yard, to wait in patience for the fire, with which he was threatned. "Proceed," cried the curate. "This that comes next," said the barber, "is Amadis of Greece; and I believe all the authors on this shelf are of the same family." "To the yard then, with all of them," replied the curate; "for, rather than not burn queen Pintiquiniestra, and the shepherd Darinel with his Eclogues, together with the unintelligible and bedevilled discourses of his author, I would even consume the father who begat me, should he appear in the figure of a knight-errant." "I am of your opinion," said the barber. "And I," cried the niece. "Since that is the case," said the housekeeper, "to the yard with them immediately." Accordingly they delivered a number into her hands, and she out of tenderness for the stair-case, sent them all out of the window.

"Who may that tun-like author be?" said the curate. "This here," answered the barber, "is Don Olivante de Laura." "The very same," replied the curate, "who composed the Garden of Flowers, and truly it is hard to determine, which of his two books is the most true, or rather which of them is least false; all that I know is, that he shall go to the pile for his arrogance and folly." "He that follows," says the barber, "is Florismarte of Hircania." "What! Signor Florismarte?" replied the curate: "in faith then he must pre-

pare for his fate; notwithstanding his surprizing birth, and mighty adventures, and the unparalelled stiffness and sterility of his stile. Down with him, mistress housekeeper, and take this other along with you also." "With all my heart, dear sir," replied the governante, who executed his commands with vast alacrity.

"He that comes next," said the barber, "is the knight Platir." "That is an old book," said the clergyman, "but, as I can find nothing in him, that deserves the least regard, he must e'en keep the rest company." He was accordingly doomed to the flames, without farther question. The next book they opened was entitled, The Knight of the Cross, which the curate having read; "the ignorance of this author," said he, "might be pardoned on account of his holy title; but, according to the proverb, the devil skulks behind the cross, and therefore let him descend into the fire." Master Nicolas taking up another book, found it was the Mirror of Chivalry. "Oh, ho," cried the curate, "I have the honour to know his worship; away with Signor Rinaldos de Mont-alban, with his friends and companions, who were greater thieves than Cacus, not forgetting the Twelve peers, together with Turpin, their candid historian. Though truly, in my opinion, their punishment ought not to exceed perpetual banishment, because they contain some part of the invention of the renowned Matteo Boyardo, on which was weaved the ingenious web of the christian poet Ludovico Ariosto; to whom, should I find him here speaking in any other language than his own, I would pay no regard; but, if he talks in his own idiom, I will place him on my head in token of respect." "I have got him at home," said the barber, in Italian, "but I don't understand that language." "Nor is it necessary you should," replied the curate; "and here let us pray heaven to forgive the captain, who has impoverished him so much, by translating him into Spanish, and making him a Castilian. And indeed, the same thing will happen to all those who pretend to translate books of poetry into a foreign language; for, in spite of all their care and ability, they will find it impossible to give the translation the same energy, which is found in the original. In short, I sentence this book, and all those which we shall find treating of French matters, to be thrown and deposited in a dry well, until we can determine at more leisure what fate they must undergo, except Bernardo del Carpio, and another called Roncesvalles, which if they fall into my hands, shall pass into those of the housekeeper, and thence into the fire, without any mitigation."

This was approved of as an equitable decision, and accordingly confirmed by the barber, who knew the curate to be such a good christian, and so much a friend to truth, that he would not be guilty of an equivocation for the whole universe. The next volume he opened was Palmerin d'Oliva; and hard by him stood another called Palmerin of England, which was no sooner perceived by the licentiate, than he cried, "Let that Oliva be hewn in pieces, and burned so, as not so much as a cinder of him shall remain; but let the English Palmerin be defended, and preserved as an inestimable jewel, and such another casket be made for him as that which Alexander found among the spoils of Darius, and destined as a case for the works of Homer. That book, neighbour, is venerable for two reasons: first, because it is in itself excellent; and secondly, because it is said to have been composed by an ingenious king of Portugal. All the adventures of the castle of Miraguarda are incomparable, and contrived with infinite art: the language perspicuous and elegant, and the characters supported with great propriety of sentiment and

decorum. I propose, Mr. Nicolas, saving your better judgment, to exempt this book and Amadis de Gaul from the flames, and let all the rest perish without farther inquiry."

"Pardon me, neighbour," replied the barber, "I have here got in my hand the renowned Don Bellianis." "Even he," answered the priest, "with the second, third, and fourth parts, stands very much in need of a little rhubarb to purge his excessive choler, and ought to be pruned of that whole castle of fame, and other more important impertinencies. For which reason, let the sentence be changed into transportation, and according as he reforms he shall be treated with lenity and justice. In the mean time, friend Nicolas, keep him safe in your house out of the reach of every reader." "With all my soul!" answered the barber; and without giving themselves the trouble of reading any more titles, they ordered the housekeeper to dismiss all the large books into the yard.

This direction was not given to a person who was either doting or deaf, but to one who was much more inclined to perform that office than to compose the largest and finest web that ever was seen. Taking up therefore seven or eight at a time, she heaved them out of the window, with incredible dispatch. While she was thus endeavouring to lift a good many together, one of them chanced to fall at the feet of the barber, who being seized with an inclination of knowing the contents, found upon examination, that it was called a history of the famous knight Tirante the White. "Heaven be praised!" cried the curate aloud, "that we have discovered Tirante the White in this place; pray give it me, neighbour; for in this book I reckon I have found a treasure of satisfaction, and a rich mine of amusement. Here is the famous Godamercy * of Mont-alban, and his brother Thomas of Mont-alban, and the knight Fonseca, as also an account of the battle fought between Alano and the valiant Detriante, together with the witticisms of the young lady, Joy of my Life, with the amorous stratagems of the widow Quiet, and her highness the empress, who was enamoured of her squire Hippolito. I do assure you, upon my word, Mr. Nicolas, that in point of stile, this is the best book that ever was written. Here the knights eat, sleep, and die in their beds, after having made their wills, with many circumstances, that are wanting in other books of the same kind. Notwithstanding, the author who composed it, certainly deserved to be sent to the galleys for life, for having spent his time in writing so much nonsense. Take, and read him at home, and you shall find what I say is true." "Very like," replied the barber; "what shall we do with these small books that remain?"

"These," said the curate, "cannot be books of chivalry, but must be poems." Accordingly, opening one, he found it was the Diana of George de Monte-mayor, and taking it for granted that all the rest were of the same kind, said, "These books do not deserve to be burnt with the rest; for they neither are, nor ever will be guilty of so much mischief, as those of chivalry have done; being books of entertainment, and no ways prejudicial to religion." "Pray, sir," said the niece, "be so good as to order these to be burnt with the rest; for my uncle will no sooner be cured of his knight-errantry, than, by reading these, he will turn shepherd, and wander about the groves and meadows piping and singing. Nay, what is worse, perhaps turn poet, which, they say, is an infectious and in-

---

* In the original *Quirieleyson*, from the two Greek words κύριε ἐλέησον signifying, Lord have mercy.[1]

curable distemper." "The young woman is in the right," said the curate, "and therefore it won't be amiss to remove this temptation and stumbling-block out of our friend's way. Since we have, therefore, begun with the Diana of Monte-mayor, I am of opinion, that we should not burn him, but only expunge what relates to the sage Felicia, and the inchanted water, together with all the larger poems, and leave to him, a God's-name, all the prose, and the honour of being the ringleader of the writers of that class."

"This that follows," said the barber, "is called Diana the second, of Salmantino, and this other that bears the same name, is written by Gil Polo." "Let Salmantino," replied the curate, "increase the number of those that are already condemned to the yard; but, let Gil Polo be preserved as carefully as if it was the production of Apollo himself. Proceed, friend Nicolas, and let us dispatch; for, it grows late." "This here book," said the barber, opening the next, "is called the ten books of the Fortune of Love, the Production of Antonio Lofrasco, a Sardinian poet." "By my holy orders!" cried the curate, "since Phoebus was Apollo, the muses the daughters of Jove, and bards delighted in poetry, there never was such a pleasant and comical performance composed, as this, which is the best and most original of the kind, which ever saw the light: and he who has not read it, may assure himself, that he has never read any thing of taste: reach it me, neighbour; it gives me more pleasure to have found this, than if I had received a cassock of Florence-silk."

Accordingly he laid it carefully by, with infinite pleasure, and the barber proceeded in his task, saying, "Those that come next, are the Shepherd of Iberia, the Nymphs of Henares, and the Undeceptions of jealousy." "Then there is no more to do," said the priest, "but to deliver them over to the secular arm of the house-keeper; and do not ask me, why? else we shall never have done." "Here comes the Shepherd of Filida." "He is no shepherd," cried the curate, "but a very elegant courtier; and therefore preserve him as a precious jewel." Then the barber laid hold of a very large volume, which was entitled the treasure of poetry. "If there was not so much of him he would be more esteemed," said the licentiate; "that book ought to be weeded, and cleared of certain meannesses, which have crept into the midst of its excellencies: take care of it, for the author is my friend, and deserves regard for some other more heroic and elevated works, which he has composed." "And this," continued the barber, "is a collection of songs by Lopez Maldonado." "That author is my very good friend also," replied the curate, "and his own verses out of his own mouth are the admiration of every body: for he chants them with so sweet a voice, that the hearers are inchanted. His eclogues are indeed a little diffuse, but there cannot be too much of a good thing. Let them be preserved among the elect: but, pray what book is that next to it?" When the barber told him, it was the Galatea of Miguel de Cervantes; "that same Cervantes," said he, "has been an intimate friend of mine, these many years, and is, to my certain knowledge, more conversant with misfortunes than with poetry. There is a good vein of invention in his book, which proposes something, though it concludes nothing. We must wait for the second part, which he promises, and then perhaps his amendment may deserve a full pardon, which is now denied: until that happens, let him be close confined in your closet."

"With all my heart," replied the barber; "but here come three more together, the Araucana of Don Alonzo de Ercilla, the Austriada of Juan Rufo Jurado de Cordova, and the Monserrato of Christoval de Virues, a Valentian poet." "These three books," said the

curate, "are the best epic poems in the Castilian language, and may be compared with the most renowned performances of Italy. Let them be kept as the inestimable pledges of Spanish poetry." The curate grew tired of examining more books, and would have condemned all the rest, contents unknown,[2] if the barber had not already opened another, which was called the Tears of Angelica. "I should have shed tears for my rashness," said the curate, "hearing the name, if I had ordered that book to be burned: for, its author was one of the most celebrated poets not only of Spain, but of the whole world, and in particular, extremely successful in translating some of the metamorphoses of Ovid."

## CHAPTER VII.

## The second sally of our worthy knight Don Quixote de la Mancha.

While they were busied in this manner, Don Quixote began to cry aloud: "This way, this way, ye valiant knights, now is the time to shew the strength of your invincible arms, that the courtiers may not carry off the honour of the tournament." The scrutiny of the books that remained, was deserted by the curate and barber, who hastened to the author of this noisy exclamation, and it is believed, that all were committed to the flames, unseen, unheard, not even excepting the Carolea, and Lyon of Spain, together with the exploits of the emperor, composed by Don Luis d'Avila, which were, doubtless, among those committed to the fire, tho' perhaps, had the curate seen them, they would not have undergone so severe a sentence.

When they arrived in Don Quixote's chamber, they found him on the floor, proceeding with his rhapsody, and fencing with the walls, as broad awake as if he had never felt the influence of sleep. Laying hold on him, by force they reconveyed him to his bed, where, after having rested a little, he returned to his ravings, and addressed himself to the curate in these words: "Certainly, my lord, archbishop Turpin, we who are called the twelve peers of France, will be greatly disgraced, if we allow the court-knights to win the victory in this tournament, after we the adventurers have gained the prize in the three preceding days." "Give yourself no trouble about that consideration, my worthy friend," said the curate; "for, providence may turn the scale, and what is lost to-day may be retrieved to-morrow. In the mean time, have a reverend care of your health, for you seem to be excessively fatigued, if not wounded grievously." "I am not wounded," replied the knight; "but, that I am battered and bruised, there is no manner of doubt: for, the bastard Don Orlando has mauled me to mummy, with the trunk of an oak; and all out of mere envy, because he saw, that I alone, withstood his valour. But, may I no longer deserve the name of Reynaldos de Mont-alban, if, when I rise from this bed, I do not repay him in his own coin, in spite of all his enchantments. Mean while, bring me some food, which is what I chiefly want at present, and let me alone, to take vengeance for the injury I have received."

In compliance with his desire, they brought him something to eat, and left him again to his repose, not without admiration of his madness and extravagance. That very night, the housekeeper set fire to, and consumed, not only all the books that were in the yard, but also every one she could find in the house; and no doubt many were burned, which deserved to have been kept as perpetual archives. But, this, their destiny, and the laziness of the inquisitors would not allow: so that, in them was fulfilled the old proverb, *a saint may sometimes suffer for a sinner.* Another remedy, which the curate and barber prescribed for the distemper of their friend was, to alter and block up the closet where his books had been kept; that upon his getting up, he should not find them, and the cause being taken away, the effect might cease; and that upon his enquiry, they should tell him, an enchanter had carried them off, closet and all: this resolution was executed with all imaginable dispatch, during the two days that Don Quixote kept his bed.

The first thing he did, when he got up, was to go and visit his books, and not finding the apartment where he had left it, he went from one corner of the house to the other, in quest of his study. Coming to the place where the door stood, he endeavoured, but in vain, to get in, and cast his eyes all around, without uttering one syllable: but, after he had spent some time in this sort of examination, he enquired of his housekeeper whereabouts he might find his book-closet. She being well instructed, readily answered, "What closet, or what nothing is your worship in search of? There are neither books nor closet in this house; for, the devil himself has run away with both." "It was not the devil," cried the niece, "but, an enchanter that conveyed himself hither in a cloud, one night after your worship's departure, and alighting from a dragon on which he was mounted, entered the closet, where I know not what he did, but having staid a very little while, he came flying thro' the roof, leaving the whole house full of smoke. And when we went to see what he had done, we could neither find books nor closet: only, the housekeeper and I can very well remember, that when the old wicked conjurer went away, he cried in a loud voice, that for the hatred he bore to the master of those books and closet, he had done that mischief, which would afterwards appear: he said also, that his name was the sage Munaton." "You mean Freston," said Don Quixote. "I do not know," answered the housekeeper, "whether it was Freston or Friton; but this I am certain of, his name ended in ton." "The case then is plain," said the knight; "that same sage enchanter is one of my greatest enemies; who bears me a grudge, because he knows, by the mystery of his art, that the time will come when I shall fight, and vanquish in single battle a certain knight whom he favours, in spite of all he can do to prevent my success: and for this reason, he endeavours to give me every mortification in his power; but, let me tell him, he won't find it an easy matter to contradict, or evade what heaven has decreed." "Who ever doubted that?" said his niece; "but, what business have you, dear uncle, with these quarrels? Would it not be better to live in peace at home, than to stray up and down the world in search of superfine bread, without considering that many a one goes out for wool, and comes home quite shorn." "My dear niece," replied Don Quixote, "you are altogether out of your reckoning. Before I be shorn, I will pull and pluck off the beards of all those who pretend to touch a single hair of my mustacho."

The two women did not choose to make any farther answer, because they perceived, that his choler was very much inflamed. After this transaction, however, he staid at

home fifteen days in great tranquillity, without giving the least sign or inclination to re-
peat his folly; during which time, many infinitely diverting conversations passed be-
tween him and his friends, the curate and the barber: wherein he observed that the world
was in want of nothing so much as of knights-errant, and that in him this honourable
order was revived. The clergyman sometimes contradicted him, and sometimes as-
sented to what he said, because, without this artful conduct, he would have had no
chance of bringing him to reason.

About this time too, the knight tampered with a peasant in the neighbourhood, a very
honest fellow, if a poor man may deserve that title, but, one who had a very small quan-
tity of brains in his skull. In short, he said so much, used so many arguments to persuade,
and promised him such mountains of wealth, that this poor simpleton determined to
follow, and serve him in quality of squire. Among other things, that he might be dis-
posed to engage chearfully, the knight told him, that an adventure might one day hap-
pen, in which he should win some island in the twinkling of an eye, and appoint him
governor of his conquest. Intoxicated with these, and other such promises, Sancho
Panza (so was the countryman called) deserted his wife and children, and listed himself
as his neighbour's squire.

Thus far successful, Don Quixote took measures for supplying himself with money,
and what by selling one thing, mortgaging another, and making a great many very bad
bargains, he raised a tolerable sum. At the same time, accommodating himself with a
target, which he borrowed of a friend, and patching up the remains of his vizor as well
as he could, he advertised his squire Sancho of the day and hour in which he resolved to
set out, that he might provide himself with those things which he thought most neces-
sary for the occasion: above all things, charging him to purchase a wallet. Sancho prom-
ised to obey his orders, and moreover, said he was resolved to carry along with him an
excellent ass which he had, as he was not designed by nature to travel far on foot.

With regard to the ass, Don Quixote demurred a little, endeavouring to recollect
some knight-errant who had entertained a squire mounted on an ass; but, as no such in-
stance occurred to his memory, he was nevertheless, determined to allow it on this occa-
sion, on a supposition, that he should be able to accommodate him with a more hon-
ourable carriage, by dismounting the first discourteous knight he should meet with. He
also laid in a store of linen, and every thing else in his power, conformable to the advice
of the innkeeper.

Every thing being thus settled and fulfilled, Panza, without taking leave of his chil-
dren and wife; and Don Quixote, without bidding adieu to his niece and housekeeper,
sallied forth from the village, one night, unperceived by any living soul, and travelled so
hard, that before dawn they found themselves secure from all search, if any such had
been made: Sancho Panza journeying upon his ass, like a venerable patriarch, with his
wallet and leathern bottle, longing extremely to see himself settled in the government
of that island which was promised to him by his master.

The knight happened to take the same route, and follow the same road in which he
travelled at his first sally thro' the field of Montiel, over which he now passed with much
less pain than formerly, because it was now early in the morning, the rays of the sun were
more oblique, consequently he was less disturbed by the heat. It was hereabouts that

Sancho first opened his mouth, saying to his master, "Sir knight-errant, I hope your worship will not forget that same island which you have promised me, and which I warrant myself able to govern, let it be as great as it will." To this remonstrance Don Quixote replied, "You must know, friend Sancho Panza, that it was an established custom among the ancient knights-errant, to invest their squires with the government of such islands and kingdoms as they had laid under their subjection; and I am firmly resolved, that such a grateful practice shall never fail in me, who, on the contrary, mean to improve it by my generosity: for, they sometimes, nay generally, waited until their squires turned grey-haired, and then after they were worn out with service, and had endured many dismal days, and doleful nights, bestowed upon them the title of count, or marquis, at least, of some valley or province, more or less: but, if heaven spares thy life and mine, before six days be at an end, I may chance to acquire such a kingdom as shall have others depending upon it, as if expresly designed for thee, to be crowned sovereign in one of them. And thou oughtest not to be surprized, that such incidents and accidents happen to knights-errant, by means never before known or conceived, as will enable me even to exceed my promise." "In that case," replied Sancho Panza, "if I should ever become a king, by any of those miracles which your worship mentions, my duck Juana Gutierez would also be a queen, and each of my daughters an infanta." "Certainly," said the knight: "who doubts that?" "That do I," said the squire; "for certain I am, that tho' it were to rain kingdoms upon the earth, not one of them would sit seemly on the head of Mary * Gutierez; your worship must know, she is not worth a farthing for a queen; she might do indeed for a countess, with the blessing of God, and good assistance." "Recommend the matter to providence," replied Don Quixote, "which will bestow upon thee what will be best adapted to thy capacity; but, let not thy soul be so far debased, as to content itself with any thing less than a vice-royalty." "That I will not," answered Sancho, "especially as I have a powerful master in your worship, who will load me with as much preferment as I can conveniently bear."

## CHAPTER VIII.

## Of the happy success of the valiant Don Quixote, and the dreadful and inconceivable adventure of the wind-mills, with other incidents worthy to be recorded by the most able historian.

In the midst of this their conversation, they discovered thirty or forty wind-mills all together on the plain, which the knight no sooner perceived than he said to his squire, "Chance has conducted our affairs even better than we could either wish or hope for; look there, friend Sancho, and behold thirty or forty outrageous giants, with whom I

---

* How comes Juana to be so suddenly metamorphosed into Mary?[1]

intend to engage in battle, and put every soul of them to death, so that we may begin to enrich ourselves with their spoils; for, it is a meritorious warfare, and serviceable both to God and man, to extirpate such a wicked race from the face of the earth." "What giants do you mean?" said Sancho Panza in amaze. "Those you see yonder," replied his master, "with vast extended arms; some of which are two leagues long." "I would your worship would take notice," replied Sancho, "that those you see yonder are no giants, but wind-mills; and what seem arms to you, are sails; which being turned with the wind, make the mill-stone work." "It seems very plain," said the knight, "that you are but a novice in adventures; these I affirm to be giants, and if thou art afraid, get out of the reach of danger, and put up thy prayers for me, while I join with them in fierce and unequal combat." So saying, he put spurs to his steed Rozinante, without paying the least regard to the cries of his squire Sancho, who assured him, that those he was going to attack were no giants, but innocent wind-mills: but, he was so much possessed with the opinion that they were giants, that he neither heard the advice of his squire Sancho, nor would use the intelligence of his own eyes, tho' he was very near them: on the contrary, when he approached them, he called aloud: "Fly not, ye base and cowardly miscreants, for, he is but a single knight who now attacks you." At that instant, a breeze of wind springing up, the great sails began to turn; which being perceived by Don Quixote, "Tho' you wield," said he, "more arms than ever belonged to the giant Briareus, I will make you pay for your insolence." So saying, and heartily recommending himself to his lady Dulcinea, whom he implored to succour him in this emergency, bracing on his target, and setting his lance in the rest, he put his Rozinante to full speed, and assaulting the nearest wind-mill, thrust it into one of the sails, which was drove about by the wind with so much fury, that the lance was shivered to pieces, and both knight and steed whirled aloft, and overthrown in very bad plight upon the plain.

Sancho Panza rode as fast as the ass could carry him to his assistance, and when he came up, found him unable to stir, by reason of the bruises which he and Rozinante had received. "Lord have mercy on us!" said the squire, "did not I tell your worship to consider well what you were about? did not I assure you, they were no other than windmills? indeed no body could mistake them for any thing else, but one who has windmills in his own head!" "Prithee, hold thy peace, friend Sancho," replied Don Quixote; "the affairs of war are, more than any thing, subject to change. How much more so, as I believe, nay, am certain, that the sage Freston who stole my closet and books, has converted those giants into mills, in order to rob me of the honour of their overthrow; such is the enmity he bears me; but, in the end, all his treacherous arts will but little avail against the vigour of my sword." "God's will be done!" replied Sancho Panza, who helped him to rise and mount Rozinante that was almost disjointed.

While they conversed together upon what had happened, they followed the road that leads to the pass of Lapice, for in that, which was a great thoroughfare, as Don Quixote observed, it was impossible but they must meet with many and divers adventures. As he jogged along, a good deal concerned for the loss of his lance, he said to his squire, "I remember to have read of a Spanish knight called Diego Perez de Vargos, who having broken his sword in battle, tore off a mighty branch or bough from an oak, with which he performed such wonders, and felled so many Moors, that he retained the name of

Machuca, or the feller, and all his descendants from that day forward, have gone by the name of Vargos and Machuca. This circumstance I mention to thee, because, from the first ash or oak that I meet with, I am resolved to rend as large and stout a bough as that, with which I expect, and intend to perform such exploits, as thou shalt think thyself extremely happy in being thought worthy to see, and give testimony to feats, otherwise incredible." "By God's help," says Sancho, "I believe that every thing will happen as your worship says, but pray, Sir, sit a little more upright; for you seem to lean strangely to one side, which must proceed from the bruises you received in your fall." "Thou art in the right," answered Don Quixote; "and if I do not complain of the pain, it is because knights-errant are not permitted to complain of any wound they receive, even tho' their bowels should come out of their bodies." "If that be the case, I have nothing to reply," said Sancho, "but God knows, I should be glad your worship would complain when any thing gives you pain: this I know, that for my own part, the smallest prick in the world would make me complain, if that law of not complaining does not reach to the squires as well as the knights." Don Quixote could not help smiling at the simplicity of his squire, to whom he gave permission to complain as much and as often as he pleased, whether he had cause or no; for, as yet, he had read nothing to the contrary, in the history of knight-errantry.

Then Sancho observing that it was dinner-time, his master told him, that for the present he had no occasion for food; but, that he his squire might go to victuals when he pleased. With this permission, Sancho adjusted himself as well as he could, upon his ass, and taking out the provision with which he had stuffed his wallet, he dropped behind his master a good way, and kept his jaws agoing as he jogged along, lifting the bottle to his head, from time to time, with so much satisfaction, that the most pampered vintner of Malaga might have envied his situation.

While he travelled in this manner, repeating his agreeable draughts, he never thought of the promise which his master had made to him, nor considered it as a toil, but rather as a diversion, to go in quest of adventures, how dangerous soever they might be: in fine, that night they passed under a tuft of trees, from one of which Don Quixote tore a withered branch to serve instead of a lance; and fitted to it the iron head he had taken from that which was broken: all night long, the knight closed not an eye, but mused upon his lady Dulcinea, in order to accommodate himself to what he had read of those errants who had passed many sleepless nights in woods and desarts, entertaining themselves with the remembrance of their mistresses.

This was not the case with Sancho Panza, whose belly being well replenished, and that not with plantane water, made but one nap of the whole night, and even then, would not have waked, unless his master had called to him, notwithstanding the sun-beams that played upon his face, and the singing of the birds, which in great numbers, and joyous melody, saluted the approach of the new day. The first thing he did when he got up, was to visit his bottle, which finding considerably more lank than it was the night before, he was grievously afflicted, because in the road that they pursued, he had no hopes of being able in a little time to supply its defect. Don Quixote refusing to breakfast, because, as we have already said, he regaled himself with the savoury remembrance of his mistress, they pursued their journey towards the pass, which after three days travelling,

they discovered. "Here," cried Don Quixote, "here, brother Sancho Panza, we shall be able to dip our hands up to the elbows in what is called adventure; but, take notice, al-tho' thou seest me beset with the most extreme danger, thou must by no means, even so much as lay thy hand upon thy sword, with design to defend me, unless I am assaulted by vulgar and low-born antagonists, in which case, thou mayest come to my assistance; but, if they are knights, thou art by no means permitted or licensed, by the laws of chivalry, to give me the least succour, until thou thyself hast received the honour of knighthood *." "As for that matter," replied Sancho, "your worship shall be obeyed to a tittle, for, I am a very peaceable man, and not at all fond of meddling with riots and quar-rels. True indeed, in the defence of my own person, I shall not pay much regard to the said laws, seeing every one that is aggrieved is permitted to defend himself by all the laws of God and man." "I say nothing to the contrary," replied Don Quixote, "but, in the af-fair of assisting me against knights, thou must keep thy natural impetuosity under the rein." "That will I," answered Sancho, "and keep your honour's command as strictly as I keep the Lord's-day."

While they were engaged in this conversation, there appeared before them two bene-dictine monks mounted upon dromedaries, for, their mules were not much less, with their travelling spectacles, and umbrellas; after them came a coach, accompanied by four or five people on horseback, and two mule-drivers on foot. In this carriage, it was afterwards known, a Biscayan lady was travelling to Seville to her husband, who was bound to the Indies with a rich cargo.

Don Quixote no sooner perceived the fryars (who, tho' they travelled the same road, were not of her company) than he said to his squire, "If I am not very much mistaken, this will be the most famous adventure that ever was known; for, those black apparitions on the road, must doubtless be enchanters, who are carrying off in that coach, some princess they have stolen; and there is a necessity for my exerting my whole power in redressing her wrongs." "This will be worse than the wind-mills," cried Sancho, "for the love of God! Sir, consider, that these are Benedictine fryars, and those who are in the coach can be no other than common travellers. Mind what I say, and consider what you do, and let not the devil deceive you." "I have told thee already, Sancho," replied Don Quixote, "that with regard to adventures, thou art utterly ignorant: what I say is true, and in a moment thou shalt be convinced."

So saying, he rode forward, and placed himself in the middle of the highway thro' which the fryars were to pass, and when he thought them near enough to hear what he said, he pronounced, in a loud voice, "Monstrous and diabolical race! surrender this in-stant, those high-born princesses, whom you carry captives in that coach: or prepare to receive immediate death, as a just punishment for your misdeeds." The fryars immedi-

---

* Here Don Quixote seems to have been too scrupulous: for, tho' no squire was permitted to en-gage with a knight on horseback, yet they were allowed, and even enjoined, to assist their masters when they were unhorsed or in danger, by mounting them on fresh steeds, supplying them with arms, and warding off the blows that were aimed at them. Davy Gam, at the battle of Agincourt, lost his life in defending Henry V. of England, and St. Severin met with the same fate in warding off the blows that were aimed at Francis I. of France, in the battle of Pavia.[1]

ately stopped short, astonished as much at the figure, as at the discourse of Don Quixote: to which they replied, "Sir knight, we are neither diabolical nor monstrous, but innocent monks of the order of St. Benedict, who are going this way about our own affairs; neither do we know of any princesses, that are carried captives in that coach." "These fawning speeches," said Don Quixote, "shall not impose upon me, who know too well what a treacherous pack you are"; and without waiting for any other reply, he put spurs to Rozinante, and couching his lance, attacked the first fryar with such fury and resolution, that if he had not thrown himself from his mule, he would have come to the ground extremely ill-handled, not without some desperate wound, nay, perhaps stone dead. The second monk, who saw how his companion had been treated, clapped spurs to the flanks of his trusty mule, and flew thro' the field even swifter than the wind.

Sancho Panza seeing the fryar on the ground, leaped from his ass with great agility, and beginning to uncase him with the utmost dexterity, two of their servants came up, and asked for what reason he stripped their master? The squire replied, that the cloaths belonged to him, as the spoils that Don Quixote his lord had won in battle: but, the others, who did not understand raillery, nor know any thing of spoils and battles, seeing Don Quixote at a good distance, talking with the lady in the coach, went to loggerheads with Sancho, whom they soon overthrew, and without leaving one hair of his beard, mauled him so unmercifully, that he lay stretched upon the ground, without sense or motion. Then, with the utmost dispatch, the fryar mounted, as pale as a sheet, and almost frightened to death, and who no sooner found himself on horseback, than he galloped towards his companion, who tarried at a good distance, to see the issue of this strange adventure. However, being joined again, without waiting for the conclusion of it, they pursued their journey, making as many crosses as if the devil had been at their backs.

Don Quixote, in the mean time, as we have already observed, was engaged in conversation with the lady in the coach, to whom he expressed himself in this manner: "Beautiful lady, you may now dispose of your own person according to your pleasure, for the pride of your ravishers lyes level with the ground, being overthrown by this my invincible arm; and that you may be at no difficulty in understanding the name of your deliverer, know that I am Don Quixote de la Mancha, knight-errant, adventurer and captive of the unparalelled, and beautiful Donna Dulcinea del Toboso; and the only acknowledgment I expect for the benefit you have received, is, that you return to that place, and presenting yourself before my mistress, tell her what I have performed in behalf of your liberty." This whole address of the knight, was overheard by a Biscayan squire, who accompanied the coach, and who seeing, that he would not allow the carriage to pass forward, but insisted upon their immediate returning to Toboso, rode up to Don Quixote, and laying hold of his lance, spoke to him thus in bad Castilian, and worse Biscayan:[2] "Get thee gone, cavalier, go to the devil, I zay, vor, by the God that made hur, if thou wilt not let the coach alone, che will kill thee dead, as zure as che was a Biscayan." The knight understanding very well what he said, replied with great composure; "If thou wast a gentleman, as thou art not, I would chastise thy insolence and rashness, wretched creature." "I not a gentleman," replied the Biscayan in great choler; "by God in heaven! thou liest, as I am a Christian; if thou wilt throw away thy lance, and

draw thy sword, che will soon zee which be the better man *. Biscayan by land, gentle-
man by zea, gentleman by devil, and thou liest, look ye, in thy throat, if thou zayest oth-
erwise." "Thou shalt see that presently, as Agragis said," replied Don Quixote, who
throwing his lance upon the ground, unsheathing his sword, and bracing on his target,
attacked the Biscayan with full resolution to put him to death †.

His antagonist, who saw him approach, fain would have alighted from his mule,
which being one of the worst that ever was let out for hire, could not much be depended
upon: but, he scarce had time to draw his sword; however, being luckily near the coach,
he snatched out of it a cushion which served him as a shield, and then they flew upon
each other as two mortal enemies. The rest of the people who were present, endeav-
oured, but in vain, to appease them; for, the Biscayan swore, in his uncouth expressions,
that if they did not leave him to fight the battle, he would certainly murder his mistress,
and every body who should pretend to oppose it. The lady in the coach, surprized and
frightened at what she saw, ordered the coachman to drive a little out of the road, to a
place from whence she could see at a distance this rigorous engagement. In the course
of which, the Biscayan bestowed such a huge stroke upon the shoulder of Don Quixote,
that if it had not been for the defence of his buckler, he would have been cleft down to
his girdle. The knight feeling the shock of such an unconscionable blow, exclaimed
aloud: "O Dulcinea! lady of my soul, thou rose of beauty, succour thy knight, who, for
the satisfaction of thy excessive goodness, is now involved in this dreadful emergency."
To pronounce these words, to raise his sword, to secure himself with his target, and at-
tack the Biscayan, was the work of one instant; for, he was determined to risk his all upon
a single stroke. His antagonist, who saw him advance, and by this time, was convinced
of his courage by his resolution, determined to follow his example; and covering him-
self with his cushion, waited his assault, without being able to turn his mule either on
one side or the other: for, she was already so jaded, and so little accustomed to such pas-
time, that she would not move one step out of the way.

Don Quixote then, as we have said, advanced against the cautious Biscayan, his sword
lifted up with an intention to cleave him through the middle: the Biscayan waited his at-
tack in the same posture, being shielded with his cushion. The frightened by-standers
stood aloof, intent upon the success of those mighty strokes that threatened each of the
combatants; and the lady in the coach, with the rest of her attendants, put up a thousand
prayers to heaven, and vowed an offering to every image, and house of devotion in
Spain, provided God would deliver the squire and them from the imminent danger in
which they were: but the misfortune is, that in this very critical instant, the author of the
history has left this battle in suspence, excusing himself, that he could find no other ac-

---

* The literal meaning of the Spanish, is, Thou shalt soon see who is to carry the cat to the water,
or rather, in the corrupted Biscayan phrase, "The water, how soon thou wilt see, that thou carriest
to the cat."[3]
† This behaviour of Don Quixote, was exactly conformable to the rules of chivalry; which, tho'
they hindered a knight from fighting in armour with a squire, did not prevent him from giving
satisfaction to an inferior, at sword and target; and every squire who was aggrieved, had a right to
demand it.[4]

count of Don Quixote's exploits, but what has already been related. True it is, that the second author of this work, could not believe that such a curious history was consigned to oblivion; nor, that there could be such a scarcity of curious virtuosi in La Mancha, but that some papers relating to this famous knight should be found in their archives or cabinets: and therefore, possessed of this opinion, he did not despair of finding the conclusion of this delightful history, which indeed he very providentially lighted upon, in the manner which will be related in the second book.

# THE

# LIFE and ATCHIEVEMENTS

## Of the Sagacious HIDALGO

## DON QUIXOTE DE LA MANCHA.

## PART I. BOOK II.

### CHAPTER I.

#### The conclusion and consequence of the stupendous combat between the gallant Biscayan, and the valiant knight of La Mancha.

In the first book of this history, we left the valiant Biscayan and renowned Don Qui-
xote with their gleaming swords brandished aloft, about to discharge two such furi-
ous strokes, as must (if they had cut sheer) have cleft them both asunder, from top to toe,
like a couple of pomegranates; and in this dubious and critical conjuncture, the delicious
history abruptly breaks off, without our being informed by the author, where or how
that which is wanting may be found.

I was not a little concerned at this disappointment; for, the pleasure I enjoyed in the
little I had read, was changed into disgust, when I reflected on the small prospect I had
of finding the greater part of this relishing story, which, in my opinion, was lost: and yet
it seemed impossible, and contrary to every laudable custom, that such an excellent
knight should be unprovided with some sage to undertake the history of his unheard-of
exploits; a convenience which none of those knights-errant who went in quest of ad-
ventures ever wanted, each of them having been accommodated with one or two ne-
gromancers, on purpose to record not only his atchievements, but even his most hidden
thoughts and amusements. Surely then such a compleat errant could not be so unlucky
as to want that, which even Platil, and other such second-rate warriors enjoyed.

I could not therefore prevail upon myself to believe that such a spirited history was
left so lame and unfinished, but laid the whole blame on the malignity of time, which
wastes and devours all things, and by which, no doubt, this was either consumed or con-
cealed: on the other hand, I considered, that as some books had been found in his li-
brary, so modern as the Undeceptions of Jealousy, together with the Nymphs and Shep-
herds of Henares; his own history must also be of a modern date, and the circumstances,
tho' not committed to writing, still fresh in the memory of his neighbours and towns-

men. This consideration perplexed and inflamed me, with the desire of knowing the true and genuine account of the life and wonderful exploits of our Spanish worthy Don Quixote de la Mancha, the sun and mirrour of Manchegan chivalry, the first who in this our age, and these degenerate times, undertook the toil and exercise of errantry and arms, to redress grievances, support the widow, and protect those damsels who stroll about with whip and palfrey, from hill to hill, and from dale to dale, on the strength of their virginity alone: for, in times past, unless some libidinous clown with hatchet and morrion, or monstrous giant, forced her to his brutal wishes, a damsel might have lived fourscore years, without ever lying under any other cover than that of heaven, and then gone to her grave as good a maiden as the mother that bore her. I say, therefore, that for these and many other considerations, our gallant Don Quixote merits incessant and immortal praise; and even I myself may claim some share, for my labour and diligence in finding the conclusion of this agreeable history; tho' I am well aware, that if I had not been favoured by fortune, chance or providence, the world would have been deprived of that pleasure and satisfaction which the attentive reader may enjoy for an hour or two, in perusing what follows: the manner of my finding it I will now recount.

While I was walking, one day, on the exchange of Toledo, a boy coming up to a certain mercer, offered to sell him a bundle of old papers he had in his hand: now, as I have always a strong propensity to read even those scraps that sometimes fly about the streets, I was led by this my natural curiosity, to turn over some of the leaves: I found them written in Arabic, which not being able to read, tho' I knew the characters, I looked about for some Portugeze Moor who should understand it; and indeed, tho' the language had been both more elegant and ancient, I might easily have found an interpreter. In short, I lighted upon one, to whom expressing my desire, and putting the pamphlet into his hands, he opened it in the middle, and after having read a few lines, began to laugh; when I asked the cause of his laughter, he said it was occasioned by a whimsical annotation in the margin of the book: I begged he would tell me what it was, and he answered, still laughing, "What I find written in the margin, is to this purpose: 'This same Dulcinea so often mentioned in the history, is said to have had the best hand at salting pork of any woman in la Mancha.'"

Not a little surprised at hearing Dulcinea del Toboso mentioned, I immediately conjectured that the bundle actually contained the history of Don Quixote: possessed with this notion, I bad him, with great eagerness, read the title page, which having perused, he translated it extempore from Arabic to Spanish, in these words: "The history of Don Quixote de la Mancha, written by Cid Hamet Benengeli, an Arabian author." No small discretion was requisite to dissemble the satisfaction I felt, when my ears were saluted with the title of these papers, which, snatching from the mercer, I immediately bought in the lump, for half a rial; tho', if the owner had been cunning enough to discover my eagerness to possess them, he might have laid his account with getting twelve times the sum by the bargain.

I then retired with my Moor, thro' the cloysters of the cathedral, and desired him to translate all those papers that related to Don Quixote into the Castilian tongue, without addition or diminution, offering to pay any thing he should charge for his labour: his demand was limited to two quarters of rasins, and as many bushels of wheat, for

which he promised to translate them with great care, conciseness and fidelity: but, I, the more to facilitate the business, without parting with such a rich prize, conducted him to my own house, where, in little less than six weeks, he translated the whole, in the same manner as shall here be related.

In the first sheet, was painted to the life, the battle betwixt Don Quixote and the Biscayan, who were represented in the same posture as the history has already described, their swords brandished aloft, one of the antagonists covered with his shield, the other with his cushion, and the Biscayan's mule so naturally set forth, that you might have known her to have been an hireling, at the distance of a bow-shot. Under the feet of her rider, was a label, containing these words, Don Sancho de Azpetia, which was doubtless his name; and beneath our knight was another, with the title of Don Quixote. Rozinante was most wonderfully delineated, so long and raw-boned, so lank and meagre, so sharp in the back, and consumptive, that one might easily perceive, with what propriety and penetration the name of Rozinante had been bestowed upon him. Hard by the steed was Sancho Panza, holding his ass by the halter, at whose feet was a third label, inscribed Sancho Zancas, who, in the picture, was represented as a person of a short stature, swag belly, and long spindle shanks: for this reason, he ought to be called indiscriminately by the names of * Panza and Zancas; for by both these sirnames is he sometimes mentioned in history.

There were divers other minute circumstances to be observed, but, all of them of small importance and concern to the truth of the history, tho' indeed nothing that is true can be impertinent: however, if any objection can be started to the truth of this, it can be no other, but that the author was an Arabian, of a nation but too much addicted to falsehood, tho' as they are at present our enemies, it may be supposed, that he has rather failed than exceeded in the representation of our hero's exploits: for, in my opinion, when he had frequently opportunities, and calls to exercise his pen in the praise of such an illustrious knight, he seems to be industriously silent on the subject; a circumstance very little to his commendation, for, all historians ought to be punctual, candid and dispassionate, that neither interest, rancour, fear, or affection may mislead them from the road of truth, whose mother is history, that rival of time, that repository of great actions, witness of the past, example and pattern of the present, and oracle of future ages. In this, I know, will be found whatsoever can be expected in the most pleasant performance; and if any thing seems imperfect, I affirm it must be owing to the fault of the infidel its author, rather than to any failure of the subject itself: in short, the second book in the translation begins thus:

The flaming swords of the two valiant and incensed combatants, brandished in the air, seemed to threaten heaven, earth, and hell, such was the rage and resolution of those that wielded them: but, the first blow was discharged by the choleric Biscayan, who struck with such force and fury, that if the blade had not turned by the way, that single stroke would have been sufficient to have put an end to this dreadful conflict, and all the other adventures of our knight; but, his good genius, which preserved him for mightier things, turned the sword of his antagonist aside, so, that tho' it fell upon his left shoul-

---

* Panza, in Castilian, signifies Paunch; and Zancas, spindleshanks.[1]

der, it did no other damage than disarm that whole side, slicing off in its passage the greatest part of his helmet, with half of his ear, which fell to the ground, with hideous ruin, leaving him in a very uncomfortable situation. Good heavens! where is the man, who can worthily express the rage and indignation which entered into the heart of our Manchegan, when he saw himself handled in this manner? I shall only say, his fury was such, that raising himself again in his stirrups, and grasping his sword with both hands, he discharged it so full upon the cushion, and head of the Biscayan, which it but ill-defended, that, as if a mountain had fallen upon him, he began to spout blood from his nostrils, mouth and ears, and seemed ready to fall from his mule, which would certainly have been the case, if he had not laid hold of the mane: yet, notwithstanding this effort, his feet falling out of the stirrups, and his arms quitting their hold, the mule, which was frightened at the terrible stroke, began to run across the field, and after a few plunges, came with her master to the ground. Don Quixote, who sat observing him, with great tranquillity, no sooner perceived him fall, than leaping from his horse, he ran up to him with great agility, and setting the point of his sword to his throat, bad him surrender, on pain of having his head cut off. The Biscayan was so confounded by the blow and fall he had sustained, that he could not answer one syllable, and as Don Quixote was blinded by his rage, he would have fared very ill, if the ladies of the coach, who had hitherto, in great consternation, been spectators of the battle, had not run to the place where he was, and requested, with the most fervent entreaties, that his worship would grant them the favour to spare the life of their squire.

To this petition, the knight replied, with great stateliness and gravity, "Assuredly, most beautiful ladies, I am very ready to do what you desire, but, it shall be upon condition and proviso, that this cavalier promise to go strait to Toboso, and present himself, in my behalf, before the unparalelled Donna Dulcinea, that she may use him according to her good pleasure." The timorous and disconsolate ladies, without entering into the detail of what Don Quixote desired, or enquiring who this Dulcinea was, promised that the squire should obey the knight's commands in every thing. "Upon the faith of your word, then," said Don Quixote, "I will do him no farther damage, tho' he has richly deserved it at my hand."

## CHAPTER II.

## Of what further happened between Don Quixote and the Biscayan.[1]

All this time, Sancho Panza, having got up, tho' very roughly handled by the lacquies of the fryars, stood very attentively beholding the battle of his master Don Quixote, and put up ejaculatory petitions to heaven, that it would please to grant him the victory, and that he might gain by it some island, of which he himself might be made governor, in consequence of the knight's promise. Seeing therefore the battle ended,

and his master returning to mount Rozinante, he went to hold his stirrup, and before he got up, fell on his knees before him; then laying hold of his hand, and kissing it, pronounced with great fervency, "Sir Don Quixote, will your worship be pleased to bestow on me, the government of that island which you have won in this dreadful combat; for, let it be ever so great, I find I have strength enough to govern it, as well as any he who governed an island in this world." To this request, Don Quixote replied; "You must know, brother Sancho, that such as these are not adventures of islands, but frays that happen in bye-roads, in which there is nothing to be got but a broken head, with the loss of an ear: have a little patience, and we shall meet with adventures, which will enable me to make you not only a governor, but something more." Sancho made him many hearty acknowledgments for his promise, then kissing his hand again, and his coat of mail, helped him to mount Rozinante; and he himself getting upon his ass, followed his master, who set off at a round pace, and without biding adieu, or speaking one syllable to those in the coach, entered a wood that was in the neighbourhood.

Sancho followed him hard as his beast would trot; but Rozinante exerted such speed, that seeing himself left behind, he was obliged to call to his master to wait for him. The knight complied with his request, and checked his horse until he was overtaken by his weary squire; who, when he approached him: "Sir," said he, "methinks it would be the wisest course for us to retreat to some church; for, as he with whom you fought remains but in a sorry condition, 'tis odds, but they inform the * holy brotherhood of the affair, and have us apprehended: and verily, if they do, before we get out of prison we may chance to sweat for it." "Peace, Sancho," said Don Quixote, "where didst thou ever see or hear, that a knight-errant was brought to justice for the greatest homicides he had committed?" "I know nothing of your honey-seeds," answered Sancho, "nor in my life did I ever see one of them: this only, I know, that the holy brotherhood commonly looks after those who quarrel and fight up and down the country; and as to the other affair, I have no business to intermeddle in it."

"Set your heart at ease then, friend Sancho," replied Don Quixote, "for, I will deliver you from the hands of the Philistines, much more from the clutches of the brotherhood: but, tell me, on thy life, hast thou ever seen a more valiant knight than me, in any country of the known world? Hast thou ever read in story of any other who possesses, or has possessed, more courage in attacking, more breath in persevering, more dexterity in wounding, and more agility in overthrowing his antagonist?" "The truth is," answered Sancho, "I never read a history since I was born; for, indeed I can neither read nor write; but what I will make bold to wager upon, is, that a more daring master than your worship I never served in the days of my life; and I wish to God, that your courage may not meet with that reward I have already mentioned. What I beg of your worship at present, is, that you would allow me to dress that ear, which bleeds very much; for, I have got some lint, and a little white ointment in my wallet." "These would have been altogether needless," answered the knight, "if I had remembered to make a vial of the balsam of Fierabras, one single drop of which would save abundance of time and trouble."

* Santa Hermandad was a brotherhood or society instituted in Spain in times of confusion, to suppress robbery, and render travelling safe.[2]

"What sort of a vial and balsam is that?" said Sancho Panza. "It is a balsam," replied Don Quixote, "the receipt of which I retain in my memory, and he that possesses the valuable composition needs be in no fear of death, nor think of perishing by any wound whatsoever: and therefore, when I shall have made it, and delivered it into thy keeping, thou hast no more to do, when thou seest me in any combat, cut thro' the middle, a circumstance that very often happens, but to snatch up that part of the body which falls to the ground, and before the blood shall congeal, set it upon the other half that remains in the saddle, taking care to join them with the utmost nicety and exactness: then making me swallow a couple of draughts of the aforesaid balsam, thou wilt see me, in a twinkling, as whole and as sound as an apple."

"If that be the case," said Sancho Panza, "I henceforth renounce the government of that island you promised me, and desire no other reward for my long and faithful service, but that your worship will give me the receipt of that same most exceeding liquor; for, I imagine, that it will sell for two rials an ounce at least, and that will be sufficient to make me spend the rest of my days in credit and ease: but, it will be necessary to know, if the composition be costly." "I can make a gallon of it for less than three rials," replied the knight. "Sinner that I am!" cried Sancho, "what hinders your worship from teaching me to make it, this moment?" "Hold thy tongue, friend," said the knight, "I intend to teach thee greater secrets, and bestow upon thee more considerable rewards than that: but, in the mean time, let us dress my ear, which pains me more than I could wish."

The squire accordingly took out his lint and ointment; but when his master found, that his helmet was quite demolished, he had almost run stark mad: he laid his hand upon his sword, and lifting up his hands to heaven, pronounced aloud, "I swear by the creator of all things, and by all that is written in the four holy evangelists! to lead the life which the great marquis of Mantua led, when he swore to revenge the death of his cousin Valdovinos: neither to eat food upon a table, nor enjoy his wife, with many other things, which, tho' I do not remember, I here consider as expressed, until I shall have taken full vengeance upon him who has done me this injury *." Sancho hearing this invocation, "Sir Don Quixote," said he, "I hope your worship will consider, that if the knight shall accomplish what he was ordered to do; namely, to present himself before my lady Dulcinea del Toboso, he will have done his duty, and certainly deserves no other punishment, unless he commits a new crime." "Thou hast spoke very much to the purpose, and hit the nail on the head," replied Don Quixote, "therefore I annul my oath, so far as it regards my revenge, but I make and confirm it anew, to lead the life I have mentioned, until such time as I can take by force as good a helmet as this from some other knight; and thou must not think, Sancho, that I am now making a smoke of straw; for, I

---

* These ridiculous oaths or vows are not confined to romances. Philip the good duke of Burgundy, at a public banquet, vowed to God, the holy virgin, the peacock and the ladies, that he would declare war against the infidels; and a great number of persons who were present listed themselves under the same vow, and incurred voluntary penance until it should be accomplished. Some swore they would never lie upon a bed, others renounced the use of a table cloth, a third set obliged themselves to fast one particular day in the week, a fourth went without one particular piece of armour, a fifth wore his armour night and day, and many confined themselves to shirts of sackcloth and hair.[3]

know very well whom I imitate in this affair; the same thing having literally happened about the helmet of Mambrino, which cost Sacripante so dear *."

"Sir, Sir," replied Sancho with some heat, "I wish your worship would send to the devil all such oaths, which are so mischievous to the health, and prejudicial to the conscience; for, tell me now, if we should not find in many days, a man armed with a helmet, what must we do? must we perform this vow, in spite of all the rubs and inconveniencies in the way: such as to lye in one's cloaths, and not to sleep in an inhabited place, with a thousand other penances contained in the oath of that old mad marquis of Mantua, which your worship now wants to renew? Pray, Sir, consider that there are no armed people in these roads, none but carriers and carters, which, far from wearing helmets themselves, perhaps never heard of any such thing during the whole course of their lives." "There thou art egregiously mistaken," replied Don Quixote, "for, before we are two hours in these cross-ways, we shall see armed men more numerous than those that came to Albraca, in order to win Angelica the fair." "On then, and be it so," said Sancho, "and pray God we may succeed, and that the time may come, when we shall gain that island which has cost me so dear, and then I care not how soon I die." "I have already advised thee, Sancho," said the knight, "to give thyself no trouble about that affair; for, should we be disappointed in the expectation of an island, there is the kingdom of Denmark, or that of Sobrediza, which will suit thee as well as ever a ring fitted a finger, and ought to give thee more joy, because it is situated on terra firma; but, let us leave these things to the determination of time; and see if thou hast got any thing in thy wallet; for, we must go presently in quest of some castle, where we may procure a night's lodging, and ingredients to make that same balsam I mentioned; for, I vow to God! my ear gives me infinite pain."

"I have got here in my bags," said Sancho, "an onion, a slice of cheese, and a few crusts of bread; but, these are eatables which do not suit the palate of such a valiant knight-errant as your worship." "How little you understand of the matter?" answered Don Quixote. "Thou must know, Sancho, that it is for the honour of knights-errant, to abstain whole months together from food, and when they do eat, to be contented with what is next at hand; this thou wouldst not have been ignorant of, hadst thou read so many histories as I have perused, in which, numerous as they are, I have never found any account of knights-errant eating, except occasionally, at some sumptuous banquet made on purpose for them; at other times, living upon air: and tho' it must be taken for granted, that they could not altogether live without eating, or complying with the other necessities of nature, being in effect men as we are; yet we are likewise to consider, that as the greatest part of their lives was spent in travelling thro' woods and desarts, without any cook

---

* Geoffroi de Rançon having been injured by the count de la Marche, swore by the saints that he would wear his buskin like a woman, and never suffer himself to be shaved, in the manner of chivalry, until he should be revenged. This oath he scrupulously observed, until he saw his adversary with his wife and children kneeling in distress before the king, and imploring his forgiveness; then he called for a stool, adjusted his buskin, and was shaved in presence of his majesty and all the court.

The knight's forehead was commonly shaved, that in case he should lose his helmet in combat, his antagonist should have no hold by which he might be pulled off his horse.[4]

or caterer, their ordinary diet was no other than such rustic food as thou hast now got for our present occasions *: therefore, friend Sancho, give thyself no uneasiness, because thou hast got nothing to gratify the palate, nor seek to unhinge or alter the constitution of things." "I beg your worship's pardon," said Sancho, "for, as I can neither read nor write, as I have already observed, I may have mistaken the rules of your knightly profession; but, from henceforward, I will store my budget with all sorts of dry fruits for your worship, who are a knight, and for myself who am none, I will provide other more volatile and substantial food †." "I do not say, Sancho, that knights-errant are obliged to eat nothing except these fruits, but only that their most ordinary sustenance is composed of them and from certain herbs, which they know how to gather in the fields; a species of knowledge which I myself am no stranger to." "Surely," answered Sancho, "it is a great comfort to know those same herbs; for, it comes into my head, we shall one day or another, have occasion to make use of the knowledge"; and taking out the contents of his wallet, they ate together with great harmony and satisfaction; but, being desirous of finding some place for their night's lodging, they finished their humble repast in a hurry, and mounting their beasts, put on at a good rate, in order to reach some village before it should be dark: but the hope of gratifying that desire failed them with day-light, just when they happened to be near a goatherd's hut, in which they resolved to pass the night; and in the same proportion that Sancho was disgusted at not being able to reach some village, his master was rejoiced at an opportunity of sleeping under the cope of heaven, because he looked upon every occasion of this kind as an act of possession, that strengthened the proof of his knight-errantry.

## CHAPTER III.

## Of what happened to Don Quixote, while he remained with the goat-herds.

He received a very hearty welcome from the goatherds, and Sancho having, as well as he could, accommodated Rozinante and his ass, was attracted by the odour that issued from some pieces of goat's flesh, that were boiling in a kettle; but though he

---

* We read in Perceforest, that there were flat stones placed at certain distances in uninhabited parts of the country, for the use of knights-errant, who having killed a roe-buck, pressed the blood out of it upon one of these tables, by the help of another smooth stone, and then ate it with some salt and spices which they carried along with them for that purpose. This diet is called in the French romances, *Chevraux de presse, nourriture des Heraux.*[5]

† *Volatiles* in the original, signifies any things that fly; and therefore Sancho may be supposed to mean, he would provide himself with game or poultry: but the blunder which we have made him commit, seems to be more in character.[6]

longed very much, at that instant, to see if it was time to transfer them from the kettle to the belly, he checked his curiosity, because the landlord took them from the fire, and spreading some sheep-skins upon the ground, set out their rustic table without loss of time; inviting their two guests to a share of their mess, with many expressions of good will and hospitality. Then those who belonged to the cot, being six in number, seated themselves round the skins, having first, with their boorish ceremony, desired Don Quixote to sit down on a trough, which they had overturned for that purpose.

The knight accepted their offer, and Sancho remained standing, to administer the cup, which was made of horn: but, his master perceiving him in this attitude, "That thou mayest see, Sancho," said he, "the benefit which is concentred in knight-errantry; and how near all those, who exercise themselves in any sort of ministry belonging to it, are to preferment and esteem of the world, I desire thee to sit down here by my side, in company with these worthy people: and that thou may'st be on an equal footing with me, thy natural lord and master, eating in the same dish, and drinking out of the same cup that I use; for what is said of love may be observed of knight-errantry, that it puts all things upon a level."

"I give you a thousand thanks," said Sancho; "but, I must tell your worship that, provided I have plenty, I can eat as much, nay, more to my satisfaction, standing on my legs, and in my own company, than if I was to sit by the side of an emperor: and, if all the truth must be told, I had much rather dine by myself in a corner, though it should be upon a bit of bread and an onion, without all your niceties and ceremonies, than eat turky-cocks at another man's table, where I am obliged to chew softly, to drink sparingly, to wipe my mouth every minute, to abstain from sneezing or coughing, though I should be never so much inclined to either, and from a great many other things, which I can freely do, when alone: therefore, sir master of mine, I hope these honours which your worship would put upon me, as being the servant and abettor of knight-errantry, which to be sure I am, while I remain in quality of your squire, may be converted into other things of more ease and advantage to me, than those which, though I hold them as received in full, I renounce from henceforth for ever, amen." "Thou must nevertheless, sit thee down," said his master; "for, him that is humble God will exalt"; and, seizing him by the arm, he pulled him down to the seat on which he himself sat.

The goatherds, who understood not a word of all this jargon of squire and knight-errant, did nothing but eat in silence, and gaze upon their guests, who with keen appetite, and infinite relish, solaced their stomachs, by swallowing pieces as large as their fists. This service of meat being finished, they spread upon their skins great quantities of acorns, and half a cheese, harder than plaister of Paris: all this time, the horn was not idle, but went round so fast, sometimes full, sometimes empty, like the buckets of a well, that they soon voided one of the two skins of wine that hung in view.

Don Quixote having satisfied his appetite, took up an handful of the acorns, and after looking at them attentively, delivered himself to this purpose: "Happy age, and happy days were those, to which the antients gave the name of golden; not, that gold, which in these our iron-times is so much esteemed, was to be acquired without trouble, in that fortunate period; but, because people then were ignorant of those two words MINE and THINE: in that sacred age, all things were in common; no man was necessitated, in search

of his daily food, to undergo any other trouble than that of reaching out his hand, and receiving it from the sturdy oak, that liberally invited him to pull his sweet and salutary fruit. The limpid fountains and murmuring rills afforded him their savoury and transparent waters in magnificent abundance. In clefts of rocks and hollow trees, the prudent and industrious bees formed their commonwealths, offering without interest, to every hand the fruitful harvest of their delicious toil. The stately cork-trees voluntarily stripped themselves of their light extended bark, with which men began to cover their rural cottages, supported upon rustic poles, with a view only to defend themselves from the inclemencies of the weather. All was then peace, all was harmony, and all was friendship. As yet, the ponderous coulter of the crooked plough had not presumed to open, or visit the pious entrails of our first mother, who, without compulsion, presented, on every part of her wide and fertile bosom, every thing that could satisfy, sustain and delight her sons, who then possessed her. Then did the simple and beautiful shepherdesses rove from hill to hill, and dale to dale, bare-headed, in their braided locks, without any other cloaths than what were necessary to cover modestly that which modesty commands, and always has commanded, to be covered. Neither were their ornaments such as are used now-a-days, enhanced in value by the Tyrian purple, and the many ways martyred silk, but composed of verdant dock-leaves and ivy interwove together; with which they appeared, perhaps with as great pomp and contrivance, as the court-ladies of our days, dressed in all the rare and foreign fashions which idle curiosity has invented. Then were the amorous dictates of the soul expressed in sensible simplicity, just as they were conceived, undisguised by the artificial cloak of specious words. There was no fraud, no deceit, no malice intermixed with plain-dealing truth: justice then kept within her proper bounds, undisturbed and unbiassed by interest and favour, which now impair, confound, and persecute her so much: law was not then centered in the arbitrary bosom of the judge, for, at that time, there was neither cause nor contest. Damsels and decency, as I have already said, went about single, and without fear of being injured by insolence or lust; and their ruin, when it happened, was the fruit of their own will and pleasure. But, now-a-days, in this detestable age, no maid is secure, though she was concealed, and shut up in such another labyrinth as was that of Crete; for, even there, the amorous pestilence, with the zeal of mischievous importunity, would enter, either by the help of wings, or by gliding through some chink or other, and all her barricadoed chastity would go to wreck. For the security of this virtue, in process of time, when mischief grew to a greater head, the order of knight-errantry was first instituted to defend damsels, protect widows, and succour the needy and the fatherless. This order, brother goatherds, I profess, and thank you for this kind entertainment and reception, which I and my squire have received at your hands: for though, by the law of nature, all mankind are obliged to favour and assist knights-errant, during the whole course of their lives; yet, as you have received and regaled me, before you knew yourselves to be under that obligation, I think it my duty to return my most sincere acknowledgment for your hospitality."

The whole of this tedious harrangue, which might very well have been spared, was pronounced by our knight, because the acorns they presented recalled to his memory the golden age: therefore he took it in his head to make these useless reflections to the goatherds, who without answering one syllable, listened with suspence and astonishment. Sancho was also silent, but, kept his teeth employed upon the acorns, and paid

many a visit to the second wine-bag, which that the contents might be the cooler, was hung upon a cork-tree. Don Quixote was less tedious in his discourse than at his meal, which being ended, one of the goatherds said, "That your worship knight-errant, may be convinced of our readiness and good will to give you all the entertainment in our power, you shall have the pleasure and satisfaction of hearing a song from one of our companions, who will soon be here. He is an understanding young fellow, very much in love, who moreover, can read and write, and play upon the rebec *, that it will delight you to hear him." Scarce had the goatherd pronounced these words, when their ears were saluted with the sound of this instrument, and presently after appeared the musician, who was a young fellow of about twenty, or twenty two years of age, and of a very graceful appearance. His companions asked him if he had supped, and he answering in the affirmative, one of them, who had made the offer to the knight, said to him, "If that be the case, Antonio, you will do us the pleasure to sing a song, that this gentleman our guest may see, there are some even among these woods and mountains who understand music. We have already informed him of thy uncommon talents, and we desire thou wouldst shew them, in order to justify what we have said in thy praise; I therefore, earnestly beseech thee to sit down, and sing the ballad of thy love, composed by thy uncle the curate, which is so much commended in our village." "With all my heart," replied the young man, who without farther intreaty sat down upon the trunk of an ancient oak, and tuning his instrument, began in a very graceful manner to sing and accompany the following song.

I.

You love, Olalla, nay adore me;
    In spite of all your art I know it,
Although you never smile before me,
    And neither tongue nor eyes avow it.

II.

For, sure to slight a lover's passion,
    So try'd as that which lives this heart in,
Were but small proof of penetration;
    And that you are no fool is certain.

III.

Sometimes, indeed, and 'tis amazing,
    Though prov'd by evidence of twenty,
You've plainly shewn your soul was brazen,
    And eke your snowy bosom flinty.

IV.

Yet, in the midst of maiden shyness,
    Affected scorn and decent scolding,
Kind Hope appear'd with proffer'd spy-glass,
    The border of her robe unfolding.

* A sort of small fiddle of one piece, with three strings, used by shepherds.[1]

### V.

Then balance in the scales of reason,
   My love unshaken and untainted,
Unapt to change from truth to treason,
   By frowns impair'd, by smiles augmented.

### VI.

If love be courtesy refin'd,
   And you be civil to profusion,
That you will to my hopes prove kind,
   Is but a natural conclusion.

### VII.

If gratitude that breast can soften,
   Which bids to other arts defiance,
The services I've render'd often,
   Must melt your soul to kind compliance.

### VIII.

For, more than once, had you attended,
   You might have seen me wear on Monday,
My best apparel scour'd and mended,
   With which I wont to honour Sunday.

### IX.

As love delights in finery,
   And women oft are wont by tightness,
I've still endeavour'd in your eye,
   To shine the mirrour of politeness.

### X.

That I have danc'd the swains among,
   To please your pride what need I mention,
Or with the cock begun my song,
   To wake my sleeping fair's attention.

### XI.

Or that, enamour'd of your beauty,
   I've loudly sounded forth it's praises;
A task which though a lover's duty,
   The spite of other women raises.

### XII.

For, once, Teresa of the hill,
   Beneath all notice would have sunk ye,
"You think Olalla angel still,
   (Said she) but others scorn the monkey.

### XIII.

Thanks to her beads of glittering glass,
    And her false locks in ringlets curling,
And the false colour of her face,
    Which Love himself might take for sterling."

### XIV.

She ly'd, I told her in her throat;
    And when her kinsman kept a racket,
You know, I made him change his note,
    And soundly thresh'd the booby's jacket.

### XV.

Your lovely person, not your wealth,
    At first engag'd my inclination;
Nor would I now possess by stealth,
    The guilty joys of fornication.

### XVI.

The church has silken ties in store,
    Then yield thy neck to Hymen's fetters;
Behold, I put my own before,
    And trust the noose that binds our betters.

### XVII.

Else, by each blessed saint I swear,
    And Heav'n forbid I prove a lyar!
Never to quit this desart drear,
    Except in form of hooded fryar *.

Thus ended the goatherd's ditty, and though Don Quixote desired him to sing another, yet Sancho Panza would by no means give his consent, being more inclined to take his natural rest than to hear ballads; and therefore, he said to his master, "Your worship had

---

* The reader will perceive that I have endeavoured to adapt the versification to the plainness and rusticity of the sentiment, which are preserved through the whole of this ballad; though all the other translators seem to have been bent upon setting the poetry at variance with the pastoral simplicity of the thoughts. For example, who would ever dream of a goatherd's addressing his mistress in these terms?

With rapture on each charm I dwell,
    And daily spread thy beauty's fame;
And still my tongue thy praise shall tell,
    Though envy swell, or malice blame.

The original sentiments which this courtly stanza is designed to translate, are literally these:
"I do not mention the praises I have spoke of your beauty, which, though true in fact, are the occasion of my being hated by some other women."[2]

better consider where you are to lodge this night; for, the labour that these honest men undergo in the day, will not suffer them to pass the night in singing." "I understand thee, Sancho," replied the knight, "it plainly appears that the visits thou hast made to the wine-bag, demand the consolation of sleep, rather than that of music." "They agreed with us all very well, blessed be God"; replied Sancho. "I do not deny it," said the knight, "and thou mayst bestow thyself in the best manner thou canst; but it is more seemly for those of my profession to watch than to sleep: it would not be amiss, however, Sancho, to dress my ear again; for, it gives me more pain than I could wish." Sancho did as he desired: when one of the goatherds perceiving the wound, bad him give himself no trouble about it, for, he would apply a remedy that would heal it in a trice; so saying, he took some leaves of rosemary, which grew in great plenty round the hut, and having chewed, and mixed them with a little salt, applied the poultice to his ear, and binding it up carefully, assured him, as it actually happened, that it would need no other plaister.

## CHAPTER IV.

## What was related by a goatherd, who chanced to come into the hut.

In the mean time, another of the lads who brought them victuals from the village, entering the hut, said, "Do you know what has happened in our town, comrades?" When one of them answered, "How should we." "Know then," continued he, "that the famous student Chrysostom died this morning; and it is murmured about, that his death was occasioned by his love for that devilish girl Marcella, daughter of William the rich. She that roves about these plains in the habit of a shepherdess." "For Marcella, said you?" cried one. "The same," answered the goatherd, "and it is certain that, in his last will, he ordered himself to be buried in the field, like a Moor (God bless us!) at the foot of the rock hard by the cork-tree-spring; for, the report goes, and they say, he said so himself, as how the first time he saw her, was in that place; and he has also ordained many other such things, as the clergy say, must not be accomplished, nor is it right they should be accomplished; for truly, they seem quite heathenish: to all which objections his dear friend, Ambrosio the student, who also dressed himself like a shepherd, to keep him company, replies that he will perform every thing, without fail, that Chrysostom has ordered; and the whole village is in an uproar about it. But, it is believed, that every thing, at last, will be done according to the desire of Ambrosio, and all the rest of the shepherds, his friends; and that to-morrow he will be interred with great pomp in the very spot I have mentioned. I am resolved therefore, as it will be a thing well worth seeing, to go thither without fail, even though I thought I should not be able to return to the village that night." "We will do so too," replied the goatherds, "and cast lots to see which of us must stay and take care of our flocks." "You are in the right, Pedro," said one, "but, there will be no occasion to use that shift; for, I myself will stay, and take care of the

whole, and you must not impute my tarrying to virtue, or the want of curiosity, but, to the plaguy thorn that ran into my foot the other day, and hinders me from walking." "We are obliged to thee, however," answered Pedro, whom Don Quixote desired to tell him, who that same dead shepherd, and living shepherdess were.

To this question the goatherd replied, all that he knew of the matter, was, that the deceased was the son of a rich farmer, who lived in the neighbourhood of a village, in these mountains; that he had studied in Salamanca many years, at the end of which he had returned to his family with the character of a great scholar: in particular, they said, he was very knowing in the science of the stars, and what passed betwixt the sun and moon, and the heavens; for, he had punctually foretold the clipse of them both! "The obscuration of those two great luminaries," said the knight, "is called the eclipse, and not the clipse, friend." But, Pedro without troubling his head with these trifles, proceeded, saying, "he likewise, foresaw when the year would be plentiful or staril." "You mean sterile," said Don Quixote. "Sterile, or staril," replied Pedro, "comes all to the same purpose; and I say, that his father and his friends taking his advice, became very rich; for, they gave credit to his words, and followed his counsel in all things. When he would say, this year you must sow barley, and no wheat; here you must sow carabances,[1] but no barley; next year there will be a good harvest of oil; but, for three years to come there will not be a drop." "That science," replied Don Quixote, "is called astrology." "I know not how it is called," replied Pedro; "but this I know, that he knew all this, and much more. In short, not many months after he came from Salamanca, he appeared all of a sudden, in shepherd-weeds, with his woolly jacket, and a flock of sheep, having laid aside the long dress of a student. And he was accompanied by a friend of his in the same habit, whose name was Ambrosio, and who had been his fellow-student at college. I forgot to tell you, that Chrysostom the defunct was such a great man at composing couplets, that he made carols for Christmass-eve, and plays for the Lord's-day, which were represented by the young men in our village; and every body said, that they were tip-top. When the people of the village saw the two scholars, so suddenly clothed like shepherds, they were surprized, and could not guess their reason for such an odd change. About that time, the father of this Chrysostom dying, he inherited great riches, that were in moveables and in lands, with no small number of sheep more or less, and a great deal of money: of all which, this young man remained desolate lord and master; and truly he deserved it all; for, he was an excellent companion, very charitable, a great friend to good folks, and had a most blessed countenance. Afterwards, it came to be known, that his reason for changing his garb, was no other, than with a view of strolling through the woods and desarts after that same shepherdess Marcella, whose name my friend mentioned just now, and with whom the poor defunct Chrysostom was woundily in love: and I will now tell you, for, it is necessary, that you should know who this wench is; for, mayhap, nay even without a mayhap, you never heard of such a thing in all the days of your life, though you be older than * St. Paul." "Say Paul's," replied Don Quixote, offended at the goatherd's per-

* In the original Spanish, the goatherd, instead of saying as old as Sarah, says as old as Sarna, which in that language signifies the itch; but as it is impossible to preserve these mistakes in the translation, I have substituted another in its room, which I apprehend is equally natural and expressive.[2]

verting the words. "St. Paul was no chicken," replied Pedro, "and if your worship be re-
solved to correct my words every moment, we shall not have done in a twelvemonth."
"I ask your pardon, friend," said the knight; "I only mention this, because there is a wide
difference between the person of St. Paul, and a church that goes by his name: but, how-
ever, you made a very sensible reply; for, to be sure, the saint lived long before the
church was built: therefore go on with your story, and I promise not to interrupt you
agen."

"Well then, my good master," said the goatherd, "there lived in our village a farmer,
still richer than Chrysostom's father; his name was William, and God gave him, over
and above great wealth, a daughter, who at her birth was the death of her mother, the
most worthy dame in all the country. Methinks I see her now with that face of hers,
which seemed to have the sun on one side, and the moon on the other; she was an ex-
cellent housewife, and a great friend to the poor, for which reason I believe her soul is
enjoying the presence of God in paradise. Her husband died of grief for the loss of so
good a wife, leaving his daughter Marcella, young and rich, to the care of an uncle, who
has got a living in our village. The girl grew up with so much beauty, that she put us in
mind of her mother, who had a great share, and yet it was thought, it would be surpassed
by the daughter's. It happened accordingly, for when she came to the age of fourteen or
fifteen, nobody could behold her without blessing God, for having made so beautiful a
creature; and every body almost grew desperately in love with her. Her uncle kept her
up with great care; but, for all that, the fame of her exceeding beauty spread in such a
manner, that both for her person and her fortune, not only the richest people in our
town, but likewise in many leagues about, came to ask her in marriage of her uncle, with
much importunity and sollicitation. But he, who, to give him his due, was a good chris-
tian, although he wanted to dispose of her as soon as she came to an age fit for matri-
mony, would not give her away without her own consent; neither had he a view in de-
ferring her marriage, to the gain and advantage which he might enjoy in managing the
girl's fortune. And truly I have heard this spoken in more companies than one, very
much to the praise of the honest priest. For, I would have you know, sir traveller, that in
these small towns, people intermeddle and grumble about every thing. And this you
may take for certain, as I know it to be so, that a clergyman must be excessively good in-
deed, if he can oblige his flock to speak well of him, especially in country villages." "You
are certainly in the right," said Don Quixote, "and pray go on, for your story is very en-
tertaining, and you, honest Pedro, relate it with a good grace." "May I never want God's
grace," said the shepherd; "for, that is the main chance: and you must know, moreover,
that though the uncle proposed to his niece, and described the good qualities of each in
particular who asked her in marriage, desiring her to give her hand to some one, or
other, and chuse for herself; she never would give him any other answer, but that she did
not chuse to marry, for, she was too young to bear the burden of matrimony. On account
of these excuses, which seemed to have some reason in them, her uncle forbore to im-
portune her, and waited till she should have more years and discernment to make choice
of her own company; for, he said, and to be sure, it was well said, that parents should
never dispose of their children against their own inclinations. But, behold, when we
least thought of it, the timorous Marcella, one day, appeared in the habit of a shep-

herdess; and without imparting her design to her uncle, or any body in the village, for fear they might have dissuaded her from it, she took to the field with her own flock, in company of the other damsels of the village. As she now appeared in public, and her beauty was exposed to the eyes of every body, you cannot conceive what a number of rich youths, gentlemen, and farmers, immediately took the garb of Chrysostom, and went wooing her through the fields. One of these suitors, as you have heard, was the deceased, who, they say, left off loving to adore her; and you must not think, that because Marcella took to this free and unconfined way of living, she brought the least disparagement upon her chastity and good name; on the contrary, such is the vigilance with which she guards her honour, that of all those who serve and sollicit her, not one has boasted, nor indeed can boast with any truth, that she has given him the smallest hope of accomplishing his desire; for, though she neither flies, or avoids the company and conversation of the shepherds, but, treats them in a courteous and friendly manner; whenever any one of them comes to disclose his intention, let it be ever so just and holy, even marriage itself, she throws him from her, like a stone from a sling, and being of this disposition, does more damage in this country, than if a pestilence had seized it; for, her affability and beauty allures all the hearts of those that converse with her to serve and love her, but, her coyness and plain-dealing drives them even to the borders of despair; therefore, they know not what to say, but, upbraid her with cruelty and ingratitude, and give her a great many such titles, as plainly shew the nature of her disposition: and if your worship was but to stay here one day, you would hear these hills and dales resound with the lamentations of her rejected followers. Not far from this place, there is a tuft of about a dozen of tall beeches, upon every one of which, you may read engraved the name of Marcella, and over some a crown cut out in the bark, as if her lover would have declared, that Marcella wears, and deserves to wear, the crown of all earthly beauty. Here one shepherd sighs, there another complains; in one place you may hear amorous ditties; in another the dirges of despair; one lover sits musing through all the hours of the night, at the foot of some tall ash, or rugged rock, and there, without having closed his weeping eyes, shrunk up as it were, and entranced in his own reflections, he is found by the rising sun; a second, without giving respite, or truce to his sighs, exposed to the heat of the most sultry summer's sun, lies stretched upon the burning sand, breathing his complaints to pitying heaven; and over this and that, and these and those, the free, the unconcerned, the fair Marcella triumphs. We who are acquainted with her disposition, wait with impatience to see the end of all this disdain, and long to know what happy man will tame such an unsociable humour, and enjoy such exceeding beauty. As every thing that I have recounted is true to a tittle, I have no reason to doubt the truth of what our comrades said concerning the cause of Chrysostom's death; and therefore, I advise you, sir, not to fail being to-morrow at his burial, which will be well worth seeing; for, Chrysostom had a great many friends, and the spot in which he ordered himself to be buried is not more than half a league from hence."

"I will take care to be present," said the knight, "and thank you heartily for the pleasure you have given me in relating such an interesting story." "Oh! as for that," cried the goatherd, "I do not know one half of what has happened to the lovers of Marcella; but, to-morrow perhaps, we may light upon some shepherd on the road, who is better ac-

quainted with them. In the mean time you will do well to go to sleep under some cover, for the cold night-air may not agree with the hurt your jaws have received, though the remedy I have applied is such, that you have nothing else to fear."

Sancho Panza, who wished the goatherd's loquacity at the devil, earnestly intreated his master to go to sleep in Pedro's hut. This request the knight complied with, and spent the greatest part of the night in thinking of his lady Dulcinea, in imitation of Marcella's lovers; while Sancho Panza taking up his lodging betwixt Rozinante and his ass, slept soundly, not like a discarded lover, but, like one who had been battered and bruised the day before.

## CHAPTER V.

### The conclusion of the story of the shepherdess Marcella, and other incidents.

S carce had Aurora disclosed herself through the balconies of the east, when five of the six goatherds arising, went to waken Don Quixote, and told him, that if he continued in his resolution of going to see the famous funeral of Chrysostom, they would keep him company. The knight, who desired nothing better, arose, and commanded Sancho to saddle his horse and pannel his ass immediately. This order was executed with great dispatch, and they set out without loss of time. They had not travelled more than a quarter of a league, when, upon crossing a path they saw coming towards them six shepherds, clothed in jackets of black sheep-skin, and crowned with garlands of cypress, and bitter-bay, each having a club of holly in his hand. Along with them came also two gentlemen on horseback, very well equipped for travel, accompanied by three young men on foot.

When they advanced, they saluted one another, and understanding, upon enquiry, that they were all bound to the place of interment, they joined company, and travelled together. One of the horsemen said to his companion, "Signor Vivaldo, we shall not have reason to grudge our tarrying to see this famous funeral, which must certainly be very extraordinary, by the strange account we have received from these people, of the dead shepherd, and the murderous shepherdess." "I am of the same opinion," answered Vivaldo, "and would not only tarry one day, but even four or five, on purpose to see it." Don Quixote asking what they had heard of Marcella and Chrysostom, the traveller replied, that, early in the morning, they had met with these shepherds, of whom enquiring the cause of their being clothed in such melancholy weeds, they had been informed of the coyness and beauty of a certain shepherdess called Marcella, and the hapless love of many who courted her, together with the death of that same Chrysostom to whose funeral they were going. In short, he recounted every circumstance of what Pedro had told Don Quixote before.

This conversation being ended, another began by Vivaldo's asking Don Quixote, why he travelled thus in armour, in a peaceable country? To this question the knight replied, "The exercise of my profession will not permit or allow me to go in any other manner. Revels, feasting, and repose were invented by effeminate courtiers; but, toil, anxiety, and arms are peculiar to those whom the world calls knights-errant, of which order I, though unworthy, and the least, am one." He had no sooner pronounced these words, than all present took him for a madman: but, in order to confirm their opinion, and discover what species of madness it was, Vivaldo desired to know what he meant by knights-errant. "What!" said Don Quixote, "have you never read the annals and history of England, which treat of the famous exploits of Arthur, who, at present, in our Castilian language, is called King Artus, and of whom, there is an ancient tradition, generally believed all over Great-Britain, that he did not die, but was, by the art of inchantment, metamorphosed into a raven: and, that the time will come, when he shall return, and recover his scepter and throne: For which reason, it cannot be proved, that from that period to this, any Englishman has killed a raven. In the reign of that excellent king was instituted that famous order of chivalry, called the Knights of the Round-Table; and those amours punctually happened, which are recounted of Don Lancelot of the Lake, with queen Ginebra, by the help and mediation of that sage and venerable duenna Quitaniona; from whence that delightful ballad, so much sung in Spain, took its rise:

> For never sure was any knight
> So serv'd by damsel, or by dame,
> As Lancelot, that man of might,
> When he at first from Britain came:[1]

With the rest of that most relishing and delicious account of his amours, and valiant exploits. From that time, the order of knight-errantry was extended, as it were, from hand to hand, and spread thro' divers and sundry parts of the world, producing, among many other worthies celebrated for their atchievements, the valiant Amadis de Gaul, with all his sons and nephews even to the fifth generation; the couragious Fleximarte of Hircania, the never-enough to be commended Tirante the white, and he whom, in this our age, we have as it were seen, heard, and conversed with, the invincible and valorous knight Don Belianis of Greece. This, gentlemen, is what I meant by knight-errant; and such as I have described, is the order of chivalry, which, as I have already told you, I, tho' a sinner, have professed, and the very same which those knights I mentioned, professed, I profess also. On which account, I am found in these desarts and solitudes, in quest of adventures, fully determined to lift my arm, and expose my person to the greatest danger that my destiny shall decree, in behalf of the needy and oppressed."

By this declaration, the travellers were convinced that the knight had lost his wits, and easily perceived the species of folly which had taken possession of his brain, and which struck them with the same surprize that always seized those who became acquainted with our knight. Vivaldo, who was a person of discretion, and a great deal of archness, in order to travel agreeably the rest of the road which they had to go, till they should come to the place of interment, wanted to give him opportunity of proceeding in his ex-

travagance, and in that view, said to him: "Sir knight-errant, methinks your worship professes one of the strictest orders upon earth, nay, I will affirm more strict than that of the Carthusian friars."

"The order of the Carthusians," answered Don Quixote, "may be as strict, but, that it is as beneficial to mankind, I am within a hair's breadth of doubting; for, to be plain with you, the soldier who executes his captain's command, is no less valuable than the captain who gave the order: I mean, that the monks pray to God for their fellow-creatures in peace and safety; but, we soldiers and knights put in execution that for which they pray by the valour of our arms, and the edge of our swords; living under no other cover than the cope of heaven, set up in a manner as marks for the intolerable heat of the sun in summer, and the chilling breath of frosty winter: we are therefore God's ministers, and the arms by which he executes his justice upon earth; and as the circumstances of war, and what has the least affinity and concern with it, cannot be accomplished without sweat, anxiety and fatigue; it follows, that those who profess it, are doubtless more subject to toil than those who in rest and security implore the favour of God for persons who can do nothing for themselves: not, that I would be thought to say, or imagine, the condition of a knight-errant is equal to that of a recluse monk; I would only infer from what we suffer, that it is without doubt more troublesome, more battered, more famished, more miserable, ragged and lousy; for, the knights-errant of past times, certainly underwent numberless misfortunes in the course of their lives: and if some of them came to be emperors by the valour of their arms, considering the blood and sweat it cost them; in faith, it was a dear purchase: and if those who attained such a supreme station, had been without their sage enchanters to assist them, they might have been defrauded of their desires, and grievously baulked of their expectations."

"I am very much of your opinion," answered the traveller; "but, there is one thing among you knights-errant, that I cannot approve of, and that is, when any great and dangerous adventure occurs, in which you run a manifest risk of losing your lives, in the instant of engagement, you never think of recommending your souls to God, as every christian ought to do on such occasions; but, on the contrary, put up your petitions to your mistresses, with as much fervour and devotion as if they were your deities; a circumstance which in my opinion smells strong of paganism." "Sir," replied Don Quixote, "that practice must in no degree be altered; and woe be to that knight-errant who should do otherwise; for, according to the practice and custom of chivalry, every knight, when he is upon the point of atchieving some great feat, must call up the idea of his mistress, and turning his eyes upon her with all the gentleness of love, implore, as it were, by his looks, her favour and protection in the doubtful dilemma in which he is about to involve himself: nay, even tho' no body should hear him, he is obliged to mutter between his teeth, an ejaculation, by which he heartily and confidently recommends himself to her good wishes: and of this practice we have innumerable examples in history; but, I would not have you think, that we are to forbear recommending ourselves to God also; there will be time and opportunity enough for that duty, in the course of action."

"But, nevertheless," said the traveller, "I have still one scruple remaining, which is, that I have often read of a dispute between two knights, which proceeding to rage, from one word to another, they have turned about their steeds, to gain ground for a good career,

and then, without any more ceremony, returned to the encounter at full gallop, recommending themselves to their mistresses by the way; and the common issue of such an engagement is, that one of them is thrown down over his horse's crupper, stuck thro' and thro' with his adversary's lance, while the other, with difficulty, avoids a fall by laying hold of his horse's main: now, I cannot comprehend how the dead man could have time to recommend himself to God, in the course of so sudden an attack; surely, it would have been better for his soul, if, instead of the words he uttered in his career, he had put up a petition to heaven, according to the duty and obligation of every Christian; especially, as I take it for granted, that every knight-errant has not a mistress, for, all of them cannot be in love." "That's impossible," answered Don Quixote. "I affirm, that there never could be a knight-errant without a mistress; for, to be in love is as natural and peculiar to them, as the stars are to the heavens. I am very certain that you never read an history that gives an account of a knight-errant without an amour; for, he that has never been in love, would not be held as a legitimate member, but some adulterate brood, who had got into the fortress of chivalry, not thro' the gate, but over the walls, like a thief in the night."

"Yet, notwithstanding," said the traveller, "I have read that Don Galaor, brother of the valiant Amadis de Gaul, never had any known mistress to whom he could recommend himself: and he was not disregarded, but looked upon as a very valiant and famous knight." "Signor," answered our hero Don Quixote, "one swallow makes not a summer: besides, to my certain knowledge, that knight was privately very much in love; indeed he made love to every handsome woman who came in his way; for, that was his natural disposition, which he by no means could resist: in short, it is very well attested, that he had one mistress, whom he enthroned, as sovereign of his heart, and to whom he recommended himself with great caution and privacy, because he piqued himself upon being a secret knight."

"Since then it is essential to every knight to be in love, we may conclude that your worship being of that profession, is no stranger to that passion; and if you do not value yourself upon being as secret a knight as Don Galaor, I earnestly entreat you, in behalf of myself, and the rest of the company, to tell us the name, country, station and qualities of your mistress, who must think herself extremely happy in reflecting that all the world knows, how much she is beloved and adored by so valiant a knight as your worship appears to be."

Here, Don Quixote uttered a grievous sigh, saying: "I am not positively certain, whether or not that beauteous enemy of mine takes pleasure in the world's knowing I am her slave; this only I can say, in answer to the question you asked, with so much civility, that her name is Dulcinea; her native country a certain part of La Mancha called Toboso; her station must at least be that of a princess, since she is queen and lady of my soul; her beauty supernatural, in that it justifies all those impossible and chimerical attributes of excellence, which the poets bestow upon their nymphs; her hair is of gold, her forehead the Elysian fields, her eyebrows heavenly arches, her eyes themselves suns, her cheeks roses, her lips of coral, her teeth of pearl, her neck alabaster, her breast marble, her hands ivory, her skin whiter than snow, and those parts which decency conceals from human view, are such, according to my belief and apprehension, as discretion ought to inhance above all comparison."

"I wish we knew her lineage, race, and family," replied Vivaldo. To this hint the knight answered, "She is not descended of the antient Caii, Curtii, and Scipios of Rome, nor of the modern Colonas and Ursini, nor of the Moncadas and Requesenes of Catalonia, much less of the Rebellas and Villanovas of Valencia; or the Palafaxes, Nucas, Rocabertis, Corellas, Lunas, Alagones, Urreas, Fozes and Gurreas of Arragon, or the Cerdas, Manriquez, Mendozas and Gusmans of Castile, or the Alencastros, Pallas and Menesis of Portugal: but, she sprung from the family of Toboso de La Mancha, a lineage, which tho' modern, may give a noble rise to the most illustrious families of future ages; and let no man contradict what I say, except upon the conditions expressed in that inscription placed by Cerbino under the trophy of Orlando's arms.

> That knight alone these arms shall move,
> Who dares Orlando's prowess prove *.

"Altho' I myself am descended from the † Cachopines of Laredo," said the traveller, "I won't presume to compare with that of Toboso de La Mancha; tho', to be plain with you, I never before heard of any such generation." "How, not heard!" replied Don Quixote. The rest of the company jogged on, listening with great attention to this discourse, and all of them, even the very goatherds, by this time, were convinced, that our knight's judgment was grievously impaired. Sancho alone believed that every thing his master said was true; because he knew his family, and had been acquainted with himself from his cradle. The only doubt that he entertained, was of this same beautiful Dulcinea del Toboso; for, never had such a name or such a princess come within the sphere of his observation, altho' he lived in the neighbourhood of that place.

While they travelled along, conversing in this manner, they perceived about twenty shepherds descending thro' a cleft made by two high mountains. They were all clad in jackets of black sheep-skin, and each of them crowned with a garland, which was composed, as it afterwards appeared, partly of cypress, and partly of yew: six of the foremost carried a bier; upon which they had strewed a variety of branches and flowers. And this

---

* When a knight challenged the whole world, he wore an emprize, consisting of a gold chain, or some other badge of love and chivalry; and sometimes this emprize was fixed in a public place, to attract the attention of strangers; when any person accepted the challenge for a trial of chivalry, called the combat of courtesy, he touched this emprize; but, if he tore it away, it was considered as a resolution to fight the owner to extremity or outrance. The combat of courtesy is still practised by our prize-fighters and boxers, who shake hands before the engagement, in token of love.

But no defiance of this kind could be either published or accepted without the permission of the prince, at whose court the combatants chanced to be. Accordingly we are told by Oliver de La Marche, that the lord of Ternant having published a defiance at the court of Burgundy, in the year 1445, Galiot asked the duke's permission to touch the challenger's emprize; which being granted, he advanced and touched it, saying to the bearer, while he bowed very low, "Noble knight, I touch your emprize, and, with God's permission, will do my utmost to fulfil your desire either on horseback or on foot." The lord of Ternant humbly thanked him for his condescension, said he was extremely welcome, and promised to send him that same day a cartel, mentioning the arms they should use.[2]

† Cachopines is the name given to the Europeans by the Indians of Mexico.[3]

was no sooner perceived by one of the goatherds, than he said, "These are the people who carry the corps of Chrysostom, and the foot of that mountain is the place where he ordered himself to be interred."

Upon this information, they made haste, and came up just at the time that the bearers having laid down the body, began to dig the grave with pick-axes on one side of a flinty rock. They received our travellers with great courtesy, and Don Quixote, with his company, went towards the bier, to look at the dead body, which was covered with flowers, clad in shepherds weeds, and seemingly thirty years old. Notwithstanding he was dead, they could plainly perceive, that he had been a man of an engaging aspect, and genteel stature; and could not help wondering at the sight of a great many papers both sealed and loose, that lay round him in the coffin.

While the new-comers were observing this phænomenon, and the shepherds busied in digging a grave, a wonderful and universal silence prevailed, till such time as one of the bearers said to another: "Consider, Ambrosio, if this be the very spot which Chrysostom mentioned, that his last will may be punctually fulfilled." "This," answered Ambrosio, "is the very place in which my unhappy friend has often recounted to me the story of his misfortunes. Here it was, he first beheld that mortal enemy of the human race; here also did he first declare his amorous and honourable intention; and here, at last, did Marcella signify her disgust and disdain, which put an end to the tragedy of his wretched life: and in this place, as a monument of his mishap, did he desire to be deposited in the bowels of eternal oblivion."

Then addressing himself to Don Quixote, and the travellers, he thus proceeded: "This corse, gentlemen, which you behold with compassionate eyes, was the habitation of a soul, which possessed an infinite share of the riches of heaven: this is the body of Chrysostom, who was a man of unparalelled genius, the pink of courtesy and kindness; in friendship, a very phœnix, liberal without bounds, grave without arrogance, gay without meanness; and, in short, second to none in every thing that was good, and without second in all that was unfortunate. He loved, and was abhorred; he adored, and was disdained; he implored a savage; he importuned a statue; he hunted the wind; cried aloud to the desart; he was a slave to the most ungrateful of women; and the fruit of his servitude was death, which overtook him in the middle of his career: in short, he perished by the cruelty of a shepherdess, whom he has eternised in the memory of all the people in this country; as these papers, which you gaze at would shew, if he had not ordered me to commit them to the flames as soon as his body shall be deposited in the earth."

"You will use them then with more cruelty and rigour," said Vivaldo, "than that of the author himself: seeing it is neither just nor convenient to fulfil the will of any man, provided it be unreasonable. Augustus Cæsar would have been in the wrong, had he consented to the execution of what the divine Mantuan ordered on his death-bed. Wherefore, signor Ambrosio, while you commit the body of your friend to the earth, you ought not likewise to consign his writings to oblivion; nor perform indiscreetly, what he in his affliction ordained: on the contrary, by publishing these papers, you ought to immortalize the cruelty of Marcella, that it may serve as an example in time to come, and warn young men to shun and avoid such dangerous precipices: for, I, and the rest of this company, already know the history of that enamoured and unhappy friend, the nature

of your friendship, the occasion of his death, together with the orders that he left upon his death-bed: from which lamentable story, it is easy to conclude, how excessive must have been the cruelty of Marcella, the love of Chrysostom, the faith of your friendship, and the check which those receive, who precipitately run thro' the path exhibited to them by idle and mischievous love. Last night, we understood the death of Chrysostom, who, we were informed, was to be buried in this place; and therefore, out of curiosity and concern, have turned out of our way, resolving to come, and see with our eyes, what had affected us so much in the hearing: and in return for that concern, and the desire we felt in remedying it, if it had been in our power, we intreat thee, O discreet Ambrosio! at least, for my own part, I beg of thee not to burn these papers, but, allow me to pre-serve some of them."

Accordingly, without staying for an answer, he reached out his hand, and took some of those that were nearest him: which Ambrosio perceiving, said, "Out of civility, signor, I will consent to your keeping what you have taken up; but to think that I will fail to burn the rest, is a vain supposition." Vivaldo being desirous of seeing the contents, immediately opened one, intitled, A song of despair: which Ambrosio hearing, said, "That is the last poem my unhappy friend composed; and that you may see, signor, to what a pass his misfortunes had reduced him, read it aloud, and you'll have time enough to finish it before the grave be made!" "That I will do with all my heart," said Vivaldo, and every body present being seized with the same desire, they stood around him in a circle, and he read what follows, with an audible voice.

A SONG of Despair.[4]

I.

Since then, thy pleasure, cruel maid!
   Is, that thy rigour and disdain
Should be from clime to clime convey'd;
   All hell shall aid me to complain!
The torments of my heart to tell,
   And thy atchievements to record,
My voice shall raise a dreadful yell,
   My bowels burst at every word:
Then listen to the baleful sound
   That issues from my throbbing breast,
Thy pride, perhaps, it may confound,
   And yield my madd'ning soul some rest.

II.

Let the snake's hiss and wolf's dire howl,
   The bull's harsh note, the lyon's roar,
The boding crow and screeching owl,
   The tempest rattling on the shore,
The monster's scream, the turtle's moan,
   The shrieks of the infernal crew,

Be mingled with my dying groan,
  A concert terrible and new!
The hearer's senses to appall,
  And reason from her throne depose;
Such melody will suit the gall
  That from my burning liver flows!

### III.

Old Tagus with his yellow hair,
  And Betis with her olive wreath,
Shall never echo such despair,
  Or listen to such notes of death,
As here I'll utter and repeat,
  From hill to dale, from rock to cave,
In wilds untrod by human feet,
  In dungeons dreary as the grave.
The beasts of prey that scour the plain,
  Shall thy more savage nature know,
The spacious earth resound my strain;
  Such is the privilege of woe!

### IV.

Disdain is death, and doubt o'erturns
  The patience of the firmest mind;
But, jealousy still fiercer burns,
  Like all the flames of hell combin'd!
The horrors of that cursed fiend,
  In absence to distraction rage,
And all the succour hope can lend,
  The direful pangs will not assuage.
Such agonies will surely kill;
  Yet, 'spite of absence, doubts and scorn,
I live a miracle, and still
  Those deadly flames within me burn!

### V.

Hope's shadow ne'er refresh'd my view,
  Despair attends with wakeful strife;
The first let happier swains pursue,
  The last my consort is for life.
Can hope and fear at once prevail,
  When fear on certainty is fed?
To shut mine eyes will nought avail,
  When thunder bursts around my head.
When cold disdain in native dye,
  Appears, and falsehood's cunning lore

Perverts the tale of truth, shall I
   Against despondence shut the door?

### VI.

O jealousy! love's tyrant lord,
   And thou soul-chilling, dire disdain!
Lend me the dagger and the cord,
   To stab remembrance, strangle pain.
I die bereft of hope in death,
   Yet still those are the freest souls,
(I'll vouch it with my latest breath)
   Whom love's old tyranny controuls.
My fatal enemy is fair,
   In body and in mind, I'll say,
And I have earn'd the woes I bear:
   By rigour love maintains the sway.

### VII.

With this opinion let me fall
   A prey to unrelenting scorn;
No fun'ral pomp shall grace my pall,
   No laurel my pale corse adorn.
O thou! whose cruelty and hate
   The tortures of my breast proclaim,
Behold how willingly to fate
   I offer this devoted frame.
If thou, when I am past all pain,
   Should'st think my fall deserves a tear,
Let not one single drop distain
   Those eyes so killing and so clear.

### VIII.

No! rather let thy mirth display
   The joys that in thy bosom flow;
Ah! need I bid that heart be gay
   Which always triumph'd in my woe.
Come then, for ever barr'd of bliss,
   Ye, who with ceaseless torment dwell,
And agonising, howl and hiss
   In the profoundest shades of hell;
Come, Tantalus, with raging thirst,
   Bring, Sysiphus, thy rolling stone,
Come, Titius, with thy vulture curst,
   Nor leave Ixion rack'd, alone:

### IX.

The toiling sisters too, shall join,
   And my sad, solemn dirge repeat,

When to the grave my friends consign
   These limbs deny'd a winding sheet;
Fierce Cerberus shall clank his chain,
   In chorus with chimæras dire:
What other pomp, what other strain
   Should he who dies of love, require?
Be hush'd my song, complain no more
   Of her whose pleasure gave thee birth;
But let the sorrows I deplore
   Sleep with me in the silent earth.

This ditty of Chrysostom was approved by all the hearers; but, he who read it observed, that it did not seem to agree with the report he had heard of Marcella's virtue and circumspection; inasmuch as the author complained of jealousy, absence, and suspicion, which tended to the prejudice of her morals and reputation. To this objection Ambrosio, as one that was acquainted with the most secret sentiments of his friend, answered, "Signor, for your satisfaction in this point, it is necessary you should know, that the forlorn shepherd composed this song in the absence of Marcella, from whose presence he had gone into voluntary exile, in order to try if he could reap the usual fruits of absence, and forget the cause of his despair; and as one in that situation is apt to be fretted by every circumstance, and invaded by every apprehension, poor Chrysostom was harassed by groundless jealousy and imaginary fears, which tormented him as much as if they had been real; for which reason, this circumstance ought not to invalidate the fame of Marcella's virtue, against which, exclusive of her cruelty, arrogance, and disdain, envy itself hath not been able to lay the least imputation."

"That may be very true," replied Vivaldo, who being about to read another of the papers he had saved from the flames, was diverted from his purpose by a wonderful vision, for such it seemed, that all of a sudden presented itself to their eyes. This was no other than the shepherdess Marcella, who appeared upon the top of the rock, just above the grave they were digging, so beautiful that she surpassed all report. Those who had never seen her before, gazed with silent admiration; nor were the rest who had been accustomed to see her, less astonished at her appearance. But, no sooner did Ambrosio perceive her, than with indignation in his looks, he cried:

"Comest thou hither, fierce basilisk of these mountains! to see if the wounds of this unhappy youth, whom thy cruelty hath slain, will bleed at thy approach? or art thou come to rejoice in the exploits of thy barbarity, and from the top of that mountain behold, like another Nero, to the flames which thy impiety hath kindled? or inhumanly trample on this unfortunate corse, as the unnatural daughter insulted the dead body of her father Tarquin? Tell us, at once, the cause of thy approach, and deign to signify thy pleasure, that I, who know how devoutly Chrysostom obeyed thee, when alive, may, now that he is dead, dispose his friends to yield the same obedience."

"I come not," answered Marcella, "for any of the purposes you have mentioned, Ambrosio; but, rather personally to demonstrate how unreasonably people blame me for their own affliction, as well as for the death and sufferings of Chrysostom. I beg therefore, that all present will give me the hearing, as it will be unnecessary to spend much

The Burial of Chrysostom.

time, or waste many words, to convince those that are unprejudiced, of the truth. Heaven, you say, hath given me beauty, nay, such a share of it, as compels you to love me, in spite of your resolutions to the contrary; from whence you draw this inference, and insist upon it, that it is my duty to return your passion. By the help of that small capacity which nature has bestowed upon me, I know that which is beautiful is lovely; but, I can by no means conceive, why the object which is beloved for being beautiful, is bound to be enamoured of it's admirer: more especially, as it may happen that this same admirer is an object of disgust and abhorrence; in which case, would it be reasonable in him to say, 'I love thee because thou art beautiful, and thou must favour my passion, although I am deformed?' But, granting the beauty equal on both sides, it does not follow, that the desires ought to be mutual; for, all sorts of beauty do not equally affect the spectator; some, for example, delighting the eye only, without captivating the heart. And well it is for mankind, that things are thus disposed; otherwise, there would be a strange perplexity and confusion of desires, without power of distinguishing and choosing particular objects; for, beauty being infinitely diversified, the inclination would be infinitely divided, and I have heard, that true love must be undivided and unconstrained; if this be the case, as I believe it is, why should I constrain my inclination, when I am under no other obligation so to do, but your saying that you are in love with me? Otherwise, tell me, if heaven that made me handsome, had created me a monster of deformity, should I have had cause to complain of you for not loving me? Besides, you are to consider, that I did not choose the beauty I possess; such as it is, God was pleased of his own free will and favour to bestow it upon me, without any solicitation on my part. Therefore, as the viper deserves no blame for its sting, although it be mortal, because it is the gift of nature; neither ought I to be reviled for being beautiful: for, beauty in a virtuous woman, is like a distant flame, and a sharp sword afar off, which prove fatal to none but those who approach too near them. Honour and virtue are the ornaments of the soul; without which the body, though never so handsome, ought to seem ugly: if chastity then be one of the virtues which chiefly adorns and beautifies both body and soul, why should she that is beloved, lose that jewel for which she is chiefly beloved, meerly to satisfy the appetite of one who, for his own selfish enjoyment, employs his whole care and industry to destroy it? I was born free, and to enjoy that freedom, have I chosen the solitude of these fields. The trees on these mountains are my companions; and I have no other mirrour than the limpid streams of these crystal brooks. With the trees and the streams I share my contemplation and my beauty: I am a distant flame and a sword afar off: those whom my eyes have captivated my tongue has undeceived; and if hope be the food of desire, as I gave none to Chrysostom or to any other person, so neither can his death nor that of any other of my admirers, be justly imputed to my cruelty, but, rather, to their own obstinate despair. To those who observe that his intentions were honourable; and that therefore I was bound to comply with them, I answer, when he declared the honesty of his designs in that very spot where now his grave is digging, I told him, my purpose was to live in perpetual solitude, and let the earth alone enjoy the fruits of my retirement, and the spoils of my beauty: Wherefore, if he, notwithstanding this my explanation, persevered without hope, and sailed against the wind; it is no wonder that he was overwhelmed in the gulph of his rashness. Had I cajoled him,

I should have been perfidious; had I gratified his inclination, I should have acted contrary to my own reason and resolution. But, because he persisted after I had explained myself, and despaired before he had cause to think I abhored him, I leave you to judge whether or not it be reasonable to lay his misfortune at my door. Let him whom I have deceived complain, and let him despair to whom I have broke my promise: if I call upon any man, he may depend upon me; if I admit of his addresses, he may rejoice in his success; but, why should I be stiled a barbarous homicide by him whom I never soothed, deceived, called, or admitted? Hitherto heaven has not thought fit that I should love by destiny; and the world must excuse me from loving by election. Let this general declaration serve as an answer to all those who sollicit me in particular, and henceforward give them to understand, that whosoever dies for me, perishes not by jealousy or disdain, for, she who never gave her love, can never give just cause of jealousy; neither ought her plain-dealing to be interpreted into disdain. Let him who terms me a fierce basilisk, shun me as an evil being; if any man thinks me ungrateful, let him refuse his services when I ask them. If I have disowned any one, let him renounce me, in his turn; and let him who has found me cruel, abandon me in my distress: this fierce basilisk, this ungrateful, cruel, supercilious wretch, will neither seek, serve, own, nor follow you in any shape whatever. If Chrysostom perished by the impatience of his own extravagant desire, why should my innocent reserve be inveighed against? If I have preserved my virginity in these desarts, why should he that loves me, wish to see me lose it among mankind! I have riches of my own, as you all know, and covet no man's wealth. I am free, and will not be subjected: I neither love nor hate any man: I do not cajole this one; nor teize that, nor do I joke with one or discourse with another; but amuse myself with the care of my goats, and the innocent conversation of the shepherdesses belonging to the neighbouring villages. My desires are bounded by these mountains; or if my meditation surpasses these bounds, it is only to contemplate the beauty of the heavens, those steps by which the soul ascends to it's original mansion." So saying, without waiting for any reply, she turned her back, and vanished into a thicket on a neighbouring mountain, leaving all that were present equally surprized with her beauty and discretion.

Some of the bystanders being wounded by the powerful shafts that were darted from her fair eyes, manifested an inclination to follow her, without availing themselves of the ingenuous declaration they had heard; which being perceived by Don Quixote, who thought this a proper occasion for exercising his chivalry, in defence of distressed damsels; he laid his hand upon the hilt of his sword, and in a lofty and audible voice, pronounced, "Let no person, of whatsoever rank or degree, presume to follow the beautiful Marcella, on pain of incurring my most furious indignation. She has demonstrated, by clear and undeniable arguments, how little, if at all, she is to be blamed for the death of Chrysostom; and how averse she is to comply with the desires of any of her admirers; for which reason, instead of being pursued and persecuted, she ought to be honoured and esteemed by all virtuous men, as the only person in the universe who lives in such a chaste and laudable intention." Whether it was owing to these menaces of the knight, or to the advice of Ambrose, who desired them to perform the last office to their deceased friend, not one of the shepherds attempted to stir from the spot, until the grave being finished, and the papers burnt, the body of poor Chrysostom was interred, not

without abundance of tears shed by his surviving companions. The grave was secured
by a large fragment of the rock which they rolled upon it, 'till such time as a tomb-stone
could be made, under the direction of Ambrose, who was resolved to have the follow-
ing epitaph engraved upon it.

> The body of a wretched swain,
>     Kill'd by a cruel maid's disdain,
> In this cold bed neglected lies.
>     He liv'd, fond hapless youth! to prove
> Th' inhuman tyranny of love,
>     Exerted in Marcella's Eyes.

Having strewed the place with a profusion of flowers and branches, every body pres-
ent condoled, and took leave of the afflicted executor; and Don Quixote bad farewell to
his kind landlords, as well as to the travellers, who would have persuaded him to ac-
company them to Sevil, which, they said, was a city so well adapted for adventurers, that
they occurred in every street, nay at the corner of every blind alley. Our hero thanked
them most courteously for their advice, and the inclination they expressed to give him
pleasure; but, assured them, he neither could nor would set out for Sevil, until he should
have cleared these desarts of the robbers and banditti, of whom they were reported to
be full.

The travellers seeing him thus laudably determined, importuned him no further, but,
taking leave of him anew, pursued their journey, during which they did not fail to dis-
cuss the story of Marcella and Chrysostom, as well as the madness of Don Quixote, who,
on his part, resolved to go in quest of the shepherdess, and offer her all the service in his
power: but, this scheme did not turn out according to his expectation; as will be related
in the course of this faithful history, the second book of which is here concluded.

# THE

# LIFE and ATCHIEVEMENTS

## Of the Sage and Valiant KNIGHT

# DON QUIXOTE DE LA MANCHA.

# BOOK III.

### CHAPTER I.

## Wherein is recounted the unlucky adventure which happened to Don Quixote, in meeting with certain unmerciful Yanguesians.

The sage Cid Hamet Benengeli relates, that Don Quixote, having bid adieu to his entertainers, and to all who were present at the funeral of the shepherd Chrysostom, entered, with his squire, the same wood to which Marcella had retreated; where, when they had wandered about upwards of two hours, without seeing her, they chanced to find themselves in a delightful spot, overgrown with verdant grass, and watered by a cool and pleasant stream; which was so inviting as to induce them to stay in it, during the heat of the day, that now began to be very sultry; the knight and squire therefore, dismounting, and leaving the ass and Rozinante at pleasure to regale themselves with the rich pasture, emptied their knapsack, and without any ceremony, attacked the contents, which they ate together like good friends, laying aside all vain distinction of master and man.

Sancho had been at no pains to tether Rozinante, secure as he thought, in knowing him to be so meek and peaceable, that all the mares in the meadows of Cordova could not provoke his concupiscence. Chance, however, or the devil, who is not often found napping, ordered it so, as that a drove of Gallician fillies, belonging to certain Yanguesian carriers, happened, at that very instant, to be feeding in that very valley; for, it being the custom of these people to halt and refresh themselves and their beasts in places where there is plenty of water and grass, they could not have lighted on a more convenient spot than that where Don Quixote chanced to be. It was then that Rozinante, seized with an inclination to solace himself with some of those skittish females, no sooner had them in the wind, than deviating from his natural disposition and accustomed deliberation, without asking leave of his lord and master, he went off at a small trot, to communicate his occasions to the objects of his desire. But they, it seems, more fond of their

pasture, than of his addresses, received him so uncivilly with their hoofs and teeth, that in a twinkling, his girth was broke, his saddle kicked off, and he himself remained in cuerpo.[1] But, what he chiefly suffered was from the carriers, who seeing violence offered to their mares, ran to their assistance with long staves, which they exercised upon him so unmercifully, that he fell prostrate to the ground, almost battered to death.

The knight and Sancho seeing their steed thus bastinadoed, made all the haste they could to his rescue; the former addressing the latter in this manner, "I perceive, friend Sancho, that these are no knights, but fellows of low degree and infamous descent: this particular I mention, because thou mayest now assist me, in taking just vengeance upon them, for the injury they have done to Rozinante before my face." "What a devil of vengeance can we pretend to take," answered the squire, "when they are more than twenty, and we but two? nay, I believe, if it was put to the trial, no better than one and a half." "I myself am worth an hundred of such vagabonds," cried Don Quixote; and, without uttering another syllable, he unsheath'd his sword, and assaulted the Yanguesians, being seconded by Sancho, who suffered himself to be rouzed and encouraged by the example of his master: and indeed the knight lent the first he met with such a hearty stroke, as laid open a leathern jacket he wore, together with a large portion of his shoulder.

The carriers seeing themselves thus maltreated by two men only, took the benefit of their numbers, and ran to sustain one another with their staves, then surrounding the two assailants, began to drum upon their carcases with infinite eagerness and dexterity. True it is, at the second application, Sancho fell to the earth: a misfortune that also happened to his master; who, in spite of all his own address, together with the assistance of his good friend, soon found himself stretched at the feet of Rozinante, who had not as yet been able to rise: from whence we may learn, what furious execution is often done by pack-staves, when managed by the hands of such enraged clowns.

The carriers perceiving the havock they had made, thought proper to load again with all dispatch, and pursue their journey, leaving our adventurers in miserable plight and doleful dilemma. The first that recovered the use of his senses, was Sancho Panza, who finding himself laid along by the side of his master, pronounced, with a weak and lamentable voice, "Sir Don Quixote! ah Sir Don Quixote!" "What wouldst thou have, brother Sancho?" replied the knight, in the same feeble and complaining tone. "I wish," resumed Sancho, "your worship would, if it be possible, comfort me with a couple of gulps of that same balsam made by fairy blas,[2] if you have got any of it about you: perhaps it may be serviceable in bruises and broken bones, as well as in wounds and running sores." "Would to God I had it here, unfortunate wight that I am!" cried Don Quixote, "but I swear to thee Sancho, on the faith of a knight-errant, that e'er two days pass, if some mischievous accident does not intervene, I will have it in my possession, if my hands do not very much misgive me." "In how many days does your worship think we shall be able to move our feet?" said the squire. "With regard to myself," answered the battered knight, "I really cannot fix any number of days; but this I know, that I alone am to blame for what has happened, in condescending to use my sword against antagonists, who were not dubbed and knighted like myself. I therefore firmly believe, that as a punishment for having transgressed the laws of chivalry, the God of battles hath permitted me

to receive this disgraceful chastisement: for which reason, brother Sancho, it is proper that thou shouldst be apprised of what I am going to say, as it may be of great importance to the safety of us both: whenever thou shalt see us insulted or aggrieved for the future, by such rascally scum, thou shalt not wait for my drawing upon them, for I will in no shape meddle with such unworthy foes; but, lay thy hand upon thy sword, and with thy own arm, chastise them to thy heart's content: but should any knights make up to their defence and assistance, then shall I know how to protect thee, and assault them with all my might; and thou art already convinced, by a thousand amazing proofs, how far extends the valour of this my invincible arm." So arrogant was the poor knight become, by his victory over the valiant Biscayan.

This wholesome advice, however, was not so much relished by Sancho, but that he replied, "Sir, I am a quiet, meek, peaceable man, and can digest any injury, be it never so hard; for, I have a wife and small children to maintain and bring up: wherefore, let me also apprize, (since I cannot lay my commands upon your worship) that I will in no shape whatever, use my sword against either knight or knave; and that henceforward, in the sight of God, I forgive all injuries, past, present, or to come, which I have already received, at this present time suffer, or may hereafter undergo, from any person whatsoever, high or low, rich or poor, gentle or simple, without exception to rank or circumstance."

His master hearing this declaration, answered, "I wish the grievous pain I feel in this rib, would abate a little, so as that I could speak for a few moments with ease, and convince thee of thy damnable error, Panza. Hark ye me, sinner! suppose the gale of fortune, which hath been hitherto so adverse, should change in our favour, and swelling the sails of our desire, conduct us safely, without the least impediment, into the haven of some one of those islands which I have promised thee: what would become of thy wretched affairs, if, after I had won and given it into thy possession, thou shouldst frustrate my intention, by thy lack of knighthood, ambition, valour and courage to revenge thy wrongs, or defend thy government? for, I would have thee to know, that in all new conquered kingdoms or provinces, the friends of their natural masters are never so quiet or reconciled to their new sovereign, as to dispel all fear of some fresh insurrection, to alter the government again, and as the saying is, Try fortune once more: it is therefore requisite, that the new possessor should have understanding to govern, resolution to punish, and valour to defend himself, in case of any such accident."

"In this last accident which hath befallen us," said Sancho, "I wish the Lord had pleased to give me that same understanding and valour your worship mentions: but, I protest, upon the word of a poor sinner, that I am at present more fit for a searcloth[3] than such conversation. See if your worship can make shift to rise, and then we will give some assistance to Rozinante, tho' it be more than he deserves; for, he was the principal cause of all this plaguy ribroasting: never could I believe such a thing of Rozinante, who, I always thought, was as chaste and sober a person as myself: but, this verifies the common remark, that you must keep company a long time with a man, before you know him thoroughly; and that there is nothing certain in this life. Who could have thought, that those huge back-strokes your worship dealt so heartily to the unlucky traveller, would be followed, as it were, post haste, by such a mighty tempest of blows, as just now

discharged itself upon our shoulders." "Thy carcase, Sancho," said Don Quixote, "was formed for enduring such rough weather; but, my limbs were tenderly nursed in soft wool and fine linen; and therefore must feel more sensibly the pain of this discomfiture: and if I did not believe (believe, said I) if I were not certain, that all these inconveniencies are inseparably annexed to the exercise of arms, I would lie still where I am, and die with pure vexation."

To this protestation, the squire replied, "Seeing these misfortunes are the natural crops of chivalry, pray good your worship, do they happen at all times of the year, or only fall at an appointed season; because, in my simple conjecture, two such harvests will leave us altogether incapable of reaping a third, if God, of his infinite mercy, will not be pleased to send us extraordinary succour." "Thou must know, friend Sancho," answered Don Quixote, "that the life of a knight-errant is subject to a thousand dangers and mishaps; but then, he enjoys the self-same chance of being a king or emperor, as experience demonstrates to have been the case of divers and sundry knights, the history of whose lives I am perfectly well acquainted with; and I could not relate, if this pain would give me leave, the fortunes of some, who, by their valour alone, have risen to that supreme degree: and those very persons, both before and after their success, have undergone various calamities and affliction; witness the valiant Amadis de Gaul, who saw himself in the power of his mortal enemy Arcalaus the enchanter, of whom it is positively affirmed, that while the knight was his prisoner, he caused him to be bound to a pillar in his court-yard, and gave him two hundred stripes with the reins of his horse's bridle. There is likewise a certain secret author of no small credit, who relates that the knight of the sun was caught in a trap in a certain castle, and falling, found himself tied hand and foot in a deep dungeon below ground, where was administred unto him, one of those things they call glysters, composed of sand and water, which had well nigh cost him his life; and if he had not been succoured in that perilous conjuncture, by a sage who was his good friend, the poor knight would have fared very ill. Wherefore, what hath happened to me, may easily pass unheeded, among those much greater affronts, that such worthy people have undergone: besides, I would have thee know, Sancho, that it is never reckoned an affront, to be wounded by those instruments which are casually in the hands of our enemies; for, it is expresly mentioned in the laws of duelling, that if a shoemaker beats a man with the last he has by accident in his hand, the man cannot properly be said to be cudgelled, altho' the said last was made of wood. This particular I mention, that thou mayst not suppose us affronted, altho' we have been mauled in this unlucky fray; for, the weapons with which those men threshed us so severely, were no other than their own packstaves; and so far as I can remember, there was neither tuck, poignard nor sword among them."

"They did not give me time," answered Sancho, "to make any such observation; for scarce had I laid my fingers upon my * Toledo, when there rained a shower of cudgels upon my poor shoulders, that banished the light from my eyes, and strength from my feet, and laid me flat upon the spot where I now lie, not so much concerned about think-

---

* Tizona, which is the word in the original, is a romantic name given to the sword that belonged to Roderick Diaz de Bivar, the famous Spanish general against the Moors.[4]

ing whether this drubbing be an affront or not, as about the intolerable pain of the blows, which remain imprinted upon my memory as well as upon my carcase." "Notwithstanding all this complaining," said the knight, "I aver, brother Sancho, that there is no remembrance which time does not efface, nor pain that death does not remove": "And pray, what greater misfortune can there be," answered Sancho, "than that which nothing but time can remove, or death put a stop to? If this mishap of ours were such a one as might be cured with a couple of snips of cerecloth, it would not be altogether so vexatious; but, so far as I can see, all the plaister of an hospital, will not be sufficient to set us cleverly on our legs again."

"Truce with thy reflections," replied Don Quixote, "and collecting strength out of weakness, as I will endeavour to do, let us rise and examine Rozinante's case; for, in all appearance, the poor beast hath not suffered the least part of the misfortune." "That is not to be wondered at," said the squire, "he being a knight-errant also; but, what surprises me most is, that my dapple should get off without paying his score, when we are scored all over." "Destiny, when one door is shut, always leaves another open, as a resource in all calamities," said Don Quixote: "this I observe, because thy ass will now supply the place of Rozinante, and carry me from hence to some castle, where my wounds may be cured; more especially, as such carriage will be no dishonour to chivalry; for, I remember to have read, that the good old Silenus, tutor and companion of the jolly God of mirth and wine, entered the city of the hundred gates, lolling at his ease upon a most comely ass." "It may be very true, that he rode upon an ass," replied Sancho, "but, there is some difference, I apprehend, between riding and lying across the beast like a bag of dirt." To this observation, the knight answered, "Those wounds which are received in battle, may well give, but can never deprive one of honour: therefore, friend Sancho, do as I bid thee, without further reply; get up as well as thou can'st, and lay me upon dapple just as thou shalt find most convenient, that we may be gone before night comes to surprise us in this unfrequented place."

"And yet," said Sancho, "I have heard your worship remark, that it is usual for knights-errant to sleep upon commons and heaths, the greatest part of the year; ay, and to be thankful for their good fortune in being able so to do." "Yes," said the knight, "when they can do no better, or are in love; and this is so true, that there was a knight who lay upon a bare rock, exposed to the sultry noon and midnight damps, with all the inclemencies of the weather, during two whole years, before his mistress knew any thing of the matter: this was no other than Amadis, who, assuming the name of Beltenebros, took up his quarters upon the naked rock,[5] for the space of either eight years, or eight months, I really do not remember which; only that he remained doing penance in that place, for some disgust shewn to him by his dame Oriana: but, truce with this conversation, Sancho, and make haste, before such another accident can happen to thy beast, as that which hath already befallen Rozinante."

"Odds my life! that would be the devil indeed," cried Sancho, who uttering thirty ah's! and sixty oh's! together with a hundred and fifty ola's! and curses upon him who had brought him to that pass, raised himself up, tho' he could not for his soul stand upright, but in spite of all his efforts, remained bent like a Turkish bow, and in that attitude, with infinite labour, made shift to equip his ass, which had also gone a little astray, presum-

ing upon the excessive licence of the time; he then lifted up Rozinante, who, could he have found a tongue to complain with, would certainly have surpassed both his master and Sancho, in lamentation: in short, the squire disposed of Don Quixote upon the ass, to whose tail Rozinante was tied; then taking his own dapple by the halter, jogged on sometimes faster, sometimes slower, towards the place where he conjectured the high road to lie: and indeed, they had not exceeded a short league, when by good luck, which now seemed to take the management of their affairs, they arrived at the highway, and discovered an inn, which, to Sancho's great grief, was mistaken for a castle by the joyful knight. This difference of opinion, begat an obstinate dispute that lasted until they arrived at the place, into which Sancho immediately conveyed his cargo, without further expostulation.

## CHAPTER II.

## The adventure that happened to this sagacious knight at the inn, which he mistook for a castle.

The innkeeper seeing Don Quixote laid athwart the ass, asked what was the matter? To which interrogation, Sancho replied, "Nothing but a few bruises which my master has received in a fall from a rock in this neighbourhood." The landlady, who differed in disposition from most of your innkeepers wives, being naturally charitable and sympathizing with the calamities of her fellow-creatures, came running to the relief of the battered knight, and brought her daughter, who was a very handsome girl, to assist in taking care of her guest. There was, in the same house, a servant maid from the Asturias, remarkable for her capacious countenance, beetle-brow'd, flat-nosed, blind of one eye, and bleared in the other; true it is, the gentility of her shape made amends for her other defects: she was something short of seven hands from head to foot, and moreover, encumbered so much by her shoulders, that she was obliged to contemplate the dust beneath her feet, oftner than she could have wished.

This comely creature, with the assistance of the other damsel, made up a sort of a sorry bed for our hero in a garret, which gave evident tokens of having been formerly an hay-loft, and in which, at that time, a certain carrier had taken up his quarters, in a bed of his own making, a little on one side of our knight's: and tho' his couch was composed of the pannels and furniture of his mules, it had greatly the advantage over Don Quixote's, which consisted only of four rough boards, supported on two benches of unequal height, covered by a mattress so thin, it might have passed for a quilt, and full of knots, so hard as to be mistaken for peeble-stones, had not the wool appeared thro' divers openings; with a couple of sheets made of bull's hide, and a blanket so bare, that you might have counted every thread, without losing one of the reckoning.

In this wretched bed, Don Quixote having laid himself down, was anointed from head

to foot by the good woman and her daughter, while Maritornes (that was the Asturian's name) stood hard by holding a light. The landlady, in the course of her application, perceiving the knight's whole body black and blue, observed that those marks seemed rather the effects of drubbing than of a fall; but, Sancho affirmed she was mistaken; and that the marks in question, were occasioned by the knobs and corners of the rocks, among which he fell: "And now I think of it," said he, "pray madam, manage matters so as to leave a little of your ointment, for it will be needed, I'll assure you; my own loins are none of the soundest at present." "What! did you fall too?" said she. "I can't say I did," answered the squire, "but, I was so infected, by seeing my master tumble, that my whole body akes as much as if I had been cudgelled without mercy." "That may very easily happen," cried the daughter! "I myself have often dreamed that I was falling from a high tower, without ever coming to the ground; and upon waking, have felt myself bruised and battered, as if I had actually got a great fall." "Ah, mistress!" replied the squire, "here is the point; I, without dreaming at all; but, on the contrary, being as broad awake as I am this precious minute, found almost as many marks upon my own shoulders, as you have observed upon those of my master Don Quixote." "What is the name of that knight?" said the Asturian. "Don Quixote de la Mancha," answered the squire, "he is a knight-adventurer; and one of the greatest and most valiant that have been seen in this world for many ages." "And what is a knight-adventurer?" resumed the wench. "Are you such a suckling as not to know that?" cried Sancho; "well, I'll tell you, mistress of mine, a knight-adventurer is a thing, that, before you can count a couple, may be kicked, and be crowned: to-day, he is the most despicable and beggarly wretch upon earth, and to-morrow, he will have a brace of kingdoms to bestow upon his squires." "Methinks," said the landlady, "seeing you appertain to such a great man, you ought to be a count at least." "All in good time," replied Sancho, "we have not been out a month in search of adventures, and have found none worth naming; besides, people sometimes go in quest of one thing, and meet with another: indeed, if my master Don Quixote gets well of this drubbing—(fall, I mean) and I myself escape without being crippled, I won't barter my hopes for the best lordship in Spain."

The knight, having listened attentively to this whole conversation, sat up in his bed as well as he could, and taking his landlady by the hand, "Believe me, beautiful lady," said he, "you may account yourself extremely happy, in having within your castle my person, as your guest, such a guest, that if I praise him not, it is on account of the common saying, that Self-commendation is in effect self-dispraise. My squire, however, will intimate who I am; while I content myself with assuring you, that I will, to all eternity, preserve engraven upon the tables of my memory, the benevolence you this day vouchsafed unto me, that I may be grateful for the favour, as long as life shall remain. And, oh! that it pleased yon Heaven supreme, that love had not so vanquished and enslaved my heart, to the triumphant eyes of that beautiful ingrate, whom I now mention between my teeth, but that the charms of this amiable young lady, could be the authors of my freedom."

The good woman, her daughter, and the gentle Maritornes, were astonished at this rhapsody, which they understood as much as if it had been delivered in Greek; tho' they could easily comprehend, that the whole of it tended to compliment and proffers of ser-

vice: as they were therefore altogether unaccustomed to such language, they gazed at him with admiration, as a person of a different species from other men, and having thanked him for his courtesy, in their tapster-phrase, left him to his repose; while the Asturian Maritornes administred to Sancho, who had as much need of assistance as his master.

She and the carrier had made an assignation to divert themselves that night; nay, she had given her word, that as soon as the company should be quiet, and her master and mistress asleep, she would visit him in the dark, and give him all the satisfaction he desired; and indeed it is recorded, for the honour of this good creature, that she never failed to perform her promises of that kind punctually, altho' they had been made in the midst of a heath, and out of the hearing of all evidence; for, she valued herself much upon her gentility, and did not look upon it as any affront, to be servant at an inn, because, she observed, disappointments and misfortunes had reduced her to that condition.

The bed of Don Quixote, which we have described so hard, so narrow, crazy and uncomfortable, stood foremost, and exactly in the middle of this ruinous hay-loft; hard by, had Sancho taken up his quarters upon a rush-mat, covered with a rug, which seemed to be manufactured of hemp rather than wool; and last of all was the carrier's couch, composed, as we have already said, of the pannels and furniture of his two best mules; for, he had no less than twelve plump, sleek and notable beasts, being one of the richest carriers in Arevalo, according to the report of the author of this history, who makes particular mention of him, and says he knew him perfectly well; nay, some go so far as to affirm, that he was his distant relation: be this as it will, Cid Hamet Benengeli was a most curious historian, and punctual to admiration, as appears from what hath been related, which, tho' in itself mean and trivial, he would by no means pass over in silence. This ought to serve as an example to those important and weighty historians, who recount events so succinctly and superficially, that the reader can scarce get a smack of them; while the most substantial circumstances are left, as it were, in the inkhorn, thro' carelessness, ignorance and malice. A thousand times blest be the authors of Tablante and Ricamonte, and he that compiled that other book, in which are recounted the atchievements of Count Tomillas! How punctually have they described the most minute particular! But to return to our story.

The carrier having visited his cattle, and given them their night's allowance, stretched himself upon his pannels, in expectation of the most faithful Maritornes; while Sancho, plaistered all over, and huddled up in his kennel, endeavoured with all his might to sleep; but, the aching of his ribs would by no means allow him to enjoy that satisfaction; and Don Quixote, for the same uncomfortable reason, lay like a hare with his eyes wide open. A profound silence reigned throughout the whole house, in which there was no other light, than a lamp stuck up in the passage; and this wonderful quiet, together with those reflections which always occured to our knight, relating to the events continually recorded in the books of chivalry, that first disordered his understanding: I say, those reflections suggested to his fancy, one of the strangest whims that ever entered a man's imagination. This was no other than a full persuasion that he was arrived at some famous castle, for, as we have before observed, all the inns he lodged at seemed castles to

him; and that the landlord's daughter was the governor's only child, who, captivated by his genteel appearance, was become deeply enamoured of him, and had actually promised to come, without the knowledge of her parents, and pass the best part of the night in bed with him. Believing therefore, this chimera (which was the work of his own brain) to be a firm and undoubted fact, he began to reflect with extreme anxiety, upon the dangerous dilemma into which his virtue was like to be drawn; and resolved, in his heart, to commit no treason against his mistress Dulcinea del Toboso; even tho' queen Ginebra herself, and the lady Quintaniona should make him a tender of their favours.

While his mind was engrossed by these extravagant fancies, the hour of assignation arrived, and an unlucky hour it was for him, when the kind Asturian, barefoot and in her smock, having her hair tucked up under a fustian night-cap, entered the apartment in which the three guests were lodged, and with silence and caution, directed her steps towards the nest of her beloved carrier. But, scarce had she got within the door, when her approach was perceived by our knight, who sitting up in his bed, in spite of his plaisters and the aching of his ribs, stretched forth his arms to receive this beautiful young lady, who, on her part holding in her breath, moved softly on her tiptoes, groping her way with her hands before her.

While she thus crept along, in quest of her lover, she chanced to come within arms length of Don Quixote, who laid fast hold of her by the wrist, and without her daring to speak a syllable, pulled her towards him, and made her sit down upon his bed; he then felt her smock, which tho' made of the coarsest canvas, to him seemed a shift of the finest and softest lawn; the string of glass beads she wore about her wrist, in his apprehension, outshone the brightest oriental pearl: her hair, which bore some resemblance to a horse's mane, he mistook for threads of pure Arabian gold, that even eclipse the splendor of the sun; and her breath, which doubtless smelled strong of broken meat and garlick, his fancy converted into an aromatic flavour, proceeding from her delicate mouth: in short, his imagination represented her in the same form and situation with that of a certain princess, recorded in one of his books, who came to visit a wounded knight of whom she was enamoured; with all the other embellishments there described. Nay, such was the infatuation of this poor gentleman, that he was not to be undeceived, either by the touch, the breath, or any other circumstance of this honest wench, tho' they were powerful enough to discompose the stomach of any body but a rampant carrier.

But, our knight believed he folded in his arms the goddess of beauty, and straining her in his embrace, began to pronounce, in a soft and amorous tone, "Would to heaven! I were so circumstanced, beautiful and high-born lady! as to be able to repay the transcendent favour bestowed upon me, in the contemplation of your amazing charms: but, it hath pleased fortune, that never ceases to persecute the virtuous, to lay me upon this bed, so bruised and battered, that even, if it was my desire to gratify yours, I should find it utterly impossible; how much more so, when that impossibility is linked to another still greater? I mean, the plighted faith I have vowed to the peerless Dulcinea del Toboso, the sole mistress of my most hidden thoughts: did not that consideration interpose, I should not be such a simple knight, as to let slip this happy occasion which your benevolence hath tendered to my choice."

Maritornes, sweating with vexation, to find herself thus pinioned, as it were, by the knight, whose discourse she neither heeded nor understood; endeavoured, without answering a syllable, to disengage herself from his embrace: while the honest carrier, whose lewd desires kept him awake, and made him perceive his doxy from the moment she entered, listened attentively to every thing that Don Quixote said, and being jealous that the Asturian had broke her promise to him, in order to keep it with another, crept nearer the bed of his rival, to wait the issue of this rhapsody, the meaning of which he could not comprehend: observing, however, that the wench struggled to get loose, and that the knight endeavoured to detain her, he could not relish the joke, but, lifting his arm on high, discharged such a terrible blow upon the lanthorn jaws of the enamoured Don, as bathed his whole countenance in blood; and not satisfied with this application, jumped upon his ribs, and travelled over his whole carcase, at a pace, somewhat exceeding that of a brisk trot, until the bed, which was none of the strongest, either in materials or foundation, unable to sustain the additional weight, sunk to the ground with both; and made such a hideous noise in its fall, as waked the innkeeper, who immediately concluded that Maritornes was concerned in the adventure, because she made no answer when he called.

On this supposition he arose, and lighting a candle, went directly to the place where he had heard the scuffle: mean while, the poor wench, confused and affrighted at the approach of her master, who was a fellow of a most savage disposition, retreated to the kennel of Sancho Panza, who slept in spite of all this din, and nestling in beside him, wound herself up like a ball, and lay snug. The landlord now entered the apartment, and crying with a loud voice, "Where have you got, strumpet? to be sure, these must be your jades tricks, with a vengeance": Sancho started, and feeling a prodigious weight upon him, thought he was labouring under the night-mare; and beginning to lay about him on all sides, chanced, in the course of his efforts, to bestow divers cuffs on Maritornes, who feeling herself thus belaboured, forgot the care of her reputation, and returned the squire's compliments so heartily, that sleep forsook him whether he would or not: without knowing the person who treated him so roughly, he raised himself up, as well as he could, and going to loggerheads with Maritornes, a most furious and diverting skirmish ensued.

By this time, the carrier, perceiving by the light the situation of his mistress, ran to her assistance; and the landlord followed the same course, tho' with a very different intention, namely, to chastise the maid; being fully persuaded, that she was the sole cause of all this uproar: and so, as the saying is, The cat to the rat, the rat to the rope, the rope to the gallows. The carrier drummed upon Sancho, Sancho struck at the maid, the maid pummelled him, the innkeeper disciplined her; all of them exerted themselves with such eagerness, that there was not one moment's pause. But to crown the joke, the landlord's candle went out, and the combatants being left in the dark, such a circulation of blows ensued, that wheresoever the fist fell, there the patient was disabled.

There chanced to lodge at the inn, that night, a trooper belonging to the ancient holy brotherhood of Toledo, who also hearing the strange noise of this fray, arose, and seizing his tipstaff, together with the tin-box that contained his commission, entered the apartment in the dark, calling aloud, "Keep the peace, in the king's name. Keep the

Vol. 1. Nº 4. Page 92.

F. Hayman inv. et pinxt.                         I. S. Müller sculpt.

Maritornes and Sancho Panza Fighting in Bed.

peace in the name of the holy brotherhood." The first he encountred was the forlorn Don Quixote, who lay insensible on his demolished bed, with his face uppermost; so that groping about, he happened to lay hold of his beard, and cried, "Assist, I charge you, the officers of justice": but, perceiving that the person he held neither stirred nor spoke, he concluded that he must be dead, and that the people within were the assassins. In this persuasion, he raised his voice, crying, "Shut the gates of the inn, that none may 'scape, for, here is a man murthered." This exclamation, which astonished them all, was no sooner heard, than every one quitted his share in the battle; the landlord retreated to his own chamber, the carrier sneaked to his panniers, and the damsel to her straw: while the unfortunate knight and squire were left on the spot, unable to move from the places where they lay. The trooper letting go of the beard of Don Quixote, went out for a light to search for and apprehend the delinquents; but, in this design, he was disappointed; the landlord having purposely extinguished the lamp, when he retired to his apartment: so that he was obliged to have recourse to the embers, at which, with great industry and time, he made shift to light another candle.

## CHAPTER III.

Containing the sequel of those incredible grievances which the valiant Don Quixote, and his trusty squire Sancho Panza, underwent at the inn, which, for their misfortune, the knight mistook for a castle.

About this time, Don Quixote recovering the use of his tongue, began to call in the same feeble tone with which he spoke, the preceding day, when he lay stretched in the pack-staff valley, "Art thou asleep, friend Sancho? friend Sancho, art thou asleep?" "God's my life!" replied Sancho, full of peevishness and pain, "how should I be asleep, seeing all the devils in hell have been upon me, this whole night?" "That thou mayest assure thyself of," answered the knight, "for, either I understand nothing at all, or this castle is inchanted. Thou must know, Sancho, but what I am going to disclose to thee, thou shalt swear to keep secret till after my death." "I do swear," said Sancho. "This secrecy I insist upon," replied his master, "because, I would by no means take away the reputation of any person." "Well then," cried the squire, "I swear to keep it secret till the days of your worship be past and gone; and God grant that I may be at liberty to reveal it to-morrow." "Have I done you so much mischief, Sancho," said Don Quixote, "that you wish to see me dead so soon?" "It is not for that," replied the squire, "but, because I am an enemy to all secrets, and would not have any thing rot in my keeping." "Be that as it may," said the knight, "I will trust greater things to thy love and fidelity: Know, therefore, that this very night, I have been engaged in a most rare and wonderful adventure, which, that I may briefly relate, take notice, that a little while ago, I was visited

by the constable's daughter, than whom a more beautiful and gracious young lady is scarce to be found on this terraqueous globe. How shall I paint to thee, the comeliness of her person? how delineate the acuteness of her understanding? or, how shall I describe those mysterious charms, which, that I may preserve the fealty I have sworn to my own sovereign mistress Dulcinea del Toboso, I must pass over in sacred silence! I shall only tell thee, that heaven itself was jealous of the happiness which fortune had put into my power; or, perhaps, which is more probable, this castle, as I have already observed, is enchanted: for, while I was engaged with her, in a most delightful and amorous conversation, an unseen hand, belonging, doubtless, to the arm of some monstrous giant, descended, I know not whence, upon my jaws, leaving my whole face bathed in gore; and afterwards bruised me in such a manner, that I am infinitely worse, than I was yesterday, when the carriers maltreated us, as thou knowest, for the excesses of Rozinante; from whence, I conjecture, that the treasure of this fair damsel's beauty, is guarded by some enchanted Moor, and not destined for my possession." "Nor for mine, neither," cried Sancho, "for, I have been drubbed by five hundred Moors, so unmercifully, that the pack-stave threshing was but cakes and gingerbread,[1] to what I now feel: so, that I see no great cause you have to brag of that rare adventure, which hath left us in this comfortable pickle. Indeed your worship was not so badly off, because you had that same incomparable beauty in your arms: but, what had I, except the hardest knocks, which, I hope, I shall ever feel in my born days? Cursed am I, and the mother that bore me; for, though, I neither am knight-errant, nor ever design to be one, the greatest part of the mischief that betides us, for ever, falls to my share." "It seems then, thou hast suffered too," said Don Quixote. "Woe be unto me and my whole pedigree!" cried Sancho, "have I not been telling you so all this time?" "Give thyself no concern about that matter," answered the knight, "for, now I am determined to prepare that precious balsam, which will cure us both, in the twinkling of an eye."

About this time, the officer of the holy brotherhood, having made shift to light his candle, came back to examine the person whom he supposed murthered; and Sancho, seeing him approach in his shirt and woollen night-cap, with a very unfavourable aspect, and a light in his hand, said to his master, "Pray, sir, is that the enchanted Moor returned * to spend the last drop of his vengeance upon us." "That cannot be the Moor," answered Don Quixote, "for, enchanters never suffer themselves to be seen." "If they won't allow themselves to be seen," cried the squire, "they make no bones of letting themselves be felt; that my shoulders can testify." "And mine too," said the knight: "but, we have no sufficient reason to believe that he whom we now see, is the inchanted Moor."

Mean while, the trooper drawing nearer, and hearing them talk so deliberately, remained some time in suspence; then observing Don Quixote, who still lay on his back, unable to stir, on account of his bruises and plaisters, he went up to him, saying, "How do'st do, honest friend?" "I would speak more submissively," answered the knight, "were I such a plebeian as you; is that the language used in this country to knights-errant, you blockhead?" The officer finding himself treated with so little ceremony, by such a mis-

* Literally, What is left in the bottom of his inkhorn.[2]

erable wight, could not bear the reproach, but, lifting up the lamp, oil and all, discharged it upon Don Quixote's pate, which suffered greatly in the encounter, and the light being again extinguished, slipped away in the dark. Things being in this situation, "Sir," said Sancho Panza, "without doubt, that was the enchanted Moor, who keeps the treasure for other people, and the fisty-cuffs and lamp-leavings for us." "It must be so," replied the knight, "but, we must not mind those affairs of enchantment so much, as to let them ruffle or inflame us; because they being invisible and fantastical, do what we can, we shall never be able to take vengeance upon the authors of them: get up therefore, Sancho, if thou canst, and desire the constable of this castle, to supply me with some oil, wine, salt and rosemary; that I may prepare the salutiferous balsam, which, really, I believe, I stand in great need of, at present, for, the wound, which the phantome hath given me, bleeds apace."

Accordingly, the squire made shift to rise, notwithstanding the intolerable aching of his bones, and creeping in the dark, towards the innkeeper's bed-chamber, happened to meet with the trooper, who stood listening, to know the intention of his adversary. "Signor," cried he, "whosoever you are, do us the benefit and favour to assist us with some rosemary, salt, wine and oil, in order to cure one of the most mighty knights-errant upon earth, who lies in that bed, desperately wounded by the hands of an inchanted Moor that frequents this inn." The officer hearing such an address, concluded that the man had lost his senses; and it being by this time, dawn, opened the inn-gate, and calling to the landlord, told him what this honest man wanted. The innkeeper having provided Sancho with the ingredients, he immediately carried them to his master, who lay, holding his head between his two hands, and complaining very much of the effect of the lamp, which, however, had done no further damage than that of raising a couple of large tumors upon his pate; that which he took for blood, being no other than sweat forced out by the anguish and pain he had undergone. In short, he made a composition, by mixing the materials together, and boiling them a good while, until he found he had brought the whole to a due consistence; then he asked for a vial to contain the balsam; but, as there was none in the house, he resolved to cork it up in a tin oil-flask, of which the landlord made him a present. Which being done, he repeated over it, more than fourscore pater-noster's, with the like number of ave-maria's, salve's and credo's, accompanying every word with the sign of the cross, by way of benediction: and this whole ceremony was performed in presence of Sancho, the innkeeper and officer; the carrier having very quietly gone to take care of his beasts.

This precious balsam being thus composed, the knight was determined to make instant trial of the efficacy, with which he imagined it endued; and accordingly swallowed about a pint and a half of what remained in the pot, after the oil-flask was full, which had scarce got down his throat, when he began to vomit in such a manner, as left nothing in his stomach; and a most copious sweat breaking out upon him, in consequence of the violent operation, he desired they would wrap him up warm, and leave him to his repose. They complied with his request, and he fell into a profound sleep that lasted three hours, at the end of which awaking, he found himself exceedingly refreshed, and so well recovered of his bruises, that he seemed perfectly well: and implicitly believed that he had now made sure of the balsam of Fierabras, which while he possessed, he might, with

the utmost confidence and safety, engage in the most perilous quarrels, combats and havock, that could possibly happen.

Sancho Panza seeing his master recovered to a miracle, begged he would bestow upon him, the sediment of the pot, which was no small quantity: and his request being granted, he laid hold of it with both hands, and setting it to his head, drank off, with strong faith and eager inclination, almost as much as his master had swallowed before. But, the poor squire's stomach chanc'd to be not quite so delicate as that of the knight, and therefore, before he could discharge a drop, he suffered such pangs and reachings, such qualms and cold sweats, that he verily believed his last hour was come, and in the midst of his wamblings and affliction, cursed the balsam and the miscreant that made it. Don Quixote perceiving his situation, said, "I believe that all this mischief happens to thee, Sancho, because thou art not a knight; for, I am persuaded, that this liquor will be of service to none but such as are of the order of knighthood." "If your worship knew so much," cried Sancho, "woe be unto me and my whole generation! Why did you allow me to taste it?" At this instant, the potion began to operate, and the poor squire to un-load at both ends, with such fury, that the mat upon which he had thrown himself, and the sheet that covered him, were soon in a woeful pickle: he sweated and shivered with such violent motions and fits, that not only he himself, but every body present, thought he would have given up the ghost.

This tempest of evacuation, lasted near two hours, at the expiration of which, he found himself far from being relieved like his master, but, on the contrary, so much fa-tigued that he was not able to stand. The knight, as we have already observed, finding himself in good health, and excellent spirits, longed fervently to depart in quest of ad-ventures, thinking every minute he spent in that place, was an injury to the world in general, and to those miserable objects who wanted his favour and protection; espe-cially, as he was now in possession of the certain means of safety and confidence, in that efficacious balsam he had made. Prompted by these suggestions, he himself saddled Rozinante, and with his own hands put the pannel upon the beast of his squire, whom he also assisted in getting on his cloaths, and mounting his ass. He then bestrode his own steed, and laying hold of a pitchfork that stood in a corner of the yard, appropri-ated it to the use of a lance; while all the people in the house, exceeding twenty persons, beheld him with admiration: the landlord's daughter being among the spectators, he fixed his eyes upon her, and from time to time, uttered a profound sigh, which seemed to be heaved from the very bottom of his bowels; and which, in the opinion of all those who had seen him anointed over night, was occasioned by the aching of his bones.

He and his squire, being by this time mounted, he halted at the gate, and calling to the innkeeper, pronounced, in a grave and solemn tone; "Numerous and mighty are the favours, sir constable, which I have received in this castle of yours, and I shall think my-self under the highest obligation, to retain a grateful remembrance of your courtesy, all the days of my life. If I can make you any return, in taking vengeance on some insolent adversary, who hath, perhaps, aggrieved you; know, that it is my province and profes-sion, to assist the helpless, avenge the injured, and chastise the false: recollect, therefore, and if you have any boon of that sort to ask, speak the word; I promise by the order of knighthood which I have received, that you shall be righted and redressed to your heart's

content." "Sir knight," replied the innkeeper, with the same deliberation, "I have no occasion for your worship's assistance, to redress any grievance of mine; for, I know how to revenge my own wrongs, when I suffer any: all I desire, is, that you will pay the score you have run up in this inn, for provender to your cattle, and food and lodging to yourself and servant." "It seems then, this is an inn," answered the knight. "Aye, and a well respected one," said the landlord. "I have been in a mistake all this time," resumed Don Quixote, "for, I really thought it was a castle; and that none of the meanest, neither: but, since it is no other than a house of public entertainment, you have nothing to do, but excuse me from paying a farthing; for, I can by no means, transgress the custom of knights-errant, who, I am sure, as having read nothing to the contrary *, never paid for lodging, nor any thing else, in any inn or house whatsoever, because they had a right and title to the best of entertainment, in recompence for the intolerable sufferings they underwent, in seeking adventures by night and by day, in winter as well as summer, on foot and on horseback, exposed to hunger and thirst, to heat and cold, and to all the inclemencies of heaven, as well as the inconveniencies of earth." "All this is nothing to my purpose," said the innkeeper, "pay me what you owe, and save all your idle tales of knight-errantry, for those who will be amused with them; for my own part, I mind no tale but that of the money I take." "You are a saucy publican and a blockhead to boot," cried Don Quixote, who putting spurs to Rozinante, and brandishing his pitch-fork, sallied out of the inn, without opposition; and was a good way off, before he looked behind to see if he was followed by his squire.

The landlord, seeing the knight depart without paying, ran up to seize Sancho, who told him, that since his master had refused to discharge the bill, he must not expect any money from him, who being the squire of a knight-errant, was, as well as his master, bound by the same laws, to pay for nothing in taverns and inns. The publican, irritated at this answer, threatned, if he would not pay him, to indemnify himself, in a manner that should not be so much to the squire's liking: but, Panza swore by the laws of chivalry his master professed, that he would not pay a doit, though it should cost him his life; for, he was resolved, that the honourable and ancient customs of knight-errantry, should not be lost through his misbehaviour; neither, should those squires, who were to come into the world after him, have occasion to complain of his conduct, or reproach him with the breach of so just a privilege.

As the unfortunate Sancho's evil genius would have it, there were among the company

---

* Don Quixote seems in this place to have forgot one adventure of his great pattern, Orlando, who, while he accompanied Angelica in her flight from Albracca, happened to intrude upon the king of the Lestrigons, as he sat at dinner in a valley; and being in great want of victuals, accosted his most savage majesty in these words, recorded by Boyardo, or rather Berni, in his poem intitled Orlando Innamorato.

> Poichè fortuna a quest'ora ne mena
> Da voi, vi prego, che non vi despiaccia,
> O pe' nostri danari o in cortesia,
> Che noi cenium con voi di compagnia.

Thus humbly requesting, that he would either for love or money, give them a bone to pick.[3]

that lodged that night, in the house, four clothiers of Segovia, three pin-makers from the great square of Cordova, and a couple of shopkeepers from the market-place of Sevil; all of them, brisk jolly fellows, and mischievous wags. These companions, as if they had been inspired, and instigated by the same spirit, came up to the squire, and pulled him from his ass; then, one of them fetching a blanket from the landlord's bed, they put Sancho into it, and lifting up their eyes, perceived the roof was too low for their purpose; therefore determined to carry him out into the yard, which had no other ciel-ing than the sky: there placing Panza in the middle of the blanket, they began to toss him on high, and divert themselves with his capers, as the mob do with dogs at Shrove-tide. The cries, uttered by this miserable valet, were so piercing as to reach the ears of his master, who halting to listen the more attentively, believed that some new adventure was approaching, until he clearly recognized the shrieks of his squire: he immediately turned his horse, and with infinite straining, made shift to gallop back to the inn; but, finding the gate shut, rode round in search of some other entrance; and when he ap-proached the yard-wall, which was not very high, perceived the disagreeable joke they were practising upon his squire, who rose into the air, and sunk again with such grace and celerity, that if his indignation would have allowed him, I verily believe the knight himself would have laughed at the occasion. He attempted to step from his horse upon the wall, but, was so bruised and battered, that he could not move from his seat; and therefore, situated as he was, began to vent such a torrent of reproachful and opprobri-ous language, against Sancho's executioners, that it is impossible to repeat the half of what he said. This, however, neither interrupted their mirth nor their diversion, nor gave the least truce to the lamentations of Sancho, who prayed and threatned by turns, as he flew. Indeed, nothing of this sort, either could or did avail him, until, leaving off, out of pure weariness, they thought fit to wrap him up in his great coat, and set him on his ass again. The compassionate Maritornes seeing him so much fatigued, thought he would be the better for a draught of water, which, that it might be the cooler, she fetched from the well; and Sancho had just put the mug to his lips, when his draught was re-tarded by the voice of his master, who cried aloud, "Son Sancho, drink not water, drink not that which will be the occasion of thy death, my son; behold this most sacred bal-sam, (holding up the cruze of potion in his hand) two drops of which will effectually cure thee." At these words, the squire eyed him, as it were, askance, and in a tone still more vociferous, replied, "Perchance your worship has forgot that I am no knight; or may be, you want to see me vomit up all the entrails I have left, after last night's quandary. Keep your liquor for yourself, and may all the devils in hell give you joy of it; and leave me to my own discretion." He had no sooner pronounced these words, than he began to swal-low, and perceiving at the first draught, that the cordial was no other than water, he did not chuse to repeat it; but, desired Maritornes to bring him some wine. This request she complied with very chearfully, and paid for it with her own money, for, it was reported of her, that although she was reduced to that low degree in life, she actually retained some faint sketches and shadows of the christian.

Sancho having finished his draught, clapped heels to his ass, and the inn-gate being thrown wide open, sallied forth, very well satisfied with having got off, without paying any thing, although he had succeeded at the expence of his shoulders, which were, in-

deed his usual sureties. True, it is, the landlord had detained his bags for the reckoning; but, these Sancho did not miss, in the confusion of his retreat. As soon as he was clear of the house, the innkeeper would have barricadoed the gate, had he not been prevented by the blanket-companions, who were of that sort of people, who would not have valued Don Quixote a farthing, even if he had been actually one of the knights of the Round-Table.

## CHAPTER IV.

In which is recounted the discourse that passed between Sancho Panza and his master Don Quixote; with other adventures worthy of record.

S ancho made shift to overtake his master, so haggard and dismayed, that he was scarce able to manage his beast; and when the knight perceived his melancholy situation, "Honest Sancho," said he, "I am now convinced beyond all doubt, that this castle or inn is enchanted; for, those who made such a barbarous pastime of thy sufferings, could be no other than phantomes and beings belonging to the other world. I am confirmed in this opinion, from having found, that while I was by the wall of the yard, a spectator of the acts of thy mournful tragedy, I could neither climb over to thy assistance, nor indeed move from Rozinante, but, was fixed in the saddle by the power of enchantment; for, I swear to thee, by the faith of my character! if I could have alighted from my steed, and surmounted the wall, I would have revenged thy wrongs, in such a manner, that those idle miscreants should have remembered the jest to their dying day: altho' I know, that in so doing, I should have transgressed the laws of chivalry, which, I have often told thee, do not allow a knight to lift his arm against any person of an inferior degree, except in defence of his own life and limbs, or in cases of the most pressing necessity." "So would I have revenged myself," said Sancho, "knighted or not knighted; but, it was not in my power; tho' I am very well satisfied, that those who diverted themselves at my cost, were no phantomes, nor enchanted beings, as your worship imagines, but men made of flesh and bones, as we are, and all of them have christian names, which I heard repeated, while they tossed me in the blanket: one, for example, is called Pedro Martinez, another Tenorio Hernandez, and the innkeeper goes by the name of Juan Palameque the left-handed: and therefore, signor, your being disabled from alighting and getting over the wall, must have been owing to something else than enchantment. What I can clearly discern from the whole, is, that these adventures we go in search of, will, at the long run, bring us into such misventures, that we shall not know our right hands from our left: and therefore, in my small judgment, the best and wholesomest thing we can do, will be to jog back again to our own habitation, now while the harvest

is going on, to take care of our crops, and leave off sauntering from * post to pillar, and falling out of the frying-pan into the fire, as the saying is."

"How little art thou acquainted, Sancho," replied Don Quixote, "with the pretensions of chivalry! hold thy tongue and have patience; for, the day will soon arrive, on which thy own eyes shall judge what an honourable profession it is: pray, tell me, now, what greater satisfaction can there be in this world, or what pleasure can equal that of a conqueror, who triumphs over his adversary in battle? None sure!" "That may be," answered the squire, "tho' I know nothing of the matter. This only I know, that since we have taken up the trade of knights-errant, your worship, I mean, for, as to my own part, I have no manner of title to be reckoned in such an honourable list, we have not gained one battle, except that with the Biscayan; and even there, your worship came off with half an ear, and the loss of one side of your helmet: from that day, to this good hour, our lot hath been nothing but cudgelling upon cudgelling, pummelling upon pummelling; except the advantage I have had over your worship, in being tossed in a blanket by inchanted Moors, whom I cannot be revenged of, in order to know how pleasant a pastime it is, to overcome one's enemy, as your worship observes." "That is the very grievance, Sancho, under which both you and I labour," said Don Quixote; "but, for the future, I will endeavour to procure a sword tempered with such masterly skill, that he who wears it, shall be subject to no kind of enchantment: and who knows, but accident may furnish me with that which Amadis possessed, when he stiled himself the knight of the flaming sword; and truly it was one of the most excellent blades that ever a warrior unsheath'd; for, besides that sovereign virtue it contained, it cut keen as a razor, and no armour, tho' ever so strong or enchanted, could stand before its edge." "I am so devilishly lucky," said Sancho, "that if the case was really so, and your worship should light on that same sword, it would, like the precious balsam, be of no service or security to any but your true knights; and we that are squires might sing for sorrow." "Thou must not be afraid of that," replied the knight, "heaven will surely deal more mercifully with thee."

In such conversation, Don Quixote and his squire jogged along, when the former descrying on the road in which they travelled, a large and thick cloud of dust rolling towards them, turned to Sancho, saying, "This, O Sancho! is the day that shall manifest the great things which fortune hath in store for me! This, I say, is the day, on which the valour of this arm shall be displayed as much as upon any other occasion; and on which, I am resolved to perform deeds that shall remain engraven on the leaves of fame to all posterity! Seest thou that cloud of dust before us? The whole of it is raised by a vast army, composed of various and innumerable nations that are marching this way." "By that way of reckoning there must be two," said Sancho, "for right over against it, there is just such another." Don Quixote immediately turned his eyes, and perceiving Sancho's information to be true, was rejoiced, beyond measure; firmly believing that what he saw, were two armies in full march to attack each other, and engage in the middle of that spacious plain; for, every hour and minute of the day, his imagination was engrossed by

* In the original from Ceca to Mecca; a phrase derived from the customs of the Moors, who used to go in pilgrimage to these two places. Ceca was in the city of Cordova.[1]

those battles, inchantments, dreadful accidents, extravagant amours and rhodomon-
tades, which are recorded in books of chivalry; and indeed every thing he thought, said,
or did, had a tendency that way.

As for the dust he now saw, it was raised by two flocks of sheep which chanced to be
driven from different parts into the same road, and were so much involved in this cloud
of their own making, that it was impossible to discern them until they were very near.
The knight affirmed they were armies, with such assurance, that Sancho actually be-
lieved it, and said to his master, "And pray now, good your worship, what must we do?"
"What," answered Don Quixote, "but assist and support that side which is weak and dis-
comfited? Thou must know, Sancho, that yonder host which fronts us, is led and com-
manded by the mighty emperor Alifanfaron sovereign of the great island of Trapoban;
and that other behind us, belongs to his mortal enemy the king of the Garamanteans,
known by the name of Pentapolin with the naked arm, because he always goes to battle
with the sleeve of his right arm tucked up." "But why are those chieftains so mischie-
vously inclined towards each other?" said Sancho. "The cause of their enmity," replied
the knight, "is this: Alifanfaron, who is a most outrageous pagan, is enamoured of Pen-
tapolin's daughter, a most beautiful and courteous lady, who being a christian, her father
will by no means betroth her to the infidel prince, unless he shall first renounce the law
of his false prophet Mahomet, and become a convert to the true faith." "Now, by my
whiskers!" cried Sancho, "king Pentapolin is an honest man, and I am resolved to give
him all the assistance in my power." "In so doing, thou wilt perform thy duty, Sancho,"
said his master, "for, to engage in such battles as these, it is not necessary to be dubbed
a knight." "That I can easily comprehend," replied the other, "but, where shall we secure
the ass, that we may be sure of finding him after the fray is over; for, I believe it is not
the fashion now-a-days, to go to battle on such a beast." "True," said the knight, "and I
think the best way will be to leave him to his chance, whether he be lost or not; for, we
shall have such choice of steeds, when once we have gained the victory, that Rozinante
himself will run some risk of being exchanged for another: but, observe and listen at-
tentively; I will now give thee a detail of the principal knights that serve in these two
armies; and that thou mayest see and mark them the better, let us retire to yon rising
ground, from whence we can distinctly view the line of battle in both." They accord-
ingly placed themselves upon a hillock, whence they could easily have discerned the two
flocks of sheep which Don Quixote metamorphosed into armies, had not the dust they
raised confounded and obscured the view: but, nevertheless, beholding in his imagina-
tion, that which could not otherwise be seen, because it did not exist, he began to pro-
nounce with an audible voice:

"That knight whom thou seest with yellow armour, bearing in his shield, a lion
crowned and crouching at the feet of a young lady, is the gallant Laucalco lord of the sil-
ver bridge; that other beside him, who wears armour powdered with flowers of gold, and
bears for his device three crowns argent in a field azure, is the amorous Micocolembo
grand duke of Quiracia; and he upon his right hand, with those gigantic limbs, is the
never to be daunted Brandabarbaran de Boliche, sovereign of the three Arabias, who
comes armed with a serpent's skin, and instead of a shield, brandishes a huge gate,
which, it is said, belonged to the temple that Samson overthrew, when he avenged him-

self of his enemies at his death: but, turn thine eyes, and behold, in the front of this other army, the ever conquering and never conquered Timonel de Carcajona, prince of New-biscay, whose arms are quartered azure, vert, argent and or; and the device in his shield, a cat or, in a field gules with the letters Miau, which constitute the beginning of his lady's name; and she, they say, is the peerless Miaulina, daughter of Alfeniquen duke of Al-garve: the other, who loads and oppresses the loins of that fiery Arabian steed, with ar-mour white as snow, and a shield without device, is a noviciate knight of the French na-tion, called Pierre Papin baron of Utrique: the third, who strikes his iron rowels into the flanks of that spotted, nimble * Zebra, is the potent duke of Nerbia, espartafilardo of the wood, who bears in his shield for a device, a bunch of asparagus, with an inscription sig-nifying, By Destiny I'm dogged."

In this manner did he invent names for a great many knights in either army, to all of whom also he gave arms, colours, mottos and devices, without the least hesitation, being incredibly inspired by the fumes of a distempered fancy; nay, he proceeded without any pause, saying, "That squadron forming in our front, is composed of people of divers na-tions: there be those who drink the delicious waters of the celebrated Xanthus, with the mountaneers who tread the Masilican plains; and those who sift the purest golden ore of Arabia felix: there also, may be seen the people who sport upon the cool and famous banks of the translucent Thermodonte; and those who conduct the yellow Pactolus in many a winding stream; the promise-breaking Numidians; the Persians for their archery renowned; the Parthians and the Medes who combat as they fly; the Arabians famed for shifting habitations; the Scythians cruel as they are fair; the thick-lipp'd race of Æthiopia, and an infinite variety of other nations, whose looks I know and can dis-cern, tho' I cannot recollect their names. In that other squadron march those men, who lave in the crystal current of the olive-bearing Betis; those whose visages are cleaned and polished with the limpid wave of the ever rich and golden Tagus; those who delight in the salutiferous draughts of Genil the divine; those who scour the Tartesian fields, that with fat pasture teem; those who make merry in the Elysian meads of Herezan; the rich Manchegans crowned with ruddy ears of corn; those cloathed in steel the bold remains of ancient Gothic blood; those who bathe in Pisuerga famous for its gentle current; those who feed their flocks upon the spacious meads of the meandring Guadiana, cele-brated for its secret course; those who shiver with the chill blasts of the woody Pyrenees, and those who feel the snowy flakes of lofty Appenine: in fine, whatever nations Europe imbosoms and contains."

Heaven preserve us! what provinces did he mention! what nations did he name; be-stowing, with wonderful facility, those attributes that belonged to each; being all the while, absorpt, and, as it were, immersed in the contents of his deceitful books. Sancho Panza listened attentively to his master, without uttering one syllable; and from time to time, turned his eyes from one side to another, to see if he could discern those knights and giants who were thus described: but, not being able to discover one of them, "Sir," said he, "your worship may say what you please, but, the devil a man, giant or knight that you have mentioned is there; at least, I can see none: perhaps indeed the whole is

* Zebra is a beautiful creature, native of Arabia, vulgarly called the wild ass.

enchantment, like the phantomes of last night." "How say'st thou?" replied Don Quixote, "do'st thou not hear the neighing of steeds, the sound of clarions, and noise of drums?" "I hear nothing," answered Sancho, "but abundance of bleating of ewes and lambs." And truly, that was the case: for, by this time, the two flocks were pretty near them. "Thy fear," said Don Quixote, "hinders thee from seeing and hearing aright; for, one effect of terror, is to disturb the senses, and make objects appear otherwise than they are: if thou art, therefore, under such consternation, retire on one side, and leave me alone; for, I myself, am sufficient to bestow victory on that cause which I espouse." So saying, he clapped spurs to Rozinante, and putting his lance in the rest, darted down from the hillock like lightning. In vain did Sancho bellow forth, "Turn, signor Don Quixote: good your worship turn! so help me God! those are ewes and lambs you are going to attack! woe be to the father that begat me! will you not turn? What madness possesses you! Consider, here are no giants, nor knights, nor cats, nor arms, nor shields quartered or whole; nor inverted azures, and the devil knows what: was there ever such distraction? sinner that I am!"

The knight, however, did not regard this exclamation: on the contrary, he rode on, bauling aloud, "So ho, knights! you that attend and serve under the banners of the valiant emperor Pantapolin with the naked arm, follow me in a body, and you shall behold, how easily I will avenge him on his adversary Alifanfaron of Trapoban." Having uttered these words, he rushed into the thickest of the squadron of sheep, and began to lay about him, with as much eagerness and fury, as if he had been actually engaged with his mortal enemies. The herdsmen and shepherds who were driving the flock, called to him to forbear; but, finding their admonition had no effect, they ungirded their slings, and began to salute his ears with stones, the least of which was as large as an ordinary fist: but he, far from minding their missiles, rode about the field, crying, "Where art thou, proud Alifanfaron? face me, if thou darest; I am but a single knight, who want to prove thy prowess, hand to hand, and sacrifice thy life for the injury thou hast done to Pentapolin Garamanta." Just as he pronounced these words, he received a pebble on his side, that seemed to have buried a couple of his ribs in his belly; and gave him such a rude shock, that he believed himself either dead or desperately wounded: then remembring his specific, he pulled out the cruze, and setting it to his mouth, began to swallow the balsam; but, before he had drank what he thought a sufficient dose, there came another such almond, so plum upon his hand and cruze, that after having shivered the pot to pieces, it carried off in its way, three or four of his grinders,[2] and shattered two of his fingers in a grievous manner: in short, so irresistible were both the applications, that the poor knight could not help tumbling from his horse. The shepherds immediately came up, and believing him actually dead, gathered together their flock with all imaginable dispatch, and taking their dead, which might be about seven in number, upon their shoulders, made off without any further inquiry.

All this time Sancho remained upon the hill, beholding, with amazement, the madness of his master, tearing his beard, and cursing the hour and minute on which it was his fate to know him: and now seeing him fallen, and the shepherds gone, he descended to his assistance, when finding him still sensible, tho' in a miserable situation, "Did not I warn you, signor Don Quixote," said he, "to turn, and assure you that those you went

to attack were no armies, but flocks of innocent sheep?" "How strangely can that miscreant enchanter, who is my enemy, transmography things to thwart me? Know, Sancho, that it is a very easy matter for negromancers to make us assume what shapes they please; and the malicious wretch who persecutes me, envying the glory I should have gained in this battle, hath doubtless metamorphosed the squadrons of the foe, into flocks of sheep: but, thou shalt do one thing, I intreat thee, Sancho, in order to be undeceived and convinced of the truth; mount thy ass, and follow them fair and softly; and, when they are at a convenient distance from hence, thou wilt see them return to their former shapes, and ceasing to be sheep, become men again, right and tight as I at first described them; but, do not go at present, for, I have occasion for thy service and assistance: come hither, and see how many teeth I have lost; methinks, there is not one left in my whole jaw."

Sancho accordingly approached so near, as to thrust his eyes into his master's mouth, just at the time when the balsam began to operate in his stomach, which, with the force of a culverin, discharged its contents full in the beard of the compassionate squire. "Holy virgin!" cried Sancho, "what is this that hath befallen me? without doubt this poor sinner is mortally wounded, since he vomits blood." But, considering the case more maturely, he found, by the colour, taste and smell, that it was not blood, but the balsam he had seen him drink: and such was the loathing he conceived at this recognition, that his stomach turned, and he emptied his bowels upon his master; so that both of them remained in a handsome pickle. Sancho ran to his ass, for a towel to clean them, and some application for his master's hurt, but, when he missed his bags, he had well nigh lost his senses; he cursed his fate again, and determined with himself to leave the knight, and return to his habitation, even tho' he should lose his wages for the time he had already served, as well as his hopes of governing the island of Promise.

At this juncture, Don Quixote arose, and clapping his left hand to his cheek, in order to prevent his teeth from falling out, with the right laid hold of the bridle of Rozinante, who, like a faithful and affectionate servant, had never stirred from his master's side; and went up to the place where his squire stood, leaning upon his ass, with one hand applied to his jaw, in the posture of a person who is exceedingly pensive: the knight perceiving him in this situation, with manifest signs of melancholy in his countenance, "Know, Sancho," said he, "that one man is no more than another, unless he can do more than another. All those hurricanes that have happened to us, prognosticate that we shall soon have fair weather, and that every thing will succeed to our wish: for, it is impossible that either good or bad fortune should be eternal; and therefore it follows, that our adversity having lasted so long, our prosperity must be now at hand. Be not grieved then, at the misfortunes that happen to me, since no part of them falls to thy share." "Not to my share!" answered Sancho, "mayhap then, he whom they tossed in a blanket, yesterday, was not the son of my father: and the bags that are lost to-day, with all the goods in them, belonged to some other person." "What! hast thou lost the bags, Sancho!" cried Don Quixote. "Yes, sure," said the other. "At that rate, then, we have no victuals to eat?" resumed the knight: "That would certainly be the case," answered the squire, "if the meadows did not furnish those herbs you say, you know, with which, unfortunate knights like your worship, are wont to make up such losses." "Yes, but for all that," replied Don

Sancho Panza Examining Don Quixote's Mouth.

Quixote, "I could at present relish a luncheon of brown bread, or a loaf with a couple of red herrings, better than all the herbs described by Dioscorides, even with the annotations of doctor Laguna; but, nevertheless, mount thy beast, honest Sancho, and follow me: God, who provides all things, will not be wanting to us; more especially, as we are employed in his immediate service: he faileth not to provide for the gnats of the air, the insects of the earth, the spawn of the sea; and is so beneficent, as to cause the sun to shine upon the good and bad, and sendeth rain to the wicked as well as to the righteous." "Your worship," said Sancho, "is more fit to be a preacher than a knight-errant." "Knights-errant," replied his master, "ever had, and ought to have, some knowledge of every thing: nay, some there have been in times past, who would stop to make a sermon or discourse upon the highway, with as much eloquence, as if they had taken their degrees at the university of Paris: from whence, it may be inferred, that the lance was never blunted by the pen, nor the quill impeded by the lance." "What your worship observes, may be very true," said Sancho, "but, in the mean time, let us leave this place, and endeavour to get a night's lodging in some house or other, where God grant there may be neither blankets nor blanketeers, nor phantomes, nor enchanted Moors; else, may the devil confound both hook and crook!"

"Implore the protection of God, my son," answered the knight, "and lead me where thou wilt: for this once, I leave our lodging to thy care; but, reach hither thy hand, and feel with thy finger, how many teeth I have lost on this right side of my upper jaw, which is the place that gives me the greatest pain." Sancho introduced his fingers, and having carefully examined his gums, "How many teeth," said he, "was your worship wont to have in this place?" "Four, besides the dog-tooth," answered Don Quixote, "all of them sound and whole." "Consider what your worship says?" replied Sancho. "I say four, if not five," resumed the knight; "for, in all my life, I never lost tooth or fang, either by worm, rheum or scurvy." "At present," said the squire, "in that part of the lower jaw, your worship has but two grinders and a half; and above, neither half nor whole; all is smooth as the palm of my hand." "Cruel fortune!" cried Don Quixote, hearing this melancholy piece of news, "would they had rather demolished a limb, so it had not been the sword arm: for, I would have thee to know, Sancho, that a mouth without grinders, is like a mill without a millstone; and a * tooth is worth a treasure; but, such mischances always attend us who profess the strict order of chivalry: get up, friend, and lead the way, and I will follow at thy own pace." Sancho complied with his desire, and took the way that seemed most likely to lead to some accommodation, without quitting the high road, which was thereabouts very much frequented. While they jogged on softly, because the pain in Don Quixote's jaws would not suffer him to be quiet, or exert himself in pushing forward, Sancho being desirous of entertaining and diverting him with his discourse, said, among other things, what will be rehearsed in the following chapter.

---

* I have endeavoured to preserve an alliteration in tooth and treasure, after the example of Cervantes, who seems to have intended it, in the words *Diente* and *Diamante*.[3]

## CHAPTER V.

An account of the sage discourse that passed between Sancho
and his master: the succeeding adventure of the corpse,
with other remarkable events.

"In my opinion, my good master, all the misventures, which have this day happened
to us, are designed as a punishment for the sins committed by your worship, in ne-
glecting to fulfil the oath you took, not to eat off a table-cloth, nor solace yourself with
the queen; together with all the rest that follows, which your worship swore to observe,
until such time as you could carry off that helmet of Malandrino, or how d'ye call the
Moor? for I don't remember his right name." "Thou art very much in the right," said
Don Quixote: "to deal ingenuously with thee, Sancho, that affair had actually slipt out
of my remembrance; and thou mayest depend upon it, that affair of the blanketing hap-
pened to thee, for the fault thou wast guilty of, in omitting to put me in mind of it, in
time: but, I will make an attonement; for, there are methods for compounding every
thing, in the order of chivalry." "Did I swear any thing?" replied Sancho. "Your not hav-
ing sworn is of no importance," said Don Quixote; "it is enough that I know you to be
concerned as an accessary; and whether that be the case or not, it will not be amiss to
provide a remedy." "Well then," replied the squire, "I hope your worship will not forget
this, as you did the oath: perhaps the phantoms may take it in their heads again, to di-
vert themselves with me, and even with your worship, if they find you obstinate."

In this and other such discourse, night overtook them in the midst of their journey,
before they could light on or discover any house where they could procure lodging; and
what was worse, they were almost famished: for, in their bags, they had lost their whole
buttery and provision; nay, to crown their misfortune, an adventure happened to them,
that without any exaggeration, might have actually passed for something preternatural.
Though the night shut in very dark, they continued travelling, Sancho believing, that
as they were in the king's highway, they should probably find an inn, at the distance of a
league or two.

Jogging on therefore, under cloud of night, the squire exceeding hungry, and the mas-
ter very well disposed to eat, they descried upon the road before them a vast number of
lights, that seemed like moving stars, approaching them. Sancho was confounded at
the sight, the meaning of which, even Don Quixote could not comprehend: the one
checked his ass, the other pulled in his horse's bridle, and both halted, in order to gaze
attentively at the apparition of the lights, which seemed to increase the nearer they
came. This being perceived by the squire, he began to quake like quicksilver;[1] and the
hair bristled up on Don Quixote's head: nevertheless, recollecting himself a little,
"Without doubt, Sancho," said he, "this must be a vast and perilous adventure, in which
I shall be obliged to exert my whole strength and prowess." "Woe is me!" cried Sancho,
"if perchance this should be an adventure of phantoms, as I am afraid it is, where shall I

find ribs for the occasion?" "Phantoms or not phantoms," said the knight, "I will not suffer them to touch a thread of thy cloaths: if they made merry at thy expence before, it was owing to my incapacity to climb over the yard wall: but, at present, we are in an open field, where I can manage my sword, as I please." "But, if they should benumb and bewitch you, as they did in the morning," said the squire, "what benefit shall I receive from being in the open field?" "Be that as it will," replied Don Quixote, "I beseech thee, Sancho, be of good courage; and thou shalt soon know by experience, how much I am master of that virtue." Sancho accordingly, promised to do his best, with God's assistance: then they both stept to one side of the road, and began to gaze again with great attention: while they were thus endeavouring to discern the meaning of the lights, they perceived a great number of persons in white: which dreadful vision entirely extinguished the courage of Sancho Panza, whose teeth began to chatter, as if he had been in the cold fit of an ague; and this agitation and chattering increased, when they saw them more distinctly: for, first and foremost appeared about twenty persons on horseback, all of them cloathed in white, with each a lighted flambeau in his hand, muttering in a low and plaintive tone. Behind them, came a litter covered with black, followed by six mounted cavaliers in deep mourning, that trailed at the very heels of their mules, which were easily distinguished from horses, by the slowness of their pace.

This strange vision at such an hour, and in such a desart place, was, surely, sufficient to smite the heart of Sancho with fear, and even make an impression upon his master; and this would have been the case, had he been any other than Don Quixote: as for the squire, his whole stock of resolution went to wreck. It was not so with his master, whose imagination clearly represented to him, that this was exactly an adventure of the same kind with those he had read in books of chivalry: that the close litter was a bier, in which was carried some dead or wounded knight, the revenge of whose wrongs was reserved for him alone: wherefore, without canvassing the matter any further, he set his lance in the rest, fixed himself in his seat, and with the most genteel and gallant deportment, placing himself in the middle of the road, through which they were indispensibly obliged to pass; he raised his voice, and called to them as they approached:

"Halt, knights, whosoever ye are, and give an account of yourselves: whence come ye? whither go ye? and what are you carrying off in that bier? for, in all appearance, you have either done or received an injury: and it is necessary and convenient that I should know it, in order to chastise you for what you are now doing, or revenge the wrong you have already done." "We are at present, in a hurry," replied one of the phantomes in white; "the inn we intend to lodge at is far off, and we cannot stay to give such a tedious account as you desire." So saying, he spurred on his mule; while Don Quixote, mightily incensed at this reply, laid hold of his bridle, saying, "Stand, and answer the questions I have asked, with more civility; otherwise, I will give battle to you all."

The mule being skittish, was frightened in such a manner, at being seized by the bridle, that rearing on her hind feet, she fell backward upon her rider; and a servant on foot, seeing his master fall, began to revile Don Quixote, whose choler being already provoked, he couched his lance, and without hesitation, attacked one of the mourners, who soon fell to the ground, most miserably mauled: then wheeling about, upon the rest, it was surprizing to see with what dispatch he assaulted and put them to the rout!

while Rozinante acted with such agility and fury, that one would have sworn, at that instant, a pair of wings had sprung from his back. All the squadron arrayed in white, was composed of timorous and unarmed people, who were fain to get out of the fray, as soon as possible, and began to fly across the plain, with their lighted torches, like so many maskers in carnival time. The mourners being involved and intangled in their long robes, could not stir out of the way: so that Don Quixote, without running any risk, drubbed them all round, and obliged them at length to quit the field, much against their inclination; for, they actually believed he was no man, but a devil incarnate, who lay in wait to carry off the dead body that was in the litter.

All this while Sancho stood beholding with admiration the courage and intrepidity of the knight; saying within himself, "This master of mine is certainly as strong and valiant as he pretends to be."

Mean while, Don Quixote, by the light of a torch that lay burning on the ground, perceiving the first whom the mule overthrew, rode up to him, and clapping the point of his lance to the poor man's throat, commanded him to yield; otherwise, he would put him to death. To this declaration the other answered, "Methinks I am already sufficiently quiet; for, one of my legs is broke, so that I cannot stir: I beseech your worship, therefore, if you be a christian, not to kill me, as in so doing, you will commit the horrid sin of sacrilege; for, I am a licentiate, and have taken holy orders." "If you are an ecclesiastic, what the devil brought you here?" cried Don Quixote. "The devil indeed I think it was," answered the overthrown priest: "You will have to do with worse than the devil," said the knight, "if you refuse the satisfaction I at first demanded." "That is easily granted": replied the other, "and in the first place, your worship must know, that tho' I just now called myself a licentiate, I am no more than a batchelor: my name is Alonzo Lopez; I was born at Alcovendas; and now come from the city of Baeça, in company with eleven other priests, who are those who fled with the torches: we are convoying to Segovia that litter, which contains the corpse of a gentleman who died in Baeça, where it was deposited till now, (as I was saying) that we are carrying his bones to be interred at Segovia, which was the place of his nativity." "And who killed him?" said Don Quixote. "God himself," replied the batchelor, "by means of a pestilential calenture that seized him!" "At that rate," resumed the knight, "the Lord hath saved me the trouble of avenging his death, as I would have done, had he been slain by any mortal arm; but, considering how he died, there is nothing to be done, except to shrug up our shoulders in silence: for, this is all that could happen, even if I myself should fall by the same hand; and I desire your reverence would take notice, that I am a knight of La Mancha, called Don Quixote, whose office and exercise it is, to travel thro' the world, redressing grievances, and righting wrongs *." "I do not know how you can call this behaviour righting wrongs," said the batchelor: "I am sure you have changed my right into wrong, by breaking my leg, which will never be set to rights again so long as I live; and the grievances you have redressed for me, have been to aggrieve me in such manner, as that I shall never cease to grieve at my misventure, in meeting with you, while you was in search of ad-

---

* Knights engaged themselves, by oath, to protect the widow and the orphan, to redress all injuries, and in a special manner, to defend the characters of ladies by force of arms.[2]

*Vol.1. pag. 111.*

*F. Hayman inv.*     *S. Ravenet Sculp.*

Don Quixote Threatening to Kill the Unhorsed Bachelor with His Lance.

ventures." "All things do not equally succeed," observed the knight; "it was the misfor-
tune of you and your companions, Mr. Batchelor Alonzo Lopez, to travel in the night,
with these surplices and lighted flambeaus, singing all the way, before people clad in
deep mourning, so that you seemed a company of ghosts broke from the other world;
therefore, I could not help performing my duty in attacking you: and I would have be-
haved in the same manner, had I actually known you to be really and truly the inhabi-
tants of hell; for, such indeed I thought you were." "Since my hard fate would have it so,"
said the batchelor, "I intreat your worship, Sir knight-errant, who have been the cause
of an unlucky errand to me, to help me in getting from under the mule, which keeps one
of my legs fast jammed between the stirrup and the saddle." "I might have talked on till
morning," said the knight; "why did not you inform me of your distress sooner?"

He then called aloud to Sancho, who was in no hurry to hear him, but busy in rum-
maging a sumpter mule which those honest priests brought along with them, well fur-
nished with provisions. Having made a bag of his great coat, into which he crammed as
much of their victuals as it would hold, he loaded his ass with the bundle, and then run-
ning up to his master, helped to free Mr. Batchelor from the oppression of his mule, on
which, having mounted him, with a torch in his hand, Don Quixote advised him to fol-
low the rout of his companions; and desired him to beg their pardon in his name, for the
injury he had done them, as it was not in his power to avoid it. Sancho likewise inter-
posing, said, "If in case the gentlemen should want to know, who the valiant hero is, who
put them to flight, your worship may tell them, that he is the famous Don Quixote de
la Mancha, otherwise sirnamed the Knight of the rueful Countenance."

Thus dismissed, the batchelor pursued his way; and the knight asked what had in-
duced Sancho, now, rather than at any other time, to stile him the Knight of the rueful
Countenance. "Truly," answered Sancho, "I have been looking at you some time, by the
light of that torch the unfortunate traveller held in his hand; and in good faith, your
worship cuts the most dismal figure I have almost ever seen; and it must certainly be oc-
casioned either by the fatigue you have undergone in this battle, or by the want of your
teeth." "That is not the case," replied his master; "but, the sage who is destined to write
the history of my exploits, hath thought proper that I should assume some appellation,
by the example of former knights, one of whom took the title of the Flaming Sword; an-
other, of the Unicorn; a third, of the Ladies; a fourth, of the Phoenix; a fifth, of the
Griffin; a sixth, called himself the Knight of death: and by these epithets and symbols,
they were known all over the face of the earth; and therefore, I say, that the fore-
mentioned sage hath now put it into thy thoughts, and directed thy tongue to call me
the Knight of the rueful Countenance; an appellation that henceforward I adopt: and
that it may suit me the better, I am resolved to have a most woeful figure painted upon
my shield, with the first opportunity." "There is no occasion," said Sancho, "to throw
away time and money on such a device; your worship has nothing more to do, but un-
cover your face; and I'll warrant, those who behold it, will call it a rueful one, without
your having recourse to pictures and shields to explain your meaning; and you may be-
lieve I tell you nothing but the truth, when I maintain, tho' it be but in jest, that hunger
and the want of teeth, makes your worship look so ill-favouredly, that we may very well
save the expence of a rueful picture."

Don Quixote could not help laughing at the pleasantry of Sancho, tho' he actually de-
termined to assume that name, and have his shield and target painted according to his
fancy. "I know, Sancho," said he, "that I have incurred the sentence of excommunica-
tion, for having laid violent hands on consecrated things, according to the canon; 'Si
quis suadente diabolo, &c.'³ yet, you know, I touched them not with my hands, but with
my lance; and even then, never dreamed of injuring priests, or of giving the smallest of-
fence to the church, which I respect and adore, like a faithful catholic and christian as I
am; but, on the contrary, took them for phantomes and beings of another world: but,
the case being as it is, I remember what happened to the Cid Ruy Diaz, who broke to
pieces the chair of a certain king's ambassador, in presence of his holiness the pope; for
which outrage he was excommunicated; and that very day, the worthy Rodrigo de Vi-
var, behaved like a valiant and honourable knight."

The batchelor being gone, as we have observed, without answering one word, Don
Quixote expressed a desire of examining the litter, to see if it really contained a corpse;
but, Sancho would by no means consent to this inquiry; saying, "Your worship has al-
ready finished this perilous adventure, with less damage to yourself, than I have seen you
receive in any other; but, the people whom you have conquered and overthrown, may
chance to recollect that they were vanquished by a single man, and be so much ashamed
and confounded at their own cowardice, as to rally, and if they find us, give us our belly-
full. Dapple is at present very comfortably furnished, there is an uninhabited mountain
hard by, hunger is craving, we have nothing to do, but retreat thither at a gentle trot;
and, as the saying is, 'the dead to the bier, and the living to good chear.'" With these
words, he took the lead with his ass, and the knight thinking there was a good deal of
reason in what he said, followed him very peaceably, without making any reply.

When they had travelled a little way between two hills, they found themselves in a
spacious and retired valley, where they alighted; Sancho unloaded the ass, they sat down
on the green turf, and with hunger for their sauce, dispatched their breakfast, dinner,
afternoon's luncheon and supper at one meal; solacing their stomachs out of more than
one basket, which the ecclesiastical attendants of the defunct, who seldom neglect these
things, had brought along with them on their sumpter mule: but, another misfortune
befel them, which in Sancho's opinion was the worst that could happen; they had not
one drop of wine to drink, nor indeed of water to cool their throats, so that they were
parched with thirst: then, the squire perceiving the meadow where they sat, was over-
grown with green and tender grass, made the proposal which may be seen in the fol-
lowing chapter.

## CHAPTER VI.

Of the unseen and unheard-of adventure atchieved by the valiant Don Quixote de la Mancha, with less hazard than ever attended any exploit performed by the most renowned knight on earth.

"This grass, my good master, proves beyond all contradiction, that there must be some spring or rivulet hereabouts, by which it is watered; and therefore, we had better proceed a little farther, until we find wherewith to allay this terrible thirst, which is more painful and fatiguing than hunger alone." This advice appearing rational to Don Quixote, he took hold of Rozinante's bridle, and Sancho leading Dapple by the halter, after he had loaded him again with the fragments of their supper, they began to move farther into the meadow, at a venture, for the night was so dark, they could not distinguish one object from another: but, they had not gone two hundred paces, when their ears were saluted with a prodigious noise of water, that seemed to rush down from some huge and lofty rocks: they were infinitely rejoiced at the sound, when, halting to listen, that they might know whence it came, they were all of a sudden surprised with another kind of noise, that soon damped the pleasure occasioned by the water, especially in Sancho, who was naturally fearful and faint-hearted: I say, they heard the sound of regular strokes, accompanied with strange clanking of iron chains, which, added to the dreadful din of the cataract, would have smote the heart of any other but Don Quixote with fear and consternation.

The night, as we have already observed, was dark, our travellers happened at this time to be in a grove of tall trees, whose leaves, moved gently by the wind, yielded a sort of dreary whisper: so, that the solitude of the place, the darkness of the night, the noise of the water, and rustling of the leaves, concurred to inspire them with horror and dismay: the more so, as the strokes were continued, the wind sighed on, and the morning was far off; and all these circumstances were aggravated by their ignorance of the place in which they were. But, Don Quixote encouraged by his own intrepid heart, mounted Rozinante, braced his shield, and brandishing his lance, "Friend Sancho," cried he, "know that I was born by heaven's appointment, in these iron times, to revive the age of gold, or, as it is usually called, the golden age. I am he, for whom strange perils, valiant deeds, and vast adventures are reserved! I am he, I say, ordained to re-establish the knights of the round table, the twelve peers of France, with the nine worthies! he, whose feats shall bury in oblivion, the Platirs, Tablantes, Olivantes, and Tirantes, the Febuses and Belianises, together with the whole tribe of knights-errant who lived in former times: performing such mighty and amazing deeds of arms, as will eclipse their most renowned acts! Consider well, thou true and loyal squire, the darkness and the solemn stillness of this night, the indistinct and hollow whispering of these trees, the dreadful din of that water we came to seek, which seems to rush and rumble down from the lofty mountains of the moon; together with these incessant strokes that strike and wound our ears: all

those circumstances united, or each singly by itself, is sufficient to infuse fear, terror and dismay, into the breast of Mars himself; much more in him who is altogether unaccustomed to such adventures and events. Yet, all I have described are only incentives that awaken my courage, and already cause my heart to rebound within my breast, with desire to atchieve this adventure, howsoever difficult it may appear to be! Therefore, straiten Rozinante's girth, recommend thyself to God, and wait for me in this place, three days at farthest, within which time, if I come not back, thou may'st return to our village, and, as the last favour and service done to me, go from thence to Toboso, and inform my incomparable mistress, Dulcinea, that her captive knight died in attempting things that might render him worthy to be called her lover."

When Sancho heard these last words of his master, he began to blubber with incredible tenderness. "I cannot conceive," said he, "why your worship should attempt such a terrible adventure: it is now dark, and no body sees us; therefore, we may turn out of this road and avoid the danger, tho' we should not taste liquor these three days; and if no body sees us, we run no risk of being accused of cowardice: besides, I have heard the curate of our town, whom your worship knows very well, remark, in his preaching, 'he that seeketh danger perisheth therein': therefore it must be a sin to tempt God by engaging in this rash exploit, from whence there is no escaping without a miracle: and heaven hath wrought enow of them already, in preserving you from being blanketted as I was, and bringing you off conqueror, and sound wind and limb, from the midst of so many adversaries as accompanied the dead man: and if all this will not move you, nor soften your rugged heart, sure you will relent, when you consider, and are assured, that your worship will be scarce gone from hence, when I shall, thro' pure fear, yield my life to any thing that may chuse to take it. I left my habitation, wife and children, to come and serve your worship, believing it would be the better, not the worse for me so to do: but, as greediness bursts the bag, so is the bag of my hopes bursten; for, when they are at the highest pitch, in expectation of that curst unlucky island your worship has promised me so often; I find, in lieu of that, you want to make me amends, by leaving me in this desert, removed from all human footsteps: for the love of God! dear master, do me not such wrong; or, if your worship is resolved to attempt this atchievement, at any rate, at least delay it till morning, which, according to the signs I learned when I was shepherd, will appear in less than three hours; for the muzzle of the bear *, is at top of his head, and shews midnight in the line of the left paw."

"How can'st thou perceive," said Don Quixote, "that line or head, or muzzle thou talkest of; when the night is so dark, that there is not a star to be seen?" "It is so," answered Sancho, "but, fear hath many eyes; and I can at present behold things that are hid within the bowels of the earth; much more those that appear in the firmament above: a man of sound judgment, like me, can easily foretell, that it will soon be day." "Let it come when it will," answered Don Quixote, "it shall not be said of me, either now, or at any other time, that I was diverted by tears and intreaties, from doing what I owed to the customs of chivalry: I therefore, beseech thee, Sancho, to hold thy peace;

* In Castilian, Boçina signifies a cornet or hunting-horn, to which the Spaniards suppose the constellation of Ursa Minor bears some resemblance.[1]

for, God who has put it in my heart, to attempt this dreadful and unseen adventure, will doubtless, take care of my safety, and comfort thee in thy affliction: thy business at present, is, to gird fast Rozinante, and remain in this place; for, dead or alive, I will soon return."

Sancho finding this was the final resolution of his master; and how little all his tears, advice, and intreaties availed; determined to make use of stratagem to detain the knight, if possible, till morning: with this purpose, under pretence of adjusting the girth of Rozinante, he fair and softly, without being perceived, tied two of the horse's feet together, with the halter of his ass, in such a manner, that when Don Quixote attempted to depart, he found it impossible, because his steed could move no otherwise than by leaps. The squire perceiving the success of his invention, "Sir," said he, "you may see that heaven, melted by my tears and prayers, hath ordained that Rozinante shall not stir; and if you obstinately persist in spurring and driving him on, you will only give offence to providence, and, as the saying is, kick against the pricks."

The knight actually despaired of making him go forward, because the more he goaded his horse, the less was he inclined to stir; and therefore, without guessing a tittle of the ligature, thought proper to submit, and wait with patience, either till morning, or such time as Rozinante should recover the use of his limbs; believing for certain, that his disappointment was owing to another cause, than the craft of his squire, to whom he said: "Since Rozinante is incapable of moving, I am content to wait for the dawn, tho' I cannot help lamenting its delay." "You shall have no cause for lamentation," answered Sancho, "I will entertain your worship with telling stories till day, unless you chuse to alight, and take a nap on the soft grass, according to the custom of knights-errant, that you may find yourself refreshed when day breaks, and ready to undertake the unconscionable adventure that awaits you." "Talk not to me, of alighting or sleeping," said Don Quixote, do'st thou imagine me to be one of those knights who seek their repose, in times of danger? Sleep thou, who wa'st born to sleep, or follow thy own inclinations; for my own part, I will behave as becomes a person of my pretensions." "Let not your worship be offended; for, that was not my intention when I spoke," answered Sancho, who coming close to him, laid hold of the saddle before and behind, and stood embracing his master's left thigh, without daring to stir a finger's breadth from the spot; such was his consternation inspired by the strokes, which all this time, sounded alternately in his ears.

Then Don Quixote claiming his promise of entertaining him with some story; "I would, with all my heart," said Sancho, "if the dread of what I hear, would allow me; but, nevertheless, I will try to force out one story, which, if I hit it aright, without letting it slip thro' my hands, is the best tale that ever was told; therefore, I would have your worship be attentive, for thus I begin.

"There was, so there was; the good that shall fall, betide us all; and he that seeks evil, may he meet with the devil. Your worship may take notice, that the beginning of antient tales, is not just what came into the head of the teller: no, they always began with some saying of Cato the censer of Rome,[2] like this of 'He that seeks evil, may he meet with the devil.' And truly it comes as pat to the purpose, as the ring to my finger, in order to persuade your worship to remain where you are, without going in search of evil, in any

manner of way; or else to turn into another road, since we are not bound to follow this in which we have been surprized with fear and terror." "Follow thy story, Sancho," said Don Quixote, "and as to the road we have to follow, leave the care of that to me." "To proceed then," said Sancho: "In a certain village of Estremadura, there lived a certain goat-shepherd. I mean, one that kept goats; and this shepherd or goat-herd, as the story goes, was called Lope Ruyz; and it came to pass, that this Lope Ruyz fell in love with a shepherdess whose name was Torralva; which shepherdess, whose name was Torralva, was the daughter of a rich herdsman; and this rich herdsman."—

"If thou tellest thy tale in this manner," cried Don Quixote, "repeating every circumstance twice over; it will not be finished these two days: proceed therefore, connectedly, and rehearse it, like a man of understanding: otherwise, thou hadst better hold thy tongue." "In my country," answered Sancho, "all the old stories are told in this manner; neither can I tell it in any other; nor is it civil in your worship, to desire I should change the custom." "Take thy own way," said the knight, "and since it is the will of fate, that I should hear thee, pray go on."

"Well then, good master of mine," proceeded Sancho, "that same shepherd, as I have already remarked, fell in love with the shepherdess Torralva, who was a thick, brawny wench, a little coy, and somewhat masculine; for, she wore a sort of mustachios: me-thinks, I see her now, for all the world." "Then thou knewest her?" said the knight. "Not I," answered the squire, "but the person who told me the story, said it was so true and certain, that if ever I should chance to tell it again, I might affirm upon oath, that I had seen it with my own eyes—And so, in process of time, the devil, who never sleeps, but wants to have a finger in every pye, managed matters in such a manner, that the shepherd's love for the shepherdess, was turned into malice and deadly hate: and the cause, according to evil tongues, was a certain quantity of small jealousies she gave him, exceeding all bounds and measure. And such was the abhorrence the shepherd conceived for her, from that good day forward, that, in order to avoid the sight of her, he resolved to absent himself from his own country, and go where he should never set eyes on her again. Torralva finding herself despised by Lope, began to love him more than ever." "That is the natural disposition of the sex," said Don Quixote, "to disdain those who adore them, and love those by whom they are abhorred: but, proceed Sancho."

"It so fell out," said Sancho, "that the shepherd put his resolution in practice, and driving his goats before him, travelled through the plains of Estremadura, towards the kingdom of Portugal. Torralva having got an inkling of his design, was soon at his heels, following him on foot, aye, and barefoot too, with a pilgrim's staff in her hand, and a wallet at her back, in which, as the report goes, she carried a bit of a looking-glass, a broken comb, and a kind of vial of wash for her complexion: but, howsomever, whether she carried these things or not, I shall not at present, take upon me to aver: but only say what is recorded, that the shepherd came with his flock to the river Guadiana, which at that time was very high, having almost forsaken its channel: and finding at the place, neither boat nor bark to carry himself and his flock to the other side, he was very much in the dumps, because he saw Torralva behind him, and knew what he must suffer, from her tears and complaints: but, looking about, he at last perceived hard by him, a fisherman in a boat that was so small, as to contain only one person and one goat: nevertheless,

they struck up a bargain, by which the man was to ferry over the shepherd with his three hundred goats. Accordingly, the fisherman took one goat into the boat, and carried it over; then he returned and carried over another, then he returned again to fetch another. Pray good your worship, keep an exact account of the goats, as the fisherman ferried them over; for, if one only should be lost in the reckoning, the story will break off, and it will be impossible for me to relate one word more. To be short then, I say, the landing-place on the other side being full of mud and slippery, was a great hindrance to the fisherman in his going and coming; but, however, he returned for the other goat, and then for some more, and then for another."

"Suppose them all passed over at once," said Don Quixote; "for, if thou goest backwards and forwards in this manner, thou wilt not have them all ferried over in a year." "How many have already passed?" said the squire, "How the devil should I know?" answered the knight. "Did not I tell you to keep a good account?" said Sancho, "now before God! the tale is ended, and it is impossible to proceed." "How can that be?" replied Don Quixote, "is it so essential to the story, to know the number of goats as they passed, so precisely, that if I misreckon one, thou canst not proceed?" "Certainly, sir," said Sancho, "I can proceed in no manner of way: for, when I desired your worship to tell me what number of goats had passed, and you answered you did not know, at that instant, the whole of the story that remained untold, vanished from my remembrance; and, upon my conscience! it was very curious and entertaining." "At that rate then, the story is at an end?" said Don Quixote. "As much at an end," replied the squire, "as the mother that bore me."

"In good sooth," resumed the knight, "thou hast related the strangest fable, tale, or story that ever was invented; and finished thy relation in such a manner, as never was, or will be heard again in this world: but nothing else was to be expected from thy sound judgment: and indeed, it is a matter of no admiration with me; because, I take it for granted that these incessant strokes have disordered thy understanding." "Not unlikely," said Sancho; "but, this I know, that there is no more to be said of the tale, which ended in that place, where the mistake began, about the passage of the goats." "In good time, end it according to thy own pleasure," replied the knight, "and now let us see if Rozinante will move." So saying, he began again to spur, and the horse to leap, without moving from his station, so effectually had Sancho fettered him.

About this time, whether it was owing to the coolness of the morning that approached, or to his having supped upon something that was laxative; or, which is more probable, to the operation of nature; Sancho was seized with an inclination and desire of doing that which could not be performed by proxy; but, such was the terror that had taken possession of his soul, that he durst not move the breadth of a nail-paring from his master's side: at the same time, it was as impossible for him, to resist the motion of his bowels; and therefore, to compromise the matter, he slipp'd his right hand from the hinder part of the saddle, and without any noise, softly undid the slip knot by which his breeches were kept up: upon which, they of themselves fell down to his heels, where they remained like a pair of shackles; he then gathered up his shirt behind, as well as he could; and exposed his posteriors, which were none of the smallest, to the open air: this being done, and he imagined it was the chief step he could take to deliver himself from the

pressing occasion and dilemma, in which he was, another difficulty still greater oc-
curred, namely, that he should not be able to disencumber himself without noise: he
therefore, began to fix his teeth close, shrug up his shoulders, and hold in his breath with
all his might. But, notwithstanding these precautions, he was so unlucky in the issue, as
to produce a rumbling sound very different from that which had terrified him so much.
It did not escape the ears of Don Quixote, who immediately cried, "What noise is that,
Sancho?" "I know not, sir," said the squire, "it must be some new affair, for adventures
and misventures never begin with trifles." He tried his fortune a second time, and with-
out any more noise or disorder, freed himself from the load which had given him so
much uneasiness. But, as Don Quixote's sense of smelling, was altogether as acute as
that of his hearing, and Sancho stood so close to him, that the vapours ascended towards
him, almost in a direct line, he could not exclude some of them from paying a visit to
his nose. No sooner was he sensible of the first salutation, than in his own defence, he
pressed his nose between his finger and thumb, and in a snuffling tone, pronounced,
"Sancho, thou seemest to be in great fear." "I am so," answered the squire; "but, how
comes your worship to perceive my fears now, more than ever?" "Because, at present,
thou smellest more than ever, and that not of amber," replied the knight. "That may be,"
said Sancho; "but, I am not so much to blame as your worship, who drags me at such
unseasonable hours, into these uninhabited places." "Retire three or four steps farther
off, friend," resumed Don Quixote, stopping his nose all the time, "and henceforth take
more heed of thy own person, and remember what thou owest to mine; for, I find, the
frequent conversation I maintain with thee, hath engendered this disrespect." "I'll lay a
wager," replied Sancho, "that your worship thinks I have been doing something I ought
not to have done." "The more you stir it, friend Sancho," said the knight, "the more it
will stink."

In this and other such discourse, the master and his squire passed the night; but, San-
cho perceiving the day begin to break apace, with great care and secrecy, unbound Roz-
inante, and tied up his breeches. The beast, which was naturally none of the briskest,
seemed to rejoice at his freedom, and began to paw the ground; for, as to curvetting,
with his leave be it spoken, he knew nothing of the matter. Don Quixote finding him so
mettlesome, conceived a good omen from his eagerness, believing it a certain presage
of his success in the dreadful adventure he was about to atchieve. Aurora now disclosed
herself, and objects appearing distinctly, Don Quixote found himself in a grove of tall
chesnut-trees, which formed a very thick shade. The strokes still continuing, though he
could not conceive the meaning of them, he, without further delay, made Rozinante feel
the spur; then turning to take leave of Sancho, commanded him to wait three days at
farthest, as he had directed before; and if he should not return before that time was ex-
pired, he might take it for granted, that God had been pleased to put a period to his life,
in that perilous adventure; he again recommended to him, the embassy and message he
should carry from him, to his mistress Dulcinea; and bade him give himself no uneasi-
ness about his wages; for, he had made a will, before he quitted his family, in which he
should find his services repaid, by a salary proportioned to the time of his attendance:
but, if heaven should be pleased to bring him off from that danger, safe, sound and free;
he might, beyond all question, lay his account with the government of the island he had

promised him. Sancho, hearing these dismal expressions of his worthy master, repeated, began to blubber afresh, and resolved not to leave him, until the last circumstance and issue of the affair.

From these tears, and this honourable determination of Sancho Panza, the author of this history, concludes, that he must have been a gentleman born, or an old christian at least. His master himself was melted a little at this testimony of his affection, but not so much, as to discover the least weakness: on the contrary, disguising his sentiments, he rode forward towards the place, from whence the noise of the strokes and water seemed to come; Sancho following on foot, and, according to custom, leading by the halter his ass, which was the constant companion of his good and evil fortune. Having travelled a good way, among those shady chesnut-trees, they arrived in a small meadow lying at the foot of a huge rock, over which a stream of water rushed down with vast impetuosity. Below, appeared a few wretched huts, that looked more like ruins than houses, and they observed that from them proceeded the horrible din of the strokes which had not yet ceased.

Rozinante being startled at the dreadful noise of the strokes and water, Don Quixote endeavoured to sooth him, and advanced by little and little, towards the huts, recommending himself in the most earnest manner, to his mistress, whose favour he implored in the atchievement of that fearful enterprize: neither did he omit praying to God for his protection. Sancho, who never stirred from his side, thrust his neck as far as he could, between the legs of Rozinante, in order to discover the objects that kept him in such terror and suspence; and when they had proceeded about an hundred paces farther, at the doubling of a corner, stood fully disclosed to view, the very individual and un-doubted cause of this tremendous sound, and terrible noise, which had filled them with such doubts and consternation, all night long.

This was no other, be not offended gentle reader, than six fulling-hammers, which by their alternate strokes, produced that amazing din. Don Quixote was struck dumb with astonishment at the sight; Sancho looked at him, and found his head hanging down upon his breast, and other manifest signs of his being out of countenance. The knight, in his turn, looked at the squire, and saw his mouth shut, his cheeks puffed up, with other symptoms of his being ready to burst with laughing: this comical situation of the squire, in spite of all his own melancholy, obliged the master to begin; and Sancho no sooner beheld the severity of the knight's features, relaxed, than he opened the flood-gates of his mirth, which broke forth with such violence, that he was under the necessity of supporting his sides with both fists, that they might not be rent to pieces by the convulsion. Four times did he exhaust, and as often renew the laugh with the same impetuosity as at first; for which, Don Quixote already wished him at the devil, more especially, when he heard him pronounce, by way of sneer, "Know, friend Sancho, that I was born by heaven's appointment, in these iron times, to revive the age of gold, or the golden age! I am he, for whom strange perils, valiant deeds, and vast adventures are reserved!" And in this manner he proceeded, repeating all or the greater part of the knight's exclamation, when they first heard the terrible noise.

Don Quixote finding that Sancho made a jest of him, was so much ashamed and pro-voked, that, lifting up his lance, he bestowed upon him two or three thwacks, which, had

they fallen upon his head, as they lighted on his shoulders, would have saved his master the trouble of paying his salary, unless it might be to his heirs. Sancho feeling his joke turned into such disagreeable earnest, which, he was afraid, might not be as yet over, addressed himself to his master with great humility, saying, "Good your worship forbear; before God I was only in jest." "Tho' you was in jest," answered Don Quixote, "I was not quite so merrily disposed: come hither, Mr. Joker; don't you think, that if, instead of fulling-hammers, these had been some very dangerous adventure, I have shewn courage enough to undertake and atchieve it? Am I, who am a knight, obliged, forsooth, to distinguish sounds, and know which proceed from fulling-mills, and which do not? especially as it may be the case, and it really is so, that I never saw one before; tho' it is otherwise with thee, base plebeian as thou art, who wast born and bred up among them: but, see if thou can'st metamorphose these six hammers into so many giants, and bring them within arm's length of me, one by one, or all together; and if I don't make them lie with their heels uppermost, make a jest of me, as much as you please."

"Enough, dear master," replied Sancho, "I confess I have exceeded a little, in my pleasantry; but, pray, tell me, now that we are at peace again, as God shall deliver your worship from all succeeding adventures, as safe and sound as you have been extricated from this; is not the terror with which we were seized, a thing to be laughed at, and repeated? I mean my own terror, for, as to your worship, I know you are an utter stranger to terror and dismay!" "I do not deny," answered Don Quixote, "that what hath happened to us, is ridiculous enough; but, nevertheless, it ought not to be repeated; because every body has not discretion to take things by the right handle." "I am sure," replied Sancho, "that your worship knows how to handle your lance, with which, while you wanted to handle my head, you happened to salute my shoulders; thanks be to God, and my own activity, in avoiding the blow: but, all that, when it is dry, will rub out;[3] and I have often heard it said, 'He that loves thee well, will often make thee cry': nay, it is a common thing for your gentry, when they have said a harsh thing to a servant, to make it up with him, by giving him a pair of cast breeches; tho' I don't know what they use to give after having beaten him, unless it be the practice of knights-errant, after blows, to give islands or kingdoms on the mainland."

"Who knows," said Don Quixote, "but the dice may run that way, and all that thou hast mentioned, come to pass: I ask pardon for what is past, since you are resolved to be more discreet for the future; and as the first emotions are not in a man's own power, I must apprize thee henceforward, to be more reserved, and abstain from speaking so freely to me; for, in all the books of chivalry I have read, and they are almost infinite, I never found that any squire talked so much to his master as thou hast talked to thine: and really, both you and I are very much to blame; thou, in regarding me so little, and I in not making myself regarded more: was not Gandalin, squire of Amadis de Gaul, count of the firm island? and yet we read of him, that he always spoke to his master, cap in hand, with an inclination of his head, and his body bent in the Turkish manner. What need I mention Gasabal, squire to Don Galaor, who was so reserved, that in order to express the excellence of his surprising silence, his name is mentioned but once, in the whole course of that equally vast and true history. From what I have said, Sancho, thou art to draw this inference, that there is a necessity for maintaining some distinction, between

the master and his man, the gentleman and his servant, and the knight and his squire: wherefore, from this day forward, we are to be treated with more respect and less provocation; for, if ever I am incensed by you again, in any shape whatever, the pitcher will pay for all: the favours and benefits I have promised, will come in due time, and if they should fail, your wages at least, will be forthcoming, as I have already informed you."

"All that your worship observes, is very just," said Sancho; "but, I should be glad to know, since, if the benefits come not in time, I must be fain to put up with the wages, what was the hire of a knight-errant's squire in those days: and whether they agreed by the month or the day, like common labourers." "I do not believe," answered Don Quixote, "that they were retained for hire, but depended altogether on favour; and tho' I have bequeathed a sum to thee, in my will, which I have left signed and sealed at home, it was done in case of the worst; for, one does not know how chivalry may succeed in these calamitous times: and I would not have my soul punished in the other world, for so small a matter; for, let me tell thee, Sancho, in this, there is not a more dangerous course, than that of adventures." "That I know to be true," answered the squire, "since the noise of a fulling-mill could daunt and disturb the heart of such a valiant knight-errant as your worship: but, this I assure you of, that from this good hour, my lips shall never give umbrage to your worship, in turning your affairs to jest again; but, on the contrary, honour you as my natural lord and master." "In so doing," replied Don Quixote, "thou shalt live long upon the face of the earth; for, after your father and mother, you ought to respect your master as another parent."

## CHAPTER VII.

### Of the sublime adventure, and shining acquisition of Mambrino's helmet; with other accidents that happened to our invincible knight.

About this time, some rain beginning to fall, Sancho proposed that they should shelter themselves in the fulling-mill; but, Don Quixote had conceived such abhorrence for it, on account of what was past, that he would by no means set foot within its walls: wherefore, turning to the right-hand, they chanced to fall in with a road different from that in which they had travelled the day before: they had not gone far, when the knight discovered a man riding with something on his head, that glittered like polished gold: and scarce had he descried this phænomenon, when turning to Sancho, "I find," said he, "that every proverb is strictly true; indeed, all of them are apophthegms dictated by experience herself, the mother of all sciences; more especially, that which says, 'Shut one door, and another will soon open': this I mention, because, if last night, fortune shut against us the door we sought to enter, by deceiving us with the fulling-hammers; to-day, another stands wide open, in proffering to us, another greater and more certain adventure, by which, if I fail to enter, it shall be my own fault, and not imputed to my ig-

norance of fulling-mills, or the darkness of the night. This I take upon me to say, because, if I am not egregiously mistaken, the person who comes towards us, wears upon his head the very helmet of Mambrino, about which I swore the oath which thou may'st remember."

"Consider well what your worship says, and better still what you do!" said Sancho. "I should not chuse to meet with more fulling-mills, to mill us and maul us altogether out of our senses." "The devil take the fellow," cried Don Quixote, "what affinity is there between a fulling-mill and a helmet?" "Truly, I know not," answered the squire; "but, in good faith, if I were permitted to speak freely, as usual, I could perhaps give such reasons as would convince your worship, that you are mistaken in what you say." "How can I be mistaken, scrupulous traitor?" replied Don Quixote: "seest thou not yonder knight who rides this way, upon a dapple steed, with a golden helmet on his head?" "What I perceive and discern," said Sancho, "is no other than a man upon a grey ass, like my own, with something that glitters on his head." "And that is the very helmet of Mambrino," replied the knight: "stand aside, and leave me alone to deal with him; thou shalt see, that without speaking a syllable, in order to spare time, this adventure will be concluded by my acquisition of the helmet I have longed for so much." "Yes, I will take care to get out of the way," answered Sancho; "and God grant," cried he as he went off, "that this may turn out a * melon rather than a milling." "I have already warned thee, brother," said the knight, "not to mention, nor even so much as think of the mill again: else by heaven! I'll say no more, but mill the soul out of thy body."

Sancho was fain to hold his tongue, dreading the performance of his master's oath, which had already struck him all of a heap. The whole affair of the helmet, steed, and knight, which Don Quixote saw, was no more than this: in that neighbourhood, were two villages, one of them so poor and small, that it had neither shop nor barber: for which reason, the trimmer of the larger that was hard by, served the lesser also, in which, at that time, there was a sick person to be blooded, and another to be shaved; so that this barber was going thither with his brass bason under his arm: but, as it chanced to rain while he was on the road, that he might not spoil his hat, which probably was a new one, he sheltered his head under the bason, which being clean scoured, made a flaming appearance, at the distance of half a league; and, as Sancho had observed, he rode upon a grey ass, which gave occasion to Don Quixote to believe he was some knight with a helmet of gold, mounted upon a dapple steed; for, he accommodated every thing he saw, with incredible facility, to the extravagant ravings of his disordered judgment. When he, therefore, saw this unlucky knight approach, without the least expostulation, he put Rozinante to full speed, and couching his lance in the rest, resolved to run him thro' the body at once; but, when he was almost up with him, without checking the impetuosity of his career, he cried aloud, "Defend thyself, wretched caitiff, or voluntarily yield what so justly belongs to me."

The poor barber, who neither dreaded nor dreamed of any such demand, seeing this phantom coming full speed upon him, could find no other means to defend himself

* Oregano, in the original, signifies sweet marjoram, as if Sancho had wished his master might find a nosegay, rather than a bloody nose.[1]

from the stroke of the lance, than to throw himself down over the buttocks of his ass; then getting up, before he had scarce touched the ground, with the nimbleness of a stag, he began to fly across the plain so swift, that the wind itself could not overtake him: but, he left his bason upon the spot, with which Don Quixote was satisfied, saying, "The pagan hath acted with discretion, in imitating the beaver, which, seeing itself chaced by the hunters, tears off with its teeth, by natural instinct, those parts for which it is pursued." Then, he ordered Sancho to take up the helmet, which the squire having examined all round, "Egad!" said he, "It is a special good bason, well worth a piece of eight, if it be worth a farthing"; and gave it to his master, who putting it on his head, and turning it round and round, without being able to find the vizor, said, "Without doubt, the pagan for whom this renowned helmet was first forged, must have had a most capacious head: but the worst of it is, that, one half is wanting."

When Sancho heard him call the bason a helmet, he could not refrain from laughing, but, remembring the indignation of his master, checked his mirth all of a sudden; and when Don Quixote asked what he laughed at, replied, "I can't help laughing when I think of the huge head of the pagan who owned that helmet, which looks for all the world like a barber's bason." "Why, truly, Sancho," said he, "I imagine that this very individual inchanted helmet, by some strange accident or other, must have fallen into the hands of some body who did not know its inestimable value, but, seeing it was made of the purest gold, melted down one half of it for sale, and left the other in this shape, resembling, as thou sayest, a barber's bason: but, be that as it may, since I am satisfied of its real worth and identity, the transmutation is of small consequence; for, I will order it to be repaired in the first village where we can find a blacksmith, in such a manner as to be unexcelled, nay even unequalled by that which Vulcan forged and finished for the God of war: mean while, I will wear it in this manner; for, it is still better than nothing at all, and will be sufficient to defend me from any shower of stones that may chance to fall."

"Yes, if they come not out of slings, as was the case in the skirmish between the two armies; when they demolished your worship's grinders, and broke the cruze which contained that blessed balsam, which made me vomit up my liver and lights." "That loss gives me not much uneasiness," answered the knight, "because thou knowest, Sancho, I retain the receipt of it in my memory"; "So do I," replied the squire. "But, Lord, let me never stir from the place where I now stand, if ever I either make or meddle with it for the future; especially, as I hope I shall never have occasion for it again, being resolved, with the assistance of my five senses, to avoid being hurt myself, and also to refrain from hurting any person whatsoever. As to another bout of blanketing, I have little to say: such misfortunes are not easily prevented; but, when they happen, there is nothing else to be done, but to shrug up our shoulders, hold in our breath, shut our eyes, and leave ourselves to the determination of chance and the blanket."

"Thou art a bad christian, Sancho," said Don Quixote, when he heard these words, "for, once you receive an injury, you never forget it; but, know it is peculiar to noble and generous minds to overlook such trifles: hast thou got a leg lamed, a rib fractured, or thy head broke in the prosecution of that jest, that thou canst not forget it? for, the affair, when duly considered, was no more than jest and pastime: had I not understood it

*Vol. 1. pag. 126.*

Hayman delin.                                              Ravenet sculp.

Don Quixote Taking the Barber's Basin for Mambrino's Helmet.

so, I should have returned e'er now, and done more mischief in revenging thy quarrel, than the Grecians did, for the rape of Helen, who, if she lived in this age, or if my Dulcinea had flourished in her time, would not have been so renowned for beauty." Here he fetched a profound sigh, and sent it to the clouds. "Let it pass then for a joke," said Sancho, "since there is no likelihood of its being revenged in earnest: but, I know what sort of jokes and earnests those are; and I believe they will scarce slip out of my memory, while they remain engraven on my shoulders. But, setting this aside, I wish your worship would tell me, what I shall do with this dapple steed so like a grey ass, which was abandoned by that caitiff, whom your worship overthrew: for, by the swiftness of his heels when he ran away, he seems to have no thoughts of returning; and by my whiskers 'tis an excellent beast!"

"It is never my custom," said Don Quixote, "to plunder those I overcome; neither is it according to the laws of chivalry, to take from them their horses, and leave them on foot, unless the conqueror hath lost his own during the engagement; in which case, we are allowed to take the horse of the vanquished, as the lawful spoils of war: wherefore, Sancho, leave that horse or ass, or what thou wilt, where he now stands, and perhaps his master, perceiving we are gone, will return and find him." "God is my witness," answered Sancho, "I should be glad to carry him off, or at least exchange him for my own, which seems to be the worst of the two: truly, the laws of chivalry are too confined; and since they do not extend to the exchange of one ass for another, I would fain know if they allow me to change the furniture of the one for that of the other?" "I am not quite clear in that particular," replied the knight; "and in such a dubious case, till such time as we can get better information, I think thou mayest exchange the furniture, if the necessity for so doing be extreme." "It is so extreme," said Sancho, "that if it were for my own particular wearing, I could not want it more." Thus provided with a licence, he made the exchange of caparisons, and equiped his beast with such finery, that he looked ten per cent. the better.

This exploit being performed, they went to breakfast on the remains of what they had plundered from the sumpter-mule, and quenched their thirst with the water from the fulling-mills, without turning their heads that way, so much did they abhor them, on account of the dread which they had inspired. The rage of hunger and anxiety being thus appeased, they mounted, and without following any determined course (for, it is the practice of true knights-errant, to keep no certain road) they left the choice of their route to the will and pleasure of Rozinante, which was always a rule to his master, as well as to the ass that followed whithersoever he led, like a trusty friend and companion. In consequence, therefore, of his determination, they returned into the high-road, in which they travelled at random, without any particular scheme.

While they thus jogged on, "Sir," said Sancho to his master, "I wish your worship would allow me to confer a little with you; for, since you imposed that severe command of silence upon me, divers things have perished in my stomach, and this moment, I have somewhat at my tongue's end, which I would not for the world have miscarry." "Speak then," said Don Quixote, "and be concise in thy discourse; for, nothing that is prolix can relish well." "I say, Sir," answered Sancho, "that for some days past, I have been considering how little is to be got and saved, by going in quest of those adventures your wor-

ship hunts after, thro' these cross-paths and desarts, where, tho' you conquer and atchieve the most perilous exploits, there is no body present to be witness of your prowess; so that it may remain in everlasting silence, contrary to the intention, and prejudicial to the merits of your worship: wherefore, in my opinion, with submission to your better judgment, our wisest course would be to go into the service of some emperor or great prince, who hath a war upon his hands, in whose service, your worship may have occasion to shew your personal valour, your great strength and greater understanding; which being perceived by the king we serve, he cannot chuse but reward every one according to his deserts; neither will there be wanting some person to write the history of your worship's exploits, for a perpetual memorial: I shall not mention my own, because they cannot exceed the bounds of a squire's province; tho' this I will venture to say, that if it was customary in chivalry, to recount the atchievements of our fraternity, I don't think mine might be inserted between the lines of the book."

"Thou art not much in the wrong," replied Don Quixote; "but, before it comes to that issue, a knight must travel up and down the world as a probationer, in quest of adventures, until, by his repeated atchievements, he shall have acquired a sufficient stock of fame; so that when he arrives at the court of some mighty monarch, he may be immediately known by his works; in that case, as soon as he shall be seen to enter the gates of the city, all the boys will surround and follow him, shouting and crying, 'behold the knight of the Sun, or the Serpent,' or of any other badge under which he hath performed his great exploits. 'Behold,' they will say, 'the man who vanquished in single combat, the mighty giant Brocabruno; and delivered the great Mamaluke of Persia, from the strange enchantment that prevailed over him, for the space of nine hundred years.' Thus shall they proceed, recounting his exploits from mouth to mouth, until, surprised at the noise of the children and populace, the king of that country shall appear at one of the palace-windows; and no sooner behold the knight, than knowing him immediately by his armour, or the device upon his shield, he will certainly exclaim, 'So ho, there! let all the knights belonging to my court, go forth and receive the flower of chivalry that comes yonder.'

"At this command, all of them will come out, and the king himself advance to meet him on the middle of the stair-case, where he will embrace him most affectionately, giving him the kiss of friendship and welcome; then taking him by the hand, will he conduct him to the queen's closet, where he will find her majesty with the princess her daughter, who is one of the most beautiful and accomplished young ladies, that ever was seen in the known world. In this interview, she will immediately fix her eyes upon the knight, who at that instant shall be gazing at her, and each will appear to the other, something supernatural: without knowing how, or wherefore, they will find themselves presently caught and intangled in the inextricable net of love, and be infinitely concerned, because they have no opportunity of conversing together, and of disclosing the reciprocal anxiety of their thoughts: after this audience, he will, doubtless, be carried to some apartment of the palace richly furnished, where, after they shall have taken off his armour, they will clothe him in a rich scarlet robe brought for the purpose; and, if he made a fine appearance in armour, he will look infinitely more genteel in his doublet: at night, he will sup at the same table with the king, queen and infanta, upon whom he will

fix his eyes, as often as he can, without being perceived by the by-standers; while she will practise the same expedient, with equal sagacity; for, as I have already observed, she must be a young lady of vast discretion.

"The table being uncovered, there will enter at midnight thro' the hall-door, a little, deformed dwarf, followed by a beautiful lady, guarded by two giants; and he will propose a certain adventure, contrived by a most antient sage, which whosoever shall finish, will be deemed the most valiant knight in the whole world: then the king will order every warrior in waiting, to attempt it, but all of them shall fail, except the stranger knight, who will perform and accomplish it very much to his own credit, as well as to the satisfaction of the princess, who will think herself extremely happy, and well requited for having placed her affections so worthily. What is better still, this king or prince, or whatever he is, being at that time engaged in a most obstinate war with a potentate of equal strength, his guest, after having staid a few days at court, begs leave to go and serve him in the field; and the king granting his request with pleasure, the knight most politely kisses his hand for the great honour he hath done him: that same night, he goes to take his leave of his mistress the infanta, thro' the rails of a garden adjoining to the chamber in which she lies; where they have already, at different times, enjoyed each other's conversation, by the means of a damsel, who being the infanta's confidante, is privy to the whole amour: on this occasion, he will sigh most pitiously, she will actually faint away, the damsel will run for water; and the knight will be extremely concerned, because the day begins to break, and he would not for the world, be discovered, to the prejudice of his lady's reputation. In fine, the princess recovers, and reaches her fair hand thro' the rails to the knight, who kisses it a thousand times, and bathes it with his tears: then is concerted between them, some method, by which he is to inform her of his good or bad success; and the infanta intreats him to return as soon as possible: he swears solemnly to comply with her request, kisses her hand again, and bids her farewell with such affliction as well nigh deprives him of life: from thence he retreats to his chamber, throws himself upon the bed, but cannot sleep, so grieved is he at parting; he rises early in the morning, goes to take leave of the king, queen and infanta; their majesties accordingly, bid him farewell, after having informed him, that the princess is indisposed, and cannot see company: the knight imputing her disorder to her sorrow for his departure, is pierced to the soul, and well nigh betrays his own anxiety. The confidante being present all the while, takes notice of every circumstance, which she imparts to her lady, who listens with tears in her eyes, and observes that nothing gives so much uneasiness as her ignorance of the knight's pedigree, and her impatience to know whether or not he is of royal extraction: the damsel assures her, that so much politeness, gentility and valour as he possessed, could never be united except in a dignified and royal disposition: the afflicted infanta consoles herself with this observation, and endeavouring to regain her serenity, that she may not give cause of suspicion to her parents, in two days, appears again in public.

"The knight having set out for the army, comes to battle, overcomes the king's adversary, takes many towns, makes diverse conquests, returns to court, visits his mistress in the usual manner, and the affair being concerted between them, demands her in marriage, as the reward of his service: her father refuses to grant the boon, on pretence of

not knowing who this hero is; but, nevertheless, either by stealth or some other way, the infanta becomes his wife; and at last, the king is overjoyed at his good fortune, when this knight proves to be the son of a valiant monarch of some unknown country, for, I suppose, it could not be found in the map. The father dies, the infanta succeeds, and in two words, the knight becomes king: this then is the time to reward his squire, and all those who helped him to ascend the throne. The squire, accordingly, is married to a damsel belonging to the infanta, who doubtless, must be she that was privy to her amour, and daughter of some powerful duke."

"This is what I want," cried Sancho, "and what with fair play I shall obtain; for, all that you have mentioned, will exactly happen to your worship, under the title of the Knight of the rueful Countenance." "Never doubt it, Sancho," replied Don Quixote; "for, in the same manner, and by the same steps I have recounted, knights-errant rise, and have risen to the rank of kings and emperors. Our only business now is, to look out for some christian or pagan king who is at war, and hath a beautiful daughter; but, there will be time enough to think of that, since, as I have already told thee, renown must be acquired elsewhere, before we repair to court: nay, another difficulty occurs, namely, that tho' we should find a king at war, who has a beautiful daughter, after I shall have acquired incredible glory thro' the whole universe; I do not know how it can be proved that I am of royal extraction, or even second cousin to an emperor: and no king will grant his daughter to me in marriage, until he is first thoroughly satisfied in that particular, tho' my famous exploits should merit a much more valuable reward: wherefore, on account of this defect, I am afraid I shall lose that which the prowess of my arm may well deserve. True it is, I am a gentleman of an ancient and honourable family, not without property, possession, and a title, to the revenge of the five hundred * Sueldos; and it is not impossible, that the sage ordained to write my history, may furbish up my parentage and pedigree in such a manner, as to prove me descended in the fifteenth or sixteenth generation from a king: for, I must tell thee, Sancho, there are two sorts of pedigree in the world; one that brings and derives its original from princes and monarchs, which time hath defaced by little and little, till at last, it ends in a point, like a pyramid: the other owes its beginning to people of mean degree, and increases gradually to nobility and power; so, that the difference is, the one was once something, but is now nothing; and the other was once nothing but is now something! Perhaps, therefore, I may be one of the first mentioned division; and my origin, upon inquiry, be found high and mighty; a circumstance that ought to satisfy the king, who is to be my father-in-law: and if it should not have that effect, the infanta will be so enamoured of me, that in spite of her father, she will receive me as her lord and husband, even tho' she were certain of my being the son of a porter; but should she be shy, then is the time to carry her away by force, to any corner of the earth I shall chuse for my residence, until time or death shall put an end to the resentment of her parents."

* The Spaniards of old paid a tribute of 500 Sueldos or pieces of coin to the Moors, until they were delivered from this imposition by the gallantry of the gentlemen or people of rank, from which exploit a Castilian of family, used to express the nobility and worth of his extraction, by saying he was of the revenge of the Sueldos.[2]

"And here," cried Sancho, "nothing can be more pat to the purpose, than what some of your unconscionable fellows often say, 'Who would beg a benison, that for the taking may have * venison?' tho' it would still be more proper, if they had said †, 'Better thieve than grieve.' This I observe, that in case the king, your worship's father-in-law, should not prevail upon himself to give you the infanta his daughter, you may, as your worship says, steal and convey her off by main force: but, the misfortune is, that while the peace is on the anvil, and before you come to the peaceable enjoyment of your kingdom, the poor squire may chew his cud in expectation of his recompense, unless that confidante damsel, who is to be his spouse, should make her escape with the princess, and be content to join her evil fortune to his, until such time as heaven shall ordain it otherwise; for, I believe his master may very safely give her away in lawful marriage." "That thou mayest depend upon," said Don Quixote. "Since it is so, then," answered Sancho, "we have nothing to do, but recommend ourselves to God, and let fortune take its own course." "The lord conduct it," replied the knight, "according to my desires and thy necessity; And small be his grace, who counts himself base." "A God's name be it so," said Sancho, "for my own part, I am an old Christian, and therefore fit to be a lord." "Ay, to be greater than a lord," answered Don Quixote, "and even if thou wast not so well qualified, it would be of no signification ‡; because, I being king, can confer nobility upon thee, without putting thee to the expence of purchasing, or of subjecting thyself to any kind of servitude: for, in creating thee an earl, behold thou art a gentleman at once; and let people say what they will, in good faith! they must call thee, your Lordship, if it should make their hearts ake." "And do you reckon that I should not know how to give authority to the portent?" said the squire. "Patent, thou would'st say, and not portent," replied the knight. "It may be so," answered Sancho; "but I insist upon it, that I should demean myself very decently: for, once in my lifetime, I was beadle of a corporation, and the gown became me so well, that every body said, I had the presence of a warden: then what shall I be when I am cloathed in a ducal robe, all glittering with pearls, like a foreign count? Upon my conscience, I believe people will come an hundred leagues on purpose to see me." "You will make a very good appearance," said Don Quixote; "but, thou must take care to keep thy beard close shaved; for, it is so thick, matted and unseemly, that unless thou hast recourse to the razor, every second day at least, they will see what thou art, a gunshot off." "What else have I to do," said the squire, "but to hire a barber and keep him constantly in the house; and if I find occasion for it, even make him follow me, as a master of the horse follows one of your grandees."

"How do'st thou know," said Don Quixote, "that our grandees are attended by their masters of horse?" "That you shall be satisfied in," answered the squire: "heretofore, I was a whole month at court, where I saw a very little gentleman, who they told me, was a very great lord, passing to and fro, and a man following him a horseback, turning ever and anon as he turned, as if he had been the nobleman's own tail: when I asked why the

---

* Literally, Never beg, when you can take.[3]
† In the original, A snatch from behind a bush, is better than the prayer of good men.[4]
‡ This seems to have been intended as a stroke of satire, against those princes who sell nobility to the highest bidder, without any regard to the merit of the purchaser.

man did not overtake the other, but always kept behind him; they answered that he was his master of horse, and that it was a fashion among the great, for each to be attended by an officer of that name. Ever since that time, I have remembred their office so distinctly, that now, I believe I shall never forget it." "I think thou art very much in the right," said Don Quixote, "in resolving to carry thy barber along with thee; for, customs come not altogether, because they were not invented all at once: therefore, thou mayest be the first earl that ever went attended by a shaver; and truly, it is an office of greater confidence to trim the beard, than to saddle the horse." "Leave that affair of the barber to my management," said Sancho, "and be it your care to make yourself a king, and me an earl with all convenient speed." "That shall be done," replied the knight, who lifting up his eyes, perceived that which shall be recounted in the succeeding chapter.

## CHAPTER VIII.

### Don Quixote sets at liberty a number of unfortunate people, who, much against their wills, were going a journey that was not at all to their liking.

Cid Hamet Benengeli, the Arabian and Manchegan author, recounts in this solemn, sublime, minute, pleasant and fanciful history, that the conversation between the renowned Don Quixote, and his squire Sancho Panza, as related in the foregoing chapter, was no sooner concluded, than the knight lifting up his eyes, beheld upon the road before him, about twelve men on foot, strung together, like beads, with a great iron chain fastened to their necks, and he perceived shackles upon the arms of each. They were conducted by two men on horseback, and the like number on foot: the horsemen armed with firelocks, and the foot with javelins and swords. Sancho seeing them advance, "That," said he, "is the chain of slaves compelled by the king to work in the gallies." "How! compelled!" cried the knight, "is it possible the king compels people into his service?" "I don't say so," answered Sancho; "those people are condemned for their crimes, to serve in the king's gallies, on compulsion." "In short," replied Don Quixote, "be that as it will, they go not voluntarily, but are driven by force." "Certainly," said Sancho. "Since that is the case," resumed his master, "here the execution of my office is concerned: to annul force, and bring succour to the miserable." "Pray, good your worship take notice, that justice; which is the king himself, never uses violence nor severity to such people, except as a punishment for their crimes."

By this time, the chain of galley-slaves being come up, Don Quixote, with much courtesy, desired the guards would be pleased to inform him of the cause or causes for which those people were treated in that manner: one of the horsemen replied, that they were slaves belonging to his majesty, going to the galleys, and that was all he could say,

or the inquirer had occasion to know of the matter. "Nevertheless," resumed the knight, "I am desirous of knowing from each in particular, the occasion of his misfortune." To these he added other such courteous intreaties to induce them to satisfy his desire, that the other man on horseback said, "Though we have got along with us, the register and certificate of the sentence of each of those malefactors, we have no time at present to take it out and give you the reading of it: but, if you have a mind to go and question themselves, they will answer every thing you ask, to the best of their knowledge; for, they are a set of miscreants who delight in recounting as well as in acting their roguery."

With this permission, which he would have taken, if they had not granted it, Don Quixote approached the chain, and asked of the foremost, for what offence he travelled in that equipage. "Only for being in love," answered the criminal. "For that only!" replied the knight. "If they condemn people for being in love, I might have been tugging in the galleys long ago." "But my love," answered the slave, "was quite different from what your worship imagines. I fell deeply in love with a basket crammed full of white linnen, and locked it so fast in my embrace, that if justice had not tore it from my arms, by force, I should not have quitted it willingly, to this good hour: the thing being flagrant, there was no room for putting me to the torture, and therefore the cause was soon discussed: my shoulders were accommodated with a cool hundred, I was advised to divert myself three years in the Gurapas; and so the business ended." "Pray what are the Gurapas?" said Don Quixote. "The Gurapas are the galleys," answered the thief, who was a young fellow, about twenty years of age, and said he was a native of Piedrahita.

The knight put the same question to the second, who seemed so overwhelmed with grief and melancholy, that he could not answer one word; but, the first saved him the trouble by saying, "This man, sir, goes to the gallies for being a canary-bird: I mean, for his skill in vocal music." "What!" said the knight, "are people sentenced to the gallies for their skill in music?" "Yes, sir," answered the other, "for, nothing is worse than to sing in the heart-ach." "On the contrary," said Don Quixote, "I have always heard it observed, that Music and Play, will fright Sorrow away." "But here," replied the slave, "the case is quite different; for, he that sings but once, will have cause to weep for ever." Don Quixote saying he could not comprehend his meaning, one of the guards explained it: "Sir," said he, "to sing in the heart-ach, is a term used by these miscreants, to express a criminal, who confesses under the torture: and it having been applied to that delinquent, he owned his crime, which was horse-stealing; accordingly, having received two hundred lashes, he was condemned for six years to the gallies: and he appears always pensive and sad, because his brother rogues who keep him company, continually maltreat, upbraid, despise and scoff at him, for having confessed out of pure pusillanimity: for, say they, No, contains as many letters as Ay; an offender is very lucky, when his life or death depends upon his own tongue, and not upon the evidence of witnesses: and truly, I think they are not far mistaken."

"I am of the same opinion," said Don Quixote, and passing on, repeated his former question to the third, who with great readiness and alacrity, answered, "I am going to pay a visit of five years to lady Gurapas, for having wanted ten ducats." "I will give twenty with all my soul," replied the knight, "to ease you of your misfortune." "That,"

resumed the slave, "is like giving money to a man perishing with hunger at sea, where there is no food to be bought. I say this, because had I been master in time of those twenty ducats your worship now offers, I would have anointed the secretary's pen, and quickened my lawyer's invention with them, to such good purpose, that I should be now, standing at liberty, in the square of Zocodover in Toledo, and not dragging like a hound to the gallies; but, heaven is above. —Patience and—that is enough."

Don Quixote then advanced to the fourth, who was a man of a venerable aspect, with a long, white beard hanging down to his girdle; and he no sooner heard the knight ask the cause of his being in that situation, than he began to weep bitterly, without answering one word; but, the fifth criminal lent him his tongue, saying, "That honourable gentleman is going to the gallies for four years, after having made his public appearance on horseback with great solemnity." "That is, I suppose," said Sancho, "after having been exposed to public shame *." "Even so," replied the slave, "and that punishment was inflicted upon him, for being an ear-broker,[2] or rather, a broker for the whole body: to be plain with you; the gentleman was convicted of pimping, and giving himself out for a conjurer." "Were it not for the addition of his conjuring scheme," said Don Quixote, "he is so far from deserving to row in the gallies for pure pimping, that it rather † entitles him to the command of them, as general in chief: for, if the office of a pander was well regulated, it would be a most honourable and necessary employment, in a well-ordered commonwealth; reserved for people of birth and talents, and, like other places of trust, laid under the inspection of proper comptrollers, and limited to a certain number, like the brokers of merchandize: such a regulation would prevent many mischiefs, which are now occasioned by that employment's being in the hands of idiots or simple wretches, such as silly women, pages and buffoons, without either age or experience; who, upon the most urgent occasions, when there is need of the most important contrivance, let the morsel freeze between the dish and the mouth, and can scarce distinguish betwixt their right hands and their left. I could proceed, and advance many arguments to prove how advantageous it would be in a commonwealth, to make proper distinctions in the choice of those who exercise such a necessary employment; but, this is no place to settle that affair in; and one day, I may chance to recommend it to the consideration of those who can both discern and provide a suitable remedy for this defect. I shall only at present observe, that the compassion I feel, at sight of these grey hairs, and that venerable countenance in distress for having been a pander, is extinguished by the additional crime of sorcery, though I am well apprised, that there are no conjurers in the world, who can force or alter the will, as some weak-minded people imagine; for, the inclination is free, and not to be enslaved by any incantation whatsoever. The practice of some simple women, and knavish impostors, is to compose poisonous mixtures, to deprive people of their senses, under pretence of causing them to be beloved: it being a thing impossible, as I have said, to compel the will." "What your honour says, is very true," replied this

---

* A crime that is punished by the pillory in England, is in Spain expiated by the convict's being mounted upon an ass, in a particular dress, and led through the streets by a crier who proclaims the transgression.[1]

† This is a good hint for a reforming legislature.

good old man; "and really, sir, as to the affair of conjuring, I am not guilty: tho' I cannot deny that I have been a pimp; but, I never thought I was to blame in that capacity, because my whole intention was, that all the world should enjoy themselves, and live in peace and quiet, without quarrels and anxiety. Yet, the uprightness of my intention was of no service in preventing my being sent to a place from which I shall never return, oppressed as I am with years and a violent strangury, that will not allow me a moment's rest." So saying, he began to weep again, as before; and his tears raised the pity of Sancho to such a degree, that he took a rial out of his bosom, and gave it in charity to the distressed senior.

Then Don Quixote addressed himself to the next, who answered his question, not with less, but infinitely more vivacity, than that of the former; saying, "I trudge in this manner, for having jested a little extravagantly with two of my female cousins; and with two more, who, tho' not related to me, were in the same degree of blood to each other: in short, I jested with them so long, that in the end, there was such an intricate increase of kindred as no casuist could unravel. Every thing was proved against me, I had neither interest nor money, and ran some risk of having my windpipe stopt; but they only condemned me for six years to the galleys; I submitted to the sentence, as the punishment of my crime: youth is on my side, life may be long, and time brings every thing to bear: if your worship, sir knight, will part with any small matter for the comfort of poor wretches like us, God will requite you in heaven, and we upon earth, will take care to petition him for long life and health to your worship, that you may be as happy, as by your goodly appearance, you deserve to be." The person who spoke in this manner, appeared in the dress of a student, and one of the guards said he was a great orator and excellent latin scholar.

After all these, came a man of a good mein, about thirty years of age, who squinted so horribly, that his eyes seemed to look at each other: he was equipped in a very different manner from the rest; his foot being loaded with a huge chain that went round his whole body, and his neck adorned with two iron rings, to one of which the chain was fastened; and the other was called a keep-friend, or friend's-foot; from which descended to his middle, a couple of iron bolts fitted with a pair of manacles for his arms, secured by a large padlock, in such a fashion, as to hinder him from lifting up his hands to his mouth, and to disable him from bending his head to his hands. Don Quixote inquiring, why that man was more fettered than all the rest; one of the guards answered, "Because he is a greater rogue than all the rest put together, and so daring a villain, that although he is shackled in that manner, we are under some apprehension that he will give us the slip." "What crime has he committed," said the knight, "that deserves no greater punishment than that of going to the gallies?" "He goes for ten years," replied the guard, "which is a kind of civil death: but, you need not inquire any further, when you know that this honest gentleman is the famous Gines de Passamonte, alias Ginesello de Parapilla." "Softly, Mr. Commissary," said the slave, hearing these words, "don't transmography names and sirnames in that manner: Gines is my name, and not Ginesello, and Passamonte the title of my family: not Parapilla, as your worship says; let every body turn about and look at home, and he will have business enough." "Speak with less insolence, Mr. Thief above sterling," replied the commissary, "or else I shall make you hold your peace with a vengeance." "It appears by this oppression," answered the galley-slave,

"that God's will must be done; but, one day, some body shall know whether or not my name is Ginesillo de Parapilla." "An't you called so, you lying vagabond?" said the guard. "Yes, yes, I am so called," answered Gines; "but, I will make them change that name, or their skins shall pay for it, if ever I meet them in a place I don't chuse at present to name. Sir knight, if you have any thing to bestow, pray let us have it, and the Lord be with you, for you only tire us with enquiring about other people's affairs; if you want to be informed of my history, know, I am that Gines de Passamonte whose life is written by these ten fingers."

"He tells nothing but the truth," said the commissary; "for, he has actually written his own history, as well as could be desired, and pawned the manuscript in jail, for two hundred rials." "Ay, and I shall redeem it," said Gines, "if it were for as many ducats." "What! Is it so entertaining?" said Don Quixote. "Yes," answered Gines, "it is so entertaining, that woe be unto Lazarillo de Tormes, and all who have written or shall write in that manner. What I can affirm of mine, is, that it contains truths, and such ingenious and savoury truths, as no fiction can equal." "And what is the title of your book?" said the knight. "The life of Gines de Passamonte," replied the other. "Is it finished?" said Don Quixote. "How can it be finished," answered the author, "when my natural life is not yet concluded? I have already written my whole history from my birth till the last time I was sent to the gallies." "You have visited them before now, then?" said the knight. "For the service of God and the good of my country, I have already served in them, during the space of four years, and know the difference between the biscuit and the bull's pizzle," answered the thief; "and my journey to them now, gives me no great pain, for, there I shall have time to finish my book, and set down a great many things I have to say: there being spare time enough in the gallies of Spain, for that purpose which does not require much leisure, as I have every circumstance by heart." "You seem to be an ingenious fellow," said Don Quixote. "And unfortunate," answered Gines; "for, genius is always attended by evil fortune." "Evil fortune ought to attend villains like you," said the guard. "I have already desired you, Mr. Commissary, to proceed fair and softly," answered Passamonte; "your superiors did not give you that rod to maltreat us poor wretches, but, to conduct and carry us to the place of our destination, according to his majesty's command: and by the life of—but 'tis no matter. The spots we received in the inn, may, one day, be rubbed out in the washing. Mum's the word. Let us live while we can, speak while we may, and at present pursue our journey; for, this joke has already lasted too long."

The commissary lifted up his rod, in order to give a proper reply to the threats of Passamonte; but, Don Quixote interposing, begged he would not chastise him; because it was not to be wondered at, if one whose limbs were so shackled, should take such liberties with his tongue: then addressing himself to the prisoners, "From all that you have told me, dear brethren," said he, "I clearly perceive, that although you ought to be chastised for your crimes, the punishment you are going to suffer, is not much to your liking; on the contrary, you make this journey very much against your inclination: and perhaps, the pusillanimity of one of you under the torture, this man's want of money, and that other's scarcity of friends, and last of all, the partiality of the judge, may have been the cause of your perdition, in depriving you of that justice, your several cases intitled you to. Which consideration now operates within me, suggesting, persuading and even compelling me to shew in your behalf, the end and aim for which heaven sent me into

this world, and made me profess the order of knight-errantry, by which I am bound by oath, to succour the needy and oppressed; but, because I know, that one maxim of prudence, is, not to do that by foul means, which can be accomplished by fair, I beseech Mr. Commissary and the guards to unchain and let you depart in peace: the king will not want people to serve him on better occasions; and I think it is very hard to enslave those whom God and nature have made free. Besides, gentlemen soldiers," added the knight, "those poor people have committed no offence against you; and every body hath sins to answer for. There is a God in heaven, who will take care to chastise the wicked and reward the righteous; and it is not seemly, that honest men should be the executioners of their fellow-creatures, on account of matters with which they have no concern. This favour I entreat in a mild and peaceable manner; and if you grant my request, will thank you heartily: whereas, if you refuse to do quietly what I desire, this lance and sword, with the valour of my invincible arm, shall make you do it on compulsion."

"A fine joke, truly!" replied the commissary: "he has brought his harangue to a very merry conclusion; desiring us to set at liberty the king's prisoners, as if we had authority to grant, or he to demand, their discharge. I wish your worship would go about your business, and set to rights that bason on your skull, without going in quest of a cat with three feet." "You are a cat and a rat and a scoundrel to boot," replied the knight, attacking him with such wonderful dispatch, that he had not time to put himself in a posture of defence, so was thrown from his horse, dangerously wounded by a thrust of the knight's lance. And it happened luckily that this was one of the two who had firelocks. The rest of the guard were at first astonished and confounded at this unexpected assault; but they soon recollected themselves, and the horsemen drawing their swords, while those on foot handled their javelins, set upon Don Quixote in their turn, who waited for them with vast composure; and doubtless, he would have fared ill, if the galley-slaves, seeing a fair occasion offered, of gaining their liberty, had not made shift to obtain it, by breaking the chain with which they were fettered. Such was the confusion, that the guards, between their endeavours to detain the slaves who were unbound, and their efforts against Don Qn Quixote who assaulted them, could do nothing at all effectual. Sancho, for his part, assisted in disengaging Gines de Passamonte, who being the first that leapt free and disencumbered, on the plain, attacked the wounded commissary, and robbed him of his sword and musket, with which, pointing at one, and taking aim at another, without firing, however, in a trice, there was not one of the guards to be seen; for they made the best of their way, not only from Passamonte's firelock, but also from the shower of stones which was rained upon them by the rest of the slaves, who had by this time disengaged themselves.

Sancho was infinitely grieved at this event, representing to himself, that those who fled would instantly give notice of the affair to the holy brotherhood, which, upon the tolling of a bell, would immediately sally forth in search of the delinquents. This supposition, he suggested to his master, whom he intreated to depart forthwith, and conceal himself somewhere in the neighbouring mountain. "That may be a very good expedient," said the knight; "but I know what is proper for me to do at present." He then called to the slaves who were all in confusion, and after they had plundered and stripped the commissary to the skin, they assembled around him in a circle, in order to receive his commands, and he accosted them in this manner: "It is the duty of honest men, to

be thankful for benefits received; and one of the sins that gives the greatest offence to God, is ingratitude. This truth, I observe, gentlemen, because you must be sensible, by manifest experience, of that which you have received from me; as an acknowledgment for which, it is my will and pleasure, that you set out immediately, loaded with that chain from which I have delivered your necks, and, repairing to the city of Toboso, there present yourselves before the lady Dulcinea del Toboso, and tell her, that her knight of the rueful countenance, hath sent you to her, with his hearty commendations. You shall also punctually recount to her, every circumstance of this famous adventure, even to the granting you that liberty you so ardently wished for: and this duty being performed, you may go, a God's name, whithersoever ye list."

To this command, Gines de Passamonte, in the name of all the rest, answered, "What your worship commands, most worthy deliverer, is of all impossibilities, the most impossible to fulfil. For, we must by no means travel in a body, but, single and divided, and each by himself endeavour to abscond within the bowels of the earth, in order to avoid the holy brotherhood, which will, doubtless, come out in search of us. But your worship may, and it is but justice you should, change that service and tribute intended for my lady Dulcinea del Toboso, into a certain number of Ave-maria's and Credo's, which we will say for your prosperity; and this is a duty we can fulfil, by night as well as by day, in motion and at rest, and in peace as well as in war: but, to suppose that we will now return to the flesh-pots of Ægypt, I mean to the carriage of our chain, and take the road to Toboso, is to suppose that it is now midnight, tho' it wants little more than two hours of noon: and indeed, to expect this condescension of us, is like expecting pears from an elm."

"Then by heavens!" said Don Quixote in a rage, "Don Son of a whore, Don Ginesillo de Parapilla, or whatsoever is thy name, you shall go alone, with your tail between your legs, and carry the whole chain upon your own shoulders." Passamonte, who was none of the most passive people in the world, having already smoaked the knight's weak side, from the mad action he had committed in giving them their freedom, and finding himself treated by him in this haughty manner, tipt the wink to his companions, who retiring with him, at a little distance, began to shower forth a number of stones upon their deliverer, that he could not contrive how to cover himself with his shield: and poor Rozinante minded the spur no more, than if he had been made of brass. Sancho retired behind his ass, which sheltered him from the storm of hail, that descended on them both: but, his master could not screen himself so well, as to avoid an infinite number of pebble-shot, which took place upon different parts of his body, some of them with such force, that he came tumbling to the ground; and no sooner was he fallen, than the student set upon him, and snatching the bason from his head, made a most furious application of it to the knight's shoulders, and then dashed it upon the ground with such force, that it went into a thousand pieces. They likewise stripped him of a * jacket he wore above his armour, and would even have taken his hose, had not his greaves been in

* It was the custom of knights to wear a coat of arms made of some rich stuff figured in a particular manner. The duke of Brabant being called in a hurry to the battle of Agincourt, took a trumpeter's banner, and making a hole through the middle, put it over his head, and wore it as his coat of arms.[3]

their way: they plundered Sancho of his great coat, leaving him in his doublet and hose, and dividing the spoils of the battle among them, each took his own separate route, more anxious to escape the holy brotherhood which they dreaded, than to load themselves with the chain again, and go to present themselves before the lady Dulcinea del Toboso.

The ass and Rozinante, Sancho and Don Quixote, were the only persons remaining on the field. Dapple, with his head hanging down in a pensive attitude, and every now and then shaking his ears, as if he imagined the hurricane of stones that whizzed about them, was not yet over; Rozinante lying stretched upon the ground, to which, like his master, he was humbled by a pebble: Sancho in his doublet, terrified at the thoughts of the holy brotherhood; and Don Quixote excessively out of humour, at seeing himself so ill requited by those people whom he had served in such an essential manner.

## CHAPTER IX.

Of what befel the renowned Don Quixote in the brown mountain; being one of the most surprising adventures, which is recounted in this true history.

Don Quixote finding himself so evil entreated, said to his squire, "I have always heard it observed, Sancho, that benefits conferred on base-minded people, are like drops of water thrown into the sea. Had I taken thy advice, I might have avoided this vexation: but, now the affair is over, we must have recourse to patience, and take warning for the future." "Yes," replied Sancho, "your worship will take warning, as sure as I am a Turk: but, since you allow, that if you had taken my advice, you would have avoided this misfortune, take my advice now, and you avoid a greater still; for, I give you notice, that all your errantry will stand you in little stead, against the holy brotherhood, who don't value all the knights-errant in the universe three farthings: and, in faith, this minute, methinks I hear their arrows buzzing about my ears." "Thou art naturally a coward, Sancho," said the knight; "but, that thou mayest have no reason to say I am obstinate, and never follow thy counsel, for once thou shalt prevail: I will retreat from the danger thou dreadest so much; but, it shall be on condition, that thou shalt never, either in life or death, hint to any person whatsoever, that I retired, and avoided this peril, thro' fear, but meerly in compliance with thy earnest request: for, to say otherwise, would be to propagate falshood; and from this hour to that, and from that hour to this, I give thee the lie, and affirm thou liest, and wilt lie as often as thou shalt say or think any such thing: make no reply, therefore; the very thought of my being supposed to abscond, or retreat from danger, especially from this, as it implies some sort of shadow of fear, inspires me with such courage, that here am I alone, ready to remain and expect not only

the holy brotherhood, which thou hast mentioned with fear and trembling, but also the brothers of the twelve tribes of Israel, those of the seven Maccabees, with Castor and Pollux, and all the brethren and brotherhoods in the universe." "Sir," replied Sancho, "to retreat is not to fly, nor is it prudent to tarry when the danger over-balances the hope: and it is always the practice of wise people, to reserve something for to-morrow, without venturing all upon one cast; and you must know, that tho' I be a rustic and a clown, I have all my lifetime had a small share of what is called good conduct: wherefore, you need not repent of having taken my advice, but mount Rozinante, if you can; if not, I will lend you my assistance, and follow me; for, this noddle of mine tells me, that at present we have more need of heels than of hands."

Don Quixote accordingly mounted, without the least reply, and Sancho leading the way, upon his ass, they took refuge in that part of the brown mountain which was nearest, the squire intending to go quite across to Viso or Almodovar de Campo, after they should have lurked for some days amongst the rocks, that they might not be found, in case the holy brotherhood should come in search of them: he was encouraged to this resolution, by seeing, that in the * scuffle with the galley-slaves, the provisions his ass carried had escaped untouched; a circumstance that, in his opinion, amounted to a miracle, considering what the thieves had taken, and how narrowly they had searched.

That evening, they arrived in the very heart of the Sierra Morena †, where Sancho proposed to spend the night, and even to pass a few days, at least stay as long as their store should last: accordingly they took up their lodging between two rocks, in the midst of a great number of cork-trees: but, fate, which, according to the opinion of those who do not enjoy the light of the true faith, guides, conducts and disposes all things after its own way, ordained that Gines de Passamonte, that famous robber and cheat, who had been delivered from the chain, by the valour and madness of Don Quixote; I say, fate ordained that he, impelled by the fear of the holy brotherhood, which he did not dread without good reason, happened likewise to take refuge in those mountains; and even to be carried by this fear to the same place whither the same principle had directed Don Quixote and Sancho Panza, just time enough to know who they were, notwithstanding their being gone to sleep. As the wicked are always ungrateful, and necessity puts them to their shifts, and the present convenience overcomes the prospect of future quiet; Gines, who was neither grateful nor good-natured, resolved to steal Sancho's ass, undervaluing Rozinante, as a subject that he could neither pawn nor sell: accordingly, while the squire was asleep, he stole Dapple, and before morning, was gone far enough to elude all pursuit.

The appearance of Aurora that rejoices the earth, had a quite contrary effect upon Sancho Panza, who missing his Dapple, and searching for him in vain, began to utter the most woeful lamentation that ever was heard; and Don Quixote waked by the noise, heard him exclaiming in this manner: "O Son of my bowels! born in my house, the play-

---

* This is an oversight of the author, who seems to have forgot, that Sancho lost his wallet at the inn, and was robbed by the galley-slaves of the great coat or cloak, in which he carried the remains of that provision he had taken from those who attended the dead body towards Segovia.[1]
† A chain of dusky mountains that divide Castile from Andaluzia.[2]

fellow of my children, the delight of my spouse, the envy of my neighbours, and comforter of my cares! in short, the half of my sustenance: for, with six and twenty maravedis which thou hast daily earned, did I defray one half of my family expence!" Don Quixote hearing this complaint, and being informed of the cause, consoled Sancho with all the arguments in his power, and begging him to have patience, promised to give him a bill of exchange, on sight of which, he should receive three asses out of five, which the knight had left at home. Sancho being comforted with this declaration, dried up his tears, moderated his sighs, and returned a thousand thanks to Don Quixote for his generosity. As they sauntered among the rocks, the knight's heart was rejoiced to see places so well adapted to those adventures he was in quest of; for, they recalled to his remembrance, those wonderful events which had happened to knights-errant among such rocks and solitudes: he went on, musing on these subjects, and indeed so wrapt up, and engrossed by them, that he minded nothing else: while Sancho's only care, now that he thought he travelled in safety, was to satisfy his appetite with what remained of the spoils of the clergy: he therefore jogged on leisurely, after his master *, sitting side-ways on his ass, and replenishing his own bags, out of that which contained the provision; and while he was thus employed, would not have given a farthing for the best adventure that could happen.

Chancing, however, to lift up his eyes, he perceived his master had stopt, and was endeavouring, with the point of his lance, to raise some bundle that lay upon the ground: he therefore hastened up to him, in order to lend his assistance, should it be found necessary, and arrived just as the knight had turned up with his lance, a pillion with a portmanteau fixed to it, all rotted and consumed by the weather: but so heavy, that Sancho was obliged to alight, in order to take them up. His master having ordered him to examine the contents of the portmanteau, he obeyed with great alacrity, and tho' it was shut with a chain and padlock, there were so many holes in it, that he soon reached the inside, where he found four shirts of fine holland, with other provision of linnen, equally fashionable and clean, together with a pretty large heap of crowns of gold, wrapt up in a rag, which he no sooner perceived, than he cried in a rapture, "Blessed be heaven for granting us one advantageous adventure!" then continuing his search, he found a pocket-book richly garnished, which Don Quixote desired to have, bidding him keep the money for his own use. Sancho kissed his hand for the favour, and taking the linnen out of the portmanteau, crammed it into the bag that held their provision.

The knight having considered the whole affair, "Sancho," said he, "I am of opinion, and I cannot possibly be mistaken, that some bewildered traveller, in his passage over these mountains, has been set upon by robbers, who having slain him, must have dragged his body to be buried in this unfrequented place." "That cannot be the case," answered the squire; "for, if they had been robbers, they would not have left the money behind them." "Thou art in the right," said Don Quixote; "and I cannot guess nor conceive what the matter can have been. Let us see if there be any thing written in this pocket-book, by which we may trace out and come to the certainty of what we want to

---

* Here Cervantes hath been caught napping by the critics, who observe, that Sancho could not be mounted on the ass which was but just now stolen by Gines Passamonte.[3]

know." He opened it accordingly, and the first thing he found was the rough draught, tho' very legible, of a sonnet, which he read aloud for the benefit of Sancho, in these words:

I.

L ove either cruel is or blind;
        Or still unequal to the cause,
Is this distemper of the mind,
        That with infernal torture gnaws.

II.

But Love's a god, and cruelty
        In heavenly breasts can never dwell:
Then say, by what authority,
        I'm doom'd to feel the pains of hell?

III.

Of all my sufferings and my woe,
        Is Chloe then the fatal source?
Sure ill from good can never flow,
        Nor so much beauty gild a curse.

IV.

With hopeless misery weigh'd down,
        I'll seek for quiet in the grave;
For when the malady's unknown,
        A miracle alone can save.

"From such rhime," said Sancho, "there is no information to be got, unless by that clue *, we could come to the bottom of the affair." "What clue do'st thou mean?" said the knight. "The clue your worship mentioned just now in the sonnet," answered the squire. "I mentioned no clue," replied Don Quixote, "but Chloe, which is without doubt, the name of the lady of whom the author of these verses complains: and really he must have been a very ingenious poet, or else I know very little of the art." "Then your worship understands crambo?" said the squire. "Better than you imagine," answered the knight, "as you will see when you carry from me a letter to my mistress Dulcinea del Toboso, written in verse from top to bottom: for, thou must know, Sancho, that all or the greatest part of the knights-errant who lived in former ages, were very much addicted to poetry and music; these two qualities, or rather gifts of nature, being annexed to all errants in love: tho' the truth is, their couplets were rather sprightly than elegant." "I wish your worship would read on," said Sancho; "perhaps you may find something more to our

---

* As it is impossible to preserve the original blunders of Sancho, who mistakes Fili or Phillis, for Hilo that signifies a thread, we are obliged to substitute another, by changing Phillis into Chloe, which Sancho, in English, might have as naturally mistaken for a clue, and by this expedient, the sense of the passage is not hurt, and but very little altered.[4]

satisfaction." Accordingly the knight, having turned over the leaf, "Here is prose," said he; "and seems to be a letter." Sancho asking if it was upon business, his master replied, "In the beginning there was nothing but love." "Pray, Sir," cried Sancho, "read it aloud; for I am highly delighted with matters of love." "With all my heart," answered Don Quixote, who raising his voice, in compliance with the squire's request, read what follows:

"Thy false promises, together with the certainty of my misfortune, have exiled me to a corner of the world, from whence thou wilt hear an account of my death, before this my complaint shall reach thine ears. Thou hast cast me off, ungrateful as thou art! in favour of one, who, tho' he is richer, is not a more deserving lover than me: for, if virtue were the wealth that is most esteemed, I should have no cause to envy the happiness of others, or to bewail my own mishap. What thy beauty had raised, thy behaviour has overthrown: by the first I mistook thee for an angel; by the last I discovered thee to be a woman. Mayest thou live in peace, fair authoress of my misfortunes; and heaven grant that the deceit of thy husband may never be disclosed, that thou mayest never repent of what thou hast done, nor I enjoy the revenge I do not desire."

Don Quixote having read this letter, observed that nothing else could be inferred either from it, or the verses, but that the author was some despairing lover. Then perusing the rest of the book, he found more verses and letters, some legible, and others not intelligible; but, the substance of them all, was composed of complaints, lamentations, suspicions, desires, disgusts, favours and disdain, some of which were extolled, and others deplored. While Don Quixote examined the book, Sancho rummaged the portmanteau, without leaving a corner in that or the pillion, which he did not search, pry into and overhaul: no seam was left unript, no lock of wool unpicked, that nothing might be lost thro' negligence and want of care; so much was his cupidity awakened, by finding the money, which amounted to more than an hundred crowns: and tho' he reaped no other fruit from his industry, he thought himself abundantly requited for his capers in the blanket, his vomit of the balsam, the benediction of the pack-staves, the fisty-cuffs of the carrier, the loss of his bags, the robbery of his great coat, with all the hunger, thirst and fatigue he had undergone in the service of his worthy master, who had made him more than amends, by his generous present of this windfall.

The knight of the rueful countenance was impatient to know the owner of the portmanteau; conjecturing by the sonnet, the letter, the gold, and the fine linnen, that he must be some lover of quality, whom the disdain and barbarity of his mistress had driven to some desperate end: but, as in that uninhabited and rocky place, there was no body who could give him the information he wanted, he resolved to penetrate still farther into the mountain, without taking any other road than what Rozinante should chuse for his own conveniency, still confident of meeting with some strange adventure among these briars and brambles.

As he went on, entertaining himself with these reflections, he perceived, upon the top of a hill, right before him, a man skipping from bush to bush, and rock to rock, with wonderful agility: his body seemed naked, his beard black and bushy, his hair long and matted, his feet unshod, his legs bare, and his thighs covered with breeches, which to all appearance, were of crimson, but so ragged, that his skin appeared thro' many different holes, while his head was without any sort of covering. Notwithstanding the nimbleness

with which he passed, all these minute circumstances were seen and remarked by the knight of the rueful countenance, who in vain, attempted to follow him; those rough roads being quite unpassable by the feeble Rozinante, which was naturally phlegmatic and tender-footed. However, Don Quixote concluded that this must be the owner of the pillion and portmanteau, and determined within himself to find him out, altho' he should travel a whole year thro' the mountains, for that very purpose. With this view, he ordered Sancho to alight, and take a short cut over one part of the mountain, while he should go round the other; that by this expedient, they might come up with the man who had so suddenly vanished from their sight. "That proposal I can by no means comply with," answered the squire; "for, if I stir but an inch from your worship, fear instantly lays hold on me, and assaults me in a thousand horrid shapes and visions; and let this serve to apprise you, that henceforward, I will not budge a finger's breadth from your presence." "Be it so," said he of the rueful countenance; "and I am very glad that thou can'st avail thyself of my courage, which shall never fail thee, even if thy soul should fail thy body: follow me therefore, step by step, or at thy own leisure, and use thine eyes like two spy-glasses: we will take a compass round this little mountain, and perhaps we may meet again with that man, who is certainly no other than the owner of what we found." To this observation, Sancho replied, "Methinks we may save ourselves that trouble; for, if upon finding him, he should prove to be the owner of the money, I must of course, make restitution: therefore we had better spare all this fruitless search, and keep it bona fide, until the true owner, appear of himself, without all this intricate inquiry; and before that happens, perhaps I shall have spent the whole, and then I shall be discharged by law." "In that notion thou art mistaken, Sancho," resumed the knight; "for, as we have already good grounds to believe that he is the owner, it is our duty to find him out, and restore what we have taken: and tho' we should not find him, the strong reason we have to believe that it belongs to him, will make us equally guilty in detaining it, as we should be, if it really did. Wherefore, friend Sancho, do not give thyself any uneasiness about the inquiry; because, if we find him, I shall be freed from a great deal of anxiety." So saying, he put spurs to Rozinante, and Sancho followed in his usual manner. Having surrounded[5] part of the mountain, they found in a brook that watered the foot of it, a dead mule saddled and bridled, and half consumed by the dogs and crows: another circumstance which confirmed them in the opinion, that he who fled from them was master both of the mule and portmanteau.

While they were looking at this object, they heard a shepherd's whistle, and presently on the left appeared a good number of goats, and behind them, on the top of the mountain, they descried the goatherd, who seemed to be a man in years. Don Quixote calling aloud, intreated him to come down; and he in the same tone, asked what had brought them to that place, which was seldom trodden except by the feet of goats, wolves, and other wild beasts that harboured thereabouts? Sancho bade him come down, and they would tell him what had brought them thither; upon which, the goatherd descended, and coming up to Don Quixote, "I'll wager," said he, "that you are looking at the hireling mule, which lies dead in that bottom, where in good sooth it hath lain full six months. Pray, have you met with its master?" "We have met with nothing," answered the knight, "but a pillion and portmanteau, which we found not far from hence." "I have often seen

the same things," replied the goatherd, "but would never touch nor go near them, being afraid of some misfortune; or of being questioned for theft; for, the devil is very cunning, and raises blocks under our feet, over which we stumble, and very often fall, without knowing how or wherefore." "That is the very thing I say," answered Sancho, "though I saw them also, I would not go within a stone's throw of them: there I left them, and there they remain as they were; for, I don't chuse to steal a dog with a collar about his neck *."[6] "Prithee, honest friend," said Don Quixote, "dost thou know who the owner of these things is?" "All that I can say of the matter," answered the goatherd, "is, that it may be about six months, more or less, since there came to our hut, which is about three leagues from hence, a very genteel young man of a comely appearance, riding upon that very mule that now lies dead, with the same pillion and portmanteau which you say, you found. He asked what part of the mountain was the most woody and concealed, and we told him, that it was this very spot where we now are; and it is so, for if you go half a league farther into the mountain, you will perhaps, find it a very difficult matter to return: and I marvel much, how you have got so far, for, there is neither high-road, nor by-path that leads to this place. But, as I was saying, the young man hearing our reply, turned his mule, and rode towards the place to which we had directed him, leaving us all very much pleased with his appearance, though not a little surprized at his question, and the speed with which we saw him ride back into the heart of the mountain: from that time we saw no more of him, till a few days after, when he sprung upon one of our shepherds on the road, and without saying why or wherefore, beat and bruised him unmercifully; after which, he went to the sumpter-ass, and, carrying off all the bread and cheese that was on his back, with surprizing nimbleness, ran back again to the thicket. As soon as we understood this particular, several of us goatherds went in search of him, through the most wild and unfrequented part of the mountain, for the space of two days, at the end of which, we found him lying in the hollow of a large cork-tree. He came out to us, in a very civil manner, with his cloaths all torn, and his face so tanned and disfigured by the sun, that we should scarce have known him, had not his cloaths, tattered as they were, which we had before taken particular notice of, assured us that he was the person we went in search of. He saluted us very courteously, and in a few words, though very well chosen, bade us not wonder at seeing him in that condition; for, he was obliged in that manner, to do penance, which had been injoined him, on account of his manifold sins and transgressions. We earnestly begged to know who he was, but that he never could be prevailed upon to tell: we desired him also, whenever he should have occasion for food, without which he could not live, to tell us where we should find him, and we would bring it to him, with great care and affection; or, if that was not to his liking, we desired him to ask it civilly, without taking it by force. He thanked us kindly for our tenders of service, begged pardon for the assaults he had committed, and promised for the future, to ask it for God's sake, without giving offence to any person whatsoever. With regard to the place of his habitation, he said he had no

---

* Methinks it is inconsistent with the character of the knight, to allow Sancho to tell such a fraudulent untruth in his hearing; nor is Panza's behaviour, on this occasion, much for the honour of his simplicity.

other than that which chance presented every night when it grew dark; and concluded his discourse with such piteous lamentation, that our hearts must have been made of flint, if we could have heard it without shedding tears, considering the woeful change he had undergone, since we saw him at first: for, as I have already observed, he was a genteel, comely youth, and by his courteous and polite discourse, shewed himself to be a person of good birth, and excellent breeding: and though we who heard him were only home-bred country people, the gentility of his carriage was easily perceived by our clownish ignorance. In the midst of this conversation that past between him and us, he grew silent all of a sudden, and nailed, as it were, his eyes to the ground, for a considerable space of time, during which, we remained in suspence and no small concern, to see the effect of this stupefaction; for, by his staring at the ground for a good while, without moving his eye-lids, then shutting them close and biting his lips, and then drawing up the skin of his forehead, we could easily perceive that he was seized with some fit of madness; and he soon confirmed the truth of our opinion; for, he sprung up with surprizing force, from the ground on which he had thrown himself, and attacked the person who was next to him, with such rage and resolution, that if we had not taken him off, he would have beaten and bit him to death: crying aloud all the time, 'Ha, treacherous Fernando! Now shalt thou pay for the injury thou hast done me. These hands shall tear out thy heart, in which all kinds of wickedness, particularly fraud and deceit, are harboured and dwell!' To these he added other expressions, tending to reproach that Fernando with treachery and baseness. When we had got our friend out of his clutches, with no small trouble, he went off without speaking another word, and ran at full speed among these shrubs and brambles, so as that it was impossible for us to follow him. From these things, we conjectured that his madness comes upon him by fits, and that some person of the name of Fernando must have done him some deadly wrong, which hath driven him to distraction. Indeed, this conjecture has been since confirmed by his different behaviour on diverse occasions, when he hath met with our shepherds, from whom he hath sometimes begged part of their provision, and at other times, hath taken it by force; for when the fit of lunacy is upon him, though they offer it of their own free will, he will not accept of it peaceably, without coming to blows; but, when he is in his right senses, he begs it for God's sake, in a very courteous and civil manner, and returns many thanks for the favour, accompanied with abundance of tears. And truly, gentlemen," added the goatherd, "I and four more country lads, two of them my own servants, and the other two friends of mine, yesterday resolved to go in search of him, and after having found him, to carry him, either by force or fair means, to the city of Almodavar, which is about eight leagues from hence; and there have him cured, if he be curable; or learn of him, when he is in his senses, who he is, and whether or not he has any relations, to whom we may give an account of his misfortune. This, gentlemen, is all I can say, in answer to the questions you asked; and you may take it for granted, that the owner of the goods you found, is the very same person whom you saw skip about, half-naked, with such agility." For, Don Quixote had said that they had seen a man in that condition, leaping from rock to rock.

The knight was very much surprized at this information of the goatherd, which making him still more impatient to know who this unfortunate lunatic was, he determined

with himself to put his former design in execution, and go in quest of him, through the whole mountain, without leaving a cave or corner unsearched until he should find him. But, accident was more his friend on this occasion, than he could either imagine or expect. For, at that instant, the young man of himself, appeared in the cleft of a rock hard by the place where they stood; and came towards them, muttering something to himself, which they could not have understood, had he been near, much less, as he was at some distance from them. His equipage was just as it has been described; but, as he approached, Don Quixote perceived that his buff doublet, though torn to rags, still retained the perfume; from whence he concluded, that the person who wore such dress, could not be a man of the lowest rank. When he came up, he saluted them very politely, though with a hoarse mistuned voice; and the salutation was returned with no less courtesy by Don Quixote, who alighting from Rozinante, with genteel and graceful deportment, went and embraced the stranger, whom he strained within his arms a good while, as if he had been a very old acquaintance. The other, who might have been called the tatterdemalion of the distracted, as Don Quixote was stiled the knight of the rueful countenance, after having submitted to this embrace, stept back, and laying his hands on the shoulders of the knight, stood looking attentively in his face, in order to recollect him; no less astonished, perhaps, at the figure, mien and armour of Don Quixote, than this last was surprised at his forlorn appearance. At length, the first who broke silence after the embrace was the ragged youth, who spoke what you may read in the following chapter.

## CHAPTER X.

## The continuation of the adventure in the Sierra Morena.

The history relates, that Don Quixote listened with vast attention to the shabby knight of the mountain, who began the conversation thus: "Assuredly, signor, though I have not the honour to know who you are, I thank you heartily for those expressions of kindness with which you treat me; and wish I were in such a situation as would enable me to repay this courteous reception with something more than meer good-will: but my hapless fortune affords me nothing to offer in return for the civilities that are shewn me, except a hearty inclination to make a more adequate satisfaction." "My will and desire," answered Don Quixote, "to serve you is so strong, that I was determined not to quit these mountains, until I had found you, and learned of yourself, whether or not, the grief you manifest in this strange course of life, could be alleviated by any kind of remedy, for which, had need required, I would have searched with all possible diligence: and had your misfortune been such as shut up all the avenues to advice and redress, I was resolved to join your lamentations, and bemoan your misery to the utmost of my power; for, in all my misfortunes, the greatest consolation is a sympathis-

ing friend: and if this my friendly intention deserves the least return of civility, I intreat you, signor, by that courtesy which I see you so eminently possess, and moreover, conjure you by that object, which of all others in this life, you have most loved, or are most in love with, to tell me who you are, and inform me of the cause that brings you to live and die in this solitude, like the brute beasts among which you dwell, so different from that rank and situation, to which your appearance and person declare you are intitled. And I swear by the order of chivalry which I have received, unworthy sinner that I am! and by the profession of a knight-errant, that if you comply with this my request, I will serve you with that earnestness which my duty obliges me to express; either in remedying your mishap, if it admits of remedy; or in condoling you, as I have already promised." The knight of the wood, hearing him of the rueful countenance talk in this manner, could do nothing for some time, but gaze, and stare and survey him from head to foot; at length having examined him thoroughly, he said, "If you have got any food, for God's-sake spare me a little; and after I shall have eaten it, I will do as you desire, in return for the civility you now shew me."

Sancho immediately pulled from his bag, and the goatherd from his scrip, some victuals to appease the hunger of the tatterdemalion, who swallowed what they gave him, like a frantic person, with such hurry that he left not the interval of an instant between one mouthful and another, but seemed to devour rather than eat, without either speaking or being spoke to by the spectators. His repast being ended, he beckoned them to follow, and conducted them to a verdant spot of grass, at the turning of a rock, a little way from the place where they were; and, sitting down on the green turf, they followed his example; not a word being spoke all the time, until the ragged knight, after having adjusted himself in his seat, began in this manner: "If you desire, gentlemen, that I should, in a few words, inform you of the immensity of my misfortunes, you must give me your promise that you will not by any question, or otherwise, interrupt the thread of my doleful story; for, if you should, that instant I will break off the narration." This warning recalled to the knight's memory, the story recounted by his squire, which still remained unfinished, because he had not kept an exact account of the goats, as they passed the river. But, to return to the tattered knight, "I give you this precaution," added he, "because, I would briefly pass over the detail of my misfortunes, the remembrance of which brings fresh addition to my woe; and the fewer questions you ask, the sooner shall I have finished the relation; although, in order to satisfy your curiosity to the full, I will not fail to mention every material circumstance." Don Quixote promised, in behalf of himself and the company, to avoid all manner of interruption, and the stranger thus assured, began in these words:

"My name is Cardenio, the place of my nativity one of the best cities in this province of Andalusia, my family noble, my parents rich, and my misfortunes so great, that no doubt, they have been lamented by them, and even felt through my whole kindred, though all their wealth would not alleviate my woe; for, the goods of fortune are but of little service against those ills inflicted by the hand of heaven. In the same country lived, shall I call her, a paradise, which love had adorned with all the charms I could desire to possess; such was the beauty of Lucinda, a young lady as well born and rich as I, though more fortunate, and endowed with less constancy than what was due to my honourable

intentions. This Lucinda did I admire, love and adore even from my most tender years; and she made me all the returns of love and inclination, that I could expect from her infant age. Our parents were not ignorant of our mutual affection, which gave them no offence, because they foresaw that if it should encrease with our years, it could have no other issue than marriage; an union which the equality of our age and fortune seemed to point out. Mean while, our passion growing up with our age, Lucinda's father thought himself obliged to forbid me his house; imitating, in that particular, the parents of Thisbe, whom the poets have celebrated so much. This prohibition, added flame to flame, and wish to wish; for, though our tongues were restrained, they could not silence our pens, which commonly express the sentiments of the heart with more liberty, because the presence of the beloved object often confounds the most determined intention, and puts to silence the most undaunted tongue.

"Good heaven! what letters did I write! what chaste endearing answers did I receive! what songs did I compose, inspired by love that displayed the soul unmasked, inflamed each soft desire, regaled the fancy and indulged the wish! in fine, my patience being exhausted, and my heart almost consumed with the desire of seeing her, I resolved to execute the scheme which seemed most favourable for my love and pretensions; and this I put in practice, by demanding her in marriage of her father, who thanked me for the honour I intended him, by this proposal of marrying into his family, but said, as my own father was alive, it was properly his business to make the demand; for, unless his consent and inclination were obtained, Lucinda was not a person either to be given or taken in marriage, by stealth. I thanked him, in my turn, for his politeness, and thinking there was a great deal of reason in what he said, assured myself that my father would readily agree to the proposal, whenever I should make it. I therefore, flew instantly to disclose my sentiments to him on that subject, and entering the closet where he was, found him reading a letter, which before I could speak a syllable, he put into my hand, saying, 'By this letter, Cardenio, you will see how much duke Ricardo is inclined to do you service.' This duke Ricardo, as you must know, gentlemen, is a grandee of Spain, whose estate lies in the best part of this province. I took and read the letter, which was so extremely kind, that I myself should have blamed my father, had he refused to comply with what he requested in it: this was, to send me immediately to his house, he being desirous that I should live as the companion, not the servant, of his eldest son; and he would take care of my fortune, in such a manner as should manifest the esteem he had for me. Having read the letter, I was struck dumb at knowing the contents; especially, when I heard my father pronounce, "Two days hence, Cardenio, you shall set out, according to the pleasure of the duke; and you ought to thank God for having opened an avenue, through which you may arrive at that fortune I know you deserve." To this declaration he added other advices, as became a prudent father, and I, the night before I departed, finding means to speak with Lucinda, told her what had happened; nay, I even imparted it to her father, intreating him to wait a few days, without disposing of her to any other, until I should know in what manner Ricardo wanted to employ me. He gave me his promise accordingly, and she confirmed it by a thousand vows and anxious sighs.

"I at length arrived at the seat of duke Ricardo, by whom I was so well received and kindly entertained, that Envy presently began to do her office, possessing the old ser-

vants with the opinion, that every expression of favour I received from the duke, was prejudicial to their interest. But he who was most rejoiced at my residing there, was the duke's second son Fernando, a gay, genteel, liberal and amorous youth, who, in a short time, was pleased to honour me with such intimacy of friendship as became the subject of every body's discourse; and though the elder brother loved and favoured me also, he did not carry his favour and affection to such a pitch. Now, as all secrets are communicated between friends, and the confidence in which I lived with Fernando was soon changed into friendship, he imparted to me, his most secret thoughts, and among other things, a love-affair that gave him a good deal of disquiet. In short, he had an inclination for a country-maid, who was his father's vassal: her parents were very rich, and she herself so beautiful, reserved, modest, and discreet, that nobody who knew her could determine in which of these qualifications she most excelled. These accomplishments of this fair maiden inflamed the desires of Don Fernando to such a pitch, that he resolved, as the easiest conquest over her virtue, to promise he would marry her; for, he found it impossible to gratify his wish, in any other way. I, prompted and bound by my friendship, endeavoured to dissuade and divert him from his purpose, by the strongest arguments and most lively examples I could produce; but, finding them all ineffectual, I resolved to communicate the whole affair to his father duke Ricardo.

"Don Fernando having abundance of cunning and discernment, suspected my intention; and was afraid, that the obligation he saw I was under, as a faithful servant, would not allow me to conceal an affair so prejudicial to the honour of the duke my master: he therefore, in order to divert and deceive me, observed, that he could find no better remedy to remove the beauty that enslaved him, from his remembrance, than that of absence for a few months; and therefore desired that we should go to my father's house, upon pretence, as he would tell the duke, of seeing and purchasing some fine horses in our town, which produces the best in the world. Scarce had he uttered this proposal, when, prompted by my love, exclusive of his prudent intention, I approved of it, as one of the best concerted schemes that could be imagined; and was rejoiced at meeting with such a fair conjuncture and occasion of returning to my dear Lucinda. Induced by this motive and desire, I applauded his pretence, and inforced his proposal, advising him to execute his plan with all speed; for, absence would certainly do it's office, in spite of the most established inclination. At that very time, as I afterwards understood, he had enjoyed the country-maid, under the title of her husband, and waited for an opportunity of owning it with safety to himself, being afraid of the duke's resentment, in case he should discover his folly. It happened afterwards, that as love in young people is, for the most part, nothing but appetite, whose only aim is pleasure; and this being enjoyed, what seemed love, vanishes, because it cannot exceed the bounds of nature; whereas real love is bounded by no such limits: I say, as soon as Don Fernando enjoyed the country-girl, his desires were appeased and his raptures abated; and if at first, he pretended to seek a cure for them, in absence, he now, earnestly desired to be absent, that he might avoid any further gratification.

"The duke having given him leave, and ordered me to attend him, we arrived at our habitation, where he was received by my father, in a manner, suitable to his rank and family. I went instantly to visit Lucinda, whose presence, in a moment, rekindled all my

desires, which indeed were neither dead nor decayed within me; and, to my infinite misfortune, I made Don Fernando acquainted with my love, because I thought, by the laws of that intimate friendship with which he honoured me, I ought to conceal nothing from him. I therefore praised the beauty, grace, and discretion of Lucinda, in such a manner, as excited his curiosity to see such an accomplished young lady. Prompted by my evil genius, I gratified his desire, shewing her to him one night, by the light of a taper, at the window, from which I used to converse with her. At sight of her he absolutely forgot all the beauties he had formerly seen; he was struck dumb with wonder; he seemed to lose all sense, became absent and pensive; and, in short, enamoured of her to that degree which you will perceive in the course of my unhappy story. And, the more to inflame his desire, which he concealed from me, and disclosed to heaven alone, he happened one day to find a letter which she had written, desiring me to ask her in marriage of her father; so prudent, modest and tender, that upon perusing it, he said, 'In Lucinda alone are concentered all the charms of beauty and understanding, which are divided among the rest of her sex.' True it is, and I will now confess it, that although I knew how justly Fernando applauded Lucinda, I was vexed at hearing these praises proceed from his mouth, and began to dread, and suspect his inclination; for, he was eternally talking of her, and always turned the discourse upon her, even when he was obliged to bring her in by the head and shoulders: a circumstance that waked a sort of jealousy within me; not, that I imagined aught could alter the faith and affection of Lucinda, yet, notwithstanding, my destiny made me dread the very thing that confidence ensured. Don Fernando always contrived means to read the letters I sent to Lucinda, together with her answers, on pretence of being highly pleased with the good sense they contained; and it once happened, that she having desired me to send her a book of knight-errantry, in which she took great delight, called Amadis de Gaul."

Don Quixote no sooner heard him mention this book, than he said, "Had you told me, in the beginning of your story, that your mistress Lucinda was an admirer of books of chivalry, you would have had no occasion to use any other argument to convince me of her sublime understanding; which I should not have deemed quite so extraordinary as you have represented it, had she wanted relish for that sort of reading: wherefore, you need not spend any more words with me, in extolling her beauty, virtue and good sense; for, upon the knowledge of her taste only, I pronounce her to be the most beautiful and discreet lady in the universe: I wish, however, that you had sent along with Amadis de Gaul, the worthy Don Rugel of Greece; for, I know your mistress Lucinda would have been greatly pleased with Darayra and Garaya, together with the judicious sayings of the shepherd Darinel, and those admirable verses of his eclogues, sung and represented by him with such grace, spirit and discretion; but, the time will come when that omission may be rectified; indeed the fault may be repaired as soon as you shall please to accompany me to the place of my habitation, where I can supply you with more than three hundred books, which are the feast of my soul, and entertainment of my life: though now I recollect, not one of them remains in my possession; thanks to the malice of wicked and envious enchanters. But, I hope you will be so good as to forgive me for having contradicted my promise of not interrupting your story; for, when the subject turns upon chivalry or knights-errant, I can no more forbear interposing, than the rays of the

sun can cease to warm, or those of the moon to wet: but, I ask pardon, pray proceed with your story; for, that is most to the purpose at present."

While Don Quixote was talking in this manner, Cardenio hung his head, and fell into a profound reverie; and tho' the knight repeated his request, would neither lift up his head, nor answer one word. At length, after a long pause, looking up, "You cannot," said he, "beat it out of my thoughts; nor is there any person upon earth, who can persuade me to the contrary; and he must be a blockhead, who imagines or believes otherwise, than that the villain master Elisabat, carried on a criminal correspondence with queen Madasima." "By heaven, 'tis false!" cried Don Quixote, with great indignation and impetuosity, as usual; "that report is the effect of malice, or rather meer wantonness. Queen Madasima was a most royal dame, and it is not to be presumed, that a princess of her rank would confer favours upon a meer quack doctor. Whosoever thinks otherwise, lies like a very great scoundrel; and I will prove him such, either on horseback or afoot, armed or disarmed, by night or by day, as will most suit his inclination." Cardenio stood all the while, looking attentively at him, and being, by this time, seized with the paroxysm of his madness, could not proceed with his story; neither, if he had proceeded, would Don Quixote have listened to it, for he was offended at what he had heard to the prejudice * of queen Madasima, whose reputation interested him as much as if she had been actually his own mistress: such wonderful impression had those profane books made on his imagination!

I say, then, Cardenio being by this time, under the influence of his distraction, and hearing himself called liar and scoundrel, with other terms of reproach, could not relish the joke; but, snatching up a large pebble that lay near him, aimed it so successfully at Don Quixote's breast, that he fell fairly on his back with the blow. Sancho Panza, seeing his master treated in this manner, attacked the madman with his clenched fist; but, the lunatic received him with such a blow, as knocked him down to the ground at once, and then getting upon him, mauled his carcase to his heart's content; while the goatherd, who attempted to defend him, met with the same fate. Having thus mastered and pummelled them all round, he left off, and, with great composure, retreated to the thickets from whence he came. Sancho then arose, and enraged to find himself handled in this manner, for nothing, ran to take vengeance on the goatherd, saying that he was to blame for the whole, because he had not informed him, that the man had intervals of madness; which had they known, they might have guarded against them. The goatherd affirmed, that he had apprised them of what might happen; and if they had not heard him, it was no fault of his. The squire replied, the goatherd retorted, and, in conclusion, they went by the ears together, and pulled each other's beards with such fury, that there would not have been a single hair left on either chin, had not Don Quixote interposed. Sancho grappling stoutly with his adversary, cried, "Give me leave, Sir knight of the rueful countenance; this is no armed knight, but a plebeian like myself, of whom I can securely take satisfaction for the injury he has done me, by fighting with him hand to hand, like a man of honour." "True," said Don Quixote; "but, the cause of what hath hap-

---

* Queen Madasima, a lady in Amadis de Gaul, attended by one Elisabat a surgeon, with whom she travels, and lies in woods and desarts.[1]

Vol. 1. Nº 6. Page 159.

F. Hayman Invet Del.

J.S. Ravenet Sculpt.

Don Quixote and Sancho Felled by Cardenio.

pened, cannot be justly imputed to him." Peace accordingly ensued, and the knight asked the goatherd again, if there was a possibility of finding Cardenio; for, he was extremely desirous of hearing the conclusion of his story. The goatherd repeated what he had said before, that he did not certainly know whereabouts he resided; but, if they should stay long in these parts, they could not fail of finding him either mad or sober.

## CHAPTER XI.

### Of the strange adventures that happened to the valiant knight of la Mancha, in the Sierra Morena, where he did penance, in imitation of Beltenebros.

D on Quixote having taken leave of the goatherd, and mounted Rozinante again, commanded Sancho to follow him; and the squire bestriding his ass, obeyed with great reluctance: as they advanced at leisure, into the most rocky parts of the mountain, Sancho longed to death for an opportunity of talking, and waited impatiently till his master should begin, that he might not transgress his orders; but, being utterly unable to keep silence any longer, "Sir Don Quixote," said he, "be pleased to give me your blessing, and grant me leave to return immediately to my wife and children, with whom, at least, I can talk and prattle my fill; for, in commanding me to travel with you, thro' these desarts, night and day, without opening my lips when I am disposed to speak, your worship buries me alive: if it were the will of heaven, that beasts spoke as they did in the days of Hyssop,[1] I should be the less uneasy, because I would converse with my ass, at pleasure; and that would be some comfort to me in my misfortunes; but, it is a very hard case, and what I cannot bear with patience, to travel in search of adventures all my life, and find nought but ribroastings, blankettings, robberies, and fistycuffs; and after all, be obliged to sew up our mouths, without daring to bring up what lies upon our stomachs, more than if we were dumb."

"I understand thee, Sancho," replied the knight; "thou art impatient until I take off the interdiction I have laid upon thy tongue: I take it off, then—say what you please, on condition, that this repeal shall last no longer than our stay in this mountain." "Be it so," said Sancho; "to-day I will speak; to-morrow, God's will be done: and the first use I make of this safe conduct, is to ask why your worship was in such a passion, about that queen Magimasa, or how d'ye call her? or of what signification was it to you, whether that same Abat[2] was her sweetheart or not? Had your worship overlooked that circumstance that you had no concern in, I firmly believe the madman would have gone on with his story, and you would have saved yourself the pebble-shot, with more than half a dozen of kicks and cuffs."

"In faith, Sancho," answered Don Quixote, "if thou knowest, as I do, what an hon-

ourable and princely lady that queen Madasima was, thou wouldest say, I had great patience in forbearing to demolish the mouth from whence such blasphemy proceeded; for, sure 'tis no less to say, or even think, that a queen should take a surgeon to her bed. The truth of the story is this, that master Elisabat, whom the lunatic mentioned, was a man of prudence and discernment, and served the queen in quality of tutor and physician; but, to suppose that there was any indecent familiarity between them, is a piece of folly that deserves to be severely chastised: and to convince thee that Cardenio knew not what he said, thou mayest remember he was deprived of his senses, when he took notice of that circumstance." "This I'll venture to say," replied the squire, "that the words of a madman are not to be minded; for, if fortune had not stood your worship's friend, and directed to your breast the pebble that was aimed at your head, we should have been in a fine condition, for your having quarrelled about that lady, whom heaven confound: you may depend upon it, Cardenio would have been acquitted on account of his madness."

"Every knight-errant," said Don Quixote, "is obliged to quarrel with those who are out of their senses, as well as those who are in them, if they asperse the honour of women, whatsoever they might be. How much more then, in behalf of princesses of such high quality and accomplishments as adorned queen Madasima, for whom I have a particular affection, on account of her admirable qualifications; for, over and above her beauty, she had a great share of prudence and resignation in her calamities, which were manifold: and the advice and company of master Elisabat, were of great service in encouraging her to bear her afflictions with patience and equanimity. From hence, the ignorant and malicious vulgar took occasion to say, and suppose, that she admitted of his caresses: but, they lie—I say again, all those who either say or think so, lie in their throats, and I will tell them so two hundred times over." "As for my own part," said Sancho, "I neither say nor think any such thing; those that do may dine upon it: if they were too familiar, by this time they have answered for it to God. I prune my own vine, and know nothing about thine. I never meddle with other people's concerns. He that buys and denies, his own purse belies; as the saying is. Bare I was born, and bare I remain: and if I lose nothing, as little I gain. If he did lie with her that is no matter of mine. Many people hunt the hare without ever finding the scut; for, 'Till you hedge in the sky, the starlings will fly. And evil tongues will not refrain from God himself."

"Good heaven!" cried Don Quixote, "what fooleries art thou stringing together, Sancho! pray, what relation have these old saws to the subject of our conversation? I charge thee to hold thy peace, and henceforth entertain thyself with spurring up thy ass, and leave off talking of things which do not concern thee: or, let thy whole five senses be convinced, that every thing I have done, am doing, or will do, is highly reasonable, and in exact conformity with the laws of chivalry, which I understand better than any knight that ever professed the order." "Yes, Sir," replied Sancho, "to be sure it is an excellent law of chivalry, to stroll about bewildered in these mountains, where there is neither highroad nor by-path, in search of a madman, who, after we have found him, will perhaps take it in his head to finish what he left undone; not of his story, but of your worship's pate and my ribs, which he may chance to break in a thousand shivers."

"I say again, Sancho," resumed the knight, "hold thy peace; for, I would have thee

know, that I am not detained in this place, so much by the desire of finding the lunatic, as of performing in it, an exploit by which I shall acquire everlasting renown through-out the whole known world; and put the stamp of perfection upon the wonderful efforts of knight-errantry." "And will this exploit be attended with much danger?" said Sancho. "No," answered he of the rueful countenance, "tho' the dice may run so as to produce bad instead of good fortune: but, the whole will depend upon thy diligence." "Upon my diligence!" cried the squire. "Without doubt," answered his master; "for, if thou wilt re-turn speedily, from the place to which thou must be sent, my affliction will soon be at an end, and my glory will speedily begin: and, that I may no longer keep thee in sus-pence about the meaning of my words, know, Sancho, that the celebrated Amadis de Gaul was one of the most perfect knights-errant. One of them, said I? he alone, was the only, single, chief and superior of all his contemporaries. Contempt and shame upon Bellianis, and all those who say he equalled him in any one particular; for, by this light, they are all egregiously deceived! I say, moreover, when a painter desires to become fa-mous in his art, he endeavours to imitate the originals painted by the most noted artists; and the same maxim holds in every other science and exercise that adorns a common-wealth: therefore, he who wants to attain the virtues of prudence and equanimity, must endeavour to imitate the character of Ulysses, in whose person and sufferings Homer has drawn an excellent picture of wisdom and patience, as Virgil, in the person of Æneas, represents the piety of an affectionate son, and the sagacity of a wise and valiant general: not, that they are described and set forth exactly as they were, but, as they ought to have been; as examples of virtue to posterity. In the same manner, Amadis shone like the north-star, the lucifer and sun of all valiant and amorous knights; and therefore, must be imitated, as a pattern, by all those who serve under the banners of love and chivalry. Now, this being the case, friend Sancho, I find that the knight-errant who ap-proaches the nearest to this great original, will bid fairest for attaining the perfection of chivalry: and one of the circumstances in which that knight gave the highest proofs of his worth, prudence, valour, patience, constancy and love, was his retiring to the poor rock,[3] when he was in disgrace with his mistress Oriana, there to do penance under the feigned name of * Beltenebros; an appellation certainly very significant and proper to the way of life he had voluntarily chosen. As it is therefore, more easy for me to imitate him in this, than in cleaving giants, beheading serpents, slaying dragons, overthrowing armies, scattering navies, and dissolving enchantments; and as this solitude is so well adapted to such designs, I am resolved to seize occasion by the forelock, which she now so complaisantly presents."

"In reality," said Sancho, "what is your worship resolved to do in this remote place?" "Have I not already told thee," replied the knight, "that I am determined to imitate Amadis, in acting the desperado, the lunatic and madman: to copy also after the valiant Don Roldan, when he discovered, in a fountain, certain marks by which he was con-vinced that Angelica the fair had committed uncleanness with Medoro. A piece of in-formation attended with such grief and anxiety, that he ran mad, tore up the trees by the roots, sullied the waters of the transparent springs, slew shepherds, destroyed flocks, set

* The Beautiful obscure.[4]

fire to cottages, demolished houses, dragged mares along the ground, and performed a thousand other insolent feats worthy to be inserted in fame's eternal record: and because I do not propose to imitate Roldan, or Orlando or Rotolando, for he went by all these names, literally in all the extravagancies he thought, said and did, I will copy his outlines as well as I can, in the most essential parts of his character; nay, perhaps, I may content myself with the sole imitation of Amadis, who, by his tears and sighs alone, acquired as much fame as the other, with all the mischief he did." "If I apprehend the matter aright," said Sancho, "the knights who played such mad pranks were provoked, and had some reason to act these fooleries and penance: but, what cause hath your worship to turn madman? With what lady are you in disgrace? or by what signs are you given to understand that the lady Dulcinea del Toboso has been playing the rogue either with Moor or Christian?" "This is the point," answered Don Quixote, "and refinement of my design: a knight who turns madman, because he cannot help it, can claim no merit from his misfortune; but, the great matter is, to run distracted without cause, and give my lady reason to conceive what I could do were I moistened, when I can do so much, being dry. More especially, as I have sufficient cause in the long absence to which I am doomed by my ever-darling mistress Dulcinea del Toboso; for, according to the words of the shepherd Matias Ambrosio,[5] which thou mayest have heard,

> In absence of my charming fair,
> I suffer all those ills I fear.

Wherefore, friend Sancho, you need not throw away your time unprofitably, in advising me to refrain from an imitation at once so admirable, rare and happy: mad I am, and mad I shall be until thou returnest with the answer of a letter which I propose to send by thee to my lady Dulcinea: and if it be such as I am intitled to by my love and fidelity; my distraction and penance will end: but, should it be otherwise, I shall run mad in earnest, and consequently be insensible of my misfortune: wherefore, let her answer be as it may, it will extricate me from the doubts and affliction in which thou leavest me; because, if it be favourable, I shall enjoy it in my right senses; and if it be unfavourable, my frenzy will not feel it.

"But, tell me, Sancho, hast thou taken care of Mambrino's helmet, which I saw thee take up, after that ungrateful vagabond endeavoured in vain to break it in pieces: a circumstance that proves the excellency of its temper?" To this exclamation, Sancho replied, "'Fore God! Sir knight of the rueful countenance, I cannot suffer nor bear with patience, some things which your worship says; for, they make me imagine, that all you have mentioned about chivalry, and acquiring kingdoms and empires, and giving away islands, with other favours and presents, according to the practice of knights-errant, is nothing but puffs of falshood, and the meer effect of piction or fiction, or what d'ye call it: for, who that hears your worship call a barber's bason the helmet of Mambrino, and sees you continue in that error so many days, but will believe, that he who affirms such nonsense, must be very much crazed in his understanding? The bason, which is all bruised and battered, I have put up in my bag, in order to be mended at home, and used for the service of my own beard, if ever, by the grace of God, I come to see my wife and family again." "Heark ye, Sancho," said Don Quixote, "by the same oath you swore, I

swear again, that thou hast the most slender understanding that any squire in this world does, or ever did possess! is it possible, that after all thy travelling in my company, thou art not convinced that every thing belonging to knights-errant, appears chimera, folly and distraction, being metamorphosed into the reverse of what it is, by the power of a tribe of enchanters who attend us, changing, converting and restoring each particular, according to their pleasure; and the inclination they have, to favour or annoy us: for which reason, what seems a barber's bason to thee, I can easily discern to be the helmet of Mambrino, and perhaps to a third, it will assume a quite different appearance; and I cannot but admire the providence of the sage who is my friend, in making that which is really and truly Mambrino's helmet, appear a bason to the rest of mankind, because it is of such inestimable value, that if it was known, the whole world would combine to ravish it from me; but, as it appears to them no more than a barber's bason, they never attempt to obtain it. This was plainly the case with the villain, who having endeavoured to break it in pieces, left it on the ground, when he went off; whereas, had he known what it was, in good faith, he would not have quitted it so easily. Keep it therefore with care, my friend, for, at present, there is no occasion for it; on the contrary, I shall strip off all my armour, and remain naked as I was born, in case I be inclined to imitate the penance of Roldan, rather than that of Amadis."

Conversing in this manner, they arrived at the foot of a high mountain, that stood alone, as if it had been cut out from the rest that surrounded it. A gentle rill murmured by the skirts of it, winding along a meadow so green and fertile, that it ravished the spectator's eye; while a number of forest-trees that grew around, together with some delicious herbs and flowers, conspired to make the place enchanting. This was the scene in which the knight of the rueful countenance chose to do penance; and therefore he no sooner perceived it, than he began to exclaim aloud, as if he had actually lost his senses; "This is the spot, ye heavens! which I chuse and appoint my residence, while I bewail that misfortune to which you yourselves have reduced me. This is the place, where the tears from these eyes, will increase the waters of that little brook; and where my profound and uninterrupted sighs will incessantly move the leaves of these mountain-oaks, in witness and testimony of the pangs which my tormented heart endures. O ye rural deities, whosoever ye are, who take up your mansion in this uninhabited place, give ear to the complaints of an unhappy lover, whom a tedious absence and imaginary doubts have brought to lament among these craggy hills, and bemoan the cruel disposition of that ungrateful fair, who is the end and perfection of all human beauty! O ye nymphs and dryads, who are wont to inhabit the hills and groves (so may no nimble and lascivious satyrs, by whom you are beloved, tho' loved in vain, disturb your sweet repose) help me to bewail my mishap; or at least disdain not to hear my moan! O Dulcinea del Toboso! Light of my darkness! Glory of my affliction! North-star of my inclinations! and planet of my fortune! as heaven shall pour upon you the blessings which you ask; consider the place and condition to which your absence hath exiled me, and put such a period to my woe, as my fidelity shall seem to deserve! O ye solitary trees, who henceforth are to bear me company in this retreat, convince me, by the gentle waving of your boughs, that my presence gives you no disgust: and thou, my squire, the agreeable companion of my good and evil fortune, faithfully retain in thy remembrance, what thou

shalt see me do, that thou mayest recount and rehearse every circumstance to the lovely cause of all my distraction!" So saying, he alighted, and taking off the bridle and saddle from Rozinante, gave him a slap on the buttocks, pronouncing these words: "He who is a slave himself, bestows freedom upon thee, O steed, as excellent in thy qualities as unlucky in thy fate! go wheresoever thou wilt; thou bearest engraven on thy forehead, that thou wast never equalled in swiftness, either by Astolpho's Hypogriff, or the renowned Frontino that cost Bradamante so dear."

Sancho, hearing this apostrophe, "My blessing," cried he, "be upon him, whose industry now saves us the trouble of taking the halter from the head of Dapple *, who, in good faith, should not want slaps on the buttocks, nor abundance of fine things said in his praise: but, if he was here, I would not consent to his being turned loose, there being no reason for so doing; for, he was never acquainted with love and despair, no more than I who was his master, while it pleased God I should be so: and truly, Sir knight of the rueful countenance, if this departure of mine, and distraction of your worship are really to take place, you had better saddle Rozinante again, to supply the want of Dapple; by which means a great deal of time will be saved in my going and coming; whereas, if I make the journey on foot, I know not when it will be performed; for, in short, I am a very sorry walker." "I say, be it so, then, Sancho," answered Don Quixote. "I approve of thy proposal; and assure thee, that thou shalt set out in three days, during which I would have thee take notice of what I shall do for her sake, that thou mayest be able to give her a full account of my behaviour." "What more can I see," said Sancho, "than I have seen already?" "You are pretty perfect in your story," answered the knight; "but, as yet, I have not torn my cloaths, scattered my armour, and dashed my head against the rocks, nor performed many other things of this sort, which thou wilt behold with admiration." "For the love of God, Sir," cried Sancho, "take care how you dash your head against the rocks; for, you may chance to meet with such an one as will at the first push put the finishing stroke to this whole scheme of penance; and I should think, that as knocks on the head are absolutely necessary to complete the work, your worship might content yourself, seeing the whole affair is a sham, a counterfeit and a joke; I say, your worship might content yourself with ramming your skull against water, or some soft thing, like a cotton bag; and leave it to my care to tell my lady, that your worship went to loggerheads with the point of a rock, a thousand times harder than adamant." "Friend Sancho," replied the knight, "I am obliged to thee, for thy kind intention; but, thou must know, that what I do is not a sham, but a very serious matter; for, to behave otherwise were to transgress the orders of chivalry, which forbid us to lie, under pain of being degraded; and you know, that to substitute one thing instead of another, is downright telling a lie: wherefore, my knocks on the head must be real, hard and effectual, and not sophisticated or imaginary; and it will be necessary to leave me some lint for my wounds, since, it was the will of fate that we should lose the balsam."

"It was a much greater misfortune," said the squire, "to lose the ass, and with him the lint and all; but I beseech your worship, not to talk of that accursed drench, the sole mention of which not only turns my stomach, but even my very soul; and I beseech you

---

* Lo! Sancho's ass hath disappeared again![6]

moreover, to suppose we have past those three days, which you have appointed for shewing me your mad pranks; for, I take them all for granted, and will tell wonders of them to my lady. Write the letter, therefore, and dispatch me forthwith; because, I am impatient till I return and deliver your worship, from that purgatory in which I leave you." "Purgatory call you it, Sancho?" replied Don Quixote: "it rather deserves the name of hell, or something worse, if worse can be." "I have heard," said the squire, "that from hell there is no retention."[7] "I know not," replied the knight, "what you mean by retention." "Retention," answered Sancho, "signifies, that whosoever goeth to hell, neither will nor can come back again. The contrary of which shall happen to your worship, or my feet will misgive me, provided I carry spurs to quicken Rozinante: and set me once face to face before my lady Dulcinea, at Toboso, I will tell her such stories of the folly and madness, for they are both the same thing, which your worship hath committed, and will then be committing, that though I should find her harder than a cork-tree, I will make her as pliant as a glove, and with her sweet and honeyed answer, return through the air, like a witch, and deliver your worship from this purgatory that appears like hell, though it be not really so, because there are some hopes of getting out of it; whereas those who are actually in hell can have no such expectation; and I dare say, your worship will not advance any thing to the contrary."

"That is all very true," said he of the rueful countenance; "but, how shall we make shift to write this letter?" "Ay, and the bill for the colts"; added Sancho. "That shall be inserted in the letter," answered his master; "and I think, as there is no paper to be had in this place, the best thing we can do, will be to write, in the manner of the ancients, on the leaf of a tree, or on waxen tables, though, I believe, those will be as difficult to be found as the paper. But, now, I remember what will do well and excellently well for our purpose: I will write it in the pocket book which belonged to Cardenio, and thou shalt take care to have it fairly transcribed in the first place where thou canst find a schoolmaster or parish-clerk to copy it. But, by no means employ a scrivener, who may write it in such an unintelligible court-hand, that Satan himself could not understand it." "But what is to be done about the signing of it?" said Sancho. "Love-letters are never signed," replied Don Quixote. "True," resumed the squire, "but all bills must be subscribed; and if this of yours, were to be copied, they would say the subscription was counterfeit, and I might go whistle for my colts." "The bill shall be subscribed with my own hand, in the pocket-book, which my niece shall no sooner see, than she will comply with the order, without any further objection: and with regard to the letter, instead of my subscription, thou shalt cause to be inserted, 'Yours, till death, the knight of the rueful countenance.' And though it be written by another hand, it is of small importance, because, now, I remember, Dulcinea can neither read nor write, nor ever set eyes on any writing or letter of mine; for, our mutual love has been altogether platonic, without extending farther than a modest glance; and even that so seldom, that I can safely swear, in twelve years, during which I have loved her more than the light of these eyes, which will one day be closed in dust, I have not seen her more than four times, and even in these four times, perhaps, she has not perceived me looking at her more than once. Such is the restraint and reserve, in which her father Lorenzo Corchuelo and her mother Aldonza Nogales, have brought her up!"

"Ah, ha!" cried Sancho, "is the daughter of Lorenzo Corchuelo, whose other name is Aldonza Lorenzo, the same with the lady Dulcinea?" "Yes," answered the knight, "and she deserves to be lady of the whole universe." "I know her perfectly well," said Sancho; "and this will venture to say, in her behalf, that she will pitch the bar, as well as e'er a lusty young fellow in the village. Bless the sender! she is a strapper, tall and hale wind and limb, and can lift out of the mire any squire or knight-errant, who shall choose her for his sweet-heart. Ah! the whore's-chick! what a pair of lungs and voice she has got! I heard her one day, hollow from the belfrey to some young fellows of her acquaintance, who were at work in a cornfield of her father's; and, though it was at the distance of half a league, they heard her as plain as if they had been right under the steeple; and what is better still, she is not at all coy, but behaves herself civilly; and jokes, and romps, and plays the rogue with any body. Now, sir knight of the rueful countenance, I say that your worship not only has cause to run mad for her, but even to despair and hang yourself; and I am sure nobody that heard it, but would say you had done extremely well; even though the devil should run away with you: and truly, I wish I were now upon my way, meerly to see her; for, I have not beheld her these many days; and, surely, she must be greatly altered; for, the sun and weather does very much damage to the face of a woman, who is always at work in the field. To tell you the truth, sir Don Quixote, I have hitherto lived in great ignorance with respect to my lady Dulcinea, whom I verily believed to be some princess, that your worship was in love with; or a person of such rank as to deserve the rich presents you sent to her; namely, the Biscayan and galley-slaves, with many others whom you conquered in the course of your numberless victories, both before and since I have been your squire. But, when one considers the affair, what benefits can my lady Aldonza Lorenzo—I mean, my lady Dulcinea del Toboso, reap from your worship's sending, or having sent those, whom you overcome in battle, to fall upon their knees before her? especially, as they might chance to come, at a time, when she is busy, carding flax and threshing corn; in which case, they would be ashamed to see her, and she laugh and be out of humour at their arrival." "I have frequently observed, before now, Sancho," said Don Quixote, "that thou art an everlasting babler, and, though of a shallow understanding, thy bluntness borders often on severity; but, to convince thee of thy own ignorance and my discretion, thou shalt give ear to a short story which I will relate.

"Know then, that once upon a time, a certain handsome widow, young, free, wealthy, and, above all, good-humoured, fell in love with a thick, squat, brawny lay-brother, belonging to a neighbouring convent; the superior of which being informed of the affair, said to the widow, one day, by way of brotherly reproof, 'I am amazed, madam, and not without cause, that a lady of your rank, beauty and fortune, should bestow your affection upon such a low, simple, clownish fellow; when there are so many masters, graduates, and divines in the convent, among whom your ladyship may choose, as one picks pears, saying, This I like, that I loath.' The lady answered, with great freedom and vivacity, 'Signor, you are very much deceived, and very old-fashioned in your opinion, if you think I have made a bad choice in that fellow, who seems so simple: for, in that particular which I admire, he is as much of a philosopher, nay, more than Aristotle himself.' In like manner, Sancho, Dulcinea del Toboso is as proper for my occasions as the highest princess upon earth. All the poets, who have celebrated ladies, under names which

they invented at pleasure, had not really such mistresses as they describe. Dost thou imagine, that all the Amaryllises, Silvias, Phillises, Dianas, Galateas, Alidas, and other names so often met with, in romances, poems, barbers shops, and on the stage, actually belonged to ladies of flesh and blood, who were adored by those who sing, and have sung their praises? No surely; but, on the contrary, are, for the most part, feigned and adopted as the subjects of verse, that the poets may be thought men of amorous and gallant dispositions. Wherefore, let it suffice, that I imagine and believe the worthy Aldonza Lorenzo, to be beautiful and modest: and, as to her pedigree, it is a matter of small importance; there is no necessity for taking informations on that head, as if she were to be invested with some order of knighthood, and I take it for granted, that she is the noblest princess in the universe; for, thou must know, Sancho, if it be a thing of which thou art ignorant, that the two qualities, which above all others, inspire love, are beauty and reputation: and these two is Dulcinea in consummate possession of; for, in beauty, she excels all women, and is equalled by very few, in point of reputation. And, to conclude, I imagine that all I have said is true without exaggeration or diminution. I paint her in my fancy, according to my wish, as well in beauty as in rank; unexcelled by Helen, unrivalled by Lucretia, or any other heroine of ages past, whether Grecian, Roman or Barbarian; and let people say what they will, if I am blamed by the ignorant, I shall be acquitted by the most rigid of those who are proper judges of the case." "I say," answered Sancho, "that your worship is very much in the right, and I am no better than an ass: but I know not why I should mention the word ass; for, one ought not to talk of halters in the house of a man who was hanged. But give me the letter, and farewell 'till I return."

Don Quixote pulled out the memorandum-book, and, stepping aside, with great composure, began to write the letter, which when he had finished, he called to Sancho, saying, he wanted to read it to him, that he might retain it in his memory, in case he should lose it by the way; for, every thing was to be feared from his evil fortune. "Your worship," answered Sancho, "may write it down, two or three times in the book, and I will take special care to convey it safely; but, it is folly to suppose, that I can retain it in my memory, which is so bad, that I have many a time forgot my own name; but, notwithstanding, pray, Sir, read it to me; I shall be hugely rejoiced to hear it; for, it must certainly be curiously penned." "Listen then, and I will read it," said Don Quixote, who began as follows.

Don Quixote's letter to Dulcinea del Toboso.

Sovereign and sublime princess,

He who is wounded by the edge of absence, and whose heart is stuck full of the darts of affliction, most divine Dulcinea del Toboso! wishes thee that health which he is not doomed to enjoy. If I am scorned by thy beauty, if thy virtue affords me no relief, if thy disdain completes my misfortune; albeit, I am inured to suffering, I can ill support the misery I bear, which hath not only been excessive, but also of long duration. My trusty squire Sancho will give thee an ample relation, O ungrateful beauty and lovely foe! of the situation in which I remain on thy account: if it be thy will to succour me, I am thy slave; if not, use thy pleasure; for, the end of my life will satisfy thy cruelty and my desire. Thine till death,

<div align="right">The Knight of the rueful countenance.</div>

"By my father's soul!" cried Sancho, "this is the highest thing I ever heard. Odds-niggers![8] how your worship writes whatsoever you please, and how curiously you con-clude, 'The knight of the rueful countenance.' I verily believe your worship is the devil himself, and knows every thing." "All that knowledge," replied the knight, "is necessary for the employment I profess." "Why then," said the squire, "be so good as to write on the other leaf, the order for the three colts, and be sure to subscribe distinctly, that when it is presented, your hand-writing may be known." "With all my heart," said Don Qui-xote, who, having written the order, read it aloud in these terms.

Dear Niece,

Please deliver to Sancho Panza, my squire, or order, at sight of this my first bill of colts, three of the five, which I left at home in your custody: which three colts I order you to pay, in return for the like number received of him: and this bill, together with his receipt, shall be a sufficient acquittance to you.

Given in the heart of the brown mountain, the twentieth and second of August, this pres-ent year.

Sancho liked the form, and desired his master to sign it. "There is no occasion for my signing it," said Don Quixote, "with any thing but my cypher, which is sufficient not only for three, but three hundred asses." "As to that, I will take your worship's word; and now give me leave to go and saddle Rozinante, which when I have done, and received your blessing, I intend forthwith to depart, without staying to see you play any foolish tricks, though I will affirm, I have beheld you perform so many, that she will desire to hear no more of the matter." "At least, Sancho," said the knight, "I would have thee, be-cause there is a necessity for it, stay and see me stript, and perform a dozen or two of mad pranks, which I can easily finish in half an hour; for, when thine eyes shall have been witnesses of some things I will act, thou mayst safely swear to what additions thou shalt make in thy report; and I assure thee, thou wilt not relate the half of what I intend to atchieve." "For the love of God! dear Sir," cried Sancho, "let me not see your worship naked: for, it will give me so much uneasiness, that I shall not be able to refrain from weeping; and, my head aches already, with the sorrow I felt last night, about Dapple; so, that I cannot bear to be set a mourning again: wherefore, if it be your worship's plea-sure, that I should see some of your mad actions, pray dispatch them in your cloaths; and let them be such as will stand you in most stead: for my own part, I think there is no occasion for any such thing; and if you dispense with them, it will save time, and send me back the sooner with such news as your worship desires and deserves. For, if my lady Dulcinea is not prepared to send a reasonable answer, I solemnly protest, I will extract a favourable reply out of her maw, by kicking and cuffing. What! is it to be born that such a renowned knight-errant as your worship, should run mad without why or where-fore, on account of a —— I would not have her ladyship compel me to speak, or, egad, I shall blab things by the dozen, even tho' they should spoil the market. I am a rare fel-low at that sport. I find she knows little of my temper, otherwise, i'faith! she would take care to give me no offence." "In good faith! Sancho," said Don Quixote, "thou seemest to be as mad as myself." "Not quite so mad," replied the squire, "but a little more cho-leric; but, enough of that. What eatables has your worship got to live upon till my re-

turn? will you go to the high-road, and rob the shepherds, like Cardenio?" "Let not that give thee any concern," answered the knight; "though I had store of provisions by me, I should eat nothing but the herbs and fruits which this meadow and these trees afford: the perfection of my design consisting in abstaining from food, and in encountering other hardships." "Your worship must know," said Sancho, "that I am afraid I shall not find my way back again, to this concealed and unfrequented place, in which I leave your worship." "Take good notice of the marks," answered the knight, "and I shall endeavour to remain always near this very spot: nay, I will take care to ascend the highest rocks hereabouts, that I may have a chance of descrying thee afar off, in thy return. But, the best scheme for preventing thy being bewildered, will be, to cut down some of the furze that grows here in great plenty, and drop bunches of it, at small distances on the way, until thou shalt reach the flat country: and they will serve as land marks to guide thee hither in thy return, like the clue of Theseus,[9] in the labyrinth of Crete."

"I will take your advice," said Sancho; who accordingly cutting a large bundle, begged his master's blessing, and took his leave, not without many tears on both sides. Then mounting Rozinante, whom Don Quixote strongly recommended to his care, commanding him to pay as much regard to the steed as he would shew for his own person; he set out for the plain, scattering, by the way, the furze he had cut, according to the direction of his master. In this manner, then, did he begin his journey, notwithstanding the incessant importunities of Don Quixote, who sollicited him to stay and see some of his extravagancies: but, he had not travelled above an hundred yards, when he returned, saying, "I confess your worship was in the right, when you observed, that, in order to my swearing with a safe conscience that I have seen you perform mad pranks, it would be necessary for you to play some in my presence; although, in my opinion, I have seen a pretty good sample already in your staying here by yourself." "Did not I tell thee so, Sancho?" said Don Quixote: "wait a little, and I will finish them in a twinkling." So saying, he stript off his breeches in a great hurry, leaving his posteriors covered by the tail of his shirt alone, and without further ceremony, cut a couple of capers,[10] and a like number of tumbles, with his head down and his heels up, disclosing particulars, which shocked the modesty of Sancho so much, that, in order to avoid the sight of them, a second time, he turned Rozinante, fully satisfied and pleased, that he might now honestly swear he had left his master distracted. We will, therefore, let him pursue his journey, till his return, which was more speedy than could be expected.

## CHAPTER XII.

### A continuation of the refinements in love, practised by Don Quixote, in the brown mountain.

B ut, to return to the account of what the knight of the rueful countenance executed when he found himself alone: the history relates, that, having performed the capers and tumbles, naked, from the waist downward, and perceived that Sancho was gone, without waiting to see more of his extravagancies, he climbed to the top of a high rock, and there revolved what he had often reflected upon, without coming to any conclusion; namely, whether it was better and more for his purpose, to imitate Orlando in his out-rageous, or Amadis in his melancholy madness. "It is not to be wondred at," said he within himself, "if Orlando was such a stout and valiant knight as he is represented; for, he was actually enchanted, and invulnerable by every weapon but the point of a pin, thrust into his foot, upon which, he always wore a shoe with seven soles of iron: though that precaution did not avail him, against Bernardo del Carpio, who being informed of the contrivance, strangled him in his arms at the battle of Roncevalles: but, the circum-stance of his valour apart, let us consider that of his losing his senses, which actually hap-pened, when he found the tokens in the fountain, and received the information of the shepherd, by which he learned that Angelica had slept more than two afternoons with Medoro, the little Moor, with curled locks, who was Agramante's page; and truly, if he was convinced in his own mind, that his mistress had misbehaved in that manner, it was no great feat to run mad upon the discovery. But, why should I imitate him in his mad-ness, when the occasion is not similar; for, my Dulcinea del Toboso, I dare swear, never in all the days of her life, beheld one Moor in his own likeness; and is this day, as much a virgin as the mother that bore her; I should therefore, do her a manifest injury, in imag-ining otherwise, and adopting that kind of madness which possessed Orlando Furioso. On the other hand, I am sensible that Amadis de Gaul, without losing his senses, or act-ing the madman, acquired as much, or more, fame than he, in the character of a lover; for, according to the history, all that he did, when he found himself in disgrace with his mistress Oriana, who banished him from her presence during pleasure, was to retire, in company of a hermit, to the poor rock, where he contented himself with bemoaning his misfortune, until heaven sent him succour, in the midst of his great necessity and afflic-tion. If this circumstance, therefore, be true, as I know it is, why should I now take the trouble of stripping myself naked, or give umbrage to these trees, which have done me no harm! or what reason have I to defile the pure stream of these rivulets, which, when I want it, will yield me pleasant drink! Flourish then the memory of Amadis! and let him be imitated as much as possible, by Don Quixote de la Mancha, of whom may be said, that which is * recorded of another; 'If he did not atchieve great things, at least, he died

---

* Probably alluding to the epitaph of Phaeton.[1]

　　Hic situs est Phaethon, currus auriga paterni,
　　Quem si non tenuit, magnis tamen excidit ausis.

in attempting them.' And, though I am not banished nor disdained by my Dulcinea, let it suffice, as I have already said, that I am absent from her. Come then, let us begin: re-cur to my remembrance, ye feats of Amadis, and initiate me in the imitation of your fame: I know his chief exercise was prayer, and in that too, will I follow his example." So saying, he composed a rosary of the large galls of a cork-tree, which he strung together, instead of beads; but, he found an unsurmountable difficulty, in the want of an hermit to confess and console him: wherefore, he entertained himself in strolling about the meadow, writing and engraving verses on the barks of trees, and the smooth sand: all of them on the subject of his own melancholy, or in praise of his mistress Dulcinea: but, after he was found in this place, none, except the following, remained intelligible and entire.

### I.

Ye trees and herbs, so green and tall,
  That shade this meadow, and adorn,
If you rejoice not at my thrall,
  Give ear unto a wretch forlorn;
Nor, let my grief, though loud invade
  Your peace; but, by Don Quixote, be a
Self-offer'd tax of sorrow, paid
  In absence of his Dulcinea
                del Toboso.

### II.

These are the rocks, to which he's driven
  By her who seems not much to care for
The truest lover under heaven:
  And yet he knows not why nor wherefore.
By love toss'd like a tennis-ball,
  A cask of tears, will not defray a
Whole day's expence of grief and gall,
  In absence of his Dulcinea
                del Toboso.

### III.

Among these craggy rocks and brambles,
  He hangs, alas! on sorrow's tenters;
Or curses, as alone he rambles,
  The cruel cause of his misventures.
Unpitying love, about his ears,
  With scourge severe began to play a
Most dreadful game that made his tears
  Flow for his absent Dulcinea
                del Toboso.

These verses, with the addition of del Toboso, to the name of Dulcinea, afforded infinite diversion to those who found them: for, they concluded Don Quixote had imag-ined, that, if he named her without this title, the stanza could not possibly be under-

stood; and this was really the case, as he afterwards owned. Many other ditties did he compose; but, as we have already observed, none but these three stanzas could be decyphered and read. In this amusement, in sighing, invoking the fawns and silvans of those woods, the nymphs of the brooks, with the damp and doleful echo to hear, console and resound his complaints; and, in culling plants to sustain nature, he employed himself till the return of Sancho, who, had he stayed three weeks, instead of three days, the knight of the rueful countenance would have been so emaciated and disfigured, that he could not have been known by the mother who bore him.

However, it will not be amiss to leave him, engrossed by his sighs and poetry; in order to recount what happened to Sancho Panza, in the execution of his embassy. Having reached the highway, this trusty messenger took the road to Toboso, and next day arrived at the very inn where he had met with the disgraceful adventure of the blanketting. He no sooner perceived the unlucky house, than he fancied himself cutting capers in the air again; and was very loath to enter, although it was then dinner-time, and he was very much instigated by the desire of tasting something hot, as he had lived for a great many days past on cold victuals only. This inclination compelled him to ride close up to the inn, where, while he was sitting in suspence, and hesitating whether or not he should enter, two persons happened to come to the door, and knowing him immediately, the one said to the other, "Pray, Mr. Licentiate, is not that man on horseback, our neighbour Sancho Panza, who, as the housekeeper told us, went out with our adventurer, in quality of squire?" "The very same," answered the licentiate, "and that is the individual horse of our friend Don Quixote." And no wonder they should know him so easily; for, they were no other than the curate and barber of the knight's town, by whom the scrutiny and trial of his books were held. Having therefore, recognized Sancho Panza and Rozinante, and being impatient to hear news of Don Quixote, they ran up to the squire, and the curate called him by name, saying, "Friend Sancho, where is your master?" Sancho, who recollected them also, resolved to conceal the place and condition in which he had left his master; and therefore, answered, that the knight was in a certain place, employed about a certain affair of the utmost importance, which he durst not disclose for the eyes that stood in his head. "That pretence will not do, Sancho," said the barber; "if you refuse to tell where he is, we shall imagine, as indeed we do, that you have robbed and murdered him, and taken possession of his horse; so, that in good sooth, you must either produce him, or in this very spot, we will—" "You have no occasion," cried Sancho interrupting him, "to threaten people in this manner; I am not the man to rob or murder any person: every man must fall by his own fortune, or by the will of God that created him: my master is sound and safe, doing penance in the midst of that mountain, to his heart's content." He then, without pausing, in a breath, informed them of the condition in which he left him, recounted all the adventures which had happened to him, and told them of the letter he was carrying to my lady Dulcinea del Toboso, who was no other than Lorenzo Corchuelo's daughter, with whom his master was up to the ears in love.

They were astonished at what the squire related, and tho' well acquainted with the particular species of Don Quixote's madness, this instance afforded fresh admiration: they desired Sancho to shew them the letter for the lady Dulcinea del Toboso; and he

told them it was only a rough draught, written on the leaf of a pocket-book; and that his master had ordered him to get it transcribed on a sheet of paper, with the first convenient opportunity. The curate promised to transcribe it in a fair legible hand, and again desiring a sight of it, Sancho put his hand in his bosom, in search of the book, which, however, he could not find; and indeed, had he fumbled till this time, it would have been to no purpose: for, he had left it with Don Quixote, who had forgot to give, as he, to ask it of him, before he set out. Sancho missing his charge, grew pale as death, and searching again his whole body with great eagerness, could find nothing; upon which, without more ado, he laid hold of his beard with both hands, and plucked one half of it from his chin; then, with vast dispatch and precipitation, belaboured his face and nose in such a manner, as left the whole covered with blood. The curate and barber seeing him make so free with his own person, asked what had happened to him, that made him handle himself so roughly? "What has happened to me?" cried the squire. "I have lost and let slip thro' my fingers, in an instant, three ass colts, each of which was as tall as a tower." "By what means?" resumed the barber. "I have lost," answered Sancho, "the pocket-book, in which was written the letter for Dulcinea, together with an order signed by my master's own hand, desiring his niece to deliver to me, three colts out of four or five which he has at home." At the same time, he told them how he had lost Dapple. The curate comforted him, by saying, that when he returned, his master would renew the order, and give him a bill upon paper, as the custom is, for, those written in pocket-books are never accepted or paid.

With this assurance, Sancho consoled himself, observing, since that was the case, he should not give himself much uneasiness about the loss of the letter, which, as he retained it by heart, he could cause to be transcribed where and when he pleased. The barber desired him to repeat it, telling him they would transcribe it; upon which, Sancho began to scratch his head, in order to recollect it, standing sometimes on one foot, sometimes on the other. One while, he fixed his eyes upon the ground, then lifted them up to heaven; at last, after a most tedious pause, during which he gnawed off the half of one of his nails, and kept his hearers in the most impatient suspense; "'Fore God! Mr. Licentiate," said he, "I believe the devil has run away with every word that I remembered of this letter: tho' I am positive it began with 'subterrene and sublime princess!'"[2] "It could not be subterrene," said the barber, "but superterrene or sovereign." "You are in the right," resumed Sancho: "then, if my memory does not fail me, it went on with 'the smitten, the sleepless and the sore, kisses your hands, most ungrateful and unregarded beauty': and something or other of health and distemper which he wished her; running on at this rate, till he concluded with, 'Yours, till death, the knight of the rueful countenance.'"

The hearers were not a little diverted with this specimen of Sancho's memory, which they applauded very much; desiring him to repeat the letter again, twice over, that they might retain it, until they could have an opportunity of transcribing it. He accordingly renewed his efforts, repeated it three times; and as often recited three thousand absurdities. He likewise gave them an account of every thing which had befallen his master; but mentioned not a syllable of the blanketting that had happened to himself, in that very inn which he refused to enter: nay, he gave them to understand, that his master, as

soon as he could bring him a favourable dispatch from my lady Dulcinea del Toboso, would put himself in the way of becoming an emperor or monarch at least, according to the plan settled between them. This he represented as a very easy matter; considering the valour of his person, and strength of his arm: and told them, that this design would be no sooner accomplished, than the knight would bestow upon him in marriage, (for by that time, he must of necessity be a widower) one of the maids of honour to the empress; a fine young lady, and heiress of a vast and wealthy estate upon the main land, without any oilands or islands, which he did not much care for.

Sancho uttered this piece of wrong-headed information with such composure, wiping his nose from time to time, that his townsmen could not help admiring anew the madness of Don Quixote, which, like a whirlpool, had sucked in and swept along with it, the understanding of this poor simpleton. They did not chuse to fatigue themselves with endeavours to convince him of his error, but, as they believed it was not prejudicial to his conscience, resolved, for their amusement, to encourage him in his folly: with this view, they advised him to pray to God, for long life and health to his master; and observed, that it was a thing both likely and feasible, that he should, in process of time, become an emperor, at least, an archbishop, or attain some station of equal dignity. To this encouragement, Sancho replied, "Gentlemen, if fortune should bring matters about, so as that my master should incline to be an archbishop rather than an emperor, I should be glad to know what archbishops-errant bestow upon their squires." The curate told him, that they commonly gave them some simple benefice, curacy, or the office of sacristan, with a good yearly income, besides the fees of the altar, which are usually reckoned at as much more. "In order to fill an employment of that kind," answered Sancho, "the squire must be unmarried, and at least capable of assisting at mass; and if that be the case, what will become of me, who have not only the misfortune to be married, but am also ignorant of the first letter of the A, B, C; should my master take it in his head to be an archbishop, rather than an emperor, according to the custom of knights-errant?" "Don't make yourself uneasy about that matter, friend Sancho," said the barber; "for, we will intreat and advise your master, nay, even make it an affair of conscience, for him to become an emperor rather than an archbishop, as a station more suited to his disposition, which is more warlike than studious." "I was of the same opinion," resumed Sancho, "but, now, I'll venture to say, he has a capacity for every thing: and what I intend to do, is to beseech our Lord to direct his choice to that station which will be most for his own honour and my advantage." "You speak like a sensible man," said the curate; "and in so doing, will act the part of a good christian: but, our present business is to think on some means of putting an end to this useless penance your master has imposed upon himself; and in the mean time, go into dinner." Sancho desired them to enter, saying he would wait for them at the door, and afterwards tell them why he did not go in, and wherefore it was not proper for him so to do: but, begged they would be so good as to bring out something hot for himself, and some barley for Rozinante. They accordingly went in, and in a little time, the barber brought him out, a mess of hot victuals. After they had both maturely deliberated about the means of accomplishing their design, the curate fell upon a scheme, extremely well adapted to the taste of the knight, as well as to their purpose. He proposed to cloath himself in the dress of

a lady-errant, and that the barber should disguise himself as well as he could, in the likeness of a squire; which being done, they should go to the place where Don Quixote was, and the priest, on pretence of being a damsel in distress, should beg a boon, which he, as a valiant knight-errant, could not help granting: this boon should be a request, that he would accompany her to a certain place whither she would conduct him, there to redress an injury she had received from a discourteous knight; and the boon should be attended with a humble supplication, that he would not desire her to take off her mask, nor ask any question about her affairs, until he should have done her justice upon her adversary. And as he firmly believed that Don Quixote would comply with any request made in that stile, he hoped by these means, to withdraw him from the mountain, and conduct him to his own habitation, where they would endeavour to find some remedy for his strange disorder.

## CHAPTER XIII.

How the curate and barber set out on the execution of their plan; with other events worthy to be recorded in this sublime history.

This scheme of the curate was so well relished by the barber, that they began to put it in execution immediately; by borrowing of the landlady a petticoat and tucker, for which the priest left a new cassock in pawn: while the barber made an artificial beard of the tail of a pyed ox, in which the innkeeper used to stick his comb. When the hostess asked what occasion they had for these things, the curate gave her a brief account of Don Quixote's madness, and explained the use to which they intended to put the disguise, in order to disengage him from the mountain where he then was. The innkeeper and his wife immediately discovered that this lunatic was no other than their quondam guest, who was author of the balsam, and master of the blanketted squire; and recounted to the curate, every thing that had happened, not even forgetting the circumstance which Sancho was at such pains to conceal. In short, the landlady dressed up the curate in a most curious manner: she put upon him a cloth petticoat flounced and furbelowed, with a broad border of black velvet; and a close jerkin of green velvet, garnished with robings of white sattin, which, together with the petticoat, seemed to have been made in the reign of king Bamba *: he would not suffer himself to be coifed, but covered his head with a quilted linnen night-cap, which he always carried about with him; and bound his forehead with a garter of black taffety, making a sort of a mask with the other, which effectually concealed his countenance and beard. Over all, he flapped his beaver,

---

* Bamba or Wamba, king of the Visigoths in Spain, mounted the throne in the year 672, and was famous for his success against the Arabians, as well as for his attachment to the christian religion, as a proof of which he retired into a monastery, and resigned the kingdom to Ervige.[1]

which was so broad, that it might have served for an umbrella; and wrapping himself up in his cloak, mounted his mule, sitting sideways like a woman: while the barber bestrid his own beast, with his beard flowing down to his girdle, of a white and red colour, being made, as we before observed, of a pyed ox's tail.

Thus equipped, they took leave of every body present, even the kind Maritornes, who promised, tho' a sinner, to mumble a whole rosary over, in prayers to God, for the good success of that arduous and christian design they had undertaken: but, scarce had they sallied from the inn, when the curate began to think he was to blame for disguising himself; it being in his opinion, indecent for a priest to appear in such a maner, how much soever depended upon their success. He therefore proposed, that he should exchange characters with the barber, who might act the part of the damsel in distress, while he took that of the squire, which he thought, did not so much profane the dignity of the cloth: and unless his neighbour would agree to this proposal, he assured him, that he was resolved to go no farther, even if the devil himself should carry off Don Quixote. At that instant, Sancho chanced to come up, and seeing them in such a garb, could not refrain from laughing: in short, the barber assented to every thing the other proposed, and the plan being thus altered, the curate began to instruct him touching his behaviour and speech to Don Quixote, in order to move and induce him to accompany them, and quit that place he had chosen for the scene of his vain and extravagant penance. The barber told him, that without his lessons, he knew very well how to demean himself in the character; and as he did not chuse to put on the dress till they should be near Don Quixote, he folded it up with great care; the priest adjusted his beard, and both together proceeded on their journey, under the direction of Sancho Panza, who, by the way, related to them what happened between his master and the madman, whom they met with in the brown mountain; concealing nevertheless, the circumstance of the portmanteau, and its contents; for, notwithstanding his simplicity, our youth was as covetous as wiser people.

Next day, they came to the broom boughs, which Sancho had strewed, in order to ascertain the place where he had left his master; he no sooner therefore perceived his marks, than he told them that was the entrance into the mountain, and desired them to put on their dresses, if they were necessary towards the deliverance of his master: for, they had already assured him, that their travelling in such disguise, was of the utmost importance, in disengaging the knight from that disagreeable course of life he had chosen: and they had charged him, not to tell his master, that he knew who they were; and if he should ask, as doubtless he would, whether or not he had delivered the letter to Dulcinea, they advised him to answer in the affirmative, and tell him, that as she could not read it, she had sent her answer by word of mouth, commanding him, on pain of her displeasure, to appear in her presence, with all convenient speed, on an affair of the utmost consequence to him: for, with this answer, and other speeches they intended to make, they did not at all doubt of reconciling him to a better way of life, and prevail upon him, immediately to begin his career towards being an emperor or king; and as to the office of archbishop, Sancho had nothing to fear. The squire listened to these directions, which he carefully deposited in his memory, thanking them heartily for their intention to advise his master to accept of an emperor's crown, rather than an archbishop's mitre, as he was very sensible that emperors could do more for their squires

than archbishops-errant. He also proposed to go before, in search of his master, and impart to him this answer of his lady, which, he assured them, would be sufficient to bring him out of the mountain, without their being put to any further trouble. They approved of his opinion, and resolved to stay where they were until he should return with the news of his having found Don Quixote: accordingly, Sancho proceeded towards the heart of the mountain, leaving them in a spot watered by a small purling brook, and shaded in a most cool and agreeable manner, by some rocks, and trees that grew around it.

It being then the month of August, when the heat in those parts is excessive, and three in the afternoon, which is the hottest time of the day, they were the more charmed with the situation, which was so inviting, that they chose it for the place of their residence, until Sancho should return. While they lay at their ease, under the covert of this shade, their ears were saluted with the sound of a voice, which, tho' unaccompanied by any instrument, sung so sweet and melodiously, that they were struck with astonishment; little expecting to meet with such a delicious warbler in that unfrequented place: for, tho' it is usually said, that the woods and mountains abound with shepherds, who sing most inchantingly, that report is rather the fiction of poets than the voice of truth: besides, the verses which they heard, were not composed in the rustic phrase of clowns, but, in a polite and courtly strain; as may be perceived by the song itself, which follows:

I.

Ah! what inspires my woeful strain?
Unkind disdain!
Ah! what augments my misery?
Fell jealousy!
Or, say, what hath my patience worn?
An absent lover's scorn!
The torments then that I endure,
No mortal remedy can cure:
For every languid hope is slain
By absence, jealousy, disdain!

II.

From love, my unrelenting foe,
These sorrows flow!
My infant glory's overthrown,
By fortune's frown;
Confirmed in this my wretched state,
By the decrees of fate!
In death alone, I hope release
From this compounded, dire disease;
Whose cruel pangs to aggravate,
Fortune and love conspire with fate!

III.

Ah! what will mitigate my doom?
The silent tomb!

> Ah! what retrieve departed joy?
> Inconstancy!
> Or say, can ought but frenzy, bear
> This tempest of despair?
> All other efforts, then, are vain,
> To cure this soul-tormenting pain,
> That owns no other remedy
> Than madness, death, inconstancy.

The hour, the season, and the solitude, conspired with the agreeable voice of the singer, to increase the wonder and satisfaction of the hearers, who listened for some time, in expectation of something else: but, the silence having continued a good while, they resolved to go in quest of the person who sung so enchantingly: and were just going to set out on this design, when they were arrested by the same voice, which again saluted their ears with this other song:

### I.

> O sacred friendship! mild and gay,
>   Who to the regions of the blest
> Hath soar'd; and left mankind a prey
>   To fraud, in thy resemblance drest.

### II.

> Auspicious, hear, and hither send
>   Thy sister truth, with radiant eyes,
> To brand the false professing friend,
>   Detected in the fair disguise.

### III.

> Or, come thyself, and reinspire
>   The purpose candid and humane;
> Else peace and order will retire,
>   While horror and confusion reign.

This sonnet was concluded with a most profound sigh, and the curate and barber began again to listen for more; but, finding the music converted into mournful sobs and interjections, they were determined to know who this melancholy person was, who sung so well, and groaned so piteously. They had not gone many paces with this intent, when turning the point of a rock, they perceived a man of the same make and appearance that Sancho described, when he related the story of Cardenio: he did not seem surprised at sight of them, but, stood with his head reclining upon his breast, in a very pensive posture, without lifting his eyes to look at them, after their first sudden appearance. The curate, who was a well-spoken man, concluding from the description, that this must be he whose misfortune he had been apprised of, went up, and in a short but pathetic address, exhorted and intreated him to quit that miserable course of life, which was the greatest of all misfortunes, and altogether perverted the end of his being. Cardenio,

being at that time in one of his lucid intervals, intirely free of that frantic paroxysm which used so utterly to deprive him of his senses, and seeing two people so differently dressed from those he commonly met with in that solitude, could not help being somewhat surprised; especially, when he heard him talk of his misfortune as a circumstance with which they were well acquainted; for, the curate had mentioned it in the course of his expostulation: and therefore he answered in this manner, "I plainly perceive, gentlemen, that heaven, which is careful in succouring the good, and sometimes, even the bad, hath sent, tho' I little deserve such favour and condescension, diverse people into this unfrequented solitude, so remote from all commerce and society; in order to convince me by just and various arguments, how unreasonably I act in leading this kind of life, which they have endeavoured to make me exchange for a better; and, as they know not the reasons I have, to think that, in quitting this situation, I shall be plunged into a worse; they have perhaps looked upon me as a person of very shallow understanding, or, which is still a conjecture more unfavourable, a downright madman; and truly, it is not to be wondered at, if that was really the case: for I can easily conceive, that my misfortunes operate so intensely upon my imagination, and impair my faculties so much, that sometimes, in spite of all my endeavours to the contrary, I become like that rock, void of all sentiment and knowledge; and am convinced of my infirmity too late, when people shew me the marks of what I have done, while I was under the influence of that terrible transport: then all that I can do, is to bewail my distemper, curse my lot in vain, and in excuse of my madness, relate my sufferings to all who express the least desire of hearing them; that those of sounder judgment, knowing the cause, may not wonder at the effects; and if they cannot prevent, at least pardon my frenzy; converting their indignation at my extravagance, into compassion for my woes: and if you, gentlemen, are come with that intention which hath brought others to this place, before you proceed with your prudent admonitions, I intreat you to hear the detail of my misfortunes, which you do not yet know, and then, perhaps, you will save yourselves the trouble which you might otherwise take, in consoling an affliction that admits of no consolation."

The two friends, who desired nothing else, than to hear from his own mouth, the cause of his misfortune, earnestly begged he would recount it, and promised to attempt nothing contrary to his own inclination, in the way of remedy or comfort. Thus assured, the melancholy gentleman began his distressful story, nearly in the same words and circumstances which he had used a few days before, to Don Quixote and the goatherd, when he was interrupted, in the affair of Mr. Elisabat, by the knight's punctuality in asserting the decorum of chivalry, as the particulars of that quarrel have been already related: but, now he remained fortunately free from his paroxysm, and, of consequence, had time to finish the narration which was imperfect before. When he therefore came to the circumstance of the letter which Don Fernando had found between the leaves of Amadis de Gaul *, he said he remembered the contents, and accordingly repeated them in these terms:

---

* There is no such letter mentioned in his conversation with Don Quixote.[2]

Lucinda to Cardenio.

"I every day discover new qualities in Cardenio, which oblige and compel me to esteem him the more. If you are inclined to extricate me out of all suspence, you may effectuate your purpose, without the least prejudice to my honour; for, my father, who is well acquainted with your virtues, loves me dearly, and far from tyrannizing over my affections, will chearfully grant that which is so justly your due, if your passion is such as I wish and believe it to be."

"I resolved, as I have already told you, to demand Lucinda in marriage, upon the receipt of this letter, which not only confirmed Don Fernando's high opinion of her prudence and virtue, but also inflamed him with the desire of ruining my hopes, before I should be able to bring them to maturity. I told this faithless friend, Lucinda's father expected that mine should propose the match; and that I durst not communicate my desire to him, lest he should refuse to comply with it: not, that he was ignorant of Lucinda's rank, virtue, beauty and qualifications, which were sufficient to ennoble any other family in Spain; but, because I understood he was averse to my being married, until he should see what duke Ricardo would do in my behalf: in short, I told him that I would not venture to propose it, being afraid not only of this ill consequence, but also of many others which I could not foresee; although I had a strong impression upon my mind, that my wishes would never be completed. In answer to this declaration, Don Fernando undertook to manage the affair, and prevail upon my father to propose the match to Lucinda's parents. O villain! more ambitious than Marius, more cruel than Cataline, more savage than Sylla, more fraudulent than Galalon, more treacherous than * Vellido, more vengeful than Julian, and more covetous than Judas! cruel, false, vindictive traitor! what injuries had'st thou suffered from this poor credulous wretch, who with such confidence disclosed to thee, the most secret recesses of his soul! what offence had he given? what words had he uttered, or what advice had he offered, that did not directly tend to thy honour and advantage? But, unhappy that I am! wherefore should I complain? seeing it is a thing certain, that when once the tide of misfortune heaped up by one's malignant stars, begins to descend with violence and fury, no earthly mound can oppose, nor human industry divert its course. Who could imagine, that such an illustrious, accomplished, young gentleman as Don Fernando, who lay under obligations for the services I had done him, and was powerful enough to obtain the gratification of his wish, whithersoever his amorous inclination pointed, should plague himself, as I may say, in attempts to rob me of my single lamb, even before I had possessed it.

"But, let us lay aside these vain and unprofitable reflections, and rejoin the broken thread of my unfortunate story. Well then: Don Fernando perceiving that my presence would be an obstruction to the execution of his false and perfidious design, resolved to send me back to his elder brother, on pretence of getting money to pay for six horses, which he purposely bought that very day he undertook to speak to my father; in order to have an excuse for sending me away, that he might, in my absence, the more easily

* Who murdered Sancho I. king of Castile, while he was engaged in the siege of Zamora.³

succeed in his villainous intention. Was it possible for me to prevent this treachery, or indeed conceive his design! no, surely. On the contrary, I offered, with the utmost alacrity, to set out forthwith, so pleased was I with the purchase he had made. That very night I had a private conversation with Lucinda, in which I told her the scheme I had concerted with Don Fernando, and bade her rest assured in the hope that our just and honourable desires would soon be gratified. She, as little suspicious of Don Fernando's perfidy as I was, intreated me to return with speed, believing that our wishes would be completed, as soon as my father should mention the affair to her's. I don't know upon what account, her eyes were filled with tears, when she pronounced these words; and something that seemed to swell in her throat, prevented her from uttering another syllable, though she looked as if she had something more to say. I was confounded at this new circumstance, which had never happened before: in all our former conversations, which my good fortune offered, or my diligence effected, there had been nothing but joy and satisfaction, without any mixture of tears, sighs, jealousy, dread or suspicion; all my discourse used to consist of acknowledgments to heaven, for having bestowed upon me such a mistress, whose beauty I extolled, and whose virtue and good sense I admired: while she returned the compliment, by praising those qualities in me, which she, in the partiality of her fondness, deemed worthy of applause: besides, we used to entertain each other with an account of a thousand trifling accidents that happened among our neighbours and acquaintance: and the heighth of my vivacity never amounted to more than the seizing of one of her delicate, white hands, and pressing it to my lips, through the narrow distance betwixt the rails that divided us. But, on that night, which preceded the fatal day of my departure, she wept, sighed and sobbed, and left me filled with confusion and surprize, and terrified at such unusual and melancholy marks of grief and affliction, in my Lucinda. But, I was flattered by my hopes, which ascribed the whole to the strength of her passion, and that sorrow which is commonly produced by the absence of a beloved object. In fine, I set out, pensive and sad, my imagination tortured with suspicions and doubts, which my reflection could neither digest nor explain: a sure presage of the melancholy fate that awaited me.

"I arrived at the place of my destination, and delivered my letters to Don Fernando's brother, who received me kindly, but, far from dispatching me immediately, desired me, to my infinite regret, to wait eight whole days in a place where his father should not see me; because his brother had writ to him, to send the money without the knowledge of the duke. But, this was altogether an invention of the false Fernando, whose brother had money enough, and could have sent me back the very same day on which I arrived. This was such an order as I was scarce able to obey; for, I thought it impossible to support life for so many days, in the absence of Lucinda, considering the sorrow in which I had left her. Yet, notwithstanding, I resolved to do my duty like a faithful servant, though I very well foresaw, that my obedience must be at the expence of my peace. Four days of the eight were not yet elapsed, when a man came in search of me, and gave me a letter, the superscription of which I no sooner beheld, than I knew it to be written by Lucinda's own hand. I opened it with fear and trembling, believing, that there must be something very extraordinary in the case, which induced her to write to me in my absence; con-

sidering that while I was present, she had been so sparing of her pen *. But, before I read a syllable, I asked the messenger, who had put it into his hands; and how long he had been upon his journey? He answered, that passing through a certain street, about noon, he was stopt by a very beautiful young lady, who called to him from a window, saying, with great earnestness, while the tears trickled from her eyes; 'Brother, if you are a christian, as you seem to be, I intreat you, for God's sake, to carry this letter to the place and person for whom it is directed; they are both well known; and in so doing, you will render a piece of service acceptable to the Lord. That you may not want conveniencies upon the road, here is something to defray the expence of your journey.' So saying, she threw down a handkerchief, in which were tied an hundred rials, this gold ring, and the letter I have delivered. Then, without waiting for a reply, she went from the window, after having seen me take up the handkerchief and the letter, and make signs that I would do as she desired. Accordingly, finding myself so well paid for the trouble I should be at, and seeing, by the direction, that you was the person to whom it was sent, (and I know you perfectly well;) induced, moreover, by the tears of that beautiful young lady, I resolved to trust no other messenger, but come and deliver it with my own hand; and in sixteen hours, which are past, since I received it, I have travelled to this place, which, as you know, is about eighteen leagues from our town. While I listened attentively to the information of this grateful and extraordinary courier, my legs shook under me, in such a manner, that I could scarce stand upright. At length, however, I ventured to read the letter, which contained these words:

"The promise which Don Fernando made, to prevail upon your father, to propose a match to mine, hath been performed more to his inclination than your advantage. Know, Cardenio, that your pretended friend asked me in marriage for himself: and, my father, swayed by the advantage which he thinks Don Fernando has over you in point of fortune, hath given his consent so much in earnest, that two days hence, the nuptials are to be celebrated so privately, that none but heaven and some people in the family, are to be present at the marriage. My situation you may guess. If it be in your power, return with all speed, and the event of this affair will shew whether I love you tenderly or not. Heaven grant that this may come to your hand, before mine shall be presented to him who so ill performs the duty of a friend."

"This, which was the sum of what the letter contained, made me set out immediately, without waiting for any answer, or the money for which I had come. For, by that time, I plainly perceived, that it was not the purchase of the horses, but his own treacherous intention, which had induced Don Fernando to send me out of the way. The indignation I conceived against him, together with the fear of losing the jewel which I had ac-

---

* The original *pues presente pocas vezes lo hazia*, signifies, since while I was present she did it very seldom. This at first sight appears a solicism, and the petulant critick will exclaim, "What occasion had she to write to her lover who was present, unless she had lost the faculty of speech?" But the seeming absurdity will vanish, when we reflect that by *present*, he means, in the same city with his mistress, to whom however, according to the custom of Spain, he had little or no access but by literary correspondence.⁴

quired, and treasured up with such unwearied services and care, added wings to my speed, and conveyed me to the place of my habitation, just at the hour and minute proper for my going to visit Lucinda. I entered the town privately, and leaving my mule at the house of the honest man who brought the letter; I went to the rail, which was the constant witness of our love, and there was so far favoured by fortune, as to find Lucinda. We knew each other presently: though not as we ought to have known each other. But, who is he, who can arrogate praise to himself, for having fathomed and discerned the capricious sentiments and fickle disposition of woman? surely no man on earth— But, this apart. Lucinda, perceiving me, 'Cardenio,' said she, 'I am now in my bridal dress, and this moment expected in the hall, by the traitor Don Fernando, my covetous father, and some other people, who shall bear witness to my death, sooner than to my marriage. Be not confounded, my friend, but, endeavour to be present at the sacrifice, which, if I cannot prevent by my declaration, I wear a dagger concealed, which can obstruct a more vigorous determination, and, by putting an end to my life, begin to convince thee of the sincere passion I have always entertained, and still retain for my Cardenio.' Afraid I should want time to answer her, I replied with great hurry and confusion, 'Let your words be verified by your deeds, madam. If you have a dagger to assert your love, I wear a sword to defend it; or, should fortune prove our foe, to rid myself of life.' I believe she did not hear all that I said, because she was called away, in a hurry, to the bridegroom who waited for her.

"Thus deepened the night of my distress; thus set the sun of my happiness! I remained without light to my eyes, or reflection to my mind for some time: I could neither resolve to enter her father's house, nor remove to any other place; at length, however, considering of what consequence my presence might be, in case any thing extraordinary should happen, I recollected myself, as well as I could, and went in, without being perceived, as I was well acquainted with all the passages and corners of the house, and was favoured by the confusion which then prevailed in it, on account of the nuptials. Thus entering, unseen, I found means to conceal myself in the hollow of a window in the hall, that was covered by the meeting of two pieces of tapestry, from behind which I could, without being perceived, observe every thing that happened.

"How shall I describe the throbbings and palpitations of my heart, the images that occurred to my fancy, the reflexions that I made, while I remained in that situation! they were such, as I neither can nor ought to describe. Let it suffice to say, the bridegroom came into the hall, without any other ornaments than his usual dress, attended by a first cousin of Lucinda, in quality of bridesman, no other person being present, except some servants of the family. A little while after, Lucinda came in, from her closet, accompanied by her mother and two waiting-women; and as richly dressed and adorned as her rank and beauty deserved, or as the perfection of gaiety and gallantry could invent. The suspence and transport of my soul, would not allow me to observe and mark the particulars of her dress; I could only take notice of the colours, which were carnation and white; and the blaze of jewels that adorned her, which was even excelled by the singular beauty of her golden locks, that struck the eye with more splendor than all the precious stones, together with the light of four torches that burned in the hall. O memory! thou mortal enemy of my repose! to what purpose dost thou now represent to my fancy, the unparallelled beauty of that adorable foe? cruel remembrance! rather recal to my view

the particulars of what then happened, that incensed by such a manifest injury, I may take vengeance, if not upon her, at least upon my own life. But you, gentlemen, must be tired with these digressions: though my misfortune is such as neither can, nor ought to be superficially or succinctly related; because, every circumstance, in my opinion, requires a full discussion." The curate answered, that far from being tired, they were very much entertained by those minute particulars, which he thought deserved as much attention as the principal events of the story.

"I say then," resumed Cardenio, "that the parties being assembled in the hall, the curate of the parish entered, and taking them both by the hand, in order to perform his function, he said, 'Madam Lucinda, are you willing to take Don Fernando here present, for your lawful spouse, as holy mother church ordains?' At this question, I thrust out my whole head and neck from behind the tapestry, and with the utmost attention and disorder of soul, listened to Lucinda's answer, which I expected, as either the sentence of my death or confirmation of my life. O! that I had then boldly advanced, and called aloud, 'Ah Lucinda! Lucinda! take care what you do; reflect upon your duty to me, remember you are mine, and can never belong to any other husband. Consider, that my life must end the moment you answer, Yes. Ha! treacherous Don Fernando! robber of my glory! death of my life! what are thy intentions! what wouldst thou have! remember that, as a christian, thou canst not fulfil thy desires; for I am Lucinda's husband, and she is my lawful wife!' Fool that I am! now, when I am absent, and far removed from the danger, I can reflect upon what I ought to have done. Now, that I am robbed of all that was dear to my soul! accursed by the robber, on whom I might have taken vengeance, had my heart supplied me with courage, as it now affords inclination to complain. In fine, as I then acted like a booby and a coward, it is but reasonable, that I should now die of madness, sorrow and shame. The priest waited for the reply of Lucinda, who declined it a good while; and when I expected she would either unsheath her dagger to vindicate her love, employ her tongue in the cause of truth, or utter some ingenious fraud that should tend to my advantage, I heard her pronounce with a weak and faultering voice, 'Yes, I will.' Don Fernando repeated the same words, and the ring being put upon her finger, they were united in the indissoluble bond of marriage: then he embraced his new-married spouse, who laying her hand on her heart, fainted away in the arms of her mother. It now remains to describe my own situation, when I heard and saw my hopes thus baffled by Lucinda's breach of promise; and found myself rendered incapable of ever retrieving the happiness I had that instant lost: I remained without sense or reflection, abandoned, as I thought, by heaven, and a declared enemy to that earth on which I lived. The air refused breath for my sighs, the water denied moisture for my tears, fire alone increased within me, to such a degree, that I was scorched with jealousy and rage! Lucinda's swooning threw the whole company into confusion, and her mother opening her breast to give her air, found in it, a folded paper, which Don Fernando taking, read by the light of one of the torches, and then sat down in a chair, and leaned one side of his head upon his hand, in a pensive attitude, without minding the remedies they were applying for the recovery of his spouse.

"I seeing the whole family in confusion, ventured to come out, cost what it would, resolving, should I be seen, to do some desperate action, that would convince the whole

world of my just indignation, in chastising the false Don Fernando, and the fickle, faint-
ing traitress. But fate, that reserved me, if possible, for greater misfortunes, ordained
that I should then abound in reflection, which hath since failed me; and resolve rather
than take vengeance upon my greatest enemies, who, as they had no suspicion of me,
were then at my mercy, to turn upon myself that resentment which they so justly de-
served to feel; and, perhaps, with more rigor than I should have exercised upon them,
had I, at that time, sacrificed them to my rage, because sudden death is infinitely more
easy than that which is lengthened out by lingering torments. In short, I quitted the
house, and went to the place where I had left my mule, which being saddled, I mounted
her, and without taking leave of my host, sallied out of town, dreading, like another Lot,
to look behind me. When I found myself alone in the open field, shrouded by the dark-
ness of the night, and invited by the silence, to complain, without caution, or fear of
being overheard or known, I raised my voice, and gave a loose to my indignation, in
venting curses upon Lucinda and Don Fernando, as if those vain exclamations could
have atoned for the injury they had done me. I bestowed upon her the epithets of cruel,
false, perfidious and ungrateful, but, above all, avaricious; since the wealth of my rival
had shut the eyes of her love, detached her from me, and swayed her inclination towards
him to whom fortune had shewn herself more kind and liberal. Yet, in the midst of these
reproaches and invectives, I could not help excusing her, observing, it was no wonder,
that a damsel educated under restraint, in the house of her parents, bred up, and always
accustomed to obey them, should comply with their will and pleasure, in marrying a
young gentleman of such wealth, rank and qualifications, that her refusal might have
been thought to proceed either from want of sense, or a passion for some other man,
which would have been a suspicion equally prejudicial to her virtue and reputation: then
I argued on the other side of the question, saying, had she owned that I was her husband,
her parents would have seen she had not committed an unpardonable crime in making
such a choice: since, before the offer of Don Fernando, they themselves could not have
desired, had their desires been bounded by reason, a better match than me for their
daughter; and consequently, before she complied with that compulsive injunction of
giving her hand to another, she might have told them, that she had already given it to
me; in which case, I would have appeared and confirmed the truth of every thing she
should have feigned for the occasion: In fine, I concluded that superficial love, slender
understanding, vast ambition and thirst after grandeur, had obliterated in her memory,
those professions by which I had been deceived, cherished and supported in the un-
shaken hope of my honourable desires.

"In this exclamation and anxiety, I travelled all night, and in the morning found my-
self in one of the passages to this mountain, in which I proceeded three days more, with-
out high-road or by-path, till I stopt at a small meadow, that lies either on the right or
left of these rocks; there I enquired of some goatherds, whereabouts the most craggy
part of the mountain, was; and, according to their directions, thither I rode, resolving
to put an end to my life. When I arrived among those ragged rocks, my mule fell down
dead of weariness or hunger; or, as I rather believe, to disencumber herself of such a use-
less load as then burthened her; and I remained on foot, quite spent and famished, with-
out having or desiring any support. In this situation, I know not how long I continued

stretched upon the ground: but, at length, I got up without feeling any cravings of hunger, and found myself in the midst of some shepherds, who, doubtless, had relieved my necessity. Indeed they told me in what condition I had been found, uttering such incoherent and extravagant expressions, as clearly demonstrated, that I had lost my senses. Since that time, I have frequently perceived my intellects so crazy and unsound, that I perform a thousand mad actions, tearing my cloaths, bellowing through these unfrequented places, cursing my fate, and repeating, in vain, the beloved name of my fair enemy, without any connected sentences, or indeed any other intent than that of putting an end to my life by violent outcries; and when I recover the use of my senses, I find myself so weak and exhausted, that I scarce can move. My usual habitation is the hollow of a cork-tree, large enough to contain this miserable carcass; the cow and goatherds who frequent these mountains, maintain me out of charity, by leaving food upon the road, or rocks, on which they think I may chance to find it: and, even while I am deprived of my understanding, natural instinct teaches me to distinguish this necessary nourishment, awakening my appetite and desire of seizing it for my use. They tell me too, when they meet with me in one of my lucid intervals, that at other times, I sally out upon the highway, and take it by force, from the shepherds, as they are bringing it from their cots, although they offer it of their own accord. In this manner, I lead my woeful and wretched life, until heaven shall be pleased to put a period to it, or give me grace to forget the beauty and falshood of Lucinda, together with the wrong I have suffered from Don Fernando. If this shall happen before I die, my intellects will return into their right channel; otherwise, there is nothing to be done, but to supplicate heaven to have mercy on my soul: for, I find I have neither virtue nor strength to extricate myself out of this extremity into which I was voluntarily plunged.

"This, gentlemen, is the bitter story of my misfortune: tell me, if you think it could have been rehearsed with less concern than I have shewn; and pray, give yourselves no trouble in offering to me such persuasions and advice, as your reason prompts you to think will do me service: for, they can have no other effect upon me, than the prescription of a celebrated physician, upon a patient who will not receive it. I will have no health without Lucinda, and since she, who is, or ought to be, mine, hath attached herself to another, I, who might have been the child of happiness, am now the willing votary of woe. She, by her inconstancy, wants to fix my perdition, and I welcome it, in order to gratify her desire; and be an example to posterity, of one who wanted that consolation, which almost all the wretched use; namely, the impossibility of receiving comfort: a consideration that increases my misery, which, I fear, will not end, even with death."

Thus did Cardenio wind up the long thread of his amorous and unfortunate story; and, just as the curate was about to give him his best advice and consolation, he was prevented by a voice that saluted his ears, and in mournful accents pronounced what will be rehearsed in the fourth book of this narration; for, in this place, the third is concluded by the sage and attentive historian Cid Hamet Benengeli.

# THE

# LIFE and ATCHIEVEMENTS

## Of the Sage and Valiant KNIGHT

## DON QUIXOTE de la Mancha.

## BOOK IV.

### CHAPTER I.

### Of the new and agreeable adventure that happened to the curate and barber, in the brown mountain.

Thrice happy and fortunate was that age which produced the most audacious knight Don Quixote de la Mancha, in consequence of whose honourable resolution, to restore and revive the lost, and, as it were, buried order of knight-errantry; we of these times, barren and unfruitful of sprightly amusements, enjoy the agreeable entertainment, not only of his own true and delightful adventures; but, also the intervening episodes, which are no less real, artful and delicious, than the main history itself, the twisted, reeled and ravelled thread of which is continued thus.

Just as the curate was ready to offer some consolation to Cardenio, he was prevented by a voice that saluted his ears in these mournful accents: "Would to God! I could find a place to serve as a private tomb for this wearisome burthen of life, which I bear so much against my inclination! this very spot will yield me what I ask, if I can trust the solitary appearance of these mountains. Alas! how much more agreeable is the company of these rocks and thickets, which give me opportunities of complaining to heaven, than that of faithless man! since nature hath not created one of whom I could reasonably expect advice in difficulty, comfort in affliction, or remedy in distress!"

This exclamation was distinctly overheard by the priest and his company, who concluding that the person who spoke must be hard by, arose to make further inquiry, and had not gone twenty paces, when behind the fragment of a rock they perceived a boy sitting under an ash-tree, in the habit of a peasant, whose face, as he stooped in order to wash his feet in a brook that murmured by him, they could not then survey. Their approach they managed with softness and silence, while his whole attention was employed in bathing his legs, that seemed two crystal pillars, which had been produced among the pebbles in the rill. They were surprised at the whiteness and beauty of his feet, which

they could not believe had been formed to tread the clods, and follow the cattle or plough, as his dress would have seemed to intimate; and the curate, who went foremost, finding himself still unperceived by the youth, made signs to the rest to crouch down, or hide themselves behind a neighbouring rock. This being done, all three stood gazing attentively at the apparition, which was clad in a double-skirted grey jacket, girt about the middle with a white napkin, and wore breeches and hose of the same cloth, with a grey hunting-cap upon his head; the hose being pulled up to the middle of his leg, which actually seemed of white alabaster. Having washed his delicate feet, he wiped them with an handkerchief, which he took out of his cap, and in so doing, lifted up his head, shewing to the by-standers, a face of such exquisite beauty, that Cardenio said in a whisper, to the curate, "Since that is not Lucinda, it can be no earthly, but some celestial being!" The youth taking off his cap, and shaking his head, a large quantity of hair, that Apollo himself might envy, flowed down upon his shoulders, and discovered to the spectators, that the supposed peasant was no other than a woman, the most delicate and handsome that the curate and barber had ever beheld; or even Cardenio, had he not seen and been acquainted with Lucinda, who alone, as he afterwards owned, could contend with her in beauty. Her golden locks fell down in such length and quantity, as not only covered her shoulders, but also concealed every other part of her body except her feet: and, instead of a comb, she made use of her hands, which, if her feet looked like crystal in the brook, appeared among her hair like moulds of drifted snow. All these circumstances increasing the desire of the bye-standers, to know who she was, they resolved to shew themselves, and at the stir they made in advancing, the beauteous phantome raised her head, and parting her locks with both hands, to see what occasioned the noise she heard, no sooner perceived them than she started up, and, without staying to put on her shoes, or tie up her hair, seized a bundle that lay by her, and betook herself to flight, full of consternation and surprize: but, she had not run six yards, when her delicate feet, unable to bear the roughness of the stones, failed under her, and she fell to the ground. This accident being perceived by the other three, they ran to her assistance, and the curate approaching her first, "Stay, madam," said he, "whosoever you are; those whom you see have no other design than that of doing you service: therefore, there is no necessity for your attempting such a precipitate flight, which neither your own feet nor our inclination will allow." To this address she made no reply, being quite astonished and confused; but, the priest taking her by the hand, proceeded in this manner: "Madam, tho' your dress concealed, your hair hath discovered manifest signs, that it must be no slight cause which hath shrouded your beauty in such unworthy disguise, and brought you to this solitude, where it is our fortune to find you; and to offer, if not a certain remedy for your misfortune, at least our best advice: for, no grievance can harrass or drive the afflicted to such extremity, while life remains, as to make them shut their ears against that counsel which is given with the most humane and benevolent intention. Wherefore, madam, or sir, or what you please to be, recollect yourself from the confusion in which the sight of us hath thrown you, and tell us the particulars of your good or evil fortune, in full assurance of finding us altogether, or each by himself, disposed to sympathize with your affliction."

While the curate pronounced these words, the disguised damsel stood wrapt in at-

Dorothea Bathing Her Feet in the Stream.

tention, gazing at them all round, without moving her lips, or uttering one syllable, like a country villager gaping at rarities which he had never seen before: but, the priest inforcing what he had said, with other arguments to the same effect, she heaved a profound sigh, and broke silence, saying, "Since these solitary mountains have not been able to conceal me, and my loose dishevelled hair allows me not to disguise the truth, it would be in vain for me to feign such things as your reason could not believe, tho' your courtesy might excuse them. On that supposition, I thank you, gentlemen, for your humane offer, which lays me under the obligation of giving you all the satisfaction you desire; tho' I am afraid, that the relation I shall make of my misfortunes, will, instead of compassion, excite your disgust; for, you will find it impossible either to cure my woes, or teach me to bear them with fortitude: but, nevertheless, that my reputation may not suffer in your opinion, as you have discovered me to be a woman, and a young one, alone, and in this disguise; circumstances, which considered either together or apart, might prejudice my good name in this world; I will freely disclose to you, those things, which, if possible, I would have willingly concealed."

All this preamble was uttered in a breath by the beautiful apparition, with such volubility of tongue, and sweetness of voice, that they admired her good sense as much as her beauty; and repeating their proffers of service, as well as their intreaties, that she would perform her promise; she, without further importunity, put on her shoes with great modesty, adjusted her hair, and sat down in the midst of her three hearers, upon a seat in the rock, where, after having endeavoured to repress a few tears that started in her eyes, she, with a clear and deliberate voice, began the story of her life, in this manner:

"In this province of Andalousia, there is a place, from whence a certain duke, one of those who are called grandees of Spain, derives his title: he hath two sons, the eldest of whom is heir to his estate, and, in all appearance, to his good qualities; but, the younger inherits nothing that I know, but the treachery of Vellido and falsehood of Galalon. To this nobleman my parents are vassals, and tho' low in pedigree, so considerable in wealth, that if their descent was equal to their fortune, they would have had nothing more to desire; nor I the mortification of seeing myself in this distress: for, I believe my misfortunes proceed from their defect in point of birth, which tho' not so mean as to make them ashamed of their origin, is not splendid enough to overthrow my conjecture about the source of my affliction: in short, they are farmers, of a plain honest family, without the least intermixture of moorish blood, but, as the saying is, old, rusty christians;[1] ay, and so rusty, that by their riches and opulent way of living, they are gradually acquiring the title of gentlefolks, nay of quality too; tho' what they prized above all riches and title, was their happiness in having me for their daughter; and therefore, as they had no other child to inherit their estate, and were naturally the most affectionate of parents, I was beloved and indulged by them, with the utmost degree of parental fondness. I was the mirrour in which they beheld themselves, the staff of their age, and shared with heaven their whole attention and desires, with which, as they were pure and unblemished, my own perfectly corresponded: and therefore, I was mistress of their affection as well as their wealth. By my advice, they received and dismissed their servants: the tale and account of what was both sowed and reaped, passed thro' my hands. I man-

aged the oil-mills, the vineyards, the herds and flocks, the beehives, and every thing that such a rich farmer as my father, may be supposed to possess: in short, I was steward and mistress, and acted with such care and oeconomy, that I should not find it easy to exaggerate the pleasure and satisfaction which my parents enjoyed. Those parts of the day that remained, after I had given all due attention to the herdsmen, overseers, and other day-labourers, I employed in exercises equally decent and necessary for young women, such as lace-making, needle-work, and spinning; and, if at any time, I interrupted these employments, in order to recreate the mind, I entertained myself with some religious book, or diversified my amusement with the harp; being convinced by experience, that music lulls the disordered thoughts, and elevates the dejected spirits. Such was the life I led in my father's house; and if I have described it too minutely, it is not thro' ostentation, in order to display our riches, but, with a view of manifesting how innocently I forfeited that happy situation, and incurred the misery of my present state. While I passed my time in these occupations, my retirement was such as almost equalled that of a nunnery; being seen by no body, as I thought, but the servants of the family; for, I went to mass early in the morning, accompanied by my mother and the maids; and veiled with such reserve, that my eyes scarce beheld the ground on which I trod; yet, nevertheless, I was perceived by those of love, or rather libertinism, which even exceeds the lynx in penetration, and then possessed the faculties of Don Fernando, younger son of the duke whom I have already mentioned."

She no sooner mentioned the name of Don Fernando, than Cardenio changed colour, and began to sweat with such agitation, that the curate and barber perceiving it, were afraid he would be seized with one of those fits of distraction which, as they had heard, assaulted him from time to time: but, after some drops of sweat had burst out upon his skin, he remained quiet, and looking earnestly at the farmer's fair daughter, immediately guessed who she was; while she, without observing the emotions of Cardenio, went on with her story, in these words: "And he no sooner beheld me, than, as he afterwards protested, he deeply felt the power of love, which indeed his behaviour clearly evinced: but, to shorten the account of my misfortune, which is lengthened beyond all comfort, I will pass over in silence, the industrious schemes that Don Fernando planned, for opportunities of declaring his passion: he bribed every servant in the family, and even made presents and proffers of service to my relations: there was nothing but gaiety and rejoicing all day long in our street; and all night, it was impossible to sleep for serenades. The letters which, thro' an unknown channel, came to my hand, were without number, filled with the most amorous flights and professions, and vows and promises in every line: but, all these efforts, far from soothing, hardened me against him, as much as if he had been my mortal foe; and all the stratagems he practised, in order to subdue my coyness, had a quite contrary effect: not, that I was disgusted at the gallantry of Don Fernando, or enraged at his importunities; for, I felt a certain kind of pleasure, in being courted and beloved by such a noble cavalier: neither did I take umbrage at seeing myself praised in his letters; for, it is my opinion, that all women, let them be never so homely, are pleased to hear themselves celebrated for beauty: but, to all these artifices, I opposed my own virtue, together with the repeated advices of my parents, who plainly perceived the passion of Don Fernando; because he himself took

no care to conceal it from the world. They assured me, that in my virtue and prudence alone, they confided and deposited their own honour and reputation: they bade me consider the inequality between Don Fernando and me, which was a convincing proof that his love, tho' he himself asserted the contrary, tended more to his own gratification than my advantage; and said, if I could throw any obstruction in his way, to make him quit his unjust pretensions, I should be married immediately, according to my own choice, either to one of the principal persons of our own town, or to some gentleman in the neighbourhood, as I had abundance of lovers, attracted by their wealth and my reputation. With these assurances, the truth of which I could not doubt, I fortified my integrity, and would never send any reply to Don Fernando, that could in the most distant manner, flatter him with the hope of accomplishing his wish: but, all my reserve, which he ought to have looked upon as the effect of disdain, served only to whet his libidinous appetite, which is the true name of the passion he professed; for, had it been genuine love, you would not now be listening to my story, which I should have had no occasion to recount.

"In fine, Don Fernando got notice that my parents intended to bestow me in marriage, that they might deprive him of all hope of possessing me, or, at least, provide me with more guards to protect my virtue; and this piece of news alarmed him so much, that he put in practice an expedient to retard the dreaded match. One night, while I sat in my apartment, attended by my maid only, the doors being all fast locked, that thro' negligence my virtue might not be in danger, without knowing or comprehending the means of his conveyance, he appeared before me, in the midst of this reserve, precaution, solitude, silence and retreat! At sight of him, I was so much confounded, that the light forsook my eyes, and my tongue denied it's office; so that being deprived of the power of utterance, I could not cry for help, neither, I believe, would he have suffered me to exclaim; for, he instantly seized me in his arms, my confusion being such, that I had not strength to defend myself, and began to pour forth such protestations, that I cannot conceive how falsehood is able to ape truth so exactly. The traitor's tears gave credit to his words, and his sighs confirmed the honesty of his intention. I being a poor young creature by myself, altogether unexperienced in those affairs, began, I know not how, to believe his false professions; but, not so as to be moved to weak compassion, either by his vows or artful sorrow; on the contrary, my first surprise being over, I recollected my dissipated spirits, and with more courage than I thought myself possessed of, said to him, 'Signor, if, instead of being within your arms, as I now am, I was in the paws of a fierce lion, and my deliverance entirely depended upon my doing or saying any thing prejudicial to my virtue, it would be as impossible for me to comply with these terms, as it is impossible for that which is, to lose its existence: wherefore, tho' you keep my body confined within your arms, I am in full possession of my soul, with all her chaste desires, which are intirely opposite to yours, as you will plainly perceive, if you resolve to proceed in gratifying your wishes by force. I am your vassal, but not your slave: the nobility of your blood neither has, nor ought to have, the power of dishonouring or despising the lowliness of mine; and my character is as precious to me, tho' I am but a plebeian farmer's daughter, as yours can be to you, who are a nobleman and cavalier. All your strength shall not effect your purpose; neither am I to be influenced by your riches,

deceived by your words, or melted by your sighs and tears. Any of these expressions in a man, to whom my parents should give me in marriage, would gain my consent and reciprocal inclination; nay, if my honour were safe, I could sacrifice my satisfaction, and voluntarily yield what you, signor, now attempt to obtain by force: this I observe, that you may rest assured, I will never grant any favour to him who is not my lawful spouse.'"

"'If that be your sole objection, charming Dorothea' (for, that is the name of this wretched creature), said the perfidious cavalier, 'behold I here present my hand, in pledge, of being yours for ever; and may heaven, from which nothing is concealed, together with that image of the blessed virgin, bear witness to the sincerity and truth of this declaration.'" Cardenio, when she called herself Dorothea, was surprised anew, and confirmed in his first conjecture; but, unwilling to interrupt the story in which he expected to hear the issue of what he already knew, he only said, "Is your name Dorothea, madam? I have heard of one of that name, to whose misfortunes yours bear a great resemblance: but pray proceed; the time will come when I shall tell you such things as will equally excite your terror and affliction." Dorothea, surprised at the discourse of Cardenio, as well as at his strange and ragged attire, intreated him, if he knew any thing of her affairs, to communicate it immediately; saying, that if fortune had left her any thing of value, it was the courage to endure any disaster that might befall her; tho' she was almost certain, that what she had already suffered, could admit of no addition. "Madam," replied Cardenio, "I would not be the means of impairing that fortitude, by telling you what I know, if my conjecture be right; neither is there any opportunity lost, nor is it of any consequence to you, whether you hear it or not." "Be that as it will," answered Dorothea, "I will go on with the sequel of my story. Don Fernando addressing himself to the image he found in my apartment, invoked the blessed virgin to bear witness to our nuptials, and avowed himself my husband with the most binding and solemn oaths: tho', before he proceeded so far, I desired him to reflect upon what he was going to do, and consider how much his father might be incensed at his conduct, when he should find him married to the daughter of his own farmer and vassal. I cautioned him against being blinded by my beauty, such as it was, telling him it would be far from being a sufficient excuse for his error; and begged, if he had any love and regard for me, he would manifest it, in leaving me to a fate more adequate to my rank and circumstances; observing, that such unequal matches were seldom blessed with a long duration of those raptures with which they begin.

"All these reflections I repeated to him, with many more which I do not remember; but, they had no effect in diverting him from the prosecution of his purpose; for, he was like a man who, in making a bargain, never boggles at the price of the commodity, because he never intends to pay it. At the same time, I held a short conference with my own breast, saying within myself, 'Neither shall I be the first, who by marriage, has risen from a low station, to rank and grandeur; nor will Don Fernando be the first nobleman whom beauty, or rather blind affection, hath induced to share his greatness with a partner of unequal birth. Since therefore, I neither make a new world nor a new custom, it is but reasonable in me to embrace this honour that fortune throws in my way; and altho' the affection he professes should not survive the accomplishment of his wish, I shall nevertheless, in the sight of God, remain his true and lawful wife. Besides, should I treat

him with disdain, I see he is determined to transgress the bounds of duty, and avail himself of force; in which case, I shall be dishonoured and inexcusable in the opinion of those who do not know how innocently I have incurred their censure; for, where shall I find arguments to persuade my parents, that this cavalier entered my apartment, without my knowledge and consent?'

"All these reflexions, which my imagination revolved in an instant, began to sway me towards that which (tho' I little thought so) proved my ruin; especially when aided and inforced by the oaths of Don Fernando, the powers he called to witness, the tears he shed, and, in short, by his genteel carriage and agreeable disposition, accompanied by such marks of real passion, as might have melted any other heart as soft and unexperienced as mine. I called my maid to be a joint evidence with the powers of heaven; Don Fernando repeated and confirmed his oaths; took other saints to witness his integrity; imprecated a thousand curses on his head, in case he should fail to fulfil his promise; had recourse to sighs and tears again, straining me still closer in his arms, from which he had never released me: by these means, and the departure of my maid, I forfeited that name, and he became a false and finished traitor.

"The morning that succeeded this night of my misfortune, did not arrive so soon, I believe, as Don Fernando could have wished; for, when once a man hath satisfied his rage of appetite, his chief inclination is to quit the scene of his success. This I observe, because Don Fernando seemed impatient to be gone, and, by the industry of my maid, who had conducted him to my chamber, found himself in the street before day: when he took his leave, he told me, tho' not with such violence of rapture as he had expressed on his first coming, that I might depend upon his honour, and the sincerity of the oaths he had sworn, as a further confirmation of which, he took a ring of value from his finger, and put it upon mine: in short, he vanished, leaving me in a situation which I can neither call joyful nor sad. This I know, that I remained in a state of confusion and perplexity, and, as it were, beside myself, on account of what had happened; but I either wanted courage or memory to quarrel with my maid for the perfidy she had been guilty of, in conducting Don Fernando to my apartment: indeed, I could not as yet determine, whether the adventure would redound to my advantage or misfortune. I told him, at parting, that now I was his wife, he might see me every night, by the same means he had used to procure this first interview, until he should think proper to make our marriage public: but, excepting the following night, I could never set eyes on him, either in the street or at church, during a whole month which I spent in the utmost anxiety of expectation; altho' I knew he was in town, and almost every day employed in the chace, an exercise to which he was greatly addicted. Those were doleful and distracting hours and days to me, for, then I began to doubt, and afterwards to disbelieve the faith of Don Fernando: then was my maid exposed to those rebukes for her presumption, which she had never heard before: then was I obliged to husband my tears, and wear composure on my countenance, that I might not give occasion to my parents, to ask the cause of my discontent; and be put to the trouble of inventing falsehoods to deceive them. But, all this constraint was banished by an event, the knowledge of which trod down all other respects, put an end to all my prudent measures, and by destroying my patience, published my misfortune to the world. This was no other than a report that soon after prevailed

in our town, by which I learned that Don Fernando was married, in a neighbouring city, to a young lady of exceeding beauty, and distinguished birth, tho' her parents could not give her a portion suitable to such a noble alliance. I understood her name was Lucinda, and that several surprising accidents had happened at their nuptials."

Cardenio hearing Lucinda's name, tho' he said nothing, shrugged up his shoulders, bit his lips, contracted the skin of his forehead, and discharged from his eyes two fountains of tears: but, notwithstanding, Dorothea continued her story, saying, "This melancholy piece of news no sooner reached my ears, than, instead of freezing, it inflamed my heart with such rage and fury, that I had well nigh run out into the streets, and published aloud the falsehood and treachery he had practised upon me: but, my rage was restrained for that time, by a plan which I conceived, and actually put in execution that very night. I dressed myself in this garb, which I received from one of the swains belonging to the house, to whom I disclosed my whole misfortune, intreating him to attend me to the city, where I understood my adversary was. After having disapproved of the attempt, and blamed my resolution, seeing me determined, he offered to keep me company, as he said, to the world's end: that moment I packed up my woman's dress in a pillow-case, together with some jewels and money, as a resource in time of need; and in the dead of that very night, without giving the least hint to my perfidious maid, left my father's house, and accompanied by my servant, and a thousand strange imaginations, set out for that city on foot, winged with the desire of finding Don Fernando; and resolved, tho' I could not prevent what was already done, to demand with what conscience he had done it.

"In two days and an half, I arrived at the city, and enquiring for the house of Lucinda's parents, the first person to whom I put the question, told me more than I desired to hear. He directed me to the house, and related every incident which had happened at his daughter's wedding; a story so public, that it was become the common town-talk. He said, that on the night of their nuptials, after she had pronounced the Yes, by which he became her husband, Lucinda was seized with a violent fit; that Don Fernando opening her breast to give her fresh air, found in it a paper written with her own hand, importing that she could not lawfully espouse Fernando, being already the wife of Cardenio, who, as the man told me, was one of the principal cavaliers of that town; and that she had now pronounced the fatal Yes, meerly because she would not swerve from the obedience she owed to her parents: in short, he said the contents of the paper plainly gave them to understand, that she intended to make away with herself, immediately after the ceremony, induced by the reasons which were there contained; and this resolution was confirmed by a poignard which they found concealed in some part of her dress. Don Fernando perceiving, by what happened, that Lucinda had baffled, scorned and undervalued his addresses, ran to her before she had recovered the use of her senses, and with the poignard they had found, would have stabbed her to the heart, had he not been prevented by her parents and the rest of the company. It was, moreover, reported that Don Fernando immediately retired; and that Lucinda continued in a fit, till next day. When she recovered from her swoon, she declared to her father and mother, that she was the true and lawful wife of that same Cardenio, who, it seems, was present at the ceremony; and who, when he saw her actually married, contrary to his former belief and firm ex-

pectation, quitted the city in despair, having first left a writing, that declared the wrong she had done him, and signified his intention, to banish himself for ever from the society of mankind. All this transaction was so notorious and public in the city, as to furnish discourse for every body; and the subject was not diminished when it was known, that Lucinda was not to be found either in her father's house, or in any other part of the town, which was searched all over by her parents, who had almost run distracted, not knowing what other method they should take to retrieve her. This information revived my hopes a little, for, I was better pleased to have missed Don Fernando than to have found him married to another; thinking, that every gate of comfort was not yet shut against me; and that heaven, perhaps, had thrown that impediment in the way of his second marriage, with a view of making him reflect upon what he owed to the first; and reminding him of his being a christian, consequently more interested in the care of his soul than in any other human concern. All these things I revolved in my imagination, and as I had no real comfort, consoled myself with the most feeble and distant hope, in order to support a life which I now abhor.

"While I remained in this city, undetermined what course to take, as I could not find Don Fernando; I heard a public cryer describe my person and dress, and offer a considerable reward to any one that should discover where I was. Nay, it was said, that I had seduced from my father's house, the young man who attended me; a circumstance that touched me to the very soul: finding my credit fallen so low, that they were not satisfied with publishing my escape, but, must needs also mention my attendant, a creature so mean and unworthy of my attention and regard; as soon as I heard myself proclaimed, I quitted the town, accompanied by my servant, who already began to give marks of staggering in his promised faith and fidelity; and that night, reached the most woody part of this mountain, urged by the fear of being discovered: but, as it is commonly observed, one mischance invites another, and the end of one misfortune is often the beginning of a worse; this was literally my case: my trusty servant, who had hitherto behaved with such zeal and fidelity, seeing me in this solitary place, and instigated by his own villainy, rather than any beauty of mine, attempted to avail himself of the opportunity which he thought this desart offered; and with great impudence, contempt of heaven, and disregard to me, began to talk of love; when, finding that I rejected his immodest proposals with just indignation and disdain, he laid aside intreaties for the use of those who might please to use them, and began to employ force for the accomplishment of his will: but, just heaven, who seldom or never abandons the righteous intention, favoured and assisted mine so effectually, that with the little strength I have, and no great trouble, I pushed him over a precipice, unknowing whether or not he survived the fall; then, as nimbly as my weariness and terror would allow, I penetrated farther into the mountain, without any other thought or intention, than that of keeping myself concealed from my father, and those whom he had employed to find me out.

"I know not how many months I have lived in this place, where I met with a grazier, who took me into his service, and carried me to his house, which stands in the very heart of the mountain. Him I have served all this time, in quality of a cowherd, endeavouring to be always in the field, that I might the more easily conceal that hair which hath now so unexpectedly discovered my sex: yet, all my care and industry were vain; for, my mas-

ter having found me out to be a woman, was seized with the same desire that took pos-
session of my own servant: but, fortune with the evil, does not always send the remedy;
for, I could neither find rock nor bog, by which I might have disabled my master, as
I had before punished my man; and therefore, as the least inconvenience, I have left
his house, and chosen to hide myself again among these thickets, rather than try my
strength against him, in defence of my innocence. I say, I returned to these woods, in
hopes of finding a place in which I might, without impediment, implore heaven with
sighs and tears, to have compassion upon my misery, and give me industry and grace to
overcome it, or quit my being in this solitude, without leaving behind me the least trace
or remembrance of this forlorn wretch, who, without any fault of her own, hath af-
forded so much matter for conversation and censure both at home and abroad."

## CHAPTER II.

### Of the beautiful Dorothea's discretion; with other pleasant and entertaining particulars.

"This, gentlemen, is the genuine detail of my tragic story: consider, therefore, and
judge whether or not, I have sufficient cause to heave more sighs than I have
vented, utter more complaints than you have heard, and shed more tears than have
flowed from mine eyes; and when you shall have deliberated upon the quality of my mis-
fortune, you will perceive how vain all consolation must be; as the disease admits of no
remedy. I only ask what you easily can, and ought to grant, namely, that you would in-
form me where I can pass my life, without being harrassed by the surprize and fear of
being found by those who are in search of me. For, though I am well assured, that my
parents, out of their great love and affection, would receive me again into their favour,
such is the shame and confusion I feel at the bare thought of their having altered their
opinion to my prejudice, that I would rather conceal myself from their sight for ever,
than appear in their presence, under the suspicion of having acted contrary to the ex-
pectations they entertained from my virtue." So saying, she left off speaking, and her
face was overspread with a blush that plainly denoted the sentiments and confusion of
her soul. Those who had heard her story, were equally surprized and afflicted at her mis-
fortune; to which the curate was going to offer some consolation and advice, when Car-
denio took her by the hand, saying, "It seems then, madam, you are the beauteous
Dorothea, only daughter of Cleonardo the rich!" She was astonished to hear her father's
name pronounced by one of such a miserable appearance; for we have already observed,
how wretchedly Cardenio was cloathed, and said to him, "And who are you, brother,
who know so well my father's name, which, if I remember aright, I have not once men-
tioned in the whole course of my unfortunate story?"

"I am," replied Cardenio, "that unfortunate man, to whom, as you have observed, Lu-

cinda said she was married. I am that miserable Cardenio, whom the villainy of him who reduced you to your present situation, hath brought to this deplorable condition in which you now see me, ragged, half-naked, destitute of all human comfort, and, which is still worse, deprived of my understanding, except at certain short intervals which I enjoy by the permission of heaven. I, Dorothea, am the person who was present at the perfidy of Don Fernando, and heard Lucinda pronounce the fatal Yes, by which she accepted him for a husband. I am he who wanted resolution to wait the issue of her swoon, or stay and see the result of that paper which was found in her bosom: for, my soul could not sustain the shock of such accumulated misfortune; and therefore, I quitted the house, already abandoned by my patience, and leaving a letter with my host, whom I charged to deliver it into Lucinda's own hand, betook myself to these desarts, with an intention here to finish the life which from that instant I have abhorred as my most inveterate foe. But, fate hath not been pleased to grant my wish, contenting itself with having deprived me of my judgment, with a view, perhaps, of reserving me for better fortune; which I begin to hope, may proceed from this lucky meeting with you, since, if that which you have recounted be true, as I believe it is, there is a possibility that heaven may have in store for us both, a more favourable termination of our disasters, than we imagined; for, supposing that Lucinda, who is already my wife, as she hath openly declared, cannot be married to Don Fernando, nor he lawfully wed her, being already espoused to you, I think we have room to hope, that heaven will one day, restore what mutually belongs to us; as it is neither alienated, ruined, nor irretrievable. And since this consolation still remains, sprung from hopes that are not very remote, and founded on expectations which are not the effects of a disordered imagination, I entreat you, madam, in the purity of your sentiments, to change your present resolution, as I intend to alter mine, and accommodate yourself to the hopes of better fortune; for, I swear upon the faith of a gentleman and a christian, that I will never abandon you, until I see you in the arms of Don Fernando, whom, if I cannot by reasonable arguments, bring to a true sense of his duty towards you, I will then use that privilege to which every gentleman is intitled, and, in single combat, demand satisfaction for the injury he has done you, without minding my own wrongs, which I will leave to the vengeance of heaven, that I may the sooner revenge yours upon earth."

This speech of Cardenio put an end to the surprize of Dorothea, who being at a loss how to thank him for his kind and generous offer, stooped in order to kiss his feet; but, this piece of condescension he would by no means allow. The priest answering for both, approved of Cardenio's declaration, and, in a particular manner, intreated, advised and persuaded them to accompany him to the village where he lived, in order to provide themselves with what they wanted; and there consult some scheme either for finding Don Fernando, or for carrying Dorothea back to her parents, or, in short, for doing that which should seem most necessary and convenient. Cardenio and Dorothea thanked him for his courteous offer, which they immediately embraced; and the barber, who had been silent and attentive all this time, having joined the curate in his compliments and hearty proffers of service, briefly recounted the cause which had brought them thither; namely, the strange madness of Don Quixote; observing, that they were then waiting for the return of his squire, whom they had sent in quest of his master. Cardenio immedi-

ately, as if it had been the faint impression of a dream, recollected and related the quar-
rel which had happened between the knight and him, though he could not remember
the cause of the dispute.

At that instant they heard and recognized the voice of Sancho, who not finding them
in the place where he had left them, hollowed aloud; upon which, they went to meet
him, and inquiring about Don Quixote, were told by the squire, that he found him
naked to the shirt, wan, meagre, half-famished, and sighing for his mistress Dulcinea;
that, when he (Sancho) told him she had commanded him to quit that place, and go im-
mediately to Toboso, where she waited with impatience to see him, he had answered,
that he was determined never to appear before her, until he should have performed such
atchievements as would render him worthy of her favour; and Sancho observed, that if
this resolution should hold, it was possible he might never attain to the rank of an em-
peror, as he was in duty bound, nor even to that of an archbishop, which was the least
he could expect. He desired them, therefore, to consider some means of disengaging the
knight from his solitude. The priest bad him be under no concern, for, they would fall
upon a method to remove his master, whether he would or no.

Then he explained to Cardenio and Dorothea, the plan they had laid, to cure Don
Quixote of his madness, or, at least, bring him back to his own house. This Dorothea no
sooner understood, than she told him, that she was more proper than the barber for act-
ing the part of the distressed damsel; especially, as she had cloaths along with her, that
would answer the purpose; and bad them trust to her, for representing every part of the
character, which should be necessary towards the success of their design; for, she had
read a great many books of chivalry, and was perfectly well acquainted with the stile in
which afflicted damsels were wont to beg boons of knights-errant. "If that be the case,"
said the curate, "let us not delay the execution of our scheme: for, without doubt, heaven
seems to favour my endeavours; not only, in opening a door, so unexpectedly, towards
the cure of your misfortunes, but also in making you subservient in facilitating our suc-
cess." Dorothea then pulled out of her pillow-case, a gown and petticoat of very rich
stuff, with a beautiful green mantelet, and opening a little casket, took out a rich neck-
lace and other jewels, with which she instantly dressed herself to such advantage, that
she appeared like a lady of the first rank and fortune. All these and other ornaments, she
said, she had carried off from her father's house, in case of what might happen; though
hitherto, she had met with no opportunity of using them. Every one present was
charmed with her graceful mien, easy deportment, and exceeding beauty; and passed
sentence on Don Fernando, as a person of little taste and discernment, for having aban-
doned such excellence. But, the admiration of Sancho was superior to that of all the rest;
for, he actually thought, and indeed it was true, that in all the days of his life, he had
never seen such a beautiful creature; and accordingly, asked the curate, with great ea-
gerness, who that handsome lady was, and what she looked for in these by-places.
"Friend Sancho," answered the curate, "that handsome lady, to say no more of her, is
heiress, in the direct male line, of the kingdom of * Micomicon, come hither to beg as a
boon of your master, that he would redress a wrong and grievance done to her by a dis-

* As if he had said Ape-land: *Mico* signifying an ape.[1]

courteous giant: for, such is the fame and reputation of that excellent knight Don Qui-
xote, through the whole extent of Guinea, as to induce this princess to come from
thence in quest of him." "Blessed quest!" cried Sancho, "and happy finding, say I! espe-
cially, if my master should be so fortunate as to right the wrong, and redress the griev-
ance, by killing that son of a whore of a giant that your worship mentions: and kill him
he certainly will, if they should once meet, provided he be not a phantome; for, you must
know, my master has no power over phantomes. But, one thing among many others, I
must beg of you, Mr. Licentiate, and that is, to put my master out of conceit of an arch-
bishopric, for, I am afraid his inclination leans that way, and advise him to marry this
princess out of hand, a match which will make it impossible for him to receive holy or-
ders; and therefore he will the more easily arrive at the seat of empire, and I at the end
of my wish. For, I have carefully considered the affair, and by my reckoning, I shall not
find my account in his being an archbishop, as I am altogether unfit for the church, by
reason of my being married; and for me, who have a wife and children, to be petition-
ing for dispensations to hold livings, would be an endless task. Wherefore, signor, the
point is this: let my master immediately take to wife that same lady, whose name I do
not know; for, indeed, I never saw her grace before this blessed minute." "She is called
the princess Micomicona," replied the curate, "because, her kingdom being Micomicon,
'tis plain her name must be Micomicona." "Yes, to be sure," said Sancho, "I have known
several people take a sirname and addition from the place of their nativity, calling them-
selves, for example, Pedro d'Alcala; Juna de Ubeda, Diego de Valladolid; and I suppose
they have the same custom in Guinea, where the queens take their names from the king-
doms they rule." The priest confirmed Sancho's opinion, and promised to use his utmost
influence to promote the marriage of the knight. With this assurance Sancho rested as
much satisfied as the other was surprized at his simplicity, when he perceived how care-
fully he cherished, in his imagination, the same extravagant whims that possessed his
master, who, he firmly believed, would one day become an emperor.

By this time, Dorothea being mounted on the curate's mule, and the barber's face ac-
commodated with the ox's tail, by way of beard, they desired Sancho to guide them to
the place where Don Quixote was, and cautioned him against pretending to know the
licentiate and his companion, assuring him that his master's becoming an emperor en-
tirely depended upon his professing ignorance of their persons. Yet neither the curate
nor Cardenio would accompany them; because the presence of this last might recal to
the knight's memory, the quarrel which had happened between them; and it was not yet
proper that the priest should appear: for which reasons, they let the rest proceed by
themselves, and they followed at a small distance, after the curate had given her cue to
Dorothea, who desired him to make himself perfectly easy on her account; for, she
would act the part assigned to her, without having the least occasion for a prompter, in
the true stile and spirit of knight-errantry.

Having travelled about three quarters of a league, they discovered Don Quixote al-
ready cloathed, though still unarmed, sitting in the midst of a labyrinth of rocks, and
Dorothea no sooner understood it was he, in consequence of Sancho's information,
than she whipt up her palfrey, close attended by the well-bearded barber, who, when she
approached the knight, threw himself from his mule, and ran to help his lady to alight.

But, she, dismounting with great agility, went and fell upon her knees before Don Quixote, whom, in spite of his repeated endeavours to raise her, she accosted in these words:

"Never will I rise from this posture, most valiant and invincible knight, until your benevolence and courtesy grant me a boon, which will not only redound to the honour and applause of your own person, but also to the advantage of the most injured and disconsolate damsel that ever the sun beheld; and, if the valour of your mighty arm corresponds with the voice of your immortal fame, you are obliged to favour the unfortunate, who, attracted by the odour of your celebrated name, come from far distant regions, in quest of your assistance." "Beauteous lady," replied Don Quixote, "I will not answer one word; nor hear one circumstance of your affairs, until you rise from the ground." "I will not rise, signor," answered the afflicted damsel, "until I shall have obtained from your condescension, the boon I beg." "I condescend and grant it," resumed the knight, "provided in so doing, I act neither to the detriment nor derogation of my king, my country, and her who holds my heart and liberty enslaved *." "Your compliance, worthy signor," replied the mourning lady, "shall in no ways affect the exceptions you have made."

At that instant Sancho, came up, and whispered softly in his master's ear; "Your worship may safely grant the boon she asks, which is a meer trifle; no more than slaying a giantish sort of a fellow; and she who begs it, is the high and mighty princess Micomicona, queen of the great empire of Micomicon in AEthiopia." "Whosoever she is," answered Don Quixote, "I will do what I am in duty bound to perform, and act according to the dictates of my own conscience, and conformable to the order I profess." Then turning to Dorothea, "Rise, most beautiful lady," said he, "the boon you ask is granted." "Then, what I ask is this," resumed the damsel, "that your magnanimity would immediately accompany me to the place from whence I came, and promise to attempt no other adventure, nor grant any other request, until you shall have taken vengeance on a traitor who hath usurped my crown, contrary to all right human and divine." "I grant your request, madam," answered Don Quixote: "henceforth you may dispel that melancholy with which you are depressed, and let your fainting hope resume new strength and vigour; for, with the assistance of God and this my arm, you shall, in a short time, see yourself restored to your kingdom, and seated on the throne of your royal ancestors, in defiance and despite of all those evil-designing persons who mean to oppose you: let us set hands to the work then, for, according to the common observation, Delay breeds danger."

* When a knight had once granted a boon in this manner, it was impossible for him to retract, let the request be never so extravagant. We are told by Joinville, that the queen of St. Lewis, being big with child, and in the utmost terror of falling alive into the hands of the infidels at Damietta in Ægypt, fell upon her knees before an old knight turned of fourscore, and conjured him to grant her boon: The old man having promised to comply, on the faith of his knighthood, she told him the favour she so pressingly sollicited, was, that he would cut off her head, before she should fall into the hands of the enemy, provided the Saracens should become masters of the town. The senior answered without hesitation, that she might depend upon his sword; and owned he had taken that resolution even before she signified her request.[2]

*Vol.1. Nº 9. Page 211.*

*F. Hayman inv. et Pinx.*                                                    *G. Scotin Sculp.*

Dorothea Received by Don Quixote as the Princess Micomicona.

The distressed damsel struggled with great perseverance, to kiss his hand; but, Don Quixote, who was in all respects a well-bred knight, would by no means allow such humiliation; on the contrary, raising her up, he embraced her with great politeness and cordiality, ordering Sancho to secure Rozinante's girths, and help him to arm with all expedition. The squire taking down the armour, which hung on a tree, in the manner of a trophy, and adjusting the horse's girths, in a twinkling, equipped his master, who finding himself armed, "Now," said he, "let us go, in the name of God, to the assistance of this high-born lady." The barber, who was all this time on his knees, at infinite pains to preserve his gravity and his beard, the fall of which, perhaps, would have utterly ruined their laudable design, when he found the boon was granted, and saw with what eagerness the knight undertook to fulfil it, rose up, and, with the assistance of Don Quixote, helped his lady upon her mule again; then her protector bestrode Rozinante, and he himself mounted his own beast, while Sancho Panza being left on foot, felt the loss of Dapple, anew: but, this he contentedly bore, believing that his master was now in the right road, and almost at the very point of being an emperor; for, he assured himself that the knight would wed that princess, and so become king of Micomicon at least: the only uneasiness he felt, was, on account of that kingdom's being in the land of negroes, so that all his servants and vassals must be black; but, his imagination supplied him with a remedy for this inconvenience, and he said within himself, "Suppose my vassals are negroes, what else have I to do, but transport them to Spain, where I can sell them for ready money, with which I may purchase some title or post that will maintain me, at my ease, all the days of my life! No, to be sure, sleep on, void of all invention or ability to dispose of your ware, and sell thirty or ten thousand slaves in the turning of a straw. Before God! I'll make them fly, little and big, or just as I may; and, blacks as they are, turn them all into whites and yellows. Let me alone to suck my own fingers." With these conceits he was so much engrossed, and so well satisfied, that he actually forgot the pain of travelling on foot.

Cardenio and the curate saw every thing that passed from behind some rushes where they were hid, and could fall upon no method of joining them conveniently, until the priest, who was an excellent schemer, thought of an expedient for the purpose: having a pair of scissars about him, he cut off the beard of Cardenio, with infinite dispatch, and giving him a grey jacket, with his own black cloak, he himself remaining in his doublet and hose, the tattered cavalier was so much altered in point of appearance, that he would scarce have known himself had he looked in a glass. Although the others were jogging on, while they disguised themselves in this manner, they easily reached the highway, before the knight and his company, whose beasts were retarded by the bushes and rockyness of the ground: and taking their station just at the mouth of the entrance to the mountain, no sooner perceived the knight and his attendants come forth, than the curate looked earnestly at him a good while, as if he had been recollecting a person whom he knew, then ran to him with open arms, crying aloud, "Blessed be this meeting with the mirror of chivalry, my worthy compatriot Don Quixote de la Mancha, the flower and cream of gentility, the protector and physician of the distressed, and quintessence of knights-errant!" So saying, he embraced the left knee of Don Quixote, who being astonished at the words and action of the man, began to consider his features with great

attention, and at length, recollecting him, was struck dumb with admiration, at seeing him in that place, and made many efforts to alight, which when the priest opposed, "Give me leave, Mr. Licentiate," said he, "it is not seemly, that I should remain on horseback, when such a reverend person as you travels on foot." "I will, by no means," answered the curate, "consent to your alighting; since, on horseback, your mighty arm hath atchieved the greatest exploits and adventures that this age hath seen: it shall suffice for me, who am but an unworthy priest, to get up, with permission, behind this gentleman who travels in your worship's company; and then I shall imagine myself mounted upon Pegasus, a Zebra, or that fiery courser that carried the famous moor Muzaraque, who still lies enchanted in the vast mountain Zulema, at a little distance from the great Compluto." "I did not think of that expedient, Mr. Licentiate," resumed the knight, "but, I know that my lady the princess will, out of regard to me, be pleased to order her squire to accommodate you with the saddle of his mule, and he himself may ride upon the crupper, if the beast will carry double." "I believe she will," said the princess; "and I am sure, there will be no occasion to lay my commands upon my squire, who is too courteous and polite, to suffer an ecclesiastic to travel on foot, when it is in his power to provide him with a beast." "Your majesty is in the right," answered the barber, who instantly alighting, complimented the curate with the saddle, which was accepted without much intreaty.

But, the misfortune was, when the squire attempted to get up behind, the mule, which was an hireling, consequently mischievous, lifted up her hind legs, and kicked with such fury, that had they lighted on the head or breast of Mr. Nicholas, he would have had reason to curse the hour on which he set out in quest of Don Quixote: such, however, was his confusion, that he came to the ground, and his beard being neglected, fell off; so that he could find no other method to prevent a discovery, than to clap both hands to his face, with great expedition, and roar out that his teeth were demolished. Don Quixote, seeing that huge mass of beard torn from the jaw, without blood, and lying at a good distance from the squire's face; "Good heavens!" cried he, "what a wonderful phaenomenon is this! the beard is taken off and shaved as clean by the heel of the mule, as if it had been done by the hand of a barber." The curate, seeing the risk he ran of being detected in his scheme, snatched up the tail, and running with it to Mr. Nicholas, who still lay bellowing for help, pulled his head to his breast with one jerk, and clapping it on again, muttered some words, which he said, were an infallible charm for fixing on beards, as they should presently see; accordingly, when the affair was adjusted, he quitted the squire, who now seemed as well bearded and as sound as ever: a circumstance that, above measure, surprized the knight, who begged, that the curate, at a proper opportunity, would impart to him the charm which, he imagined, must contain more virtues than that of cementing beards; because it was plain, that where the hair was torn off, the skin and flesh must be lacerated and hurt; and if the application could heal these wounded parts, it was good for something more than meer mustachios. The curate confirmed his conjecture, and promised to disclose the secret to him, with the first proper opportunity: then it was agreed, that the priest should mount the mule by himself, and, with the other two, ride her by turns, until they should arrive at the inn, which was about two leagues off.

Don Quixote, the princess, and the curate being thus mounted, and Cardenio, the barber, and Sancho Panza following on foot, the knight told the damsel, that her highness might conduct him whithersoever she pleased; but, before she could make any reply, the priest interposed, saying, "Towards what kingdom is your majesty journeying? I am much mistaken in my notions of kingdoms, if you are not bound for Micomicon?" She, who had been well instructed in her cue, concluding, that she must answer in the affirmative, said, "Yes, signor, that is the place of my destination." "Then you must pass through our village," answered the curate, "and take your route to Carthagena, where your highness may happily embark, and if you meet with no hurricane, but be favoured with a fair wind and smooth sea, in something less than nine years, you may get sight of that vast lake Meona, I mean Meotis, which is a little more than one hundred days journey from your majesty's kingdom." "Your worship must be mistaken," said the princess, "for, two years are not yet elapsed, since I set out from thence; and though the weather has been always bad, I have already obtained what I so much longed after, namely, the sight of signor Don Quixote de la Mancha, whose fame reached mine ears, as soon as I landed in Spain, and induced me to come in quest of him, that I might sollicit his courtesy, and trust my righteous cause to the valour of his invincible arm." "Enough, madam," said Don Quixote; "spare your encomiums; for, I am an utter enemy to all sorts of adulation; and although you are not to be suspected of flattery, my chaste ears are always offended at that kind of discourse. What I can safely affirm, is this: Whether I have valour or not, here is he, valiant or pusillanimous, who will exert himself to the last drop of his blood, in the service of your highness. But, this apart; pray, Mr. Licentiate, what cause hath brought you hither alone, where I am really astonished to find you so ill attended, and so slightly cloathed."

"In that particular you shall soon be satisfied," answered the curate: "your worship must know that I and our friend Mr. Nicholas the barber, set out for Sevil, to recover a sum of money, which was sent to me by a relation of mine that went to the Indies, a good many years ago: no less than sixty thousand pieces of eight in good silver, which make no inconsiderable sum; and yesterday, passing through this place, we were set upon by four highwaymen, who stripped us even to our very whiskers, and that in such a manner as obliged the barber to wear artificial ones; and you may see, pointing to Cardenio, how they have despoiled the face of this young man who accompanied us; and the cream of the story is, that, according to the public report, which prevails in this neighbourhood, those who robbed us were galley-slaves, that, almost in this very place, were set at liberty by a man so valiant, as to let them all loose, in spite of the commissary and his guards. Without all doubt, he must have been deprived of his senses, or as great a villain as any of those he freed, or some person void of all conscience and feeling, who could thus turn loose the wolf among the lambs, the fox among the poultry, and the flies among the honey-pots; defrauding justice, and rebelling against his king and rightful sovereign, by acting contrary to his just commands, in depriving the gallies of their hands, and putting in confusion the holy brotherhood, which hath continued so many years in undisturbed repose: in short, he hath done a deed that may tend to the perdition of his own soul as well as body."

Sancho had before, recounted to them, the adventure of the galley-slaves, which he

had atchieved with so much glory; and therefore, the curate urged it home, in order to observe the behaviour of Don Quixote, who changed colour at every word, without daring to own himself the deliverer of that worthy crew. "Those," added the priest, "were the persons who rifled us; and God of his infinite mercy forgive the man who prevented the punishment they so richly deserved."

## CHAPTER III.

The pleasant artifice practised to extricate our enamoured knight from the most rigorous penance he had imposed upon himself.

Scarce had the curate pronounced this apostrophe, when Sancho blundered out, "Then, in good faith, Mr. Licentiate, he who performed this exploit was no other than my master; not, that I neglected to tell and advise him beforehand, to consider what he was about, and think what a sin it would be to let loose those who were going to the gallies, for the most grievous enormities." "You blockhead," cried Don Quixote incensed, "it neither concerns, nor belongs to knights-errant, to examine whether the afflicted, the enslaved and oppressed, whom they meet on the highway, are reduced to these wretched circumstances by their crimes, or their misfortunes; our business is only to assist them in their distress, having an eye to their sufferings, and not to their demerits. I chanced to light upon a string of miserable and discontented objects, in behalf of whom, I acted according to the dictates of my religion, without minding the consequence; and he who takes umbrage at what I have done, saving the sacred character and honourable person of Mr. Licentiate, is, I insist upon it, utterly ignorant of chivalry, and lies like the base-born son of a whore; and this assertion I will make good with my sword, in the most ample manner." So saying, he fixed himself in the stirrups, and cocked his beaver; the barber's bason, which he mistook for Mambrino's helmet hanging useless at the saddle-bow, until the damage it received from the galley-slaves could be repaired.

Dorothea, who was equally prudent and witty, understanding that every body present, except Sancho, diverted themselves with the extravagant humour of Don Quixote, was willing to have her share of the entertainment, and accordingly, perceiving that his indignation was raised, "Sir knight," said she, "I hope your worship will remember your promise to me, by which, you are restricted from engaging in any other adventure, howsoever pressing it may be. Subdue your resentment therefore, and be assured, that had Mr. Licentiate known the galley-slaves were set at liberty by that invincible arm, he would have taken three stitches in his mouth, and bit his tongue three times, rather than have uttered one word that should redound to the prejudice of your worship." "That I swear I would have done," said the curate, "ay, and have plucked off one of my whiskers to boot." "Madam," answered the knight, "I am silent. I will restrain the just indignation

which begins to rise within me, and proceed in the utmost peace and quiet, until I shall have fulfilled the boon I promised to your highness: but, in recompence for this my kind intention, I beseech you, if it be not too much trouble, to make me acquainted with the nature of your misfortune; and tell me the number, quality and condition of those persons on whom I am to take just satisfaction and full vengeance, in your behalf." "With all my heart," answered Dorothea, "tho' I am afraid of tiring you with a recital of my woes and misfortunes." The knight assured her, that would be impossible; and she resumed, "Well then, be so good as to favour me with your attention."

At these words, Cardenio and the barber went up close to her, in order to hear what story she, in her discretion, would invent; and Sancho Panza, who was as much deceived as his master, followed their example. After she had seated herself firmly in the saddle, cleared her pipes with a hem or two, and made other preliminary gestures, she, with great sprightliness, thus began:

"In the first place, gentlemen, you must know, that my name is——" Here she made a full stop, having forgot how the curate had christened her: but, this defect was soon remedied; for, immediately conceiving the cause of her hesitation, he said, "It is no wonder, madam, that your highness is disturbed and disordered at the recollection of your misfortunes, which are often so great, as to impair the memory to such a degree, that the afflicted cannot even remember their own names: this effect they have had upon you, madam, who have forgot that you are the princess Micomicona legitimate heiress of the great kingdom of Micomicon. With the assistance of this hint, your highness will easily recal the whole thread of your story, to your sorrowful remembrance." "You are in the right," replied the damsel; "and I believe I shall be able to bring my true narrative to a happy conclusion, without further prompting.

"The king, my father, whose name was Tinacrio the sage, foresaw, by his profound skill in magic, that my mother, who was called queen Zaramilla, would die before him, and that, as he himself must quit this life soon after, I should be left an helpless orphan: but, this consideration, he said, did not give him so much pain and confusion, as the certain foreknowledge, that a monstrous giant, lord of a great island that bordered on our kingdom, called Pandafilando of the gloomy aspect: (for, it is affirmed, that altho' his eyes are, like any other person's, placed in the middle of his face, he always looks askance, as if he squinted; and this obliquity the malicious tyrant practises, in order to surprise and intimidate those who behold him:) I say, my father foresaw by his art, that this giant, informed of my being an orphan, would invade me with a great army, and deprive me of my whole kingdom, without leaving so much as a village for my retreat; and that nothing could prevent this ruin and misfortune, unless I would consent to marry him: tho', so far as he could learn, it would never come into my thoughts, to make such an unequal match: and truly his conjecture was well founded; for, it never entered into my head, to wed this giant, or other person, howsoever tall and unmeasurable he might be. My father, therefore, advised me, that when, after his death, I should get notice that Pandafilando was beginning to invade my kingdom; I should not stay to put myself in a posture of defence, which would prove my destruction, but, freely leave him the possession of my realms, if I was resolved to avoid my own death, and to prevent the total destruction of my good and faithful subjects; for, it would be impossible to defend my-

self against the infernal force of the giant: but, that I should immediately set out for Spain, where I would find a remedy for all my misfortunes, in the person of a certain knight-errant, whose fame would be, at that time, spread over the whole kingdom, and whose name, if I right remember, would be Don Hacksot or Kicksot."[1] "Don Quixote, your ladyship would say," cried Sancho interposing, "alias the knight of the rueful countenance." "The very same," replied Dorothea; "he told me moreover, that this knight would be a tall man, with a long meagre visage, and have on his right side, below his left shoulder, or thereabouts, a grey mole garnished with hairs, which bear some resemblance to a hog's bristles."

Don Quixote hearing this circumstance, said to his squire, "Come hither, son Sancho, and help me to strip; for, I want to see if I am actually the knight of whom that sage king foretold." "Why should your worship strip?" said Dorothea. "In order to satisfy myself about that mole which your royal father mentioned." "You need not give yourself that trouble," said Sancho, "I know your worship hath just such a mole on the middle of your back-bone, which is a sign of strength." "That assurance is sufficient," resumed Dorothea, "for, among friends, we ought not to stand upon trifles; and it is of very little consequence whether the mole be upon the shoulder or the back-bone; provided there is really such a mark on any part of your body, which is all composed of the same flesh: without doubt, my worthy father was right in every thing he prognosticated; and I have exactly followed his directions, in recommending my cause to the protection of signor Don Quixote, who is certainly the individual knight my father described; since his features correspond with his fame, which fills not only Spain, but, likewise the whole province of la Mancha *; for, scarce had I landed at Ossuna, than hearing of his vast exploits, my mind suggested that he must be the very person I came in quest of." "How could your highness," said Don Quixote, "land at Ossuna, which is not a sea-port."

Before she had time to make a reply, the curate took the task upon himself, saying, "The princess must mean, that after she landed at Malaga, Ossuna was the first place in which she heard of your worship." "That was my meaning," said Dorothea. "There is nothing more plain," answered the priest, "and now, your majesty may proceed." "I have nothing more to say," resumed the princess, "but that, at length, destiny has been so favourable to me, in my finding Don Quixote, I reckon, and look upon myself as queen again, and mistress of my whole realms, since out of his great courtesy and magnificence, he hath promised, in consequence of the boon I asked, to go with me, whithersoever I shall conduct him; and my intention is no other than to bring him face to face, with Pandafilando of the gloomy aspect, that he may, by putting him to death, restore me to the possession of that which he so unjustly usurps: and all this will literally happen, as it was prophesied by my worthy father Tinacrio the sage, who hath also left it written in Chaldean or Greek characters, for, I cannot read them, that if the knight mentioned in the prophecy should, after having cut off the giant's head, demand me in

---

* This is a diverting example of the Bathos, not unlike that anticlimax repeated in the art of sinking.[2]

Nor Alps, nor Appenines could keep us out,
Nor fortified redoubt!

marriage, I must instantly accept of him as my lawful husband, without the least hesita-tion, and give him immediate possession of my person and throne."

Don Quixote hearing this circumstance, cried, "What d'ye think now, friend Sancho? d'ye hear what passes? and did not I tell thee as much? Observe now, whether or not, we have not a queen to marry, and a kingdom to govern." "Adzookers! it is even so," cried the squire, "and plague upon the son of a whore who refuses to marry her, as soon as Mr. Pandahilado's weazond[3] is cut: then, what a delicate morsel the queen is! odd! I wish all the fleas in my bed were such as she!" So saying, he cut a brace of capers, with marks of infinite satisfaction, then running up, and taking hold of the bridle of Dorothea's mule, made her halt, while he, falling down on his knees before her, besought the princess to let him kiss her hand, in token of his receiving her as his queen and mistress. Which of the company could behold the madness of the master, and the simplicity of the man, without laughing! Dorothea actually gave him her hand, and promised to make him a grandee, as soon as, by the favour of heaven, she should be restored to the possession of her kingdom; and he thanked her in terms which redoubled the mirth of all present.

"This, gentlemen," added the damsel, "is my story, and nothing now remains, but to tell you, that of all the people who attended me when I left my own country, not one sur-vives, except this well-bearded squire; all the rest having perished in a dreadful storm that overtook us after we were within sight of land: he and I miraculously floated to the shore on two planks; and indeed the whole course of my life, as you may have observed in my narration, hath been full of mystery and wonder. If I have in any thing exceeded the bounds of credibility, or been less accurate than I ought, I hope you will impute it to that cause assigned by the Licentiate, in the beginning of my story, namely, the con-tinual and extraordinary affliction which often impairs the memory of the unfortunate." "But, mine shall not be impaired, most high and virtuous lady!" said Don Quixote, "by all the misfortunes I shall undergo in your service, let them be never so great and un-precedented: therefore, I again confirm the boon I have promised, and swear to attend you even to the world's end, until I get sight of that ferocious adversary of yours, whose proud head I hope to slice off, with the assistance of God, my own arm, and the edge of this (I will not say good) sword; thanks to Gines de * Passamonte who run away with my own": (this last apostrophe he muttered between his teeth, and then proceeded, aloud, saying) "And after I shall have deprived him of his head, and put you in peaceable pos-session of your throne, you shall be at free liberty to dispose of your person, according to your own will and pleasure; for, while my memory is engrossed, my will enslaved, and my understanding subjected to her who——I say no more, but, that it is impossible I should incline, or have the least thought towards marrying any other person, tho' she were a perfect phoenix."

Sancho was so much disgusted at this last declaration of his master, refusing the mar-riage, that raising his voice, he cried, with great indignation, "Signor Don Quixote, I vow and swear your worship is crazy, else you would never boggle at marrying such a

* If the knight was robbed of his own sword by Gines; where did he find that which he wore on this occasion?[4]

high-born princess as this! Do you imagine that fortune will offer such good luck at every turn, as she now presents? or pray, do you think my lady Dulcinea more handsome than the princess? I am sure she is not half so beautiful, and will even venture to say, that she is not worthy to tie her majesty's shoe-strings. How the plague shall I ever obtain the earldom I expect, if your worship goes thus a fishing for mushrooms at sea?[5] Marry her, marry her, in the devil's name, without much ado; lay hold on this kingdom that drops, as it were, into your hand; and, after your coronation, make me a marquis or lord lieutenant, and then the devil, if he will, may run away with the rest."

Don Quixote was enraged, when he heard such blasphemies uttered against his mistress Dulcinea, and lifting up his lance, without speaking a syllable, or giving the least notice of his intention,[6] discharged two such hearty blows upon the squire, as brought him instantly to the ground, and had not Dorothea called aloud, and begged of him to forbear, would certainly have murdered poor Sancho on the spot. "Do you think, (said he, after some pause) you plebeian scoundrel, that I will always stand with my hands in my pockets; and that there is nothing to be done, but for you to misbehave, and for me to forgive you? I'll teach you better manners, you excommunicated rascal, for such to be sure you are, else you would not wag your tongue against the peerless Dulcinea. Don't you know, you grovelling beggarly villain, that were it not for the valour with which she inspires this arm, I should not have enough to kill a flea? Tell me, you viperish scoffer, what you think hath won this kingdom, cut off the giant's head, and made you a marquis, for all this I look upon as already done and determined? Is it not the valour of Dulcinea that makes use of my arm as the instrument of her exploits? In me she fights and overcomes; in her I live, breathe, and have my being. O thou whoreson, ungrateful ruffian, who seest thyself raised from the dust of the earth, to the rank of nobility, and repayest the obligation by slandering thy benefactress."

Sancho, was not so roughly handled but he heard every syllable that his master spoke, and starting up as nimbly as he could, ran behind Dorothea's palfrey, from whence, he said to the knight, "Pray, Sir, if your worship is determined against marrying this great princess, is it not plain, that the kingdom cannot be yours; and if that be the case, what favours can you bestow upon me? this is what I complain of. I would your worship would, once for all, marry this queen, who is, as it were, rained down from heaven upon us; and then you may converse with my lady Dulcinea, according to the custom of some kings who keep concubines. As to the affair of beauty, I will not intermeddle, but, if the truth may be told, I like them both very well, tho' I never saw my lady Dulcinea in my life." "How! not seen her? blasphemous traitor!" cried Don Quixote; "have you not just brought a message from her?" "I say," answered Sancho, "that when I saw her, I had not an opportunity of examining the particulars of her beauty and good qualities one by one; but altogether, she pleased me very much." "Now, Sancho," said Don Quixote, "I exculpate thee, and thou must forgive what I did in my wrath; for, no man can command the first emotions of his passion." "That I can plainly perceive," answered the squire, "and therefore, the desire of speaking is always the first motion in me; and truly, when once my tongue begins to itch, I cannot for my blood keep it within my teeth." "For all that, friend Sancho," said the knight, "I would have you consider before you speak; for, tho' the pitcher goes often to the well——I need not mention what follows." "In good

time," replied the squire, "there is a God above, who sees the snare, and will judge which of us is most to blame; I in speaking, or your worship in doing evil." "Let there be no more of this, Sancho," said Dorothea, "but run and kiss your master's hand, and beg his pardon; and henceforth, set a better guard upon your praise, and disparagement: above all things, beware of saying any thing to the prejudice of that lady Tobosa, whom I know by nothing else than my inclination to serve her: and if you put your trust in God, you will not fail of acquiring some estate, by which you will live like a prince."

Sancho took her advice, and, hanging his head, went to beg a kiss of his master's hand, which was granted with great solemnity of deportment; nay, the knight gave him his blessing also, desiring he would attend him while he rode on a little before the rest of the company, that he might have a better opportunity of asking a few questions, and conversing with him about affairs of the utmost importance. Sancho obeyed the order, and the two having advanced a good way before the rest, "Since thy return," said Don Quixote, "I have had neither time nor convenience, to enquire about many particular circumstances of thy embassy, with the answer thou hast brought: and now, that fortune favours us with a fit opportunity, thou must not deny me the pleasure I shall receive from thy agreeable information." "Your worship," answered the squire, "may ask as many questions as you please: I shall make every thing come out as clear as it went in: but, I intreat your worship, dear Sir, not to be so revengeful for the future." "Why do'st thou call me revengeful?" said the knight. "Because," resumed the squire, "those blows I was just now honoured with, were more owing to the quarrel the devil picked between us, t'other night, than to any thing I said against my lady Dulcinea, whom I love and reverence as a relic, tho' she be not one, merely, because she appertains to your worship." "No more of these reflexions, on thy life," said Don Quixote; "else thou wilt give me fresh umbrage: I freely forgave thee at that time, and thou knowest, that, according to the common observation, Every new fault, deserves a new penance."

While this conversation passed between them, they perceived a man riding towards them on an ass; and, when he came a little nearer, discerned him to be a gypsie: but, Sancho Panza, who sent his soul abroad with his eyes, to examine every ass that appeared, no sooner beheld the rider, than he recognised Gines de Passamonte, and by the thread of the gypsie discovered the clue of his own ass; for, it was actually Dapple that carried Passamonte, who, for the better convenience of selling the beast, had disguised himself in the dress of a gypsie, whose language, with many others, he could speak as fluently as his mother tongue. Sancho saw and recollected him, and no sooner had he seen and recollected him, than he bellowed forth, "Ah villain Ginesillo! restore my goods—give me back the comfort of my life—rob me not of my heart's content—give me my ass—give me my darling—fly, thief—skip, robber; and seek not to preserve that which is none of thy own."

There was no need of all this exclamation and reproach; for, Gines leaped off at the first word, and at a pretty round trot, which might have passed for a gallop, made the best of his way, and vanished in a twinkling. Sancho running to his ass, embraced it with great affection, saying, "How hast thou been, my dear Dapple? my trusty companion and joy of my eyes!" Then kissed and caressed it as if it had been a christian; while Dapple very peaceably received these demonstrations of love and kindness, without an-

swering one word. The whole company wished him joy of his recovery; particularly Don Quixote, who assured him, that altho' he had retrieved Dapple, the promise of the three colts should not be annulled; and Sancho thanked him for his generosity.

While the master and man were conversing by themselves, the curate told Dorothea, that she had behaved with great discretion in her story, both with regard to the matter and brevity of it, as well as the resemblance it bore to those legends that are found in books of chivalry. She observed that she had employed a good part of her leisure time in reading such romances, but, being ignorant of the situation of different provinces and sea-ports, she had spoke at random, when she mentioned her landing at Ossuna. "I thought so," resumed the priest, and made all haste to adjust matters by what I said: "but, is it not very strange, to see with what facility this poor unfortunate gentleman swallows all those lies and fictions, meerly, because they are delivered in the stile and manner of his nonsensical books?" "So very strange and singular," said Cardenio, "that I question if there be any genius whatever so fertile as to frame such a character by the meer force of invention." "And what is a very remarkable circumstance," replied the curate, "waving those extravagancies which this worthy gentleman utters upon the subject of his disorder, he can discourse upon other topics with surprising ability, and appears to be a man of great knowledge and intellects: so that, if you do not touch upon chivalry, his hearers must look upon him as a person of excellent understanding."

While they were engaged in this conversation, Don Quixote proceeded in his with Sancho, to whom he said, "Come, friend Sancho, let us forget what is past, with regard to animosity, and tell me, without any ingredient of rancour and resentment, where and how you found Dulcinea? What was she doing? What did she say? What answer did she make? How did she look when she read my letter? Who transcribed it for her perusal? These particulars, and every other circumstance of the affair, which you think worthy to be known, asked and answered, I expect you will explain, without seeking to increase my pleasure with false additions, much less to diminish it by malicious omission." "Signor," answered Sancho, "if the truth must be told, no body transcribed the letter; because I had no letter to be transcribed." "That is very true," replied the knight; "for, two days after thy departure, I found the pocket-book in which it was written; a circumstance that gave me infinite pain, as I could not conceive what thou wouldst do, when the mistake should appear; indeed I always imagined thou wouldst have returned hither immediately upon the discovery." "That would certainly have been the case," said the squire, "if, when your worship read it to me, I had not retained it in my memory, so perfect as to be able to dictate it to a parish clerk, who, as I repeated, transcribed it so exactly, that he said, in all the days of his life, tho' he had read many letters of excommunication, he had never seen such a clever letter as yours." "And dost thou still retain it," said Don Quixote. "No, Sir," replied Sancho. "For, after I had put it into her hand, I thought there was no further occasion to retain it, and therefore let it slip out of my remembrance; or, if any part remains, it is that of the subterrene—I mean sovereign lady, and the conclusion, Yours till death, the knight of the rueful countenance; with about three hundred souls, and lives, and pigsnies, which I set down in the middle."

## CHAPTER IV.

The savoury conversation that passed between Don Quixote
and his squire Sancho Panza; with many other incidents.

"All this is pretty well; proceed," said Don Quixote: "how was that queen of beauty employed, when you arrived? I dare say, you found her stringing pearls, or embroidering some device for this her captive knight, with threads of gold." "No, truly," answered the squire; "I found her winnowing two bushels of wheat, in the yard." "Then you may depend upon it," resumed the knight, "the grains of that wheat, were converted into pearls by the touch of her hand: and didst thou observe, my friend, whether it was of the finer or common sort?" "Why neither," said Sancho, "it seemed to be as it were, red wheat." "But, since it was winnowed by her fair hands," answered Don Quixote, "I dare affirm, it will make the whitest bread in Spain. Go on with thy information. When the letter was delivered did she not kiss it, and place it upon the crown of her head, in token of respect? did she not perform some ceremony worthy of such a letter? pray how did she receive it?" "When I presented the letter," answered Sancho, "she was in a main hurry, winnowing a large heap of wheat that was in her sieve; and said to me, 'Friend, lay down the letter on that sack; for I can't pretend to read it, until I have made an end of my work.'" "Discreet lady!" cried the knight; "her intention certainly was to read it at her leisure, that she might recreate herself with the contents.—Proceed, Sancho—and while she was thus employed, what conversation passed between you? what questions did she ask concerning me? and what answers didst thou make? Recount the whole, without leaving one syllable untold."[1]

"She asked me no questions," replied the squire; "but, I told her, how I had left your worship doing penance for love of her, skipping among those rocks, naked from the waste, upwards, like a meer savage, sleeping on the bare ground; neglecting to eat your food like a christian, or to comb your beard like a decent man, but whining, and weeping, and cursing your fortune." "If you said I cursed my fortune, you misrepresented me," said Don Quixote; "for, I bless my fate, and will bless it all the days of my life, for having made me worthy to aspire to the love of such an high lady as Dulcinea del Toboso." "High indeed!" answered Sancho, "for, in faith she is a good hand taller than I am." "How, hast thou been measured with her, Sancho?" said the knight. "I'll tell you how," answered the squire; "while I was helping her to lay a load of corn upon an ass, we came so close together, that I could easily perceive she over-topped me by a full hand." "That may be true," said Don Quixote; "tho' her tallness is accompanied and adorned by a myriad of mental graces. But, this you will not deny, Sancho, that while you was so near her, your nostrils were regaled by a sabaean odour, an aromatic fragrance, a certain delicious sensation, for which there is no name. I mean a scent, a perfume, such as fills the shop of some curious glover." "All that I can say," answered Sancho, "is, that I was sensible of a sort of rammish smell, which I believe, was owing to her being in a muck sweat with hard work." "That is impossible," cried the knight; "thy sense must have been

depraved; or that smell must have proceeded from thy own body; for, I am perfectly well acquainted with the odour of that rose among briars, that lilly of the valley, that liquid amber." "It may be so," said Sancho: "I have often known such smells come from myself, as then seemed to come from my lady Dulcinea: but that is not to be wondered at; because, as the saying is, every fiend may stink of brimstone." "Well then," added Don Quixote, "she hath now winnowed the wheat, and sent it to the mill, how did she behave after she had read my letter." "The letter," answered Sancho, "was not read at all: for, as she could neither read nor write, she chose to rend and tear it to pieces, rather than give it to any body who might publish her secrets, in the village; saying, she was very well satisfied with the information I gave her, by word of mouth, concerning your worship's love for her, and the extraordinary penance I left you doing on her account. Finally, she bad me tell you, that she kissed your worship's hands, being much more desirous of seeing than writing to you, and therefore she intreated and commanded your worship, by these presents, to quit this desart, and leave off playing the fool, and forthwith set out on your journey to Toboso, provided that something else of greater importance should not happen; for, she longed very much for a sight of your worship: and laughed heartily when I told her, that you had taken the name of the knight of the rueful countenance. When I asked, if the Biscayan had been lately with her, she answered, 'Yes'; and that he was very much of a gentleman: but, when I inquired about the galley-slaves, she said, she had as yet, seen none of them."

"Hitherto, all goes well," said the knight; "but, pray tell me, what jewel she gave you at parting, for the news you had brought of me her lover; for, it is an ancient practice and custom among knights-errant and their mistresses, to bestow upon their squires, damsels or dwarfs, who bring them news of each other, some rich jewel, as a reward and acknowledgment for the message." "It may be so," said Sancho, "and I think it an excellent custom; but, that must have been in times past: for, in this age, it is customary to give nothing but a piece of bread and cheese, which was all the present I received from my lady Dulcinea, who reached it over the yard wall, when I took my leave; by this token, that the cheese was made of ewe's milk." "She is liberal to excess," said the knight; "and if she omitted giving thee a jewel, it must certainly have been owing to her not having any by her; but all in good time *: I shall see her soon, and then every thing will be set to rights. Yet, there is one thing, Sancho, which overwhelms me with astonishment. You seem to have travelled thro' the air; for, you have spent little more than three days in your journey; though Toboso is more than thirty leagues distant from hence. From this extraordinary expedition, I conjecture, that the sage, who is my friend, and interests himself in my affairs, and such there certainly is, and must be, else I should be no true knight-errant: I say, this enchanter must have assisted thee in thy journey, tho' thou didst not perceive it; for, some there are of that class, who will take up a knight-errant while he is asleep in his bed, and without his knowing any thing of the matter, he shall awake next morning in some place more than a thousand leagues from the house where he took up his lodging the night before; and without such sudden transportations, it

---

* Literally, Sleeves are good even after Easter, i.e. Though a good thing comes late, it is never unseasonable.[2]

would be impossible for knights to succour each other in distress; as they frequently do. A knight-errant, for example, happens to be fighting in the desarts of Armenia, with some fierce dragon, dreadful goblin, or rival knight; and being worsted, and just at the point of being slain, behold, when he least expects it, there suddenly appears in a cloud or fiery chariot, another knight, a friend of his, who, but a minute before, resided in England, and who assists and delivers him from death; and that same knight, finds himself supping at his ease, in his own house, which is often two or three thousand leagues from the field of battle: and all this is effected by the industry and art of sage inchanters, who take those valiant knights under their protection.

"Wherefore, friend Sancho, I can easily believe, that thou hast in so little time, travelled from hence to Toboso and back again; because, as I have already observed, some friendly sage must have carried thee through the air, though thou didst not perceive it." "Not unlikely," replied the squire, "for, in good faith, Rozinante went like a gypsy's ass, with quicksilver in his ears." "With quicksilver," cried the knight; "ay, and a legion of demons to boot, who are beings that travel themselves, and make other people travel as fast as they please, without tiring.

"But, waving this subject, how do'st thou think I ought to regulate my conduct, now that my mistress commands me to appear in her presence! for, although I find myself obliged to comply with her orders, I am utterly incapacitated by the boon I have granted to this princess: and, I am bound, by the laws of chivalry, to fulfil my promise, before I indulge my inclination. On one hand, I am persecuted and harrassed by the desire of seeing Dulcinea; on the other, I am incited and invited by my honour, and the glory I shall acquire in this enterprize. I am therefore determined to travel with all expedition, until I arrive at the place where the giant resides, and when I shall have restored the princess to the peaceful possession of her kingdom, after having shortned the usurper by the head, I will return to the rays of that beauty which enlightens my thoughts; and excuse myself in such a manner as to obtain her forgiveness, as she will plainly perceive, that my delay tended to the increase of her glory and fame: seeing all my reputation in arms, past, present or to come, proceeds from her favour and inspiration." "Lord!" cried Sancho, "how your worship is concerned about a parcel of potsheards.[3] Pray tell me, sir, do you intend to make this journey for nothing; and to let such a rich and noble marriage as this slip through your fingers, while the dowry is no less than a kingdom, which, I have actually heard, is more than twenty thousand leagues, round, plentifully stored with every thing that is needful for the sustenance of mortal man, and larger than Portugal and Castile put together? Hold your tongue, a God's name, and take shame to yourself, for what you have said: pardon my freedom, take my advice, and marry in the first place where we can find a curate; or make use of our friend the licentiate, who will buckle you handsomely. Take notice, therefore, that I am of an age to give good counsel, and this that I offer will fit you to a hair; for, a bird in hand is worth two in the bush; and, as the saying is, He that hath good in his view, and yet will not evil eschew, his folly deserveth to rue."

"Sancho," answered Don Quixote, "if thou advisest me to marry, with a view of seeing me king, after I shall have killed the giant, that I may have an opportunity of rewarding thee with what I have promised, thou must know, that I can easily gratify thy

wishes, without wedding the princess; for, before I engage in the combat, I will covenant, that provided I come off conqueror, and decline the marriage, I shall have it in my power to dispose of one part of the kingdom, as I shall think proper; and to whom should I give it but to thee?" "That is very plain," replied the squire; "but, I beseech your worship to make choice of the sea-coast, because, if I should happen to dislike the country, I may ship off my black slaves, and sell them as I have already hinted. Wherefore, without troubling yourself, at present, about my lady Dulcinea, I would have you go and slay the giant, and conclude that affair, from which, before God! we shall certainly reap much honour and advantage." "I tell thee, Sancho," said Don Quixote, "thou art in the right, and I will follow thy advice, so far as it regards my attendance upon the princess, before I visit Dulcinea. But, say not a word to any body, even those of our company not excepted, of this conversation; for, as she is so reserved and careful of concealing her sentiments, it would be inexcusable in me, if I, or any other thro' my means, should disclose them." "Since that is the case," said the squire, "why does your worship command all those that are vanquished by your arm, to go and present themselves before my lady Dulcinea? You may as well give it under your hand, that you are her true and trusty lover: for, if you compel them to fall upon their knees before her, and say they are sent by your worship, to pay homage to her, how is it possible, that the sentiments of either you or her can be concealed?"

"What an ignorant and simple fellow thou art!" resumed the knight, "canst thou not see that all this redounds to her praise and exaltation?—Thou must know, that in our stile of chivalry, it is deemed a great honour for a lady to be admired by a great many knights, whose wishes extend no farther than to the desire of serving her for her own sake, without expecting any other reward for their great and manifold services, than the glory of being admitted into the number of her knights." "In like manner," said Sancho, "I have heard a priest in the pulpit, observe, that we must love our Saviour for his own sake, without being moved thereto, by any fear of punishment or hopes of applause: though, for my own part, I am inclined to love and serve him, on account of his power." "Now, the devil take the clown!" cried Don Quixote, "he sometimes makes such shrewd observations, that one would think he had actually studied!" "And yet, upon my conscience," answered the squire, "I know not so much as my letters." At that instant, master Nicholas calling aloud to them, to stop a little, that the rest might have time to drink at a spring which they found in the way; Don Quixote turned back, to the no small satisfaction of Sancho, who was already tired with telling lies, and afraid of being detected by his master; for, although he knew that Dulcinea was the daughter of a peasant at Toboso, he had never seen her in his life. By this time Cardenio had put on the cloaths which Dorothea wore, when they found her, and though they were none of the most elegant, he made a much better figure than with his tattered dress, which he now threw away. The whole company sat down by the spring, where, while they appeased the keen hunger that possessed them all, with what the curate had brought from the inn, a lad chanced to pass that way, who, looking earnestly at the whole company, at length ran up to Don Quixote, and embracing his knees, began to blubber most heartily, saying, "Ah! signor, don't you know me? look at me again; I am that same individual young man, called Andrew, whom your worship delivered from the tree to which I was tied." The

knight recollected his features, and taking him by the hand, addressed himself to the company, in these words:

"That you may see of what importance knight-errantry is, to redress the wrongs and grievances which are daily committed by the insolent and wicked wretches who live upon this earth, know, that as I passed by a wood some time ago, I heard the screams and woeful cries of some afflicted creature, in the utmost distress; and, in consequence of my oath and obligation, riding towards the place from which the lamentation seemed to come, I found this very young man tied to an oak tree; and, I am glad from my soul, that he is here in person, to bear witness to the truth. I say, he was bound to an oak, naked from the waist, upwards; and, a peasant, who, I afterwards understood, was his master, stood scourging him with the reins of a bridle. When I enquired into the cause of this barbarous treatment, the rustic answered, that he only whipped his own servant, for being guilty of some neglect that savoured more of knavishness than simplicity. The boy protested he had done nothing but asked his wages: to this affirmation, the master replied, by some asseverations which I have forgot, but, though I heard his excuses, I would not admit of them. In short, I ordered the peasant to untie the youth, and made him swear, that he would carry him home, and pay him his wages in ready cash, nay, and pay him in rials that should be perfumed. Is not this literally true, son Andrew? didst thou not observe, with what authority I commanded, and with what humility he promised to comply with every thing that I imposed, suggested and desired? Answer without perturbation, or doubt, and tell this honourable company what passed, that they may see, and be convinced, of what use it is, as I said, to have knights-errant continually upon duty."

"All that your worship hath told, is very true," answered the young man; "but, the end of the business was quite the reverse of what you imagined." "How! the reverse!" cried the knight; "has not the peasant paid thee thy wages?" "Far from paying me my wages," said Andrew, "your worship was no sooner out of the wood, and we by ourselves again, than he bound me a second time, to the same oak, and lashed me so severely that I remained like St. Bartholomew, flead alive; and, at every stripe, he jeered and scoffed and made game of your worship in such a manner, that if it had not been for the excessive pain I felt, I could not have refrained from laughing at what he said. In short, he treated me so cruelly, that 'till this very day, I have been in the hospital, for the cure of the wounds I received from that mischievous farmer: and, truly your worship was the cause of all that I suffered; for, if you had followed your own road, without going where nobody called you, or meddling with other people's affairs, my master would have been satisfied with giving me a cool dozen or two, and then loosed and paid me my due. But, when your worship abused him so unseasonably, and called him so many bad names, his choler was inflamed, and as he could not be revenged upon you, as soon as you was gone, he discharged the storm of his wrath upon me, in such a manner, that I shall never be my own man again."

"The misfortune," said the knight, "was in my leaving him, before I had seen thee paid; for, I ought to have known, by long experience, that no peasant will keep his word, if he thinks it his interest to break it. But, thou mayst remember, Andrew, that I swore, if he did not perform his promise, I would return, and search for him, until he should

be found, even if he should hide himself in the whale's belly." "Very true," replied Andrew; "but that threat signifies nothing." "Thou shalt presently see what it signifies," resumed Don Quixote, who getting up hastily, ordered Sancho to bridle Rozinante, who was following their example, in refreshing himself with grass.

When Dorothea asked what he intended to do, he replied, he was going in quest of the peasant, to chastise him for his villainous behaviour, and make him pay Andrew to the last farthing, in despite and defiance of all the rustics upon earth. To this declaration, she answered, by desiring him to consider that, according to the promised boon, he could not engage in any enterprize, until her affair should be finished; and since this stipulation was known to himself better than to any other person, she intreated him to repress his resentment, till his return from her kingdom. "That is very true," resumed the knight, "and Andrew must wait with patience for my return, as your majesty observes; but, I repeat my oath and my promise, never to desist until I shall have seen his wages paid, and his injuries revenged." "I don't trust to those oaths," said Andrew, "and would rather, at present, have wherewithal to bear my expences to Sevil, than all the revenge in the world: be so good, if you have any victuals, to give me something to eat upon my journey, and the Lord be with your worship and all knights-errant, who, I wish, may always err as much in their own affairs, as they have done in mine." Sancho, taking a luncheon of bread and cheese from the store, gave it to the young man, saying, "Here, brother Andrew, take this: and now we have all shared in your misfortune." When Andrew asked, what share of it had fallen to him, he replied, "That share of bread and cheese which I have given you: and God knows whether I shall not feel the loss of it; for, you must know, friend, that we squires of knights-errant are subject to many a hungry belly, with other misfortunes which are more easily felt than described."

Andrew accepted of the bread and cheese, and seeing that no body offered him any thing else, made his bows, and as the saying is, took his foot in his * hands. True it is, before he departed, he addressed himself to Don Quixote, saying, "For the love of God! Sir knight-errant, if ever you meet me again, spare yourself the trouble of coming to my assistance, even tho' you should see me cut into minced meat, but leave me to my misfortune, which cannot be so great, but that it may be increased by the succour of your worship, whom God confound, together with all the knights-errant that ever were born." Don Quixote started up, in order to chastise him, but, he ran away with such nimbleness, that no body attempted to pursue him; and the knight was so ashamed of his exploit, that the company were at great pains to contain their laughter, to prevent his being quite out of countenance.

---

* Literally, Took the road in his hands.[4]

CHAPTER V.

## Which treats of what happened to Don Quixote and his company at the inn.

Their sumptuous meal being ended, they saddled their beasts, and without meeting any thing worthy of mention, arrived next day at the very inn which was so much the dread and terror of Sancho; but, unwilling as he was to enter, he could not avoid going into it. The innkeeper, his wife, daughter and Maritornes, seeing Don Quixote and Sancho at the gate, went out to receive them, with great demonstrations of joy; and the knight returned their compliments with grave deportment and solemn approbation, desiring them to prepare a better bed for him than that which he had occupied before. To this demand, the landlady answered, that, provided he would pay better than he did before, he should lye like a prince: he promised to see her satisfied, and they immediately made up a tolerable bed, in the same garret where he had formerly lodged, in which, he laid himself down, very much disordered, both in body and mind. He was no sooner locked up in his chamber, than the landlady attacked the barber, and seizing him by the beard, cried, "By my faith! you shall no longer use my tail for a beard. Give me my tail, I say, for, it is a shame to see how my husband's thing is bandied about for want of it; I mean the comb that he used to stick in my tail." But, the barber would not part with it, for all her tugging, until the priest desired him to restore it; because there was no further occasion for the disguise, as he might now appear in his own shape, and tell the knight, that after he had been robbed by the galley-slaves, he had fled to that inn; and if he should enquire for the princess's gentleman usher, they would tell him, she had dispatched him away before her, to advertise her friends and subjects, that she was upon the road, accompanied by the deliverer of them all. Thus satisfied, the barber willingly restored the landlady's tail, and every thing else they had borrowed, with a view of disengaging Don Quixote from the mountain; and all the people of the inn were astonished at the beauty of Dorothea, as also at the genteel mien of the swain Cardenio. The curate ordered them to get ready something to eat; and the innkeeper, in hope of being well paid, dressed, with all dispatch, a pretty reasonable dinner, but, they did not think proper to waken Don Quixote, who, they believed, stood at that time more in need of sleep than of food.

The discourse at table, in presence of the innkeeper, his wife, daughter, Maritornes, and all the other lodgers, happening to turn upon the uncommon madness of the knight, and the condition in which they found him; the hostess recounted to them, what had happened in her house, between him and the carrier; then looking round the room, and seeing Sancho was not present, she told the whole story of the blanketting, to the no small entertainment of the company. The curate observing that Don Quixote's understanding was disordered by the books of chivalry he had read, the innkeeper replied, "I cannot conceive how that is possible; for, really, in my opinion, they are the best reading in the world: I have now in my custody two or three of them, together with some

other papers, which, I verily believe, have preserved not only my life, but also that of many others: for, in harvest time, a great number of reapers come hither, to pass the heat of the day; and there being always, one among them, who can read, he takes up a book, and we to the number of thirty or more, forming a ring about him, listen with such pleasure, as were enough to make an old man grow young again; at least, I can say for myself, when I hear him read of those furious and terrible strokes that have been given by certain knights, I am seized with the desire of being at it myself; and could listen to such stories whole nights and days without ceasing." "I wish you would, with all my heart," replied the wife; "for, I am sure, I never enjoy a quiet minute in the house, except when they are reading, and then you are so bamboozled with what you hear, you forget to scold for that time." "That is the very truth of the matter," said Maritornes; "in good faith, I myself am hugely diverted, when I hear those things; they are so clever, especially when they tell as how yon t'other lady lay among orange trees, in the embraces of her knight, while a duenna half dead with envy and surprize, kept sentry over them——odd! all these things make my chops water."

"And what is your opinion of the matter, my young mistress?" said the priest to the innkeeper's daughter. "Truly, signor, I don't well know," she replied; "but, listen among the rest, and really, tho' I do not understand it, I am pleased with what I hear: yet, I take no delight in those strokes that my father loves; but, in the lamentations made by the knights, when they are absent from their mistresses, which in good sooth, often make me weep with compassion." "Then you would soon give them relief, if they mourned for you, my pretty maid?" said Dorothea. "I don't know what I should do," answered the girl; "but, this I know, that some of those ladies are so cruel, their knights call them lions, tygers, and a thousand other reproachful names. Jesus! I can't conceive what sort of folks those must be, who are so hard-hearted and unconscionable as to let a man of honour die, or lose his senses, rather than take the least notice of him: why should they be so coy? if their suitors court them in an honest way, let them marry, and that is all the men desire." "Hold your peace, child," said the landlady; "methinks, you are too well acquainted with these things: young maidens, like you, should neither know nor speak so much." The daughter said, as the gentleman asked her the question, she could do no less than answer him; and the curate demanding a sight of the books, "With all my heart," replied the innkeeper, who going to his own chamber, brought out an old portmanteau secured with a chain, which being opened, the priest found in it three large volumes, and some manuscripts written in a very fair character.

The first book they opened appeared to be Don Cirongilio of Thrace, the second, Felixmarte of Hyrcania, and the third was the history of that great captain Goncalo Hernandes de Cordova, with the life of Diego Garcia de Paredes. The curate having read the titles of the two first, turned to the barber, saying, "We now want our friend's housekeeper and cousin." "Not at all," answered Mr. Nicholas, "I myself can convey them to the yard, or rather to the chimney, where there is actually a special good fire." "What! you intend to burn these books, then?" said the innkeeper. "Only these two," answered the curate, pointing to Don Cirongilio and Felixmarte. "I suppose then," resumed the landlord, "my books are heretic and flegmatic?" "You mean schismatic, honest friend, and not flegmatic," said the barber. "Even so," replied the landlord; "but, if any of them

be burnt, let it be the history of that great captain, together with Diego Garcia; for, I would rather suffer you to commit my son to the flames, than to burn e'er a one of the rest." "Heark ye, brother," said the curate, "these two books are stuffed with lies, vanity and extravagance; but, that of the great captain is a true history, containing the exploits of Goncalo Hernandez de Cordova, who, by his numerous and valiant atchievements, acquired all the world over, the epithet of the great captain, a renowned and splendid appellation, merited by him alone: and that Diego Garcia de Paredes was a noble cavalier, born in the city of Truxillo in Estremadura, a most valiant soldier, and endowed with such bodily strength, that with a single finger, he could stop a mill-wheel in the heat of its motion; and being once posted at one end of a bridge, with a two-handed sword, he alone prevented a vast army from passing over it: he performed a great many actions of the same kind, which he himself hath recounted with all the modesty of a gentleman who writes his own memoirs; whereas, had they been committed to writing, by any other free and dispassionate author, they would have eclipsed all the Hectors, Achilleses and Orlandos that ever lived." "You may tell such stuff to my grannam," said the innkeeper. "Lord! how you are surprised at the stopping of a mill-wheel! before God! I advise your worship to read, as I have done *, the history of Felixmarte of Hyrcania, who, with a single backstroke, cut five giants thro' the middle, as easily as if they had been made of beans, like the figures with which the boys divert themselves.[2] Another time, he engaged a most infinite and powerful army, consisting of a million and six hundred thousand soldiers, all armed capapee, whom he totally routed, as if they had been flocks of sheep. Then what shall we say of the most excellent Don Cirongilio of Thrace, who was so valiant and couragious, as may be seen in the book of his history, that while he was sailing on a river, a fiery serpent rose above the water, which he no sooner saw, than leaping on its back, he fastened himself astride upon its scaly shoulders, and seized it by the throat, with both hands, so forcibly, that the serpent feeling itself well nigh strangled, could find no other remedy but to dive into the profound, with the knight, who would not quit his hold, and when he descended to the bottom, he found himself in a palace situated in the midst of a garden that was wonderfully pleasant; and then the serpent turned itself into an ancient man, who told him such things as you would rejoice to hear——Say no more, signor, if you was to hear it, you would run stark mad for joy——so that, a fig for your great captain, and that same Diego Garcia you talk of."

Dorothea hearing this harrangue, whispered to Cardenio, "Our host wants not much to make the second edition of Don Quixote." "I think so too," answered Cardenio; "for, by his discourse, he seems to take it for granted, that every thing which is recounted in these books, is neither more nor less than the truth; and all the capuchins in Spain will not be able to alter his belief." "Consider, brother," resumed the curate, "that there never was upon earth, such a person as Felixmarte of Hyrcania, nor Don Cirongilio of Thrace, nor any other of such knights as are celebrated in books of chivalry. The whole is a fiction composed by idle persons of genius, for the very purpose you mentioned, namely pastime, which was the aim of your reapers; for, I swear to you, no such knights

---

* It will appear in the sequel, that the landlord could not read at all: nevertheless, he might boast of what he could not do.[1]

ever existed, nor were any such exploits and extravagancies ever performed in this world." "You must throw that bone to some other dog," replied the landlord, "as if I did not know that two and three make five; or where my own shoe pinches. Your worship must not think to feed me with pap, for, egad I am no such suckling: a good joke, faith! You would make me believe that all the contents of these books are madness and lies, al-tho' they are printed by licence from the king's council; as if they were persons who would wink at the printing of such lies, battles and enchantments as turn people's brains."

"Friend," replied the curate, "I have already told you, that they are designed for the amusement of our idle hours; and as in every well-governed commonwealth, the games of chess, billiards and tennis, are licensed for the entertainment of those who neither can nor ought to work; in like manner, those books are allowed to be printed; on the supposition, that no body is so ignorant as to believe a syllable of what they contain; and if I was now permitted, or the company required it, I could give some hints towards the improvement of books of chivalry, which perhaps might be both serviceable and enter-taining; but, I hope, the time will come, when I may have an opportunity of imparting my suggestions to those who can convert them to general use: mean while, Mr. Publi-can, you may depend upon the truth of what I have said; take your books away, and settle the affair of their truth or falsehood, just as your own comprehension will permit; much good may they do you, and God grant that you may never halt on the same foot of which your lodger Don Quixote is lame." "I hope," answered the innkeeper, "I shall never be mad enough to turn knight-errant, as I can easily perceive that the customs now-a-days are quite different from those in times past, when, as it is reported, those famous heroes travelled about the world."

Sancho, who had come into the room, about the middle of this conversation, was very much confounded and perplexed, when he heard them observe, that there was no such thing as knight-errantry in the present age, and that all the books of chivalry were filled with extravagance and fiction: he therefore determined within himself, to wait the issue of his master's last undertaking; and if it should not succeed as happily as he expected, to leave him, and return, with his wife and children, to his former labour.

When the innkeeper took up the portmanteau with the books, in order to carry them away, "Stay," said the curate, "until I examine these papers which are written in such a fair character." The landlord accordingly pulled out a manuscript, consisting of eight sheets of paper, intitled, in large letters *, The novel of the Impertinent Curiosity. The priest having read three or four lines, to himself, said, "Really the title of this novel pleases me so much, that I have a strong inclination, to peruse the whole." To this ob-servation, the innkeeper replied, "then your reverence may read it aloud; for, you must know, the reading of it hath given great satisfaction to several lodgers at this inn, who have earnestly begged the copy: but, that request I would not comply with, because I think of restoring it to the right owner, as I expect that the person who left the port-manteau with the books and papers, in a mistake, will return, on purpose to fetch them;

* The original, which is *Curioso impertinente*, signifies one who is impertinently curious, not a cu-rious impertinent.[3]

or, you know, he may chance to travel this way, on other business; and tho' I should miss them heavily, in faith, they shall be restored; for, tho' an innkeeper, I am still a christian." "Friend," said the curate, "you are very much in the right; but for all that, if I like the novel, you shall give me leave to transcribe it." "With all my heart," replied the landlord. While this discourse passed between them, Cardenio having taken up the manuscript, and begun to read, was of the curate's opinion, and intreated him to read it aloud, that the whole company might hear it. "I will," answered the priest, "if you think we had not better spend the time in sleeping than in reading." "For my own part," said Dorothea, "it will be a sufficient refreshment for me, to listen to some entertaining story; for, my mind is not composed enough to let me sleep, even if I stood in need of repose." "If that be the case," resumed the curate, "I will read it out of curiosity, at a venture, and perhaps, it will yield us some entertainment into the bargain." Master Nicholas earnestly joined in the request, and Sancho himself expressed a desire of hearing it; upon which, the licentiate finding he should please the whole company, as well as himself, "Well then," said he, "listen with attention, for the novel begins in this manner":

## CHAPTER VI.

## The novel of the impertinent curiosity.

In Florence, a rich and celebrated city of Italy, situated in the province called Tuscany, lived Anselmo and Lothario, two wealthy and noble cavaliers, so strictly united in the bands of amity, that every body who knew them, called them by way of excellence and epithet, the Two Friends: and indeed, being both batchelors, and their age and education so much alike, it was not to be wondered at, if a reciprocal affection sprung up between them: true it is, Anselmo was rather more addicted to amorous pastime than Lothario, whose chief delight was in hunting; yet, upon occasion, Anselmo could quit his own amusements to pursue those of his friend; and Lothario could postpone his favourite diversion, in order to practise that of Anselmo: in this manner, their inclinations proceeded so mutually, that no clock ever went with more regularity. Anselmo happened to fall desperately in love with a young lady of rank and beauty, in the same city, descended from such a noble family, and so amiable in herself, that he determined, with the approbation of his friend, without which he did nothing, to demand her of her parents, in marriage; and accordingly, put his resolution in practice. Lothario was intrusted with the message, and concluded the affair so much to the satisfaction of his friend, that in a very little time, Anselmo saw himself in possession of his heart's desire; and Camilla thought herself so happy in having obtained such a husband, that she was incessant in her acknowledgments to heaven and Lothario, by whose mediation her happiness was effected.

During the first two days after marriage, which are commonly spent in feasting and

mirth, Lothario, as usual, frequented the house of his friend, with a view of honouring his nuptials, and endeavouring, as much as in him lay, to promote the joy and festivity attending all such occasions: but, the wedding being over, and the frequency of visits and congratulations abated, he began carefully and gradually to absent himself from Anselmo's house, thinking, as every prudent person would naturally conclude, that a man ought not to visit and frequent the house of a friend after he is married, in the same manner as he had practised, while he was single; for, tho' suspicion should never find harbour with true and virtuous friendship, yet the honour of a married man is so delicate, as to be thought subject to injury, not only from a friend, but even from a brother. Anselmo perceived Lothario's remissness, and complained of it loudly, saying, that if he had thought his marriage would have impaired their former correspondence, he never would have altered his condition; and begged, that as by the mutual friendship which inspired them while he was single, they had acquired such an agreeable title as that of The Two Friends, he would not now suffer that endearing and celebrated name to be lost, by a scrupulous adherence to meer form and punctilio. He therefore intreated him, if he might be allowed to use the expression, to be master of his house, and to come in and go out as formerly, assuring him that the inclinations of Camilla, in that respect, were exactly conformable to his own; and that, knowing the perfect friendship which subsisted between them, she was extremely mortified at his late shyness.

To these and many other arguments used by Anselmo, to persuade his friend to frequent his house as usual, Lothario answered with such prudence, force and discernment, that the other was convinced of his discreet conduct; and it was agreed betwixt them, that Lothario should dine with him twice a week, besides holidays; but, notwithstanding this agreement, he resolved to comply with it no further than he should see convenient for the honour of Anselmo, which was dearer to him than his own. He said, and his observation was just, that a man on whom heaven hath bestowed a beautiful wife, should be as cautious of the men he brings home to his house, as careful in observing the female friends with whom his spouse converses, abroad: for, that which cannot be performed, nor concerted in the street or the church, or at public shews and diversions, with which a husband must sometimes indulge his wife, may be easily transacted in the house of a female friend or relation, in whom his chief confidence is reposed. Wherefore, Lothario observed,[1] that every married man had occasion for some friend to apprize him of any omission in her conduct; for, it often happens, that he is too much in love with his wife, to observe, or too much afraid of offending her, to prescribe limits to her behaviour, in those things, the following or eschewing of which, may tend to his honour or reproach: whereas, that inconvenience might be easily amended by the advice of a friend. But, where shall we find such a zealous, discreet trusty friend, as is here required? I really know not, except in Lothario himself, who consulting the honour of Anselmo, with the utmost care and circumspection, was at great pains to contract, abridge and diminish the number of the days on which he had agreed to frequent his house; that the idle vulgar, and prying eyes of malice, might not indulge their love of slander, when they perceived a genteel young man of such birth, fortune, and accomplishments as he knew himself possessed of, go into the house of such a celebrated beauty as Camilla; for, although his virtue and honour might be a sufficient check to the

most malevolent tongue, he would not expose his own character, or that of his friend, to the smallest censure; and therefore, employed the greatest part of those days on which he had agreed to visit Anselmo, in such things as he pretended, were indispensable: so that when they were present, a great deal of time was consumed by the complaints of the one, and the excuses of the other. One day, however, as they were walking through a meadow, near the suburbs of the city, Anselmo addressed himself to Lothario in these terms:

"You believe, my friend Lothario, that I can never be thankful enough to heaven, for the blessings I enjoy, not only in the most indulgent parents, and in the abundance of those things which are called the goods of nature and fortune; but, also in a friend like you, and a wife like Camilla; two pledges which I esteem, if not as highly as I ought, at least, as much as I can. Yet, though I possess all those benefits which usually constitute the happiness of mankind, I find myself one of the most disgusted and discontented men alive. I have been for these many days, so harassed and fatigued with such an odd unaccountable desire, that I cannot help being amazed at my infatuation, for which I often blame and rebuke myself, endeavouring to suppress and conceal it from my own reflexion: but, I find it as impossible to keep the secret, as if I had industriously published it to the whole world; and since it must actually be disclosed to some body, I would have it deposited in the most secret archives of your heart; in full confidence, that by the diligence which you, as a trusty friend, will exert in my behalf, when you know it, I shall soon see myself delivered from that anxiety to which it hath reduced me; and by your assiduity be raised to a pitch of joy, equal to the degree of vexation which my own folly hath intailed upon me."

Lothario was astonished at this discourse of Anselmo, as he could not comprehend the meaning of such a long preface and preamble; and endeavoured, by revolving every thing in his imagination, to find out what this desire could be, that preyed so much upon the spirits of his friend; but, finding himself always wide of the mark, he was willing to ease himself immediately of the excessive pain his suspence occasioned; and with this view, told Anselmo, that he did a manifest injury to the warmth of his friendship, in going about the bush, seeking indirect methods to impart his most secret thoughts, since he was well assured, that he might entirely depend upon him, either for advice to suppress, or assistance to support them. "I am well convinced of the truth of what you say," answered Anselmo; "and in that confidence will tell you, my friend, that the desire with which I am possessed, is to be certain, whether or not my wife Camilla is as virtuous and perfect as I believe her to be: and this truth I shall never be fully persuaded of, until the perfection of her nature appear upon trial, as pure gold is proved by fire: for, it is my opinion, that there is no woman virtuous, but in proportion to the sollicitation she hath withstood; and, that she only is chaste, who hath not yielded to the promises, presents, tears and continual importunities of persevering lovers. And pray, where is the merit in a woman's being chaste, when nobody ever courted her to be otherwise? what wonder, that she should be reserved and cautious, who has no opportunity of indulging loose inclinations, and who knows her husband would immediately put her to death, should he once catch her tripping? Wherefore, I can never entertain the same degree of esteem for a woman who is chaste out of fear, or want of opportunity, as I would for her who

hath triumphed over perseverance of solicitation: so that, for these and many other reasons I could urge to sanction and enforce my opinion, I desire that my wife Camilla may undergo the test, and be refined in the fire of importunate addresses, by one possessed of sufficient accomplishments to inspire a woman with love; and, if she comes off, as I believe she will, victorious, in the trial, I shall think my own happiness unparalelled. I shall then, be able to say, that my wishes are fulfilled; and that she hath fallen to my lot, of whom the wise man saith, 'Who hath found her?' And even, if the contrary of what I expect, should happen, the satisfaction of seeing my opinion confirmed, will help me to bear with patience that which would otherwise prove such a costly experiment. Supposing then, that nothing you can say, in opposition to this desire of mine, can avail in diverting me from my purpose, I expect and intreat that you, my friend Lothario, will condescend to be the instrument with which I execute this work of my inclination. I will give you proper opportunities, and supply you with every thing I see necessary for solliciting a woman of virtue, honour and disinterested reserve: and, what, among other things, induces me to entrust you with this enterprize, is the consideration, that should Camilla's scruples be overcome, you will not pursue your conquest to the last circumstance of rigour, but only suppose that done, which for good reason, ought to remain undone; so that I shall be injured by her inclination alone, and my wrongs lie buried in the virtue of your silence, which, I know, in whatever concerns my welfare, will be eternal as that of death. Wherefore, if you would have me enjoy what deserves to be called life, you will forthwith undertake this amorous contest, not with lukewarmness and languor, but with that eagerness and diligence which corresponds with my wish, and the confidence in which I am secured by your friendship."

Such was the discourse of Anselmo, to which Lothario listened so attentively, that, except what he is already said to have uttered, he did not open his lips, until his friend had finished his proposal; but, finding he had nothing more to alledge, after having, for some time, gazed upon him as an object hitherto unseen, that inspired him with astonishment and surprize: "I cannot be persuaded, Anselmo," said he, "but what you have said was spoke in jest, for, had I thought you in earnest, I should not have suffered you to proceed so far, but, by refusing to listen, have prevented such a long harangue. Without doubt, you must either mistake my disposition, or I be utterly unacquainted with yours; and yet, I know you to be Anselmo, and you must be sensible that I am Lothario: the misfortune is, I no longer find you the same Anselmo you wont to be, nor do I appear to you the same Lothario as before; your discourse favours not of that Anselmo who was my friend; nor is what you ask, a thing to be demanded of that Lothario who shared your confidence. Good men, as a certain poet observes, may try and avail themselves of their friends, Usque ad aras;[2] I mean, not presume upon their friendship, in things contrary to the decrees of heaven. Now, if a heathen entertained such ideas of friendship, how much more should they be cherished by a christian, who knows, that no human affection ought to interfere with our love to God: and, when a person stretches his connexions so far, as to lay aside all respect for heaven, in order to manifest his regard for a friend he ought not to be swayed by trifles or matters of small consequence, but by those things only on which the life and honour of a friend, depend. Tell me then,

Anselmo, which of these is in danger, before I venture to gratify your wish, by comply-
ing with the detestable proposal you have made? Surely, neither: on the contrary, if I
conceive you aright, you are desirous, that I should indefatigably endeavour to deprive
you and myself also, of that very life and honour, which it is my duty to preserve: for, if
I rob you of honour, I rob you of life; since a man without honour, is worse than dead;
and I being the instrument, as you desire I should be, that entails such a curse upon you;
shall not I be dishonoured, and of consequence, dead to all enjoyment and fame. Lis-
ten, with patience, my friend Anselmo, and make no answer, until I shall have done with
imparting the suggestions of my mind, concerning the strange proposal you have made;
for, there will be time enough for you to reply, and me to listen in my turn." "With all
my heart," cried Anselmo; "you may speak as long as you please."

Accordingly, Lothario proceeded, saying, "In my opinion, Anselmo, your disposition
is at present like that of the Moors, who will not suffer themselves to be convicted of the
errors of their sect, by quotations from the holy scripture, nor with arguments founded
on speculation, or the articles of faith; but, must be confuted or convinced by examples
that are palpable, easy, familiar, and subject to the certainty of mathematical demon-
stration: for instance, if from equal parts, we take equal parts, those that remain are
equal. And if they do not understand this proposition verbally, as is frequently the case,
it must be explained and set before their eyes, by manual operation, which is also in-
sufficient to persuade them of the truth of our holy religion. The self-same method
must I practise with you, whose desire deviates so far from every thing that bears the
least shadow of reason, that I should look upon it as time mispent, to endeavour to con-
vince you of your folly, which is the only name your intention seems to deserve: nay, I
am even tempted to leave you in your extravagancy, as a punishment for your prepos-
terous desire: but, I am prevented from using such rigour by my friendship, which will
not permit me to desert you in such manifest danger of perdition. But, to make this af-
fair still more plain, tell me, Anselmo, did not you desire me to sollicit one that was re-
served, seduce one that was chaste, make presents to one that was disinterested, and as-
siduously court one that was wise? Yes, such was your demand. If you are apprised, then,
of the reserve, virtue, disinterestedness and prudence of your wife, pray, what is your
aim? if you believe that she will triumph over all my assaults, as undoubtedly she will,
what fairer titles can you bestow upon her, than those she possesses already? or how will
she be more perfect after that trial, than she is at present? You either do not believe she
is so virtuous as you have represented her, or know not the nature of your demand. If
you think she is not so chaste as you have described her, you should not hazard the trial,
but rather, according to the dictates of your own prudence, treat her as a vicious woman:
if you are satisfied of her virtue, it would be altogether impertinent to make trial of that
truth, which from the test, can acquire no additional esteem. From whence we may rea-
sonably conclude, that for men to execute designs which are clearly productive of more
hurt than benefit, is the province of madness and temerity; especially, when they are not
incited or compelled to these designs by any sort of consideration; but, on the contrary,
may at a greater distance, perceive the manifest madness of their intention. Difficulties
are undertaken, either for the sake of God, of this world, or of both. The first are in-

curred by holy men, who live the life of angels here on earth; the second, by those who traverse the boundless ocean, visiting such a diversity of climates and nations, with a view of acquiring what are called the goods of fortune: and such undertakings as equally regard God and man, fall to the share of those valiant soldiers, who no sooner behold, in the wall of an adverse city, a breach, though no bigger than that which is made by a single cannon ball, than, laying aside all fear, and overlooking with unconcern, the manifest danger that menaces them, winged with desire of signalizing their valour in behalf of their king, country and religion, throw themselves, with the utmost intrepidity, into the midst of a thousand deaths that oppose and await them. These are the enterprizes which are generally undertaken, and, though full of peril and inconvenience, attended with glory, honour and advantage; but that which you have planned, and purpose to put in execution, neither tends to your acquiring the approbation of God, the goods of fortune, nor the applause of mankind: for, granting that the experiment should succeed to your wish, it will make you neither more happy, rich, or respected than you are; and should it turn out contrary to your expectation, you will find yourself the most miserable of all mortals. It will then, give you little ease to reflect, that your misfortune is unknown: for, the bare knowing it yourself, will be sufficient to plunge you in affliction and despair. As a confirmation of this truth, you must give me leave to repeat the following stanza, written by the celebrated poet Lewis Tansilo, at the end of the first part of the tears of St. Peter.

> When Peter saw the approach of rosy morn,
>     His soul with sorrow and remorse was torn,
> For, though from ev'ry mortal eye conceal'd,
>     The guilt to his own bosom stood reveal'd:
> The candid breast will self-accusing, own
>     Each conscious fault, tho' to the world, unknown:
> Nor, will th' offender 'scape internal shame,
>     Though unimpeach'd by justice or by fame.

"Wherefore, secrecy will never assuage your grief, but, on the contrary, you will incessantly weep, not tears from your eyes, but drops of blood, from your heart, like that simple doctor, whom our * poet mentions, who made trial of the vessel, which the prudent Reynaldo, with more discretion, refused to touch: and although this be a poetical fiction, it nevertheless contains a well-couched moral worthy of notice, study and imitation; especially, as what I am going to say will, I hope, bring you to a due sense of the great error you want to commit.

"Tell me, Anselmo, if heaven or good fortune had made you master and lawful possessor of an exquisite diamond, the brilliancy of which was admired by all the lapidaries

---

* Ludovico Ariosto, author of Orlando Furioso, to which poem Cervantes frequently alludes. Here, however, he seems to have forgot the passage he meant to cite: for, the person who proffered the cup to Rinaldo, was no doctor. In Canto 43, of the *Orlando Furioso*, mention is made indeed of one *Anselmo*, who was a doctor of law; but, not at all concerned in the enchanted cup: yet, it must be owned, that Dr. Anselmo had recourse to an astrologer, in order to know whether his wife preserved her chastity in his absence.[3]

who had seen it, and unanimously allowed to be the most perfect of it's kind; an opinion, which, as you knew nothing to the contrary, was exactly conformable to your own; would it be wise or pardonable in you, to put that jewel betwixt an anvil and a hammer, and by meer dint of blows and strength of arm, try if it was as hard and perfect as it had been pronounced? for, supposing that the diamond should resist the force of this foolish experiment, it would thereby acquire no addition of value or fame; and if it should be broke to pieces, a thing that might easily happen, would not all be lost? Yes, for certain; and the owner be universally deemed a fool. Consider then, my friend, that Camilla is an exquisite diamond, not only in your estimation, but in that of every one who knows her, and it would be highly unreasonable to expose her to the least possibility of being broke; for, even should she remain intire, her reputation will receive no increase; but, should she fail in the trial, reflect upon what you must feel, and the reason you will then have to complain of yourself, for having been the fatal cause of her perdition and your own despair. Consider, that no jewel upon earth is comparable to a woman of virtue and honour; and, that the honour of the sex consists in the fair characters they maintain. Since, therefore, the reputation of your wife is already as high as it possibly can be, why would you bring this truth into question? Remember, my friend, that woman is an imperfect creature, and that, far from laying blocks in her way, over which she might stumble and fall, we ought to remove them with care, and clear her paths from all obstructions, that she may, without trouble, proceed smoothly, in attaining to that perfection which she may still want, namely, immaculate virtue. We are informed by naturalists, that the ermin is a little animal, covered with a fur of excessive whiteness, and that the hunters use this artifice to catch it: being well acquainted with the places through which it chuses to pass in its flight, they daub them all over with mud, and as soon as they get sight of the creature, drive it directly thither. The ermin finding itself thus barricadoed, stands still, and is taken; chusing captivity, rather than by passing through the filth, to stain and sully the whiteness of its fur, which it prizes above liberty, and even life itself. A chaste and virtuous wife is like the ermin, her character being more pure and white than drifted snow; but he, who would guard and preserve it, must use a method quite different from that which is practised upon the little animal, and beware of clogging her way with the mud of entertainments, and the addresses of importunate lovers; lest perhaps, nay, without a perhaps, she should not possess such virtue and resolution as are sufficient of themselves, to surmount those obstructions. It is therefore necessary to remove them, and place before her, the purity of virtue, and the beauty of an unblemished reputation. A virtuous woman also resembles a bright transparent mirrour, which is liable to be stained and obscured by the breath of those who approach too near it. A virtuous woman, like reliques, ought to be adored at a distance. She ought to be preserved and esteemed as a beautiful garden full of flowers and roses, the owner of which will suffer nobody to handle them or pass through it, permitting them only, to enjoy its fragrance and beauty afar off, through the iron rails that surround it. In fine, I will repeat a few verses that I just now recollect, from a modern comedy, because they seem to have been composed upon the very subject of our present discourse. A sage old man advising his friend, who is blessed with an handsome daughter, to lock her up, and watch over her with the utmost vigilance and care, among other reasons, cautions him with these.

I.

Woman is form'd of brittle ware;
Then, wherefore rashly seek to know
What force, unbroken she will bear,
And strike, perhaps, some fatal blow.

II.

Though easily to fragments tore,
'Twere equally absurd and vain,
To dash in pieces on the floor,
What never can be join'd again.

III.

This maxim, then, by facts assur'd,
Should henceforth be espous'd by all;
Where'er a Danae lies immur'd,
The tempting show'r of gold will fall.

"All that I have hitherto suggested, Anselmo, regards yourself; and now it is but reasonable you should hear something that concerns me; and if I should be prolix in my observations, you must excuse me, because it is absolutely necessary to expatiate on the subject, in order to extricate you from the labyrinth in which you are involved, and from which you desire to be disengaged by my assistance. You consider me as your friend, and yet, seek to deprive me of my honour; a desire opposite to all friendship or regard; nay, even endeavour to make me rob you of your own. That you want to destroy mine, is plain; for, Camilla finding herself exposed to my sollicitations, as you desire, will certainly look upon me as a man void of all principle and honour; because I attempt to succeed in a design so contrary to the dignity of my own character, and the friendship subsisting between us. That you desire I should rob you of yours, is not to be doubted; because Camilla, seeing herself importuned by my addresses, will think I must have observed some levity in her conduct, which hath encouraged me to disclose my vitious inclinations, and think herself dishonoured accordingly; so that you will be as much concerned in her dishonour, as if it was your own. Hence springs the common observation that the husband of a lewd woman, though he neither knows, nor hath given the least occasion for the misconduct of his wife; and, though his misfortune was neither owing to his want of prudence or care, is notwithstanding pointed at, and distinguished by a name of scandal and reproach; being looked upon, by those who know the frailty of his wife, with an eye of disdain, instead of compassion, which he certainly deserves, as his disgrace proceeds not from any fault of his, but from the loose inclinations of his worthless spouse. I will now explain the reason, why the husband of a bad woman is justly dishonoured, though he neither knows, nor hath been in any shape accessory to her back-slidings; and you must hear me with patience, because my remarks will, I hope, redound to your own advantage.

"When God created our first parent in the terrestrial paradise, we are told by the holy scripture, that he was thrown into a deep sleep, during which, the Almighty took a rib

from his left side, and of this, Eve being formed, Adam no sooner awoke and beheld her, than he cried, 'This creature is flesh of my flesh and bone of my bone.' Nay, God himself, pronounced, 'For this shall a man leave father and mother, and they two shall be one flesh.' Then was instituted the divine sacrament of marriage, consisting of such ties as death alone can unbind; and endowed with such miraculous virtue and power, as to unite two different persons in one flesh; nay, what is still more wonderful, to combine two souls, so as to produce but one will; provided the union be happily effected. From hence, it follows, that the flesh of the wife being the same with that of the husband, whatever stains or blemishes are imbibed by the first, must equally affect the other, although, as I have already observed, he is, in no manner, accessory to the misfortune. Wherefore, as the whole person is affected by the pain of the foot or any other member of the human body; and the head, though no way concerned in the cause, be a fellow-sufferer with the ancle when it is hurt; by the same rule, an husband, being a part of the same whole, must bear a share of his wife's dishonour; for, as all the honours and disgraces of this life proceed from flesh and blood; the infamy of a vicious woman, being of the same origin, must be shared by her husband, who ought to be looked upon as a dishonoured person, though he be utterly ignorant of the guilt. Reflect, therefore, Anselmo, on the danger into which you bring yourself, by seeking to disturb the peace and tranquillity of your virtuous wife. Reflect upon the vanity and impertinence of that curiosity, which prompts you to awaken and stir up those humours, that now lie tamed and quiet in the bosom of your chaste spouse. Consider, that in this rash adventure, your gain must be very small, but your loss may be so great, that I leave it unmentioned, because I want words to express its estimation. On the whole, if what I have said, be insufficient to divert you from your mischievous design, I desire you will chuse some other instrument of your misfortune and disgrace; for, I will not undertake the office, though, by my refusal, I should even lose your friendship, which is dearer to me than any thing upon earth."

Here the virtuous and prudent Lothario left off speaking, and Anselmo remained in such confusion and perplexity, that, for some time, he could not answer one word: at length, however, he broke silence, saying, "I have listened, my friend Lothario, as you may have perceived, with great attention to all you had to say, and by your arguments, examples and comparisons, am fully convinced, not only of your great discretion, but also of that perfection of friendship to which you have attained; I see also, and own, that in refusing your counsel, and following my own, I avoid the good and pursue the evil. This truth being acknowledged, you must consider me as a person afflicted with that infirmity, which induces some women to swallow earth, chalk, coals, and other things of a worse nature, which, if loathsome to the sight, how much more disagreeable must they be to the taste. Wherefore, there is an absolute necessity for using some method of cure, which you may easily effect, by beginning to sollicit the love of Camilla, though coldly and feignedly; and sure, she cannot be so frail as to surrender her virtue at the first encounter. With this slight attempt I shall rest satisfied, and you fulfil the duty of friendship, not only in giving me new life, but also, in dissuading me from being the cause of my own dishonour. Nay, you are obliged to comply with my request, by this other consideration, that, determined as I am to put my design in execution, you ought

not to allow me to communicate this extravagant resolution to any other person, lest I run the risk of losing that honour which you endeavour to preserve: and, as to your suffering in the opinion of Camilla, by attempting to seduce her, that is a reflection of small importance, because, when her integrity is proved, you can soon inform her of our whole contrivance, consequently, regain and repossess the former place you held in her esteem. Since therefore, by adventuring so little, it is in your power to give me so much satisfaction; I hope, you will not refuse the office, even if it was attended with more inconvenience; for, I have already told you, that I shall look upon the affair as concluded, whenever you shall have made the first attempt."

Lothario seeing him fixed in his resolution, even after he had exhausted all his rhetoric to dissuade him from it; and fearing he would execute his threat of imparting his unhappy design to some other person, determined to prevent a greater misfortune, by complying with his desire: purposing, however, to manage the business in such a manner, as to satisfy Anselmo, without altering the sentiments of his wife. With this view, he told Anselmo, that he should have no occasion to communicate his intention to any other man; for he, Lothario, would undertake the affair, and begin when he pleased. Anselmo, embracing his friend with great tenderness and affection, thanked him as much for his compliance, as if he had granted him some vast favour; and it was concerted between them, that Lothario should begin the enterprise the very next day, when Anselmo would give him time and opportunity of being alone with Camilla, that he might speak to her with freedom; and also supply him with money and jewels, that with such presents he might promote his suit: he, moreover, advised him to attempt her by music, and write verses in her praise; or, if that would be too much trouble for the gallant, he himself would compose them for the purpose. Lothario undertook every thing, but with a very different intention from what Anselmo supposed; and the agreement being made, they returned to the house of this last, where they found Camilla waiting with great anxiety, for her husband, who had that day tarried longer than usual, abroad. Lothario soon after, went home to his own lodgings, leaving his friend as happy as he himself was perplexed how to contrive a scheme for bringing this affair to a fortunate issue: but, that night, he fell upon an expedient to deceive Anselmo, without giving offence to his wife.

Next day, he went to dine with his friend, and was very kindly received by Camilla, who entertained him with great cordiality, as her husband's intimate companion. Dinner being ended, and the table withdrawn, Anselmo rising up, desired Lothario to stay with Camilla till his return from an indispensible piece of business, that would detain him an hour and an half. Camilla intreated him to defer it until another time, and Lothario offered to go along with him; but, he was deaf to both, pressing Lothario to let him go, while he should wait at his house till he came back, for he wanted to talk with him upon a subject of the last importance; at the same time, desiring Camilla to keep Lothario company till his return: in short, he so well feigned the necessity, or rather folly, of his absence,⁴ that no body could have suspected the deceit. He accordingly went out, and left Camilla and his friend by themselves; for, the rest of the family had gone to dinner: so that Lothario seeing himself within the lists, according to Anselmo's desire, with his fair enemy, whose beauty alone was powerful enough to overcome a whole

squadron of armed knights, it may be easily conceived what reason he had to fear: yet all he did, was to lean his head on his hand, while his elbow rested upon the arm of the chair in which he sat, and after having begged pardon for his ill-manners, to tell Camilla, he would take a nap till Anselmo's return. She said, he would be more at his ease in a couch than in the chair, and advised him to walk into a chamber where he would find one. This offer, however, he declined, and slept where he was till the return of his friend, who finding Camilla in her own apartment, and Lothario asleep, concluded, that by his long stay, he had given them time, not only to speak, but also to take their repose; and was impatient for Lothario's waking, that he might carry him out to walk, and inquire about his own fortune.

Every thing succeeded to his wish: when his friend awoke, they went forth together, and he put every question to him that his curiosity suggested: Lothario answered, that thinking it improper to explain himself, on the first occasion, he had done nothing but praised Camilla's beauty, which, together with her discretion, he told her, engrossed the conversation of the whole city: this, he imagined, was the most prudent beginning, as it might prepossess her in his favour, and dispose her to listen to him another time, with pleasure; being the same artifice which is practised by the devil, who, when he would seduce those who are on their guard, transforms himself from an imp of darkness into an angel of light, and flattering them with specious appearances, at length discovers his cloven foot, and succeeds in his design, provided his deceit be not detected in the beginning. This declaration was altogether satisfactory to Anselmo, who said he would give him the same opportunity every day, without quitting the house, in which he would employ himself so artfully, that Camilla should never suspect his design. Many days passed, in which, tho' Lothario never opened his mouth on the subject to Camilla, he told Anselmo that he had made many efforts, but, could never perceive in her the least tendency to weakness, or obtain the least shadow of hope; on the contrary, that she had threatened, if he did not lay aside his wicked design, to disclose the whole affair to her husband. "Very well," said Anselmo, "hitherto she is proof against words; we must now try whether or not she can resist works also: to-morrow, you shall have two thousand crowns in gold, for a present to her; and as much more to purchase jewels for a bait: these are things with which all beautiful women are captivated; for, be they ever so chaste, they love finery and gay apparel; if she withstands that temptation, I will rest satisfied, and give you no further trouble."

Lothario promised to go thro' with the enterprize, now that he had begun, tho' he was persuaded he should be fatigued and baffled in the execution. Next day, he received four thousand crowns, and as many perplexities along with them; for, he did not know what lie he should next invent: however, he determined to tell his friend, that Camilla was as invincible to presents as to words; and that he should give himself no further vexation, since all his endeavours were thrown away to no purpose: but, fortune, which conducted matters in another manner, ordained, that Anselmo, one day, after having, according to custom, left Lothario and his wife by themselves, and gone to his own chamber, should peep thro' the key-hole, and listen to their conversation: it was then, he perceived, that in half an hour and more, Lothario did not speak one word; neither would he have opened his mouth, had he remained a whole age in the same situation.

From hence he concluded, that every thing his friend had told him of Camilla's replies, was meer fiction: but, to be still more assured, he came out of his chamber, and calling Lothario aside, asked what news he had, and how Camilla stood affected to him? He replied, that he was resolved to drop the business intirely; for, she had checked him with such bitterness and indignation, that he had no mind to return to the charge. "Ah Lothario! Lothario," said Anselmo, "how much you have failed in the duty of friendship, and abused the confidence I have reposed in your affection! I have been all this time, looking thro' the key-hole of that door, and perceived that you have not spoken one word to Camilla; from whence, I suspect, that your first declaration is yet to come; and if that be the case, as without doubt it is, wherefore have you thus deceived me; and in so doing, prevented me from other means to satisfy my desire?" He said no more, but this was sufficient to cover Lothario with shame and confusion; who thinking his honour concerned, in being convicted of a lie, swore to Anselmo, he would, from that moment, take the charge of giving him the satisfaction he required, without the least equivocation, as he might perceive, by watching him narrowly; tho' there would be no occasion for using such diligence, because, his future behaviour in that affair, would acquit him of all suspicion.

Anselmo gave credit to his protestation, and that his opportunities might be more secure, and less subject to interruption, resolved to absent himself from his own house, for eight days, during which he proposed to visit a friend who lived in a village not far from the city; and whom he desired to invite him to his house with the most earnest intreaties, that he might excuse himself to Camilla for his absence—Unfortunate and imprudent Anselmo! what art thou doing? what art thou contriving and concerting? consider that thou art acting against thyself, planning thy own dishonour and perdition. Your wife Camilla is virtuous and sober, and you possess her at present, in quiet; enjoying uninterrupted pleasure: her inclinations never ramble beyond the walls of your own house; you are her paradise upon earth, the goal of her desires, the accomplishment of her wishes, and the standard by which she measures her will, adjusting it, in all respects, according to your pleasure and the directions of heaven. Since the mine of her honour, beauty, modesty and virtue, yields thee, without trouble, all the riches which it contains, or thou can'st desire; why would'st thou, by digging in search of a new and unheard-of treasure, risk the fall or destruction of the whole, which is sustained by the feeble props of female constancy? remember, it is but just, that he who builds on impossibilities, should be denied the privilege of any other foundation; as the poet hath better expressed it, in the following couplets:

> In death, I sought new life to find,
>     And health, where pale distemper pin'd:
> I look'd for freedom in the jail,
>     And faith where perjuries prevail:
> But fate supreme, whose stern decree
>     To sorrow match'd my destiny,
> All possible relief withdrew;
>     Because th'impossible I kept in view.

Next day, Anselmo went to the country, after having told Camilla, that, in his absence, Lothario would take charge of the family; and dine with her every day; he therefore, desired her to treat him with all the respect due to his own person. Camilla, being a woman of honour and discretion, was disgusted at this order, and bad him consider how unseemly it was, for another man to sit at the head of his table in his absence; at the same time, begging, that if his directions proceeded from his diffidence in her capacity, he would for once put her management to the trial, and be convinced, by experience, that she was equal to a more important charge. Anselmo replied, that such was his pleasure, and her province was to bow the head and obey; upon which, she, tho' unwillingly, submitted. Next day he set out accordingly, and Lothario went to his house, where he met with a very kind and honourable reception from Camilla, who never gave him an opportunity of being alone with her, but was always surrounded by her servants, generally attended by her own maid, whose name was Leonela, for whom her mistress had a particular affection, because they had been brought up together from their infancy, in the house of Camilla's parents, and when she married Anselmo, she accompanied her to his house in quality of waiting-woman.

During the first three days, Lothario did not declare himself, altho' he had opportunities immediately after the table was uncovered, while the servants were at dinner, which Camilla always ordered them to finish with all expedition. Nay, she gave directions to Leonela, to dine every day, before the cloth was laid for herself, that she might always be in waiting; but her maid's thoughts were too much engrossed by her own amusements, the enjoyment of which required such time and opportunity, as often hindered her from obeying the commands of her mistress; so that she frequently behaved as if she had received orders to leave them alone—But, the dignified presence of Camilla, the gravity of her countenance, and awfulness of person were such, as effectually bridled Lothario's tongue: yet the energy of virtue, in having this very effect, redounded the more to the disadvantage of them both; for, tho' his tongue was restricted, his thoughts had a full and free opportunity of contemplating, at leisure, the charms both of her mind and person, which were sufficient to captivate not only an heart of flesh, but, even a statue of stone.

Lothario, by gazing at her, during those opportunities, beheld how worthy she was to be beloved; and this conviction, began gradually to sap his regard for his friend; so that he made a thousand resolutions to quit the city, and go where he should never more be seen by Anselmo, or be exposed to danger from the beauty of his wife; but, all these were baffled by the pleasure he had already felt, in seeing and admiring her charms: he constrained himself, and combated his own inclinations, in order to expel and efface that satisfaction; when he was alone, he condemned his own madness, and reproached himself as a false friend and worthless christian; he made a thousand reflections and comparisons between himself and Anselmo, and they all terminated in this conclusion, that the madness and rash confidence of his friend, greatly exceeded his own infidelity; and that, if he could excuse himself to heaven, for what he intended to do, as easily as to mankind, he had no reason to dread any punishment for the crime: in short, the beauty and other accomplishments of Camilla, together with the opportunity which the igno-

rant husband put into his hands, intirely overthrew the integrity of Lothario; who, giving way at once, to the dictates of his passion, began, at the end of three days, during which he had been at continual war with his desires, to address himself to Camilla with such disorder, and amorous discourse, that she was utterly astonished, and rising up, went to her own chamber, without answering one word: but, this coyness did not abate Lothario's hope, which always increases with a man's love; on the contrary, he redoubled his efforts, while she, perceiving him behave so wide of expectation, did not well know what conduct to espouse: but, thinking it would be both unseemly and unsafe in her, to grant him another opportunity, she determined that very night, to send a message to her husband, and actually dispatched a servant to him, with the following letter:

## CHAPTER VII.

### The continuation of the novel called the Impertinent curiosity.

"It is a common observation, that an army without a general, and a garrison without a chief, make but a very indifferent appearance: but, I say, that a young married woman without a husband, makes a worse, especially when his absence is not the effect of absolute necessity: for my own part, I find myself so uneasy, and unable to support our separation, that if you do not return immediately, I must go and pass my time at my father's house; tho' I should leave yours without a guard; for, I believe, he that you left, if he was designed for that purpose, hath more regard to his own pleasure than to your advantage; and since you are wise, I have nothing more to say, nor is it proper I should."

When Anselmo received this letter, he was convinced that Lothario had begun the enterprize, and that his wife had behaved according to his wish; rejoiced beyond measure at this information, he answered by a verbal message, that she should, by no means, leave the house; for, he would return in a very little time. Camilla was astonished at this reply, which perplexed her more than ever; as she durst neither stay in her own house, nor go to her father's; for, in staying at home, she endangered her honour, and in going to her parents, she transgressed the commands of her husband. In fine, she resolved upon that which was worst of all; namely, to remain where she was, determined not to avoid Lothario, that the servants might not observe her situation; and she was already sorry for what she had written to Anselmo, being afraid he would imagine Lothario had perceived some levity in her conduct, which encouraged him to lay aside the decorum he ought to have preserved. Confident of her own virtue, she trusted to God and her conscious prudence, by the help of which she thought she could, in silence, resist all the solicitations of Lothario, without giving her husband any further information, lest it should involve him in some trouble or dangerous dispute: nay, she was even industrious in inventing some excuse for Lothario, in case Anselmo should ask the reason that induced her to write such a letter.

With these sentiments, which were more honourable than prudent and advantageous, she, next day, sat listening to Lothario, who exerted himself in such a manner, as to shake her fortitude, which, with all her virtue, was barely sufficient to hinder her eyes from giving manifest indications of the amorous compassion that his tears and addresses had awakened in her breast. All this tenderness, which Lothario observed, inflamed his passion the more; and thinking there was a necessity for shortening the siege, while this opportunity of Anselmo's absence, lasted; he assaulted her pride with the praises of her beauty; for, nothing sooner succeeds in overthrowing the embattelled towers of female vanity, than vanity itself, employed by the tongue of adulation: in short, he so assiduously undermined the fortress of her virtue, and plied it with such irresistible engines, that tho' she had been made of brass, she must have surrendered at mercy: he wept, intreated, promised, flattered, feigned and importuned, with such earnest expressions of love, as conquered all her reserve; at last, he obtained a complete triumph, which, tho' what he least expected, was what of all things, he most ardently desired: she yielded—the chaste Camilla yielded! But, what wonder? since even Lothario's friendship gave away. A clear and incontestible proof, that love is to be conquered by flight alone; and that no person whatever, ought to engage such a powerful adversary, hand to hand; because nothing but force divine can subdue that human power.

Leonela alone was privy to the weakness of her mistress, which the two new lovers and false friends could not possibly conceal from her knowledge: and Lothario did not choose to tell Camilla, the contrivance of Anselmo, who had given him the opportunity of accomplishing his design; that she might not undervalue his love, by supposing, that he courted her by accident, without being at first, really enamoured of her charms. Anselmo returning in a few days, did not perceive the loss of that, which, tho' he preserved with the least care, he prized above all other possessions: but, going in quest of Lothario, whom he found in his own lodging, after a mutual embrace, he desired he would tell him the news that must determine his life or death. "The news which I have to give you, my friend," said Lothario, "are these: you have a wife who truly deserves to be the pattern and queen of all good women. The expressions I used to her were spent in the air, my promises were despised, my presents rejected, and some tears that I feigned, most heartily ridiculed: in short, Camilla is the sum of all beauty, and the casket in which are deposited honour, affability, modesty, and all the qualifications that dignify and adorn a woman of virtue. Here, take back your money, which I have had no occasion to use: the chastity of your spouse is not to be shaken by such mean considerations as those of promises and presents: be satisfied, Anselmo, and make no more unprofitable trials; since you have dry-shod crossed the sea of those doubts and suspicions, which are and may be entertained of women, seek not to plunge yourself anew into the dangerous gulf of fresh difficulties, by using another pilot to make a second trial of the strength and tightness of the vessel, which you have received from heaven, to perform the voyage of this life: but, consider yourself as in a safe harbour, where you ought to secure yourself with the anchor of sound reflection, and remain until you are called upon to pay that tax from which no human rank can exempt you."

Anselmo was infinitely rejoiced at this information of Lothario, which he believed as implicitly as if it had been pronounced by an oracle: but, nevertheless, he besought him

to continue his addresses, merely for curiosity and amusement, tho' not with the same eagerness and diligence which he had used before: he desired him to write verses in praise of Camilla, under the name of Chloris, promising to tell his wife, that he, Lothario, was in love with a lady whom he celebrated under that fictitious name, in order to preserve the decorum due to her character: and he assured him, that if Lothario did not choose to take the trouble of making verses, he himself would compose them for the occasion. "You shall not need," said Lothario; "the muses are not quite so averse, but they visit me sometimes: you may tell Camilla what you have mentioned, concerning my pretended love; and as for the verses, if not adequate to the subject, they shall, at all events, be the best I can make."

This agreement being concerted between the impertinent husband and treacherous friend, Anselmo returned to his own house, and asked Camilla, what she wondered he had not mentioned before; namely, the meaning of that letter which she had dispatched to him in the country. She answered, that she then fancied Lothario looked at her with more freedom than he used to take when Anselmo was at home; but, now she was undeceived, and convinced of its being no more than mere imagination; for, he had of late, avoided all occasions of being alone with her. Anselmo said she might make herself intirely easy, from that quarter; for, he knew that Lothario was in love with a lady of fashion in the city, whom he celebrated under the name of Chloris; and even, if he was free of any such engagements, there was nothing to be feared from the honour of Lothario, and the friendship subsisting between them. If Camilla had not been previously advertised by her secret gallant, of this supposed love of Chloris, with which he intended to hoodwink her husband, that he might sometimes indulge himself in her own praise, under the cover of that name; she would, without doubt, have been distracted with jealousy, but, thus instructed, she heard him without surprise or concern.

Next day, while they were at dinner, Anselmo intreated his friend to repeat some of the verses he had composed in praise of Chloris, who being utterly unknown to Camilla, he might securely say what he pleased: "Tho' she were of her acquaintance," answered Lothario, "I should not think myself bound to conceal my passion; for, when a lover praises the beauty, and at the same time, bewails the cruelty of his mistress, her reputation can suffer no prejudice: but, be that as it will, I own, I yesterday wrote a song on the ingratitude of Chloris, which you shall hear.

I.

When night extends her silent reign,
　　And sleep vouchsafes the world to bless,
To heav'n and Chloris, I complain
　　Of dire and affluent distress.

II.

When Phoebus, led by rosy morn,
　　At first, his radiant visage shews,
With tears, and sighs and groans, forlorn,
　　My soul the bitter plaint renews.

III.

When from his bright meridian throne,
    The dazzling rays descend amain,
With aggravated grief I moan,
    And night brings back the woeful strain.
Thus, to my vows and pray'rs, I find
    My Chloris deaf, and heav'n unkind.

The song was approved by Camilla, and much more so by her husband, who ap-
plauded it to the skies, and observed that the lady must be excessively cruel who could
resist such a true and pathetic complaint. "What!" said Camilla, "is every thing true that
we are told by the poets when they are in love?" "What they rehearse as poets," answered
Lothario, "is not always truth; but, what they affirm as lovers, is always from the heart."
"You are certainly in the right," replied Anselmo, with a view of supporting and giving
sanction to Lothario's sentiments, in the opinion of Camilla, whose indifference about
her husband's artifice was now equal to her love for his pretended friend. Pleased there-
fore, with his performances, because she very well knew that his inclinations and com-
positions were inspired by, and addressed to her, who was the true Chloris, she desired
him, if he had any more songs or verses, to repeat them. "I have another," said Lothario,
"but, I believe, it is not so good; or rather, it is less tolerable than the last. However, you
shall judge for yourself—here it is.

I.

Yes, cruel maid! I welcome death,
    And tho' I perish undeplor'd,
Thy beauty, with my latest breath,
    Shall be applauded and ador'd.

II.

Tho' lost in dark oblivion's shade,
    Bereft of favour, life and fame,
My faithful heart, when open laid,
    Will shew thine image and thy name.

III.

These reliques I preserve with care,
    My comfort in disastrous fate;
For, steel'd and whetted by despair,
    My love, new force acquires from hate.
Unhappy those! who darkling, sail
    Where stars and ports and pilots fail.

This song was commended as much as the first, by Anselmo, who in this manner,
added link to link of the chain with which he enslaved himself, and secured his own dis-
honour; for, then Lothario disgraced him most, when he thought himself most hon-
oured, and every step that Camilla descended towards the very center of contempt, she,

in the opinion of her husband, mounted to the very summit of virtuous reputation: about this time, happening to be alone with her maid, "I am ashamed, dear Leonela," said she, "when I consider how I have undervalued myself; for, I ought to have made Lothario employ a great deal of time, in purchasing the intire possession of my favours, which I so willingly surrendered at once; and I am afraid that he will look upon my sudden yielding as the effect of levity, without reflecting upon the violence of his own addresses, which it was impossible to resist." "Let not that give you the least disturbance, madam," answered Leonela; "for, there is no reason why a thing should lose its estimation, by being freely given, if it is actually good in its kind and worthy of esteem; nay, it is a common saying, that he who gives freely, gives twice." "There is also another common observation," replied Camilla, "that which is easily got, is little valued." "You are not at all affected by that observation," resumed Leonela; "for, love (they say) sometimes flies, sometimes walks, runs with one, creeps with another, warms a third, burns a fourth, wounding some, and slaying others. In one moment, it begins, performs and concludes its career; lays siege in the morning to a fortress, which is surrendered before night, there being no force that can withstand its power. This being the case, what cause have you to be alarmed or afraid? This was the power that assisted Lothario, by making use of my master's absence, as the instrument of his success; and what love had determined, must of necessity have been concluded during that period, before Anselmo could, by his return, prevent the perfection of the work. Opportunity is the best minister for executing the designs of love; and is employed in all his undertakings, especially in the beginning of them. This I know to be true, more by experience than hearsay; and I shall one day tell you, madam, that I am a girl of flesh and blood, as well as your ladyship. Besides, your ladyship did not yield until you had discerned in the looks, sighs, protestations, promises and presents of Lothario, his whole soul undisguised, and adorned with such virtues as rendered him worthy of your love. Let not, therefore, these scrupulous and whining reflexions harrass your imagination; but, assure yourself, that Lothario's love and yours are mutual: so, that you may think yourself extremely happy, in being caught in the amorous snare by a man of worth and honour, who not only possesses the four qualities beginning with * S, which ought to be the case of all true lovers, but also, a whole alphabet of accomplishments. Listen, and you shall hear how cleverly I will recount them. He is, in my simple opinion, amiable, benevolent, courageous, diverting, enamoured, firm, gay, honourable, illustrious, loyal, mettlesome, noble, obedient, princely, qualified, rich, and the S. S. as I have already observed. Then, he is trusty, vigilant, the X does not suit him, because it is a harsh letter; Y stands for youth, and Z for zeal, in his attachment to you."

Camilla laughed at the alphabet of her maid, whom she found more knowing in the affairs of love than she had pretended to be; and this knowledge indeed she confessed, disclosing to her mistress an intrigue that she carried on with a young man of a good family in town. Camilla was disturbed at this information, fearing that her honour ran some risk from their correspondence; and when she pressed her to confess, whether or not it had been brought to the last extremity, she, without the least symptom of shame,

---

* *Sensato, Secreto, Sobrepusado, Senzero,*—Sensible, secret, surpassing and sincere.[1]

answered in the affirmative: for, it is very certain, that the failings of mistresses divest their servants of all modesty; because, seeing their ladies trip, they think themselves intitled to halt, without being at the trouble to conceal their defect. Camilla, thus circumstanced, could fall upon no other expedient than that of cautioning her maid against betraying her to the person who was her gallant, and beseeching her to keep her own intrigue secret, that it might not fall under the observation of Anselmo and Lothario.

Leonela promised to be upon her guard, but managed her affairs with so little discretion, that she confirmed Camilla in the apprehension of losing her reputation by the carelessness of her maid; for, the bold and immodest Leonela, seeing that her lady's conduct was not the same as formerly, had the assurance to introduce and conceal her lover in the house, conscious, that although her mistress should perceive, she durst not detect him, in that situation. Among other disadvantages incurred by the slips of women of fashion, they become slaves to their own servants, and find themselves obliged to connive at their impudence and vice.

This was the very case of Camilla, who, though she more than once, observed Leonela engaged with her gallant, in one of the chambers, far from reprimanding her on that score, she gave her opportunities of concealing him, and did all she could to prevent his being seen by her husband. But, all their caution could not screen him from the notice of Lothario, who, perceiving him come out of the house, one morning at break of day, and not knowing who he was, at first mistook him for a phantome; but, seeing him run away, and seek to hide himself with care and concern, he soon changed that simple opinion for another which would have ruined them all, had not Camilla found out an expedient to prevent their destruction. He was so far from thinking, that this man, whom he saw coming out of Anselmo's house, at such an unseasonable hour, had gone in on Leonela's account, that he did not even remember there was such a person in the world; on the contrary, he was firmly persuaded, that Camilla, who yielded so easily to his addresses, had acted in the same manner, to some other person: for, this additional misfortune attends a loose woman, that she loses her credit even with the man by whose importunities and intreaties her honour was subdued: nay, he believes that she will be more easily won by another than by him, and implicitly credits every suspicion that may arise from that unjust inference. On this occasion, Lothario's good sense failed, and all his caution seemed to vanish; since, regardless of every thing that was right or reasonable, without further examination, he hied him to Anselmo before he was up, where, impatient and blind with the jealous fury that preyed upon his entrails, and inflamed with the desire of being revenged upon Camilla, who had given him no offence, he expressed himself thus:

"You must know, Anselmo, that for some days past, I have had a continual struggle with myself, endeavouring to suppress that which I no longer, either can or ought to conceal from your knowledge. The fortress of Camilla is at last surrendered, and submitted entirely to the dominion of my will. This I have delayed imparting to you, until I should be certain, whether her compliance was owing to some transient flash of affection, or to the desire of trying the sincerity of those addresses which, by your own direction, were carried on: and, I likewise concluded, that if she was a woman of honour and virtue, as we both imagined, she would, ere now, have given you an account of my

sollicitation. But, finding that still undone, I take it for granted, she means to keep her promise of giving me an interview in the wardrobe, the very next time you go to the country": (And here it was where Camilla actually used to entertain him) "but I should not wish that you would run precipitately into any scheme of vengeance. However, as the crime is committed in thought only, before an opportunity offers of performing that promise, Camilla may change her mind, and repent of her weakness. Wherefore, as you have hitherto, in whole, or in part, followed my advice, I hope you will treasure up and observe one which I shall now offer, that you may, without the least possibility of being deceived, carefully and cautiously satisfy yourself, so as to take such measures as your prudence shall suggest. You may pretend that you are going, as usual, for two or three days, to the country, and, in the mean time, conceal yourself in the wardrobe, where you will find tapestry and plenty of other things for the purpose: from thence, you, with your own eyes, as I with mine, will observe the conduct of Camilla, and if unhappily you should find more cause to fear than to hope, you may in person, revenge your own wrongs, with silence, safety and discretion."

Anselmo was thunderstruck at this declaration of Lothario, which came upon him when he least expected it; for, he already looked upon Camilla as a conqueror in the fictitious assaults of his friend, and had actually begun to enjoy the glory of her triumph. After having stood silent for a long time, with his eyes fixed upon the ground, "Lothario," said he, "you have acted up to the expectation of my friendship: I will adhere to your advice in every thing: do what you please; I hope you will keep this unexpected affair as secret as the nature of it requires."

His false friend promised to observe the caution, but soon as he quitted the apartment, repented of every thing he had said, reflecting how foolishly he had proceeded, and that he might have punished Camilla by means less cruel and dishonourable. He cursed his own folly, condemned his precipitation, and endeavoured to find out some expedient to undo what he had done, or, at least, bring it to some favourable issue. At length, he resolved to disclose the whole to Camilla, as there wanted not opportunities of being with her alone; and that very day, being together, she made use of the first that happened, addressing herself to him in this manner: "Know, my dear Lothario, that my heart is ready to burst with one affliction, which is so grievous, that it will be a wonder if I survive it: Leonela is arrived to such a pitch of impudence, that, every night she introduces a gallant into the house, and remains with him till morning, very much at the expence of my reputation, as the field is left open for any malicious construction, upon seeing a man come out of my house, at such unseasonable hours: and the misfortune is, I dare neither chide nor chastise her for her audacity; for, her being privy to our correspondence, puts a bridle in my mouth, obliging me to be silent on the subject of her folly, from which, I fear, some mischance will befal us."

When Camilla began this discourse, Lothario imagined it was an artifice to deceive and persuade him, that the man he had seen coming out of the house had been there on Leonela's account only; but, seeing his mistress weep, and in the utmost affliction, intreat him to find out some remedy for this inconvenience, he was convinced of the truth, and covered with shame and remorse for what he had done: nevertheless, he desired Camilla to make herself easy, and promised to fall upon some method to curb Leonela's

insolence. He then told her what, instigated by the rage of jealousy, he had disclosed to Anselmo, who, by his appointment, was to conceal himself in the wardrobe, that he might have an incontestible proof of her infidelity: he begged pardon for his madness, with advice how to remedy it, and to extricate himself from the labyrinth in which he was involved by his own imprudence. Camilla was astonished at the discourse of Lothario, whom she chid and reprimanded with great reason and resentment, for the groundless suspicion which had driven him to such a mad and mischievous resolution. But, women having naturally more invention than man can boast of, either for a good or bad occasion, though sometimes, they fail in premeditated schemes; Camilla instantly thought of a cure for this seemingly incurable dilemma, and bad Lothario prevail upon her husband to conceal himself in the appointed place, the very next day; for, she hoped to reap such advantage from his concealment, as that, for the future, they should enjoy each other, without the least fear or interruption. She, therefore, without disclosing to her lover, the whole of her plan, desired him to take care, when Anselmo was hid, to come at Leonella's call, and answer every question she should ask, in the same manner as he would reply, if he did not know that her husband was within hearing. Lothario insisted upon knowing the particulars of her scheme, that he might with more security and success perform his cue; but, Camilla assured him, he had nothing to do but answer her questions with truth and sincerity; being unwilling to make him previously acquainted with her design, lest he should disapprove of that which to her seemed so necessary, and recommend another, which, perhaps, she might not think so effectual. Accordingly, Lothario took his leave; and next day, Anselmo, under pretence of going to his friend's country-house, set out, but soon returned to his hiding-place; Camilla and her maid having purposely given him an opportunity of getting in unseen. There he remained in a state of perturbation, which may be easily conceived to harrass the breast of a man who expected to see with his own eyes, the bowels of his honour dissected, and found himself on the brink of losing that supreme bliss which he thought he possessed in his beloved Camilla.

She and her maid, by this time, certified of his being there, went to the wardrobe, which Camilla no sooner entered, than heaving a profound sigh, "Dear Leonela," said she, "rather than execute the design which I conceal from your knowledge, that you may not endeavour to prevent it, would it not be better for you to take this poignard of Anselmo, and plunge it in my unfortunate bosom? Yet, do not, Leonela; for it were unreasonable, that I should be punished for another's crime; I want, first, to know what the daring and licentious eyes of Lothario have discerned in my conduct, that should encourage him to declare a passion so guilty as that which he hath owned, so much to my dishonour and the prejudice of his friend. Go to that window, Leonela, and beckon to him, for, doubtless, he is now in the street, expecting to succeed in his wicked intention: but, I shall first, execute mine, which is equally honourable and severe." "Alas, madam!" answered the cunning and well-instructed Leonela, "how do you intend to use that fatal poignard? are you determined to take away your own life, or that of Lothario? by sacrificing either the one or the other, you will intirely ruin your own reputation. You should rather stifle your wrongs, than give that wicked wretch an opportunity of finding us here alone: consider, madam, that we are but weak women, and he a determined

man, who, blinded by his guilty passion, may, by force deprive you of that, which you value more than life, before you can execute your purpose upon him. A plague upon my master Anselmo, for allowing that impudent fellow, to be so free in his house! besides, madam, should you kill him, as I believe you intend to do, what shall we do with him, after he is dead?" "Nothing, my friend," replied Camilla, "but, let Anselmo bury him; for, he ought to take pleasure in the task of interring his own infamy. Go and beckon to him, I say, for every moment I delay my just revenge seems to injure afresh that fidelity which I owe to my husband."

All this conversation was overheard by Anselmo, whose sentiments were entirely changed by what Camilla said: and when he understood that she intended to kill Lothario, he was inclined to come out and discover himself, in order to prevent the deed: but, he was diverted from that resolution by the desire of seeing the issue of his wife's gallant and virtuous determination; purposing, however, to appear seasonably enough for the safety of his friend.

About this time Camilla, throwing herself upon a couch, was seized with a violent fit, during which Leonela wept bitterly, exclaiming, "Ah, woe is me! must I then see, expiring in these unfortunate arms, the flower of human virtue, the queen of excellent wives, the pattern of chastity!" with other epithets of the same kind, which no body could have heard, without esteeming her the most faithful and afflicted damsel upon earth, and her mistress another persecuted Penelope. Camilla, having soon recovered from her fit, said to her woman, "Why don't you go and call this the most faithful friend that ever was seen by the day, or shrouded by the night? make haste, go, run, fly; let not the fire of my rage be consumed by your delay, and the just vengeance I mean to take, evaporate in curses and unsubstantial threats." "I go," answered Leonela, "but, you must first give me that poignard, lest, in my absence, you do a deed to make all those who love you weep to the end of their lives." "Go, dear Leonela," replied her mistress, "and fear nothing: for, although, in your opinion, I may be rash and even unreasonable in thus resenting the affront upon my honour; I shall not behave like that Lucretia, who, 'tis said, killed herself, though innocent, without having first punished the villainous cause of her misfortune. If I must die, I will at least fall, fully revenged of him who is the occasion of my being here, to bewail his audacious behaviour, which, I am sure, proceeded from no misconduct of mine."

Many intreaties did she use, before Leonela would go and call Lothario, but, at length, she prevailed; the maid went out to seek him, and, in her absence, Camilla uttered the following soliloquy: "Good heaven! would it not have been more prudent to dismiss Lothario, as usual, than to give him this occasion of thinking me vitious and immodest, even though that opinion can only last until I have an opportunity of undeceiving him? Yes, certainly: but, I shall not think myself revenged, nor the honour of my husband sufficiently vindicated, if he escapes so smooth and clean from this snare into which his wicked inclinations have decoyed him. Let the traitor pay with his life, for the enterprize of his lascivious desire;—the world shall know, if ever the affair be made public, that Camilla not only preserved her affection for her husband, inviolate, but also took vengeance on the man who sought to impair it. Yet, methinks, I ought to disclose the whole to Anselmo: but, I have already touched upon the subject, in the letter I sent

to him when he was in the country; and his omitting to apply a remedy to the evil I then hinted at, must certainly be owing to his own integrity, and unsuspecting heart, which would not suffer him to believe, that the breast of such a constant friend, could harbour one thought to the prejudice of his honour: indeed, this was my own opinion, until his behaviour became intolerably licentious, and his presents, promises and tears, fully manifested his guilty purpose. But, wherefore these reflections? does a gallant resolution stand in need of hesitating advice? No!—traitor, avaunt! hither vengeance! enter, thou false, perfidious wretch, come, quick, be speedy, die, and let the consequence be what it will! Pure and unspotted I came into the possession of him whom heaven appointed to be my husband and my lord! and equally pure shall I leave his embrace, tho' bathed in my own chaste blood, and embrued in the tainted gore of the falsest friend that ever friendship saw!" So saying, she brandished the drawn dagger in her hand, and stalked across the room with such disordered steps and violent gestures, that she seemed to have lost her senses, and looked more like a desperate ruffian than a delicate wife.

All this transport and agitation was perceived, with astonishment, by Anselmo, where he stood concealed behind the tapestry: he thought he had now seen and heard enough to dispel suspicions of a stronger kind, than those he entertained; and even wished that the proof might proceed no farther, by Lothario's failing to keep the appointment; for, he was afraid that some sudden, unlucky accident might happen—being therefore, on the point of shewing himself, and running to embrace and undeceive his wife, he was prevented by seeing Leonela return with his friend, whom Camilla no sooner beheld, than drawing a line before her, with the dagger, she said, "Take notice, Lothario, if you attempt to pass this line, or even approach it, the moment I perceive your intention, I will plunge the poignard in my breast. Without offering the least reply therefore, to this declaration, I desire you will listen to some questions I mean to ask, which you may answer as you shall think proper: in the first place, tell me, Lothario, if you know my husband Anselmo, and what station he maintains in your opinion? and then be as explicit in your sentiments of me: answer without perturbation or difficulty; for, the questions I ask, are easily solved."

Lothario was not so ignorant, but that he had conceived her design, from the moment of her desiring him to advise Anselmo to conceal himself; and therefore, his replies were so seasonable, and corresponded so exactly with her aim, that this fiction had all the air of the most genuine truth. "Beauteous Camilla," said he, "I did not imagine you had sent for me, with a view of asking questions so foreign to the purpose for which I come: if you mean to delay the promised bliss, you might have protracted the assignation to a more distant term; for, the nearer the prospect of enjoyment is, the more grievous will the disappointment be: but, that you may have no cause to complain of my refusing to answer your demands, I will own that I know your husband Anselmo, with whom I have been intimate from our most tender years. Of the friendship (as you know) subsisting between us, I will say nothing, that I may not bear witness to the wrong which love, the powerful excuse of greater crimes, compels me to commit: you too I know, and rate as high as you can possibly be in his esteem; for a prize of less value I should not have acted so unbecoming my own character, or transgressed those laws of perfect friendship, which I have broken and violated, at the instigation of that mischievous and irresistible power."

"Since thou art self-convicted so far," replied Camilla, "thou mortal enemy to all that merits love! with what face darest thou appear before her who is the mirrour that reflects him, and in which thou oughtest to have seen how little reason and encouragement thou hadst to wrong his honour: but, unfortunate that I am! I have found out the cause that induced thee to forget thyself so far; it must have been some lightness of carriage in me; immodesty I will not call it, because it could not be the effect of deliberate determination, but must have proceeded from a neglect of some of those forms which women often inadvertently omit, before those whom they think they can entertain without ceremony. Otherwise, tell me traitor, when did I ever answer thy addresses with any word or sign that could awaken in thy breast, the least glimpse of hope to accomplish thy infamous aim? did I not always reject and reprove thy amorous protestations with rigour and severity? and when were thy promises and presents believed and accepted? But, as I think no person could long persevere in such a flagitious intention, without being supported by some sort of hope, I am willing to lay the blame of your impertinence at my own door; since, without doubt, some failure of care in me, hath enabled you to exert yours so long; and therefore, I will inflict upon myself, the punishment that your crime deserves: but, that you may see, in being thus inhuman to myself, it was impossible for me to deal mildly by you, I have invited you hither, to be witness of the sacrifice I mean to offer to the injured honour of my noble husband, whom you have aggrieved to the utmost of your power, I myself being accessory to the wrong, because I have not industriously enough avoided all occasion, if I gave you any, of favouring and countenancing your wicked inclinations. I say, the suspicion I have, that some levity of mine engendered such frantic sentiments in your bosom, gives me the utmost pain, and prompts me to chastise my indiscretion with my own hands, rather than make my fault more public, by submitting to another executioner: but, if I must perish, my fall shall be accompanied with the death of him whose blood will satisfy the vengeance which I already in some measure enjoy, when I consider that, wheresoever I go, I shall have before mine eyes, the victim I offered to the most disinterested justice, in punishing the wretch who hath reduced me to this despair."

So saying, she assaulted Lothario with incredible force and agility, manifesting such eagerness to plunge the poignard in his breast, that he himself doubted whether her endeavours were feigned or real, and was actually obliged to exert his whole strength in defending himself from Camilla, who acted this strange imposture so much to the life, that, in order to give it the greater appearance of truth, she resolved to colour it with her own blood; for, seeing, or feigning that she could not touch Lothario, she cried, "Tho' fate denies me the full satisfaction of my just desire, it cannot rob me of one part of my revenge." With these words, struggling to disengage her dagger-hand, which was held by Lothario, she at last succeeded, and directing her poignard to a part of her body, which she thought she might slightly wound without danger, she sheathed it between her shoulder and left breast, and fell upon the floor, as in a swoon. Leonela and Lothario were astonished and confounded at this event, and still dubious whether or not Camilla was in earnest, when they saw her stretched upon the ground, and bathed in her own blood. Lothario ran, in the utmost fright and consternation, to draw forth the dagger;

but, perceiving what a superficial wound she had made, he recovered of the terror which had begun to seize him, and could not help admiring anew, the uncommon sagacity, prudence, and discretion of the beautiful Camilla: that he might, therefore, proceed in the part he had to act, he began to make a long and sorrowful lamentation over the body, as if she had been really dead, imprecating a thousand curses, not only upon himself, but also upon him who was the original cause of this disaster: and as he knew that Anselmo was listening, said such melancholy things, that whosoever had heard him, would have pitied his case as much as that of Camilla, tho' they had believed her actually dead.

Leonela lifted her up, and laying her on the bed, earnestly intreated Lothario to find some person who would cure her privately; and begged he would advise her, with regard to what she should tell Anselmo, about her lady's wound, in case he should return before she was cured: he said, she might tell him what she pleased, for, he was then in no condition to give any profitable advice about the matter: he only desired her to fall upon some method of staunching the blood; and declared, that for his own part, he would go where man should never see him. He accordingly departed, with the appearance of infinite grief and anxiety, and, when he found himself alone, in a private place, crossed himself with amazement, at the invention of Camilla, and the artful behaviour of her maid: he could easily conceive that Anselmo was, by this time, thoroughly convinced of his having a second Portia for his wife; and was impatient to see him, that they might together extol her behaviour, which, tho' imposture, had more appearance of truth than any thing of the same kind that had ever been practised.

Leonela, as she was desired, stopt her lady's blood, of which there was just enough to give credit to her artifice; and washing the wound with a little wine, bound it up as well as she could, uttering such sorrowful expressions all the time, as would have been sufficient, without any previous lamentation, to persuade Anselmo that his wife was the mirror of chastity. Leonela's complaints were joined by those of her mistress, who taxed herself with cowardice and pusillanimity, in having lost the best opportunity she should ever have of parting with that life which she abhorred. She consulted her maid about disclosing the whole affair to her beloved spouse; but, this scheme Leonela opposed, observing that it would lay her master under an obligation of taking vengeance on Lothario; a satisfaction he could not enjoy, without exposing himself to great danger; and that a virtuous woman, far from seeking to involve her husband in quarrels, was in duty bound to keep him free of all such disputes, by every method in her power. Camilla seemed to approve of her maid's prudence, and promised to follow her advice; but, said it would be necessary, at all events, to invent some excuse to Anselmo, about the wound which he could not fail of observing. Leonela assuring her, that she could never tell a lie even in jest, the mistress replied, "What shall I do then, child? for, I would not attempt to frame and maintain a falsehood, even tho' my life depended upon it: since, therefore, we know not how to extricate ourselves otherwise, we must e'en discover the naked truth, rather than run the risk of being detected in a lie." "Don't give yourself any further uneasiness, madam," said Leonela, "by to-morrow morning I shall have found some expedient: perhaps the wound being where it is, may be concealed from his view, and heaven vouchsafe to favour our upright and honourable intention. Compose your-

self, dear madam, endeavour to calm the perturbation of your spirits, that my master may not perceive your disorder; and leave the consequence to my care, and that of heaven, which never fails to favour the righteous design."

Anselmo listened with the utmost attention to this tragedy, of the death of his honour, which was represented with such exquisite and surprising address, that the actors seemed really transformed into the very characters they feigned: he longed impatiently for night, and an opportunity of escaping unseen, that he might fly to his worthy friend Lothario, and receive his congratulation upon the precious jewel he had found in this vindication of his wife's virtue: they took care to furnish him with the occasion he wanted, and he, without letting it slip, ran immediately in quest of Lothario: it would be difficult to describe the eagerness of his embraces, at meeting, or to recount the expressions he used in the overflowings of his satisfaction, and the extravagant praises he bestowed on Camilla. All these Lothario heard, without being able to manifest the least signs of joy; his reflexion taxed him with the deceit he had practised, and the injury he had done his unsuspecting friend. Anselmo took notice, that he did not seem to participate in his pleasure, but, believed his concern proceeded from the thoughts of having been the occasion of Camilla's wound: he therefore, among other things, told him to make himself easy on that score; for, the hurt must certainly have been very slight, as they had agreed to conceal it from his knowledge; and since there was no bad consequence to be apprehended, he hoped, for the future, to enjoy, in mirth and good humour, the friendship of his dear Lothario, by whose industry and mediation, he now saw himself raised to the most sublime pitch of human felicity: at the same time he signified, that his desire and design was to pursue no other amusement than that of composing verses in praise of Camilla, that should transmit to latest posterity the remembrance of her worth.

Lothario commended his laudable determination, and promised to contribute all that lay in his power towards the rearing of such an illustrious edifice: so that Anselmo being the most agreeably deceived of any man that ever lived, led by the hand, to his own house, the very man who, tho' in his opinion, the instrument of his glory, was the total perdition of his fame. Camilla received him with a countenance expressing resentment, but, a soul brimful of joy; and their secret correspondence continued uninterrupted for a few months, at the end of which, the wheel of fortune having performed a full circle, the intrigue, which had been hitherto so artfully concealed, was discovered, and Anselmo's Impertinent Curiosity cost him his life.

## CHAPTER VIII.

## The conclusion of the Impertinent Curiosity.[1]

A little more of this novel remained to be read, when Sancho came running in great confusion, from the garret where his master Don Quixote lay, bawling aloud, "Come hither, gentlemen! make haste to the assistance of my master, who is this precious minute engaged and grappled in the toughest battle that ever my eyes beheld! Egad! he has given that same giant, the enemy of my lady the princess of Micomicona, such a back-stroke, as hath sliced off his head, as smooth and clean as the skin of a turnip." "What do you mean, brother?" said the curate, closing the book, "are you in your right wits, Sancho? how the devil can your master be fighting with a giant who is two thousand leagues from hence?"

That instant, they heard a great noise in the apartment, and Don Quixote pronounced aloud, "Stay, villain, robber, caitiff, here I have thee, and thy scymitar shall not avail." Then he began to strike furiously at the walls; and, Sancho exclaimed, "Don't stand here listening, but, go in and part the fray, or lend your assistance to my master; tho' I believe that will be needless by this time; for, the giant is certainly dead, and giving an account to God, of his wicked and mispent life: nay, I saw, with my own eyes, his blood running about the floor, and his head cut off, lying on one side, as large as a winebag." "May I be hanged," cried the innkeeper, at these words, "if this Don Quixote, or Don Devil, has not cut open one of the skins filled with red wine, that stood at his bed's head, and the wine that ran out is mistaken by this simple fellow for blood!"

So saying, he rushed into the apartment, with the whole company at his heels, and found the knight in a very ludicrous situation: he appeared in his shirt, which was too scanty before, to cover his thighs, and still shorter behind, by six inches at least, and displayed a pair of long lank legs, imbrowned with hair, and not extremely clean; his head was covered with a little, red, greasy night-cap,[2] belonging to the landlord; round his left arm he had wrapped the blanket of his bed, to which Sancho, for good reasons known to himself, bore an inveterate grudge; and in his right, he wielded his drawn sword, with which he laid about him at a furious rate, talking as if he was actually at blows with the giant: but, what was very surprising, his eyes were shut all the time, and he was fast asleep, dreaming of this encounter; for, his imagination was so much engrossed by the adventure he had undertaken to atchieve, as to make him dream that he was already arrived in the kingdom of Micomicon, and engaged in a single combat with his gigantic adversary, instead of whom, he hacked the wine-bags so furiously, that the whole room was afloat with their contents.

The innkeeper no sooner perceived this havock, than incensed to the last degree, he assaulted Don Quixote with his clenched fists, and began to pummel him so severely, that if the curate and Cardenio had not interposed, he would soon have put an end to the adventure of the giant: yet, for all that, the poor knight did not awake, until the barber, fetching a kettle of cold water from the well, soused him all over; even then, tho'

F. Hayman inv. et delin.                    C. Grignion sculp.

Don Quixote Attacking the Wine Bags in His Sleep.

sleep forsook him, he did not recollect the situation he was in; and Dorothea seeing him so slight and airily equipt, did not choose to be a spectator of the combat between her adversary and protector. Mean while, Sancho went about the room, prying into every corner, and searching for the giant's head, which, when he could not find, "I knew," said he, "that every thing goes by enchantment in this house: the last time I was in this very spot, I received a great many thwacks and thumps, without seeing a soul, or being able to guess from whence they came; and now this head is vanished, tho' I saw it cut off with mine own eyes, and the blood spout out of the body, like water from a fountain." "What do'st thou talk of blood and fountains, thou enemy of God and his saints!" cried the innkeeper, "don't you see, rascal, that there is no blood or fountain, but, the skins that are pierced, and the red wine that swims about the room? I hope the soul of him who pierced them, will swim in hell!" "I know nothing of the matter," replied Sancho; "but that, on account of my not finding the head, I shall see my earldom dissolve like salt in water."

Thus the squire, tho' awake, was more extravagant than Don Quixote in his dream: such an impression had his master's promises made upon his imagination. The phlegmatic temper of the squire, together with the mischievous disposition of the knight, well nigh distracted the landlord, who swore, that they should not now, as formerly, go away without paying; and that all the privilege of their errantry should not exempt them, from paying both reckonings, to the last farthing for the damage they had done, even to the bits of leather for botching the wine-skins that were cut. The curate, by this time, had got hold of the hands of Don Quixote, who, believing he had now finished the adventure, and was, in presence of the princess Micomicona, fell upon his knees, before the priest, saying, "Renowned princess, your highness may henceforth live secure of what that misbegotten wretch can do; and I, from this day forward, am acquitted of my promise, which is now, by the assistance of heaven above, and the favour of her for whom I live and breathe, happily and fully performed." "Did not I tell you so?" cried Sancho, hearing these words. "You see I am not drunk, and may take notice that my master hath put the giant in pickle—the holidays will certainly come round,[3] and the earldom fit me to a hair."

Who could refrain from laughing at the follies of the master and man? they occasioned abundance of mirth to every one present, except the landlord, who cursed himself to the devil. At length the barber, curate and Cardenio, with no small difficulty, put the knight to bed again, where he fell asleep in an instant, like one who had been excessively fatigued: they left him to his repose, and went out to console Sancho for his disappointment in losing the giant's head; but, they found it a harder task to pacify the innkeeper, who was driven almost to despair, by the sudden death of his wine-bags: besides, the landlady began to cry, in a whimpering tone, "In an unlucky minute and evil hour did this knight-errant enter my doors; for, I am sure, I never beheld him, without paying dearly for the sight! The last time he was here, he refused to defray a whole night's expence of supper, lodging, straw and barley, for himself and his squire, his horse and his ass; saying that he was a knight-errant, forsooth; (God send him and all other knights-errant upon errands that will tend to their sorrow!) and therefore, was not obliged to pay for any thing, because it was not ordained in the registers of chivalry:

then, this gentleman coming after him t'other day, borrowed my tail, and tho' I have got it again, it is a good penny the worse for the wearing, the hair being plucked off in such a manner as makes it unfit for my husband's purpose; and to finish and conclude the whole, my bags are broke, and my wine spilt: (would I could see his heart's blood in the same condition!) but, he must not think to get off so easily, for by the bones of my father, and my mother's soul! they shall pay for every thing upon the nail; or, may I never be called by my own name again, or believed to be my father's own child!"

These, and other expressions of the same kind, were uttered, with great bitterness, by the landlady; and her faithful servant Maritornes joined in the exclamation, while the daughter held her peace, and, from time to time, smiled at their indignation, which at last was appeased by the curate, who promised to give them satisfaction, to the best of his power, for the loss they had sustained in bags and wine, and, in particular, for the damage done to the tail, which they valued so highly: and Dorothea comforted Sancho, by telling him, that as soon as ever it should appear that his master had actually cut off the giant's head, and she should find herself in quiet possession of her kingdom, she would bestow upon him the best earldom in her gift. The squire was consoled by this promise, and assured the princess, that he was certain he had seen the giant's head, by the same token, that he had a huge beard that flowed down to his middle; and that the whole was now vanished, because every thing in that house was performed by enchantment, as he had found by woeful experience, the last time he had lodged in that apartment. Dorothea said she was of the same opinion, desiring he would give himself no uneasiness, for, every thing would be for the best, and succeed to his heart's content. The quiet of the house being thus re-established, the curate wanted to read the remaining part of the novel, which, he perceived, already drew near a close; and Cardenio, Dorothea and the rest, intreating him to finish the story, he, with a view of pleasing them as well as himself, proceeded in these words:

Anselmo being now satisfied of his wife's virtue, enjoyed himself without the least disturbance or care; while Camilla, in order to disguise her real sentiments, affected always to frown upon Lothario, who, as a further sanction to this stratagem, desired Anselmo to excuse him from coming to his house, since it was plain that Camilla was disgusted at his presence: but, the infatuated Anselmo would by no means comply with this request; so that this unhappy husband was, in a thousand shapes, the author of his own dishonour, while, in his own opinion, he was laying up a store of happiness and reputation.

About this time, Leonela's desire of gratifying her own loose wishes, carried her to such a pitch of imprudence, that she gave her wantonness the rein, without the least caution; conscious that her mistress would conceal her conduct, and even advise her how to carry on the intrigue with the least danger of being detected. At length, however, Anselmo, one night, heard somebody walking in her apartment, and endeavouring to get in and see who it was, found the door shut against him. This circumstance increasing his desire, he made a violent effort, and the door flew open; upon which he entered, and seeing a man leap out of the window, into the street, ran hastily to lay hold or get sight of him; but, he was disappointed in both, by Leonela, who hanging upon her master, cried, "Hold, dear Sir, be not surprized, nor seek to pursue the person who is fled; he was here on my account, and is as good as my wedded husband."

Anselmo would give no credit to her words, but, blinded with passion, drew his poignard to stab Leonela, whom he commanded to reveal the truth, on pain of immediate death. She, terrified by his threats, answered, without knowing what she said, "Spare my life, good Sir, and I will disclose things of greater importance than you imagine." "Speak then," cried Anselmo, "or thou shalt instantly die." "At present," replied Leonela, "I am in such perturbation, that I cannot possibly make a distinct confession—delay your vengeance till to-morrow morning, and then you shall hear something that will strike you with astonishment; mean while, be assured that he who leapt out of the window, is a young man of this city, who has given me a promise of marriage."

Anselmo being somewhat pacified by this declaration, resolved to grant the respite she demanded; tho' he never dream'd of hearing any thing to the prejudice of Camilla, of whose virtue he was satisfied and secure: he, therefore, quitted the room in which, however, he locked up Leonela, telling her, she must continue in that place, until she should have made this promised discovery: then going to Camilla, informed her of every thing that had passed, together with the promise her maid had made of discovering things of great importance. It is almost needless to say that Camilla was disturbed at this information; the terror that took possession of her was such, that believing, with good reason too, Leonela would actually disclose to Anselmo, every circumstance of her infidelity, she had not resolution enough to wait the issue of her suspicion; but, that very night, while her husband was asleep, collected the best of her jewels, with some money, and getting out of the house, without being perceived, fled to Lothario, and recounted what had happened; at the same time, beseeching him to put her in a place of safety, or accompany her to some retreat, where they should be secure from the search of Anselmo.

Such was the confusion of Lothario, at the news of this unexpected event, that he could not answer one syllable, nor for some time, resolve upon what was to be done. At length, he proposed to carry Camilla to a monastery, the abbess of which was his first cousin; and his mistress consenting to the proposal, he conducted her thither, with all the dispatch which the nature of the case required, and leaving her to the care of his relation, quitted the city that very night, without imparting the cause of his absence to any living soul.

Next morning, soon as it was day, Anselmo, without perceiving that Camilla was gone, so eagerly did he long to hear this confession of her maid, arose and went directly to the room in which he had confined her; but, he no sooner opened the door, and entered the apartment, than he perceived the sheets of the bed tied together, hanging out at the window; a manifest proof that Leonela had lowered herself down into the street, by means of that contrivance: he then returned, with a good deal of chagrin, to communicate his disappointment to Camilla, whom, when he could not find, he was seized with the utmost consternation, especially, as none of the servants could give the least account of her departure: but, chancing, in the course of his inquiry, to find the coffers open, and the best part of her jewels carried off, he began to comprehend his disgrace; and concluded, that Leonela was not the cause of his misfortune.

Dispirited with this reflexion, he did not stay to dress, but went, in a most disconsolate situation, to give an account of his mishap, to his friend Lothario; and, when he un-

derstood from his servants, that their master had gone out in the night, and carried all his ready money along with him, he had well nigh lost his senses. To crown his misery, he returned to his own house, which was deserted by all his servants, and found himself the most solitary being in nature: he knew not what to think, say or do, and his judgment began to be impaired; for, upon recollection, he perceived that he was in an instant, deprived of wife, friend and servants, renounced by heaven, and, what he felt more deeply than any other part of his disaster, destitute of honour, by the misconduct of Camilla, from which he dated his utter destruction. At length, after a long internal struggle, he resolved to go to the country-house of his friend, where he had been, when he furnished the opportunity of planning his own ruin. Accordingly, having locked his door, he mounted his horse, and almost fainting under the burthen of his woes, set out for that place: but, scarce had he travelled one half of the way, when harrassed by his shocking reflexions, he was obliged to alight and tie his horse to a tree, at the root of which, he threw himself down, giving vent to the most lamentable sighs that ever were heaved: there he remained till the twilight, about which time, perceiving a man coming on horseback from the city, after salutation, he asked what news were stirring at Florence?—"The strangest," replied the citizen, "that have been heard these many days: it is publicly reported, that Lothario, the intimate friend of Anselmo the rich, who lived at St. John's, hath this last night, carried off the wife of his friend, who is also missing. This discovery was made to the governor by Camilla's maid, who was detected in letting herself down by a sheet, from one of the windows of Anselmo's house: in short, I do not know the particulars exactly; but, the whole city is astonished at this event, which they could never have expected from the intimacy of the two gentlemen, who were so strictly united in the bands of amity, as to acquire the title of the Two Friends." "Do you know what road Lothario and Camilla have taken?" said Anselmo. "That is not yet discovered," replied the traveller; _tho' the governor hath used great diligence in the inquiry." Anselmo wished him a good even; and the citizen having returned the compliment, proceeded on his journey.

This unhappy news reduced this ill-fated husband to the verge of death as well as distraction: he mounted, however, as well as he could, and arrived at the house of his friend, who had not as yet heard of his misfortune; but, seeing him so exhausted, ghastly and pale, imagined he had met with some grievous disaster. Anselmo begged to be put to bed immediately, and furnished with pen, ink and paper: thus provided, he was left alone, and the chamber lock'd, at his own desire: then, the remembrance of his misfortune began to be so heavy upon his soul, that he plainly perceived his end approaching, and being desirous of declaring the cause of his strange and sudden death, he took up the pen; but, before he could execute his design, his breath failed him, and he expired, a victim to that sorrow which was occasioned by his own impertinent curiosity. His friend finding it grow late, and that Anselmo had not called, went into his chamber, to enquire about his health: there he found him lying upon his face, one half of his body in bed, and the other on the table, with a pen in his hand, and a written paper lying open before him.

The gentleman, having spoke to him, without receiving an answer, took him by the hand, and feeling him cold and stiff, concluded he was dead. Surprized and concerned

to the last degree, he called up his family to be witnesses of this melancholy event, and knowing the paper to be Anselmo's own hand-writing, read the contents, in these words: "I am deprived of life by my own impertinent curiosity: if the news of my death reach Camilla's ears, let her know that I forgive her infidelity; for, she was not bound to perform miracles, nor I under any necessity of expecting them at her hands: since therefore, I have been the contriver of my own dishonour, there is no reason that——" So far he had written, but life had forsaken him, before he could finish the sentence. Next day, his friend sent an account of his death to his parents, who were already informed of his mischance, as also of the convent to which Camilla had retreated; and where she now lay at the point of accompanying her spouse in his last, indispensible journey; not so much on account of Anselmo's death, as in consequence of the information she received concerning her absent lover: it was said, that tho' she was now a widow, she would neither quit the convent, nor take the veil: but, in a little time, the news arrived of Lothario's being killed in a battle which was fought between the renowned captain Goncalo Fernandez de Cordova, and monsieur de Lautrec, in the kingdom of Naples, whither this too late repenting friend had made his retreat. This event was no sooner known, than Camilla professed herself nun, and, in a few days, yielded up her life a prey to grief and melancholy. Such was the untimely end to which they were all brought, from a beginning of whim and indiscretion!

"This novel," said the curate, "is not amiss; but, I cannot think the story is true, and if it be feigned, the author has erred in point of invention; for, it cannot be supposed, that any husband would be so mad as to try this dangerous experiment of Anselmo: had it been related of a gallant and his mistress, it might have passed; but, with regard to a husband and his wife, it is altogether improbable: however, the manner of narrating it is not disagreeable."

## CHAPTER IX.

### An account of other strange adventures that happened at the inn.

At that instant, the landlord standing at the inn-door, exclaimed, "There's a noble company: odd! if they halt here, we shall sing for joy." "What company?" said Cardenio. "Four men," replied the innkeeper, "who ride with short stirrups,[1] each of them equiped with lance, target and mask;[2] with a lady on a side-saddle, dressed in white and veiled, and two attendants on foot." When the priest asked if they were near, he answered, "So near, that they are already at the gate."

Dorothea hearing this information, put on her veil, and Cardenio withdrew into Don Quixote's apartment. Immediately the whole company, announced by the landlord, entered the inn yard, and the four horsemen, who were persons of genteel mien and carriage, instantly alighting, went to help the lady from her horse; when one of them, tak-

ing her in his arms, placed her in a chair that stood by the door of the room, in which
Cardenio had concealed himself. All this time, neither she nor they took off their masks,
nor uttered one syllable; but, when she was seated, she heaved a profound sigh, and let
her arms fall down on each side, like a person fainting with weakness. While the foot-
men led the horses into the stable, the curate, being curious to know who those persons
were, so remarkable in their silence and dress, went up and put the question to one of
the lacquies, who answered, "Truly, signor, we are as ignorant in that particular as you
are; tho' they seem to be people of condition, especially he who took the lady in his
arms, because all the rest behave to him with great respect, following his directions in
every thing, with the utmost punctuality." "And, pray who may the lady be?" said the
priest. "We know as little of her as of the men," replied the lacquey; "for, during the jour-
ney, I have never once beheld her face; I have often heard her sigh bitterly, and utter
piercing groans, in every one of which, she seemed to yield her very soul: but, it is not
to be wondered at, that we should know so little of their affairs; my companion and I
having attended them two days only: for, meeting us on the road, they intreated and per-
suaded us to accompany them as far as Andalousia, promising to pay us handsomely for
our trouble." "Have you never heard one of them named?" resumed the curate. "Never
once," answered the young man; "they travel with surprising silence; nothing is heard
but the sobs and sighs of the poor lady, which move us to compassion: we firmly believe,
that she is forced upon this journey; and gather from her dress, that she is a nun, or
which is more probable, going to take the veil, and finding herself very little inclined to
that way of life, is melancholy at the prospect."

The curate said nothing was more probable, and leaving the lacquey, returned to
Dorothea, who, by this time, out of natural sympathy with the affliction of the masked
lady, had approached and accosted her in these words: "What is the matter with you,
dear madam? If you labour under any indisposition which the practice and experience
of women can relieve, my assistance is heartily at your service." To this kind offer no re-
ply was made by the sorrowful lady, who, notwithstanding the other's repeated in-
treaties, would not open her mouth; until the person, who, by the lacquey's information,
was chief of the company, addressing himself to Dorothea, said, "Do not fatigue your-
self, madam, in making proffers of service to that woman, who cannot be grateful for
any favour she receives; nor importune her for any reply, unless you desire to hear some
falsehoods proceed from her lips." "My lips," said the hitherto silent lady, "were never
profaned with falsehood; on the contrary, my present misfortune is owing to my sin-
cerity and my abhorrence of lies. Of this assertion, you yourself are too sensible; since
your own perfidy and falsehood are the effects of my constancy and truth."

These words were distinctly overheard by Cardenio, who was only separated from
them by the door of Don Quixote's chamber; and they no sooner reached his ears, than
he cried aloud, "Good heaven! What do I hear! What voice is that which struck my
sense!" The lady being exceedingly surprized at that exclamation, turned about her
head, and not seeing the person that pronounced it, started up and ran towards the
apartment from whence it seemed to come; but, was prevented by her conductor, who
would not suffer her to move one step farther. In the disorder occasioned by her
struggle, her mask droped off, and discovered a countenance of incomparable and

amazing beauty, even tho' disguised with paleness and horror; for, her eyes rolled about to every corner which her sight could reach, with such eagerness and wildness, that she looked like a woman possessed.

Dorothea, and all present, were infinitely concerned at these symptoms, the meaning of which they could not understand: mean while, the cavalier was so busied in holding her fast by the shoulders, that he could not attend to his mask, which also fell to the ground: and Dorothea lifting up her eyes towards him, as he held the lady in his arms, perceived that this cavalier was no other than her own husband, Don Fernando. No sooner did she recognize his features, than fetching a long and melancholy sigh from the very bottom of her soul, she fell backward in a swoon, and if the barber had not been at hand to support her, would have certainly come to the ground: the curate ran instantly to take off her veil, that he might sprinkle water on her face, which was immediately known by Don Fernando, who held the other lady in his arms, and was thunderstruck at the sight: he would not, however, quit Lucinda, who struggled to get loose; she and Cardenio having by this time, recognized each other by their mutual exclamations: he had also overheard the groan uttered by Dorothea, when she fainted, and believing that it proceeded from Lucinda, rushed out of his apartment in a fright, when the first object he beheld was Don Fernando clasping her in his arms. This nobleman knew him immediately, and all three, namely, Lucinda, Cardenio, and Dorothea, were struck dumb with astonishment, and seemed insensible of what had happened; gazing in silence, at one another.

Dorothea directed her eager view to Don Fernando, who stared at Cardenio, whose eyes were fixed upon Lucinda, who looked wishfully at him; but, the first that broke silence, was this last, who addressed herself in these words to Don Fernando: "Suffer me, signor, in regard to your own character, since you are deaf to every other consideration, to cleave to that wall of which I am the ivy, to avail myself of that prop from which you could not disengage me, with all your importunities, promises and threats. Behold how heaven, by unusual and mysterious means, hath brought me to my true and lawful husband: and since you know, by dear-bought experience, that nothing but death can expel his image from my breast, let this plain demonstration, since all other attempts are vain, convert your love into rage, your friendship into hate, and instantly deprive me of life, which I shall yield with pleasure in the presence of my legal lord, who will then, perhaps, be convinced of the fidelity I preserved to the last moment of my existence."

In the mean time Dorothea, being recovered from her swoon, had listened to Lucinda's declaration, by which she discovered her situation and name: but, perceiving that Don Fernando neither quitted his hold, nor answered one word to her sollicitation, she exerted her whole strength in falling down on her knees before him, and having shed a large quantity of tears from her beautiful eyes, accosted him in these words: "My dear lord! if your eyes were not dazzled and obscured by the rays of that sun which you hold eclipsed within your arms, you would perceive that she who thus kneels before you, is the unhappy (so long as you are pleased she should be so) and forlorn Dorothea—I am that humble country-maiden whom your generosity or passion vouchsafed to raise to the honour of calling you her own. I am she who, continued within the bounds of modesty, lived a contented life, until moved by your importunities, and seemingly upright

addresses, she opened the gates of her reserve, and surrendered to you the keys of her freedom. An offering but ill requited, as plainly appears by that hard fate, in consequence of which, I am found in this place, and also find you in your present situation. Nevertheless, I would not have you imagine that I came hither, induced by any dishonourable motives; but, that the sorrow conceived at seeing myself forsaken and forgotten by you, was the sole cause of my retreat. You desired I should be your own, and that desire you accomplished so effectually, that altho' your inclinations may be changed, it is impossible you should cease to be mine. Consider, my lord, that my unparallelled affection may counterbalance the beauty and birth of her, for whom I am abandoned: you cannot be the fair Lucinda's husband, because you are already mine, nor she become your wife, while she appertains to Cardenio; and it will be a much easier task, if you reflect upon it, impartially, to recal your love for her who adores you, than to gain the affection of one by whom you are abhorred. You sollicited my unsuspecting heart, you importuned my integrity, you was not ignorant of my lowly station, and know in what manner I yielded to your will; so, that you have no subterfuge, nor the least room to say you was deceived. If this be the case, as doubtless it is, and you be a christian as well as a gentleman, why do you, by such evasions, delay to make the end as happy as the beginning of my fortune? If you will not receive me as what I really am, your lawful wife, at least, admit me into the number of your slaves; for, in whatever shape I belong to you, I shall account myself fortunate and blessed: do not, therefore, by renouncing me intirely, give scandal an opportunity of impeaching my honour. Make not my parents miserable in their old age; their faithful services to your father merit a more kind return: if you think your blood will be debased, in mixing with mine, consider, that almost all the great families on earth have undergone the same intercourse, and that the woman's quality in no manner affects illustrious descents: besides, true nobility consists in virtue, and in that I shall have the advantage over you, if you deny and oppose the justice of my claim. In fine, the last argument I shall use is this, whether you are pleased or displeased with your destiny, I am your lawful wife: witness your own words, which neither are, nor ought to be false, if you value yourself on that, for which you undervalue me; witness your handwriting, and heaven above, to the testimony of which you appealed, for the performance of your promise: and if all these should fail, your conscience will never cease whispering to you, amidst your pleasures, in vindication of this truth, which will disturb your most exalted enjoyments."

This supplication, enforced with other arguments, was pronounced so feelingly by the afflicted and weeping Dorothea, that tears of sympathy were shed by all present, the companions of Don Fernando not excepted; he himself listened without answering one word, until she had made an end of her address, and begun to utter such woeful sighs and groans, as were almost sufficient to melt an heart of brass. Lucinda stood gazing upon her with equal compassion for her sorrow, and admiration of her beauty and good sense; nay, she would have gone and offered her all the consolation in her power, had she not still been kept fast locked in the arms of Don Fernando, who, full of confusion and surprize, after having for a good while fixed his eyes upon Dorothea, with great attention, opened his arms, and leaving Lucinda at liberty, said, "You have conquered, beauteous Dorothea—The victory is yours; for, so many truths conjoined are surely irresistible."

Lucinda was so faint and weak, that when Don Fernando quitted her, she would have fallen to the ground, had it not been for Cardenio, who had placed himself behind her ravisher, that he might not be known *: but now, laying aside all fear, and resolving to adventure every thing, he sprung to the assistance of Lucinda, and catching her in his arms, "If," said he, "it be the will and pleasure of pitying heaven, that you should find repose, my faithful, constant and charming Lucinda! I think you can enjoy it no where so securely, as in these arms, which now receive, and formerly encircled you, when fortune was pleased that I should call you mine."

At these words, she gazed upon him with great eagerness; she had before begun to recognize his voice, and now, recollecting his features, like a person deprived of judgment, who disregards all decency and form, she threw her arms about his neck, and joining her lips to his, "Yes, my dear Cardenio," said she, "you are the real lord of this your slave, in spite of adverse fate, and all those threats, tho' greater than they are, that persecute my life, which now depends on yours alone."

An unexpected sight was this, to Don Fernando, and all the by-standers, who were not a little surprized at what they saw. While Dorothea observing her husband change colour, and signify an inclination of being revenged upon Cardenio, by laying his hand upon his sword, ran, with incredible agility, and clasping his knees, which she kissed, held him so firmly embraced that he could not move, saying, while the tears incessantly trickled from her eyes, "What means my only refuge, to do on this unexpected occasion? Your own wife is now kneeling before you, and she whom you desire to wed is in the arms of her lawful husband; consider whether it be just or possible for you to undo that which heaven hath done; why should you seek to unite yourself with one who, disdaining all opposition and inconvenience, and confirmed in her own constancy and truth, even before your eyes, lets fall from hers, a shower of tenderness into the bosom of her lawful spouse? For the sake of God and of yourself, I intreat and beseech you, that this remarkable recognition may not only fail to increase your indignation, but even diminish it in such a manner, that these two lovers may, without any impediment from you, enjoy each other as long as heaven will permit them to live. In this self-denial you will manifest the generosity of your noble and illustrious soul, and convince the world, that you are governed more by reason than by appetite."

While Dorothea pronounced these words, Cardenio, though he held Lucinda in his arms, kept his eyes still fixed upon Don Fernando, with full resolution, if he attempted any thing to his prejudice, to defend himself as well as he could, against his adversary and all his adherents, although it should cost him his life. But, this young nobleman's friends, together with the curate and barber, not forgetting honest Sancho Panza, who were present at the whole affair, interposed, and making a circle about him, begged earnestly, that he would be pleased to consider the tears of Dorothea, and if what she alleged was true, as they firmly believed it was, no longer suffer her to be defrauded of her just and reasonable hope. They desired him to observe, that in all appearance, it was not by accident, but the immediate direction of providence, that they had all met together,

* But it appears, p. 265, that he was already known both to Fernando and Lucinda. *Aliquando bonus dormitat homerus.*[3]

Dorothea Pleading with Don Fernando as He Draws His Sword against Cardenio.

so unexpectedly in this place: and the curate entreated him to reflect, that death alone could divide Lucinda from Cardenio; that though they might be parted by the edge of the sword, they would look upon death as the greatest blessing that could befal them; and that, in a case of this kind, which admitted of no other remedy, it would be his wisest course, to constrain and conquer his own passion, and demonstrate the generosity of his heart, by permitting, of his own free-will, these two lovers to enjoy that state of happiness which heaven had ordained for their lot: that he should contemplate Dorothea's beauty, which far from being excelled, was equalled in few or none; and to her beauty, add the consideration of her humility and excessive love; above all, take notice, that if he valued himself upon being a gentleman and a christian, he could do no less than perform the promise he had given, and in so doing, act in conformity to the will of God, and satisfy the discreet part of mankind, who are very sensible, that it is the prerogative of beauty, even in a low estate, when accompanied with virtue, to be lifted up to the highest rank, without any disparagement to the person who thus raises it to an equality with himself; and since the irresistible force of inclination must prevail, provided there be nothing criminal in the means, he is not to be blamed who acts according to its dictates.

To these arguments were added so many of the same sort, that the valiant heart of Don Fernando, nourished by illustrious blood, relented, and he was overcome by the force of that truth which, however inclined, he could not deny. The signal of his surrender, and yielding to this reasonable and just proposal, was his stooping down and embracing Dorothea, to whom he said, "Rise, madam; it is not just, that she who reigns in my soul, should lie prostrate at my feet. If hitherto, I have given small proof of what I now profess, perhaps, my omission hath been owing to the appointment of heaven, that by giving you an opportunity of manifesting the sincerity of your love, I might know how to esteem you according to your deserts. I beg, therefore, you will not upbraid me with my misconduct and unkind neglect; since the same force and occasion that attached me to you, was the cause of my endeavour to disengage myself. That you may be convinced of the truth, behold and contemplate the eyes of the now contented Lucinda, in which you will find an excuse for all my errors: and, since she hath found and attained her heart's desire, and my utmost wish is fulfilled in thus retrieving you, may she live in peace and quiet, for many happy years, with her Cardenio, and may heaven grant the same felicity to me with Dorothea."

So saying, he embraced her again, pressing his lips to hers with such tenderness, that it required his greatest efforts to forbear giving, with his tears, indubitable signs of his affection and remorse. But, those endeavours did not succeed with Lucinda, Cardenio, and every other person present, who began to weep so plentifully, either at their own happiness, or the satisfaction of their friends, that one would have thought some grievous misfortune had happened to the whole company. Even Sancho blubbered, though he afterwards owned, that his sorrow proceeded from seeing that Dorothea was not, as he imagined, the queen of Micomicon, from whom he expected such favours.

This universal admiration and thaw having lasted some time, Cardenio and Lucinda fell upon their knees before Don Fernando, whom they thanked for his generosity in such polite terms, that he scarce knew what answer to make, but, raised and embraced

them both, with demonstrations of uncommon courtesy and affection. Then asking Dorothea, how she had come to that place so distant from her own home, she, with great elegance and brevity, repeated what she had before recounted to Cardenio: and her husband and his company were so pleased with her narration, that they wished it could have been spun out to a much greater length: so gracefully did she relate her own misfortunes.

Her task being finished, Don Fernando informed them of what had happened to him, in the city after he found, in Lucinda's bosom, the paper in which she declared herself Cardenio's wife. Seeing that she could not possibly be his, he said, he was determined to put her to death, and would actually have executed his purpose, had not her parents interposed. He then quitted the house, full of shame and resentment, resolving to revenge himself with the first opportunity; and next day, understood that she was gone off, without any body's knowing whither she had directed her flight. At length, however, in a few months, he got notice, that she was in a certain monastery, where she intended to spend her whole life, if she could not enjoy it in the company of Cardenio. He no sooner received this intimation, than choosing these three gentlemen for his companions, he went strait to the place of her residence, but, without speaking to her, or making himself known, lest the monastery should be more strictly guarded on his account. He waited therefore until, one day, he found the porter's lodge open, when leaving two of his friends to secure the door, he entered the monastery, with the other, in quest of Lucinda, whom he found in the cloisters, talking with a nun; and snatching her off, without giving her a moment's time for recollection, carried her instantly to a place where they provided themselves with necessaries for their journey. This exploit they were enabled to perform with safety, because the monastery stood in the middle of a field at a good distance from any village or town. He said, Lucinda no sooner perceived herself in his power, than she fainted away, and when she recovered the use of her senses, did nothing but weep and sigh, without speaking one word; so that, accompanied with silence and tears, they had arrived at that inn, which he looked upon as the heavenly goal where all earthly misfortunes are happily terminated.

## CHAPTER X.

## A continuation of the history of the renowned princess Micomicona; with other pleasant adventures.

Sancho heard every thing that passed, with no small anxiety of mind, seeing the hopes of his preferment vanish into smoke, the beautiful princess Micomicona transformed into Dorothea, the giant into Don Fernando, and his master in a sound sleep, little dreaming of what had happened. Dorothea could not persuade herself, that all her good fortune was not a dream; Cardenio entertained the same opinion, which was also

embraced by Lucinda; while Don Fernando gave thanks to heaven for its favour, in extricating him from that labyrinth of perplexity, in which he was at the point of losing his reputation and soul. In fine, every person present was well satisfied, and rejoiced at the happy issue of such intricate and desperate affairs. The curate represented every thing in the right point of view, with great discretion, and congratulated the parties concerned, on the felicity they had acquired; but, she whose joy was most vociferous was the landlady, who loudly exulted in the promise of Cardenio and the curate, who had undertaken to pay her with interest, for the damage she had sustained on Don Quixote's account. Sancho alone, as we have already observed, was afflicted, unfortunate and sad, and going to his master who was just awake, said, with a lamentable tone, "Sir knight of the rueful countenance, your worship may now sleep as long as you please, without giving yourself the trouble of slaying the giant, or restoring the princess to her throne—that whole affair is already brought to conclusion."

"I really believe what you say," answered the knight; "for, I have been engaged with the giant, in the most obstinate and outrageous combat that I believe I shall ever fight in all the days of my life: with one backstroke, slam went his head to the ground; and discharged such a quantity of blood, that it ran like rills of water, along the field." "Or rather like red wine, your worship should say," replied the squire; "for, I must inform you, if you do not already know it, that the dead giant is no other than a wine-bag, and the blood, eighteen gallons of good red wine, which was contained in its belly: the head you cut off is the whore my mother, and the whole affair is gone to the devil." "What does the lunatic mean?" said Don Quixote, "are you in your right senses, Sancho?" "Rise, sir," resumed the squire, "and see what a fine piece of work you have made, and what a score you have run. You shall behold the queen converted into a private lady, called Dorothea, with many other strange events, at which, if you take them right, you will be hugely astonished." "I shall not wonder at any thing of that kind," replied his master; "for, thou may'st remember, the last time we were in this house, I told thee, that every incident which happened was conducted and brought about by inchantment; so that we need not be surprised, if the same power should prevail at present." "I should be of your worship's opinion," answered Sancho, "if my blanketting had been of the same stamp: but that was not the case; for, it was really and truly a substantial tossing. This very innkeeper, whom we saw to-day, held a corner of the blanket, and canted me into the air with great strength and nimbleness, passing a thousand waggish jokes, and laughing at me all the while; from whence I concluded, simple and sinner as I am, that as I knew their persons, there was no inchantment in the case, but, abundance of bruising and bad fortune." "Well, heaven will make thee amends," said the knight: "mean while, reach me my cloaths; for, I want to go forth, and examine those events and transformations which thou hast mentioned."

While Sancho was helping him to dress, the curate gave Don Fernando and his company, an account of Don Quixote's madness, and the artifice they had used to disengage him from the poor rock to which he imagined himself exiled by the disdain of his mistress. He also recounted all those adventures that Sancho had imparted to him, at which they were not a little surprized, and laughed immoderately; agreeing in opinion with every body who knew the knight, that it was the strangest extravagance that ever entered

a disturbed imagination. The priest, moreover, observed, that since the good fortune of Dorothea obstructed the progress of their design, there was a necessity for inventing another plan that should bring him home to his own house. Cardenio proposed that they should prosecute the scheme they had already begun; and Lucinda would act and represent the part of Dorothea. "No," said Don Fernando, "that must not be, Dorothea shall still proceed with her own invention; for, as it cannot be far from hence to the habitation of that honest gentleman, I shall be glad to contribute towards his cure." And when he understood that they would arrive in two days, at his house; "Were it farther off," said he, "I should go with pleasure, to assist in such a laudable design."

At that instant Don Quixote came forth, armed at all points, with Mambrino's helmet, battered as it was, upon his head, his shield braced upon his arm, and his pole or lance in his hand. Don Fernando and his companion were amazed at this strange apparition, when they beheld such a rueful length of face, so withered and tawny; together with his ill-sorted armour, and the solemnity of his gait. They gazed upon him, in silent expectation of what he would say; while he, with infinite gravity of aspect, fixing his eyes upon Dorothea, accosted her in these words: "Fair lady, I am informed by this my squire, that your greatness is annihilated, and your quality undone, by being changed from your former rank of queen and sovereign princess, into the condition of a private damsel. If this hath been done by the negromancy of the king your father, who is, perhaps, afraid that I should not be able to give you the assistance required; I say, he neither knows, nor ever did know, the half of that art which he professeth; and that he is but little conversant in the history of chivalry; for, had he read and perused it with such leisure and attention as I have bestowed upon that subject, he would have found that, on every occasion, knights of much less reputation than I possess, have atchieved much more difficult enterprizes than this; it being a matter of small moment to kill a pitiful giant, let him be as arrogant as he will: for not many hours ago, I saw myself engaged with one—but I chuse to be silent, rather than have my veracity called in question, though time, that unmasks all things, will shew, when we least expect it—"

"That you was engaged with wine-bags, and not with a giant," cried the innkeeper, who was silenced by Don Fernando, and forbid to interrupt the knight's discourse, in any shape whatever. So that Don Quixote proceeded, saying, "In fine if the father of your disinherited highness hath performed this metamorphosis on your person, for the causes I have mentioned, I hope you will give no credit to such considerations; for, there is no danger upon earth, through which my sword will not open a way, and by laying the head of your adversary in the dust, in a few days, invest yours with that crown to which you have an undoubted right."

Here Don Quixote left off speaking, in expectation of a reply from the princess, who knowing it was Don Fernando's pleasure that she should continue the deceit, until the knight could be brought back to his own house; answered with equal gravity and grace, "Whosoever hath told you, most valiant knight of the rueful countenance, that I am changed and transformed from what I was, has not adhered to the truth, in his information: indeed I am somewhat changed by certain fortunate events which have happened even beyond my own expectation; but, nevertheless, I have not ceased to be what I was, nor altered that resolution which I have always maintained, of taking the advan-

tage of your valiant and invincible arm. Wherefore, dear sir, be so good as to do justice to the honour of the father who begat me, and look upon him as a man of sagacity and foresight; since, by the science he possessed, he found such an easy and effectual path to the cure of my misfortune: for, I firmly believe, that were it not for you, I should not now be so happy as I am, as the greatest part of these gentlemen can truly witness. Nothing then remains, but that we set out to-morrow, because we could not propose to travel far to-day; and as for the success on which my hopes are built, I leave it entirely to God and the worth of your heroic breast."

Don Quixote hearing these words, turned to Sancho, in the most violent indignation, saying, "I protest, sirrah! You are the most malicious little slanderer in Spain. Say, you rascal—you vagabond! did not you tell me just now, that the princess was transformed into a private gentlewoman called Dorothea; and that the head, which I know I cut from the giant's shoulders, was the whore your mother: with many more foolish particulars, which threw me into the greatest confusion that ever I felt since I was born? By heaven! (here he turned up his eyes and bit his lips) I have a strong inclination to commit such slaughter upon thee, as will be an * instructive warning to all the lying squires who shall henceforward attend knights-errant, in the course of their adventures."

"Pray be pacified, good your worship," cried Sancho, "I may very possibly be deceived in what concerns the change of my lady princess Micomicona; but as to the giant's head being a wine-bag, and the blood no other than good red wine, I am not mistaken, as I shall answer to God! for, the skins that were slashed are still to be seen, by your worship's bedside, and the whole room is flooded with the wine. But the proof of the pudding, is in the † eating of it: you will be convinced when Mr. What-d'ye-call him our landlord here makes out a bill of the damage he has suffered. As to the rest, I am rejoiced from my soul to find that the queen's majesty is the same as usual; because it concerns me, as well as any other neighbour's child." "I tell thee, Sancho," replied Don Quixote, "thou art distracted; forgive me, that is enough." "Enough in all conscience," said Don Fernando, "there is nothing more to be said on this subject. I think the princess judges very prudently in deferring her journey till to-morrow; because the day is already far advanced: let us therefore, spend this night in agreeable conversation, and at the approach of day, we will in a body attend the gallant Don Quixote, that we may be witnesses of the unheard-of exploits which he will, doubtless, perform in the course of this vast enterprize he hath undertaken." "It is my duty and resolution to serve and attend you," answered the knight: "and I have the most grateful sense of your favour and good opinion, which I shall endeavour to justify, though it should cost me my life, or even more—if more I can pay."

Many compliments and proffers of service passed between Don Fernando and Don Quixote; but, they were interrupted by the arrival of a traveller, who, by his garb, seemed to be a christian slave, lately escaped from Barbary: for, he was clad in a coat of

---

* In the original, As will put salt in thy skull.[1]

† Literally, You shall see when the eggs are fried. A phrase alluding to the story of a thief, who having stole a frying pan, and being asked by the owner what he carried under his cloak, replied, You will see when the eggs are fried. Metaphorically, Time will discover.[2]

blue cloth, wanting a collar, with short skirts and half-sleeves; his britches and cap were of the same stuff; and he wore date-coloured buskins, with a Moorish scymitar slung in a shoulder-belt, across his breast. He was followed by a woman dressed in the moorish habit, mounted upon an ass; with a veil over her face, a brocaded bonnet on her head, and a mantle that flowed from her shoulders to her heels. The man was robust, and well-proportioned, seemingly turned of forty, with a brownish complexion, large whiskers, and a well-furnished beard: in short, his mien was so genteel, that if he had been properly dressed, they would have taken him for a man of birth and quality.

Soon as he entered the gate, he called for a private apartment, and seemed very much concerned, when he understood that all the rooms of the inn were engaged: however, he went to the lady in moorish dress, and lifted her off in his arms. Upon which Lucinda, Dorothea, the landlady, her daughter, and Maritornes, flocked around her, their curiosity being excited by the novelty of the garb, which none of them had ever seen before; and Dorothea, who was always good humoured, mannerly and discreet, concluding that both she and her conductor were chagrined at their want of a chamber, spoke to her thus: "Be not uneasy, madam, at your want of accommodation here; it is the inconvenience of almost all inns: but, if you will be pleased to partake with us, pointing to Lucinda, perhaps you will find that, in the course of your journey, you have been fain to put up with harder fare." The veiled lady made no answer, but, only rising from her seat, signified her thanks, by crossing her hands upon her bosom, bending her body and bowing her head; so that, from her silence, they conjectured that she must be a native Moor, and that she could not speak any christian language.

Her attendant, who had hitherto been employed in something else, perceiving that the company had made a circle about his companion, who could make no replies to their interrogations, said to them, "Ladies, this young woman understands little or no Spanish, and speaks no language but that of her own country; so that she is incapable of answering any questions you may have asked." "We have asked no questions," said Lucinda, "but only made her an offer of our company, for this night, with a share of our lodging, and what accommodation is to be had; and this we tender with that hearty good will which obliges us to serve all strangers, especially those of our own sex who stand in need of our assistance." "Dear madam," replied the conductor, "in her name and in my own, I return you a thousand thanks; and highly esteem your proffered favour, which, on this occasion, and from such persons as your appearance proclaims you to be, must certainly be very kind and condescending." "Signor," said Dorothea, "is this lady christian or Moor? By her silence and her dress, we are induced to believe that she is not what we could wish her to be." "In her body and dress," replied the stranger, "she is a Moor, but altogether a christian in her soul; for, she longs ardently to be a professed convert to our faith." "Then she is not baptized?" resumed Lucinda. "She has had no opportunity," said the captive, "since she quitted Algiers, which is her native country; and hitherto hath never been in such imminent danger of her life, as to make it necessary, before she is instructed in all the ceremonies enjoined by our holy mother church: but, if it please heaven, she shall be baptized very soon, with decency suitable to the quality of her person, which is greater than either her dress or mine seems to declare."

This intimation raised the curiosity of all the spectators, to know who this Moor and captive were; but, no body chose to ask the question, at that time, which seemed more proper for reposing themselves than relating the history of their lives. Dorothea taking her by the hand, seated the stranger close by her side, and intreated her to take off the veil: she looked at her conductor, as if she wanted to know what the lady desired, and he told her, in Arabic, that they intreated her to be uncovered; at the same time, advising her to comply with their request. She accordingly unveiled herself, and discovered a face so amiable, that Dorothea thought her handsomer than Lucinda, who, in her turn, gave her the preference to Dorothea; and all present concluded, that if any creature upon earth could vie with them in beauty, it was this moorish lady, who in the opinion of some of the company excelled them both in certain particulars. As beauty, therefore, has the privilege and energy to conciliate minds and attract affections, every body present were seized with an inclination to serve and cherish the charming Moor. Don Fernando asked her name of the captive, who answered Lela Zorayda: this she no sooner heard, than understanding the question which had been put to the christian, she pronounced with great eagerness and sweetness of concern, "No, no Zorayda; Maria, Maria"; signifying that her name was Maria, and not Zorayda: these words, with the affecting manner in which they were expressed, brought tears from the eyes of some of the hearers, especially the women, who are naturally tender and compassionate. Lucinda embraced her affectionately, saying, "Yes, yes, Maria, Maria": and to this, the Moor replied, "Yes, yes, Maria—Zorayda Macange"; which, in the Arabic, signifies No.

Mean while it grew late, and the innkeeper, by order of Don Fernando's attendants, prepared, with great diligence and care, as good a repast as he could possibly provide: so that, when supper-time arrived, they sat down altogether, at a long hall table; for, there was neither a round nor square one in the house: they forced the head and principal seat, in spite of all his excuses, on Don Quixote, who desired that the princess Micomicona might sit by the side of her protector: next to her, Lucinda and Zorayda placed themselves, being fronted by Fernando and Cardenio, at whose left hand sat the captive and the other gentlemen, while the curate and the barber took their station close to the ladies. In this manner they supped with vast satisfaction, which was still increased, when Don Quixote leaving off eating, and inspired by the same spirit that moved him to harrangue among the goatherds, began the following dissertation: "Verily, gentlemen, if it be duly considered, great and unexpected events are seen by those who profess the order of knight-errantry. What inhabitant of this earth, if he should now enter the gates of this castle, and behold us seated in this manner, could conceive or credit that we are what we are? Who could imagine, that this lady on my right hand, is the great queen whom we all know her to be, and that I am the knight of the rueful countenance, so celebrated by the voice of fame? Now, there is no manner of doubt, that this exercise and art exceeds all others hitherto invented by man, and that it ought to be more esteemed, because it is more exposed to danger. Away with those who give letters the preference over arms: I affirm, that such people, whosoever they are, know not what they say; for, the sole reason to which they adhere, in this decision, is, that the labour of the body is exceeded by that of the mind; and that the profession of arms is altogether as

corporeal as the exercise and office of a common day-labourer, that requires nothing more than bodily strength; as if that which is called soldiership, by us who profess it, did not include acts of valour which none but persons of uncommon genius could execute: or, as if the toil of a warrior who has the charge of an army, or commands in a town that is besieged, doth not affect the mind as well as the body: is it to be supposed, that by meer corporeal strength, he can penetrate and discover the intention of the enemy? To anticipate designs, baffle stratagems, surmount difficulties, and prevent the mischief that is to be dreaded, are all efforts of the understanding, in which the body hath no share: if the profession of arms, therefore, requires genius, as well as that of letters; let us see which of the two requires most mental toil: and this question may be determined, by considering the end and aim of each; for, that occupation deserves the highest esteem, which hath the noblest purpose in view—the end and scope of letters. I speak not here, of that divine learning, whose aim is to raise and conduct the soul to heaven; to an end so infinite, no intention whatever can be compared: I speak of human learning, the ultimate end of which is, to regulate distributive justice, render to every one his due, and to understand and protect the equitable laws; an aim certainly generous, and highly commendable! yet not so deserving of the most sublime praise as the profession of arms, the object and the end of which is peace, the greatest good that mortals can enjoy; for, the first blessed news which this world and mankind heard, were those pronounced by the angels, on that night which was our day, when they sung in the air, 'Glory be to God on high, and on earth, peace and goodwill towards men': and the salutation, which the best master, either in heaven or upon earth, taught his adherents and favourites; which was to say, when they entered any house, 'Peace be to this house.' Nay, he himself, at different times, said, 'My peace I give unto you. My peace I leave with you. Peace be among you.' A jewel and legacy well worthy of him who left it! a jewel, without which there can be no felicity, either on earth or in heaven! This peace is the genuine aim of war; for, arms and war are the same; and this being taken for granted, the end of war is nobler than that of learning: wherefore, let us next consider the bodily toil sustained by each, that we may see on which side the ballance lies, in that particular."

In this sensible manner did Don Quixote continue his discourse, from which no body that heard him could distinguish that he was mad: on the contrary, his audience consisting chiefly of gentlemen, to which title the profession of arms is annexed, they listened with great pleasure, while he proceeded thus:

"The hardships of a student, I say, are these; first of all, poverty, (not that all students are poor, but that we may suppose the worst that can happen); and when I have named his indigence, the whole of his misfortune is mentioned; for, he that is poor can enjoy nothing that is good, but must endure necessity in all its forms, sometimes hunger, sometimes cold, sometimes nakedness, and often, all three together: nevertheless, his necessity is not so great, but that he eats, tho' perhaps later than usual, or, tho' he may feed upon the leavings of the rich, or, which is the greatest misery to which a scholar can be reduced, go a sopping *, as they term it: then they are always admitted to some charitable person's fire-side or chimney-corner, where, if they cannot warm themselves ef-

---

* Alluding to the charity given at the gates of monasteries.[3]

fectually, they may at least defy the cold; and at night, they sleep under cover. I need not descend to minute particulars, such as want of linen, scarcity of shoes, flimsy and thread-bare cloaths, nor the surfeits which they so eagerly incur, when their good fortune sets a plentiful table in their way. By this path, rough and difficult as I have already described it, after many tumblings, slidings, risings and fallings, they, at last, attain to the wished degree, which being gained, we have seen many who have passed with a favourable gale of fortune, thro' these quicksands and straits of Scylla and Charybdis: I say, we have seen many such, command and dictate to the world, from a chair of state; their hunger being changed into satiety, their cold into refreshment; their rags into gay apparel; and the matts on which they lay, to the richest damask and finest holland: a recompence which their merit most justly enjoys! but, their labours, when fairly stated and compared, are infinitely short of the warrior's, as I shall now clearly demonstrate."

## CHAPTER XI.

### The sequel of Don Quixote's curious discourse, on the subjects of learning and war.

The knight proceeded thus: "Since we began with the student, representing his poverty in all its circumstances, let us see if the soldier be more wealthy: and we shall find that poverty itself is not poorer; for, he is restricted to his miserable pay, which comes always late, if ever, or to what he can plunder by force, with the imminent danger of his life and conscience; and frequently, his nakedness is such, that his slashed buff doublet serves him instead of coat, shirt, and all other parts of apparel. In a winter campaign, while he remains in the open field, he has nothing to mitigate the severity of the cold, but his own breath, which as it proceeds from an empty place, must, I believe, be cold, contrary to all the rules of nature: but, stay till the approach of night, when, it is to be hoped, his bed will make amends for all these inconveniencies; and this, if it be not his own fault, will never offend in point of narrowness, for, he may measure as many feet of ground as he thinks sufficient, and there tumble about at pleasure, without any danger of discomposing the sheets: then, instead of the day and hour of receiving the degrees of his art, comes the day of battle, in which his head is adorned with the doctoral tossle, made in form of a pledgit to stuff the wound made by some ball, which, perhaps, hath gone thro' his temples, or left him maimed of a leg or arm: and even if this should not happen, but, merciful heaven guard and preserve him safe and sound, he continues as poor as ever: he must risk himself in several more rencounters and battles, and be victorious in each, before his circumstances be bettered; but, these miracles rarely happen. Tell me, gentlemen, have you considered what a small proportion those who make their fortunes by war bear to those who perish in the field? Doubtless, you must answer, that there is no sort of comparison; that the slain are scarce to be num-

bered, while the living who are recompenced for their services, may be comprehended within three figures of * arithmetic. The case of the learned, is quite the reverse †: for, one way or another, they are all provided; so that, tho' the toil of a soldier is greater, his reward is much less. To this observation, it may be replied, that it is far more easy to reward two thousand scholars than thirty thousand soldiers; for, the first are recompensed with offices which must, of course, be bestowed on people of their profession; whereas, the others can enjoy no reward, except a share of the property belonging to their master whom they serve; even this impossibility strengthens my asseveration.

"But, waving that consideration, which would lead us into a most intricate labyrinth, let us return to the pre-eminence which arms have over learning: a point hitherto undecided, of such force are the reasons alledged on both sides of the question: one of which in favour of the last is, that without letters, the profession of arms could not be supported, because there are laws to which war itself is subject; and all laws fall within the province of letters and learned men. To this observation, the partizans of the other opinion reply, that no laws could be maintained without arms, which preserve the constitution, defend kingdoms, guard cities, scour the highways, and clear the seas of piratical corsairs. In short, that without arms, all republics, kingdoms, monarchies, cities, journeys by land, and voyages by sea, would be exposed to the horror and confusion that attend unbridled war, while it continues in all its licentious privilege and force. It is a general and established maxim, that every thing ought to be esteemed in proportion to what it costs: now, to become eminent in letters, costs the student much time, watching, hunger, nakedness, vertigoes, indigestion, and their consequences, which are in part mentioned above: but, to acquire, in a regular manner, the character of a good soldier, a man must undergo all these inconveniencies in an incomparably greater degree; because, he is every moment in danger of losing his life. What fear of indigence and poverty can seize and harrass the student's apprehension, equal to that which must possess the soldier besieged in a fortress, who being placed centinel or guard in some ravelin or ‡ cavalier, perceives the enemy at work undermining the very spot whereon he stands; without daring to stir from his post, or avoid the danger by which he is so imminently threatened? All he can do, is to give notice of what passes, to his captain, who must endeavour to baffle the foe by some countermine, while he remains upon the place in terror, and expectation of being suddenly whirled aloft into the clouds without wings, and of falling thence head-long into the profound abyss: if this danger seems inconsiderable, let us see whether it be equalled or exceeded in the grappling of two gallies, by

---

* *i.e.* Do not amount to 1000, which is a number expressed by four figures.[1]

† The literal translation is, "For, from the skirts, (for I would not mention the sleeves)." The Spaniards, instead of the English phrase, by Hook or by Crook, use this of "From the sleeves or the skirts"; derived from the practice of taylors, who are supposed to cabbage from those parts of the habit in which there is the greatest quantity of cloth: but, the knight's exception of sleeves, on this occasion, seems to have proceeded from a supposition that poor scholars are generally provided for in the church, and consequently wear cassocks, which descend to their heels.[2]

‡ Cavalier is an artificial mount, raised in a fortress for the convenience of scouring a field, or opposing a commanding work of the enemy.[3]

their prows, in the midst of the extended ocean; when they are locked and fastened into each other, and the soldier hath not an inch more than two feet of the beak to stand upon, while he sees himself threatened and opposed by as many ministers of death as there are cannon in the enemy's vessel, and these within a spear's length of his body; and is sensible, that if his feet should chance to slip, he would instantly visit the profound bosom of the sea: yet, nevertheless, with an intrepid heart, incited and transported by honour, he bears the brunt of their whole artillery, and endeavours by that narrow passage to board the adverse vessel: and, what is very much to be admired, is, that as soon as one falls, never to rise again till the general resurrection, another occupies his place, and should he also drop into the sea, which, like an enemy, gapes to devour him, another and another still succeeds, without the smallest intermission: an instance of gallantry and boldness the greatest to be found in all the extremities of war. Happy were the ages past, while strangers to those infernal instruments of artillery, the author of which is, I firmly believe, now in hell, enjoying the reward of his diabolical invention, that puts it in the power of an infamous coward to deprive the most valiant cavalier of life; for, often in the heat of that courage and resolution that fires and animates the gallant breast, there comes a random ball, how or from whence no man can tell, shot off, perhaps, by one that fled and was afraid at the flash of his own accursed machine, and, in an instant, puts an end to the schemes and existence of a man who deserved to live for ages. This very consideration makes me almost own, that I am sorry for having chosen this profession of a knight-errant in this detestable age; for, tho' no danger can daunt my resolution, it gives me some uneasiness to think that powder and shot may deprive me of the opportunity of making myself famous and renowned thro' the whole globe, for the valour of my arm, and the keenness of my sword: but, let the will of heaven be fulfilled; if I accomplish my aim, I shall be more esteemed, because I have faced more danger than ever was incurred by the knights-errant in ages past."

While the rest of the company were employed in eating, this long harangue was uttered by Don Quixote, who never thought of swallowing a morsel; tho' Sancho frequently put him in mind of eating his supper, observing, that he would afterwards have time enough to say what he pleased. The hearers were moved with fresh concern, at seeing a man who, in every other subject, seemed to have a large share of sense and discernment, lose it so irrecoverably, whenever the discourse turned upon the cursed mischievous theme of chivalry. The curate observed, that there was a great deal of reason in what he had advanced in favour of arms; and that he himself, tho' a graduate, consequently a man of letters, was entirely of the knight's opinion. Supper being ended, and the table uncovered, while the landlady, her daughter and Maritornes were busied in fitting up the garret of Don Quixote de la Mancha, in which it was determined the three ladies should pass the night by themselves; Don Fernando intreated the captive to recount the story of his life, which he imagined must be both uncommon and entertaining, from the specimen they had already seen, in his arriving thus equiped, in company with the fair Zorayda. To this request the stranger answered, that he would willingly obey his command, tho' he was afraid the company would not find the relation to their liking; but, nevertheless, rather than fail in point of obedience, he was ready to make it. The curate and whole company thanked him for his complaisance, and joined in the re-

quest; and he seeing himself besought by so many, said there was no occasion for in-treaties, where they might so effectually command: "Lend me your attention therefore, and you shall hear a true story, perhaps unequalled by those fictions which are usually adorned with all the curious and profound artifice of composition."

At this preamble, all present, adjusted and composed themselves; and he perceiving the general silence in which they waited for the performance of his promise, began in this manner, with a grave and agreeable voice.

## CHAPTER XII.

## In which the captive recounts his life and adventures.

"In a certain place, among the mountains of Leon, my family had its origin; more be-holden to the liberality of nature than to the smiles of fortune: tho' amidst the nar-rowness of circumstances, which prevails in that country, my father had the reputation of being rich, and really was so, had he possessed the art of preserving, as he practised the means, of spending his estate. This liberal and profuse disposition was owing to his having been a soldier in his youth: the army being a school, in which the miser becomes generous, and the benevolent man grows prodigal; for, a covetous soldier is a monster which is rarely seen. My father exceeded the bounds of liberality, and bordered upon those of prodigality; a disposition of very little service to a married man who has chil-dren to succeed him in rank as well as name: and he had no less than three; all of them sons, already at an age to choose for themselves. The old gentleman finding it impos-sible, as he said, to resist the bent of his inclination, was resolved to deprive himself of the means that induced and enabled him to spend so lavishly, by giving up his estate; as without money, Alexander himself must have seemed frugal.

"One day, therefore, calling us all three together into his chamber, he delivered him-self in these or the like words. 'Sons, to say I love you, is no more than to say and know you are my own children: though it would seem that I do not love you, by my squander-ing away the fortune which is your due: but, that you may be henceforward convinced that I love you like a true parent, rather than seek your destruction like a stepfather, I am resolved to execute a plan which I have formed a good while ago, and digested with the most mature deliberation. You are now of an age to chuse settlements for yourselves, or at least, to pitch upon employments which, in your riper years, may conduce to your honour and advantage. My intention is to divide my estate into four equal parts, three of which you shall receive among you, in equal shares, without the least difference or distinction, and the fourth I will reserve for my own sustenance and support, while heaven shall be pleased to protract the days of my life. But, after you have received your portions, I should be glad to find you inclined to follow the paths which I shall propose. We have a saying in Spain, which, I believe, is very true, as indeed all proverbs are, be-

cause they are short sentences dictated by long and sage experience: that which I mean, contains no more than these words: "The church, the court, or the sea"; as if it more fully expressed the following advice, He that would make his fortune, ought either to dedicate his time to the church, go to sea as a merchant, or attach himself to the court: for it is commonly observed, that, "The king's crumb is worth the baron's batch." This I mention, because I wish and desire that one of you would follow letters, another merchandize, and a third serve his sovereign in the field, since it is difficult to obtain an office at court: and, although much wealth cannot be expected, there is a great deal of valour and reputation to be acquired in war. In eight days I will give each of you his share, in ready money, without defrauding you of one farthing, as you will see by my distribution. Tell me, therefore, if you are willing to follow my advice in what I have proposed?' said my father, addressing himself to me as the eldest. After having dissuaded him from parting with his estate, and desired him to spend as much of it as he pleased, observing, that we were young men, and capable of making our own fortunes, I concluded with saying, I would obey his will, and, for my own part, chuse to serve God and my king, in adhering to the exercise of arms. My second brother made the same offer, proposing to set sail for the Indies, and employ his stock of ready money in traffic. The youngest, and I believe the wisest, said he would qualify himself for the church, by going and finishing his studies at Salamanca.

"We having thus agreed in the choice of our different employments, our father embraced us all affectionately, and within the time he had proposed, performed his promise of giving us our portions, which, to the best of my remembrance, amounted to three thousand ducats each: for, an uncle of ours paid ready money for the whole estate, that it might not be alienated from the family. In one day, all three took leave of our worthy father, when I, thinking it a piece of inhumanity to leave him so straitned in his old age, prevailed upon him to accept two thousand of the three I had received, as the remainder was sufficient to accommodate me with all the necessaries of a soldier. Each of my brothers, induced by my example, gave him back one third of their shares, so that he remained possessed of four thousand ducats in cash, and the value of three thousand more in land, which he did not chuse to sell. At length, I say, we took leave of him, and that uncle whom I have mentioned, not without great concern and many tears on all sides; they charging us to seize every opportunity of making them acquainted with our adventures, either in prosperity or adversity. Having given this promise, and received their embraces and blessing, one took the road to Salamanca, another went to Sevil, and I set out for Alicant, where I understood there was a ship taking in a lading of wool for Genoa. Two and twenty years are now elapsed since I left my father's house; and during all that time, though I have written several letters, I never received the least information concerning him or my brothers. What hath happened to myself within that period, I will now briefly relate.

"Embarking at Alicant, I had a favourable passage to Genoa, from whence I went to Milan, where I provided myself with arms and some gay military furniture. Then I departed for Piedmont, with a resolution of inlisting in the service; and being upon the road to Alexandria de la Paglia, was informed that the great duke of Alva was on his march into Flanders. Upon receiving this intimation, I changed my design, attended

him to the Low Countries, served in all his campaigns, and was present at the death of the counts Egmont and Horn. There I obtained an ensign's commission in the company of a famous captain of Guadalajara, whose name was Diego de Urbina: but, after I had been some time in Flanders, the news arrived of the league between his holiness pope Pius the fifth of happy memory, and the Spanish monarchy, against their common enemy the Turk, who about that time had, by means of his fleet, made a conquest of the famous island of Cyprus, which was under the dominion of the Venetians: a most lamentable and unfortunate loss. It was certainly known that the most serene Don John of Austria, natural brother to our good king Philip, was to be general of this league; and the vast preparations for this war were publickly reported. All these rumours raised and excited within me the desire and resolution of being present in a campaign of such expectation; and though I had strong hopes, and indeed, certain promises of being promoted to the rank of a captain, as soon as a vacancy should happen, I chose to quit that prospect, and go, as I actually did, to Italy; and luckily for me, Don John of Austria was then at Genoa, just going to embark for Naples, in order to join the Venetian fleet, which he afterwards found at Messina. In short, I served in that most happy campaign, and was advanced to the rank of captain of foot, which honourable post I obtained more by good fortune than merit; and that day which was so fortunate for Christendom, on which the world was convinced of the error they had espoused in believing the Turks invincible by sea; on that day, I say, when the Ottoman pride and insolence was humbled and broke, among so many happy christians there present, (and sure those who fell were happier than the living victors!) I alone was unfortunate; for, instead of receiving a naval crown, which would have been my reward, had I lived in the Roman ages, on the night that succeeded that glorious day, I found myself a captive loaded with chains; and this was the cause of my misfortune: Uchali king of Algiers, a bold and fortunate corsair, having attacked and mastered the capitan galley of Malta, in which there remained only three knights alive, and these desperately wounded; the vessel commanded by John Andrea Doria, in which my company was stationed, hastened to her relief, and I doing my duty on that occasion, leaped into the enemy's ship, which disengaging herself immediately from our galley that was grappled with her, my soldiers were prevented from following their officer, and I found myself alone among my foes, whom, by reason of their numbers, I could not resist; therefore was obliged to submit, after having been almost covered over with wounds: and Uchali, as you have heard, gentlemen, having saved himself with his whole squadron, I remained his prisoner, the only sad person amidst the general joy, and captive among so many that were set free; for, full fifteen thousand christians who came into the action, chained to the Turkish oars, that day recovered their long wished-for liberty.

"I was carried to Constantinople, where Selim the grand Turk, created my master general of the sea, for having done his duty in the battle, and as a proof of his valour, brought off the high standard of Malta. Next year, which was that of seventy-two, I rowed in the capitan galley of the three lanthorns, at Navarino, where I saw and observed the christians lose the opportunity of taking the whole Turkish fleet in the harbour, for, all the Levantines and Janizaries belonging to it laid their account with being attacked in port, and had actually got in readiness their knapsacks and passamaques,

which are a kind of shoes, in order to go on shore, and seek their safety in flight, without waiting for the assault; such was the consternation that prevailed among them! But, heaven ordained things to happen in another manner, not through any error or neglect of the general who commanded the expedition, but on account of the sins of Christendom, it being the will and permission of God, that we should never want executioners to chastise us. In short, Uchali retreated to Modon, which is an island almost contiguous to Navarino, where he disembarked his men, fortified the mouth of the harbour, and remained until Don John set sail on his return. In this expedition, the galley called the prize, commanded by a son of the famous corsair Barbarossa, was taken by the capitan galley of Naples, called she-wolf, the commander of which was that thunderbolt of war, that father of his soldiers, that fortunate and invincible chief, Don Alvaro de Basan, marquis of Santa Cruz; and I cannot help mentioning what happened at the taking of this prize: the son of Barbarossa was so cruel, and treated his captives so inhumanly, that when the rowers perceived the she-wolf ready to board, and in a fair way of taking her, they quitted their oars all at once, and seizing the captain, who stood upon the * stentrel, calling to them to row lustily, they tossed him forwards from bench to bench, and beat him so severely as he went along, that before he passed the main-mast, his soul passed into hell. Such was his barbarity, as I have already observed, and such the revenge which their hatred to him inspired.

"We returned to Constantinople, and during the following year, which was seventy-three, understood that Don John had taken Tunis, wrested that whole kingdom from the Turks, and put Muley Hamet in possession of the whole; thus cutting off all the hopes of restoration from Muley Hamida, the most valiant and most cruel Moor of his time. The grand signor was deeply affected with this loss, and practising that sagacity which is peculiar to all those of his family, clapt up a peace with the Venetians, who were much more desirous of it than he. Next year, being seventy-four, he attacked the goleta[2] and fort, which Don John had left half-finished, near Tunis: and on all these occasions I was present, being tied to the oar, without the least hope of freedom, especially by ransom; for, I was resolved not to write to my father, an account of my misfortune. At length, the goleta and fort were both lost, having been besieged by seventy-five thousand Turkish soldiers, regularly paid, and upwards of four hundred thousand Moors and Arabs from the other parts of Africa; this multitude being provided with a vast quantity of warlike stores and ammunition, and attended with such a number of pioneers, that, by throwing handfuls of earth, they might have covered both the places they came to besiege. The goleta, which had been counted impregnable, was first taken; not through any fault of the besieged, who performed all that men could do, in its defence; but, because experience shewed that trenches could be made with ease in that loose sand, under which, though water was commonly found at the depth of two spans, the Turks, at that time, dug as many fathoms, without finding one drop; and so filling a vast number of sacks, raised their works so high as to overlook the fort; then mounting this cavalier with cannon, kept such a firing as rendered it impossible for the garrison to make any longer defence. It was a common opinion, that our troops ought not to have shut themselves

* The stentrel or estanterol is a post that supports the awning of the poop.[1]

up in the goleta, but, opposed the disembarkation in the plain: however, those who talk in that manner, speak at random, and must be persons of small experience in such affairs: for, if the whole garrison, in both places, scarce amounted to seven thousand soldiers, how could such a small number, though ever so valiant, take the field, and, at the same time, defend the forts against such a multitude of foes! and how could the forts be possibly maintained without supplies, in an enemy's country, when they were hemmed in by such a numerous and obstinate army? But, others thought, and I am of the same opinion, that heaven manifested a particular grace and favour to Spain, in permitting them to destroy that rendezvous and pretence of mischief, that sink, spunge and devourer of infinite sums of money, which were there unprofitably spent, without serving any other purpose than that of preserving the memory of its being the most happy conquest of the invincible Charles the Vth: as if it was necessary for those stones to support his fame, which is already immortal. The fort was also yielded; though the Turks won it by inches; for, the garrison behaved with such gallantry and resolution, that in two and twenty general assaults, the enemy lost upwards of twenty-five thousand men; and of the three hundred Spanish soldiers that remained alive, they did not make one prisoner who had not been wounded during the siege: a clear and certain proof of the obstinate valour with which the places were defended. A small fort or tower that stood in the middle of the lake, under the command of Don Juan Zanoguera, a Valentian knight and celebrated soldier, surrendered upon terms: but, Don Pedro Puertocarrero, general of the goleta, was made prisoner; and though he did all that man could do, in defence of the place, he was so deeply affected by the loss of it, that he died of grief, on the road to Constantinople, whither they were carrying him captive. The general of the fort, whose name was Gabrio Cerbellon, a Milanese gentleman, a great engineer and excellent soldier, was likewise taken prisoner; and in these two forts perished many persons of note, among whom was one Pagan d'Oria, a knight of St. John, a gentleman of a most generous disposition, as appeared from his excessive liberality to his brother the famous Juan Andrea d'Oria; and what made his death still more lamentable was, that he perished by the hands of some Arabs, to whom, seeing the fort already lost, he trusted himself, relying upon their promise to carry him disguised in a moorish dress, to Tabarca, which is a small port or settlement belonging to the Genoese who fish for coral on that part of the coast; but, those perfidious Arabs cut off his head, which they carried to the general of the Turkish navy, who fulfilled upon them our Castilian Proverb, which imports, that though we love the treason we abhor the traitor; for, it was reported, that he ordered them all to be hanged, because they had not brought him alive.

"Among the christians, who were taken in the fort, was one Don Pedro de Aguilar, a native of some town in Andalousia, who had been an ensign in the garrison, a soldier of great worth and rare endowments, particularly blessed with a happy talent for poetry. This circumstance I mention, because it was his fate to belong to our galley, where he was my companion at the oar and fellow-slave; and before we departed from that harbour, he composed two songs, by way of epitaph, upon the goleta and the fort. As I have them both by heart, I believe it will not be disagreeable to the company, if I repeat them."

When the captive mentioned Don Pedro de Aguilar, Don Fernando looked at his companions, who smiled, and when the stranger was going to repeat the songs, one of

the three, said to him, "Before you proceed, I beg the favour to know what became of that Don Pedro de Aguilar?" "All that I know of the matter," replied the captive, "is, that after having staid two years at Constantinople, he made off in the habit of an * arnaut, with a Greek spy; but, I do not know whether or not he obtained his liberty; though I believe he succeeded; for, about a year after, I saw the same Greek at Constantinople, but, I had not an opportunity to inquire about the success of their scheme." "Then I can satisfy you in that particular," resumed the cavalier; "Don Pedro is my brother, and now lives at home, in good health and easy circumstances, blessed with a wife and three hopeful sons." "Thanks be to God for the great mercies bestowed upon him!" answered the captive, "for, in my opinion, there is no happiness on earth equal to that of liberty regained." "Besides," said the gentleman, "I retain in my memory the songs which my brother composed." "Be so good then," replied the stranger, "as to entertain the company with them; for, doubtless, you can repeat them more perfectly than I can." "With all my heart," said the cavalier, "that upon the goleta runs thus."

## CHAPTER XIII.

## The continuation of the captive's history.

I.

Ye happy shades, whose deeds renown'd
    Have freed you from encumbring clay;
From this low scene where woes abound,
    Ascending to eternal day.

II.

With glorious zeal your bosoms glow'd,
    Your bodies brav'd excessive toil;
Your blood with that of pagans flow'd,
    To drench the hostile, barren soil.

III.

Your lives, but not your courage fail'd,
    Death sealed your just victorious claim:
Enjoy, still honour'd and bewail'd,
    Immortal happiness and fame.

"These are the very words which I remember," said the captive. "And, if my memory does not fail me," replied the gentleman, "the other upon the fort is this."

* A Dalmatian trooper.[3]

### I.

L o! from yon ruins on the desart plain,
    Oppress'd with numbers, in th'unequal fight,
Three thousand souls of christian warriors slain,
    To happier regions, wing'd their joyous flight.

### II.

Yet, not before, in vain, they had essay'd
    The force and vigour of their dauntless arms;
'Til wearied and reduc'd, though undismay'd,
    They welcom'd death encompass'd with alarms.

### III.

On Afric's coast, as records tell,
    The scene of past and present woes,
More valiant bodies never fell,
    More spotless spirits never rose.

The songs were not disliked, and the captive rejoicing at the good fortune of his comrade, proceeded thus, in his narration:

"The goleta and forts being taken, the Turks ordered the first to be dismantled, the other being quite demolished before it was surrendered; and, that this might be done with the less trouble and greater dispatch, it was undermined in three parts; but, they could, by no means, blow up the old walls, which seemed to be the weakest part, while that which was executed by Fratin, was destroyed with great facility. In short, the victorious fleet returned in triumph to Constantinople, where, in a few months, happened the death of my master Uchali, who went by the name of Uchali Fartax, which, in the language of that country, signifies the Scabby Renegado; for, such he actually was, and it is a custom among the Turks, to bestow epithets upon people, derived either from some defect or virtue inherent in them: this method they practise, because they have but four families distinguished by particular names, and these are descended from the house of Ottoman; so, that the rest, as I have observed, adopt some appellation either from the blemishes of the body, or the virtues of the mind. This leper, therefore, tugged at the oar, during fourteen years, as slave to the grand signor, and when he was turned of thirty-four, apostatized, out of resentment against a Turk, who struck him at the oar, renouncing his religion, that he might be able to revenge the affront. Such was his gallantry and conduct, that without practising those vile steps and methods by which the sultan's favourites are raised, he was promoted to the throne of Algiers, and afterwards, created general at sea, which is the third post in the empire. He was a native of Calabria, a man of good morals, and behaved with great humanity to his slaves, who, to the number of three thousand, were at his death, in consequence of his last will, divided between his renegadoes, and the grand signor, who is also coheir with the children of all his deceased subjects. I fell to the share of a Venetian, who had been a common sailor, when he was taken; and Uchali had such an affection for him, that he enjoyed the greatest share of his favour, and became the most cruel renegado that ever was known. This man,

whose name was Azanaga, acquired great riches, and even succeeded to the crown of Algiers, to which place I accompanied him from Constantinople, with some degree of satisfaction, at the thoughts of being so near my own country; not that I intended to send home an account of my unhappy fate, but, to see if fortune would not prove more favourable at Algiers than at Constantinople, where I had laid a thousand schemes for my escape, without having an opportunity of putting one of them in execution: but, I was in hope of finding at Algiers some other more effectual means of obtaining that which I so ardently desired; for, the hope of gaining my liberty never forsook my breast: on the contrary, when all my plans, efforts and expectations miscarried; far from abandoning myself to despair, I endeavoured to find out some new expedient, which tho' ever so frail and unsubstantial, served to support my spirits, and flatter my imagination. Thus I made shift to live within a house or prison, called a bath, in which the Turks confine the christian captives, whether belonging to the king, or private persons, or of that class, which they call magazine-slaves; these are the captives of the council, who serve the state in public works, and other kinds of day-labour; and find great difficulty in obtaining their freedom, because they belong to the community, and have no particular master with whom they can treat concerning their ransom, even tho' they can command money for the purpose.

"In these baths, as I have already said, some private persons lodge their slaves, especially when their ransom is agreed upon; and there they remain secure, and at their ease, until it arrives. Neither do the king's captives, who are to be ransomed, go out to work, with the rest of the crew, except when the money is delayed, and then, that they may be induced to write with more importunity, they are sent out with the rest, to cut wood, an office of no small mortification and toil. As they knew I had been a captain, I, in vain, assured them, that I had neither interest nor money; they put me into the number of those who were to be ransomed, loading me with a chain, rather to denote my condition than to secure my person; so, that I spent my time in that bath, among a great many cavaliers and people of fashion, who were thus marked and designed for ransom; and tho' we were sometimes, nay, almost always exposed to hunger and nakedness, nothing gave us so much pain, as to hear and see, upon every occasion, the new and unheard-of cruelties which my master exercised upon the christians. He was every day, hanging one, impaling another, maiming a third, upon such slight occasions, frequently without any cause assigned, that the Turks themselves owned he acted thus out of meer wantonness of barbarity, as being naturally of a savage disposition, and an inveterate enemy to the whole human race. The person who used the greatest freedom with him, was a Spanish soldier, called such-a-one de Saavedra,[1] who, tho' he did many things which those people will not soon forget, in attempting to regain his liberty, he never gave him one blow, nor ordered him once to be chastised, nor even chid him with one hasty word; and yet the least of all his pranks was sufficient, as we thought, to bring him to the stake: nay, he himself was more than once afraid of being impaled alive. If time would permit, I could here recount some of that soldier's actions, which, perhaps, might entertain and surprize you more than the relation of my own story.

"But, to return to the thread of my narration: just over the yard of our prison were the windows of a rich and principal Moor; but, according to the custom of the country, they

were rather like peep-holes than windows, and even these covered with very thick and close lattices. One day I chanced to be on the terrass of our jail, with three of my companions, passing the time, in trying which of us could leap farthest, in our shackles, the rest of the christians being gone out to work; I casually lifted up my eyes, and perceived a cane with a handkerchief tied to it, held out at these little openings I have mentioned, and waving to and fro, as if by way of signal for some of us to go and catch it. This object was no sooner observed, than one of my companions ran hastily to the place that was directly under it, to see if the cane would be dropped, or what would be the consequence: but, when he arrived, it was pulled up, and moved from one side to another, as if a man should signify his dissent from any proposal, by shaking his head: when the christian returned, the cane was lowered again, with the same motion as at first; upon which, another of our company tried the experiment, but succeeded no better than the first; a third went, and miscarried like the other two. Observing their disappointment, I was resolved to try my fortune also; accordingly, I had no sooner placed myself under the cane, than it was dropped, and fell down within the bath, just at my feet. I snatched it up immediately, and untied the handkerchief, in which I found a knot containing ten zianiys, which are pieces of bad gold, current among the Moors, each of them valued at ten rials of our money. It would be superfluous to say that I rejoiced at this windfall: indeed my joy was equal to my surprize; for, I could not conceive from whence that present could come, especially to me; the circumstance of the cane's being refused to every other person, plainly shewing that the favour was intended for me. I pocketted this lucky sum, broke the cane, returned to the terrass, and looked at the window, thro' which appeared a very white hand, that opened the lattice, and hastily shut it again: from this circumstance we understood, or at least imagined, that we owed the present to some lady who lived in that house; and, in token of thanks, made our obeisance in the moorish manner, by bowing the head, bending the body, and crossing the hands upon the breast. Soon after this ceremony, a small cross made of cane, was held out at the window, and immediately withdrawn: a signal which confirmed us in the opinion, that we were befriended by some christian woman, who lived as a slave in that house; but, this supposition was changed, when we reflected upon the whiteness of the hand, and the bracelets which we had perceived; and then, we concluded that she must be one of those christian renegades whom their masters frequently take to wife, and even think themselves fortunate in having such an opportunity; for, they esteem them much more than the women of their own nation: but, all our conjectures were wide of the truth.

"From this day forward, our whole entertainment was, to gaze at the window, as the north, in which the star of the cane had appeared: but, full fifteen days elapsed, before we had another glimpse either of that or the hand, or indeed, of any other signal: and during this interval, tho' we endeavoured by all the means in our power, to learn who lived in that house, and whether or not there was a christian renegado in it, we never could get any other information but, that it belonged to a rich Moor of great note, called Agimorato, who had been alcayde of Pata, an office of great honour among that people: but, when we least expected another shower of zianiys, the cane re-appeared all of a sudden, with another handkerchief, and a larger knot than before; and this occurrence happened as formerly, when none but ourselves were in the bath: we made the usual exper-

iment; each of my three companions, going towards it, as at first, without success until I approached, and then it was immediately dropped. I untied the knot, within which I found forty crowns in Spanish gold, and a paper written in Arabian characters, with a large cross at the head of the page: I kissed the sacred sign, put up the money, returned to the terrass, where we made our obeisance, the hand appearing again, I made signs that I should read the letter, and then the window was shut. We were equally pleased and perplexed at this event; for, none of us understood Arabic, and altho' our impatience to know the contents of the paper was very great, the difficulty of finding an interpreter was still greater: at length, I determined to trust a renegade, a native of Murcia, who had professed himself my friend, and given me such pledges of his fidelity, as obliged him to keep any secret I should think proper to impart; for, those renegades who intend to return to Christendom usually carry about with them certificates signed by the principal captives, attesting, in the most ample form they can devise, that such a renegade is an honest man, who hath always been obliging to the christians, and is desirous of making his escape with the first opportunity. Some there are who procure these testimonials with a good intention; others use them occasionally, as the instruments of their craft; for, going to rob and plunder on the christian coast, if they should chance to be shipwrecked or taken, they produce their certificates, and observe, that these papers will shew the real design of their coming on a cruize with Turks, which was no other than to take the first occasion of returning to their native country: by these means, they escape the first fury of resentment, and are reconciled to the church, without suffering the least damage; but, when they see their opportunity, they return to Barbary, and reassume their former way of life; whereas, those who procure recommendations with a good design, make use of them accordingly, and remain in peace among the christians. Such a renegado was this friend, who had obtained certificates from all my companions, conceived in the strongest terms of confidence and applause; for which, had he been detected, the Moors would have burned him alive. I knew that he could both speak and write the Arabian tongue; but, before I would disclose the whole affair, I desired him to read that paper which I had found by chance in a corner of my cabbin. He opened it accordingly, and having pored and perused it a good while, muttering between his teeth, I asked if he understood the contents? He answered in the affirmative, bidding me, if I chose to have the literal meaning, furnish him with pen and ink, that he might translate it the more exactly. I accordingly accommodated him with what he desired, and when he had made an end of the translation at his own leisure, he said, 'This that I have written in Spanish, is the literal meaning of that moorish paper; and you are to take notice, that wheresoever you meet with the words Lela Marien, they signify our lady the blessed virgin.'

"The paper contained these words, 'When I was a child, my father had a woman slave, who, in my own language, taught me the christian worship, and told me divers things of Lela Marien. This christian died, and I am sure her soul did not go to the fire, but to Ala; for, I saw her twice after her death, and she advised me to go to the land of the christians, where I should see Lela Marien, by whom I was beloved. I know not which way to go: many christians I have seen from this window, but, not one who seems so much a gentleman as yourself. I am very beautiful and young, and have a great deal of money

in my possession: if thou can'st find out any method of carrying me to thy country, thou shalt there be my husband, if thou art so inclined; but, if that be contrary to thy inclination, I shall not be uneasy, for Lela Marien will provide me with a spouse. I write this with my own hand: let no body read it, but such as you can trust. Beware of the Moors, for, they are altogether deceitful: therefore, I am very much concerned, for, I would not have it disclosed to any person whatever; because, if it should come to my father's ears, he would instantly cause me to be sunk in a well, and covered with stones. I will fasten a thread to the cane, to which thou may'st tie thine answer; and if thou hast not a proper person to write for thee in Arabic, let me know by signs, for, Lela Marien will help me to understand them. May she and Ala preserve thee, by means of this cross, which I often kiss, according to the direction of my deceased slave.'

"You may easily conceive, gentlemen, whether or not, we were surprized and rejoiced at the contents of this paper. Indeed, the symptoms of joy and admiration appeared so plain, in our behaviour, that the renegado suspected it was not found by accident, but, actually written and addressed to one of our company. He accordingly intreated us to tell him, if his conjecture was true; protesting that we might safely trust to his fidelity, and assuring us, if we would favour him with our confidence, he would venture his life in procuring our freedom. So saying, he pulled from his bosom, a crucifix of metal, and with many tears, swore by the God represented under the form of that image, in whom he, though a wretched sinner, fully and faithfully believed, that he would be trusty and secret in every thing we should please to communicate; for, he firmly believed, and as it were, prognosticated, that by means of her who had written the paper, we should all obtain liberty, and he accomplish that which he had so much at heart, namely, his readmission into the bosom of his holy mother church, from which he, thro' his ignorance and guilt, had been, like a rotten member, divided and cut off. This declaration he made with so many tears and signs of repentance, that we unanimously agreed to entrust him with the affair, and accordingly, gave him an account of every thing that had happened, without suppressing one circumstance; and shewed him the window at which the cane had appeared; so that from thence he took his mark of the house, resolving to inform himself, with great care and caution, of the name and quality of those who lived in it. Mean while, we were all of opinion, that there was a necessity for answering the billet; and there being a person present, who could perform that office, the renegado that instant wrote in Arabic what I dictated, which was literally as I shall now repeat; for, of all the material circumstances of that affair, not one hath escaped my memory, which will retain them all to my last breath. In short, this was the answer which I sent to the beautiful Moor.

'My dear lady!

 Mayest thou be protected by the true Ala, and that blessed Mary the real mother of God, who, because she loves thee hath put it into thy heart to go to the land of christians: beseech her therefore, that she will be pleased to teach thee how thou mayest obey her commands; for, she is so benevolent, that she will grant thy request. For my own part, and in behalf of those who are my fellow-prisoners, I promise to serve thee with our whole power, even unto death. Fail not to write and give me notice of what thou shalt resolve to do; and I will always answer thy letters; for, the great Ala hath favoured us with the friendship of a christian cap-

tive, who can speak and write thy language, as thou wilt perceive by this paper: wherefore, thou mayest communicate thy will and pleasure to us, without fear. As to thy offer of becoming my wife, when thou shalt be safely settled in the land of the christians, I pledge myself thine, on the faith of a good christian; and know that those of our religion perform their promises more punctually than the Moors. God, and his mother Mary, take my dear lady into their holy protection.'

"This letter being written and sealed, I waited two days, until the bath was empty, and then went to the usual place on the terrass, to look for the cane, which, in a little time appeared. I no sooner perceived the sign, though I could not see who made it, than I held up the letter to make her understand, that she should fasten a thread to the cane; but, that was already done, and I tied the paper to it, accordingly. In a little time, our star appeared again, loaded with the white flag of peace; which being dropt, I took it up, and found, in different coins of gold and silver, to the amount of fifty crowns, which increased our satisfaction fiftyfold, and confirmed us in the hope of obtaining our freedom. That same night our renegade returned, and told us, he was informed the house was inhabited by that same Moor I have mentioned under the name of Agimorato, who was excessively rich, and had only one daughter to inherit his whole fortune; that by the current report in the city, she was the most beautiful woman in Barbary; and that many of the viceroys, who went thither, had demanded her in marriage, but she would never yield her consent; he likewise understood that she had once a christian slave, who had died some time ago: so, that all these circumstances agreed with the contents of her letter. We then consulted with the renegado, about the means of transporting ourselves, with the moorish lady, into Christendom; and, at length, we came to the resolution of waiting for another intimation from Zorayda, which is the name of her who now desires to be called Maria; for, we plainly perceived, that by means of her and no other, we should be enabled to surmount all the difficulties that occurred.

"Having come to this determination, the renegado bad us give ourselves no uneasiness, for, he would either procure our liberty or forfeit his own life. The bath being full of people, during four days, no cane appeared all that time, at the end of which the usual solitude prevailing, we perceived it with a handkerchief so pregnant as to promise a most happy birth. I stood under it; the whole was dropped as usual, and I found in the handkerchief another paper, with one hundred crowns in gold, without any mixture of other coin. The renegade being then present, we carried him to our cabin, where we desired him to read the letter, which he interpreted in these words:

'I know not, dear sir, how to give directions about our passage into Spain; nor hath Lela Marien told me, though I have earnestly implored her assistance. But, what may be easily effected is this: I will, from this window, furnish you with a great quantity of money, so, that you may ransom yourself and your companions, and going to the land of the christians, purchase a bark, with which you may return for the rest; and you will find me in my father's garden, which is by the gate of Barbazon, close to the sea-side. There I shall be during the whole summer, with my father and servants, and from thence you may, in the night, carry me to the bark, without fear. But, remember thou shalt be my husband; otherwise I will pray to Marien to chastise thee. If thou canst depend upon no other person for purchasing the bark, ransom thyself for that purpose. I know thou wilt be more apt than any other body to return, because

thou art a gentleman and a christian. Be sure to inform thyself well, about the garden. When I see thee walking where thou art at present, I shall know the bath is empty, and provide thee with more money.

Ala preserve thee, my dear gentleman.'

"These were the contents and purport of the second paper, which being read in presence of us all, each proposed himself as the person to be ransomed, promising to go and return with the utmost punctuality; I likewise offered myself for that purpose. But, the renegado opposed the proposal, saying, that he could by no means consent that one should be set free, before we had all obtained our liberty; because experience had taught him, how ill those who are free, perform the promises they have made in their captivity: for, prisoners of note had often practised the expedient of ransoming one of their number, to go to Valencia or Majorca, with money to purchase an armed bark, and return for his companions; but, they never saw his face again: for, having once obtained his own liberty, the dread of losing it again, by returning, blots all manner of obligations out of his remembrance. As a confirmation of the truth of what he alleged, he briefly recounted a case which had lately happened to some christian gentleman, attended with the strangest circumstances ever known even in these parts, where the most uncommon and surprizing events occur almost every day. In short, he told us, the most practicable and prudent scheme was, to give him the money we should receive for our ransom, with which he would purchase a bark at Algiers, under pretence of becoming merchant, and trading to Tetuan, and the other places on that coast; and that being master of the vessel, he would soon contrive the means of disengaging us from the bath, and getting us all on board: especially if the moorish lady should perform her promise in supplying us with money sufficient to pay ransom of our whole company; in which case, being no longer slaves, we might embark with the greatest ease and safety, even at noon-day. The greatest difficulty that occurred, was the backwardness of the Moors, to allow a renegade to purchase or command a vessel, unless it be a large cruizer for pirating; because they suspect, especially, if he be a Spaniard, that his sole motive in buying a small bark, is to make his escape into Christendom: but, he undertook to remedy that inconvenience, by giving a share of the bark and profits of the merchandize to a Tangarin Moor; by which means, he should be master of the bark, and of consequence, have it in his power to accomplish the whole affair.

"Although, in the opinion of me and my companions, there was no better plan than that of sending to Majorca for a bark, as the moorish lady had proposed, we durst not contradict the sentiments of the renegade, lest, he, being disobliged by our acting contrary to his intention, should make a discovery of our correspondence with the fair Moor, and endanger not only our lives, but also that of Zorayda, for which we would have willingly sacrificed our own. We therefore, determined to rely upon God and the renegado; and immediately wrote an answer to Zorayda, importing, that we would adhere in every thing to her advice, which was as prudent as if it had been dictated by Lela Marien; and that it depended solely upon her, either to hasten or to retard the negotiation: pledging my faith anew, to become her spouse. In consequence of this intimation, the very next day, when the bath happened to be empty, she at different times, by means

of the cane and handkerchief, transmitted two thousand crowns in gold, with a paper signifying, that on the first juma, which is Friday, she should set out for her father's garden, but, before her departure, supply us with more money; and desired us to inform her, if we should find that insufficient; for, she would give us as much as we could desire, her father having such vast sums, that he would never be sensible of what she took, especially as all his keys were in her possession. We immediately accommodated the renegado with five hundred crowns, for the purchase of the bark: with eight hundred more I ransomed myself, depositing the money with a Valentian merchant then residing at Algiers, who bargained for my ransom with the king, and obtained my freedom, upon giving his word to pay the money, on the arrival of the first ship from Valencia; for, if he had paid it immediately, the king would have suspected that the ransom had been some time at Algiers, and that the merchant had hitherto detained it for his own convenience. In short, my master was so contentious, that I durst, by no means, disburse the money at once. On the Thursday before the fair Zorayda removed to her father's country-house, she gave us another thousand crowns, and apprized us of her departure; intreating me, as soon as I should be ransomed, to make myself acquainted with her father's garden, and find some opportunity of going thither to see her. I answered, in a few words, that I would obey her in every thing, desiring she would fervently recommend us to Lela Marien in all those prayers which she had learned of the slave.

"This affair being transacted, means were concerted for ransoming my three companions; lest, seeing me at liberty and themselves confined, since I had money enough to procure their freedom, they should be chagrined, and tempted by the devil, to do something to the prejudice of Zorayda: for, although their honour and integrity might have secured me against any such apprehension, I would not run the smallest risk, and therefore took care they should be ransomed by the same canal through which my liberty was obtained; depositing the whole sum required, in the merchant's hands, that he might, with more certainty and confidence, act the part of their bondsman; though we never disclosed to him our secret commerce with Zorayda, for fear of what might happen.

## CHAPTER XIV.

### The continuation of the captive's adventures.

"Before fifteen days had elapsed, our renegado had purchased a stout vessel, capable of containing thirty persons at least; and to secure what he had done with a favourable pretext, he made a voyage to a place called Sargel, about thirty leagues from Algiers, towards the coast of Oran, where there is a great traffic of dried figs: and he made two or three trips of this kind, in company with the Tagarin Moor already mentioned. The Moors of Arragon are, in Barbary, called Tagarins, and those of Grenada

go by the name of Mudajares; though these last are, in the kingdom of Fez, called Elches, being the people whom the king chiefly uses in his wars. I say then, in every passage, the renegado brought his bark to an anchor in a small creek, within two bow-shots of Agimorato's garden; and there purposely employed himself and his moorish rowers in practising the * Zala; or attempted that in jest, which he intended to execute in earnest. He went frequently to Zorayda's garden, on pretence of asking fruit, which he always received from her father, though he did not know him: but although, as he afterwards owned, he wanted to speak with Zorayda, and tell her that he was the person appointed by me, to carry her off to the land of the christians, that she might be satisfied and secure of his fidelity; he never had an opportunity of executing his design: for, the moorish women avoid the sight of their own countrymen and the Turks, unless when they are commanded to appear, by their parents and husbands; though they talk and converse with christian captives, even more freely than decency allows. I should have been very much concerned, had he spoke with her, because it would, perhaps, have given her great uneasiness, to see renegades entrusted with the affair; but God, who ordained all for the best, gave him no opportunity of fulfilling his well-meaning intention.

"Perceiving how securely he traded to and from Sargel, and anchored when, where, and how he pleased, his partner submitting to his direction, in all things; and that I being ransomed, there was nothing wanted but some christians to row, he desired me to pick out those who should accompany me, exclusive of my friends who were ransomed, and bespeak them for the Friday following, which he had appointed for the day of our departure. Seeing him thus determined, I spoke to a dozen Spaniards, all of them ablebodied rowers, and people who could easily get out of the city: and indeed, it was no small difficulty, to find so many at that conjuncture; for, no fewer than twenty gallies being then out upon the cruize, almost all the rowers were employed, so that I should not have found those I have mentioned, had not their master staid at home, that summer, to finish a vessel which he had on the stocks. All I said to them was, that next Friday in the evening, they should slily slip out of the city, one by one, and betake themselves to Agimorato's garden, where they should wait my coming; and I directed every one by himself, if he should meet with other christians at the rendezvous, to say nothing, but, that I had ordered him to wait for me in that place.

"This point being settled, another precaution still more necessary, remained untaken; this was to advertise Zorayda of the situation of our affairs, that she might be prepared and guarded against surprize, at our sudden assault, before she could think it possible that the christian bark was arrived. Resolved, therefore, to see and speak with her, if possible, one day before our departure, I went to the garden, on pretence of gathering some herbs; and the first person I met was her father, who spoke to me in a language used through all Barbary, and even at Constantinople, between the captives and the Moors; it is neither Arabic nor Castilian, nor indeed peculiar to any nation, but a mixture of different tongues, by which we make shift to understand each other. I say, he asked in this sort of jargon, who I was, and what I wanted in his garden? I answered, that I was a slave belonging to Arnaute Mami, who I knew to be an intimate friend of his;

* *Zala* or *Sala*, is the moorish salutation.[1]

and that I wanted a few herbs for a sallad. In consequence of this answer, he inquired whether or not I was to be ransomed, and what my master demanded for my freedom? And while we were thus conversing together, the fair Zorayda came out into the garden. She had already perceived me from a window of the house, and, as the moorish women make no scruple of shewing themselves to christians, with whom, as I have already observed, they are not at all shy, she, without any hesitation, walked towards the place, where I was standing with her father, who no sooner saw her, than he called at a distance, desiring her to come up. It would be a difficult task for me, at present, to describe the exceeding beauty, the genteel mien, the gay and rich ornaments with which my beloved Zorayda then presented herself before mine eyes: I shall only observe, that the pearls about her beauteous neck and ears, outnumbered the hairs of her head. On her ancles, which were bare, according to the custom of the country, she wore carcaxes, (by which name the bracelets for the feet are called in the Morisco language,) of the purest gold, set with such a quantity of diamonds, that she afterwards told me, her father valued them at twenty thousand ducats; and those she wore upon her wrists were of equal richness. The pearls, though in such a vast number were extremely fine; for, the greatest pride and magnificence of the moorish women lie in pearls and embroidery; consequently, there is a greater quantity of pearls and seed-pearl, in Barbary, than in all the other nations of the world, and Zorayda's father had the reputation of possessing the greatest number and the best in Algiers, together with a fortune of two hundred thousand Spanish crowns, of all which she, who is now mine, was once mistress. Whether, with the assistance of all these ornaments, she appeared beautiful or not, and what she must have been in her prosperity, may be conjectured by what remains after the great fatigues she hath undergone; for, it is well known, that the beauty of some women hath its days and seasons, and is diminished or increased according to the circumstances that happen; being improved or impaired, nay, often totally destroyed, by the passions of the mind. In short, she approached in all the pomp of dress, and all the excess of beauty; at least to me, she seemed the most beautiful creature I had ever seen, which circumstance, joined to the obligations I lay under, made me look upon her as an angel sent from heaven, for my delight and deliverance. When she came up, her father told her, in their own language, that I was a captive belonging to his friend Arnaute Mami, and had come for a sallad; upon which she took up the discourse, and in that jumble of languages before mentioned, asked if I was a gentleman; and why I did not ransom myself? I answered, that I was already ransomed, and that she might see in what esteem I was with my master, by the sum he received for my freedom, which was no less than fifteen hundred sultanins. To this observation, she replied, 'Truly, if thou hadst belonged to my father, he should not have parted with thee for twice the sum; for, you christians always dissemble, and call yourselves poorer than you really are, with a view of imposing upon the Moors.' 'That may be sometimes the case, madam,' said I, 'but I adhered to the truth, in bargaining with my master, and will deal honestly with all mankind.' She then asked how soon I intended to depart; and I answered, 'To-morrow, I believe: there is a French ship in the harbour, to sail in the morning, and I have some thoughts of taking my passage on board of her.' 'Had not you better stay till the arrival of a vessel from Spain,' said Zorayda, 'than trust yourself with the French, who are no good friends of yours?' 'No,

madam,' answered I, 'though, as there is a Spanish ship expected, if she arrives immedi-
ately, I believe I shall wait for her: but, it is more likely that I shall sail to-morrow; for,
the desire I have to see myself in my native country, with those I love, is too strong to
let me wait for any other convenience, let it be ever so good.' 'Without doubt,' said Zo-
rayda, 'thou art married in thy own country, and therefore desirous of being with thy
wife.' 'I am not yet wedded,' I replied; 'but, under promise of being married at my re-
turn.' 'And is the woman beautiful to whom thou hast pledged thy faith?' said she. 'So
beautiful,' answered I, 'that to compliment her, and tell thee the truth, she is the exact
resemblance of thyself.'

"Her father laughed heartily at this declaration, saying, 'Truly, christian, she must be
very handsome indeed, if she resembles my daughter, who is the most beautiful woman
in this kingdom; look at her, and thou wilt see whether or not I speak truth.'

"In the greatest part of this conversation, Agimorato served as interpreter for his
daughter, he being better acquainted with this spurious language, which, tho' she un-
derstood a little, in consequence of its being much spoke among the Moors, she ex-
plained her meaning by signs, oftener than by words.

"While we were engaged in this and other such conversation, a Moor ran towards us,
crying aloud, that four Turks having got thro' the pales, or leaped over the garden-wall,
were gathering the fruit, tho' it was not yet ripe. At this information the old man and
Zorayda started; for, the Moors are commonly, and as it were naturally, afraid of the
Turks, especially the soldiers, who are so insolent and imperious to their moorish sub-
jects, that they treat them worse than if they were slaves. Accordingly, the father said to
Zorayda, 'Daughter, retire to the house, and lock thyself up, while I go and talk to those
dogs; and thou, christian, (turning to me) gather thy herbs, and depart in peace; and Ala
send thee safe into thy own country.' I made my obeisance, and he went in search of the
Turks, leaving me alone with Zorayda, who pretended to go homeward, according to
her father's desire; but, no sooner was he out of sight, among the trees of the garden,
than she came back, with her eyes drowned in tears, saying, 'Amexi, christiano, amexi!'
the signification of which address, is, 'Thou art going away, christian, thou art going
away!' 'Yes, madam,' answered I 'but, by no means without you: on the next Juma expect
me, and be not afraid when you see us; for, we shall certainly go to the land of the chris-
tians.' I made shift to express myself in such a manner, that she understood this, and
every thing else that I said; and throwing her arm about my neck, began to walk towards
the house, with a slow and faultering pace: but, it pleased fortune, which might have
proved very unlucky, had not heaven otherwise ordained, that while we walked in this
attitude, with her arm about my neck, we were observed by her father, on his return
from having sent away the Turks; and we immediately perceived ourselves discovered.
Nevertheless, Zorayda prompted by her discretion and presence of mind, would not
take her arm from my neck; but, on the contrary, coming closer to me, let her head drop
upon my bosom, and her knees sink under her, as if she was fainting: while I seemed to
support her with a sort of strained civility.

"The father seeing his daughter in this situation, ran towards us with great concern,
and asked what was the matter: but, she making no reply, 'Doubtless,' said he, 'she hath
fainted with the fright occasioned by the insolence of those dogs.' Then, taking her out

of my arms, he supported her in his own; while she, fetching a deep sigh, the tears still continuing in her eyes, repeated, 'Amexi, christiano, amexi': 'Begone christian, begone.' 'There is no necessity for the christian's departure,' said the father, 'he hath done thee no harm; and as the Turks are gone already, be not disturbed: thou hast no cause to be uneasy; for, as I have already said, the Turks, at my intreaty, went out as they had come in.' 'Indeed, sir,' said I, 'they have discomposed her very much, as you observe; but, since she desires me to go, I will not stay to give offence. Peace be with you. I will, with your permission, return to this garden, for herbs, if they should be wanted; for, my master says there are none better to be found in any other place.' 'Thou mayest come as often as thou wilt,' answered Agimorato: 'what my daughter says, is not out of resentment against thee, or any other christian; but, instead of bidding the Turks begone, she applied the words to thee, or else thought it was time for thee to go and gather thy herbs.' I then took leave of them both; and she, as if her soul had been rent from her body, went away with her father, while I, on pretence of culling my sallad, went round the whole garden, at my pleasure, observing all the entries and outlets, together with the strength of the house, and every convenience that might tend to facilitate our purpose.

"Having thus reconnoitred, I went and communicated my observations to the renegado, and the rest of my companions, longing eagerly for the hour of seeing myself in peaceable possession of the blessing which fortune presented in the beauteous and charming Zorayda. At length, the intervening time elapsed, and the long wished-for day and period arrived, when all of us, following the order and plan which had been often canvassed, and at last settled, after the most mature deliberation; our desires were happily accomplished. On the Friday, after I had spoke with Zorayda, Morrenago, which was the renegade's name, anchored his bark, at night-fall, opposite to the place where my charming mistress resided; and the christians who were to row, in consequence of my directions, lay already concealed in different corners, all around the place, waiting for me with impatience, joy and desire of attacking the vessel which was in view; for, they were ignorant of our confederacy with the renegade, and believed that they must win and maintain their liberty, by force of arms, in killing all the Moors who belonged to the bark: wherefore, as soon as I and my companions appeared, those who were hid came and joined us immediately, about the time when the city-gates were shut; so that not a soul was to be seen in the fields. Being all met together, we were in some doubt, whether we should go immediately for Zorayda, or first of all secure the moorish rowers belonging to the bark. While we hesitated on this point, the renegado arriving, asked what we waited for; observing, that now was the time, the Moors being altogether unguarded, and the greatest part of them actually asleep: we told him the subject of our doubt; upon which, he assured us, that it was of the greatest consequence to make ourselves first masters of the bark, a precaution which might be easily taken, without running the least hazard; and then we could go in quest of Zorayda, with greater security. His advice was unanimously approved; and therefore, without further delay, we followed him as guide to the vessel, into which he leaped, and drawing a scymitar, called in the moorish language, "Let none of you stir, on pain of death." The christians were at his back in an instant; while the Moors being naturally pusillanimous, hearing their master talk in this manner, were seized with consternation, and as there were few or no

arms on board, suffered themselves, without the least resistance, to be fettered by the christians, who performed this office with infinite dexterity and dispatch, threatening to put them all to the sword, if any one of them should raise his voice, or attempt to make the least noise.

"This scheme being executed, we left one half of our number to guard them, and with the rest, using the renegado still as our guide, went to Agimorato's garden-door, which fortunately opened with as much ease as if it had not been locked; so that, without being perceived, we proceeded to the house with great silence and composure. The adorable Zorayda, who stood waiting for us, at a window, no sooner perceived people at the door, than she asked, with a low voice, if we were Nazarini, which in their language, signifies christians. I replied in the affirmative, desiring her to come down: when she knew my voice, she made no delay, but, without answering one syllable, came down in a moment, opened the door, and appeared so beautiful and richly dressed, as to surpass all description. Transported at the sight, I took her hand and kissed it most devoutly: the renegado, and my two companions, did the same, and the rest, tho' ignorant of the occasion, followed our example, thinking we expressed our thanks, and acknowledgments to her as the instrument of our deliverance. The renegado asked, in the Moresco tongue, if her father was in the house? and she assuring him, that he was asleep in his own apartment; 'Then it will be necessary,' said Morenago, 'to wake and carry him off, together with every thing of value, in this agreeable habitation.' 'Touch not my father,' said she, 'and take my word for it, there is nothing valuable in this house but what I have secured, which is enough to make you all rich and happy: stay a little, and thou shalt see.'

"So saying, she went back into the house, protesting she would immediately return, and desiring us to make no noise. I then asked the renegade what had passed between them, and when he told me, charged him to do nothing that should be disagreeable to Zorayda, who soon returned with a coffer so full of golden crowns, that she could scarce support the weight: but, our evil fortune ordained that her father should wake in the interim, and hear a noise in the garden; upon which, he started up, and running to the window, no sooner perceived that we were all christians, than he began to bawl, in Arabic, with vast vociferation, 'Christians! christians! thieves! thieves!' and his cries threw us all into the utmost terror and confusion: however, the renegado seeing the danger we were in, and how much it imported him to atchieve the enterprize, without being detected, ran up to Agimorato, with infinite agility, being accompanied with some others of our company, as I could not leave Zorayda, who by this time had fainted in my arms: in short, those who entered the house managed him so well, that in a moment they brought him down, with his hands tied, and an handkerchief in his mouth, to hinder him from crying, threatening all the while, that if he presumed to speak, it would cost him his life. His daughter covered her eyes, that she might not see her father in that condition; while he was astonished at sight of her, little thinking how willingly she had put herself in our power; and our feet being then more necessary than our hands, we, with great industry and dispatch, returned to the vessel, where we were expected with impatience by those we had left, who had begun to fear we had met with some mischance.

"Before two hours of the night had elapsed, we were all safe on board, where we untied the hands of Zorayda's father, and took the handkerchief out of his mouth; tho' the

renegado commanded him again to be silent, on pain of death. Seeing his daughter also in our power, he began to sigh most bitterly, more especially as he perceived her lie quietly in my arms, without resisting, complaining, or the least appearance of constraint: but, he was fain to hold his tongue, lest the renegado should put his repeated threats in execution. Zorayda now seeing us embarked, and on the point of manning the oars, while her father and the other Moors remained fettered, as prisoners among us, bade the renegado desire, in her name, that I would be so good as to dismiss the Moors, and set her father at liberty; for, she would rather throw herself into the sea, than behold a parent, who loved her so much, dragged into captivity on her account. Morrenago having made me acquainted with her request, I consented to the proposal; but, he said it was by no means expedient, because, should we leave them there, they would instantly alarm both town and country; so that some light frigates would be sent out in pursuit of us, and then we should be so beset, both by sea and land, that it would be impossible for us to escape: he proposed, therefore, to set them at liberty, on the first christian land he should make. We were all of the same opinion, which was also embraced by Zorayda, to whom he imparted the reasons which hindered us from complying immediately with her desire: then each of our valiant rowers laid hold of his oar with joy, silence, and alacrity, and recommending ourselves to the protection of God, we took our departure, directing our course towards the island of Majorca, which was the nearest christian land; but, the north wind beginning to blow, and the sea becoming rough, it was impossible to steer our course, and we were obliged to row along shore, towards Oran, not without great apprehension of being discovered from the town of Sargel, which lies upon that coast, about sixty miles from Algiers; we were also afraid of meeting, in those parts, with some of the galleys which frequently come thither from Tetuan, to trade; tho' each of us singly, and all of us together, presumed, that if we could fall in with a merchant vessel not fitted out, or manned for a corsair, far from losing our liberty again, we should make ourselves masters of a ship in which we might perform our voyage with more security. While we thus coasted along, Zorayda lay with her head in my bosom, that she might not see her father in distress; and I could hear her imploring Lela Marien to assist us in our design.

"When we had rowed about thirty miles, day breaking, discovered that we were about three gun-shots distant from the shore of a desart country, where not a soul appeared to detect us: but, for all that, we plied hard to get a little farther off to sea, which was now somewhat calmer; and having made about two leagues, directed the men to row by turns, that we might refresh ourselves with the provisions, of which we had plenty in the bark; but, the rowers said, it was then no time to be idle, and desired the rest to bring them victuals, which they would eat while at work, protesting that they would by no means quit their oars: this hint was accordingly taken, and a fresh gale springing up, we were obliged to lay aside our oars, and make sail directly for Oran; for, it was impossible to follow any other course. All this was done with great expedition, we sailed at the rate of eight miles in an hour, without any other dread than that of falling in with some corsair. We ordered some victuals to be given to the Moors, who were consoled by the renegado's telling them, that they were not slaves, and should have their freedom with the first opportunity: the same declaration he made to Zorayda's father, who answered, 'I

might expect any other favour from your generosity and courteous behaviour, O christians! but, you must not think me so simple as to believe you will give me my freedom; for, you would never have run such risque in depriving me of it, with a view of restoring it so liberally; especially, when you know who I am, and the advantage you may reap from my ransom, which, if you will now propose, I here promise to pay your utmost demand, for myself and this unhappy daughter, or for her alone, who is the better part of my soul.'

So saying, he wept with such bitterness, as moved us all to compassion, and obliged Zorayda to lift up her eyes, when seeing the tears trickle down from his aged cheeks, she was melted, and rising from the place where I supported her, went to embrace her father; then joining her face to his, the two uttered such a tender lamentation, as drew tears of sympathy from the eyes of almost all those who heard it; but, when Agimorato perceived her so gaily dressed, with all her jewels about her, he said with some surprize, in their language, 'What is the meaning of this finery, my child? Last night, before this terrible misfortune happened, I saw thee in thy ordinary and common dress; but, now, tho' thou had'st neither time, nor any happy tidings to solemnize with such ornaments and finery, I see thee decked in all the richest apparel I could contrive or bestow upon thee, while fortune was much more favourable than at present! Answer me in this particular, at which I am more concerned and surprized, than at the mishap which hath befallen us.' The renegado interpreted to us all that the Moor said to his daughter, who made no answer to his question: but, when he saw on one side of the bark, the coffer in which she used to keep her jewels, which he knew he had left at Algiers, when he moved to his country-house, he was still more confounded, and asked how that casket had fallen into our hands, and what it contained? To this question the renegado replied, without waiting for Zorayda's answer; 'You need not weary yourself, signor, in putting so many questions to your daughter; for, I can satisfy you, in one word: know then, that Zorayda is a christian; that she hath filed off our chains, and converted our captivity into freedom; that she came hither of her own accord, and is now, I believe, as well satisfied with her present condition as one delivered from darkness to light, from death to life, and from affliction to triumph.' 'Daughter,' cried the Moor, 'is that which he affirms, true?' 'Yes,' replied Zorayda. 'That thou art actually a christian, and the very person who hath put thy father into the hands of his enemies?' resumed the old man. 'I am a christian, 'tis true,' said Zorayda, 'but, not the person who reduced you to this situation; for, my desire never extended so far as either to leave or render you unhappy, my sole intention being to provide for my own welfare.' 'And how ha'st thou provided for it, my child?' replied the father. 'Put that question to Lela Marien,' said she, 'who will inform you better than I can.'

"Scarce had these words reached the ears of Agimorato, than, with incredible agility, he darted himself headlong into the sea, where, without all doubt, he must have perished, had not his large intangling robes helped to keep him afloat. Zorayda shrieking, begged we would save her father; upon which we all exerted ourselves, and laying hold of his upper garment, pulled him on board, already half drowned, and deprived of all sensation; when she was so much affected with his condition, that she uttered a most tender and doleful lamentation over him, as if he had been actually dead. Having turned

him upon his face, a great quantity of water ran out of his mouth, and he recovered the use of his senses, in the space of two hours, during which, the wind shifting, we were driven towards the shore, and by main dint of rowing, kept from running aground; but, by good fortune, we arrived in a creek formed by a small cape or promontory, known among the Moors by the name of Cava Rumia, which signifies, The wicked christian woman; there being a tradition among them, that * Cava, on whose account they lost their possessions in Spain, is interred in that place; for, Cava, in their language, implies a Wicked Woman, and Rumia signifies Christian: so that they look upon it as a bad omen, when they are obliged, by necessity, to drop anchor here, and except, in cases of emergency, they never attempt it: tho' to us, it was by no means the shelter of a wicked woman, but a secure harbour in stormy weather. Having placed centinels on shore, without quitting our oars, we made another meal of what the renegado had provided; and prayed heartily to God and the blessed Virgin, to favour and assist us, in bringing such a fortunate beginning to a happy conclusion. We then determined, at the intreaty of Zorayda, to set her father and the Moors, whom we had fettered, on shore, because she had not resolution enough, nor could her tender disposition endure to see her parent and countrymen in the condition of captives; we accordingly promised to gratify her desire, at our departure, since we ran no risk in setting them at liberty, in that uninhabited place.

"Our prayers were not so vain as to be rejected by heaven, that sent a favourable wind and a smooth sea, inviting us to proceed with alacrity in the voyage we had undertaken. This we no sooner perceived, than unbinding the Moors, we put them all on shore, one by one, to their no small astonishment; but, when we came to dismiss Zorayda's father, who by this time had recovered the intire use of his senses, 'Christians,' said he, 'do you think that bad woman rejoices at my freedom, thro' filial piety? No, surely, but meerly to be rid of the check which she would receive from my presence, in seeking to gratify her vicious desires. Do not imagine that she hath been induced to change her religion, because she believes that the christian faith is preferable to ours. No; she hath apostatized, because she understood that, in your country, she might indulge her loose inclinations more freely than in her own.' Then turning to Zorayda, while I and another christian held him fast, that he might not commit some desperate action, he said, 'O infamous wretch, and ill-advised maiden! what blindness and distraction hath prompted thee to put thyself in the power of these dogs, who are all our natural foes? Cursed be the hour in which thou wast engendered! and cursed be the gaiety and indulgence in which I brought thee up!'

"Perceiving that there was no likelihood of his ending his exclamations for some time, I presently set him on shore, where he proceeded with his reproaches, imprecations and complaints, imploring the mediation of Mahomet with Ala, to confound, overwhelm and destroy us; and when we had sailed out of hearing, we could perceive him act his despair, pulling his beard, and rolling himself upon the ground; nay, once he raised

---

* Cava or Caba, daughter of count Julian, count of Ceuta, was violated by Roderick king of Spain, and, in order to revenge this injury, the father called the Saracens into that kingdom, in the year 712.[2]

his voice in such a manner, that we could distinctly hear him pronounce, 'Return, my beloved daughter! return to the shore; I forgive all that is past: leave with these men the money which they already have in their possession, and return to comfort thy disconsolate father, who, if thou forsakest him, will lie down and breathe his last upon this barren sand!' This pathetic address was heard by Zorayda, who lamented his affliction with the utmost sensibility, tho' she could make no other reply than this, 'Ala grant, my dear father, that Lela Marien, who was the cause of my conversion, may console you in your distress! Ala knows I could not do otherwise than I have acted, and that these christians owe nothing to any particular good-will I bore them; for, if I had not assisted and accompanied them in their escape, but remained at home with you, it would have been impossible for me, in consequence of the earnest sollicitations of my own soul, to execute that which, in my opinion, is as righteous as it is infamous and wicked in yours.' But, these words never reached the ears of her father, whom, by this time, we could not perceive: I therefore endeavoured to console my amiable mistress, while the rest were intent upon our voyage, which was so much favoured by a fair wind, that we laid our accounts with being next day on the coast of Spain.

"But, as good fortune seldom comes pure and single, unattended or unpursued by some troublesome and unexpected circumstance, it was ordained by heaven, perhaps in consequence of the curses imprecated by the Moor upon his daughter; for, such curses are to be dreaded, let the parent be what he will. I say, heaven ordained, that when we were a good way off at sea, with a flowing sheet, three hours of the night being already spent, the oars lashed up, because the fair wind made it unnecessary to use them, and the moon shining with remarkable brightness; we perceived a large round vessel with all her sails out, steering a little upon the wind, right athwart our hause, and so near that we were obliged to shorten sail, that she might not run foul of us, while she claped[3] her helm aweather that we might have time to pass: those upon deck hailed us, asking who we were, whence we came, and whither bound: but, as they spoke in French, the renegado said, "Let no man answer; these are French privateers, who make prize of every thing that falls in their way."

"Thus cautioned, we made no reply, but sailed on, leaving the ship a little to windward, when all of a sudden, they discharged two pieces of cannon, loaded, in all appearance, with chain-shot; for, one of them cut away our mast in the middle, which, with the sail, fell overboard into the sea; and the other coming a moment after, took us amidships, and laid the side of the bark intirely open, without doing any other mischief. Seeing ourselves going to the bottom, we began to cry aloud for assistance, beseeching the people in the ship to save us from perishing: then they brought to, and hoisting out their boat or pinnace, it was instantly manned by a dozen of Frenchmen, well armed with their muskets, and lighted match, who rowing up to us, and seeing how few we were, as also, that our bark was on the point of foundering, took us in, observing that this misfortune had happened, because we had been so uncivil as to refuse an answer to their hail: while the renegado, without being perceived, took up the coffer in which Zorayda's treasure was contained, and threw it into the sea. In short, we went on board with the French, who, when they had informed themselves of every thing we could impart, for their purpose; as if they had been our enemies, plundered us of all that we had, taking

from Zorayda the very bracelets she wore upon her ancles: but, their behaviour to her gave me the more anxiety, as I was afraid that, after having pilfered all her rich and precious jewels, they would proceed to rob her of that which was of greater value, and which she herself esteemed infinitely more than all the rest: but, the desires of those people extend no farther than to money, and with that they can never satiate their avarice, which then engrossed them so much, that they would even have robbed us of the wretched garments we wore in our captivity, if they could have applied them to any sort of use: nay, some among them, proposed to wrap us altogether in a sail, and throw us into the sea; because they intended to trade in the ports of Spain, under pretence of being Bretons, and if they carried us thither alive, their depredation would be discovered and themselves chastised accordingly. But, the captain, who had with his own hands rifled my beloved Zorayda, said, he was satisfied with the prize he had got, and resolved to touch at no port in Spain, but, pass the streights of Gibraltar in the night, or take the best opportunity of so doing that should occur, and return to Rochelle, from whence he had sailed on the cruize: they, therefore, agreed to give us their boat, with what necessaries we should want, to finish the little that remained of our voyage: this promise they actually performed next day, at a small distance from the Spanish coast, at sight of which, all our poverty and vexation vanished from our remembrance, as if we had never endured them; such is the transport occasioned by liberty regained! It might be about noon when we were put into the boat, with two casks of water and some biscuit, and the captain, moved to compassion at the distress of the lovely Zorayda, gave her to the amount of forty crowns in gold, and would not suffer his soldiers to strip her of the cloaths which she now wears: so that at parting, instead of complaining of the hard usage we met with, we thanked them kindly for the benefit we had received at their hands. They steered right before the wind for the streights, while we, without minding any other compass than that of the land that appeared ahead, plied our oars so vigorously, that at sun-set, we were near enough to conclude, that we could easily reach the shore before the night should be far advanced; but, that night being dark, without any moon-shine, and every body on board ignorant of the coast, some of our company judged it unsafe to row ashore; while others insisted upon our running that hazard, even if we should land among rocks, or in some uninhabited part of the country, that we might be secured from the just apprehension of meeting with some rovers from Tetuan, who are frequently, in the beginning of the night, in Barbary, and in the morning, on the Spanish coast, where having taken a prize, they return the same day, and sleep at home in their own houses. Of these contrary opinions we chose that of rowing gently towards the shore, with intent, if the smoothness of the sea would permit, to land at the first convenient place; in consequence of this resolution, a little before midnight, we arrived at the foot of a huge and lofty mountain, tho' not so rocky towards the sea but that there was a little space left, for commodious landing: the boat being run ashore, and all of us disembarked, we kissed the ground, and, with tears of unutterable joy, returned sincere thanks to our gracious Lord, for his unparalelled protection vouchsafed to us in the voyage: then we took out the provision, and dragging her on shore, ascended a vast way up the mountain; not being as yet able to quiet our apprehensions, or persuade ourselves, tho' it actually was so, that the soil we trod was christian ground. The day broke

much later than we could have wished, and about this time we gained the summit of the mountain, purposing to look from thence for some village or shepherd-huts; but, altho' we viewed the whole country around, we could neither discern village, house, highway, path, nor the least trace of human footsteps. Nevertheless, we determined to penetrate farther into the country, since it could not be long, before we should discover some person who would give us information: but what gave me the greatest concern, was to see Zorayda travelling on foot, among the flinty rocks; for, tho' I sometimes took her on my shoulders, she was much more fatigued with seeing me weary, than refreshed by finding herself exempted from walking; and therefore would not allow me to take any more trouble of that kind, but, proceeded with infinite chearfulness and patience, while I led her by the hand, all the way.

"In this manner, we had gone about a quarter of a league, when our ears were saluted by the sound of a small sheep-bell, which was a sure sign of a flock's being somewhere not far off; looking therefore, attentively, to discover it, we perceived a young shepherd, sitting with great composure at the root of a cork-tree, smoothing a stick with his knife: when we called to him, he raised his head, and started nimbly up, and as we afterwards understood, the renegade and Zorayda, who were in moorish dress, being the first objects that presented themselves to his eyes, he thought all the corsairs of Barbary were upon him, and running with incredible swiftness, into a wood that grew near the place where he was, he began to cry as loud as he could bawl, 'The Moors! the Moors are landed! the Moors, the Moors! to arms, to arms!' This exclamation threw us all into perplexity, but, reflecting that his cries would alarm the country, and that the cavalry of the coast would immediately come and see what was the matter; it was agreed, that the renegade should pull off his turkish robes, and put on a slave's jacket, with which one of our company accommodated him, tho' he himself remained in his shirt. This being done, we recommended ourselves to God, and followed the same road which we saw the shepherd take, expecting every moment, to see ourselves surrounded by the cavalry of the coast. Neither were we deceived in our expectation; for, in less than two hours, having crossed those thickets, and entered a plain on the other side, we descried about fifty horsemen riding briskly towards us, at a hand-gallop; upon which we halted, until they should come up: but, when they arrived, and, instead of the Moors they came in quest of, beheld so many poor christian captives, they were utterly confounded, and one of them asked, if we were the people who had been the occasion of a shepherd's calling to arms? I answered in the affirmative, and being desirous of telling him who we were, whence we came, and what had happened to us, one of our company knew the horseman who accosted us, and without giving me time to speak another word, said, 'Thanks be to God, gentlemen, for having conducted us to such an agreeable part of the country; for, if I am not mistaken, the ground we now tread belongs to Velez Malaga; and, if the years of my captivity have not impaired my remembrance, you, signor, who ask that question, are Pedro Bustamante, my uncle.'

"Scarce had the captive pronounced these words, when the cavalier threw himself from his horse, and ran to embrace the young man, saying, 'Dear nephew of my life and soul! I now recollect thee: thy supposed death has been mourned by myself, my sister thy mother, and all thy relations, who are still alive; for, heaven hath been pleased to

spare their lives, that they might enjoy the pleasure of seeing thee again: I knew thou wast at Algiers, and from the information of thy habit, and that of all your company, I guess you have made a miraculous escape.' 'Your conjecture is true,' replied the young man, 'and we shall have time to recount the particulars.' As soon as the horsemen understood we were christian captives, they alighted, and each of them made a tender of his horse, to carry us to the city of Velez Malaga, which was about a league and a half from the place where they found us. Some of them went to bring the boat round to the city, after we had told them where she lay; others took us up behind them; and Zorayda rode with the christian's uncle. All the people came out to receive us, being apprized of our arrival, by one of the troopers who had pushed on before; not that they were surprized at the sight of captives freed, or Moors in captivity; for, the inhabitants on that coast, are accustomed to see great numbers of both: but, they were amazed at the beauty of Zorayda, which was at that instant in full perfection; the fatigue of her journey, cooperating with the joy she felt in seeing herself in a christian country, without the fear of being lost, having produced such a bloom upon her countenance, that, unless I was then prejudiced by my affection, I will venture to say, the world never produced, at least, I had never seen, a more beautiful creature.

"We went directly to church, to make our acknowledgments to God for his mercies; and as soon as Zorayda entered, she said she perceived some faces that resembled Lela Marien: we told her these were the images of the blessed virgin; and the renegado, as well he could, informed her of their signification, that she might adore them, as if each was actually the person of Lela Marien, who had spoke to her; so that, having naturally a good understanding, with a docile and discerning disposition, she easily comprehended what he said upon the subject. From thence, they conducted us to our lodgings in different families of the town; the renegado, Zorayda and I, being invited by the christian who escaped with us, to the house of his father, who was moderately provided with the good things of this life, and treated us with the same affection he expressed for his own son. Six days we tarried at Velez, during which, the renegado having informed himself of what was necessary for him to do, went to the city of Grenada, there, by means of the holy inquisition, to be readmitted into the bosom of our most sacred church: the rest of our company departed, each for his own home; leaving Zorayda and me by ourselves, destitute of every thing but the few crowns which she received from the courtesy of the French corsair. With part of these I bought the animal on which she arrived at this inn, and hitherto have cherished her with the affection of a parent, and the service of a squire, without using the prerogative of a husband: we are now upon the road to the place of my nativity, to see if my father be still alive, and if either of my brothers has been more fortunate than myself; tho', as heaven hath made Zorayda my companion for life, fortune could not have possibly bestowed upon me any other favour which I should have valued at so high a rate. The patience with which she bears the inconveniencies attending poverty, and the zeal she manifests to become a christian, is so great and extraordinary, as to raise my admiration, and engage me to serve her all the days of my life: but, the pleasure I take in this office, and in the prospect of seeing her mine, is disturbed and perverted, by reflecting, that possibly, in my own country, I shall not find a corner in which I can shelter the dear object of my love; and that time or death

may have made such alterations in the fortune and lives of my father and his other children, that I shall scarce meet with a soul that knows me.

"This, gentlemen, is the substance of my story; whether or not it be agreeable and uncommon, I leave to the decision of your better judgment; assuring you that I wish I could have related it more succinctly, though the fear of tiring you, hath made me suppress a good number of circumstances."

## CHAPTER XV.

### Of what further happened at the inn, with many other particulars worthy to be known.

Here the captive left off speaking; and Don Fernando said to him, "Really, signor captain, the novelty of your strange adventures is equalled by your agreeable manner of relating them. Your whole story is uncommon, surprizing, and full of incidents that keep the hearers in admiration and suspence: and such is the pleasure we have received from it, that though the narration should have continued till to-morrow morning, we should rejoice at your beginning it anew."

When this compliment was passed, Cardenio,[1] and all the rest of the company, offered to serve him to the utmost of their power, with such affectionate and sincere expressions of friendship, that the captain was extremely well satisfied of their good will. Don Fernando, in particular, promised, that if he would go home with him, his brother the marquis should stand godfather to Zorayda; and that he, for his part, would accommodate him in such a manner, that he should return to the place of his nativity with that authority and ease to which he was intitled by his birth and merit. The captive thanked him in the most courteous manner, but declined accepting any of his generous offers.

It was now night, when a coach arrived at the inn, attended by some men on horseback, who demanded lodging: and the landlady made answer, that there was not in the whole house an handful of room unengaged. "Be that as it will," said one of the horsemen, who had entered the gate, "there must be some found for my lord judge." At mention of that name the hostess was disturbed, saying, "Signor, the greatest difficulty is my want of beds: but, if his lordship hath brought one along with him, as I suppose he hath, he is very welcome to come in; I and my husband will quit our own apartment to accommodate his worship." "Be it so," said the attendant. By this time, a person had alighted from the coach, who, by his garb immediately shewed the nature of his rank and office; for, his long robe with high sleeves tucked up, plainly distinguished him to be a judge, as the servant had affirmed. He led by the hand a young lady seemingly sixteen years of age, dressed in a riding suit, and so sprightly, beautiful and genteel, as to raise the admiration of all who beheld her: so, that those who had not seen Dorothea, Lucinda and Zorayda then present, would have thought it a very difficult task to find another woman of equal beauty. Don Quixote seeing the judge and young lady as they

entered, pronounced with great solemnity, "Your worship may securely enter and recreate yourself in this castle, which, though narrow and inconvenient, there is no narrowness and inconvenience in this world, but what will make room for arms and letters, especially, if they have for their guide and conductor, such beauty as that which accompanies the letters of your worship, in the person of that amiable young lady, to whom, not only castles ought to open and unfold their gates, but, also rocks divide, and mountains bow their heads at her approach. Enter, I say, this paradise, where you will find stars and suns to accompany that heaven which you have brought hither. Here you will find arms in perfection, and beauty in excess."

The judge marvelled greatly at this address of the knight, whom he earnestly considered, no less surprized at his figure than his words, without knowing what reply to make, so much was he confounded at both; when he was relieved by the appearance of Lucinda, Dorothea, and Zorayda, who, upon hearing the news of their arrival, and the landlady's description of the young beauty, had come out to welcome and receive her: the beauteous ladies of the inn welcomed this beauteous damsel; while Don Fernando, Cardenio, and the curate, paid their compliments to the judge, in the most civil and polite terms. He was more and more astonished at what he saw and heard, though he could easily perceive that his fellow-lodgers were persons of rank and consequence: but, the mien, visage, and figure of Don Quixote, baffled all his conjectures. Compliments having thus passed on all sides, and the conveniencies of the inn being duly considered, it was agreed, as before, that all the ladies should sleep together in the fore-mentioned apartment, and the men sit in another room to guard them. The judge was very well satisfied, that his daughter (for such the young maiden was) should lodge with the other ladies, she herself willingly consenting to the proposal; and what with the innkeeper's narrow bed, and the half of that which the judge brought along with him, they made shift to pass the night more agreeable than they expected.

The captive, who, from the first moment he beheld the judge, felt his heart throb with a sort of intimation, that this was his own brother; asked of one of the servants that attended him, his master's name, with the place of his nativity. The footman replied, that his name was the licentiate Juan Perez de Viedma; and born, as he had been informed, in the mountains of Leon. This information, together with what he himself had before observed, confirmed him in the opinion, that he was his brother, who, by his father's advice, had followed his studies. Transported with this discovery, he called aside Don Fernando, the curate, and Cardenio, to whom he imparted the affair, and assured them that the judge was his own brother, by the servant's report, so far on his way to the West Indies,[2] in quality of supreme judge of Mexico. He understood also, by the same canal, that the young lady was his daughter, whose birth had cost the mother her life; and that he was very much enriched by his wife's fortune, which had been settled on the children of the marriage. The captive, therefore, consulted them about the method he should take to make himself known, or rather to be assured before-hand, whether, upon the discovery, his brother would be ashamed of his poverty, or receive him with the bowels of affection. "Leave that task to my conduct, signor captain," said the curate; "though there is all the reason in the world, to believe that you will meet with a brotherly reception: for the virtue and prudence that appear in his courteous demeanour give no indications of his being proud and unnatural; but, rather declare, that he knows how to consider the

accidents of fortune, in the right point of view." "Nevertheless," replied the captain, "I would not willingly disclose myself of a sudden, but, prepare him by some round-about insinuation." "I have already told you," answered the curate, "that I will manage the affair to your mutual satisfaction." By this time, the cloth * being laid, and every body sat down to table, except the captive, and the ladies, who supped in their own apartment, the curate addressed himself to the judge, saying, "I had once a comrade of your lordship's name at Constantinople, where I was a slave for many years. He was one of the bravest soldiers, and best officers in the Spanish infantry; but, his misfortunes were equal to his valour and ability." "Dear sir," cried the judge, "what was that officer's name?" "He was called Ruy Perez de Viedma," replied the priest; "and a native of some town in the mountains of Leon. He told me a circumstance that happened between his father, two brothers and himself, which, had it not been affirmed by a person of his veracity, I should have looked upon as one of those tales which old women tell by the fireside in winter: for, he said his father divided his estate equally among his three sons, whom he, at the same time, enriched with advice more salutary than any that ever Cato gave. This I know, the choice he made of going into the army succeeded so well, that in a few years, by his gallant behaviour, and without any other assistance than that of his extraordinary virtue, he rose to be captain of foot, and saw himself in the streight road of becoming a field-officer, very soon: but there, where he had reason to expect the smiles of fortune, she proved most unkind, he having lost her, with his liberty, on that glorious day of the battle of Lepanto, in which it was found by so many christians. I was taken in the goleta, and, after various vicissitudes, we happened to be fellow-slaves at Constantinople, from whence he was transported to Algiers, where he met with one of the strangest adventures that ever was known."

Then the curate briefly recapitulated the story of Zorayda, to which the judge listened with more attention than ever he had yielded on the bench †. But, the priest brought it no farther than the period when the French corsairs plundered the christians who were in the bark; describing the poverty and distress to which they had reduced his comrade and the beautiful Moor; and observing that he did not know what further befel them, nor whether they had arrived in Spain, or been carried into France.

The captain stood at some distance, behind, listening to what the curate said, and observing the emotions of his brother, who seeing that the curate had made an end of his story, uttered a profound sigh, saying, while the tears gushed from his eyes, "O signor! if you knew how nearly I am concerned in what you have related, you would not wonder at these tears, which, in spite of all my fortitude and discretion, trickle from mine eyes. That valiant captain whom you have mentioned is my father's eldest son, who, being more brave and noble-minded than my youngest ‡ brother and me, chose the honourable exercise of arms, which was one of the three paths proposed by our father, in his advice, as you seem to have been informed by your companion in adversity. I followed

---

* This is the second time they have sat down to supper in one night. Vide p. 145 [275].[3]

† A judge in Spanish is called *Oydor*, i.e. Hearer, and the original literally translated, is, "The hearer was never so much an hearer before."[4]

‡ Cervantes seems to have forgot that the judge was the youngest of the three brothers, the second having gone to the Indies.[5]

that of letters, in which God hath been pleased to reward my diligence with that station which you see I now maintain; my younger brother is at present in Peru, so rich, that his remittances to my father and me, have made large amends for the small sum he carried with him at first; and even enabled the old gentleman fully to indulge his liberal disposition, impowering me also to prosecute my studies, with more honour and decency, until I acquired the post I now enjoy. My father is still alive, though daily pining with the desire of hearing from his eldest son, and putting up petitions to heaven, incessantly, that his own eyes may not be closed for ever, until he shall have seen those of his first-born in life. What gives me a great deal of surprize is, that a person of his discretion should, in the midst of such trouble and affliction, or even in his prosperity, omit writing to his father; for, if he, or either of us, had known his situation, he should have had no occasion to wait for the miracle of the cane, in obtaining his liberty; but, at present, the uncertainty of his fate, gives me the greatest concern, as it is doubtful, whether those French have set him at liberty, or taken away his life, to conceal their robbery. This apprehension will convert the joy and satisfaction with which I undertook my journey, into melancholy and despondence. O my dear brother! would to heaven, I knew where thou art, that I might go and free thee from all trouble and affliction, though at the expence of my own. Who shall carry the news of thy being alive to our aged father; that, although thou art shut up in the deepest dungeon of Barbary, thou mayst be delivered by my brother's riches and my own! O generous and lovely Zorayda! who shall requite thy benevolence to my brother, be present at the regeneration of thy soul, and assist at the nuptials which would afford such pleasure to us all!"

These, and many other exclamations, the judge pronounced with such symptoms of sorrow, at the news he had received of his brother, that all the hearers sympathized with him, in the expressions of his grief. The curate, seeing every thing succeed to his own expectation, and the captain's desire, was unwilling to protract the judge's anguish, and the impatience of the whole company; so, rising from the table, and going into the other apartment, he led out Zorayda, who was followed by Lucinda, Dorothea and the young lady lately arrived, then, taking in his other hand the captain, who stood waiting to see what he intended, he went into the room, where the judge and the rest of the gentlemen sat, and presenting them both, said, "Dry your tears, my lord judge, and enjoy the completion of your wish; behold your worthy brother, and virtuous sister in law: this is captain Viedma, and that the beautiful Moor who behaved so generously to him in his distress: the French corsairs have reduced them to this extremity, that you may have an opportunity of displaying the liberality of your noble breast."

The captain ran to embrace his brother, who kept him off with both hands fixed on his shoulders, that he might consider him the more attentively; but, no sooner did he recollect his features, than he flew into his arms, and shed a flood of tears of joy, while the greatest part of those who were present wept in concert at the affecting scene. The expressions of both the brothers, and their mutual demonstrations of affection, are, I believe, scarce to be conceived, much less described. They briefly recounted their adventures to each other, and manifested the genuine flame of fraternal affection. There, the judge embraced Zorayda, making her a tender of all his wealth; there he commanded his daughter to receive her with open arms; there the mutual caresses of the beautiful christian and lovely Moor renewed the tears of the whole company; there Don

Quixote silently observed these surprizing accidents, which he wholly attributed to the chimeras of knight-errantry; there it was concerted that the captain and Zorayda should return to Sevil with his brother, from whence they could advertise their father of the liberty and arrival of his son; that the old gentleman being still able to undertake such a journey, might come and be present at the baptism and nuptials of his daughter in law; as it would be impossible for the judge to go far out of his way, because he was informed that, in a month, the flota would set sail from Sevil, for New-Spain; and it would be extremely inconvenient for him, to lose his passage. In short, the whole company were exceedingly rejoiced at the captive's good fortune; and two thirds of the night being already exhausted, they agreed to retire and repose themselves during the remaining part of it; while Don Quixote undertook to guard the castle from the assaults of any giant or wicked adventurer that might possibly covet the vast treasure of beauty which it contained. Those of his acquaintance thanked him for his courteous offer, and afterwards gave an account of his strange disorder to the judge, who was not a little diverted with the detail of his extravagance. Sancho Panza alone was distracted at their sitting up so late; though, in point of lodging, he was better accommodated than all the rest, for, he made his bed of the furniture of his ass, which cost him so dear, as will hereafter be seen.

The ladies having retired to their apartment, and every other person disposed of himself as tolerably as he could, Don Quixote went out to keep guard at the castle-gate, according to his promise; and a little before morning, the ladies were serenaded by a voice so clear and well-tuned, as to attract the attention of them all, especially of Dorothea, who was awake, and lay in the same bed with Donna Clara de Viedma, the judge's daughter. Nobody could imagine who the singer was, the voice being single, and unaccompanied by any instrument, and seeming to come sometimes from the stable and sometimes from the court-yard. While they listened with equal surprize and attention, Cardenio came to the door, saying, "You that are not asleep, take notice, and you will hear the voice of a mule-driver, who chaunts most enchantingly." When Dorothea told him that they had heard it already, he went away, while she, employing her whole attention, when he began to sing again, could plainly distinguish the following words.

## CHAPTER XVI.

## The agreeable story of the young muleteer, with many other strange incidents that happened in the inn.

I.

Toss'd in a sea of doubts and fears,
   Love's hapless mariner, I sail,
Where no inviting port appears,
   To screen me from the stormy gale.

II.

At distance view'd, a chearing star
   Conducts me through the swelling tide;
A brighter luminary, far,
   Than Palinurus e'er descry'd.

III.

My soul attracted by it's blaze,
   Still follows where it points the way,
And while attentively I gaze,
   Considers not how far I stray.

IV.

But female pride, reserv'd and shy,
   Like clouds that deepen on the day,
Oft shroud it from my longing eye,
   When most I need the genial ray.

V.

O lovely star, so pure and bright!
   Whose splendour feeds my vital fire,
The moment thou deny'st thy light,
   Thy lost adorer will expire!

Here the musician pausing, Dorothea thought it was pity Clara should not hear such an excellent voice; therefore, by gently jogging, she waked her, saying, "I ask pardon, my dear Clara, for disturbing you, but, my intention in so doing, was to regale you with one of the best voices that ever you heard." Clara, being still half asleep, did not at first understand what she said, which, at her desire, Dorothea repeated; and the young lady listened accordingly: but, scarce had she heard two lines of the song, which was now resumed, when she began to tremble as violently as if she had been seized with a severe fit of the ague, saying, while she hugged Dorothea, "Ah! dear lady of my life and soul, why did you wake me? the greatest favour that fortune could at present bestow, would be to keep both my eyes and ears fast shut, that I might neither see nor hear that unfortunate musician." "What do you mean, my dear child?" answered Dorothea; "consider what you say, he that sings is a young muleteer." "Ah, no!" replied Clara, "he is a young gentleman of great fortune, and so much master of my heart, that unless he quits it of his own accord, it shall remain eternally in his possession." Dorothea was surprized at this passionate declaration of such a young creature, who seemed to have so much more sensibility than could be expected from her tender years; and said to her, "Truly, Donna Clara, you talk in such a manner, that I do not understand you. Pray, explain yourself, and tell me the meaning of those expressions, about fortune and heart, and that musician, whose voice hath thrown you into such disorder; but say no more at present, for, I would not, by attending to your transports, lose the pleasure of hearing the singer, who now seems to be tuning his voice, and preparing to give us another song." "With all my

heart," said Clara, stopping her ears with her fingers, to the further admiration of Dorothea, who listening attentively, heard the musician proceed in these words:

I.

Aspiring hope, thou, unconfin'd,
    Pursu'st th'imaginary path,
Thro' woods, and rocks, and waves combin'd,
    Defying danger, toil, and death.

II.

No laurel shall adorn his brow,
    No happiness the sluggard crown,
Who tamely can to fortune bow,
    And slumber on th'inglorious down.

III.

The joys unmatch'd bestow'd by love,
    Can never be too dearly priz'd,
For, undeny'd examples prove
    What's cheaply bought, is soon despis'd.

IV.

Success, by the consenting fair,
    Is oft to perseverance given;
Then wherefore should my soul despair
    Of mounting from this earth to heaven.

Here the voice ended; and Clara's sighs beginning afresh, kindled Dorothea's curiosity to know the cause of such agreeable music and grievous lamentation; she therefore, now desired to hear what her bed-fellow had before proffered to impart: then Clara, fearful of being overheard by Lucinda, crept close to Dorothea, and applying her mouth to her ear, so that she could securely speak without being perceived, "Dear madam," said she, "that singer is the son of an Arragonian gentleman, who is lord of two towns, and when at court, lives opposite to my father's house; and although our windows are covered with canvas in winter, and lattices in summer, I know not how this young gentleman, while he prosecuted his studies, got sight of me, either at church, or somewhere else, and in short, being smitten, disclosed his passion from the windows of his own apartment, by so many tears and significant expressions, that I believed him sincere, and even loved him in my turn, without knowing the nature of my own desires. Among other signs, he made that of joining his hands, giving me to understand that he would take me to wife; and tho' I should have been extremely glad to comply with that proposal, as I was alone and motherless, I had no body to consult, and therefore let it rest, without granting him any other favour, except (when his father and mine were abroad) that of lifting up the canvas or lattice, that he might have a more perfect view of my person; and this conde-scension always transported him so much, that I was afraid he would have run stark mad with joy: in the midst of this commerce, the time of my father's departure drew near, of

which being informed, tho' not by me, for I never had an opportunity of telling him, he fell sick, as I understand, of grief; so that, when we set out, I could not see him, as I wished, to indulge one parting look: but, having travelled two days, just as I entered the place at which we lodged last night, I perceived him standing at the gate, disguised so naturally in the habit of a muleteer, that it would have been impossible for me to know him, had not his image been so deeply imprinted on my soul. The sight of him filled me with joy and surprize; and he gazed upon me by stealth, unperceived by my father, from whom he always conceals his face, when he crosses the road before me, or is obliged to appear at the inns where we lodge: knowing therefore who he is, and that he travels on foot, undergoing so much hardship and fatigue for love of me, I am half dead with grief and anxiety, and wheresoever he sets his feet, there I fix my pitying eyes: I know not what he intends by thus following me, nor how he could manage to escape from his father, who loves him tenderly, because he has no heir but him; and the young gentleman deserves all his affection, as you will perceive when you see him. I can moreover assure you, what he sings is the product of his own head; for, I have been told that he is a great scholar, and an excellent poet: every time I behold him, or hear him sing, I start and tremble from head to foot, being afraid that he will be known by my father, and thus our mutual love be discovered; for, tho' I never spoke to him in my life, my passion is so violent, that without him I shall not be able to live. This, dear madam, is all I can say concerning that musician whose voice hath given you such pleasure; and is alone sufficient to convince you, that he is not a muleteer, but the lord of towns and hearts, as I have described him."

"Enough, Donna Clara: (said Dorothea kissing her with great affection) say no more; but, wait with patience till the approach of a new day, when, I hope in God, to manage matters so well, as to bring such a virtuous beginning to an happy end." "Ah, madam!" replied the young lady, "what happy end can be expected, seeing his father is a man of such rank and fortune, that he would think me unworthy to be the servant, much less the wife of his son? and as to marrying him without my own father's consent, I would not do it for the whole universe. All I desire is, that the young gentleman would return; perhaps his absence, and the length of the journey we have undertaken, will alleviate the uneasiness I at present feel, tho' I must own, I believe that remedy will have small effect. I cannot conceive what the deuce is the matter with me; nor how this same love got entrance into my heart, considering how young we both are; for, I really believe we are of the same age, and my father says, that till Michaelmas next, I shall not be sixteen." Dorothea could not help laughing at these innocent observations of Donna Clara, to whom she said, "Let us sleep, my dear, during the little that I believe remains of the night: God will grant us a new day, and if my skill fails me not, every thing will succeed to our wish."

They accordingly went to rest, and a general silence prevailed over the whole house, in which there was not a soul awake, except the innkeeper's daughter and her maid Maritornes, who, by this time, being acquainted with the extravagant humour of Don Quixote, and knowing that he was then without the gate, keeping guard in arms, and on horseback, determined to play some trick upon him, or at least, divert themselves in listening to his folly.

The inn chancing to have no window nor opening towards the field, but a hole thro' which they took in their straw; this pair of * demi-ladies there took their station, and observed Don Quixote, who sat on horseback, leaning upon his lance, and breathing from time to time such profound and doleful sighs, as seemed to tear his very soul: they likewise heard him pronounce, in a soft, complacent and amorous tone, "O my dear mistress, Dulcinea del Toboso! thou perfection of beauty, scope and sum total of discretion, cabinet of good humour, depository of virtue, and lastly, the idea of all that is useful, chaste and delectable in this life! in what art thou at present, employed? Art thou reflecting upon thy captive knight, who voluntarily subjects himself to such dangers, with the sole view of serving thee? Give me some information of my love, thou three-faced luminary! who now, perhaps, with envious eyes, beholdest her walking thro' some gallery of her sumptuous palace, or leaning over some balcony, revolving in her mind, how, without imparing the delicacy of her honour, she may assuage the torments that this heart endures on her account; how she may crown my sufferings with glory; my care with comfort; in fine, my death with new life, and my service with reward: and thou sun, who by this time must be busy in harnessing thy steeds to light the world, and enjoy the sight of her who is the sovereign of my soul, I intreat thee to salute her in my behalf; but, in thy salutation, beware of touching her amiable countenance, else I shall be more jealous of thee than ever thou wast of that nimble ingrate, who made thee sweat so much along the plains of Thessaly, or banks of Peneus; for, I do not remember thro' which thou ran'st, so jealous and enamoured."

So far had the knight proceeded in this piteous exclamation, when the innkeeper's daughter whispered softly, "Sir knight, will your worship be pleased to come this way?" Hearing this invitation, he lifted up his eyes, and by the light of the moon, which was then in full splendor, perceived them beckon to him from the straw-hole, which he mistook for a window, adorned with gilded bars, suitable to the grandeur of such a magnificent castle as the inn appeared: then, his crazy imagination instantly suggested, as before, that the beauteous damsel, daughter of the constable, being captivated by his person, intended again to sollicit his love. On this supposition, that he might not seem discourteous or ungrateful, he turned Rozinante, and riding up to the hole, no sooner perceived the two lasses, than he said, "I am extremely concerned, most beautiful lady, that you have fixed your amorous inclinations where it is impossible they should meet with that return which is due to your rank and qualifications; but, you ought not to impute your disappointment to any fault in me, whom love hath rendered incapable of yielding my heart to any other but to her, who at first sight took absolute possession of my soul. Pardon my refusal, honoured madam, and retire to your apartment, without seeking to explain your sentiments more fully, that I may not appear insensible or ungrateful; and if your love can find in me the power of giving you any other sort of satisfaction, you may freely command my service; for, I swear by that absent and amiable enemy of mine, to gratify your wish immediately; even if you should desire to have a lock of Medusa's hair, which was altogether composed of snakes, or the rays of the sun confined in a vial."

---

* In the original Demi-Donzellas, equivalent to the modern term Demireps.[1]

"Sir knight," answered Maritornes, "my lady has no occasion for either of these things." "What then is your lady's pleasure, discreet duenna?" resumed the knight. "Only the favour of one of your beautiful hands," replied Maritornes, "with which she may, in some measure, indulge the longing desire that brought her to this straw-hole, so much to the danger of her reputation, that if she should be detected by her father, the first slice of his indignation would cost her an ear at least." "I would fain to see him take that liberty," said Don Quixote; "but, he will take care to refrain from any such acts of barbarity, unless he has a mind I should bring him to the most calamitous exit that ever happened to a father, for having laid violent hands upon the delicate members of his en-amoured daughter."

Maritornes concluding that he would certainly grant the request, and having already determined on what she was to do, ran down to the stable, and laid hold of the halter belonging to Sancho's ass, with which she instantly returned, just when Don Quixote had made shift to set his feet on the saddle that he might reach the gilded window, at which he imagined the wounded damsel was standing: presenting therefore, his hand, "Receive, madam," said he, "that hand, or rather that chastiser of all evil-doers; receive, I say, that hand, which was never touched by any other woman, not even by her who is in possession of my whole body. I do not present it to be kissed; but, that you may con-template the contexture of its nerves, the knittings of the muscles, the large and swelling veins; from whence you may conjecture what strength must reside in the arm to which it belongs." "That we shall see presently," said Maritornes, who having made a running knot on the halter, fixed it upon his wrist, and descending from the hole, made fast the other end to the bolt of the hay-loft door. The knight feeling the roughness of this bracelet, said, "Your ladyship seems to rasp rather than to clasp my hand: do not treat it so cruelly; for, it is not to blame for what you suffer, from my inclination; nor is it just that such a small part should bear the whole brunt of your indignation: consider that one who is such a friend to love, ought not to be so attached to revenge."

All these expostulations of Don Quixote were uttered in vain; for, as soon as Mari-tornes had tied him up, she and her companion, ready to expire with laughing, left him fastened in such a manner, that it was impossible for him to get loose: thus, while he stood on Rozinante's back, with his whole arm thrust up into the straw-hole, and fast tied to the bolt of the door, he was in the utmost apprehension and dread, that if his horse should make the least motion to either side, he must lose his support, and the weight of his whole body hang by one arm; so that he durst not venture to stir; tho' he might have expected from the patience and peaceful disposition of Rozinante, that he would stand motionless for a whole century. In short, finding himself thus tucked up, and the ladies vanished, he imagined that the whole had been effected by the power of enchantment, which he had experienced once before, in that same castle, when he was belaboured by the enchanted Moor of a carrier; and cursed, within himself, his want of conduct and discretion, in entering a second time that fortress in which he had fared so ill at first; it being a maxim among knights-errant, that when they prove an adventure, without success, they conclude it is reserved for another, and therefore think it unnec-essary to make a second trial. Nevertheless, he pulled with intention to disengage his arm, but, he was so well secured, that all his efforts were ineffectual: true it is, he pulled

with caution, that Rozinante might not be disturbed; and tho' he had a longing desire of sitting down upon the saddle again, he found that he must either continue in his present upright posture, or part with his hand: then, he began to wish for the sword of Amadis, against which no enchantment could prevail; then cursed his fortune; then exaggerated the loss which the world would sustain, while he remained enchanted, as he firmly believed himself to be; then he reflected anew upon his beloved Dulcinea del Toboso; then he called to his trusty squire; Sancho Panza, who, stretched upon the pannel of his ass, and buried in sleep, at that instant, retained no remembrance of the mother that bore him; then he implored the assistance of the two sages Lirgando and Alquise; then he invoked his good friend Urganda, for succour in his distress; and, in fine, the morning found him in that situation, so distracted and perplexed, that he roared aloud like a bull, without expecting that the day would put an end to his disaster, which he thought would be eternal, believing himself actually inchanted: and this opinion was confirmed, by his seeing that Rozinante scarce offered to stir; for, he was persuaded, that in this manner, without eating, drinking, or sleeping, he and his horse would continue until the evil influence of the stars should pass over, or some other sage of superior skill disengage them from their enchantment.

But for once he was mistaken in his calculation; for, day had scarce begun to dawn, when four men on horseback arrived at the inn, well mounted and accoutred with carbines hanging at their saddle-bows: the knight perceiving from the place, where, in spite of his misfortune, he still kept guard, that they thundered for entrance at the gate, which was still shut, called, in an arogant and haughty tone, "Knights or squires, or whosoever you are, you have no business to make such a noise at the gate of this castle; for, it is very plain, that either the people within are asleep, or unaccustomed, at these hours, to open the fortress, which you cannot enter before the sun rise. Retire, therefore, and wait until the day be farther advanced, and then we shall see whether or not you have any title to be admitted."

"What the devil of a fortress or castle is this, that we must observe such ceremony!" said one of the company: "if you are the innkeeper, order some body to open the door: we are all travellers, and only want to bait, that we may forthwith proceed on our journey; for, we are in haste." "Gentlemen," replied Don Quixote, "do you think I resemble an innkeeper?" "I don't know what you resemble," answered the other; "but this I know, that you talk nonsense, in calling this inn a castle." "A castle it is," cried the knight, "and one of the best in this province; nay, at this very instant, it contains those who have wore crowns on their heads, and wielded sceptres in their hands." "Or rather the reverse," said the traveller: "that is, the sceptre on the head, and the crown in the hand \*; but, perhaps, there may be within some company of strollers who frequently wear these crowns and sceptres you mention; for, otherwise, in such a sorry inn, without any sort of noise or stir, I cannot believe that any persons of such note would lodge." "You know little of the world," replied Don Quixote, "since you are so ignorant of the events that happen in knight-errantry."

The other horsemen being tired with this dialogue that passed between the knight

---

\* Alluding to the delinquents, who were branded and marked with these figures.[2]

and their companion, began again to knock and bawl with such vociferation, that the landlord and all the persons in the inn, waking, rose to see who called so furiously: about this time, one of the horses belonging to the travellers, drew near and smelled at Rozinante, who sad and melancholy, with his ears hanging down, stood supporting his outstretched master, without stirring; but, at length, being made of flesh, tho' he seemed to have been carved out of a block, he was sensible of the civility, and turned about to repay the compliment to the courteous stranger; and scarce had he moved one step, when both his master's feet sliping from the saddle, he would have tumbled to the ground, had not he hung by his arm, which endured such torture in the shock, that he verily believed it was cut off by the wrist, or torn away by the shoulder. He was suspended so low, that the tops of his toes almost touched the ground; a circumstance that increased his calamity; for, feeling how little he wanted of being firmly sustained, he stretched and fatigued himself with endeavouring to set his feet upon the ground, like those wretches who, in undergoing the strappado, being hoisted up a very little space, increase their own torment by their eager efforts to lengthen their bodies, misled by the vain hope of reaching the ground.

## CHAPTER XVII.

### A continuation of the surprising events that happened in the inn.

D on Quixote actually made such a hideous outcry, that the innkeeper opened the door, and ran out to see what was the matter; while the strangers that remained without were no less astonished at his bellowing. Maritornes being also waked by the same noise, conjectured what might be the case, and going straight to the hay-loft, without being perceived, untied the halter that sustained him, so that the knight came to the ground, in sight of the landlord and strangers, who running up, asked what was the matter with him, and wherefore he cried so violently? Without answering one word, he loosed the tether from his wrist, and rising up, mounted Rozinante, braced his target, couched his lance, and making a pretty large circuit in the field, returned at a half gallop, pronouncing with great emphasis, "If any person whatever sayeth, that I have justly suffered enchantment, I here, with the permission of my lady princess Micomicona, give him the lie, challenge and defy him to single combat."

The travellers were amazed at his words; but, their astonishment abated, when the innkeeper told them who Don Quixote was, observing that they ought not to mind what he did, because he was disordered in his brain: they then asked if he had seen a youth about fifteen years of age, dressed like a young muleteer, with such and such marks, giving an exact description of Donna Clara's lover. The landlord answered, there were so many people in his house, that he could not possibly distinguish the person for whom they enquired; but, one of them perceiving the judge's coach, "He must certainly be

here," said he; "for this is the coach, which they say he followed: let one of us stay at the door, and the rest go in to search for him; it will also be proper that one go round the whole house, to prevent his escaping over the yard-wall." This plan being agreed upon, two of them entered the inn, another remained at the door, and the fourth rode round the house to reconnoitre; while the landlord observing every thing that passed, could not conceive the meaning of all this care and diligence, altho' he believed they were in search of the youth whom they had described. By this time, it was clear day-light, and upon that account, as well as in consequence of Don Quixote's roaring, all the company were awake, and got up, especially Donna Clara and Dorothea, who had sleeped very little that night; the first being disturbed and alarmed, by reflecting that her lover was so near, and the other kept awake by the desire of seeing this pretended muleteer.

Don Quixote seeing that none of the travellers took the least notice of him, or made any answer to his defiance, was transported with rage and vexation; and if he could have recollected any law of chivalry, authorising a knight-errant to undertake another enter-prize, while he was under promise and oath, to abstain from any adventure, until that in which he was engaged already, was atchieved; he would have assaulted them all together, and forced them to reply, contrary to their inclination: but, thinking it was neither ex-pedient nor just to begin a new enterprize, until he had re-established the princess Mi-comicona on her throne; he chose to be silent, waiting to see the effects of that diligence practised by the new comers, one of whom found the youth they came in quest of, sleep-ing by the side of a muleteer, and little dreaming that any body was in search of him; much less that he was in any danger of being discovered. The man, however, shook him by the arm, saying, "Truly, signor Don Lewis, this is a very suitable dress for one of your quality; and the bed in which you now lie, extremely well adapted to the tenderness and delicacy in which your mother brought you up."

The youth rubbed his sleepy eyes, and looking stedfastly at the person who held him by the arm, no sooner perceived that he was one of his father's servants, than he was so much surprised and confounded, that for a good while, he could not speak one word: while the domestic proceeded, saying, "At present, Don Lewis, there is nothing else to be done, but, to exert your patience, and return home, if you are not resolved that your father and my lady shall visit the other world; for, nothing else can be expected from their anxiety at your absence." "How did my father get notice that I travelled this road, and in this habit?" said Don Lewis. "A student," replied the servant, "to whom you im-parted your intention, was so much moved by the sorrow that took possession of your parents, the moment you were missed, that he disclosed your scheme to your father, who instantly dispatched four of his domestics in search of you; and we are all here, at your service, infinitely rejoiced that we have now an opportunity of returning speedily, and carrying you back to the longing eyes of those by whom you are so much beloved." "That may depend upon my own will and the appointment of heaven," said the young nobleman. "What should you will, or heaven ordain, but your immediate return, which indeed you cannot possibly avoid."

All this conversation was overheard by the muleteer with whom Don Lewis lay, who got up immediately, and going to Don Fernando, Cardenio, and the ladies, who were al-ready dressed, told them how the man called his fellow-servant Don, and communi-

cated every thing that passed between them, concerning the domestic's proposal of con-
ducting him home again, and the youth's refusal to comply with his desire. This infor-
mation, together with the knowledge of that sweet voice with which heaven had en-
dowed him, excited in all the company, a desire of knowing more particularly who he
was, and even of assisting him, should they offer any violence to his inclination: for this
purpose, therefore, they repaired to the place where he still stood, talking and disputing
with his father's servant. At the same time, Dorothea coming out of her apartment, fol-
lowed by Donna Clara, in the utmost confusion, called Cardenio aside, and briefly re-
lated to him, the story of the musician and the judge's daughter: and he in his turn, in-
formed her of what passed on the arrival of his father's servants. This, he spoke not so
softly, but that he was overheard by Clara, who was so much affected at the news, that if
Dorothea had not supported her, she would have fallen to the ground: but, Cardenio de-
sired them to retire into their apartment, saying, he would endeavour to set every thing
to rights, and they accordingly followed his advice. Mean while, the four, who had come
in quest of Don Lewis, stood round him in the inn, persuading him to return, without
loss of time, and console his melancholy father; but, he assured them, he could by no
means comply with their request, until he had finished an affair, upon which his hon-
our, life and soul depended. Then the domestics began to be more urgent, protesting
they would, in no shape, return without him; and declaring, that if he would not go will-
ingly, they should be obliged to carry him off, by force. "That you shall never do,"
replied Don Lewis, "unless you carry me off, dead: and indeed you may as well kill me,
as force me away, in any shape."

Most of the people in the house were now gathered together to hear the dispute, par-
ticularly Cardenio, Don Fernando, his companions, the judge, curate, barber, and Don
Quixote, who thought it was no longer necessary to guard the castle. Cardenio being al-
ready acquainted with the young man's story, asked what reason the domestics had to
carry off the youth, contrary to his own inclination? "Our motive," replied one of the
four, "is to retrieve his father's life, which is in danger of being lost, on account of this
young gentleman's absence." To this declaration Don Lewis answered, "There is no rea-
son why I should here give an account of my affairs; I am free, and will return, if I please;
otherwise, none of you shall compel me into your measures." "Your honour will, I hope,
hear reason," said the servant; "or if you should not, it will be enough for us to execute
our errand, as we are in duty bound."

Here the judge desiring to know the whole affair from the bottom, the man having
lived in the same neighbourhood, knew him, and replied, "My lord judge, don't you
know that young gentleman is your neighbour's son, who hath absented himself from
his father's house, in a dress altogether unbecoming his quality, as your lordship may
perceive?" Then the judge looking at him more attentively, recollected his features, and
embracing him, said, "What a frolick is this, Don Lewis? or what powerful cause hath
induced you to come hither in a garb so ill suited to your rank and fortune?" The tears
gushing into the young man's eyes, he could not answer one word to the judge, who de-
sired the four domestics to make themselves easy, for, all would be well; then taking Don
Lewis by the hand, he led him aside, and asked again, the cause of his coming in that
manner.

While he was employed in this and other questions, they heard a great noise at the inn-door, occasioned by two men, who had lodged all night in the house, and who see-ing every body intent upon knowing the business of the four last comers, resolved to march off without paying their reckoning: but, the innkeeper, who minded his own af-fairs, more than those of any other person, stopped them on the threshold, demanded his money, and upbraided them for their evil intention, with such abusive language, as provoked them to answer by dint of fists, which they began to employ so dextrously, that the poor landlord found himself under the necessity of calling aloud for assistance. His wife and daughter seeing no body so idle, consequently so proper for the purpose, as Don Quixote, the damsel addressed him in these words; "Sir knight, I beseech your worship, by the valour which God hath given you, to go to the assistance of my poor fa-ther, whom two wicked men are now beating to a jelly." To this request the knight replied, with great leisure and infinite phlegm, "Beautiful young lady, I cannot, at pres-ent, grant your petition, being restricted from intermeddling in any other adventure, until I shall have accomplished one, in which my honour is already engaged: all that I can do for your service, is this; run and desire your father to maintain the combat as well as he can, and by no means allow himself to be overcome, until I go ask permission of the princess Micomicona, to succour him in his distress; and, if I obtain it, be assured that I will rescue him from all danger." "Sinner that I am!" cried Maritornes, who was then present, "before your worship can obtain that permission, my master will be in the other world." "Allow me, madam," answered Don Quixote, "to go and sollicit the licence I mention, which if I obtain, I shall not make much account of his being in the other world, from whence I will retrieve him, though all its inhabitants should combine to op-pose me; at least, I shall take such vengeance on those who have sent him thither, as will give you full and ample satisfaction."

So saying, he went and kneeled before Dorothea, begging, in the stile and manner of knight-errantry, that her highness would be pleased to give him permission to run and assist the constable of the castle, who was, at that time, involved in a very grievous dis-aster. The princess having very graciously granted his request, he braced on his target, unsheathed his sword, and ran to the gate where the two guests still continued pum-melling the landlord; but, as soon as he beheld them, he stopped short, as if suddenly surprized, and when Maritornes and her mistress asked what hindered him from giving assistance to their master and husband, "I am hindered," answered the knight, "by a law, which will not permit me to use my sword against plebeians; but, call hither my squire Sancho, for to him it belongs, and is peculiar to engage in such vengeance or defence."

This transaction happened on the very field of battle, while kicks and cuffs were dealt with infinite dexterity, to the no small prejudice of the innkeeper's carcase, and the rage of his wife, daughter, and Maritornes, who here half-distracted at seeing the cowardice of Don Quixote, and the distress of their lord and master. But, let us here leave him awhile; for, he shall not want one to assist him; or else, let him suffer with patience, and hold his tongue as becomes those who rashly undertake adventures which they have not strength to atchieve; and let us retreat backwards, about fifty yards, to see what answer Don Lewis made to the judge, whom we left inquiring the cause of his travelling on foot in such a mean habit. The youth, squeezing both his hands with great eagerness, in

token of the excessive grief that wrung his heart, and shedding a flood of tears, replied to this question, "Dear sir, I can give you no other reason, but that from the first moment that fortune made us neighbours, and heaven ordained that I should see Donna Clara, your daughter and my delight, I, that instant, made her mistress of my heart; and if your inclination, my real lord and father, does not oppose my happiness, this very day she shall be my lawful wife: for her I forsook my father's house, and disguised myself in this manner, with a resolution to follow whithersoever she should go, directing my views towards her, like the arrow to its mark, and the needle to the pole; though she knows no more of my passion than what she may have understood from the tears which, at a distance, she hath often seen me shed. You yourself, my lord, know the rank and fortune of my father, whose sole heir I am: if you think that a motive sufficient for venturing to make me perfectly happy, receive me immediately as your son; and though my father, prompted, perhaps, by other views, should be disobliged at the blessing which I have chosen for myself, it is in the power of time to work greater changes and alterations than human prudence can foresee."

Here the enamoured youth left off speaking, and the judge remained in the utmost suspense; not only, admiring the discretion with which Don Lewis had disclosed his passion, but also finding himself perplexed about the resolution he was to take, in such a sudden and unexpected affair. He therefore made no other reply for the present, but, to desire he would make himself easy, and detain his servants a day longer, that he might have time to consider what steps it would be most proper to take, for the satisfaction of all concerned. Don Lewis kissed his hands by force, and even bathed them with his tears; a circumstance sufficient to melt an heart of marble, much more that of the judge, who, being a man of prudence, had already conceived all the advantages of such a match for his daughter; though he wished it could be effected, if possible, with the consent of the young man's father, who, he knew, had some pretensions to a title for his son.

By this time peace was re-established between the innkeeper and his two lodgers, who being persuaded by the arguments and exhortations of Don Quixote, more than by his threats, had paid their reckoning to the last farthing; and the servants of Don Lewis waited the result of the judge's advice, together with their master's resolution; when the devil, who is ever watchful, so ordered matters, that the barber should just then enter the inn; that very barber from whom Don Quixote had retrieved Mambrino's helmet, and Sancho Panza taken, the furniture of his ass, which he had exchanged for his own. This individual shaver, as he led his beast to the stable, perceived Sancho employed in mending something that belonged to the pannel, and knowing him at first sight, assaulted the squire in a trice, crying, "Ha! Don thief, I have caught you at last. Restore my bason and pannel, with all the furniture you stole from me."

Sancho seeing himself so suddenly attacked, and hearing the reproachful language of his antagonist, with one hand laid fast hold on the pannel, and with the other bestowed upon the barber such a slap in the face, as bathed his whole jaws in blood. But, for all that, he would not quit the pannel which he had also seized; on the contrary, he raised his voice so high as to alarm the whole company, and bring them to the scene of contention, crying, "Justice! help in the king's name! this robber wants to murder me, because I endeavour to recover my own property." "You lie," answered the squire, "I am no

robber; my lord Don Quixote won these spoils fairly in battle." The knight coming up, among the rest, beheld, with infinite satisfaction, his squire so alert in offending and defending, and looking upon him from thenceforward as a man of valour, resolved, in his heart, to have him dubbed with the first opportunity, confident that on him the order of knighthood would be very well bestowed. Among other things alledged by the barber in the course of the fray, "Gentlemen," said he, "that pannel belongs as much to me as my soul belongs to God; for, I know it as well, as if it had been produced by my own body; and though I had all the mind in the world, my ass, which is now in the stable, would not suffer me to tell a falshood: since you will not take my word, pray go and try it upon his back, and if it does not fit him to a hair, I shall give you leave to call me the greatest liar upon earth. Besides, the very same day on which they took my pannel, they also robbed me of a new brass bason never hanselled, that cost me a good crown *."

Don Quixote hearing this, could contain himself no longer, but interposed between the combatants, whom he parted, and depositing the pannel on the ground, to be publickly viewed until the truth should appear, addressed himself thus, to the spectators, "Gentlemen, you may now clearly and manifestly perceive how this honest squire errs in his judgment, by calling that a bason, which was, is, and shall be, Mambrino's helmet: a piece of armour I won in fair and open battle, and now possess by the just laws of conquest. With regard to the pannell I will not intermeddle: all that I can say of the matter, is, that my squire Sancho having asked permission to take the trappings of that coward's horse, and adorn his own with them, I gave him leave, and he took them accordingly; though I can give no other reason for their being now converted into a pannel, but, that such transformations frequently happen in the events of chivalry: yet, as a confirmation of what I say, run, friend Sancho, and bring hither the helmet, which this honest man calls a bason."

"'Fore God!" answered Sancho, "if your worship has no better proof of our honourable doings than what you mention, Mambrino's helmet will turn out a bason, as certainly as this honest man's trappings are transmographied into a pannel." "Do what I order," replied the knight; "sure I am, every thing in this castle cannot be conducted by inchantment." Sancho went accordingly, and fetched this bason or helmet of Mambrino, as his master called it, which Don Quixote taking in his hand, said, "Behold, gentlemen, with what face this plebeian can affirm that this is a bason, and not the helmet I have mentioned: now, I swear by the order of knighthood I profess, that this is the individual helmet which I took from him, without the least addition or diminution." "Without all manner of doubt," said Sancho; "for since my master won it, to this good hour he hath used it but in one battle, when he delivered those mischievous galleyslaves; and, if it had not been for that same bason-helmet, he could not have come off so well: for, there was a deadly shower of stones rained upon his pate in that storm."

---

* Literally, "Lady of a crown."[1]

## CHAPTER XVIII.

The decision of the doubts concerning Mambrino's helmet and the pannel; with a full and true account of many other adventures.

"Gentlemen," said the barber, "pray, favour me with your opinion, concerning what is affirm'd by these gentlefolks, who so obstinately maintain that this is not a bason but a helmet." "And if any one affirms to the contrary," replied Don Quixote, "I will make him sensible that he lies, if he be a knight; and if a plebeian, that he lies a thousand times." His own townsman, who was present all the while, being well acquainted with the knight's humour, resolved to encourage him in his extravagance, and carry on the joke for the diversion of the company: with this view, he addressed himself to the other shaver, saying, "Mr. Barber, or whosoever you are, you must know that I am of the same profession: I have had a certificate of my examination these twenty years; and know very well, all the instruments of the art, without excepting one: I was moreover, a soldier in my youth, consequently can distinguish an helmet, a morrion, and a casque, with its beaver, together with every thing relating to military affairs; I mean, the different kinds of armour wore by soldiers in the field: I say, under corrections, and still with submission to better judgment, that the object now in dispute, which that worthy gentleman holds in his hand, is not only no barber's bason, but also, as far from being one as black is from white, or falshood from truth. I likewise aver that tho' it is an helmet, it is not entire." "You are certainly in the right," said Don Quixote, "for it wants one half, which is the beaver."

The curate, who by this time, understood the intention of his friend, seconded this asseveration which was also confirmed by Cardenio, Don Fernando, and his companions; and the judge himself would have bore a part in the jest, had he not been engrossed by the affair of Don Lewis; but, that earnest business kept him in such perplexity of thought, that he could give little or no attention to the joke that was going forward.

"Good God!" cried the barber, with amazement, "is it possible that so many honourable persons should pronounce this bason to be a helmet! an assertion sufficient to astonish a whole university, let it be never so learned. Well: if that bason be an helmet, I suppose the pannel must be a horse's trappings too, as this gentleman says." "To me it seems a pannel," replied the knight: "but, as I have already observed, I will not pretend to decide whether it be the pannel of an ass, or the furniture of a steed." "Don Quixote has no more to do but speak his opinion," said the curate; "for, in affairs of chivalry, all these gentlemen, myself, and even the ladies, yield to his superior understanding." "By heaven! gentlemen," cried the knight, "so many strange accidents have happened to me, twice that I have lodged in this castle, that I will not venture positively to affirm the truth of any thing that may be asked relating to it; for, I imagine that every thing in this place is conducted by the power of inchantment. The first time I passed the night in this place, I was harrassed extremely, by an enchanted Moor that resides in the castle, while Sancho was almost as roughly handled by some of his attendants; and this very night I was

suspended by one arm, for the space of two hours, without knowing how or wherefore I incurred that misfortune. For me therefore, to give my opinion in a case of such perplexity, would be a rash decision: with regard to the helmet which they say is a bason, I have already expressed my sentiments; but, dare not give a definitive sentence, by declaring, whether that be a pannel, or horse's furniture. That I leave to the judgment of the good company; who, not being knights as I am, perhaps are not subjected to the enchantments of this place, but, enjoying their faculties clear and undisturbed, can judge of these things, as they really and truly are, not as they appear to my imagination." "Doubtless," replied Don Fernando, "signor Don Quixote manifests his own prudence, in observing, that to us belongs the determination of this affair, which, that it may be the better founded, I will, in private, take the opinions of this company, one by one, and then openly declare the full result of my inquiry."

To those who were acquainted with the knight's humour, this proposal afforded matter of infinite diversion; but, the rest being ignorant of the joke, looked upon it as a piece of downright madness: this was particularly the opinion of the domestics belonging to Don Lewis, which was even espoused by himself and three travellers just arrived, who seemed to be troopers of the holy brotherhood, as indeed they were; but, he that almost ran distracted, was the barber whose bason was, even in his own sight, transformed into Mambrino's helmet, while he expected every moment that his pannel would be certainly declared the rich trappings and furniture of a horse. Every body laughed to see Don Fernando going about with great gravity, collecting opinions in whispers, that each might privately declare, whether that jewel, about which there had been such obstinate disputes, was the pannel of an ass, or the furniture of a steed. Having received the answers of all those who knew Don Quixote, he pronounced aloud, "Truly, honest friend, I am quite tired with asking so many opinions; for, every one to whom I put the question, affirms it is downright distraction to call this a pannel, which is certainly the furniture of a horse, and that too of an excellent breed. Therefore you must e'en have patience; for, in spite of you and the testimony of your ass to boot, an horse's furniture it must remain, as you have failed so egregiously in the proof of what you alledge." "May I never taste the joys of heaven!" cried the transported barber, "if you are not all deceived; and so may my soul appear before God, as this appears to me, a meer pannel, and not the furniture of an horse! but, thus * might overcomes—I say no more, neither am I drunk, being fresh and fasting from every thing but sin."

The company laughed as heartily at the simplicity of the barber as the extravagance of the knight, who upon this decision, said, "Nothing now remains, but that every one should take his own again; and may † St. Peter bless what God bestows." One of the four servants belonging to Don Lewis now interposed, saying, "If this be not a premeditated joke, I cannot persuade myself that people of sound understanding, such as all this company are or seem to be, should venture to say and affirm, that this is no bason, nor that a pannel; yet, seeing this is both said and affirmed, I conceive there must be some mys-

---

* The original would be more literally translated, by saying, "The law's measure is the king's pleasure."[1]

† A bridal benediction.[2]

Vol. I. pag. 352.

The Barber Confounded by the Assurances of Don Quixote, Don Fernando
and the Rest that His Basin is a Helmet.

tery in thus insisting upon a thing so contrary to truth and experience; for, by God! (an oath he swore with great emphasis) all the people on earth shall never make me believe that this is not a barber's bason, or that not the pannel of an he-ass." "Why not of a she-ass?" said the curate. "That distinction makes no difference," said the servant, "nor has it any concern with the dispute, which is occasioned by your saying that it is not a pannel at all."

At the same time, one of the troopers, who had entered and been witness to the quarrel and question, could no longer contain his choler and displeasure at what he heard, and therefore said, in a furious tone, "If that is not a pannel, my father never begat me; and he that says, or shall say the contrary, must be drunk." "You lie, like an infamous scoundrel," replied Don Quixote, who lifting up his lance, which he still kept in his hand, aimed such a stroke at the trooper's skull, that if he had not been very expeditious in shifting it, he would have been stretched at full length upon the ground, on which the weapon was shivered to pieces: the rest of the troop, seeing their companion so roughly handled, raised their voices, crying for help to the holy brotherhood: the innkeeper being of that fraternity, ran in for his tipstaff and sword, and espoused the cause of his brethren; the domestics surrounded Don Lewis, that he might not escape in the scuffle; the barber seeing the house turned topsy turvy, laid hold again of the pannel, which was at the same time seized by Sancho; Don Quixote attacked the troopers sword in hand; Don Lewis called to his servants to leave him, and go to the assistance of Cardenio and Don Fernando, who had ranged themselves on the side of Don Quixote; the curate exhorted, the landlady screamed, the daughter wept, Maritornes blubbered, Dorothea was confounded, Lucinda perplexed, and Donna Clara fainted away; the barber pummelled Sancho, who returned the compliment; one of the servants presuming to seize Don Lewis by the arm, that he might not run away, the young gentleman gave him such a slap in the face, as bathed all his teeth in blood; the judge exerted himself in his defence. Don Fernando having brought one of the troopers to the ground, kicked his whole carcase to his heart's content: the landlord raised his voice again, roaring for help to the holy brotherhood; so that the whole inn was a scene of lamentation, cries, shrieks, confusion, dread, dismay, disaster, back-strokes, cudgelling, kicks, cuffs, and effusion of blood. In the midst of this labyrinth, chaos, and composition of mischief, Don Quixote's imagination suggested, that he was all of a sudden involved in the confusion of Agramonte's camp; and therefore pronounced, with a voice that made the whole inn resound, "Let every man forbear, put up his sword, be quiet and listen, unless he be weary of his life."

On hearing this exclamation, all the combatants paused, while he proceeded thus: "Did not I tell you, gentlemen, that this castle was enchanted, and doubtless, inhabited by a whole legion of devils; as a proof of which, you may now perceive, with your own eyes, how the discord and mutiny in Agramonte's camp is translated hither: behold, in one place, we fight for a sword; in another, for a horse; in a third, for an eagle; and in a fourth, for a helmet; in short, we are all by the ears together, for we know not what. Advance therefore, my lord judge, and Mr. curate, and in the persons of Agramonte and king Sobrino, re-establish peace among us; for, by Almighty God! it were wicked and absurd, that persons of our importance should be slain in such a frivolous cause."

The troopers, who did not understand the knight's stile, and found themselves very

severely treated by Don Fernando, Cardenio, and their companions, would not be pacified; but, it was otherwise with the barber, who, in the scuffle, had lost both his pannel and beard: Sancho, who like a faithful servant, minded the least hint of his master, willingly obeyed; and the servants of Don Lewis were fain to be quiet, seeing how little they had got by concerning themselves in the fray; the innkeeper alone, insisted upon their chastising the insolence of that madman, who was every moment throwing the whole house into confusion; at length, the disturbance was appeased, the pannel remained as an horse's furniture, till the day of judgment, the bason as an helmet, and the inn as a castle, in Don Quixote's imagination.

Every thing being thus amicably composed, by the persuasion of the judge and priest, the servants of Don Lewis began again to press him, with great obstinacy, to set out with them for his father's house immediately; and while he expostulated with them, the judge consulted with Don Fernando, Cardenio, and the curate, about what he should do on this occasion; imparting to them the declaration Don Lewis had made: at last, it was agreed that Don Fernando should tell the servants who he was; and express a desire, that Don Lewis should accompany him to Andalousia, where his brother the marquis should entertain him according to his rank and merit; for, he well knew the young gentleman was fixed in the determination of being cut to pieces, rather than return to his father, at that time. The domestics being informed of Don Fernando's quality, and understanding the resolution of Don Lewis, determined amongst themselves, that three of them should return and give the father an account of what had happened, while the fourth should attend the young gentleman, until they should either come back for him, or know his father's pleasure.

In this manner was that accumulation of quarrels appeased, by the authority of Agramonte and prudence of king Sobrino; but, the enemy of concord and rival of peace, being thus foiled and disappointed, and seeing how little fruit he had reaped from the labyrinth of confusion in which he had involved them, determined to try his hand once more, and revive discord and disturbance anew; and these were the means he practised for this purpose: the troopers apprised of the quality of those with whom they had been engaged, were fain to be quiet, and retreat from the fray, concluding that whatever might happen, they would have the worst of the battle; but, one of them who had been pummelled and kicked by Don Fernando, recollected that among other warrants for apprehending delinquents, he had one against Don Quixote, issued by the holy brotherhood, on account of his having set the galley-slaves at liberty, as Sancho had very justly feared: this coming into his head, he was resolved to assure himself, whether or not the knight's person agreed with the description; and pulling out of his bosom, a bundle of parchment, he soon found what he sought, and beginning to spell with great deliberation (for, he was by no means an expert reader) between every word he fixed his eyes upon the knight, whose physiognomy he compared with the marks specified in the warrant, and discovered beyond all doubt, that he was the very person described: no sooner was he thus convinced, than putting up the parchment, and holding the warrant in his left hand, he with his right seized Don Quixote so fast by the collar, that he could scarce fetch his breath, roaring aloud, "Help, in the name of the holy brotherhood; and that you may see my demand is just, read that warrant for apprehending this highwayman."

The curate, upon perusing the warrant, found what the trooper said was true, and that the description exactly agreed with the person of Don Quixote, who seeing himself so unworthily treated by such a ragamuffin, was incensed to the highest degree, so that every bone in his body trembled with rage; and he made shift to fasten on the trooper's throat with both hands, so violently, that if his companions had not come to his assistance, he would have quitted his life before the knight had quitted his hold. The innkeeper being obliged to succour his brethren, ran immediately to their assistance; his wife seeing her husband re-engaged in the quarrel, exalted her voice anew; Maritornes and the daughter squalled in concert, imploring heaven and the by-standers for help: Sancho perceiving what passed, "By the Lord!" cried he, "what my master says about the enchantments of this castle is certainly true; for, it is impossible to live an hour in quiet, within its walls."

Don Fernando parted the knight and trooper, to their mutual satisfaction; unlocking their hands, which were fast clinched in the doublet-collar of the one, and the windpipe of the other: but, for all that, they did not cease demanding their prisoner, and the assistance of the company, in binding and delivering him to their charge, agreeable to the service of the king, and the order of the holy brotherhood, in whose behalf they repeated their demand of favour and assistance, to secure that felon, robber and thief. Don Quixote smiled at hearing these epithets, and with much composure, replied, "Come hither, ye vile and base-born race! Do you call it the province of an highwayman, to loose the chains of the captive, and set the prisoner free; to succour the miserable, raise the fallen, and relieve the distressed? Ah! infamous crew! whose low and grovelling understanding renders you unworthy, that heaven should reveal to you the worth that is contained in knight-errantry, or make you sensible of your sin and ignorance, in neglecting to revere the very shadow, much more the substance of any knight. Come hither, ye rogues in a troop, and not troopers; ye robbers licensed by the holy brotherhood; and tell me what ignorant wretch he was, who signed a warrant of caption against such a knight as me? who did not know that we are exempted from all judicial authority, and that a knight's own sword is his law, he being privileged by his valour, and restricted only by his will and pleasure? Who was the blockhead, I say, who does not know, that no gentleman's charter contains so many rights and indulgencies as adhere to a knight-errant, the very day on which he is dubbed, and devotes himself to the painful exercise of arms? What knight-errant ever paid tax, toll, custom, duty or excise? What taylor ever brought in a bill for making his cloaths? What governor ever made him pay for lodging in his castle? What king did ever neglect to seat him at his own table? What damsel ever resisted his charms, or refused to submit herself intirely to his pleasure and will? And in fine, what knight-errant ever was, is, or will be, whose single valour is not sufficient to annihilate four hundred troopers, should they presume to oppose him?"

## CHAPTER XIX.

In which is concluded the notable adventure of the troopers;
with an account of the surprising ferocity of our worthy knight
Don Quixote.

W hile Don Quixote harrangued in this manner, the curate was employed in per-
suading the troopers, that he was a man disordered in his judgment, as they
might perceive both by his words and actions, and therefore they ought not to proceed
any further in the affair; for, even if they should apprehend him, he would soon be dis-
missed as a person non compos. To this observation, the man who had the warrant
replied, that it was not his business to judge of Don Quixote's madness, but, to obey the
orders of his superiors; and that if he was apprehended once, they might discharge him
three hundred times over, if they would. "For all that," said the priest, "you must not
carry him off, at present, nor do I believe he will suffer himself to be so treated."

In short, the curate talked so effectually, and the knight himself acted such extrava-
gancies, that the troopers must have been more mad than he, if they had not plainly per-
ceived his defect; therefore they thought proper to be satisfied, and even performed the
office of mediators betwixt the barber and Sancho Panza, who still maintained the fray
with great animosity; for, the troopers, as limbs of justice, brought the cause to an arbi-
tration, and decided it in such a manner, as left both parties, if not fully satisfied, at least
in some sort content with the determination, which was, that the pannels should be ex-
changed, but the girths and halters remain as they were. With regard to Mambrino's
helmet, the curate, unperceived by Don Quixote, took the barber aside, and paid him
eight rials for the bason, taking a receipt in full, that cleared the knight from any suspi-
cion of fraud, from thence forward, for ever, amen.

These two quarrels, which were of the greatest importance of any that happened,
being luckily composed, it remained, that three of the servants belonging to Don Lewis
should return, and the fourth accompany his master to the place whither Don Fernando
intended to conduct him; and as good luck and favourable fortune had already begun to
quell the spirit of discord, and smooth all difficulties, in behalf of the lovers and heroes
in the inn, they were resolved to proceed in such a laudable work, and bring every thing
to a happy conclusion; for, the domesticks were satisfied with what Don Lewis pro-
posed; a circumstance that gave such pleasure to Donna Clara, that every body who be-
held her face might have discerned the joy of her soul. Zorayda, tho' she did not well
understand the incidents she had seen, was sorrowful and gay, by turns, according as she
perceived the company affected, particularly her Spaniard, upon whom her eyes and
heart were always fixed. The innkeeper, who took particular notice of the full satisfac-
tion which the barber had received from the curate, demanded payment of Don Qui-
xote, of the reckoning, as well as for the damage he had done to the bags, and the loss of
his wine, swearing that neither Rozinante or Sancho's ass, should stir from the stable,

until he should be satisfied to the last farthing *. The curate pacified the landlord, and Don Fernando paid the bill, altho' the judge very frankly offered to take that upon himself: in this manner, universal concord was restored; so that, the inn no longer represented the disorder in Agramonte's camp, but, rather the peace and quiet that reigned in the time of Octavius Caesar: and this blessing was generally ascribed to the laudable intention and great eloquence of the priest, together with the incomparable generosity of Don Fernando.

Don Quixote now finding himself freed and disentangled from so many broils, in which both he and his squire had been involved, thought it high time to proceed on his journey, in order to finish that great adventure to which he had been summoned and chosen: he therefore, with determined purpose, went and fell upon his knees before Dorothea, who refusing to hear him in that posture, he rose, in obedience to her will, and expressed himself in this manner: "It is a common proverb, beauteous princess, that diligence is the mother of success; and in many important causes, experience hath shewn, that the assiduity of the sollicitor hath brought a very doubtful suit to a very fortunate issue; but, the truth of this maxim is no where more evinced than in war, where activity and dispatch anticipate the designs of the enemy, and obtain the victory, before he has time to put himself in a posture of defence. This I observe, most high and excellent princess, because, in my opinion, our stay in this castle is unprofitable and prejudicial, as we may one day perceive, when it is too late; for, who knows but, by means of secret and artful spies, your enemy, the giant, may get notice that I am coming to destroy him; and taking the opportunity of our delay, fortify himself in some impregnable castle, against which all my diligence, and the strength of my indefatigable arm, will not avail: wherefore, most noble princess, let us, as I have already observed, prevent his designs by our activity, and set out immediately, in the name of good fortune, which your highness shall not long sigh for, after I shall have come within sight of your adversary."

Here the knight left off speaking, and, with great composure, expected the answer of the beautiful infanta, who, with a most princely air, and in a stile perfectly well suited to his address, replied in this manner: "I thank you, Sir knight, for the desire you express, to assist me in my necessity, like a true knight, whose duty and province it is, to succour the fatherless and distressed; and heaven grant that your desire and my expectation may be fulfilled, that you may see there are grateful women upon earth. With regard to my departure, let it be as speedy as you please: my will is altogether included in yours; dispose of me, therefore, according to your own pleasure; for, she who hath once invested you with the charge and defence of her person, and solely depends upon your valour, for being re-established on her throne, would act preposterously, in seeking to contradict what your prudence shall ordain." "In the name of God, then," cried Don Quixote, "since a princess humbles herself thus, before me, I will not let slip the opportunity of raising her up, and placing her upon the throne of her ancestors: let us depart immediately; for, the desire of seeing you restored, the length of the journey, and the common

---

* It were to be wished, for the honour of Spanish innkeepers, that Cervantes had caused mine host to restore Sancho's wallet, which he had detained on the day of the blanketting; as such restitution would have increased the general satisfaction.[1]

reflexion, 'that delays are dangerous,' act as spurs upon my resolution; and since, heaven hath not created, nor hell ever seen an object that could strike me with terror and consternation, go, Sancho, saddle Rozinante, prepare the queen's palfrey, and get ready your own ass, while we take leave of the constable, and these noble personages, and set forward on our journey, without loss of time."

Here Sancho, who was present all the time, shook his head, saying, "Ah, master, master! there are more tricks in town than you dream of;[2] with submission to the honourable lappets,[3] be it spoken." "What tricks can there be either in town or city, that can redound to my discredit, rascal?" cried the knight. "Nay, if your worship be in a passion," replied the squire, "I will keep my tongue within my teeth, and not mention a syllable of what, as a trusty squire, and faithful servant, I am bound to reveal to my master." "Say what thou wouldst," answered Don Quixote, "so thy words have no tendency to make me afraid; for, in being susceptible of fear, thou shewest the baseness of thy own character, as I, in being proof against all sorts of terror, preserve the dignity of mine." "As I am a sinner to God," cried Sancho, "that is not the case; but, this I know for truth and positive certainty, that this lady, who calls herself queen of the great kingdom Micomicon, is no more a queen than my mother; for, if she were what she pretends to be, she would not be nuzzling into a corner with one of this company, at every snatch of an opportunity."

Dorothea's face was overspread with a blush, at these words of Sancho; for, sooth to say, her husband Don Fernando had several times, as he thought, unperceived, made free with her lips, as earnest of that reward his affection deserved; and in so doing, he was observed by Sancho, who thought that such condescension in her looked more like the behaviour of a courtezan than that of such a mighty princess; so, that she neither could nor would answer one word to this charge, but, suffered him to proceed in these words: "This, dear master, I make bold to mention, because, if after we have travelled the Lord knows how far, and passed many weary days and bitter nights, he that is taking his recreation in this inn should gather the fruit of all our labour; we need not be in such a perilous hurry to saddle Rozinante, prepare the palfrey, and get ready the ass; but, had better remain in peace where we are, and as the saying is, 'While we enjoy our meal let every harlot mind her spinning-wheel.'"

Gracious heaven! what a torrent of indignation entered the breast of Don Quixote, when he heard these indecent expressions of his squire: such, I say, was the rage that took possession of his faculties, that with a faultering voice and stammering tongue, while his eyes flashed lightening, he exclaimed, "O villainous, inconsiderate, indecent and ignorant peasant! thou foul-mouthed, unmannerly, insolent and malicious slanderer! darest thou utter such language against these honourable ladies in my presence? darest thou entertain such disgraceful and audacious ideas in thy confused imagination? Get out of my sight, monster of nature, depository of lies, cupboard of deceit, granary of knavery, inventor of mischief, publisher of folly, and foe to that respect which is due to royalty; go, nor presume to see my face again, on pain of my highest displeasure!" So saying, he pulled up his eye-brows, distended his cheeks, looked round him, and with his right foot, stamped violently upon the floor, in consequence of the wrath that preyed upon his intrails.

Sancho was so shrunk and terrified at these words and furious gestures, that he would have been glad, if the earth had opened that instant, under his feet, and swallowed him up; and not knowing what else to do, he sneaked off from the presence of his incensed master; but, the discreet Dorothea, who was so well acquainted with Don Quixote's humour, in order to appease his indignation, accosted him thus: "Sir knight of the rueful countenance, let not your wrath be kindled by the nonsense which your good squire hath uttered; for, perhaps, he might have had some sort of reason for what he said: and as from his good understanding and christian conscience, he cannot be suspected of a design to bear false witness against any person whatever, it is to be supposed, and indeed I firmly believe, that every thing in this castle, as you, Sir knight, have observed, being conducted by means of enchantment, Sancho, thro' that diabolical medium, must have seen what he affirms, so much to the prejudice of my honour and reputation." "I swear by Almighty God!" cried Don Quixote, "that your highness hath hit upon the true cause! and the eyes of that poor sinner Sancho, have been fascinated by some delusive vision, of what could not possibly be real; for, unless he had been misled by enchantment, such is the innocence and simplicity of that miserable wretch, that I know he neither could nor would invent a slander against any living soul." "That certainly is, and shall be the case," said Don Fernando; "for which reason, signor Don Quixote ought to pardon and restore him to the bosom of his favour, Sicut erat in principio,[4] before those illusions impaired his understanding."

The knight promised to forgive him accordingly; upon which, the curate went in quest of Sancho, who came in with great humility, and falling on his knees, begged leave to kiss his master's hand: this favour was granted by Don Quixote, who also gave him his benediction, saying, "Thou wilt now, son Sancho, be convinced of the truth of what I have so often told thee, that all things in this castle are performed by the power of enchantment." "I believe so too," replied the squire, "except in the affair of the blanketting, which really happened in the ordinary course of things." "Thou must not imagine any such thing," answered the knight; "for, had that been the case, I should have revenged thy cause at the time, and even now would do thee justice; but, neither at that time, nor now, could I, or can I find, any persons to chastise as the cause of thy disaster."

The company being desirous of knowing the affair of the blanket, the landlord gave a very minute detail of Sancho's capering, to the no small diversion of all present, except the squire himself, who would have been very much out of countenance, had not the knight assured him anew, that the whole was effected by enchantment: tho' the folly of Sancho never rose to such a pitch, but that he firmly believed, without the least mixture of doubt or delusion, that his blanketting had been performed by persons of flesh and blood, and not by phantoms or imaginary beings, according to the opinion and affirmation of his master.

Two days had this illustrious company already passed at the inn, from whence thinking it now high time to depart, they concerted matters in such a manner, as that, without putting Dorothea and Don Fernando to the trouble of returning with Don Quixote to the place of his habitation, in order to carry on the scheme concerning the restoration of queen Micomicona, the curate and barber were enabled to execute their design of carrying him to his own house, where endeavours might be used, for the cure of his

disorder. In consequence of this plan, they agreed with the master of an ox-waggon, who chanced to pass that way, for transporting the knight in the following manner: having made a sort of wooden cage, capacious enough to hold Don Quixote at his ease, Don Fernando, with his companions, the servants of Don Lewis, together with the troopers and inn-keeper, by order and direction of the curate, covered their faces and disguised themselves, some in one shape, some in another, so as to appear, in Don Quixote's eyes, quite different from the people he had seen in the castle. Thus equipped, they entered, with all imaginable silence, into the chamber where he lay asleep and fatigued with the toil he had undergone in the skirmishes already described; and laying fast hold on him, while he securely enjoyed his ease, without dreaming of such an accident, tied both his hands and feet so effectually, that when he waked, in surprize, he could neither move, nor do any other thing but testify his wonder and perplexity at sight of such strange faces. He then had recourse to what his distempered imagination continually suggested, and concluded that all these figures were phantomes of that inchanted castle; and that he himself was, without all question, under the power of incantation, seeing he could not even stir, in his own defence: and this conceit was exactly foreseen by the curate, who was author of the whole contrivance. The only person of the whole company who remained unaltered, both in figure and intellect, was Sancho, who, though his lack of understanding fell very little short of his master's infirmity, was not so mad but that he knew every one of the apparitions, though he durst not open his mouth, until he should see the meaning of this assault and capture of the knight, who likewise expected, in silence, the issue of his own misfortune.

Having brought the cage into his apartment, they enclosed him in it, and fixed the bars so fast, that it was impossible to pull them asunder; then taking it on their shoulders, in carrying it out, they were saluted by as dreadful a voice as could be assumed by the barber (I do not mean the owner of the pannel) who pronounced these words: "O knight of the rueful countenance! afflict not thyself on account of thy present confinement, which is necessary towards the more speedy accomplishment of that great adventure in which thy valour hath engaged thee; and which will be atchieved when the furious Manchegan lion is coupled with the white Tobosian dove, their lofty necks being humbled to the soft matrimonial yoke. From which unheard-of conjunction, the world shall be blessed with courageous whelps, who will imitate the tearing talons of their valiant fire; and this will happen, e'er the pursuer of the fugitive nymph shall have twice performed his visit through the resplendent constellations, in his natural and rapid course. And O! thou the most noble and obedient squire that ever wore sword in belt, beard on chin, or smell in nostril, be not dismayed nor discontented at seeing the flower of knight-errantry thus carried off before thine eyes; for, if it please the creator of this world, soon shalt thou be so exalted and sublimed, as that thou wilt not even know thyself; neither shalt thou be defrauded of the fruit of those promises which thy worthy lord has made in thy behalf; and I assure thee, in the name of the sage Fibberiana *, that thy salary shall be faithfully paid, as in effect thou wilt see: follow, therefore, the footsteps of the valiant and inchanted knight; for, it is necessary that you should

* A word of equal signification with *Mentironiana*, from *Menteroso*, a liar.[5]

proceed together, to the end of your career; and as I am not permitted to declare myself more explicitly, I bid you heartily farewel, and will return I well know whither." Towards the end of this prophecy, he raised his voice to the highest pitch, and then sunk it gradually, to such a faint and distant tone, that even those who were privy to the joke, were tempted to believe what they had heard.

Don Quixote remained very much comforted by this prophecy, the meaning of which he no sooner heard than comprehended; interpreting the whole into a promise, that he should one day see himself joined in the just and holy bonds of matrimony with his beloved Dulcinea del Toboso, from whose fortunate womb would proceed those whelps (meaning his sons) which would perpetuate the glory of la Mancha. In this persuasion, therefore, and firm belief, he raised his voice, and heaving a profound sigh, replied, "O thou! whosoever thou art, whose prognostication sounds so favourably in mine ears, I beg thou wilt, in my name, beseech the sage inchanter who takes charge of my affairs, that he will not leave me to perish in the confinement which I now suffer, until I shall have seen the accomplishment of those joyful and incomparable promises which thou hast uttered in my behalf. So shall I glory in the hardships of this prison, and bear with pleasure, these chains with which my limbs are fettered; and instead of comparing the boards on which I lie, to the rough, uncomfortable field of battle, consider them as the soothing down of the most happy and luxurious marriage-bed. With respect to the consolation of Sancho Panza, my squire, I confide in his virtue and affection, which will not allow him to forsake me either in prosperity or adversity; for, should his evil fortune, or my unhappy fate, hinder me from bestowing upon him the island, or some equivalent, according to my promise; at least, he shall not lose his wages, specified and bequeathed to him in my will that is already made; a recompence which, though proportioned to my own slender ability, comes far short of his great and faithful services."

Here the squire bowed, in the most respectful manner, and kissed both his hands, as he could not make his compliments to one of them apart, they being fast bound together. Then the apparitions taking the cage upon their shoulders, carried it to the waggon, in which it was immediately fixed.

## CHAPTER XX.

### An account of the strange manner in which Don Quixote was enchanted; with other remarkable events.

Don Quixote seeing himself thus encaged, and placed upon a cart, could not help saying, "Many very grave histories have I read, concerning knights-errant; but, never did I read, see, or hear, that enchanted knights were transported in this manner, at such a pace as these lazy, slow-footed animals seem to promise; for, they used always to be carried through the air, with surprizing swiftness, wrapt up in some dark and dusky

cloud, or in a fiery chariot, or mounted on a hypogriff, or some such creature: so that, before God! I am utterly confounded at my own fate, in being thus transported on a waggon drawn by oxen. But, perhaps the chivalry and enchantments of this age follow a different path from that which was pursued of old; and, as I am a new knight on the face of the earth, and the first who revived the long forgotten order of errantry; perhaps, they may have also newly invented other kinds of incantation, and other methods of conveying those whom they inchant. What is thy opinion of the matter, son Sancho?" "I know not what my opinion is," replied the squire, "because I am not so well read in the scriptures of errantry as your worship: but, for all that, I will venture to affirm, ay and swear to it, that these apparitions who strole about us, are not altogether catholic." "Catholic! my * stars!" answered the knight, "how can they be catholic, when they are all devils who have assumed fantastical shapes, and come hither on purpose to perform this deed, and leave me in my present situation? but, that thou mayest be † convinced of the truth of what I alledge, endeavour to touch and feel them, and thou wilt perceive that they have no other bodies but forms of condensed air, consisting of nothing but meer semblance." "'Fore God! sir," cried Sancho, "I have made that trial already, and that same devil who goes about so busy, is well provided with good substantial flesh, and has another property widely different from what is reported of evil spirits, all of whom, they say, stink of brimstone and other bad smells; whereas, he is so well scented with amber, that you may perceive it, at the distance of half a league." Sancho made this remark on Don Fernando, who, being a man of fashion, probably wore scented linnen. "Marvel not at that circumstance, friend Sancho," replied the knight, "for thou must know that devils are a set of very sagacious beings, and although they bring smells along with them, they themselves being spirits, can produce no smell; or if any odour proceeds from them, it cannot be agreeable, but rather stinking and unwholsome, because they carry their hell about them, wheresoever they are, and their torments admit of no kind of alleviation: now, sweet smells being agreeable and delicious, cannot possibly proceed from beings which are productive of nought but evil: therefore if, in thy opinion, that devil smells of amber, either thy senses are perverted, or he wants to impose upon thy understanding, by making thee believe that he is not an inhabitant of hell."

Don Fernando and Cardenio overhearing this dialogue between the master and squire, were afraid of Sancho's stumbling upon the discovery of their whole plot, in which he seemed already to have made great progress; therefore, determined to hasten their departure, and calling the landlord aside, ordered him to saddle Rozinante, and put the pannel on Sancho's ass. This task he performed with great dispatch, while the curate agreed to give the troopers so much a day, for attending Don Quixote to the town where he lived. Cardenio having fastened the target to one side of the pummel of Rozinante's saddle, and the bason to the other, made signs for Sancho to mount his ass, and lead his master's steed by the bridle, and then stationed two of the troopers, with their

* In the original *mi padre!* my father! which I have changed for an exclamation more frequently used in our language.[1]
† In the text, the knight is guilty of a palpable solecism, in desiring Sancho to touch and feel that which, he himself expresly observes, was subject neither to touch or feeling.

carbines, on each side of the waggon. But, before it began to move, the landlady, her daughter, and Maritornes, came out to take leave of Don Quixote, feigning themselves extremely affected with his misfortune; upon which he said to them, "Weep not, worthy ladies; all these disasters are incident to those who choose my profession, and if I were not subject to such calamities, I should not deem myself a renowned knight-errant; for, these things never happen to knights of little fame and reputation, who are never regarded, scarce even remembred on the face of the earth. It is quite otherwise with the valiant, whose virtue and valour is envied by many princes and rivals, who endeavour, by the most perfidious means to destroy them; but, nevertheless, virtue is so powerful, that of herself she will, in spite of all the negromancy possessed by the first inventor Zoroaster, come off conqueror in every severe trial, and shine refulgent in the world, as the sun shines in the heavens. Pardon me, beauteous ladies, if I have given you any disgust, through neglect or omission; for, willingly and knowingly, I never offended a living soul; and pray to God to deliver me from this prison in which I am confined by some malicious inchanter: for, if I regain my liberty, the favours I have received from your courtesy, in this castle, shall never escape my remembrance, but always be acknowledged with gratitude, service and respect."

While the knight made these professions to the ladies of the castle, the curate and barber took their leave of Don Fernando and his companions, the captain and his brother, and all the happy ladies, especially Dorothea and Lucinda: they embraced each other, and agreed to maintain a correspondence by letters, Don Fernando giving the curate a direction by which he might write to him an account of the knight's future behaviour and fate, than which, he protested, nothing could yield him more pleasure; and promising, for his own part, to inform the priest of every thing which he thought would conduce to his satisfaction, relating to his own marriage, the baptism of Zorayda, the success of Don Lewis, and the return of Lucinda to her father's house: the priest having assured him, that he would obey his commands with the utmost punctuality, they embraced again, and repeated their mutual proffers of service. The innkeeper coming to the curate, put into his hand a bundle of papers, which he said he had found in the lining of the portmantua, along with the novel of the Impertinent Curiosity; and since the owner had not returned that way, he desired the priest to accept of them; for, as he himself could not read, he had no occasion for such useless furniture: the curate thanked him for his present, which he immediately opened, and found written in the title page, Rinconete and Cortadilla[2] *; a novel: from hence he concluded, that since the Impertinent Curiosity was an entertaining story, this might also have some merit, as being probably a work of the same author; and on this supposition put it carefully up, intending to peruse it, with the first convenient opportunity: then he and his friend the barber mounting their beasts, with their faces still disguised, that they might not be known by Don Quixote, jogged on, behind the waggon, and the order of their march was this: first of all proceeded the cart, conducted by the driver, and guarded on each side by the troopers with their carbines, as we have already observed; then followed Sancho Panza upon his ass, leading Rozinante by the bridle; and in the rear of all, came the curate and

* Written by Cervantes himself.[3]

the barber masked, and mounted on their trusty mules, with a grave and solemn air, marching no faster than the slow pace of the oxen would allow; while the knight sat within his cage, his hands fettered and his legs outstretched, leaning against the bars, with such silence and resignation, that he looked more like a statue of stone than a man of flesh and blood: in this slow and silent manner they had travelled about a couple of leagues, when they arrived in a valley, which the wagoner thinking a convenient spot for his purpose, proposed to the curate, that they should halt to refresh themselves, and let the oxen feed; but, the barber was of opinion, that they should proceed a little farther to the other side of a rising-ground, which appeared at a small distance, where he knew there was another valley better stored with grass, and much more agreeable than this in which the waggoner proposed to halt. The advice of Mr. Nicolas was approved, and they jogged on accordingly.

About this time, the curate chancing to look back, perceived behind them, six or seven men well mounted, who soon overtook them, as they did not travel at the phlegmatic pace of the oxen, but, like people who rode on ecclesiastic mules, and were desirous of spending the heat of the day at an inn that appeared within less than a league of the waggon: these expeditious strangers coming up with our slow travellers, saluted them courteously, and one among them, who was actually a canon of Toledo, and master of those who accompanied him, observing the regular procession of the waggon, troopers, Sancho, Rozinante, the curate and barber, and in particular, Don Quixote encaged and secured as he was, could not help asking why, and whither they were conveying that man in such a manner? tho' he had already conjectured, from the badges of the troopers, that he must be some attrocious robber or delinquent, the punishment of whom belonged to the holy brotherhood. One of the troopers, to whom the question was put, answered, "Signor, the gentleman himself will tell you the meaning of his travelling in this manner; for our parts, we know nothing at all of the matter." The knight overhearing what passed, said to the strangers, "Gentlemen, if you are skilled and conversant in matters of knight-errantry, I will communicate my misfortune; otherwise there is no reason why I should fatigue myself with the relation."

By this time, the curate and barber having perceived the travellers in conversation with the knight, came up, in order to prevent their plot from being discovered, just as the canon had begun to answer Don Quixote in these words: "Truly, brother, I am better acquainted with books of chivalry than with the summaries of Villalpando; so that, if there be nothing else requisite, you may freely impart to me as much as you please." "A God's name then," said Don Quixote, "if that be the case, you must know, signor cavalier, that I am enchanted in this cage, thro' the envy and fraud of mischievous negromancers; for, virtue is always more persecuted by the wicked than beloved by the righteous: a knight-errant I am, tho' none of those whose names fame never enrolled in her eternal records; but, of that number, whom maugre, and in despite of Envy herself, and all the magi whom Persia ever produced, with the brachmans of India, and gymnosophists of AEthiopia, will leave their names engraved on the temple of immortality, as examples and patterns to succeeding ages, by which all knights-errant may see what steps they must follow, if they wish to attain the height and honourable summit of arms."

Here the curate interposing, said, "Signor Don Quixote speaks no more than the

truth; he is inchanted in that waggon, not on account of his own crimes or misde-
meanours, but thro' the malice of those who are disgusted at virtue, and offended at val-
our: this, signor, is the knight of the rueful countenance, whose name perhaps you have
heard, and whose valiant exploits, and mighty atchievements, will be engraved on
durable brass; and carved in eternal marble, in spite of the unwearied efforts of malice
to cancel, and of envy to obscure them."

The canon hearing such a stile proceed, not only from the prisoner's mouth, but also
from the lips of him who was free, had well nigh crossed himself with astonishment, and
could not conceive what had befallen him, while his whole company were seized with
the same degree of amazement: but, Sancho Panza, who was near enough to hear what
passed, being willing to undeceive the strangers, said to them, "Gentlemen, whether
what I am going to say, be ill or well taken, I must tell you the case is this: my master
Don Quixote is no more enchanted than the mother that bore me; he enjoys his right
wits, eats, drinks, and does his occasions, like other men, and as he himself was wont to
do, before he was encaged: now, if this be the truth of the matter, how can any man per-
suade me that he is enchanted? since I have heard divers persons observe, that those who
are enchanted, neither eat, sleep, nor speak; whereas, my master, if he is not hindered,
will talk like thirty barristers." Then turning to the curate, he proceeded thus: "Ah
Mr. curate, Mr. curate! you think I don't know you, and imagine that I cannot dive into
the meaning of these new enchantments; but, you are mistaken: I know you very well,
for all your masking, and can smell out your plots, disguise them as you will; in short,
as the saying is, Just are virtue's fears, where envy domineers; and bounty will not stay,
where niggards bear the sway. Damn the devil, if it had not been for your reverence, my
master, by this time, would have been married to the princess Micomicona, and I should
have been an earl, at least; for, less I could not expect, either from the generosity of my
lord of the rueful countenance, or from the greatness of my own services: but, now I see
the truth of what is commonly said, that fortune turns faster than a mill-wheel; and that
those who were yesterday at top, may find themselves at bottom to day. It grieves me,
on account of my poor wife and children, who, instead of seeing their father come
home, in the post of governor or viceroy of some island or kingdom, as they had great
reason to expect, will behold him returning in the station of a common groom: all this
I have observed, Mr. curate, for no other reason, but to prevail upon your fathership, to
make a conscience of the ill treatment my master receives at your hands; and consider
that God may call you to account in the next world, for this captivity of my lord Don
Quixote, and for all the succours and benefits that are prevented by his being thus
confined."

"Snuff me these candles, (cried the barber, hearing the squire's declaration) why, sure
Sancho you belong to your master's fraternity; by the Lord! I find you ought to keep
him company in his cage, and undergo the same sort of enchantment, so much are you
infected with the humour of his chivalry: in an unhappy moment were you got with
child by his promises, and in an evil hour did that island you harp so much upon, take
possession of your skull." "I am not with child by any person whatever," answered San-
cho, "nor will I suffer any king in Christendom to beget a child upon my body; for, tho'
I be a poor man, I'm an old christian, and owe no man a farthing: if I long for an island,

others long for things that are worse, every one being the son of his own works: the lowest mortal may come to be pope, much more governor of an island, especially as my master may gain more than he knows well what to do with. Mr. barber, you had better think before you speak: there is something else to do than shaving of beards; and * one Pedro may differ from another: this I say, because we know one another; and you must not think to palm false dice upon me: with regard to the enchantment of my master, God knows the truth, and there let it lie; for, as the saying is, the more you stir it, the more it will—you know what." The barber durst not make any reply, lest Sancho's simplicity should discover what he and the curate were so desirous of concealing; and the priest being under the same apprehension, desired the canon to ride on with him, a little before the waggon, promising to disclose the mystery of the encaged knight, with other particulars that would yield him some diversion: the canon put on accordingly, with his servants, listening attentively to every thing the curate was pleased to communicate, concerning the rank, employment, madness, and manners of Don Quixote; for, he briefly recounted the cause and beginning of his disorder, with the whole progress of his adventures, until he was secured in the cage, by their contrivance, that they might carry him home to his own house, and endeavour to find some cure for his distemper.

The canon and his servants were astonished anew, at hearing the strange story of Don Quixote, which being finished, the Toledan replied, "Truly, Mr. curate, I am firmly persuaded that those books of chivalry are very prejudicial in the commonwealth; for, though I have been induced by a false taste and idle curiosity, to read the beginning of almost every one that hath been printed, I never could prevail upon myself to read any one of them from the first to the last page; because, in my opinion, they are all of the same stamp, without any essential difference; and indeed that kind of composition seems to fall under that species of writing called the Milesian fables, which are no other than extravagant tales calculated for meer amusement, without any tendency to instruction: on the contrary, the scope of your apologues, is to convey instruction and delight together. Now, though the principal intention of those books is to delight and entertain the reader, I do not see how they can answer that end, being, as they are, stuffed with such improbable nonsense: for, the pleasure that the soul conceives, is from the beauty and harmony of those things which are contemplated by the view, or suggested by the imagination; so, that we can receive no pleasure from objects that are unnatural and deformed. And what beauty, symmetry or proportion can be observed in a book, containing the history of a youth of seventeen, who, with one back-stroke, cuts through the middle a giant like a tower, with as much ease as if he had been made of paste; and in the description of a battle, after having observed, that there are no less than a million of combatants on the side opposite to that which the hero of the piece espouses, we must, in despite of common sense, believe, that such a knight obtained the victory, by the single valour of his invincible arm. Then, how shall we account for the confidence with which some queen, empress, or orphan heiress, throws herself into the protection of an unknown knight-errant? What mind, if not wholly barbarous and uncultivated, can be pleased with an account of a huge tower full of knights, sailing upon the sea, like

* Equivalent to our saying, "Every jack is not a good-fellow."[4]

a ship before the wind; being over-night, upon the coast of Lombardy, and next morning arrived in the dominions of Prester John, in the Indies, or in some other country which Ptolemy never discovered, nor Marcus Polus ever saw? If to this observation, it be answered, that the authors of those books do not pretend that the stories they contain, are true; and therefore, they are under no necessity of adhering to such niceties of composition: I reply, that fiction is always the better, the nearer it resembles truth, and agreeable in proportion to the probability it bears, and the doubtful credit which it inspires. Wherefore, all such fables ought to be suited to the understanding of those who read them, and written so, as that by softening impossibilities, smoothing what is rough, and keeping the mind in suspence, they may surprize, agreeably perplex, and entertain, creating equal admiration and delight; and these never can be excited by authors who forsake probability and imitation, in which the perfection of writing consists. I have never as yet seen, in any book of chivalry, an intire body of a fable, with all its members so proportioned, as that the middle corresponds with the beginning, and the end is suitable to both; on the contrary, one would think the author's intention is commonly to form a chimera or monster, instead of a figure well proportioned in all its parts. Besides, their stile is usually harsh, their atchievements incredible, their amours lascivious, their courtesy impertinent, their battles tedious, their dialogue insipid, their voyages extravagant, and, in short, the whole void of all ingenuity of invention; so that they deserve to be banished as useless members from every christian commonwealth."

The curate, who had listened with great attention, hearing the canon talk so sensibly, looked upon him as a man of excellent understanding, and assented to every thing he said, observing that, in consequence of his being of the same opinion, and of the grudge he bore to such books of chivalry, he had burned a great number of those that belonged to Don Quixote. He then gave him a detail of the scrutiny which had been made, distinguishing such as he spared, from those that he condemned to the flames.

The traveller laughed heartily at this account of such an extraordinary trial, saying, that notwithstanding what he had advanced to the disadvantage of such books, there was one thing in them which he could not but approve; namely, the subject they presented for a good genius to display itself, opening a large and ample field in which the pen might, at leisure, expatiate, in the description of shipwrecks, tempests, battles and encounters; painting a valiant general with all his necessary accomplishments, sage and penetrating into the enemy's designs; eloquent and effectual, either in persuading or dissuading his soldiers, ripe in council, prompt in execution, and equally brave in standing or in giving an assault. One while, recounting a piteous, tragical story; at another time, describing a joyful and unexpected event; here, a most beautiful lady endued with virtue, discretion and reserve; there, a christian knight possessed of courtesy and valour; in a third place, an outrageous boasting barbarian; and in a fourth, a polite, considerate gallant prince; not forgetting to describe the faith and loyalty of vassals, together with the grandeur and generosity of great men. The author may also shew himself an astrologer, geographer, musician, and well skilled in state-affairs; nay, if he be so minded, he will sometimes have an opportunity of manifesting his skill in negromancy and magic: he may represent the cunning of Ulysses, the piety of Æneas, the valour of Achilles, the misfortunes of Hector, the perfidy of Sinon, the friendship of Euryalus, the

liberality of Alexander, the ability of Caesar, the clemency and candour of Trajan, the fidelity of Zopyrus, the wisdom of Cato, and finally, all those qualifications which constitute the perfection of an illustrious hero; sometimes, uniting them in one, sometimes dividing them into several characters; and the whole being expressed in an agreeable stile and ingenious invention, that borders as near as possible, upon the truth, will, doubtless, produce a web of such various and beautiful texture, as when finished, to display that perfection which will attain the chief end and scope of such writings, which, as I have already observed, is to convey instruction mingled with delight. Besides, the unlimited composition of such books gives the author opportunities of shewing his talents in epics, lyrics, tragedy and comedy, and all the different branches of the delicious and agreeable arts of poetry and rhetoric: for, epics may be written in prose as well as verse.

### CHAPTER XXI.

## In which the canon prosecutes the subject of knight-errantry, and makes other observations worthy of his genius.

"Mr. canon," said the curate, Awhat you have observed, is extremely just; and therefore those authors deserve the greater reprehension, who have composed such books, without the least regard to good sense or the rules of art, by which they might have conducted their plans, and rendered themselves as famous in prose as the two princes of Greek and Latin poetry are now in verse." "I, myself," replied the canon, "have been tempted to write a book of chivalry, observing all the maxims and precautions I have now laid down: nay, to tell you the truth, no less than an hundred sheets of it are already written; and, in order to try if my own opinion of it was well founded, I have communicated my performance to a great many people, who are passionately fond of that kind of reading, not only, men of learning and taste, but also ignorant persons, who chiefly delight in extravagant adventures; and I have been favoured with the agreeable approbation of them all: nevertheless, I have not proceeded in the work; because, I not only thought it foreign to my profession, but, likewise concluded, that the world abounds much more with fools than people of sense; and though an author had better be applauded by the few that are wise, than laughed at by the many that are foolish, I was unwilling to expose myself to the uninformed judgment of the arrogant vulgar, whose province it principally is, to read books of this kind: but, what contributed most, to my laying aside the pen, and indeed all thoughts of bringing the work to a conclusion, was, a reflection I made upon the comedies of the present age. If, said I to myself, our modern plays, not only those which are formed upon fiction, but likewise such as are founded on the truth of history, are all, or for the greatest part, universally known to be monstrous productions, without either head or tail, and yet received with pleasure

by the multitude, who approve and esteem them as excellent performances, though they are far from deserving that title; and if the authors who compose, and the actors who represent them, affirm, that this and no other method is to be practised, because the multitude must be pleased; that those which bear the marks of contrivance, and produce a fable digested according to the rules of art, serve only for entertainment to four or five people of taste, who discern the beauties of the plan, which utterly escape all the rest of the audience; and that it is better for them to gain a comfortable livelihood by the many, than starve upon reputation with the few; at this rate, said I, if I should finish my book, after having scorched every hair in my whiskers, in poring over it, to preserve those rules and precepts already mentioned, I might fare at last, like the * sagacious botcher, who sewed for nothing, and found his customers in thread.[1] I have sometimes endeavoured to persuade the players, that they were mistaken in their maxims; and that they would bring more company to their house, and acquire much more reputation, by representing regular comedies, than such absurd performances; but, I always found them so obstinately bigotted to their own fancies, that no evidence or demonstration could alter their opinion in the least. I remember, I once said to one of those pragmatic fellows, 'Don't you recollect, that a few years ago, three tragedies were acted, composed by a celebrated poet of this kingdom; and that they raised admiration, pleasure and surprize, in all who saw them exhibited, gentle as well as simple, ignorant as well as learned, and brought more money to the actors than thirty of the best that have since appeared?' 'Doubtless,' answered the player, 'you mean, Isabella, Phillis, and Alexandria?' 'The very same,' said I; 'and pray take notice, whether or not they are composed according to rule, or failed to please every body, because they were regular? Wherefore, the fault does not lie in the multitude's demanding absurdities, but, in those who can represent nothing else; for, there is nothing absurd in the play of Ingratitude Revenged, nor in Numantia, the Merchant Lover, the Favourable Female Foe, nor in some others which were composed by poets of genius, to their own reputation, and the advantage of those who represented them.' I made use of many more arguments, by which he seemed to be confuted, though not so much satisfied or convinced, as to retract his erroneous opinions."

"Mr. canon," said the curate, interrupting him in this place, "the subject you have touched upon awakes in me an old grudge I have bore to our modern plays, even equal to that I entertain against books of chivalry. Comedy, according to Tully, ought to be the mirrour of life, the exemplar of manners, and picture of truth; whereas those that are represented in this age, are mirrours of absurdity, exemplars of folly, and pictures of lewdness; for, sure nothing can be more absurd, in a dramatic performance, than to see the person, who in the first scene of the first act, was produced a child in swaddling-cloaths, appear a full grown man with a beard, in the second; or to represent an old man active and valiant, a young soldier cowardly, a footman eloquent, a page a counsellor, a king a porter, and a princess a scullion. Then, what shall we say concerning their management of the time and place, in which the actions have, or may be supposed to have, happened? I have seen a comedy, the first act of which was laid in Europe, the second in

* A Spanish proverb, applicable to a great many modern projectors and reformers.

Asia, and the third was finished in Africa; nay had there been a fourth, the scene would have shifted to America, so that the fable would have travelled through all the four divisions of the globe. If imitation be the chief aim of comedy, how can any ordinary understanding be satisfied with seeing an action that passed in the time of king Pepin and Charlemagne, ascribed to the emperor Heraclius, who being the principal personage, is represented, like Godfrey of Bulloign, carrying the cross into Jerusalem, and making himself master of the holy sepulchre; an infinite number of years having passed between the one and the other. Or, when a comedy is founded upon fiction, to see scraps of real history introduced, and facts misrepresented both with regard to persons and times; not with any ingenuity of contrivance, but with the most manifest and inexcusable errors and stupidity: and what is worst of all, there is a set of ignorant pretenders, who call this the perfection of writing; and say that every attempt to succeed by a contrary method is no other than a wild-goose chace *. Again, if we consider those plays that are written on divine subjects, how many false miracles do they contain? how many apocryphal events misunderstood by the author, who frequently confounds the operations of one saint with those of another? nay, in prophane subjects, they have the assurance to work miracles, for no other respect or consideration, but because they think such a miracle will make a very decent appearance in such a place; and, as they term it, attract the admiration of the vulgar, and bring them in crowds to the play: but, all this redounds to the prejudice of truth, the contempt of history, and scandal of our Spanish wits; so that the authors of other nations, who punctually observe the unities of the drama, conclude, that we are barbarous and ignorant, from our absurd and preposterous productions. Neither is it a sufficient excuse, to say, that the intent of all well-governed commonwealths, in permitting public plays to be acted, is to entertain the common people with some honest recreation, in order to divert those bad humours which idleness usually engenders; and that, since this end is answered by any play whatever, either good or bad, there is no occasion to cramp and limit the authors or actors to the just laws of composition; the purpose of the legislature being, as I have said, accomplished without any such restriction. To this suggestion, I answer, that the same end, without any sort of comparison, will be much better answered by good than bad comedies; for, after having seen an artful and well-digested play represented, the hearer will go away, delighted with the comic parts, instructed by the serious, and agreeably surprized with the incidents; collecting information from the dialogue, precaution from the deceits of the fable, experience from the examples exhibited, affection for virtue, and indignation for vice. All these sensations, I say, will a good comedy excite in the spectator's mind, let it be never so stupid and uncultivated; for, of all impossibilities, it is the most impossible, that a comedy, thus perfect in all its parts, should not yield more entertainment, satisfaction, and delight, than one that is defective in each particular, as the greatest part of our modern pieces are. Neither is this want of correctness always to be laid to the author's charge; for, there are some poets among us who are perfectly well acquainted with the rules of writing, and could easily avoid any such errors of composition; but as their pieces are made for sale, they say, and it is very true, that the players would not purchase

---

* *Buscar Gullerias*, signifies to seek dainties.[2]

them, if they were of any other stamp: so that the author is fain to accommodate himself to the demand of the actor who pays him for his work. The truth of this observation evidently appears in a great number of comedies, which have been composed by a most happy genius of these * kingdoms, with so much wit, pleasantry, elegance of versification, genteel dialogue, sententious gravity, and finally, with such elocution and sublimity of stile, that the whole world resounds with his fame: yet, in suiting himself to the false taste of the actors, he hath not been able to bring them all to the requisite point of perfection. Others again, are so inconsiderate in their productions, that after representation, the players have been frequently obliged to fly, and abscond, for fear of chastisement, on account of having exhibited something to the prejudice of royal heads, or dishonour of noble families: now, all these inconveniencies, with many more that I do not choose to mention, might be prevented, if there was at court, some person of taste and learning, appointed to examine every dramatic performance before its appearance on the stage; and this precaution should affect not only the plays composed in Madrid, but, all pieces whatever to be represented within the monarchy of Spain; for, without the approbation of this licenser, signed and sealed, no magistrates should allow any production to be acted within the bounds of his jurisdiction. In consequence of this expedient, the actors would take care to submit every play to the censure of the examiner, that they might afterwards represent them with safety; and the authors would employ more caution and study in their compositions, knowing that they must pass the rigorous examination of an intelligent judge: in this manner, good comedies would be produced, and the aim of such writings happily accomplished, to the entertainment of the people, and the credit of Spanish wits; while the actors would represent them with security and advantage, and the state be exempted from the trouble of chastising such delinquents. And if the same licenser, or any other person, were invested with the charge of examining books of chivalry, before they see the light, some performances of that sort would certainly appear in all the perfection you have described, enriching our language with the delightful and precious treasure of eloquence; while the old romances would be entirely eclipsed by the light of the new, that would furnish rational amusement not only for the idle, but also for those who are most industrious; seeing, it is impossible for the bow to continue always bent, or that feeble nature can subsist, without some innocent recreation."

Thus far had the canon and curate proceeded in their conversation, when the barber coming up to them, said to his townsman, "Mr. Licentiate, this is the place in which I proposed to halt, that the oxen might have fresh pasture in abundance." The curate approved of the hint, and communicated their intention to the canon, who resolved to stay with them, being invited by the situation of a delicious valley that presented itself to his view; that he might, therefore, enjoy the agreeable spot, together with the conversation of the curate, for whom he had already conceived an affection, and be more particularly informed of Don Quixote's exploits, he ordered his domestics to proceed to an inn, which was not far off, and bring from thence victuals sufficient for the whole company; for he was resolved to spend the afternoon where he was. One of the servants told him

* Lopez de Vega Carpio.³

that the sumpter-mule, which by that time had reached the inn, carried provision enough, and that they should want nothing but barley for the beasts. "If that be the case," said the canon, "carry the rest to the inn, and bring the sumpter-mule hither."

Mean while, Sancho perceiving that he might now speak to his master without being overheard by the curate and barber, of whom he was suspicious, approached the cage, and thus addressed himself to the knight: "Truly, Sir, in order to disburthen my conscience, I must tell you something concerning this same enchantment. These people, with masks on their faces, are no other than the curate and barber of our town, who, I verily believe, have contrived to carry you off, in this manner, out of pure envy and spite, because your worship has got the heels of them in your famous atchievements: now, this being supposed, it follows, as plain as the nose upon my face, that you are not enchanted, but rather fooled and bamboozled. As a proof of which, I desire to ask you one question, which if you answer, as I do believe you will, your worship may clap your ten fingers on the trick, and perceive that you are not enchanted, but that your whole brain is turned topsy-turvy." "Ask what you will, son Sancho," replied Don Quixote, "I will freely answer, and satisfy your doubts to the best of my power: with regard to your saying, that those who attend us, are our friends and townsmen the curate and barber, so, indeed, they may appear to your eye; but, that they are really and effectually so, you must, by no means, believe; on the contrary, you are to conclude, that if they resemble our friends, the enchanters, who can assume what form they please, have taken that appearance and resemblance, to mislead your credit, and bewilder your imagination in such a labyrinth of perplexity, that even the clue of Theseus would not extricate your thoughts: besides, they may have done it with a view of confounding my judgment, that I might not be able to guess from what quarter my misfortune proceeds; for, if on one hand, you affirm, that I am attended by the barber and curate of our town; and on the other, I find myself encaged, though I am sensible, that nothing but supernatural force could suffice to confine me thus, what would you have me say or think, but, that the manner of my enchantment exceeds every thing I have read in all the histories that treat of inchanted knights? Wherefore, set your heart at rest, and take it for granted, that these are as far from being the persons you have mentioned as I am from being a Turk. With respect to thy desire of asking me questions, I repeat my promise of answering, even if thy interrogation should last till to-morrow morning." "God's blessed mother!" cried the squire with great vociferation, "is it possible that your worship can be so thick-skulled and brainless, as not to perceive the truth of what I alledge, and see that this imprisonment and misfortune is more owing to malice than enchantment? But, seeing it is so, I will venture to prove, beyond all contradiction, that you are no more enchanted than my ass: tell me, therefore, as God shall deliver you from this mischance, and as you hope to see yourself in the arms of my lady Dulcinea, when you least expect any such good luck—." "Truce with thy conjuration," said the knight, "and ask what thou wilt; I have already promised to answer with the utmost punctuality." "That is my request," answered Sancho; "and what I want to know, is, that your worship will tell me, without eking or curtailing God's precious truth, but, in honest simplicity of heart, as it ought to be, and always is told those who, like your worship, profess the occupation of arms, under the title of knights-errant—." "I tell thee," cried the knight, interrupting him, "I

will not in the least prevaricate: dispatch then, Sancho, for, truly, I am quite tired with so many salvos, sollicitations and preambles." "I make so bold," replied the squire, "because I am well aware of my master's goodness and sincerity, which being as it were to the purpose, I ask, (with reverence be it spoken) whether or not, since you have been confined, and as you suppose, inchanted in this cage, your worship hath felt any motion or desire to undam either way, as the saying is?" "I do not know what you mean by undamming," answered Don Quixote; "you must be more explicit, Sancho, if you expect an answer to the purpose." "Is it possible," said the squire, "that your worship should be ignorant of the meaning of the word undamming, which is the first thing the boys learn at school? Well then, you must know, I wanted to ask if you never had any inclination to do that which no body else can do for you." "Now I understand thee, Sancho," said the knight; "verily, I have had divers calls of that nature, one of which is at present very importunate: pray, fall upon some method to disembarrass me; for, I believe all is not so sweet and clean as it ought to be."

## CHAPTER XXII.

### The sage conversation that passed between Sancho Panza and his master Don Quixote.

"Ha!" cried Sancho, "have I caught you at last? this is what I wanted to know, with all my heart and soul; come on, sir, there is no denying of what is commonly said, when any person is in the dumps, I know not what is the matter with such an one; he neither eats, drinks, nor sleeps, nor answers to the purpose, when he is spoke to; sure the man must be enchanted: from whence we are to conclude, that those who are enchanted neither eat, drink, sleep, nor do their natural occasions, as I have observed; but, this is not the case with such as are disturbed with the inclination that your worship at present feels, drinking when they can get liquor, eating when they can lay hold on food, and giving plain answers to every question that is asked." "Thou art in the right," replied Don Quixote: "but, I have already told thee, that there are different kinds of enchantment; and time may have so intirely altered the fashion, that those who are under the power of enchantment in this age may, like me, retain the use of their faculties, tho' it was quite otherwise of old; so, that there is no arguing or drawing consequences, against the different practice of different times. I am sensible and certain of my being enchanted; and that is sufficient for the quiet of my conscience, which would give me great uneasiness, if I had the least doubt about my fate, and allowed myself to be in this cage, like an idle coward, deceitfully withholding my succour from a great number of the needy and oppressed, who, at this very hour, must be in the most absolute and extreme necessity, from the want of my aid and protection." "Nevertheless," answered the squire, "for your more abundant satisfaction, your worship, methinks, might try to escape from

this prison; for my own part, I'll be bound not only to give my assistance, but even to work your deliverance, and then you may endeavour to remount your trusty Rozinante, who trudges along as melancholy and sad as if he was enchanted also. This being performed, let us try our fate once more, in quest of adventures; and if they do not turn out to our expectation, it will be time enough to return to the cage, in which, I promise, on the faith of a true and loyal squire, to shut myself up with your worship, if perchance, thro' your ill fortune or my folly, this that I mention, should not succeed." "I am content to follow thy counsel, brother Sancho," replied the knight, "and whenever thou shalt perceive a proper conjuncture for effecting my deliverance, I will implicitly obey thee in every thing; but, thou wilt soon find thyself deceived in thy opinion of my mishap."

This conversation between the knight-errant and the erring squire, lasted until they arrived at the place in which the curate, canon and barber, who had already alighted, waited for them. The waggoner immediately unyoking his oxen, turned them loose in that verdant and delicious spot, the coolness of which was extremely inviting, not only to enchanted people, like Don Quixote, but also to persons of intelligence and discretion, like his squire, who besought the curate to let his master come out of the cage, for a few minutes; because, without such permission, the prison would not be quite so clean as the decency of such a knight required. The curate understanding what he meant, told him that he would willingly grant his request, were he not under some apprehension, that his master, finding himself at liberty, would play one of his old pranks, and be gone where men should never see his face again. "I will be bound for his good behaviour," answered Sancho: "And I also," said the canon, "especially, if he will promise, on the word of a knight, not to stir from our presence, until he shall have obtained our consent."

"I will: (cried the knight, who overheard all that passed) the more so; as one who, like me, is enchanted, cannot be at liberty to make use of his own person; for, the enchanter can so utterly deprive him of all motion, that he shall not be able to stir from the place, for three whole ages; and if he should make his escape, would whisk him back thro' the air, in a twinkling." This being the case, he said, they might very safely uncage him, especially as such indulgence would redound to the benefit of the whole company; for, he protested, that if they did not comply with his present necessities, he should be obliged to incommode their sense of smelling, unless they removed to a greater distance, from the place of his confinement.

The canon, confiding in his word and honour, took him by the hands, tied as they were, and helped him to descend from his cage: then the knight being infinitely rejoiced at his momentary deliverance, stretched every joint in his body, and going up to Rozinante, gave him a slap on the buttocks, saying, "I still hope in God and his blessed mother, thou flower and mirrour of steeds! that in a short time, we shall both obtain our heart's desire; thou prancing under the agreeable pressure of thy lord, and I mounted upon thy trusty back, exercising the employment for which heaven sent me into the world." Having pronounced this apostrophe, he retired with Sancho to a remote place, from whence he returned much eased and comforted, and more desirous than ever of executing the project of his squire. The canon could not help gazing upon him, being struck with admiration, at the strange unaccountable symptoms of his disorder; for, in

all his conversation and replies, he gave evident proofs of an excellent understanding, and never lost himself\*, except on the subject of chivalry, as we have formerly observed: he was therefore touched with compassion for his infirmity, and when the whole company were seated on the grass, waiting for the return of the sumpter-mule, addressed himself to the knight in this manner:

"Is it possible, good sir, that the idle and unlucky reading of books of chivalry, can have so far impaired your judgment, as that you should now believe yourself inchanted, and give credit to other illusions of the same kind, which are as far from being true as truth is distant from falsehood? Is it possible that the human understanding can suppose that ever this world produced that infinite number of Amadises, with the whole crowd of famous knights, so many emperors of Trebisond, Fleximartes of Hyrcania, palfreys, damsels, serpents, dragons, and giants; so many incredible adventures, enchantments of different kinds, battles, dreadful encounters, magnificence of apparel, enamoured princesses, squires created earls, witty dwarfs, billets, amorous expressions, valiant ladies, and finally, such extravagant events as are contained in books of knighterrantry? For my own part, when I read a performance of that sort, without reflecting that it is a legend of vanity and lies, my imagination is a little amused, but, as soon as I begin to consider it in the right point of view, I dash the volume against the wall, and would even commit it to the flames, (if I should chance to be near a fire) as a criminal richly deserving such punishment, on account of its falsehood and imposture, so contrary to nature, and bewildered from the tract of common sense; and as an inventor of new sects and preposterous ways of life; misleading and inducing the ignorant vulgar to believe the absurdities which it contains: nay, so presumptuous are such productions as to disturb the minds of gentlemen of birth and education, as may be too plainly perceived by their effects upon you, signor, whom they have reduced to such a pass, as to make it necessary that you should be cooped up in a cage, and transported from place to place, on a waggon, like a lion or tyger, exhibited as a shew, for money. Go to, signor Don Quixote, have pity upon yourself, return into the bosom of discretion, and put those happy talents which heaven hath been pleased to bestow upon you, to a better use; employing your genius in other studies, which may redound to the increase of your honour, as well as to the good of your soul; or, if swayed by your natural inclination, you are still desirous of reading the histories of exploits and atchievements, you may have recourse to the book of Judges, in the holy scripture; and there you will find real miracles of might, and actions equally valiant and true. Portugal produced a Viriatus, Rome a Caesar, Carthage an Hannibal, Greece an Alexander, Castile a count Fernan Gonçales, Valencia a Cid, Andalusia a Gonzalo Fernandez, Estremadura a Diego Garcia de Paredes, Xerez a Garcia Perez de Vargas, Toledo a Garcilasso, Sevil a Don Manuel de Leon; the history of their valiant exploits will afford entertainment, instruction, surprize and delight, to readers of the most sublime conception. Such study as this would be worthy of the good sense of signor Don Quixote, who would thus become learned in history, enamoured of virtue, improved in worth, bettered in morals, brave without rashness, cautious without cowardice; while the whole would redound to the

---

\* Literally, Never lost the stirrups.[1]

honour of God, his own particular emolument, and the renown of La Mancha, from whence I understand his family and origin is derived."

Don Quixote listened with infinite attention to this harrangue; and even after he perceived it was finished, looked stedfastly at the canon for some time, before he answered in these words: "Signor Hildalgo, if I am not mistaken, the scope of your discourse was to convince me that there never were knights-errant in this world; that all the books of chivalry are false, deceitful, unprofitable, nay, mischievous in a commonwealth; that I have been much to blame in reading, more so in believing, and most of all in imitating the characters they describe, by following the most painful profession of knight-errantry; and lastly, you deny that ever there was an Amadis, either of Gaul or Greece, or that any one of that vast number of knights recorded in those writings had any real existence." "You have exactly summed up my allegations," said the canon. "You were likewise pleased to add," resumed the knight, "that such books had done me infinite prejudice, impaired my judgment, and reduced me to the necessity of being confined in a cage; and that I would do well to amend and alter my course of studies, and to use performances which contain more truth, instruction, and delight." "That," said the canon, "was my precise meaning." "Why, then," cried Don Quixote, "in my opinion, the person impaired in his judgment, and inchanted, is no other than your worship, who have presumed to utter such blasphemies against an order so well received in the world, and established as truth, that he who like you denies it, deserves the same punishment you inflicted upon those books that gave you disgust; for, to say that there never was such a person as Amadis, or any other of those adventurous knights, with whom history abounds, is like an endeavour to persuade people, that frost is not cold, that the sun yields no light, and the earth no sustenance. Will any earthly eloquence make a man believe that story of the infanta Floripes, and Guy of Burgundy, is false; or, that of Fierabras, with the bridge of Mantible, which happened in the time of Charlemagne, and I vow to God! is as true as that the sun shines at noon-day? If this be a lie, you may also affirm, that there never was such an event as the Trojan war, nor such persons as Hector and Achilles, or the twelve peers of France, or Arthur king of England, who to this day survives in the likeness of a raven, and is every moment expected to reascend his throne. People may as well venture to say, that the history of Guarino Mezquino, and the suit of St. Grial,[2] are pure fiction; and look upon the amours of Don Tristan and queen Iseo, with those of Ginebra and Lancelot, as altogether apocryphal; tho' there are people who almost remember to have seen the duenna Quintanona, who was the best wine-skinker in Great Britain: this is so true, that I myself have heard my grandmother by the father's side, often say, when she happened to see a duenna with a reverend * biggen,[3] 'Grandson, there is a person very like the duenna Quintanona.' From whence I conclude, that she must either have known her personally, or at least, seen some picture of that venerable matron: then, who can deny the history of Peter of Provence, and the fair Magalona, since, to this day, may be seen, in the royal armoury, the very peg that turned the wooden horse upon which the valiant Peter travelled thro' the air; by the same token, that it is something larger than the pole of a coach, and stands near the

* Toca, which is the original word, signifies a woman's coif, veil or handkerchief.

saddle of Babieca: nay, at Roncevalles, you may see Orlando's horn, as big as a weaver's beam. From all which circumstances we may justly infer, that the twelve peers, the Peters, the Cids, with all those who were called knights-errant, actually existed, according to the records of their fame: otherwise, they may as well deny, that the valiant Portugeze, Juan de Merlo was a knight-errant; tho' it is well known, that he went to Burgundy, and fought in the city of Ras, with the famous lord of Charne, called Monseigneur[4] Pierre, and afterwards in the city of Basil, with Monseigneur Henrique de Remestan; gaining the victory in each of these combats, with abundance of honourable fame: neither, I suppose, will they credit the defiance and adventures that were also atchieved in Burgundy, by those valiant Spaniards Pedro Barba and Guttierre Quixada, (from whom I am lineally descended on the father's side) who conquered the sons of the count de St. Paul: nay, let them likewise refuse to own that Don Fernando de Guevara went in quest of adventures into Germany, where he fought with Messire[5] George, a knight of the houshold to the duke of Austria; and say that the justs and tournaments at Suero de Quinones, and the pass, were meer illusion, as well as the enterprizes of Monseigneur Lewis de Falses, against Don GonHalo de Guzman, a Castilian knight; together with many other exploits performed by christian warriors belonging to these and other foreign realms, so authentic and true, that (I repeat my asseveration) he who denies them is void of all reason and common sense."

The canon was struck with admiration, when he heard Don Quixote utter such a medley of fiction and truth; and perceiving that he was intimately acquainted with every circumstance regarding and concerning the atchievements of knight-errantry, answered him in these words: "Signor Don Quixote, I cannot deny but what you have said, is partly true, particularly that which regards the Spanish knights: I grant also, that there was an order called the twelve peers of France, but cannot believe that they performed all those exploits recounted by archbishop Turpin; for, the truth is, they were a set of knights, chosen by the kings of France, under the title of the twelve Peers, because they were all equal in point of virtue, rank and valour: at least, if they were not, they ought to have been possessed of this parity of qualifications; for, it was an association resembling the modern orders of St. Jago and Calatrava, which suppose that every member is valiant, virtuous and noble; and as we now say, a knight of St. Juan or Alcantara, in those days, they said a knight of the twelve peers; because those who professed that military order were equal, in all respects, and twelve in number: that there were such persons as the Cid and Bernardo del Carpio, I make no question; but, whether or not they performed all those exploits which are ascribed to them, is, I believe, extremely doubtful: with respect to the peg of count Peter, which, you say, stands by the saddle of Babieca, in the royal armoury, to my shame be it spoken, I am either so ignorant or short-sighted, that altho' I have seen the saddle, I could never observe the peg, large as you have been pleased to describe it." "But, there it certainly is," replied the knight; "and what makes it the more remarkable, it is said to be kept in a case of calves leather, that it may not rust." "It may be so," said the canon; "but, by my holy orders! I do not remember to have seen any such thing: yet, granting it to be in that place, I am not therefore bound to believe the stories that are recounted of so many Amadises, and such a rabble of knights: nor is it reasonable, that a person of honour, like you, endowed with so many happy tal-

ents, should give credit to such extravagant rhodomontades as are related in the lying legends of knight-errantry."

## CHAPTER XXIII.

## Of the sage contest between Don Quixote and the canon, with other events.

"A good jest, truly!" replied Don Quixote, "that books printed with the licence of kings, and approbation of those who are appointed to examine them, read with universal delight, celebrated by great and small, rich and poor, knights and plebeians, the learned and illiterate; finally, by persons of all ranks and degrees whatever, should contain nothing but lies; notwithstanding the appearance of truth which they maintain, in mentioning the father, mother, country, relations, condition, birthplace; and in giving an exact journal of the exploits peculiar to every individual knight: cease therefore, good sir, to vent such blasphemy, and believe, that in this particular, I advise you to act according to the dictates of good sense: read them again, and you will see what pleasure you will reap for your pains; for, what can be more entertaining than to see, as it were, before our eyes, a vast lake of boiling pitch, thro' which an infinite number of serpents, snakes, and alligators, with many other kinds of fierce and terrible creatures, are continually winding and writhing along; then to hear a most dismal voice that seems to issue from the middle of this pitchy pool pronounce, 'O knight! whosoever thou art, that now standest gazing at the dreadful lake, if thou wouldst enjoy the bliss that is concealed beneath these sable waves, display the valour of thy dauntless breast, and dart thyself amidst these black and burning billows; otherwise, thou art not worthy to behold the mighty wonders deposited and contained within the seven castles of the seven nymphs that dwell below this sullen flood.' Scarce hath the sound of this dismal voice ceased to vibrate on his ear, when the knight, without the least hesitation, or reflecting upon the danger he incurs, nay, without putting off his heavy armour, but, recommending himself to God and his mistress, plunges at once into the burning lake; and when he neither cares nor knows what will be his fate, finds himself in the midst of a delightful plain, by which the Elysian fields are infinitely excelled: there the heaven seems more transparent, and the sun shines with new lustre; the eye is entertained with an agreeable forest of tall and leafy trees, whose verdure delights the view, while the ear is regaled with the sweet and artless notes of an infinite number of little painted warblers that hop from bough to bough: here, he perceives a brook, whose refreshing waters, clear as liquid crystal, run murmuring on the yellow sand and glistening pebbles, that emulate the purest pearls and heaps of sifted gold. In one place, springs an artificial fountain adorned with variegated jasper and polished marble; in another, rises a rustic grotto, in which the small shells of the muscle, and the white and yellow twisted domes of the

352 History & Adventures of the Renowned Don Quixote

snail, placed in beauteous disorder, and mixed with bits of shining crystal and counterfeit emeralds, compose such an agreeable variety, that nature seems to be excelled by imitative art. In a third place, all of a sudden, appears a strong castle or magnificent palace, the walls of massy gold, the battlements of diamond, the gates of hyacinth, and finally, the workmanship so admirable, as infinitely to excel the materials which are no less than adamant, carbuncles, rubies, pearls, emeralds and gold. Nay, after having thus feasted his eyes, there still remains for him to see a fair bevy of damsels coming out at the castle-gate, dressed in such gay and splendid attire, that were I to describe it minutely, as it is represented in the history, I should never have done. Then, she who appears the principal, takes by the hand the undaunted knight who threw himself into the boiling lake, and silently leading him into the rich castle or palace, strips him as naked as he was when his mother bore him, and bathes him in water of an agreeable temperature, then anoints his whole body with aromatic essences, and puts upon him a shirt of the finest lawn, all scented and perfumed; then comes another damsel, and throws over his shoulders a mantle, which, at least, is usually valued at the price of a whole city, or more. After all this ceremony, what a sight it is, when, as they relate, he is conducted into another hall, in which a table is furnished with such elegance as to excite his admiration and suspence! when they sprinkle upon his hands water distilled from amber and odoriferous flowers! when he is seated upon a chair of ivory, and attended by all those damsels who serve him in amazing silence! when he is allured by such a variety of dishes, and so savourily cooked, that the appetite is confounded in its choice! then to hear music, during his repast, without seeing the minstrel, or knowing from whence the sound proceeds; and, after he has refreshed himself, and the table is uncovered, while he lolls at ease upon his chair, perhaps, picking his teeth, according to custom, he is surprized with the sight of another young lady, much more beautiful than any of the former, who enters the hall, and, sitting down by the knight, begins to tell him whose castle that is, and how she is enchanted within it, relating other circumstances which create wonder in him, and raise the admiration of those who read the story. I need not further expatiate on this subject, since, from what hath been said, it plainly appears, that any part whatever, of the history of any knight-errant whatever, must yield pleasure and surprize to any reader whatsoever. Believe me, therefore, good sir, and as I have already hinted, take the trouble of reading those books, and you will see what effectual antidotes they are against melancholy, and how they improve the disposition, when it is bad. For, my own part, I can safely aver, that since I professed the order of knight-errantry, I have been valiant, courteous, liberal, well-bred, generous, civil, daring, good-humoured, and a patient endurer of toils, captivities and inchantment; and tho' I so lately found myself shut up in a cage, like a madman, I hope, by the valour of this my arm, provided heaven shall favour, and fortune cease to oppose me, in a few days, to see myself sovereign of some kingdom, when I shall be enabled to demonstrate the gratitude and generosity which reside within my breast: for, truly, signor, a poor man is incapable of exerting the virtue of liberality, let him possess it in never so eminent a degree; and that gratitude which is restrained to good-will alone, is like faith without works; no more than the ghost of virtue. Wherefore, I wish fortune would speedily furnish me with an opportunity of making myself an emperor, that I may exercise the virtues of my heart, in be-

stowing benefits on my friends, especially on my poor squire Sancho Panza, one of the best men in the world, whom I intend to create an earl, in consequence of a promise which he obtained from me, long ago; though I fear he wants capacity to manage his estate."

These last words being overheard by Sancho, he said to his master, "Signor Don Quixote, I wish you would take the trouble to give me that same earldom, which is as firmly promised by your worship as expected by me, and I will undertake to find ability to manage it; or, if I should find myself at a loss, I have heard it often said, that there are certain persons who farm the estates of great noblemen, at so much a year, and take charge of the whole, while the owner lolls at his ease, enjoying his income, without troubling his noddle about any other affairs. Now, I would live in the very same manner, minding the cares of this world as little as possible, but, leaving off all sorts of business, enjoying my rents, like any duke, and let the world wag." "Brother Sancho," said the canon, "that is to be understood only of the spending your income; but, the lord of a great estate must have regard to the administration of justice, which requires ability, sound judgment, and principally an upright intention; for, if this be wanting in the beginning, the middle and end will always be involved in error: and therefore, heaven usually assists the righteous intent of the simple, while it confounds the wicked aims of the cunning." "I know nothing of these philosophies," answered the squire; "but, this I know, that I wish to God I had this earldom, as soon as I should find understanding to manage it; for, I have as big a soul as my neighbours, and as much body as he that has more; and would be as much a king in my own estate, as any he that wears a head: and so being, I would do what I pleased; and doing what I pleased, I should please myself; and pleasing myself, I should be satisfied; and in being satisfied, I should have nothing more to desire; and having nothing more to desire, there would be an end; so, let the earldom come a God's-name: I wish we could see it, as one blind man said to another." "These are no bad philosophies, as you call them, Sancho," said the canon; "but, for all that, there is much to be said on the subject of earldoms." "I know not what more can be said," replied Don Quixote, "for, my own part, I do no more than follow the example transmitted to me by the great Amadis de Gaul, who created his squire earl of the Firm Island; and therefore, I may, without scruple of conscience, bestow the same honour on Sancho Panza, who is one of the best squires that ever served knight-errant." The canon was amazed at the methodical madness of Don Quixote, manifested in his description of the knight of the Lake; and in the impression which the false adventures of chivalry had made upon his imagination: neither was his wonder diminished, when he considered the folly of Sancho, who so ardently desired the possession of that island which his master had promised to give him, as the reward of his services.

By this time the canon's servants had returned from the inn, with the sumpter-mule; and, instead of a table, spread a carpet on the green grass, under the shade of some trees, where the company seating themselves all round, went to dinner, that the waggoner might not lose the opportunity of such a convenient situation, as we have already observed. While they thus enjoyed themselves, their ears were struck with a sudden noise, and the sound of a bell, issuing from the midst of some briars and thickets, that surrounded the place where they sat; and immediately appeared a beautiful she-goat, her

skin speckled with spots of white, black and grey, followed by the goatherd, who, in his rustic dialect, called to her to stop and return to the fold. The fugitive goat trembling with affright, came towards the company, and there stopped, as if to implore their protection; while her keeper, seizing her by the horns, accosted her in these words, as if she had been possessed of sense and understanding: "Ah! you spotted wanton, what a rambler you have become of late; the wolves will feast upon you one day—what is the matter with you, my pretty child? yet what else can it be, but, that you are a female, and consequently inconstant! a plague upon your disposition, and all those you resemble; return, return my darling; and if you are not so happy, at least, you will be more secure in the fold, among your companions; for, if you who ought to watch over and guide the rest, stray about in this imprudent manner, what must become of them?"

These words of the goatherd, diverted those who heard them, especially the canon, who said to him, "I beseech you, brother, to pacify yourself, and be not in such a hurry to drive back your goat, which being a female, as you observe, will follow her natural disposition, in spite of all you can do to oppose it. Take this morsel, and assuage your choler with a cup of wine, and in the mean time, the goat will repose herself."

So saying, he presented to him, on the point of a fork, the hind quarter of a cold rabbit, which was thankfully accepted by the goatherd, who having taken a long draught, and composed himself, said to the company, "Gentlemen, you must not take me for a simpleton, because I talk to this animal as if it were a rational creature; for, really, there is a mystery concealed beneath the words I have uttered. I am a peasant, 'tis true, yet not so rustic, but, that I know how to converse with men as well as beasts." "I firmly believe what you say," replied the curate, "for, I myself have experienced that the mountains produce learned men, and that philosophers are to be found within the shepherd's cot." "At least," resumed the goatherd, "the cottage may contain those who are warned by woeful experience; and to convince you feelingly, that what I alledge is true, I, though undesired, and self-invited, saving the good pleasure of this good company, intreat a moment's hearing, while I recount a true story, which will confirm what that gentleman (pointing to the curate) and myself have observed."

To this proposal Don Quixote replied: "As this affair seems to bear something of the shadow of an adventure, I, for my part, will gladly give you the hearing, brother; and so will all those gentlemen who are persons of taste, and lovers of curious novels, that surprize, delight and entertain the sensible hearer; for, I hope your story will certainly produce these agreeable effects: begin then, friend; we are all attention." "By your leave," cried Sancho, "I will e'en betake myself, with this piece of pasty, to yonder brook, and lay in store for three days; for, I have heard my master Don Quixote observe, that the squire of a knight-errant ought to eat as often and as much as he can; because they are frequently so bewildered in woods and forests, that it will take them six whole days to disengage themselves; and if a man's belly or his bags be not well-lined with provision, there he may stay, as he often does, till he withers into perfect mummy." "You are in the right, Sancho," said the knight, "go where you will, and eat as much as you please; for, my own part, my grosser appetite is satisfied, and now I want refreshment for the mind, which I shall enjoy in listening to this honest countryman's story." "We shall all share in the repast," replied the canon, who intreated the peasant to perform his promise.

Then the goatherd gave the goat which he held by the horns, two slaps on the but-
tocks, saying, "Lie down by my side, you speckled nanny; we shall have time enough to
return to the fold." The creature seemed to understand his meaning; for, he was no
sooner set, than she lay down very quietly, and looking in his face, gave him to under-
stand that she was attentive to what he was going to say; upon which, he began his story,
in these words:

### CHAPTER XXIV.

## The story which the goatherd recounted to the conductors
## of Don Quixote.

"Three leagues from this valley stands a village, which, tho' small, is one of the rich-
est in all this country; and therein dwelt a farmer in great repute: and albeit, re-
spect follows worldly wealth, he was more beloved for his virtue than respected for his
riches; but, what he regarded as the best part of his good fortune, (as he himself was wont
to say) was a daughter he had, of such exceeding beauty, rare discretion, modesty and
grace, that every one who saw and knew her, marvelled at the happy talents with which
heaven and nature had enriched her body and her soul: in the cradle she was handsome,
and continually increased in beauty, till at the age of sixteen, she was a most enchanting
creature: the fame of her charms, began to spread over all the neighbouring villages; but,
what need I say the neighbouring villages! it extended to distant cities, and even made
its way into the king's court, filling the ears of all sorts of people, who came from all
parts, to see her, as if she had been some great curiosity, or miracle-working image. Her
father watched over her with great care, and she took great care of herself; for, truly, a
maiden's own prudent reserve is a better guard upon her conduct than all the bolts and
spies and padlocks upon earth. The father's wealth, and the daughter's beauty moved a
great many people both of town and country, to demand her in marriage; but he, like
one who has the disposal of a rich jewel, was perplexed in his mind, and could not de-
termine in favour of any one of the infinite number that solicited his consent. Among
the croud of her suitors, I was one, who conceived great and flattering hopes of success;
because her father knew me to be his townsman, of an honest family, in the flower of my
age, rich in wealth, and in point of understanding not very poor. She was also courted
by another young man of our town, who was in every respect my equal; so, that her fa-
ther was perplexed, and wavered in his choice; because he thought his daughter would
be well bestowed upon either of us: wherefore, in order to deliver himself from this sus-
pence, he resolved to communicate our demands to Leandra, (for, that is the name of
this wealthy maiden, who hath made me miserable;) and since we were equal in all
qualifications, to refer the whole affair to the choice and decision of his beloved daugh-
ter. An example worthy to be followed by every father in the settlement of his children:

not that I would have parents leave them to their own choice, in things that are manifestly wicked and base; but, first propose a number of prudent schemes, out of which they may be allowed to fix upon that which is most to their liking. I know not to which of us Leandra gave the preference; this only I know, that her father put us off, on pretence of his daughter's tender years, in general terms, which neither laid him under any obligation, nor gave us any cause of complaint. I think proper to tell you, that I am called Eugenio, and my rival Anselmo, that you may be acquainted with the names of the persons principally concerned in this tragedy, which is still depending; tho' one may easily foresee, that it must have a melancholy end.

"But, to return to my story: just about that time, there came to our town one Vincent de la Rosa, the son of a poor labouring man that lived in the village; this Vincent, who was just returned from being a soldier in Italy, and other foreign parts, had been carried away, when he was a boy about twelve years of age, by a captain that chanced to march thro' the town with his company; and now, after an absence of another dozen of years, he returned, in the garb of a soldier, pinked up in a thousand colours, and bedecked with a power of glass toys and slender chains of steel. To-day, he dressed himself out in one gay suit; to-morrow in another: but, all his finery and gewgaws were of little weight or value. The labouring people, who are naturally malicious, nay, when idleness gives them opportunity, downright malice itself, observed and took an exact account of all his ornaments and fine apparel, and found that he had no more than three suits of different colours, with garters and hose; but, he found means to disguise them by such inventions, that one who had not been at the pains to detect him, would have sworn that he had appeared in more than ten different dresses, and in upwards of twenty plumes of feathers; and you must not think it impertinent or foolish in me, to give you this account of his cloaths, because they bear a considerable share in the story. He used to seat himself upon a stone, under a tall poplar that grew in our market-place, and there keep us all gaping around him, at the exploits which he recounted: if you would take his word for it, there was not a country on the face of the earth, which he had not seen, nor a battle in which he had not served; he had killed a greater number of Moors than ever Tunis or Morocco produced; and by his own account, fought more single combats than were ever maintained by Gante, Luna, Diego Garcia de Paredez, and a thousand more whom he named, gaining the victory in each, without losing one single drop of his blood: then, he would shew the marks of wounds, which tho' not to be distinguished, he gave us to understand, were the effects of musket-shot he had received in different actions and encounters: finally, with incredible arrogance, he used to thou his own equals, even those who knew his extraction, and say that his own arm was his father, his family the work of his own hands, and being a soldier, he owed nothing even to the king himself: with all this boasting, he knew something of music, and could thrum upon the guitarre, so as that some people said he made it speak; but, his talents did not end here, for, he was also a piece of a poet, and wrote ballads a league and a half long, upon every silly trifle that happened in the village. Well then, this soldier whom I have described, this Vincent de la Rosa, this Braggadocio, this gallant, this musician, and poet, was often seen and observed by Leandra from the window of her apartment, that looked towards the market-place: she was captivated by the tinsel of his gaudy cloths, and enchanted by his ballads;

for, he gave away twenty copies of each that he composed; the feats he related of himself, reached her ears; in short, (as the devil himself must certainly have ordained) she fell in love with him, even before he had the presumption to make any attempt upon her heart; and as in the affairs of love, every thing is easily accomplished by the man who is already in possession of the woman's affection, Leandra and Vincent soon came to a right understanding; and before any one of her numerous admirers had the least inkling of her inclination, she had already gratified it, by leaving the house of her loving and indulgent father, (mother had she none) and running away with the soldier, who triumphed in that enterprize, and more effectually than in any one he had ever undertaken.

"This event filled not only the whole village, but likewise all who heard of it, with admiration: I, for my part, was amazed, Anselmo astonished, the father overwhelmed with sorrow, and the relations with shame. Justice, however, being sollicited, the troopers immediately took the road, examined every copse and thicket thereabouts, and after a search of three days, found the giddy Leandra in the cave of a mountain, naked to the smock, and stripped of a great quantity of money and precious jewels, which she had carried off when she made her escape: when she was brought back to the presence of her afflicted father, and questioned about her misfortune, she frankly owned that Vincent de la Rosa had imposed upon her; that, under promise of marriage, he had persuaded her to forsake her father's house, promising to conduct her to Naples, which, he said, was the most beautiful and flourishing city in the whole world; that she inadvertently, and fondly believed his false professions, and robbing her father, put herself under his protection that same night she was missed, when he carried her to a rocky mountain, and confined her in the cave where she was found: she likewise affirmed that the soldier, without making any attempt upon her virtue, had stripped her of all she had, and left her in that forlorn condition; a circumstance that surprised all who heard it, the soldier's continence being so incredible; but, she insisted upon it with such earnest asseverations, that the disconsolate father was in some sort comforted, making little account of the money he had lost, since his daughter was allowed to keep the jewel which, when once lost, there is no hope of retrieving.

"The same day that Leandra appeared, her father removed her from our eyes, and shut her up in a monastery of a neighbouring town, hoping that time would efface some part of the bad opinion his daughter had incurred: the tender years of Leandra serve as an excuse for her misconduct, especially with those who are not concerned in the affair; but, those who know her discretion and good sense, do not ascribe her fault to ignorance, but to meer levity, and the natural disposition of women, which is always injudicious and imperfect. Leandra being thus secured, Anselmo's eyes were blind to every thing that could yield him pleasure; and mine remained in darkness, without the least glimpse of light to direct them to any agreeable object: the absence of Leandra increased our affliction, and exhausted our patience; we cursed the soldier's finery, and exclaimed against her father's want of care; at length, we agreed to quit the village, and repair to this valley, where he feeding a vast flock of sheep, which are his own property, and I tending a numerous fold of goats, which are also mine, we spend our lives under the cool shade of lofty trees, and give vent to our passion, either by singing, in concert,

the praise or dispraise of the beautiful Leandra, or each by himself, sighing in the lonely grove, and ejaculating his complaint to heaven. In imitation of us, many more of Leandra's lovers have betaken themselves to these rugged mountains, and the exercise of the same employment; so that this spot seems to be transformed into a pastoral Arcadia, every field being crowded with shepherds and folds, and every corner resounding with the name of the fair Leandra. One curses and calls her fickle, inconstant and immodest; a second condemns her credulity and lightness of behaviour; a third acquits and forgives her, while she is arraigned and reproached by a fourth; some celebrate her beauty; others find fault with her disposition: in short, she is censured and adored by them all; nay, to such a pitch hath their extravagance risen, that some of them complain of her disdain, tho' they never spoke to her; and others, in their lamentations, pretend to feel the rage of jealousy, which is a passion she never inspired; for, as I have already mentioned, her fault was known before her inclination was suspected: there is not the hollow of a rock, the margin of a rill, nor the shade of a tree, that is not occupied by some shepherd recounting his misfortune to the winds; wherever an echo can be formed, it repeats the name of Leandra; the hills resound with Leandra; the rivulets murmur Leandra: in short, Leandra keeps us all enchanted and perplexed, hoping we know not how, and dreading we know not what. Among the wrongheaded society, he that shews the least, tho' he has the greatest share of judgment, is my rival Anselmo, who notwithstanding all the cause he has to be dissatisfied, complains of absence only, tuning his lamentation to the sound of a rebec, which he touches with admirable skill, in verses that shew the excellence of his genius: I follow a more easy, and in my opinion, a wiser course; namely, to inveigh against the levity of the female sex; their fickleness, their double dealing, their rotten promises, their broken faith; and finally, their want of judgment in bestowing their affections. These, gentlemen, are my reasons for the discourse you heard me address to my goat, whom (because she is a female) I despise, altho' she be the best of the fold; this is the story I promised to recount; and if I have been prolix in the narration, I shall not be brief in what service you shall please to command: hard by is my cottage, in which I have plenty of new milk, and most savoury cheese, with abundance of the fruit in season, no less agreeable to the taste than to the view."

## CHAPTER XXV.

# Of the quarrel that happened between Don Quixote and the goatherd, with the curious adventure of the disciplinants, which the knight happily atchieved with the sweat of his brow.

This story of the goatherd gave infinite pleasure to all that heard it, especially to the canon, who observed, with admiration, his manner of relating it, as distant from the rustic phrase of a peasant as near approaching to the polite stile of a courtier; and therefore, he said the curate had justly observed, that the mountains sometimes produced learned men. Every body made proffers of service to Eugenio, but, he that shewed himself most liberal in compliment, was Don Quixote, who said to him, "Truly, brother goatherd, were it possible for me to undertake any new adventure, I would forthwith set forward in your behalf, and deliver Leandra from that monastery, in which she is, doubtless, detained against her will, in spite of the abbess and all that should oppose my design; and would put her into your hands to be treated according to your good will and pleasure, so far as is consistent with the laws of chivalry, by which all damsels are protected from wrongs: tho' I hope in God, that a malicious enchanter shall not so far prevail, but, that he may be excelled in power, by another of a more righteous disposition; and then, you may depend upon my favour and assistance, according to the duty of my profession, which is no other than to succour the wretched and the weak."

The goatherd stared at Don Quixote, and being struck with admiration at his rueful aspect and dishevelled locks, said to the barber who sat near him, "Signor, pray, who is that man who looks and talks so wildly?" "Who should it be," answered the barber, "but the renowned Don Quixote de la Mancha, the redresser of grievances, the righter of wrongs, the protector of damsels, the terror of giants, and thunderbolt of war?" "That discourse," replied the peasant, "puts me in mind of those books which treat of knights-errant, who were commonly distinguished by such titles as you bestow on that man: but, I suppose, you are pleased to be merry, or else, the apartments of this poor gentleman's skull are but indifferently furnished."

"You are a most impudent rascal! (cried the knight, overhearing what he said) it is your skull that is unfurnished and unsound; but, mine is more pregnant than the abominable whore that brought you forth." So saying, he snatched up a loaf, and flung it at the goatherd with such fury, that he levelled his nose with his face.

Eugenio, who did not understand raillery, finding himself maltreated in earnest, without any respect for the carpet, table-cloth or company, leaped upon the knight, and laying hold of his collar, with both hands, would certainly have strangled him, if Sancho Panza had not that instant sprung to his master's assistance, and pulling his antagonist backwards, tumbled him over upon the table, where plates, cups, victuals, wine, and all went to wreck. Don Quixote finding himself disengaged, arose, and in his turn, got upon the goatherd, who being battered by the master, and kicked by the man, was creeping

about on all four, in quest of a table-knife, with which he intended to take some bloody revenge; but, was prevented by the canon and curate; the goatherd, however, managed matters so, as that he got the knight under him, when he rained such a shower of kicks and cuffs upon his carcase, that our hero's countenance was as much overflowed with blood as his own: the curate and canon were ready to burst with laughing, the troopers capered about with joy, and the whole company halloo'd, according to the practice of the spectators, when two dogs are engaged; Sancho Panza alone was distracted, because he could not get out of the clutches of one of the canon's servants, who hindered him from assisting his master. In fine, when every body was thus regaled and rejoiced, except the combatants, who worried each other, they heard a trumpet utter such a melancholy note, that they could not help turning their heads, and looking towards the place from whence the sound seemed to come; but, he on whom it made the greatest impression was Don Quixote, who, tho' lying under his antagonist, very much against his inclination, and more than sufficiently pummelled, said to the goatherd, "Brother devil, (for, sure thou canst be nothing else, who hast strength and valour sufficient to overcome my efforts) I beg a truce for one hour only; because the doleful sound of that trumpet which salutes our ears, seems to summon me to some new adventure."

The goatherd being by this time heartily tired of drubbing, as well as of being drubbed, immediately complied with his request, and Don Quixote starting up, directed his view towards the place whence the sound seemed to issue, where he descried a great number of people dressed in white, like disciplinants, coming down the side of a neighbouring hill. That year the heavens had withheld refreshing showers from the earth; and thro' all the villages of that district the people instituted processions, disciplines and prayers, beseeching God to open the fountains of his mercy, and favour them with rain: for this purpose, the inhabitants of a neighbouring village were then going in procession, to a holy hermitage, built on an eminence that skirted the valley; and Don Quixote seeing the strange dress of disciplinants[1] *, without recollecting that he had frequently seen such habits before, concluded the whole to be an adventure, which it was the province of him as a knight-errant, to atchieve: what served to confirm him in this notion, was an image cloathed in black, which was carried before them, and which he supposed to be some princess, whom those discourteous robbers were carrying off by force.

This whim no sooner entered his brain, than he ran with great agility to Rozinante, who was feeding very quietly, and taking the bridle and shield, which hung upon the pummel of the saddle, clapt the bit in his mouth, in a twinkling, and demanding his sword from Sancho, mounted his steed, and braced his target, calling aloud to the company, "Now, honourable gentlemen, ye shall perceive the importance of those who profess the order of knight-errantry! now, I say, ye shall, in the deliverance of that excellent lady, who is at present a captive, behold how much knight-errants ought to be esteemed."

So saying, he clapt heels to Rozinante, (spurs he had none) and at a hand-gallop, (for, we do not find in this true history, that ever Rozinante went full speed) rode up to at-

---

* Persons hired to whip themselves on such occasions.[2]

tack the disciplinants. Tho' the canon, curate and barber made efforts to detain him, they found it impracticable; he was even deaf to the cries of Sancho, who bauled with great vociferation: "Where are you going, signor Don Quixote? what devil possesses and provokes you to act against our catholic faith! take notice—a plague upon me! take notice that this is no other than a procession of disciplinants, and that lady carried on the beer the blessed image of the immaculate virgin! Consider, signor, what you are about; for, sure I am you do not know!"

In vain did Sancho strain his lungs: his master was so intent upon overtaking the apparitions, and setting the lady in black at liberty, that he heard not one syllable; nor if he had, would he have returned, even if the king had commanded him so to do. When he approached the procession, he stopped Rozinante, who was already out of breath, and with a hoarse disordered voice, pronounced, "You there, who, perhaps, disguise yourselves for no good, stop, and give ear to what I am going to say."

Those who carried the image were the first that halted, and one of the four priests who sung the litanies, observing the strange aspect of Don Quixote, the leanness of Rozinante, with other ridiculous circumstances belonging to both, answered in these words: "Friend, if you have any thing to say, speak quickly; for, these our brethren are all this while scourging their own flesh, and we cannot, nor is it reasonable we should, tarry to hear any thing that cannot be comprehended in two words." "I will comprehend what I have to say in one," replied the knight; "and it is this: I command you, instantly to set free that beautiful lady, whose tears and melancholy deportment clearly demonstrate that you are carrying her off, contrary to her inclination, after having done her some notorious wrong; and I, who was born to redress such grievances, will not suffer you to proceed one step farther, until she shall have obtained that liberty she deserves."

From these words, concluding that he must be some madman, all of them began to laugh very heartily; and their mirth acting as a train of gunpowder to the knight's choler, he drew his sword, and without uttering another word, attacked the bearers, one of whom, leaving his share of the load to his companions, opposed himself to this aggressor, brandishing a fork or pole, on which (when they were wearied) they supported the bier. Don Quixote, with a furious backstroke, cut this implement in two; but, with the piece which remained in the hand of the defendant, received such a thwack upon the shoulder above his sword-arm, that his buckler was unable to sustain the shock of such a rude assault, and down came the poor knight, in a most lamentable condition.

Sancho Panza, who came puffing after his master, seeing him fall, called aloud to his antagonist to forbear; for, he was a poor enchanted knight, who had never done the least harm to man, woman, or child: but, the peasant's forbearance was not owing to this exclamation of the squire, so much as to the situation of Don Quixote, who neither moved hand nor foot; so that believing he had done his business, he hastily gathered up his frock, and fled through the field, as nimble as a buck. By this time, the whole company were come up to the place where Don Quixote lay; and those belonging to the procession, seeing so many people running towards them, accompanied by the troopers with their cross-bows, began to be in dread of some mischievous event, and formed themselves into a circle around the image; then the disciplinants lifting up their hoods, and wielding their scourges, and the priests their long tapers, waited the assault, with full de-

termination to defend themselves, and, if possible, act offensively against all who should attack them. But, fortune disposed of things more favourably, than they expected; for, all that Sancho did, was to throw himself upon the body of his master, who, he believed, was actually dead, and utter the most doleful and ludicrous lamentation that ever was heard. The curate was immediately known by a brother of the cloth, who belonged to the procession, and this acquaintance dispelled the apprehension which both squadrons had begun to conceive. Our licentiate told his friend, in a few words, who Don Quixote was, upon which he and the whole croud of disciplinants went to see whether or not the poor knight was dead, and heard Sancho Panza, with tears in his eyes, lamenting in these words: "O! Flower of chivalry, who, by the single stroke of a cudgel hast finished the career of thy well-spent life! O! thou honour of thy family, thou glory of la Mancha, ay, and of the whole world, which being deprived of thee, will soon be filled with evil doers, who will prosper without fear of chastisement for their wicked deeds! Oh! thou wast more liberal than all the Alexanders that ever lived! for, thou gavest me, for eight months service, only, the best island that ever the sea surrounded. Oh! thou wast humble with the haughty, and haughty with the humble, tempting dangers, enduring disgraces, in love without cause, imitating the good, scourging the wicked, a professed enemy to every thing that was base; in short, a knight-errant, and that is every thing in one word!"

The cries and groans of Sancho revived his master, and the first words he pronounced were these: "He who is condemned to live absent from thee, most amiable Dulcinea! is subjected to much greater hardships than these. Friend Sancho, help to lay me on the inchanted car, for, I am incapable of pressing Rozinante's saddle, this whole shoulder being crushed to pieces." "That I'll do very willingly, dear master," replied the squire, "and let us return to our own habitation, in company of these gentlemen, who wish you well; and there we will lay a scheme for another sally, which, I hope will be more fortunate and creditable." "You are in the right, Sancho," replied Don Quixote, "and it will be very prudent in us to let the malign influence of the stars pass over."

The canon, curate and barber approved of his intention, and being extremely diverted with the squire's simplicity, conveyed the knight to his former situation in the waggon. The procession was formed anew, and set forwards accordingly; the goatherd took his leave of the company, the troopers being unwilling to go farther, were paid by the curate for their trouble; the canon having intreated the priest to inform him by letter, of Don Quixote's fate, with regard to the continuation or cure of his extravagance, bad him farewel, and proceeded on his journey; in short, there was a general separation, till at length the curate, barber, Don Quixote and Panza were left by themselves, with the trusty Rozinante, who, with the patience of his master, bore and beheld every thing that passed.

The waggoner yoking his oxen, accommodated the knight with a truss of hay, and with his usual phlegm jogged on, according to the priest's directions, till, at the end of six days, they arrived at their own village, which they entered about noon; and it chancing to be Sunday, the market-place through which they were obliged to pass was crouded with people, who running to see what was in the cage, recognized their townsman, and were struck with astonishment. A boy ran immediately to his housekeeper and niece, whom when he informed of their master's arrival, in a most meagre, withered condition, stretched upon a truss of hay, in a waggon; it was a piteous thing to hear the cries that were uttered by these worthy ladies, who buffetted themselves through vexa-

tion, and vented bitter curses against the wicked books of chivalry; which lamentations, buffetings and curses were repeated with greater violence than ever, when they saw the knight enter his own gate.

Sancho Panza's wife, who had got intimation, that he was gone with Don Quixote in quality of his squire, hearing of their return, ran strait to her husband, and the first question she asked, was, Whether or not the ass was in good health? when the squire answered, that the ass was in better health than his master, "Thanks be to God," cried she, "for that and all his other mercies. But, now tell me, friend, what good you have got by your squireship? Have you brought home a new petticoat for me, or shoes for your children?" "I have brought no such matters, my dear," replied Sancho, "but, things of greater consideration and importance." "I am glad of that, with all my heart," said the wife; "pray, shew me these things of greater consideration and importance, that the sight of them may rejoice my heart, which hath been so sad and discontented all the weary time of your being away." "You shall see them at home," answered Sancho; "and heark'ee, wife, make yourself easy for the present, for, an it please God, that we set out again in quest of adventures, you shall speedily behold your husband an earl, or governor of an island; I don't mean your common islands, but, one of the best that ever was seen." "The Lord in heaven grant it, husband! for I am sure we have need enough of such windfalls: but, tell me, what is an island; for, truly, I know not the meaning of the word." "Honey was not made for the mouth of an ass," said the squire; "you shall see what it is, all in good time, my dear; ay, and admire to hear all your vassals call you, my lady." "What is that you say, Sancho, of ladies, islands, and vassals?" cried Joan Panza; for, that was the name of the squire's wife, though she was not related to Sancho before marriage, but, it is the custom in la Mancha, for the women to take the names of their husbands. "Don't be in such a hurry to know every thing, Joan," replied the squire; "it is sufficient that I tell thee nothing but truth; let this therefore stop that mouth of thine: mean time, however, I care not if I tell thee, that it is one of the most pleasant occupations in the world, for an honourable person like me, to be squire to a knight-errant, when he is in quest of adventures. True it is, the greatest part of them do not fall out quite so much to one's liking as one could wish; for, out of an hundred in which we are engaged, ninety-nine are generally cross and unfortunate. That I know by experience, having been sometimes threshed and sometimes blanketted: but, howsomever, it is a curious pastime to be always in expectation of adventures, crossing huge mountains, searching woods, climbing rocks, visiting castles, lodging at inns, where we live at rack and manger, and the devil a farthing to pay."

While this conversation passed between Sancho and his wife, the housekeeper and niece received Don Quixote, whom they undressed and put to bed in his old chamber, while he eyed them askance, without being able to comprehend where he was. The curate laid his injunctions on the niece, to cherish her uncle with great tenderness, and charged them both, to take especial care, that he might not escape again, giving them an account of the trouble they had been at, in bringing him back to his own house. Here they raised their voices again, in concert, renewing their curses upon the books of chivalry, and beseeching heaven to confound the authors of such madness and lies, to the lowest pit of hell: in short, they were half distracted with the apprehension of losing him again, as soon as his health should be re-established; and this was actually the case.

But, the author of this history, although he inquired with the utmost curiosity and diligence, concerning the actions of Don Quixote, in his third sally, could never find any satisfactory and authentic account of them; only, fame hath preserved some memoirs in la Mancha, by which it appears, that Don Quixote, when he set out the third time, went to Saragossa, where he was present at a most celebrated tournament, in which, many things happened to him worthy of his genius and valour: but, with regard to his death and burial, he could obtain no information, and must have remained entirely ignorant of that event, had he not luckily met with an old physician, who had in his custody a leaden box, which he said he found under the foundation of an ancient hermitage that was repairing. This box contained some skins of parchment, on which were written in Gothic characters, and Castilian verse, many of our knight's exploits, with a description of Dulcinea's beauty, Rozinante's figure, Sancho's fidelity, and Don Quixote's own funeral, celebrated by divers epitaphs, and panegyrics on his life and morals. All that could be read and fairly copied, are those which are here inserted by the faithful author of this new and surprising history, who, in recompence for the immense trouble he has undergone in his inquiries, and in examining the archives of la Mancha, that he might publish it with more certainty, desires the reader to favour him with the same credit which intelligent persons give to those books of chivalry that pass so currently in the world; and herewith he will rest fully satisfied; and perhaps, be animated to search after, and find out other histories, if not as authentic, at least as full of invention and entertainment.

The verses which were written in the first skin of parchment found in the leaden box, were these.

The academicians of Argamasilla, a town of la Mancha, on the life and death of the valiant Don Quixote de la Mancha, hoc scripserunt.[3]

Monicongo, academician of Argamasilla, on the sepulture of Don Quixote.

### EPITAPH.

The bully that la Mancha deck'd
   With spoils that shame the Cretan Jason,
Whose judgment ripe, and wit uncheck'd
   The trumpet of renown shall blason;
That arm, whose valour did extend
   To Gaeta, from remote Cathay,
That muse which did the welkin rend
   With verse which brazen plates display;
Who Amadis left far behind,
   And deem'd Galaor a meer baby,
Whose valour with such lustre shin'd,
   As shew'd ev'n Belianis shabby;
He that on Rozinante rode,
   Now mingles with this clay-cold clod!

Paniguado,[4] academician of Argamasilla, in praise of Dulcinea del Toboso.

SONG.[5]

> The maid you see with cheeks so blouzy,
>     High-chested, vigorous and frouzy,
> Dulcinea, fam'd Toboso's princess,
>     Don Quixote's gen'rous flame evinces:
> For her, on foot, he did explore
>     The sable mountain o'er and o'er,
> Through many a weary field did halt,
>     And all through Rozinante's fault.
> Hard fate! that such a dame should die
>     In spite of him and chivalry;
> That he, whose deeds ev'n stones proclaim,
>     Should mourn a disappointed flame!

Caprichoso, a most ingenious academician of Argamasilla, in praise of Rozinante the renowned steed of Don Quixote de la Mancha.

> On a proud trunk of adamant,
>     Whose bloody branches smell'd of war,
> La Mancha's frantic wight did plant
>     His standard glitt'ring from afar.
> There hung his arms; there gleam'd his sword,
>     That won't to level, hack and hew,
> Yet shall the wond'ring muse afford
>     For new exploits, a stile that's new.
> Let Gaul of Amadis be proud,
>     Greece boast the champions she hath bore;
> Don Quixote triumphs o'er the croud
>     Of all the warlike knights of yore.
> For, neither Gaul nor Greece can vye
>     With fam'd La Mancha's chivalry.
> Ev'n Rozinante wears the bay;
>     Let Brilladore and Bayard bray *.

Burlador, an Argamasillan academician, on Sancho Panza.

SONG.

> Here Sancho view of body small,
>     But great in worth, in action clear,
> The best and simplest squire of all
>     The world e'er saw, I vow and swear.
> An earl he surely might have been,
>     Had not this knavish age of brass,

---

* The horse of Orlando Furioso was called Brigliadoro; as Bayardo was the name of the steed belonging to Ruggiero, the second, if not the first hero in Ariosto's incomparable poem.[6]

With insolence and envious spleen,
Conspir'd against him and his ass;
That ass! on which he gently trotted
At gentle Rozinante's tail:
Vain man! with flatt'ring hope besotted,
How, in a dream, thy prospects fail!

Cachidiablo, academician of Agramasilla, on the sepulture of Don Quixote.

EPITAPH.

On Rozinante's back
    The knight that whilome travel'd,
Thro' highway, path, and track,
    Is here bemir'd and gravel'd:
And eke as stiff as he,
    The block of Sancho Panza,
A trusty squire, perdie!
    As ever mortal man saw.

Tiquiloc, academician of Agramasilla, on the sepulture of Dulcinea del Toboso.

Here lies Dulcinea once so plump,
    But, now her fat all melts away;
For death, with an inhuman thump,
    Has turn'd her into dust and clay,
Of a true breed she surely sprung,
    And wanted not external grace;
Don Quixote's heart with love she stung,
    And shone the glory of her race.

These were all the verses which could be read; the rest being worm-eaten were delivered to an academician, that he might attempt to unravel their meaning, by conjecture. This task, we understand, he has performed with infinite pains and study, intending to publish them to the world, in expectation of the third sally of Don Quixote.

"Forse altri canterà con miglior plettro."[7]

END of the FIRST PART.

# The History
# and Adventures
# of the Renowned
# Don Quixote

## VOLUME TWO

THE

# HISTORY and ADVENTURES

OF THE RENOWNED

# DON QUIXOTE.

Tranflated from the SPANISH of

## MIGUEL DE CERVANTES SAAVEDRA.

To which is prefixed,

Some ACCOUNT of the AUTHOR's LIFE.

By T. SMOLLETT, M.D.

Illuftrated with Twenty-eight new Copper-Plates, defigned by HAYMAN,
And engraved by the beft ARTISTS.

---

IN TWO VOLUMES.

---

VOL. II.

---

LONDON:

Printed for A. MILLAR, over againft Catherine-Street, in the Strand;
T. OSBORN, T. and T. LONGMAN, C. HITCH and L. HAWES, J. HODGES,
and J. and J. RIVINGTON.
MDCCLV.

Title Page of First Edition, Volume 2, 1755.

Heavens! with what eagerness must thou be waiting for this prologue, courteous reader, whosoever thou art, gentle or simple, in hope of finding it replete with resentment, reproaches and revenge, against the author of the second Don Quixote: him, I mean, who 'tis reported, was ingendered at Tordesillas, and brought forth in Tarragona. But, truly, I have no intention to give thee that satisfaction; for, although injuries may awaken indignation, in vulgar breasts; mine, I hope, will always be an exception to that rule. Thou wouldst be glad, perhaps, to find me bestowing upon him, the epithets of ass, blockhead, and insolent coxcomb; but such low revenge never once entered my imagination; his own conscience will sufficiently chastise him: let him therefore chew the cud of remorse, and digest it if he can. I own, I cannot help feeling the unjust reproach, when he taxes me with lameness, and old age, as if it had been in my power to retard the lapse of time; or that I had been maimed in some tavern-brawl, and not on the most glorious occasion that ever the past or present age beheld, or posterity can ever hope to see. If my wounds do not brighten in the eyes of every spectator, they are, at least, esteemed by those who know where they were acquired *, and who think, that a soldier who falls in battle makes a much more noble appearance than he who saves himself by flight. This opinion is so rooted within my own breast, that, were such an impossibility proposed and effected, I would rather be lame, as I am, with the share I had in that stupendous action, than sound of body, without the honour of having been there. The wounds that appear in a soldier's countenance and bosom, are so many stars to guide the rest of mankind to the heaven of honour, and the desire of honest praise; and it ought to be observed, that an author does not write with his grey hairs, but according to the dictates of his understanding, which is usually improved by years and experience. I perceive also, that he calls me envious; and, as if I were utterly ignorant, is at the pains to describe the nature of envy; though I protest, of the two kinds, I only harbour that which is pure, virtuous and noble. This being the case, as it undoubtedly is, I have not the least inclination to inveigh against any priest, especially one who bears the office of familiar to the holy inquisition; and, if what he says be advanced in behalf of him whose cause he seems to espouse, he is altogether mistaken, in my opinion, of that person, whose genius I adore: I admire his works, together with his continual occupation in the practice of virtue: but I am actually obliged to this honourable author, for saying, that my novels † are more satirical than exemplary, though he owns they are good of their kind; for, without being exemplary, they cannot possibly be good.

I suppose, gentle reader, thou art, by this time, of opinion, that I walk with great circumspection, and scrupulously confine myself within the bounds of modesty, conscious that it is inhuman to heap affliction on the afflicted; and that this gentleman's must needs be very great, since he dares not appear in the open field, and in the face of heaven, but conceals his name, and dissembles his country, as if he had been guilty of high treason:

---

* The battle of Lepanto.[1]                    † Novelas Exemplares.

tell him, therefore, in my name, if ever thou shouldst chance to find him out, that I do not at all think myself injured by what he has done; for, well do I know, what temptations the devil spreads before us; and that one of his most effectual snares, is to make a man believe, that he has capacity to write a book, by which he shall obtain an equal share of money and reputation. In confirmation of what I say, I will, with thy good leave and favour, tell thee a short story.

There was in Sevil, a certain madman, seized with the most diverting whim that ever entered the brain of a lunatic. He used to walk with a hollow cane, pointed at one end; and whenever he met with a dog in the street, or in any other place, he clapped his foot on one of the creature's hind legs, pulled up the other with his hand, and applying, as well as he could, the pipe to his posteriors, instantly blew him up as round as a ball: this operation being performed, he clapt him twice on the belly, and dismissed the patient, saying, very gravely to the mob, that never failed to gather round him, "Gentlemen, I suppose now, you think it is an easy matter to blow up a dog."[2] In like manner, I say, "I suppose your worship thinks it an easy matter to write a book." If this story should not be to his liking, be so good, friendly reader, as to tell this other, which also relates to a dog and a madman.

There was another ideot in Cordova, who had a trick of carrying upon his head, a piece of marble, or heavy stone; and, as often as he perceived any dog off his guard, he would approach him slily, and let fall plum upon his head. This was no joke to the poor dog, who used to run barking and howling, the length of three whole streets, before he ventured to look behind. But, among others he, one day, happened to discharge his burthen on a capmaker's favourite dog; down went the stone upon his head, the injured beast set up the howl; the master seeing what passed, was filled with indignation, snatched up his measure, and sallying out upon the lunatic, did not leave a whole bone in his skin, saying at every blow he bestowed, "Dog! rascal! use my spaniel in this manner! did not you see, barbarous villain, that my dog was a spaniel!" Thus repeating the word, Spaniel, a great many times, he beat the aggressor into jelly.

The madman being documented, sneaked off, and kept his chamber a whole month; at the end of which, he returned to his former pastime, with a greater stone than ever, and coming up to a dog that lay asleep, considered him with great attention; but was afraid of discharging the stone, saying, "'Ware spaniel!" In short, all the dogs he afterwards met with, whether curs or mastiffs, were in his opinion, spaniels; so that he never ventured to repeat his experiment.—Now, this may be the fate of our historian, who will not choose to open the flood-gates of his wit again, in composing books, which, if bad, are harder than stone.

Tell him, likewise, that I value not his threats a farthing; when he says, that his performance will deprive me of bread; but, answer him, with a quotation from the famous interlude of the Perendenga: "To four and twenty, live my lord, and Christ be with us all." Long live the great count de Lemos, whose well-known christian generosity supports me, against all the strokes of adverse fortune; and long life to the transcendent charity of the most illustrious archbishop of Toledo, Don Bernardo de Sandoval y Rojas; if there was not one printing-press in the whole world, or if more books were published against me than there are letters in the couplets of Mingo Rebulgo;[3] these two

princes, unsollicited by any adulation or other kind of praise, on my part, but purely out of their own benevolence, have been pleased to honour me with their countenance and favour, in which I think myself infinitely more happy and rich, than if I had been conducted to the highest pinnacle of fortune, in the ordinary way. Honour may be enjoyed by a poor, but never by a vicious man: nobility may be clouded by indigence, but never altogether obscured; for, virtue shining by its own internal light, even through the inconveniencies and crannies of poverty, will recommend itself to the esteem of high and princely minds, and of consequence obtain their favour and protection. Thou need'st say no more to him; nor will I give thee any farther trouble, except to observe, that thou art to consider this Second part of Don Quixote, as a work of the same artificer, and composed of the same materials with the first, in which I present the knight at full length; and, in short, exhibit him dead and buried; that no man, for the future, may presume to raise fresh evidence against him; those already examined, being sufficient for the purpose. The more so, as a man of honour has already given an account of his ingenious follies, without any intention to resume the subject: for, there may be too much even of a good thing; and the scarcity of those things which are in themselves indifferent, often brings them into some degree of estimation. I had almost forgot to tell thee, that thou mayst expect the Persiles, which I am now finishing, together with the Second Part of Galatea.

# APPROBATION.[1]

By order of signor doctor Gutierrez de Cetina, vicar-general of the city of Madrid, where his majesty keeps his court, I have perused the Second Part of the Sage Knight, Don Quixote de la Mancha, written by Miguel de Cervantes Saavedra; in which I can find nothing unworthy of a zealous christian, or deviating from that respect which is justly due to good example and moral virtue. On the contrary, the performance contains much erudition, and profitable amusement; not only in the well-supported sequel of his design, to extirpate those vain and lying books of chivalry, which had already, too far, spread their infection; but, also in the purity of his Castilian language, unadulterated with insipid affectation, which every man of sense abhors; and in his manner of correcting the vicious, who generally feel the point of his satire. Yet, he so wisely observes the laws of christian rebuke, that the patient, labouring under the infirmity which he intends to cure, may, in such sweet and palatable medicine, even without his own knowledge, or the least hindrance and loathing, swallow down an effectual detestation for vice; so, that he will find himself at once delighted and reformed, in consequence of an art which is known to few. There are many authors, who not knowing how to blend and mix instruction with delight, have seen all their tedious labours miscarry; because, not being able to imitate Diogenes, as a learned philosopher, they have presumed licentiously, not to say obscurely, to mimic him as a cynic, giving ear to slander, and inventing things that never happened; by which means, they enlarge the vicious capacity of those whom their harsh reproofs stigmatize; and, perhaps, strike out new paths of lewdness hitherto unknown: so that, instead of reformers, they become teachers and abettors of vice. In this manner, they grow hateful to men of sense, and lose all their credit, if they had any, with the people who refuse to encourage their writings: while the vicious, are rather hardened than amended by their rash and imprudent corruption; for, the knife and caustic are not proper for all kinds of tumors, some of which are more successfully treated by soft and gentle remedies, by the application of which, the experienced and learned physician often attains his end of discussing them; a period much more eligible than that which is obtained by the barbarity of steel.

The writings of Miguel de Cervantes have met with a very different reception, not only from our nation, but likewise from strangers; who, as if he was something miraculous, are inflamed with the desire of seeing the author of those books which have met with such general applause, on account of the decency and decorum, as well as the agreeable sweetness of his stile, in Spain, France, Italy, Germany, and Flanders. This I can, with great truth, affirm, that on the twentieth and fifth day of February, in this year of God one thousand six hundred and fifteen, I attended my master, his grace Don Bernardo de Sandoval y Rojas, cardinal archbishop of Toledo, when he returned the visit of the French ambassador, who came to treat about a double match, between the princes and princesses of France and Spain; and several gentlemen of that country, belonging to the embassy, who were equally sensible and well-bred, as well as lovers of the Belles Lettres, in their conversation with me, and the other chaplains of the cardinal,

desired to know what books of genius were in highest esteem among us: I chanced to mention this performance, which was then under my examination; but, no sooner did they hear the name of Miguel de Cervantes, than they began to expatiate upon the high esteem in which France, and the neighbouring kingdoms, held his production; namely, the Galatea, which one of them could almost repeat; with the novels, and the first part of Don Quixote. Such were the commendations they bestowed upon them, that I offered to introduce them to the author, whom they honoured with a thousand demonstrations of regard. They were curious to know his age, profession, quality and fortune; and when I found myself obliged to tell them he was a soldier and a gentleman, oppressed with poverty and old age; one of them replied in these very words, "What! does not Spain load such a man with riches, and maintain him out of the public treasury?"— Another of those gentlemen, hearing this observation, interposed, saying, with great vivacity, "If necessity compels him to write, God grant that he may never enjoy affluence; but, in being poor, enrich the world with his works."

I believe, this will be thought rather too much for a certificate; and some will say, that I have even encroached upon the bounds of flattery: but, the truth of my allegation, disproves that suspicion, and acquits me of the charge; besides, in this age, adulation is bestowed upon none but those, who are in a capacity of greasing the fist of the flatterer; who, though he praises in fulsome fiction, expects to be rewarded in substantial truth.

Madrid, Feb. 27.
1615.

<div align="right">The Licentiate MARQUES TORRES.</div>

## The Ordinary LICENCE.[1]

BY order and command of the lords of council, I have caused to be examined, the book specified in this petition; which book contains nothing to the prejudice of religion or morals; but, on the contrary, is fraught with much lawful amusement, blended with moral philosophy: wherefore, it may be allowed to be printed.

Madrid, Nov. 5.
1615.

<div align="right">Doctor GUTIERREZ de CETINA.</div>

# APPROBATION.

By order and command of the lords of council, I have perused the Second part of Don Quixote de la Mancha, written by Miguel de Cervantes: a book that contains nothing to the prejudice of our holy catholic faith, or sound morals; on the contrary, much honest recreation, and agreeable amusement, such as the antients judged not only allowable, but convenient for the commonwealth: even the severe Lacedemonians erected a statue to the goddess of laughter; and the Thessalians instituted festivals to the same power, according to Pausanias, quoted by Vossius, Lib. II. De signis eccles. cap. 10. for exhilarating the melancholy, and raising the dejected spirits; as observed by Tully, in his first book, de Legibus; and by the poet, who says, "Interpone tuis interdum gaudia curis."[1] Which maxim hath been the guide of this author, who has mingled fiction with truth, delight with instruction, and morals with pleasantry; disguising the hook of reproof, with the bait of sprightly entertainment, and fulfilling the sequel of his well-executed scheme, to depreciate and expel the books of chivalry, from the mischievous contagion of which he hath purged these kingdoms, with admirable diligence and dexterity. In short, it is a work worthy of that great genius which is the honour and ornament of our nation, and the envy and admiration of strangers. This is my opinion, with submission, &c.

Madrid, March 17.
1615.

JOSEPH de VALDIVIELSO.

# THE

# LIFE and ATCHIEVEMENTS

## Of the Sage Knight

# DON QUIXOTE DE LA MANCHA

# PART II. BOOK I.

### CHAPTER I.

## Of the behaviour of the curate and barber, with regard to Don Quixote's infirmity.

Cid Hamet Benengeli, in the second part of this history, containing the third sally of Don Quixote, relates that the curate and barber forbore to visit him for a whole month, that they might not revive and recal to his imagination, the remembrance of things past; but, during all that time, they frequently went to see the housekeeper and niece, on whom they laid strong injunctions to cherish the knight with great care and tenderness, and treat him with such comfortable food as should be most agreeable to his stomach and brain, in which, they reasonably supposed that his whole disorder lay. The ladies assured them, it was their chief study, which they would prosecute with all imaginable care and satisfaction; for, they began to perceive that their master, at certain intervals, gave tokens of being in his right wits. This information afforded great pleasure to the two friends, who now concluded they had acted wisely, in bringing him home, on the enchanted waggon, as hath been recounted in the last chapter of the first part of this sublime and punctual history; and determined to pay him a visit, that they might be convinced of his amendment, which they deemed almost impossible: tho' they agreed to avoid, with great care, the subject of chivalry, that they might run no risk of ripping up the wound so lately closed.

In short, they entered his chamber, and found him sitting upon his bed, in a waistcoat of green bays, and a red Toledan night-cap, so meagre, shrunk and withered, that he looked like an AEgyptian mummy: he received them very courteously, and when they enquired into the state of his health, spoke of his indisposition and himself with great judgment and elocution. Their conversation happening to turn on what is called reasons of state, and modes of administration, they amended certain abuses, and condemned others, reforming one custom, and banishing another; as if each of the three

had been a new legislator, a modern Lycurgus, or regenerated Solon; and in such a man-
ner did they furbish up the commonwealth, that one would have imagined they had
committed it to a forge, and brought out another quite different from that which they
put in. Don Quixote spoke on every subject that was handled, with such discretion, as
actually convinced the two examiners, that he was quite sound, and had recovered the
right exercise of his judgment; while the niece and housekeeper, who were present all
the time, thought they could never be thankful enough to God, when they heard their
master talk so sensibly. But, the curate altering his first resolution, which was, to avoid
the subject of chivalry, now determined to make an experiment, by which he should be
thoroughly satisfied, whether the knight's cure was real or imaginary; with this view, he,
from one thing to another, came to mention some news from court, and among other
pieces of intelligence, said he was certainly informed that the Turk had taken the sea,
with a powerful armament, tho' his design was not known, nor could it be guessed
where the expected storm would burst: but, that these preparations, which keep us al-
most constantly in arms, had alarmed all christendom; and that his majesty had ordered
the coasts of Naples and Sicily, with the island of Malta, to be provided against all at-
tempts. To this intimation Don Quixote replied, "His majesty has acted like a most pru-
dent warrior, in providing for the safety of his dominions, that the enemy may not find
them unprepared; but, if he would take my advice, I would furnish him with an expedi-
ent, which, I believe, our sovereign at present little thinks of."

The curate no sooner heard these words, than he said within himself, "Lord have
mercy upon thee, poor Don Quixote! if I am not mistaken, thou art just going to cast
thyself headlong, from the highest pinnacle of madness, into the profound abyss of thy
folly." But the barber, who immediately adopted the same suspicion, asked the knight
what that expedient was, which he thought should be put in practice, by way of preven-
tion; observing that it was, perhaps, such a scheme as deserved to be inserted in the list
of those impertinent advices usually offered to crowned heads. "Mine Mr. shaver," said
Don Quixote, "will be pertinent, not impertinent." "I don't say otherwise," replied the
barber, "I only made that observation, because experience hath shewn, that all, or the
greatest part of those projects which have been offered to his majesty, are either impos-
sible, extravagant, or prejudicial to the state." "My scheme," answered the knight, "is
neither impossible nor extravagant, but, on the contrary, the most easy, just, brief and
expeditious, that ever projector conceived." "Methinks your worship is very slow in de-
livering it, signor Don Quixote," said the priest. "I should not choose," answered the
knight, "to have what I say here, carried by to-morrow morning, to the ears of the lords
of the council; by which means, another may reap the credit and reward of my labour."
"For my own part," cried the barber, "I here give my word, before God! never to dis-
close what your worship shall impart, either to king or knave, or any mortal man: an
oath I learned in the romance of the curate, who, in the preface, gives the king notice of
the robber that stole his hundred ducats, and ambling mule." "I am not acquainted with
the story," said Don Quixote, "but, the oath is a good oath, because I am convinced, that
Mr. Nicholas is an honest man." "Be that as it will," replied the curate, "I will be bound
for him, and undertake, that with regard to this affair, he shall speak no more than if he
was actually dumb, on pain of whatever penalty you shall think proper to inflict." "And

who will be security for you, Mr. curate?" said the knight. "My profession," answered
the priest, "by which I am bound to keep secrets." "Body of me!" cried Don Quixote,
"his majesty has nothing to do, but, to issue a proclamation, commanding all the
knights-errant in Spain to assemble at his court, by such a day; and altho' not more than
half a dozen should come, among these one may be found, who is alone sufficient to
overthrow the whole Turkish power. Pray, gentlemen, give attention, and take me along
with you: is it such a new thing, for a single knight to cut in pieces a whole army of two
hundred thousand men, as if they had but one common throat, or were made of ginger-
bread? How many histories are there, think you, filled with such marvellous exploits?
Unfortunate it is for me, (I will not say, for any other) that the renowned Don Belianis
is not now alive, or some knight of the innumerable race of Amadis de Gaul; for, if any
one of them was now living, to confront the Turks, in good sooth, I should not choose
to farm their conquests; but, God will provide for his own people, and produce some
champion, who, if not equal in valour to former knights-errant, at least, will be inferior
to none of them in point of courage * —Heaven knows my meaning—I will say no
more." "Lack-a-day! (cried the niece, when she heard this insinuation) I'll be hanged, if
my uncle is not resolved to turn knight-errant again." "A knight-errant," replied Don
Quixote, "I will live and die; and the Turks may make their descents or ascents, when
they will, with all the power they are masters of—I say again, heaven knows my mean-
ing"—Here the barber interposing, "Gentlemen," said he, "I beg you will give me leave
to tell a short story of what once happened at Sevil; it comes so pat to the purpose, that
I have a strong inclination to relate it." Don Quixote and the curate granted his request,
and the rest yielded him attention, when he began in these words:

"There was in the mad-house at Sevil, a certain lunatic, whom his relations had sent
thither, on account of the defect in his judgment: he had taken his degrees in the canon
law, at Ossuna, and many were of opinion, that if he had acquired them at Salamanca, he
would not have been a bit the wiser: this graduate, having been confined some years,
took it in his head, that he was quite well, and restored to his right wits; and in this imag-
ination, wrote to the archbishop, earnestly intreating him, with many sensible argu-
ments, to give order that he should be extricated from the misery in which he lived;
since, thro' the mercy of God, he had recovered his lost judgment, tho' his relations kept
him still in confinement, that they might enjoy his estate, and in despite of truth, were
resolved that he should be mad to the day of his death. The archbishop, persuaded by
the many sensible and pathetic letters he received, ordered one of his chaplains to go to

---

* Ridiculous as this scheme may seem to be, such an expedient has actually succeeded in practice.
During the captivity of John king of France, his dominions were ravaged by above one hundred
thousand peasants, who under the name of Jacqieers, assembled in arms to exterminate the noblesse,
and among other horrid outrages, murdered every gentleman that fell in their way. The dutchess of
Normandy and Orleans, together with three hundred ladies of rank, retired for protection to
Meaux, where they were surrounded, and would have actually perished by the swords of these ban-
ditti, had they not been rescued by the count de Foix, and the captal of Buch, who hearing of their
distress, hastened to their relief, with no more than sixty knights; and, without hesitation, attacked
that furious multitude with such bravery and vigour, that they were soon routed and dispersed.[1]

the rector of the mad-house, and inquire into the truth of what the licentiate alledged, and even to talk with himself, that if he should find him quite recovered, he might bring him away, and set him at liberty. The chaplain obeyed the command of his grace, and the rector assured him that the man was still mad; for, although he would very often talk like a person of excellent understanding, at the long run, he commonly broke out into folly and nonsense, as absurd as the first part of his discourse was rational and discreet: however, he himself might make the experiment, by conversing with the licentiate. The chaplain accordingly went to his apartment, and talked with him a whole hour and more, during which time, the lunatic did not utter one vague or incoherent sentence, but, on the contrary, spoke so judiciously, that the chaplain could not help believing him quite sound of intellect: among other things, he told him the rector was his enemy, and pronounced him still distracted, tho' with lucid intervals, that he might not lose the presents which he received from his relations; so, that the greatest cause of his misfortune was no other than his own affluent estate, which to enjoy, his adversaries craftily pretended to doubt of the mercy which the Lord had vouchsafed him, in re-converting him from a beast into a man: in short, he talked so effectually, as to render the rector suspected, to prove his relations covetous and unnatural, and himself so discreet, that the chaplain determined to carry him forthwith to the archbishop, that his grace might be personally satisfied of the truth. With this laudable intention, he desired the rector to order the licentiate to be dressed with the cloaths in which he entered the house; the rector again advised him to consider what he was about, for, the licentiate was without all question, still distracted: but, these cautions and counsels had no effect in dissuading the chaplain from carrying him off, and the rector seeing the archbishop's order, was obliged to obey; so, that the licentiate received his own cloaths, which were decent and new. Seeing himself thus divested of the badge of his disorder, and habited again, like a person of sound intellects, he besought the chaplain, that he would be so charitable as to allow him to go and take leave of his companions in affliction; the other granted his request, and said he would accompany him, in order to see the patients; upon which, they went up stairs, followed by several persons who chanced to be then present. The licentiate going to the gate of a cell, in which there was a furious madman, tho' at that time he was calm and quiet, said to him, 'Brother, have you any commands for me: I am going to my own house; for, God of his infinite goodness and mercy, without any desert of mine, hath been pleased to restore unto me the use of my reason, and I am now perfectly recovered; so, that there is nothing impossible to the power of the Almighty: put therefore your hope and trust in him, who, as he hath restored me to my former state, will grant the same indulgence to you, if you confide in his protection—I will take care to send you some cordial food, and be sure, at all events, to eat it, for, you must know, I conclude from experience, that all our disorder proceeds from an empty stomach, and the brain's being filled with wind. Take heart, brother, take heart; for, despondence under misfortune consumes the constitution, and hastens the stroke of death.' This discourse being overheard by another lunatic, who was confined in a cell opposite to that of the furious patient, he started up stark naked from an old matt on which he lay, and roared aloud, 'Who is that going away so sober and so sound?' The licentiate replied, ''Tis I, brother, who am going home, being under no necessity of tarrying longer in this

place; thanks be to heaven for the signal favour I have received!' 'Take care what you say, Mr. licentiate, and let not the devil deceive you,' answered the madman: 'halt a little, stay where you are, and spare yourself the trouble of being brought back.' 'I know that I am perfectly recovered,' said the licentiate, 'and shall have no further occasion to visit the Stations *.'² 'You recovered!' cried the other, 'good! we shall see—adieu—but, I swear by Jupiter, whose majesty I represent on earth, that, for the transgression this day committed in Sevil, by discharging you from the house, as a person of sound judgment, I will take such vengeance as shall be a monument of wrath, for ever and ever, amen. Do'st thou not know, pitiful licentiate, that all this is in my power, being as I have already observed, Jove the thunderer, who wield the flaming bolts, with which I use to threaten, and can destroy the universe? But, with one evil only, will I chastise this ignorant people: I will not suffer one drop of rain to fall upon the city, nor its confines, nor indeed, in any part of this district, for the space of three whole years, reckoning from the day and minute in which this dreadful menace is made. Thou free! thou sound! thou recovered! and I mad! I distracted and confined! I will sooner hang myself than rain one spoonful.' The bye-standers were very attentive to the vociferous exclamations of this madman, when our licentiate turning to the chaplain, and taking him by the hand, said, 'Dear sir, give yourself no uneasiness or concern about what he says; for, if he who is Jupiter, withholds refreshing showers from the earth, I who am Neptune, the father and god of waters, will rain as often as I please, should there be occasion for it, in consequence of the privilege I possess.' To this promise, the chaplain replied, 'Nevertheless, signor Neptune, it will not be politic to incense signor Jupiter; therefore, your worship will be so good as to stay where you are, till some other day, when we may have more leisure and convenience to remove you.' The rector and the rest of the company could not help laughing, the chaplain was out of countenance, the licentiate was stripped, and sent back to his cell, and so ends my story.'

"And this is the story, Mr. barber," said Don Quixote, "which came so pat to the purpose, that you could not help relating it? Ah! My shaver, Mr. shaver, he must be blind indeed, that cannot see through the bottom of a sieve; is it possible, your worship does not know that comparisons in point of genius, virtue, beauty and descent, are always odious and ill received? I, Mr. barber, am not Neptune god of waters, neither do I set up for being thought a wise man, knowing that I am not so; the sole end of my labours is to convince the world of its error, in not seeking to renew those most happy times, when the order of knight-errantry exerted itself in full perfection; but, this depraved age of ours is unworthy of tasting that felicity which was enjoyed by those ages, when knights-errant undertook the charge, and burdened their shoulders with the defence of kingdoms, the protection of damsels, the relief of wards and orphans, the chastisement of the proud, and the promotion of the humble. The greatest part of your modern knights rustle in damasks, brocades, and other rich and splendid attire, instead of rattling in coats of mail: no knight now sleeps in the open field, exposed to the inclemency of the weather, armed at all points, capapee: no warrior, in this degenerate age, sits on

* A certain number of churches through which they made circuits, uttering an appointed prayer at each.

horseback, and without disengaging his feet from the stirrups, but, leaning upon his lance, endeavours to take, as it were, a snatch of sleep, after the example of former knights-errant: no champion, now-a-days coming out of some dreary wood, immediately enters another rocky wilderness, thro' which he reaches the barren and deserted coast of the rough and stormy sea, where finding, in some creek, a crazy boat without oars, sails, mast or tackle, he intrepidly throws himself into it, and launches out upon the implacable billows that whirl him aloft to heaven, and then sink him to the profound abyss, while his unshaken soul defies the storm: then, when he dreams of no such matter, he finds himself three thousand leagues and more from the place where he embarked, and leaping ashore on some remote and unknown country, atchieves adventures worthy to be written, not on parchment, but on brass: but, now, sloth triumphs over activity, idleness over toil, vice over virtue, arrogance over valour, and the theory over the practice of arms, which obtained and shone resplendent in those golden ages that produced knights-errant. Pray, tell me, who could be more honourable and valiant than the famous Amadis de Gaul? who more discreet than Palmerin of England? who more insinuating and pliant than Tirante the white? who more gallant than Lisuarte of Greece? who more hacked and hacking than Don Belianis? who more intrepid than Perion of Gaul? or, who more daring than Felixmarte of Hyrcania? who more sincere than Esplandian? who more desperate than Cirongilio of Thrace? who more brave than Rodamont? who more prudent than king Sobrino? who more bold than Reynaldo? who more invincible than Roldan? and who more gallant and courteous than Rogero, from whom (according to Turpin, in his Cosmographia) the present dukes of Ferrara are descended. All these, and many more which I could name, Mr. curate, were knights-errant, and the very light and glory of chivalry: these, or such as these, are the champions proposed by my scheme, which, should it take place, would effactually serve his majesty's purpose, spare an infinite expence, and the Turk would even tear his own beard in despair: in that case, I would tarry where I am, since the chaplain would not think fit to enlarge me, and if Jupiter, as the barber said, would not rain, here am I ready to frustrate his intent: this I mention, that Mr. bason there, may know I understand his meaning." "Verily, signor Don Quixote," said Mr. Nicholas, "I meant no harm, so help me God! my intention was good, and therefore, your worship ought not to be displeased." "Whether I am displeased or not," replied the knight, "I myself know best."

Here the curate interposing, said, "Tho' I have hitherto scarce opened my mouth, I cannot be easy under a scruple which tears and gnaws my conscience, and which arose from what signor Don Quixote hath just now asserted." "In greater matters, Mr. curate may command me," answered the knight: "out with your scruple, then; for scruples of conscience are very uncomfortable companions." "With your good permission," replied the priest, "this it is: I can, by no means persuade myself that the whole tribe of knights-errant, whom your worship have named, were really and truly earthly persons of flesh and blood; on the contrary, I imagine, all these things are fictions, fables, and lying dreams, recounted by men who are awake, or rather, by those who are half a sleep." "That," said Don Quixote, "is another error incident to many people, who do not believe that any such knights ever existed; and I have, on divers and sundry occasions, en-

deavoured to dissipate that almost general mistake, by the light of truth: sometimes, indeed, I have not succeeded in my attempts; however, I have frequently gained my point, by supporting it on the shoulders of demonstration; and truly, the case is so clear, that I could almost affirm, I have with my own eyes, beheld Amadis de Gaul, who was a tall man, of a fair complexion, well furnished with a black beard, his aspect something between mild and severe, concise of speech, slow to anger, and soon appeased. In the same manner, methinks, I could delineate and paint all the knights-errant that ever were recorded in history; for, according to the ideas formed by reading these histories, and by comparing their exploits and dispositions, sound philosophy may discover their lineaments, statures, and complexions." "Signor Don Quixote," said the barber, "how large do you think the giant Morgante must have been?" "As to the affair of giants," answered the knight, "there are different opinions; some affirming, and others denying the existence of any such beings: but the holy scriptures, which surely cannot fail one atom, in point of truth, put that affair beyond all dispute, in relating the story of that Philistine Goliah, who was seven cubits and an half in height; a most amazing stature! Besides, in the island of Sicily, several thigh and shoulder-bones have been dug up, so large as to manifest, that the persons to whom they belonged must have been huge giants, as tall as high towers; and this can be proved by mathematical demonstration: but, nevertheless, I will not pretend to ascertain the size of Morgante; tho' I believe he was not very tall, because, I find in the history which gives a particular account of his exploits, that he often slept under a roof; now, if there was any house capacious enough to receive him, his magnitude could not be very extraordinary." "No, surely," said the curate, who being diverted with his extravagant assertions, asked his opinion, concerning the looks and persons of Reynaldo de Montalvan, Don Orlando, and the rest of the twelve peers of France, who were all knights-errant. "With regard to Reynaldo," answered Don Quixote, "I will venture to say, he was broad-visaged, of a ruddy complexion, with large rolling eyes, full of punctilio, excessively choleric, and a friend to robbers and vagabonds. As for Roldan, or Rotolando, or Orlando, for, he is mentioned in history by all these names, it is my opinion, and I affirm, that he was of a middling stature, broad-shouldered, somewhat bandy-legged, of a dark complexion and carotty beard, hairy all over, with a frowning aspect, sparing of speech, though very affable and well-bred." "If Roldan was not more comely than you have represented him," replied the curate, "I do not wonder that Angelica the fair disdained and deserted him, for the gallantry, mirth and pleasantry of the little smock-faced Moor, to whose embraces she yielded; and surely, she was in the right, to prefer the smoothness of Medoro to the roughness of Roldan." "That same Angelica, Mr. curate," said the knight, "was an unsettled, rambling young woman that longed after novelties, and left the world as full of her impertinent actions as of the fame of her beauty. She undervalued a thousand noblemen, a thousand valiant and discreet admirers, and contented herself with a yellow-haired page, who had neither fortune nor reputation, but that of being grateful to his friend. The renowned Ariosto, who sung the praises of her beauty, either not daring or not designing to rehearse what happened to her after her base intrigue, because he deemed it a theme not extremely honourable for his muse, dropped her at these lines:

Another bard may sing in loftier lay,
How he obtain'd the scepter of Cathay.

And truly, this was a sort of prophecy; for, the poets are also called vates, which, in Latin, signifies diviners, and it was plainly verified in the event, an Andaluzian bard having since that time sung in verse her tears and lamentation, as the most famous and sublime genius of Castile hath celebrated her beauty."

"Pray tell me, signor Don Quixote," said the barber, "among all those authors who have written in her praise, hath not some one or other composed a satire against my lady Angelica?" "I firmly believe," replied the knight, "that if Sacripante or Roldan had been bards, they would have made the damsel smart severely, it being natural and peculiar to poets, who are disdained and rejected by their false mistresses, whether real or imaginary, to revenge themselves by satires and lampoons; a resentment altogether unworthy of generous breasts; but, hitherto I have not met with any such defamatory verses against the lady Angelica, tho' she made strange confusion in the world." "That is a wonder, indeed," said the curate, when hearing the housekeeper and niece, who had sometime before quitted the company, bawling aloud in the yard, they ran out to see what was the occasion of such noise.

## CHAPTER II.

The notable fray that happened between Sancho and Don Quixote's niece and housekeeper; with other diverting incidents.

The history relates, that the noise which Don Quixote, the curate and barber heard, was occasioned by the niece and housekeeper scolding at Sancho, who struggled to get in and see his master, while they defended the door. "What does the swag-bellied lurcher want in this house?" said the housekeeper, "get you home, brother; it was you and none but you, that turned my poor master's brain, inticing him from his own home, to strole about the highways." To this apostrophe Sancho replied, "Housekeeper of satan! 'tis my brain that's turned; 'twas I that was inticed to strole about the highways, and not thy master; for, he carried me a rambling: so that you have reckoned without your host. 'Twas he that wheedled me from my own house, with the promise of an island, which I expect to this good hour." "Devil choak thee with islands, thou cursed cormorant!" cried the niece, "and pray, what is an island; is it any thing to eat, thou gorbellied glutton, ha?" "No, not to eat, but to govern," answered Sancho, "and a fat government it is. Better than four cities, or the places of any four of the king's alcaldes." "Be that as it will," said the housekeeper, "thou shan't set foot in this house, thou bag of mischief and bundle of malice! go, and look after thy own family, fatten thy hogs, and let us hear no more of these islands or oyl-lands."

The curate and barber were highly entertained with this dialogue; but, Don Quixote, fearing that Sancho would open his budget, and disburthen himself of some mischievous load of folly, by blabbing things not much to his credit, called him in, bidding the women hold their tongues, and give him entrance. Sancho being accordingly admitted, the curate and barber took their leave of Don Quixote, whose recovery they despaired of, seeing him so unalterably fixed in his folly, and so wholly possessed with the frantic spirit of knight-errantry. "You shall see, neighbour," said the curate to the barber, "that when we least think of it, this poor gentleman will make another sally." "That I make no doubt of," answered the barber, "but I don't wonder so much at the madness of the knight as at the simplicity of the squire, who believes so devoutly in this island, that, I think, all the invention of man could not extract it from his skull." "God mend them!" replied the curate; "mean while, let us keep a strict eye over their behaviour, and observe the operation of their joint extravagance; for, the madness of the master seems to have been cast in the same mould with the foolishness of the man, and, in my opinion, the one without the other would not be worth a farthing." "True," said the barber, "and I should be glad to know what they are now talking of." "I dare say," replied the curate, "the niece and housekeeper will give us a good account of their conversation; for, they are none of those who can resist the opportunity of listening."

In the mean time, Don Quixote having shut himself up in his apartment with Sancho, said, "It gives me much concern, Sancho, to hear thee say, as thou dost, that I enticed thee from thy cottage, when thou knowest that I, at the same time, quitted my own house: together we set out, lived and travelled together; sharing the same fortune and the same fate. If thou hast been once tossed in a blanket, I have been bruised an hundred times, and this is the only pre-eminence I enjoyed." "And that's but reasonable," replied Sancho, "according to your worship's own remark, that misfortune belongs more to knights-errant, than to their squires." "There you are mistaken, Sancho," said Don Quixote; "for the Latin adage says, Quando caput dolet, &c." "Nay," quoth Sancho, "I understand no lingo but my mother-tongue." "The meaning," said his master, "is, When the head akes, all the members are affected. I therefore, as thy lord and master, am thy head, and thou as my servant art a part of me; so, that whatever mischief has happened, or may happen to me, ought to extend to thee likewise, in the same manner as I bear a share in all thy sufferings." "So it ought to be," said Sancho; "but when I, as a member, was tossed in a blanket, my head sat peaceably on the other side of the wall, and beheld me vaulting in the air, without feeling the least uneasiness; and since the members are obliged to ake with the head, I think it is but just, that the head should ake with the members." "How canst thou affirm, Sancho," replied Don Quixote, "that I felt no pain while thou wast tossed in the blanket? Say, or think so no more; for, I was, at the time, more afflicted in mind than thou in body.

"But let us wave this subject for the present; and, time will, no doubt, offer an opportunity of considering it more maturely, and of setting every thing to rights; and tell me, friend Sancho, how am I spoke of in this place? what say the vulgar? what character do I bear among the gentry? and how am I treated by the knights? what is their opinion of my valour, exploits and courteous behavior? and how do they relish the design I have undertaken of raising and restoring to the world the long-forgotten order of

knight-errantry? In short, Sancho, I desire that thou wilt inform me of every thing thou hast heard on this subject, without adding to the good, or subtracting from the evil; it being the duty of faithful servants to represent the truth to their masters, in its own native form, neither exaggerated by adulation, nor diminished by any other vain respect; and let me tell thee, Sancho, if the naked truth was always conveyed to the ears of princes, undisguised by flattery, we should see better days, and other æras would deserve the name of the iron age, more than the present, which would be justly looked upon as the age of gold. Remember this advice, Sancho, and inform me with honesty and discretion, of all that thou knowest, in regard to what I have asked." "That I will with all my heart, sir," answered Sancho, "on condition that your worship won't be offended with the truth, since you desire to see it in its nakedness, just as it came to my knowledge." "I shall not be offended in the least," replied Don Quixote; "speak therefore, freely, without going about the bush."

"Well then," said the squire, "in the first place, you must know that the common people think your worship a stark, staring madman, and me a most notorious fool; the better sort say, that scorning the rank of a private gentleman, you have put Don before your name, and dubbed yourself a knight, with a small garden, a few acres of land, and a doublet clouted on both sides. The knights forsooth are affronted that your small gentry should pretend to vie with them, especially those needy squires who sole their own shoes, and darn their black hose with green silk." "That observation," said Don Quixote, "cannot affect me, for I always wear good cloaths, and never appear patched. My doublet may, indeed, be torn, but then it is by my armour, not by time." "Touching the valour, courtesy, adventures and design of your worship," said Sancho, "there are different opinions. Some say he is mad, but a diverting madman; others allow that he is valiant, but unlucky; a third set observe, that he is courteous, but impertinent; and in this manner we are handled so severely, that neither your worship nor I have a whole bone left." "You see, Sancho," said Don Quixote, "that whenever virtue shines in an eminent degree, she always meets with persecution. Few or none of the celebrated heroes of antiquity could escape the calumnies of malice: Julius Cæsar, a most daring, wise and valiant general, was accused of being ambitious, and not over cleanly in his customs or apparel: Alexander, who by his atchievements acquired the name of Great, was said to be a drunkard: and Hercules, renowned for his labours, reported to have been lewd and effeminate: Don Galaor, brother of Amadis de Gaul, was grumbled at for being excessively quarrelsome, and Amadis himself ridiculed as an arrant whiner. Therefore, son Sancho, among so many aspersions thrown upon such great men, I may well overlook what is said against me; since it is no worse than what thou hast repeated." "That's the very thing, body of my father!" replied Sancho. "What is there any thing more?" said his master. "More!" cried the squire, "the tail is yet unflea'd.[1] What you have heard is but cakes and gingerbread;[2] but, if your worship would know all the backbitings we suffer, I will this moment bring hither one, who can inform you of every circumstance, without losing a crumb; for, last night, the son of Bartholomew Carrasco arrived from Salamanca, where he has been at his studies, and got a batchelor's degree; and when I went to welcome him home, he told me there was a printed book of your worship's history, in which you go by the name of 'The ingenious squire Don Quixote de la Man-

cha'; and that I am mentioned in it, by my own name of Sancho Panza, as well as my lady
Dulcinea del Toboso, with other things that passed between you and me only; at hear-
ing of which, I crossed myself through fear, wondring, how they should come to the
knowledge of the historian." "You may depend upon it, Sancho," said Don Quixote, "the
author of our history must be some sage enchanters; for nothing is hid from writers of
that class." "How can he be a sage enchanter," said Sancho; "when batchelor Sampson
Carrasco (for that's the name of him who told me) says the author of our history is called
Cid Hamet Bean-and-jelly?" "That name is moorish," replied Don Quixote. "Very
like," said the squire, "for I have often heard, that the Moors are very fond of beans and
jellies."[3] "Thou must certainly be mistaken, Sancho," said Don Quixote, "in the sirname
of that Cid, which in Arabic, signifies Signor." "Very possible," answered the squire, "but
if your worship desires to see the batchelor, I will bring him hither in a twinkling."
"Thou wilt oblige me very much, my friend," said Don Quixote, "for what thou hast
told me has bred such doubts and suspence within me, that I cannot eat a morsel with
any satisfaction, until I am informed of the whole affair." "Then I'll go seek him," replied
Sancho, who, leaving his master, went in quest of the batchelor, with whom he returned
in a little time, and a most pleasant dialogue ensued.

## CHAPTER III.

## The ludicrous conversation that passed between Don Quixote, Sancho Panza, and the batchelor Sampson Carrasco.

Don Quixote remained extremely pensive, in expectation of the batchelor Sampson
Carrasco, from whom he hoped to hear news of himself, in print, according to
Sancho's information; though he could hardly persuade himself, that there could be
such a history extant; the blood of his enemies whom he had slain, being scarce, as yet,
dry upon the blade of his sword; and yet they would have his high atchievements already
recorded in printed books. He therefore imagined that some sage, either friend or foe,
had cast them off, by the power of inchantment: if a friend, in order to aggrandize and
extol them above the most distinguished exploits of knight-errantry; if an enemy, to an-
nihilate and depress them beneath the meanest actions that ever were recorded of any
squire. "Although," said he, within himself, "the deeds of squires are never committed
to writing; and, if my history actually exists, seeing it treats of a knight-errant, it must,
of necessity, be pompous, sublime, surprizing, magnificent, and true." This reflection
consoled him a little: but he became uneasy again, when he recollected that his author
was a Moor, as appeared by the name of Cid; and that no truth was to be expected from
that people, who are all false, deceitful, and chimerical. He was afraid that his amours
were treated with some indecency, that might impair and prejudice the honour of his
lady Dulcinea del Toboso, wishing for nothing more than a true representation of his

fidelity, and the decorum he always preserved, in refusing queens, empresses and damsels of all ranks, thus keeping the impulse of his passions under the rein. Tossed therefore, and fluctuating on these and many other fancies, he was found by Sancho and Carrasco, whom the knight received with great courtesy.

The batchelor, though his name was Sampson, was not very big, but a great wag, of a pale complexion and excellent understanding; he was about the age of four and twenty; had a round visage, flat nose, and capacious mouth, all symptoms of a mischievous disposition, addicted to jokes and raillery; as appeared, when he approached Don Quixote, before whom he fell upon his knees, saying, "Permit me to kiss your most puissant hand, signor Don Quixote de la Mancha, for by the habit of St. Peter, which I wear, though I have received no other orders than the first four, your worship is one of the most famous knights-errant that ever were, or ever will be, within the circumference of the globe! Blest be Cid Hamet Benengeli, who wrote the history of your greatness! and thrice blest that curious person who took care to have it translated from the Arabic into our mother tongue, for the entertainment of mankind!" Don Quixote raising him up, said, "'Tis true, then that there is a history of me, and that the sage who composed it is a Moor." "So true, signor, (said Sampson) that to my certain knowledge, there are twelve thousand volumes of it, this day, in print; let Portugal, Barcelona, and Valencia, where they were printed, contradict me, if they can. It is even reported to be now in the press at Antwerp; and I can easily perceive, that there is scarce a nation or language into which it will not be translated." "One of the things," said Don Quixote on this occasion, "which ought to afford the greatest satisfaction to a virtuous and eminent man, is to live and see himself celebrated in different languages, and his actions recorded in print, with universal approbation; I say with approbation, because to be represented otherwise, is worse than the worst of deaths." "In point of reputation and renown," said the batchelor, "your worship alone, bears away the palm from all other knights-errant; for, the Moor in Arabic, and the Christian in his language, have been careful in painting the gallantry of your worship to the life; your vast courage in encountring dangers, your patience in adversity, your fortitude in the midst of wounds and mischance, together with the honour and chastity of your platonic love for my lady Donna Dulcinea del Toboso."

Here Sancho interposing, said, "I never heard my lady called Donna Dulcinea, but simply the lady Dulcinea del Toboso; so that there the history is wrong." "That is no material objection," answered Carrasco. "No, sure," replied the knight; "but tell me Mr. batchelor, which of my exploits is most esteemed in this history?" "As to that particular," said the batchelor, "there are as many different opinions as there are different tastes. Some stick to the adventure of the windmills, which to your worship appeared monstrous giants; others, to that of the fulling-mills: this reader, to the description of the two armies, which were afterwards metamorphosed into flocks of sheep; while another magnifies that of the dead body, which was carrying to the place of interment at Segovia: one says, that the deliverance of the galley-slaves excels all the rest; and a second affirms, that none of them equals the adventure of the Benedictine giants, and your battle with the valiant Biscayner." Here Sancho interrupting him again, said, "Tell me, Mr. batchelor, is the adventure of the Yanguesians mentioned, when our modest

Rozinante * longed for green pease in December." "Nothing," replied Sampson, "has es-
caped the pen of the sage author, who relates every thing most minutely, even to the ca-
pers which honest Sancho cut in the blanket." "I cut no capers in the blanket," answered
Sancho; "but in the air, I grant you, I performed more than I desired." "In my opinion,"
said Don Quixote, "there is no human history that does not contain reverses of fortune,
especially those that treat of chivalry, which cannot always be attended with success."
"Nevertheless," resumed the batchelor, "some who have read your history, say, they
should not have been sorry, had the author forgot a few of those infinite drubbings
which, in different encounters, were bestowed on the great Don Quixote." "But in this,
consists the truth of history," said the squire.

   Don Quixote observed, that they might as well have omitted them; for those inci-
dents, which neither change nor affect the truth of the story, ought to be left out, if they
tend to depreciate the chief character. "Take my word for it," said he, "Æneas was not
so pious as Virgil represents him, nor Ulysses so prudent as he is exhibited by Homer."
"True," said Sampson, "but it is one thing to compose as a poet, and another to record
as an historian: the poet may relate or rehearse things, not as they were, but as they
ought to have been; whereas, an historian must transmit them, not as they ought to have
been, but exactly as they were; without adding to, or subtracting the least tittle from the
truth." "Since this moorish gentleman has told all the truth," said Sancho, "I don't doubt
that among the drubbings of my master, he has mentioned mine also; for, they never
took the measure of his shoulders, without crossing my whole body; but at this I ought
not to wonder, since, as he observes, when the head aches, the members ought to have
their share of the pain." "You are a sly rogue, Sancho," replied Don Quixote, "and I find
you don't want memory, when you think proper to use it." "If I had all the mind in the
world," said Sancho, "to forget the blows I have received, the marks, which are still fresh
upon my carcase, would by no means allow me."

   "Hold your peace, Sancho," said the knight, "and don't interrupt Mr. batchelor,
whom I intreat to proceed, and let me know, what more is said of me in this same his-
tory." "Ay, and of me too," cried Sancho, "who, they say, am one of the principal per-
sonages of it." "You mean persons and not personages, friend Sancho," said Sampson.
"What! have we got another reprimander of words?" said the squire; "since it is come
to this, we shall never have done." "Plague light on me! Sancho," replied the batchelor,
"if you are not the second person of the history; and there are many who would rather
hear you speak than the first character in the book; tho' some there be also, who say you
are excessively credulous, in believing there could be any foundation for the govern-
ment of that island, which was promised to you by signor Don Quixote, here present."
† "There is no time lost," said Don Quixote, "while thou art advancing in years, San-
cho, age will bring experience; and then thou wilt be more qualified and fit to govern
than thou art at present." "'Fore God! Sir," said Sancho, "the island which I cannot gov-
ern with these years, I shall never govern, were I as old as Methusalem: the mischief is,

---

* *Pedir cotufas en el golfo*, signifies to look for tartuffles in the sea, a proverb applicable to those who
are too sanguine in their expectations, and unreasonable in their desires.[1]
† *Aun ay sol en las bardas——*. There is still sun-shine on the wall.——i.e. It is not yet too late.[2]

that this same island is delayed I don't know how; not that I want noddle to govern it." "Recommend it, Sancho," said Don Quixote, "to the direction of heaven, which does all for the best, and may perhaps exceed your expectation; for, not a leaf can move upon a tree, without the permission of God." "True," said Sampson, "if it be the will of God, Sancho shall not want a thousand islands, much less one to govern." "I have seen governors in my time," quoth Sancho, "who, to my thinking, did not come up to the sole of my shoe, and yet they were called your lordship, and served in plate." "Those were not governors of islands," replied Sampson, "but of other governments more easily managed; for, such as govern islands, ought, at least, to have some grammatical knowledge." "I know very well how to * cram," said Sancho, "but as to the matted cawl, I will neither meddle nor make, because I don't understand it: but, leaving this government in the hands of God, who will dispose of me the best for his own service, I am, Mr. Batchelor Sampson Carrasco, infinitely pleased and rejoiced that the author of our history has spoke of me in such a manner as not to give offence; for, by the faith of a good squire! if he had said any thing of me, that did not become an old christian as I am, the deaf should have heard of it." "That were a miracle indeed!" answered Sampson. "Miracle or no miracle," said Sancho, "let every man take care how he speaks or writes of honest people, and not set down at a venture, the first thing that comes into his jolterhead."

"One of the faults that are found with the history," added the batchelor, "is, that the author has inserted in it, a novel intituled The Impertinent Curiosity. Not that the thing itself is bad, or poorly executed; but, because it is unseasonable, and has nothing to do with the story of his worship signor Don Quixote." "I'll lay a wager," cried Sancho, "that this son of a cur has made a strange hodge-podge of the whole." "Now, I find," said the knight, "that the author of my history is no sage, but some ignorant prater, who, without either judgment or premeditation, has undertaken to write it at random, like Orbaneja the painter of Ubeda, who being asked what he painted, answered, 'just as it happens'; and when he would sometimes scrawl out a mishapen cock, was fain to write under it in Gothic letters, This is a Cock; and my history being of the same kind, will need a commentary to make it intelligible." "Not at all," answered Sampson, "it is already so plain, that there is not the least ambiguity in it: the very children handle it, boys read it, men understand, and old people applaud it: in short, it is so thumbed, so read, and so well known by every body, that no sooner a meagre horse appears, than they say, 'There goes Rozinante'; but those who peruse it most, are your pages: you cannot go into a nobleman's antichamber, where you won't find a Don Quixote, which is no sooner laid down by one, than another takes it up, some struggling, and some intreating for a sight of it: in fine, this history is the most delightful and least prejudicial entertainment that ever was seen: for, in the whole book, there is not the least shadow of a dishonourable word, nor one thought unworthy of a good catholic." "To write otherwise," said Don Quixote, "were not to publish truth, but to propagate lies; and those historians who deal in such, ought to be burnt like coiners of false money: but, I cannot imagine what

---

* Finding it impossible to translate the original pun or blunder, I have substituted another in its room, on the word Grammatical, which I think has at least an equally good effect.[3]

induced the author to avail himself of novels and stories that did not belong to the subject, when he had such a fund of my adventures to relate: he doubtless stuck to the proverb *, so the gizzard is crammed, it matters not how; for, truly, had he confined himself to the manifestation of my reveries, my sighs, my tears, my benevolence, and undertakings; he might have compiled a volume larger, or as large as all the works of † Tostatus bound together: really, Mr. batchelor, according to my comprehension, it requires great judgment and a ripe understanding to compose histories, or indeed any books whatever; for, to write with elegance and wit is the province of great geniuses only: the wittiest person in the comedy is he that plays the fool; for, he must be no simpleton, who can exhibit a diverting representation of folly. History is a sacred subject, because the soul of it is truth, and where truth is, there the divinity will reside; yet there are some who compose and cast off books, as if they were tossing up a dish of pancakes."

"There is no book so bad," said the batchelor, "but you may find something good in it." "Doubtless," replied the knight, "but it frequently happens, that those who have deservedly purchased and acquired great reputation by their writings, lose it all, or at least, forfeit a part of it in printing them." "The reason," said Sampson, "is, that printed works are perused with leisure, consequently their faults easily observed; and the greater the reputation of the author is, the more severely are they scrutinized: men celebrated for their genius, great poets, and illustrious historians, are, for the most part, if not always envied by those whose pleasure and particular entertainment consists in criticising the works of others, without having obliged the world with any thing of their own." "That is not to be wondered at," said Don Quixote, "for there are many theologicians who make but a poor figure in the pulpit, and yet are excellent in discerning the faults and superfluities of those who preach well." "That is all true, signor Don Quixote," said Carrasco, "and I could wish that those censurers were either a little more compassionate, or something less scrupulous, than to insist upon such blemishes of the work they decry, as may be compared to little spots in the sun, and as aliquando bonus dormitat Homerus,[6] consider how long the author watched, in order to display the light of his performance, with as little shade as possible: perhaps too, those things which disgust them, are no other than moles, that sometimes add to the beauty of the face on which they grow: and therefore I affirm, that he who publishes a book, runs an immense risk; because, it is absolutely impossible to compose such an one as will please and entertain every reader." "I believe, few will relish that which treats of me," said the knight. "Quite the contrary," answered Sampson, "for as stultorum infinitus est numerus,[7] the number of those who are delighted with your history, is infinite; tho' some accuse the author's memory as false or faulty, because he has forgot to tell who the thief was that stole Sancho's Dapple, of whom there was not a word mentioned: we can only infer from the his-

* The original is De paja, y di heno, el jergan lleno; i.e. The bed is filled, tho' it be with hay and straw.[4]
† Alphonsus Tostatus, bishop of Avila, was said to have known every thing that could be known. He made a figure at the council of Basil; wrote twenty-seven volumes; and dying in the fortieth year of his age, was interred of the church of Avila, with this epitaph:

*Hic stupor est mundi, qui scibile discutit omne.*[5]

tory, that he was stolen; and by-and-by, we find the squire mounted on the same beast, without knowing how he was retrieved: they say likewise, that he has omitted telling what Sancho did with those hundred crowns which he found in the portmanteau, in Sierra Morena; and which are never mentioned, tho' many people desired to know what use he made of them; and this is one of the chief defects in the work."

"Mr. Sampson," answered the squire, "I am not in an humour at present, to give accounts and reckonings of that affair; for, I feel a certain qualmishness in my stomach, and if I don't recruit it with a couple of draughts of old stingo, I shall be in most grievous taking *: I have the cordial at home, and my dame waits for me; but, when I have filled my belly, I will return and satisfy your worship, and all the world, in whatever they shall desire to ask, both with regard to the loss of my beast, and the spending of the hundred crowns." So, without expecting a reply, or speaking another word, he hied him home, while Don Quixote desired and intreated the batchelor to stay and do penance with him. The batchelor accepted the invitation, and stayed; a pair of pidgeons was added to the knight's ordinary; he talked of nothing but chivalry, at table, and Carrasco encouraged the discourse: the repast ended, they took their afternoon's nap, Sancho returned, and the former conversation was renewed.

## CHAPTER IV.

### In which Sancho Panza satisfies the doubts, and answers the questions of batchelor Sampson Carrasco; with other incidents worthy to be recited and known.

Sancho returning to his master's house, resumed the former conversation, to gratify Mr. Sampson, who said he wanted to know, when, in what manner, and by whom his ass had been stolen: "You must know, then," said he, "that very night we fled from the holy brotherhood, and got into the brown mountain, after the misventuresome adventure of the galley-slaves, and the corpse that was carrying to Segovia, we took up our quarters in a thicket, where my master and I, being both fatigued, and sorely bruised in the frays we had just finished, went to rest, he leaning upon his lance, and I lolling upon Dapple, as if we had been stretched upon four feather-beds: I, in particular, slept so sound, that the thief, whosoever he was, had an opportunity of coming and propping me up with four stakes, fixed under the corner of my pannel, on which I was left astride; so that he slipt Dapple from under me, without my perceiving it in the least." "And this no difficult matter, nor new device," said Don Quixote; "for, the same thing happened

* In Spanish, *Me pondra en la Espina de Santa Lucia;* i.e. Will put me on St. Lucia's thorn: applicable to any uneasy situation.[8]

to Sacripante, at the siege of Albraca, where, by this contrivance, his horse was stolen from between his legs, by the famous robber Brunelo *." "When morning came," proceeded Sancho, "I no sooner began to stretch myself, than the stakes gave way, and down I came to the ground, with a vengeance: I looked for my beast, and finding he was gone, the tears gushed from my eyes, and I set up a lamentation, which, if the author of our history has not set down, you may depend upon it, he hath neglected a very excellent circumstance: a good many days after this mischance, as I chanced to be travelling with my lady the princess Micomicona, descrying a person riding towards me, in the habit of a gypsie, I immediately knew my own ass, and discovered the rider to be Gines de Passamonte, that impostor and notorious malefactor, whom my master and I delivered from the galley-chain."

"The error lies not in that part of the history," replied the batchelor, "but, consists in the author's saying that Sancho rode on the same ass, before it appears, that he had retrieved him." "As to that affair," said the squire, "I can give you no satisfactory answer, perhaps, it was an oversight in the historian, or owing to the carelessness of the printer." "Doubtless it was so," replied Sampson, "but, what became of those hundred crowns? were they laid up, or laid out?" "I laid them out," answered Sancho, "in necessaries for my own person, my wife and children; and those crowns were the cause of my gossip's bearing patiently, my ramblings and rovings in the service of my lord and master Don Quixote; for, if after such a long absence, I had come home without my ass, and never a cross in my pocket, I might have expected a welcome the wrong way. Now, if you have any thing else to ask, here I am, ready to answer the king in person; and it matters not to any person, whether I did or did not bring them home, or whether I spent them or lent them; for, if the blows I have received in our peregrinations, were to be repaid with money, rated at no more than four maravedis apiece, another hundred crowns would not quit one half of the score: therefore, let every man lay his hand upon his heart, and not pretend to mistake an † hawk for a hand-saw; for, we are all as God made us, and great many of us much worse."

"I will take care," said Carrasco, "to apprize the author of the history, that if it should come to another edition, he may not forget to insert what honest Sancho observes, as it will not a little contribute to raise the value of the work." "Mr. batchelor," said the knight, "did you in reading it, perceive any thing else that ought to be amended?" "There might be some things altered for the better," replied Carrasco; "but, none of such consequence as those already mentioned." "And pray," resumed Don Quixote, "does the author promise a second part?" "Yes," said Sampson, "but, he says, he has not yet found it, nor does he know in whose possession it is; so, that we are still in doubt, whether or not it will see the light: on that account, therefore, and likewise, because some people say that second parts are never good, while others observe, that too much already hath been written concerning Don Quixote, it is believed that there will be no second part; tho' there is a third sort more jovial than wise, who cry, 'Quixote for ever!

* As related in the famous poem of *Orlando Inamorato*, composed by *Boyardo*, of which the *Orlando Furioso* of *Ariosto* is the continuation.[1]

† In the original, "Black for white."[2]

let the knight engage, and Sancho Panza harrangue; come what will, we shall be satisfied.'" "And how does the author seem inclined?" said the knight. "How?" answered Carrasco, "to set the press agoing, as soon as he can find the history, for which he is now searching with all imaginable diligence; thereto swayed by interest, more than by any motive of praise." "Since the author keeps interest and money in his eye," said Sancho, "it will be a wonder if he succeeds; for, he'll do nothing but hurry, hurry, like a taylor on Easter-eve; and your works that are trumped up in a haste, are never finished with that perfection they require: I would have Mr. Moor take care, and consider what he is about; for, my master and I will furnish him with materials, in point of adventures and different events, sufficient to compose not only one, but an hundred second parts. What! I suppose the honest man thinks we are now sleeping among straw; but, let him lift up our feet, and then he will see which of them wants to be shod: all that I shall say, is, if my master had taken my advice, we might have been already in the fields, redressing grievances, and righting wrongs, according to the use and custom of true knights-errant."

Scarce had Sancho pronounced these last words, when their ears were saluted by the neighing of Rozinante, which Don Quixote considered as a most happy omen, and determined in three or four days, to set out on his third expedition: accordingly, he declared his intention to the batchelor, whose advice he asked with regard to the route he should take. Sampson said, that in his opinion, he ought to direct his course towards the kingdom of Arragon, and go to Saragossa, where, in a few days, was to be held a most solemn tournament on the festival of St. George; there he would have an opportunity of winning the palm from the Arragonian knights, which would raise his reputation above that of all the champions upon earth: he applauded his design, as a most valiant and honourable determination, and begged he would be more cautious in encountring dangers, because his life was not his own, but the property of all those who had occasion for protection and succour in distress.

"That is the very thing I repose, Mr. Sampson," said the squire, "for, my master thinks no more of attacking an hundred men in arms, than a hungry boy would think of swallowing half a dozen * pippins: body of the universe! Mr. batchelor, if there are times for attacking, there are also seasons for retreating: the cry must not always be, 'St. Jago † ! close, Spain'; especially as I have heard, and if I remember aright, my master himself has often observed, that valour lies in the middle, between the extremes of cowardice and rashness: this being the case, I would not have him fly without good reason, nor give the assault when he is likely to be overpowered by numbers; but, above all things, I give my master notice, that if he carries me along with him, it shall be on condition, that he fight all the battles himself, and I be obliged to do nothing, but tend his person, that is, take care of his belly, and keep him sweet and clean; in which case, I will ‡ jig it away, with pleasure; but, to think that I will put hand to sword, even against base-born plebeians,

---

* Literally *Badeas*, a kind of water melon.[3]
† This is the cry uttered by the Spaniards when they charge in battle.[4]
‡ *Baylar el agua delante*, is a phrase applicable to those who do their duty with alacrity, taken from the practice of watering the courts in Spain, an office which the maids perform with a motion that resembles dancing.[5]

with cap and hatchet, is a wild imagination: for my own part, Mr. Sampson, I do not pretend to the reputation of being valiant, but, of being the best and loyalest squire that ever served a knight-errant; and if my master Don Quixote, in consideration of my great and faithful services, shall be pleased to bestow upon me one of those many islands which his worship says, will fall in his way, I shall very thankfully receive the favour; and even, if he should not keep his word, here stand I, simple as I am, and one man must not depend upon another, but, trust in God alone: besides, the bread I eat, without a government, mayhap will relish better than the dainties of a governor; and how do I know, but the devil may, in these governments, raise some stumbling-block, over which I shall fall and beat out my grinders? Sancho I was born, and Sancho will I die; but, nevertheless, if by the favour of providence, I could fairly and softly, without much risk or anxiety, obtain an island, or some such matter, I am not such a ninny as to throw it away; for, as the saying is, When the heifer is offered, be ready with the rope; and when good fortune comes to thy door, be sure to bid it welcome."

"Brother Sancho," said the batchelor, "you have spoke like a professor; but, for all that, put your trust in God, and signor Don Quixote, who instead of an island will give you a whole kingdom." "The one as likely as the other," answered Sancho; "tho' I dare venture to assure signor Carrasco, that the kingdom, which my master shall bestow upon me, will not be put into a rotten sack; for, I have felt my own pulse, and find myself in health sufficient to rule kingdoms and govern islands, as I have, upon many other occasions, hinted to my master." "Consider, Sancho," said the batchelor, "that honours often change the disposition; and, perhaps, when you come to be governor, you will not know the mother that bore you." "That may be the case," answered the squire, "with those who were born among mallows; but, not with me, who have got four inches of old christian suet on my ribs: then, if you come to consider my disposition, you will find I am incapable of behaving ungratefully to any person whatever." "God grant it to be so," said the knight; "but, this will appear when you arrive at the government, which methinks, I have already in mine eye."

He then intreated the batchelor, if he was a poet, to favour him with a copy of verses on his intended parting from his mistress Dulcinea del Toboso, and desired that every line might begin with a letter of her name, so that the initials being joined together, might make Dulcinea del Toboso. Carrasco, tho' he owned he was not one of the famous poets of Spain, who were said to be but three * and an half, promised to compose such an acrostic as he desired, which, by the by, he foresaw, would be no easy task, because the name consisted of seventeen letters, and if he should make four stanzas of four lines each, one must be left out; or should they be composed of five, called decimas or roundelays, three letters would be wanting to complete the number: however, he would endeavour to sink one letter as much as he could; so that in four stanzas, the name Dulcinea del Toboso should be included. "That must be done, at all events," said Don Quixote; "for, if the name be not plain and manifest, no woman will believe that she was the

* Alonzo de Ercilla, author of the Araucana, Juan Ruso de Cordova, author of the Austriada, Christopher Verves de Valentia, author of the Montserrate, and as for the half, Cervantes in all probability meant himself.[6]

subject of the poem." This affair being thus settled, as also the time of their departure, which was fixed at the distance of eight days, Don Quixote charged the batchelor to keep it secret, especially from the curate, Mr. Nicholas, his niece and housekeeper, that they might not obstruct his honourable and valiant determination. Carrasco having promised to observe this caution, took his leave of the knight, whom he begged to favour him, on every occasion, with an account of his good or evil fortune, and Sancho went home, to provide every thing necessary for their expedition.

## CHAPTER V.

### Of the sage and pleasant dialogue between Sancho Panza and his wife Teresa Panza, with other incidents worthy to be most happily recorded.

The translator says, he looks upon this chapter as apocryphal, because it represents Sancho Panza speaking in a stile quite different from that which might be expected from his shallow understanding, and making such ingenious observations, as he thinks it impossible he should know; but, he would not leave it out, that he might punctually perform the duty of a faithful translator, and therefore proceeds in these words:

Sancho returned to his own house, in such high spirits, that his wife perceived his gaiety at the distance of a bowshot, and could not help saying, "What is the matter, friend Sancho, that you seem so joyful?" To this question the squire answered, "An it please God, wife, I should be very glad, if I were not so joyful as I seem to be." "Truly, husband," replied * Teresa, "I don't understand you, and cannot conceive what you mean, by saying, you should be very glad, an it pleased God, you were not so joyful; for, simple tho' I be, I am always glad with what makes me joyful." "Mark me, Teresa," said the squire, "I am rejoiced, because it is determined that I shall return to the service of my master Don Quixote, who is going to make a third sally in quest of adventures, and I must accompany him in his expedition; for, so my destiny will have it, together with the comfortable and lovely hope of finding another hundred crowns like those I have expended; on the other hand, sorry am I to part with thee and my children; and if God would permit me to eat my bread, dry-shod at home, without dragging me over clifts and cross-paths: (and this might be done at a small expence, if he would only say the word) it is plain, that my joy would be more firm and perfect; whereas, that which I feel at present, is mingled with the melancholy thoughts of leaving thee, my duck: wherefore, I justly said I should be glad, an it pleased God, I were less joyful." "Verily, Sancho," said his wife,

* Sancho's wife has already been mentioned under the names of Juana and Mary, and now she is called Teresa.

"ever since you made yourself a member of knight-errantry, you talk in such a round-about manner, that there is no understanding what you say." "Let it suffice," answered the squire, "that I am understood by God, who is the understander of all things; and there let it rest: mean while, take notice, gossip, it will be convenient for you to tend Dapple for these two or three days, with special care; let his allowance be doubled, that he may be enabled to carry arms, and look out for the pannel and the rest of the tackle; for, we are not going to a wedding, but, to traverse the globe, and give and take dry blows with your giants, dragons and hobgoblins, and hear nothing but hissing, roaring, bellowing and bleating; and all this would be but flowers of lavender, were it not our doom to encounter with Yanguesians and enchanted Moors." "I very well believe, that squires-errant do not eat the bread of idleness," replied Teresa; "and therefore, husband, I shall continually pray to our Lord, to deliver you from such misfortunes." "I tell thee, wife," said Sancho, "if I did not expect to see myself in a little time governor of an is-land, I should drop down dead upon the spot." "By no means, dear husband," cried Teresa, "let the hen live, tho' she have the pip; and I hope you will live, tho' the devil run away with all the governments upon earth: without a government, did you come from your mother's womb; without a government have you lived to this good hour; and with-out a government shall you go or be carried to your grave, in God's own time: there are many in the world, who have no governments, and yet, for all that, they live and are numbered among the people. Hunger is the best sauce, and as that is never wanting among the poor, they always relish what they eat; but, take care, Sancho, if you come to a government, that you do not forget me and your children: consider, Sanchico has al-ready fifteen good years over his head, and that it is time for him to go to school, if, in case his uncle the abbot has a mind to breed him to the church: consider too, that your daughter Mary Sancha will not break her heart if we marry her; for, I am much mistaken if she does not long for a husband, as much as you do for a government, and the short and the long of it is, you had better have your daughter ill buckled as a wife than well kept as a concubine."

"Take my word for it," answered Sancho, "if by the blessing of God, I come to any sort of government, I intend, my dear, to match Mary Sancha so high, that no body shall come near her, without calling her, your ladyship." "Never think of that, Sancho!" cried Teresa, "match her with her equal; which will be more prudent than to raise her from clogs to pattens, from good fourteen-penny hoyden grey, to farthingales and petticoats of silk, and from Molly and thou, to Donna and my lady such-a-one: the girl's head would be quite turned, and she would be continually falling into some blunder, that would discover the coarse thread of her home-spun breeding." "Shut that foolish mouth of thine," said Sancho; "in two or three years practice, quality and politeness will be-come quite familiar to her; or, if they should not, what does it signify? let her first be a lady, and then happen what will." "Meddle, Sancho, with those of your own station," replied Teresa, "and seek not to lift your head too high; but, remember the proverb that says, When your neighbour's son comes to the door, wipe his nose and take him in.[1] It would be a fine thing, truly, to match our Mary with a great count or cavalier, who would, when he should take it in his head, look upon her as a monster, and call her coun-try wench, and clod-breaker's and hemp-spinner's brat: that shall never happen in my

life-time, husband; it was not for that, I brought up my child: do you find a portion, and as to her marriage, leave that to my care; there is Lope Tocho, old John Tocho's son, a jolly young fellow, stout and wholesome, whom we all know, and I can perceive that he has no dislike to the girl: besides, he being our equal, she will be very well matched with him; for, we shall always have them under our eye, and the two families will live together, parents and children, sons and sons-in-law, and grandsons, and the peace and blessing of God will dwell amongst us: wherefore you shall not match her in your courts and grand palaces, where she will neither understand nor be understood." "Heark ye, you beast and yoke-fellow for Barabbas!" replied Sancho, "why wouldst thou, now, without rhime or reason, prevent me from matching my daughter, so as that my grand-children shall be persons of quality? remember, Teresa, I have often heard my elders and betters observe, He that's coy when fortune's kind, may, after seek, but never find. And should not I be to blame, if, now that she knocks at my door, I should bolt it against her? Let us therefore, take the advantage of the favourable gale that blows."

It was this uncommon stile, with what Sancho says below, that induced the translator to pronounce the whole chapter apocryphal.

"Can't you perceive, animal, with half an eye," proceeded Sancho, "that I shall act wisely, in devoting this body of mine to some beneficial government that will lift us out of the dirt, and enable me to match Mary Sancha according to my own good pleasure: then thou wilt hear thyself called Donna Teresa Panza, and find thyself seated, at church, upon carpets, cushions and tapestry, in despite and defiance of all the small gentry in the parish; and not be always, in the same moping circumstances, without increase or diminution, like a picture in the hangings: but, no more of this; Sanchica shall be a countess, tho' thou should'st cry thy heart out." "Look before you leap, husband," answered Teresa; "after all, I wish to God, this quality of my daughter may not be the cause of her perdition: take your own way, and make her dutchess or princess, or what you please; but, I'll assure you, it shall never be with my consent or good will: I was always a lover of equality, my dear, and can't bear to see people hold their heads high, without reason. Teresa was I christened, a bare and simple name, without the addition, garniture and embroidery of Don or Donna; my father's name is Cascajo, and mine, as being your spouse, Teresa Panza, tho' by rights, I should be called Teresa Cascajo: but, As the king minds, the law binds:[2] and with that name, am I contented, tho' it be not burthened with a Don, which weighs so heavy, that I should not be able to bear it; neither will I put it in the power of those who see me dressed like a countess or governor's lady, to say, 'Mind Mrs. porkfeeder, how proud she looks! it was but yesterday, she toiled hard at the distaf, and went to mass, with the tail of her gown about her head, instead of a veil; but, now, forsooth, she has got her fine farthingales and jewels, and holds up her head, as if we did not know her.' If God preserve me in my seven or five senses, or as many as they be, I shall never bring myself into such a quandary: as for your part, spouse, you may go to your governments and islands, and be as proud as a peacock; but, as for my daughter and me, by the life of my father! we will not stir one step from the village; for, The wife that deserves a good name, stays at home, as if she were lame; and the maid must still be ado-ing, that hopes to see the men come a wooing. You and Don Quixote may therefore, go to your adventures, and leave us to our misventures; for, God will better our condition,

if we deserve his mercy; tho', truly, I cannot imagine who made him a Don; I am sure, neither his father nor grandfather had any such title." "I tell thee, wife," replied the squire, "thou hast certainly got some devil in that carcase of thine: the Lord watch over thee, woman! what a deal of stuff hast thou been tacking together, without either head or tail? What the devil has your Cascajos, jewels, proverbs and pride, to do with what I have been saying? Heark ye, you ignorant beast; for such I may call thee, as thou hast neither capacity to understand my discourse, nor prudence to make sure of good fortune, (when it lies in thy way) were I to say, that my daughter shall throw herself from the top of a steeple, or go strolling about the world, like the Infanta Donna Uraca; thou would'st have reason to contradict my pleasure: but, if in two turnings of a ball, and one twinkling of an eye, our good fortune should lay a title across our shoulders, and raising thee from the stubble, set thee in a chair of state, under a canopy, or lay thee upon a sofa, consisting of more velvet * almohadas, than there are Moors in all the family of the Almohadas in Morocco; wherefore would'st not thou consent, and with me, enjoy the good-luck that falls?" "I'll tell thee wherefore, husband," replied Teresa, "because, as the saying is, What covers, discovers thee: the eyes of people always run slightly over the poor, but, make an halt to examine the rich; and if a person so examined was once poor, then comes the grumbling, and the slandering; and he is persecuted by back-bitters, who swarm in our streets like bees." "Give ear, Teresa, and listen to what I am going to say," answered Sancho; "for, mayhap, thou hast never heard such a thing in all the days of thy life: and I do not now pretend to speak from my own reflection, but, to repeat the remarks of the good father who preached last Lent, in our village: he said, if I right remember, that all objects present to the view, exist, and are impressed upon the imagination, with much greater energy and force, than those which we only remember to have seen. (The arguments here used by Sancho, contributed also, to make the translator believe this chapter apocryphal; because they seem to exceed the capacity of the squire, who proceeded thus) From whence it happens, that when we see any person magnificently dressed, and surrounded with the pomp of servants, we find ourselves invited, and as it were compelled to pay him respect; altho' the memory should, at that instant, represent to us, some mean circumstances of his former life; because, that defect, whether in point of family or fortune, is already past and removed, and we only regard what is present to our view; and if the person whom fortune hath thus raised from the lowness of oblivion, to the height of prosperity, be well-bred, liberal and courteous, without pretending to vie with the ancient nobility; you may take it for granted, Teresa, that no body will remember what he was, but, reverence what he now is; except the children of envy, from whom no thriving person is secure." "I really do not understand you," said Teresa, "you may do what you will; but, seek not to distract my brain with your rhetorick and harranguing; for, if you be revolved to do what you say—." "You must call it resolved, woman, and not revolved," cried Sancho. "Never plague yourself to dispute with me, husband," answered Teresa; "I speak as God pleases, and meddle not with other people's concerns: if you are obstinately bent upon this same government, I desire you will carry your son Sancho along with you, and from this hour, teach him the art of that

* Almohada signifies a cushion.[3]

profession; for, it is but reasonable that the sons should inherit and learn the trade of their fathers." "As soon as I have obtained my government," said Sancho, "I will send thee money for him by the post; as, by that time, I shall have plenty; for, there are always people in abundance, that will lend to a governor who has no money of his own; and be sure you cloath him in such a manner, as to disguise his present condition, and make him appear like what he is to be." "Send you the money," answered Teresa, "and I will dress him up, like any branch of palm *." "Well then," said Sancho, "we are agreed about making our daughter a countess—." "That day I behold her a countess," cried the wife, "I shall reckon her dead and buried; but, I tell you again, you may use your pleasure; for, we women are born to be obedient to our husbands, tho' they are no better than blocks."

So saying, she began to weep as bitterly as if she had actually seen her daughter laid in her grave: Sancho consoled her, by saying, that altho' she must be a countess, he would defer her promotion as long as he could. Thus ended the conversation, and the squire went back to Don Quixote, to concert measures for their speedy departure.

## CHAPTER VI.

### Of what passed between Don Quixote, his niece and housekeeper, being one of the most important chapters of the whole history.

While this impertinent conversation passed between Sancho Panza, and his wife Teresa Cascajo, Don Quixote's niece and housekeeper were not idle; for, collecting from a thousand symptoms, that their master wanted to give them the slip a third time, and return to the exercise of his unlucky knight-errantry, they endeavoured, by all possible means, to divert him from his extravagant design: but, all they could say, was like preaching to the desart, or hammering cold iron. However, among many other arguments, the housekeeper said to him, "As I hope to be saved, dear master, if your worship will not settle at home in your own house, but are resolved to stray about the mountains and valleys, like a troubled ghost, in quest of what you term adventures, but what I call mischances, I will complain in person, and raise up my voice to God and the king, that they may apply some remedy to your disorder." To this declaration the knight replied, " Mrs. housekeeper, how God will accept of thy complaints I know not, neither can I guess in what manner his majesty will answer thy petition: this only I know, that if I were king, I would excuse myself from answering that infinite number of impertinent memorials which are daily presented; for, one of the greatest of the many fatigues that attend royalty, is, that of being obliged to listen and reply to all petitions; therefore, I would not have his majesty troubled with any affair of mine." "Pray, sir," said the house-

---

* Alluding to the bough that is adorned and carried in procession on Palm-sunday.[4]

keeper, "are there no knights at court?" "Yes, there are many," answered Don Quixote; "and it is reasonable, that there should be always a good number in attendance, to adorn the court, and support the pomp and magnificence of majesty." "Would it not be better, then, for your worship," replied the matron, "to be one of that number, and serve your king and master, quietly and safely at court?" "You must know, good woman," said Don Quixote, "all knights cannot be courtiers, neither can or ought all courtiers to be knights-errant; there ought to be plenty of both, and tho' we are all knights, there is a great difference between the one sort and the other: your courtiers, without crossing the thresholds of their own apartments, travel over the world, in maps, gratis, and never know what it is to suffer either heat, cold, hunger or thirst, in their journey; whereas, we real knights-errant measure the whole globe with our own footsteps, exposed night and day, on horseback and afoot, to the summer's sun and winter's cold, and all the inclemencies of the weather: we not only, seek to see the picture, but the person of our foe, and on all emergencies and occasions, attack him, without paying any regard to the trifling rules of challenges, whether, for example, his sword and lance be shorter or longer than our own; whether he wears about him any relick or secret coat of mail; or whether the sun and wind be equally divided; with other ceremonies of that nature, which are usually observed in duelling, and which, tho' I know them punctually, thou art little acquainted with: thou must also know, that a good knight-errant, tho' he sees ten giants, whose heads not only touch, but overtop the clouds, with legs like lofty steeples, and arms resembling the masts of vast and warlike ships; while each eye, as large as a mill-wheel, beams and burns like a glass furnace, is by no means confounded or abashed; but, on the contrary, with genteel demeanour and intrepid heart, approaches, assaults, and if possible, vanquishes and overthrows them in a twinkling, tho' they are armed with the shell of a certain fish, said to be harder than adamant; and instead of a sword, use a keen scymitar of damasked steel, or a huge club armed with a point of the same metal, as I have seen on a dozen different occasions. All this I have mentioned, good woman, that thou mayest see what difference there is between knights of different orders; and every prince ought, in reason, to pay greater respect to this second, or rather, this first species of knights-errant, among whom, as we read in history, there have been some who were the bulwarks, not only of one, but of many kingdoms."

"Ah, dear Sir," cried the niece, interrupting him, "consider that all those stories of knights-errant are nothing but lies and invention; and every one of the books that contain them, deserves, if not to be burnt, at least, to wear a * Sanbenito, or some other badge, by which it may be known, for an infamous perverter of virtue and good sense." "By the God that protects me!" cried the knight, "were't thou not undoubtedly my niece, as being my own sister's child, I would chastise thee in such a manner, for the blasphemy thou hast uttered, that the whole world would resound with the example! How! shall a pert baggage, who has scarce capacity enough to manage a dozen lace-bobbins, dare to wag her tongue in censuring the histories of knights-errant? What would signor Amadis say to such presumption? But, surely he would forgive thy arrogance; for, he was the most humble and courteous knight of his time, and besides, the particular champion

---

* A dress put upon convicted heretics.

and protector of damsels; but, thou mightest have been heard by another who would not treat thee so gently; for, all are not affable and well bred: on the contrary, some there are extremely brutal and impolite; all those who call themselves knights, are not intitled to that distinction, some being of pure gold, and others of baser metal, notwithstanding the denomination they assume. But, these last cannot stand the touchstone of truth: there are mean plebeians, who sweat and struggle to maintain the appearance of gentlemen; and on the other hand, there are gentlemen of rank who seem industrious to appear mean and degenerate: the one sort raise themselves either by ambition or virtue, while the other abase themselves by viciousness or sloth; so that we must avail ourselves of our understanding and discernment, in distinguishing those persons, who, tho' they bear the same appellation, are yet so different in point of character." "Good God!" said the niece, "that your worship should be so learned, that even, if need were, you might mount the pulpit, or go a preaching in the streets, and yet remain in such woeful blindness, and palpable folly, as to persuade the world that you are a valiant, and vigorous righter of wrongs, when you are old, feeble, and almost crippled with age; but, above all things, to give yourself out for a knight, when you are no such thing, for, tho' rich gentlemen may be knighted, poor gentlemen like you, seldom are."

"There is a good deal of truth in what thou hast observed, cousin," replied Don Quixote; "and I could tell thee such things, concerning families, as would raise thine admiration; but, these I suppress, that I may not seem to mix what's human with what's divine: take notice, however, my friends, and be attentive to what I am going to say: all the families in the world, may be reduced to four kinds, which are these; one that from low beginnings, hath extended and dilated to a pitch of power and greatness; another, that from great beginnings hath continued to preserve and maintain its original importance; a third, that from vast beginnings hath ended in a point, diminishing and decaying from its foundation, into an inconsiderable point like that of a pyramid, which, in respect of its base, is next kin to nothing; a fourth, and that the most numerous, had neither a good foundation, nor reasonable superstructure, and therefore sinks into oblivion, unobserved; such are the families of plebeians and ordinary people. The first, that from low beginnings, hath mounted to power and greatness, which it preserves to this day, is exemplified in the house of Ottoman, that from an humble shepherd, who gave rise to it, attained that pinnacle of grandeur on which it now stands: the second sort of pedigree, that without augmentation hath preserved its original importance, is exhibited in the persons of many princes, who are such by inheritance, and support their rank without addition or diminution, containing themselves peaceably within the limits of their own dominions: of those who, from illustrious beginnings, have dwindled into a point, there are a thousand examples, in the Pharaohs and Ptolemeys of Ægypt, the Caesars of Rome, with all the tribe, if they may be so called, of your Median, Assyrian, Persian, Greek and barbarian princes, monarchs, and great men. All these families and states, together with their founders, have ended in a very inconsiderable point; since, at this day, it is impossible to trace out one of their descendants, or, if we could, he would be found in some base and low degree. I have nothing to say of the plebeians, who only serve to increase the number of the living, without deserving any other fame or panegyric. From what I have said, I would have you infer, my precious Wiseacres, that there is a great

confusion of pedigrees, and that those only appear grand and illustrious, whose representatives abound with virtue, liberality and wealth: I say, virtue, liberality and wealth, because, the vicious great man is no more than a great sinner; and the rich man, without liberality, a meer covetous beggar; for, happiness does not consist in possessing, but in spending riches, and that, not in squandering them away, but, in knowing how to use them with taste: now, a poor knight has no other way of signalizing his birth, but, the practice of virtue, being affable, well bred, courteous, kind, and obliging, a stranger to pride, arrogance, and slander, and, above all things, charitable; for, by giving two farthings chearfully to the poor, he may shew himself as generous as he that dispenses alms by sound of bell: and whosoever sees him adorned with these virtues, altho' he should be an utter stranger to his race, will conclude that he is descended of a good family. Indeed, it would be a sort of miracle to find it otherwise; so that praise is always the reward of virtue, and never fails to attend the righteous. There are two paths, my children, that lead to wealth and honour; one is that of learning, the other that of arms: now, I am better qualified for the last than for the first, and, (as I judge from my inclination to arms) was born under the influence of the planet Mars; so that I am, as it were, obliged to choose that road, which I will pursue, in spite of the whole universe: you will therefore fatigue yourselves to no purpose, in attempting to persuade me from that which heaven inspires, fortune ordains, reason demands, and above all things, my own inclination dictates: knowing, as I do, the innumerable toils annexed to knight-errantry, I am also well acquainted with the infinite benefits acquired in the exercise of that profession: I know the path of virtue is very strait, while the road of vice is broad and spacious; I know their end and issue is different: the wide extended way of vice conducts the traveller to death; while the narrow, toilful path of virtue, leads to happiness and life—not that which perisheth, but, that which hath no end; and I know, as our great Castilian poet observes,

> By these rough paths of toil and pain,
> Th' immortal seats of bliss we gain,
> Deny'd to those who heedless stray
> In tempting pleasure's flow'ry way."

"Ah! woe is me!" cried the cousin, "my uncle is a poet too! he knows every thing, and can do every thing: I'll wager, if he should turn bricklayer, he could build a house like any cage." "I do assure thee, niece," replied Don Quixote, "if those knightly sentiments did not wholly engross my attention, there is not a thing on earth that I could not make; nor a curiosity that should not go thro' my hands, especially bird-cages and toothpicks."

Here the conversation was interrupted by a knocking at the gate, which, as they found upon enquiry, was made by Sancho, whose presence was no sooner intimated, than the housekeeper ran away to hide herself, that she might avoid the sight of him whom she abhorred: the niece, therefore, opened the door, and his master came out to receive him with open arms; then shutting themselves up together, another dialogue passed, no ways inferior to the former.

## CHAPTER VII.

## Of what passed between Don Quixote and his squire; with other surprising incidents.

The housekeeper seeing that her master and Sancho were locked up together, immediately guessed the subject of the conversation; and imagining, that the result of this consultation would be a third sally, she put on her veil, and full of trouble and anxiety, went in quest of the batchelor Sampson Carrasco, thinking, that as he was a well-spoken man, and her master's new friend, he might persuade him to lay aside such an extravagant design: accordingly, she found him taking a turn in his own yard, and fell upon her knees, before him, in a cold sweat, occasioned by her vexation. Carrasco seeing her appear with such marks of sorrow and consternation, said, "What is the matter, Mrs. housekeeper? what hath befallen you? something seems to have harrowed up your very soul!" "Nothing at all, dear Mr. Sampson," cried the housekeeper, "only my master is breaking out——he is certainly breaking out!" "How breaking out?" said Sampson, "is any part of his body unsound?" "Where should he break out," replied the other, "but thro' the gate of his madness? my meaning, dear batchelor of my soul! is, that he is going to make another sally, (and that will be the third) searching up and down the world for what he calls adventures, tho' I cannot imagine why they should have that * name: the first time, he returned so battered and bruised, that they were fain to lay him across an ass, like a sack of oats, because he could not sit upright: the second time, he was brought home in a waggon, stretched and cooped up in a cage, in which he imagined himself inchanted, in such a woeful plight, that he could scarce be known by the mother that bore him, so lank and meagre, with his eyes sunk into the very lowest pit of his brain; so that before I could bring him to any tolerable degree of strength, I expended more than six hundred new laid eggs, as God and all the world know, as well as my hens, that will not suffer me to tell a lie." "That I verily believe," said the batchelor; "your hens are so good, plump and well bred, that they would rather burst than say one thing and mean another: well then, Mrs. housekeeper, nothing else hath happened, neither have you met with any other misfortune, but, the apprehension of what your master Don Quixote will do?" "Nothing else," said she. "Give yourself no trouble then," resumed the batchelor, "but go home a God's name, and get ready something hot for my breakfast; and in your way, repeat St. Apollonia's prayer, if you can; I will follow, in a little time, and then you shall see wonders." "Dear heart!" cried the housekeeper, "St. Apollonia's prayer, say you? that I should repeat if my master had the tooth-ach, but, lack-a-day! his distemper lies in his skull." "I know what I say," answered Sampson: "take my advice, Mrs. housekeeper, and do not pretend to dispute with me; for, I would have thee to know that I am a batchelor of Salamanca; there's no higher batcheleering than that." She

---

* The original, *ventura*, signifies good luck as well as adventures.[1]

accordingly moved homeward, while Sampson went to communicate to the curate that which will be in due time disclosed.

While Don Quixote and Sancho were closetted together, there passed between them, a conversation which the history recounts with great punctuality and truth. "Signor," said the squire, "I have at length traduced my wife to consent that I shall attend your worship wheresoever you please to carry me." "Say reduced, and not traduced, Sancho," replied the knight. "I have once or twice, if my memory serves me," said Sancho, "in-treated your worship, not to correct my words, if you understand my meaning; and when you can't make it out, I desire you would say, Sancho, or devil, I don't understand thee: then, if I fail in explaining myself, you may correct me as much as you please; for, I am so fossil." "I do not understand thee now," cried Don Quixote, "nor can I compre-hend what thou wouldst be at, in saying I am so fossil." "So fossil," said the squire; "that is, whereby, as how I am just so." "Nay, now, thou art more and more unintelligible," replied the knight. "If your worship does not understand me now," answered Sancho, "I know not how to express it; for, I am already at my wit's-end, and Lord have mercy upon me." "O! now I conceive thy meaning," said the knight; "thou would'st say thou art so docil, gentle and tractable, as to comprehend every thing I say, and retain whatsoever I shall teach thee." "I'll lay a wager," said the squire, "that from the beginning, you knew my meaning by my mumping, but wanted to confound me, by leading me into a thou-sand more blunders." "It may be so," said the knight, "but in reality what says Teresa?" "Teresa," answered Sancho, "says I must be sharp with your worship. Fast bind, fast find: he that shuffles does not always cut;[2] and that a bird in hand is worth two in the bush: now, I know that a wife's counsel is bad, but he that will not take it is mad." "So say I," replied Don Quixote; "proceed, friend Sancho, you speak like an oracle to-day." "Why then, the case is this," resumed Sancho, "your worship very well knows we are all mor-tal, here to-day, and gone to-morrow; for, the lamb goes as fast as the dam; and no man in this world can promise himself more hours of life than God is pleased to grant him; because death is deaf, and when he knocks at the door of life is always in a hurry, and will not be detained either by fair means or force, by scepters or mitres, as the report goes, and as we have often heard it declared from the pulpit." "All this is very true," said the knight; "but, I cannot guess what you drive at." "What I drive at," answered Sancho, "is that your worship would appoint me a certain monthly salary for the time I shall serve you, to be paid out of your estate; for, I don't chuse to depend upon recompences that come late or low, or never. God will protect me with my own. In short, I would know, what I have to trust to, whether little or much; for, the hen clucks though but on one egg; many littles make a mickle; and he that is getting aught, is losing nought. True it is, if it should happen, which I neither believe nor expect, that your worship can give me that island you have promised me so long, I am not so greedy or ungrateful, but, that I will suffer my rent to be appraised, and my salary deducted in due portion." "To be sure, friend Sancho," said the * knight, "all portions ought to be proportioned." "I un-derstand you," replied the squire, "I should have said proportion, instead of portion; but, that is of no signification, since my meaning is comprehended by your worship." "Ay,

---

* I have substituted this play upon the word proportion, in lieu of Sancho's blundering on *Rata.*[3]

and so thoroughly comprehended," said Don Quixote, "that I have penetrated into the inmost recesses of thy thoughts, and perceive the mark at which those innumerable shafts of thy proverbs are aimed. Look you, Sancho, I would appoint thee a salary, if I could find in any history of knights-errant, one precedent, by which I might discover, or have the least glimpse of what they used to give monthly or yearly; but, I have carefully perused all, or the greatest part of those histories, and cannot remember to have read, that any knight-errant ever paid a certain salary to his squire. I only know, that all of them trusted to favour, and when it was least in their thoughts, provided their masters chanced to be fortunate, they found themselves rewarded with an island, or something equivalent, and at least, were honoured with rank and title. If, with these hopes and expectations, you are willing to return to my service, do it a God's name; but, if you think I will unhinge and deviate from the ancient customs of chivalry, you are grievously mistaken: wherefore, friend Sancho, you may go home again, and declare my intention to your wife Teresa, and if she is pleased, and you are willing to depend upon my favour, bene quidem, if not, let us shake hands and part; while there are pease in the dovehouse, I shall never want pigeons; and remember, my child, that it is better to be rich in hope, than poor in possession; and that a good claim is preferable to bad pay. I talk in this manner, Sancho, to shew that I can pour forth a volley of proverbs as well as you; and finally, I must and will give you to understand, that if you do not choose to serve me on these terms, and share my fortune, whatsoever it may be, I pray God may prosper and make a saint of you; for my part, I shall not want squires more obedient and careful, though less troublesome and talkative than your worship."

When Sancho heard this firm resolution of his master, the sky began to lour, and down flagged the wings of his heart in a moment; for, he had believed, that the knight would not set out without him, for all the wealth in the world. While he thus remained pensive and dejected, in came Sampson Carrasco, followed by the niece, who was very desirous to hear, with what arguments he would dissuade her uncle from going again in quest of adventures. Sampson, who was a notable wag, no sooner entered, than embracing the knight, as at first, he pronounced with an audible voice, "O flower of knight-errantry, resplendent sun of arms, thou glory and mirror of the Spanish nation! may it please the Almighty, of his infinite power, that if any person or persons shall raise any impediment to obstruct thy third sally, they may never extricate themselves from the labyrinth of their desires, or accomplish what they so unjustly wish!" Then turning to the duenna, "Mrs. housekeeper," said he, "you need not now repeat St. Apollonia's prayer; for, I know it is the precise determination of the stars, that signor Don Quixote shall again execute his new and lofty plan; and I should greatly burden my conscience, if I forbore to intimate, and desire, that this knight will no longer withhold and detain the force of his valiant arm, and the virtue of his heroic soul; because, by his delay, he retards the righting of wrongs, the protection of orphans, the honour of maidens, the favour of widows, the support of wives, with many other things of that nature, which regard, concern, depend upon, and appertain to the order of knight-errantry. Courage! signor Don Quixote, beautiful and brave; may your worship and grandeur set out, before to-morrow morning; and if any thing be wanting to forward your expedition, here am I, ready to make it good with my person and fortune; and if need be, to serve your magnificence in quality of squire; an office in the execution of which I should think myself extremely happy."

Don Quixote hearing this proffer, turned to Sancho, saying, "Did not I tell thee, San-
cho, that I should not want for squires? Take notice who it is that offers to attend me;
who, but the unheard-of batchelor Sampson Carrasco, the perpetual darling and delight
of the court-yards belonging to the Salamancan schools, sound of body, strong of limb,
a silent sufferer of heat and cold, hunger and thirst, and endued with all those
qualifications which are requisite in the squire of a knight-errant; but, heaven will not
permit me, for my own satisfaction, to break and demolish this pillar of learning, this
urn of sciences, and to hew down such an eminent branch of the liberal arts. No, let this
new Sampson stay at home, and honour the place of his nativity, together with the grey
hairs of his ancient parents; while I make shift with any sort of squire, since Sancho will
not vouchsafe to go along with me."

"Y—yes, I do vouchsafe!" cried Sancho, blubbering, "it shall never be said of me,
dear master, that when the victuals were eaten up, the company sneaked off; I am not
come of such an ungrateful stock; for, all the world, and especially my own townsmen
know, what sort of people the Panzas were, of whom I am descended; besides, I have
perceived, and am sensible, by many good works, and more good words, that your wor-
ship is actually inclined to do for me; and, if I have haggled more than enough about my
wages, it was to please my wife, who, if she once takes in hand to persuade me to any
thing, no cooper's adze drives the hoops of a barrel as she drives at her purpose, until she
hath gained it; but, after all, a man must be a man, and a woman a woman: now, I being
a man every inch of me, when, or wheresoever I please to shew myself, (that I cannot
deny) I am resolved to be master in my own house, in spite of the devil, the world and
the flesh; and therefore, your worship has no more to do but prepare your will, with the
codicil, so as that it cannot be rebuked; and then let us take our departure, that we may
not endanger the soul of Mr. Sampson, whose conscience, he says, prompts him to per-
suade your worship, to make a third sally through the world; and here I promise again,
to serve your worship, faithfully and lawfully, as well as, and better, than all the squires
that ever attended knights-errant, either in past or present time."

The batchelor was astonished at hearing the manner and conclusion of Sancho's
speech; for, although he had read the first part of his master's history, he never believed
him so diverting as he is there represented; but, now, hearing him talk of the will and
codicil that could not be rebuked, instead of revoked, he was convinced of the truth of
what he had read, and confirmed in the opinion of his being one of the most solemn sim-
pletons of the present age; saying, within himself, two such madmen as the master and
his squire, are not to be paralelled upon earth. In fine, Don Quixote and Sancho were
reconciled, and embraced each other; and, in consequence of the opinion and assent of
the great Carrasco, whom they looked upon as an oracle, it was determined that they
should depart in three days, during which they would have time to provide themselves
with necessaries for the journey, and find a compleat helmet for the knight, who insisted
upon carrying one along with him, into the field. Sampson, accordingly, undertook to
accommodate him, saying, he could command an helmet that was in the possession of
a friend of his; though the brightness of the metal was not a little obscured by the rust
and mould which it had contracted.

Innumerable were the curses which were vented against the batchelor, by the house-
keeper and niece, who tore their hair, and scratched their faces, and like the hired

mourners, formerly in use, lamented the departure, as if it had been the death of their master. But, Sampson's view in persuading him to another sally, was to execute a design which he had concerted with the curate and barber; as will appear in the sequel. In short, during those three days, Don Quixote and Sancho furnished themselves with every thing they thought they should have occasion for: the squire pacified his wife, the knight appeased his niece and house-keeper; and on the evening of the fourth day, without being perceived by any living soul but the batchelor, who insisted upon accompanying them half a league out of town, they set out, and took the road to Toboso; Don Quixote mounted on his trusty Rozinante, and Sancho throned upon his old friend Dapple, with a pair of bags well-lined with belly-timber, and a purse of money, which his master deposited in his hands, in case of accidents in their expedition.

Sampson embracing the knight, intreated him to write an account of his good or evil fortune, that he might congratulate or sympathize with him, as the laws of friendship require. Don Quixote assured him, he would comply with his request; the batchelor returned to the village, and the other two pursued their way towards the great city of Toboso.

## CHAPTER VIII.

### An account of what happened to Don Quixote, in his journey to visit his mistress Dulcinea del Toboso.

"Blessed be the almighty Ala!" saith Cid Hamet Benengeli, in the beginning of this chapter; and this benediction he repeats three times, in consequence of finding Don Quixote and Sancho in the field again; observing, that the readers of this agreeable history may assure themselves that, from this period, the exploits of the knight and his squire begin. He therefore persuades them to forget the former adventures of our sage hero, and fix their attention upon those which are to come; and which now begin in the road to Toboso, as the others took their origin in the field of Montiel; and truly his demand is but reasonable, considering the fair promise he makes. Thus therefore he proceeds:

Scarce had Samson left Don Quixote and Sancho by themselves, when Rozinante began to neigh, and Dapple to bray most melodiously; a circumstance which was looked upon by both our adventurers, as a fortunate signal, and most happy omen; though, to deal candidly with the reader, the brayings of the ass exceeded in number the neighings of the horse; from whence Sancho concluded, his fortune would surmount and overtop that of his master. But, whether or not he founded his belief on his knowledge in judicial astrology, I cannot determine, the history being silent on that subject; yet, certain it is, he had been heard to say, when he stumbled or fell, that he wished he had not stirred over his own threshold; for, nothing was to be got by a stumble or fall but a torn shoe,

or a broken bone; and truly, simple as he was, he had some reason for making that observation.

"Friend Sancho," said Don Quixote, "the night is so far advanced, that we shall not be able to reach Toboso by day-light; yet, thither I am determined to go, before I engage in any other adventure, that I may receive the benediction and good leave of the peerless Dulcinea, by the help of which I shall certainly atchieve, and happily perform the most perilous exploits; for, nothing in this life exalts the valour of knights-errant so much as the favour of their mistresses." "I am of the same way of thinking," replied the squire; "but, I believe your worship will find some difficulty in seeing her in a proper place for courtship, or indeed, for receiving her blessings, unless she throws it over the pales of the yard through which I saw her for the first time, when I carried the letter that gave an account of the folly and mad pranks I left your worship committing in the heart of the brown mountain." "Didst thou then actually imagine," said Don Quixote, "that those were the pales of a yard, over or through which thou sawest that paragon of gentleness and beauty? Certainly they could be no other than galleries, arcades or corridores, such as belong to rich and royal palaces." "It may be so," answered Sancho, "but, either my memory fails me very much, or, to me they seemed no better than the pales of a farmer's yard." "Be that as it will," resumed Don Quixote, "thither we will go, and at any rate get sight of her; for, be it through pales, windows, crannies, or the rails of a garden, so the least ray of that sun of beauty reach mine eyes, it will enlighten my understanding, and fortify my heart, in such a manner, that I shall remain the unequalled phenix of valour and discretion." "Truly, sir," said the squire, "when I saw that same sun of my lady Dulcinea del Toboso, it was not so bright as to send forth any rays at all; but, the case was, the wheat that her ladyship was winnowing, as I told you before, raised such a cloud of dust about her, as quite darkened her countenance." "Wilt thou still persist, Sancho," replied the knight, "in saying, thinking, believing, and affirming, that my mistress Dulcinea was employed in such a mean office, so wide of all that is, or ought to be practised by persons of rank, who are created and reserved for other exercises and amusements, that denote their quality at the distance of a bow-shot. Thou seemest to forget, O Sancho! those verses of our poet, in which he paints the labours that, in their crystal bowers, engrossed the four nymphs, who, raising their heads above the waves of their beloved Tagus, sat down to work in the verdant meadow, those rich and silken webs, which, as the ingenious poet describes, were with gold and pearls adorned and interweaved. In this manner my mistress must have been employed when thou sawest her; but, some wicked inchanter, envious of my happiness and fame, converts and perverts every thing that yields me pleasure, into shapes and figures different from its real appearance; and in that history of my atchievements which, they say, is printed, if the author be some sage, who is an enemy to my success, I am afraid, he hath confounded one thing with another, and clogged every fact with a thousand falshoods; straying from his subject, to recount actions quite foreign to the skilful detail of a true history. O envy! thou root of infinite mischief, and canker-worm of virtue! The commission of all other vices, Sancho, is attended with some sort of delight; but, envy produces nothing in the heart that harbours it, but rage, rancour and disgust." "So say I, master," answered Sancho; "and I suppose, in this legend or history of us, which batchelor Carrasco says he

has seen, my reputation goes like a jolting hackney-coach, and is tossed about, as the saying is, like a tennis-ball. Though in good faith, I never spoke an ill word of any inchanter whatsomever; nor am I rich enough to stir up envy in any living soul: true it is, I am a little waggish, and have a small spice of knavery at bottom; but, all this is crowned and covered with the broad cloak of my simplicity, which is always natural, and never affected. And if there was nothing else but my believing, as I always do, firmly and sincerely in God, as well as in all that is owned and believed by the holy Roman catholic church; and my being a mortal enemy, as I certainly am, to the Jews; the historians ought to have mercy on me, and use me tenderly in their writings: but, let them say what they will, I, naked was born, and naked remain; and if I lose nothing, as little I gain: though provided I see myself mentioned in a book, and circulate through the world from hand to hand, I don't value what they can say of me, a fig's end."

"That observation," said Don Quixote, "puts me in mind of what happened to a famous poet of this age, who having composed a severe satire against the court-ladies, omitted to insert one in particular, by name, so that it was doubtful whether or not she was implied in any part of the performance. The lady, thus neglected, complained to the poet, asking what he had seen in her character, unworthy of being described among the rest, and desiring him to enlarge the satire, that she might be included in the supplement, or look to himself. The author complied with her request, lashing her in terms not fit to be named; and she was perfectly well satisfied with the fame of being infamous. Of a piece with this ambition was that reported of the shepherd, who set fire to the celebrated temple of Diana, reckoned one of the wonders of the world, with no other view than to render his name immortal; and although there was a severe edict, prohibiting all persons whatever from making mention of his name, either by word or writing, that he might not accomplish his aim, it is very well known at this day, that his name was Erostratus. This likewise bears an affinity to that occurrence which passed at Rome, between that great emperor Charles the Vth, and a certain knight. The emperor went to visit the famous temple of the rotunda, which was of old called the Pantheon, but is now more happily named the church of All-saints, the most entire edifice that remains of heathen Rome, and which most of all evinces the grandeur and magnificence of its founders. It is built in the shape of half an orange, of a vast extent, and very well lighted, though it has but one window, or rather a round lanthorn at its top, from whence the emperor considered the inside of the structure, being attended by a Roman knight, who described the excellence and ingenious contrivance of that vast and memorable work, and after they had descended, said to him, 'Sacred sir, a thousand times was I seized with an inclination to clasp your majesty in my arms, and throw myself down from the lanthorn, in order to eternize my name.' 'I thank you,' replied the emperor, 'for having resisted such a wicked suggestion, and henceforward, will never give you an opportunity of repeating such a proof of your loyalty; avoid my presence, and never presume to speak to me again.' But, notwithstanding this severe command, he conferred upon him some extraordinary favour. My meaning, Sancho, is, that the desire of fame is a most active principle in the human breast. What, do'st thou imagine was the motive that prevailed on Horatius to throw himself from the bridge, armed at all points, into the depth of the river Tyber? what induced Mutius to burn his hand and arm? what impelled

Curtius to dart himself into the flaming gulph, which opened in the midst of Rome? what prompted Caesar to pass the Rubicon, in spite of all the unfavourable omens that appeared? and, to give you a more modern instance, what consideration bored the ships, and left on shore, encompassed with enemies, those valiant Spaniards, in the new world, under the conduct of the most courteous Cortez? All these, and many other great and various exploits, are, were and shall be performed, in consequence of that desire of fame, which flatters mortals with a share of that immortality which they deem the merited reward of their renowned atchievements: although, we catholic christian knights-errant, ought to pay greater attention to that glory which is to come, and eternally survives within the etherial and celestial mansions, than to the vanity of that fame which is obtained in this present, perishable state, and which, considered in its longest duration, must end at length, with the world itself, which hath its appointed period. Wherefore, Sancho, our works must not exceed the limits prescribed by the christian religion, which we profess. We must, in slaying giants, extirpate pride; get the better of envy by benevolence and virtue; resist anger with patience and forbearance; conquer gluttony and sloth by temperance and watchfulness; luxury and lewdness by our fidelity to those whom we constitute mistresses of our inclination; and idleness by travelling through all parts of the world, in quest of opportunities to evince ourselves not only christians, but, moreover, renowned knights. Thus, Sancho, thou seest the means of acquiring that superlative praise which produces fame and reputation."

"All that your worship hath hitherto said," replied the squire, "I understand perfectly well; but, for all that, I wish you would dissolve me one doubt, which hath this moment struck me in the noddle." "Thy meaning is resolve, Sancho," said the knight; "in good time, out with it, and I will give thee satisfaction, as far as my own knowledge extends." "Tell me, then, signor," proceeded Sancho, "where now are all those Julys and Augusts, and adventuresome knights who died so long ago?" "The heathens," answered Don Quixote, "are doubtless, in hell, and the christians, if they were good catholics, either in purgatory or in heaven." "Right," said the squire; "let us next enquire, if the tombs that contain the bodies of that sort of gentry are lighted with silver lamps; or the walls of their chapels adorned with crutches, winding-sheets, periwigs, legs and eyes made of wax: if not, pray in what manner are they adorned?" To this question, Don Quixote answered, "that the sepulchres of the heathen heroes were, for the most part, sumptuous temples: the ashes of Julius Caesar were placed upon the top of a stone-pyramid, of vast dimensions, still to be seen at Rome, under the name of St. Peter's obelisk: the emperor Adrian's tomb was a building as large as a good village, formerly called Moles Adriani, but, at present, the castle of St. Angelo; and queen Artemisia buried her husband Mausolus in a monument that was accounted one of the seven wonders of the world. But none of these sepulchres, nor any other belonging to the heathens, were adorned with shrouds, offerings, or marks to denote the sanctity of the persons there buried." "So I perceive," said Sancho, "and now tell me, whether it be more meritorious to slay a giant, or raise up the dead to life again?" "The answer is plain," replied the knight, "it is more meritorious to reanimate the dead." "Then, I have caught you fairly," cried the squire; "he who revives the dead, restores sight to the blind, straightens the crooked, heals the sick; before whose tomb the lamps continually burn; whose chapels are filled with de-

vout people who adore his relics upon their knees: I say, he shall have more fame in this world, and that which is to come, than all the heathen emperors and knights-errant that ever lived have left, or will leave behind them." "I am very sensible of the truth of what you alledge," answered the knight. "Now, this fame, this grace, this prerogative, or what you call it," resumed the squire, "is vested in the bodies and relics of the saints; and with the approbation and licence of our holy mother-church, they have their lamps, tapers, shrouds, crutches, pictures, periwigs, eyes and legs, whereby the devotion of the people is increased, and their own christian fame promulgated: the bodies and relics of saints are carried upon the shoulders of kings, who kiss the very fragments of their bones, with which they enrich and adorn their most precious altars and oratories." "What would'st thou have me infer from all this?" said Don Quixote. "My meaning," replied Sancho, "is, that we should turn saints immediately, and so with the greater dispatch acquire that fame which we are in search of; and pray, take notice, signor, it was but yesterday, or t'other day, as one may say in comparison, that they canonised and beatified two bare-footed friars; and people now think it a great happiness to be allowed to touch and kiss the iron chains with which they girded and tormented their poor bodies, and which are in greater esteem than the sword of Orlando, which, as the report goes, is kept in the armoury of our lord the king, whom God in heaven bless: wherefore, dear master, it is better to be an humble friar of any order whatever, than the most valiant knight that ever breathed; for, with God, two dozen of disciplines will more avail than as many thousand back-strokes, whether they be bestowed on giants, dragons or hobgoblins." "All this is very true," answered Don Quixote, "but, we cannot all be friars, and various are the paths by which God conducts the good to heaven. Chivalry itself is a religious order, and some that were knights are now saints in glory." "True," resumed the squire, "but, I have often heard it observed, that there are more friars than knights in heaven." "The reason," said the knight, "is, because there is a greater number of monks than of the other order." "And yet there are many knights-errant," replied the squire. "There is indeed a good number," answered Don Quixote, "but very few that deserve the name."

In this, and other such discourse, they passed that night and the following day, without encountring any thing worthy of being mentioned; a circumstance that chagrined our knight not a little. Next day, however, in the twilight, they descried the great city of Toboso, at sight of which, Don Quixote's spirits were exhilarated, and Sancho's depressed, because he did not know where to find the house of Dulcinea, whom he had never seen, neither had his master ever beheld this peerless princess; so that the one suffered perturbation from the desire of seeing her, and the other because he had not seen her; and indeed, Sancho could not contrive how to manage the affair, when his master should send him to Toboso. In fine, Don Quixote resolved to enter the city, in the dark; and with this view, they tarried in a grove of oaks, not far from the gate, till the night was advanced; then entered the town, where they met with things which amount to things indeed.

CHAPTER IX.

Which contains what you will see in the perusal of it.

It was midnight, or thereabouts, when Don Quixote and Sancho leaving their covert, entered the city of Toboso, which was then in profound silence, all its inhabitants being asleep, and lying with outstretched legs, as the saying is. The night was clear, tho' Sancho wished it otherwise, that in the darkness he might find an excuse for his imposition; and nothing was heard in the whole town but the barking of dogs, which thundered in Don Quixote's ears, and very much disturbed the heart of Sancho: yet, from time to time, they were saluted by the braying of asses, the grunting of hogs, and the mewing of cats; which different notes being augmented by the stillness of the night, were considered as ill omens by the enamoured knight, who, nevertheless, said to his squire, "Son Sancho, lead on to the palace of Dulcinea, whom, perhaps, we shall find awake." "Body of the sun!" cried Sancho, "what palace should I lead to? when I saw her highness she was in a very small cottage." "Then she must have been retired," answered the knight, "to some small apartment of her castle, to divert herself with her damsels, according to the use and custom of princesses and ladies of rank." "Signor," said the squire, "since your worship, in spite of all that I can say, will have my lady Dulcinea's house to be a castle, is this an hour to find the gate open? and will it be decent for us to throw the whole family into confusion and uproar, by making a racket, and demanding entrance, at this time of night? Do you think we are going to a bawdy-house, like your fornicators, who rap and knock, and enter at any hour of the four and twenty?" "First of all, let us fairly find the castle," replied the knight, "and then I will tell thee what is to be done; and take notice, Sancho, for either mine eye-sight fails me, or that great shadowy building before us is the palace of Dulcinea." "Advance then," answered Sancho, "perhaps it may be so; and yet, tho' I should see it with mine eyes, and touch it with my hands, I will believe it as much as I believe it is now twelve a clock at noon."

Don Quixote, however, proceeded, and having gone about two hundred paces, came up with the building that produced the shadow, and perceiving it an high steeple, found it was no castle, but in reality the principal church in town. "We are arrived at the cathedral, Sancho," said he. "So I perceive," replied the squire, "and God grant we be not arrived at our graves! for, it is no good sign to be strolling about churchyards, at these hours: besides, I have already told your worship, (if my memory serves me right) that my lady's house stands in a blind alley." "The curse of God light on thee, for a blockhead as thou art!" cried Don Quixote, "where didst thou ever hear of castles and royal palaces built in blind alleys?" "Signor," answered Sancho, "every country has its own customs; and perhaps, it is the custom here, in Toboso, to raise palaces and grand edifices in blind alleys; I therefore humbly beseech your worship to let me search all the streets and alleys I shall meet with; and who knows but in some corner I may light on this same castle, which I wish the dogs had devoured, before it had brought us to such perplexity and confusion." "Talk respectfully, Sancho, of those things that appertain to my mistress,"

said the knight; "let us spend our holyday in peace, and not throw the helve after the hatchet." "Well, I will be pacified," answered the squire, "tho', how can I endure your worship should expect that I who have seen my lady's house but once, should know it always, and even find it out, in the middle of the night, when you yourself are at a loss, tho' you must have seen it a thousand times." "You distract me, Sancho," cried Don Quixote: "hark ye, heretick, have not I told you a thousand times, that in all the days of my life, I never saw the peerless Dulcinea, nor ever crossed the threshold of her palace, being only enamoured by hearsay, and the great reputation of her beauty and discretion?" "I hear your worship say so now," replied Sancho, "and tell you in my turn, that if you have not seen her, no more have I." "That is impossible," resumed the knight, "at least, you told me, you had seen her winnowing wheat, when you brought back an answer to the letter with which I sent you to her habitation." "Truly, signor, you must not depend upon that," answered Sancho, "for, you must know, my seeing her, and bringing back the answer, was also, upon hearsay; and I am as incapable of giving any account of the lady Dulcinea as I am of pulling the moon by the nose." "Sancho! Sancho!" said Don Quixote, "there is a time for jesting, and a time when jokes are very unseasonable; tho' I say, I have never seen, or spoke with the mistress of my soul, there is no reason for thy making the same declaration, which thou knowest is so contrary to the truth."

While they thus conversed together, they perceived a person passing that way, with a couple of mules, and by the noise of a plough-share which they dragged along, justly concluded that he was a peasant who had risen before day, to go to labour: they were not mistaken; it was actually a labourer, who went along singing the ballad of Ronscevalles [1]*; which the knight no sooner heard than he exclaimed, "Let me die, Sancho! if any thing lucky will befall us to-night; don't you hear what that peasant is singing?" "Yes," said Sancho, "but, what has the defeat at Ronscevalles to do with our affair? if he had sung the ballad of Calaynos, it would have been the same thing with regard to our good or evil fortune."

Don Quixote said to the peasant, who was by this time come up, "Can you tell me, honest friend, and the blessing of God attend you, in what part of this city stands the palace of the peerless princess Donna Dulcinea del Toboso?" "Signor," answered the young man, "I am a stranger, and have been but a few days in town, in the service of a rich farmer, whose lands I till; but, in that house that fronts you live the curate and sexton of the parish, and either or both can give your worship an account of that same princess; for, they keep a register of all the inhabitants of Toboso; tho', I believe, there is no such thing as a princess in the whole place: there are indeed many ladies of fashion, and every one may be a princess in her own house." "She whom I ask for, must be one of these," said the knight. "It may be so," answered the peasant, "but, I shall be overtaken by the morning." So saying, he drove on his mules, without waiting for any more questions.

Sancho, seeing his master in suspence, and over and above dissatisfied, "Signor," said he, "day begins to break, and it will not be altogether convenient, to let the sun find us here in the street; we had better quit the city, and look out for some wood in the neigh-

* Like our Chevy-chase.[2]

bourhood, where your worship may enjoy the cool shade; and I will return by day, and search every hole and cranny in Toboso for this house, castle, or palace of my lady, and it will be very unfortunate indeed, if I cannot find it; and if I have the good luck to meet with her ladyship, I will tell her where and how I have left your worship, in expectation of her contriving some means whereby you may visit her, without any prejudice to her honour and reputation." "Sancho," cried Don Quixote, "thou hast uttered a thousand sentences within the compass of a few words; the counsel thou hast given me I relish, and most willingly receive: come, my son, let us go in quest of some thicket, where I may embower myself, while thou shalt return to seek, see and talk with my mistress, from whose courtesy and discretion I hope to receive more than miraculous favours."

Sancho burned with impatience to see his master fairly out of town, that he might not detect the falsehood of the answer which he pretended to bring from Dulcinea, while he remained in the brown mountain; he therefore pressed him to depart, and, about two miles from the city, they found a thicket or wood, where Don Quixote took up his residence, while Sancho went back to commune with Dulcinea; and, in the course of his embassy, met with adventures that demand new credit and fresh attention.

## CHAPTER X.

## Gives an account of the stratagem which Sancho practised, in order to enchant the lady Dulcinea; with other circumstances equally ludicrous and true.

The author of this stupendous history, when he comes to relate what is contained in this chapter, says, he would have willingly passed it over in silence, because he was afraid that it would not be believed; for, here, the madness of Don Quixote soars to the highest pitch of extravagance that can be imagined, and even, by two bow-shots, at least, exceeds all credit and conception: yet, notwithstanding this jealousy and apprehension, he has recounted it in the same manner as it happened, without adding to the history, or detracting one tittle from the truth, undervaluing the risk he runs of being deemed apocryphal; and surely, he was in the right, for, truth may bend, but will never break, and always surmounts falsehood, as oil floats above water. Wherefore, he proceeds in the narrative, saying:

Don Quixote having taken his station in the forest, grove, or wood, near the great city of Toboso, ordered Sancho to go back to town, and not return to his presence, before he should have spoken to his mistress, and begged, in his name, that she would be pleased to grant an interview to her captive knight, and deign to bestow upon him her blessing, thro' which he might expect the most happy issue to all his attempts and enterprizes.

The squire, having undertaken to execute this command, and to bring back as favourable an answer as he had brought the first time; "Go, my son," said the knight, "and be not confounded when you find yourself beamed upon by that resplendent sun of beauty, which is the object of your inquiry: happy thou, above all the squires that ever lived! Be sure to retain in thy memory, every circumstance of thy reception: observe if she changes colour, while thou art delivering my message; if she is discomposed, and under confusion at the mention of my name; whether she sinks upon her cushion, or happens, at the time, to be seated under the rich canopy of her authority:[1] if she be standing, take notice whether or not, she sometimes supports herself on one foot, sometimes on the other; and if she repeats her answer more than once, changing it from kind to harsh, from sour to amorous; and if she lifts up her hand to adjust her hair, altho' it be not disordered; finally, son, mark all her gestures and emotions; and if thou bringest me an exact detail of them, I shall be able to divine her most abstruse sentiments, touching the concerns of my passion; for, know, Sancho, if thou art still to learn, among lovers, the least gesticulation in their external behaviour, while the conversation turns upon their amours, is, as it were, a messenger that brings a most certain account of what passes within the soul. Go, friend, and enjoy thy fate, so much more favourable than thy master's; and return with much more success than that which I dread and expect in this cruel solitude, where I now remain." "I go," replied Sancho, "and will return in a twinkling; therefore, good your worship, do encourage that little heart of yours, which, at present, must be no bigger than a hazle-nut; and consider, as the saying is, a stout heart flings misfortune; where you meet with no hooks, you need expect no bacon; and again, the hare often starts, where the hunter least expects her. This I observe, because, tho' we did not find the palace and castle of my lady, in the night; now that it is day, I hope to stumble upon it, when I least expect to see it, and if so be, I once catch it, let me alone with her." "Sancho," said the knight, "God grant me better fortune in my desires than you have in the application of the proverbs you utter."

This was no sooner said, than Sancho switching Dapple, quitted the knight, who remained on horseback, resting his legs upon his stirrups, and leaning upon his lance, his imagination being engrossed by the most melancholy suggestions. Here let us leave him, and proceed with Sancho Panza, who parting from his master, in equal perplexity and confusion, no sooner found himself clear of the wood, than looking back, and perceiving that Don Quixote was not in sight, he alighted from his ass, and sitting down at the root of a tree, began to catechise himself, in these words: "Brother Sancho, be so good as to let us know, where your worship is going? are you in search of some stray beast? No truly! What then is your errand? why, really, I am going in search of a thing of nought, a princess, God wot, and in her, the sun and the whole heaven of beauty. And pray, where may you expect to meet with this that you mention, Sancho? where, but in the great city of Toboso. Well, and, by whose order are you going upon this enquiry? by order of the renowned knight Don Quixote de la Mancha, the righter of wrongs, who gives thirst to the hungry, and food to those that are dry. All this is mighty well; but, do you know the house, Sancho? my master says, it must be some royal palace, or stately castle. But have you never once seen this same princess? neither I nor he ever set eyes on her. And do you think it will be well bestowed, if the inhabitants of Toboso, getting

notice that you are come with an intention to wheedle away their princesses, and disturb their dames, should break every bone of your skin, and grind your ribs to a paste, with pure cudgelling? Verily, they would not be much to blame, unless they considered, that I do nothing but execute my master's command, and being only a messenger, am not in fault: never trust to that, Sancho; for the Manchegans are as choleric as honourable, and will not suffer themselves to be tickled by any person whatever. Ecod! if you are once smoaked, you will come but scurvily off. Bodikins! since that be the case, why should I plague myself seeking a cat with three legs, for another man's pleasure? besides, you may as well seek for a magpye in Rabena, or a batchelor in Salamanca, as for Dulcinea in Toboso: the devil, and none but the devil, has sent me on this fool's errand!"

The result of this soliloquy was another that broke out in these words: "There is a remedy for every thing but death, under whose yoke we must all pass, will we nill we, when this life is at an end: this master of mine, as I have perceived by a thousand instances, is mad enough to be shackled among straw; and truly, I am not much behind him in folly: nay, indeed I am more mad than he, seeing I serve and follow him, if there be any truth in the proverb that says, Tell me your company, and I will tell you your manners: and the other, Not he with whom you was bred, but he by whom you are fed.[2] Now he being, as he certainly is, a madman, ay, and so mad, as for the most part to mistake one thing for another, affirming white to be black, and black to be white; as plainly appeared, when he took the windmills for giants, the mules of the friars for dromedaries, the flocks of sheep for opposite armies; and a great many other things in the same stile: I say, it will be no difficult matter to make him believe, the first country-wench I shall meet with, to be his mistress Dulcinea: and if he bogles at swallowing the cheat, I will swear lustily to the truth of what I affirm; and if he swears also, I will swear again; and if he is positive, I will be more positive; so, that come what will, my obstinacy shall always exceed his. Perhaps, by this stubborn behaviour, I shall get rid of all such troublesome messages for the future; when he finds what disagreeable answers I bring: or, perhaps, which I rather believe, he will think that one of those enchanters, who, he says, bear him a grudge, hath transmographied her shape, in order to vex and disquiet him."

Sancho having found out this expedient, was quite calm and satisfied in his mind, and thinking he had brought the business to a good bearing, remained where he was till the evening, that Don Quixote might think he had sufficient time to execute his orders, and return. Every thing succeeded so well to his wish, that when he got up to mount Dapple, he descried three country-wenches riding from Toboso, towards the place where he stood, upon three young he or she-asses, for, the author does not declare their sex; tho', in all likelihood, they were of the female gender; as your village-maidens commonly ride upon she-asses; but, this being a circumstance of small importance, we shall not give ourselves any trouble to ascertain it.

In short, Sancho no sooner perceived the wenches, than he rode back at a round trot, to his master, whom he found sighing bitterly, and pouring forth a thousand amorous complaints: the knight seeing him arrive, "Well, friend Sancho," said he, "is this day to be marked with a white or black stone?" "Your worship," answered the squire, "had better mark it with red ochre, like the titles on a professor's chair, that it may be seen the better, by those who look at it." "At that rate," replied Don Quixote, "thou bringest me

good news." "So good," answered Sancho, "that your worship has nothing to do, but, to mount Rozinante, and gallop into the plain, where you will see my lady Dulcinea del Toboso, and two of her damsels, coming this way, to pay you a visit." "Gracious God!" cried the knight, "what is that you say, friend Sancho? Take care how you deceive me, endeavouring, by feigned joy, to enliven my real sadness." "What should I get, by deceiving your worship?" said the squire; "besides, you can easily be satisfied of the truth of what I say; make haste, signor, come and see our mistress the princess, arrayed and adorned; in short, as she ought to be: her damsels and she are all one flame of gold; all covered with pearls, diamonds, rubies, and brocard, more than ten hands deep; their hair flowing loose about their shoulders, like so many sun-beams waving with the wind; and moreover, they are mounted on three pyed bellfreys, that it would do one's heart good to see them." "Palfreys you mean, Sancho," said the knight. "There is no great difference," answered the squire, "between palfreys and bellfreys; but, be that as it will, they are the finest creatures one would desire to see, especially my lady Dulcinea, who is enough to stupify the five senses." "Come then, my son," replied Don Quixote, "and as a gratuity for bringing this piece of news, equally welcome and unexpected, I bestow upon thee the spoils of the first adventure I shall atchieve; and if thou art not satisfied with that recompence, I will give unto thee the foals that shall this year be brought forth by my three mares, which thou knowest we left with young upon our town-common." "I stick to the foals," cried the squire, "for, as to the spoils of our first adventure, I question whether or not they will be worth accepting."

By this time, they were clear of the wood, and in sight of the three country-maidens; when the knight lifting up his eyes, and surveying the whole road to Toboso, without seeing any thing but them, began to be troubled in mind, and asked Sancho, if the ladies had got out of town when he left them. "Out of town?" said Sancho. "What! are your worship's eyes in the nape of your neck, that you don't see them coming towards us, glittering and shining like the sun at noon?" "I see no body," replied the knight, "but three country-wenches riding upon asses." "God deliver me from the devil!" cried the squire, "is it possible that three bellfreys, or how-d'ye-call-ums, white as the driven snow, should appear no better than asses, in your worship's eyes? By the lord! I'll give you leave to pluck off every hair of my beard, if that be the case." "Then I tell thee, Sancho," said his master, "they are as certainly he or she-asses as I am Don Quixote, and thou Sancho Panza, at least, so they seem to me." "Hold your tongue, signor," replied Sancho, "and never talk in that manner, but, snuff your eyes, and go and make your reverence to the mistress of your heart, who is just at hand."

So saying, he advanced towards the damsels, and alighting from Dapple, seized one of their beasts by the halter; then fell upon his knees, before the rider, to whom he addressed himself in this manner: "Queen, princess and dutchess of beauty, will your highness and greatness be pleased to receive into grace and favour your captive knight, who sits there, stupified to stone, utterly confounded and deprived of pulse, at seeing himself in presence of your magnificence: I am Sancho Panza his squire, and he is the perplexed and down-trodden knight Don Quixote de la Mancha, alias the knight of the rueful countenance."

By this time, Don Quixote having placed himself on his knees, by Sancho, gazed with

Sancho Panza Presenting the Country Wench as Dulcinea to Don Quixote.

staring eyes, and troubled vision, upon the object which the squire called queen and princess; and perceiving nothing but a country-wench's visage, and that none of the most agreeable, for, it was round and flat-nosed, he remained in the utmost confusion and surprise, without daring to open his lips. The other two damsels were equally astonished at seeing a couple of such different figures kneeling before their companion, whom they had detained; but she, breaking silence, pronounced, in a most ungracious and resentful manner: "Get out of the way, and let us pass, for, we are in a hurry." To this apostrophe, Sancho replied, "O princess and universal lady of Toboso! do not your magnificent bowels yearn, to see upon his marrowbones before your sublimated presence, the very pillar and prop of knight-errantry?" One of the other two hearing this pathetic remonstrance, bauled aloud, "Would I had the currying that ass's hide of thine:[3] mind, forsooth, how your small gentry come and pass their gibes upon us country-folks; as if we could not give them as good as they bring; go about your business, friend, and leave us to mind our'n, and so God b'w'ye."

Here the knight interposing, said, "Rise, Sancho, I can plainly perceive that fortune, not yet tired of persecuting me, hath barred every avenue by which any comfort could arrive at the miserable soul that this carcase contains: and thou! the essence of every thing that is desirable in nature, thou sum of human perfection, and sole remedy of this afflicted heart, by which thou art adored! altho' that malicious enchanter, my inveterate enemy, hath spread clouds and cataracts before mine eyes, to them and them only changing and transforming thy unequalled beauty into the appearance of a poor country-wench; if he hath not also altered my figure into that of some frightful spectre horrid to thy view, deign to look upon me with complacency and love; because thou mayest perceive, by this submissive posture I have assumed, even before thy person thus disguised, the humility with which my soul adores thy charms." "You may go kiss my grannam," cried the damsel, "I'm a fine madam, truly, to hear such gibberish; we should be more obliged to you, if you would get out of our way, and let us go about our own affairs."

Sancho accordingly quitted his hold, leaving her free to go whither she would, and highly pleased with the issue of his stratagem. The suppositious Dulcinea no sooner found herself at liberty, than pricking her palfrey with a goad which was in the end of a stick she had in her hand, the creature galloped across the field with great speed, and feeling the application more severe than usual, began to plunge and kick in such a manner, that my lady fell to the ground. Don Quixote perceiving this accident, ran with great eagerness to raise her up, and Sancho made haste to adjust and gird on the pannel, which had got under the ass's belly. This affair being set to rights, the knight went to lift his enchanted mistress in his arms, and place her on her seat again; but she, starting up from the ground, saved him that trouble, for, retreating a few paces backward, she made a small run, and clapping both hands upon the crupper, leaped upon the pannel as nimble as a falcon, seating herself astride, like a man.

"By St. Roque!" cried Sancho, "my lady mistress is as light as a hawk, and can teach the most dextrous horseman to ride; at one jump, she has sprung into the saddle, and without spurs, makes her palfrey fly like any Zebra; and truly, her damsels are not a whit behind; for, they go scouring along, as swift as the wind." This was actually true, for, Dulcinea was no sooner remounted, than the other two trotted after her, and at last dis-

appeared, after having gone more than half a league, at full speed, without once look-ing behind them.

Don Quixote followed them with his eyes, until they vanished; then, turning to his squire, "Sancho," said he, "thou seest how I am persecuted by enchanters, and mayest perceive how far the malice and grudge they bear me, extend; seeing they have deprived me of the pleasure I should have enjoyed at sight of my mistress in her own beauteous form. Surely, I was born to be an example of misery; the very mark and butt for all the arrows of misfortune; nay, thou art also to observe, Sancho, that those traitors were not contented with a simple metamorphosis of my Dulcinea, but, have transformed and changed her into the base and homely figure of that country-wench; robbing her, at the same time, of that which is so peculiar to ladies of fashion, I mean that sweet scent which is the result of their living among flowers and perfume; for, know, my friend, when I went to lift Dulcinea upon her palfrey, as thou sayest it was, tho' to me, it seemed nei-ther more nor less than a she-ass, I was almost suffocated and poisoned with a whiff of undigested garlic!"

"O! ye miscreants!" cried Sancho, "O! ye malicious and mischievous inchanters! would to God, I could see you all strung by the gills, like so many haddocks! much you know, much you can, and much more will you still be doing. Was it not enough, ye knaves, to change the pearls of my lady's eyes into a couple of cork-tree galls, and her hair of shining gold into the bristles of a red cow's tail; and, in short, to transmography every feature of her countenance, without your meddling with the sweetness of her breath, by which we might have discovered what was concealed beneath that bark of homeliness: tho' to tell the truth, I saw not her homeliness, but beauty, which was ex-ceedingly increased by a mole upon her upper lip, something like a whisker, consisting of seven or eight red hairs, like threads of gold, as long as my hand." "According to the correspondence which the moles of the face have with those of the body," said Don Qui-xote, "Dulcinea must have just such another on the brawny part of her thigh, of the same side; but, hairs of such a length are, methinks, rather too long for moles." "I do assure your worship," answered Sancho, "they seemed as if they had come into the world with her." "I very well believe what you say, my friend," replied the knight; "for, nature hath bestowed nothing on Dulcinea but what is perfectly finished; wherefore, if thou had'st seen an hundred such moles; in her, they would be so many moons and resplendent stars: but, tell me, Sancho, that which you adjusted, and which to me seemed a pannel, was it a plain pad, or a side-saddle?" "It was a great side-saddle," answered the squire, "so rich that half the kingdom would not buy it." "And why could not I see all this?" said the knight. "I say, again, Sancho, and will repeat it a thousand times, that I am the most unfortunate of men."

The rogue Sancho, finding his master so dextrously gulled, and hearing him talk in this mad strain, could scarce refrain from laughing in his face: in fine, a good deal more of this sort of conversation having passed between them, they remounted their beasts, and took the road to Saragosa, where they expected to arrive time enough to be present at the solemn festival yearly celebrated in that famous city; but, before they accom-plished their journey they met with adventures, which, for their variety, novelty and greatness, deserve to be read and recorded, as in the sequel.

<center>CHAPTER XI.</center>

## Of the strange adventure which befel the valiant Don Quixote, with the cart or waggon containing the parliament of death.

D on Quixote jogged along, exceedingly pensive, his thoughts being ingrossed by the scurvy trick which the enchanters had played him, in transforming his mistress Dulcinea into the disagreeable figure of a country-wench; and he could not conceive what remedy he should find for restoring her to her former shape: so much was he absorpt in this reflection, that he insensibly dropt the reins upon the neck of Rozinante, who being sensible of the liberty he enjoyed, at every two steps turned aside to take a pluck at the inviting pasture with which those fields abounded. At length, Sancho Panza rouzed him from this fit of musing, saying, "Signor, melancholy was not made for beasts, but for men; and yet, if men encourage melancholy too much, they became no better than beasts: good your worship be contented, mind what you're about, take hold of Rozinante's reins, rouse up, awake, and shew that gaiety which all knights-errant ought to have. What the devil is the meaning of all this faint-heartedness? Sure you don't know whether we are here or in France! let Satan rather run away with all the Dulcineas upon earth; for, the health of one single knight is of more value than all the inchanted persons or transformations that ever were known." "Peace, Sancho," cried Don Quixote, with a voice that was none of the faintest. "Peace, I say, and utter not such blasphemies against that inchanted lady, of whose disgrace and misfortune I am the sole cause; for, from the envy of my wicked foes, her mischance hath sprung." "So say I," answered Sancho, "for, he that hath seen her before, let him look at her now, and her fortune deplore." "Well mayest thou make that observation, Sancho," said the knight, "seeing thou sawest her in the full perfection of her beauty; as the inchantment did not extend so far as to disturb thy vision, or conceal her charms from thy view: no! against me alone, and my longing eyes, was the force of its poison directed! Yet, nevertheless, Sancho, I cannot help observing that you made but an indifferent picture of her beauty; for, if I rightly remember, you likened her eyes to pearls: now, eyes resembling pearls are more peculiar to dead whitings than to living beauties; and, in my conjecture, Dulcinea's must be rather like green emeralds, arched over with two celestial rainbows: those pearls, therefore, must be compared to her teeth, which, without doubt, you have mistaken for her eyes." "Nothing more likely," answered the squire, "for, I was as much confounded by her beauty as your worship by her ugliness: but, let us recommend this whole business to God, who fore-ordains every thing that is to happen in this vale of tears; in this evil world of ours, where scarce any thing is to be had, without a mixture of falshood, knavery, and sin. One thing, dear sir, of all others, gives me the greatest pain, and that is, to think what method is to be fallen upon, when your worship, after having vanquished some giant or knight, shall command him to go and present himself before the beauty of the lady Dulcinea; where will this poor giant, or this poor miserable object of an vanquished knight, find out the person to whom he is sent? Methinks

I see them strolling up and down, and gaping about thro' the streets of Toboso, in quest of my lady Dulcinea; and if they should stumble upon her in their way, they would no more know her than they would know my father." "Sancho," resumed Don Quixote, "perhaps the enchantment will not extend so far as to disguise Dulcinea to the eyes of those vanquished giants and knights who shall present themselves before her; and in one or two of the first whom I shall conquer and send thither, we will make the experiment, commanding them to return and give me an account of what shall happen to them, with regard to that affair." "Truly, Signor," said Sancho, "I heartily approve of your worship's scheme, because, by this artifice, we will soon learn what we want to know; and if so be, that she is only concealed from your worship, you are the most unfortunate person of the two; for, as my lady Dulcinea enjoys good health and satisfaction, we will comfort ourselves, and make the best of a bad bargain, going about in quest of adventures, and leaving the rest to time, who is the best physician for these and other greater calamities."

Don Quixote would have replied, but was prevented by the appearance of a sort of waggon that crossed the road, full of the strangest figures that can be imagined, and conducted by a frightful demon that drove the mules. The cart being altogether open, without tilt or cover, the first figure that struck the eyes of Don Quixote, was death itself in human shape; next to which appeared an angel, with broad painted wings: on one side, stood an emperor with a crown (seemingly) of gold, upon his head; and hard by death, was the god Cupid, with his bow, quiver and arrows, but without the bandage on his eyes: there was likewise a knight armed capapee, except that he wore neither helmet nor head-piece, but a hat adorned with a plume of variegated feathers. Besides these, there were other personages of different countenance and dress; so that the whole groupe appearing of a sudden, discomposed our hero a little, and filled the heart of Sancho with fear; but, Don Quixote soon recollected himself, and rejoiced, because he looked upon it as some new and perilous adventure. On this supposition, and with an effort of courage capable of encountring the greatest danger, he placed himself before the wain, and with a loud and threatening voice, pronounced, "Driver, coachman, devil, or whatsoever thou art, tell me, strait, whither thou art going, and who those people are whom thou drivest in that carriage, which looks more like Charon's bark than any modern vehicle." The devil stopping his waggon, very courteously replied, "Signor, we are players belonging to the company of Angulo el Malo, and have, this morning, which is the octave of Corpus Christi, been representing, in a village on the other side of yon hill, the piece called the Parliament of death, which we are going to act over again, this very evening, in that other village now in sight; we therefore travel in our habits, to save ourselves the trouble of undressing and dressing anew: this young man plays the part of death, that other represents an angel; the woman, who is the author's wife, acts the queen; he with the plume of feathers is our hero; the emperor you may distinguish by his gilded crown; and I am the devil, which is one of the best characters in the performance; for, I myself, am the chief actor of this company. If your worship is desirous of knowing any thing else concerning our affairs, question me freely, and I will answer with the utmost punctuality, for, being a devil, I understand every thing."

"By the faith of a knight-errant!" said Don Quixote, "when I first descried the waggon, I thought myself on the eve of some great adventure; and now I affirm, that a man

ought to examine things with more senses than one, before he can be assured of the truth: proceed, my honest friends, a God's name, in order to exhibit your entertainment, and if I can serve you in any respect, you may command my endeavours, which shall be heartily and freely exerted for your advantage; for, from my childhood, I have been a great lover of masques and theatrical representations."

While this conversation passed between them, they chanced to be overtaken by one of the company, dressed in motley, hung round with a number of morrice-bells, with a pole in his hand, to the end of which were tied three blown ox-bladders. This merry-andrew advancing to Don Quixote, began to fence with his pole, beating the ground with his bladders, and skipping about, so that his bells rung continually; till at length, Rozinante being disturbed at the uncommon apparition, took the bridle between his teeth; and the knight being unable to restrain him, began to gallop across the plain with more nimbleness than could have been expected from the bones of his anatomy. Sancho seeing his master in danger of falling, leaped from Dapple, and ran with all dispatch to give him all possible assistance, but, before he came up, the knight was overthrown close by Rozinante, who had come to the ground with his lord; and this was the usual end and consequence of all his frolicksome adventures. Scarce had Sancho quitted his beast, to run to the assistance of his master, when the bladder-shaking devil jumped upon Dapple, and began to belabour him with his rattle; so, that being frightened at the noise, rather than with the smart of the application, he took to his heels, and flew towards the village where they intended to perform. Sancho seeing, at the same time, the career of Dapple, and his master's fall, scarce knew which of these misfortunes he ought first to remedy: but at length, as became a loyal servant and trusty squire, his love for his master prevailed over his tenderness for the beast; tho' every time he saw the bladders raised aloft, and discharged upon Dapple's buttocks, he felt the pangs and tortures of death, and would rather have received every thwack upon the apple of his own eye, than have seen it fall upon the least hair of his ass's tail.

In this state of perplexity and tribulation, he arrived at the place where Don Quixote lay, in very indifferent plight, and helping him to mount Rozinante, "Signor," said he, "the devil has run away with Dapple." "Which devil?" cried the knight. "He with the bladders," answered the squire. "I will retrieve him," replied Don Quixote, "even if he should conceal him, in the darkest and deepest dungeon in hell: follow me, Sancho, the waggon moves slowly, and the mules shall atone for the loss of Dapple." "There is no occasion for putting ourselves to that trouble," said the squire, "good your worship be pacified; for, I see the devil has quitted my ass, and returned to the rest of his crew." This observation was actually true, Dapple and his new rider had come to the ground, in imitation of the knight and Rozinante; upon which the devil trudged on foot to the village, and the ass returned to his right owner. "For all that," said Don Quixote, "it will not be amiss to punish the troop, for that devil's incivility, tho' it should be in the person of the emperor himself." "I hope your worship's imagination will harbour no such thoughts," answered Sancho; "take my advice, and never meddle with players, who are a set of people in such high favour with the public, that I have known an actor taken up for two murders, and yet scape scot free: your worship must know, that being the ministers of mirth and pleasure, they are favoured, protected, assisted, and esteemed by every body;

especially if they belong to the king's company, or to some grandee; in which case, all, or most of them, look like princes in their manners and dress." "Nevertheless," replied the knight, "that farcical devil shall not escape unpunished, or applaud himself for what he has done, tho' all mankind should appear in his favour."

So saying, he rode towards the waggon, which was, by this time, pretty near the village; and called aloud, "Stay, my merry men, halt a little, and I will teach you how to treat the asses and cattle belonging to the squires of knights-errant." Don Quixote hollowed so loud as to be heard and understood by the people in the waggon, who judging, by his words, the intention of the speaker, death instantly jumped out of the cart, and was followed by the emperor, the devil-driver, and the angel, with the queen and Cupid in their train: in short, the whole company armed themselves with stones, and drawing up, in order of battle, stood without flinching, to receive the assailant, at point of pebble.

The knight perceiving them arranged in such a formidable squadron, their arms lifted up in a posture that threatened a powerful discharge of stones, checked Rozinante, and began to consider in what manner he should attack them, with least hazard to his person. During this pause, Sancho came up, and seeing him bent upon assaulting such a well-compacted brigade, "It will be the height of madness," said he, "to attempt any such adventure: consider, dear Sir, that there is no kicking against the pricks; and that there is no armour upon earth sufficient to defend your body from such a shower, unless your worship could creep into a bell of brass: you ought also to remember, that it favours more of rashness than of true valour, for one man to attack a whole army, in which death and emperors fight in person, being aided and assisted both by good and evil angels; and if that consideration will not prevail upon you to be quiet, you ought to be diverted from your purpose, by knowing certainly, that among all those enemies, in the appearances of kings, princes, and emperors, there is not so much as one single knight-errant." "Now, indeed," cried Don Quixote, "thou hast hit upon the sole reason that can and ought to dissuade me from my determined design: I neither can nor ought to draw my sword (as I have told thee, on many other occasions) against any person who hath not received the honour of knighthood: to thee, Sancho, it belongs, if so thou art inclined, to take vengeance for the injury done to Dapple, while I, from hence, will assist and encourage thee with salutary advice." "Signor," answered the squire, "there is no occasion to take vengeance of any person whatever; for, it is not the part of a good christian to revenge the wrongs he hath suffered: besides, I will prevail upon my ass to leave the affair to my inclination, which is to live peaceably all the days that heaven shall grant me in this life." "Since that is thy determination," replied the knight, "honest Sancho, discreet Sancho, christian and sincere Sancho, let us leave these phantomes, and go in quest of adventures more dignified and substantial; for, this country seems to promise a great many, and those very extraordinary too."

He accordingly turned his horse, Sancho went to catch Dapple, while death, with his whole flying squadron, returned to their waggon, and proceeded on their journey. Thus, was the dismal adventure of the waggon of death happily terminated by the wholesome advice which Sancho Panza gave to his master, who, next day, met with another equally surprizing, in the person of an enamoured knight-errant.

## CHAPTER XII.

# Of the strange adventure that happened to the valiant Don Quixote, in his encounter with the knight of the mirrours.

The night that followed the rencounter with death, Don Quixote and his squire passed among some tall and shady trees; the knight, by Sancho's persuasion, having eaten of what was found in the store that Dapple carried. During this meal, Sancho said to his master, "What a fool should I have been, signor, if I had chosen, by way of gratification, the spoils of your worship's first adventure, instead of the three foals? Verily, verily, a bird in hand is worth two in the bush." "But, for all that," answered Don Quixote, "had'st thou suffered me to attack them, as I intended, thou would'st have enjoyed, among the spoils, the emperor's golden crown, with Cupid's painted wings, which I would have stript off, against the grain, and put into thy possession." "The sceptres and crowns of your stage-emperors are never made of pure gold, but, of tin or tinsel," replied the squire. "True," said the knight, "the ornaments of comedy ought not to be rich and real, but feigned and artificial, like the drama itself, which I would have thee respect, Sancho, and receive into favour, together with those who represent and compose it; for, they are all instruments of great benefit to the commonwealth, holding, as it were, a looking-glass always before us, in which we see naturally delineated all the actions of life; and no other comparison whatever represents to us more lively, what we are, and what we ought to be, than comedy and her attendants: for example, hast thou never seen a play acted, in which kings, emperors, popes, knights, ladies, and many other characters were introduced? One acts the ruffian, another the sharper, a third the merchant, a fourth the soldier, a fifth the designing fool, and a sixth the simple lover; but, the play being ended, and the dresses laid aside, all the actors remain upon an equal footing." "Yes, I have seen all this," answered Sancho. "Then the very same thing," said the knight, "happens in the comedy and commerce of this world, where one meets with some people playing the parts of emperors, others in the characters of popes, and finally, all the different personages that can be introduced in a comedy; but, when the play is done, that is, when life is at an end, death strips them of the robes that distinguished their stations, and they become all equal in the grave." "A brave comparison!" cried Sancho, "tho' not so new but I have heard it made on divers and sundry occasions, as well as that of the game of chess, during which every piece maintains a particular station and character; but, when the game is over, they are all mixed, jumbled and shaken together in a bag, like mortals in the grave." "Sancho," resumed the knight, "every day you become less simple and more discreet." "Yes," said the squire, "some small portion of your worship's discretion must needs stick to me; as lands which are, in their own nature, sapless and barren, being well dunged and cultivated, come to yield excellent fruit: my meaning is, that your worship's conversation hath fallen like dung upon the barren desart of my understanding, which being cultivated by the time of my service and communication, will, I hope, produce blessed fruit, such as shall not disgrace, nor stray

from the path of that good breeding which your worship hath bestowed on my narrow capacity."

Don Quixote could not help smiling at the affected terms in which Sancho delivered himself, tho' what he said of his own improvement was actually true; for, at certain times, he talked to admiration; and yet, when he attempted to argue, or speak in a polite stile, his efforts always, or for the most part, ended in precipitating himself from the pinnacle of simplicity to the depth of ignorance; his chief talent lying in his memory, which never failed to furnish him with proverbs that he lugged into his discourse, whether they were pat to the purpose or not, as may be seen and observed thro' the whole course of this history.

In this, and other such conversation, the greatest part of the night elapsed, when Sancho began to be inclined to let fall the portcullices of his eyes, as he termed it, when he wanted to go to sleep; he therefore unpannelled Dapple, to let him graze among the rich pasture with which the place abounded; but, Rozinante's saddle he would not remove, in consequence of his master's express order, which was never to unsaddle his steed while they were in the field, or did not sleep under cover; it being an ancient, established custom, observed by all knights-errant, in these cases, to take the bridle out of the horse's mouth, and hang it upon the pummel of the saddle, but, to leave the saddle itself untouched. This expedient was accordingly practised by Sancho, who turned Rozinante loose with Dapple; and between these two animals such a strict, reciprocal friendship subsisted, that, according to tradition from father to son, the author of this true history wrote particular chapters on this very subject; but, in order to preserve the decency and decorum which belongs to such an heroic composition, omitted them; though sometimes he seems to neglect this precaution, and writes, that these two friends used to approach and scrub each other, most lovingly, and after they had rested and refreshed themselves, Rozinante would stretch his head more than half a yard over Dapple's neck, while the two were wont to stand in this posture, with their eyes fixed upon the ground, three whole days together, at least, till they were parted, or compelled by hunger, to go in quest of sustenance: nay, it is confidently reported, that the author hath compared their mutual attachment to the friendship of Nisus and Euryalus, or that which subsisted between Pylades and Orestes. If this be the case, we may, with admiration, conceive how firm the fellowship of those two pacific animals must have been; to the utter confusion of mankind, who so little regard the laws of friendship and society, according to the common saying, There is no trust in profession; the staff will turn into a spear; and as the song goes *, The modes of the court, so common are grown, that a true friend can hardly be met:[1] let no man imagine the author went out of his road, in comparing the friendship of brutes with that of the human species; for, men have received valuable hints, and learned many things of importance from beasts, such as the clyster from storks, gratitude and the use of vomits from dogs, vigilance from the crane, foresight and frugality from the ant, honesty from the elephant, and loyalty from the horse.

* As the original quotation is a fragment that will not complete the sense, I have taken the liberty to make the allusion altogether English.

In fine, Sancho went to sleep, at the root of a cork-tree, and Don Quixote began to slumber under an oak, but being, in a very little time, awaked by a noise behind him, he started up, and employing both eyes and ears to distinguish whence it proceeded, he perceived two men on horseback, one of whom, letting himself drop, as it were, from the saddle, said to the other, "Alight my friend, and unbit the horses; for this place seems to abound with pasture for them, and with silence and solitude, which are the necessary food of my amorous thoughts." He had no sooner pronounced these words, than he threw himself upon the ground, and his armour rattled as he fell, furnishing Don Quixote with a manifest proof of his being a knight-errant: he therefore approached Sancho, who was asleep, and shaking him by the arm, with no small difficulty, brought him to himself; saying, in a low voice, "Brother Sancho, here is an adventure." "God grant it may be a good one," answered the squire, "and pray, signor, whereabouts may her ladyship be?" "Where?" said Don Quixote, "turn thine eyes this way, and behold lying upon the grass, a knight-errant, who, by what I have already observed, cannot be over and above easy in his mind; for, I saw him throw himself upon the ground, with evident marks of vexation, and heard his armour clatter in his fall." "But how has your worship found that this is an adventure?" replied the squire. "I will not positively say that it is altogether an adventure," answered the knight, "but rather the beginning of one; for, thus they usually commence: but, hark! he seems to tune a lute or rebeck, and by his hawking and hemming, I suppose he is going to sing." "In good faith, it is even so," said Sancho, "and he must be some knight-errant in love." "All knights-errant are so," resumed Don Quixote, "but, let us listen, and by the thread of his song, discover the clue of his thoughts; for, from the abundance of the heart the tongue speaketh."

Sancho would have made some reply, but was prevented by the voice of the knight of the wood, which was neither very sweet nor disagreeable; and listening with surprize, they heard him sing the following song:

### I.

Subjected to thy sov'reign will,
　Ah, cruel maid! my fate decree:
The sentence, tho' inhuman still,
　Shall never be declined by me.

### II.

Say, that my death thy joy would move,
　My breath with freedom I'll resign—
Or wouldst thou listen to my love,
　The God himself shall whisper mine.

### III.

This heart, thy vassal whilst I live,
　Like ductile wax, and diamond hard,
Thy stamp will yieldingly receive,
　And keep th' impression unimpair'd.

The knight of the wood finished this complaint with an ah! that seemed to be heaved from the very bottom of his soul, and soon after exclaimed, in a sorrowful tone, "O thou most beautiful and ungrateful woman upon earth! is it possible, that the most serene Casildea de Vandalia, has doomed this her captive knight to consume and exhaust himself in continual peregrinations, in harsh and rugged toils? Is it not enough, that I have established the fame of thy beauty above all comparison, by the extorted confession of all the knights of Navarre, Leon, Tartesia, Castile, and finally of La Mancha?"

"Not so, neither," cried Don Quixote interposing; "for I, who am of La Mancha, never made any such acknowledgment; neither could I, or ought I to make a confession so prejudicial to the beauty of my own mistress: therefore, Sancho, this knight must certainly be disordered in his judgment; but, let us listen, perhaps he will explain himself." "Very like," answered the squire, "he seems to be in the humour of complaining for a whole month."

But, this was not the case; for the knight of the wood, hearing people talk so near him, proceeded no farther in his lamentation, but starting up, called with a courteous and sonorous voice, "Who is there? are you of the number of happy or afflicted?" "Of the afflicted," replied Don Quixote. "Come hither, then," resumed the stranger, "and depend upon it, you will find the very essence of sorrow and affliction."

Don Quixote hearing him speak in such civil and pathetic terms, went towards him, with Sancho at his back, when the complaining knight took him by the hand, saying, "Sit down, Sir knight, for, that you are one of those who profess knight-errantry, I am convinced by finding you in this place, accompanied by solitude and the dews of night, which are the peculiar companions of those who belong to our order."

To this address, Don Quixote replied, "I am a knight of that order you mention; and tho' melancholy, mischance and misfortune have taken up their habitation in my soul, they have not been able to banish from it that compassion which I feel for the unhappy. From the soliloquy you just now uttered, I gather that your misfortunes are of the amorous kind; I mean, that they proceed from the passion you entertain for that beautiful ingrate whom you named in your complaint." While this conversation passed, they sat down together upon the grass, with all the marks of amity and good fellowship, as if at break of day they had not been doomed to break each other's head. "Perchance, Sir knight," said the stranger, "you are in love?" "By mischance I am so," answered Don Quixote, "tho' the vexation that proceeds from well-placed affection, ought rather to be deemed a benefit than misfortune." "True," said the knight of the wood, "if our judgment and reason are not disturbed by disdain, which if exerted severely, seems akin to revenge." "I never was disdained by my mistress," replied Don Quixote. "No indeed, (cried Sancho, who stood hard by) my lady is as meek as a lamb, and as soft as butter."

The stranger knight asked if that was his squire, and the other answering in the affirmative, "I never saw a squire," said he, "that like him, durst intrude upon his master's conversation; at least, I can say so much for mine, who, tho' as tall as his father, was never known to open his lips, when I was engaged in discourse." "In good faith!" cried Sancho, "I have spoke, and will speak again before as good a man as—but, let that rest— the more you stir it, the more it will—."

Here the other squire took hold of Sancho by the arm, saying, "Let you and I go some where, and talk our bellies full, in our own way, and leave our masters at liberty to recount their amours; for, sure I am, the night will be spent before they are done." "With all my heart," replied Sancho, "and I will tell your worship who I am, that you may see whether or not I am qualified to be ranked among your talking squires." They accordingly retired together, and between them passed a conversation every bit as merry as that of their masters was grave.

### CHAPTER XIII.

## In which is continued the adventure of the knight of the wood; with the sage, uncommon and agreeable dialogue that passed between the two squires.

The knights and their squires being thus parted, the first entertained each other with the story of their loves, while the last indulged themselves with a reciprocal account of their own lives; but, the history first of all records the conversation of the domestics, and then proceeds to relate what passed between the masters. The squires, therefore, having chosen a situation, at a convenient distance from the knights, he of the wood accosted Sancho in these words: "Signor, this is a troublesome life that we squires to knights-errant lead: in good sooth, we earn our bread with the sweat of our brows, which is one of the curses that God denounced against our first parents." "It may also be said," replied Sancho, "that we earn it with the frost of our bodies; for, no creatures on earth suffer more heat and cold than the miserable squires of knight-errantry; and even that, would be more tolerable, if we had any thing good to eat; for, hearty fare lightens care, as the saying is; but we often pass a whole day, nay sometimes two, without ever breaking our fast, except upon the winds of heaven." "All this," said the other, "may be endured, with the hope of reward; for, if the knight-errant is not extremely unfortunate, his squire must, in a very little time, see himself recompensed with the handsome government of some island, or with the possession of a profitable earldom." "For my own part," answered Sancho, "I have already told my master, that I shall be satisfied with the government of an island, which he has been so noble and generous as to promise me, divers and sundry times." "And I," said the stranger, "am contented with a canonship, which my master has already bespoke for me, on account of my faithful services." "It seems then, your master must be an ecclesiastical knight," replied Sancho, "seeing he can provide for his squire in the church: but as for mine, he is a meer layman; tho' I remember, that certain very wise persons (and yet, I believe, not very honest at bottom) advised him to procure for himself an archbishopric; but he would be nothing but an emperor: and I was then in a grievous quandary, for fear he should take it in his head to

be of the church; in which case, I should not have been qualified to hold a benefice; for, your worship must know, tho' I look like a man, I am no better than a beast at church matters." "Verily," said he of the wood, "your worship mistakes the matter quite: your governments of islands are not at all desirable; some are vexatious; some are beggarly; others attended with much melancholy and fatigue: in short, the most creditable and orderly brings along with it a load of care and inconvenience, that lies heavy on the shoulders of the unhappy person whose lot it is to bear it: it would be abundantly better for us who undergo this accursed slavery, to return to our own homes, and there amuse ourselves with more agreeable pastimes; such, for example, as hunting or fishing; for, what squire is there on earth, so poor as to want a horse, a couple of hounds, and a fishing-rod, wherewith to entertain himself at his own habitation?"

"For my own part," answered Sancho, "I want none of these conveniencies: true it is, I have not a horse, but then, I am in possession of an ass, which is worth my master's steed twice over: God let me never see a joyful easter, if I would truck with him for four bushels of barley to boot; you may laugh, if you will, at the price I set upon Dapple, (for that is the colour of my beast) then, I should never be in want of hounds; for, there are plenty, and to spare, in our town, and you know nothing is so relishing as to hunt at another's expence." "Really and truly, signor squire," resumed the stranger, "I am fully resolved and determined to quit those knights-errant, with all their crazy pranks, and betake myself to my own town, where I will bring up my children; for, thank God, I have three, like as many oriental pearls." "And I have a couple," said Sancho, "that may be presented to the pope in person; especially, my daughter, whom I breed up to be a countess, by the blessing of God, tho' it be contrary to her mother's inclination." "And of what age may this young lady be, whom you are breeding for a countess?" said the squire of the wood. "Fifteen years, or thereabouts," answered Sancho; "but, she is as tall as a spear, fresh as an April morn, and strong as a porter." "These are qualifications, not only for a countess, but even for the nymph of the green-wood tree," said the other: "ah the whore-son baggage! what a buxom jade she must be." Sancho, nettled at this epithet, replied, "She is no whore; neither was her mother before her; nor shall either of them be so, an please God, whilst I live: so, I think you might talk more civilly; for, considering your worship has been bred among knights-errant, who are, as it were, courtesy itself, methinks your words might be better chosen." "How little are you acquainted with the nature of commendation, signor squire!" answered he of the wood: "don't you know, that when any cavalier, at a bull-feast, wounds the bull dexterously, or when any person behaves remarkably well, the people exclaim, How cleverly the son of a whore has done it! and that which looks like reproach, is on such occasions, a notable commendation. Take my word, signor, you ought to renounce all children, if their behaviour does not intitle the parents to such praise." "I do renounce them," answered Sancho; "at that rate, and for that reason, your worship may call my wife and daughter as many whores as you please; for, both in word and deed, they richly deserve the name; and that I may see them again, I beseech God to deliver me from this mortal sin, which will be the case, if he delivers me from this dangerous employment of squire, which I have incurred a second time, being seduced and inticed by a purse of one hundred ducats, which I found one day in the midst of the brown mountain; and the devil continually sets before mine eyes,

here and there and every where, a bag full of doubloons, which, at every step, me thinks I have fast in my clutches, hugging it in my arms, and carrying it home to my own house, where I purchase mortgages and estates, and live like any prince, and while I please my-self with these notions, I bear, without murmuring, all the toils and fatigues I undergo, in the service of the wiseacre my master, who, I know, is more of a madman than a knight."

"So that, according to the proverb," replied the stranger, "covetousness bursts the bag. But, if you talk of wiseacres, there is not a greater in the universe than my master, who is one of those concerning whom people say, He is burthened, like an ass, with an-other man's load: for, truly, he is turned mad, that another knight may turn wise, and is going about in quest of that which, when he hath found it, may hit him in the teeth." "And pray, is he in love?" said Sancho. "Yes," replied the other, "he is enamoured of one Casildea de Vandalia, the most fickle dame that ever was seen; but, her cruelty is not the foot that he halts upon at present: he has got other crotchets of greater importance grumbling in his gizzard, which ere long will more plainly appear." "There is no road so smooth," resumed Sancho, "but you'll meet with rubs and hollows in it. Other people use beans, but I boil whole kettles full. Madness is always more accompanied and fol-lowed after, than discretion: but, if it be true, as it is commonly alledged, that company in affliction lessens the weight of it, I shall comfort myself by reflecting that your wor-ship serves a master who is as distracted as mine." "Distracted, I grant you," said he of the wood, "but valiant, and still more mischievous than valiant or distracted." "That is not the case with my master," replied Sancho, "he has nothing at all mischievous about him; on the contrary, is as dull as a beetle,[1] and knows not what it is to harm man, woman or child, or harbour the least malice, but seeks to do good unto all mankind: a child may persuade him that it is night at noon; and indeed for that very simplicity, I love him as my own bowels, and cannot find in my heart to leave him, notwithstanding all the mad pranks he is guilty of." "But, for all that, signor and brother of mine," said the stranger, "if the blind lead the blind, they are both in danger of falling into the ditch: we had much better retire fair and softly, and return to our own habitations; for, they who go in search of adventures do not always find them to their liking."

About this time Sancho began to hawk a kind of dry spitting, which being observed by the charitable squire of the wood, "Methinks," said he, "we have talked till our tongues cleave to the roofs of our mouths; but, I have got something that will agreeably moisten them, at my saddle-bow." He accordingly got up, and going aside to his horse, soon returned with a large leathern bottle of wine, and a pye half a yard long; and this is really no exaggeration; for, it contained a whole fed rabbit, so large, that when Sancho felt it, he took it for a whole goat, or large kid at least, crying, as soon as he perceived it, "How? does your worship usually carry such provision as this, about with you?" "What d'ye think?" answered the other: "d'ye take me for a hackney squire *? I carry a better cupboard on my horse's crupper than e'er a general on his march."

---

* Literally, *a squire of wool and water*, an allusion to a custom among the Spaniards, who sometimes have domestics to attend them to mass, and sprinkle them with holy water: these are generally shabby fellows, who have very poor appointments.[2]

Sancho fell to, without staying for intreaty, and swallowed, in the dark, huge mouth-fuls, with as much ease as if it had been flummery, saying between whiles, "Yes indeed, your worship is a true and loyal squire, well dammed and gristed,³ as the saying is, grand and magnificent withal, as plainly appears from this banquet, which, if it did not come hither by the art of enchantment, at least seems so to have done: this is not the case with such an unlucky poor devil as me, who carry nothing in my bags but a piece of cheese, hard enough to knock out a giant's brains, accompanied by three or four dozen of car-robes,⁴ and as many hazzle-nuts; thanks to the niggardliness and opinion of my master, and the rule he observes, by which knights-errant must maintain and support them-selves with nothing but dried fruits, and the herbs of the field." "In good faith, brother!" resumed he of the wood, "my stomach was not made for your sweet thistle, wild pear and mountain roots: let our masters please themselves with their own opinions and rules of chivalry, and live according to their meagre commands: for my own part, I always carry some cold pasty, happen what will, and this bottle hanging at my saddle-bow, which I love so devoutly, that I kiss and embrace it almost every minute." So saying, he handed it to Sancho, who lifting it up to his mouth, stood gazing at the stars a whole quarter of an hour, and when his draught was out, he hung his head on one side, pro-nouncing with a long sigh, "Ah whoreson! how catholic it is!" "You see now," said he of the wood, hearing Sancho's whoreson, "how you have praised the wine, by giving it such a title." "I am sensible," replied Sancho, "and confess that it is no disparagement to any body to be called the son of a whore, when it is understood in the way of commenda-tion: but, tell me, signor, by the life of what you best love, is not this wine from Cividad Real?"

"You have an excellent taste," answered he of the wood, "it comes from no other part, I'll assure you, and has, moreover, some good years over its head." "Let me alone for that," said Sancho, "you'll never catch me tripping in the knowledge of wine, let it be never so difficult to distinguish: is it not an extraordinary thing, signor squire, that I should have such a sure and natural instinct in the knowledge of wine, that give me but a smell of any sort whatever, and I will tell you exactly its country, growth and age, to-gether with the changes it will undergo, and all other circumstances appertaining to the mystery. But, this is not to be wondered at; for, by my father's side, I had two kinsmen who were the most excellent tasters that La Mancha hath known for these many years; as a proof of which, I will tell you what once happened to them: a sample of wine was presented to them, out of a hogshead, and their opinions asked, concerning the con-dition and quality, that is the goodness or badness of the liquor to which it belonged: one of them tasted it with the tip of his tongue; the other did no more but clap it to his nose: the first said the wine tasted of iron; the other affirmed it had a twang of goats leather: the owner protested the pipe was clean, and the contents without any sort of mixture that could give the liquor either the taste of iron, or the smell of goats leather: nevertheless, the two famous tasters stuck to the judgment they had given; time passed on, the wine was sold, and when the pipe came to be cleaned, they found in it a small key, tied to a leathern thong. By this your worship may perceive whether or not one who is descended from such a race may venture to give his opinion in cases of this nature." "Therefore, I say," replied the stranger, "that we ought to quit this trade of going in

quest of adventures, and be contented with our loaf, without longing for dainties: let us return to our own cottages where God will find us, if it be his blessed will." "I will serve my master till he arrives at Saragossa," said Sancho, "and then we shall come to a right understanding."

In fine, the two honest squires talked and drank so copiously, that sleep was fain to tie up their tongues, and allay their drought, which it was impossible to remove: each, therefore, grasping the bottle, which by this time was almost empty, fell asleep, with the morsel half chewed in his mouth. In this situation we will leave them for the present, and relate what happened between the knight of the wood, and him of the rueful countenance.

## CHAPTER XIV.

## Wherein the adventure of the knight of the wood is continued.

In the course of the conversation that passed between the two knights, the history relates, that he of the wood said to Don Quixote, "Finally, sir knight, you must know, my destiny, or rather, my choice, led me to place my affection on the peerless Casildea de Vandalia. I call her peerless, because she has no equal, either in point of stature, quality, fortune or beauty. Now this lady, in return for all my virtuous inclination, and amorous desires, like the stepmother of Hercules, employs me in many various toils and dangers, promising, at the conclusion of each, that with the next my cares shall be finished; but, thus she goes on, stringing one labour to another, without number, and I know not which will be the last that is to produce the accomplishment of my wishes. At one time she commanded me to go and challenge that famous giantess of Sevil, called * Giralda, who is so valiant and strong (her body being made of brass) and who, without shifting her station, is the most changeable and fickle female in the whole world: I came, saw and conquered; fixing her motionless to one point, for, during a whole week, the wind blew from the north. Another time, she ordered me to weigh the ancient figures called the valiant bulls of † Guisando; an enterprize more suitable to porters than to knights: nay, she even commanded me to throw myself headlong into the gulph of Cabra, an adventure equally new and dangerous, and bring to her a particular account of what is concerted in that dark and deep abyss. I fixed the inconstant Giralda, weighed the bulls of Guisando, precipitated myself into the gulph, and brought to light the secrets of its abyss; and yet my hopes are dead——ah how dead! while her cruelty and disdain are still alive——ah how much alive! In short, to conclude, she ordered me to tra-

---

* A brass statue on a steeple at Sevil, serving for a weather-cock.[1]
† These are stone statues of bulls, erected by the Romans at Guisando, a town in Castile; all the inscriptions are effaced, except the name of A. Quintus Cæcilius, Consul II.[2]

verse all the provinces of Spain, and compel every knight-errant in the kingdom to confess that she is preferable, in point of beauty, to all the women upon earth; and that I am the most valiant and amorous knight in the world. In consequence of this command, I have travelled over the greatest part of Spain, and vanquished many knights who have presumed to contradict my assertion: but, I value and applaud myself chiefly, for having conquered, in single combat, that so renowned knight Don Quixote de la Mancha, and made him confess, that my Casildea is more beautiful than his Dulcinea. Now, in that single conquest, I deem myself superior to all the knights in the universe; for, that same Don Quixote hath vanquished all his cotemporaries; and I, in conquering him, have transferred and conveyed to my own person, all his honour, glory, and reputation; the victor being always honoured in proportion to the fame of his vanquished foe; wherefore, the innumerable atchievements of the said Don Quixote are placed to my credit, as if they were the effects of my own personal prowess."

Don Quixote was astonished at hearing the knight of the wood talk in this manner, and was a thousand times tempted to give him the lie: nay, you lie was at the very tip of his tongue; but, repressing his indignation as well as he could, that he might make the stranger's own tongue convict him of falshood, he replied very calmly, "That your worship, sir knight, may have vanquished the greatest part of the knights-errant in Spain, and even in the whole world, I do not pretend to question, but, that you have conquered Don Quixote de la Mancha, I doubt very much; perhaps, it might be another who resembles him, though there are few such." "How! not conquer him?" cried he of the wood; "now, by yon canopy of heaven, under which we sit, I engaged, overcame, and subjected that very individual Don Quixote: he is a tall, meagre, long-legged, lanthorn-jawed, stalking figure; his hair inclining to grey, his nose hooked and aquiline, with long, straight, black mustachios: in his excursions he assumes the name of the knight of the rueful countenance; and is attended by a peasant, called Sancho Panza, who serves him in quality of squire; he presses the loins, and governs the reins of a famous steed hight Rozinante; and in fine, he avows, as mistress of his heart, one Dulcinea del Toboso, formerly known by the name of Aldonza Lorenzo; in like manner, my own mistress, whose name is Casilda, being a native of Andalousia, is now distinguished by the appellation of Casildea de Vandalia. If all these proofs are not sufficient to evince my veracity, here is my sword, which shall make a convert of incredulity itself."

"Have a little patience, sir knight," said Don Quixote, "and give ear unto what I am going to say. You must know, that same Don Quixote you mention, is the dearest friend I have upon earth; so that I may say, I love him as well as my own individual person; now, your description of him is so punctual and exact, that I should never doubt but he is actually the person you have vanquished, did I not see with my eyes, and, as it were, feel with my hands, the impossibility of the fact; and yet, as divers enchanters are his enemies, particularly one who persecutes him incessantly, some one among them may have assumed his figure, and allowed himself to be overcome, in order to defraud the knight of that fame which his gallant exploits had collected and acquired thro' the whole known world: in confirmation of this conjecture, I must also tell you that but two days ago, those perverse enchanters transformed the shape and person of the beautiful Dulcinea del Toboso, into that of a mean and plebeian country-wench: so that Don Quixote must

have also undergone a transformation. And, if all this is not enough to ascertain the truth of what I say, here is Don Quixote himself, who will maintain it by force of arms, on horseback or on foot, or in any shape you please."

So saying, he started up, and grasping his sword, stood waiting for the resolution of the knight of the wood, who with great deliberation, replied: "A good paymaster needs no pawn, signor Don Quixote; he, who could vanquish you when you was transformed, may well hope to reduce you in propria persona; but, as it is unseemly for knights to perform their exploits in the dark, like robbers and ruffians, let us wait for day, that the sun may shine upon our works; and let this be the condition of our combat, that the vanquished shall comply with the will of the victor, and do every thing that he shall desire; provided his commands be such as a knight-errant can decently obey."

Don Quixote assured him, that he was extremely well satisfied with the condition and proviso; upon which, they went in quest of their squires, who were found snoring in the very same attitudes in which sleep had surprized them. They wakened, and ordered them to get their horses ready; for by sun-rise they intended to engage in a most unparalleled and bloody single combat. Sancho was astonished and confounded at this piece of news; despairing of his master's safety, when he recollected what the other squire had told him, concerning the valour of the knight of the wood. The two squires, however, without pretending to make any words, went to look for their cattle, and found the three steeds with Dapple (for they had smelled each other out) very sociably met together. While they were thus employed, "Brother," said he of the wood to Sancho, "you must know that it is customary with your warriors of Andalousia, when they are godfathers in any quarrel, not to stand idle, with their arms across, while their godsons are engaged. This I hint, by way of apprizing you that, while our masters are at it, we must exchange a few dry blows too." "That custom, signor squire," answered Sancho, "may pass current with those ruffians and warriors you mention; but, that it prevails among the squires of knights-errant, I can by no means believe, at least, I have never heard such a custom mentioned by my master, who knows all the ordinances of chivalry by rote. Besides, granting it to be fact, and expresly ordained, that the squires must go to loggerheads while their masters are engaged; I will by no means comply with it, but pay the penalty incurred by peaceable squires, which I am sure cannot exceed a couple of pounds of wax; and that will not cost me so much as the pence I should expend in the cure of my head, which I would lay my account with having split and divided into two halves; and moreover, it is impossible that I should fight, because I have got no sword, and never wore one in my born days." "I know a very good remedy for that inconvenience," said the stranger: "here are a couple of linen bags, of the same size; you shall take one, and I the other, and play away upon each other with equal arms." "With all my heart," answered Sancho; "that sort of exercise will serve to dust our jackets, without hurting our skins." "Not quite so neither," resumed the other, "for, that the bags may not flap in the air, we will clap into each, half a dozen clear, smooth pebbles, of equal weight and magnitude; so that we may thwack one another, without hurt or damage." "Body of my father!" cried Sancho, "mind what sable furs and flakes of carded cotton he would line the bags withal, to prevent them from grinding our skulls, and making a paste of our bones! Hark ye, master of mine, I'll have nothing to do with them, though they

were stuffed with balls of silk; let our masters fight as they shall think proper, but, for our parts, let us drink and live quietly; for, old father time will take care to rid us of our lives, without our seeking occasions to throw them away before the appointed season, at which, being ripe, they drop off of their own accord." "But, for all that," replied he of the wood, "we must have a bout, if it should not last half an hour." "By no means," said Sancho. "I shall not be so uncivil and ungrateful, as to have any difference, let it be never so small, with a person at whose cost I have both eaten and drank; besides, who the devil, do you think, can fight in cool blood, without any sort of anger or provocation?" "I know how to remove that objection," resumed the stranger: "before we begin the battle, I will come up fairly and softly, and give your worship two or three such hearty boxes on the ear, as will lay you flat at my feet, and awaken your choler, though it should sleep sounder than a dormouse." "Against that expedient," answered Sancho, "I know another twice as good: for, I will lay hold on a good cudgel, and before your worship comes to awaken my choler, give your own such a lullaby of dry beating, that it shall never wake but in the next world, where you'll have reason to know that I am not a man who will suffer his nose to be handled by any person whatsomever; wherefore, let every one look to his own affairs. Though it would be the wisest course for every man to let his own choler lie still and sleep: for, nobody knows the heart of his neighbour, and some who go out for wool, come home quite shorn. God himself bestowed his blessing upon peace, and curse upon contention; for, if a cat that is confined, provoked and persecuted, turns into a lion, the Lord knows, what I, who am a man, may turn into: I therefore, signor squire, give your worship notice, that all the mischief and damage which shall proceed from our quarrel, must be charged to your account." "Mighty well," replied the stranger, "we shall see what is to be done, when God sends us morning."

Now, a thousand kinds of painted birds began to warble from the trees, and in their various and sprightly notes seemed to welcome and salute the fresh and joyous morn, which already through the gates and balconies of the east, disclosed her beauteous visage, while from her hair distilled an infinite number of liquid pearls, in which delicious liquor, the herbs being bathed, seemed to sprout and rain a shower of seed-pearl, upon the earth. The willows shed savoury manna, the fountains laughed, the brooks murmured, the woods rejoiced, and the meadows adorned themselves at her approach.

But, scarce had the light of day rendered objects distinguishable, when the first thing that presented itself to the eyes of Sancho Panza, was the nose of his brother squire, which was so large as almost to overshadow his whole body. It is actually said to have been of excessive magnitude, crooked in the middle, and studded all over with warts of a mulberry-colour, like the fruit called berengena; and it hung down two fingers-breadth below his mouth. The size, colour, warts and curvature of this feature, rendered the face so frightful and deformed, that Sancho no sooner beheld it than he began to shake in every limb, like a child troubled with convulsions, and resolved, in his heart, to endure two hundred buffetings, before his choler should be awaked, so as to fight with such an hobgoblin.

Don Quixote surveying his antagonist, found his vizor already down, and closed in such a manner, as effectually concealed his face; but he perceived him to be a muscular man, of a middling stature. Over his arms, he wore a loose coat or cassock, to all ap-

pearance of the finest cloth of gold, powdered with a number of small moons formed of the brightest looking-glass, which had a most magnificent, gay and shewy effect. Over his helmet waved a great quantity of green, yellow and white plumes; and his lance, which leaned against a tree, was excessively long and large, armed with above an hand's breadth of pointed steel. All these particulars were observed and considered by Don Quixote, who concluded from what he saw and observed, that the said knight must be a person of Herculean strength. Nevertheless, far from being afraid, like Sancho Panza, he with the most gallant intrepidity, thus addressed himself to the knight of the mirrours: "I intreat you, by your courtesy, sir knight, if your eager desire of fighting hath not destroyed that quality, to lift up your beaver a little, that I may see, whether or not the grace of your countenance corresponds with the gallantry of your demeanour." "Signor cavalier," replied he of the looking-glasses, "whether you are victor or vanquished in this enterprize, you will have time and opportunity more than sufficient to consider my visage: my reason for not satisfying your desire at present, is, that I should deem it a notable injury to the beautiful Casildea de Vandalia, to spend so much time as it would take to lift up my beaver, before I compel you to confess what you know I pretend to maintain." "Yet, while we mount our steeds," said Don Quixote, "you may easily tell me if I am that same Don Quixote, whom you pretend to have overcome." "To that question I answer," said he of the mirrours, "that you are as like the knight I overcame, as one egg is like another; but, as you say, you are persecuted by inchanters, I will not venture to affirm, whether or not you are the same person." "That is enough," replied Don Quixote, "to convince me that you are mistaken: nevertheless, to persuade you beyond all possibility of doubt, let us have recourse to our horses, and in less time than you would have taken to lift your beaver, if God, my mistress, and my arm avail me, I shall see your face, and you will see I am not that conquered Don Quixote whom you suppose me to be."

Thus breaking off the conversation, they mounted their horses, and Don Quixote turned Rozinante, in order to take a sufficiency of ground for returning to encounter his antagonist; while he of the mirrours took the same precaution. But, the first had not proceeded twenty paces, when he was called back by the other, and the two meeting again half-way, "Take notice, sir knight," said he of the looking-glasses, "the condition of our combat is, that the conquered, as I have already observed, must be at the discretion of the conqueror." "I know it," answered Don Quixote, "provided the commands imposed upon the vanquished be such as do not transgress the bounds of chivalry." "So I understand the conditions," answered he of the mirrours.

At that instant, the strange nose of the squire presented itself to the eyes of Don Quixote, who was no less astonished than Sancho, at the sight; insomuch, that he took him for some monster or new-fashioned man, such as are not commonly found in this world. Sancho, seeing his master set out, in order to take his career, would not stay alone with nozzle, being afraid, that one flirt of such a snout in his face, would determine the quarrel, and lay him stretched along the ground, either through fear or the severity of the blow: he therefore, ran after his master, and laying hold of one of Rozinante's stirrups, when he saw him ready to turn, "I beseech your worship, dear master," cried he, "before you turn to begin the combat, help me in climbing this cork-tree, from whence I may

behold, more to my liking than from the ground, your worship's gallant encounter with that same knight." "I rather believe, Sancho," said Don Quixote, "that thy motive for clambering up, is to see the bull-fight from a scaffold, without any danger to thyself." "The truth is," answered Panza, "the outrageous nose of that squire fills me with such astonishment and affright, that I dare not tarry along with him." "It is such indeed," replied the knight, "that were I any other than what I am, I should be scared at it's appearance: come, therefore, and I will help thee to ascend to the place you mention."

While Don Quixote stopped until Sancho should get up into the cork-tree, the knight of the mirrours took as much ground as he thought necessary, and imagining that Don Quixote had done the same, without waiting for sound of trumpet, or other signal, he turned his horse, which was not a whit superior to Rozinante, either in fleetness or appearance, and at his full speed, which was a middling trot, rode forwards to encounter his antagonist; but, seeing him busy in the exaltation of Sancho, he pulled in the reins, and halted in the middle of his career; a circumstance that gave infinite joy to his steed, which was already so tired, that he could not move another step. Don Quixote perceiving his enemy approaching with such speed, drove his spurs stoutly into the meagre flanks of Rozinante, and made him spring forwards in such a manner, that the history says, this was the only occasion on which he was ever known to gallop, for at all other times his swiftest pace was no other than a downright trot; and with this hitherto unseen fury, he arrived at the spot where the knight of the mirrours sat thrusting his spurs rowel-deep into the sides of his horse, without being able to move him one finger's breadth from the place where he had made his halt. In this confusion and dilemma, Don Quixote found his antagonist embroiled with his horse and embarrassed with his lance, which, either through want of knowledge or of time, he had not as yet fixed in the rest. Our Manchegan, who never minded these incumbrances, safely and without the least danger to his own person, encountered him of the mirrours with such vigour, as to bring him, very much against his inclination, to the ground, over the crupper of his horse, with such a fall, that he lay without sense or motion, to all appearance bereft of life.

Sancho, no sooner saw him unhorsed, than sliding down from the cork-tree, he ran down to his master, who having alighted from Rozinante, stood over the knight of the mirrours, untying his helmet, in order to see, whether or not he was actually dead, and to give him air, in case he should be alive. Then it was, he saw—who can relate what he saw, without creating admiration, wonder and affright in those who hear it? He saw, says the history, the very face, the very figure, the very aspect, the very physiognomy, the very effigies, the very perspective of the bachelor Sampson Carrasco; and this he no sooner beheld, than raising his voice, he cried, "Come hither Sancho, and behold what thou shalt see, but not believe; quick, my child, and contemplate the power of magic: here thou wilt see what those wizzards and inchanters can do." Sancho accordingly approached, and seeing the face of batchelor Carrasco, began to cross and bless himself a thousand times.

Mean while, the overthrown knight, giving no signs of life, Sancho said to Don Quixote, "In my opinion, master, right or wrong, your worship should thrust your sword through the jaws of this miscreant, who seems to be the batchelor Sampson Carrasco, and in him, perhaps you may slay one of those enchanters who are your enemies." "That

*Vol. II. pag. 80.*

*F. Hayman inv.t et delin.*

*G. Scotin Sculp.t*

Don Quixote Prevented by the Squire of the Nose from Killing the Knight of the Mirrors.

is no bad advice," said the knight; "for, the fewer enemies the better." So saying, he drew his sword, in order to put in execution the advice and counsel of Sancho, when the squire belonging to the knight of the mirrors, came up without his frightful nose, and cried aloud, "Take care what you do, signor Don Quixote; he who lies at your feet is your friend the batchelor Sampson Carrasco, and I am his squire."

Sancho seeing him, without his original deformity, "and the nose?" said he. "I have it here," replied the other, who putting his hand in his right side pocket, pulled out a pasteboard nose, covered with varnish, such as we have already described. Sancho, having considered him more and more attentively, broke out into a loud exclamation of wonder, crying, "Blessed virgin watch over me! Sure this is not my neighbour and gossip Tommy Cecial?" "The very same, (answered the unsnouted squire) Tummas Cecial I am, your own friend and gossip, Sancho Panza, and I will presently tell you by what round-about conduits, tricks and mischievous stories I have been brought hither; in the mean time, supplicate and beseech your master's worship, not to treat, maltreat, wound or slay the knight of the looking-glasses, who now lies at his feet; for, without all doubt, he is no other than our townsman, the inconsiderate and ill-advised batchelor Sampson Carrasco."

About this time, the knight of the mirrors came to himself, and Don Quixote perceiving he had recovered the use of his senses, clapped the point of his naked sword to his throat, saying, "Knight, you are a dead man, if you do not instantly confess that the peerless Dulcinea del Toboso excels your Casildea de Vandalia, in beauty; and in the next place, you must promise, (provided you escape with life from this contention and overthrow) to go to the city of Toboso, and present yourself before her, in my name, that she may dispose of you according to her good pleasure; and if she leaves you at your own disposal, you shall return in quest of me; for the tracts of my exploits will serve as a guide to conduct you to the place where I shall be, and give me an account of what hath passed between you; these conditions being conformable to what we agreed upon before the combat, and not deviating from the customs of knight-errantry." "I confess," said the vanquished knight, "that the clouted dirty shoe of the lady Dulcinea del Toboso, excels the dishevelled, tho' shining locks of Casildea; I promise to go and return from her to your presence, and give you a full and particular detail of what you demand." "You must, in like manner, confess, and believe," added Don Quixote, "that the knight whom you overcame neither was, nor could be Don Quixote de la Mancha, but some other who resembled him; as I confess and believe, that although you appear to be the batchelor Sampson Carrasco, you are not really he, but another cloathed in his appearance, with which my enemies have invested you, in order to arrest my arm, and restrain the impetuosity of my rage, so as that I may bear the glory of my conquest with moderation." "I confess, judge and perceive in all respects, as you believe, judge and perceive," answered the discomfited knight; "and I beseech you allow me to rise, if the severity of my fall, which hath put me in a miserable plight, will permit me to get up."

He was accordingly assisted in rising, by Don Quixote and his own squire Tommy Cecial, from whose person Sancho could not withdraw his eyes, while he asked a thousand questions; the answers to which manifestly shewed, that he was really and truly the

individual Tommy Cecial, whom he pretended to be: but, the apprehension which Sancho had conceived, from what his master said touching the enchanters, who had metamorphosed the knight of the mirrours into the batchelor Carrasco, hindered him from giving credit to the truth of what he saw with his own eyes. Finally, both master and man remained under the influence of that deception, while he of the mirrours, with his squire, in exceeding bad humour and evil plight, took his leave of Don Quixote and Sancho, to go in quest of some place where he might beplaister and besplinter his ribs. Don Quixote and Sancho returned to the prosecution of their journey, in which the history leaves them, to explain the mystery of the knight of the looking-glasses, and his snouted squire.

## CHAPTER XV.

# Which gives an account and information of the knight of the mirrours, and his squire.

D on Quixote went on his way rejoicing; he gloried, he triumphed in the importance of his conquest, imagining the knight of the mirrours to be the most redoubtable of all knights that had yet ever appeared; and what afforded him likewise great matter of comfort was, that this knight, having engaged himself by the ties of honour, from which he could not deviate, without forfeiting his title to the order, he conceived hopes of hearing soon from Dulcinea, and of being certainly informed whether the enchantment of that princess still continued; tho' indeed, it happened, that he and the knight of the mirrours thought, at that time, differently upon this subject; inasmuch as the latter was solely intent upon thinking how he should repair the damage done to his carcase.

And here the historian informs his readers, that when Sampson Carrasco advised Don Quixote to resume the profession of knight-errantry, it was in consequence of mature consultation between him, the curate, and the barber, when they deliberated upon the means of keeping him in peace and quiet at home, so that his brains, for the future, should not be disturbed in pursuit of those wild extravagancies; the result of which was, that the only way to cure the frenzy of this unhappy man, was at present not to check his ungovernable obstinacy, but, to humour it, and encourage him to go out again, as they saw it was impossible to prevent him; that Sampson should arm himself, and take an opportunity of meeting and challenging him, as a knight-errant; that he should settle the terms with him; that the vanquished should be at the disposal of the conqueror; that, in consequence of this agreement, Don Quixote, when overcome, (which they looked upon as a matter of little doubt and difficulty) should be ordered to return home, and not to pass the bounds of his own village, for the space of two years, without the good-will and permission of the other; that no doubt this he would religiously comply with,

as not daring to violate the laws of the order; and that there might be hopes, he would either in that space of time, be naturally cured of those extravagant follies, or they might find out some method of diverting his mind from the farther pursuit of them. Carrasco undertook the affair very readily; and this Thomas Cecial, an intimate friend and companion of Sancho, and a queer sort of fellow, proffered his service to go upon the expedition, in the quality of squire. Sampson got himself accoutred in the manner you have read, and Cecial appeared in the terrors of that tremendous paste-board nose, to disguise himself from Sancho; and being thus equipped, they followed him so close, that they were very near coming up with him at the adventure of the waggon of death; they met him however in the wood, where ensued what the attentive reader must already be acquainted with; and where, had it not been for Don Quixote's heated imagination, which hurried him into the belief that the batchelor was not the batchelor, signor Sampson Carrasco would have been effectually stopped in the progress of his university degrees, and would not even have found a nest where he expected a flight of sparrows.

Thomas Cecial, finding the unhappy success that attended their undertaking; said, "Mr. Carrasco, I cannot in my conscience see why we ought to complain; it is one thing to undertake, but another thing to finish: we looked upon Don Quixote as mad, and ourselves as hugely wise; but, behold the end! we take our march back again, both from a fool's errand, and you most handsomely drubbed to boot, while he pursues his journey in safety and triumph: and I should really be curious to know which is the greatest fool, he who is made so by nature, or he who makes himself one?" "There is this difference," replied the batchelor, "between a natural and a wilful fool, that the former will always remain so, the latter may cease to be so when he has a-mind." "As that is the case," said Thomas, "I think I have been a monstrous fool in coming here to attend you as your squire; and therefore, that I may be so no longer, I will this instant hie me to my own habitation." "In that particular, you may do what seems good unto you," replied Sampson, "but, as for me, I see not the place of my dwelling, until I shall have taken bodily vengeance upon Don Quixote: 'tis not now from motives of charity or benevolence; no, 'tis revenge, and the anguish of my ribs, that prompt me to persevere in attempting the work of his reformation."

They entertained one another in this manner, till they came to a village, where they had the good fortune to find a bone-setter, who put the batchelor's ribs somewhat to rights; and Cecial took the route for his own village, leaving Carrasco deep in his meditations, projecting schemes of revenge. In due time, the history will again mention him, but, at present, let us share with Don Quixote in the transports of his joy.

CHAPTER XVI.

## What happened to Don Quixote, with a grave gentleman of La Mancha.

Don Quixote, as we have observed, went on his way, glorying in his success. From that day, he dated himself the most renowned and invincible of all knights that had ever yet gone thro' a course of labours on this our earth: he looked upon all dangers, all difficulties that possibly could come in his way, as already vanquished, already overcome: he now valued not a rush the machinations of the most powerful enchanters. The very traces of former misfortunes, those drubbings out of number he had undergone, in discharging the functions of knighthood, were now quite obliterated from his memory. He thought no more of the shower of stones which had so sorely afflicted his jaw-bones, nor the mortifying ingratitude of the galley-slaves; nor did he think any more of the pack-staves of the Yanguesian carriers, who had the hardiness to make his sides resound like the dusting of a carpet: in short, the idea he conceived of his own felicity was so great, that could I, said he to himself, but accomplish the great point of delivering my celestial princess from the power of enchantment, I should not envy the glory that ever was or will be purchased by any knight in the universe.

He was lost in these reveries, when Sancho interrupted him, "Signor, you will hardly believe what a fool I am, but, it is an actual truth, that I cannot keep myself from thinking on that horrid and unmeasurable nose of my neighbour Tom Cecial." "And dost thou really believe," replied the other, "that the knight of the mirrours was Sampson Carrasco; and that thy old companion, Thomas Cecial, was his squire?" "As to that affair, I can say nothing to it," answer'd Sancho, "only one thing I am positive in, that no one but himself could have given me such an account of my house, my wife and my children; and as to his face, when that nose was slipt off, it was the very individual face of Thomas Cecial, just as I have beheld it many a time, when we were next door neighbours in our village: and as for his voice, I will take my oath, it is the same to a tittle." "Come, Sancho," said Don Quixote, "let us reason cooly upon this head: what probability is there, that Sampson Carrasco should come, as a knight-errant, armed cap-a-pee, to offer me combat? Am I his enemy, or did I ever give him occasion to bear resentment against me? Do you imagine I am his rival, or that he has entered into the profession of chivalry, as envying the glory I have acquir'd by arms?" "But, then, Sir," answer'd Sancho, "what account can we give of the resemblance of that same knight and his squire to Sampson Carrasco, and my old friend Thomas Cecial? And if it be enchantment, as your worship says, were there no other two in the world but them, whose likeness they could assume?" "It is all design," answered the other, "and the contrivance of those cursed enchanters who persecute me, who easily foreseeing I should be victorious in the combat, changed the form of their vanquished knight into that of the batchelor, that the friendship I have for him might check the fury of my sword, and shield him against the effects of my just indignation; and by that means save the life of him who, by treachery and artifice, had

attempted to take away mine. But, what further proof need there be of the power of those enchanters, to change the appearance of human countenances, the fair into the deformed, and the deformed into the fair, than what thou thyself hast lately found by certain experience? Thou, who not two days since, beheld the peerless Dulcinea, in all the charms and lustre of perfect beauty, while at the same time she appeared to me an ugly rustic wench, with blear'd eyes, and stinking breath: and doubtless, if the wicked magician could effect such a diabolic enchantment as that, it is not to be wondered at, if he did the like by Carrasco and Thomas Cecial, to rob me of the glory of my victory: however, this is my consolation, that the prowess of my arm hath prevailed against my enemy, whatever shape he has assum'd." "It is God alone who knows the truth of all things," answered Sancho, who well knowing, that the transformation of Dulcinea was the effect of his own enchantments, upon that account was not quite convinced by his master's arguments, but durst not mutter the least word, lest something should have dropped from him, by which he might have betrayed himself.

While they were discoursing in this manner, a gentleman, mounted in the jockey-fashion, on a fine flea-bitten mare, came up with them, dressed in a riding-coat of fine green cloth, faced with murry-coloured velvet, and a hunting-cap of the same; his furniture of a piece, murry-coloured and green: he had a belt of green and gold, at which hung a Moorish scymitar, and his buskins were wrought in the same manner: his spurs were not gilt, but so finely varnished with green, that as they were more of a piece with the rest of his dress, they looked better than if they had been pure gold. When this gentleman overtook them, he saluted them with great politeness, and was spurring on, in order to pass them, when Don Quixote calling to him, said, "Signor, if you are not in haste, and are going this way, I should be exceeding glad to join company with you." "Sir," answered the other, "I should not have been in such haste to pass you, but was afraid your horse might be unruly, in the company of my mare." "If that be all," answered Sancho, "you may stop your mare when you please, with great safety; ours is the most sober and most discreet horse in the world, and has more breeding than ever to let his naughtiness get the better of him, upon such occasions, and never transgressed in this particular but once, and then my master and I both suffered severely in the flesh for it: I say once more, your worship may stop; for, if your mare was served up in a dish, our steed would not so much as smell to her." Upon this assurance, the gentleman stop'd, and look'd with amazement at the air and appearance of Don Quixote, who rode without his helmet, which hung like a wallet before Sancho, at the pummel of his ass's pannel: and, on the other hand, Don Quixote beheld him with no less attention, conceiving him to be some person of figure and distinction. The traveller seem'd to be a man about fifty; he had some, tho' few grey hairs; his features were sharp, and in his looks appeared neither levity nor moroseness: in short, his appearance bespoke him a man of consequence. He looked with a kind of astonishment at Don Quixote, as having never beheld such a phoenomenon before; the lankness of the horse, and the tall stature of the person that rode him, the sepulchral meagerness of his aspect, his solemn gravity, the strangeness of his armour, all together forming such a composition as perhaps had never before been seen in that country.

Don Quixote observed with what attention the traveller considered him, and by the

surprize he saw him in, guessing what he wanted to know, as he was himself the very flower of civility, and of excessive complaisance, he was resolved to be before hand with him, and save him the trouble of asking any question: "Signor," said he, "I am not at all surprised to find, that with amazement you contemplate this my appearance, so new to you, and so different from that of other mortals; but, your wonder will cease, when I have told you that I am of the fraternity of those knights whom people distinguish by the title of adventure-hunters. I have left my native home, mortgaged my all, bid adieu to ease and pleasure, and cast myself upon fortune, to dispose of me as she shall think proper; my design being to awaken the lost and decayed spirit of knight-errantry: it is now some time since I entered upon the resolution of accomplishing this aim, during which period, I have suffered a variety of fortune, tossed about from one adventure to another, sometimes triumphant, at other times not so successful, until I have in a great measure fulfil'd my design, having relieved many disconsolate widows, afforded protection to many distressed damsels, and been of aid and assistance to divers married women and fatherless children, the true duty and intent of our order; so that, by numberless exploits becoming a christian hero, I am now celebrated in print through almost all the nations of the habitable globe. Thirty thousand copies of my renowned history are already in the hands of the public, and, if heaven does not think proper to put a stop to it, in all likelihood, there will be a thousand times as many more. In one word, Sir, I am Don Quixote de la Mancha, otherwise stiled the knight of the rueful countenance; and tho' I own it is illiberal to sound one's own praises, yet am I sometimes obliged to do it; but then, never unless when no one is by to do it for me; so that, signor, after what I have told you, neither my lance nor my shield, my horse nor my squire, the wanness of my countenance, nor the lankness of my person, and all my whole composition together, ought any more to affect you with surprize, since you know the profession I am of, and the order I belong to."

There Don Quixote stoped to give the traveller an opportunity of reply; but, he was so long before he opened his mouth, that it seemed as if he could make no answer; however, after a long pause, "Sir knight," said he, "you was not mistaken, when, by the surprize you saw me in, you guessed the desire I had to be informed; but, I am still as much surprised as ever, and tho' what you say may be right, that my knowing who you are ought to have made my wonder cease, it is yet far from having that effect upon me: can it be possible, that there are indeed now in the world knights-errant really existing, and that there are published accounts of real adventures? I should never have once dreamed that there was such a thing upon earth as any one who assisted married women and orphans, relieved widows, and protected damsels, if I had not had this opportunity of being convinced by now seeing you; and heaven be praised, that this noble history of your real and glorious atchievements is in print, as it must efface and discredit those numberless romances about knights-errant, who never had being, and with which the world was so pestered and abused, to the apparent corruption of the mind of the readers, and the discredit of real and true history." "As to that circumstance, Sir, there is much to be said, and you must not be too rash in believing, that the histories of knight-errantry are all fable." "Is there any one," answered the traveller, "who makes a doubt of it?" "I do, for one," answered Don Quixote; "but, we will drop that subject for the pres-

ent, as I doubt not but if we continue any time travelling together, I shall be able, by the blessing of God, to convince you of your error, and to shew you that you are prejudiced only by the number of those who have entertained a notion, that such accounts are fictitious."

These last words of Don Quixote gave the gentleman in green a suspicious idea of his understanding; he had a notion that he must be disordered in his senses, and was expecting some other proof of it; but, without entering into farther discourse, Don Quixote desired his companion to let him know who he was, as he himself had given an account of his life and situation. To which request the gentleman replied, "Sir knight of the rueful countenance, I am a gentleman born in a village where, if it pleases God, we shall all dine to-day; my fortune is better than moderate, and my name Don Diego de Miranda. I pass my time chearfully, with my wife, my children, and my friends; my usual diversions are fishing and hunting, but, I neither keep hounds nor hawks, all I have are some decoy-partridges, and a good ferret. My library consists of about some six dozen of Spanish and Latin books; some are books of history, others of piety, for, as to books of chivalry, I have not yet allowed them to come under my roof; I am more inclined to the reading of profane than religious authors, if the subjects they treat of are of an innocent nature, if the stile is engaging, and the incidents affecting and surprizing; but, indeed, Spain produces mighty few performances of this sort. I live in terms of good neighbourhood with all about me; sometimes I go to their houses, sometimes I invite them to mine; my table is neat and clean, and sufficiently affluent, without extravagance. I slander no one, nor do I allow backbiters to come near me; my eyes pry not into the actions of other men, nor have I any impertinent curiosity to know the secrets of their lives. I go to mass every day, and the poor man partakes of my substance; I make no ostentation in the good I do; that I may defend myself against the attacks of hypocrisy and vain-glory, well knowing, that the best fortified heart is hardly proof against those sly deceivers. As far as I have an opportunity, I am a reconciler of differences among my neighbours: I particularly pay my devotions to the blessed mother, and have an entire dependance on the mercies of God our Saviour."

Sancho had listened with uncommon attention to what the gentleman in green, said; and this discourse seemed to him of such exalted piety and virtue, that he immediately conceived such a man must be endowed with the power of working miracles; fully persuaded of the truth of this supposition, he threw himself off his ass, ran up to the gentleman, seized his right stirrup, and with a heart overflowing with devotion, and eyes full of tears, fell a kissing his feet. Which humility, when the traveller perceived, "What is the matter, friend," said he, "what is the meaning of these embraces?" "Pray let me alone," said Sancho, "for in my life before, excepting your worship, did I never know a saint mounted on horseback." "I have no title to be thought so," answered the gentleman; "on the contrary, I am a miserable sinner; but, the simplicity of your behaviour, my friend, shews, that you yourself must be a very good man." Upon this declaration, Sancho quitted him, and again remounted Dapple, having by his behaviour unbended the solemn gravity of his master into a smile, and encreased the wonder of Don Diego.

Don Quixote then made enquiry into the number of children he had, informing him at the same time, that the ancient sages, who were not enlightened with the knowledge

of the true God, reckoned the gifts of fortune and nature, abundance of friends and encrease of dutiful children, as constituting part of the supreme happiness. "Sir," answered Don Diego, "I have one son, and if I had none, should, peradventure, think myself happier than I am; not that he is very bad, but because he does not come up to what I would wish him to be. He is now eighteen years of age, six of which he has spent at Salamanca, studying Greek and Latin, and when I would have had him apply to something else, I found him so dipt in poetry, if that deserves the name of science, that I could not prevail upon him to take to the study of the law, which was what I wanted he should do; nor, would he apply to divinity, the first and noblest of all sciences. I was desirous to make him the honour and ornament of his family, as we live in an age, and under a monarch, where useful and virtuous learning is so amply recompensed; for, what is learning without virtue? No better than pearls on a dung-hill. He will spend whole days in examining whether such a verse in Homer's Iliad be expressed with propriety, whether such an epigram of Martial is to be construed into a lewd sense or not, and whether such a verse in Virgil will bear this or that meaning. In a word, these authors, with Horace, Persius, Juvenal, and Tibullus, engross the whole of his time and conversation. As to the modern authors of his own country, he seems to have no great relish for them, though, notwithstanding his seeming disregard, he is now busied in making a kind of commentary upon four verses, which, I believe, are designed as a subject for a prize in the schools."

To this information, the other answered, "Signor, children are to be considered as part of the bowels of the parents, and be they good or bad, we must treat them as such, and cherish them accordingly. It is incumbent upon parents, to lead them betimes into the paths of decency and virtue, to instil into them sound principles, and train them up in christian discipline, that by these means they may be the stay of their declining years, and an honour to their own descendants. I am not against using persuasion to encline them either to the study of this or that science, but, look upon using force as altogether unwarrantable; more especially as the young gentleman does not study in view of getting his livelihood, he being so fortunate as to have that secured by inheritance; then I think he should be indulged in pursuing whatever his genius or inclination mostly prompts him to; and though in poetry, there is more pleasure than utility, it generally does honour to the person who has a vein for it. I liken poetry to a young, tender, and beautiful virgin, whom many other virgins, that is, all the other sciences, are assiduous to ornament, enrich and embellish; now, as she makes use of them all, so likewise does she reflect a lustre upon them all. But then, this tender virgin is not to be handled roughly, she is not to be dragged thro' the streets, exposed in public places, or stand as a prostitute at the gates of palaces. She is a kind of alchemy of such rare virtue, that whoever knows the nature of her composition may change her into pure gold of inestimable value; whoever would keep her, must narrowly look after her; she must not be indulged in the indecency of obscene satyr, nor allowed to run into insipid sonnets. And though she may enjoy the profits arising from heroic poetry, weeping tragedy, or laughing comedy, yet the muse must not be venal; no buffoons must have any thing to do with her, and she must be kept sacred from the unhallowed multitude, who neither know nor esteem those hidden treasures she carries about her. And think not that by the multitude,

I only mean the common rank of men; no, under that class I number all who are strangers to real knowledge, be they peers or be they princes. But, whoever is possessed of these qualifications I have been mentioning, and with them, attempts the study and execution of poetry, I say, his name will be famous, and held in veneration, wherever politeness extends its influence. As to what you say of your son's not esteeming the poetry of his own country, I don't think he is quite right in that opinion, and for this reason: the mighty Homer did not write in Latin, because he was a Greek; nor Virgil in Greek, for the same reason that he was a Roman; and in general, every one of the ancient poets wrote in the language of his own country, and did not seek for another to clothe the majesty of his ideas. As this is the case, I think it should be a prevailing maxim in all countries; nor should we undervalue the German poet for writing in his own language, nor the Castilian, nor even the Biscayan, for writing in his; but, perhaps, your son does not dislike Spanish poetry, but Spanish poets, as being destitute of the knowledge of other languages or sciences, that might contribute to cultivate, assist and enliven their own natural genius; and even this prejudice may be carried too far; for, the maxim, that a poet is born with his talent, is certainly just; that is, a real poet comes forth a poet into the world, and with this natural endowment implanted in him by his Creator, produces, without the help of study or cultivation, such things as verify that of the poets when they say, Est Deus in nobis.[1] One so born a poet, if he cultivates his genius by the assistance of art, must be much better, nay, greatly preferable to him who, without natural fire, attains to the knowledge of the rules only; for, it is obvious, that as art does not exceed nature, but, serves to polish and bring it to perfection; so art assisting nature, and nature so assisted by art, form the accomplished poet. To conclude, signor, my advice is, that your son should be allowed to follow the bent of his own inclination, and, as he must be already an exceeding good scholar, having mastered the learned languages, which may be looked upon as having mounted the first steps in his progress to the seat of the sciences, by the assistance of that knowledge he will be able, without more help, to climb to the top of human literature, which as much adorns and sets off a gentleman as a mitre does a bishop, or the long robe the counsel learned in the law. If you find him writing satires injurious to private characters, burn his works and rebuke him; but, if he composes discourses, that comprehend for their subject of satire, vice in general, as Horace did with so much elegance, then commend him; for, though it be unlawful to mark and single out particular persons, it is allowable to write against particular vices; for example, to write against envy, or to lash the envious, and so of others. Here are some poets indeed, who, rather than baulk their fancy of saying a smart thing, will risque being sent to the isles of Pontus. As the manners, so will the verses be; if the former are chaste the latter will be so likewise; writing is the interpreter of the mind, which will always produce what is consonant to its own native conceptions; and when kings, and the great men of the earth, once see this wonderful gift of poetry employed on subjects of wisdom, virtue and dignity, they bestow marks of honour, esteem and munificence upon the poet, they crown him from the leaves of that tree, which is proof against the glancing thunderbolt, emblematically denoting, that such as wear that crown ought to be secure against all hurt or offence."

The traveller wondered so much at Don Quixote's discourse, that he began to be stag-

ger'd in his mind, whether he was a madman or not. But, as this conversation did not altogether hit Sancho's taste, he had, in the midst of it, gone out of the road, to beg a little milk of some shepherds who were milking ewes hard by, and the gentleman in green, who seemed very fond of the good sense and ingenious conversation of Don Quixote, was going to renew their dialogue, when the Don, suddenly lifting up his eyes, saw a carriage with the king's colours meeting them upon the road, and taking this for some new adventure, called to Sancho to bring his helmet. Sancho, hearing the voice of his master, left the shepherd in great hurry, and mounting Dapple, arrived where Don Quixote was, to whom there happened a very terrible and tremendous adventure.

## CHAPTER XVII.

Which sets before the reader that highest and most exalted pinnacle, which the incredible magnanimity of Don Quixote ever did, or ever could arrive at, with the happy issue of the adventure of the lions.

The history then proceeds to inform us, that when Don Quixote called upon Sancho to bring him his helmet, he, Sancho, was deep in bargain with the shepherds about some curds; and finding himself summoned in such violent haste by his master, was at a prodigious loss what to do with them, for he had paid for them, and could not bear the thought of losing his purchase; in this extremity he had recourse to his master's helmet, in which he safely stowed them, and hugging himself in this lucky thought, away he trotted to receive the commands of his lord and master, who desired him to deliver his helmet; "For," said he, "if I know aught of adventures, that which I descry yonder will prove such a one as will oblige me to have recourse to arms."

Don Diego, upon hearing this declaration, looked about him every where, but, could discover nothing except a carriage coming towards them, with two or three flying flags, by which he guessed the carriage might be loaded with some of the king's money, and mentioned this observation to Don Quixote, who minded not what he said, his brain wandering so upon adventures, that every thing must be one, and nothing but a series of one adventure upon the back of another; he therefore answered the gentleman to this effect: "Sir, forewarned and forearmed is half the day; I am not now to learn that I have enemies of all kinds, visible and invisible; neither know I the time, the place, the hour, nor under what appearance they will attack me." With these words turning about, he demanded his helmet of Sancho, who not having time to disengage the curds from it, was obliged to deliver it with that lining in the inside to his master, who took it, and without farther examination, clapped it in a great hurry upon his head, which pressing and squeezing the curds, the whey began to ooze down his beard; and this circumstance so startled him, that he called out to Sancho, "What can this mean; is my skull softening

or my brains melting, or do I sweat from head to foot? Surely, this I can say, that if I do sweat, it is not through fear, though I am fully persuaded this will prove a most terrible adventure. If you have got anything, let me have it to wipe me, for this deluge of sweat blinds my eyes." Sancho replied not, but gave him a cloth, and with it sent up his thanks to the Almighty, that his master had not found out what it was. Don Quixote, after rubbing himself, took off his helmet, to see what it was that sat so cool upon his head, and, perceiving something white and clotted, put it to his nose and snuffed at it: "By the life of my lady Dulcinea del Toboso," cried he, "thou hast put curds into my helmet, thou traitor, thou ill-bred squire!" To which apostrophe, Sancho answered with great unconcern and tranquillity, "If they are curds let me have them to eat, but, the devil ought rather to eat them, for, I am sure it must be he who put them there. I offer to defile your worship's helmet! in good troth, I can perceive, by the help of that understanding God has given me, that I am not without my enchanters too, who are at me, as a sort of member and limb of your worship; and I'll be sworn, have put that nastiness there, to instigate your worship to wrath against me, and stir up your worship to anoint my ribs in the manner your worship was wont to do. But, this time, they have missed their aim, I trow, as I can depend upon the just sentence of my master, who will easily weigh with himself, that I had neither curds, cream, nor any such stuff; and that if I had, it was more likely I should have crammed them into my own guts than put them into his worship's helmet." "All this is possible"; cried Don Quixote: and all this the other gentleman saw, and saw with astonishment, more especially, when our hero, after having clean'd his head, beard, chops, and helmet, clap'd the latter upon his skull, and fixing himself in his seat, tried whether or not his sword could be easily drawn; then grasping his spear, "Now," cried he, "happen what will happen, here am I determined for the combat, should the prince of the evil spirits set himself in battle array against me."

By this time, the carriage with the streamers was come up, attended only by the driver (who rode one of the mules) and a man who sat upon the fore-part of it. Don Quixote wedged himself directly in their way, and called out, "Whither, my brethren, are you bound? what carriage is this? what does it contain? what ensigns are those display'd?" To which interrogations, the waggoner replied, "The carriage itself belongs to me, and within are two savage lions, which the general of Oran sends to court to his majesty; the streamers are the ensigns of our lord the king, to shew that what is here contained belongs to the crown." "Are these lions large?" answered Don Quixote. "So large," replied the man, who sat upon the fore-part of the waggon, "that lions of a more monstrous size never came from Barbary into this kingdom. I am their keeper, and have had several under my charge before now, but never any so big as they; there is a male and a female, the he is in the first cage, and the female in the other; they are now ravenous with hunger, having had no food to-day, and therefore I must entreat you to get out of the way, as we must make haste to the place where they are to be fed." To which intreaty, Don Quixote answer'd with half a smile, "What are your lion whelps to me, and at this time of day too! are lion whelps brought against me? I'll make those who sent them hither, yes—by the holy God! I'll make them see whether I am a man to be scared by lions. Come, honest friend, get off, and as you are their keeper, open the cages and turn them out; for, in the midst of this plain, will I make the savage beasts of the wilderness know

who Don Quixote de la Mancha is, in defiance of the enchanters who have sent them against me."

"Ah ha!" said Don Diego to himself, "I think our knight of the rueful countenance has now given us a pretty incontestable sample of what he is, these curds have certainly soaked his skull, and suppurated his brains." Then Sancho came up to Diego, and said, "For God's sake, signor, take care that my master's worship does not encounter these lions, or belike, we shall all of us be tore to pieces." "What," answered he, "is your master then really so much out of his wits, that you believe and dread he will engage these savage monsters?" "He is not out of his wits," replied Sancho, "but prodigious bold."

"I'll make him give over," answered the other: then going up to Don Quixote, who was pressing the keeper to open the cages, he said, "Signor, gentlemen of the order of knights-errant, ought to go upon adventures that have a probability of success, not such as are quite desperate; for, that courage which is almost temerity, savours rather of madness than true fortitude. Besides, these lions do not come with any hostile design against you; no, they think of nothing less; they are going to be presented to the king, and as they are on their way to court, I think they should not be stopped in their journey." "Pray, good signor," said Don Quixote, "if you will please to get away from hence, and look after your ferrets and decoy-partridges, do, and leave every one to mind his own business; this is my business, and it behoves me to know whether or not these lions come against me." Then turning to the keeper, "Sirrah," said he, "if you do not immediately open the cages, I swear by the living God, I will this instant pin you to the place where you sit."

The carter, seeing the obstinate resolution of this armed phantom, who addressed him, begged for the sake of charity, he would let him take off his mules, and get with them out of danger, before the lions were uncaged, "For should my cattle be slain," said he, "I am undone for ever, having nothing to depend upon for bread but this cart and these mules." "Man of little faith," said Don Quixote, "alight, take off thy mules, and do what thou wilt, but thou shalt quickly see thou hast laboured in vain, and that thou mightest have spared thyself this unnecessary trouble." The carter then got off, and unharnessed in great hurry, and the keeper spoke aloud, "I call all present to witness that I am forced, against my will, to open the cages, and let loose the lions; and I here declare, that this gentleman is chargeable with, and answerable for, all the harm they shall do, as also for my salary and perquisites over and above. And now, gentlemen, pray take care of yourselves, and get out of the way, for, as to me, I know they will do me no harm." Don Diego again urged him to forbear attempting so extravagant an action, alledging it was tempting of God to think of going about such a desperate undertaking. The other replied, that he knew what he did; and Don Diego once more desired him to think well of what he was about, as he was certain that he deceived himself. "Signor," said Don Quixote, "if you do not care to be a spectator of what you think will be a tragical adventure, set spurs to your mare, and provide for your own safety." Sancho, upon this intimation, fell a blubbering, and earnestly besought him not to think of entering upon this adventure; "For, in comparison of this," said he, "the windmills, the terrible adventure of the fulling-mill hammers, nay, all the exploits your worship has performed during the course of your life, are but custards and puff-paste.[1] Consider, sir," continued he, "that

there can be no enchantment in this cage; I myself have peeped through the cage, and there I saw the claw of a real living lion; and sure I am that the beast that owns such a claw, must be bigger than a mountain." "Be he large or small," answered Don Quixote, "thy fear would magnify him to the bigness of one half of the globe. Begone, leave me; if I die, you know our old agreement; repair to Dulcinea. I say no more." He spoke several other things, which shewed he was determined on what he was about, and that all attempts to dissuade him were in vain.

Don Diego would willingly have stopped him, but had neither weapons nor armour equal to the other's, and besides, did not think it prudent to engage with a man who was frantic; for, by this time, he was convinced that Don Quixote was so in all respects; who still pressing the keeper, and repeating his threats, Don Diego clap'd spurs to his mare, Sancho applied his heels to Dapple, the carter put forward his mules, and all endeavoured to get as fast out of the way as they could, before the beasts were let loose. Sancho deplored the fate of his master, who he believed was just going to be sacrificed by the lions; he bewailed his own hard fortune, and cursed the hour when he thought of serving him again; however, amidst the intenseness of his grief, he ceased not to punch and jog on his ass, that he might get from the cart as far as possible. The keeper seeing that these runaways were now safe, at a sufficient distance, renewed his expostulations with Don Quixote, who said, "I hear you, friend, but, give yourself no more trouble with arguments or entreaties, it will all signify nothing; and therefore I desire you will make haste."

While the keeper protracted the time in opening the first grate, Don Quixote considered with himself, whether he had best alight for the combat, or continue on the back of Rozinante; and determined, at last, to fight on foot, lest his steed might take fright at the sight of the lions. Accordingly he leaped upon the ground, threw away his lance, braced his shield, and drew his sword; in which attitude, approaching with great steadiness, he placed himself just before the cart, recommending himself, with great devotion, first to the protection of the Almighty, and then to his mistress Dulcinea del Toboso.

We must observe that, at this place, the author of this history breaks out into pathetic exclamations, expressing himself to this purpose, "O Don Quixote de la Mancha! renowned for fortitude, brave beyond human expression, thou mirrour, in which all heroes of the earth may contemplate their own perfections! thou second and other Don Manuel de Leon, glory and ornament of Spanish knights! how shall I find words worthy to relate this matchless atchievement: by what power of argument shall I make it gain credit among future generations? for, what encomiums ever so exalted, even beyond hyperbole, can there be, but what thou deservest? On foot thou stood'st, collected within thy magnanimous self, with a sword far from being sharp, with a shield far from bright and shining; there, I say, did'st thou stand waiting and expecting two of the fiercest lions that were ever yet engendered in the dens of Libya. I want words wherewithal to embellish thy great atchievements; let thy own exploits then be the harbinger of thy praises, O heroic Manchegan!"

The author here breaks off his exclamation, and proceeds in the recital of the history, saying,

The keeper seeing Don Quixote fixed in this posture, and finding himself under a ne-

cessity of letting loose the he-lion, to avoid the resentment of this enraged and intrepid hero, flung the door of the first cage open, where the lion appeared lying, of a monstrous bigness and terrifying aspect: he immediately turned himself round in the cage, put out one of his paws, and stretched himself at full length, yawned and gaped with great composure, and then, with a tongue of about half a yard long, clean'd his face and eyes, after which he thrust his head out of the cage, and stared around him with eyes like firebrands; a sight sufficient to have struck a damp into the most intrepid heart: but, Don Quixote only fixed his eyes attentively upon him, wishing for the minute he would leap out of the cart, that he might engage, and cut him in pieces; to such an unaccountable degree had his frenzy work'd up his disturbed imagination. But, the lion, naturally generous, and more inclinable to be gentle than rough, heeded not his bravadoes or flourishing; on the contrary, after having looked around him, as we have observed, turned about, and shewing our hero his back-side, with great composure and tranquillity, laid himself down again to rest; which circumstance, Don Quixote perceiving, ordered the keeper to rouse him by blows, and oblige him to come forth: "Nay that I won't," answered he; "for, should I enrage him, he would immediately tear me to pieces: come, Sir knight, be contented with what you have done, which is all that can be expected from any man's courage, and give over tempting fortune any more. The door of his cage is open, and he may come forth, or not, as he pleases, but, as he has not come out now, he will not all day. The intrepidity of your worship's valour is sufficiently vouched; I apprehend the bravery of no combatant needs do more than challenge his adversary, and await him in the field; and if the enemy won't meet him, the imputation of cowardice lies with him, and the crown of victory devolves upon the other." "You say true," said Don Quixote; "shut the door, my friend, and let me have, under your hand, in the best manner you are able to draw it, a certificate of what you have now seen; for, I think it is highly fitting mankind should know that you open'd the lion's cage; that I waited for him, and he came not out; that I waited for him again, and he came not out; and that again he laid himself down. I am not bound to do any more; so enchantments avaunt, and God prosper truth, justice and noble chivalry: shut the door therefore, and I will wave a signal for those who have run off, to return, and have an account of this action from your own mouth."

The keeper obeyed; and Don Quixote clapping upon the point of his lance the cloth Sancho had given him to wipe off the curds, called out to them, who were still pursuing their flight, and at every step, all in a body, turning about their heads, and Don Diego leading them on; but, Sancho chancing to espy the signal of the linen cloth, "I'll be bound to be crucified," said he, "if my master has not got the better of the lions, for he now calls to us." They all stopped, and perceived it was Don Quixote who made the sign; upon which the violence of their terrors somewhat abated, and they approached nearer and nearer, by degrees, till they could distinctly hear the voice of Don Quixote calling to them; at last, they came back to the cart, and Don Quixote said to the carter, "Harness your mules again, my friend, and go on in your journey; and, Sancho, give him and the keeper two crowns of gold, as a recompence for the time I have detained them." "That I will most willingly do; but where are the lions, dead or alive?" Then the keeper very circumstantially, and dividing his discourse with great propriety, gave an account

of the issue of this adventure, exaggerating, with all his might, and all the power of rhetorick he could muster up, the courage of Don Quixote, at sight of whom, said he, the lion overawed, would not, or rather durst not, venture out of the cage, though I held the door open a considerable time; and that upon remonstrating to the great knight, that it was tempting of God, to provoke the lion so far as to oblige him to come out by force, as he wanted him to have done, and was going to make him do, whether he would or not, his honour had suffered the cage door to be shut. "Sancho," said Don Quixote, "what dost thou think now, can enchantments avail ought against true courage? They may indeed, and with ease, stand in the way of my good fortune, but, of valour and res- olution they never can deprive me." Sancho gave the crowns to the people; the carter harnessed his mules, and the keeper kissed Don Quixote's hand for his liberality, and promised, when he arrived at court, he would give an account of this heroic atchieve- ment to his majesty himself. "Should the king," said Don Quixote, "perchance enquire who performed it, tell him, it was the knight of the lions; for, I am determined, that, from this time forward, the title I have been hitherto distinguished by, of knight of the rueful countenance, shall be changed, barter'd and sunk, into that of knight of the lions; and in this alteration, I imitate the example of knights-errant of old, who, as they pleased, altered their designations, as it best suited their purposes."

The carriage went forward, Don Quixote, Sancho, and the traveller in green pursued their journey; and, during all this time, Don Diego de Miranda was so attentive to re- mark and observe the actions of Don Quixote, that he had not opened his mouth, but looked upon him as a man whose good sense was blended with a strange sort of mad- ness: the reason was, he knew as yet nothing of the first part of his history; had he read that, his amazement at the knight's words and actions would have vanished, as it would have clear'd up to him the nature of his frenzy; but, as he knew not that, he was at times divided in his opinion, sometimes believing him in his senses, and at other times think- ing him frantic; because, what he spoke was sensible, consistent, and genteelly ex- pressed, but, his actions discovered all the symptoms of wildness, folly, and temerity. "For, what greater sign of disorder," said he to himself, "can there be, than for a man to clap on a helmet full of curds, and then take it into his head, that some magician had liquified his skull, and what more certain proof of fool-hardiness and wild frenzy, than for a person, in spite of all that can be said to him, to resolve to engage lions."

Don Quixote interrupted these reflections and soliloquy of his fellow-traveller, by saying, "Signor Don Diego de Miranda, I don't doubt but that, in your judgment, I must pass for an extravagant madman; and indeed no wonder, for, to be sure, my actions would seem to declare me such; but, at the same time, I must beg leave to say to you, that I am not so disordered, or so bereft of understanding, as to you I may have seemed. The gay cavalier, who in burnished armour, before the ladies prances over the lists, makes a gallant appearance. The adventrous knight too shews off to great advantage, when in the midst of the spacious square, in view of his prince, he transfixes the furious bull. And a noble appearance make those knights, who, in military exercises, or such like, are the life, spirit, and even honour of their prince's court. But, a much more noble figure than all these makes the knight-errant, who in the solitudes of the desert, thro' the almost impervious passages of the forest, and over the craggy mountains, goes in

quest of perilous adventures, to bring them to a successful issue, and that only to obtain glory, honour, and an immortal name. A knight-errant, I say, makes a more glorious appearance, when he assists the widow in some solitary plain, than the courtier knight, when he lavishes his gallantry on a town-lady. All cavaliers have their different spheres, in which they act: let the courtier pay his attendance to the ladies; adorn the court of his prince with the splendor of his equipage, entertain gentlemen of inferior fortunes with the hospitality of his sumptuous table; let him propose matches of different exercise, and direct the justs and tournaments; let him shew himself splendid, liberal and munificent; and above all, approve himself a good christian; in acting thus, he will discharge the duties that belong to him. But for the knight-errant, let him explore the most hidden recesses of the universe, plunge into the perplexities of the labyrinths; let him, at all times, not be afraid of even impossibilities; in the barren, wasteful wilderness, let him defy the scorching rays of the solstitial sun, and the piercing chillings of the nipping frost. Lions must not frighten him, phantoms must not terrify him, nor dragons dismay him; for, in searching after such, engaging with, and getting the better of all difficulties, consists his true and proper occupation. It being my fortune then to be of this last order, I cannot, consistent with that, avoid engaging in whatever I deem to be part of the duty of my calling; and for these reasons, tho' I knew, that encountring the lions was in itself an act of the greatest temerity, yet it immediately belonged to my profession: I am very sensible that true fortitude is placed between the two extremes of cowardice and fool-hardiness, but then, it is better valour should mount even to an over daring hardiness, than be debased to pusillanimity; for, as the prodigal is more likely to become truly generous than the miser, so will the over courageous sooner be brought to true valour, than the coward to be courageous at all; and in undertaking adventures, I assure you, Don Diego, it is much better to overdo than underdo, and much better does it sound in the ear of him to whom it is related, that a knight is daring and presumptuous, than that he is pusillanimous and faint-hearted."

"Signor Don Quixote," answered Diego, "I think all you have said is consonant to the rule of right reason; and I am of opinion, that if the laws and statutes of true chivalry were lost, they would be found deposited and faithfully recorded in your breast: but, if you please, we will put on, for it grows late; let us get towards my house and village, that you may have some rest, and taste of some refreshment after your late fatigue, which, if it does not weary the body, must be heavy upon the mind, the labours of which often affect the body likewise." "I accept of your invitation, Don Diego," said the other, "as a favour and mark of politeness." And hastening forward a little quicker than they had done before, they arrived about two in the afternoon at the habitation of Diego, on whom Don Quixote bestowed the appellation of knight of the green surtout.

# THE

# LIFE and ATCHIEVEMENTS

## Of the Sage and Valiant KNIGHT

# DON QUIXOTE DE LA MANCHA.

# BOOK II.

### CHAPTER I.

## Of what befel Don Quixote, at the castle or house of the knight of the green surtout; with other out-of-the-way matters.

Don Quixote found, that Diego's house, like the houses of most country gentlemen, was large and roomy; with the arms of the family over the great gates, cut out in rough stone; the buttery was in the yard, the cellar was under the porch, and around were placed divers jars, which jars being of the manufactory of Toboso, recalled the memory of the metamorphosed and inchanted Dulcinea; upon which, without reflecting on what he said, or before whom, he poured out his sighs and tears: "O dearest pledges," said he, "which now I find in bitterness of sorrow, but sweet and ravishing when heaven's high will ordained it so; O jars of Toboso, which have recalled into my mind, the dear idea of my greatest sorrow!" This exclamation was overheard by the young poet, Diego's son, who, along with his mother, had come down to receive Don Quixote. Both mother and son were struck with his uncouth figure, and he, alighting from Rozinante, with great good breeding, begged leave to kiss the lady's hands. To which intreaty, Don Diego added, "Madam, receive, with your usual politeness, signor Don Quixote de la Mancha, knight-errant, whom I here introduce to you as a gentleman of the brightest parts and most intrepid courage of any in the world." Donna Christina (for that was the lady's name) received him with all the marks of respect and esteem, and Don Quixote overpaid them in polite and mannerly acknowledgements; the same kind of intercourse passed between him and the young scholar, whom he took by his conversation to be a gentleman of vivacity and acuteness.

The author here minutely describes Don Diego's house, gives an inventory of the furniture usually contained in the house of rich country gentlemen: but, the translators of this history have thought it advisable not to mention these and other such particular

matters, as being rather foreign from the main scope of this history, in which truth has more energy than needless and languid digressions.

Don Quixote was conducted into a hall, where Sancho disarmed him; after which, he remained in his other accoutrements, a pair of wide waloon breeches, and a shamoy-leather doublet, stained with the rust of his armour; his band was collegian, neither starched nor laced, his buskins of the colour of dates, and his shoes of waxed leather: he girded upon his thigh his trusty sword, which hung at a belt of seal's skin, for, it is believed he had been for some years troubled with an imbecillity in his loins; and over all these was a long cloak of good grey cloth; but, before he stirred any further, he applied to his face five or six pitchers (the precise number not being exactly ascertained) of fair water, which nevertheless still ran off exhibiting a whey colour; and it was undoubtedly owing to the irregular appetite of Sancho, and his having made the bargain for these nasty curds, that his master was now scoured so white and so clean. In this equipment, as here described, and with a gallant air and address, Don Quixote walked into another hall, where the young gentleman of the house was waiting to receive and entertain him, till dinner should be got ready; for, as to the lady, Donna Christina, she was busy in ordering matters so, upon the arrival of this noble guest, as to let it be seen she knew what reception to give those who came to visit under her roof.

While Don Quixote was unarming, Don Lorenzo (that was the name of Diego's son) took the opportunity of that leisure time to ask his father, who that knight was he had brought home to them; "for," said he, "his name and uncouth figure, and your telling us, at the same time, that he is a knight-errant, puzzle both my mother and me prodigiously." Said Don Diego, "I know not what answer to make you; all I can say is, I never saw a madman act more franticly, and have heard him talk so very sensibly, as gave the lie to all his actions: but, I would have you enter into conversation with him, and sound the depth of his understanding; you have sense enough, and therefore I would have you form a judgment of him according to your own observation; to say the truth, I myself am more inclined to believe him distracted than otherwise."

Upon this intimation, Don Lorenzo went to entertain Don Quixote, as we have mentioned, who, among other discourse, said to Lorenzo, "signor Don Diego de Miranda, your father has been pleased to inform me a little of your great genius and good judgment, and particularly that you are a great poet." "A poet in some sense, I may be," said Lorenzo; "but a great one did I never so much as dare, even in my own imagination, to think myself: true it is, I am a little fond of poetry, and of reading the good poets; but, don't at all for that reason merit the title my father is pleased to bestow upon me." "I love your reserve," said Don Quixote; "for, poets are usually far removed from modesty, each thinking himself the greatest in the world." "No rule holds universally," answered Lorenzo, "and there may be one who is really a great poet, and yet does not think himself so." "There must be very few such," answered the other; "but, pray, Sir," continued he, "what verses are those you are about, which your father says make you so anxious and studious? for, if it be commenting upon some theme, I know somewhat of the art of paraphrasing, and should be glad to see what your performance is; and if they are designed as a poetical prize, let me advise you to obtain the second, for the first is decreed in view of interest, or in favour of the great quality of some person; but, merit carries the sec-

ond: so that, according to the general practice of our universities, the third becomes the second, and the first the third: but, notwithstanding this acceptation, the name of the first makes a great shew." "So far surely," said Lorenzo to himself, "this gentleman shews no sign of a disturbed understanding; but we'll go on: Your worship, I presume, has been long at the schools; pray, Sir, what sciences have you addicted yourself to?" "That of knight-errantry," replied Don Quixote; "a science equally sublime as your poetry, and in my humble opinion, even mounted a few steps above it." "That science," answered Lorenzo, "I am hitherto a stranger to; it has not yet come within the extent of my knowledge." "It is a science," answered the other, "that includes in itself virtually, most, if not all the other sciences in the world; for, he who professes it, must be a civilian, and know the laws both of distributive and commutative justice, to determine, with equity and propriety, what lawfully and properly belongs to every individual: he must be a good divine and casuist, that he may, with clearness and precision, defend the principles of the christian faith, which he professes, as often as he shall be required so to do: he ought to be a physician, and particularly a botanist, that, in the midst of desarts and wildernesses, he may know those herbs that are of efficacy in curing wounds; for a knight-errant cannot at every turn have recourse to a surgeon. He ought to be an astronomer, to distinguish by the stars the time of the night, together with the climate and part of the globe on which he chances to be: he must be learned in the mathematics, for which he will frequently have occasion; and besides being adorned with all the theological and cardinal virtues, he ought to descend to other minute branches of science; I say, for example, he must know how to swim like an herring,[1] to shoe an horse, to mend a saddle and bridle. And, returning to what we have observed above, he must preserve his fealty to God and his mistress: he must be chaste in thought, decent in speech, liberal in action, valiant in exploits, patient in toil, charitable with the needy; and finally, an asserter of truth, even though the defence of it should cost him his life. Of all these great and small qualities is a good knight-errant composed; so, that Signor Don Lorenzo may judge, whether it be a snivelling science which is learned and professed by a knight-errant; and whether it may not be compared with the sublimest which are taught in college and schools." "If that be the case," replied Don Lorenzo, "I affirm, that it has the advantage over all others." "How!" cried Don Quixote, "if that be the case!" "What I would say," resumed Lorenzo, "is, that I doubt whether there ever were or are knights-errant adorned with so many virtues." "I have often said what I am now going to repeat," answered Don Quixote, "that the greatest part of the world believes there never were knights-errant; and, in my opinion, if heaven does not work a miracle to prove that they both did and do exist, whatever trouble may be taken, will fail of success, as I know by repeated experience: I will not therefore, spend time at present, in refuting and rectifying the error in which you and many others are involved; but my intention is to pray that heaven will extricate you from your mistake, and give you to understand how advantageous and necessary knights-errant have been to the world in past ages, and how useful they might be to the present, were it the custom to sollicit their assistance: but, now, for the sins of mankind, idleness, sloth, gluttony and extravagance prevail and triumph." Here Don Lorenzo said within himself, "Now hath our guest given us the slip; but, nevertheless, he is a whimsical madman, and I should be an idle fool, if I thought otherwise."

In this place their discourse was interrupted by a call to table; and Don Diego asked his son, what he had fairly extracted from the genius of his guest? To this question he replied, "All the best physicians and writers that the world contains, will not extract him fairly from the blotted sheet of his madness; but, he is a party-coloured maniac, full of lucid intervals." They sat down to eat, and their repast was such as Don Diego had said upon the road he was wont to bestow upon his friends whom he invited, neat, plentiful and savoury; but, what yielded more satisfaction to Don Quixote, was, the wonderful silence that prevailed over the whole house, which in this particular resembled a monastery of carthusians.

The cloth being removed, grace said, and hands washed, Don Quixote earnestly desired that Don Lorenzo would repeat the verses designed for the literary contest; and the young gentleman answered, "Rather than appear one of those authors, who when they are requested to rehearse their works, refuse to grant the favour; and, on the other hand, disgorge them upon those who have no inclination to hear them, I will repeat my gloss, from which I expect no reward, as I composed it solely with a view to exercise my genius." "It was the opinion of an ingenious friend of mine," said Don Quixote, "that no man ought to fatigue himself in glossing upon verses; because, as he observed, the gloss could never come up to the text; and very often, or indeed, almost always, the gloss was foreign to the original proposition; besides, the laws of the gloss were extremely narrow, restricting the paraphraser from the use of interrogation; and, 'Said he,' or, 'I will say'; as well as from changing verbs into nouns, and altering the sentiment; with other ties and shackles incurred by those who try their fortune in this way, as you yourself undoubtedly know." "Verily, signor Don Quixote," cried Don Lorenzo, "I am very desirous of intraping your worship in false Latin; but, it is not in my power; for you slip through my fingers like an eel." "I do not know," answered the knight, "what you mean by saying I slip through your fingers." "I will explain myself some other time," replied Don Lorenzo, "mean while your worship will be pleased to hear the paraphrase and the text, which run thus."

<div align="center">

THE TEXT.

C ould I the moments past renew,
    Though fate should other joys deny;
Or bring the future scenes to view,
    In time's dark womb that rip'ning lie.

THE GLOSS.

A s all things perish and decay;
    So did the happiness I mourn,
On silent pinion fleet away;
    Ah! never-never to return.
At fortune's feet forlorn I lie:
    Would she again propitious strew
Her favours, who more blest than I,
    Could I the moments past renew.

</div>

No pleasure, palm or wreath I claim,
   No wealth or triumph seek to find;
For, all my wish and all my aim
   Is to retrieve my peace of mind.
Ah, fortune! thy returning smile
   Would change to bliss my destiny,
And ev'ry gloomy thought beguile,
   Though fate should other joys deny.

Fond wish! impossible and vain,
   No pow'r on this terrestrial ball
Can time's unwearied foot detain,
   Or his accomplish'd flight recall.
He forward flies, nor looks behind;
   And those miscarriage will pursue,
Who hope the fugitive to bind,
   Or bring the future scenes to view.

Perplex'd with hopes and fears I live,
   Though death at once would ease my pain;
What folly then for me to grieve,
   Who can that easy cure obtain?
No! yet a wiser course I'll steer,
   Resolv'd my fortune still to try,
Until those happier days appear,
   In time's dark womb that rip'ning lie.

Don Lorenzo no sooner concluded his paraphrase, than Don Quixote starting up, took the young gentleman by the right hand, and raising his voice even almost to a hollow, pronounced, "Now by the heaven of heavens! noble youth, you are the best poet in the world, and deserve to be crowned with laurel, not by Cyprus or Gaeta, as an author said, whom God pardon, but by the academy of Athens, did it now subsist, and by those of Paris, Bologna and Salamanca, which are still in being. Heaven grant, that those judges who deny you the first prize, may be transfixed by the arrows of Apollo, and that the muses may never deign to cross the thresholds of their doors. Signior, let me hear, if you please, some of your more majestic verses, that I may be thoroughly acquainted with the pulse of your admirable genius." Is it not diverting, to observe, that Don Lorenzo was pleased with the applause of Don Quixote, although he considered him as a madman? O influence of flattery, how far do'st thou extend! and how unlimited are the limits of thy agreeable jurisdiction! This truth is verified in the behaviour of Lorenzo, who, in compliance with the desire and intreaty of the knight, repeated this sonnet, on the fable or story of Pyramus and Thisbe.

SONNET.

Fair Thisbe's charms what bulwarks could withstand!
   They pierc'd ev'n to her gallant lover's soul;
And Cupid hasten'd from the Cyprian strand,
   To view the narrow pass by which they stole.

> Here silence spoke, and through that narrow breach,
>    Which ev'n the timid voice durst not essay,
> Th'intrepid souls to perfect union stretch;
>    Inspir'd, impower'd by love's almighty sway.
> Th'ill-fated pair to death untimely came,
>    With flow'ry pleasure's tempting bait intic'd:
> By the same poignard, monument and fame,
>    At once destroy'd, enclos'd, immortaliz'd.

"Blessed be God!" cried Don Quixote, when he had heard the sonnet of Don Lorenzo, "That amidst the infinite number of consumptive poets that now exist, I have found one consummate, as your worship has plainly evinced yourself, by the art and execution of those stanzas."

The knight was sumptuously regaled in the house of Don Diego, for the space of four days, at the expiration of which, he thanked his entertainer for the noble treatment he had received from his hospitality, and begged leave to depart; for, as it did not become knights-errant to devote much time to ease and banquetting, he was desirous of fulfilling the duty of his profession, in seeking adventures, with which he understood that country abounded, and in which he hoped to employ the time till the day of the tournament of Saragossa, whither he was bound: but, first of all he was resolved to enter the cave of the Montesinos, about which so many strange stories were recounted all over that neighbourhood, that he might investigate and discover the origin and real springs of the seven lakes of Ruydera. Don Diego and his son applauded the glorious design, and desired he would supply himself with whatever their house or fortune could afford; for, they would, with the utmost good will perform that service which they equally owed to his personal valour and honourable profession. At length arrived the day of his departure, as joyful to the knight as dismal and unfortunate to Sancho Panza, who had lived so much at his ease amidst the plenty of Don Diego's house, that he could not, without reluctance, return to the hunger that prevails in dreary forests, and to the poverty of his ill-provided bags, which, however, he now took care to fill and stuff with what he thought most necessary for his occasions.

At parting, Don Quixote addressing himself to Don Lorenzo, "I know not," said he, "whether I have already told your worship, but if I have, let me now repeat the intimation, that when you are inclined to take the shortest and easiest road to the inaccessible summit of the temple of fame, you have no more to do, but to leave on one side the path of poetry, which is pretty narrow, and follow that of knight-errantry, which, though the narrowest of all others, will conduct you to the throne of empire, in the turning of a straw." With this advice, did the knight, as it were, sum up the process of his madness, which, however, was still more manifest in this addition. "Heaven knows what pleasure I should feel in the company and association of Don Lorenzo, whom I would teach, by my own example, to spare the fallen, and trample the haughty under foot; virtues annexed to the order I profess: but, as his tender years do not require such tutorage, nor would his laudable exercises permit him to pursue my steps, I shall content myself with assuring his worship, that being a poet, he may certainly acquire renown, if he will conduct himself rather by the opinion of others, than his own; for, no parent ever thought

his own offspring ugly, and this prejudice is still more strong towards the children of the understanding."

Both father and son admired anew the strange medley of Don Quixote's discourse, in which so much discretion and madness were jumbled together; and were astonished at the wilfulness and obstinacy with which he was so wholly bent upon the search of his misadventurous adventures, that constituted the very aim of all his desires. Nevertheless, they repeated their offers of service and civility, and with the good leave of the lady of the castle, Don Quixote and Sancho set out on Rozinante and Dapple.

### CHAPTER II.

In which is recounted the adventure of the enamoured shepherd, with other truly diverting incidents.

A little way Don Quixote had travelled from the habitation of Don Diego, when he was joined by two persons dressed like ecclesiastics or students, and a couple of labouring men mounted upon asses: behind one of the students was a bundle wrapped up in green buckram, seemingly consisting of some linnen and two pair of coarse thread stockings; while the other was encumbered with nothing but a couple of new black fencing foils, with their buttons. The countrymen carried other things, which discovered and gave notice, that they were on their return from some great town, where they had made a purchase, and were bringing it home to their own village; and they, as well as the students, were seized with that admiration which was incident to all those who for the first time beheld Don Quixote; indeed they burned with curiosity to know what sort of a creature he was, so different in appearance from other men.

The knight saluted them courteously, and understanding their road was the same route that he designed to follow, made a proffer of his company, at the same time begging they would slacken their pace, as their beasts travelled faster than his horse. In order to facilitate their compliance with his request, he briefly told them who he was, made them acquainted with his office and profession, which was chivalry, and observed that he was going in quest of adventures, through all parts of the world; giving them to understand, that his proper name was Don Quixote de la Mancha, and his apellative, the knight of the lions.

All this information was Greek or gibberish to the countrymen, but not to the students, who immediately discovered the weakness of Don Quixote's brain; nevertheless, they beheld him with admiration, and one of them, in a respectful manner, accosted him thus: "If your worship, sir knight, follows no determined road, as those who go in quest of adventures, seldom do, be so good as to accompany us, and you will be an eye-witness of one of the most splendid and opulent weddings that ever were celebrated in La Mancha, or in many leagues around." When Don Quixote asked, if it was the marriage of any

prince, which he so highly extolled, the other replied, "It is no other than the bridal of a farmer and a country-maid; he the richest of all this neighbourhood, and she the comeliest that ever man beheld. The preparations are new and extraordinary; for, the marriage is to be celebrated in a meadow adjoining to the village of the bride, who, by way of excellency, is called Quiteria the beautiful, and the bridegroom is known by the apellation of Camacho the rich: she is but eighteen, and he turned of twenty, so that they are extremely well-matched; though some curious persons, who remember all the pedigrees in the world, are pleased to say, that her family has in that respect the advantage of Camacho's: but now-a-days these circumstances are altogether overlook'd; for, wealth is able to repair a number of flaws. In a word, Camacho is liberal, and has taken it in his head to overshadow and cover the whole meadow in such a manner, that the sun will find some difficulty in penetrating, so as to visit the verdant plants with which the ground is adorned. He has likewise bespoke choice dancers, both with swords and morrice-bells; for, there are people in the village who can jingle and snap to perfection; not to mention your shoe-slappers,[1] a power of whom are summoned to the nuptials: but, none of those things I have mentioned, or of a great many circumstances I have left untold, are likely to render the marriage so memorable as the behaviour which is on this occasion expected from the rejected Basilius.

"This Basilius is a neighbouring swain, and townsman of Quiteria, and there is nothing but a partition-wall between his house and that of her parents, whence Cupid took occasion to renew the long forgotten loves of Pyramus and Thisbe; for, Basilius became enamoured of Quiteria, even from his tender years, and she smiled upon his passion with all manner of honourable indulgence; insomuch, that the love of the two children Basilius and Quiteria furnished entertainment and discourse for the whole village. As their age increased, Quiteria's father resolved to forbid Basilius the usual access he had to his house; and, to free himself from all sorts of jealousy and suspicion, proposed a match between his daughter and the rich Camacho, thinking it would not be so well to give her away to Basilius, to whom fortune had not been so kind as nature; though, to tell the truth, without envy or affection he is the most active young man we know, an expert pitcher of the bar, an excellent wrestler, and great judge of hand-ball, he runs like a deer, leaps nimbler than a goat, plays at nine-pins as if he used inchantment, sings like a sky-lark, touches the guitarre so as to make it perfectly speak, and handles a foil like the best fencer in the world." "For that sole accomplishment," cried Don Quixote, "the young man deserves not only to be married to the beautiful Quiteria, but even to Queen Ginebra herself, were she now alive, in spite of Sir Lancelot, and all those who should endeavour to oppose the match." "Let my wife alone for that," said Sancho Panza, who had hitherto travelled in silent attention, "she, good woman, would have every body match with his equal, sticking to the old proverb, that says, Let every goose a gander choose. What I would willingly see, is the marriage of this worthy Basilius, for, he has already got my good-will, with that same lady Quiteria; and God grant them peace and plenty, and rest their souls in heaven (his meaning was quite the reverse) who prevent lovers from marrying according to their inclinations." "If that was always the case," replied Don Quixote, "parents would be deprived of that election and jurisdiction they possess, to marry their children when, and how, they shall think proper; and, if every

daughter was at liberty to indulge her own inclination in the choice of an husband, one would perhaps choose her father's servant, and another place her affection upon some gaudy coxcomb, whom she might chance to see passing along the street, even though he should be a disorderly ruffian: for, love and affection easily blind the eyes of the understanding, which are so necessary towards the settlement of one's condition in life; and, as we are apt to commit very important mistakes in the article of matrimony, it requires great caution as well as the particular favour of heaven, to succeed in the choice of a wife. A prudent man, who is resolved to undertake a long journey, will, before he sets out, endeavour to find a safe, quiet, and agreeable fellow-traveller. Then why should not the same pains be taken by the man who is going to travel through the whole journey of life? especially, in the choice of a companion for bed, board, and every other purpose for which the wife is subservient to the husband; a man's own wedded wife is not like a commodity which, being once bought, may be bartered, exchanged, or returned, but is an inseparable appendage that lasts for life.

"Marriage is a noose, into which, if the neck should happen to slip, it becomes inexplicable as the gordian knot, and cannot be undone till cut asunder by the scythe of death. Much more could I add upon this subject, if I were not prevented by the desire I have to know, whether Mr. licentiate has any thing further to entertain us with relative to the history of Basilius." To this hint, the other (call him scholar, batchelor or licentiate) replied, "I have not any thing material to add, but that from the time he understood Quiteria was to be married to Comacho the rich, he was never seen to smile, or heard to speak consistently; he is thoughtful and melancholy, talks to himself: all which are undoubted symptoms of a disordered mind. He scarce either eats or sleeps; and what little he does eat is fruit; when he sleeps at all, it is upon the bare ground, and in the open air, like the beasts of the field. He every now and then looks up to heaven; at other times, like one stupid, fixes his eyes on the ground, and seems as if he was a cloathed statue with the drapery flowing to the gales of the wind: in a word, he gives such indications of a fatal passion, that we believe for certain, when Quiteria to-morrow pronounces the word Yes, she will in that seal the sentence of his death."

"God will order things better," said Sancho, "for, he inflicts the wound, and will also perform the cure. No one knows what may happen; there are a great many hours between this and to-morrow, and in one hour, even in a moment, down comes the house: I have myself seen sun-shine and rain at the same time; a man goes to bed well at night, but cannot bestir himself next morning. Let me know, the best of ye, if any man can brag of having put a spoke in fortune's wheel? no one, to be sure; and between the Yes and No of a woman, I would not venture to thrust the point of a pin, and that for a weighty reason, because there would not be room for it: if you will only allow me one thing, that Quiteria loves Basilius, I'll yet engage to give him a wallet-full of good luck; for, I have been told, that love wears a pair of spectacles, which spectacles make copper look like gold, and poverty appear to be riches, and specks in the eyes to seem pearls." "A curse on thee!" cried Don Quixote, "what is it thou would'st be at? once thou art set in to stringing thy proverbs, none but Judas, with whom I wish thou wert, can have patience to hear thee out! Say animal, what knowest thou about spokes or wheels, or any other thing whatsoever?" "O! since you do not understand me," answered the squire, "no

wonder you think it nonsense what I say; but that signifies nothing, I understand my-self, nor have I said many nonsensical things yet, only your worship always plays the cricket upon my words and actions." "God confound thee, thou confounder of all lan-guage!" said Don Quixote. "Cricket! I suppose thou meanest critic." "As to that matter, Sir," said Sancho, "be not too severe upon me; you know I was neither bred at court, nor studied at Salamanca, to know when I am right in the letter of a word; and, as I hope for mercy from God, I think it unreasonable to expect that the Sayagues * should speak in the same manner as the Toledans; tho', for that matter, there are Toledans who are not more nice than other folks at the work of speaking properly." "Very true," said the li-centiate, "for how should a man, whose business is in the tan-yards, and in the Zocodover †, speak so good language as they who do nothing but walk from morning to night in the cloysters of the cathedral? and yet they are all Toledans: on the other hand, purity, propriety, elegance and perspicuity are to be found among polite people of sense, tho' they be natives of Majalahonda: I say people of sense, because so great a number of people are not so, and sense is the foundation of good language, assisted by custom and use. I must tell you, gentlemen, it has pleased God, for my sins, that I have studied the canon-law at Salamanca, and I pique myself a little, on being able to con-verse in clear, easy, and expressive language." "If you had not piqued yourself more upon your dexterity at these good-for-nothing foils you carry about with you, than upon your knowledge in languages, instead of lagging the hindmost, you might have been at the head of your class," said the other student. "I tell you, Mr. batchelor, that you are the most prejudiced man in the world, in that respect, for treating dexterity at the sword as a matter of no signification." "It is no prejudice with me, it is a confirmed opinion and truth," replied Corchuelo; "and if you please to make the experiment, I will convince you. You carry foils now along with you, and an opportunity offers; I'll shew you that I have nerves and strength, backed with such courage as will prove sufficient to demon-strate to you, that my opinion is not the effect of prejudice: get off your ass, and try your measured distances, your wheelings, your longes and art of defence; and I'll engage with only the plain rustic skill I have, to make you see the stars at noon-day; for, I trust under God, the man is yet unborn who can make me turn my back; nor have I met with any man whom I will not oblige to give ground." "As to turning your back or not turning your back, that is none of my business," replied the master of the science; "tho' it is not impossible but that the first spot you fix your foot on may prove your burying-ground: I mean, it is possible you may be left dead there, for slighting the noble science of defence." "That we shall see presently," replied Corchuelo, jumping hastily upon the ground, and snatching with great fury one of the foils, which the other carried upon his ass.

    Here Don Quixote cried out, "Not so, by heavens! I will be umpire of this fencing match, and judge of this long controverted dispute." So saying, he alighted from Rozi-nante, and grasping his lance, planted himself in the very middle of the road, just as master licentiate, in a masterly posture, and regular advances, was making towards

* Poor people that live about Zamora.[2]
† Zocodover, a square in Toledo, like Smithfield, where cattle are sold.[3]

Corchuelo, who ran at him with fire, as the saying is, flashing from his eye; while the two country fellows, without dismounting, sat still as spectators of this most deadly tragedy. Corchuelo assailed him every way with high strokes, low strokes, backstrokes, cuts, thrusts, slashes out of number, and as thick as hail; in short, he fell upon the licentiate, like an enraged lion, but was checked a little, in the career of his fury, by a smart push in the mouth from the licentiate's foil, who made him kiss the button, tho' with less devotion than if it had been a relic. In a word, the licentiate, by skilful and well planted thrusts, counted the buttons of his cassock, and went thro' it so often, that it hung in rags like the tails of the polypus: twice was Corchuelo's hat struck off, and so spent was he, that in rage and spite, and furious choler, he flung the foil into the air with so much force, that one of the countrymen, who went to fetch it, being a kind of scrivener, declared upon oath, that it went near three quarters of a league; which affidavit being preserved, has been, and is, a testimony to demonstrate, that art prevails over strength.

Corchuelo quite tired out, sat down, and Sancho going up to him, "Mr. batchelor," said he, "if you will be ruled by me, from henceforth challenge no one to fence, but dare them to wrestle and pitch the bar, since now you are of a proper age and strength for that exercise; for, I have heard say of these fencers, that they can thrust you the point of a sword thro' the eye of a needle." "I am now convinced," answered Corchuelo, "and am taught by experience, a truth I could not otherwise have believed."

So getting up, he went and embraced his adversary, and they were now better friends than ever. The company not being willing to wait for the scrivener, who was gone after the foil, imagining he might be too long absent, resolved to put forward as fast as they could, that they might arrive early at Quiteria's village, whither they were all going. As they travelled on their way, the licentiate demonstrated to them the excellencies of the noble science of defence, by such convincing arguments, drawn from the nature of truth and mathematical certainty, that every one was convinced of the usefulness of the science; and Corchuelo particularly was made a convert, and entirely cured of his obstinacy.

The night was just fallen, and before they came to the village it seemed as if something like a heaven full of an infinite number of bright stars was between them and it: they likewise heard an harmonious but mix'd sound of flutes, tambourines, psalters, cymbals, drums, and bells. As they came nearer, they perceived the boughs of an arbour, which was made on one side of the entrance into the village; and this all flaming with lights, which were not in the least disturbed by the wind; for, the evening was so calm, that there was not a breath of air, so much as to move a leaf upon a tree. But, the life and spirit of the wedding consisted in the musicians, who, in bands ranged up and down that delightful place, some singing, some dancing, and others playing upon the different instruments. In a word, it looked as if joy and delight were sporting and playing thro' this meadow: a great many were employed in raising scaffolds, that they might view from them more commodiously the plays and dances which were to be in that place, to solemnize the nuptials of Camacho the rich, and the obsequies of Basilius. Don Quixote refused to enter the village, tho' both the batchelor and the countryman invited him; but he pleaded what he thought a sufficient excuse, the custom of knights-errant to sleep in fields and forests, rather than in towns, tho' under gilded roofs; and therefore he turned

a little aside, grievously against the will of Sancho, who had not yet forgotten the good lodgings he had enjoyed at the house of Don Diego.

## CHAPTER III.

## An account of the wedding of Camacho the rich, and what happened to Basilius the poor.

The fair Aurora had hardly allowed Phoebus time to dry up the liquid pearls that hung upon his golden locks, when Don Quixote shaking from his limbs the drowsy fetters of sloth, got upon his legs, and called to Sancho Panza, who lay stretched along, and snoring, which situation his master seeing before he awak'd him, broke out into this soliloquy: "Happy thou, and blessed beyond the fate of other mortals, who neither envying nor envied, sleepest sound, with unconcern of soul! Enchanters neither persecute, nor enchantments terrify thee: sleep on, I say again, and a hundred times more I say, sleep on; no jealousies on account of a mistress torture thee with perpetual watchings; no anxious cares of paying debts awake thee; no sollicitude how thou must to-morrow provide for thyself and little ones, breaks in upon thy slumbers. Ambitious views create thee no disquiet, nor the vain pomp of this empty world occasions thee any disturbance; thy concern is center'd within the bounds of taking care of thy ass; for, as to taking care of thy person, that is laid upon my shoulders, a charge and burthen that both nature and custom have laid upon masters; the servant sleeps, while the master is awake, and thinking how he shall maintain him, advance him in life, or do him some service. The uneasiness that arises from seeing the heavens, as it were, hard as brass, locked up, and refusing rain to cherish the earth, brings no anxiety upon the servant but upon the master, who, in the days of dearth and famine, is bound to provide for him who served him in the time of abundant and plentiful harvest."

To all this effusion Sancho answered not one word; for, he was fast asleep, nor would have waked when he did, but that his master jogged him with the butt-end of his lance. He waked yawning and drowsy; and turning his face every way, "Umph," said he, "from yonder shady bower, if my nostrils deceive me not, proceeds rather the steam and savour of broiled rashers of bacon, than the fragrance of thyme and jessamine. O my conscience, weddings that begin in this savoury manner, must needs, in truth, be magnificent and abundant." "Thou epicure," said Don Quixote, "have done, and let us go see this wedding, and what will be the fate of the slighted Basilius." "Let his fate be as it pleases," quoth Sancho; "what, he poor and marry Quiteria! A pretty fancy truly, for one not worth a groat to think of matching so high; 'tis my opinion, a man who is poor ought to bless God for what he finds, and not be diving to find troufles at the bottom of the sea.[1] I'll lay a limb, that Camacho can cover this same Basilius from head to foot with sixpenny pieces; and if this be so, as it certainly is, Quiteria would be a pretty lady of a

bride indeed, to refuse all the fine cloaths and fine things that, I warrant you, Camacho has given her already, and can give her still more; and to prefer, instead of them, a pitch of the bar truly, and a pass at the foils, which, it seems, make up Basilius's riches. Go into a tavern for a pint of wine, and see if they will take a pitch of the bar, or a clever push of the foils, in lieu of the reckoning: as for your abilities, and your refinements and graces, that will bring in none of the ready; count Dirlos may have them for me; but, when they happen to take their resting-place on a man who has wherewithal, O then, I wish no better than that my life may shew off as well as they do. Upon a good foundation a good house may be raised, and the very best bottom and best foundation of any, is wealth." "O!" cried Don Quixote, "have done, have done with this harrangue; I do from my soul believe, if one would but suffer thee to go on, thou wouldst lose both thy eating and sleeping in talking." "Was your worship possessed of a good memory," replied Sancho, "you would remember certain articles stipulated between us, before we sallied forth upon this expedition; one of which was, that I was to talk as much as I pleased, provided it was not scandal against my neighbour, or derogating from your worship's authority; and I imagine, that nothing I have hitherto said, is a breach of this agreement." "I remember no such agreement," said Don Quixote; "but, allowing it to be so, it is my pleasure you should give over, and come attend me; for, now the instruments we heard last evening send their cheering sounds through the vallies; and beyond all doubt the nuptials will not be put off to the sultry heat of the noon-day, but be solemnized in the fresh cool of the morning."

Sancho did as he was commanded, and putting on Rozinante's saddle and Dapple's pannel, they both mounted, and gently walked their beasts into the artificial shade. The first object that presented itself to the eyes of Sancho, was an entire bullock spitted whole, upon an elm, roasting by a fire of wood of the size of a middling mountain, and round it six pots, but not such pots as are cast in common moulds, for, they were half jars, and each of them contained a whole shamble of meat; whole sheep found room in them and were stowed as commodiously as if they had been so many pigeons. There was an innumerable quantity of cased hares, and ready-plucked fowls that hung about the branches of the trees, ready to be swallowed up in these receivers; and an infinite number of wild fowl, with vast quantities of venison, were likewise hanging about the trees, for the air to cool them. Sancho himself told above threescore skins, which, as it was afterwards discovered, were full of rich wines, every skin containing about twenty four quarts. Loaves of the whitest bread were piled up like heaps of wheat on a threshing-floor; and such a quantity of cheese ranged in the form of bricks, as seemed a wall; two cauldrons of oil, larger than a dyer's vat, were ready for frying their fritters and pan-cakes; and when fried, they took them out with strong peels, and dipped them in another pot that stood by full of prepared honey. The cooks, men and women, amounted to above fifty, clean, good-humoured, and all busy; in the belly of the roasting bullock, were sewed a dozen sucking pigs, to make it tender and savoury. Spices of all sorts, which seemed to have been bought by wholesale and not by retail, stood in a vast chest. In short, the preparations for the wedding were indeed in a rustic taste, but in such plenty and profusion as might have feasted an army.

Sancho looked at every thing, attentively considered each particular and was in rap-

tures with the whole. But, his whole heart and affections were chiefly captivated by the flesh-pots; out of them he would have been glad, with all his heart, to have filled about a moderate barrel. Then the wine-skins made his bowels yearn; and after these the contents of the frying-pans, if vessels of such immoderate size may be so called. He could hold out no longer; it was not in the power of his nature to contain himself; therefore, up he went to one of the cooks, who was busy, and addressing himself to him with a humble and hungry air, begged that he might be permitted to sop a luncheon of bread in one of the pots. To which request the cook replied, "Hunger does not preside over this day, thanks be to Camacho the rich; even alight, and see if thou canst find any where a ladle, and skim out a fowl or two, and much good may it do thy good heart." "I see no ladle," said Sancho. "God forgive me all my sins!" cried the cook, "what a poor helpless thing thou art, stay." So saying, he laid hold of a kettle, and dipping it at once, into one of the half-jar pots, brought up three pullets, and a couple of geese. "Here," said he, "eat, make a breakfast of this scum, and see if you can stay your stomach with it, till dinner-time." "I have nothing to put it in," said Sancho. "Then, take ladle and all," replied the cook; "for, Camacho's riches and good fortune are sufficient to supply every thing."

While Sancho Panza passed his time in this manner, Don Quixote was attentive in observing about a dozen of his countrymen, who entered in at one side of this spacious arbour, mounted upon beautiful mares, each of them accoutred with rich and gay caparisons, and hung round with little bells. They were clad in holiday apparel, and coursed round the meadow in a body, and, in regular careers, several times, with a joyous moorish shout, flourishing, and crying out, "Long live Camacho and Quiteria, he as rich as she is fair, and she the fairest of the universe." Which exclamation, Don Quixote hearing, said within himself, "It is evident they never have beheld the beauty of my Dulcinea del Toboso; had they ever been blessed with a sight of her transcendant charms, they would be more sparing in their praises of this their Quiteria."

Some time after there entered, at different parts of the arbour, different sets of dancers; one of whom consisted of twenty-four sword dancers, all of them clean, well-made jolly swains, clad in fine, white linen, and white handkerchiefs embroidered with silk of various colours. One of those who were mounted upon the mares asked a youth, who led the band of the sword-dancers, whether any of his companions had received any hurt? "As yet," replied the other, "we are all safe and sound, thanks be to God, no one is wounded"; and immediately upon that mixed among his companions with so many twistings and windings, and with such dexterity, that though Don Quixote had been used to behold such dances, he never saw any he approved so much. Another dance likewise pleased him prodigiously; that was another chorus of twelve most beautiful damsels, of such an age, that none appeared under fourteen, nor did any seem to be quite eighteen; they were all clad in green stuff of Cuença, their locks were, some plaited, some flowing loose, and all so fine and flaxen, as to rival those of Phoebus himself, and crowned with garlands of roses of jessamine and of woodbine. This beautiful bevy was led up to the dance by a venerable old man and an ancient matron, both more airy and agile than could be expected from their years. A bagpipe of Zamora was their music, and with modesty in their looks and countenances, and lightness of foot, they danced and tripped it away the prettiest in the world. After these, entered an emblem-

atic dance of eight nymphs divided into two bodies: the god of love led one, and Interest the other; Cupid with his wings, his bow, his quiver and arrows; Interest clad in gold, and silk of rich and various colours. The nymphs, attendants on Cupid, had their names displayed in white parchment, and capital letters on their backs: the first was named Poetry, the second Discretion, the third Pedigree, the fourth Bravery. The attendants on Interest were likewise characterised: the first was Liberality, the second Bounty, the third Treasure, the fourth Quiet possession. The whole masque was preceded by a wooden castle, drawn by savages clad in ivy and hemp died green, and so savage they looked that they had almost frightened Sancho. On the front and on each of the four sides of this machine were inscribed these words, "The castle of discretion." Four able musicians played on the tabor and the pipe. Cupid, who began the dance, after he had made two movements, lifted up his eyes, and bent his bow against a damsel that stood upon the battlements of the castle, to whom he pronounced this address:

> I am the god whose pow'r extends
>    Through the wide ocean, earth, and sky;
> To my soft sway all nature bends,
>    Compell'd by beauty to comply.
> Fearless, I rule, in calm and storm,
>    Indulge my pleasure to the full,
> Things deem'd impossible perform,
>    Bestow, resume, ordain, annul.

Having repeated these stanzas, he shot an arrow to the top of the castle, and retired to his station. Then Interest advanced, and performed other two movements; after which the tabors were silent, and the power rehearsed these lines:

> My pow'r exceeds the might of Love;
>    For, Cupid bows to me alone,
> Of all things fram'd by heav'n above,
>    The most respected, sought, and known.
> My name is Interest, mine aid
>    But few obtain, though all desire,
> Yet, shall thy virtue, beauteous maid,
>    My constant services acquire.

Interest retiring, was succeeded by Poetry, who, after having performed his motions like the rest, fixed his eyes upon the lady of the castle, and said,

> Let Poetry, whose strain divine
>    The wond'rous pow'r of song displays,
> His heart to thee, fair nymph, consign,
>    Transported in melodious lays:
> If haply, thou wilt not refuse
>    To grant my supplicated boon,
> Thy fame shall, wafted by the muse,
>    Surmount the circle of the moon.

Poetry disappearing, Liberality advanced from the side of Interest, and, after several movements, repeated these lines:

> My name is Liberality,
>   Alike beneficent and wise,
> To shun wild prodigality,
>   And sordid avarice despise.
> Yet, for thy favour lavish grown,
>   A prodigal I mean to prove,
> An honourable vice, I own,
>   But, giving is the test of love.

In this manner, all the figures of the two squadrons advanced and retired, every one performing his movements, and repeating his verses, some of which were elegant, and others foolish enough; but those we have inserted, were all that Don Quixote could retain, although his memory was very tenacious: then mixing altogether in the dance, they winded and turned with great ease, grace and agility. Cupid, in passing shot arrows at the castle, while Interest battered it with round gilded earthen pots: at length, after the dance had continued a good while, this last pulled out a large purse made of Roman cat-skin, to all appearance full of money, and throwing it at the castle, the boards seemed to be disjoined by the blow, and immediately fell asunder, leaving the damsel quite discovered and defenceless; then Interest, with the figures of his train, advancing, and throwing a great gold chain about her neck, seemed bent upon taking and dragging her into captivity. This design being perceived by Cupid and his partisans, they made an effort to release her, and all their motions were performed by the sound of the tabors, to which they danced and capered in concert. Then the savages interposing, and effecting an accommodation, refitted and rejoined the boards of the castle with admirable dispatch, the damsel enclosed herself anew; and thus the dance was finished, to the infinite satisfaction of the spectators.

Don Quixote asked one of the nymphs, what author had contrived and composed this entertainment; and being told it was the production of the parson, who had a rare noddle for such conceits, "I'll lay a wager," said he, "that this same batchelor or curate is more a friend of Camacho than of Basilius; and that he is better acquainted with satire than prayer; for, he has very artfully interwoven in this masque the talents of Basilius, and the wealth of his rival." Sancho Panza overhearing this observation, "My cock is the king," said he, "and I hold fast by Camacho." "Then am I convinced," replied the knight, "that Sancho is one of the low-born peasants, who cry, Long life to the conqueror." "I know not," resumed the squire, "what sect I am of; but, this I know perfectly well, that I shall never skim from the flesh-pots of Basilius, such a delicate scum as this, that I have taken from the boilers of Camacho." With these words, he produced a kettle full of geese and pullets, and seizing a bird, began to eat with great glee and satisfaction; saying, in defiance of the talents possessed by Basilius, "Thou art worth just as much as thou hast, and hast just as much as thou art worth. There are only two families in the world, as my grannam was wont to observe, the have-somethings and the have-nothings: though she stuck always to the former; and now-a-days, my good master, we

are more apt to feel the pulse of property than of wisdom. An ass with golden trappings, makes a better appearance than an horse with a pack-saddle. Therefore, I say again, I hold fast by Camacho, the plentiful scum of whose pots contains geese, hens, hares, and coneys, while that of Basilius, if it comes to hand, or even if it should only come to the feet, is no better than dish-washings."

"Sancho," cried Don Quixote, "hast thou finished thy harangue?" "It shall be finished," replied the squire, "as I see your worship is displeased with it; though, if your disgust has not fallen in the way, I had cut out work enough for three days." "Grant heaven," said the knight, "that I may see thee dumb before I die." "At the rate we follow," answered Panza, "before your worship dies, my mouth will be crammed with clay, and then I may chance to be so dumb that I shall not speak another word to the end of the world, or at least, till the day of judgment." "Even should that be the case," replied Don Quixote, "I say unto thee O Sancho! thy silence will never counterbalance what thou didst, dost, and wilt say, during the course of thy life: moreover, according to the nature of things, the day of my death will happen before thine; so that I have no hope of ever seeing thee silent, even while thou art drinking or sleeping, and that is the greatest favour I could expect."

"In good sooth, signor," said the squire, "there is no trusting to * Mrs. Ghostly, I mean death, who gobbles up the goslin as well as the goose; and as I have heard our curate observe, tramples down the lofty turrets of the prince, as well as the lowly cottage of the swain. That same lady who is more powerful than coy, knows not what it is to be dainty and squeamish, but eats of every thing, and crams her wallet with people of all nations, degrees and conditions: she is none of your labourers that take their afternoon's nap, but, mows at all hours, cutting down the dry stubble as well as the green grass; nor does she seem to chew, but rather swallows and devours every thing that falls in her way; for, she is gnawed by a dog's hunger that is never satisfied; and though she has no belly, plainly shews herself dropsical, and so thirsty as to drink up the lives of all the people upon earth, just as one would swallow a draught of cool water." "Enough, friend Sancho," cried the knight, interrupting him in this place, "keep thyself well, now thou art in order, and beware of stumbling again; for, really a good preacher could not speak more to the purpose than thou hast spoken upon death, in thy rustic manner of expression: I say unto thee, Sancho, if thy discretion was equal to thy natural parts, thou mightest ascend the pulpit, and go about teaching and preaching to admiration." "He is a good preacher, who is a good liver," answered Panza; "and that is all the divinity I know." "And that is sufficient," said the knight; "yet I shall never understand or comprehend, as the fear of God is the beginning of wisdom, how thou, who art more afraid of a lizard than of thy maker, should be so wise!" "Signor," replied Sancho, "I desire your worship would determine in your own affairs of chivalry, without taking the trouble to judge of other people's valour or fears; for my own part, I am as pretty a fearer of God as one would desire to see in any neighbour's child: wherefore, I beseech your worship,

* In the original there is a play upon the words *Descarnada, Cordero* and *Carnero,* which I have endeavoured to imitate, by substituting goose in the room of mutton, which is the literal meaning of the text.[2]

let me discuss this same scum; for, every thing else is idle chat, of which we shall be able to give a bad account in the other world." So saying, he renewed his attack upon his kettle, with such keen appetite as awakened that of his master, who would have certainly joined in the assault, had not he been prevented by that which we must now relate.

## CHAPTER IV.

## Which continues to treat of Camacho's wedding, and other incidents.

While Don Quixote and Sancho were engaged in the conversation, related in the preceding chapter, they heard a great noise and shouting, raised by a company mounted on mares, galloping in full cry, to meet the young couple, who came, surrounded by a thousand kinds of instruments, and accompanied by the curate, the relations, and all the creditable people of the neighbouring villages, in their holiday cloaths. Sancho seeing the bride, exclaimed with marks of admiration, "I'faith! she looks more like one of your gay court-dames than a plain country maid. Now, by the biggest beads of my rosary! instead of a tin * brooch, her breast is bedizened with rich coral, and her hoyden-grey is turned into thirty-piled velvet, and body o'me! the trimming is not of white linnen but of silk and sattin; then handle me her hands set off with what? jewels of jet? no! let me never thrive, if they an't decked with rings of gold! aye, and of massy gold, paved with pearls as white as a curd, every one of which is worth a jew's eye. O the whoreson baggage! and such hair! if it is not false, I never saw any so long and so fair in my born-days. Do but mind how buxom, straight and tall she is, and see whether she may not be compared to a moving palm-tree, loaded with clusters of dates; for, nothing can be more like the gew-gaws and toys that hang from her hair and neck. By my salvation! the damsel is well covered, and might pass through all the banks of Flanders." Don Quixote, though he smiled at the rustic praises of his squire, owned that, exclusive of his mistress Dulcinea del Toboso, she was the most beautiful female he had ever seen.

Nevertheless the fair Quiteria was paler than usual; and this change of complexion must have been owing to the bad night which brides always pass, in adorning themselves for the approaching day of their nuptials. The company repaired to a theatre erected at one side of the meadow, and ornamented with carpets and boughs, where the ceremony was to be performed, and from whence they were to see the masques and other diversions; and they had just arrived at the place, when their ears were saluted with a noise behind them, and a voice that pronounced, "Stay a little, hasty and inconsiderate people." In consequence of this address, they turned about, and perceived it was uttered

* The *Patina* was a small consecrated plate which the Spanish women, especially those of an inferior rank, wore upon their breasts.[1]

by a man cloathed in a loose black coat, interspersed with crimson flames, crowned, as they soon perceived, with a chaplet of funereal cypress, and holding in his hand a truncheon of uncommon size. As he approached, he was known to be the gallant Basilius; at sight of whom they were surprized, and waited in suspence to see the issue of his exclamation, dreading some mischance from such an unseasonable visit. At length, wearied and breathless, he came up to the bride and bridegroom, and thrusting in the ground his staff that was pointed with steel, he fixed his eyes upon Quiteria, and with a pale aspect, and hoarse, quavering voice, pronounced these words: "Thou well knowest, ungrateful Quiteria, that, according to the holy faith we profess, thou canst not espouse another husband, while I am alive; nor art thou ignorant, that while I waited until time and diligence should meliorate my fortune, I never sought to deviate from that decorum which thy honour required I should preserve; yet, thou, disburthening thyself of all the obligations which thou owest to my honest passion, hast made another person master of what is justly mine; a man, whose wealth is not only subservient to his good fortune, but even renders him superlatively happy; which happiness, that he may enjoy to the full (not that I think he deserves it, but because it is the will of heaven to bestow it) I will, with my own hands, remove the impossibility, or inconvenience that may obstruct it, by taking myself out of the way. Long live, long live Camacho the rich, with Quiteria the ungrateful, to enjoy many quiet and happy years; and death be the portion of the poor Basilius, whose poverty clipped the wings of his fortune, and laid him in an untimely grave."

So saying, he laid hold of the staff which he had stuck in the earth, and drew from it a middling tuck, which was concealed in it as in a scabbard; then fixing that which may be called the hilt on the ground, he threw himself with great activity and resolution upon the point, which in an instant, came out bloody at his shoulder, leaving the unhappy youth weltring in gore, and stretched upon the ground, transfixed with his own weapon. His friends immediately ran to his assistance, pierced with affliction at his misery and lamentable fate, and Don Quixote dismounting, flew to his relief, held him in his arms, and found that he had not as yet expired. They were inclined to withdraw the tuck, but, the curate, who was present, gave his opinion that it should not be withdrawn before he had confessed himself, because his death would be the immediate consequence of pulling out the weapon. Mean while Basilius recovering a little, said in a faint and piteous tone, "Ah, cruel Quiteria! wouldst thou, in this last and fatal agony, bestow upon me thy hand in marriage, I should deem my rashness exculpated, seeing by that I should acquire the happiness of calling thee my own." The curate, hearing this address, exhorted him to employ his attention upon the health of his soul, rather than upon such carnal pleasures, and earnestly pray to God to pardon his sins, and in particular this last desperate determination. To this remonstrance Basilius replied, that he would by no means confess, until Quiteria should first grant him her hand, a favour which would set his heart at rest, and give him spirits to undergo his confession.

Don Quixote hearing the petition of the wounded man, declared, in an audible voice, that Basilius requested nothing but what was just and reasonable, and besides very practicable, and that signor Camacho's honour would suffer no more in wedding Signora Quiteria as the widow of Basilius, than in receiving her from her father's own hands; for,

here nothing was required but the monosyllable of assent, which could have no other effect than the trouble of pronouncing it, as the bridal bed must also be the tomb of such a marriage. Camacho heard the whole, which kept him in such confusion and suspence, that he knew not what to say or do: but the friends of Basilius were so clamorous in solliciting him to consent to Quiteria's giving her hand in marriage to the hapless youth, whose soul would otherwise perish in despair, that he was persuaded, and as it were compelled to say, that if his bride would grant that favour, he should be satisfied, as it would only for a moment delay the accomplishment of his desires. Immediately they surrounded Quiteria, whom with tears, intreaties, and other pathetic remonstrances, they pressed to give her hand to poor Basilius; but she, more obdurate than marble, and more inflexible than a statue, neither could, would, or desired, to answer one word; nor would she have made the least reply, had not the curate desired her to come to a speedy determination, for, the soul of Basilius being already between his teeth, would not afford long time for hesitation.

Then the beautiful Quiteria, without speaking one syllable, but seemingly disordered, sad and sorrowful, advanced to the place where Basilius lay, with his eyes already fixed, breathing short and thick, murmuring the name of Quiteria, and, to all appearance, dying rather like an heathen than a christian. The bride at length approaching and kneeling before him, desired by signs he would hold out his hand; then Basilius unfixing his eyes, and stedfastly gazing upon her, "O Quiteria!" said he, "thou art become kind at a time when thy kindness must serve as a sword to finish my unfortunate life; seeing I have not strength enough left to obtain that glory which thou wouldst confer in calling me thine, or to suspend the grief that comes so fast to cover mine eyes with the dismal shades of death: what I request, O fatal star of my destiny! is, that thy consent to this exchange of vows may not be a meer compliment to deceive me anew, but that thou wilt confess and declare, there is no restraint upon thy inclination, while thy hand is given and delivered to me as thy lawful husband; for, it would be cruel to use deceit and dissimulation with one in such extremity, who has always behaved to thee with such sincerity and truth." Having pronounced these words, he fainted away, so that all the by-standers thought his soul would forsake his body in that swoon: but, when he retrieved the use of his faculties, Quiteria all blushing with modesty, took hold of his right hand, saying, "No force upon earth would be sufficient to biass my will; and therefore, with all the freedom of inclination, I give thee my hand as thy lawful wife, and receive thine on the same terms, if thou bestowest it with the same good will, undisturbed and unconfounded by the calamity into which thou hast been hurried by thy own precipitate conduct." "I do," answered Basilius, "without either disorder or confusion; but, on the contrary, with all the clearness of understanding with which heaven hath thought proper to endow me, I give and deliver myself for thy true and faithful husband." "And I take thee for such," replied Quiteria, "whether thou mayest live many years, or now be hurried from mine arms to the grave." "Considering how desperately this spark is wounded," said Sancho Panza, "methinks he talks woundily; make him lay aside his courtship, and mind his soul, which seems to be in his tongue rather than between his teeth."

The hands of Basilius and Quiteria being joined, the tender-hearted curate, with

T. Hayman inv. et del:                                J. S. Muller Sculp:

Quiteria Wedded to Basilio while He Feigns to be Dying of a Wound.

tears in his eyes, pronounced the nuptial benediction, and fervently prayed, that God would grant forgiveness and repose to the soul of the bridegroom, who no sooner perceived the ceremony was performed, than he nimbly sprung upon his legs, with incredible activity, withdrew the tuck which was sheathed in his body, to the admiration of the bystanders, some of whom, being more simple than curious, began to cry aloud, a miracle! a miracle! But, Basilius replied, "No miracle! no miracle! but sheer industry! nothing but industry!" The curate, confounded and astonished, ran up to feel the wound with both his hands, and found that the blade, instead of passing through the body of Basilius, had run through an iron tube fitted to the part, and full of blood, which, as they afterwards understood, was prepared so as to retain its fluidity; in a word, the curate and Camacho, with almost all the company, found themselves fairly outwitted. The bride, however, expressed no mortification at the deceit; on the contrary, hearing somebody observe, that such a marriage, obtained by fraud, could not be valid, she said she confirmed it anew. From which circumstance every one concluded, that the stratagem had been contrived and executed with her privity and consent. This supposition enraged Camacho and his adherents to such a degree, that they referred their revenge to the prowess of their hands, and unsheathing a great many swords, assaulted Basilius, in whose favour almost an equal number were instantly produced. Don Quixote taking the lead on horseback, well armed with his lance and shield, made the whole company give ground; while Sancho, who had no delight or comfort in such exploits, retired to the jars from which he had extracted his agreeable scum, looking upon that place as a sacred sanctuary and respected retreat. The knight exclaimed, in an audible voice, "Forbear, gentlemen, forbear; it is unjust to revenge the grievances of love; for, in this particular love and war are the same: and, as in the last, it is lawful and customary to use feints and stratagems against the enemy, so likewise, in amorous contests and competitions, all sorts of tricks and contrivances are allowed in attaining the accomplishment of the lover's desire, provided they do not tend to the disparagement or dishonour of the beloved object. Quiteria was fated to Basilius, and Basilius to Quiteria, by the just and favourable determination of heaven. Camacho is rich, and may purchase his pleasure, when, where, and how his inclination shall require; whereas, Basilius has but this one poor sheep, of which he ought not to be deprived by any person, how powerful soever he may be: for, those whom God hath joined, no man shall put asunder; and he who attempts it must first pass through the point of this lance." So saying, he brandished it with such strength and dexterity, as filled the hearts of those who did not know him with fear and consternation; and the disdain of Quiteria made such a deep impression upon the imagination of Camacho, that he shook her from his heart in an instant: so that the persuasions of the curate, who was a prudent and well-meaning priest, pacified and quieted him and his partizans, who, in token of peace, sheathed their weapons, blaming the inconstancy of Quiteria more than the contrivance of Basilius; and Camacho himself observed, that if she loved Basilius before marriage, the same love would have continued after it; and that he had more reason to thank heaven for having lost, than he should have had for obtaining, such an help-mate.

    Camacho and those of his train, being thus consoled and appeased, the friends of Basilius took no step to disturb their peace; and Camacho the rich, in order to shew how

little he resented or thought of the trick which had been played upon him, desired that the entertainments might proceed as if he was really to be married: but, Basilius with his bride and followers refusing to partake of them, set out in a body for the place of his habitation; for, the poor who are virtuous and discreet will always find people to honour, attend, and support them, as well as the rich with all their parasites and companions. In consequence of their earnest intreaty, they were accompanied by Don Quixote, whom they esteemed as a prodigy of valour and integrity; and nothing was cloudy but the soul of Sancho, when he found it impossible to enjoy the splendid banquets and diversions of Camacho, that lasted till night: he, therefore, in a fretful and melancholy mood, followed his master, who joined the troop of Basilius; leaving behind the flesh-pots of AEgypt, although he still retained them in his fancy; and the half-finished scum of his kettle inhanced the glory and abundance of the benefit he had lost: so that, pensive, sullen and sad, yet without hunger or dismounting from Dapple, he silently trudged after the heels of Rozinante.

## CHAPTER V.

In which is recounted the vast adventure of the cave of Montesinos, in the heart of La Mancha, which was happily atchieved by the valiant Don Quixote.

Great and manifold were the treats and particulars of respect paid to Don Quixote by the new-married couple, who thought themselves greatly obliged by the readiness he had shewn to defend their cause, and looked upon his discretion to be equal to his valour; indeed, they esteemed him a perfect Cid in arms, and a Cicero in elocution. Honest Sancho regaled himself three days at their expence, during which it was known that the contrivance of the fictitious wound had not been communicated to Quiteria, but was hatched by the ingenuity of Basilius himself, in hope of meeting with that success which, as we have seen, he actually attained: true it is, he confessed he had imparted his design to some of his friends, that they might, in case of necessity, favour his intention, and facilitate the execution of his deceit.

"Whatsoever hath virtue for its ultimate aim," said Don Quixote, "neither can or ought to be called deceit; and surely no aim can be more excellent than the union of two lovers in the holy bands of marriage." He observed, that the greatest enemy of love is hunger and necessity; for, love is altogether sprightly, joyous, and satisfied, especially when the object of desire is in possession of the lover, whose fierce and declared adversaries are want and inconvenience. He made these observations with a view to persuade signor Basilius to quit the exercise of those talents he possessed, which, tho' they acquired reputation, would not earn a farthing of money, and to employ his attention in

augmenting his estate by legal and industrious means, that never fail the prudent and the careful. The poor man of honour (if a poor man can deserve that title) possesses, in a beautiful wife, a jewel; and when that is taken away, he is deprived of his honour, which is murthered: a beautiful and chaste woman, whose husband is poor, deserves to be crowned with laurel and palms of triumph; for, beauty alone attracts the inclinations of those who behold it, just as the royal eagle and soaring hawk stoop to the savoury lure; but, if that beauty is incumbered by poverty and want, it is likewise attacked by ravens, kites, and other birds of prey; and if she who possesses it firmly withstands all these as- saults, she well deserves to be called the crown of her husband. "Take notice, dearest Basilius," added the knight, "it was the opinion of a certain sage, that there was but one good wife in the whole world; and he advised every husband to believe she had fallen to his share, and accordingly be satisfied with his lot. I myself am not married, nor hith- erto have I entertained the least thought of changing my condition; nevertheless, I will venture to advise him who asks my advice, in such a manner, that he may find a woman to his wish: in the first place, I would exhort him to pay more regard to reputation than to fortune; for, a virtuous woman does not acquire a good name, meerly by being virtu- ous; she must likewise maintain the exteriors of deportment, for, the honour of the sex suffers much more from levity and freedom of behaviour in public, than from any pri- vate misdeeds. If thou bringest a good woman to thy house, it will be an easy task to pre- serve and even improve her virtue; but, shouldest thou choose a wife of a different char- acter, it will cost thee abundance of pains to mend her; for, it is not very practicable to pass from one extreme to another: I do not say it is altogether impossible, tho' I hold it for a matter of much difficulty."

Sancho hearing these remarks, said to himself, "This master of mine, whenever I chance to utter any thing pithy or substantial, will say I might take a pulpit in hand, and travel thro' the world, teaching and preaching to admiration; now, I will say for him, that when he begins to string sentences, and give advice, he might not only take one pulpit in hand, but, even a couple on each finger, and stroll about the market-towns. Wit, whither wouldst thou? May the devil fetch him for a knight-errant! he knows but every thing; I thought for certain, he could be acquainted with nothing but what relates to his chivalries; but, he pecks at every thing, and throws his spoonful in every man's dish."

His master overheard him murmuring in this manner, and asking what he grumbled at, "I don't grumble," answered Sancho, "I was only saying to myself, I wished I had heard those remarks of your worship, before I married; in which case, I might now, per- haps, remark in my turn, The loosened ox is well licked."[1] "What, is Teresa such a bad wife?" said the knight. "Not very bad," answered the squire, "but, then she is not very good; at least, not so good as I could wish." "You are in the wrong, Sancho," said Don Quixote, "to disparage your wife, who in effect is the mother of your children." "As to that matter," replied Sancho, "we are not at all in one another's debt; for, she can dis- parage me fast enough, especially when she takes it in her head to be jealous, and then Satan himself could not endure her."

In a word, they stayed three days with the new-married couple, during which they were treated and served like the king's own person; and here Don Quixote desired the nimble-wristed licentiate, to provide him with a guide to direct his steps to the cave of

Montesinos, which he had a longing desire to explore, that he might investigate with his own eyes the truth of those wonderful stories that were reported of it, through the whole neighbourhood. The licentiate promised to accommodate him with a first cousin of his own, a famous student deeply read in books of chivalry, who would willingly conduct him to the very mouth of the cave, and point out the lakes of Ruydera, so famous, not only in the province of La Mancha, but also through the whole kingdom of Spain: and he likewise observed, that he would find his conversation very entertaining; for, he was a lad who knew how to compose books for the press, and even dedicate them to princes. At length, this cousin arrived upon an ass big with foal, whose pannel was covered with a piece of tawdry tapestry or carpet: Sancho saddled Rozinante, put Dapple in order, stowed his wallet, which was reinforced by the cousin's, likewise very well stored; then recommending themselves to God, and taking leave of the company, they set out, choosing the shortest road to the famous cave of Montesinos.

While they travelled along, Don Quixote addressing himself to the student, asked what was the nature and quality of his exercises, studies and profession? To this question, the other answered, that his profession was humanity; and that his exercise and study consisted in composing books for the press, of great emolument, and no less entertainment to the public; that one of them was intituled, The book of Liveries, in which he had described seven hundred and three liveries, with their colours, mottos, and cyphers: "From these," said he, "your courtiers may extract and assume such devices as will suit their fancies, in times of festivity and rejoicing, without going about begging from any person whatever, or cudgelling their brains, as the saying is, in order to invent what will suit their several desires and dispositions; for, I insert those that will fit the jealous, the disdained, and the forgotten and absent, so exactly, that the just will far exceed the number of the gentiles.[2] I have likewise finished another book which I propose to call, The Metamorphoses; or, The Spanish Ovid, of an invention equally new and agreeable; for, there, in imitation of Naso, I give a burlesque description and history of the Giralda of Sevil, the Angel of La Madalina, the Conduit of Vecinguerra at Cordova, the Bulls of Guisanda, the Sierra Morena, the Fountains of Leganitos, and the Lavapies of Madrid, not forgetting those of the Piojo, the Golden Pipe and the Priora, with their allegories, metaphors and transformations, which at once surprize, instruct and entertain. I have a third performance, which I denominate, The supplement to Polydore Virgil, which treats of the invention of things, and is a work of great study and erudition; for, many things of great importance, which Polydore has omitted, I examine and explain, in a most elegant stile: he, for example, has forgot to let us know who was the first person troubled with a defluxion or rheum, and who was first anointed for the cure of the French distemper: now, these two questions I resolve, in the most accurate manner, upon the authority of above five and twenty authors; so your worship will perceive whether I have laboured to good purpose, and composed a book that will be useful to the world in general."

Sancho having listened very attentively to this narration, "Tell me, signor," said he, "so may God lend an helping hand to the printing of your books; tell me, if you know, and surely you know every thing, who was the first man that scratched his own head; for my own part, I firmly believe it must have been our father Adam." "Certainly," answered

the student; "for, Adam without doubt had a head and hair upon it; now, that being the case, and he being the first man in the world, he must have scratched it sometimes." "I am of the same opinion," resumed Sancho, "but now, pray tell me who was the first tumbler?" "Verily, brother," resumed the scholar, "I cannot determine that point, until I shall have studied it, and study it I will, upon my return to the place where I keep my books; so that I shall satisfy you the next time we meet; for, I hope this will not be the last time of our meeting." "Then I desire you will give yourself no trouble about the matter," said Sancho; "for, I have already found out the solution of my question: know, signor, that the first tumbler must have been Lucifer, who, when he was thrown and ejected from heaven, came tumbling down to the bottomless pit." "Friend," cried the student, "you are certainly in the right." "That question and answer," said Don Quixote, "is none of thy own; thou must have learned them from some other person, Sancho." "Hold your tongue, signor," replied the squire; "for, in good faith! if I begin to question and answer, I shall not have done till morning: yes, as to the matter of asking like a fool, and answering like a simpleton, I have no occasion to crave the assistance of my neigh-bours." "Thou hast said more than thou art aware of," answered Don Quixote; "for, some people there are who fatigue themselves in learning, and investigating that which, when learned and investigated, is not worth a farthing either to the memory or under-standing."

In this and other such relishing discourse they passed that day, and at night took up their lodging in a small village, from whence, as the scholar told the knight, the distance to the cave of Montesinos did not exceed a couple of leagues; and he observed, that if Don Quixote was really determined to explore the cavern, it would be necessary to pro-vide ropes, by which he might be lowered down to its bottom. The knight said, that al-though he should descend to the abyss, he would see the bottom, for which purpose, he purchased about a hundred fathoms of rope. Next day, about two o'clock in the after-noon, they arrived at the cave, and found the mouth broad and spacious, tho' overgrown with thorns, weeds, brambles and brakes, so thick and intricate, that it was almost quite covered and concealed: at sight of the place all three alighted; the student and Sancho immediately began to fasten the rope strongly about the knight, and while they were thus employed in cording and girding him, Sancho addressing himself to the adven-turer, "Dear master," said he, "consider what your worship is about: seek not to bury yourself alive, and to be used like a bottle of wine, let down to cool in some well; for, it neither concerns nor belongs to your worship to be the surveyor of that pit, which must be worse than a dungeon." "Tie the knot, and hold thy tongue, friend Sancho," answered Don Quixote, "for, such an enterprize as this was reserved for me alone." Then the guide interposing, "I intreat your worship, signor Don Quixote," said he, "to consider attentively and examine, as it were, with an hundred eyes, every circumstance within this cave, where, perhaps, there may be things which I shall insert among my transfor-mations." "The cymbal," answered Sancho, "is in the hands that can play it to the utmost nicety."

This discourse having passed, and the ligature being made, not over the knight's ar-mour, but his doublet, "We have been guilty of an inadvertency," said Don Quixote, "in coming hither unprovided with a small bell, which, had it been tied to me with the same

cord, would, with its sound, have given you notice, as I descended, of my being alive: but, as it is now impossible to be accommodated, I commit myself to the hands of God, who will conduct me." Then falling upon his knees, he, in a low voice, preferred a prayer to heaven, beseeching God to assist and crown him with success, in this seemingly perilous and new adventure. His ejaculation being finished, he pronounced in a loud voice, "O! thou mistress of my deeds and motions, the most resplendent and peerless Dulcinea del Toboso! if the prayer and petition of this thy adventurous lover can possibly reach thine ears, I conjure thee, by thy unheard-of beauty, to grant my request, which is no other than that thou would'st not now deny me thy favour and protection, when I stand so much in need of both; for, I am just upon the brink of darting, plunging and ingulphing myself into the profound abyss that opens wide before me, on purpose that the world may know there is nothing so impossible that I will not attempt and execute, under the wings of thy favour."

So saying, he approached the pit, where he found it would be impracticable to slip down, or make way for entering, without the strength of arms and back-strokes; he therefore, unsheathing his sword, began to lay about him, and mow down the bushes that grew around the mouth of the cave, out of which an infinite number of huge crows and daws, affrighted at the noise and disturbance, sallied forth with such force and velocity, as laid the knight upon his back; and had he been as superstitious as he was a good catholic, he would have looked upon this irruption as a bad omen, and excused himself from visiting the bowels of such a dreary place: at length he rose, and seeing that the flight of crows, and other birds of night, was now over, (for a number of bats had likewise come forth) he put the rope in the hands of Sancho and the scholar, desiring them to lower him down to the bottom of that dreadful cavern, which, when he entered, Sancho gave him his benediction, and making a thousand crosses over him, exclaimed, "God and the rock of France, together with the trinity of Gaeta, be thy guides, thou flower, and cream, and scum of knights-errant: there thou goest, bully of the globe, heart of steel, and arm of brass! I say again, God be thy guide, and bring thee back safe, sound, and without deceit, to the light of this life, which thou art now forsaking to bury thyself in that obscurity." Almost the same prayer and deprecation was uttered by the scholar; while Don Quixote called aloud for rope, and afterwards for more rope, which they gave him by little and little. By that time the voice, which ascended through the windings and turnings of the cave, ceased to vibrate on their ears, they had already uncoiled the hundred fathoms, and were inclined to hoist him up again, as they had no more cord to spare: they stayed, however, about half an hour, at the expiration of which they began to pull up the rope, which seemed to have no weight attached to it, and came up with such ease, that they imagined the knight was left below; a supposition, in consequence of which the squire wept most bitterly, while he pulled with great eagerness, in order to discover the truth; but, when they had coiled up about fourscore fathoms, they felt the weight again, and were exceedingly rejoiced: finally, at the distance of ten fathoms, they distinctly perceived Don Quixote, to whom Sancho addressed himself, saying, "Dear master, I wish your worship an happy return; we began to think you had tarried below to breed."

To this welcome the knight answered not a word. When they pulled him up, they per-

ceived his eyes were shut, and that, to all appearance, he was fast asleep; then he was laid upon the ground, and untied; but still he did not awake: however, by dint of turning, jogging, shaking and moving, they, after some time, brought him to himself, when yawning hideously, as if he had awoke from a profound and heavy sleep, he looked around with amazement, and pronounced, "God forgive you, friends, for having withdrawn me from the most delightful prospect and agreeable life that ever mortal saw or enjoyed: in effect, I am now fully convinced, that all the pleasures of this life fleet away like a shadow or a dream, or fade like the flowers of the field. O unfortunate Montesinos! O deeply wounded Durandarte! O hapless Belerma! O weeping Guadiana! and you forlorn daughters of Ruydera, who by your waters shew the copious floods of tears that fall from your beauteous eyes."

The scholar and Sancho hearing these words, which Don Quixote seemed to heave with immense pain from his very intrails, begged he would explain the meaning of what he had said, and inform them of what he had seen in that infernal gulph. "Infernal, call you it?" said the knight; "pray give it a better epithet, for, that it surely does deserve, as you will presently perceive." Then he desired they would give him something to eat, for, he was excessively hungry: they, spreading the carpet upon the grass, produced the buttery of their bags, when all three sitting around them, in love and good fellowship, made one meal serve for supper and afternoon's luncheon, which being finished, and the cloth taken away, "My sons," said Don Quixote, "let no man stir, but listen with your whole attention to that which I am going to rehearse."

## CHAPTER VI.

Of the wonderful incidents recounted by the extravagant Don
Quixote, who pretended to have seen them in the profound cave
of Montesinos; from the greatness and impossibility of which,
this adventure has been deemed apocryphal.

It might be about four o'clock in the afternoon, when the sun retiring behind a cloud, so as to emit a scanty light and temperate rays, gave Don Quixote an opportunity of relating coolly and comfortably to his two illustrious hearers the particulars he had seen in the cave of Montesinos; and he accordingly began to recite what follows:

"About twelve or fourteen fathoms below the mouth of this dungeon, there is a concavity on the right hand, wide enough to contain a large waggon with its cattle, and illuminated by a small stream of light that descends through corresponding cracks and crannies, which open at a distance on the surface of the earth: this spacious cavity I perceived, when I was tired and out of humour at finding myself hanging and descending by a rope, through that dark and dreary dungeon, without knowing any certain or de-

termined way; I therefore resolved to enter it, and repose myself a little, and called to you to leave off lowering the rope, until I should give you further notice; but, I suppose you did not hear me, so that I gathered up the cord you let down, and making it into an heap or coil, sat down upon it, in a very pensive mood, to consider how I should descend to the bottom, having no person to support my weight. While I sat musing on this misfortune, I was, all of a sudden, overpowered by a most profound sleep, and without dreaming of the matter, or knowing how, or wherefore, I awoke, and found myself in the midst of the most beautiful, charming and delightful meadow that nature should create, or the most fertile imagination conceive. I rubbed and wiped my eyes, so as to see that far from sleeping I was broad awake: nevertheless, I felt my head, and fumbled in my bosom, in order to be assured, whether it was really my identical self, or some unsubstantial phantom and counterfeit; but the touch, the reflection and connected discourse I held with myself, concurred to convince me, that I was the same at that time as I find myself at present. Then was my view regaled with a sumptuous palace or castle, with walls and battlements of clear, transparent crystal, and two large folding-gates, which opening, there came forth, advancing towards me, a venerable old man, clad in a long cloak of purple bays, that trailed upon the ground: his shoulders and breast were girded with a collegiate scarf of green sattin; his head was covered with a black Milan cap; and his beard, white as the drifted snow, descended to his middle. He wore no arms, but held in his hand a rosary of beads as large as walnuts, though the tens were as big as ostrich-eggs; and his deportment, air, gravity, and dignified presence, filled me with surprize and veneration. Coming up to me, the first thing he did was to hug me closely in his arms, then he said, 'Long, very long, most valiant knight Don Quixote de la Mancha, have we, who are inchanted in these solitudes, expected thy arrival, that thou mayest inform the world of what is contained and concealed in this profound cavern, which is called the cave of Montesinos; an adventure hitherto reserved on purpose to be atchieved by thy invincible heart and most stupendous courage. Follow me, illustrious signor, and I will shew thee the wonders that lie hid in this transparent castle, of which I am governor and perpetual warder, as being that identical Montesinos from whom the cavern takes its name.' No sooner had he told me who he was, than I asked if it was true, what the world above related of him, namely, that he had, with a small dagger cut out the heart of his great friend Durandarte, and carried it to the lady Belerma, according to his own desire, while he was in the agonies of death. He answered, every circumstance was true, except that of the dagger; for, it was neither a dagger, nor small in its dimensions, but a polished poignard as sharp as an awl."

Here Sancho interposing, observed, that such a poignard must have been made by Raymond de Hozes of Sevil. "I do not know who was the maker," said the knight, "but it could not be that sword-cutler; for, Raymond de Hozes was living t'other day; whereas, many years are elapsed since the battle of Roncesvalles, where that misfortune happened; but, this inquiry is of no importance; nor does it disturb or alter the truth and evidence of the story." "No, surely," cried the scholar, "pray, good your worship Don Quixote proceed; for, I listen to your narration with infinite pleasure." "And I feel no less in recounting it," answered the knight.

"Well then, the venerable Montesinos led me into the crystalline palace, where, in a

low hall, cool beyond conception, and lined with alabaster, stood a monument of marble of exquisite workmanship, upon which I perceived a knight lying at full length, I do not mean a statue of bronze, marble or jasper, such as we commonly see on other tombs, but a man of real flesh and bones: he held his right hand, which being muscular and hairy, denoted the great strength of the owner, over the region of the heart, and before I had time to ask any questions, Montesinos seeing me astonished, and gazing attentively at the sepulchre, 'this is my friend Durandarte,' said he, 'the flower and mirrour of all the valiant and enamoured knights of his time: here he is kept enchanted, as well as myself, and many others of both sexes, by Merlin that French enchanter, who is said to have been begotten by the devil; though, for my own part, I believe he is not really the devil's son, but that, according to the proverb, he knows one point more than the devil. How or for what reason he enchanted us, nobody knows, but time will discover the mystery; and, in my opinion, that time is not far off: what surprizes me is, I know as certainly as the sun shines, that Durandarte breathed his last in my arms, and after he was dead, I with my own individual hands took out his heart, which must certainly have weighed a couple of pounds; for, according to the observation of naturalists, the man who has a large heart is endowed with more valour than he whose heart is of smaller dimensions: this being the case, and the knight certainly dead, how comes he, even at this day, to sigh and complain, from time to time, as if he was actually alive?"

"He had no sooner pronounced these words than the wretched Durandarte cried, in a loud voice, 'O cousin Montesinos! the last favour I requested of you, was, that when my soul should quit my body, you would extract my heart either with poignard or dagger, and carry it to Belerma.' The venerable Montesinos hearing this apostrophe, kneeled before the piteous knight, and with tears in his eyes, replied, 'Already, signor Durandarte, my dearest cousin! already have I executed what you commanded me to perform, on that unlucky day of our defeat; I extracted your heart as well as I could, without leaving the smallest particle of it in your breast; I wiped it with a lace handkerchief, and set out with it, full gallop for France, after having first committed you to the bosom of the earth, with such a flood of tears as was sufficient to bathe and wash my hands of the blood they had contracted by raking in your bowels; and as a surer token, dear cousin of my soul! at the first place I reached, in my way from Roncesvalles, I sprinkled your heart with a little salt, that it might not acquire a bad smell, and continue, if not quite fresh, at least tolerably sweet, until it could be presented to the lady Belerma, who, together with you and me, and your squire Guadiana, the duenna Ruydera, her seven daughters and two nieces, and many others of your friends and acquaintance, have been long enchanted in this place by the sage Merlin; and, although five hundred years are elapsed, not one of us, is dead; though we have lost Ruydera with her daughters and nieces, who, by weeping, are, through the compassion of Merlin, converted into so many lakes, which, in the world above, and in the province of La Mancha, are called the lakes of Ruydera; the Seven Sisters, belong to the king of Spain, and the Two Nieces to the knights of a very holy order, called St. John. Your squire Guadiana bewailing likewise your misfortune, was changed into a river of the same name, which, when it reached the surface of the earth, and saw the sun of the other sky, was so grieved at the thoughts of leaving you, that he sunk down into the bowels of the globe; but, as it was

not possible for him to resist his natural current, he from time to time rises up, shewing himself to the sun and to the nations: he receives a reinforcement from the waters of the forementioned lakes, with which, and many others that join his stream, he enters Portugal in majesty and pomp. Nevertheless, wheresoever he runs, he discovers a sullen melancholy, and does not pique himself upon breeding within his channel, fish of dainty relish and esteem; but only such as are coarse and unsavoury, and widely different from those of the golden Tagus. What I now say, my dear cousin, I have often expressed, and as you make no reply, I conclude you either do not hear or do not give credit to my words: a circumstance which, as heaven doth know, overwhelms me with affliction. I will at present, make you acquainted with one piece of news, which, if it does not alleviate your sorrow, can, surely, in no shape, tend to its augmentation. Know then, here stands in your presence (open your eyes and behold him) that great knight of whom so many things have been prophesied by the sage Merlin; that Don Quixote de la Mancha, I say, who has renewed, and with greater advantages than in times past, raised again from oblivion the long forgotten chivalry, by the means and favour of whom, perhaps, we ourselves may be disinchanted; for great men such great atchievements are reserved.' 'And, if that should not be the case,' replied the afflicted Durandarte, in a faint and languid tone; 'and if that should not be the case, cousin, I say, Patience, and shuffle the cards.' Then turning himself upon one side, he relapsed into his usual silence, without speaking another word.

"At that instant hearing a great noise of shrieks and lamentations, accompanied with doleful sighing and dismal sobbing, I turned about, and saw through the crystal walls into another apartment, through which a procession passed, consisting of two files of most beautiful damsels in mourning, with white turbans on their heads, in the Turkish manner; in the rear of these came a lady, for such, by her stately demeanour, she seemed to be, cloathed like the rest in black, with a veil so full and long that it kissed the ground: her turban was twice as large as the largest of the others, her eye-brows met above her nose, which was flattish; her mouth was large, but her lips retained the colour of vermilion: her teeth, which she sometimes disclosed, were thin and ill-set, though white as blanched almonds, and in her hand she held a fine linen cloth, in which, as near as I could guess, was an heart so dried and shrivelled that it seemed to be of perfect mummy. Montesinos gave me to understand, that all those of the procession were domestics of Durandarte and Belerma, enchanted in that place, together with their lord and lady; and that the last who carried the heart in the napkin, was Belerma herself, who, with her damsels, never failed to appear in that procession four days in the week, and sing, or rather howl dirges over the body, and the woeful heart of his cousin; and that, if she now seemed a little homely, or not quite so beautiful as fame reported her, the change proceeded from the bad nights and worse days she passed in that state of enchantment, as I might perceive in her large wrinkles and wan complexion; nor did that yellowness and those furrows proceed from any irregularity in the monthly disorder incident to women; for, many months and even years had passed since she had the least shew of any such evacuation; but, solely from her anguish of her heart, occasioned by that which she holds incessantly in her hand, and which renews and recals to her memory the misfortune of her ill-fated lover: had it not been for that mischance, scarce would she have

been equalled in beauty, sprightliness, and grace, even by the fair Dulcinea del Toboso, celebrated as she is not only in this country, but also thro' the whole universe.

"'Softly, signor Don Montesinos,' said I, interrupting him at this period, 'be so good as to tell your story as it ought to be told; for, you know all comparisons are odious, and therefore there is no occasion to compare any person with another; the peerless Dulcinea del Toboso is what she is, and the lady Donna Belerma is likewise what she is and has been, and there let the matter rest.' To this remonstrance he replied, 'Pardon me, signor Don Quixote; I confess I have been to blame, and egregiously erred, in saying, the lady Dulcinea would scarce equal the lady Belerma; seeing, my having known by certain guesses that your worship is the knight of Dulcinea, was sufficient to have induced me to bite off my tongue, rather than compare her with any thing but heaven itself.' Such satisfaction from the great Montesinos allayed the disgust that my heart received in hearing Belerma compared with my mistress."

"I marvel much," said Sancho, "that your worship did not fall upon the old hunks, and break every bone in his skin; ay, and pull his beard in such a manner as not to leave one single hair." "By no means, friend Sancho," answered the knight, "it would not have become me to behave in that manner; for, we are all obliged to respect our seniors, although they are not knights; but more especially those who are really of that quality, and besides in a state of inchantment. This I know full well, that there was nothing left unpaid on either side, in the course of the questions and answers that passed between us."

Here the scholar interposing, "I cannot conceive," said he, "signor Don Quixote, how your worship, in such a short time as that you have spent below, could see so many things, and ask and answer such a number of questions." "How long is it since I descended," said the knight. "Little more than an hour," replied the squire. "That's impossible," resumed Don Quixote; "for night fell, and morning dawned, and darkness and light succeeded each other three times; so that, by my reckoning, I must have remained three days in those sequestered shades, which are hidden from our view." "My master must be in the right," said Sancho, "for, as all those things have happened by inchantment, perhaps, what appeared but one hour to us, might seem three days and nights to your worship." "It may be so," answered the knight. Then the student asking, if his worship had eaten any thing in all that time; "I have not tasted one mouthful," said he, "nor had I the least sensation of hunger." "And do those who are inchanted, eat?" resumed the scholar. "They do not eat," answered Don Quixote, "nor do they void the larger excrements, though, it is supposed, that their nails, beards and hair are always growing."

Here Sancho desired to know, if ever those inchanted gentry enjoyed the benefit of sleep? To which interrogation his master replied, "No, surely, at least in those three days that I passed among them, neither they nor myself once closed an eye." "Here then," said the squire, "we may conveniently thrust in the proverb, Tell me your company, and I'll tell you your manners. While your worship keeps company with inchanted people, who are always fasting and watching, it is no great wonder, if you neither eat nor sleep while you are among them; but, really, signor, your worship must forgive me, if I say, that of all you have told us, God take me, I was going to say the devil, if I believe one circumstance." "How!" cried the scholar, "then signor Don Quixote must have lied; who, even if we could entertain such a supposition, has not had time to compose and contrive such

a number of fables." "I do not believe that my master tells lies," answered Sancho. "What then is thy conception?" said the knight. "I conceive," replied Sancho, "that Merlin, or those magicians who have enchanted the whole rabble, which your worship hath seen and discoursed with below, have likewise stuffed your noddle or memory with all that nonsense which you have already recounted, as well as what you have left untold." "That might be the case," said Don Quixote, "but, I assure you it is not so at present; for, what I have recounted I saw with my own eyes, and touched with my own hands. But, what wilt thou say, when I now tell thee, that among an infinite number of other wonderful things, which I shall relate hereafter, in the course of our travels, as they do not all belong to this place, Montesinos shewed me three country-wenches leaping and skipping like so many goats through those delightful plains; and scarce had I set eyes on them, when I recognized them to be the peerless Dulcinea, and those two individual young women, with whom we spoke in the neighbourhood of Toboso. When I asked Montesinos if he knew them, he answered in the negative, but said he took them to be some inchanted ladies of quality; for, they had appeared but a few days in that meadow; nor ought I to wonder at that circumstance, forasmuch as in the same place there were many ladies of the past and present age, enchanted in different and strange forms, among whom he recollected queen Ginebra, and her duenna Quintanona, who was skinker[1] to Lancelot, when he came from Britain." Sancho hearing his master talk in this manner, was ready to run distracted, or burst with laughing; for, knowing the truth of the feigned inchantment of Dulcinea, of which indeed he himself had been the author and evidence, he was convinced, beyond all doubt, that his master was stark staring mad; and in that persuasion exclaimed, "In evil hour, accursed season and unlucky day, my dear master, did your worship go down to the other world; and in a mischievous moment did you meet with signor Montesinos, who has sent you back in such a woeful condition. Well was your worship here above, in your sound judgment such as God had bestowed upon you, saying sentences, and giving counsel at every turn, and not as at present, venting a heap of the greatest nonsense that was ever conceived." "I know thee too well, Sancho," answered Don Quixote, "to mind what thou sayest." "And I, in like manner," replied the squire, "know you too well to regard what you say: wound me or confound me, or kill me if you will, for what I have said, and what I mean to say, if your worship does not mend and correct your own speeches; but, now we are at peace, pray tell me how or by what token you came to know our lady mistress, and if you spoke to her, what answer she made?"

"I knew her again," replied the knight, "by the same cloaths she wore when thou thyself did'st shew her to my astonished eyes: I likewise addressed myself to her, but, she answered not a syllable; on the contrary, she turned about and fled so swiftly, that an arrow would not have overtaken her: nevertheless, I wished to follow, and would certainly have pursued her, had not Montesinos advised me not to fatigue myself; for, it would be to no purpose, and besides, it was time for me to return to the light above. He likewise told me that, in process of time, he would give me notice in what manner he, Durandarte, Belerma, and all the rest, in those sequestred shades, were to be disinchanted. But, what of all I saw and observed, gave me the greatest pain, was this: while I was engaged in this conversation with Montesinos, one of the hapless Dulcinea's companions came

up to me, unperceived, and with tears in her eyes, thus accosted me, in a low and whim-
pering voice, 'My lady Dulcinea del Toboso kisses your worship's hands, and begs your
worship will be pleased to let her know how your worship does: moreover, being in great
necessity, she supplicates your worship, in the most earnest manner, to be pleased to
lend her, upon this her new cotton under-petticoat, half a dozen rials, or any small mat-
ter your worship can spare, which, upon her honest word, shall be restored in a very
short time.' This message filled me with surprize and concern; and turning to the sage,
'Is it possible, signor Montesinos,' said I, 'that people of condition are exposed to ne-
cessity, in a state of enchantment?' To this question he replied, 'Take my word for it,
signor Don Quixote de la Mancha, that which we call necessity is known in all states,
extending to all conditions, prevailing among every class of people, and not even spar-
ing those who are enchanted: and since signora Dulcinea del Toboso sends to beg these
six rials, and the pledge seems to be well worth the money, you had better let her have
them; for, she must certainly be in great trouble.' 'The pledge I will not touch,' said I,
'nor indeed can I comply with her request; for, I have not above four rials'; which I gave
her, and these were the very individual pieces which I received from thee, Sancho,
t'other day, in order to give away in charity to the poor I might meet with on the road.
'Sweetheart,' said I, 'tell your lady that her distress affects me to the very soul, and I wish
I were as rich as Fouckar * to remove it; let her know, that I neither can, nor will enjoy
health, while deprived of her agreeable presence and improving conversation; and that
I fervently and earnestly beg her goodness will be pleased to indulge with her company,
this her captive servant and afflicted knight. Tell her also that, when least she dreams of
any such matter, she shall hear that I have made a vow, like that which was sworn by the
marquis of Mantua, to revenge his cousin Valdovinos, when he found him at the last
gasp, in the middle of the mountain; namely, that he would not eat from off a table-
cloth, together with some whimsical additions, until he should have revenged his death;
and, in like manner, I will swear never to be quiet, but traverse the seven divisions of the
globe, more punctually than did the infant Don Pedro[3] † of Portugal.' 'All that and
much more you owe to my lady,' said the damsel, who, taking the rials, instead of curt-
seying, cut a caper in the air two yards high."

"O holy God!" cried Sancho with a loud voice, "is it possible that those inchanters
and inchantments should have such power to change the good sense of my master into
such nonsensical madness! O signor! signor! for the love of God, look to yourself, have
some respect for your own honour, and give no credit to those vanities, which have di-
minished and disturbed your senses." "Thy regard for me, Sancho, makes thee talk in

---

* Fouckar was a very rich merchant of Augsburg, and a great favourite of Charles V. who owed him
a very considerable sum. It is reported of him, that when the emperor lodged at his house, in his
return from Tunis, the fire in his chamber was of cinnamon, and his landlord lighted it with his im-
perial majesty's own obligation, thereby cancelling an immense debt. The wealth of these traders,
for there were two brothers, became proverbial, and it was usual to say of any very opulent person,
"He is as rich as a Fouckar."[2]
† This was the great patron of the Portuguese discoveries along the coast of Africa to the cape of
Good Hope.

that manner," answered the knight: "and as thou art not experienced in the events of this world, every thing that is uncommon, to thee seems impossible; but, the time will come, as I have already observed, when I shall recount some circumstances which I saw below, that will compel thee to believe what I have now related, the truth of which neither admits of dispute or reply."

## CHAPTER VII.

In which are recounted a thousand fooleries, equally impertinent and necessary to the true understanding of this sublime history.

He who translated this sublime history from the original, composed by its first author Cid Hamet Benengeli, says, that coming to the chapter which treats of the adventure of the cave, he found this observation written on the margin, in the handwriting of the said Hamet.

I cannot conceive or persuade myself that the valiant Don Quixote literally saw and heard all that is recounted in the foregoing chapter, for this reason: all the adventures in which he has hitherto been engaged, are feasible and likely to have happened; but, this of the cave I can by no means believe true, in any circumstance, because it is so wide of all reason and probability; then to suppose that Don Quixote would tell lies, he who was the truest gentleman and most noble knight of his time! It is not possible! He certainly would have suffered himself to be shot to death, rather than deviate one tittle from the truth: besides, I consider that he explained and recounted the adventure so circumstantially, that he could not be supposed to have contrived extempore such a large concatenation of extravagancies; but, after all, should the adventure seem apocryphal, the blame cannot be laid to my door, and therefore I give it to the public, without affirming it either to be true or false. Reader, if thou hast discernment, thou mayest judge for thyself; for it is neither my duty, not is it in my power, to do more: tho' it is held for certain, that the knight, on his death-bed, retracted the whole, saying he had invented the story, because it seemed to agree and quadrate with those adventures he had read in his books.

Then the Arabian proceeds in the history, to this effect:

The scholar was equally astonished at the presumption of Sancho Panza, and the forbearance of his master, and concluded that the satisfaction he derived from having seen his mistress Dulcinea del Toboso, even tho' enchanted, had produced that milkiness of temper, which was now so remarkable; had not this been the case, Sancho's freedom and remarks were such as would have brought a wooden shower upon his shoulders; for, he was downright impertinent to his master, to whom the student thus addressed himself: "For my own part, signor Don Quixote de la Mancha, I look upon this as the happiest journey I ever performed; for, in the course of it, I have made four valuable acquisitions: In the first place, I have gained the acquaintance of your worship, which I deem a piece

of singular felicity. Secondly, I have been made acquainted with what is locked up and contained in the cave of Montesinos, together with the metamorphoses of Guadiana, and the lakes of Ruydera; transmutations that will aptly fill a place in the Spanish Ovid which I have in hand. Thirdly, I have discovered the antiquity of card-playing, which, at least, must be as old as the time of Charlemagne, as may be gathered from the words which your worship heard Durandarte pronounce, when, at the end of that long harrangue of Montesinos, he awoke and said, Patience, and shuffle the cards. For, that phrase and manner of speaking he could not have learned during his enchantment, but certainly, when he was alive and well in France, during the reign of the said Charlemagne; and this investigation comes pat to the purpose, for the other book which I am composing, I mean the Supplement to the Polydore Virgil, on the invention of antiquities; for, I take it for granted, he has forgot to insert in his book the discovery of card-playing, which I will now explain, and doubtless it will be a very material circumstance, especially when confirmed by such a grave and authentic evidence as signor Durandarte. Fourthly and lastly, I have now ascertained the source of the Guadiana, hitherto unknown among the nations."

"You have indeed, good reason to be satisfied," replied the knight; "but, I should be glad to know, if, by God's assistance, you should obtain a license for printing those books (which is a matter of doubt with me) to what patron you intend they should be dedicated?" "There are plenty of lords and grandees in Spain," answered the scholar, "to whom they may be dedicated." "But a very few," said Don Quixote; "not, but that a great many deserve dedications, but, because few will receive them, that they may not lay themselves under the obligation of making such a recompense as may seem due to the labour and courtesy of authors: one prince, indeed, I know, who supplies the defect of the rest, with such advantages, that if I durst presume to describe them, I might perhaps excite envy in many noble hearts: but, let that circumstance rest till a more convenient season; and, in the mean time, let us endeavour to find someplace where we may procure a night's lodging." "Not far from hence," replied the student, "is an hermitage, where lives an anchorite, who is said to have been a soldier, and bears the character of being a good christian, and moreover, a very discreet and charitable man: adjoining to the hermitage is a little house, built by the labour of his own hands, which, tho' narrow, is large enough to receive travellers." "Can that same hermitage produce any poultry?" said Sancho. "There are few hermitages destitute of that provision," answered the knight; "for, the anchorites of these days, are not like those who dwelt in the desarts of Egypt, cloathing themselves with palm leaves, and subsisting on the roots of the earth. And here I would not be understood to extol one sort, in order to depreciate another; for, the penitence now in use does not come up to the rigour and austerity of those times: nevertheless, they are all good, at least, so I suppose them to be; and even should the stream run foul, the hypocrite, who cloaks his knavery, is less dangerous to the commonwealth than he who transgresses in the face of day."

This conversation was interrupted by the appearance of a man coming towards them on foot, walking fast, and switching a mule loaded with lances and halberts: when he came up, he saluted them, and passed on at a good pace, and Don Quixote perceiving his hurry, "Honest friend," said he, "pray stop a little, for you seem to go faster than your

mule could wish." "Signor," answered the man, "I cannot tarry at present, because these arms of which I have the charge, are to be used to-morrow morning, so that I cannot possibly stay; therefore adieu: but, if you desire to know for what purpose they were procured, at the inn which is beyond the hermitage I have some thoughts of taking my night's lodging, and if you are travelling the same road, there you will find me, and there you shall hear strange tidings; so, once more I bid you farewel." So saying, he whipped up the mule in such a manner, that Don Quixote had not time to ask another question concerning those strange tidings, which he promised to relate; but, being extremely curious, and continually fatigued with the desire of learning novelties, he ordered his company to set off that instant, and proceed to the inn, without touching at the hermitage, where the scholar wished to pass the evening. In compliance with the knight's desire, all three mounted their beasts, and followed the direct road to the inn, which they reached a little before the twilight. The student however proposed that they should call and take a draught at the hermitage: Sancho Panza hearing this proposal, immediately turned Dapple's head towards it, being followed by Don Quixote and the scholar: but, his ill luck seemed to have ordained, that the hermit should not be at home, as they were told by an under hermit whom they found in the place. When the squire demanded a flask of his best and dearest, he answered, that his master had no wine, but if he chose a pitcher of his cheapest water, he should have it with all his heart. "If I had chosen water," said Sancho, "there is plenty of wells upon the road, from which I might have quenched my thirst. O the wedding of Camacho! and the abundance of Don Diego's house! how often shall I lament the loss of you?"

When he had uttered this ejaculation, they quitted the hermitage, and pushed on towards the inn, and having rode forwards a little way, they overtook a lad who travelled the same road, at his own leisure: he carried a sword over his shoulder, that supported a bundle of cloaths, which seemed to consist of troussers, a cloak and shirt; for, he wore a velvet jacket with some slips of sattin, and the shirt hanging out: he had silk stockings, and square-toe'd shoes, in the court fashion: his age seemed to be about eighteen or nineteen; he had a sprightly countenance, and an agility in his person; he amused himself in singing couplets to beguile the fatigue of travelling, and when they overtook him, had just finished one, which the student remembered to have run in this strain:

> To the wars my necessity drags me away,
> But, if I had money, at home I would stay.

The first who accosted him was Don Quixote, saying, "You travel very light, young gentleman; pray, good now, whither may you be going?" To this interrogation the youth replied, "I travel so light on account of poverty, and the heat of the weather; and I am going to the wars." "The heat may be a very good reason," resumed the knight; "but how should poverty be the cause of your travelling in that manner?" "Signor," answered the youth, "I carry in this bundle a pair of velvet trunk breeches, fellows to this jacket, which, if I wear out in the country, they will do me no credit in town, and I have not wherewithal to purchase a reinforcement: for this reason, therefore, and the benefit of the free air, I travel as you see me, until I get up with some companies of foot, which are quartered at a town about twelve leagues from hence; there I shall inlist among them,

and there will not be wanting some baggage-waggon, in which I may proceed to the place of embarkation, which they say is to be Carthagena; and I would much rather have the king for my lord and master, and serve him in his wars, than be the lacquey of some scoundrel at court." "And have you obtained any post?" said the scholar. "Had I served a grandee of Spain, or some person of quality," replied the youth, "I should certainly have got something of that kind; for, this is the advantage of being in good service, that a man is frequently preferred from the back of his master's chair to a pair of colours, a company, or some handsome provision: but, it was my unhappy fate to be always in service of the poor, idle rascals or foreigners, who give such a miserable and consumptive allowance of board wages, that one half was expended in the starching of a ruff; and it would be looked upon as a miracle, if any such page-adventurer should obtain a tolerable provision." "And pray, friend," said Don Quixote, "is it possible, that during all the years you have been in service, you never had livery?" "Yes," answered the page, "I have had two; but, as he who quits a convent, before he professes, is stripped of his habit, and obliged to resume his own cloathes; so was I served by my masters, who, after having transacted the business that brought them to court, returned to their own homes, and took back the liveries, which they had given me out of meer ostentation."

"A very scandalous * Espilorcheria indeed! as the Italians call it," said Don Quixote; "but, notwithstanding, you may think yourself very happy in having left the court with such a laudable intention; for, there is nothing upon earth more productive of honour and profit, next to the service of God, than the service of the king, our natural lord and master; especially in the exercise of arms, by which more honour, if not more wealth, is acquired than by learning itself; for, as I have divers and sundry times observed, although a greater number of families has been raised by learning than by arms, yet those founded upon arms rise, I don't know how, above their fellows, with a kind of natural splendour, by which all others are outshone: and what I am now going to say, I desire you will lay up in your remembrance; for, it will be of much comfort and utility to you, in the midst of all your sufferings: never entertain a thought of what adversity may happen, for the worst is death; and provided it comes with honour, it is the greatest happiness to die. Julius Caesar, that valiant emperor of Rome, being asked which was the most agreeable death, answered, 'that which is sudden, unexpected, and unforeseen': and tho' this reply savoured of the pagan, ignorant of the knowledge of the true God, nevertheless, with regard to his being freed from the pangs of human infirmity, he said well: for, supposing you should be slain in the first action or skirmish, either by a cannon ball, or the explosion of a mine, what does it signify? we must all die, and there is an end of the whole; and, according to Terence, a dead soldier who falls in battle, makes a much nobler appearance than one who lives by running away: the good soldier acquires reputation in proportion to the obedience he pays to his captain, or those who have a right to command him; and pray, take notice, child, a soldier had much better smell of gunpowder than of civet; and if old age overtake you in that noble employment, tho' you should be covered over with wounds, paralytic, or lame, it can never overtake you without such honour as poverty cannot diminish; especially now that provision is to be made

* A knavish trick.[1]

for the maintenance and relief of old disabled soldiers; for, it is not reasonable that they should be treated like negro slaves, to whom, when they are old and incapable of service, their masters often give their freedom, driving them from their houses, and, under the title of liberty, leaving them still slaves to hunger, which nothing but death can dispel. This is all I have to say at present, therefore get up, and ride behind me to the inn, where I shall treat you with a supper, and, in the morning, you may pursue your journey, which I pray God may be as fortunate as your intention is good."

The page excused himself from riding behind the knight, tho' he embraced his invitation to supper at the inn; and Sancho said within himself, "Lord comfort thee for a master! Is it possible that a man who can utter so many good things, should affirm that he has seen all that impossible nonsense which he has told of the cave of Montesinos? But, time is the trier of all things."

In such discourse they arrived at the inn, just as it grew dark, and Sancho was not a little rejoiced to find that his master took it to be a real inn, and not a castle, according to his usual whims. They had scarce entered when Don Quixote inquired of the landlord about the man with the lances and halberts, and understood he was in the stable, providing for the accommodation of his beast; an example which was followed by the student and Sancho, who preferred Rozinante to the best manger and stall of the whole stable.

### CHAPTER VIII.

In which is set forth the braying adventure, and the diverting atchievement of the puppets, with the memorable responses of the divining ape.

Don Quixote would not stay till his bread was baked, as the saying is, so impatient was he to hear and know the strange tidings that were promised by the arms-carrier, in quest of whom he forthwith went to the place where the landlord said he was; and having found him, desired he would by all means gratify him with a circumstantial account of those things he had mentioned on the road. "The account of my strange tidings," answered the man, "I shall give when I am more at leisure, and not at work as I am at present: if your worship will give me time to take care of my beast, I will tell you such things as you will be surprized to hear." "They shall not be delayed on that account," said the knight, "for, I myself will lend you an helping hand." He accordingly winnowed the corn and cleaned the manger; so that the man, induced by his humility, could do no less than grant his request, with good will: sitting down therefore, in a hollow of the wall, close by Don Quixote, who, with the scholar, page, Sancho Panza, and the inn-keeper, composed his council and audience, he began to relate what follows:

"You must know, gentlemen, that in a village at the distance of four leagues and an half from this inn, it came to pass, that a certain alderman, through the craft and malice of a servant wench, which I have not time to explain, lost an ass; and tho' the said alderman used all possible means to find him, he found it impossible to succeed: fifteen days had the ass been missing, according to public fame and report, when the owner was, in the market-place, accosted by another alderman of the same town, who said, 'Hansel me for my good news, neighbour; your beast has appeared.' 'That I will, neighbour, and heartily,' answered the other; 'but, let us know where he has appeared.' 'Upon the mountain,' replied the finder: 'I saw him this morning, without pack-saddle or any sort of furniture; and so lean, that it was piteous to behold him. I would have driven him before me, and brought him home; but, he is so wild and shy, that when I went near him, he took to his heels, and ran into the most concealed part of the mountain: if you choose it, we two will go in quest of him; stay till I house my own beast, and I'll return presently.' 'I shall be much obliged to you,' said he of the strayed ass; 'and I shall endeavour to repay you in the same coin.' With these very circumstances, and in the self-same manner that I relate the affair to you, it is told and related by all those who have entered into the true spirit of the case.

"In conclusion, the two aldermen walked hand in hand to the mountain, and coming to the place and spot where they expected to find the ass, they found him not: nor could they get one glimpse of him, altho' they searched all about over and over. Perceiving that he was not likely to appear, 'Heark ye, neighbour,' said the alderman who had seen him, 'there is a contrivance come into my head, by which we shall certainly discover this animal, even though he should be concealed in the bowels of the earth, much more if he is in this mountain; and that is this, I have a marvellous knack at braying, and if you have any turn that way, you may conclude the business is done.' 'Any turn, neighbour!' cried the other: 'by the Lord! I will not yield in point of braying to the best man alive, not even to an identical ass.' 'We shall see presently,' answered the second alderman; 'for, my intention is that you should go to one side of the mountain, and I to the other, so as to walk round it quite, and every now and then you shall bray, and I will bray; and it cannot be but that the ass will hear, and answer, if he is on this mountain.' To this proposal the owner replied; 'Neighbour, it is an excellent scheme, and worthy your great genius.' So parting, according to agreement, it came to pass that both brayed almost at the same time, and each being deceived by the other's braying, ran forward in hopes of finding the ass; when perceiving their mistake, 'Neighbour,' said the loser, 'is it possible that was not my ass which brayed just now?' 'No: it was I,' answered the other. 'Agad, then,' cried the owner, 'there is not the least difference in point of braying, between you and an ass! for, in my life did I never hear or see such a resemblance.' 'That compliment and approbation,' answered the contriver, 'would be much better bestowed upon yourself than upon me, neighbour; for, by the God that made me! you would give two heats of advantage to the biggest and best brayer in Christendom; for, the sound you produce is deep, sonorous, within proper time and compass, and the falls frequent and sharp; in a word, I own myself overcome, and yield you the palm and banner of that rare talent.' 'By the mass!' said the owner, 'I will from hence forward have a higher opinion of my own ability, and believe I know something, since I really possess such a gift; for, although I

always thought I brayed tolerably well, I never imagined I excelled so much as you say I do.' 'I therefore tell you,' replied the other, 'that many rare talents are lost in this world; and that they are ill-bestowed upon those who cannot turn them to advantage.' 'Ours,' said the owner, 'except in such cases as this, that we have now in hand, can be but of little service, and even in this, God grant it may turn it to account.'

"After these mutual compliments they parted a second time, and began to bray again; but still they were deceived and met as before, until, by way of counter-signal, from which they might know one another, they agreed to bray twice in a breath: accordingly, they doubled their brayings, and encompassed the whole mountain, without being favoured with the least answer, or sign from the strayed ass; and indeed, no wonder the poor, unfortunate animal did not answer; for they found him in the remotest part of the wood, almost devoured by the wolves. The owner seeing him in this plight, 'I marvelled much,' said he, 'that he did not answer, for had he been alive and heard you, he must have brayed again, else he had been no ass; but, as I have had the pleasure of hearing you bray so melodiously, neighbour, I think my trouble well-bestowed, even although I have found him dead.' ''Tis in good hands, neighbour,' replied the other; 'for in chanting the clerk is not a whit inferior to the curate.'

"Having made these mutual remarks, they returned to the village, equally hoarse and disconsolate, and recounted to their friends, neighbours, and acquaintance, what had happened to them, in their searching for the ass, extolling one another to the skies for the talent of braying; so that every circumstance of the story was related among the neighbouring villages; and the devil, who is never at rest, but, always glad of an opportunity to sow discord and scatter quarrels, raising lies in the wind, and huge chimeras from little or no foundation, so ordered matters, that the people of the other villages, when they saw any person belonging to our town, began to bray, as if to hit him in the teeth with the braying of our aldermen. The story was taken up by the boys, which was all one as if it had fallen into the hands and mouths of all the devils in hell; and the braying was circulated from one town to another in such a manner, that the natives of the village of Braywick are as well known and distinguished as a Blackamoor from a Spaniard; and this joke has become so serious, that our townsmen have frequently gone forth in arms and regular order, to give battle to the jokers, without any regard to king or rook, or fear or shame; I believe that to-morrow or next day, the men of Braywick will take the field once more against the people of another village within two leagues of us, who are our chief persecutors; and that we may be well provided for the occasion, I have purchased the lances and halberts you have seen. Now these are the strange tidings which I said I would relate; and if you do not think them so, I have no other worth your hearing."

Thus the honest man concluded his story, and at that instant came into the house, a man cloathed in a doublet, breeches and hose of shamoy leather, who said with a loud voice, "So ho, Mr. Landlord, have you got any lodging for the fortune-telling ape, and the puppet-shew of the deliverance of Melisendra." "Odd's bodikins!" cried the innkeeper, "master Peter is here! we shall have rare doings i'faith!" We forgot to observe, that the left eye, and half of the cheek of this master Peter was cover'd with a patch of green silk, from whence it was supposed all that side of the face laboured under some

infirmity. Be that as it will, the innkeeper proceeded, saying "Welcome, good master Peter; but, where is the ape and the puppet-shew? for I see neither." "They are at hand," answered the owner of the shamoy-suit; "but I came before, to know whether or not we could have lodging?" "The duke d'Alva himself should be turned out to make room for master Peter," said the landlord; "bring hither your ape and your shew, for, there is company in the house that will pay for a sight of them." "In good time then," replied the wearer of the patch: "I will lower the price, and think myself well paid, if they defray the expence of my lodging; mean while, I'll go and lead hither the cart that contains my puppets and my ape."

So saying, he went out, and Don Quixote inquiring who this master Peter was, with the puppet-shew and ape; the landlord replied, "This is a famous puppet-shew man, who has long travelled through La Mancha and Arragon, representing the story of Melisendra, who was delivered by the famous Don Gayferos, one of the most entertaining and best represented histories which have been for many years seen in this kingdom; he likewise carries along with him an ape of the rarest talent that ever was known among apes, or conceived among men; for, if you ask any question, it listens attentively to what you say, then leaping upon its master's shoulders, and clapping its mouth to his ear, it gives an answer, which master Peter immediately explains. Of things that are past, it says much more than of those that are to come, and though it does not hit the truth exactly in every thing, it errs but seldom; so that we are inclined to believe it is inspired by the devil. Every question costs a couple of rials, provided the ape answers, I mean, supposing the master answers for the ape, after it has whispered in his ear: wherefore, master Peter is thought to be woundy rich; indeed he is a gallant man, as they say in Italy, and excellent companion, and lives the pleasantest life in the world; he talks as much as any six, and drinks more than a dozen, and all at the expence of his tongue, his ape, and his puppet-shew."

Just as he spoke these words, master Peter returned with the cart that contained his puppets and the ape, which was a very large animal, without a tail: his buttocks were like felt, but not ugly withal; and Don Quixote no sooner beheld him than he asked, "Pray, Mr. Fortuneteller, what have we got in the net? what fortune awaits us? Behold, here are my two rials." So saying, he ordered Sancho to give them to Mr. Peter, who answered in the name of the ape, "Signor, this animal gives no response or intelligence concerning what is to come; he is only acquainted with the past, and knows something of the present." "Rabbit it!" cried Sancho, "I would not give a doit to be told of the past; for, who knows that better than myself, and to pay for being informed of what I know, would be downright folly: but, since he knows the present, here are my two rials; and tell me, good your apeship, how my wife Teresa Panza is at present employed?" Master Peter refused to take the money, saying, "I will not receive a premium per advance, until it is preceded by service." Then clapping his hand twice upon his left shoulder, the ape, with one skip, leaped upon it, and laying its mouth to his ear, began to mow and chatter with great eagerness: having made this motion, which continued as long time as one would take in repeating the creed, with another skip he leaped upon the ground. Immediately master Peter, with infinite hurry, threw himself on his knees, before Don Quixote, and hugging his shins exclaimed, "These legs I embrace, as I would embrace the pillars of Hercules,

O thou celebrated reviver of the already forgotten order of knight-errantry! thou never enough to be applauded cavalier Don Quixote de la Mancha, the soul of the dejected, the prop of the falling, the shield of those that are fallen, the staff and comfort of all the unhappy!" Don Quixote was alarmed, Sancho thunderstruck, the scholar surprised, the page confounded, the Braywick carrier amazed, the landlord astonished, and, in a word, admiration prevailed among all those who heard the words of the shewman; while he proceded, saying "And thou, worthy Sancho Panza, the best squire of the bravest knight in the universe, be merry and rejoice; for thine agreeable helpmate, Teresa, is in good health, and this very moment employed in dressing a pound of flax; by the same token, there stands at her right-hand a broken mouthed pitcher, containing a good sup of wine, with which she comforts herself while she is at work." "That I can easily believe," answered Sancho; "for, she is a rare one, and if she was not a little given to jealousy, I would not exchange her for the giantess Andandona, who, as my master says, was a very proper and complete housewife; and truly my Teresa is one of those who will live to their hearts content, even though their heirs should pay for it."

"I am now convinced," said Don Quixote, "that he who reads and travels much will see and learn a great deal. This observation I make, because no arguments would have been sufficient to persuade me that there are apes in the world, endowed with the gift of divination, as I have this day seen with my own eyes; for I am the very Don Quixote named by that good animal, which, however, has expatiated rather too much in my praise; but, be that as it may, I give thanks to God who bestowed upon me a mild and compassionate disposition, ever inclined to do good to all mankind, and harm to no person whatever." "If I had money," said the page, "I would ask signor ape, what will be the success of my present peregrination?" To this hint, master Peter, who had rose from his prostration, replied, "I have already told you, that this creature does not answer for what is to come; if he did, your want of money would be no objection; for, in order to serve Don Quixote here present, I would willingly forfeit all the interested views in the world; and now, as in duty bound, I will, for his amusement, set up my shew, and divert all the people in the house, without fee or reward." The landlord, hearing this declaration, was rejoiced beyond measure, and pointed out a proper place for the exhibition of his entertainment, which was prepared in a twinkling.

Don Quixote was not very well satisfied with the divinations of the ape, as he did not think it natural for such an animal to divine, in things either past, present, or to come; and therefore, while master Peter was busy in setting up his shew, he retired, with his squire, to a corner of the stable, where they could confer together without being overheard, and spoke to this effect: "Heark ye, Sancho, I have considered this wonderful talent of the ape, and, according to my notion, this same master Peter, its owner, must certainly have made a secret or express pact with the devil." "Nay, if it be the devil's pack," answered Sancho, "it must be a very dirty pack; but, what signifies such a pack to master Peter?" "Sancho," replied the knight, "you do not understand my meaning: what I would say is, that he must certainly have made some concert with the devil, who hath infused this talent into the ape, by which he gains his livelihood; and when he becomes rich, he must yield him his soul, which is the aim of that universal enemy of mankind; and what confirms me in this opinion is, that the ape answers no questions but such as

regard the past and present time: now the devil's understanding reaches no farther; what is to come he knows only by conjecture, and that, not always; for, it is the attribute of God alone, to know times and seasons: to him there is neither past nor future, but, all things are ever present to his eyes. This being the case, as doubtless it is, the ape certainly speaks from the inspiration of the devil; and I am surprized it hath not been accused and examined by the holy office, which would soon discover by virtue of whom it presumes to divine; for, surely this ape is no astrologer; nor did he or his master ever raise, or were capable of raising, those figures called judicial, which are now so common in Spain, that every pitiful little hussy, page, and even cobler, has the impudence to raise an horoscope, as readily as a knave of trumps, from the ground, ruining and disgracing, by their ignorance and falsities, the wonderful truth of that noble science. One lady I myself knew, who having inquired of one of those pretenders, whether a little bitch she had would have puppies, how many, and of what colour they would be? Mr. Astrologer, after having raised his figure, replied, that the bitch would bring forth three puppies, one of a green, another of carnation, and the third of a mixed colour, provided the bitch would take the dog between the hours of eleven and twelve at noon or night, on Saturday or Monday. Notwithstanding this prediction, the bitch died in three days of a surfeit; and yet Mr. Figure-caster was still esteemed in the place, a most infallible astrologer, as almost all those fellows are." "Nevertheless," answered Sancho, "I wish your worship would desire master Peter to ask his ape, if what happened to your worship in the cave of Montesinos, is really true; as for my own part, begging your worship's pardon, I cannot for the blood of me help thinking it was all a flam and a lie, or at least no better than a dream." "It may be so," replied Don Quixote; "but, I will take thy advice; for, truly, I myself have some sort of scruples about the matter."

Here he was interrupted by the arrival of Mr. Peter, who came to tell him that the shew was ready, and invite him to come and see it; for, it would be well worth his trouble. Then the knight imparted his sentiments, desiring he would ask the ape whether or not certain incidents that happened in the cave of Montesinos were dreams or realities; for to him the whole seemed to be a mixture of both. Master Peter, without answering one word, went and brought the ape into the presence of Don Quixote and Sancho, and thus accosted it; "Look ye, Mr. Ape, this knight wants to know, whether certain things that happened to him in a place called the cave of Montesinos, be true or false." Then making the usual signal, the creature leaped upon his left shoulder, and seemingly whispered something in his ear. In consequence of this communication, "The ape," said master Peter, "declares, that part of what your worship saw and underwent in that same cave, is false, and part is likely to be true; and this, and nothing else, is all he knows touching that interrogation: but, if your worship desires to be further informed, he will, next Friday, answer all the questions you can ask; at present, his virtue has left him, and will not return till Friday, as I have already observed." "Signor," said Sancho to his master, "did not I always affirm your worship should never make me believe that all, or even the half of those accidents you pretended to have met with in the cave was true?" "The event will shew," answered Don Quixote; "for, there is nothing that time, the discoverer of all things, will not bring to light, even tho' it should be hidden in the bowels of the earth. Let that suffice for the present; and now we will go and see the puppet-shew of honest

master Peter, which I really believe will be productive of some novelty." "Of some!" cried master Peter; "my shew is productive of sixty thousand: why, I tell your worship, signor Don Quixote, there is nothing equal to it in the whole world; but Operibus credite & non verbis:[1] let us begin presently, for it grows late, and we have a great deal to do, to say, and to shew."

In consequence of this request, Don Quixote and Sancho repaired to the place where the puppet-shew was set up, and set forth with a great number of little wax-lights, which made a most resplendent appearance. Master Peter withdrew within the curtain, in order to play the figures of the piece; and on the outside sat a boy, who was his servant, to interpret and explain the mysteries of the shew, holding a wand, with which he pointed out the puppets as they entered. All the people of the inn being seated, some fronting the stage, and Don Quixote with Sancho, the page and the scholar, accommodated with the best places, the drugoman[2] began to pronounce that which will be heard and seen by those who will take the trouble to read or peruse the following chapter.

## CHAPTER IX.

### In which is continued the diverting adventure of the puppet-shew; with other matters really entertaining enough.

Universal silence prevailed among Tyrians as well as Trojans, that is, all the spectators of the shew, sat in silent expectation, suspended as it were on the mouth of him who was appointed to expound the wonders of the piece; when their ears were saluted with sound of atabals, trumpets, and artillery, that issued from behind the scene; and this noise being soon over, the boy thus began in an audible voice: "This true history, which will now be represented before the honourable company, is literally extracted from the French Chronicles and Spanish ballads, which may be heard every day repeated in the streets by man, woman, and child. It exhibits the manner in which signor Don Gayferos accomplished the deliverance of his spouse Melisendra, who was a captive in Spain, detained by the Moors in the city of Sansuenna, which was formerly the name given to what we now call Saragossa; and pray, gentlemen, take notice, Don Gayferos is playing at tables, according to the old song:

> Now Gayferos, at tables playing,
> Of Melisendra thinks no more.

"And that personage who next appears, with a crown on his head and a sceptre in his hand, is the emperor Charlemagne, the supposed father of Melisendra, who, vexed at the indolence and carelessness of his son-in-law, comes forth to chide him; and observe with what vehemence and keenness he seems to scold; one would imagine he intended to give him half a dozen raps on the pate with his sceptre; nay, some authors say, that he

actually did bestow them, ay, and that with very good will: after having said abundance of things concerning the risk his honour would run, if he did not effect the deliverance of his spouse, he is reported to have added these words, 'I have said enough, look to it.' Behold, gentlemen, how the emperor turns about and walks off, leaving Don Gayferos in a fume, who, in the impatience of his anger, throws away the table and pieces, and calls hastily for his armour, desiring his cousin Orlando to lend him his sword Durindana. Don Orlando will not comply with his request, but offers to attend him, in his difficult enterprize; however, the provoked hero will not accept of his offer; on the contrary, he says his own single arm is sufficient to deliver his wife, even tho' she were concealed in the profoundest centre of the earth. So saying, he goes in to arm, that he may be able to set out with all expedition. Gentlemen, turn your eyes to the tower that appears yonder, and suppose it one of the towers belonging to the castle of Saragossa, now called Aljaferia. That lady who stands in the balcony in the Moorish dress is the peerless Melisendra, who from thence hath often cast her longing eyes towards the road to France, and consoled herself in her captivity, by thinking on the city of Paris and her valiant lord. Observe likewise a new incident, the like of which, perhaps, you have never seen before: don't you see that Moor stealing along silently and softly, step by step, with his finger on his mouth, behind Melisendra? Now mind how he prints a kiss in the very middle of her lips, and with what eagerness she spits, and wipes them with the sleeves of her shift, lamenting aloud, and tearing, for anger, her beautiful hair, as if it had been guilty of the transgression. Behold, now, that venerable Moor in yon gallery; he is Marsilius the king of Sansuena, who, having perceived the insolence of the Moor, altho' he was his own relation, and a great favourite, orders him to be apprehended, and carried through the principal streets of the city, with the criers before, and the rods behind, with which he is to receive two hundred stripes: and here you shall see the sentence executed, almost as soon as the crime is committed; for, among the Moors, there is no copy of a writ, trial or delay, as in our courts of justice."

Here Don Quixote interposing, said, with a loud voice, "Boy, boy, follow your story in a right line, without falling into curves and crosses; for, there is not so much proof and counter-proof required to bring truth to light." "Sirrah (cried Mr. Peter, from behind the curtain) none of your vagaries, but follow the gentleman's counsel, which is good and wholesome: sing your plain song, without counter-points; for, you may spin the thread so fine as to break it." "I shall obey your orders," answered the boy, who proceeded, saying,

"That there figure a-horseback, wrapped up in a cloak of Gascony, is the very individual Don Gayferos, to whom his own lady, by this time, revenged of the presumptuous and enamoured Moor, talks with more seeming composure from the battlements of the tower, supposing him to be some traveller, and between the two passeth that whole discourse and conversation, recorded in the ballad, which says,

> Sir knight, if you to France do go,
> For Gayferos enquire:

together with what follows, which I shall not at present repeat, because prolixity ingenders disgust: let it suffice that you see how Gayferos discovers himself, and that we learn from the joyful gestures of Melisendra, that she recognizes her husband; especially as

we now see her let herself down from the balcony, in order to get a-horseback behind her loving spouse: but, as ill luck would have it, the border of her under-petticoat has caught hold of one of the iron spikes of the balcony, and there she hangs dangling, without being able to reach the ground: but, you see how compassionate heaven brings relief in the most pressing emergencies; for, Don Gayferos comes to her assistance, and without minding whether or not the rich petticoat may be torn, seizes his lady, and, by main force, brings her to the ground; then with one jerk, sets her upon the crupper of his horse, astride like a man, bidding her hold fast, and throw her arms around his neck, so as to cross them on his breast, that she may be in no danger of falling; for, my lady Melisendra was not used to ride in that manner: you likewise perceive how the horse, by his neighing, expresses the satisfaction he feels in carrying the valiant and beautiful burthen of his lord and mistress: you see how they turn about, and quitting the city, take the road to Paris, with equal eagerness and joy. Go in peace, ye peerless pair of faithful lovers; may you arrive in safety at your desired country, without fortune's raising any obstruction to your happy journey; and may the eyes of your friends and kindred behold you enjoy in peace all the days of your life, which I hope will exceed the age of Nestor!" Here Mr. Peter interposing again, called aloud, "None of your flourishes, sirrah: seek not to entangle yourself; for, all affectation is naught." The interpreter, without answering a syllable, went on in this manner. "There were not wanting some idle eyes which nothing can escape, and they, perceiving the descent and flight of Melisendra, gave notice of it to king Marsilio, who straight gave orders for sounding to arms: and behold the hurry and commotion of the city, occasioned by the sound of bells that ring in every minoret."

"It cannot be," cried Don Quixote. "In what regards the bells, Mr. Peter is guilty of an impropriety; for the Moors use no bells, but attabals or kettle-drums, and a kind of dulcimers, like those belonging to our waits; so that the circumstance of ringing bells in Sansuenna, is a downright absurdity." Mr. Peter hearing this observation, left off ringing, and answered, "Signor Don Quixote, your worship must not mind such trifles, nor seek for that perfection which is not to be found. How many plays do you see every day represented, full of impropriety and absurdities? yet they happily run their career, and are heard, not simply with applause, but even with universal admiration. Proceed boy, and let people talk; for, provided I fill my pocket, I don't care if there should be more improprieties than there are atoms in the sun." "You are in the right," replied the knight; and thus the boy went on:

"Behold what a number of resplendent cavalry marches out of the city in pursuit of the two catholic lovers: what a sound of trumpets, tinkling of dulcimers, and rattling of drums and kettle-drums! I am afraid they will overtake and bring them back tied to their horse's-tail, and that would be a most dismal spectacle."

Don Quixote, seeing such a number of Moors, and hearing this uproar, thought it was incumbent upon him to assist the fugitives; and therefore, starting up, he pronounced with a loud voice, "Never while I breathe will I consent that such an injury should be done in my presence to a knight so famous, daring and enamoured as is Don Gayferos: desist, ye base born plebeians; seek not to follow and punish him, but, face me in battle, if you dare." With these words and actions he unsheathed his sword, and springing up to the puppet-shew, began with incredible agility and fury to lay about him among the

Moorish puppets, demolishing some, beheading others, maiming this, and hacking that; and in the course of this exercise, he fetched such a back-stroke, that had not Mr. Peter stooped and squatted down with great expedition, he would have sliced off his head as easily as if it had been made of ginger-bread. This unfortunate shew-man exalting his voice, "Hold, for the love of God! signor Don Quixote," said he, "and take notice, that those whom you overthrow, kill and destroy, are not real Moors, but poor, harmless, little figures of paste; consider, sinner that I am! you are ruining me, by depriving me of my livelihood." Notwithstanding this remonstrance, the knight continued to play away in a perfect shower of back-strokes, fore-strokes, outside and inside, that fell as thick as hail; so that, in less than a couple of credos, he brought the whole shew to the ground, all the tackle and figures being hewed down, and dismembred; king Marsilio himself sorely wounded, and the crown, together with the head of the emperor, cleft in twain. The whole audience was involved in confusion: the ape fled to the roof of the house, the scholar trembled, the page was seized with consternation, and Sancho Panza himself overwhelmed with terror and dismay, for, as he swore after the hurricane subsided, he had never before seen his master in such a frantic rage.

The puppet-shew being thus intirely demolished, Don Quixote became a little more composed, saying, "I wish I had before me, at this very moment, those who either do not, or will not believe that knights-errants are of any benefit or service to mankind, that they might see what would have become of the worthy Don Gayferos, and the beautiful Melisendra, had not I been present on this occasion: certainly, by this time, they would have been overtaken by those dogs, who would have done them some grievous injury: let knight-errantry, therefore, live and flourish above all things upon the face of the earth." "In a happy hour, let it live (cried Mr. Peter in a languid tone) and let me die, who am so unfortunate, that I may say with king Rodrigo, 'Yesterday I was lord of Spain, and now there is not one battlement I can call my own.' Half an hour, yea not half a minute is elapsed, since I saw myself in possession of kings and emperors; my stables, coffers and bags were filled with an infinite number of horses, and other gay particulars, and now I find myself quite desolate and abased, poor and beggarly, and, which is worst of all, deprived of my ape, who, in good faith, will make my teeth sweat, before he returns to me his lawful master; and all this misfortune I have suffered from this here Sir knight, who is said to protect orphans, rectify wrongs, and perform other charitable actions, but, in me alone, his generous intention has failed; blessed and praised be the highest heaven above! In a word, the knight of the rueful figure is he by whom I and mine are disfigured and undone."

Sancho Panza melted at this piteous lamentation: "Do not weep, Mr. Peter," said he, "do not whine so piteously, or thoul't break my heart; for, I'd have thee know, my master Don Quixote is such a catholic and scrupulous christian, that provided he be convinced of having done thee wrong, he knows how to make amends, and will satisfy and repay thee with double interest." "If signor Don Quixote," replied the shew-man, "will make some atonement for the deeds by which he has undone me, I shall rest satisfied, and his worship's conscience will be at peace; for, that man cannot expect salvation who witholds the effects of his neighbour against his will, and refuses to make restitution." "You are in the right," said Don Quixote; "but, as yet I do not know that I withhold any

Don Quixote Attacking the Puppet Show.

of your effects, Mr. Peter." "How! none of mine? (cried the shew-man) and these unfortunate remains that lie extended on the hard and barren pavement, were they not thus scattered and annihilated by the invincible force of that redoubted arm? to whom but me did their unhappy bodies belong? and with what but them did I procure a comfortable subsistence?" "Now," cried Don Quixote, "I am fully convinced of what I have on divers occasions believed; namely, that those enchanters, by whom I am persecuted, take pleasure in presenting realities to my view, and then changing and metamorphosing them into such figures and forms as they choose to bestow: believe me, gentlemen, to me every thing that has passed appeared a true and literal concurrence of real facts; and the figures represented, seemed to be really and truly the very individual persons of Melisendra, Don Gayferos, Marsilio, and Charlemagne: in consequence of that belief, my wrath was provoked, and, in order to fulfil the function of a knight-errant, I resolved to favour and assist the fair fugitive; in the execution of which resolved, I have done what you see. If the exploit has turned out contrary to my expectation, the blame ought not to lie with me, but with those miscreants by whom I am persecuted: nevertheless, as I have committed an error, although it did not proceed from malice aforethought, I stand by my own award condemned in costs: let Mr. Peter make out his own bill of the figures that are demolished, and I promise it shall be paid on the spot, in good and lawful current coin of this kingdom." The shew-man hearing this declaration, made a profound bow, saying, "I expected no less from the unheard-of christianity of the valiant Don Quixote de la Mancha, the unflinching auxiliary and support of the whole tribe of needy and forlorn vagabonds: Mr. Landlord, and the great Sancho, shall act as moderators and appraisers between your worship and me, with regard to what the injured figures are or might be worth."

The innkeeper and squire having undertaken this office, Mr. Peter lifted up the headless Marsilio king of Saragossa, saying, "You see how impossible it is to reinstate this king in his former situation; and therefore, with submission to better judgments, I think I must be allowed four rials and an half, on account of his death and final perdition." The knight desiring him to proceed, "Then," said he, "for this dreadful gash from top to bottom (taking up the cloven emperor Charlemagne) I cannot be thought exorbitant, if I demand five rials and a quarter." "That's no small matter," said Sancho. "Nor a great deal too much," replied the landlord. "Split the difference, and set him down at five rials." "Let him have the whole five and the quarter," said Don Quixote; "for, in such a notable misfortune, a quarter more or less is a meer trifle: and pray, dispatch, Mr. Peter, for, it is now supper-time, and I begin to feel some symptoms of a keen appetite." "For that figure without a nose, and deprived of one eye, which is the beautiful Melisendra," proceeded Peter, "I demand two rials and twelve maravedis." "The devil's in't," cried the knight, "if Melisendra is not by this time, with her husband, at least upon the frontiers of France; for, the horse on which they were mounted, seemed to fly rather than tread the ground; so that there is no reason for your selling me a cat instead of a coney, that is, in presenting me with a noseless Melisendra, when, in all probability, that lady is now enjoying herself at leisure with her husband in France. God give every man joy of his own, Mr. Peter, and let us all endeavour to walk tightly and rightly; and now you may proceed." Mr. Peter perceiving Don Quixote beginning to warp and return to his old biass, resolved to be even with him, and with that view, said, "This cannot be Melisen-

dra, but must be one of her waiting-women, for whom I shall think myself very well payed, and rest satisfied with threescore maravedis." In the same manner did he set prices on many other maimed figures; so that, after they were moderated by the two arbitrators to the satisfaction of both parties, the whole sum amounted to forty rials and three quarters, which being disbursed by Sancho, Mr. Peter demanded another brace of rials for the trouble he should have in catching the ape. "Let him have them, Sancho," said Don Quixote, "not for catching the ape, but the juice of the grape *: and I would not give two hundred as a reward to any person who would certify that the lady Donna Melisendra, and her lord Don Gayferos, are now safe among their friends in France." "No person upon earth can resolve that question sooner or better than my ape," replied Mr. Peter; "but, the devil himself cannot catch him at present, tho' I imagine, hunger and affection will compel him to return to me sometime to-night; and if God will send us a new day, we shall see what can be done." In fine, the hurricane of the puppet-shew being quite blown over, the whole company supped together in peace and good fellowship, at the expence of Don Quixote, who was liberal to excess.

Before day-break, the lance and halbert-carrier set out for his village, and early in the morning the scholar and the page came to take their leave of Don Quixote, the first intending to return to his own home, and the other to pursue his journey, for the comfort of which, the knight made him a present of a dozen rials. Mr. Peter, having no inclination to reinvolve himself in any sort of dispute with Don Quixote, to whose disposition he was no stranger, arose before the sun, and packing up the remains of his puppets, together with his ape, sallied forth also in quest of further adventures. The innkeeper, who knew not Don Quixote, was equally astonished at his madness and liberality: finally, Sancho paid him handsomely, by his master's order, and the two bidding him farewell about eight a clock in the morning, left the inn, and betook themselves to the road, in which we will leave them, having now a proper opportunity to recount other incidents appertaining and necessary to the illustration of this famous history.

## CHAPTER X.

In which the reader will discover who Mr. Peter and his ape were; together with Don Quixote's bad success in the braying adventure, which did not at all turn out according to his wish and expectation.

Cid Hamet, author of this sublime history, begins this chapter with these words; "I swear, as a catholic christian": and upon this occasion, the translator observes, that Cid Hamet being a Moor, as he certainly was, in swearing as a catholic christian means

---

* In the original there is a miserable pun upon the words *Mono* and *Mona*, the first of which signifies an ape, and the other drunkenness.[1]

no more than that, as a catholic christian, when he makes oath, swears he will speak the truth, and nothing but the truth, in like manner he would adhere to it, as a catholic christian adheres to his oath, in what he intended to write concerning Don Quixote, especially in disclosing the mystery of Mr. Peter, and the fortune-telling ape, whose talent attracted the admiration of all that country. He then proceeds to observe, that he who has read the first part of this history, cannot but remember that same Gines de Passamonte, whom, together with his fellow-slaves, Don Quixote set at liberty near the brown mountain; a benefit for which he was ill-thanked, and worse requited by that mischievous and immoral crew. This Gines de Passamonte, whom Don Quixote called Ginesillo de Parapilla, was the very thief who stole Sancho's Dapple, and as, through the fault of the printers, neither the time nor the manner of that conveyance is described, in the first part of the book, many people ascribed this error of the press to want of memory in the author: but, in short, stolen he was by Gines, even while Sancho was sitting sleeping on his back, by means of the same contrivance and expedient that was used by Brunelo, who, while Sacripante lay at Albraca, withdrew his horse from between his legs; and Sancho afterwards retrieved him, as we have already related. Gines then, afraid of being overtaken by justice, that was in quest of him, to chastise him for his numberless tricks and transgressions, which were so manifold and remarkable as to fill a large volume of his own composing, resolved to remove himself into the kingdom of Arragon, to cover his left eye with a patch, and profess the occupation of playing puppets, and performing feats of legerdemain, which he understood to great perfection: he afterwards happened to fall in company with some christians, just delivered from bondage in Barbary, of whom he purchased that ape, which he taught to leap upon his shoulder, at a certain signal and whisper, or seem to whisper in his ear. Having so far succeeded, before he entered any place with his puppet-shew and ape, he took care to inform himself at the next village, or of any person whom he could conveniently pump, of the particular accidents that had happened in that place, with all their circumstances, which, he retained by dint of a tenacious memory. The first thing he did, was to represent his puppet-shew, the subject of which he extracted sometimes from one story, and sometimes from another; but, it was always full of mirth and entertainment, and well known: and this being ended, he propounded the talents of his ape, telling the audience that he could disclose the past and present; but, with regard to the future, he pretended no knowledge: for every response he demanded two rials, tho' sometimes he afforded them cheaper, just as he felt the pulse of his consulters; and as he sometimes came to families, the anecdotes of which he knew, even tho' they would spend no money upon questions, he would make the signal to the ape, and then say he had communicated this and that circumstance, which tallied exactly with what had really happened. By these means, he acquired the credit of infallibility, and drew the whole country after him; at other times, as he had abundance of cunning and penetration, he would answer in such a manner, that the responses agreed perfectly well with the questions; and there being no body to hamper him, by inquiring and sifting into the bottom of this pretended divination of the monkey, he found means to make monkeys of all his followers, and fill his bags at the same time. As soon as he entered the inn, he knew Don Quixote and Sancho, and this recognition enabled him to excite the admiration of the knight, squire, and all the by-

standers: but, his art would have cost him dear, had Don Quixote lowered his hand a little, when he decapitated king Marsilio, and destroyed his whole cavalry, as we have related that adventure in the preceding chapter.

So much for Mr. Peter and his ape: and now, returning to Don Quixote de la Mancha, we must observe, that after having departed from the inn, he resolved, in the first place, to visit the banks of the river Ebro, and all the circumjacent country, before he should enter the city of Saragossa, as the length of time between this period and the tournaments permitted him to make such an excursion. With this resolution, he proceeded in the road, through which he travelled two days, without encountring any thing worth relating, until on the third, as he ascended a rising-ground, his ears were saluted with a mighty noise of kettle-drums, trumpets, and muskets, which he at first imagined might proceed from some company of soldiers marching that way: in order, therefore, to view them, he spurred up Rozinante, and when he reached the top of the rising-ground, saw below, as near as he could guess, above two hundred men, equipped with different kinds of arms, such as lances, cross-bows, partisans, halberts, pikes, a few muskets, and a great number of targets. He rode down the hill, and drew so near this squadron, that he could distinguish their colours, and observe their devices, particularly a banner or pendant of white sattin, in which was painted to the life, an ass of the small Sardinian breed, with his head raised, his mouth open, and his tongue lolling out, as if in the very act and attitude of braying, and surrounded by this motto, in capital letters,

> It is no children's play,
> When brother bailiffs bray.

From this symbol Don Quixote gathered, that those people belonged to the village of Braywick; and this discovery he communicated to Sancho, whom he likewise made acquainted with the motto of the standard; observing, at the same time, that he, by whom they were informed of the adventure, had committed a mistake, in saying the brayers were aldermen; for, according to this couplet, they must have been bailiffs. To this observation, Sancho replied, "Signor, in that circumstance, there is nothing to be mended; for, those who were aldermen when they brayed, might very well in time come to be bailiffs of the corporation, consequently they may be mentioned with both titles; especially as it is of small signification to the truth of the story, whether the brayers were aldermen or bailiffs, provided they really conjunctly and severally did bray; for, a bailiff is as likely to bray as an alderman."

Finally, conjecturing and understanding that the people who were ridiculed, had come forth to fight those who had ridiculed them, and carried the joke beyond the bounds of reason and good neighbourhood, Don Quixote approached their line of battle, to the no small chagrin of Sancho, who was never fond of interposing on such occasions; and they were immediately received by the whole squadron, who believed the knight was come to espouse their quarrel. Then Don Quixote lifting up his vizor, with graceful ease and courteous demeanour, advanced to the standard of the ass, where he was environed by the chiefs of the army, who gazed at him with that admiration incident to all those who beheld him for the first time. The knight perceiving them looking at him so attentively, without speaking or asking any question, resolved to take advantage

of their silence, and breaking his own, began in this manner, with an audible voice, "Worthy gentlemen, I beg, in the most earnest manner, that you will not interrupt a discourse I intend to make, until you perceive it becomes insipid, and disgusting; in which case, I will, upon the least sign, put a seal upon my lips, and a gag upon my tongue."

All the spectators assured him, he might say what he pleased, and they would willingly give him the hearing; so that, thus licensed, he proceeded to this effect: "I, gentlemen, am a knight-errant, whose exercise is that of arms, and whose profession is to assist the needy, and favour those who want favour and protection. Some days ago I was informed of your disgrace, and the motives which have induced you to arm at every turn, in order to take vengeance on your enemies; and having once and again revolved your affair in my mind, I find that, according to the laws of duel, you are in the wrong to suppose yourselves affronted: for, no individual can affront a whole community, unless they are accused of treason by the lump, because the person guilty of the said treason, is not known, consequently cannot be challenged by himself. Of this practice, we have an instance in Don Diego Ordonnez de Lara, who challenged the whole town of Zamorano, because he did not know that Vellido Dolfos alone was the traitor who had slain his king; he, therefore, defied the whole body of inhabitants, and to the whole body of them did the answer and revenge belong: though, indeed, signor Don Diego bordered upon extravagance, and exceeded the bounds of defiance; for, he had not sufficient reason to challenge the dead, the water and the bread, or those who were yet unborn, as well as other minute matters therein set forth: but, let that pass, When choler once is born *, the tongue all curb doth scorn—I mean a bridle to restrain it. This being the case, then, that one single person cannot affront an intire kingdom, province, city, society, or corporation, it plainly appears, that you have no just cause to come forth, in order to take vengeance for that which was not really an affront: for, it would be a good joke indeed, if the inhabitants of a town called Clockwell, should take it in their heads, at every turn, to slay every person that might ask, What † i'st a clock? Or if the cheesemongers, fruiterers, whale-bone-sellers, soapboilers, and those of other names and appellations that are in the mouth of every boy, and hackneyed among the vulgar; I say, it would surely be a good joke, if all those people, who are distinguished by their different callings, should be ashamed and incensed at such simple provocations, and be always making sacbuts of their swords, in every trifling quarrel: no, no; God neither likes, nor will he suffer such unjustifiable revenge. Prudent men, and well-ordered commonwealths, ought to take up arms, unsheath their swords, and risque their persons, lives and fortunes, for four causes only. Firstly, to defend the catholic faith; Secondly, in self-defence, which is justified by the laws of God and nature; Thirdly, in behalf of one's honour, family and fortune; and Fourthly, in the service of his majesty, when he is engaged in a just war: and if we would add a fifth cause, (which indeed, ought to be ranked as the second) is the de-

---

* Literally, "When choler quits the mother, the tongue has then no father."[1]

† I have ventured to deviate a little from the precise meaning of the original, which the reader will own to be very insipid, when he reads the literal translation: "For, it would be good, if the inhabitants of the town of Reloxa, (signifying a watch or clock) should, at every turn, slay those that call them so."[2]

fence of one's country. To these principal causes, may be annexed some others, both just and reasonable, which may oblige us to have recourse to arms: but, to take them up for childish trifles, and things that are rather subjects of laughter and diversion than of serious revenge, seems to denote a total defect of reason and discretion; especially as unjust vengeance (and surely no vengeance can be just) is diametrically opposite to that holy law we profess, by which we are enjoined to do good to our enemies, and love those by whom we are abhorred: a command which, tho' seemingly difficult, is not really hard to be observed, except by those who have less of God than of this world, and more of the flesh than of the spirit; for, Jesus Christ, the true God and true man, who never lied, who neither was nor is capable of falsehood, as being our eternal lawgiver, tells us, that his yoke is easy, and his burden is light: therefore, he would not impose a command which we could not possibly fulfil; and consequently, good gentlemen, you are obliged by laws divine and human, to be appeased."

At this period, Sancho said within himself, "The devil run away with me, if this master of mine is not a downright thologister![3] at least, if he is not, no two eggs were ever more alike." Don Quixote having taken breath a little, and finding his audience still attentive, was inclined to prosecute his harrangue, and would certainly have pursued the subject, had not he been prevented by the archness of Sancho, who during his master's pause, took it in hand, saying, "My master, Don Quixote de la Mancha, who, at one time, went by the name of the knight of the rueful countenance, but is at present called the knight of the lions, is a very learned gentleman, that understands Latin and Castilian like a perfect batchelor of arts. In all his sermons and exhortations, he proceeds like a very able soldier, as having all the laws and ordinances of what you call duel, at his finger's end: therefore, you have no more to do but let yourselves be guided by his counsel; and if you go wrong, the blame shall lie upon my shoulders; especially, as he hath already told you, that it is meer madness to be angry without any cause but that of a man's braying. I remember, when I was a boy, I brayed whensoever and wheresoever I pleased, without lett or molestation; ay, and so prettily and naturally, that I was always answered by all the asses of the common; yet, for all that, I did not cease to be the son of my parents, who were most worthy people; and tho', for this talent, I was envied by more than enow of the gravest folks in the parish, I valued not their envy two farthings: and that you may see I speak nothing but the truth, wait a little and give me the hearing, for the art of braying is like that of swimming, which, when once learned, is never forgot."

So saying, he clapped his fingers to his nostrils, and began to bray so stoutly, that all the neighbouring vallies re-echoed the sound. But, one of those who stood next him, supposing the squire made himself merry at their expence, lifted up a pole that was in his hand, and bestowed it upon him with such good will, that Sancho, in spite of all his efforts, came to the ground.

Don Quixote seeing his squire so roughly handled, attacked the aggressor lance in hand; but, such a number of people interposed, that he found it impossible to take vengeance: on the contrary, perceiving a cloud of stones ready to pour upon him, and being threatened by a vast number of presented cross-bows and muskets, he wheeled Rozinante about, and galloped off as fast as the steed could carry him; recommending himself heartily to the protection of God, that he might be delivered from that danger;

and in the apprehension that some ball would enter at his shoulders, and make its exit through his breast, he held in his breath at every step, in order to know whether or not he was wounded. But, those who composed the squadron, being satisfied with his flight, did not shoot after him; and as for Sancho, they laid him across upon his beast, as soon as he recovered the use of his senses, and allowed him to follow his master: not that he was able to manage the ass; but, Dapple followed the footsteps of Rozinante, from whom he could not bear to be parted, tho' but for a moment. The knight having rode a good way, turned his horse's head, and seeing Sancho following, waited for his coming up, as he perceived no body attempted to pursue him.

The warriors of Braywick kept their ground till night, and as their adversaries did not think proper to give them battle, returned to their own town, with joy and satisfaction; and had they known the ancient custom of the Greeks, they would have erected a trophy on the spot.

## CHAPTER XI.

## Of things related by Benengeli, which he who reads them attentively, will know.

When a brave man flies, he must have discovered some odds or foul play; and it is the business of prudent captains, to reserve themselves for better occasions. This maxim was verified in Don Quixote, who, by giving way to popular fury, and the evil intention of that incensed squadron, took to his heels, and, without paying the least regard to Sancho, or the danger in which he left him, moved off to such a distance as he judged sufficient for his own security. He was followed by Sancho lying across the ass, as we have already observed, who, by that time he was brought up to his master, had just recovered the use of his senses, and fell from Dapple at the feet of Rozinante, all battered and bruised, and in an agony of pain.

The knight dismounting to search his wounds, no sooner perceived he was sound from head to foot, than he thus accosted him in angry tone: "In evil hour, you must understand braying, sirrah! Where did you learn it was convenient to talk of halters in the house of a man that was hanged? To the tenor of braying, what bass could you expect but the basting of a cudgel? You have reason to thank God that, instead of receiving a benediction with a pole, you have not been crossed with a scymitar." "I am at present in no condition to answer," said Sancho; "for, methinks I talk through my shoulders; let us mount and depart from this place, and I shall make an end of my braying; though I shall never be weary of telling as how knights-errant run away, and leave their honest squires beaten to chaff and pounded to cinders, in the power of their enemies." "There is a wide difference between flying and retreating," answered Don Quixote; "for you must know, Sancho, that valour which is not founded on the base of discretion, is termed temerity

or rashness; and the atchievements of a rash person ought to be ascribed rather to good fortune than courage. I own, therefore, I have retreated, but not fled, and in so doing have imitated a great number of valiant chiefs, who reserved themselves for more dignified occasions: and of these instances histories are full, but I omit rehearsing them at present, because the recital would be of no advantage to thee, or entertainment to myself."

By this time Sancho, being set upon his ass again by Don Quixote, who likewise mounted Rozinante, they jogged along softly, in order to shelter themselves in a grove that appeared at the distance of a quarter of a league; and the squire every now and then heaving up a most profound ah! accompanied with piteous groans, his master desired to know the cause of such bitter ejaculations. To which question the squire replied, that from the extremity of his rump to the nape of his neck, he felt such intolerable pain as was like to deprive him of his senses. "The cause of that pain," said Don Quixote, "must doubtless be this; as the pole or staff by which you have suffered was long and large, it extended over thy whole back, comprehending all those parts that now give you pain; and if it had reached still farther, the pain would have been more extensive." "'Fore God," cried Sancho, "your worship has taken me out of a huge uncertainty, and resolved the doubt in delicate terms. Body o'me! was the cause of my pain so mysterious, that there was a necessity for telling me, I feel pain in those parts that were cudgelled? Had my shins ached, there might have been some reason for guessing at the cause of their aching; but, surely there is no great witchcraft required to tell me that my back aches, because it was crossed with a quarter-staff. In good faith! sir master of mine, our neighbour's care hangs by a hair. Every day I see more and more how the land lies, and how little I have to expect from keeping your worship's company; for, if you left me to be cudgelled at this time, we shall, upon a hundred different occasions, return to our late blankettings and other such toys; and though this misfortune has fallen upon my shoulders, the next may light upon my eyes. Abundantly better should I have done, but, I am such a barbarian, that in all the days of my life, I never did well; I say again, abundantly better should I have done, had I returned to my house, my wife, and my children, and maintained and brought them up with what Providence should please to bestow; rather than lag after your worship in this manner, through roadless roads and pathless paths, drinking bad liquor and eating worse food; then when I come to sleep, 'Brother squire, measure out seven feet of ground; and if you choose to be more at your ease, take as much more, for the laddle is in your own hand, and lay yourself out to your heart's desire.' Would to God I could see the first man who meddled with knight-errantry burnt to a cinder; at least the first booby who chose to be squire to such wiseacres as all former knights-errant must have been. Of the present, I say nothing; as your worship is one of the number, I hold them in respect, because I am sensible, that in speeching and understanding, you know a point more than the devil himself."

"I would venture to lay a good wager, Sancho," said Don Quixote, "that now while you are permitted to speak without the least hindrance, you feel no pain in any part of your body. Proceed, child, and out with every thing that comes into your head, or tarries at your tongue's end; for, provided you are free from pain, I shall convert into pleasure that disgust which proceeds from your folly and impertinence; and if you are so

much bent upon returning to your house, your wife and your family, God forbid that I should oppose your resolution. You have some of my money in your hands; recollect how long it is since we set out on this my third sally; then reckon what you might and should have earned monthly, and be your own paymaster." "When I worked for Thomas Carrasco, father of Batchelor Sampson, who is your worship's acquaintance," answered Sancho, "I earned two ducats a month, besides my victuals: with your worship I know not what I can earn, though well I know that the squire of a knight-errant has a much more troublesome office than that of a farmer's servant; for, in fact, we who serve husbandmen, let us work never so hard through the day, and happen what will, have a hot supper out of the pot at night, and lie in a good bed, which I have never enjoyed since I have been in your worship's service, except for that short space of time that we stayed in the house of Don Diego de Miranda; and bating the good chear I found among the scum of Camacho's kettle, and my eating, drinking and sleeping at the habitation of Basilius, all the rest of the time I have slept on the hard ground, under the cope of heaven, exposed to what you call the inclemencies of the weather, living upon cheese-parings and crusts of bread, and drinking cold water, sometimes from the brooks and sometimes from the springs we met with in the public roads through which we travelled."

"Allowing," said Don Quixote, "that all you have mentioned is true, how much more do you think I ought to give you than that which you received from Thomas Carrasco?" "With the addition of two rials a month," replied Sancho, "I shall think myself well paid, that is, with regard to my wages; but, as to some satisfaction for your worship's word and promise of making me governor of an island, methinks it would be but fair and honest to add six rials more; and that, altogether, will come to thirty." "Very well reckoned," answered the knight; "now, according to the tale of wages you have mentioned, calculate fairly and exactly what I am indebted to you, for the five and twenty days that are elapsed since our departure from our own village, and, as I said before, be your own paymaster." "Body o'me!" cried Sancho, "your worship is quite out in your reckoning; for, in regard to the promise of the island, we must compute from the day in which your honour made the said promise to this blessed hour." "How long then, has that same promise been made?" said Don Quixote. "If my memory does not fail me," answered the squire, "it must be above twenty years, a few days over or under." Here, the knight slapping his forehead with his hand, began to laugh heartily, saying "Why my stay in the Sierra Morena, with the whole course of our peregrinations, has scarce employed two months; and wilt thou say I have promised thee that island these twenty years? Now I perceive thy intention is to keep, in lieu of wages, all my money that is in thy hands; and, if that be the case, and thou really lookest upon it with an eye of desire, I give thee the whole sum from this moment, and much good may it do thee; for, provided I find myself rid of such a wretched squire, I shall think myself happy, though poor and pennyless. But, tell me, thou prevaricator of all the squirely ordinances of chivalry! where hast thou seen or read that any squire of a knight-errant ever presumed to bargain with his master, touching a certain monthly salary for his service? Launch out, launch out, you ruffian, vagabond and hobgoblin, for such you are, launch out, I say, into the Mare magnum[1] of chivalry; and if you find that any squire ever attempted to say or even to think what thou hast here uttered, I will give thee leave to nail the passage on my forehead, and pinch the

sign of the four nipples on my face,[2] by way of additional mortification. Turn, immediately, the reins or the halter of your ass, and return to your house, your wife and your family; for, one step farther thou shalt not travel with me. O bread ill-bestowed! O promise misapplied! O wretch that favourest more of the beast than of the man! At this juncture, when I was on the eve of raising thee to such a station as would have ennobled thee, even in spite of thy wife, thou seek'st to leave me! Now, thou art going away, when I had firmly and unalterably resolved to make thee lord of the best island in the universe! In a word, as thou thyself hast observed upon other occasions, An ass's mouth was not made for honey, &c. An ass thou art, an ass wilt thou be, ay, and thou wilt die like an ass, when the course of thy life is finished; for, I am convinced that thy days will reach their utmost period, before thou shalt learn and know what a beast thou art."

Sancho looked woefully at his master, while he poured forth these reproaches, from which the squire felt such compunction, that the tears started in his eyes, and he replied in a faint, whimpering tone, "My good master, I confess that, in order to be really and truly an ass, I want nothing but a tail, which, if your worship will furnish me with, I shall think it well bestowed, and serve you as a beast of burthen all the days of my life. Good your worship, forgive and look upon my green years with compassion; and consider that I know very little; and if I speak a great deal of nonsense, it does not proceed from malice but infirmity; and those who sin and kiss the rod, find favour in the sight of God." "I should have been surprised, Sancho," said the knight, "if thou hadst not seasoned thy discourse with some proverbial expression. Well, then, for the present, I forgive thee, in hope of thy amendment, and on condition that thou wilt not henceforward betray such a sordid and selfish disposition, but, endeavour to enlarge thy heart, fortify and encourage thy mind, to wait the accomplishment of my promises, which, though it may not speedily happen, is nevertheless far from being impossible." Sancho said he would do his endeavour, and follow his advice, even tho' he should gather strength from feebleness.

Then they betook themselves to the covert of the grove, where the knight accommodated himself at the root of an elm, and the squire retreated to the foot of a beech; for, these and other such trees never want feet, though they are always destitute of hands. Sancho passed the night in great trouble; for the cold air augmented the pain of his bruises; whereas, Don Quixote amused himself with his incessant meditations. Nevertheless, both master and man gave way to the operations of sleep, and at the approach of morn, prosecuted their way to the banks of the renowned Ebro, where they were involved in an adventure that will be recounted in the succeeding chapter.

## CHAPTER XII.

## Of the famous adventure of the inchanted bark.

B
y dint of travelling at a very deliberate pace, for the space of two days after they quitted the grove, Don Quixote and Sancho arrived at the river Ebro, the sight of which afforded infinite pleasure to the knight, who eagerly contemplated the amenity of its banks, the transparency of its water, the tranquillity of its course, and the abundance of its crystal stream, the joyous prospect of which renewed in his remembrance a thousand amorous thoughts that chiefly turned upon what he had seen in the cave of Montesinos; for, although master Peter's ape had declared, that part of those circumstances was true, and part of them false, he inclined more to the belief that they were altogether real, while Sancho, on the contrary, looked upon the whole detail as one continued lie.

As they jogged on in this manner, their view was saluted by a small boat, without oars, or any other tackle, close to the river-side, and made fast to a tree that grew on the bank. Don Quixote looking around him, without perceiving any living soul, alighted immediately from Rozinante, commanding Sancho to quit the back of Dapple, and tie both beasts securely to the trunk of a poplar or willow that grew upon the spot. When the squire desired to know the cause of this sudden descent and ligation, "You must know, Sancho," said the knight, "that this vessel is here on purpose, without a possibility of any other design, to call and invite me to embark, that I may be conveyed to the succour of some knight or other necessitous personage of high degree, who must certainly be involved in some dire disasters; for, this is the very spirit of books of chivalry, and the practice of those inchanters concerning whom they treat, who, when any knight in distress cannot be delivered by their art, but solely by the prowess of another errant, though perhaps at the distance of two or three thousand leagues or more, they snatch him up in a cloud, or provide him with a vessel, in which he embarks, and in the twinkling of an eye he is transported either through the air, or by sea to the place where his assistance is required: this bark, therefore, O Sancho, is brought hither for the like purpose, as sure as it is now day; and before the day be spent, take and secure Dapple and Rozinante together, and let us commit ourselves to the direction of God; for, even the barefooted carmelites shall not dissuade me from embarking." "Since that is the case," answered Sancho, "and your worship is resolved, at every turn, to plunge into these (I know not whether I should call them, mad) vagaries, I have nothing to do but bow and obey, according to the proverb, If you obey the commands of your lord, you may sit as a guest at his board. Nevertheless, in order to disburthen my conscience, I must give your worship notice, that in my opinion this same bark has nothing to do with enchanted people, but belongs to some fishermen of this river, in which they catch the best shads in the world."

This remonstrance was made, while he tied the cattle, which he could not leave to the protection of inchanters, without being grieved to the very soul. But, the knight ex-

horted him to banish his anxiety on account of the animals, which would be carefully maintained and protected by the same sage destined to transport their riders through roads and regions of such longitude. "I do not understand what you mean by logickhood," said the squire; "for, I never heard such a word before, in the whole course of my life." "By longitude, I mean length," answered the knight, "but, I do not at all wonder that thou shouldst not understand the word; for, thou art not obliged to be acquainted with the Latin tongue, like some arrogant people who pretend to knowledge of which they are intirely ignorant." "The beasts are now secured," said Sancho, "what is next to be done?" "What!" replied Don Quixote, "but to cross ourselves and weigh anchor, I mean, to embark and cut the rope by which the vessel is made fast."

So saying, he leaped on board, whither he was followed by Sancho, and the fastening being cut, the boat edged gently off from the bank. The squire seeing himself about two fathoms from the shore, began to tremble, in the apprehension of perishing; but nothing gave him more pain than hearing Dapple raise his voice, and seeing Rozinante struggle for his freedom. "Now Dapple," said he to his master, "brays for grief at our departure; and Rozinante strives to get loose, that he may throw himself in the water and swim after us! Farewel, my dearly beloved friends, peace be with you, and may the madness that parts us be converted and undeceived, that we may be restored to your agreeable company."

Then he began to weep so bitterly, that the knight, exclaimed in a tone of rage and vexation: "Of what art thou afraid, cowardly miscreant? wherefore dost thou weep, thou heart of butter? who persecutes, who molests thee, thou soul of a garret-mouse? or what wants dost thou suffer, beggarly wretch, rolling as thou art in the very bowels of abundance? art thou peradventure, travelling barefoot over the Raphean mountains? No: seated like an archduke upon a convenient bench, thou art softly conveyed by the gentle current of this delicious river, from which, in a little time, we shall launch into the wide and extended ocean: but, indeed, we must have already entered the open sea, ay, and sailed at least seven or eight hundred leagues; and if I had here an astrolabe to take the elevation of the pole, I would tell thee exactly what way we have made; though, either I have little skill, or we have already passed, or will pass, in a very little time, the equinoctial line, that divides the globe into two equal parts." "And how far shall we have gone when we come to that same line your worship mentions?" said Sancho. "A great way," replied the knight; "for, of three hundred and sixty degrees, comprehending the whole terraqueous globe, according to the computation of Ptolemy, who was the greatest cosmographer ever known, we shall have traversed one half when we reach the equinoctial line." "'Fore God!" cried Sancho, "your worship has brought a set of rare witnesses to prove the truth of what you say. Copulation and Kiss-me-gaffer, with the addition of Tool-i'me, or some such name *."

---

* As it is altogether impossible, in a translation, literally to preserve the low humour arising from blunders upon words or sounds, I have been obliged to substitute an equivalent jingle, in the room of *Puto*, *Gafo* and *Meon*, which are Spanish words signifying a *whore*, a *catamite* and a *piss-a bed*: so that Sancho, deceived by the affinity of these sounds to *Computo*, *Cosmographo* and *Ptolomeo*, thought he had reason to say his master had produced a fair set of evidences.[1]

Don Quixote laughed at Sancho's blunders, upon the computation of the cosmographer Ptolemy, adding, "You must know, Sancho, that one of the signs by which those who embark at Cadiz for the East-Indies know they have passed the equinoctial, is the total destruction of vermin among the passengers and seamen; so that not one louse remains alive, or can be had in the whole ship, even though you should give its weight in gold; thou mayest therefore slip thy hand along thy thigh, Sancho, and if thou canst catch any thing alive, our doubt will be resolved; but if there is nothing to be found, we must certainly have passed the line." "I can hardly believe it!" answered the squire, "but, however, I will do as your worship desires; though there is no necessity for trying those experiments; for, I can see with my own eyes, that we have not moved five yards from the bank, no, nor have we driven two yards below the cattle; for, there stand Rozinante and Dapple, in the very spot where they were left; and taking aim as I do now, I vow to God, we do not move or go at the pace of a pismire." "Sancho," said the knight, "perform the investigation I have mentioned, and give thyself no trouble about any other circumstance; for, thou dost not know the meaning of colures, lines, parallels, zodiacs, eccliptics, poles, solstices, equinoxes, planets, constellations, points and measures that compose the spheres celestial and terrestrial. Wert thou acquainted with these, or even a part of them, thou would distinctly perceive what parallels we have crossed, what signs we have seen, and what constellations we have left, and are now leaving behind us. I therefore repeat my request, that thou wouldst examine and go a fishing upon thyself; for, I am persuaded thou art clean and smooth as a sheet of white paper."

Sancho, in compliance with his desire, slipped down his hand softly, and felt about his left ham; then raising his head, and looking at his master, "Either the experiment is false," said he; "or, we have not reached the place your worship mentioned, by many leagues." "What!" said the knight, "hast thou found something!" "Ay, more than one something," answered the squire; who snapped his fingers, and afterwards washed them in the river, along the current of which the boat glided softly, without the assistance of any secret power, or concealed inchanter, being conveyed by nothing but the stream, which then ran with a smooth and gentle course.

In this manner they proceeded, when they discovered some large mills, built in the middle of the river, which Don Quixote no sooner perceived, than he addressed himself to Sancho, in an exalted voice. "Behold, my friend, yonder appears the city, castle or fortress that contains some oppressed knight-errant, queen, infanta or princess in distress, for whose relief I am brought hither." "What the devil does your worship mean by a city, fortress or castle!" cried the squire; "don't you see these are mills built in the river, for grinding wheat?" "Peace, Sancho," replied the knight, "although they appear to be mills, they are in reality edifices of a very different nature: I have already told thee, that all things are transformed and changed by the power of enchantment; I do not mean, that they are really changed in any circumstance but appearance, as we have been taught by woeful experience, in the transformation of Dulcinea the sole refuge of my hope."

By this time, the boat being sucked into the middle of the stream, so as to move considerably faster than at first, was perceived by the millers, who seeing it advancing to the indraught of the wheels, came suddenly out in a body, with long poles to stop its motion; and as their faces and cloaths were bepowdered with meal, they made a frightful

figure, while they exclaimed with great vociferation, "You devils of men! where are you going? are you mad, to come and drown yourselves, or be ground to pieces by the wheels?"

Don Quixote hearing this address, "Did not I tell thee, Sancho," said he, "that we had arrived at the scene in which I must exert the prowess of mine arm. Behold, what felons and assassins come forth to try my valour; behold what a number of hobgoblins range themselves against me; behold, I say, what horrid physiognomies appear to scare and overawe us; but, you shall presently see what will happen, ye ruffians." Then, starting up, he began to threaten and revile them, exclaiming aloud, "Ye scum, ye scoundrels, ill-intentioned and worse-advised, release, I charge you, and restore to the full fruition of freedom, the person whom ye keep confined and oppressed in that fortress or jail, let him be high or low, or of what rank and quality soever he may be; for, I am Don Quixote de la Mancha, otherwise intituled the knight of the lions, destined by the appointment of heaven above, to bring this adventure to an happy issue."

So saying, he unsheathed his sword and brandished it in the air, in defiance of the millers, who hearing this rhapsody without understanding it, began to employ their poles, in order to turn aside the boat, which by this time had entered the current and canal of the wheels. As for Sancho, he fell upon his knees, and prayed devoutly that heaven would deliver him from such imminent danger; and his deliverance was accordingly effected by the alertness and dexterity of the millers, who pushed back the boat with their poles; yet, not without oversetting the vessel; so as that the knight and his squire were soused over head and ears in the water. It was well for Don Quixote that he could swim like a goose; nevertheless, the weight of his armour sunk him twice to the bottom, and had not the millers thrown themselves into the river, and weighed them up by main strength, it might have been said, Here Troy once stood *.

They were no sooner dragged ashore, rather drenched than dead of drought, than the squire humbling himself upon his knees, again clasping his hands and lifting up his eyes to heaven, uttered a very fervent petition to God, that he might be from thenceforward delivered from the frantic projects and mad attempts of his master. This ejaculation was scarce finished, when they were joined by the fishermen who were owners of the boat which was crushed to pieces by the mill-wheels; and they perceiving the wreck, began to strip Sancho, and demand indemnification of his master, who, with great tranquillity, as if nothing at all had happened, told the millers and fishermen, that he would pay for the bark with the utmost chearfulness, on condition that they would release, without ransom or security, the person or persons whom they detained in durance and oppression, within that castle.

"What does the madman mean by persons and castles," answered one of the millers, "wouldst thou carry off the customers that bring grist to our mills, forsooth?" "Enough," said Don Quixote within himself. "I might as well preach to the desart, as at-

---

* In allusion to the Speech that Virgil puts in the mouth of *Panthus Othryades*, who says to Æneas,

————*fuit Ilium, et ingens*
*Gloria Teucrorum!*²

tempt, by intreaties, to prevail upon such miscreants to do any virtuous action. In this adventure there must certainly be two powerful inchanters engaged on opposite sides, one of whom baffles the designs of the other; by one I was provided with a bark, and his antagonist overturned me in the water. Lord mend us! the world is nothing but a continual warfare of opposite machinations and deceit; for my own part, I can do no more." Then raising his voice, and fixing his eyes upon the mills, "Friends," cried he, "whosoever you are who lie confined within that prison, forgive me, that for my misfortune, as well as yours, it is not in my power to extricate you from your distress; for some other knight the adventure must be reserved." Having pronounced this apostrophe, he compounded with the fishermen, for whose boat he paid fifty rials, which Sancho disbursed with great reluctance, saying, "Two such boatfuls will sink our whole stock to the bottom."

The fishermen and millers gazed with admiration at those two figures, so different in appearance from other men; and as they could by no means understand the meaning and tendency of Don Quixote's discourse, and the questions he asked, they looked upon them as madmen, and went away. The millers retreated to their mills, the fishermen betook themselves to their cottage; the knight and squire, like beasts, returned to their beasts: and thus ended the adventure of the inchanted bark.

## CHAPTER XIII.

## Of what passed between Don Quixote and a fair huntress.

In a melancholy plight did the knight and squire reach the place where their cattle stood; indeed they were both sufficiently out of humour, especially Sancho, who was cut to the soul by the incroachment upon their capital, which to him was as precious as the apple of his eye. At length they mounted, in the most profound silence, and departed from the banks of that famous river, Don Quixote buried as it were amidst the meditations of his love, and Sancho immersed in those of his preferment, which, at that time, seemed to be at a weary distance; for, maugre all his simplicity and folly, he could easily perceive that all, or the greatest part, of his master's actions, proceeded from frenzy and distraction: he therefore resolved to take an opportunity of retreating abruptly to his own house, without expostulation, or the ceremony of taking leave. But fortune ordained that things should fall out quite contrary to his apprehensions.

Next day at sun-set, as they came out of a wood, Don Quixote extending his view over a delightful green meadow, perceived some people at the farther end of it; and as he proceeded, saw they were hawkers; approaching still nearer, he observed among them a gay lady, mounted upon a palfrey or beautiful pad as white as the driven snow, adorned with green furniture and a saddle of silver: the lady was likewise dressed in a rich habit of the same colour, as fine as finery itself. On her left-hand she carried a hawk, a circumstance

from which the knight concluded she was some lady of high rank, and mistress of all the rest; nor was he mistaken. On this supposition, therefore, he said to his squire, "Make haste, son Sancho, go and tell that lady of the palfrey and hawk, that I, the knight of the lions, send my respects to her exceeding beauty; and that, with her good leave, I will go and pay my compliments in person, and make her a tender of my service to the utmost of my power, in whatever she shall please to command: but, keep a guard upon your tongue, Sancho, and beware of thrusting in some of your proverbs, while you deliver my embassy." "To be sure, you have found me a deadly thruster," answered the squire, "that you give me such warning, as if this were the first time in my life, that I have carried embassies to ladies of high rank and augmentation." "Except that which you carried the lady Dulcinea," said the knight, "I do not know that ever you carried another, at least while in my service." "That's true," replied Sancho, "but a good paymaster never wants bail; and a dinner is easily got, where there is plenty of meat for the pot: what I mean is, that there is no occasion to tell me or advertise me of anything; for, I am never out, and have a sort of a smack of every thing." "I believe it, Sancho," said Don Quixote, "go in peace, and God be your guide."

The squire setting out accordingly, at a good rate, and spurring Dapple beyond his natural pace, came up with the fair huntress; then alighting and kneeling before her, "Beautiful lady," said he, "yonder knight, called the knight of the lions, is my master, and I am his squire, known at my own home by the name of Sancho Panza; and that same knight of the lions, tho' formerly of the rueful countenance, sends me to beg your grandeur would be pleased to allow him purposely, courteously, and consentingly, to come and gratify his desire, which is no other, as he says, and I believe, than to serve your exalted beauty and hawkingship; and in so doing, your excellency will do a thing that will redound to your own advantage, and from which he will receive the most notorious honour and satisfaction."

"Worthy squire," replied the lady, "assuredly you have delivered your embassy with all the circumstances that such embassies require: pray, rise, for it is not reasonable, that the squire of such a great knight-errant as he of the rueful countenance, whose character is well known in these parts, should remain in that posture: rise, friend, and go tell your master, that he shall be extremely welcome to command the services of me and the duke my husband, at our country-house in the neighbourhood." Sancho arose, equally astonished at the beauty, good-breeding and affability of this worthy lady; but, he was still more surprised at what she said concerning the well-known character of the knight of the rueful countenance; for, if she did not give him the appellation of the lions, it was because he had but lately assumed that epithet. "Pray, tell me, brother squire," said the dutchess, (whose title is not known) "is not your master the person whose history is printed under the name of the sage Hidalgo Don Quixote de la Mancha, who professes himself the admirer of one Dulcinea del Toboso?" "The very same, my lady," answered Sancho, "and I myself am that very squire of his who is mentioned, or ought to be mentioned, in that history, by the name of Sancho Panza, unless they have changed me in the cradle, I mean in the press." "I am extremely glad to hear it," replied the dutchess: "go, brother Sancho, and tell your master, that he is well met, and welcome to my estate; and that nothing could give me more pleasure than his arrival."

Sancho, in an excess of joy, occasioned by this agreeable answer, returned, and recounted to his master all that this lady of rank had said, extolling to the skies, in his rustic phrase, her exceeding beauty, good-humour and politeness. The knight chose one of his genteelest attitudes, fixed himself well in his stirrups, adjusted his vizor, quickened Rozinante, and with an agreeable air, advanced to pay his respects to the dutchess, who, while he approached, caused her husband to be called, and communicated the curious embassy. As they had read the first part of the history, from which they learned the extravagant humour of Don Quixote, they waited with infinite pleasure, and the most eager desire of being acquainted with the original, fully determined to gratify his humour in every thing, and treat him all the time he should stay with them, as a real knight-errant; that is, with all the ceremonies described in those books of chivalry they had read, and to which, indeed, they were greatly attached. Mean while, Don Quixote approaching with his beaver up, made a motion to alight, and Sancho made haste to hold the stirrup; but, he was so unfortunate, that in dismounting from Dapple, he slipped his foot through the noose of the stirrup-rope, in such a manner, that he could not possibly disentangle himself, but continued hanging with his face and part of his body on the ground. The knight, who never alighted without his assistance, imagining that Sancho, as usual, held the stirrup, threw himself off with a swing, and the saddle, which must have been very ill girted, and he, came to the ground together; not without great disgrace,[1] and a thousand curses, which he muttered between his teeth, against the unfortunate Sancho, whose leg was still in the stocks.

The duke seeing their distress, ordered his huntsman to assist the knight and squire; and they lifted up Don Quixote, who was very much bruised by the fall; nevertheless, he advanced as well as he could, with a limping pace, and kneeled before this noble pair: but the duke would by no means allow him to remain in that posture; on the contrary, alighting from his horse, he ran to embrace the knight, saying, "I am heartily sorry, sir knight of the rueful countenance, that the first time you touch my ground, you should be so unlucky; but, the carelessness of squires is often the cause of greater misfortunes." "This accident, valiant prince," replied Don Quixote, "cannot possibly be deemed a misfortune, though I had been plunged into the profound abyss; for, even from thence should I have been raised and extricated by the glory of seeing your grace. My squire, whom God confound, is more ready at untying his tongue, in order to utter malicious insinuations, than at tying and securing the girth of a saddle: but, whether fallen or exalted, afoot or on horseback, I shall always be devoted to your service, and that of my lady dutchess, your grace's worthy consort, the dignified queen of beauty, and universal princess of politeness." "Softly, my good signor Don Quixote de la Mancha," said the duke, "where my lady Dulcinea del Toboso reigns, no other beauty deserves applause."

By this time, Sancho Panza had disentangled himself and come up, and interposing in the discourse, before his master could make any reply, "It cannot be denied," said he, "but must always be affirmed, that my lady Dulcinea del Toboso is extremely beautiful: but the hare starts where she is least expected; for, I have heard it said, that the power called nature, is like a potter, who, if he can make one beautiful vessel, can in like manner make two, three, ay, and an hundred: this I observe, because, in good faith, my lady dutchess comes not a whit behind my lady mistress Donna Dulcinea del Toboso." Don

Vol. II. pag. 186.

F. Hayman inv.t        J. Rauenet Sculp.

Don Quixote Paying His Respects to the Duchess.

Quixote turning to the dutchess, "Your grace must know," said he, "that no knight-errant upon earth has such a prattling and freespoken squire as mine; and he will certainly verify my words, if your highness shall be pleased to make use of my service for a few days." "I have the better opinion of honest Sancho, for his being freespoken," answered the dutchess, "that is a sign of his discretion; for, pleasantry and wit, signor Don Quixote, as your worship very well knows, do not love to dwell in a reserved disposition; and therefore, since honest Sancho is frank and freespoken, I from henceforth set him down as a man of discretion." "And loquacity," added the knight. "So much the better," said the duke, "for a great deal of wit cannot be expressed in a few words; and that we may not spend more time in them, come, renowned knight of the rueful countenance—" "Of the lions, your highness must call him," cried Sancho; "the rueful countenance is no more." "Of the lions let it be then," continued the duke; "I say, come, Sir knight of the lions, to a castle I have in this neighbourhood, where you shall meet with that reception which is due to a person of your fame and character, and that respect which I and the dutchess always pay to the knights-errant who favour us with their company."

By this time Sancho, having replaced and secured Rozinante's saddle, Don Quixote bestrode that famous steed, and the duke mounting a beautiful courser, they rode towards the castle, on each side of the dutchess, who desired Sancho to keep close to her; for, she took infinite pleasure in hearing his conceits. Indeed the squire did not need intreaty, but mingling among the three, made a fourth in the conversation, to the unspeakable satisfaction of their graces, who thought themselves extremely fortunate in having an opportunity of entertaining, at their castle, such a knight-errant, and such an erring squire.

## CHAPTER XIV.

### Which treats of manifold important subjects.

S ancho rejoiced exceedingly at seeing himself, as he thought, a favourite with the dutchess; for, being a staunch well wisher to good cheer, he imagined he should find the same abundance in the castle, which prevailed in the houses of Don Diego and Basilius, and always took by the forelock every occasion of living at his ease. The history then relates, that before they reached the castle or pleasure-house, the duke riding on before, directed his servants how to behave to Don Quixote, who no sooner arrived at the gate with the dutchess, than two lacquies or grooms came forth, clad in long trailing morning gowns of fine crimson sattin, and lifting him off, said, without being heard or perceived, "Your highness must go and help my lady dutchess to dismount." The knight took the hint, and a dispute of compliments passed between them on the subject; but, at length the obstinacy of the dutchess prevailed; for, she would not quit her palfrey, or

alight, except in the arms of the duke, saying she was not worthy to load such an excellent knight with such an useless burden: at last, the duke came out to perform the office, and when they entered the court-yard, they were met by two beautiful damsels, who threw a mantle of the finest scarlet over Don Quixote's shoulders, and the corridores were instantly crowded with servants of both sexes, who exclaimed aloud, "Welcome, thou flower and cream of knights-errant"; while all, or the greatest part of them, emptied bottles of sweet water upon him, and their graces, to the admiration of Don Quixote, who now, for the first time, was sure and satisfied of his being a real, and not a fantastic knight-errant, because he saw himself treated as the knights of former ages, whose histories he had read.

Sancho quitted Dapple, and betaking himself to the dutchess, entered the castle, where, however, his conscience upbraiding him, for having left his beast alone, he made up to a reverend duenna, who with others, had come out to receive the dutchess, and accosting her in a soft voice, "Signora Gonçalez," said he, "or what's your name, madam?" "My name is Duenna Rodriguez de Grijalva," answered the gentlewoman, "what are your commands, brother?" "I wish you would do me the favour, good madam," replied the squire, "to go to the castle-gate, where you will find a dapple ass of mine, and be so good as either to send or lead him to the stable; for, the poor creature is a little timorous, and cannot bear to be alone, by any manner of means." "If the master be as wise as the man," cried the duenna, "we have brought our pigs to a fine market; get you gone, brother, with a vengeance to you, and those who brought you hither, and take care of your ass with your own hands: the duennas of this house are not used to such employments." "But, for all that," said Sancho, "I have heard my master, who is a perfect mine of history,[1] tell as how, when Lancelot came from Britain, ladies tended his own person, and duennas took care of his horse: now, with respect to my ass, I declare I would not exchange him for signor Lancelot's courser." "Heark ye, friend," replied the duenna, "if you are a jack-pudding, keep your jokes for a proper place, where they may turn to account: from me you'll get nothing but a fig for them." "Very well," said the squire, "I'll answer for its ripeness: your ladyship won't lose your game by a short reckoning." "You whoreson," cried the duenna, in a violent rage, "whether I am old or not, I must render an account to God, and not to such a garlic-eating rascal as you."

This address she pronounced in such an audible voice, that she was overheard by the dutchess, who, turning about, and seeing her woman in such wrath and trepidation, asked, with whom she was in such a passion? "With this honest fellow here," answered the duenna, "who has earnestly desired me to go and house an ass of his, that stands at the castle-gate, telling me forsooth, as an example, that the same employment was undertaken by some ladies, who took care of one Lancelot, while the duennas looked after his horse; and to crown the compliment, he tells me I am old." "I, myself," said the dutchess, "would construe that into the greatest affront that could be given: take notice, friend Sancho, that Donna Rodriguez is in the prime of her youth; and that the veil she wears is more for authority and custom, than on account of her years." "Accursed be those I have to live," cried the squire, "if I spoke to her for that reason; but, only for the great affection I bear to my ass, whom I thought I could not recommend to a more charitable person than Signora Donna Rodriguez." Don Quixote overhearing all that

Sancho Panza's Quarrel with the Duenna Rodriguez.

passed, "Is that proper discourse for this place, Sancho?" said he. "Signor," replied the
squire, "every man must speak of his wants where he finds them: here I thought of
Dapple, and here I talked of him; and if he had come into my head in the stable, there
too he should have been honourably mentioned." Here the duke interposing, "Sancho
is very much in the right," said he, "and must not be blamed for what he has said: Dapple
shall have no more to do but ask and have as much provender as he can eat; so that San-
cho may be quite easy in that respect, for, his beast shall be treated like his own person."

This conversation, which was extremely agreeable to all except Don Quixote,
brought them to the top of the stair-case, and the knight being conducted into an apart-
ment, hung with the richest tissue and brocard, was unarmed, and attended by six
sprightly damsels well instructed by the duke and dutchess in the particulars of behav-
iour which they were to observe towards Don Quixote, in order to convince him that
he was treated in all respects like a knight-errant. Thus disarmed, he remained in his
strait breeches and shamoy doublet, so long, so lank, so lean, with his lanthorn jaws kiss-
ing each other, that, if the damsels had not been very careful in preserving their gravity,
according to the precise orders they had received, they must certainly have burst with
laughing at sight of such an uncouth figure. They desired he would allow them to un-
dress and shift him; but he would not assent to this proposal, saying that knights-errant
ought to be as remarkable for decency as for valour: he therefore bade them deliver the
shirt to Sancho, with whom, shutting himself up in a chamber, furnished with a
magnificent bed, he was immediately undressed and shifted. Then being alone with his
squire, "Tell me," said he, "thou modern buffoon and ancient blockhead! was it their
province to dishonour and affront a venerable duenna, so worthy of reverence and re-
spect? Was that a time to think of Dapple? or could'st thou imagine those noble persons
would neglect the cattle belonging to guests whom they treated with such elegance? For
the love of God, Sancho, set a guard upon thy tongue, and behave so as that people may
not discover, by the thread, the coarse country web of which thou art woven: consider,
sinner as thou art, that the master is respected in proportion to the discretion and good
breeding of his servants; and this is one of the great advantages which noblemen have
over people of inferior rank: do'st thou not consider, thou plague to thyself, and vexa-
tion to me! that if they perceive thee to be a base bred clown or blundering fool, they
will take me for some cheating impostor or knight of the post? No, no, Sancho, shun
and avoid those inconveniencies; for, he who sets up for a merry-andrew, falls at the first
stumble into a disgraced buffoon: bridle thy tongue, therefore, consider and ruminate
well, before the words issue from thy mouth; and remember that we are now arrived at
a place from whence, by the favour of God, and the valour of mine arm, we shall depart,
bettered three, nay five-fold, both in fortune and in fame." Sancho promised, with re-
peated assurances, that he would rather stitch up his mouth, or bite off his tongue, than
utter one word that should not be pat to the purpose, and well considered, according to
his command; and that he might make himself perfectly easy on that score; for, by him
it should never be discovered who they were.

Don Quixote having dressed himself, girded on his sword, thrown the scarlet mantle
over his shoulders, and covered his head with a cap of green velvet, which he received
from the damsels, came forth thus equipped, into the great hall, where he found the

maidens placed in two equal rows, furnished with the implements for hands-washing, which they administered with profound respect and abundance of ceremony: then came the major-domo, attended by twelve pages, to conduct him to the table where their graces waited for him; he was accordingly surrounded by these domestics, and led with great pomp and majesty into another hall, in which appeared a table nobly decorated, with four covers. The duke and dutchess came to the door to receive him, attended by one of those grave ecclesiastics who govern the families of noblemen; who being of no birth themselves, know not how to direct those who are; who seek to measure the grandeur of the great by the narrowness of their own souls, and in attempting to make their pupils oeconomists, convert them into downright misers: such, I say, was the grave clergyman who came out to receive Don Quixote, with the duke and dutchess. After a thousand courteous compliments, they walked on each side of him to the table, where the duke complimented him with the upper end, and tho' he refused that honour, they importuned him so much, that he was obliged to comply; the clergyman sitting opposite to him, and the duke and dutchess taking their places at the sides.

Sancho, who was present at all this ceremony, being confounded and astonished at the honours which were paid to his master, and perceiving the formality and intreaties that passed between his grace and Don Quixote, about sitting at the head of the table, intruded himself as usual, into the discourse, saying, "With your honour's leave, I'll tell you a story of what happened in our village, with respect to the upper-hand in sitting."

Scarce had he pronounced these words, when the knight began to tremble with apprehension, that he was going to utter some absurdity; but, the squire seeing and understanding the cause of his master's trepidation, "Signor," said he, "your worship needs not be afraid that I shall misbehave, or say something that is not to the matter in hand; for, I have not forgot the advice I just now received from your worship, about speaking a little or a great deal, to the purpose, and not to the purpose." "I know nothing at all of the matter," answered the knight; "say what thou wilt, so thou sayest it quickly." "Well then," replied Sancho, "what I am going to say, is true, for my master Don Quixote here present, would not suffer me to tell a lie." "As for me," said Don Quixote, "you may lie as much as you please, without let or molestation: but, I advise you to consider well what you are about to say." "I have it so well considered and reconsidered, that I am as safe as he that has the repique in hand,[2] as will appear in the performance." "Your graces will do well," said Don Quixote, "to order the servants to turn out this madman, who will commit a thousand blunders." "By the life of the duke!" cried the dutchess, "I will not part with my good friend Sancho, for whom I have a very great respect, because I know him to be a person of wit and pleasantry." "Pleasant may all the days of your holiness be, for your good opinion of my deserts," said the squire; "tho' God knows, they are but slender enough: however, my story is this:

"There was an invitation given by a gentleman of our town, who was both rich and well born, as being come of the Alamos of Medina del Campo, and married to Donna Mencia de Quinones, daughter of Don Alonzo de Maranon, knight of the order of St. Jago, who was drowned in the Heradura, and occasioned a quarrel some years ago in our village, in which, if I am not mistaken, my master Don Quixote was concerned; but, this I know, mad Tom, the son of old Balvastro the blacksmith was hurt on that occa-

sion: now, Sir master of mine, is not this God's truth; speak upon your worship's hon-
our, that these noble persons may not look upon me as a chattering liar." "Hitherto," said
the clergyman, "I take you to be a chatterer rather than a liar; but, I know not what I
shall take you for in the sequel." "Thou hast produced so many witnesses and tokens,"
replied the knight, "that I cannot but say thy story looks like truth: proceed, however,
and shorten thy tale, for, thou art in the way of lengthening it out for the space of two
whole days." "He shall not shorten it," said the dutchess, "if he consults my entertain-
ment; but on the contrary, tell it in his own way, tho' it should not be finished in six days;
for, should it hold out so long, they will be some of the pleasantest I ever passed."

"Well then, my masters," proceeded Sancho, "that same gentleman, whom I know as
well as I know these two hands, for, it is not above a bowshot from his house to mine,
invited a farmer, who though not rich, was a very honest man." "Dispatch, brother,"
cried the priest, interposing, "for, at this rate, your story will reach to the other world."
"It will hardly go half as far, an it please God," answered the squire, who thus proceeded.
"So, as I was saying, the farmer going to the house of the gentleman-inviter, who is now
dead, God rest his soul! by the same token, they say he died like an angel; for my own
part, I was not present at his death, having gone a reaping to Tembleque." "As you hope
to live, son," cried the ecclesiastic, "return quickly from Tembleque, and finish your
story, without staying to inter the gentleman, unless you have a mind to bury us all!"
"Well, to come to the point," replied Sancho; "when the two came to be seated at table—
methinks I see them now more than ever." The duke and dutchess were infinitely
pleased with the disgust which the reverend ecclesiastic expressed at the tedious and cir-
cumstantial manner in which the squire related his story, while Don Quixote was almost
consumed by shame and indignation. "I say, moreover," resumed Sancho, "that the two,
as I have already observed, coming to sit down at the table, the farmer obstinately re-
fused to take the upper end, according to the desire of the entertainer; while the gentle-
man on the other hand as obstinately insisted upon his compliance, alledging that he
ought to be master in his own house; but, the farmer who piqued himself upon his po-
liteness and good-breeding, still persisted in his refusal, until the gentleman growing
angry, took him by the shoulders and thrust him into the seat, saying, 'Know, Mr. Chaff-
thresher, that wheresoever I sit, I shall always be at the head of the table.' Now this is my
tale, and I really believe it was brought in pretty pat to the purpose."

Don Quixote's brown face was speckled with a thousand different colours, at this
recital; and their graces restrained their laughter, that he might not be quite abashed at
the sarcastic insinuation of his squire. To change the discourse, therefore, and prevent
Sancho from uttering other such dangerous conceits, the dutchess addressing herself to
the knight, asked, when he had heard from the lady Dulcinea? and if he had lately sent
her any presents from the great number of giants and robbers whom he must have van-
quished? To this interrogation the knight replied, "My misfortunes, madam, though
they had a beginning, will never have an end. Giants I have vanquished; felons and rob-
bers I have sent; but, where must they find her, enchanted and transformed as she is, into
the most homely country wench that can be imagined!" "This I know," said Sancho
Panza: "to me she seemed the most beautiful creature in the whole world; at least, in
point of nimbleness and leaping, she would get the better of a professed rope-dancer; in

good faith! my lady dutchess, she skipped from the ground upon her ass, like a perfect cat." "What! have you seen her enchanted, Sancho?" said the duke. "How! I seen her?" replied the squire: "who the devil but I was the first that fell upon the plot of the inchantment; to be sure she is as much enchanted as my father."

The ecclesiastic hearing them talk of giants, felons and inchantments, began to imagine that this must be the Don Quixote de la Mancha whose history the duke took such delight in reading, that he had often reprehended his grace for being so mad as to read such nonsense; and being now confirmed in his suspicion, he said to the duke, in a very choleric tone, "Signor, your excellency is accountable to heaven for the actions of that poor man. That Don Quixote or Don Driveller, or what's his name, would not, I imagine, be such a fool, if your excellency did not administer fuel and encouragement to his madness and folly." Then addressing himself to the knight, "And, pray Mr. Wiseacre,"[3] said he, "who has stuffed your brain with the ridiculous conceit of your being a knight-errant, conquering giants and apprehending robbers? Return, in good hour (for in good hour I advise you) return to your own house, educate your children, if you have any, take care of your own concerns, and leave off strolling about the country, sucking the wind, and exposing yourself to the laughter of those who do, and those who do not, know your infirmity. Where, in evil hour, did you find that there are, or ever were, knights-errant? Where did you ever see giants in Spain, caitiffs in La Mancha, or enchanted Dulcineas, with all that tribe of absurdities that are recounted as your adventures?"

Don Quixote, who listened attentively to the discourse of this venerable person, no sooner perceived he had left off speaking, than forgetting the respect he owed to the duke and dutchess, he started up, and with an ireful aspect and glowing visage, replied— But the reply deserves a chapter for itself.

## CHAPTER XV.

### Containing Don Quixote's reply to his reprover; with other serious and diverting incidents.

D on Quixote starting up and trembling from head to foot, like quicksilver,[1] thus accosted the ecclesiastic, with an eager, yet faultring tongue: "The place and presence in which I am, and the respect which I always had and still have for the function you profess, withhold and tie up the hands of my just resentment: for these reasons, as well as because I know what all the world knows, that gownmen and women make use of no weapons but their tongues, I will, with mine, fairly engage your reverence, of whom I might have expected good advice, rather than infamous reproach, as wholsome and well-meant reproof requires far other circumstances, and ought to be conveyed in gentler terms: at least, a rebuke in public, delivered with such asperity, has exceeded all the bounds of christian reprehension, the beginning of which ought to be mild rather

The Priest Enraged with Don Quixote at the Table of the Duke and Duchess.

than severe; nor is it just to call the delinquent, in plain terms, a wiseacre and a fool, without knowing the nature of the fault for which he is reprehensible. But, pray, tell me, reverend signor, for which of the absurdities you have noted in my behaviour, do you condemn and reproach me, bidding me return to my own house, to take care of my family, my wife and children, without knowing whether I have either wife or children? What then! is there nothing required but to enter a house at random, in order to lead the master by the nose; and shall a narrow-minded pedant, on the strength of having taught a few pupils to read Latin,[2] though he has seen no more of the world than what may be contained in twenty or thirty leagues of district, presume abruptly, without permission, to give laws to chivalry, and judge of knights-errant? Is it a vain undertaking then, or is the time mispent, which we employ in travelling about the world, not in quest of its delights, but its adversities, by which good men ascend the throne of immortality? Had I been counted a fool by knights, or people of fashion, birth and generosity, I should have deemed myself irreparably affronted; but my being regarded as a madman, by bookworms who never entered or trod the paths of chivalry, I value not a farthing: a knight I am, and a knight I shall die, according to the pleasure of the Almighty. Some choose the spacious field of proud ambition; others take that of base and servile adulation; a third set follow the paths of deceitful hypocrisy; and a fourth proceed in that of true religion; but I, by the influence of my stars, pursue the narrow track of knight-errantry, for the exercise of which, I undervalue fortune in the chace of honour. I have assisted the aggrieved, redressed wrongs, chastised the insolent, overcome giants, and overthrown hobgoblins. I am enamoured, for no other reason but because it is necessary that knights-errant should be in love; and this being the case, I am not a vicious libertine, but a chaste platonic admirer. My intention I always direct to a worthy aim, namely, to do good unto all men, and harm to no creature. Whether or not he who thinks, acts and speaks in this manner, deserves to be called a fool, let your graces determine."

"Well argued, master!" cried Sancho; "'Fore God! your worship needs say no more in behalf of your own character; for, there is no more to be said, thought, or insisted upon; especially, as that gentleman denies, and he certainly has denied, that there either are, or ever were knights-errants in this world; so that he knows nothing at all of the matter!" "Brother," replied the priest, "belike you are that Sancho Panza to whom they say your master has promised an island?" "Yes, I am," said the squire, "and I hope I deserve it as well as another. I am one of whom you may say, Keep good company, and you'll learn good manners, and, I ask not where you was hatched, but where you was watched.[3] And again, Well sheltered shall he be, who leans against a sturdy tree. Now I have leaned against a good master, and accompanied him many months, and will learn to be just such another as himself; and if God pleases, and he live and I live, he will not want governments to give, nor I islands to govern." "No surely, friend Sancho," said the duke, "for I myself in the name of signor Don Quixote, will confer upon you the government of an odd island, and that not inconsiderable, which is in my possession." "Fall upon your knees, Sancho," cried Don Quixote, "and kiss his excellency's feet, for the honour he has done you." Sancho did as he was desired; and the ecclesiastic no sooner saw

the ceremony performed, than he rose from table in a violent passion, saying, "By the habit which I wear, I affirm, that your excellency is as mad as these poor sinners; what wonder that they should be frantic, when people who are in their senses, canonize their frenzy? Your excellency may enjoy their company by yourself; for, while they remain in this house, I shall stay in my own, and excuse myself from reproving what I cannot remedy." Without further speech, or eating another mouthful, he went away abruptly, in spite of all that their graces could say to detain him. Indeed, the duke said not much; for, he was hindered by the laughter which the priest's impertinent indignation had produced; however, as soon as he could resume his gravity, he addressed himself to Don Quixote, in these words:

"Sir knight of the lions, your worship has made such an ample reply, that nothing further remains to be done, by way of satisfaction, for that, which though it may seem an affront, falls by no means under that denomination; for, neither the female sex, nor the clergy, can give affronts, as your worship so very well knows." "Undoubtedly," answered the knight, "and the reason is, because those persons who cannot receive, are not capable of giving, an affront. Women, children and ecclesiastics, as they cannot defend themselves when attacked, so, neither can they be affronted; for there is this difference between an injury and affront, as your excellency well knows: an affront comes from a person who is capable of giving an affront, and when it is given, maintains it; whereas an injury may come from any quarter, unattended by an affront. For example, a man walking carelessly in the street, is assaulted and cudgelled by ten armed persons, against whom he draws his sword, and behaves like a man of honour; but, he is overpowered by the number of his antagonists, and prevented from executing his intention, which is to revenge the wrong: this man is injured not affronted. A truth which we will confirm by another example. A man comes and strikes another, whose back is turned, and then betakes himself to his heels; and the other pursues, though he cannot overtake the fugitive: the man so struck, received an injury but no affront, because an affront ought to be maintained. If he who gave the blow, though it was done by stealth, in a cowardly manner, had drawn his sword and stood facing the enemy, he who received the blow would have been both injured and affronted; injured, because he was surprized, and affronted, because he who gave the blow, maintained it by keeping his ground. And therefore, according to the punctilios of honour, I may be injured but not affronted; for, women and children do not feel those things; they can neither fly nor stand their ground: and the same rule holds good with those who are consecrated to the service of religion. Now these three classes of mankind are destitute of offensive and defensive weapons; and though nature obliges them to stand in their own defence, yet they can offend no body: and albeit I just now said I might be injured, I now affirm it cannot be in any shape; for, he who cannot receive, much less can he give an affront. For which reasons, I ought not to resent, nor do I resent the reproaches of that honest man; I only wish he had stayed a little, until I should have convinced him of his error, in thinking and saying, there never were, nor are, knights-errant upon the face of the earth; an asseveration which might have turned to his prejudice, had it been overheard by Amadis, or any one of his infinite progeny." "I'll take my corporal oath," cried Sancho, "that they would have given a back-

stroke that would have laid him open from top to toe, like a pomegranate or ripe melon: they were a rare set to endure such tickling. By my holidame! I am well assured, that if Reynaldos of Montalvan had heard this manikin's discourse, he would have given him such a slap in the mouth, that he should not have spoke another word in three long years. No, no: let him meddle with them, and he'll see how well he'll escape out of their clutches." The dutchess had well nigh died with laughing at this speech of Sancho, who, in her sentiment, was a more diverting madman than his master, and a great many people at that time were of the same way of thinking.

Finally, Don Quixote was appeased, dinner ended, and the cloth being taken away, in came four damsels, one of them with a silver ewer, another with a flask of the same metal, a third with a couple of very fine, white towels over her arm, and a fourth with her arms bare up to the elbow, and in her white hands, for, doubtless they were white, a washball of Neapolitan soap. She who carried the ewer, approaching with a genteel carriage and modest assurance, thrust it under the beard of Don Quixote, who, without speaking one word, wondered at this ceremony; from which he concluded, that it was the custom of the country to wash beards, instead of hands: he therefore stretched out his chin, as far as he could, and immediately the flask began to rain: the damsel with the soap-ball, lathered him with great expedition, raising flakes of snow, (for the suds were as white) not only upon the beard, but also over the whole face of the obedient knight, insomuch, that he was obliged to shut his eyes in their defence; while the duke and dutchess, who were not in the secret, sat impatiently waiting to see the issue of this ablution. The young she-barber having raised the lather as high as her hand, pretended the water was spent, and bade the damsel of the flask go for a fresh supply, and signor Don Quixote would have patience till her return. He accordingly waited with patience, exhibiting the strangest and most ludicrous figure that ever was conceived, to the view of numerous spectators, who seeing half a yard of neck more than moderately brown, two eyes shut, and his beard covered with lather, had need of great discretion to restrain their laughter, and it was a wonder they could smother it at any rate. As for the damsels concerned in the joke, they kept their eyes fixed on the ground, without daring to look at the duke and dutchess, who were at once agitated by mirth and indignation; and did not know, whether they should resolve upon chastising their presumption, or rewarding them for the pleasure they received in seeing the knight in such an attitude. At length the damsel returning with more water, they finished the ablution of Don Quixote; then she who carried the towels having wiped and dried him with great composure, all four at once made a most profound curtsie, and were going away. But, the duke fearing the knight would smell the joke, called to the damsel of the ewer, saying, "Come hither, and wash me too, and be sure you have water enough." The girl being very handy and acute, obeyed without hesitation, placed the ewer under his grace's chin, and when he was well washed, lathered, wiped and dried, they dropped their curtsies and retired. It was afterwards known, the duke had sworn within himself, that if they should have refused to serve him in that manner, he would have chastised them for their assurance; but they prudently scaped a scouring, by scouring his grace.

Sancho having attentively considered this ceremony of cleansing, "God's mercy!" said he within himself, "is it the custom in this country to wash the squire's beard as well

as the knight's? for God and my own conscience knows, I have need of such purification; and if they would give me the touch of a razor, the benefit would still be the greater." "What is that you mutter, Sancho?" said the dutchess. "I say, my lady," answered the squire, "I have always heard it said, that in the courts of other princes, when the cloth is taken away, water for the hands is brought in, but not suds for the beard; so that the longer we live, the more we learn: yet it is also observed, that he who lives much time will bear much misfortune; though to undergo such a purification as this may pass for a pleasure rather than a toil." "Give yourself no concern, friend Sancho," said the dutchess, "for, I will order my maids not only to wash, but also to lay you a bucking, should it be necessary." "I shall be satisfied with the lathering of my beard," replied the squire, "at least for the present; and God will ordain what is to happen in the sequel." The dutchess turning to the major-domo, "Remember," said she, "what honest Sancho desires, and gratify his inclination with the utmost punctuality." This domestic promised that signor Sancho should be obeyed in all things; and returning to dinner with the squire, left their graces and Don Quixote sitting at the table, discoursing on many and various subjects, though all of them related to chivalry and the exercise of arms.

The dutchess intreated the knight, who seemed to possess such a tenacious memory, to delineate and describe the beauty and deportment of the lady Dulcinea del Toboso, who, she concluded from what fame had proclaimed of her charms, must be the fairest creature, not only in the whole world, but even in La Mancha. Don Quixote sighing at her grace's request, "If," said he, "I could take out my heart, and lay it before your highness, in a plate upon this table, I should save my tongue the trouble of saying what is almost inconceivable, for in it your excellency would see her picture at full length: but, why should I now attempt to delineate and describe circumstantially the particular charms of the peerless Dulcinea? A burthen worthy of other shoulders than mine, and a task which ought to employ the pencils of Parrhasius, Timanthes, and Apelles, together with the chissel of Lysippus, to exhibit her image on canvas, brass and marble, as well as the Ciceronian and Demosthenian eloquence to sound her praise." "What does signor Don Quixote mean by Demosthenian," said the dutchess, "which is a word I never heard before in the whole course of my life." "Demosthenian eloquence," answered the knight, "has the same signification as the eloquence of Demosthenes, and Ciceronian means that of Cicero; for these two were the greatest orators in the whole world." "Certainly," said the duke, "and you exposed yourself by such an interrogation: nevertheless, signor Don Quixote would give us infinite pleasure, could he be prevailed upon to describe that beauty which, even in a sketch or rough draught, would certainly appear such as might excite envy in the most beautiful women of the creation." "I would assuredly comply with your grace's desire," replied the knight, "were not her idea blotted from my remembrance, by the misfortune which hath lately befallen her; a misfortune which induces me to bewail rather than describe her; for, your highness must observe, that when I went some time ago, to kiss her hands and receive her benediction, consent, and license, for this my third sally, I found her quite otherwise than I expected: I found her inchanted and transformed from a princess into a country wench, from beauty into deformity, from an angel into a demon, from a delicious perfume into a pestilential vapour, from the pink of compliment into the most clownish dialect, from

light into darkness, from a sedate young lady into a rustic romp, and finally, from Dulcinea del Toboso into a * Sayago drab." "God protect us! (cried the duke with a loud voice) who can have done such mischief to the world, in robbing it of that beauty by which it was delighted, that good humour by which it was entertained, and that modesty which did it honour?" "Who?" answered the knight, "who could it be but one of the malignant and envious tribe of enchanters, by whom I am persecuted? That accursed race, brought into the world on purpose to obscure and annihilate the exploits of the good, and to illustrate and extol the deeds of the wicked. Persecuted I have been by enchanters, persecuted I am by enchanters, and enchanters will persecute me, until I and all my lofty feats of chivalry are plunged into the abyss of oblivion: nay, they injure and wound me in that part where they know my feeling is most acute; for, to deprive a knight-errant of his mistress, is to rob him of the eyes with which he sees, the sun by which he is enlightened, and the support by which he is maintained: I have many times said, and now I repeat the observation, that a knight-errant, without a mistress, is like a tree without leaves, a building without cement, and a shadow without the substance by which it is produced."

"There is no more to be said," replied the dutchess: "nevertheless, if we are to believe the history of signor Don Quixote, which has lately been ushered into the world, with the general applause of the different nations that compose it, we must conclude (if I right remember) that your worship never saw the lady Dulcinea, and that there is no such person in being; but that it is only a fantastical mistress, begot and born in your imagination, which hath decked her with all the graces and perfection that fancy could conceive." "Much may be said on that subject," answered Don Quixote: "God knows whether or not there is such a person as Dulcinea in the world, whether she is fantastical or not fantastical; for, these things are not to be too nicely investigated: for my own part, I neither begat nor bore my mistress, altho' I contemplate her with that admiration which is due to a lady, in whom are concentred those qualities that ought to render her renowned throughout the whole world, such as beauty without blemish, gravity without pride, tenderness with chastity, affability from courtesy, courtesy from goodbreeding; and finally, dignity from birth, because nobleness of blood reflects an additional splendour upon beauty, and shews it to greater perfection than that which we find among the fairest of those who are meanly born." "Your observation is extremely just," said the duke: "but, signor Don Quixote must give me leave to mention what the history of his adventures, which I have read, obliges me to declare; namely, that tho' we grant there may be a Dulcinea, either in or out of Toboso; and that she may be beautiful to excess, as your worship has described her; yet, in respect to pedigree, she is by no means on a footing with the Orianas, the Alastrajareas, and the Madasimas, together with the rest of that class, which occurs so often in those histories that are so familiar to your worship."

"To that observation I can answer," said the knight, "that Dulcinea is the daughter of her own works; that good qualities ennoble the blood, and that a virtuous person of low

* Sayago is a district in the kingdom of Leon, the inhabitants of which were extremely poor, and very meanly cloathed.[4]

descent ought to be more esteemed than a vicious man of high degree; especially as Dulcinea possesses qualifications which may raise her to the throne of a crowned and sceptred queen; for, the merit of a virtuous and beautiful woman is sufficient to work still greater miracles, and virtually, tho' not formally, contains within itself still greater advantages." "Signor Don Quixote," said the dutchess, "every thing you say is spoken with deliberation, and, according to the proverb, you proceed with the plummet in your hand:[5] henceforth, I shall firmly believe, and make my whole family, even the duke himself, should there be occasion, believe, that Dulcinea is living at this day in Toboso; that she is beautiful, high born, and in all respects worthy to be served and admired by such a knight as signor Don Quixote; and that is the highest compliment that can be bestowed. But I cannot help forming a scruple, and entertaining a kind of grudge against Sancho Panza: the scruple arises from a particular of the history, importing, that the said Sancho, found the lady Dulcinea winnowing a sack of wheat when he carried a letter to her from your worship, by the same token it is said to have been red wheat; a circumstance that makes me doubt the nobleness of her pedigree."

To this remark Don Quixote replied, "Madam, your highness must know, that all or the greatest part of the incidents that happen to me, deviate from the ordinary limits of those adventures which occur to other knights-errant, either conducted by the inscrutable will of destiny, or effected by the malice of some envious enchanter: and it is a circumstance well known of all or the greatest part of renowned knights-errant, that one possessed the virtue of being proof against enchantment, another of being invulnerable, which was the case of the famous Orlando, one of the twelve peers of France, who, as it is recorded, could not be wounded in any other place but the sole of his left foot, and even there, with no other weapon than the point of a large pin; so that Bernardo del Carpio, who slew him at the battle of Ronscevalles, perceiving that he could make no impression upon him with steel, lifted him off the ground, and strangled him between his arms, in imitation of the manner in which Hercules destroyed Anteus, that ferocious giant said to be the son of Earth. What I would infer from what I have said, is, that I too may have some of these virtues centered in my person, tho' not that of being invulnerable; for, I have been frequently convinced by experience, that my flesh is very tender, and by no means impenetrable: nor that of being proof against enchantment; for, I once found myself cooped up in a cage, in which the whole world would not have had strength enough to inclose me, without the additional power of enchantment: but, since I freed myself from that confinement, I am apt to believe that no other will ever interrupt the course of my adventures; and therefore, those enchanters seeing that their wicked arts will not take effect upon my own person, revenge themselves on those things to which my affection is chiefly attached, and endeavour to deprive me of life, by persecuting that of Dulcinea, for whom alone I live. I therefore am persuaded, that when my squire delivered my message, they had converted her into a coarse country wench, employed in such a mean exercise as that of winnowing wheat: but, I have already said, that it could not be red wheat, nor indeed any sort of wheat, but oriental pearls; and as a proof of this asseveration, I must tell your highnesses, that when I lately went to Toboso, I could by no means find Dulcinea's palace; and the day following, while my squire Sancho beheld her in her own figure, which is the fairest in the whole

world, to me she seemed a rustic and homely country wench, without any thing sensible in her conversation; whereas she is in fact the very pink of discretion and good sense. Now, since I myself neither am, nor, in all probability, can be inchanted, she is the person inchanted, offended, changed, perverted and transformed, and in her my enemies have taken vengeance upon me; so that, for her, I shall live in perpetual affliction, until I see her restored to her former state: all this I have observed, that no body may scruple about what Sancho said of her sifting and winnowing; for, since they have transformed her in my view, no wonder they should change her form, in his. Dulcinea is a person of birth and fashion, one of the genteel families of Toboso, which are very numerous, ancient and noble, and certainly no small part of these qualifications falls to the share of the peerless Dulcinea, on whose account the place of her nativity will become famous and renowned, in future ages, as Troy is become famous by Helen, and Spain by Cava,[6] tho' with a better title and nobler fame. On the other hand, I must inform your graces, that Sancho Panza is one of the most pleasant squires that ever served a knight-errant: sometimes his simplicity is so arch, that, to consider whether he is more fool or wag, yields abundance of pleasure; he has roguery enough to pass for a knave, and absurdities sufficient to confirm him a fool; he doubts every thing, and believes every thing; and often, when I think he is going to discharge nonsense, he will utter apothegms that will raise him to the skies: in a word, I would not exchange him for any other squire, even with a city to boot; and therefore I am in doubt whether or not it will be expedient to send him to that government which your grace has been so good as to bestow upon him; although I can perceive in him a certain aptitude for such an office: so that, when his understanding is a very little polished, he will agree with any government, like the king with his customs; for, we know by repeated experience, that great talents and learning are not necessary in a governor, as there are an hundred at least, who govern like jerfaulcons, tho' they can hardly read their mother tongue: provided their intention is righteous, and their desire to do justice, they will never want counsellors to direct them in every transaction, like your military governors, who being illiterate themselves, never decide without the advice of an assessor. I shall advise him corruption to eschew, but never quit his due: and inculcate some other small matters that are in my head, which, in process of time, may redound to his own interest, as well as to the advantage of the island under his command."

Thus far the conversation had proceeded between their graces and Don Quixote, when they heard a number of people talking, and a great noise in the palace, and presently Sancho entered the hall in a fright, tucked with a dishclout by way of bib, and followed by several boys, or rather scullions, and other small gentry, one of whom brought a tray full of water, which, by its colour and filth, appeared to be dish-washings, pursuing and persecuting the poor squire, and struggling to thrust it under his chin, while another, with the same earnestness, endeavoured to lather his beard.[7] "What is the matter, fellows?" cried the dutchess, "what is the matter? what designs have you upon that worthy gentleman, hah! don't you consider he is governor elect?" To this apostrophe the barber-scullion replied, "The gentleman won't suffer himself to be washed, according to the custom and manner practised upon my lord duke and his own master." "Yes, I will," cried Sancho (in a violent passion) "but, it must be with whiter towels,

clearer suds, and cleaner hands; for, surely there is not such a difference between me and my master, as that he should be washed with angel water, and I drenched with devil's lye. The customs of different countries, and the fashions of princely courts, are no further good than as they are agreeable; but this here custom of lathering, is worse than the exercise of disciplinants *. My beard is clean enough, and needs no such scrubbing; and if any man pretends to lather me, or touch a hair of my head, (my beard I mean) saving this honourable presence, I'll drive my fist in his scull; for, these ceremonies of soap-scouring look rather like making game than making welcome." The dutchess was ready to burst with laughing at the rage and remonstrance of Sancho: but, Don Quixote was not extremely well pleased, to see his squire tucked up with such a dirty cloth, and surrounded with so many sons of the kitchen: he therefore, making a low bow to the duke and dutchess, by way of asking their permission to speak, thus addressed himself to the scullions, in a solemn tone: "So ho, you gentlemen cavaliers, I desire your worships will let the young man alone, and return to the place from whence you came, or go whithersoever you please: my squire is as cleanly as another, and those trays are as unfit for him as a narrow-necked bottle: take my advice therefore, and let him alone; for, neither he nor I understand such impertinent jokes." Here Sancho taking the word out of his master's mouth, proceeded, saying, "No, no, let them perform their clumsy joke, which I shall bear as sure as it is now night: let them fetch a comb, or what they will, to curry this beard, and if they catch any thing that should give offence to cleanliness, they shall shear me against the hair."

At this period, the dutchess still laughing, "Sancho Panza," said she, "is certainly in the right in all that he has said, and will be in the right in all that he shall say; he is already clean enough, and as he observes, has no occasion to be washed; and if he does not like the custom of the place, he shall follow his own † inclination: besides, you ministers of cleanliness have been extremely remiss and negligent, not to say presumptuous, in bringing to such a personage and such a beard, trays, wooden troughs, and dishclouts, instead of ewers and golden basons, and towels of the finest holland: but, the case is, you are base-born miscreants, and, like caitiffs as you are, cannot forbear shewing the grudge you bear to the squires of knights-errant." The whole scullion-ministry, as well as the major-domo, who came in with them, believed her grace was actually in earnest, and sneaked away in great shame and confusion, after having untied the dishclout from the neck of Sancho, who seeing himself delivered from that imminent danger, went and

---

* In Spain and Italy there is, upon every Holy Thursday, a procession of disciplinants, or people who do penance in sackcloth, carrying a flambeau in one hand, and in the other a scourge, with which they belabour their own shoulders, in such a manner, that the very street is sometimes coloured with their blood. Some of these disciplinants, however, are meer hypocrites, who, under their sackcloth, wear womens stays, buff jackets, and even plates of tin; so that they are often detected from the sound of the stroke: and at Rome nothing is more common, than to hear the people who accompany these devotees, call out, according to the report of the application, *Guippone di Buffalo! Busti di Donna!* and *Corrazini di Latta!*[8]

† *Su alma en Su Palma.* The original expression literally signifies "His soul is in his hand," *i.e.* He is at his own discretion.[9]

fell upon his knees before the dutchess, saying, "From great ladies great benefits are ex-
pected; and this that I have now received from your grace, I can in no other shape re-
pay, than in wishing I were dubbed a knight-errant, that I might spend all the days of my
life in the service of such a noble and exalted lady: a peasant I am, and Sancho Panza by
name, with a wife and family, and serve in quality of a squire; and if in any of these re-
spects I can serve your highness, I shall be more speedy in obeying than your grace in
laying your commands." "Sancho," replied the dutchess, "it plainly appears that you
have learned politeness in the school of courtesy itself: I say, it plainly appears, that you
have been bred up at the feet of Don Quixote, who is the cream of compliment, and
flower of ceremony, or, as you term it, Sarah-money: long life and prosperity to such a
master and such a pupil; one the north-pole of knight-errantry, and the other the very
star of squirish fidelity. Rise, friend Sancho, and I will remunerate your politeness, by
prevailing upon my lord duke to perform his promise of the government, with all pos-
sible dispatch."

 Here the conversation being broke off, the knight retired to take his afternoon's * nap,
and the dutchess desired Sancho, if he was not very much disposed to sleep, to go and
pass the evening with her and her women, in a very cool and pleasant apartment. San-
cho told her, that altho' it was really his custom to sleep for four or five hours every af-
ternoon, in the heat of summer, yet, for the satisfaction of her grace's goodness, he
would that day strive with all his might to keep himself awake, and obey her commands
in all things: he accordingly attended her steps; while the duke gave fresh directions for
treating Don Quixote as a real knight-errant, without deviating one tittle from the stile
in which the ancient knights are said to have been entertained.

* In Spain, the people always retired after dinner, and sleep till six a clock, whence, the afternoon's
nap is called *Siesta*.

# THE

# LIFE and ATCHIEVEMENTS

## Of the Sage Hidalgo

# DON QUIXOTE de La MANCHA.

# BOOK III.

## CHAPTER I.

### Of the pleasant conversation that passed between the dutchess, her women, and Sancho Panza; worthy to be read and remembered.

The history then relates, that Sancho did not sleep that afternoon, but, according to his promise, went, eating all the way, into the apartment of the dutchess, who took great delight in hearing his conversation, and desired him to sit close by her on a joint-stool, tho' the squire, out of pure good-breeding, begged to be excused: but, her grace told him, he should sit as a governor, and speak as a squire, for, in both capacities, he deserved the individual seat of the champion Cid Ruy Dias.

Sancho shrugging up his shoulders, obeyed and took his place, surrounded by all the damsels and duennas, who listened with profound silence and attention. Nevertheless, the dutchess was the first who began the discourse, saying, "Now that we are by ourselves, unheard by any body, I must intreat Mr. governor, to resolve certain doubts of mine, produced by the printed history of the great Don Quixote; one of which doubts is this: as honest Sancho never saw Dulcinea, I mean the lady Dulcinea del Toboso, nor conveyed to her the letter of signor Don Quixote, which remained with the memorandum book in Sierra Morena, how durst he feign an answer, and pretend that he found her winnowing wheat, a circumstance altogether ridiculous and untrue, so much to the prejudice of the peerless Dulcinea's reputation, and so ill-becoming the station and fidelity of a trusty squire?"

Without making any immediate answer to this interrogation, Sancho rose from his seat, and moving softly on his tiptoes, with his body bent, and a finger on his lips, examined the whole apartment, lifting up and looking behind the tapestry; and this scrutiny being made, returned to his stool, and replied, "Now my lady dutchess, that I am assured there is no skulker listening, and that we are not overheard by any but this good company, I will, without fear or trembling, answer all the questions of your grace;

and first and foremost, I will own I look upon my master Don Quixote as an incurable madman; although sometimes he says things, which, to my thinking, and in the opinion of all who hear them, are so sensible and well directed, that even Satan himself could not mend them: nevertheless, I am really and truly, and without any scruple, fully persuaded within myself, that he is downright distracted. Now, as I am possessed with this notion, I venture to make him believe any story, without either head or tail, like that of the answer to his letter, and another trick I played him six or eight days ago, which is not yet recorded in the history; I mean the enchantment of Donna Dulcinea, which I palmed upon him, tho' it was a tale as wild and uncertain as the hills of Ubeda *."

The dutchess desired he would recount that enchantment or deception; and he accordingly related it exactly as it happened, to the no small entertainment of the hearers; but when he was about to proceed in his discourse, her grace interposing, said, "From this recital of honest Sancho, a scruple has started in my mind, and whispers me in the ear, since Don Quixote de la Mancha is so lunatic, crazy and mad, and his squire Sancho Panza, who knows his infirmity, nevertheless serves and follows him, and even depends upon his vain promises; the said squire must, without all doubt, be more crazy and mad than his master: and if this be the case, as it certainly is, it would be no great sign of wisdom in you, my lady dutchess, to bestow an island on such a governor; for, how will he be able to govern other people, who cannot govern himself?"

"'Fore God! my lady," cried the squire, "your scruple starts in the right place: and I beg your ladyship will let it speak out in its own way; for, I know it speaks truth. Had I been wise, I should have left my master long ago; but this was my fate and my misventure: I cannot do otherwise; but follow him I must: we are of the same town; I have eaten of his bread; I have an affection for him; he returns my love, and has given me his colts; but, above all, I am constant and faithful, and therefore nothing can possibly part us but the sexton's shovel. If your highness does not choose to perform your promise of the island, God made me of a less matter, and perhaps your refusal may turn out to the ease of my conscience, for maugre all my madness, I understand the proverb that says, The pismire found wings to her sorrow: and mayhap Sancho the squire may get sooner to heaven than governor Sancho; there's as good bread baked here as in France; and by night all cats are grey; and sure the man his lot may rue who has not broke his fast by two; between man and man the maw cannot differ a span; and as the saying is, With hay or with straw we'll fill up the craw;[2] the little birds of the field have God for their steward and shield; four yards of coarse Cuenca stuff are warmer than as much of fine Segovia serge; when we leave this world and are laid in the ground, the Lord goes in as narrow a path as his labourer; and the pope's body takes up no more room than the sexton's; for, though the one be higher than the other, when we go to the pit, we must lie snug, and make it fit; or we shall be obliged to find room, though scanty is the tomb; and so good night.[3] Wherefore, I say again, if your grace will not give me the island, because I'm a fool, I shall be so wise as not to break my heart at the disappointment; and

---

* This is an expression proverbially applied to any story that is vague, inconsistent, or of dubious authority; for, the hills of Ubeda make an extensive chain, the different parts of which are differently denominated, from the different countries or districts thro' which it extends; so that the whole is not easily ascertained.[1]

I have often heard, that the devil skulks behind the cross; it is not all gold that glitters; and that from his oxen, his yokes and his ploughs, Bamba the husbandman was raised to the throne of Spain; and that from his riches, pastime and embroidery, Rodorigo was taken to be devoured by serpents, if the rhimes of old ballads do not lie."

Here Donna Rodriguez the duenna, who was one of the hearers, interposing, "Where-fore, should they lie?" said she, "for the ballad says as how they thrust king Rodorigo all alive into a tomb full of toads, lizards and snakes, and two days after, he was heard to cry with a weak and doleful voice, 'Now they eat me! now they gnaw the part in which I sinned so heinously!' And therefore the gentleman is in the right to say he would rather be an husbandman than a king, to be devoured by vermin."

The dutchess could neither help laughing at the simplicity of her duenna, nor ad-miring the discourse and proverbs of Sancho, to whom she replied, "Honest Sancho very well knows, whatsoever a knight promises must be fulfilled, even though it should cost him his life; now, my lord and husband the duke, though no errant, is nevertheless a knight; and therefore will perform his promise of the island, in spight of all the envy and malice of the world: let Sancho, then, be of good chear; for, when he least thinks of the matter, he will see himself seated in the saddle of his island and dominion, and grasp his government, which he would not exchange for one of superfine brocade; but, I charge him to mind how he governs his vassals, who, I give him notice, are all people of honest parents and approved loyalty."

"With respect to their being happy under my government," said the squire, "you need not give me any thing in charge; for, I am naturally charitable and compassionate towards the poor; and from him who can knead and bake, it is not easy to steal a cake. By my salvation, they shall not pass false dice upon me! I am an old dog, not to be taken in with *, Come hither, poor Tray. I know how to snuff my peepers upon proper occa-sions; nor will I consent to walk with cobwebs in my eyes; for I know where the shoe pinches. This I observe, because the righteous shall always have the benefit of my heart and hand, but the wicked shall have neither foot nor footing. In my opinion, every gov-ernor must have a beginning in the art and mystery of government, and perhaps, in a fortnight's administration, I shall lick my fingers after the office, and know as much of the matter as I do of day-labour, to which I was bred."

"Sancho," said the dutchess, "you are certainly in the right; for no man was ever a scholar at his birth; and bishops are made of men, and not of blocks. But to return to our former discourse about the inchantment of the lady Dulcinea; I take it for an absolute certainty, and not a bare asseveration, that Sancho's scheme of deceiving his master, and making him believe that the country-wench was Dulcinea, whom the knight could not know, because she was inchanted: I say, this scheme was altogether the invention of one of those inchanters who persecute Don Quixote; for, I know from very good authority, that the village-maiden who skipped upon the ass, was really and truly the individual Dulcinea del Toboso; and that Sancho, in thinking himself the deceiver, was in fact the person deceived: a truth of which we ought no more to doubt, than of things we never saw; for signor Sancho Panza must know, that here also we have friendly inchanters,

* In the original, And thoroughly understand *Tus, Tus;* which is an expression in Spain, to wheedle a cur.⁴

who, out of real regard, impart to us every thing that passes, truly and distinctly, without circumlocution or deceit; and therefore, Sancho may believe me, when I affirm, that the jumping wench was and is Dulcinea del Toboso, who is as much inchanted as the mother that bore her; and when we dream of no such thing, we shall see her in her own shape, and then Sancho will be undeceived."

"There is nothing more likely," cried the squire; "and now I am apt to believe my master's account of the cave of Montesinos, where he saw my lady Dulcinea del Toboso, dressed in the same manner which I described, when I enchanted her for my own amusement. Now, the whole affair must have been quite the reverse, as your ladyship observes; for it cannot be supposed that my ignorant pate could contrive, in an instant, such an ingenious stratagem; nor can I think my master such a fool as, upon my weak and meagre persuasion, to believe such an improbable device; but, for all that, my lady, your goodness ought not to take me for an evil-minded person, seeing a blockhead, like me, is not obliged to bore into the designs and knavery of abominable inchanters. I contrived the scheme, in order to escape the displeasure of my master Don Quixote, and not with any design to do him hurt; and if it has turned out otherwise, there's a judge in heaven who knows the heart." "Very true," answered the dutchess; "but, tell me now, Sancho, the story of the cave of Montesinos, which I shall be extremely glad to hear."

Then Sancho Panza recounted every circumstance of that adventure, as it hath been already related; and her grace having heard the whole, "From this incident," said she, "we may infer, that since the great Don Quixote says he beheld in that place the same country-wench whom Sancho saw in the neighbourhood of Toboso, it could be no other than Dulcinea, and that the inchanters of this country are very officious, and extremely curious." "This I will venture to say," replied Panza, "that if my lady Dulcinea del Toboso is really inchanted, 'tis her own loss, and that it is no business of mine to enter the lists with my master's enemies, who are certainly both wicked and numerous. True it is, she I saw was a country wench, for such I took her, and such I judged her to be. If that was Dulcinea, it ought not be laid to my charge, nor am I to be blackened for that reason; yet I must be lugged in at every bawdy-house bench, with Sancho said this; Sancho did that; Sancho went and Sancho came; as if Sancho were just such as they would please to make him, and not the very same Sancho Panza who has already travelled all the world over in books, as I have been informed by Samson Carrasco, who is, at least, a batcheleering person of Salamanca; and such people cannot tell an untruth, except when it comes into their heads, or will turn to their account; wherefore, nobody has any right to meddle with me; and seeing I live in good repute, and I have heard my master say, a good name is better than tuns of wealth, even shove me into this government, and they shall see marvellous things; for, he who has been a good squire will never become a bad governor."

"All that honest Sancho has uttered," said the dutchess, "is Catonian wisdom, or at least, the very essence of Michael * Verino, *Florentibus occidit annis*.[6] In a word, to speak in his own stile, A good drinker is often found under a rusty cloak." "In sober

---

* A young Florentine, of great genius, who died in the seventeenth year of his age, and was lamented by all the poets of his time.[5]

truth, my lady," answered Sancho, "I never in my life drank out of malice; from thirst I might, for, I have not the least spice of hypocrisy in my belly; I drink when I choose it, and even when I would rather be excused, because I am desired so to do, that I may not seem shy or ill-bred; for, sure he must have an heart of marble who can refuse to pledge a friend, for though I put on my shoes, I will not defile them; especially, as the squires of knights-errant usually drink water, as they are always strolling through forests, woods and meadows, and over rocks and mountains, without finding the smallest charity of wine, even though one should offer to purchase it with an eye." "I believe what you say," answered the dutchess: "at present Sancho may go to rest; and we shall afterwards talk more at large upon these subjects, and take order that with all convenient dispatch he may be, to use his own words, shoved into that same government."

Sancho kissed hands again, and begged her grace would be so good as to give directions about the entertainment of Dapple, who was the light of his eyes. When she asked, what he meant by Dapple; "My ass," replied the squire, "whom, rather than use the vulgar term, I call Dapple: when I first came to the castle, I desired madam Duenna here to take care of him; and truly, she was as much affronted as if I had called her ugly and old; though I think it would be more natural and proper for duennas to look after cattle, than to regulate rooms of state. God's my life! what a spite a gentleman of our town had to these waiting gentlewomen." "He must be some ill-bred clown," said Donna Rodriguez the duenna; "for had he been a gentleman of birth, he would have exalted them above the horns of the moon." "Enough, for the present," resumed the dutchess: "hold your tongue, Donna Rodriguez, and let signor Panza make himself perfectly easy, and leave me to take special care of Dapple, whom, as being a moveable appertaining to Sancho, I will place above the apple of mine eye." "The stable is a place good enough for him," answered the squire; "for, neither he nor I are worthy of being placed for one moment above the apple of your highness's eye; and I will as soon consent to his being disposed of in that manner, as I would to drive a dagger in my breast; for, although, as my master says, in point of courtesy, one ought to lose the game by a card too much, rather than by a card too little; in respect to asses and the apple of an eye, one ought to proceed cautiously with the compass in his hand, and measure as he goes."

"Sancho may conduct him to his government," said the dutchess, "and there entertain him to his heart's content; nay, even infranchise him from all labour." "Your grace, my lady dutchess, needs not think much of that," replied the squire; "for, I have seen more than one or two asses go to governments; and therefore it will be no new practice if I carry Dapple to mine."

This remark renewed the laughter and satisfaction of the dutchess, who having dismissed him to his repose, went to communicate the conversation to the duke; and this noble couple contrived and gave directions about the execution of a pleasant joke upon Don Quixote, which should turn out a famous incident, and be conformable in all respects to the stile of chivalry; in which they invented a number, with such propriety and discretion, that they are counted the best adventures contained in this important history.

## CHAPTER II.

Which gives an account of the information received, touching
the means for disenchanting the peerless Dulcinea del Toboso;
one of the most renowned adventures of this book.

Great was the satisfaction which the duke and dutchess received from the conversa-
tion of Don Quixote and Sancho Panza; and being confirmed in their design of
practising some jokes, which should bear a faint shadow and appearance of adventures,
they took the hint for a very extraordinary contrivance, from the knight's account of
what had happened to him in the cave of Montesinos: but, what mostly excited the ad-
miration of the dutchess, was the amazing simplicity of Sancho, who was by this time
brought to believe, as an infallible truth, the inchantment of Dulcinea, though he him-
self was the only inchanter and projector of that whole stratagem. Their graces having
given directions to the servants touching the execution of the scheme they had laid, at
the end of six days they went forth to hunt the wild boar, with as great an apparatus of
hunters and spearmen as used to attend the king in person. Don Quixote was presented
with an hunting suit, and Sancho received another of superfine green cloth; but, the
knight excused himself from accepting the present, observing that, in a few days, he
should be obliged to resume the rugged exercise of arms, and therefore could not en-
cumber himself with baggage and wardrobes; as for the squire, he took that which was
offered to him, without scruple, intending to sell it with the first opportunity.

On the morning of the appointed day, Don Quixote armed himself at all points, San-
cho put on his green suit, and mounting Dapple, which he would not exchange for the
best steed in the stable, mingled among the troop of hunters: the dutchess came forth,
very gaily caparisoned, and the knight, out of pure courtesy and good breeding, would
have held the reins of her palfrey; but the duke would not consent to his performing
such an office. At length they arrived at a wood, between two very high mountains,
where, the disposition being made, the toils set, and the people distributed in their dif-
ferent posts, the hunt began with a vast noise of hollowing and crying; and nothing
could be distinctly heard for the barking of the dogs and the sound of the horns. The
dutchess alighted, and with a pointed boar-spear in her hand, took post in a place
through which she knew the wild beasts were used to come; the duke and Don Quixote
likewise dismounting, posted themselves on each side of her grace, while Sancho stayed
in the rear, without parting from Dapple, whom he durst not quit, lest some misfortune
should happen to that darling beast.

Scarce had they set foot on ground, and taken their stations, supported by a number
of servants, when they beheld a monstrous boar, baited by the dogs and pursued by the
hunters, running towards them, gnashing his teeth and tusks, and foaming at the mouth.
The knight no sooner perceived this savage, than bracing his shield and unsheathing his
sword, he advanced to receive him; while the duke did the same with his boar-spear; but,

the dutchess would have been the foremost of the three, had she not been restrained by her lord. Sancho alone, seeing this furious animal, forsook his friend Dapple, and running full speed, in order to climb a lofty oak, found his endeavour altogether ineffectual; for, having surmounted one half of the ascent, the branch on which he stood struggling to gain the top, unfortunately gave way, and in falling, he was caught by another stump of the tree, so that he hung dangling in the air, without being able to reach the ground. Perceiving himself thus suspended, that his green suit was torn, and supposing that if the wild boar should come up, he would be able to seize him as he hung, he began to utter such doleful cries, and roar so hideously for assistance, that all those who heard his clamour, without seeing his situation, actually believed he was in the jaws of some savage beast. At length the tusky boar being pierced and killed by the number of spears that opposed him, Don Quixote turned about his head, in consequence of Sancho's cries, by which he recognized his faithful squire, whom he saw hanging from the oak, with his head downwards, and hard by he perceived Dapple, who did not forsake him in his calamity: and Cid Hamet observes, that he very seldom saw Sancho without Dapple, or Dapple without Sancho, such was the friendship and fidelity subsisting between them. Don Quixote immediately advanced and unhooked Sancho, who finding himself delivered, and fairly placed upon firm ground, examined the rent in his hunting-suit, which grieved him to the soul; for, in that dress he thought he had obtained an invaluable inheritance.

About this time they laid the mighty boar across a sumpter-mule, and covering him with sprigs of myrtle and rosemary, carried him in triumph, as the spoils of victory, to a large field-tent, pitched in the middle of the wood, where they found the cloth ready laid, and the table furnished with such a grand and sumptuous entertainment as well bespoke the wealth and magnificence of the founder. Sancho presenting to the dutchess the skirts of his torn suit, "If," said he, "this had been hare or sparrow-hunting, my coat would have been secure from this unlucky accident; for my own part, I do not know what pleasure there is in attacking an animal, which, if he can once fasten his tusks on you, will deprive you of life. I remember to have heard people sing an old ballad that says,

> May bears upon thy carcase feed,
> As erst on Fabila they did."

"That was a Gothic king," said Don Quixote, "who, in going to the chace, was devoured by a bear." "That is the very thing, I say," replied the squire; "I would not have kings and noblemen run themselves into such dangers, for the enjoyment of a diversion, which, in my opinion, hardly deserves the name, as it consists in murdering a poor beast that never committed any crime." "There, Sancho, you are mistaken," said the duke, "for, the exercise of hunting wild beasts is, of all others, the most necessary and suitable to kings and noblemen. The chace is a picture of war, comprehending schemes, feints and stratagems for taking advantage of the enemy; by this we are enabled to endure extreme cold and excessive heat, to contemn ease and undervalue sleep; our bodies acquire strength, and our limbs agility: in a word, it is an exercise that affords pleasure to numbers, and does prejudice to none; and what renders it superior to all others is, that it can-

not be enjoyed by every body, like all the other kinds of sport, except hawking, which is also peculiar to sovereigns and persons of rank: you must therefore alter your opinion, Sancho, and when you are governor, employ yourself in the chace, which you will find of incredible * service." "Surely, that cannot be," answered the squire; "a good governor will stay at home, as if he had a broken bone. It would look rarely indeed, if, when people fatigued with a journey, come to visit him upon business, he should be taking his diversion upon the hills; in that case the government would go to wreck. In good faith, my lord, such pastime is more proper for idle folks than for governors: I intend, God willing, to amuse myself with a game at cards at Easter, and with nine-pins on Sundays and holidays; for, as to these chaces or cases, they neither suit my condition nor agree with my conscience." "God grant Sancho may behave as he says he will," replied the duke; "but, there is a wide difference between saying and doing." "Let it be as wide as it pleases," cried Sancho. "A good paymaster needs no pawn; God's blessing is better than early rising; and the belly is carried by the feet, and not the feet by the belly: I mean that, with God's assistance, and a righteous intention, I shall certainly be able to govern like any goshawk; ay, ay, let them thrust their fingers in my mouth, and they shall see whether or no I can bite."

"The curse of God, and all his saints, light on thee, accursed babbler!" cried Don Quixote: "will that day never come, as I have often said, when I shall hear thee speak sensibly and distinctly, without lugging in old saws? My lord and lady dutchess, I intreat your graces to let that madman alone; otherwise he will grind your souls, not between two but two thousand proverbs, dragged in as much to the purpose and as seasonably as I wish God may give him health, or me protection, if I desire to hear them." "The proverbs of Sancho Panza," said the dutchess, "tho' more in number than those of the Greek commentator, are not the less to be esteemed for the conciseness of the apophthegms. I can safely say for myself, that they give me much more pleasure than I should receive from others, tho' better culled, and more suitable to the occasion."

In the midst of this and other such savoury conversation, they quitted the tent, to examine some snares they had laid; in which amusement the day was soon elapsed, and was succeeded by the night, which did not appear so serene and composed as it might have been expected at that season of the year, which was midsummer, but along with it came a certain *darkness visible*,[2] which greatly assisted the design of the duke and dutchess. When the night therefore began to fall, a little after the twilight, all of a sudden the four quarters of the wood seemed to be on fire, and here and there, and every where, they heard an infinite number of cornets and other warlike instruments, as if a great number of cavalry had been marching through the wood: so that the light of the flames, and the sound of those warlike instruments, dazzled and astonished the eyes and ears of the bystanders, and indeed of all the people in the wood. This noise was succeeded by innumerable *Lelilles*, or cries used by the Moors in battle; the trumpets and clarions exalted their brazen throats, the drums rattled, and the fifes resounded all together, in such a continued and alarming concert, that the man must have been utterly devoid of all sense who did not lose it in consequence of such confusion and uproar. The duke was con-

* Literally, And you shall see it will be worth a loaf that will serve an hundred.[1]

founded, the dutchess amazed, Don Quixote astonished, Sancho Panza affrighted; and, finally, even those who were let into the secret, seemed to be seized with consternation, which produced among them a most dreary silence.

During this pause, came a postilion dressed like a devil, and, instead of a cornet, blew an unmeasurable horn, which yielded an hoarse and dreadful sound. "Holla! brother courier," cried the duke, "who are you? where are you going? and what troops are those that seem to march across the wood?" To these interrogations the courier replied, in a dismal, hollow tone: "I am the devil, going in quest of Don Quixote de la Mancha: those who follow are six troops of inchanters, who bring, upon a triumphant car, the peerless Dulcinea del Toboso inchanted, accompanied by the gallant Frenchman Montesinos, to instruct Don Quixote in a certain method for disinchanting the said lady Dulcinea." "If you were the devil," answer'd the duke, "as you say you are, and your figure seems to declare, you would have distinguished that same knight Don Quixote de la Mancha, who now stands before you." "'Fore God! and upon my conscience!" cried the devil, "I did not see him: for, my thoughts are so much distracted by different avocations, that I had forgot the principal aim of my coming." "Without doubt," said Sancho, "that devil must be an honest man, and a good christian, otherwise he would not swear 'fore God! and on my conscience! Now am I fully convinced that there must be some worthy people even in hell."

Then the courier, without alighting, fixed his eyes upon Don Quixote, and pronounced: "To thee, the knight of the lions (and would I might see thee in their clutches) am I sent by the unfortunate, tho' valiant knight, Montesinos, who commanded me to desire, in his name, that thou wouldst wait on the very spot where I should find thee, because he brings along with him one Dulcinea del Toboso, in order to communicate what will be necessary towards her disinchantment: and as this message was the sole cause of my coming, there is no cause that requires my longer stay. Devils like me be with thee, and good angels guard that noble pair." So saying he sounded his dreadful horn, and rode off, without waiting for the least reply.

This address renewed the astonishment of all present, especially of Sancho and Don Quixote: of Sancho, because in despite of truth, he saw they were resolved that Dulcinea should be inchanted; and of Don Quixote, because he could not be certain of the truth of what had happened to him in the cave of Montesinos. While he was rapt in these meditations, the duke accosted him, saying, "Signor Don Quixote, do you intend to wait?" "Wherefore not?" replied the knight, "here will I wait, courageous and intrepid, tho' all hell should come to assault me." "Then for my part," cried Sancho, "if I see another devil, and hear another horn like that which passed, I should as soon wait here as in Flanders."

About this time, the night being more advanced, a number of lights began to gleam through the wood, like the dry exhalations of the earth that glide through the air, and are mistaken by ignorant people for shooting stars: their ears were likewise invaded by a frightful sound, like that occasioned by the massy wheels of waggons drawn by oxen; an harsh and grating noise, from which the very bears and wolves (if any chance to be in the way) are said to fly with terror. This uproar was succeeded by another more terrible than all the rest; for, all at once, at the four corners of the wood, there really seemed

to be four encounters or battles: in one place was heard the horrid din of cannon; in another a vast number of muskets were fired; here resounded the cries of the combatants; there the moorish *Lelilles* were repeated with vast vociferation. In a word, the cornets, horns, bugles, clarions, trumpets, drums, artillery and musketry, but above all, the dismal noise of the cars, formed all together, such a confused and horrible concert, that Don Quixote was obliged to recollect his whole courage, in order to bear it without emotion: but, Sancho's heart died within him, and down he came in a swoon upon the train of the dutchess, who received him as he fell, and, with marks of great concern, ordered her servants to throw water in his face: in consequence of this application he recovered, just as one of the waggons with the creaking wheels came up to the place where they stood. It was drawn by four lazy oxen wholly covered with black trappings, with a large lighted taper tied to each horn, and in the waggon was raised a lofty seat, on which sat a venerable old man with a beard as white as snow itself, that flowed down below his middle, and a large loose garment of black buckram: for, the waggon being stuck full of lights, it was easy to observe and distinguish every thing that it contained. It was conducted by two ugly devils clad also in buckram, with such hideous features, that Sancho no sooner saw them than he shut his eyes, that they might not encounter such frightful objects. This carriage being come up, the venerable senior rose up from his lofty seat, and pronounced aloud, "I am the sage Lirgandeo." He said no more; and the waggon proceeded. Another carriage followed in the same manner, with another old man inthroned, who ordering the waggon to stop, said, with a voice as solemn as the first, "I am the sage Alquise, the great friend of Urganda the unknown." And so the carriage proceeded. Then a third approached in the same stile: but, he who possessed this throne, instead of being old like the others, was a robust man of a very disagreeable aspect, who rising from his seat, like the other two, exclaimed in a more hoarse and diabolical tone, "I am the inchanter Arcalaus, the mortal enemy of Amadis de Gaul, and his whole race." And so the carriage passed on: but, when they had proceeded a little way, the three waggons halted; then ceased the dismal creaking of the wheels, and no other sound was heard but that of an agreeable, musical concert, which rejoiced the heart of Sancho, who took it as a good omen, and in that persuasion said to the dutchess, from whom he had not budged an hair's breadth, "My lady dutchess, where there is music there can be no harm." "As little should we expect any harm where there is light and illumination," answered the dutchess. "And yet," replied the squire, "we may be easily burnt by such torches and bonfires as these, notwithstanding all the light and illumination they produce: but, musick is always a sign of joy and feasting." "Time will shew," said Don Quixote, who overheard the conversation; and he said well, as will appear in the following chapter.

## CHAPTER III.

# Being a continuation of what was imparted to Don Quixote, touching the means for disinchanting Dulcinea; with an account of other surprizing incidents.

Moving to the sound of this agreeable music, came one of those carriages called tri-umphal cars, drawn by six grey mules covered with white linen, and upon each was mounted a * penitent of light, clad also in white, with a large lighted wax taper in his hand. The car was twice, nay thrice as large as the carriages which had passed, and the tops and sides were occupied by twelve other penitents as white as snow, with their lighted tapers: a sight that excited equal terror and surprize. Seated on a lofty throne, appeared a nymph habited in robes of silver tissue, bespangled with innumerable leaves of gold brocard; so that her dress, if not rich, was extremely gaudy: her face was covered with a delicate and transparent veil of fine tiffany, the plaits of which could not conceal the beauteous features of a young lady; and the number of lights enabled the spectators to distinguish her charms and her age, which seemed to be turned of seventeen but under twenty. Close by her appeared a figure clad in what is called a robe of state, that reached to his feet; and his head was muffled in a black veil. The cart had no sooner come opposite to the duke and dutchess, and Don Quixote, than the music of the waits, the harps, and lutes, ceased all at once; then this figure rising, threw aside his robe, and, taking off the veil, disclosed to view the horrible and uncarnate form of death; at sight of which Don Quixote was startled, Sancho overwhelmed with fear, and the duke and dutchess exhibited some affected marks of consternation.

This living death standing upright, began, with a languid voice and tongue but half awake, to repeat the following address.

> I Merlin am, by histories bely'd,
> That represent the devil as my sire:
> A falshood sanction'd by the lapse of time.
> I am the prince of magic, in whose breast
> The Zoroastric science lies intomb'd:
> The rival of invidious Time, whose wings
> Still seek to shade and darken all exploits
> Atchiev'd by the illustrious errant knights,
> For whom my friendship glows and ever glow'd.
>
> Tho' all my fellows of th'inchanting tribe,
> The magi and magicians, ever nurs'd
> A disposition barbarous and harsh,
> Mine still was tender, gentle, and humane,

* *Disciplinante de Luz*, is a cant phrase, applied to those who are exposed to public shame.[1]

A friend to all the various race of man.
In the profoundest caves of gloomy Dis,
Where my industrious spirit was employ'd
In forming mystic characters and spells,
Mine ears were wounded with the wailing cries
Of fam'd Dulcinea that matchless fair.

I learn'd her strange inchantment, and condol'd
Her transformation from a gentle nymph
To the vile figure of a rustic wench.
An hundred thousand volumes I perus'd,
Fraught with the dark and diabolic art,
Then in the horrible and ghastly trunk
Of this dry skeleton my soul enclos'd:
And now I come on purpose to impart
An easy remedy for her mishap.

O thou! the glory of all knights who wear
Impervious coats of mail and adamant:
Thou light and lanthorn, path and north and guide
Of all who quit the drousy joys of sloth,
And starting from the lazy down, embrace
Th'intolerable use and exercise
Of rude, unwieldy, sanguinary arms:
To thee I speak, great chief whose valiant deeds
So far transcend the loudest blast of fame.

Quixote, for courage and discretion fam'd,
La Mancha's mirrour and the star of Spain,
In order to recover and restore
Thy peerless mistress to her former state,
Sancho, thy faithful squire, must undergo
Three thousand and three hundred stripes, apply'd
To his posteriors, passively expos'd;
And he himself must wield the pliant scourge,
And start, and smart, and tingle with the pain.
Thus stands th'irrevocable doom, pronounc'd
By the fell authors of her dire mischance,
And on this errand, gentles, am I come.

"I vow to God!" cried Sancho at this period, "not to mention three thousand, I will as soon give myself three stabs with a dagger as three single stripes with a scourge. Now devil take such ways of disinchanting. I cannot conceive what my buttocks have to do with inchantments. Before God! if signor Merlin can find no other method for disinchanting my lady Dulcinea del Toboso, she may e'en go inchanted to her grave." "Heark ye, Don Garlick-eating rustic," said Don Quixote, "I shall take and tie you to a tree, naked as your mother bore you, and not to mention three thousand three hundred, give you six thousand six hundred lashes so well laid on, that three thousand three hundred

twitches shall not pull them off; and answer me not a syllable, or I will tear thy soul from the body."

Merlin hearing this declaration, "Not so, neither," said he: "the lashes to be received by honest Sancho must be voluntary, not upon compulsion, and at his own leisure; for, there is no time fixed for the final execution: nevertheless he is so far indulged, that he may be quit for one half of the stripes, provided he will allow the other half to be inflicted by another hand, tho' it may chance to be a little weighty." "No man's hand shall touch my flesh; neither another's, nor my own, nor weighty nor unweighed. What a plague! did I forsooth, bring my lady Dulcinea into the world, that my backside must suffer for the transgression of her eyes? My master, indeed, who is a part of her, and is continually calling her his life, his soul, his sustenance and support, may, and ought to lash himself for her sake, and take with all dispatch the necessary steps for her disin-chantment; but, for me to scourge my own body, I denounce it."[2]

Scarce had Sancho uttered this remonstrance, when the embroidered nymph who sat by Merlin's spirit, rising up, took off her transparent veil, and disclosing a face which to all the spectators seemed more than exceedingly beautiful, addressed herself in these words, directly to Sancho Panza, with a masculine assurance and a voice that was not extremely melodious, "O! ill-conditioned squire! thou soul of a pitcher, heart of cork, and bowels of flinty pebbles; had'st thou been commanded, thou nose-flaying catif, to throw thyself down from a lofty tower; had'st thou been desired, thou enemy of human species, to swallow a dozen of toads, twice the number of lizards, and three dozen of snakes; hadst thou been urged to murder thy wife and children with some sharp and ruthless scymitar, it would not have been strange to see thee shy and fearful; but, to make such objections to three thousand three hundred stripes, which there is scarce a naughty boy that does not receive every month, astounds, astonishes and affrights the compassionate bowels of all this audience, as well as of all those who shall hear it in the future course of time. Turn, O miserable, hard-hearted, animal! turn, I say, thy mulish goggle eyes[3] upon these balls of mine that emulate the glittering stars, and see how they weep thread by thread and skein by skein,[4] creating trenches, paths and furrows through the delightful meadows of my cheeks. Wilt thou not relent, thou crafty and malicious monster, at seeing me in the flower of my age (for I am still in my teens, being no more than nineteen, which is one year short of twenty) consume and pine within the bark of an homely rustic wench? in which form if I do not now appear, it is owing to the par-ticular favour of signor Merlin, who has indulged me so far, that my beauty might melt thy savage heart; for, the tears of afflicted beauty soften rocks to cotton, and transform tygers into gentle lambs. Chastise, chastise, obdurate beast, that brawny beef of thine; arrouse that slothful spirit which inclines thee to nothing but to gorge and regorge thy voracious maw, and set at liberty the beauty of my face: and if for my sake thou wilt not mollify thyself, and listen to any reasonable terms, at least relent in favour of that poor knight who stands forlorn at thy elbow; I mean, thy master, whose soul I now can see traversed in his throat, not above ten fingers breadth from his lips, waiting for nothing but thy kind or rigorous reply, in consequence of which it will either leap out of his mouth or retire to his stomach."

Don Quixote hearing these words, felt his throat, and turning to the duke, "By heaven! my lord," said he, "Dulcinea has spoke truth; for, here do I feel my soul traversed in my throat, like the nut of a cross-bow." When the dutchess asked what Sancho said to that circumstance, "I say," replied the squire, "what I have said already, that the whipping I denounce." "You must call it renounce," said the duke, "and not denounce." "I would your grace would let me alone," answered Sancho: "this is no time for me to mind niceties and letters, more or less; for, I am so confounded at those stripes which I am to receive, or execute upon myself, that I neither know what I am saying or doing: yet, I should be glad to know where my lady Dulcinea del Toboso learned that manner of asking favours. She comes to desire me to tear open my flesh with a horse-whip, and calls me soul of a pitcher, obdurate beast, and a whole rigmarole of villainous names, which the devil may suffer for me! What a plague, is my flesh made of brass? or is it any thing to me, whether she is disinchanted or no? What baskets of white linnen, shirts, caps and socks (tho' I wear none) does she bring to soften me? Nothing but abuse upon abuse; without remembering the proverb, that says, An ass loaded with gold will skip over a mountain. A generous gift the rock will rift. We must fervently pray, and hammer away. I will give thee, is good; but, Here take it, is better. Then, my master, who ought to lead me fair and softly by the hand, and persuade me with gentle words to whip myself into wool and carded cotton, declares, forsooth, that if he should once take me in hand, he will tye me naked to a tree, and double the allowance of stripes. These angry gentlemen ought to consider it is not only a squire, but a governor whom they desire to flog himself; as if it was no more than drinking after cherries. Let them learn; let them learn, with a vengeance, how to intreat and beg with good breeding; for, all seasons are not the same; and a man is not always in good humour: here am I ready to burst with vexation to see the rent in my green coat; and they must needs come and desire me to whip myself with good will, when God knows, I am as far from doing it with good will, as I am from turning * Turk."

"Nevertheless, friend Sancho," said the duke, "if your heart does not become softer than a ripe fig, you shall finger no government of mine. It would be a fine scheme indeed, if I should send to my islanders, a cruel, flinty-hearted governor, who would not melt at the tears of damsels in affliction; nor at the intreaties of wise, imperious, ancient sages and inchanters. In a word, Sancho, you must either consent to whip yourself or be whipped, or lay aside all thoughts of being a governor." "My good lord," replied the squire, "will not they give me two days to consider and determine what will be for the best?" "By no means," cried Merlin: "on this very spot, and this very instant, the business must be discussed; otherwise Dulcinea will return to the cave of Montesinos, and the appearance of a country-wench; whereas, if you comply, she will, in her present form, be transported to the Elysian fields, where she must reside until the number of the stripes be accomplished."

"Go to, honest Sancho," said the dutchess, "pluck up your spirits, and behave like a grateful squire that has eaten the bread of signor Don Quixote, who is intitled to the service and acknowledgements of us all, by his amiable disposition and sublime chivalry.

* Literally, *Cacique*, which was the appellation given to Indian princes.⁵

Say aye, my son, to this same flagellation, and let the devil fetch the devil: leave fear to the coward; for, a stout heart quails misfortune, as you very well know."

To these exhortations Sancho made no reply; but, addressing himself to Merlin, with his usual extravagance, "Good, your worship, pray tell me, signor Merlin, the meaning of one thing. A certain courier devil came here with a message to my master, from signor Montesinos, desiring him to stay in this place, until he should come up; for, he would teach him a way to disinchant my lady Dulcinea del Toboso; and hitherto we have seen no such person." To this interrogation Merlin replied, "That devil, friend Sancho, is an ignorant blockhead, and a very great knave. I sent him hither in quest of your master; not with a message from Montesinos, but from myself; for, Montesinos is still in his cave, planning, or rather expecting his disinchantment, the worst of which is still to come;[6] but, if he owes you any thing, or you have any business to transact with him, I will bring you face to face wherever you shall appoint. In the mean time, dispatch, and give your consent to this discipline, which, I assure you, will greatly redound to the advantage both of your soul and body: to your soul, from the charity of the undertaking, and to your body, as I know you are of a florid complexion, and will be the better for losing a little blood."

"What a number of leeches have we got in this world!" said Sancho, "the very inchanters are physicians; but, since every body says so, although I cannot perceive it myself, I am content to give myself three thousand three hundred lashes, on condition that I may give them when and where I shall think proper, without being confined to any certain time, or rate of allowance; and I will endeavour to discharge the debt as soon as possible, that the world may enjoy the beauty of the lady Dulcinea del Toboso, since, contrary to my former belief, she appears to be really beautiful. I likewise covenant that I shall not be obliged to fetch blood with the scourge, and that in case I should chance to be whipped by the officers of * justice, every lash so received, shall enter into the tale: Item, lest I should commit a mistake in the number, signor Merlin, who knows every thing, shall take care to reckon them, and give me to understand, how far I have fallen short, or exceeded the appointed score." "There will be no occasion to apprise you of the overplus," said Merlin; "for, as soon as the number shall be completed, the lady Dulcinea will be disinchanted, and come, out of pure gratitude, to return thanks, and even a recompence, to the charitable Sancho, for his good work. You need not, therefore, make any scruple about the superplus or the deficiency; nor will heaven allow me to defraud any person, even of a single hair." "A God's name, then," cried Sancho, "I consent in my tribulation: I say, I accept of the penance on the conditions aforesaid."

Scarce had Sancho pronounced these last words, when the music of the waits began to play again, and an infinite number of muskets was discharged, while Don Quixote, hanging about Sancho's neck, imprinted a world of kisses on his cheeks and forehead: the duke and dutchess, and all the by-standers, expressed the utmost pleasure, the car

* The other translators have interpreted *Mosqueo* into a fly flap, which is, undoubtedly, one of its meanings; but, as it likewise signifies flagellation at the cart's tail, I have taken it in this last acceptation, which, I think, heightens the humour of the passage.[7]

began to move, and the beauteous Dulcinea, in passing, bowed to their graces, and made a profound curtsie to Sancho.

About this time, the chearful smiling morn advanced; the flowrets of the field, with heads erect, diffused their fragrance; and the liquid crystal of the rills, murmuring among the variegated pebbles, went sliding on to pay its tribute to the rivers, that waited to receive their customary dues: the joyous earth, the splendid firmament, the buxom air, and light unclouded; each singly, and altogether joined, prognosticated plainly, that the day which trod upon Aurora's skirts, would be serene and fair. The duke and dutchess, extremely well satisfied with the chace, as well with the ingenious and fortunate execution of their design, returned to the castle, with full intention to perform the sequel of their jest; than which no real adventure could have given them more delight.

## CHAPTER IV.

Which gives an account of the perilous and inconceivable adventure of the afflicted Duenna, alias the countess Trifaldi; together with a letter which Sancho Panza wrote to his wife Teresa Panza.

The duke's steward was a man of humour and ingenuity, who acted the part of Merlin, and adjusted all the apparatus of the foregoing adventure; for, he composed the verses, and directed a page to represent Dulcinea: finally, under the auspices of his lord and lady, he projected another of the most agreeable and strange fancy, that could possibly be conceived.

Next day, the dutchess asking Sancho if he had begun the task of the penance which he was to undergo for the disinchantment of Dulcinea, he answered in the affirmative, and said, he had that same night given himself five lashes: but, when she inquired about the instrument with which they were inflicted, he owned they were applied with his hand. "That is rather clapping than lashing," replied her grace; "and, I take it for granted, the sage Merlin will not be content with such delicacy; it will be absolutely necessary that honest Sancho should make a scourge of briars, or use a switch that will make him feel it; for, learning is not acquired without pain, and the liberty of such an high-born lady as Dulcinea is not to be purchased for a trifle." To this remonstrance Sancho replied, "I wish your grace would lend me some convenient whip, or ragged rope's end, which would do the business without giving me a great deal of pain; for, I would have your grace to know that, although I am a labouring man, my flesh has more of the cotton than the matt weed in it; and there is no reason that I should destroy myself for another's advantage." "In good time be it," answered the dutchess; "to-morrow morning, I will give you a scourge that will fit you to an hair, and agree as well with the tenderness of your flesh, as if it was its own brother."

This affair being adjusted, "My lady," said Sancho Panza, "your highness must know, I have writ a letter to my wife Teresa Panza, giving an account of all that hath befallen me since we parted: here it is in my bosom, and wants nothing but a superscription. I wish your grace, in your great understanding, would read it; for, in my mind, it smacks of the governor; I mean, of the manner in which governors ought to write." "And, who was the inditer?" said the dutchess. "Who should indite it, sinner that I am, but myself," answered the squire. "Did you likewise write it, yourself?" replied her grace. "I did not so much as think of any such matter," said Sancho; "for, the truth is, I can neither read nor write, tho' I know very well how to set my mark." "Let us see this epistle," quoth the dutchess, "in which, I dare say, you have displayed the quality and extent of your understanding."

Then Sancho pulling an open letter from his bosom, the dutchess took and read it to this effect.

### Sancho's Letter to his wife Teresa Panza.

"If I have been finely lashed, I have been well mounted; if I have obtained a good government, it has cost me a good whipping. This, Teresa, thou wilt not now understand, but shalt learn some other opportunity. Know, Teresa, I am determined thou shalt ride in a coach, which is a resolution pat to the purpose; for, any other way of travelling is fit for none but cats. A governor's lady you shall be, and I would fain see the best of them tread upon thy heels. I have sent thee a green hunting-suit, which was a present from my lady dutchess. Make it up into a petticoat and jacket for our daughter. My master Don Quixote, as I have heard in this country, is a sensible madman and a diverting fool, and I myself am nothing short of him in these respects. We have been in the cave of Montesinos, and the sage Merlin has pitched upon me to disinchant the lady Dulcinea del Toboso, who in your parts is called Aldonza Lorenzo: with three thousand three hundred stripes, lacking five, which I am to give myself, she will be as much disinchanted as the mother that bore her. Thou shalt not mention a syllable of this to any person whatsoever; for, if you go to seek advice about your own concerns, one will say it is white, and another swear 'tis black.

A few days hence I shall set out for my government, whither I go with a most outrageous desire of getting money; and, I am told, this is the case with all new governors. I will feel the pulse of it, and give thee notice whether or no thou shalt come and live with me.

Dapple is in good health, and sends his most hearty commendations: I believe I shall not forsake him, even if they should make me the grand Turk. My lady dutchess kisses thy hands a thousand times; return the compliment with two thousand; for, as my master says, Nothing is so reasonable and cheap as good manners. It has not pleased God that I should stumble upon another portmanteau with a hundred crowns, as heretofore; but, let that give thee no uneasiness, my dear Teresa, for, he is safe who has good cards to play;[1] and what is amiss will come out in the washing[2] of this same government. One thing, I own, gives me great concern: I am told that if once I taste it, I shall be apt to eat my fingers; and should that be the case, it will be no cheap bargain; tho' the lame and the paralytic enjoy a sort of canonry, in the alms they receive. Wherefore, one way or another, thou wilt certainly be rich and fortunate. The Lord make thee so, as he very well may, and preserve for thy service thy husband the governor

From the Duke's-castle,                                    SANCHO PANZA"
July 20, 1614.

The dutchess having read the letter to an end, "In two circumstances," said she, "the honest governor is a little out of the way. First, in saying or insinuating, that the government was bestowed upon him, in return for the stripes he must undergo; whereas, he knows and cannot deny, that when my lord duke promised him the island, no body thought of any such thing as stripes in the world: secondly, he discovers an avaritious disposition, and I should not like to see him a skin-flint; for, greediness bursts the bag, and a covetous governor will do very ungoverned justice." "I did not write with that intention," answered the squire: "and if your ladyship thinks this is not a proper letter, there is nothing to do but tear it and write another, which perhaps will be still worse, if it be left to my own num-scull." "No, no," cried the dutchess, "this will do very well, and must be shewn to the duke."

Accordingly, repairing to a garden, where they were to dine that day, she communicated Sancho's epistle to the duke, who perused it with infinite pleasure. Here they went to dinner, and after the cloth was taken away, and they had entertained themselves a good while with the savory conversation of Sancho, their ears were suddenly invaded with the dismal sound of a fife, and a hoarse unbraced drum: all the company were startled at this confused, martial and melancholy musick, especially Don Quixote, whose emotion would not allow him to sit quiet. With regard to Sancho, all that can be said is, that he was driven by fear to his usual shelter, the side or skirts of the dutchess: for, the sound they heard was really and truly horrible and dreary. In the midst of this confusion and surprise, which took hold on all present, they saw two men enter the garden, in mourning-cloaks so large and long that they trailed upon the ground. These figures were employed in beating two large drums, which were likewise covered with black, and they were accompanied by a fifer as black and dismal as themselves, and followed by a personage of gigantic stature, rolled, rather than clothed with a cassoc of the blackest hue, furnished with a train of an unmeasurable length. Over this cassoc, his body was girded and crossed with a broad black belt, from which depended an immense scymiter, with hilt and sheath of the same sable colour. His face was covered with a black, transparent veil, through which appeared a huge and bushy beard as white as snow; and in walking he kept time to the sound of the drums, with great gravity and composure. In a word, his tallness, demeanour, his melancholy dress and his attendants, were sufficient to surprise, and did surprise, all those who beheld him, without knowing the nature of the scheme. With the said solemnity of personification he advanced in order to kneel before the duke, who, with the rest of the company, received him standing; but, his grace would by no means hear his address until he rose. The prodigious spectre complied with his desire and stood upright; then unveiling his face, and displaying the largest, whitest, thickest, and most stupendous beard that ever human eyes beheld, he fixed his eyes upon the duke, and in a grave, sonorous voice, extracted and discharged from his ample and dilated chest, pronounced, "Most high and mighty prince, I am Trifaldin of the snowy beard, squire to the countess Trifaldi, otherwise distinguished by the appellation of the afflicted duenna: from her I bring a message to your grace, requesting that your magnificence would be pleased to give her leave and opportunity to enter and declare in person, her mishap, which is the strangest and the newest, that ever the most hapless

imagination could conceive: and first of all, she wants to know if the valiant and invincible knight Don Quixote de la Mancha, now resides within your castle; for, in quest of him, she is come a foot and fasting, from the kingdom of Candaya to these your territories: a circumstance which might and ought to be deemed a miracle, or at least effected by the power of inchantment. She is now at the gate of this fortress or pleasure-house, and only waits for your permission to come in."

So saying, he hemmed, and with both hands stroaking his beard from top to bottom, waited with great composure for the duke's reply, which was this: "Worthy squire Trifaldin of the snowy beard, many days are passed since we have been apprised of the misfortune of my lady countess Trifaldi, on whom the inchanters have intailed the epithet of the afflicted duenna; well may you, stupendous squire, desire her to come in; and here is the valiant knight Don Quixote de la Mancha, from whose generous disposition she may securely promise herself all manner of aid and protection; and you may likewise give her to understand, in my name, that if my assistance be necessary, it shall not be wanting; for, I think myself obliged to grant it, as being a knight, to which title is annexed and belongs that maxim of assisting the fair sex with all our might, especially widowed, reduced, and afflicted duennas like her ladyship." Trifaldin hearing this declaration, bent his knee to the ground, and making a signal to the fifer and drummers to repeat the same notes and resume the same pace with which they entered, he retired from the garden, leaving the whole company astonished at his presence and deportment.

Then the duke turning to Don Quixote, "In a word, renowned knight," said he, "it is not in the power of all the clouds of ignorance and malice to conceal or obscure the light of valour and of virtue. This observation I make, because your excellency has been scarce six days in this castle, when the melancholy and afflicted come in quest of you from the most distant and sequestered countries, not in coaches or on dromedaries, but a foot and fasting, confident of finding in that most valiant arm, the remedy and cure of their toils and misfortunes: thanks to your illustrious exploits, which pervade and encircle the whole habitable globe." "My lord duke," replied the knight, "I wish that same pious ecclesiastic was here at present: he, who at your grace's table, the other day, expressed so much ill will and such an inveterate grudge to knights-errant, that he might see with his own eyes whether or not such knights are of any service in this world, or, at least, be fully convinced that the distressed and disconsolate, overwhelmed with extraordinary woes and enormous misfortunes, do not go for redress to the houses of learned men, to the mansions of parish priests, nor to the knight who never dreamed of going beyond the limits of his own estate; nor to the idle courtier who would rather inquire about news, that he might have the pleasure of repeating and retailing them, than endeavour to perform actions and exploits for others to perpetuate and record: the redress of grievances, the support of the necessitous, the protection of damsels, and the consolation of widows, are found in no set of people more than in knights-errant: that I am one of these, I return infinite thanks to heaven, and shall chearfully undergo whatever danger and disgrace may befall me in the course of such an honourable exercise. Let this duenna approach, and beg what boon she shall desire, I will commit her cause to the strength of my arm and the intrepid resolution of my aspiring soul."

## CHAPTER V.

# In which is continued the famous adventure of the afflicted duenna.

The duke and dutchess were exceedingly rejoiced to see Don Quixote's behaviour correspond so well with their design. Sancho interposing, "I wish," said he, "this madam duenna may not throw some stumbling-block in the way of my government; for, I have heard an apothecary of Toledo, who talked like any goldfinch, observe that nothing good could happen where duennas interfered. Lord help us! what a spite that same apothecary had to the whole tribe; from whence I conclude, that seeing duennas of all qualities and degrees whatsoever, are offensive and impertinent, what must those be who are afflicted, which they say is the case with this * Trifaldis or three-tailed countess? for, in my country, skirts and tails, and tails and skirts, are the same thing." "Hold your tongue, friend Sancho," said Don Quixote: "this lady who is come in quest of me from remote countries, cannot be one of those to whom the apothecary alluded, especially as she is a countess; and when ladies of that rank serve as duennas, it must be under queens and empresses; for, in their own houses they are honoured with the title of ladyship, and have other duennas in their service."

To this remark Donna Rodriguez, who was present, replied, "My lady dutchess has duennas in her service, who might have been countesses, had it pleased fortune; but, the law's measure is the king's pleasure:[2] and let no body speak disrespectfully of duennas, especially of those who are ancient and maidens; for, although I am not of that class, I can easily perceive and comprehend the advantage a maiden duenna has over one that is a widow: and he that undertakes to shear us, will have no easy task to perform." "And yet for all that," replied Sancho, "if my barber's word may be taken, you duennas require so much to be shorn that—You had better not stir the porridge tho' it stick to the pot." "The squires are always our enemies," answered Donna Rodriguez: "they are imps of the antichamber, who are every minute making a jest of us; and except when they are at prayers, which is not often the case, their whole time is spent in back-biting, disinterring our bones and interring our reputation. But, let me tell those moving blocks, that in spite of all they can do, we will live in the world, ay, in noble families, tho' we should die of hunger, and cloath our delicate or indelicate bodies with a black shroud, as they cover or shade a dunghill with tapestry, on a day of procession. In good faith! if I were allowed, and the time required it, I could demonstrate not only to those who are now present, but likewise to the whole world, that there is no kind of virtue which does not center in a duenna." "I believe there is reason, and a great deal of reason, in what the worthy Donna Rodriguez observes," said the dutchess; "but, she must wait for a proper opportunity to appear in behalf of herself and other duennas, and confute the ill opinion of that malicious apothecary, as well as to eradicate those sentiments from the breast of the mighty Sancho Panza." To this remark the squire replied: "Since the fumes of a

---

* *Faldas*, in Spanish, signifies skirts.[1]

governor have expelled the vapours of a squire, I value not all the duennas upon earth a fig's end."

They would have proceeded with this duennian conference, had not they heard again the sound of the fife and drums, which announced the entrance of the afflicted duenna. The dutchess asked the duke, if it would be proper to advance and receive her, as she was a countess and person of quality. "With regard to her being a countess, (said Sancho, before the duke could reply) it would be right for your graces to go and receive her; but, in respect to her being a duenna, I think you should not move a step." "Who taught thee to interfere in such matters?" said Don Quixote. "Who, signor?" replied Sancho, "I interfere, because I am qualified to interfere, as a squire who has learned all the punctilios of courtesy in the school of your worship, who is the most courteous and best bred knight that ever the province of courtesy produced; and in these matters, as I have heard your worship observe, the game is as often lost by a card too many as one too few; but, a word to the wise is sufficient." "It is even so as Sancho has remarked," said the duke, "let us first see a specimen of the countess, and from that sample consider what courtesy she deserves."

At that instant the fifer and drummers entered as before: and here the author concludes this short chapter, in order to begin another with the sequel of the same adventure, which is among the most remarkable of the whole history.

## CHAPTER VI.

## In which is recounted the misfortune of the afflicted duenna.

In the rear of those melancholy musicians, about a dozen duennas, divided into two files, began to enter the garden, clad in loose mourning-gowns, seemingly of milled stuff, with white veils of fine muslin, so long that nothing but the borders of the gowns were seen. After these came the countess Trifaldi, led by her squire Trifaldin of the snowy beard, and cloathed in a robe of the finest black serge, which, had it been napped, would have displayed grains as large as the best Martos * garavances. The tail or skirt, or whatsoever it is called, was divided into three parts, supported by three pages, who were likewise in mourning, making a remarkable mathematical figure, with the three acute angles formed by the three divisions, a circumstance from which all who saw this divided train, concluded that from hence she was called the countess Trifaldi, as if we should say the countess of three skirts; and this is what Benengeli affirms for truth, observing that her proper appellation was the countess de Wolf, because her country produced a great number of those animals, and if it had been famous for foxes, she would have been called my lady Fox; for, it is the custom in those countries, for people of fash-

---

* A kind of pea that grows at Martos, a town in the province of Andaluzia.[1]

ion to take their denomination from the thing or things with which their estates chiefly abound; but, this countess, in order to favour the fashion of her train, laid aside the name of Wolf, and assumed that of Trifaldi.

The twelve duennas and their lady advanced at a procession-pace, their faces covered with white veils, tho' not transparent like that of the squire Trifaldin; on the contrary, they were so close that nothing appeared through them. When the whole duennian squadron appeared, the duke and dutchess, Don Quixote, and all those who beheld the procession, stood up; and the twelve duennas halting, made a lane through which the afflicted lady advanced, without quitting the hand of Trifaldin, while their graces and Don Quixote went forwards about a dozen steps, to receive her: then she kneeled upon the ground, and with a voice that was coarse and rough, rather than smooth and delicate, pronounced this address: "I beg your graces will be pleased to wave all this courtesy to your humble * varlet—I mean your handmaid—Indeed, I am so overwhelmed with affliction, that I can hardly return a rational answer; for my strange and unheard-of misfortune hath hurried away my understanding, I know not whither, tho' it must be at a great distance, because the more I seek, the farther I am from finding it." "He must be deprived of it altogether, my lady countess," answered the duke, "who could not discover your worth from the appearance of your person, which, without further inquiry, is deserving of the whole cream of courtesy, and the very essence of polite ceremony."

So saying, he presented his hand, and raising her up, seated her in a chair close by the dutchess, who likewise received her with great respect. Don Quixote was silent, and Sancho ready to burst with curiosity, to see the faces of the countess Trifaldi and some of her duennas; but, he could not possibly gratify his desire until they unveiled themselves, of their own free will and motion. Every body was hushed, expecting who would put an end to the general silence, which the afflicted countess broke in these words, "Confident I am, O powerful lord, most beautiful lady, and most sagacious bystanders, that my most wretchedness will find a reception equally placid, generous and dolorous, within your valorous bosoms; for, such it is, as were enough to soften marble, melt the diamond, and mollify the steel of the most obdurate heart; but, before it appears in the parade of your hearing, not to say your ears, I would I were certified, whether or not the perfectionatissimo knight Don Quixote de la Manchissima, and his squirissimo Panza, are in this groupe, circle or assembly." Before any other person could reply, "Panza," cried Sancho, "is here, and likewise Don Quixotissimo; and therefore most dolorous duennissima, you may say what you think properissimo; for, we are all ready and promptissimos to be your servantissimos." Then Don Quixote, rising and addressing himself to the afflicted duenna, "If your misfortunes, distressed lady," said he, "can derive any remedy or redress, from the valour or strength of any knight-errant, here are mine, which, tho' feeble and defective, shall be wholly exerted in your behalf. I am Don Quixote de la Mancha, whose office it is to assist the necessitous of all degrees, and, this

---

* This blunder is much more natural in the Spanish, *Criado* for *Criada;* but, as in the English language, the gender is not distinguished by the termination, I have been obliged to substitute the words *varlet* and *handmaid*. Varlets were the servants of yeomen, tho' formerly squires were known by that appellation.[2]

being the case, as it really is, you have no occasion, madam, to bespeak benevolence, and seek after preambles; but, only to rehearse your misfortunes plainly and without circumlocution, and they shall be heard by those who, tho' perhaps unable to redress, will at least condole them."

The afflicted duenna hearing this declaration, attempted to throw herself at the feet of Don Quixote, nay even executed the attempt, and struggling to embrace them exclaimed, "O invincible knight! I prostrate myself before these feet and legs, which are the bases and supporters of knight-errantry: suffer me to kiss these feet on whose footsteps the cure of my misfortune solely depends. O valiant errant! whose real exploits outstrip and obscure the fabulous feats of all the Amadises, Belianises and Esplandians——"

Then turning from the knight, and seizing Sancho by the hand, "And O!" said she, "thou loyalest squire that ever served knight-errant, in the past or present age, whose virtue exceeds in length the beard of this my domestic Trifaldin, well mayest thou boast that, in attending the great Don Quixote, thou dost attend in epitome the whole tribe of knights that ever handled arms on this terrestrial ball. I conjure thee, by thy own most faithful benevolence, to be my intercessor with thy master, that he may instantly favour me, the most humble and unfortunate countess that ever was born."

To this address Sancho replied, "Whether my virtue, my lady, be as long and broad as your squire's beard, is of very little signification; so that my soul be bearded and whiskered when it leaves this life, which is the main point, I care little or nothing for beards here below. But, without all this coaxing and begging, and I will desire my master, who, I believe, has a respect for me, especially now that I am become necessary in a certain affair, to favour and assist your ladyship to the utmost of his power: your ladyship may therefore unpack and recount your griefs, that all of us may understand the nature of your misfortune."

The duke and dutchess were ready to burst with laughing at this dialogue; for, they knew the drift of the adventure, and were extremely well pleased with the acuteness and dissimulation of the countess Trifaldi, who seating herself again, began her story in these words:

"Of the famous kingdom of Candaya, situated between the great Trapobana and the South Sea, two leagues beyond Cape Comorin, Donna Maguncia was queen, as widow of king Archipiela her lord and husband, in which marriage they begat and procreated the infanta Antonomasia, heiress of the crown, which said infanta Antonomasia was bred and brought up under my care and instruction; for, I was her mother's most ancient and principal duenna. And it came to pass, in process of time, that the young Antonomasia attained the age of fourteen, with such perfection of beauty as nature could not exceed. Nay, we may even say that discretion itself was but a girl, compared to her who was equally discreet and beautiful, and surely she was the most beautiful creature upon earth, and is so still, if the invidious fates and hard-hearted sisters have not cut short the yarn of her life; but, surely they have not, for, heaven would not permit such mischief to be done on earth, as to tear the green cluster from the most beautiful vine that ever soil produced. Of this beauty, which my coarse tongue can never extol, an infinite number of noblemen, natives as well as strangers, became enamoured. Among these, a private

knight belonging to the court had the presumption to raise his thoughts to the heaven of such perfection, confiding in his youth, his gallantry, his various talents and accomplishments, and the facility and felicity of his wit; for, I must tell your graces, if you are not offended at the subject, that he touched the guitarre so nicely as to make it speak; besides, he was a poet, a great dancer, and could make birdcages so curiously, that he might have earned his bread by that employment, had he been reduced to want. Such a number of natural gifts and qualifications was enough to overthrow a mountain, much more a delicate young maiden; but, all his gaiety and gallantry, his gifts and graces, would have availed little or nothing against the fortress of my charge, if the treacherous ruffian had not practised means to reduce me first. The base robber, and lewd vagabond, began by cultivating my good-will, and corrupting my taste, that, like a disloyal governor, I might deliver up the keys of the fort which I guarded. In a word, he flattered my understanding, and obtained my consent, by presenting me with some jewels and trinkets; but, what chiefly contributed to lay me on my back, were some couplets which I heard him sing one night, while I stood at a rail that looked into an alley where he was, and which, to the best of my remembrance, were to this effect.

> A thousand shafts from my sweet foe,
> Are launched unerring to my heart,
> Yet must I not reveal the smart;
> And silence aggravates my woe!

"I thought the turn of the rhime was as smooth as pearls, and his voice as sweet as sugar-candy; and, since that time, seeing the mischief that hath befallen me, thro' these and other such verses, I have often thought, that wise and well regulated commonwealths ought to expel the poets, according to the advice of Plato; at least your lascivious writers who compose couplets, not like those of the marquis of Mantua, that entertain and draw tears from women and children; but, your pointed conceits, which like agreeable thorns, prick as it were, the very soul, and wound like lightning, leaving the garment whole and untouched. Another time, he sung the following stanza:

> Come, gentle death, so soft and sly,
> That thy approach I may not see;
> Lest I rejoice to such degree,
> That I shall not have pow'r to die.

And other tags and couplets of the same kidney, which when written, confound, and when chanted, inchant; for, when they condescend to compose a sort of verse in fashion at that time in Candaya, called roundelays, they produce a kind of palpitation in the soul, a titillation of good humour, an agitation in the nerves, and finally, a tremulous motion, like that of quicksilver, in all the senses. Therefore, I repeat it to this honourable company, that such dangerous rhymers ought to be banished to the isle of Lizzards: yet, they are not so much to blame, as the simple wretches who applaud, and the boobies who believe them. If I had adhered to the duty of a good duenna, I should not have been moved by his serenading concerts, nor believed the truth of these expressions: 'In death I live; in frost I burn; in fire I shiver; in despair I hope; tho' I depart I still re-

main"; and other impossibilities of the same strain, with which their works abound. When they promise the phoenix of Arabia, the crown of Ariadne, the locks of Apollo, the pearls of the South Sea, the gold of Tyber, and the balsams of Pancaya, they give the greatest latitude to their pens; for, it costs them but a small matter to promise what they have neither inclination nor ability to perform. But, woe is me! ah, wretched creature! whither am I straying? what madness or despair thus hurries and prompts me to re-hearse the faults of other people? me who have so much to say of my own infirmities. Woe is me again, unhappy woman! Not by his verses, but my own simplicity, was I van-quished: It was not his music that softened me; but, my own levity, inadvertency and ig-norance, opened the way, and cleared the path, for the passage of Don Clavijo, which is the name of the said knight: and therefore, I being the go-between, he was once, and often admitted into the chamber of the (by me, and not by him) misled Antonomasia, under the title of her lawful spouse; for, sinner as I am, without being her husband, he should not have come near enough to touch the sole of her slipper. No, no, marriage must go before in every business of that kind, where I am concerned: the only misfor-tune in this affair, was the inequality between Clavijo, who was but a private knight, and the infanta Antonomasia, who, as I have already said, was heiress of the kingdom. For some time, the plot was covered and concealed in the sagacity of my circumspection, until I perceived a small protuberance daily increasing in the belly of my Antonomasia, whose fears obliged us to lay our three heads together; and the result of our consulta-tion was, that before the misfortune should come to light, Clavijo should demand Antonomasia in marriage, before the vicar-general, by virtue of a contract signed by the infanta, which was indited by my ingenuity, in such strength of terms as Samson him-self could not break. The scheme was accordingly executed; the vicar perused the con-tract, and confessed the princess, who owned the whole affair, and was committed to the care of a very honourable alguazil[3] of the court."

Here Sancho interposing, "So then," said he, "there are alguazils of the court, poets and roundelays in Candaya, as well as in Spain? I swear, I think the world is every where the same! but, I beg your ladyship, madam Trifaldi, would dispatch; for, it grows late, and I die with impatience to know the end of this long-winded story." "I will comply with your request," answered the countess.

## CHAPTER VII.

In which the lady Trifaldi proceeds with her memorable
and stupendous story.

Every word that Sancho uttered gave as much pleasure to the dutchess as pain to Don Quixote, who having imposed silence on the squire, the afflicted duenna thus pro-ceeded: "At length, after innumerable questions and replies, as the infanta continued

still in her story without variation, the vicar pronounced sentence in favour of Don Clavijo, whom he declared her lawful husband; a circumstance that so deeply affected queen Maguncia, mother to the infanta Antonomasia, that we buried her in three days." "Not before she was dead, I hope," said Sancho. "No certainly," replied Trifaldin; "for, in Candaya, people do not bury the living, but the dead." "And yet, signor squire," said Sancho, "we have seen a person in a swoon buried for dead: and, in my opinion, queen Maguncia ought to have swooned rather than died; for, while there is life there is hope; and, the infanta's slip was not so great as to oblige her to take on so much. Had the young lady buckled with her own page, or any other servant of the family, as I have heard many others have done, the mischief would not have been easily repaired; but, to marry such a genteel, accomplished knight as the countess hath described;—verily, verily, although it was indiscreet, the indiscretion was not so great as people may imagine: for, according to the maxims of my master who is here present, and will not suffer me to tell a lie, as learned men are created bishops, so may knights, especially knights-errant, be created kings and emperors." "Thou art in the right, Sancho," said Don Quixote; "for, a knight-errant with two fingers-breadth of good fortune, is the very next in promotion to the greatest lord in the universe: but, pray, afflicted lady, proceed; for, I guess the bitter part of this hitherto agreeable story is still to come." "How! the bitter part to come?" replied the countess: "ay, and so bitter, that in comparison with it, gall and wormwood are sweet and savoury."

"Well then, the queen being really dead, and not in a swoon, was buried; but, scarce was she covered with the mould, and scarce had we pronounced the long and last farewel, when, 'Quis talia fando, temperet a lachrymis?'[1] all of a sudden, above the tomb, appeared upon a wooden-horse the giant Malambruno, Maguncia's first cousin, who, exclusive of his cruel disposition, was an inchanter, and by his diabolical art, in order to revenge his relation's death, and chastise the presumption of Don Clavijo, together with the folly of Antonomasia, fixed them both inchanted on Maguncia's tomb, after having converted her into a monkey of brass, and him into a frightful crocodile of some unknown substance: between them is a plate of metal, displaying an inscription in the Syrian language, which being translated into the Candayan, and afterwards into the Castilian tongue, contains this sentence: 'These two presumptuous lovers will not recover their pristine form until the valorous Manchegan shall engage with me in single combat: for his stupendous valour alone, the fates have reserved this unseen adventure.' This metamorphosis being affected, he unsheathed a vast unmeasurable scymitar, and twisting his left hand in my hair, threatened to slit my windpipe and slice off my head. I was confounded, my voice stuck in my throat, and I remained in an agony of fear: nevertheless, I made one effort, and in a faultering accent and plaintive tone, uttered such a pathetic remonstrance as induced him to suspend the execution of his rigorous revenge. In fine, he ordered all the duennas of the palace (there they are) to be brought into his presence, when, after having exaggerated our fault, reviled the disposition of duennas, their wicked schemes and contrivances, and accused them all of the crime of which I alone was guilty, he said he would not punish us with instant death, but with a more tedious penalty, by which we should suffer a civil and continued death. He had no sooner done speaking, than that very moment and instant, we all felt the pores of our

faces open, and the whole surface tingle as if pricked with the points of needles: then clapping our hands to the part, every one found her visage in the condition which you shall now behold."

So saying, the afflicted duenna and her companions, lifting up their veils, disclosed so many faces overgrown with huge beards, red, black, white and party-coloured; at sight of which, the duke and dutchess were amazed, Don Quixote and Sancho confounded, and all present overwhelmed with astonishment: as for the countess, she pursued her story in these words:

"In this manner were we punished by the felonious and ill-designing Malambruno, who covered the smoothness and delicacy of our faces with the roughness of these bristles; and would to heaven he had rather struck off our heads with his unmeasurable scymitar, than obscured the light of our countenances with this frightful bush: for, if this honourable company will but consider, and in speaking what I am now going to say, I wish I could turn my eyes into fountains; but, the consideration of our misfortune, and the oceans they have already rained, have drained them as dry as beards of corn; and therefore, I must speak without tears. I say then, whither can a duenna go with a beard upon her chin? What father or mother will condole her disgrace? or, who will give her the least assistance? for if, when her face is smoothed and martyred by a thousand cosmetic slops and washes, she can scarce find one who will favour her with affection; what must she do when her face becomes a perfect coppice of brushwood? O ye wretched duennas! my companions dear! in an unlucky minute did we see the light, and in an hapless hour were we engendred by our fathers!"

So saying, she pretended to faint away.

CHAPTER VIII.

Of circumstances appertaining and relating to this adventure
and memorable story.

Verily, and in good truth! all those who take pleasure in reading such histories, ought to manifest their gratitude to its first author Cid Hamet, for his curiosity in recounting the most trivial incident, without neglecting to bring to light the least circumstance, how minute soever it may be. He describes the thought, discloses the fancy, answers the silent, explains doubts, discusses arguments; and finally displays the very atoms of the most curious disposition. O celebrated author! O happy Don Quixote! O renowned Dulcinea! O facetious Sancho Panza! may you flourish conjunctly and severally to the end of time, for the entertainment and pastime of mankind in general!

The history relates, that Sancho seeing the Afflicted faint away, "Now, by the faith of man!" cried he, "and by the pedigree of all the Panzas my forefathers! never did I hear or see, nor did my master recount, or indeed conceive such an adventure as this. A le-

gion of devils confound thee for a giant and inchanter, accursed Malambruno! could'st thou find no other method to punish these sinners, but by clapping beards to them? Would not it have been better, at least it would have been more for their advantage, to cut off half of their noses, even tho' they should snuffle in their speech, than to encumber them with beards? I'd lay a wager too, they have not wherewithal to pay a barber." "What you say, is very true," replied one of the dozen: "we have not wherewithal to be trimmed; and therefore some of us, by way of oeconomy, make use of sticking plaister, which being applied to our faces and plucked off with a jerk, leave us as sleek and smooth as the bottom of a marble mortar: for, although there are women in Candaya who go from house to house, taking off the hair,[1] arching the eyebrows, and composing slipslops for the uses of the fair-sex, we who belonged to her ladyship would never admit them into the family, because, for the most part, they are persons who having ceased to be principals, exercise the occupation of procuress;[2] and therefore, if we are not redressed by signor Don Quixote, we must e'en carry our beards to the grave." "If I do not redress your whiskers," cried the knight, "I will leave mine among the Moors."

Here the countess Trifaldi recovering, "Valiant knight," said she, "the tingling of that promise reached mine ears while I lay in a swoon, and hath been the cause of my recovering and retrieving the use of all my senses: therefore, renowned errant and invincible knight, I again intreat you, to put your gracious promise in execution." "In me there shall be no delay," replied Don Quixote: "consider then, my lady, and tell me what I am to do: my mind is perfectly disposed for your service." "The case is this, then," answered the afflicted duenna, "from hence to the kingdom of Candaya, if you go by land, you must travel five thousand leagues, it may be one or two more or less; but, if you go through the air in a right line, you measure no more than three thousand two hundred and twenty seven. You must likewise know, Malambruno told me, that whenever fortune should furnish me with our deliverer, he would send him a steed that should be much better, and less vitious, than any of your return post-horses, as being the very individual wooden-horse upon which the valiant Peter carried off the fair Magalona: he is governed by a peg in his forehead that serves instead of a bridle, and he flies so swiftly through the air, that one would think he was transported by all the devils in hell. This steed, according to ancient tradition, was contrived by the sage Merlin, and he lent him to his friend Peter, who by means of such conveyance, performed incredible journeys, and stole, as I have observed, the fair Magalona who sat behind him, and was transported through the air, to the astonishment of all those who gaped after her from the earth. Yet he would lend him to none but his particular favourites, or such as would pay him a handsome price; and, we do not know, that he was ever mounted, from the days of the great Peter to the present time. Malambruno, by dint of art, has got and keeps him in his possession, making use of him in his journeys, which he performs in an instant, from one part of the world to another; now here, to-morrow in France, and next day in Peru: and, there is one great advantage in this horse; he neither eats nor sleeps, nor costs any thing in shoeing, and ambles through the air without wings, in such a manner, that his rider may hold a cup full of water in his hand, without spilling a single drop, his motion is so smooth and easy: for which reason, the fair Magalona delighted much in taking the air upon his back."

"As for his going smooth and easy," said Sancho, "there is my Dapple, whom (tho' he does not go through the air, but along the ground) I will match against all the amblers that ever the earth produced." All the company laughed at this observation, and the afflicted duenna proceeded: "Now, this horse, if Malambruno is actually disposed to put an end to our misfortune, will be here in less than half an hour after it is dark: for, he told me, the signal by which I should be certain of having found the knight I was in quest of, would be his sending the horse thither with all convenient dispatch." "And, pray," said Sancho, "how many persons will this horse carry?" "Two," replied the Afflicted; "one upon the saddle, and the other on the crupper, and these are commonly the knight and his squire, when there is no damsel to be stolen." "I should be glad to know, afflicted madam," resumed the squire, "what is the name of that same horse?" "His name," answered the Afflicted, "is not like that of Bellerophon's horse, which was called Pegasus, not does it resemble that which distinguished the steed of Alexander the great, Bucephalus; nor that of Orlando Furioso, whose appellation was Brilladoro; nor Bayarte,[3] which belonged to Reynaldo de Montalvan; nor Frontino, that appertained to Rugero; nor Bootes nor Peritoa, the horses of the sun; nor is he called Orelia, like that steed upon which the unfortunate Rodrigo last king of the Goths, engaged in that battle where he lost his crown and life." "I will lay a wager," cried Sancho, "that as he is not distinguished by any of those famous names of horses so well known, so neither have they given him the name of my master's horse Rozinante; a name which, in propriety, exceeds all those that have been named." "Very true," replied the bearded countess: "nevertheless, it fits him very well; for, he is called * Clavileno Aligero, an appellation that suits him exactly with his wooden substance, the peg in his forehead, and the swiftness with which he travels; so that for his name, he may be brought in competition, even with the famous Rozinante." "The name pleases me well enough," said Sancho; "but, what sort of bridle or halter must be used in managing him?" "I have already told you," answered Trifaldi, "that by turning the peg, the knight who rides, can make him travel just as he pleases, either mounting through the air, or else sweeping, and as it were brushing the surface of the earth; or, lastly, sailing through the middle region, which is the course to be sought after and pursued, in all well concerted enterprizes."

"I should be glad to see this same beast," replied the squire; "but, to think that I will mount him, either in the saddle or on the crupper, is all the same thing as to look for pears upon an elm. A fine joke, i'faith! I can scarce keep the back of my own Dapple, tho' sitting upon a pannel as soft as sattin, and they would now have me get upon a crupper of board without either pillow or cushion. By the lord! I have no intention to bruise myself, in order to take off the beard of any person whatsoever: let every beard be shaved according to the owner's fancy; for my own part, I have no notion of accompanying my master in such a long and tedious journey: for, surely I have no concern in the shaving of beards, whatever I may have in the disinchantment of Dulcinea." "Indeed, you have, my friend," answered Trifaldi, "ay, and so much, that without your presence I believe we shall do no good." "In the king's name!" cried Sancho, "what have squires to do with the adventures of their masters? What! are they to run away with all the reputation, and we

* Or in English, *Wooden Peg the winged*.[4]

to undergo all the trouble? Body o'me! would your historians but mention, that such a knight atchieved such and such an adventure, with the assistance of his squire what-d'ye-callum, without whom he could not possibly have finished the exploit; but, they drily relate, as how Don Paralipomenon of the three stars, finished the adventure of the six goblins, without even naming the squire who was present all the time, no more than if there was not such a person in the world: I therefore say again to this honourable company, that my master may go by himself, and good luck attend him; but, for my own part, I will stay where I am, and keep my lady dutchess company: and peradventure, at his return, he may find my lady Dulcinea's business well forwarded; for, I intend, at my idle and leisure hours, to whip myself to such a tune, that not a single hair shall stand before me."

"But, for all that," said the dutchess, "honest Sancho, you must attend him, should there be occasion; for, you will be sollicited by the righteous; and surely it would be a great pity, that the faces of these gentlewomen should continue overshadowed with hair, merely from your needless apprehension." "I say again, in the king's name!" cried Sancho, "if this charity should be of any benefit to release maidens, or parish-children, a man might venture to undergo some trouble; but, to take such pains in order to rid duennas of their beards! a plague upon the whole generation! I had rather see them all bearded from the highest to the lowest, tag, rag, and bobtail." "Friend Sancho," said the dutchess, "you are on bad terms with duennas, and very much infected with the opinion of that apothecary of Toledo; but, in good sooth, you are very much in the wrong: there are duennas in my house, who might serve as patterns of virtue; and here stands Donna Rodriguez, who would not suffer me to say otherwise." "Your excellency may say what you please," answered Rodriguez; "but, God knows the truth of all things, and good or bad, bearded or smooth, we duennas were born of our mothers, as well as other women; since, therefore, God sent us into the world, he knows for what, and in his mercy do I put my trust, and not in the beard of any person whatsoever——"

"'Tis very well, signora Rodriguez, madam Trifaldi, and you ladies of her company," said Don Quixote; "heaven, I hope, will look upon your misfortunes with propitious eyes, and Sancho will chearfully obey my orders: let Clavileno come, so as that I may once see myself engaged with Malambruno, and confident I am, that no rasor can shave your ladyships with more facility than my sword should find in shaving the giant's head from his shoulders: for, tho' God permits the wicked to prosper, it is but for a time." The afflicted duenna hearing this declaration, exclaimed, "Now may all the stars of the celestial regions shed their benign influence upon your worship, most valiant knight, infusing courage into your soul, and crowning your atchievements with prosperity, that you may be the shield and support of this our slighted and depressed duennian order, abominated by apothecaries, grumbled at by squires, and jeered by pages! now, ill betide the wretch who, in the flower of her youth, would not rather take the veil than become a duenna. Unfortunate duennas that we are! for, tho' we may be descended in a direct male line from Hector of Troy, our ladies will not fail to throw Thou in our teeth, even if they thought they should be crowned for it. O thou giant Malambruno, who, tho' an inchanter, art always punctual in thy promises, send hither the peerless Clavi-

leno, that our disaster may be done away; for, if our beards continue until the dogdays begin, woe be unto us!"

Trifaldi pronounced these words in such a pathetic strain, as brought tears from the eyes of all the bystanders, and even filled Sancho's to the brim; so that he resolved in his heart, to accompany his master to the utmost limits of the earth, provided his attendance should be necessary towards shearing the wool of those venerable countenances.

## CHAPTER IX.

## Of Clavileno's arrival, and the conclusion of this protracted adventure.

Mean while, night came on, and along with it the time fixed for the arrival of the famous steed Clavileno, whose delay began already to afflict Don Quixote; for, he looked upon the detention of the horse, as a sign that he himself was not the knight for whom the adventure was reserved, or that Malambruno was afraid to engage with him in single combat. But, lo, all of a sudden, four savages, clad in green ivy, entered the garden, bearing on their backs a great wooden horse, which being placed on the ground, one of the number pronounced, "Let him who has courage, mount this machine." "For my own part," said Sancho, "I do not mount; for, neither have I courage, nor am I a knight." But, the savage proceeded, saying, "Let the squire, if he has one, occupy the crupper; and, he may confide in the valiant Malambruno; for, except the sword of that giant, no other steel or malice shall offend him; and, the knight has no more to do, but to turn this peg upon his neck, and he will carry them through the air to the place where Malambruno waits for their arrival: but, lest the heighth and sublimity of the road should turn their heads, their eyes must be covered until such time as the horse shall neigh; for, that will be the signal of their having performed the journey." This intimation being given, they left the horse, and retired to the place from whence they came, with great solemnity.

The afflicted duenna no sooner beheld the steed, than addressing herself to Don Quixote, with tears in her eyes, "Valiant knight," said she, "Malambruno's promise is made good: here stands the horse, our beards are still growing, and each of us, nay every hair upon our chins, supplicate thee to shave and shear them, since there is nothing else required but to mount with thy squire, and happily begin your journey." "That will I do, my lady countess Trifaldi," replied Don Quixote, "with good will, and hearty inclination; nor will I delay the expedition, by spending time in furnishing myself with a cushion, or even in putting on my spurs, so impatient I am to see your ladyship and those duennas quite smooth and shaven." "That will not I do," cried Sancho, "neither with hearty nor heartless inclination, nor in any manner of way; and if the shaving cannot be

performed without my mounting upon the crupper, my master must look for another squire to attend him, and these ladies must find another method for smoothing their faces; for, I am no wizzard, to take delight in flying through the air: and pray, what would my islanders say, should they know that their governor was riding upon the wind? moreover, it being three thousand and so many more leagues from hence to Candaya, should the horse be tired, or the giant out of humour, we may spend half a dozen years in returning; and by that time, the devil an island or islander in the whole world will know my face. It is a common saying, that Delay breeds danger; and, When the heifer you receive, have a halter in your sleeve. The beards of these ladies must therefore excuse me: I know St. Peter is well at Rome; my meaning is, I find myself very well in this mansion, where I am treated with such respect, and from the master of which I expect so great a favour as that of being made a governor." To this remonstrance the duke replied, "Friend Sancho, the island I have promised is neither floating nor fugitive, but its roots are so deeply fixed in the bowels of the earth, that three good pulls will not remove or tear it away; and, as you are sensible, I know there is no kind of office of any importance that is not obtained by some sort of bribe, more or less, the present I expect for the government is, that you will attend your master Don Quixote, in crowning and accomplishing this memorable adventure; and, whether you return upon Clavileno with that dispatch which his speed seems to promise; or, by the cruelty of adverse fortune, you come back in the habit of a pilgrim, begging on foot, from house to house, and from one inn to another, you shall nevertheless, at your return find your island where you left it, and your islanders actuated by the same desire of receiving you as their governor, which they have always indulged: and, as for my inclination it can never change; for, to entertain the least doubt of my sincerity, signor Sancho, would be a notorious injury to the attachment I feel for your service." "Enough, my lord," cried Sancho: "I am a poor squire, and cannot bear such a load of courtesy: let my master mount, and my eyes be covered; recommend me to God; and, let me know whether, while we travel through those altitudes, I may call upon the name of the lord, or implore the protection of his angels." To this interrogation the countess replied, "You may recommend yourself to God, or to whom you will; for, Malambruno, tho' an inchanter, is nevertheless a christian, and performs his inchantments with great sagacity and caution, nor does he intermeddle in any person's affairs." "Well then," cried Sancho, "God, and the most holy trinity of Gaeta, be my guide and protection!" "Since the memorable adventure of the fulling-mills," said Don Quixote, "I have never seen Sancho so infected with fear, as upon this occasion; and, if I were as much addicted to superstition as some people are, his pusilanimity would produce some compunction in my soul: but, come hither, Sancho; for, with the permission of that noble pair, I would speak two words with you in private."

Then taking his squire aside into a tuft of trees, and grasping both his hands, "You see, brother Sancho," said he, "the long journey that awaits us; and God knows when we shall return, and what leisure or convenience our business may allow; I therefore beg thou wilt now retire to thy apartment, on pretence of fetching some necessaries for the road, and, in the twinkling of a straw, inflict upon thyself some five hundred of those three thousand three hundred lashes for which thou art engaged, and they shall stand

good in the account; for, when a thing is once begun, it is almost as good as half finished." "Before God!" cried Sancho, "your worship must be out of your senses; this is just as they say. You see me in a hurry, and ask me to marry. Now, when I am going to ride upon a wooden crupper, would your worship have me afflict my posteriors? Verily, verily, your worship was never more out of the way: at present, let us proceed and shave those duennas, and at our return, I promise to your worship on the faith of my character, to quit my score with such dispatch that your worship shall be satisfied; and I'll say no more." "Well then," answered the knight, "I will console myself, honest Sancho, with that promise, which I really believe thou wilt perform; for, surely, tho' thy head be but green, thy heart is true blue." "Green," said Sancho; "my head is not green, but black; but, even tho' it were pyebald, I would perform my promise."

After this short dialogue they returned, in order to take horse; then, the knight addressing himself to the squire, "Sancho," said he, "suffer yourself to be hoodwinked, and get up: he who sends for us from such distant regions, can have no intention to deceive us, because he could reap no glory from having deceived those who depended on his sincerity; and, although the event may turn out contrary to my expectation, the glory of having undertaken such an exploit no malice whatsoever can impair." "Come then, signor," cried the squire, "for, the beards and tears of those ladies are so imprinted in my heart, that I shall not swallow a mouthful to do me good, until I see them restored to their original smoothness. Get up, signor, and hoodwink yourself first; for, if the crupper is to be my seat, it is plain that you must mount first into the saddle." "You are in the right," replied Don Quixote; who, pulling an handkerchief from his pocket, desired the afflicted duenna to fasten it round his eyes, which, however, were no sooner covered than he took off the bandage, saying, "If I remember aright, I have read in Virgil, of the Trojan Palladium, a wooden horse offered to the goddess Pallas, the bowels of which horse were filled with armed men, who afterwards occasioned the total destruction of Troy; and, therefore, it will not be amiss, first of all, to examine the belly of Clavileno." "There is no occasion," said the afflicted duenna; "for, I am certain that Malambruno has neither treachery nor malice in his heart: your worship, signor Don Quixote, may therefore mount, without the least apprehension, and if any mischief befall you, lay it at my door." The knight reflecting that any hesitation about his personal safety would be a disparagement to his valour, mounted Clavileno without further altercation, and tried the peg, which turned with ease; and, his legs hanging down at full length, for want of stirrups he looked like a figure in some Roman triumph, painted or wrought in Flemish tapestry.

Then Sancho, very slowly, and much against his will, crept up behind, and seating himself as well as he could upon the crupper, found it so hard and uneasy, that he begged the duke would order him to be accommodated with some cushion or pillow, tho' it should be taken from my lady dutchess's sopha, or some page's bed; for, the crupper of that horse seemed to be made of marble rather than of wood.

Here Trifaldi interposing, assured him that Clavileno would bear no kind of furniture or ornament; but, said he might sit sideways like a woman, in which attitude he would not be so sensible of the hardness. Sancho took her advice, and saying Adieu, allowed his eyes to be covered; but, afterwards pulling up the bandage, and looking rue-

fully at all the people in the garden, he with tears in his eyes, besought them to assist him in that extremity with a brace of paternosters, and as many ave marias, as God should provide somebody to do as much for them in like time of need.

Don Quixote hearing this apostrophe, "How now, miscreant!" said he, "are you brought to the gallows, or in the last agonies of death, that you make use of such intreaties? Dispirited and cowardly creature! art not thou seated in the very same place which was occupied by the fair Magalona, and from which she descended, not to her grave, but, to the crown of France, if history speaks truth? And I, who sit by thy side, surely may vie with valiant Peter, who pressed the self same back now pressed by me. Shroud, shroud thine eyes, thou animal without a soul, and let not those symptoms of fear escape thy lips, at least in my presence." "Hoodwink me then," answered Sancho, "and since I must neither recommend myself, nor be recommended, to the protection of God, what wonder is it, if I am afraid we shall meet with some legion of devils who will treat us according to the * Peralvillo law?"

Their eyes being covered, and Don Quixote perceiving he was fixed in his seat, turned the peg; and, scarce had his finger touched this rudder, when the whole bevy of duennas, and all that were present, raised their voices, crying, "Heaven be thy guide, valorous knight! God be thy protection, intrepid squire! Now, now, you rise and cut the liquid sky more swiftly than an arrow! now, you begin to astonish and confound all those who gaze upon you from this earthly spot! Hold fast, valiant Sancho, for, we see thee totter; beware of falling: to fall from such an height would be more fatal than the fall of that aspiring youth whose ambition prompted him to drive the chariot of the sun his father."

Sancho hearing this exclamation, crept closer to his master, and hugging him fast in his arms, "Signor," said he, "how can we be so high as those people say we are, seeing we can hear them speak as well as if we were within a few yards of them?" "You must not mind that circumstance," answered the knight; "for, these incidents and flights being altogether out of the ordinary course of things, you may hear and see what you please, at the distance of a thousand leagues: but, do not squeeze me so hard, lest I tumble from my seat. I really cannot imagine what it is that disturbs and affrights thee; for, I swear, in all the days of my life, I never bestrid a horse of a more easy pace: indeed, he goes so smoothly that I can hardly feel him move. Dispel thy fear, my friend; for, truly the business goes on swimmingly, and we sail right afore the wind." "You are certainly in the right," answered Sancho; "for, on this side, there blows as fresh a gale as if I was fanned with a thousand pair of bellows——"

Nor was he much mistaken in his conjecture; for, the wind that blew was actually produced by one of those machines: so well had the adventure been contrived by the duke and dutchess, and their steward, that nought was wanting to render it complete. Then

---

* Equivalent to Abington law; in consequence of which, a criminal is first executed and then tried. *Peralvillo* is a village near Ciudad Real, in Castile, where the officers of the holy brotherhood execute robbers taken in *flagrante*, who require no trial. Hence the phrase *la justicia de Peralvillo, que aborcado el hombre, le haze la Pesquisa.* Peralvillo law, which begins the process after the man is hanged.[1]

the knight feeling the same breeze, "Without doubt," said he, "we must be arrived at the second region of the air, in which hail and snow are produced: meteors, thunder and lightning are ingendered in the third region: if we continue to mount at this rate, we shall in a very little time reach the region of fire; and I know not how to manage this peg, so as to put a stop to our rising, and prevent our being scorched to a cinder."

In the midst of this conversation their faces were warmed with some tow that was kindled for the purpose, at the end of a long pole, and Sancho feeling the heat, "Let me perish!" cried he, "if we are not now come to that same habitation of fire; for, a great part of my beard is already singed; and, I am resolved to uncover my eyes, that I may see whereabouts we are." "By no means," answered the knight: "remember the true story of the licentiate Toralva, who, being mounted on a cane, was conveyed thro' the air, with his eyes shut, by the devils: in twelve hours he arrived at Rome, and alighted on the tower of Nona, which is in one of the streets of that city, whence he beheld the whole tumult, assault, and death, of the constable of Bourbon; and, before morning he had returned to Madrid, where he gave an account of that transaction. He likewise affirmed, that while he travelled through the air, the devil bad him open his eyes, and he saw himself so near the body of the moon, that he could have touched it with his hand; but, he durst not look towards the earth, lest his head should have turned giddy. Let us not, therefore, uncover our eyes, Sancho; he in whose charge we are will give a good account of us; and perhaps, we are now at the very point of our elevation, from whence we shall come souse upon the kingdom of Candaya, as a saker or jerfaulcon darts down upon an heron with a force proportioned to his rise: and, although it seems to us no more than half an hour since we set out from the garden, you may depend upon it we have travelled an immense way." "As to that matter I am quite ignorant," said Sancho: "this only I know, that if madam Magallanes or Magalona took pleasure in sitting upon this crupper, her flesh must not have been very tender."

All this dialogue of the two heroes was overheard by the duke and dutchess, and the rest of the company in the garden, to whom it afforded extraordinary entertainment: at length, desirous of finishing this strange and well concerted adventure, they set fire to Clavileno's tail with some lighted flax: his belly being filled with squibs and crackers, he instantly blew up with a dreadful explosion, and Don Quixote, with his squire, came to the ground more than half singed. By this time the whole bearded squadron, with my lady Trifaldi, had vanished from the garden, and all the rest of the company were stretched upon the ground as in a trance. Don Quixote and Sancho getting on their feet, in a very indifferent condition, and looking all round, were astonished to find themselves in the same garden from which they took their flight, and to see such a number of people extended along the grass: but their admiration was still more increased, when at one corner of the garden they beheld a huge lance fixed in the ground, and tied to this lance, by two cords of green silk, a smooth, white skin of parchment, on which was the following inscription in large golden letters.

"The renowned knight Don Quixote de la Mancha, has finished and atchieved the adventure of the countess Trifaldi, alias the afflicted duenna, and her companions, solely by his having undertaken the enterprize.

"Malambruno is wholly satisfied and appeased; the chins of the duennas are smooth and clean; their majesties Don Clavijo and Antonomasia are restored to their original form; and when the squirely flagellation shall be accomplished, the white dove will be delivered from the pestilential talons of her persecutors, and find herself within the arms of her beloved turtle; for, such is the decree of the sage Merlin, the prince and prototype of all inchanters."

Don Quixote having read this scroll, at once comprehended the meaning, which related to the disinchantment of Dulcinea, and returning a thousand thanks to heaven for his success in having finished such a mighty exploit with so little danger, and reduced to their pristine form the faces of those venerable duennas who had disappeared, he went towards the place where the duke and dutchess still lay intranced, and pulling his grace by the arm, "Courage! courage, my noble lord," said he; "all is over now; the adventure is finished, without damage to the barrier, as will plainly appear by the inscription of yonder scroll."

The duke seemed to recover gradually, like one waking from a profound sleep; his example was followed by the dutchess, and all the rest who lay along the garden; and they exhibited such marks of fear and astonishment, that even almost to themselves, That seemed to have happened in earnest which they had so well acted in jest. The duke having read the inscription with his eyes half shut, ran with open arms to embrace Don Quixote, calling him the most worthy knight that any age had ever produced: while Sancho went looking about for the afflicted matron, to see if her beard was quite gone, and whether her face, without hair, was as beautiful as her gallant deportment seemed to promise. But he was told, that as Clavileno descended in a flame from the sky, the whole squadron of duennas, with Trifaldi at their head, had vanished, and their faces smack smooth as if they had been clean shaven.

Then the dutchess asking, how it had fared with Sancho in his long journey; the squire replied, "As for me, my lady, I perceived, as my master told me, that we flew through the region of fire, and I felt a strong inclination to have a peep; but, my master would not consent, when I begged his permission to uncover my eyes: nevertheless, I, who have a sort of a chip of curiosity, and an eager desire to know what I am forbid to enquire about, fair and softly, without being perceived by any living soul, pulled down upon my nose the handkerchief that covered my eyes, and by these means had a glimpse of the earth, which seemed no bigger than a grain of mustard, and the men that walked upon it almost as little as hazle nuts; so you may guess how high we must have soared by that time."

To this asseveration the dutchess answered, "Have a care, friend Sancho; from what you say, it appears that it could not be the earth, but the men walking upon it, whom you saw: for, if the earth appeared like a grain of mustard, and every man as big as a nut, it clearly follows that one man must have covered the whole earth." "Very true," said Sancho; "but, for all that, I had a side view, by which I discovered the whole globe." "Take notice, Sancho," resumed the dutchess, "it is impossible to see the whole of any thing, by a side view." "I know nothing of views," replied the squire; "this only I know, your ladyship ought to consider, that as we flew by inchantment, so might I, by inchantment, see the whole earth, and all the men upon it, in any sort of view whatsoever: and if your

ladyship will not believe me in that, no more will you believe me when I tell you, that pushing up the handkerchief towards my eyebrows, I found myself within an hand's-breadth and an half of heaven, which I'll assure your ladyship upon oath is very huge; and it came to pass, that our road lay close to the seven nanny * goats: now, I having been a goatherd in my youth, before God and my conscience! I no sooner set eyes on them, than I was seized with the inclination to divert myself a little with the pretty creatures, and if I had not done it, I believe I should have burst for vexation. Come on then, what does I? but, without saying a word to any living soul, not even to my master, fairly and softly slide down from Clavileno, and sport with the nannies, which are like violets and lillies, for the space of three quarters of an hour, and all that time the horse did not budge a step from the place."

"And while honest Sancho diverted himself with the goats," said the duke, "how was signor Don Quixote entertained?" To this interrogation the knight replied, "As all these adventures and incidents are out of the ordinary course of nature, we are not to wonder at what Sancho has told: for my own part, I can safely affirm, that I neither shoved up nor pulled down the bandage, nor did I see either heaven or earth, or sea or land. True it is, I perceived we passed through the region of the air, and even bordered upon the region of fire; but, that we travelled beyond it, I cannot believe: for, the fiery region being between the sphere of the moon and the utmost region of the air, we could not reach that firmament in which are placed the seven nannies, as Sancho calls them, without being scorched to death; and feeling we are not scorched, either Sancho lies, or Sancho dreams." "I neither lie nor dream," cried the squire: "let them ask the marks of the nanny goats; and by my answers you will perceive whether or not I speak truth." "Describe them then, Sancho," said the dutchess. "Two of them," replied Sancho, "are green, two carnation, two blue, and one motley." "This is a new breed," said the duke: "in our region of earth there are no such colours; I mean, among the nanny goats." "That is very plain," replied the squire: "there must be some difference between the goats of heaven and those upon earth." "Pray, tell me, Sancho," said his grace, "didst thou see never a † he goat among those females?" "No, my lord," answered the squire; "I have been told, none of those pass beyond the horns of the moon."

They did not choose to interrogate him further about his journey; for, they concluded that Sancho was in a fair way to travel through all the heavens above, and tell the news of each; tho' he had never stirred from the garden.

Finally, thus ended the adventure of the afflicted duenna, which afforded a fund for laughter to the duke and dutchess, not only at that time, but, during the whole course of their lives; as well as matter for Sancho to relate, had he lived whole centuries.

Don Quixote coming to the squire, whispered in his ear, "Heark ye, Sancho; since you would have us believe what you say, touching the things you saw in heaven, I desire the like credit from you, with regard to those things I saw in the cave of Montesinos. That's all."

---

* In Spain, the Pleiades are vulgarly called *Cabrillas*, nanny goats.[2]
† There is a kind of pleasantry in this question of the duke, which cannot be translated: for, the Spanish word *Cabròn*, signifies a cuckold, as well as an he goat.[3]

## CHAPTER X.

Containing Don Quixote's instructions to Sancho Panza, before he
set out for his government, with other well weighed incidents.

The duke and dutchess were so well pleased with the diverting and happy success of
the adventure of the afflicted duenna, that they resolved to proceed with the jest,
seeing what a proper subject they had to make it pass for earnest. Having, therefore,
communicated their scheme and instructions to their servants and vassals, touching
their behaviour to Sancho in his government of the promised island; on the day suc-
ceeding the flight of Clavileno, the duke desired him to prepare and make himself ready
to set out for his government, as the islanders already longed for him as much as for May
showers.

Sancho, having made his obeysance, "Since my descent from heaven," said he, "and
since from its lofty summit I have viewed the earth, and found it of such small extent,
my desire of being a governor, is much moderated: for, what grandeur can there be in
reigning over a grain of mustard seed? or what dignity and empire in governing half a
dozen of mortals no bigger than filberts? for, the whole earth seemed to contain noth-
ing more. If your lordship would be pleased to bestow upon me a small trifling space in
heaven, tho' it should not be above half a league, I would more gladly receive it than the
best island in the world." "You must consider, friend Sancho," replied the duke, "that I
have it not in my power to give away any part of heaven; no, not a nail's breadth: these
favours and benefits, are in the gift of God alone. What is in my power, I freely give you;
namely, a good island, right and tight, round and well proportioned, above measure fer-
tile, and so abounding with all good things, that if you mind your hits, you may with the
riches of earth purchase the opulence of heaven." "Well then," cried Sancho, "let this is-
land be forthcoming, and I will struggle hard, but I shall be such a governor, that in spite
of knaves, I may go to heaven; and, take notice, it is not from avarice that I desire to quit
my cottage, and raise myself to a footing with my betters; but, solely to taste and try
what it is to be a governor." "Nay, if once you taste it," said the duke, "you will be ready
to eat your fingers after the government; for, nothing is so delicious as to command and
be obeyed: certain I am, that when your master shall come to be an emperor, as will
doubtless be the case, considering the current of his affairs, it will not be in the power
of any person upon earth to tear it from him, and he will sorely grieve, and heartily rue
the time he has lost before his advancement to such an imperial station." "Indeed, my
lord," replied Sancho, "I imagine it must be a very pleasant thing to govern, even tho' it
should be but a flock of sheep." "May I be buried with you, Sancho, but you know every
thing!" answered the duke: "I hope you will turn out such a governor as your judgment
and sagacity seem to promise: but, here let that matter rest; and take notice, that, to-
morrow morning you must set out for the government of the island; and, this evening
you shall be accommodated with a convenient dress, and all other necessaries for your
departure." "They may dress me as they will," said the squire; "but, be that as it may, I

shall still be Sancho Panza." "True," replied the duke; "but, the garb ought always to be suited to the dignity and function of the profession: for, it would be a great impropriety in a lawyer to appear in the dress of a soldier, or in a soldier to wear canonicals: you, Sancho, must wear an habit that shall partly bespeak the gown, and partly the sword: for, in the island which I have bestowed upon you, letters and arms are both necessary." "As for letters," answered Sancho, "I am but indifferently stored, as I am even ignorant of the a, b, c; but, provided I remember my Christ-cross,[1] I shall be sufficiently qualified for a good governor: with regard to arms, I shall use those that may be put into my hand, until I can stand no longer, and God be my shield." "With such an excellent memory," said the duke, "Sancho can never fall into the least mistake."

Here they were joined by Don Quixote, who understanding the subject of their conversation, and the short space allotted to Sancho, to prepare for his departure, took the squire by the hand, with the duke's permission, and led him to his apartment, in order to instruct him how to behave in his office. Having entered the chamber, he locked the door, and obliging Sancho to sit down by him, spoke to this effect, in a grave and solemn tone:

"I return infinite thanks to heaven, friend Sancho, for having ordained, that, before I myself have met with the least success, good fortune hath gone forth to bid thee welcome. I, who had ballanced the remuneration of thy service in my own prosperity, find myself in the very rudiments of promotion; while thou, before thy time, and contrary to all the laws of reasonable progression, findest thy desire accomplished: other people bribe, sollicit, importune, attend levies, intreat, and persevere, without obtaining their suit; and another comes, who, without knowing why or wherefore, finds himself in possession of that office to which so many people laid claim: and here the old saying is aptly introduced, A pound of good luck is worth a tun of merit. Thou, who in comparison to me, art doubtless, an ignorant dunce, without rising early, or sitting up late, or, indeed, exerting the least industry; without any pretension more or less, than that of being breathed upon by knight-errantry, seest thyself created governor of an island, as if it was a matter of moonshine. All this I observe, O Sancho, that thou mayest not attribute thy success to thy own deserts; but, give thanks to heaven for having disposed matters so beneficially in thy behalf, and then make thy acknowledgements to that grandeur which centers in the profession of knight-errantry. Thy heart being thus predisposed to believe what I have said, be attentive, O my son, to me who am thy Cato, thy counsellor, thy north pole, and guide, to conduct thee into a secure harbour, from the tempestuous sea into which thou art going to be engulphed; for, great posts, and offices of state, are no other than a profound gulph of confusion.

"In the first place, O my son, you are to fear God: the fear of God is the beginning of wisdom; and, if you are wise you cannot err.

"Secondly, You must always remember who you are, and endeavour to know yourself; a study of all others the most difficult. This self-knowledge will hinder you from blowing yourself up like the frog, in order to rival the size of the ox: if, therefore, you succeed in this learning, the consideration of thy having been a swineherd, will, like the peacock's ugly feet, be a check upon thy folly and pride." "I own I once kept hogs, when I was a boy," said Sancho; "but, after I grew up, I quitted that employment, and took care

of geese: but, I apprehend, that matter is not of great consequence; for, all governors are not descended from the kingly race." "No, sure," answered the knight; "and, for that reason, those who are not of noble extraction, ought to sweeten the gravity of their function with mildness and affability; which, being prudently conducted, will screen them from those malicious murmurs that no station can escape. Rejoice, Sancho, in the lowness of your pedigree, and make no scruple of owning yourself descended from peasants: for, no body will endeavour to make you blush for that of which they see you are not ashamed: and value yourself more upon being a virtuous man of low degree, than upon being a proud sinner of noble birth: innumerable are those, who, from an humble stock, have risen to the pontifical and imperatorial dignity; a truth which I could prove by so many examples that you would not have patience to hear them.

"Take notice, Sancho, if you choose virtue for your medium, and pique yourself upon performing worthy actions, you will have no cause to envy noblemen and princes; for, blood is hereditary, but virtue is acquired; consequently, this last has an intrinsic value which the other does not possess.

"This being the case, as undoubtedly it is, if peradventure any one of your relations should come to visit you in your island, you must not discountenance and affront him, but, on the contrary, let him be kindly received and entertained; and, in so doing, you will act conformably to the will of heaven, which is displeased at seeing its own handywork despised; and, perform your duty to the well concerted rights of nature.

"If you send for your wife, and, indeed, those who are concerned in governing, ought not to be long without their helpmates, take pains in teaching, improving, and civilizing her: for, all that a sagacious governor can acquire, is very often lost and squandred by a foolish, rustic wife.

"If, perchance, you should become a widower, (a circumstance that may possibly happen) and have it in your power to make a more advantageous match, you must not choose such a yokefellow as will serve for an angling hook, fishing rod, or equivocating * hood: for, verily, I say unto thee, all that a judge's wife receives must be accounted for at the general clearance, by the husband, who will repay fourfold after death, what he made no reckoning of during life.

"Never conduct yourself by the law of your own arbitrary opinion, which is generally the case with those ignorant people who presume upon their own self-sufficiency.

"Let the tears of the poor find more compassion in thy breast, tho' not more justice, than the informations of the rich.

"Endeavour to investigate the truth from among the promises and presents of the opulent, as well as from the sighs and importunities of the needy.

"When equity can, and ought to take place, inflict not the whole rigour of the law upon the delinquent; for, severity is not more respected than compassion, in the character of a judge.

"If ever you suffer the rod of justice to be bent a little, let it not be warped, by the weight of corruption, but the bowels of mercy.

---

* The phrase *No quiero de tu capilla*, alludes to the practice of friars, who, when charity is offered, hold out their hoods to receive it, while they pronounce a refusal with their tongues.[2]

"If ever you should have an opportunity to judge the process of your enemy, recal your attention from the injury you have received, and fix it wholly upon the truth of the case.

"In another man's cause, be not blinded by private affection; for, the errors thus committed are generally incurable; or, if they admit of remedy, it will be greatly at the expence of your fortune and credit.

"If a beautiful woman should come to demand justice, withdraw your eyes from her tears, and your hearing from her sighs, and deliberate at a distance upon the substance of her demand, unless you have a mind that your reason should be overwhelmed by her complaint, and your virtue burried in her sighs.

"Abuse not him in word whom you are resolved to chastise in deed: for, to such a wretch, the pain of the punishment will be sufficient, without the addition of reproach.

"In judging the delinquents who shall fall under your jurisdiction, consider the miserable object Man, subject to the infirmities of our depraved nature; and, as much as lies in your power, without injury to the contrary party, display your clemency and compassion: for, although all the attributes of God are equally excellent, that of mercy has a better effect in our eye, and strikes with greater lustre than justice.

"If you observe, and conduct yourself by these rules and precepts, Sancho, your days will be long upon the face of the earth: your fame will be eternal, your reward complete, and your felicity unutterable: your children will be married according to your wish; they and their descendants will enjoy titles; you shall live in peace and friendship with all mankind: when your course of life is run, death will overtake you in an happy and mature old age, and your eyes will be shut by the tender and delicate hands of your posterity, in the third or fourth generation.

"The remarks I have hitherto made, are documents touching the decoration of your soul; and, now you will listen to those that regard the ornaments of the body."

## CHAPTER XI.

## Of the second series of instructions which Don Quixote gave to Sancho Panza.

Who that had heard this discourse of Don Quixote, would not have taken him for a person of sound judgment, and excellent disposition? but, as we have oftentimes observed, in the progress of this sublime history, his madness never appeared except when the string of chivalry was touched; and, on all other subjects of conversation, he displayed a clear and ready understanding: so that every minute, his works discredit his judgment, and his judgment his works. But, in this second set of instructions communicated to Sancho, he discovered great ingenuity, and raised his madness and discretion to a most elevated pitch.

Sancho listened with the utmost attention, and endeavoured to retain his advice, like a man who desired to preserve it, as the infallible means to promote the happy birth of that government with which he was so far gone. Don Quixote then proceeded in these terms.

"With respect to the government of your person and family, Sancho: In the first place, I charge you to be cleanly, and pair your nails; and, do not let them grow, like some people whose ignorance teaches them that long nails beautify the hand; as if that additional excrement which they neglect to cut, were really and truly the nail; whereas it more nearly resembles the talons of a lizzard-hunting wind-whiffer,[1] and is a most beastly and extraordinary abuse.

"You must never appear loose and unbuttoned; for, a slovenly dress denotes a disorderly mind; unless that looseness and negligence be the effect of cunning, as we suppose to have been the case with Julius Caesar.

"Examine sagaciously the profits of your place, and if they will afford livery to your servants, let it be rather decent and substantial than gay and tawdry; and be sure to divide it between your servants and the poor. For example, if you can cloath six pages, put three in livery, and cloath as many poor boys; and then you will have pages for heaven as well as for earth: now, this is a method of giving livery, which the vain-glorious could never conceive.

"Abstain from eating garlic and onions, lest your breath should discover your rusticity.

"Walk leisurely, speak distinctly, but not so as to seem delighted with your own discourse; for, all affectation is disagreeable.

"Dine sparingly, and eat very little at supper; for, the health of the whole body depends upon the operation of the stomach.

"Be temperate in drinking; and, consider that excess of wine will neither keep a secret nor perform a promise.

"Beware, Sancho, of chewing on both sides of your mouth, as well as of eructing before company." "I do not understand what you mean by eructing," said the squire. "By eructing," answered the knight, "I mean belching, which, tho' one of the most expressive, is at the same time one of the most vulgar terms of our language; therefore people of taste have had recourse to the Latin tongue, saying To eruct instead of To belch, and substituting eructations in the room of belchings; and, tho' some people may not understand these terms, it is of small importance; for, time and use will introduce and render them intelligible; and this is what we call enriching the language, over which the practice of the vulgar has great influence." "Truly, signor," said Sancho, "one of the advices and good counsels which I intend to remember, must be that of not belching; for, it is a fault of which I am very often guilty." "Eructing, Sancho, and not belching," replied Don Quixote. "Eructing, it shall be henceforward," answered the squire; "and, I will take care that it shall not be forgotten."

"Moreover, Sancho, you must not intermingle so many proverbs with your discourse; for, although proverbs are short sentences, you very often bring them in by the head and shoulders so preposterously, that they look more like the ravings of distraction than well chosen apothegms."

"That defect, God himself must remedy," said Sancho; "for, I have more proverbs by heart than would be sufficient to fill a large book; and, when I speak, they croud together in such a manner as to quarrel for utterance; so that my tongue discharges them just as they happen to be in the way, whether they are or are not to the purpose: but, I will take care henceforward, to throw out those that may be suitable to the gravity of my office; for, Where there's plenty of meat, the supper will soon be complete. He that shuffles does not cut. A good hand makes a short game; and, It requires a good brain, to know when to give and retain." "Courage, Sancho," cried Don Quixote, "squeeze, tack, and string your proverbs together; here are none to oppose you. My mother whips me, and I whip the top. Here am I exhorting thee to suppress thy proverbs, and in an instant thou hast spewed forth a whole litany of them, which are as foreign from the subject as an old ballad.² Remember, Sancho, I do not say that a proverb properly applied is amiss; but, to throw in, and string together, old saws helter skelter, renders conversation altogether mean and despicable.

"When you appear on horseback, do not lean backwards over the saddle, nor stretch out your legs stiffly from the horse's belly, nor let them hang dangling in a slovenly manner, as if you was upon the back of Dapple; for, some ride like jockies, and some like gentlemen.

"Be very moderate in sleeping; for, he who does not rise with the sun, cannot enjoy the day; and observe, O Sancho, Industry is the mother of prosperity; and Laziness, her opposite, never saw the accomplishment of a good wish.

"The last advice which I shall now give thee, although it does not relate to the ornament of the body, I desire thou wilt carefully remember; for, in my opinion, it will be of as much service to thee as any I have hitherto mentioned; and this it is: Never engage in a dispute upon pedigree, at least, never compare one with another; for, in all comparisons, one must of consequence be preferred to the other; and, he whom you have abased will abhor you; nor will you ever reap the least return from him whom you have extolled.

"Your garb shall consist of breeches and stockings; a full waistcoat, with skirts and hanging sleeves, and a loose coat; but, never think of wearing trunk hose, which neither become gentlemen nor governors.

"This is all that occurs to me at present, in the way of advice; but, in process of time, my instructions shall be proportioned to thy occasions, provided thou wilt take care to communicate, from time to time, the nature of thy situation."

"Signor," said Sancho, "I plainly perceive that all the advices you have given me, are sound, and good, and profitable; but, of what signification will they be, if I forget them all? Indeed, as for the matter of not letting my nails grow, or marrying another wife, in case I should have an opportunity, it will not easily slip out of my brain; but, as to those other gallimawfries, quirks and quiddities, I neither do retain them, nor shall I ever retain more of them than of last year's rain; and therefore, it will be necessary to let me have them in writing; for, tho' I myself can neither read nor write, I will give them to my confessor, that he may repeat, and beat them into my noddle, as there shall be occasion."

"Ah, sinner that I am!" exclaimed Don Quixote, "what a scandal it is for governors to

be so ignorant that they can neither read nor write. Thou must know, Sancho, that for a man to be totally devoid of letters, or left-handed, argues either that he was descended from the very lowest and meanest of people, or that he was so wicked and stubborn, that good example and judicious precepts have had no effect upon his mind or understanding. This is a great defect in thy character, and I wish thou would'st learn, if possible, to write thy name." "I can sign my name very well," answered Sancho; "for, during my stewardship of the brotherhood, I learned to make such letters as are ruddled upon packs, and those they told me, stood for my name: besides, I can feign myself lame of my right hand, and keep a secretary to sign in my room; so that there is a remedy for every thing but death. And I having the cudgel in my hand, will make them do as I command; for, He whose father is mayor—you know³—and I shall be a governor which is still better. Let them come and see, but not throw their squibs or slanders at me: otherwise they may come for wool, and go home shorn. The house itself will tell, if God loves its master well. A rich man's folly is wisdom in the world's eye: now, I being rich as being governor, and liberal withal, as I intend to be, no body will spy my defects. Make yourself honey, and a clown will have flies. You are worth as much as you have, said my grannam; and, Might overcomes right."

"O! God's curse light on thee!" cried Don Quixote: "threescore thousand devils fly away with thee and thy proverbs! A full hour hast thou been stringing them together, and every one has been like a dagger to my soul. Take my word for it, these proverbs will bring thee one day to the gallows; for these, thy vassals will deprive thee of thy government, or at least enter into associations against thee. Tell me, numscul, where didst thou find this heap of old saws? or how didst thou learn to apply them, wiseacre? It makes me sweat like a day-labourer, to utter one proverb as it ought to be applied." "'Fore God, Sir, master of mine," replied Sancho, "your worship complains of mere trifles. Why the devil should you be in dungeon with me for making use of my own: I have no other fortune or stock, but proverbs upon proverbs; and, now there are no less than four at my tongue's end, that come as pat to the purpose as pears in a basket; but, for all that, they shall not come forth; for, sagacious silence is * Sancho." "That thou art not Sancho," said the knight, "far from being sagaciously silent, thou art an obstinate and eternal babler. Nevertheless, I would fain hear those four proverbs that are so pat to the purpose; for, I have been rummaging my whole memory, which I take to be a good one, and not a proverb occurs to my recollection." "What can be better than these?" replied the squire: "Never thrust your thumb between another man's grinders; and to Get out of my house; what would you with my wife? there is no reply: Whether the stone goes to the pitcher, or the pitcher to the stone, 'ware pitcher. Now all these fit to a hair. Let no man meddle with a governor or his substitute; otherwise he will suffer, as if he had thrust his finger between two grinders; and even if they should not be grinders, if they are teeth, it makes little difference: then, to what a governor says, there is no reply to be made; no more than to, Get out of my house, what would you with my wife? And as to the stone and the pitcher, a blind man may see the meaning of it: Wherefore, let him who spies a mote in his neighbour's eye, look first to the beam in his own, that people may not say of him,

* Instead of *saintly*.⁴

The dead mare was frightened at the flea'd mule: and, your worship is very sensible that a fool knows more in his own house, than a wise man in that of his neighbour." "There, Sancho, you are mistaken," answered Don Quixote; "a fool knows nothing either in his own or his neighbour's house; because, no edifice of understanding can be raised upon the foundation of folly. But, here let the subject rest: if thou shouldst misbehave in thy government, thine will be the fault, and mine the shame: I console myself, however, in reflecting that I have done my duty, in giving thee advice, with all the earnestness and discretion in my power; so that I have acquitted myself in point of promise and obligation. God conduct thee, Sancho, and govern thee in thy government, and deliver me from an apprehension I have, that thou wilt turn the island topsy turvy; a misfortune which I might prevent, by discovering to the duke what thou art, and telling him all that paunch and corpulency of thine is no other than a bag full of proverbs and impertinence."

"Signor," replied Sancho, "if your worship really thinks I am not qualified for that government, I renounce it from henceforward for ever, amen. I have greater regard for a nail's breadth of my soul, than my whole body; and I can subsist as bare Sancho, upon a crust of bread and an onion, as well as governor on capons and partridges; for, while we sleep, great and small, rich and poor, we are equal all. If your worship will consider, your worship will find, that you yourself put this scheme of government into my head: as for my own part, I know no more of the matter than a bustard; and if you think the governorship will be the means of my going to the devil, I would much rather go as simple Sancho to heaven, than as a governor to hell-fire."

"Before God!" cried the knight, "from these last reflections thou hast uttered, I pronounce thee worthy to govern a thousand islands. Thou hast an excellent natural disposition, without which all science is naught: recommend thyself to God, and endeavour to avoid errors in the first intention; I mean, let thy intention and unshaken purpose be, to deal righteously in all thy transactions; for, heaven always favours the upright design. And now let us go in to dinner; for, I believe their graces wait for us."

## CHAPTER XII.

Giving an account of the manner in which Sancho was conducted to the government, and a strange adventure that happened to Don Quixote in the castle.

The original of the history, it is said, relates that the interpreter did not translate this chapter as it had been written by Cid Hamet Benengeli, who bewails his fate in having undertaken such a dry and confined history as that of Don Quixote; which obliged him to treat of nothing but the knight and his squire, without daring to launch

out into other more grave and entertaining episodes, and digressions. He complained, that to be thus restricted in his hand, his pen, and his invention, to one subject only, so as to be obliged to speak through the mouths of a few persons, was an insupportable toil, that produced no fruit to the advantage of the author; and that, in order to avoid this inconvenience, he had in the first part used the artifice of some novels, such as the Impertinent Curiosity, and the Captive, which were detached from the history, although many particulars there recounted are really incidents which happened to Don Quixote; and, therefore, could not be suppressed. It was likewise his opinion, as he observes, that many readers being wholly ingrossed with the exploits of Don Quixote, would not bestow attention upon novels, but pass them over either with negligence or disgust, without adverting to the spirit and artifice they contain; a truth which would plainly appear, were they to be published by themselves, independent of the madness of Don Quixote, and the simplicities of Sancho. He would not therefore insert in the second part any novels, whether detached or attached; but only a few episodes that seem to spring from those very incidents which truth presents; and, even these, as brief and concise as they could possibly be related: and since he includes and confines himself within the narrow limits of narration, tho' his abilities and understanding are sufficient to treat the whole universe, he hopes that his work will not be depreciated, and begs he may receive due praise, not for what he has written, but for what he has left unwrit. Then the history proceeds in this manner:

In the evening that succeeded the afternoon on which the knight admonished his squire, he gave him his admonitions in writing, that he might find some person to read them occasionally; but, scarce had Sancho received, than he dropped them by accident, and they fell into the hands of the duke, who communicated the paper to the dutchess, and both admired anew, the madness and ingenuity of Don Quixote. Resolving to prosecute the jest, they, that very evening, dismissed Sancho with a large retinue to the place, which he supposed to be an island; the execution of the whole scheme being left to the sagacity of the duke's steward, who was a person of great humour and discretion; for, without discretion there can be no humour. He it was who acted the part of the countess Trifaldi, with that pleasantry above related. Thus qualified, and in consequence of the instructions he received from their graces, touching his behaviour to Sancho, he had performed his part to admiration. It happened then, that Sancho no sooner beheld the said steward, than he traced in his countenance the very features of Trifaldi, and turning to his master, "Signor," said he, "the devil may fly away with me from this spot where I stand, as an honest man, and a believer, if your worship will not confess that the face of the duke's steward here present, is the very same with that of the afflicted duenna!" Don Quixote, having attentively considered the steward's countenance, replied, "There is no occasion for the devil's running away with thee, Sancho, either as an honest man or a believer; (indeed, I cannot guess thy meaning) for, sure enough, this steward's face is the very same with that of the afflicted duenna: but, nevertheless, the steward and the duenna cannot possibly be the same person; that would imply a downright contradiction, and this is no time to set on foot such inquiries, which would intangle us in the maze of inextricable labyrinths. Believe me, friend, we ought to beseech the Lord very earnestly to deliver us from those two evils of wicked wizzards, and vile inchanters."

"But, this is no joke," answered Sancho; "for, I heard him speak a little while ago, and methought the very voice of Trifaldi sounded in mine ears. At present, however, I will hold my tongue; but, nevertheless, I will keep a strict eye over him from hence forward, in order to discover some other mark either to destroy or confirm my suspicion." "Do so, Sancho," said Don Quixote; "and, he sure to send me notice of the discoveries thou shalt make in this particular, as well as of every thing that shall happen to thee in the course of thine administration."

At length, Sancho departed with a numerous attendance: he was dressed like a gown-man, with a long cloak of murrey-coloured camblet, and a cap of the same stuff: he rode upon a mule, with short stirrups,[1] and was followed by Dapple, who, by the duke's express order, was adorned with rich trappings of flaming silk; so that the governor from time to time turned about his head to contemplate the finery of his ass, with whose company he was so well content, that he would not have exchanged it for that of the German emperor.

At parting, he kissed the hands of the duke and dutchess, and asked the benediction of his master, which was given with tears, and received with a whimper.

Courteous reader, suffer honest Sancho to depart in peace and happy time, and lay thy account with two bushels of laughter, which will proceed from thy knowing how he behaved himself in office; and, in the mean time, attend to what befel his master this very night; an incident which, if it cannot excite thy laughter, will, at least, induce thee to grin like a monkey; for, the adventures of Don Quixote must be celebrated either with mirth or admiration.

It is related then, that Sancho was no sooner gone than his master became solitary, and had it been possible, would have revoked the commission, and deprived him of his government; but, the dutchess being apprised of his melancholy, desired to know the cause, observing, that if it proceeded from Sancho's absence, there was plenty of squires, duennas, and damsels in the family, who should serve him to the satisfaction of his utmost wish. "True it is, my lady dutchess," replied Don Quixote, "I feel the absence of Sancho; but, that is not the principal cause of my seeming sadness: and of all the generous proffers of your excellency, I choose to accept nothing but the good will with which they are made; for the rest, I humbly beg your excellency will consent, and permit me to wait upon myself in my own apartment." "Truly," said the dutchess, "that must not be; signor Don Quixote shall be served by four of my damsels as beautiful as roses." "With regard to me," answered the knight, "they will not be roses, but thorns to prick my very soul; and, therefore, I will as soon fly as permit them, or any thing like them to enter my chamber. If your grace would continue to bestow your favours, which, I own, I do not deserve, suffer me to be private, and make use of my own doors, that I may raise a wall between my passions and my chastity; a custom which I would not forego for all the liberality which your highness is pleased to display in my behalf: and, in a word, I will rather sleep in my cloaths, than consent to be undressed by any person whatsoever." "Enough, enough, signor Don Quixote," answered her grace; "you may depend upon it, I shall give such orders, that not even a fly, much less a damsel, shall enter your apartment: I am not a person to discompose the decency of signor Don Quixote, among whose virtues, I perceive, that of decorum shines with superior lustre. Your worship may

dress and undress yourself alone, after your own fashion, when and how you please, without lett or impediment; for, in your chamber, you will find every utensil suited to those who sleep under lock and key, without being obliged to open upon any necessary occasion. Long live the great Dulcinea del Toboso, and may her fame be extended around the whole circumference of the earth, seeing she is worthy to be beloved by a knight of such valour and chastity; and may propitious heaven infuse into the heart of Sancho Panza, our governor, a promptitude to finish his flagellation, that the world may soon reenjoy the beauty of such an excellent lady." To this compliment the knight replied, "Your highness hath spoken like yourself; for, from the mouths of such benevolent ladies nothing evil can proceed: and Dulcinea will be more fortunate, and more renowned through the world, by your grace's approbation, than by all the applause of the greatest orators upon earth."

"Well then, signor Don Quixote," answered the dutchess, "it is now supper-time, and the duke probably stays for us; let us go and sup therefore, that you may be a-bed betimes; for, your journey to Candaya was not so short, but that it must have fatigued your worship in some measure." "Madam," replied Don Quixote, "I feel no sort of weariness; and I swear to your excellency, that in my life I never crossed a better, or easier going steed than Clavileno; nor can I conceive what should induce Malambruno to deprive himself of such a light and gentle carriage, by burning it without scruple or hesitation." "As to that particular," said the dutchess, "we may suppose, that repenting of the injury he had done to the countess and her company, as well as to other people, and being sorry for the mischief he must certainly have produced as a wizzard and inchanter, he resolved to destroy all the instruments of his art: as the principal of these, which gave him the greatest uneasiness, because it had transported him from place to place in his operations, he burned Clavileno, that by means of his ashes, and the trophy of the parchment, the valour of Don Quixote might be eternized."

The knight made fresh acknowledgments of her grace's politeness, and after supper retired to his apartment, without suffering any person to accompany or minister unto his occasions; so much was he afraid of meeting with trials, which might provoke or compel him to foregoe the chastity and decorum which he had hitherto preserved for his mistress Dulcinea, ever schooling his imagination with the exemplary virtue of Amadis, the flower and mirrour of knight-errantry.

Having locked the door behind him, he undressed himself by the light of two wax tapers, and in the course of this occupation (O misfortune, ill decreed to such a personage!) forth broke—not a volley of sighs, or any thing else to discredit the purity of his politeness, but about two dozen of stitches in one stocking, which, being thus torn, resembled a lattice: a mishap which was the source of extreme affliction to our worthy signor, who, on this occasion, would have given an ounce of silver for a drachm of green silk: I say green silk; for, his stockings were of that colour.

Here Benengeli exclaims, "O poverty, poverty! I know not what should induce the great Cordovan poet to call thee an holy unrequited gift. I, tho' a Moor, am very sensible, from my correspondence with christians, that holiness consists in charity, humility, faith, poverty, and obedience; yet, nevertheless, I will affirm that he must be holy indeed, who can sit down content with poverty, unless we mean that kind of poverty to

which one of the greatest saints alludes, when he says, Possess all things as not possess-
ing them: and this is called spiritual poverty. But, thou second poverty, which is the
cause I spoke of, why wouldst thou assault gentlemen of birth rather than any other class
of people? Why dost thou compel them to cobble their shoes, and wear upon their coats
one button of silk, another of hair, and a third of glass? Why must their ruffs be gener-
ally yellow and ill starched?" (* By the bye, from this circumstance we learn the antiq-
uity of ruffs and starch.) But, thus he proceeds: "O wretched man of noble pedigree!
who is obliged to administer cordials to his honour, in the midst of hunger and solitude,
by playing the hypocrite with a tooth-pick which he affects to use in the street, tho' he
has eaten nothing to require that act of cleanliness: wretched he! I say, whose honour is
ever apt to be startled, and thinks that every body at a league's distance, observes the
patch upon his shoe, his greasy hat, and thread-bare cloak, and even the hunger that pre-
dominates in his belly."

All these reflections occurred to Don Quixote when he tore his stocking; but, he con-
soled himself for the misfortune, when he perceived that Sancho had left behind him a
pair of travelling-boots, which he resolved to wear next day: finally, he crept into bed,
where he lay pensive and melancholy, as well for the absence of Sancho, as for the ir-
reparable misfortune of his stocking, which he would have gladly mended, even with
silk of a different colour; one of the greatest marks of misery which a gentleman can ex-
hibit in the course of his tedious poverty. After having extinguished the lights, he found
the weather so hot that he could not sleep: he therefore arose again, and opened the
casement of a grated window that looked into a fine garden: then it was, that perceiving
and hearing people walking and talking together, he began to listen attentively, while
those below spoke so loud that he heard the following dialogue:

"Do not, O Emerencia, press me to sing; for, well thou knowest, that from the mo-
ment this stranger entered the castle, and mine eyes beheld his merit, instead of singing,
I can do nothing but weep: besides, my lady's sleep is rather slight than profound; and I
would not for all the wealth in the world, that her grace should find us here. Moreover,
suppose she should still sleep on, without waking, vain would be my song, unless it
should awake, and attract the attention of this new AEneas, who is arrived in my terri-
tories, in order to leave me forlorn." "Let not these suppositions have any weight with
you, my dear Altisidora," replied another voice: "the dutchess is doubtless asleep, and
every body in the house, except the lord of your heart, and watchman of your soul, who
must certainly be awake; for, I just now heard him open the casement in his apartment:
sing, therefore, my disastrous friend, in a low, sweet, and plaintive tone, to the sound of
thy harp: and should the dutchess overhear us, we will lay the blame upon the heat of
the weather." "That is not the cause of my hesitation, O Emerencia," replied Altisidora;
"but, I am afraid, that my song will disclose the situation of my heart, and I myself be
censured by those who never felt the almighty power of love, as a light and liquorish

---

* Cervantes has been frequently caught napping, and here in particular; how could this be any
proof of the antiquity of ruffs, when the adventure happened after the first part of Don Quixote
was published? But, perhaps, this is no other than an ironical animadversion upon the trifling dis-
coveries of antiquarians.

damsel: but, come what will; better have an hot face than an heavy heart." At that instant an harp was ravishingly touched; and, Don Quixote hearing the sound was struck with amazement; for, his imagination was instantly filled with an infinity of similar adventures of rails and gardens, serenades, courtships and swoonings, which he had read in his vain books of chivalry: and he concluded that some damsel of the dutchess was enamoured of him, but that modesty compelled her to keep her inclinations secret. Possessed of this notion, he began to be afraid of his virtue; but, he resolved, in his own mind, to hold out to the last; and, recommending himself with all his soul and spirit, to his mistress Dulcinea del Toboso, determined to listen to the song. With a view, therefore, to let them know he was there, he pretended to sneeze, a circumstance which not a little pleased the damsels, who desired nothing so much as that Don Quixote should hear them. Then the harp being tuned, Altisidora, after a flourish, began the following ditty.

## SONG.

O Thou! who now a-bed,
In Holland sheets art laid,
And sleep'st from night till morn,
Untouch'd by care and scorn;
The knight of greatest worth
La Mancha e'er brought forth;
More chaste an hundred-fold,
Than pure Arabian gold;
O hear an hapless maid
By cruel love betray'd!
The flame of thy two suns,
Hath scorch'd her to the bones!
Thou, seeking thy own foe,
Hast found another's woe:
Thou gav'st the wound, and sure
Wilt not refuse the cure.
O tell me, valiant youth,
(So God shall prosper truth)
Wast thou in deserts bred,
Or among mountains fed?
Did serpents give thee suck,[2]
On some bleak barren rock,
Deep in the wild recess
Of forest or morass?
Dulcinea fat and fair,
May boast her shape and air,
That in subjection hold
A tyger fierce and bold.
Her fame shall live in stanza,
From Ebro to Arlanza,
From Tagus to Henarez,
From Seine to Manganarez.

Would I her place could fill,
I'd give her for good will,
My gayest petticoat
With golden fringes wrought.
How happy then should I
In thine embraces lie!
Or on some cushion loll,
And scratch thy valiant poll.
Such joys are far above
The merits of my love;
Let me then bending low,
With rapture, kiss thy toe.
What presents would be made,
Of sattin and brocade!
I'd give thee shoes and socks,
Silk hose with silver clocks;
Of cash uncounted sums,
And pearls as big as plums,
So precious, each would sell
As perfect nonpareil.
Manchegan Nero, say,
Dost thou, aloof, survey
The flames that rage and smart
Within my love-sick heart?
A maid, I vow and swear,
Young, tender, and sincere,
As yet, I have not seen
The borders of fifteen.
My sides are not awry,
Nor lame, nor blind, am I:
My locks with ribbons bound,
Like lillies, sweep the ground:
My nose is flat, 'tis true,
And eke my mouth askew;
But, teeth as topaz fine,
Complete my charms divine:
My voice, as you may hear,
Is tuneful, sweet and clear:
My temper soft and good,
If rightly understood.
These beauties all so clever,
Are yielded to thy quiver,
And I who tell my story,
Am call'd Altisidory.

Here ended the song of the hapless Altisidora; and here began the horrour of the courted Don Quixote, who, fetching a heavy sigh, said within himself, "What an unfortunate errant am I, whom no damsel can behold without being enamoured of my

person! and, how hapless is the peerless Dulcinea del Toboso, who cannot enjoy my incomparable constancy, without a rival! Queens, what would you have? Empresses, why do you persecute her beauty? Damsels of fifteen, why do you molest such virtue? Leave, leave, I say, that wretched lady to taste, enjoy, and triumph in the lot which love hath decreed her, by subduing my heart, and captivating my soul. Take notice, enamoured tribe, that to Dulcinea alone I am sugar paste, but flint to all the rest of her sex: to her I am honey; but, gall and bitterness to such as you. In my eye, Dulcinea alone is beauteous, wise, gay, chaste, and well born; but, all others are homely, foolish, idle, and of humble birth. To be her slave, and hers alone, nature has thrown me into the world: Altisidora may weep or sing; and that lady may despair, on whose account I was pummelled in the castle of the inchanted Moor;³ Dulcinea's I am resolved to be, boiled or roasted, neat, chaste, and well bred, in spite of all the witchcraft upon earth." So saying, he shut the casement with a flap, and retired to bed in as much anxiety and concern as if some great misfortune had befallen him. There then we will leave him for the present, as we are summoned by the mighty Panza, who is impatient to begin his famous administration.

## CHAPTER XIII.

### Giving an account of the manner in which Sancho Panza took possession of his island, and began his administration.

O Thou! perpetual explorer of the antipodes, torch of nature, eye of heaven, and agreeable motive for wine-cooling jars, Timbrius here, Phoebus there, archer in one place, physician in another, father of poetry, and inventor of music; thou who always risest, but never set'st, although thou seem'st to set. Thee I invoke, O sun! by whose assistance man is by man ingendred; thee I implore, that thou would'st favour and enlighten the obscurity of my genius, and enable me to write with precision, an account of the great Sancho Panza's administration: for, without thy aid, I find myself lukewarm, feeble, and confused.

To begin then: Sancho, with his whole retinue, arrived at a town containing about a thousand inhabitants, one of the best in the duke's possession; which, they told Sancho, was called the island Barataria, either, because the name of the place was really Barataria, or because he had very * cheaply purchased the government. When he reached the gates of the town, which was walled, the magistrates came forth to receive him, the bells were set a ringing, and the inhabitants with expressions of universal joy, conducted him with vast pomp to the great church, in order to return thanks to heaven for his safe arrival:

---

* *Barato* signifies cheap.¹

then, with some ridiculous ceremonies, they delivered to him the keys of the town, and admitted him as perpetual governor of the island Barataria.

The equipage, matted beard, corpulency, and diminutive stature of the new governor, furnished food for admiration to every body who did not know the juggle of the contrivance; ay, and even to those acquainted with the mystery, who were not a few. In fine, they carried him from the church to the town-hall, and placing him upon the bench, the duke's steward addressed himself to the governor in these words: "It is an ancient custom in this famous island, my lord governor, that he who comes to take possession of it, is obliged to answer some difficult and intricate question that shall be put to him, and by his response the inhabitants feel the pulse of their new governor's genius, according to which they rejoice or repine at his arrival." While the steward pronounced this address, Sancho was contemplating a number of large letters written upon the wall that fronted his tribunal, and as he could not read, he desired to know the meaning of that painting on the wall. "In that place, my lord," replied the steward, "is written and recorded, the day on which your excellency has taken possession of this island; for, the inscription runs, On such a day and such a month, signor Don Sancho Panza took possession of this island, and long may he enjoy the government thereof." "And whom do they call Don Sancho Panza?" said the governor. "Who, but your excellency?" answered the steward; "for, this island never saw any other Panza than him who sits on that tribunal." "Take notice then, brother," replied Sancho, "the Don belongs not to me, nor did it ever belong to any of my generation. Simple Sancho is my name; so was my father called, and so my grandfather; and they were all Panzas, without addition of Don or Donna; and I begin to imagine there are as many Dons as stones in this island— but, no more of that: God knows my meaning; and peradventure, if my government lasts above three days, I shall weed out these Dons, which from their swarms must be as troublesome as vermin. But, pray, Mr. steward, proceed with your question, which I shall answer to the best of my understanding, whether the townsmen should repine or not repine."

At that instant, two men entered the hall, one in the habit of a labouring man, and the other a taylor with shears in his hand, who, approaching the bench, "My lord governor," said he, "this countryman and I are come before your lordship about an affair which I am going to explain. This honest man comes yesterday to my shop, for, saving your presence, I am an examined taylor, God be praised! and putting a remnant of cloth in my hand, 'Gaffer,' said he, 'is there stuff enough here to make me a cap?' I, having handled the piece, replied Yes: now, he supposing, as I suppose, and to be sure it was a right supposition, that I wanted to cabbage part of the stuff; grounding his suspicion on his own deceit, and the bad character of us taylors, desired I would see if there was enough for two caps; and I, guessing his thoughts, answered Yes: and so my gentleman, persisting in his first and evil intention, went on adding cap to cap; and I proceeded to answer Yes upon Yes, until the number increased to five caps: this very moment he called for them, and when I produced them, he not only refused to pay me for my work, but, even demanded that I should either restore the cloth, or pay him the price of it." "Is this really the case, brother?" said Sancho. "Yes, my lord," replied the countryman; "but, I beg

your lordship would order him to shew what sort of caps he has made." "With all my heart," cried the taylor, who, immediately pulling out his hand from under his cloak, produced five small caps fixed upon the tops of his four fingers and thumb; saying, "Here are the five caps which this honest man desired me to make; as I shall answer to God and my own conscience, there is not a scrap of the stuff remaining; and, I am willing to submit the work to the inspection of the masters of the company." All the people in court laughed at the number of caps, and the novelty of the dispute, which Sancho having considered for a few moments, "Methinks," said he, "this suit requires no great discussion; but, may be equitably determined out of hand: and therefore, my determination is, that the taylor shall lose his work, and the countryman forfeit his cloth; and, that the caps shall be distributed among the poor prisoners, without further hesitation."

If the sentence he afterwards passed upon the herdsman's purse, excited the admiration of the spectators, this decision provoked their laughter: nevertheless, they executed the orders of their governor, before whom two old men now presented themselves, one of them having a cane which he used as a walking-staff. The other making up to the governor, "My lord," said he, "some time ago, I lent this man ten crowns of gold, to oblige and assist him in an emergency, on condition that he should pay them upon demand; and, for a good while, I never asked my money, that I might not put him to greater inconvenience in repaying, than that which he felt when he borrowed the sum; but, as he seemed to neglect the payment entirely, I have demanded the money again and again, and he not only refuses to refund, but also denies that I ever lent him the ten crowns; or if I did, he says he is sure they were repayed: now, I having no witnesses to prove the loan, nor he evidence of the repayment, for, indeed, they never were repayed, intreat your lordship to take his oath, and if he swears the money was returned, I here forgive him the debt, in the presence of God." "What have you to say to this charge, honest gaffer with the staff?" said Sancho. "My lord," replied the senior, "I confess he lent me the money; and, since he leaves the matter to my oath, if your lordship will lower your rod of justice, I will make affidavit, that I have really and truly returned, and repayed the sum I borrowed." The governor accordingly lowering his wand, the defendant desired the plaintiff to hold his cane until he should make oath, because it incumbered him; then, laying his hand upon the cross of the rod, he declared that the other had indeed lent him those ten crowns which he now demanded; but, that he, the borrower, had returned them into the lender's own hand, and he supposed he dunned him in this manner, because he had forgot that circumstance. This oath being administred, the great governor asked what further the creditor had to say to the allegation of the other party? And he answered, that doubtless the defendant had spoke the truth; for, he looked upon him as an honest man, and a good christian; and, that as he himself must have forgot the particulars of the payment, he would never demand it from thence forward. Then the defendant taking back his cane, and making his obeisance, quitted the court; while Sancho seeing him retire in this manner, and perceiving the resignation of the plaintiff, hung down his head a little, and laying the forefinger of his right hand on one side of his nose, continued in this musing posture for a very small space of time: then, raising his head, he ordered them to call back the old man with the staff, who had retired: he was accordingly brought before Sancho, who said to him, "Honest friend, lend me that staff,

I have occasion for it." "With all my heart, my lord," replied the elder, reaching it to the judge: then, Sancho took and delivered it to the plaintiff, saying: "Now, go your ways a-God's name, you are fully payed." "How, my lord," said the old man, "is this cane then worth ten crowns of gold?" "Yes," replied the governor, "otherwise I am the greatest dunce in nature: and, now it shall appear, whether or not I have a noddle sufficient to govern a whole kingdom." So saying, he ordered the cane to be broke in public; and when, in consequence of his command, it was split asunder, ten crowns of gold were found in the heart of it, to the astonishment of all the spectators, who looked upon their new governor as another Solomon. When he was asked how he could conceive that the money was in the cane, he answered, that seeing the deponent give his staff to the other party before he made oath, then hearing him declare that he had really and truly re-turned the money; and lastly, perceiving that after his deposition he took back the staff, it came into his head that the money was concealed within the cane. And in this instance, we see that governors, tho' otherwise fools, are sometimes directed in their decisions by the hand of God: besides, Sancho had heard such a story told by the curate of his vil-lage, and his memory was so tenacious, in retaining every thing he wanted to remem-ber, that there was not such another in the whole island. Finally, the two old men went away; the one overwhelmed with shame, and the other miraculously repayed; the by-standers were astonished, and he whose province it was to record the sayings, actions, and conduct of Sancho, could not determine in his own mind, whether he should regard and report him as a simpleton, or as a sage.

This suit being determined, a woman came into court, holding fast by a man habited like a rich herdsman, and exclaiming with great vociferation, "Justice, my lord gover-nor! justice, which, if I find not on earth, I will go in quest of to heaven! My lord gov-ernor of my soul, this wicked man has forced me in the middle of a field, and made use of my body, as if it had been a dirty dish-clout: alack, and a-well-a-day! he has robbed me of that which I had preserved for three and twenty years, in spite of Moors and chris-tians, natives and foreigners: and, have I, who was always as hard as a cork-tree, main-tained my virtue intire, like a salamander in the midst of flames, or wool among bram-bles, to be handled by the clean hands of this Robin Goodfellow?"[2] "That must be inquired into," said Sancho, "whether the gallant's hands be clean or no." Then turning to the man, he asked what he had to say to the complaint of that woman? To this ques-tion the culprit replied with great perturbation, "My lord, I am a poor herdsman who deals in swine, and this morning went to market, saving your presence, with four hogs, and the duties and extortions, and one thing and another, ran away with almost all they were worth; and so, in my return, I lighted on this honest damsel in the road, and the devil, who will always meddle and make, and have his finger in every pye, yoked us to-gether: I payed her handsomly; but she, not satisfied, laid fast hold on me, nor would she quit her hold until she had brought me hither: she alledges I forced her; but by the oath I have taken, or am to take, she lies: and this is the whole truth, without the least crum of prevarication." Then the governor asked if he had any money about him; and when he owned he had a leathern purse with twenty ducats in his bosom, Sancho or-dered him to pull it out, and deliver the whole to the complainant. The man obeyed this command with fear and trembling; the woman received the money, and making a thou-

sand curtsies to all the bystanders, prayed God would preserve the life and health of my lord governor, who took such care of damsels and orphans in necessity. So saying, she went away, holding the purse with both hands, tho' not before she had examined the contents. Scarce had she quitted the court, when Sancho said to the herdsman, who stood with tears in his eyes, sending his heart, and many a long look after his purse, "Heark ye, friend, go after that woman, and take the purse from her, either by fair means or force, and bring it hither to me." This command was not imposed upon one that was either deaf or doating; for, he darted like lightning, in order to put it in execution: while all the spectators waited in suspence to see the issue of the suit. In a little time, the parties returned, but more closely engaged, and clinging faster together than before; she, with her petticoat tucked up, and the purse in her lap, and he struggling, to no purpose, to take it from her; so vigorously did she defend her acquisition, crying aloud, "Justice, in the name of God and his creatures! Take notice, my lord governor, of the impudence and presumption of this miscreant, who, in the very face of the people, and the middle of the street, wanted to rob me of the purse which I received by your lordship's decree." "Has he taken it from you, then?" said the governor. "Taken it from me!" replied the wench; "I'll sooner part with my life than with my purse. I should be a precious ninny indeed! otherguise cats must scratch my beard, and not such a pitiful muckworm as he. Pincers and hammers, mallets and chissels should not tear it out of my clutches; no, not the claws of a lion; my soul and body shall rather be tore asunder." "It is even so," said the man; "I submit as the weaker vessel, and own I have not strength enough to recover my purse." He quitted her accordingly. Then, the governor said to the woman, "Come hither, my virtuous and spirited dame; let me see thy purse." Which, when she delivered it, he restored to the man; and, turning to the wench, who was too forceful to be forced, "Sister of mine," quoth he, "if you had exerted the same vigour and perseverance, or even half so much, in preserving your chastity, as you have shewn in defending the purse, the force of Hercules would not have forced you. Begone, a-God's name! begone, I say, with a vengeance, and never more appear in this island, or within six leagues of it, on pain of receiving two hundred stripes. Begone immediately, you chattering, shameless impostor." The woman, terrified at his menaces, sneaked off, hanging her head and discontented; and the governor spoke to the man in these words: "Honest friend, get you home with your money, in the name of God; and, unless you are inclined to lose it again, from henceforward avoid all temptations to yoke with any woman whatsoever."

The herdsman thanked him as sheepishly as he could, and went away, and the audience were struck with admiration afresh, at the judgment and decisions of their new governor; every circumstance of which being recorded by his historiographer, was immediately communicated to the duke, who waited for the account with the utmost impatience.

But, here let honest Sancho rest a little: for, we are summoned in all haste by his master, who is greatly disturbed by the music of Altisidora.

## CHAPTER XIV.

Of the dreadful consternation, and cattish concert, to which
Don Quixote was exposed, in the course of the enamoured
Altisidora's amour.

We left the great Don Quixote wrapped up in those cogitations that were suggested by the music of the enamoured damsel Altisidora. With these companions he crept into bed; but, as if they had been fleas and vermin, they would not suffer him to sleep, or indeed enjoy a moment's repose, especially when reinforced with the reflexion of his wounded stocking. But, as time is so light and nimble, that no rub can retard his career, he galloped along upon the hours, and soon ushered in the morning, which was no sooner beheld by the knight, than he forsook the gentle down, and, being the reverse of lazy, dressed himself in his shamoy suit. He put on his travelling boots to conceal the misfortune of his hose; threw his scarlet cloak over his shoulder, cased his head in a green velvet cap trimmed with silver, slung his trusty hanging sword in his buff-belt, took up his large rosary, which always depended from his wrist, and with great port and solemnity went forth into the hall, where the duke and dutchess, already dressed, stayed for him. As he passed through a gallery, he perceived Altisidora, and the other maiden her friend, who stood waiting for his appearance; and, he was no sooner beheld by the love-sick damsel than she pretended to faint away; while her companion received her in her arms, and with all possible dispatch began to unclasp her bosom. The knight seeing her fall, approached the place where they were, saying, "I know whence these accidents proceed." And the companion replied, "I do not know whence—for Altisidora is the healthiest damsel of the whole family; and, I never knew her so much as fetch a sigh, from the first minute of our acquaintance. Ill betide all the knights-errant in the world, if they are all so shy and scornful. Signor Don Quixote, I wish your worship would leave the place; for, this poor girl will not come to herself while you stand here." To this intreaty, the knight replied, "Be so good, madam, as to order a lute to be left in my apartment; and, at night, I will, to the best of my power, console this unfortunate damsel: for, a speedy explanation in the beginning is often an effectual cure for those who are indiscreetly in love." So saying, he went away, that he might not be observed in conference with the damsels; and, scarce was he gone, when the swooning Altisidora coming to herself, said to her companion, "It will be requisite to leave the lute: for, doubtless, Don Quixote intends to entertain us with music, which cannot be bad if he is the performer." Then they went and gave an account of what had passed, and in particular of the lute, to the dutchess, who was rejoiced beyond measure, and concerted with her lord, and her women, how to execute another joke which should be more merry than mischievous. This being accordingly contrived, they with great glee waited for night; and, it came posting along in the same pace that brought in the day, which their graces spent in savoury discourse with Don Quixote. On this day, the dutchess really and truly dis-

patched one of her pages, who had acted the part of the inchanted Dulcinea in the wood, to Teresa Panza, with her husband's letter, and a bundle, which he had left on purpose to be sent home; and the messenger had particular orders to bring back a circumstantial detail of every thing that should pass between him and the governor's lady.

This step being taken, and the hour of eleven at night arrived, Don Quixote found a lute in his apartment; this he tuned, and having opened the window, perceived people walking below in the garden: he immediately ran over the strings of his instrument, making as good a prelude as he could, then hemming and clearing his pipes, he with an hoarse, tho' not untuneful voice, sung the following sonnet which he had that very day composed.

SONG.

Love, with idleness combin'd,
Will unhinge the tender mind:
But to few, to work and move,
Will exclude the force of love.
Blooming maids that would be married,
Must in virtue be unwearied:
Modesty a dow'r will raise,
And be trumpet of their praise.
A cavalier will sport and play
With a damsel frank and gay;
But, when wedlock is his aim,
Choose a maid of sober fame.
Passion kindled in the breast,
By a stranger or a guest,
Enters with the rising sun,
And fleets before his race be run:
Love that comes so suddenly,
Ever on the wing to fly,
Neither can or will impart
Strong impressions to the heart.
Pictures drawn on pictures, shew
Strange confusion to the view:
Second beauty finds no base,
Where a first has taken place:
Then Dulcinea still shall reign
Without a rival or a stain;
Nor shall fate itself controul
Her sway, or blot her from my soul,
Constancy, the lover's boast,
I'll maintain whate'er it cost:
This, my virtue will refine;
This, will stamp my joys divine.

So far had Don Quixote proceeded with his song, which was overheard by the duke and dutchess, Altisidora, and almost all the people in the castle, when all of a sudden, from the top of a corridore immediately above Don Quixote's window, came down a

cord to which above an hundred horse-bells were tied; and, after these was discharged a whole sackful of cats with smaller bells fastened to their tails. Such was the noise occasioned by the tinkling of these bells, and the meawling of the cats, that even the duke and dutchess, who invented the joke, were terrified and confounded, and Don Quixote astonished and dismayed; especially when two or three cats chanced to enter his window, and coursed up and down through his apartment, which seemed to be haunted by a whole legion of devils: for, they extinguished the lights, and ran to and fro, endeavouring to escape, while the rope with the large bells, was lowering down, and pulling up incessantly; so that the greatest part of the people in the family, who were ignorant of the scheme, listened with fear and admiration. Then Don Quixote starting up, and unsheathing his sword, began to fence with the window, exclaiming aloud, "Avaunt, malignant inchanters! avaunt, ye wizzard crew! for, I am Don Quixote de la Mancha, against whom your whole power and malice shall not avail." So saying, he laid about him among the cats which had entered his apartments; and, they sprung towards the casement, from whence two of them made their escape: but, the third finding itself hard pressed by the valour and backstrokes of the knight, flew at his face, and laid fast hold on his nose with its teeth and claws. The pain of this assault affected Don Quixote in such a manner, that he began to roar with vast vociferation, which being heard by the duke and dutchess, who guessed the cause of his cries, they ran instantly to his chamber, which they opened with a master-key; and lights being brought, they found the poor knight endeavouring with all his strength to disengage the cat from his visage. Seeing the unequal fray, made haste to part the combatants; when Don Quixote called aloud, "Let no man part us; but, leave me hand to hand, with this demon, this wizzard, this inchanter; and, I will make him sensible of the difference between him and me, who am Don Quixote de la Mancha." The cat, however, without minding his threats, stuck fast to his nose; but, at length, the duke tore it away, and threw it out at the window: so that the knight remained with his face like a sieve, and his nose in no very sound condition; tho' he was very much dissatisfied, that they would not suffer him to finish the engagement he had so obstinately maintained with that felonious inchanter.

Oil of Aparicio was immediately fetched, and Altisidora herself, with her snowy hands, applied the balsam, saying in a low voice as she bound up his wounds, "All these misadventures befal thee, hard-hearted knight, as a punishment for thy cruelty and disdain; and, God grant, thy squire Sancho may forget to scourge himself, that thy so much beloved Dulcinea may never be disinchanted, nor thou enjoy her as a wedded wife; at least, during the life of me, by whom thou art adored." To all this apostrophe Don Quixote answered not a word; but, heaving a profound sigh, laid himself along in his bed, and thanked their graces for this instance of their concern; not that he was afraid of such a cattish-inchanting, and bell-ringing crew; but, on account of the kind intention they had manifested in coming to his relief. As for the duke and dutchess, they left him to his repose, and went away extremely sorry for the unfortunate issue of their joke; for, they did not think Don Quixote would have suffered so terribly by the adventure, which cost him five days confinement in his bed; where he was engaged in another still more diverting, which, however, the historian will not at present recount, that he may return to Sancho Panza, who proceeded in his administration with equal pleasantry and solicitude.

Sancho Panza at Dinner.

## CHAPTER XV.

# Containing a further account of Sancho's behaviour in his government.

The history relates, that from the town-hall Sancho Panza was conducted to a sumptuous palace, in the great hall of which was a royal table most elegantly furnished: when the governor entered, the waits struck up, and four pages came forth and presented him with water for his hands, which he received with great solemnity; then the music ceasing, he took his place at the upper end of the table, which was accommodated with one seat only, and a cover for himself alone: while close by him stood a personage, who afterwards proved to be a physician, with a rod of whalebone in his hand. They removed a very fine white cloth that covered the fruit and a great variety of dishes: one who looked like a student, said grace; a page tucked a laced bib under Sancho's chin; and, another person, who acted the part of sewer, set a plate of fruit before the governor: but, scarce had he swallowed a mouthful; when the doctor touching the said plate with his wand, it was snatched from him in a twinkling: the sewer presented him with another dish, which the governor resolved to prove; but, before he could finger or taste it, the plate being also touched by the wand, one of the pages conveyed it away with incredible dispatch, to the amazement of Sancho, who, looking around him, asked if he must be obliged to eat like a juggler, by slight of hand?

To this interrogation, he of the wand replied: "My lord governor must, in eating, conform to the use and customs of other islands where governors reside. I, my lord, enjoy a salary as physician to the governors of this island, and take more care of their health than of my own; studying night and day, and considering the governor's constitution, that I may be able to cure him, in case he should be taken ill; but, the principal part of my office is to be present at his meals, where I allow him to eat what I think will agree with his complexion, and restrain him from that which I conceive will be hurtful and prejudicial to his stomach. I, therefore, ordered the fruit to be removed, because it is dangerously moist; and, likewise, commanded the other dish to be conveyed away, because it is excessively hot, as containing a number of spices which create thirst, and copious drinking drowns and destroys the radical moisture, which is the essence of life." "By that way of reasoning," said Sancho, "that there dish of roasted partridges, which seem to be very well season'd, will do me no harm." To this hint, the physician replied: "Of these, my lord governor shall not eat while there is breath in my body." "And, pray for what reason?" said the governor. "Because our master Hippocrates, the north star and luminary of physic, expressly says, in one of his aphorisms, Omnis saturatio mala, perdix autem pessima;[1] that is, All repletion is bad, but that with partridge worst of all." "If that be the case," said Sancho, "good Mr. doctor, pray examine all the messes on the table, so as to point out that which will do me least harm and most good, that I may eat without fear of conjuration; for, by the life of the governor, and as God shall prolong it! I am ready to die of hunger; and to deny me victuals, even tho' signor doctor should pre-

scribe fasting, and say a thousand things in its praise, will, instead of preserving my health, deprive me of life intirely." "Your lordship is very much in the right," replied the physician: "and, to begin, I would not have you touch these ragoo'd rabbits, because they are a sharp-haired food: of that veal, indeed, you might pick a little, if it was not roasted a-la-daube; but, as it is, touch it not." "The dish that smoaks yonder," said Sancho, "seems to be an Olla podrida, and considering the variety of ingredients of which these Ollas are composed, surely I cannot fail to light on something that will be both savoury and wholesome." "Absit!" cried the physician, "far from us be such a thought. There is not a more pernicious nutriment upon the face of the earth: leave your Ollas to canons, rectors of colleges, and country weddings; but, let them never appear upon the tables of governors, where elegance and neatness ought to reign. The reason is clear; at all times, in all places, and by all the learned, simple medicines are more esteemed than those that are compound: for, in the first, no mistakes can be committed; whereas, in the other, numberless errors may take place, in the quantity and proportion of the ingredients; but, what I would advise my lord governor to eat at present, in order to preserve and corroborate his health, is about an hundred confected wafers, and a few thin slices of quinces, which will sit easy on his stomach, and assist digestion."

Sancho hearing this prescription, threw himself backwards in his chair, and surveying the physician from head to foot, asked in a grave and solemn tone, what was his name, and where he had studied? To this question the other replied, "I, my lord governor, am called doctor Pedro * Positive de Bode-well, native of a place called Snatchaway, on the right-hand between Caraquel and Almodobar del Campo; and, I took my doctor's degree at the university of Osuna." To this declaration Sancho replied, in a rage, "Heark ye then, Mr. doctor Pedro Positive de Bode-ill, native of Snatchaway, which is on the right hand as we go from Caraquel to Almodobar del Campo, graduate of Ossuna, get out of my presence this instant, or by the body of the sun! I will snatch up a cudgel, and beginning with you, employ it in such a manner as not to leave a physician on the whole island; of those I mean who are ignorant fellows; as for the learned, virtuous, and discreet members of the faculty, I will place them on my head, in token of respect, and honour them as things divine. But, I say again, begone doctor Pedro Positive, or positively I will take up this chair on which I sit, and make immediate application to your skull; and, should I be called to account for it, when I resign my government, I will exculpate myself by proving that I have done service to God, in slaying a wicked physician, who was a scandal to the commonwealth. Let me have something to eat therefore, or take back your government; for, a post that will not afford victuals, is not worth a pease-cod."

The doctor was frightened at seeing the governor in such a passion, and was going to snatch himself away from his presence,[3] when, at the very instant, their ears were saluted with the noise of a post-boy's horn in the street; and, the gentleman sewer going to the window, informed the governor that there was a courier arrived from my lord duke, with some dispatches of importance. Accordingly, the messenger entered the hall, sweating,

---

* The Spanish name is *Pedro Rezio de Aguiero;* which, together with *Tirte Afuera,* the place of his nativity, I have translated into English, that the humour may be better understood.[2]

with marks of consternation in his countenance; and, taking a packet out of his bosom, delivered it into the hands of the governor, who gave it to the steward, with orders to read the superscription, which ran thus: "To Don Sancho Panza, governor of the island Barataria, to be delivered into his own hand, or that of his secretary." Sancho hearing the direction, "Who is my secretary?" said he. One of the people who were present, answered, "I am secretary, my lord; for, I can read, and write, and am a Biscayan." "Nay, with that addition," said Sancho, "you might be secretary to the emperor himself: open this packet, and see what it contains." The new-born secretary obeyed the command; and, having perused the contents, told his excellency, it was business for his private ear. Then Sancho ordered every body to quit the place, except the steward, and gentleman sewer: accordingly the rest retired, with the doctor at their head; and the secretary recited the letter to this effect:

"I have received information, signor Don Sancho Panza, that certain enemies of mine and of the island, intend one of these nights, to give you a furious assault; you will therefore be vigilant and alert, that they may not find you unprepared. I am likewise informed, by trusty spies, that four persons in disguise have entered the town, with intention to take away your life, as they dread the extent of your abilities: be upon your guard, therefore, examine every person who comes to speak with you, and taste nothing that comes in a present. I will take care to reinforce you, should you stand in need of assistance; mean while, you will act in every thing according to the good opinion I have of your understanding.

From my castle, August 16th.                    Your friend, The Duke."
    at four in the morning.

This epistle overwhelmed Sancho with astonishment, which the rest pretended to share; and turning to the steward, "What is to be done," said he, "and that immediately, is to confine doctor Positive in a dungeon; for, if any body has a design to take away my life, he is the man; ay, and by the most pitiful, and worst of all deaths; namely, hunger." "True," replied the gentleman sewer; "and, in my opinion, your lordship ought not to eat any of the victuals now on the table, for they were a present from certain nuns; and, as the saying is, The devil skulks behind the cross." "That is a truth not to be denied," said Sancho; "but, in the mean time, let me have a luncheon of bread, and about four pounds of raisins, which cannot be poisoned; for, really and truly, I cannot live without eating; and, if we must be prepared for those battles with which we are threatened, at least, let us be well fed; for, the stomach supports the heart, and not the heart the stomach. You, secretary, must write an answer to my lord duke; and tell him his commands shall be obeyed to a tittle. You shall likewise make my compliments to my lady dutchess, beseeching her, in my name, to remember to send an express, with my letter and bundle, to my wife Teresa Panza; in so doing she will lay me under great obligation, and I shall take care to be her humble servant to the utmost of my power. By the bye, you may thrust in a how d'ye to my master Don Quixote de la Mancha, that he may see I am not of an ungrateful leaven; and you, as a faithful secretary, and honest Biscayan, may add what you shall think proper, and most likely to turn out to advantage. At present, take away these things, and let me have something to eat; and I shall manage any spies, murderers, or inchanters, that may presume to attack me or my island."

Here he was interrupted by a page, who, coming into the hall, told him there was a countryman without, who wanted to speak with his lordship upon some business of the utmost importance. "Those people of business are strange fellows," said Sancho; "is it possible they are so ignorant, as not to see that this is not a proper hour for the transaction of business? Mayhap they think, we governors, and judges, are not made of flesh and blood, and therefore require no time for refreshment, any more than if we were created of marble.—As I shall answer to God! if my government holds (tho' I begin to perceive it will not be of long duration) I will sit upon * the skirts of more than one of these men of business. At present, tell that honest man to come; but, first of all, take care that he is not one of the spies or murderers." "There is no occasion, my lord," answered the page; "for, he seems to be a simple soul,⁵ and either I am very much mistaken, or he is as honest as a well weighed loaf."⁶ "While we are present," said the steward, "there is nothing to fear." "Mr. sewer," said Sancho, "now that doctor Pedro Positive is not here, might not I eat something substantial, even tho' it should be nothing better than a luncheon of bread, and an onion?" "This night your supper shall make amends for the defect of dinner, so as that your lordship shall be perfectly well pleased, and satisfied," replied the sewer. "God grant I may be so," quoth the governor.

At that instant the countryman entered the hall, of a goodly presence, and indeed one might have seen that he was an honest soul, even at the distance of a thousand leagues. The first thing he said, was, "Which of all this company is my lord governor?" "Who should be governor," replied the secretary, "but he who sits in the chair?" "Then, I humble myself before him," said the peasant; who, falling on his knees, begged leave to kiss his lordship's hand. This request, however, Sancho would not grant; but ordered him to rise, and explain his business. Accordingly, the countryman getting up, "My lord," said he, "I am a husbandman belonging to Miguel Turra, a place about two leagues from Ciudad Real." "What! have we got another Snatchaway?" cried Sancho: "proceed, brother; for I can tell you, that I am very well acquainted with Miguel Turra, which is not far from our own village." "This here then is the case, my lord," said the countryman: "By the mercy of God, I was married in peace, and in the face of the holy roman catholic church; and I have two sons now at college, the youngest of whom is to be a batchelor, and the elder is intended for a licentiate. I am a widower; for my wife died, or rather she was killed, by a wicked physician, who gave her a purge when she was big with child; and, had it pleased God, that the fruit of her womb had come to light, and had been a boy, I would have bred him up a doctor, that he might not have envied his brothers, the batchelor and licentiate." "So then," said Sancho, "if your wife had not died, or been killed, in all likelihood, you should not now be a widower." "No, my lord, by no manner of means," answered the countryman. "Agad!" cried Sancho, "we are in a thriving way. Pray, go on, brother; for, this is an hour more proper for sleep than for business." "Well then," replied the countryman, "this son of mine, who is to be bred a batchelor, became enamoured of a young lady of the same town, called Clara Paralina †,

* The original *Ponga en pretina*, signifies, I will put in my girdle.⁴
† She is in the original called *Perlerina*, which I have changed into *Paralina*, in order to preserve the subsequent play on the words.⁷

daughter of Andrew Paralino, a very wealthy yeoman; and, this name of Paralino, does not come from their pedigree, or any family descent; but, they have acquired it, because the whole race of them is Paralytic: and so, in order to improve the sound, they are called Paralino; tho', to say the truth, the young lady is a perfect oriental pearl, and, when you look at her, on her right side, seems to be a very flower of the field; on the left indeed she is not quite so amiable, being blind of an eye which she lost in the small-pox: and, although the pits in her face are very large and numerous, her admirers say that these are not pits, but graves, in which the hearts of her lovers are buried. Then she is so cleanly, that to prevent her face from being defiled, she carries her nose cocked up, as the saying is, so that it seems to be running away from her mouth: yet, for all that, she is extremely beautiful, for she has a very wide mouth, and if she did not want some ten or a dozen teeth, might pass for a very phoenix of beauty. Of her lips I shall say nothing; but, they are so thin, and delicate, that if it was the custom to reel lips, they might be made up into a skein; but, as they are of a different colour from common lips, they appear quite miraculous; for, they contain a mixture of blue, green, and orange tawny. My lord governor will pardon me, for painting so exactly the parts of her who is to be my daughter, for I love her exceedingly, and like to dwell upon the subject." "Paint what you will," said Sancho; "for my own part, I am hugely delighted with your description, and, if I had dined, should not desire a better desert than the picture you have drawn." "That shall be always at your service," replied the countryman; "and, though we are not at present known to each other, the time will come when we shall be better acquainted. And now, my lord, if I could describe her genteel deportment, and tall stature, you would be struck with admiration: but that is an impossible task, because she is so doubled, and bent, that her knees touch her mouth; and yet, for all that, one may see with half an eye, that if she could stand upright, her head would touch the cieling; and she would have given her hand in marriage to my batchelor before this time, if she could have stretched it out, but it happens to be shrunk and withered; tho', by the long channeled nails, one may easily perceive the beauty of its form and texture."

"Very well," said Sancho. "Now, brother, let us suppose you have painted her from head to foot: tell me what is your request? and come to the point, without going about the bush, through lanes and alleys, with a parcel of scraps and circumlocutions." "Well then, my lord," replied the countryman, "my request is, that you would give me a letter of recommendation to the young lady's father, intreating him to give his consent to the match, as the parties are pretty equal in the gifts of fortune, and of nature; for, to say the truth, my lord governor, my son is possessed, and scarce a day passes, but he is three or four times tormented by the foul fiend; and, in consequence of having once fallen into the fire, his face is shrivelled up like a skin of parchment, and his eyes are bleared, and run woundily: but yet, he has the temper of an angel, and if he did not beat and buffet himself, he would be a perfect saint." "Do you want any thing else, honest friend?" replied Sancho. "I did want something else," said the countryman, "but I dare not be so bold as to mention it: but, out it shall go; for, take or not take, it shall never rot in my belly. Why then, my lord, I wish your lordship would bestow three or six hundred ducats, to help to set up my batchelor; I mean, to furnish his house; for, the truth is, the young couple are to live by themselves, without being subject to the peevishness of us

old folks." "Consider if you want any thing else," said Sancho, "and speak without bashfulness or restraint." "Truly, I want nothing else," replied the countryman. Scarce had he pronounced these words, when the governor starting up, and laying hold on the chair that was under him, exclaimed, "I vow to God, you don lubberly, rascally rustic, if you don't get you gone, and abscond from my presence this instant, I will with this chair demolish your skull, you knavish son of a whore, and painter for the devil himself; is this a time to come and demand six hundred ducats? Where the devil should I find them, you stinkard? or if I had found them, why the devil should I give them to you, you idiotical scoundrel? What a pox have I to do with Miguel Turra, or any of the generation of the Paralinos? Begone, I say, or by the life of my lord duke, I'll be as good as my word: thou art no native of Miguel Turra, but some fiend sent from hell to torment me: heark ye, miscreant, I have been governor but a day and a half, and you would have me already in possession of six hundred ducats!"

The gentleman sewer made signs to the countryman to leave the place; and he accordingly quitted the hall, hanging his head, and seemingly afraid that the governor would execute his threats; for, the rogue acted his part to admiration. But, let us leave Sancho's indignation to cool, and peace attend him in his career, while we return to Don Quixote, whom we left with his face bandaged up for the cure of his cattish wounds, which were not healed in the space of eight days; and in that time an adventure happened to him, which Cid Hamet promises to recount, with that truth and punctuality he has hitherto maintained, in recording even the most trivial and minute incidents of this authentic history.

## CHAPTER XVI.

## Of Don Quixote's adventure with Donna Rodriguez, the dutchess's duenna; and other incidents worthy of eternal fame.

Exceedingly peevish and melancholy, was the sore wounded Don Quixote, with his face bandaged and marked—not by the hand of his maker, but by the claws of a cat; and indeed, such misfortunes are annexed to chivalry. Six days did he remain in his chamber, without appearing in public; and, during this time it was, that one night, while he lay watchful and awake, musing upon his disaster, and the persecution of Altisidora, he heard a key turning in the door of his apartment, and straight imagined the enamoured damsel was come to surprize his chastity, and tempt him to forego the fidelity he owed to his mistress Dulcinea del Toboso. On this supposition he pronounced with an audible voice, "No! the greatest beauty upon earth shall never have such an effect as to interfere with my adoration of her, who is impressed and engraved in the midst of my heart, and in the depth of my bowels! No, my dear mistress! whether thou art transformed into a garlic-eating wench, or as a nymph of the golden Tagus, art weaving webs

of gold and silver twist: whether thou art in the power of Merlin or Montesinos; where-soever thou mayest be, mine thou art, and, wheresoever I am, I must be thine." This ejaculation being uttered just as the door opened, he stood upright in his bed, wrapped up in a quilt of yellow silk, with a woolen night-cap on his head, his face and whiskers being bound up; the first, on account of the scratches he had received, and the last, in order to preserve the buckle;[1] and, in this equipage, he appeared the most extraordinary phantom that the imagination can conceive. His eyes were fixed upon the door, and when he expected to see the yielding, and afflicted Altisidora enter, he beheld a most reverend duenna, with a white hemmed veil, so long as to cover her from head to foot. Between the fingers of her left hand, she held a lighted candle's end, and with her right she formed a shade to keep the glare from her eyes, which were furnished with large spectacles; and, in this trim, she came treading very softly, and moving her feet with great tranquillity as she advanced. Don Quixote surveyed her from his post, and mark-ing her silence and appearance, concluded she was some hag or sorceress, come in that equipage to annoy him; and, in this opinion, he began to cross himself with great ea-gerness and devotion. The apparition advancing to the middle of the chamber, and lift-ing up its eyes, perceived the knight busily employed in these devout precautions, if he was afraid at sight of her, she was no less terrified at his figure; for, seeing him so tall and yellow, wrapped up in the quilt, and disfigured by the bandages, she cried aloud, "O Jesus! what do I see?" and in the surprise dropped the candle. Finding herself now in the dark, she attempted to make her retreat, and treading upon her own skirts in the confu-sion of her fear, she stumbled and fell to the ground: while Don Quixote, sweating with terror, began to ejaculate, "I conjure thee, O phantom, or whatever thou mayest be, to tell me who thou art, and what thou would'st have. If thou art a perturbed spirit,[2] let me know, and I will do all that lies in my power to give thee relief; for, I am a catholic chris-tian, well disposed to befriend all mankind; and, in consequence of this disposition, I received the order of knight-errantry, which I now profess; and, the exercise of that pro-fession, extends even so far as to give assistance to souls in purgatory."

The duenna, bruised as she was with her fall, hearing herself exorcised in this man-ner, guessed from her own fear, the terrors of Don Quixote, and in a low and plaintive tone replied, "Signor Don Quixote, I am no phantome, apparition, or soul in purgatory, as your worship seems to suppose, but Donna Rodriguez, chief duenna to my lady dutchess, and I come with one of those necessitous cases which your worship is wont to remedy." "Pray, tell me, signora Donna Rodriguez," said Don Quixote, "are you come in the office of a go-between? because, I would have you to know, that I am altogether unfit for any such commerce, thanks to the peerless beauty of my own mistress Dulcinea del Toboso. Finally, I say unto you, signora Donna Rodriguez, if you will suppress, and lay aside, all amorous messages, you may go and light your candle, and return; and we will discourse upon any subject you shall think proper to introduce, saving, as I have al-ready observed, all your dainty incitements." "Signor," answered the duenna, "I carry messages for no person. Your worship is but little acquainted with my character. Nor am I so stricken in years as to take to those fooleries; for, God be praised! there is still some soul in my body, and my teeth, grinders and all, are still in my head, except a very few I have lost by the rheums that are so rife in this country of Arragon: but, if your wor-

ship will wait a minute, I will go and light my candle, and return in an instant, and then I shall recount my disaster to you, as the physician of all disasters upon earth."

So saying, she, without waiting for an answer, quitted the apartment, where the knight waited for her, in the utmost suspence and concern: then being assaulted by a thousand reflections upon this new adventure, he began to think it would be very indiscreet, even so much as to dream of exposing himself to the danger of breaking his fidelity to his own mistress. "Who knows," said he to himself, "but the devil, who is equally crafty and dextrous, intends at present to seduce me by means of a duenna, after having in vain attempted me, with empresses, queens, dutchesses, marquesses, and countesses? for I have often heard it observed by a number of people of good understanding, that he will never give you an high nose, if a flat nose will serve your turn:³ and who knows but this solitude, opportunity, and silence, may waken those desires in me which are now asleep, and compel me at these years to fall, where hitherto I never so much as stumbled? In such emergencies, it is surely better to avoid than await the battle. And yet, I must certainly be deprived of my senses, to talk and think at this rate; for, it is absolutely impossible, that a long, meagre, white veiled, and spectacled duenna, should move or excite a lascivious thought in the lewdest bosom upon earth. Is there, for example, a duenna in nature, who has a tolerable person? Is there a duenna upon this our globe, who is not wrinkled, loathsome, and impertinent? Avaunt then, ye duennian tribe, unfit for any human entertainment! Praise be to that lady who is said to have had at one end of her sopha two marble duennas, with their spectacles and bobbin cushions, in the attitude of working; and these statues fulfilled the dignity of the apartment, as well as if they had been duennas of flesh and blood."

So saying, he started from his bed, with intention to lock the door, and deny admittance to signora Rodriguez; but, before he could execute his resolution, that lady had returned with a lighted wax-taper, and seeing Don Quixote so near her, with his quilt, bandages, night-cap or hood, she was again affrighted, and retired backwards a couple of paces, saying, "Am I safe, sir knight? for, your worship's getting out of bed, is no great sign of virtue, me thinks." "Madam," replied Don Quixote, "I ought to ask you the same question; and I do accordingly ask, whether or not I am safe from assault and ravishment?" "Of whom, or from whom, do you demand that security, sir knight?" said the duenna. "Of you, and from you, and you alone," answered Don Quixote: "for, I am not made of marble, nor you of brass; nor is it now ten o'clock in the forenoon, but midnight, and something more, if I am not mistaken; and we are here in a more close and secret apartment than the cave in which the treacherous, and daring Æneas, enjoyed the beautiful and tender hearted Dido: yet give me your hand, madam; for, I require no other security than my own reserve and continence, together with the appearance of that most reverend veil."

So saying, he kissed his right hand, and took hold of her's, which she presented with the like ceremony.

Here Cid Hamet, in a parenthesis, swears by Mahomet, that to have seen these two originals thus linked, and walking from the door to the bed, he would have given the best of his two jackets.

The Duenna Rodriguez Entering Don Quixote's Bedchamber.

At length Don Quixote slipped into bed, and Donna Rodriguez seated herself in a chair at some distance from it, without quitting her spectacles or candle: then the knight shrunk under the clothes, with which he covered himself in such a manner that nothing but his face appeared; and both parties having composed themselves, the first who broke silence was Don Quixote, who accosted her in these words: "Now, madam duenna Rodriguez, you may unrip, and unload, all that lies upon your sorrowful heart, and afflicted bowels; and I shall listen to your grievances with chaste ears, and redress them with generous works." "I believe as much," said the duenna; "for, from the genteel and agreeable presence of your worship, I could expect no other than such a christian reply.

"This then, is the case, signor Don Quixote; although your worship now sees me seated in this chair, in the midst of Arragon, and in the dress of a contemptible and injured duenna, I was born in the Asturias, of Oviedo, of a family which intermarried with many of the best in that province; but my niggardly fate, and the extravagance of my parents, who came to untimely want, without knowing how or wherefore, drove me to the court of Madrid, where, for the sake of peace, and in order to prevent greater misfortunes, my parents provided me with the place of needlewoman, in the service of a lady of quality; and, I would have your worship to know, that in making knitting-sheaths and plain work, no person had ever the advantage of me in the whole course of my life. As for my parents, after they had seen me settled in this place, they returned to the country, and in a few years went to heaven; for, they were exceeding good catholic christians. Mean while, I was left an orphan, stinted to the wretched salary, and pitiful wages, commonly given to such servants in great families; and so, about that time, a squire of the house fell in love with me, tho' I am sure I gave him no occasion. He was a man already well stricken in years, with a venerable beard, and of a comely appearance, and besides, as good a gentleman as the king; for, he was a mountaineer. We did not correspond so secretly but our intrigue came to the knowledge of my lady, who, waving all questions and commands, caused us to be married in peace, and in the face of our holy mother the roman catholic church. The fruit of this marriage was a daughter, who was the death of my good fortune, if any such I had: not that I died in child-bed; on the contrary, I was safely and seasonably delivered; but because, soon after that event, my poor husband died of a fright; and, if I had now time to recount the manner, I know your worship would be struck with admiration."

Here she began to weep most bitterly, and thus proceeded: "Your worship, signor Don Quixote, will pardon me for not being able to contain myself; for, as often as I remember my unfortunate husband, mine eyes run over. God be my comfort! with what dignity did he ride before my lady, on a mighty mule as black as jet: for, at that time, they did not use coaches or chairs, which, they say, are now in fashion; and the ladies always rode behind their squires. This one circumstance, however, I cannot help recounting, because it demonstrates the good breeding and punctilio of my worthy spouse. One day, as he entered the street of St. Jago, in Madrid, which is but narrow, he happened to meet a judge, preceded by two of his officers; and my good squire no sooner beheld him, than he turned his mule, in order to attend his worship. My lady, who sat behind him, said in a whisper, 'Blockhead, what are you going to do? don't you know that I am here?' while the judge, out of politeness, stopped his horse, saying, 'Pray proceed, signor; for, it is

rather my duty to attend my lady Donna Casilda'; that was the name of my mistress. Nevertheless, my husband still persisted, with his cap in hand, in his resolution to attend the judge; and my lady, enraged at his obstinacy, pulled out a large pin, or rather, I believe, a bodkin, from her tweezer-case, and thrust it into his loins; so that my poor man roared aloud, and writhed his body in such a manner, that both he and my lady came to the ground. Her two lacquies ran immediately to lift her up, and were assisted by the judge and his officers. The whole gate of Guadalajara, I mean the idle people about it, were in an uproar: my lady came home a-foot, and my husband hastened to a surgeon, declaring he was thrust through the bowels. His great courtesy soon became public, in so much that the very children mocked him in the street; for which reason, and because he was a little short-sighted, my lady dismissed him from her service; and he took his dismission so much to heart, that I am positively certain it was the cause of his death. Thus was I left a forlorn widow, with a daughter upon my hands, who, as she grew up, increased in beauty, like the foam of the sea. In a word, as I had the character of being an excellent needle-woman, my lady dutchess, who was just then married to my lord duke, carried me and my daughter, without more ado, along with her to this kingdom of Arragon; where, in process of time, my child improved in all manner of accomplishments; she sings like any sky lark, dances light as thought, cuts a caper as if she was mad, reads and writes like a school-master, and casts accounts like a miser. I say nothing of her cleanliness, for the running water is not more pure; and, if my memory does not fail me, she is now sixteen years, five months, and three days, perhaps one over or under. In a word, this maiden of mine captivated the son of a rich farmer, who lives in a village not far from hence, belonging to my lord duke; and so, the young couple meeting, I know not where nor how, he, under promise of marriage played the rogue with my daughter, and refuses to perform his promise: and although my lord duke is well acquainted with the affair; for, you must know, I complained to him—not once, but divers and sundry times, desiring he would order the young farmer to take my daughter to wife; he lends a deaf ear to my complaint, and, indeed, will scarce give me a hearing, because, forsooth, the young rogue's father is extremely rich, and lends him money; nay, becomes surety for him when he happens to be in trouble: so that he will, by no manner of means, give him the least umbrage or disgust. Now, dear sir, my request is that your worship would undertake to redress this grievance, either by intreaty or force of arms; for, as all the world says, your worship was born for such purposes, to rectify wrongs, and protect the wretched. And I beg your worship will consider the orphan state of my daughter, her gentility, her youth, and all those good qualities which, I have told you, she possesses: for, in the sight of heaven, and in my own conscience, I dare aver, that of all the damsels belonging to my lady dutchess, there is not one that comes up to the sole of her shoe: and tho' she, whom they call Altisidora, is reckoned the most sprightly and good humoured, when compared to my daughter, she does not come within two leagues of her; for, your worship must know, signor, all is not gold that glitters. This same creature Altisidora has more forwardness than beauty, and more airiness than modesty: besides, she is not over and above wholesome; her breath has such a flavour that no body can be near her; no, not for a moment; and even my lady dutchess—but, mum for that: Walls have ears, as the saying is."

"What of my lady dutchess?" cried Don Quixote. "Signora Donna Rodriguez, I con-jure you tell me, by the life of my soul." "Nay, if you conjure me in that manner," an-swered the duenna, "I cannot help telling the truth. Signor Don Quixote, your worship has, no doubt, perceived the beauty of my lady dutchess; that freshness of complexion that shines like polished steel, those cheeks of milk and crimson, with the sun on one side, and the moon on the other, and that gaiety with which she treads, or rather dis-dains the ground, seeming to diffuse health and joy wheresoever she walks. Well then, your worship must know, that she may thank God, in the first place; and, secondly, two issues in her legs, that discharge the bad humours with which the doctors say she abounds." "Blessed virgin!" cried the knight, "is it possible that my lady dutchess should have occasion for such sluices? I would hardly believe the bare-footed friars, should they make the assertion; yet, since Donna Rodriguez avers it, there is no reason to doubt: but, from those issues, surely nothing but liquid amber can flow; and, in good sooth, I am now fully convinced that the use of issues must be a matter of great importance to the preservation of health."

Scarce had Don Quixote pronounced these words, when the chamber-door flew open, with a sudden slap, which surprised and disordered the duenna to such a degree, that she dropped the candle, and in a moment the apartment was dark as a dog's mouth,[4] as the saying is. Immediately, the poor duenna felt her throat assaulted by two hands, which pressed it so close that she could not squeak, while another person, with incred-ible dispatch, and in great silence, turned up her petticoats, and with something like a slipper, began to make such application to her posterior parts, that she was in a most piteous taking. Although Don Quixote compassionated her case, he stirred not from his bed, as he did not know the nature of the assault, but lay snug and silent, in great fear that the same discipline would come round and sound to his own carcase. Nor was his apprehension altogether groundless; for, the silent executioners having severely flogged the duenna, who durst not complain, advanced to Don Quixote; and, stripping off the sheets and the quilt, pinched him so fast, and so smartly, that he could not forbear de-fending himself by dint of fist; and the whole affair was transacted in wonderful silence. The battle having lasted about half an hour, the phantoms vanished, Donna Rodriguez adjusted her petticoats, and groaning over her misfortune, sneaked away, without speaking a syllable to the knight, who remained alone, full of pains and pinches, sorrow and confusion. And here we will leave him, burning with desire to know who the per-verse inchanter was, who had used him in such a cruel manner; but, that secret shall be revealed in due season. Mean while, we are summoned by Sancho Panza; and the ex-cellent plan of our history obliges us to obey his call.

## CHAPTER XVII.

# Of what happened to Sancho Panza, in going the round of his island.

We left the great governor out of humour, and enraged at that same painting coun-try-wag, who had received his cue from the duke's steward and gentleman sewer, sent thither on purpose to make merry at his expence: nevertheless, he held out toughly against the whole combination, Rude, and brood, and simple as he stood; and addressing himself to all present, and among the rest to doctor Pedro Positive, who, after the duke's letter was read, had returned to the hall, "Now," said he, "I am fully convinced that judges and governors are, or ought to be made of brass, so as that they may not feel the impor-tunity of people of business, who expect to be heard, and dispatched, at all hours and at all seasons, come what will, attending only to their own affairs; and if the poor devil of a judge does not hear and dispatch them, either because it is not in his power, or it happens to be an unseasonable time for giving audience, then they grumble and backbite, gnaw him to the very bones, and even bespatter his whole generation. Ignorant man of busi-ness! foolish man of business! be not in such a violent hurry; wait for the proper season and conjuncture, and come not at meals and sleeping time; for, judges are made of flesh and blood, and must give to nature that which nature requires, excepting myself, un-happy wretch that I am! who cannot indulge my appetite, thanks to doctor Pedro Posi-tive Snatchaway here present, who intends that I shall die of hunger, and affirms that such a death is good living, which I pray to God may fall to the share of him and all of his kidney; I mean, bad physicians; as for the good, they deserve palms and laurels."

Every body who knew Sancho was struck with admiration at hearing him talk so el-egantly, and could not account for his improvement any other way, than by supposing that posts and places of importance enlarge the faculties of some, while they stupify the understanding of others. Finally, doctor Pedro Positive Bodewell de Snatchaway prom-ised to indulge his excellency with a plentiful supper at night, even tho' he should trans-gress all the aphorisms of Hippocrates. The governor rested satisfied with this declara-tion, waiting for the approach of night and supper with great impatience; and although time seemed to stand stock-still, the wished-for hour at length arrived, when they treated him with an hachis[1] of beef well onioned, and some calves feet not very fresh: nevertheless, he attacked these dishes with more relish than if he had been served with Milan godwits, Roman pheasants, Sorrento veal, partridges of Moron, or geese of Lava-jos: and, in the midst of supper, turning towards his physician, "Take notice, doctor," said he, "that from henceforth you need not take the trouble to provide dainties and del-icate dishes for me; they will only serve to unhinge my stomach, which is used to goats-flesh, cow-beef and bacon, with turnips and onions; and, if by accident it chances to re-ceive any of your tit-bits, it contains them with loathing, and sometimes throws them up: but, master sewer may bring me those dishes called olla podridas; and the * staler

---

* *Podrida* signifies rotten or mortified: hence the *olla podrida* is, in French, stiled *Pot-pourri*.[2]

they are, so much the better; in one of these, he may crowd and cram all the eatables he can think of, and I will thank him for his pains; nay, one day or other, I shall make him amends: and let no man play the rogue with me: either we are or we are not; let us live and eat in harmony and peace; for, when God sends the morning, the light shines upon all. I will govern this island without favour or corruption: and let every body keep a good look-out, and mind his own affairs; for, I would have you to know, the devil's in the dice *, and if you give me cause, you shall see wonders—yes, yes: make yourself honey, and the flies will bite."

"Assuredly, my lord governor," said the steward, "your lordship hath said nothing but the truth; and, I promise, in the name of all the islanders of this island, to serve your lordship with perfect love, benevolence and punctuality: for, the agreeable sample of government which your lordship hath given in the beginning, leaves us no room to do or even to conceive any thing that shall redound to the disgust and detriment of your honour." "I believe what you say," replied Sancho; "and, indeed, they must be fools to think or act any otherwise. And I say again, let the maintenance of me and my Dapple be taken care of; for, that is the main point in this business: and, when the time comes, let us go and make the round; my intention is to clear the island from all sort of filth, such as vagabonds, idlers, and immoral people: for, I would have you to know, my friends, that your idle and lazy fellows are the same in a commonwealth as drones in a bee-hive, that consume the honey which the industrious labourers have made. My resolution is to protect the farmers and handicrafts-men, maintain the prerogative of gentlemen, re-ward virtue; and, above all things, respect religion and the honour of the clergy. Tell me, my friends, what is your opinion of my plan? Does it smack of something? or do I thresh my skull to no purpose?" "My lord governor," said the steward, "your lordship speaks so much to the purpose, that I am struck with admiration, to hear a man so illiterate as your worship (for, I believe you do not know your letters) make so many observations full of sagacity, and give counsel so much above every thing that was expected from your lord-ship's capacity, by those who sent us, as well as by ourselves who are come hither. Every day produces something new: jokes are turned into earnest, and the biters are bit."

Night being come, and the governor having supped with the good leave of doctor Pe-dro, they prepared for going the round. Accordingly his excellency went forth, accom-panied by the steward, notary, gentleman sewer, and historiographer, whose office it was to record his actions; and attended by such a number of alguazils and scriveners, as would have formed a moderate squadron. Sancho walked in the middle, with his rod, and a goodly sight he was to see. Having traversed a few streets, they heard the clashing of swords, upon which hastening to the place of action, they found two men fighting, who, seeing the officers of justice, desisted, and one of them exclaimed, "Help, in God's name, and the king's! What, are people suffered to be robbed in this town, and assaulted in the very middle of the street?" "Compose yourself, honest friend," said Sancho, "and let me know the cause of this quarrel; for, I am governor." Then his adversary interpos-ing, "My lord governor," said he, "I will tell you the whole story in a few words: Your worship must know, that this gentleman has been at play in that there gaming-house

---

* Literally, *the devil's in Cantillana*, which is a town of Andalouzia, near Sevil.³

over the way, where he has won above a thousand rials, and God knows how fairly: now, I being present, decided more than once in his favour, when the bett was doubtful, against the dictates of my own conscience: he took up his winning, and when I expected he would gratify me with a crown at least, for good will, as players generally make such presents to men of honour like me, who attend in those places, ready at all adventures to support unreasonable demands, and prevent disturbance; he pocketed the cash and went away: I followed him out of humour; yet in the most courteous manner, begged he would indulge me with eight rials, as he knew me to be a gentleman without either business or fortune; for, my parents neither bred me up to the one, nor left me the other: and the rascal who, by the bye, is as great a thief as Cacus, and as arrant a sharper as Andradilla, would not give me a farthing more than four rials; so that, my lord governor, your excellency may perceive what a shameless and unconcionable rogue it is: but, in good faith, if your lordship had not come up, I would have made him disgorge his winning, and taught him how to trim the ballance." When Sancho asked what the other had to say in his own defence, he owned that as his adversary alledged, he had refused to give him more than four rials, because the plaintiff had often tasted of his bounty; and those who expect such gratifications ought to be thankful, and take chearfully what their benefactors bestow, without pretending to make peremptory demands upon those who win, unless they know them to be cheats, and that their winning is unfairly acquired. He likewise observed, that there could be no surer mark of his honour and fair play, than his having refused to comply with the demands of such a rascal; for, sharpers are always tributary to those lookers-on who know their knavery. "The remark is certainly just," said the steward: "how will your excellency please to dispose of these men?" "What must be done, is this," replied the governor: "You, Mr. winner, whether you be good, bad, or indifferent, must immediately pay to this here swash-buckler, one hundred rials; and, besides, disburse thirty more for the use and behoof of the poor prisoners: and you, sir, who have neither business, fortune, or employment in this island, take these hundred rials, and some time to-morrow, banish yourself from this island for the space of ten years, on penalty (if you disobey the sentence) of completing the term of your exile in the other world: for, in that case, I will hang you on a gibbet, at least, the executioners shall do it by my order; and let no man presume to reply, or I will chastise him severely." The one disbursed, the other received the rials: this quitted the island, that retired to his own lodgings; and the governor, who remained on the spot, said to his followers, "If my power is not very small, I will suppress those gaming-houses, which, I begin to perceive, are very prejudicial to the public." "This, at least," said the notary, "your excellency cannot suppress; for, it is kept by a person of quality, who, in the course of the year, loses a great deal more than he gets by the cards. Against petty gaming-houses of small account, which are productive of most mischief, and cover more crimes, your lordship may exert your authority; but, in the houses of noblemen, and gentlemen of rank, the noted sharpers dare not put their tricks in practice: and since the vice of gaming is become a common exercise, better play in houses of fashion than in any public gaming-house, into which an unfortunate wretch is often seduced, in the middle of the night, and, as it were, skinned alive." "Mr. notary," replied the governor, "much may be said on that subject."

Here he was interrupted by the arrival of a serjeant who had fast hold of a youth, and thus addressed himself to the governor: "This spark, my lord, was coming towards us; but, no sooner had a glimpse of the officers of justice, than he turned his back, and began to scamper off as nimbly as a fallow-deer; a sure sign of his being some sort of a delinquent: I pursued him immediately, but should never have overtaken him, had not he stumbled and fallen." "Young man," said Sancho, "what did you run for?" To this question the youth replied, "I ran, my lord, in order to avoid the tedious interrogations of justice." "What business do you follow?" "I am a weaver." "And what sort of stuff do you weave?" "Iron heads for lances, with your honour's leave." "What! you are a small wit, methinks, and set up for a joker? very well, sir, and where was you going now?" "To take the air, my lord." "And whereabout do you take the air in this island?" "Just where it happens to blow." "Good again! your answers are pat; and to be sure, you are a pretty, smart young fellow: but, hark ye, youngster, I am the air that will blow in your poop, until you are safely lodged in prison. Here, take and carry him to gaol, I will take order that he shall sleep for one night without air." "'Fore God!" cried the youth, "your honour can no more make me sleep in gaol, than you can make me king." "And wherefore cannot I make thee sleep in gaol?" replied Sancho; "is it not in my power to confine and release thee, when and where I please?" "How great soever your honour's power may be," said the young man, "it is not sufficient to make me sleep in prison." "How! not sufficient?" cried Sancho, "away with him, and let his own eyes convince him of his mistake; and lest the gaoler should practise his interested generosity upon him, I will fine him in two thousand ducats, if he suffers thee to move one step from the prison." "All this is matter of mirth," answered the youth; "for, the truth is, all the people upon earth shall not make me sleep in prison." "Tell me, devil," said Sancho, "hast thou got a familiar to release thee, and loose the chains with which I intend thou shalt be fettered?" "Now, my lord governor," replied the youth with a graceful air, "let us argue the matter, and come to the point. Suppose your excellency should order me to be carried to jail, to be loaded with chains and shackles, and thrust into a dungeon, and lay an heavy penalty upon the jailor, in case he should allow me to escape; and lastly, suppose he should perform his duty with all imaginable care and success: notwithstanding all these precautions, if I have no inclination to sleep, and can keep myself awake all night, without closing an eye, pray tell me, is all your lordship's power sufficient to make me sleep against my will?" "No, surely," said the secretary: "and the young man has made good his assertion." "Provided always," said Sancho, "that your defying sleep would be meerly for your own pleasure, without any intention to contradict mine." "No, my lord," replied the youth, "I never dreamed of any such intention." "Then, peace be with you," resumed the governor, "you may go and sleep at home, and God send you a sound sleep; for I have no design to disturb your repose: but, let me advise you, never, henceforth to crack a joke upon justice; otherwise, you may chance to light upon some of her ministers that will crack your skull."

The youth went away, the governor continued his circuit; and, he had not gone far, when two serjeants brought in a person they had taken, saying, "My lord governor, this here person that seems to be a man, is no other than a woman, and that not ugly neither, in man's cloaths." Here they held up two or three lanthorns, by the light of which they

discovered the face of a woman, seemingly about sixteen years of age, beautiful as a thousand pearls, with her hair tied up in a net of green silk and gold. Having surveyed her from head to foot, they perceived her stockings were of flesh-coloured silk, tied with garters of white taffeta, and fringes of gold embroidery; her breeches were of green cloth of gold; she had a loose coat of the same stuff, under which she wore a jacket of the finest brocade; and her shoes were white, and made like those used by men. She had no sword about her, but a very rich dagger, and upon her fingers was a great number of valuable rings: in a word, all who beheld the girl were struck with her appearance, tho' not one of them knew her face; and the inhabitants of the town, said they could not conceive who she was. But, those who concerted the jokes that were practised upon Sancho, were most struck with admiration; for this incident and salvage was not of their contriving; and therefore they stood in suspence, waiting to see the issue of the adventure; while Sancho, confounded at the girl's beauty, asked who she was, whither she was going, and what had induced her to appear in the habit of a man? She, fixing her eyes upon the ground, with the most engaging bashfulness, replied, "My lord, I cannot disclose in such a public company, what it concerns me so much to conceal. One circumstance I beg leave to communicate: I am no thief or criminal person; but, an unfortunate young lady, compelled by jealousy to trespass upon that decorum which is due to my honour and reputation."

The steward hearing these words, said to Sancho, "My lord governor, be so good as to bid the people retire, that this lady may disburthen her mind with more freedom." The governor accordingly laid his commands upon his attendants, all of whom retired, except the steward, the gentleman sewer, and the secretary; and the young lady finding they were gone, proceeded to this effect: "Gentlemen, I am the daughter of Pedro Perez Mazorca, farmer of the wool in this town, who comes frequently to my father's house." "Madam," said the steward, "this will not go down. I am very well acquainted with Pedro Perez, and know he has neither chick nor child, male or female: besides, you first say he is your father, and then add he frequently comes to your father's house." "That circumstance I likewise took notice of," said Sancho. "Well, gentlemen," replied the damsel, "I am in such confusion, that I know not what I say: but, the truth is, I am the daughter of Diego de Llana, whom you must all know." "Ay, this goes better," answered the steward: "Diego de Llana is my acquaintance, and a gentleman of rank and fortune: I know too, he has a son and daughter; tho', since he was a widower, no person in this town can pretend to say he ever saw the face of his daughter, whom her father keeps so closely shut up, that the sun himself has no opportunity to behold her; and yet, report says she is extremely beautiful." "True," said the damsel: "I am that very daughter, and whether or not fame has belyed me in point of beauty, you yourselves, gentlemen, may judge from your own observation." So saying, she began to weep most tenderly.

The secretary perceiving her distress, said to the sewer in a whisper, "Doubtless, something of consequence must have happened to this poor young lady, seeing a person of her quality, quits her own home at such an hour, and in such an equipage." "Certainly," replied the other, "that suspicion is confirmed by her tears." As for Sancho, he consoled her in the best terms he could use, and desired that she would without fear or constraint communicate what had befallen her; for, they would endeavour to remedy

The Maiden, Disguised as a Youth, Brought before Sancho.

her disaster, with great sincerity, and by all possible means. "This then is the case, gentlemen," answered the damsel, "my father had locked me up for the space of ten years, which are elapsed since my mother was committed to her grave: there is in the house a rich oratory where mass is said; and, in all that time, I have seen nothing but the sun in the heavens by day, and the moon and stars by night: I am utterly unacquainted with the streets, squares, churches, and all mankind, except my father, my brother, and Pedro Perez the wool-farmer, who, because he comes frequently to our house, I took it in my head to call my father, in order to conceal the name of my real parent: I have been very disconsolate for many days and months, on account of this confinement, and his constant refusal to let me go to church: I longed to see the world, at least the town in which I first drew breath; and, I did not think, this desire transgressed the bounds of that decorum which young women of fashion ought to preserve. When I heard of bull-feasts, darting the javelin, and plays, I desired my brother, who is a year younger than myself, to describe the nature of these and many other things which I had not seen, and he gratified my desire to the utmost of his power; but his description served only to inflame my impatience to behold those spectacles: in a word, to cut short the account of my ruin, I say, I desired and intreated my brother—would to God I had never desired or intreated him."

And here she renewed her lamentation, when the steward interposing, "Madam," said he, "be so good as to proceed, and finish the story of your adventure; for, your own words, and tears, keep us all in the utmost suspense." "I have little else to say," replied the damsel, "tho' a great many tears to shed; for, such irregular desires are always, without fail, attended by such misfortunes."

The beauty of this damsel having made an impression on the soul of the gentleman sewer, he once more held up the lanthorn to take another view, and the tears she let fall, he took to be seed-pearl, or the dewdrops of the meadow; nay, his fancy even compared them to oriental pearls, and he ardently wished that her misfortune might not appear so great as her sighs and lamentation seemed to indicate.

The governor being tired of the dilatory manner in which the girl told her story, desired she would keep them no longer in suspense; for, it was late, and they had a great part of their round still to perform. Then, she, in the midst of interrupted sobbings, and broken sighs, proceeded thus: "My misfortune, and my disaster, is nothing else than this: I begged my brother to disguise me in one of his suits, and carry me out to see the town, some night while my father should be asleep; he, importuned by my intreaties, complied with my request, and gave me this dress, while he himself put on a suit of mine which fits him to a nicety; for, he has not one hair upon his chin, and looks exactly like a very handsome girl. This night about an hour ago, little more or less, we sallied forth from our own house; and conducted by our foot-boy, and our own unruly desire, went round the whole town: but, when we wanted to return home again, we perceived a great number of people coming up, and my brother said, 'Sister, this must be the patrole; quicken your pace, put wings to your feet, and run after me; that they may not know who we are, otherwise we shall be in evil taking.' So saying, he took to his heels, and began—not to run but to fly: but, scarce had I followed him six paces, when I fell through fear, and then came the officers of justice, who brought me before your lordship, where

in consequence of my foolish and rash conduct, I find myself confounded and ashamed, before so much company." "So that after all, madam," said Sancho, "no other mishap has befallen you, nor was it jealousy that brought you from your own house, as you alledged in the beginning of your story?" "Nothing else hath happened to me, nor did I quit my own home from jealousy; but, meerly from the desire of seeing the world, which extended no farther than a wish to see the streets of this town."

The truth of this assertion was confirmed by the arrival of two other serjeants with her brother, whom they had taken in his flight. He had no other cloaths but a rich petticoat, and a manteel of blue damask laced with gold: on his head there was no cap, or any other ornament but his own hair, which was so rich and ruddy, that it looked like ringlets of gold. The governor, steward, and sewer, taking him aside, that he might not be overheard by his sister, questioned him about his being disguised in that dress; and the youth with equal bashfulness and disorder, repeated the same story which his sister had related, to the unspeakable satisfaction of the enamoured sewer.

"Gentlefolks," said the governor, "this is certainly a very childish trick, and in giving an account of your simplicity and rashness, there needed not all this weeping and wailing: had you said at first, our names are so and so, and we fell upon this contrivance to steal out of our father's house, meerly to gratify our curiosity, without any other design; the affair would have been at an end, and you might have spared all this grunting and groaning." "Very true," replied the damsel; "but, your honours must know, my confusion was so great, that I was not mistress of my own behaviour." "There is no harm done," replied Sancho; "let us go and see you safe home to the house of your father, who perhaps has not missed you as yet; and henceforward be not such a baby, or so desirous to see the world. The maid that would keep her good name, stays at home as if she was lame: A hen and a housewife, whatever they cost, if once they go gadding will surely be lost: And she that longs to see, I ween, is as desirous to be seen. This is all I shall at present say upon the subject."

The young man thanked the governor for his intended civility in seeing them home; and accordingly they took the road to their father's house, which was not far off. When they arrived at the gate, the brother threw a pebble at a casement, and immediately a maid-servant who sat up for them, came down and opened the door, at which they entered, leaving all the company in admiration at their beauty and genteel deportment, as well as at their scheme of seeing the world by night, without going out of the town: but, this they ascribed to their tender years.

The sewer's heart was transpierced by the charms of the sister, whom he resolved to demand in marriage of her father the very next day, concluding he should not meet with a denial because he was a domestic of the duke's. Even Sancho was seized with a whim and inclination to make a match between the youth and his daughter Sanchica, and he actually resolved to effectuate it in due season; taking it for granted that no man would refuse his hand to a governor's daughter.

Thus ended the round for that night, and in two days he saw the end of his government, which overthrew and destroyed all his designs, as will be seen in the sequel.

## CHAPTER XVIII.

Which declares who were the inchanters and executioners that scourged the duenna, and pinched and scratched Don Quixote; together with the expedition of the page, who carried the letter to Teresa Panza, Sancho's spouse.

Cid Hamet, the most punctual investigator of the most minute atoms belonging to this genuine history, says that when Donna Rodriguez quitted her apartment to visit Don Quixote in his chamber, another duenna, who was her bed-fellow, perceived her motions, and as all the individuals of that class are naturally disposed to enquire, to pry, and to smell into the affairs of their neighbours, she followed her so softly that honest Rodriguez knew nothing at all of the matter: and when she saw her enter Don Quixote's apartment, that she might conform to the general custom of all duennas, who are much addicted to tale-bearing, she, that instant, went and informed my lady dutchess, that Donna Rodriguez was in the knight's bed-chamber; the dutchess communicated this intelligence to the duke, and asked leave to go along with Altisidora, and see what the duenna wanted with Don Quixote: the duke granted his permission, and the two, with great caution, treading softly, step by step, went up so close to the chamber-door, as to overhear every thing that was said; and the dutchess hearing how Rodriguez divulged the secret of those healing * streams, that flowed from her body, could not bear the duenna's presumption, which was equally resented by Altisidora. Exasperated therefore, and bent upon vengeance, they burst into the apartment, where they pinched the knight, and flogged the duenna, as hath been already recited; for, affronts levelled directly against the beauty and pride of the fair-sex, wakens the indignation of the offended party to a great degree, and inspires her with the desire of revenge.

The dutchess recounted the adventure to the duke, who was extremely diverted with the particulars; and her grace resolving to proceed with her jokes, and extract entertainment from Don Quixote, dispatched the page who had acted the part of Dulcinea, in the contrivance of the disinchantment, which, by the bye, Sancho Panza had by this time forgot, so much was he engrossed by the affairs of his government—the dutchess, I say, dispatched the page to Teresa Panza, with her husband's letter, and another from her grace, together with a rosary of rich coral in a present.

The history relates, then, that the page, who was a very intelligent, acute young fellow, extremely well disposed to contribute to the entertainment of his lord and lady, set out with great satisfaction for Sancho's native place; but, before he entered the village, he saw a number of women washing linnen in a brook, and of these he asked, if they

* Literally, the *Aranjuez* of the fountains. *Fuentes* signifies, either fountains or issues; and *Aranjuez* is the name of a delightful place, about seven leagues from Madrid, famous for gardens and fountains.[1]

could inform him, whereabouts lived one Teresa Panza, wife of one Sancho Panza, squire to a certain knight called Don Quixote de la Mancha. This question was no sooner pronounced, than a girl, who was washing, starting up, "That Teresa Panza," cried she, "is my mother; and that same Sancho my honoured father, and that knight our master." "Come then, young mistress," replied the page, "conduct me to your mother; for, I bring her a letter, and a present, from that same father of yours." "That I will do with all my heart, kind sir," answered the girl, who seemed to be fourteen years of age, over or under; and, leaving the cloaths upon which she was at work, to one of her companions, without putting on her cap or her shoes; for, she was barefoot, and her hair hung about her eyes, she ran before the page's horse, saying, "Come along, good sir, our house is at this end of the village, and there you will find my poor mother in a sorrowful taking, because she has not for many days heard any news of my honoured father." "But now," said the page, "I bring her such good news, that she will have reason to bless God for this happy day." In a word, what with dancing, running and skipping, the wench arrived at the village; but, before she entered the house, she called aloud at the door, "Come out, mother Teresa, come out, pray come out; here's a gentleman, who brings letters, and other good things, from my good father."

Teresa Panza, hearing this exclamation, came forth spinning tow from a distaff, with a grey petticoat, so short that it seemed to have been cut close to the placket; a jacket of the same stuff, and an open breasted shift: she was not very old, tho' seemingly turned of forty; but, strong, hale, nervous, and tough. Seeing her daughter, with the page on horseback, "What is the matter, child?" said she: "what gentleman is that?" "The very humble servant of my lady Donna Teresa Panza," replied the page, who, throwing himself from his horse, ran with great eagerness and humility, to kneel before madam Teresa, saying, "Grant me permission to kiss your ladyship's hand, madam Donna Teresa, as the legitimate, and particular consort, of my lord Don Sancho Panza, sole governor of the island Barataria." "Nay, good sir, forbear; do not so," answered Teresa; "I am none of your court-dames; but, a poor countrywoman, a ploughman's daughter, and wife to a squire-errant, but no governor." "Your ladyship," replied the page, "is the most worthy consort of the most superlatively worthy governor; and this letter and present, is an incontestible proof of the truth of what I say." So saying, he instantly pulled from his pocket, the string of coral set in gold, and tied it round her neck; then producing a letter, "This," said he, "is from my lord governor, and this other with the necklace, from my lady dutchess who sent me hither."

Teresa was confounded, and her daughter, no less astonished, exclaimed, "I'll be hanged if our master Don Quixote be not at the bottom of all this; and surely must have given my father that same government or countship, which he promised him so often!" "You are certainly in the right," answered the page; "for, it is intirely on signor Don Quixote's account, that signor Sancho is now governor of the island Barataria, as will appear in this letter." "Pray, good gentleman, read it," said Teresa; "for, though I can spin, I cannot read so much as a crumb." "Nor I, neither," added Sanchica; "but, stay a moment, I'll go and fetch one that shall read it, either the curate himself, or the batchelor Sampson Carrasco, who will come with pleasure to hear news of my father." "There is no occasion to fetch any person whatever," said the page; "for, tho' I cannot spin, I can read,

*Vol. II . pag. 311 .*

*F. Hayman invᵗ delᵗ*    *P.ᵗ. Ravenet Sculpᵗ*

The Page Presenting Sancho's Letter to His Wife and Daughter.

and read it I shall." He accordingly read Sancho's letter from beginning to end; but, as it hath been already recited, we shall not repeat it in this place. Then he rehearsed the other, which came from the dutchess, in these words:

"Friend Teresa,
The great talents, and excellent disposition of your husband Sancho, induced and obliged me, to beg of the duke my husband, that he would confer upon him the government of one, among many islands that are in his possession; and, I understand, he governs like any jer-faulcon; a circumstance that affords great pleasure to me, and of consequence to my lord duke; and I thank heaven heartily, that I have not been deceived in choosing him for that same government; for, madam Teresa must know, it is a very hard matter to find a good governor in this world, and God make me as good a woman as Sancho is a governor. I have sent you, my dear friend, a coral necklace set in gold; and I wish, for your sake, it had been of oriental pearls: But, he that gives, tho' it were but an egg, would be sorry to see thee lame of a leg.[2] The time will come when we shall be better acquainted, and carry on a closer correspondence, and heaven knows what may come to pass. Commend me to your daughter Sanchica, and tell her from me, to keep herself in readiness; for, I mean to match her very high, when perhaps she thinks least of the matter. I am told your town is famous for fine, large acorns; pray send me two dozen, which I shall greatly esteem as coming from your hand. Write me a long letter, giving an account of your health and welfare; and, if you should want any thing, you have nothing to do but open your mouth, and it shall be measured. That God would protect you, is the prayer of

Your loving friend,
The Dutchess."

"La! now, (cried Teresa, when she heard the contents of the letter) what a kind, and plain, and humble lady! would I might live, and die, and be buried, among such ladies, and not your gentlewomen of this town, who think, forsooth, because they are gentle-folks, the wind must not touch them, and go to church in such finery, as if they were perfect queens: nay, they seem to think it a disgrace to look at a poor body; and see here now, how this worthy lady, even tho' no less than a dutchess, calls me friend, and treats me as if I were her own equal; and equal may she be to the highest steeple in all La Mancha. As to what concerns the acorns, kind sir, I'll send her a whole peck, so fair and large, that people shall come far and near, to see and admire them. For the present, Sanchica, we must look to the entertainment of this gentleman: let his horse be taken care of; fetch some eggs from the stable, and cut some rashers of bacon, and let us treat him like a prince; for, the good news he has brought, and his own good countenance, deserves every thing at our hands. In the mean time, I'll go out, and give an account of our good fortune to my neighbours, especially our father the curate, and master Nicholas the barber, who are, and always were, such friends to your father." "I will do as you desire, mother," answered Sanchica; "but remember, you shall give me one half of the string of coral; for, I don't take my lady dutchess to be such a ninny, as to send the whole for your use." "It is all thy own, daughter," replied Teresa; "but thou must let me wear it a few days about my neck; for, in faith and troth, it will rejoice my poor heart." "It will be still more rejoiced," said the page, "when you see the bundle in that portmanteau, consist-

ing of a suit of superfine cloth, which was never wore but one day at the hunting, by the governor, who sends it for the sole use of Miss Sanchica." "May he live a thousand years!" cried Sanchica, "as well as he that brings it, neither more nor less; and even two thousand, if there should be occasion."

Now Teresa going out with the letters, and the string about her neck, went along playing with her fingers upon the paper as if it had been a cymbal; and casually meeting the curate, and Sampson Carrasco, she began to caper about, saying, "In good faith, we have no poor kindred now: we have caught the governorship: ay, ay, pick me up the best gentlewoman of them all, ifack! I'll look upon her as an upstart."[3] "What is the matter, Teresa Panza?" said the curate: "what is the meaning of this rhapsody? and what papers are these?" "No rhapsody at all," replied Teresa; "but only these letters are from dutchesses and governors, and these here upon my neck are true corals: the ave-marias and pater-nosters are of beaten gold, and I am a governess." "God shield us, Teresa," cried the curate, "as we do not understand a word of what you say!" "Seeing is believing," answered the good woman, putting the letters into his hand, which, he having read, in the hearing of Sampson Carrasco, they looked at one another with astonishment. When the batchelor asked who brought those letters, Teresa desired they would go along with her to her house, and they would see the messenger, who was a comely youth, like a perfect golden pinetree, and had brought another present worth twice as much. The curate taking the string of coral from her neck, viewed and reviewed it with great deliberation; and, being satisfied the beads were real fine coral, was again struck with admiration, and exclaimed, "Now by the habit which I wear! I know not what to say, or what to think of these letters and presents: on one side I see, and even feel the worth of these corals; and on the other, I read a letter from a dutchess, who begs two dozen of acorns!" "Reconcile these things if you can," said Carrasco: "but, now let us go and see the bearer of this packet, whose information will solve all these difficulties."

They accordingly accompanied Teresa, and found the page winnowing a little barley for his beast, while Sanchica was employed in cutting rashers to fry with the eggs, for the entertainment of their guest, whose appearance and equipage gave great satisfaction to the new-comers. After the compliments of salutation had courteously passed between them, Sampson intreated him to tell them news of Don Quixote, as well as of Sancho Panza; for, although they had perused the letters of this last, and of my lady dutchess, they were still overwhelmed with confusion, and could by no means comprehend the meaning of that government, especially of an island, seeing all, or the greatest part of the islands in the Mediterranean, belonged to his majesty. To this remonstrance the page replied, "That signor Sancho Panza is a governor, there is no sort of doubt; but whether of an island or not, I do not pretend to decide: let it suffice, however, that he governs a place of above a thousand inhabitants; and with respect to the acorns, I can affirm, my lady dutchess is of such a frank and humble disposition, that her sending for acorns to a countrywoman is not to be wondered at; nay, I once knew her send, and borrow a comb of one of her neighbours; for, you must know, gentlemen, the ladies of Arragon, although as noble, are not so ceremonious and superb, as the quality of Castile, but treat their inferiors with more frankness and familiarity."

In the midst of this conversation, Sanchica coming in with her lap full of eggs, addressed herself to the page, saying, "Pray, tell me, signor, does my honoured father wear trunk-hose since he was a governor?" "I have not observed that particular," replied the page; "but, certainly he must." "My God!" cried Sanchica, "how glad I should be to see my father with trunk-hose! let me never thrive but I have, ever since I was born, longed to see father in laced trunk-breeches." "Laced hose!" said the page; "lord, madam, if he lives, and his government should hold but two months, he is in a fair way of travelling with a hood to his riding-coat." The curate and batchelor could easily perceive the page made a jest of his entertainers; but, the worth of the coral beads, and the hunting-suit which Sancho had sent, destroyed all their conjectures; for, Teresa had shewn them the green garment; nor did they fail to laugh at the ambition of Sanchica, and their mirth was not extinguished when Teresa accosting the priest, "Mr. curate," said she, "do pray cast your eyes about a little, and see if any body be going to Madrid or Toledo, that I may have an opportunity to purchase a round farthingale, right and tight, fashionable and of the best sort; for, truly and truly, I am resolved to honour my spouse's government as much as lies in my power; ay, and if they vex me, I'll go to court, and ride in my coach, like all the rest, and the best of them; for she who is married to a governor, may very well procure and maintain such a convenience." "Yea, forsooth," replied Sanchica; "and would to God it were to-day rather than to-morrow, although those who saw me seated with my lady mother in the coach, should say, Look at such a one, daughter of such a garlic-eater, how she sits, and lolls in a coach, like the pope's lady;[4] but, let them trudge in the dirt, so I ride in my coach, with my feet lifted off the ground: an ill year, and worse month, betide all the envious grumblers upon earth: and so I am warm, without and within, the mob may laugh, and the malicious grin. Speak I to the purpose, mother?" "To the purpose? yes to be sure, daughter; and all this good luck, and even more, was prophecied by my good man Sancho, and thou shalt see, daughter, it will not stop until I am a countess; for, good fortune wants only a beginning, as I have often heard it observed by thy worthy father, who is likewise the father of proverbs, When they bring thee a heifer, be ready with the halter: when they give thee a government, seize it a-God's name: when they bestow a countship, lay thy clutches upon it; and when they throw thee some good beneficial bone, wag thy tail, and snap at the favour;[5] if not, sleep on, and never answer to good fortune and preferment, when they knock at thy door." "And what do I care?" added Sanchica, "let them say what they will, when they see me exalted in all my finery, and cry, There goes Mrs. ape, with her buttocks cased in crape: and all the rest of that stuff."[6]

The curate hearing her remark, "I cannot believe," said he, "but that all the family of the Panzas are born with a bag of proverbs in their bowels; for, I have never seen one of them, who does not scatter about old saws, at all times, and in all conversations." "Your observation is very just," said the page; "for, my lord governor Sancho utters them at every step; and although many of his proverbs are not much to the purpose, they nevertheless give great pleasure, and are very much extolled by my lady dutchess and the duke." "What! and do you still, my good sir," said the batchelor, "affirm the truth of that government of Sancho; and that there is actually a dutchess who sends presents, and letters to his wife? For our parts, although we handle the presents, and have perused the

letters, we cannot believe the evidence of our senses; and imagine this is one of those things which our townsman Don Quixote supposed to have been effected by inchantment; and therefore, I own, I have an inclination to touch and feel your person, that I may know whether you are a fantastical embassador, or really a man of flesh and blood." "Gentlemen," replied the page, "all that I know of the matter is, that I am a real ambassador; that signor Sancho Panza is effectually a governor; and that my lord duke, and lady dutchess, not only could, but actually did, invest him with that government, in which I hear the said Sancho Panza behaves with vast ability. Whether or not there is any inchantment in the case, I leave you gentlemen to dispute and decide among yourselves; that this is all I know of the matter, I swear by the life of my parents, who are still alive, and whom I love and honour with the utmost reverence of affection." "What you say may be true," answered the batchelor: "but, Dubitat Augustinus."[7] "Doubt as much as you please," resumed the page: "what I have said is the naked truth, which will always swim above falshood, like oil above water; but, Operibus credite & non verbis:[8] let one of you gentlemen go along with me, and he shall see with his eyes what he will not believe upon hearsay." "I am for that jaunt," cried Sanchica: "good sir, if you will take me up behind you, I shall be glad to go and see my father's worship." "The daughters of governors," said the page, "never travel alone; but are always accompanied by coaches, and litters, and a great number of attendants." "'Fore God!" replied Sanchica, "I can travel upon a she-ass as well as in a coach: you won't find me shy or fearful." "Hold your tongue, wench," said Teresa: "you know not what you say. The gentleman is in the right; for, Every season has it's reason. When it was plain Sancho, it was plain Sancha; but now, being governor, my lady—I know not if what I say be to the purpose." "Madam Teresa has said more than she is aware of," replied the page: "but, pray, let me have some victuals, and dispatch me immediately; for, I intend to return this evening." To this remonstrance the curate answered: "Sir, you shall come and do penance with me; for, madam Teresa has more inclination than ability to entertain such a worthy guest." The page, at first, declined the invitation, but, at length, found it was his interest to consent; and the curate conducted him to his parsonage, with great pleasure, that he might have an opportunity to inquire at leisure, about Don Quixote and his exploits.

The batchelor offered to write answers to Teresa's letters; but, she did not choose that he should intermeddle in her affairs; for, she looked upon him as a wag. She, therefore, gave a roll of bread, and a couple of eggs, to a noviciate monk who could write; and he penned two letters, one for her husband, and another for the dutchess, indited by Teresa's own noddle, which are not the least entertaining that occur in this sublime history, as will be seen in the sequel.

## CHAPTER XIX.

## Of the progress of Sancho Panza's government, and other such diverting incidents.

At length arrived the morning, that succeeded the night of the governor's round, which the gentleman sewer passed without sleep, so much were his thoughts engrossed by the face, the air, and beauty of the disguised damsel; while the steward employed the time in writing an account of Sancho's conduct to his lord and lady, equally astonished at his words and actions, in which folly and discretion were strangely blended.

At last my lord governor arose, and by direction of doctor Pedro Positive, he was fain to break his fast with a little conserve, and four gulps of cold water, which Sancho would have gladly exchanged for a luncheon of bread, and a bunch of grapes; but, finding himself under compulsion, he bore his fate with grief of soul, and anxiety of stomach; Pedro Positive giving him to understand, that your slight and delicate dishes animate the genius, consequently were most proper for persons appointed to posts and offices of importance, in which corporal strength cannot avail so much as the vigour of the understanding. By this sort of sophistry Sancho was subjected to such severe hunger, that he in secret cursed the government; ay, and him who conferred it: nevertheless, in despight of hunger, and upon the strength of the conserve, he, that day, sat in judgment; and the first case that occurred was a question put by a stranger, in presence of the steward and the rest of the assistants: "My lord," said he, "a certain manour is divided by a large river—I beg your honour will be attentive; for, the case is of great consequence, and some difficulty. I say then, upon this river is a bridge, and at one end of it a gibbet, together with a sort of court-hall, in which four judges usually sit, to execute the law enacted by the lord of the river, bridge and manour, which runs to this effect: 'Whosoever shall pass over this bridge, must first swear whence he comes, and whither he goes: if he swears the truth, he shall be allowed to pass; but, if he forswear himself, he shall die upon the gallows, without mercy or respite.'

"This law, together with the rigorous penalty being known, numbers passed, and as it appeared they swore nothing but the truth, the judges permitted them to pass freely, and without controul. It happened, however, that one man's oath being taken, he affirmed, and swore by his deposition, that he was going to be hanged on that gibbet, and had no other errand or intention. The judges having considered this oath, observed, If we allow this man to pass freely, he swore to a lie, and therefore ought to be hanged according to law; and if we order him to be hanged, after he hath sworn he was going to be suspended on that gibbet, he will have sworn the truth, and by the same law ought to be acquitted. I beg, therefore, to know of your honour, my lord governor, what the judges must do with this man; for, hitherto they are doubtful and in suspence; and having heard of your lordship's acute and elevated understanding, they have sent me to intreat your honour, in their names, to favour them with your opinion in a case of such

doubt and intricacy." To this address Sancho replied, "Assuredly those judges who sent you to me, might have spared themselves the trouble; for, I am a man that may be said to be rather blunt than acute: nevertheless, repeat the business so as that I may understand it fully, and who knows but I may chance to hit the nail on the head?" The interrogator having repeated his story again and again, Sancho said, "I think I can now explain the case in the twinkling of two balls; and this it is: A man swears he is going to be hanged upon such a gibbet; if he actually suffers upon that gibbet, he swore the truth, and by the enacted law ought to be allowed freely to pass the bridge; but if he is not hanged, he swore false, and for that reason ought to suffer upon the gibbet."

"The case is exactly as my lord governor conceives it," said the messenger: "and with respect to the scope, and understanding of the matter, there is no further room for doubt or interrogation." "I say then," replied Sancho, "that part of the man which swore truth, ought to be allowed to pass, and that which told a lie, ought to be hanged; and in this manner, the terms or condition of passing will be literally fulfilled." "But, my lord governor," replied the questioner, "in that case it will be necessary to divide the man into two parts; namely, the false and the true; and if he is so divided, he must certainly die: therefore, the intent of the law will be frustrated, whereas there is an express necessity for its being accomplished." "Come hither, honest friend," said Sancho: "either I am a blockhead, or this passenger you mention has an equal title to be hanged, and to live, and pass over the bridge; for, if the truth saves him on one side, his falshood condemns him equally on the other. Now, this being the case, as it certainly is, I think you must tell the gentlemen who sent you hither, that as the reasons for condemning, and for acquitting the culprit are equally ballanced, they shall let him freely pass; for, it is always more laudable to do good than harm: and to this opinion I would subscribe if I could write my name. Nor, indeed, have I spoken my own sentiment on this occasion; but, I have recollected one, among the many precepts I received from my master Don Quixote, the night before I set out for the government of this island: he said, that when justice was doubtful, I should choose, and lean towards mercy; and it pleased God that I should now remember this maxim, which falls so pat to the present purpose." "So it does," said the steward: "and, I firmly believe, that Lycurgus himself, who gave laws to the Lacedemonians, could not have uttered a more sagacious decision than that which the great Panza has pronounced. Now let the audience end for this morning, and I will give orders that my lord governor shall dine to his heart's content." "That is my request," cried Sancho: "nothing but fair play: give me plenty of victuals, and let them load me with cases and doubts, I will soon make them vanish into smoke."

The steward kept his word; for, he had a scruple of conscience in famishing such a discreet governor; especially as he intended that night to conclude the farce with the last joke he had a commission to execute.

Well then, Sancho having dined that day, contrary to all the rules and aphorisms of doctor Snatchaway, the cloth was no sooner removed than a courier entered with a letter from Don Quixote to the governor, who desired the secretary to read it by himself; and then, if there was nothing in it which required to be kept secret, to rehearse it in an audible voice. The secretary, in obedience to his command, having perused it in secret, "It may be very safely read aloud," said he: "what signor Don Quixote writes to your

lordship, deserves to be printed, and even displayed in golden letters." This is the purport of the letter:

The letter from Don Quixote de la Mancha to Sancho Panza, governor of the island Barataria.

"Friend Sancho,

When I expected to hear of thy negligence and impertinence, I was informed of thy discretion, for which I have returned particular thanks to heaven, that can raise the poor from the dunghill, and extract wisdom from the heart of the fool. I am told thou hast governed like a man, and that thou art a man as if thou wert a beast; such is the humility of thy deportment. Take notice, Sancho, it is often convenient and necessary, for the authority of office to resist the humility of the heart; for, the ornament of the person invested with charges of dignity, ought to be conformable to what these require, and not measured according to the will of an humble disposition. Appear always well dressed; for, a may-pole when decorated, loses its original appearance: not that I advise thee to wear jewels and finery; or, as thou art a judge, to go in the habit of a soldier; but, to adorn thyself with that garb which thine office requires, and to be always clean, and neatly dressed. In order to acquire the good will of the people over whom thou art set, among other things, remember two particulars; one is to be affable to every body; but this I have mentioned upon another occasion: the other is to procure plenty of provision; for, there is nothing that gives such vexation to the poor as hunger and dearth.

"Do not issue a great number of ordinances; but, take care that those which are published be good; and, above all things, see they are maintained and put in execution; for, those ordinances, which are not observed, might as well be annulled, as they serve to demonstrate that the prince who had discretion and authority to enact them, wanted power to enforce obedience; and those laws which only intimidate, without being put in execution, resemble the king Log of the frogs, which at first terrified his subjects, by whom, however, at the long run, he was despised and insulted. Be thou a father to the virtuous, and a stepfather to the wicked. Thou must not be always rigorous, nor always gentle; but, choose the medium between these two extremities, in which lies the point of discretion. Visit the prisons, the slaughter-houses, and the markets; for, in such places the presence of the governor will be of great importance. Console the prisoners with hope of being speedily dispatched. Be a bugbear to butchers; for, then they will use honest weights; and a terror to market-women for the same reason. Beware of shewing thyself (tho' thou really shouldst be so, and yet, I believe, thou art not) a miser, a letcher, or a glutton; for, thy people, and those who have concerns with thee, knowing the biass of thine inclination, will batter thee from that quarter, until thou art overthrown into the profundity of perdition. Consider and reconsider, peruse and reperuse, the advices and instructions which I gave thee in writing, before thy departure for thy government; and, if thou observest the contents, thou wilt find in them a precious aid, that will alleviate the toils and difficulties which every moment occur to governors. Write to thy noble patrons to evince thy gratitude; for, ingratitude is the daughter of pride, and one of the vilest sins that can be committed: and the person who is grateful to his benefactor gives indication that he is also grateful to God, whose benefits are so manifold and incessant. My lady dutchess dispatched a messenger with thy hunting-suit, and another present to thy wife Teresa, and we expect her answer every moment.

"I have been somewhat indisposed, in consequence of a certain cat-clawing adventure, which I lately atchieved with some discomfiture of my nose: but, that was of no consequence;

for, if I am maltreated by one set of inchanters, I am protected by another. Let me know if the steward, who is with thee, had any concern in the adventure of the countess Trifaldi, as thou once seemedst to suspect: and give me an account of every thing that betides thee, seeing the distance between us is so small. I think of leaving, in a little time, this idle life for which I was never designed. I am like to be engaged in an affair which, I believe, will bring me in disgrace with the duke and dutchess: but, although this affects my mind, it shall not influence my conduct; for, in a word, I am resolved to comply with the duties of my profession, rather than with the dictates of their pleasure, in conformity with the old saying, Amicus Plato, sed magis amica veritas.[1] I write this sentence in Latin, because I apprehend thou hast learned that language since thou wast a governor. I commit thee to the protection of God, who is the fountain of all good; and am

<div align="center">

Thy friend,

Don Quixote de la Mancha."

</div>

Sancho listened with great attention to the letter, which was applauded for the good sense it contained, by all the hearers; then the governor rising from table, shut himself up in his apartment with the secretary, in order to compose an answer to his master, without loss of time. He desired the scribe to write what he should dictate, without the last addition or diminution. The secretary obeyed his command, and the answer was to this effect:

<div align="center">

Sancho Panza's letter to Don Quixote de la Mancha.

</div>

"The employment of my office is so severe, that I have not time to scratch my head, or even to pare my nails, which I, therefore, wear so long that God must find some remedy. This I observe, dear master of my soul, that your worship need not be confounded because I have not hitherto given you an account of my well or ill-being in this government; where, by the bye, I suffer more pinching hunger than when we two used to travel through the woods and desarts.

"My lord duke gave me notice the other day, in a letter, that certain spies had entered the island, in order to murder me; but, as yet, I have discovered none, except a doctor, who has a salary in the place, for killing all the governors that come hither. They call him doctor Pedro Positive, and he is a native of Snatchaway; so that your worship may see, by his name, what reason I have to fear I shall perish by his hands. This very doctor frankly owns, that he does not cure the distempers which are already formed, but only prevents their formation; and the medicine he prescribes, in fasting upon fasting, until the patient is clean, skin and bone, as if a consumption was not worse than a fever. Finally, he is killing me by inches with hunger; and I find myself dying of pure vexation; for, I thought, in coming to this government, I should have hot meals, and cool liquor, and regale my body in holland sheets, upon beds of down; whereas, I am come to penance like an hermit; and as I cannot even do that, I believe, at the long run, the devil will fly away with me.

"Hitherto, I have neither touched fee, nor fingered bribe; nor can I conceive the reason of such proceeding; for, I have been told, that the governors who used to come to this island, even before their entrance, always received a good sum of money, either by way of present or loan, from the inhabitants; a custom observed in other governments as well as in this.

"In going the round last night, I found a very beautiful damsel in man's cloaths, and her brother in the dress of a woman: my gentleman sewer is in love with the girl, and, as he says,

hath fixed his fancy on her for a wife, and I have chosen the youth for my son-in-law: to-day, we two will communicate our thoughts to the father of this young pair, who is one Diego de Llana, a gentleman, and as old a christian as one would desire.

"I visit the markets, according to your worship's advice, and yesterday seeing a huckster selling new nuts, I discovered that she had mixed with a bushel of the new, the same quantity of old nuts that were empty and rotten; upon which, I gave the whole to the charity boys, who know very well how to separate the good from the bad, and forbad her to enter the market for fifteen days: I was told I had done gallantly. What I can assure your worship is, that according to the report of this town, there is not a more wicked set of people than those market-women; for, they are all without shame, conscience, and moderation: and, indeed, I believe the report, from what I have seen in other corporations.

"It gives me great satisfaction to hear that my lady dutchess has written to my wife Teresa Panza, and sent the present your worship mentions: and I will endeavour to shew my gratitude in due season. I beg your worship will kiss her grace's hand, in my name, and tell her, I say, she has not thrown her favour into a rotten sack, as our deeds shall declare. I should be sorry that your worship came to any reckonings of disgust with my lord duke, and lady dutchess; for, should there be any breach between you, it is very plain, the whole would redound to my loss; and, considering the advice you gave me to be always grateful, it would not look well in your worship to be otherwise to those who have done you such favours, and treated you so nobly in their castle.

"The story of the cat-clawing I do not understand; but, do suppose, it must have been one of those unlucky frays in which your worship is often engaged with wicked inchanters; but, I shall know when we meet.

"I would fain present your worship with something, but I know not what to send, except some glyster-pipes, which are very curiously turned and mounted in this island; tho', if my office holds, it shall go hard but I will find something to send, either by hook or crook. If my wife Teresa Panza should write to me, I beg your worship will pay the postage, and forward the letter; for, I am extremely desirous to know the state of my family, my wife and children. And now, the lord deliver your worship from evil designing inchanters, and safely and peaceably quit me of this government; which I very much doubt, for, I believe, I shall leave my bones in it, so cruelly am I treated by doctor Pedro Positive.

<div align="center">Your worship's humble servant,</div>

<div align="right">Sancho Panza the governor."</div>

The secretary having sealed this letter, dispatched it with the courier; and those who executed the jokes upon Sancho, laying their heads together, contrived a scheme for dismissing him from the administration. The evening his excellency spent in making some wholesome regulations, touching the government of what he imagined to be an island. Among other things, he ordained that there should be no monopolizers of provision in the commonwealth; that wine should be imported from all parts indifferently, at the pleasure of the merchant: with this addition, that he should declare the place from whence it came, so as that a price might be set upon it, according to its worth, fame, and estimation; and he who should be detected in dashing it with water, of falsifying its name, should suffer death for the offence. He moderated the price of all kinds of hose, and particularly that of shoes, which he looked upon as exorbitant: he rated the wages of servants who went at full gallop in the road of interest:[2] he laid severe penalties upon those who should sing lewd and lascivious ballads, by night or by day: he ordered that

no blind man should sing his miracles in couplets, without an authentic testimony of the truth; it appearing that the greatest part of those sung by blind persons, are false and feigned, to the prejudice of those which are true: he made and appointed an overseer of the poor, not to persecute, but to examine whether or not they were real objects; for, sturdy thieves, and hale drunkards, often screen themselves in the shade of feigned lameness, and counterfeit sores. In a word, he made so many good regulations, that they are hitherto preserved in the place, and called the constitutions of the great governor Sancho Panza.

## CHAPTER XX.

### In which is recorded the adventure of the second afflicted, or sorrowful matron; otherwise called Donna Rodriguez.

C id Hamet recounts, that Don Quixote being now cured of his scratches, began to think the life he led in the castle was altogether contrary to the order of chivalry which he professed; and therefore he determined to beg leave of the duke and dutchess, to set out for Saragossa, as the time of the tournament approached; for, there he laid his account with winning the armour which is the reward of the victor. Accordingly, while he sat one day at table with the duke and dutchess, he began to execute his resolution in asking leave; when behold, all of a sudden, two women, as it afterwards appeared, entered the dining-room, covered with mourning from head to foot. One of them approaching Don Quixote, prostrated herself before him, and with her mouth close to his feet, uttered such melancholy, profound, and doleful groans as overwhelmed all the spectators with confusion: for, although the duke and dutchess imagined it was some joke which the servants intended to perpetrate upon the knight; yet, seeing how violently the woman sighed, groaned, and wept, they remained doubtful and in suspence, until the compassionate Don Quixote raised her from the ground, and intreated her to discover herself, by taking away the veil that concealed her rueful face. She complied with his request, and shewed herself to be what no body believed she was; for, she displayed the individual countenance of Donna Rodriguez the duenna of the house, and the other mourner was her daughter, who had been seduced by the rich farmer's son. All who knew her, were struck with admiration, and the duke and dutchess more than any body; for, although they took her to be a fool, and a person of a soft disposition, they did not think her folly could have risen to such acts of extravagance. In fine, Donna Rodriguez, addressing herself to the duke and dutchess, "I hope," said she, "your excellencies will give me leave to communicate a little with this knight; for, it is necessary I should confer with him, that I may be safely extricated from the dilemma in which I am involved by the presumption of an evil-minded clown."

The duke having assured her she was at full liberty to confer with signor Don Qui-

History & Adventures of the Renowned Don Quixote

xote as much as she pleased, she directed her voice, and her countenance to the knight, saying, "Some days are elapsed, most valiant knight, since I gave you an account of the wrong and treachery which a wicked peasant has done my dearly beloved daughter, who is this unfortunate creature now standing before you; and you promised, in her behalf, to redress the wrong she had suffered: but now, I am informed, that you are going to depart from this castle, in quest of the happy adventures God shall throw in your way; and therefore, I could wish, that before you begin your career through those paths, you would defy this inflexible rustic, and compel him to marry my daughter, and so fulfil the promise he made of being her spouse, before he first yoked with her in the way of love; for, to think my lord duke will do me justice, is the same as to look for pears upon an elm, for the reason which I explained to your worship in private: and upon these terms, the lord preserve your worship's health, and grant us his protection."

To this address Don Quixote, with great gravity and stateliness of deportment, replied, "Worthy duenna, moderate, or rather dry up your tears, and spare your sighs; for, here I undertake to redress the grievances of your daughter; though it would have been better for her, had not she so easily believed the protestations of lovers, who, for the most part, are very ready and alert to promise, but very heavy and backward in the performance: nevertheless, with the good leave of my lord duke, I will forthwith set out in quest of this perfidious youth; and having found him, defy and slay him, whensoe'er and wheresoe'er he shall refuse to perform his promise; for, the principal aim of my profession is to pardon the humble, and chastise the haughty; that is, to succour the wretched, and destroy the cruel." "Your worship," replied the duke, "needs not give yourself the trouble to go in quest of the rustic who is the subject of this worthy duenna's complaint; nor is there any occasion for your worship's asking my leave to challenge him to single combat; I consider the challenge as already given; I undertake for its being conveyed to the party, and even for its acceptance; and promise that he shall come to answer for himself in person at this castle, where I will furnish both with a listed field, and observe all the conditions that are wont, and ought to be observed in such encounters; for, justice shall be equally done to each, according to the obligation that lies on all those princes who furnish lists for combatants, within the limits of their territories." "With this security then, and the good leave of your grace," replied Don Quixote, "I now, for once renounce my gentility, humble and adjust myself to the level of the delinquent, making myself equal with him, that he may be entitled and enabled to fight with me: I therefore, tho' in his absence, challenge and defy him, for his wickedness in seducing this poor creature, who was a maid, and now through his fault is deprived of her maidenhead; and he shall either perform the promise he made of being her lawful spouse, or die, in default of the performance."

So saying, he pulled off one of his gloves, and threw it into the middle of the hall; this was taken up by the duke, who said he accepted the challenge in the name of his vassal: he likewise appointed the time at the distance of six days, and pitched upon the courtyard of the castle as the field of action: then they agreed to wear the usual arms of knights; namely, the lance, the shield, the plaited coat of mail, and all other pieces, without the least fraud, treachery or superstition, to be viewed and examined by the judges of the lists— "But, before we proceed," said the duke, "it will be necessary that this good

duenna, and that mistaken maid, should put the justice of their cause into the hands of signor Don Quixote, otherwise nothing to the purpose will be done, nor will the challenge ever come to due execution."

"I do put my cause into his hands," replied the duenna. "And I too," cried the daughter; all in tears, and overwhelmed with shame and confusion. The particulars of this affair being adjusted, and the duke having determined with himself what was to be done in the family, the mourners retired, and the dutchess ordered that for the future they should not be treated as her servants, but as ladies, adventurers come to her house to demand justice: she therefore allotted a separate apartment to themselves, and they were attended as strangers, not without the amazement of the other servants, who could not conceive what would be the issue of the folly and effrontery of Donna Rodriguez, and her indiscreet and unhappy daughter.

At this instant, in order to complete the mirth of the company, and finish their meal with more enjoyment, who should enter the hall but the page who carried the letters and presents to Teresa Panza, the wife of governor Sancho Panza? The duke and dutchess were extremely pleased at his arrival, and desirous to know the particulars of his journey, about which he was questioned accordingly. The page answered that he could not describe them in public, or in a few words; but begged their excellencies would be pleased to reserve the account for their private ear; and, in the mean time, entertain themselves with these letters. So saying, he produced two letters, and gave them to the dutchess, one superscribed in these words: "To my lady dutchess of I know not what nor where." And the other directed "To my husband Sancho Panza, governor of the island Barataria, whom God prosper many more years than myself."

The dutchess would not toast her cake, as the saying is, until she had read her letter, which having opened and perused by herself, when she perceived it might be recited aloud for the benefit of the duke and the company, she rehearsed it with an audible voice, to this effect:

### Teresa Panza's letter to the dutchess.

"I received great satisfaction, my lady, from the letter your grace was pleased to write me; for, in truth, it was what I greatly desired: the string of coral is very good, and my husband's hunting-suit comes not short of it: your ladyship's having made my spouse Sancho a governor, has given great pleasure to all our town, although there are some who cannot believe it, especially the curate, Mr. Nicholas the barber, and the batchelor Sampson Carrasco; but that gives me no trouble; for, seeing it be so, as it certainly is, let people say what they will: tho', if the truth must be told, had not the string of coral and the hunting-suit come, I should not have believed it myself; for, in our town, every body takes my husband for a noodle, and taken as he was, from governing an herd of goats, they cannot conceive what other government he can be good for. The Lord make him fit for his office, and conduct him in that way which will be most for the advantage of his children.

"For my own part, dear lady of my soul, I am resolved, with your honour's leave, to bring this happy day home to my own house, and hie me to the court, where I will loll in my coach, and burst the eyes of a thousand people who envy my good fortune: I beg therefore, your excellency will tell my husband to send me money, and let it be a round sum; for, it is very expensive living at court, where bread sells for a rial, and meat for thirty maravedis a pound; and

that is an unconscionable price. If he does not choose that I should go, let him give me notice in time; for, my feet itch to be a-travelling; and my neighbours and gossips tell me, if I and my daughter go to court, and appear in pomp and grandeur, my husband will come to be known by me, more than I by him; because, when people ask Who are these ladies in that coach? One of my servants will answer, These are the wife and daughter of Sancho Panza, governor of the island Barataria; and in this manner Sancho will be known, I shall be respected, and to Rome for every thing.

"I was vexed to the heart that this year there was no acorn harvest in our town; nevertheless, I send your highness about half a peck which I gathered one by one upon the mountain, and went thither on purpose: I could find none larger, tho' I wish they were as big as ostrich eggs.

"I hope your pomposity will not forget to write to me, and I will take care to send an answer, giving an account of my own health, and of every thing that may be worth mentioning from this place, where I remain praying to our Lord that he will preserve your grace, without forgetting me: my daughter Sanchica and my son kiss your honour's hand: and this is all at present from her who would much rather see your grace, than subscribe herself

Your humble servant,
TERESA PANZA."

Great was the satisfaction which all the hearers received from this letter of Teresa Panza, tho' the greatest share fell to the duke and dutchess; and her grace asked Don Quixote, whether or not he thought it would be proper to open the letter directed for the governor, which she imagined must be excellent in its kind. The knight said he would open it to oblige her grace, and having done so, found the contents to this purpose:

Teresa Panza's letter to her husband Sancho Panza.

"I received thy letter, dear Sancho of my soul, and I promise and swear to thee, on the faith of a catholic christian, I was within two fingers-breadth of running mad with joy; and take notice, brother, when I heard thou wast a governor, I had like to have dropped down dead with pure pleasure; for, thou knowest, they say, sudden joy kills as well as deadly sorrow: thy daughter Sanchica scattered her water about insensibly, out of meer satisfaction: thy hunting-suit lay before me, the string of corals sent by my lady dutchess was tied round my neck, the letters were in my hand, and the messenger in my presence; and yet, I imagined and believed, that all I saw and handled was a dream; for, who could conceive that a goatherd should come to be governor of islands? Thou know'st, my friend, that my mother said, One must live long to see a great deal: this I mention because I hope to see more if I live longer; for, I do not intend to stop, until I see thee a farmer, or collector of the revenue; offices which, tho' they carry those who abuse them to the devil, are, in short, always bringing in the penny.

"My lady dutchess will tell thee how desirous I am of going to court: consider of it and let me know thy pleasure; for, I will endeavour to do thee honour there by riding in my coach.

"The curate, barber, batchelor, and even the sexton, cannot believe thou art a governor, and say the whole is a deception, or matter of inchantment, like all the affairs of thy master Don Quixote. Sampson vows he will go in quest of thee, and drive this government out of thy head, as well as the madness out of Don Quixote's skull: I say nothing, but laugh in my own sleeve, look at my beads, and contrive how to make thy hunting-suit into a gown and petticoat for our daughter. I have sent some acorns to my lady dutchess, and I wish they were of

gold: send me some strings of pearl, if they are in fashion in thy island. The news of our town are these: the widow of the hill has matched her daughter with a bungling painter, who came here and undertook all sorts of brush-work; the corporation employed him to paint his majesty's arms over the door of the town-house; he demanded two ducats for the jobb, and they payed him beforehand; but, after he had laboured eight whole days, he produced nothing, and saying he could not hit upon such trifles, returned the money; and yet, for all that, he married with the character of a good workman: true it is, he hath already laid aside the pencil, and taken up the spade, and goes to the field like a gentleman. Pedro de Lobo's son has taken orders, and shaved his head, with intention to become a priest; and this circumstance being known by Minguilla, niece of Mingo Silvato, she is going to sue him upon promise of marriage: evil tongues scruple not to say she is with child by him; but, this he positively denies. This year there are no olives, nor a drop of vinegar, in the whole town. A company of soldiers marching this way, carried off three girls belonging to the village; but, I will not tell thee who they are, because perhaps they will return, and then there will not be wanting husbands who will take them with all their faults. Sanchica, by making bone-lace, clears eight maravedis a day, which she keeps in a pipkin, to be a stock to her when she grows up: but now, that she is a governor's daughter, thou wilt give her a portion without her working for it. The public fountain is dried up. A thunder-bolt fell upon the pillory, and there may they always light. I expect an answer to this epistle, and thy resolution about my going to court: and so, God preserve thee more years than I have to live, or as many; for, I should not choose to leave thee behind me in this world.

<div align="center">Thy faithful spouse,

TERESA PANZA."</div>

The letters were read with admiration, esteem, laughter, and applause; and the entertainment was crowned by the arrival of the courier who brought Sancho's epistle to Don Quixote, which, being likewise recited in public, rendered the governor's folly extremely doubtful. The dutchess retired, in order to be informed, by the page, of what had happened to him in Sancho's village; and he recounted the particulars at large, without leaving one circumstance untold: he delivered the acorns, together with a cheese, which Teresa vouched for excellent, and even preferred to those of Tronchon. This the dutchess received with excessive pleasure, in the enjoyment of which we will leave her grace, and relate in what manner concluded the government of the great Sancho Panza, the flower and mirrour of all insulary governors.

# THE

# LIFE and ATCHIEVEMENTS

## Of the Sage HIDALGO

# DON QUIXOTE DE LA MANCHA.

# BOOK IV.

### CHAPTER I.

## Of the toilful end and conclusion of Sancho Panza's government.

To think the affairs of this life will always remain in the same posture, is a wild supposition; on the contrary, every thing goes in a round: I mean, goes round. Spring succeeds winter, summer follows spring, autumn comes after summer, and winter comes in the rear of autumn; then spring resumes its verdure, and time turns round on an incessant wheel. The life of man alone runs lightly to its end, unlike the circle of time, without hope of renewal, except in another life, which knows no bounds. Thus moralizes Cid Hamet, the Mahometan philosopher, for the knowledge of the frailty, and instability, of the present life, together with the eternal duration of that which we expect, many, without the light of faith, by natural instinct have attained. But here our author makes the observation on account of the celerity with which Sancho's government was finished, consumed, destroyed, and dissolved into smoak and vapour.

This poor governor being a-bed on the seventh night of his administration, not crammed with bread and wine, but fatigued with sitting in judgment, passing sentence, and making statutes and regulations; and sleep, maugre and in despight of hunger, beginning to weigh down his eye-lids, his ears were saluted with a terrible noise of bells and cries, as if the whole island had been going to wreck.

Sitting up in his bed, he listened attentively, in hope of comprehending the meaning and cause of such a mighty uproar: however, he not only failed in his expectation; but, the noise of the cries and the bells being reinforced by that of an infinite number of drums and trumpets, he remained more terrified, confounded, and aghast than ever. Then starting up, he put on his slippers, on account of the dampness of the ground; though without wrapping himself up in his morning-gown, or in any other sort of apparel; and opening the door of his apartment, saw above twenty persons running through the gallery, with lighted torches, and naked swords in their hands, exclaiming

aloud, and altogether, "Arm! arm, my lord governor, arm! a vast number of the enemy has landed on the island; and we are lost and undone unless protected by your valour and activity."

With this clamour, fury, and disturbance, they rushed towards Sancho, who stood astonished and perplexed at what he saw and heard; and when they came up to the spot, one of them accosting him, "Arm, my lord," said he, "unless you want to perish, and see the whole island destroyed." "For what should I arm?" replied Sancho: "I neither know the use of arms, nor can I give you protection: these matters had better be left to my master Don Quixote, who, in the turning of a straw, would dispatch the whole affair, and put every thing in safety; but, for me, as I am a sinner to God, I understand nothing of these hurly burlys!" "How! my lord governor," cried another, "what despondence is this? Put on your armour, signor; here we have brought arms offensive and defensive; come forth to the market-place, and be our guide and our general, seeing of right that place belongs to you, as being our governor." "Arm me then, a-God's name!" replied Sancho: at that instant they took two large bucklers they had brought along with them, and putting over his shirt (for they would not give him time to cloath himself) one buckler before and another behind, they pulled his arms through certain holes they had made in the targets, and fastened them well together with cords, in such a manner, that the poor governor remained quite inclosed, and boarded up as streight as a spindle, without being able to bend his knees, or move one single step: and in his hands they put a lance, with which he supported himself as he stood. Having cooped him up in this manner, they desired him to march out, and conduct and animate his people; in which case, he being their north star, their lanthorn, and Lucifer, their affairs would be brought to a prosperous issue. "How should I march, unfortunate wight that I am," said Sancho, "when my very knee-pans have not room to play, so much am I cramped by those boards, which are squeezed into my very flesh? your only way is to take me up in your arms, and lay me across, or set me upright in some postern, which I will defend either with this lance or this carcase." "Come, my lord governor," replied the other, "you are more hampered by fear than by your bucklers: make haste, and exert yourself; for, it grows late, the enemies swarm, the noise increases, and the danger is very pressing."

In consequence of this persuasion and reproach, the poor governor endeavoured to move, and down he came to the ground with such a fall that he believed himself split to pieces. There he lay like a tortoise covered with its shell, or a flitch of bacon between two trays; or, lastly, like a boat stranded with her keel uppermost. Yet his fall did not excite the compassion of those unlucky wags; on the contrary, extinguishing their torches, they renewed the clamour, and repeated the alarm with such hurry and confusion, trampling upon the unhappy Sancho, and bestowing a thousand strokes upon the bucklers, that if he had not gathered, and shrunk himself up, with drawing his head within the targets, the poor governor would have passed his time but very indifferently; shrunk as he was within that narrow lodging, he sweated all over with fear and consternation, and heartily recommended himself to God, that he might be delivered from the danger that encompassed him. Some stumbled, and others fell over him; nay, one of the party stood upon him for a considerable time, and thence, as from a watch-tower, gave orders to the army, exclaiming with a loud voice, "This way, my fellow-soldiers; for, here the

enemy make their chief effort: guard this breach, shut that gate, down with those scal-ing-ladders, bring up the fire-pots, with the kettles of melted pitch, rosin, and boiling oil, barricado the streets with woolpacks." In a word, he named with great eagerness, all the implements, instruments, and munition of war, used in the defence of a city as-saulted; while the bruised and battered Sancho, who heard the din, and suffered griev-ously, said within himself, "O! would it please the Lord that the island were quickly lost, that I might see myself either dead or delivered from this distress!" Heaven heard his petition, and when he least expected such relief, his ears were saluted with a number of voices, crying, "Victory! victory! the enemy is overcome! Rise, my lord governor, and enjoy your conquest; and divide the spoil taken from the foe by the valour of your invin-cible arm."

The afflicted Sancho, with a plaintive voice, desired them to lift him up; and when they helped him to rise, and set him on his legs again, "I wish," said he, "the enemy I have conquered were nailed to my forehead: I want to divide no spoils; but, I beg, and supplicate some friend, if any such I have, to bring me a draught of wine; and that he will wipe me dry of this sweat which has turned me into water." They accordingly wiped him clean, brought the wine, untied the bucklers, and seated him upon his bed, where he fainted away through fear, consternation, and fatigue. Those concerned in the joke, now began to be sorry for having laid it on so heavy; but, Sancho's recovery moderated their uneasiness at his swooning. He asked what it was o'clock? and they answered it was day-break: then, without speaking another syllable, he began to dress himself, in the most profound silence, and all present gazed upon him with looks of expectation, im-patient to know the meaning of his dressing himself so earnestly. At length, having put on his cloaths very leisurely; for, his bruises would not admit of precipitation, he hied him to the stable, attended by all the bystanders, where, advancing to Dapple, he em-braced him affectionately, and gave him the kiss of peace upon the forehead, saying, while the tears trickled from his eyes, "Come hither, my dear companion! my friend, and sharer of all my toils and distress; when you and I consorted together, and I was plagued with no other thoughts than the care of mending your furniture, and pamper-ing your little body, happy were my hours, my days, and my years! but, since I quitted you, and mounted on the towers of pride and ambition, my soul has been invaded by a thousand miseries, a thousand toils, and four thousand disquiets."

While he uttered this apostrophe, he was employed in putting the pack-saddle on his ass, without being interrupted by any living soul; and Dapple being equipped for the road, he made shift to mount him, with great pain and difficulty: then, directing his words and discourse to the steward, secretary, sewer, doctor Pedro, and many others who were present, "Make way, gentlemen," said he, "and let me return to my ancient liberty; let me go in quest of my former life, that I may enjoy a resurrection from this present death: I was not born to be a governor, or to defend islands and cities from the assaults of their enemies: I am better versed in ploughing and delving, in pruning and planting vines, than in enacting laws, and defending provinces and kingdoms. I know St. Peter is well at Rome—that is, every one does well in following the employment to which he was bred; a sickle becomes my hand better than a governor's sceptre; and I would rather fill my belly with soupe-meagre,[1] than undergo the misery of an imperti-

nent physician who starves me to death. I would much rather solace myself under the shade of an oak in summer, and cloath myself with a sheepskin jacket in the winter, being my own master, than indulge, under the subjection of a government, with holland sheets, and robes of sables—God be with you, gentlemen; and pray tell my lord duke, Naked I was born, and naked I remain; and, if I lose nothing, as little I gain. That is, I would say, Pennyless I took possession of this government, and pennyless I resign my office; quite the reverse of what is usually the case with governors of other islands. Make way, therefore, and let me go and be plaistered; for, I believe, all my ribs are crushed, thanks to the enemies who have, this night, passed, and repassed, over my carcase."

"It must not be so, my lord governor," said doctor Positive: "I will give your worship a draught, calculated for falls and bruises, that will instantly restore you to your former health and vigour; and, with respect to the article of eating, I promise your lordship to make amends, and let you eat abundantly of every thing you desire." "Your promise comes too late," answered Sancho: "and I will as soon turn Turk as forbear going. Those are no jokes to be repeated. Before God! I will as soon remain in this, or accept of any other government, even tho' it should be presented in a covered dish, as I will fly to heaven without the help of wings. I am of the family of the Panzas, who are all head-strong, and if once they say Odds, odds it must be, tho' in fact it be even, in spite of all the world. In this stable I leave the pismire's wings, that carried me up into the clouds, to make me a prey to martlets and other birds; and now let us alight, and walk softly and securely on the ground; and if my feet are not adorned with pinked shoes of Cordovan leather, they shall not want coarse sandals of cord or rushes: Let ewe and weather go together; and, No body thrust his feet beyond the length of his sheet. Now, therefore, let me pass; for, it grows late."

To this address the steward replied, "We shall freely allow your lordship to go, although we shall be great sufferers in losing you, whose ingenuity, and christian conduct, oblige us to desire your stay; but, it is well known that every governor is obliged, before he quits his government, to submit his administration to a scrutiny; and if your lordship will give an account of yours, during the seven days² you have stood at the helm, you may depart in peace, and God be your guide." "No body can call me to an account," said Sancho, "but such as are appointed by my lord duke. Now, to him am I going, and to him will I render it fairly and squarely: besides, there is no occasion for any other proof than my leaving you naked as I am, to shew that I have governed like an angel." "'Fore God! the great Sancho is in the right," cried doctor Positive: "and, in my opinion, we ought to let him retire; for, the duke will be infinitely rejoiced to see him."

All the rest assented to the proposal, and allowed him to pass, after having offered to bear him company, and provide him with every thing he should want for the entertainment of his person, and the convenience of the journey. Sancho said he wanted nothing but a little barley for Dapple, and a piece of cheese with half a loaf for himself, the journey being so short, that he had no occasion for any better, or more ample provision. All the company embraced him, and were in their turns embraced by the weeping Sancho, who left them equally astonished at his discourse, as at his resolute, and wise determination.

## CHAPTER II.

# Which treats of matters belonging to this history, and no other whatsoever.

T he duke, and dutchess, resolved that the defiance which Don Quixote breathed against their vassal, for the cause already mentioned, should be answered: and although the young man was in Flanders, whither he had fled to avoid such a mother-in-law as Donna Rodriguez, they determined to supply his place with a Gascoon lacquey, called Tosilos, whom they beforehand minutely instructed to behave on this occasion.

Two days after these measures were taken, the duke told Don Quixote that in four days his antagonist would come and present himself in the lists, armed as a knight, and maintain that the damsel lied by one half of her beard, and even by every hair of it, if she affirmed that he had promised her marriage. The knight received these tidings with great pleasure, flattering himself he should do something to excite the admiration of the whole family; and he thought himself extremely fortunate in having found an opportunity of shewing this noble pair how far the valour of his powerful arm extended. He, therefore, with great joy, and satisfaction, waited the expiration of the four days, which, reckoned by his impatience, seemed equal to four hundred centuries.

In the mean time, let them pass, as we have already let many other matters pass, and attend Sancho, who, between merry and sad, jogged along upon Dapple, in quest of his master, whose company he preferred to the government of all the islands upon earth. Well then, he had not travelled far from the island of his government, (for, he never dreamed of being certified whether what he governed was island, city, town, or village) when he saw coming towards him six pilgrims, with their staves, of that sort which begs charity by singing. So soon, therefore, as they approached him, they made a lane; and, raising their voices together, began to sing in their language, tho' Sancho understood nothing of what they said, except the word Charity, which they distinctly pronounced; so that he immediately conceived the meaning of their outlandish song. Now, he being, according to the asseveration of Cid Hamet, extremely charitable, took out of his bags, and gave them the bread and cheese with which he had been furnished, making them understand by signs, that he had nothing else to give. They received his benefaction chearfully, pronouncing, however, the word Guelte, Guelte: to which Sancho answering, "I really do not understand what you want, good people": One of them took a purse from his bosom, and held it up, giving him to understand they wanted money. Then Sancho clapping thumb to his throat, and displaying the back of his hand, signified that he had not so much as the corner of a rial, and spurred up Dapple, in order to make his way through the midst of them. As he passed, one of them having considered him very attentively, laid hold on Dapple's halter, and clasping him round the middle, exclaimed aloud, in very good Castilian, "The Lord protect me! what is this I see? is it possible that I actually hold in my arms my dear friend, and good neighbour, Sancho Panza? Yes, doubtless; for, I am neither asleep nor drunk."

Sancho was astonished to hear his own name; and see himself embraced by a pilgrim, and a stranger, whom, tho' he silently gazed upon him with the utmost attention, he could by no means recollect. The pilgrim perceiving his surprize, "Is it possible, brother Sancho Panza," said he, "that thou dost not know thy neighbor Ricote, the Moresco shop-keeper, that lived in your town?" Then Sancho, reviewing him with greater attention, began to recal his features; and, at length, perfectly recognizing the Moor, he, without alighting, threw his arms about his neck, saying, "Who the devil could know thee, Ricote, in that disguise? Tell me who has pilgrimized thee;[1] and wherefore hast thou dared to return to Spain, where, if thou art found, and known, thou wilt suffer for thy rashness?" "If thou wilt not discover me, Sancho, I am secure," replied the pilgrim: "for, in this disguise, no body will know me. Let us quit the high-road, and remove to yon poplar grove, where my companions intend to take some refreshment, and repose; there thou shalt partake with them; for, they are a very good sort of people; and there I shall have leisure to recount every thing that has befallen me since I departed from our town, in obedience to his majesty's proclamation, which so severely threatened the unfortunate people of my nation; as, no doubt, thou hast heard."

Sancho assented to his proposal, and Ricote having spoke to the other pilgrims, they betook themselves to the tuft of poplars, at a good distance from the high-road. There they threw down their staves, laid aside their rochets, or mantles, so as to remain in their doublets; and all of them appeared to be young men of genteel persons, except Ricote, who was already advanced in years. Each had a wallet, in all appearance well provided; at least, with incentives which provoked thirst, at the distance of two leagues. They stretched themselves upon the ground, and using the grass as a table-cloth, spread upon it bread, salt, knives, nuts, crusts of cheese, and some clean bones of bacon, which, tho' they could not be eaten, were in a condition to be sucked with pleasure. They likewise produced a black dish, which they called Caviere, made of the roes of fishes, a great awakener of drought; nor did they want olives, which, though dry, and without pickle, were very savoury, and delicate: but what made the best figure in the field of this banquet, was a bottle of wine which every pilgrim drew forth from his wallet, not excepting honest Ricote, who, being transformed from a Moor into a German, or Teutonian, pulled out his bottle also, which in size might have vied with all the other five. They began to eat with infinite relish, and great deliberation, smacking their lips at every mouthful which they took with the point of a knife, tho' they ate but little; then all at once, the whole squadron together raised their arms, and bottles aloft, and joining mouth to mouth, with their eyes fixed on the firmament, they seemed to take aim at heaven. In this manner, shaking their heads from side to side, in token of the satisfaction they received, they continued a good while in the act of transfusing the contents of the bottles into their own bellies.

Sancho beheld this scene, with every part of which he was perfectly well pleased; and, in compliance with the proverb which he very well knew, importing, When thou art at Rome, follow the fashion of Rome, he begged an embrace of Ricote's bottle, and took his aim like the rest; nor was his satisfaction inferior to theirs. Four times did their bottles admit of elevation; but, the fifth was to no purpose: for, by that time, they were as clean, and as dry as a rush; a circumstance that threw a damp upon the mirth which

had hitherto prevailed. From time to time, each pilgrim in his turn shook hands with Sancho, saying, "Spaniard or German, all one, goot companion." To which compliment Sancho replied, "Goot companion, by the Lord!" and bursting out into a fit of laughter which lasted a whole hour, without remembering, at that time, the least circumstance of what had happened to him in his government; for, over the times, and seasons, of eating and drinking, care seldom holds jurisdiction. Finally, the conclusion of the wine was the beginning of sleep, which overwhelmed the whole company, and stretched them along upon the table, and cloth, they had been using. Ricote, and Sancho, were the only two who remained awake, in consequence of having eaten more, and drank less, than their fellows: then Ricote taking Sancho aside, they sat down at the root of a beech, leaving the pilgrims buried in an agreeable slumber; and without stumbling in the least upon his Morisco language, he spoke in pure Castilian to this effect:

"Well thou knowest, O Sancho Panza, my neighbour, and friend, how the edict, and proclamation, which his majesty published against those of my religion, overwhelmed us all with terror and consternation; at least, they terrified me to such a degree, that long before the time allotted to us for our removal from Spain, I thought the rigour of the penalty was already executed against me and my children. I therefore resolved, and I think, wisely, like the man who knowing he must quit the house he lives in, at such a time, provides himself with another to which he may remove—I resolved, I say, to retire by myself, without my family, and go in quest of some place to which I might carry it commodiously, without that hurry and confusion which attended the departure of my neighbours; for, I was very well convinced, and so were all our elders, that those edicts were not only threats, as some people said, but real laws, that would certainly be put in execution at the appointed time: and this truth I was compelled to believe, by knowing the base and mad designs which our people harboured; such designs that, I verily think, his majesty was divinely inspired to execute such a gallant resolution. Not that we were all guilty; for, some, among us, were firm, and stanch christians: but, they were so few in number, that they could not oppose the schemes of those who were otherwise; and it was dangerous to nurse a serpent in one's bosom, by allowing the enemy to live within the house. In a word, we were justly chastised by the sentence of banishment, mild and gentle in the opinion of some, but to us the most terrible that could be pronounced. In what country soever we are, we lament our exile from Spain: for, in fine, here we were born; this is our native country; in no clime do we find a reception suitable to our misfortunes: nay, in Barbary, and all the other parts of Afric, where we expected to be received, cherished, and entertained, we have been most injured, and maltreated: we knew not our happiness until we lost it; and so intense is the longing desire which almost all of us have to return to Spain, that the greatest part of those, and they are many, who understand the language like me, return to this kingdom, leaving their wives, and children, unprotected abroad, such is their affection for this their native soil: and now, I know, by experience, the truth of the common saying, Sweet is the love of native land.

"Leaving our town, as I have already said, I repaired to France; and, tho' there we met with a civil reception, I was desirous of seeing other countries. I, therefore, travelled into Italy, from whence I passed into Germany, where people seemed to live with more freedom: the natives do not pry with curious eyes into one another's concerns; every one

lives according to his own humour: for, in most parts of the empire there is liberty of conscience. I left a house which I hired in a village near Augsburg, and joined these pilgrims, a great number of whom are wont to come hither yearly, on pretence of visiting the sanctuaries of Spain, which are their Indies, as being productive of well known advantage, and most certain gain. They traverse the whole country; and there is not a village from which they are not dismissed with a belly full of meat and drink, as the saying is, and a rial, at least, in money; so that, at the end of their peregrination, they are above an hundred crowns in pocket, which, being changed into gold, they conceal in the hollow of their staves, or in the patches of their cloaks, or task their industry in such a manner as to carry off their purchase to their own country, in spite of the guards at the passes and gates, where they are examined and registred.

"My present intention, Sancho, is to carry off the money I have buried, which, being without the town, I can retrieve without danger; then I shall write, or take a passage from Valencia, to my wife and daughter, who, I know, are at Algiers, in order to contrive a method for transporting them to some port of France, from whence I will conduct them to Germany, where we will bear with resignation the will of heaven: for, in fine, Sancho, I am positively certain that my daughter Ricota, and my wife Francisca Ricote are real catholic christians; and, tho' I myself am not entirely of that way of thinking, I have more of the christian than the mussulman; and I incessantly pray to God to open the eyes of my understanding, that I may know how to serve him the right way. But what excites my wonder, and baffles my penetration, is the conduct of my wife and daughter, who have chosen to retire into Barbary rather than to France, where they might have lived as christians."

To this observation Sancho replied, "Why, look ye, Ricote, they were not, I suppose, at liberty to choose for themselves, inasmuch as they were carried off by your wife's brother, John Tiopieyo, who, being a rank Moor, would naturally go to the place where he himself intended to make his abode: and, I can tell you, moreover, I believe it will be in vain for you to go in search of what you left under-ground; for, we were informed that thy wife, and brother-in-law, were stripped of a number of pearls, and a great deal of money, which was carried off to be registred." "That may be very true," said Ricote: "but, I am certain, Sancho, they have not touched my hoard; for, I would not tell them where it was hid, because I dreaded some misfortune: and therefore, Sancho, if thou wilt come along with me, and assist me in taking up, and concealing it, I will gratify thee with two hundred crowns, to relieve thy necessities, which thou are sensible I know to be manifold." "I would comply with thy proposal," answered Sancho; "but I am not at all covetous; were I that way inclined, I this morning quitted an employment by which I might have been enabled to build the walls of my house of beaten gold, and in less than six months, eat out of plate: for this reason, therefore, and because I should think myself guilty of treason to my king, in favouring his enemies, I will not go along with thee, even tho' in lieu of promising me two hundred, thou shouldst here lay down four hundred crowns upon the nail." "And pray, what office is this that thou hast quitted?" said Ricote. "I have quitted the government of an island," replied Sancho: "ay, and such a one as, in good faith, you will not find its fellow in three bowshots." "And whereabouts is this island?" resumed the other. "Whereabouts?" cried Panza: "about two leagues from hence,

and it is called the island Barataria." "Spare me, spare me, good Sancho," said Ricote: "islands are far at sea; there are none upon the continent." "How? none!" replied Sancho: "I tell thee, friend Ricote, I left it but this morning, and yesterday governed in it at my pleasure, like a perfect sagittary;[2] but, for all that, I resigned my place; for, I found the office of governors is very troublesome and dangerous." "And what hast thou got by this government?" said Ricote. "I have got sense enough to know that I am fit for governing nothing but a flock of sheep," answered Sancho: "and that the wealth acquired in such governments is got at the expence of ease, sleep, and even sustenance; for, in islands the governors must eat very little, especially if they have physicians to watch over their health." "I really do not understand thee, Sancho," said Ricote: "but, every thing thou hast spoke, to me seems meer madness; for, who would give thee islands to govern, when there is plenty of men in the world, so much more capable of governing than thou? Keep thy own counsel, Sancho, and recollect thy judgment, and consider whether or not thou wilt accompany me, as I have proposed, to assist me in conveying the treasure I have hid; for, the sum is really so great, it may well be called a treasure, and I will give thee wherewithal to live, as I have already promised." "I have already told thee, Ricote, that I will not," answered Sancho: "be satisfied that by me thou shalt not be discovered, continue thy journey in happy hour, and let me proceed in mine: for, well I know, What's honestly earn'd may be easily lost, but, ill got wealth is ever at the owner's cost." "Well, I will not further importune thee," said Ricote: "but, pray tell me, Sancho, wast thou in our village, when my wife and daughter departed with my brother-in-law?" "Yes, I was," replied Sancho: "and, I can tell thee, thy daughter appeared so beautiful, that all the people in town went forth to see her, and every body owned she was the fairest creature under the sun; she went along weeping, and embraced all her friends and acquaintance; and begged of all that came to see her, that they would recommend her to God, and our lady his blessed mother. Indeed, her behaviour was so moving, that I myself, who am no blubberer, could not help shedding tears; and, in good sooth, many persons were very desirous of going after, and carrying her off, in order to conceal her; but, they were diverted from that design, by the fear of acting contrary to the king's proclamation. He that shewed himself the most passionately fond of her, was Don Pedro Gregorio, the young rich heir, who, thou knowest, was said to be in love with her. After her departure, he never more appeared in our town, and every body believed he went away, in order to carry her off; but, hitherto we have had no account of his motions." "I had always a suspicion," said Ricote, "that the young gentleman was enamoured of my daughter; but, as I confided in the virtue of my Ricota, his passion gave me no disturbance; for, thou must have heard, Sancho, that the Moorish women seldom, or never, engage in amorous intercourse with old christians; and my daughter, whose inclination, I believe, leaned more to christianity than to love, payed no attention to the importunities of that young heir." "God grant it may be so," replied Sancho: "for, it would have been to the prejudice of both: and now let me depart in peace, friend Ricote; for, this night, I intend to be with my master Don Quixote." "God be thy guide, brother Sancho," said the Moor: "I see my companions are stirring, and it is time for us to make the best of our way."

Then the two having embraced one another, Sancho mounted Dapple, Ricote supported himself with his staff, and in this manner they parted different ways.

## CHAPTER III.

## Of certain accidents that befel Sancho upon the road; and other circumstances, which to know you need only look forward.

Sancho was so long detained by Ricote, that he could not reach the duke's castle that day, tho' he was within half a league of it, and there overtaken by the night, which was dark and close; but, it being the summer season, he was not much concerned, and retired a little from the high-road, with intention to wait patiently for morning. It was, however, the pleasure of his niggard and unhappy fortune, that in seeking a place proper for his accommodation, he and Dapple tumbled into a deep, and very dark pit, among a number of old buildings. In falling, he recommended himself to God, with all his heart, in the firm persuasion that he would not stop until he reached the bottom of the profound abyss. But this apprehension was happily disappointed; for, Dapple having descended little more than three fathoms, touched the ground, and his rider found himself on his beast's back, without having sustained the least hurt or damage. He felt his body all over, and held in his breath to know whether he was sound or perforated in any part; and when he found himself safe, whole, and in catholic health, he did not fail to thank our Lord God for his protection, as he actually thought he had been shattered into a thousand pieces. He likewise felt about the sides of the pit, to know if there was any possibility of being extricated without assistance; but, he found them all smooth, and perpendicular, without any projection or cranny of which he could take the least advantage; a circumstance that greatly increased his chagrin, especially when he heard Dapple complain, in a most pathetic, and lamentable tone; and, indeed, it was no great wonder: nor did he lament out of wantonness; for, in truth, he was in a very sorry condition.

It was then that Sancho Panza exclaimed, "Alack, and a-well a-day! how unexpected are the accidents which, at every turn, befal those who live in this miserable world! who could foretel, that he who yesterday saw himself inthroned as governor of an island, giving orders to his servants and vassals, should to-day be buried in a dungeon, without a soul to remedy his misfortune, or a servant or vassal to hasten to his relief? Here I, and my poor beast, must perish by hunger, if we do not give up the ghost before that period; he, in consequence of being battered and bruised, and I, from pure sorrow and vexation. At least, I shall not be so lucky as my master Don Quixote de la Mancha, who, when he descended, and sunk into the cave of that same inchanted Montesinos, was better entertained than he could have been in his own house; so that the cloth seemed to be laid, and the bed fairly made. There he enjoyed beautiful and agreeable visions; but here, I believe, I shall see nothing but toads and serpents. Unfortunate wretch that I am! to what a pass am I brought by my fantasies and folly. From this cavern (when heaven shall be pleased to discover them) my bones, together with those of my honest friend Dapple, will be taken up smooth, and white, and bare as an atomy;[1] and, from this particular, perhaps, it will be discovered who we are, especially by those who know that Sancho Panza

never parted from his ass, nor his ass from Sancho Panza. I say again, miserable crea-
tures that we are! why would not our niggard fortune allow us to die at home, in our own
country, in the midst of our friends? where, tho' our misfortune would admit of no rem-
edy, we should not have wanted relations to grieve at our fate, and close our eyes in the
last hour of our trial!

"O my dear companion, and my friend! how ill have I rewarded thy good services!
Forgive me, honest Dapple, and intreat fortune in the best terms thou canst use, to de-
liver us from this vexatious misery in which we are equally involved; in which case, I
promise to put a crown of laurel upon thy head, so as that thou shalt look like a poet lau-
reat; and, withal, to give thee double allowance of provender." In this manner did San-
cho Panza pour forth his lamentation, to which the poor beast listened, without an-
swering one word; such was the danger and distress to which the poor animal found
himself exposed.

At length, after they had passed the whole night in miserable complaints and lamen-
tations, day broke; and, by the light and splendor of the morning, Sancho perceived,
that of all impossibilities it was the most impossible to free himself from that pit, with-
out assistance; so that he began to lament a-fresh, and roar aloud, in hope that some
body might hear his voice: but, all his cries were uttered to the desart; for, in all that
neighbourhood there was not a soul by whom he could be heard; and therefore he gave
himself up for lost. As Dapple lay with his mouth uppermost, Sancho Panza exerted
himself in such a manner as to raise his friend upon his legs, which, by the bye, could
scarce bear his weight; and, taking a piece of bread out of his wallet, which had likewise
suffered the same unfortunate fall, gave it to the poor beast, who received it very thank-
fully, and Sancho told him, as if he understood his words, "All ills are good when at-
tended with food." About this time, he discovered an hole at one side of the dungeon,
large enough to give passage to a man, provided he could bend his body, and creep
through: to this he hastened, and squeezing himself into it, perceived, within, a large ex-
tensive space, the particulars of which he could distinguish; for, through what may be
termed the roof, descended a small stream of light that illuminated the whole place,
which, as he observed, dilated and extended itself through another spacious concavity.

Sancho, having made these remarks, returned to the place where his companion
stood, and with a stone began to clear away the rubbish from the hole, which he in a
little time enlarged to such a degree that Dapple passed with ease. Then, taking the hal-
ter in his hand, he led him forwards through that cavern, in hope of finding an exit at
the other end: and sometimes he proceeded darkling, and sometimes without one ray
of light; but, always in fear and trepidation. "God Almighty protect me!" said he within
himself: "this, that is such a dismal expedition to me, would be an excellent adventure
to my master, who would look upon these depths, and dungeons, as so many flower-
gardens, and palaces of * Galiana; and expect to pass from this distress, and obscurity,
into some blooming meadow adorned with the pride of spring: whereas, I, a miserable
wretch! equally imprudent and poor-spirited, dread, at every step, that another dun-

---

* This was a Moorish princess, for whom her father built a stately palace near the Tagus, the ruins
of which remain to this day.[2]

geon, still more deep, will suddenly open under my feet, and swallow me up at once: We may bear, without a groan, the misfortune that comes alone." In venting these ejaculations, he fancied he had proceeded about half a league, when he perceived a kind of confused light, like that of day, glimmering through a passage that seemed to be the road from this to the other world.

Here Cid Hamet Benengeli, leaving the squire, returns to Don Quixote waiting with joy and transport for the combat in which he was to engage with the person who had robbed the daughter of Donna Rodriguez of her precious virtue; for, he made no doubt of redressing the grievance and disgrace which the delinquent had feloniously intailed upon the innocent damsel.

Chancing one morning to go out, in order to improve, and inure himself to that exercise of arms which he meant to practise in that combat to which in a few days he must be exposed, he, in wheeling about, or giving the charge with Rozinante, rode so near the mouth of a cavern, that if he had not vigorously pulled in the reins, he must have plunged into it, without all possibility of escape. He kept his seat, however, and at length made his retreat good; then, reapproaching the hole, he, without alighting, surveyed the depth of the cave; and, while he was thus employed, heard loud cries issuing from below; in consequence of which, listening with great attention, he could distinguish articulate sounds, and distinctly understand the following exclamation: "So ho! above there; is there any christian within hearing? or any charitable gentleman whose bowels yearn at the distress of a sinner buried alive, and an unfortunate misgoverned governor?"

Don Quixote thought he recognized the voice of Sancho Panza, at hearing which he was confounded and astonished; and raising his own voice as high as he could strain, "Who is that below," cried he, "complaining so grievously?" "Who should be here, or who complain, but the bewildered Sancho Panza, for his sins, and misfortune, appointed governor of the island Barataria, who was formerly squire to the renowned knight Don Quixote de la Mancha?" When the knight heard this declaration, his surprise redoubled, his amazement increased, and he was struck with the notion that Sancho Panza was dead, and his soul doing penance in that place. Swayed by this conjecture, he exclaimed, "I conjure thee by all that is sacred, as a catholic christian, to tell me who thou art; if a soul in punishment, let me know what I can do in thy behalf; for, as it is my profession to favour and assist the needy of this world, so likewise am I ready to succour and relieve the miserable objects of the other world, who cannot relieve themselves." "At that rate, and by your worship's discourse," answered the voice, "you should be my master Don Quixote de la Mancha; and, indeed, by the tone of your voice, I know you can be no other." "Don Quixote I am," replied the knight: "he who professes to aid and assist the living, as well as the dead, in their distresses. Tell me, therefore, who thou art, by whom I am thus held in astonishment; for, if thou art my squire Sancho Panza, and hast quitted this life, seeing the devils have not got possession of thy soul, but, through the mercy of God, thou art now in purgatory, our holy mother the roman catholic church has prayers sufficient to deliver thee from thy present pain; and I, for my part, will sollicit them in thy behalf, as far as my whole fortune will extend: I say, therefore, make haste, and declare thy name and situation." "I vow to God!" answered the voice, "and swear by the birth of whom your worship pleases, signor Don Quixote de la Man-

cha, that I am your identical squire Sancho Panza, and was never yet dead in the whole course of my life; but, I quitted my government for causes and considerations which I must have more leisure to explain; last night I fell into this dungeon, together with Dapple, who will not suffer me to tell an untruth; by the same token he stands now at my back." One would have imagined the beast understood what his master said; for, that moment, he began to bray so strenuously that the whole cave echoed with the sound. "A most unexceptionable evidence!" cried Don Quixote: "I know that note as well as if I had given it birth; and, besides, I recognize thy voice, my good Sancho; wait a little, I will ride to the duke's castle, which is hard by, and bring people to extricate thee from that dungeon into which thou hast been plunged for thy sins and transgressions." "I intreat your worship to go, for the love of God! and return speedily; for, I cannot bear to be buried here alive; and, moreover, I am ready to die with fear!"

The knight leaving him accordingly, repaired to the castle, where he recounted to the duke and dutchess the accident which had befallen poor Sancho, at which they were not a little surprised, tho' they at once comprehended how he must have fallen by the correspondence of that cavern which had been there time out of mind; but, they could not conceive how he should have quitted the government, without giving them notice of his coming. Finally, ropes and cables were provided, together with a good number of people; and Dapple, and Sancho Panza, tho' not without a good deal of trouble, were hoisted up from dungeons and darkness to the chearful light of day. "In this manner," said a student, who chanced to be among the spectators, "should all bad governors be dragged from their governments, like that poor sinner from the profound abyss, half dead with hunger, pale with fear, and, as I believe, without a penny in his pocket." Sancho, hearing this observation, replied, "Eight or ten days are now elapsed, brother growler, since I assumed the reins of government in that island which was committed to my charge; and, in all that time, I never once had my belly full, even of dry bread: I have been persecuted by physicians; my bones have been crushed by the enemy: but, I never had a bribe in view, nor did I ever receive my due. And this being the case, as it certainly is, methinks, I have not deserved to be dragged out in this manner: but, Man projects in vain; for, God doth still ordain: Heaven knows how meet it is to grant what every one pretends to want: Every season has its reason: Let no man presume to think, of this cup I will not drink: for, Where the flitch we hoped to find, not even a hook is left behind. God knows my meaning, and that's enough; I shall say no more, tho' perhaps I could speak more plainly." "Be not angry, Sancho," replied Don Quixote, "and give thyself no concern about what thou mayest hear, otherwise there will be no end of thy vexation: console thyself with a good conscience, and let them say what they will; for, it is as impracticable to tie up the tongue of malice, as to erect barricadoes in the open fields. If a governor resigns his office in good circumstances, people say he must have been an oppressor, and a knave; and if poverty attends him in his retreat, they set him down as an idiot, and fool." "For this time," answered Sancho, "I am certain they will think me more fool than knave."

Thus discoursing, and surrounded by a number of boys, and other spectators, they arrived at the castle, where the duke and dutchess waited to receive them in a gallery; but, Sancho would not go up stairs, until he saw Dapple properly accommodated in the

stable; for, he observed, the poor creature had passed the preceding night in very indifferent lodging: then he went to pay his respects to his noble patrons, before whom, falling on his knees, "According to the good pleasure of your graces," said he, "and without any merit on my side, I went to govern your island Barataria, which Naked I entered, and naked I remain; and if I lose nothing, as little I gain. Whether I have governed righteously or amiss, there are witnesses who will declare, and say whatsoever they think proper. I have explained doubts, and decided causes, though all the time half dead with hunger, because my fasting seemed good unto doctor Pedro Positive, native of Snatchaway, the island and governor's physician: we were assaulted in the night by the enemy, who put us all in great jeopardy and consternation; and the inhabitants of the island said they were delivered, and proved victorious, by the valour of my invincible arm; but, so may God deal with them as they speak truth. In a word, I have, during my administration, considered the cares and obligations that attend the exercise of power, and found them, by my reckoning, too weighty for my shoulders; they are neither fit burthens for my back, nor arrows for my quiver: and therefore, that the government might not discard me, I have thought proper to discard the government; and yesterday I left the island as I found it, with the same streets, houses and roofs, which belonged to it when I took possession. I have borrowed of no man, nor consulted my own private gain or advantage; and although my intention was to make some wholesome regulations, I did not put my design in execution, because I was afraid they would not be observed; and a law neglected is the same thing as one that never was enacted.

"I quitted the island, as I have said, without any other company than that of Dapple; I fell into a dungeon, through which I groped my way, until, this morning, by the light of the sun, I perceived a passage out of it, though not so easy but that if heaven had not sent my master Don Quixote to my assistance, there I should have remained to the day of judgment. Here then, my lord duke, and lady dutchess, is your governor Sancho Panza, who, during the ten days of his administration, has gained nothing but so much knowledge, that he would not give a farthing to be governor, not only of an island, but even of the whole world; and in this opinion, kissing your graces feet, and imitating the game of boys, who cry, Leap and away, I take a leap from the government into the service of my master Don Quixote; for, in short, tho' with him I eat my bread in terror and alarm, I at least fill my belly; and so that is full, I care not whether it be with carrots or partridge."

Here Sancho concluded his harrangue, during which the knight was in continual apprehension that he would utter a thousand absurdities; but, when he heard it finished with so few, he thanked heaven in his heart; while the duke embraced Sancho, and told him he was grieved to the soul that he had so soon left his government; but, he would find means to invest him with another office in his estate, which would be attended with less care and more advantage. He was likewise consoled by the dutchess, who gave particular orders about his entertainment, as he seemed to be sorely bruised, and in a lamentable condition.

## CHAPTER IV.

Of the dreadful and unseen battle, fought between Don Quixote
de la Mancha and the lacquey Tosilos, in behalf of the daughter
of Rodriguez the duenna.

T he duke and dutchess did not repent of the joke they had executed upon Sancho
Panza, with respect to his government, especially as the steward arrived the same
day, and gave a circumstantial detail of all the words and actions which he had said and
performed, during the term of his administration. In fine, he magnified the assault of
the island, and the terror of Sancho, and described the manner of his departure, from
the account of which they received no small pleasure and satisfaction.

The history afterwards relates, that the day appointed for the combat arrived; and the
duke, having again and again instructed his lacquey Tosilos how to manage Don Qui-
xote, so as to conquer without slaying, or even wounding the knight, ordered the
launces to be divested of their iron heads, observing to Don Quixote that christianity,
upon which he valued himself, would not allow him to let the combat be fought with
any risque, and danger of his life; and that he hoped the knight would be satisfied with
his granting a field for the lists in his territories, an indulgence contrary to the decree
of the holy council, which prohibits all such challenges: he therefore desired that the
battle might not be fought to the last extremity. Don Quixote said his excellency might
order the particulars of that affair according to his own pleasure, and that he would
punctually comply with every circumstance of the disposition.

The dreadful day then being arrived, and the duke having caused a spacious scaffold
to be erected before the court-yard of the castle, for the accommodation of the judges
of the field, and the mother and daughter, who were plaintiffs in the cause; an infinite
number of people assembled from all the neighbouring towns and villages, to see the
novelty of this battle; for, such a combat had never been seen nor heard of in that coun-
try, by either the living or the dead. The first that entered the lists was the master of the
ceremonies, in order to examine the ground; and he accordingly surveyed the whole
field, to see that there was no deceit, or any thing concealed that might occasion stum-
bling or falling: then came the duennas and took their seats, veiled down to the eyes, and
even to the bosom, with demonstrations of excessive grief. They being seated, Don
Quixote presented himself in the lists; and in a little time appeared the great lacquey
Tosilos upon a mighty steed that shook the very ground, accompanied with a number
of trumpets, his vizor being down, and his whole body stiffened with strong and shin-
ing armour; his horse seemed to be of the Freizland breed, broad built, and of a flea-
bitten colour, with a stone of wool hanging to every foot. Thus approached the valiant
combatant, well instructed by the duke how to engage the valorous Don Quixote de la
Mancha, and particularly cautioned against taking away the life of his knightly oppo-
nent; for, he was warned to avoid the first encounter as he would shun his own death,

which must have been certain had they met full shock in the midst of their career. This champion, crossing the field, and riding up to the place where the duennas were seated, began very earnestly to * contemplate the person who claimed him as her husband; while the master of the field, calling to Don Quixote, who had likewise entered the lists, and kept close to Tosilos, asked the duennas if they consented to depend on don Quixote de la Mancha for the redress of their grievances: they replied in the affirmative, declaring, at the same time, that whatever he should do in their affair they would hold as † well done, firm, and sufficient. By this time, the duke and dutchess had placed themselves in a gallery that overlooked the barriers, which were crowded with an infinite number of people, who came to see the dreadful and never beheld encounter; but, before they engaged, it was stipulated that if Don Quixote should overcome his antagonist, he, the said antagonist, should marry the daughter of Donna Rodriguez; but, should victory declare for the defendant, he should be released from the promise they pretended he had made, without giving any other satisfaction.

The master of the ceremonies having divided the sun, and stationed each combatant in his proper post, the drums began to thunder, the sound of trumpets filled the air, the earth trembled beneath their feet, and the hearts of the gazing multitude throbbed with suspence and expectation, some hoping, and others fearing, the good or bad success of the battle. Finally, Don Quixote, recommending himself with all his heart to our Lord God, and to the lady Dulcinea del Toboso, waited with impatience for the precise signal of engaging; while our lacquey, engrossed by far other sentiments, thought of nothing but what we will now explain: While he stood gazing at his female enemy, she appeared in his eyes the most beautiful creature he had ever seen in the whole course of his life, and the little blind urchin, vulgarly known by the name of Cupid, was unwilling to lose this opportunity to triumph over a lacqueyan soul, and register this subject in the list of his atchievements; he, therefore, approached him fairly and softly, and unperceived let fly an arrow two yards long, which, entering his left side, transfixed his heart: nor was it difficult to perform this exploit; for, love is invincible, and makes his entrance and exit wheresoever he chooses to pass, without being called to account by any person upon earth—I say, when they gave the signal for battle, our lacquey's soul was transported by the beauty of her, to whom, by this time, he had surrendered his liberty; and, therefore, he was not so much affected by the sound of the trumpet as his antagonist Don Quixote, whose ears it no sooner saluted, than he sprung forwards to assault his

* A critic inclined to enumerate the inadvertencies of Cervantes, might observe that Sancho pulled a piece of bread out of his wallet and gave it to Dapple, after he had given the contents of the said wallet to the pilgrims; that he tells the duke and dutchess he had governed ten days, whereas he had continued but seven days in office; and, lastly, that Tosilos contemplated the beauty of the damsel, though, we are previously told, that she was veiled down to the bosom.[1]

† In the romance of Gerard de Nevers we read, that a certain young lady, perceiving the eagerness with which that knight undertook her defence, pulled the glove from her left hand, and presented it to him, saying, "Sir knight, my body, life, lands, and honour, I commit to the protection of God and you, to whom I pray he may grant grace to obtain the victory, and deliver us from the danger in which we are now involved."[2]

adversary with all the mettle that Rozinante could exert; and his good squire Sancho seeing him begin his career, exclaimed with an audible voice, "God be thy guide, thou cream and flower of knights-errant: God grant thee the victory, seeing thy cause is the best."

Although Tosilos saw Don Quixote advancing against him, he did not budge one step from his station, but called aloud to the field-master, to whom, when he went up to see what he wanted, he thus addressed himself: "Tell me, signor, is not this combat appointed to determine whether I shall or shall not marry that lady?" To this question the other having replied in the affirmative, "Well then," resumed the lacquey, "I have a tender conscience that would be grievously burthened should I proceed in this quarrel; and, therefore, I own myself vanquished, and will forthwith take the lady to wife." The field-master was surprised at this declaration of Tosilos, and, being in the secret of the plan, knew not what answer to make; while Don Quixote, perceiving his enemy did not come on to the assault, checked Rozinante in the middle of his career. The duke, being ignorant of the cause that retarded the battle, was by the field-master informed of what Tosilos had said, at which he was extremely surprised and incensed; whereas, Tosilos, in the mean time, rode up towards the place where Donna Rodriguez was seated, and pronounced with a loud voice, "Madam, as I am willing to marry your daughter, there is no occasion to seek that by disputes and contention which I may obtain peaceably, without the danger of death." The valiant Don Quixote hearing this address, "Since that is the case," said he, "I am released and acquitted of my promise: let them marry a-God's name, and as our Lord bestows the bride, may St. Peter bless the nuptials."

The duke descending into the court-yard of the castle, and advancing to Tosilos, "Knight," said he, "is it true that you own yourself vanquished, and that instigated by your timorous conscience, you consent to marry this damsel?" When he answered, "Yes, my Lord": "He is very much in the right," cried Sancho: "Give always to the cat what was kept for the rat; and, Let it still be thy view all mischief to eschew." As for Tosilos, he began to unlace his helmet, and earnestly begged that some body would come to his assistance; for, his breath was almost gone, and he could not bear to be confined so long in such a narrow lodging. People accordingly ran to his relief; and his head being uncased, Donna Rodriguez discovered the individual countenance of our lacquey, which the daughter no sooner beheld than she cried aloud, "A cheat! a cheat! my lord duke has palmed his lacquey upon us, in lieu of my lawful husband: I demand justice of God and the king, for this malicious, not to call it knavish contrivance."

"Ladies," said Don Quixote, "give yourselves no concern; there is neither malice nor knavery in the case; or if there is, it cannot be occasioned by the duke, but by those wicked inchanters who persecute me without ceasing: envious of the glory I should have acquired in this atchievement, they have metamorphosed your husband's face into the aspect of this man, who, you say, is the duke's lacquey. Take my advice therefore, and maugre the malice of mine enemies, bestow your hand upon him; for, without all doubt, he is the very person whom you desire to obtain as an husband."

The duke, overhearing this admonition, had well-nigh vented all his indignation in laughter, saying, "The adventures that happen to signor Don Quixote are so extraordinary, that I am apt to believe this is not really my lacquey; but, let us make use of this ex-

pedient and stratagem: we will, if it be agreeable, delay the marriage a fortnight, and confine this person of whom we are doubtful, and, in that time, perhaps he will retrieve his former figure; for, surely the rancour of those wicked inchanters, who hate Don Quixote, cannot last so long; especially as such delusions and transformations avail them so little." "O my lord!" cried Sancho, "those banditti have been long accustomed to chop, change, and transmography every thing that belongs to my master: some time ago he vanquished an errant called the knight of the mirrours, and in a twinkling they transformed him into the figure of the batchelor Sampson Carrasco, a townsman and great friend of ours; as for my lady Dulcinea del Toboso, they have changed her into a homely country-wench; and, therefore, I take it for granted that this man will die and live a lacquey all the days of his life."

Here the daughter of Donna Rodriguez interposing, "Be who he will," said she, "I am obliged to him for asking me in marriage; and, I would rather be the lawful wife of a lacquey than the deluded mistress of a gentleman; although he who deluded me has no pretensions to that title." In fine, all these incidents and explanations ended in the resolution to confine Tosilos, until they should see the issue of his transformation; while, with unusual acclamation, the victory was adjudged to Don Quixote; tho' the greatest part of the spectators seemed melancholy and disappointed, because they had not seen two such hopeful combatants hew one another to pieces: in the same manner as the boys are out of humour, when the execution is prevented by the malefactor's being pardoned, either by the party or the king.

The crowd dispersed, the duke and Don Quixote returned to the castle, Tosilos was sent to prison; Donna Rodriguez and her daughter rejoiced exceedingly, when they saw, that one way or another, this affair would end in marriage, and the lover consoled himself with the same prospect.

## CHAPTER V.

Giving an account of the manner in which Don Quixote took leave of the duke; and of what passed between him and the gay and witty Altisidora, one of the dutchess's damsels.

By this time, Don Quixote thought he would do well to quit that idle way of life which he led in the castle; for, he imagined himself much to blame in living thus buried and inactive among those infinite dainties and entertainments with which he, as a knight-errant, was indulged by that noble pair; and he concluded that he would be obliged to give a severe account to heaven of this idleness and sequestration. He therefore, one day, begged leave of the duke and dutchess to depart; and they granted his request with marks of being extremely grieved at his intention. The dutchess delivered to

Sancho Panza his wife's letter, and the good squire wept bitterly when he understood the contents; saying, "Who could have thought such mighty hopes as were ingendered in the breast of my wife Teresa Panza, by the news of my government, would vanish in my returning again to the woeful adventures of my master Don Quixote de la Mancha? Nevertheless, I am pleased to find that my Teresa behaved like herself, in sending the acorns to the dutchess; for, had she failed in that particular, I should have been sorely vexed, and she would have shewn herself ungrateful: what comforts my poor heart, is, that they cannot call this present a bribe; for, I was actually in possession of the government before the acorns were sent: and it is but reasonable, that folks who receive any sort of benefit should shew their gratitude, even tho' in trifles. In effect, Naked I took possession of the government, and naked I resigned my office; therefore, I may say with a safe conscience, which is no small boast, I naked was born, and naked remain; and, if I lose nothing, as little I gain."

This conference Sancho held with his own bosom on the day of their departure: as for Don Quixote, having taken leave of their graces overnight, he, in the morning, presented himself armed in the court-yard of the castle, where he furnished a spectacle to all the people of the family, not even excepting the duke and dutchess, who viewed him from the gallery. Sancho was mounted upon Dapple, extremely well pleased with the contents of his bags, wallet or store; for, the duke's steward, who acted the part of the countess Trifaldi, had given him a small purse of two hundred crowns, to answer the emergencies of the road: but, of this supply Don Quixote was ignorant. While every individual, as we have said, stood gazing at the knight, all of a sudden, from among the other duennas and damsels of the dutchess, the gay and witty Altisidora, raising her voice, pronounced what follows, in a lamentable tone:

> Ah! hear my plaint, unlucky knight,
> Pull in thy reins and do me right,
> And prithee spare, at my request,
> The flanks of that poor, batter'd beast.
> Consider she whose heart's at stake,
> False man! is not a scaly snake;
> But, a young lambkin, meek and true,
> Just wean'd from teat of mother ewe.
> Say, monster, why undo a maid
> More beautiful than ever stray'd
> With Cynthia, huntress of the wood,
> Or Venus, native of the flood?
> But, if Æneas-like thou mean'st to fly,
> The death of Barrabas may Quixote die.
>
> Thou, robber! in thy claws hast got
> The heart and bowels, and what not,
> Of a weak virgin, heav'n befriend her!
> Mild, humble, timorous and tender.
> Three linnen night-caps hast thou stole,
> And silken garters strong and whole,

That to these legs did appertain,
These legs, as marble smooth and clean.
Thou carry'st off two thousand sighs,
Which, kindled by thy beaming eyes,
Would in a twinkling quite destroy
Two thousand cities great as Troy.
But, if Æneas-like thou mean'st to fly,
The death of Barrabas may Quixote die.

May Sancho's buttocks and his heart
Ne'er feel the ignominious smart
Prescrib'd, when he is pleased and ready
To disinchant thy favourite lady.
Since thine is the offence and blame,
Endure the punishment and shame
Which in my country, once a year,
The righteous for the wicked bear.
Be thy adventures (small and great)
Inglorious and unfortunate;
Like dreams may all thy pleasures fade,
Thy constancy oblivion shade;
And, if Æneas-like thou mean'st to fly,
The death of Barrabas may Quixote die!

May'st thou be deem'd a perjur'd devil,
Ev'n from Marchena unto Sevil;
From Loja to Granada hated,
From London Tow'r to England baited.
At draughts should'st thou attempt to play,
Or waste at ombre all the day,
May no crown'd monarch or spadille
Attend the efforts of thy skill:
When angry corn disturbs thy toe,
May blood at ev'ry paring flow;
And of each tooth the barbers draw,
The stump still fester in thy jaw:
Nay, since Æneas-like thou mean'st to fly,
The death of Barrabas may Quixote die!

While the afflicted Altisidora complained in these strains, Don Quixote surveyed her attentively, and without answering a word to her lamentation, turned to Sancho, saying, "By the age of thine ancestors! my dear Sancho, I conjure thee to tell me the truth: say, hast thou actually got the three caps, and the garters, which this enamoured damsel mentions?" To this question the squire replied: "The three caps I have; but, as to the garters, I know nothing of the matter."[1]

The dutchess was surprised at the freedom of Altisidora's behaviour; for, although she knew her to be forward, merry and frank, she did not think the girl possessed of assurance enough to attempt a scheme of this nature; and her admiration was the greater as

she had not been previously apprised of the intended joke. The duke, however, in order to reinforce the jest, addressed himself to Don Quixote in these words: "It does not look well, sir knight, that you who have met with such honourable reception and treatment in this my castle, should presume to carry off by stealth three night-caps, at least, if not a pair of garters likewise, belonging to my damsel: these are marks of a bad heart, and but ill agree with your reputation. Restore the garters to the right owner; otherwise, I challenge you to mortal combat, without any apprehension that knavish inchanters will transform or change my face, as they have practised upon my lacquey Tosilos, your last antagonist."

"God forbid," replied Don Quixote, "that I should unsheath my sword against your illustrious person, of whom I received such favours. The three night-caps shall be restored; for, Sancho owns they are in his custody: but, it is impossible to make restitution of the garters, as neither he nor I did ever receive them: and I dare say your damsel will find them, if she will take the trouble to rummage her own drawers. I, my lord duke, was never a thief, and I hope never shall, in the whole course of my life, provided God will not withdraw from me his guiding hand. The damsel, according to her own declaration, talks like an enamoured person; but, surely I am not to blame for her impertinence; and, therefore, I have no reason to ask pardon either of her or your excellency, whom I intreat to look upon me with more favourable sentiments, and beseech a-new to consent that I may prosecute my journey." "God grant your departure may be so happy," said the dutchess, "that we may always hear good news of Don Quixote's exploits. Go then, a-God's name; for, the longer you stay, your presence blows up the fire the more fiercely in the bosoms of the damsels who behold you: as for mine, I will chastise her in such a manner, that from henceforward she shall never transgress either in word or deed." "One word more, however, I beg thou wilt hear me speak, O valiant Don Quixote!" said Altisidora: "I crave pardon for having taxed you with the garters; for, as I shall answer to heaven and my own conscience, they are now upon my legs; and I have been guilty of a mistake, like the man who went in search of his ass, while he was mounted on his back." "Did not I tell you so?" cried the squire: "I should be a rare fellow, indeed, to receive and conceal stolen goods; had I been that way inclined, I might have had opportunity enough in my government."

Don Quixote bowing his head, made a profound reverence to the duke and dutchess, and all the spectators; then turning Rozinante, and being followed by Sancho upon Dapple, he set out from the castle, directing his course to Saragossa.

## CHAPTER VI.

### Shewing how adventures thronged upon Don Quixote so thick as to intangle one another.

WHEN Don Quixote found himself in the open field, free and disembarrassed from the complaints of Altisidora, he seemed to be placed in the very center of his own wish, and to enjoy a renovation of spirits, in order to prosecute anew the aim of his chivalry. Turning, therefore, to his squire, "Sancho," said he, "liberty is one of the most precious gifts which heaven hath bestowed on man, exceeding all the treasures which earth incloses or which ocean hides; and for this blessing, as well as for honour, we may and ought to venture life itself: on the other hand, captivity and restraint are the greatest evils that human nature can endure. I make this observation, Sancho, because thou hast seen the delicacies and the plenty with which we were entertained in that castle: yet, in the midst of those savoury banquets, and ice-cooled potations, I thought myself confined within the very straits of famine, because I did not enjoy the treat with that liberty which I should have felt, had it been my own; for, obligations incurred by benefits and favours received, are fetters which hamper the freeborn soul—Happy is he to whom heaven hath sent a morsel of bread, for which he is obliged to none but heaven itself."

"But, notwithstanding all that your worship hath said," replied Sancho, "we, for our parts, ought not to be ungrateful, considering the two hundred crowns of gold which the duke's steward gave me in a purse, and which as a plaister and a cordial I keep next my heart, in case of emergency; for, we shall not always find such castles where we can be entertained; on the contrary, we may, sometimes, stumble upon sorry inns, where we shall be soundly cudgelled."

With this and other such discourse, the two errants, knight and squire, amused themselves while they proceeded on their journey. Having travelled a little more than a league, they perceived upon a green spot of ground, about a dozen countrymen at dinner, with their cloaks spread under them; and, hard by, certain white sheets at some distance from one another, that seemed to cover something, above which they were raised up and stretched with great care and caution. Don Quixote approaching the men, first of all saluted them courteously, and then asked what it was that they covered so carefully with these pieces of linnen? "Signor," replied one of the countrymen, "under these sheets are carved images for an altar-piece to be set up in our town: we cover them in this manner, that they may not be sullied, and carry them upon our shoulders that they may not be broken." "If you please," replied the knight, "I should be glad to see them: they must certainly be good images which you so carefully convey." "Good!" cried the other: "ay, that the price of them will declare: I can assure you there is not one of them that does not cost above fifty ducats; and, that your worship may be convinced of the truth of what I say, stay a moment and you shall see it with your own eyes."

So saying, he left his dinner, and rising up, uncovered the first piece, which repre-

sented St. George on horseback, with his lance thrust into the throat of a serpent coiled at his feet, exhibiting all the fierceness with which that animal is usually painted; and the whole groupe looked, as the saying is, like a flame of gold.

Don Quixote, immediately recognizing the subject, "This knight," said he, "was one of the best errants that ever signalized himself in divine warfare: his name was St. George, and he was, moreover, a protector of damsels. Let us see the next," which, when displayed, appeared to be the image of St. Martin on horseback, dividing his cloak with the beggar. Don Quixote no sooner beheld it, than he said to Sancho, "This knight was also one of the christian adventurers, and, I believe, more liberal than valiant, as thou mayest perceive by this circumstance of his dividing his cloak and giving one half to the beggar; and, doubtless, this incident must have happened in the winter season, otherwise the saint was so charitable he would have given the whole." "Nay, that surely was not the case," replied the squire: "but, he held fast by the old proverb, which says, The man in wisdom must be old, who knows in giving where to hold."

Don Quixote smiled at this remark, and desired the man to lift the third cover, under which appeared the figure of the patron of Spain on horseback, with his bloody sword, trampling down and bruising the heads of the Moors. Don Quixote, seeing this representation, exclaimed, "Ah! this is a knight, and chief in the squadrons of Christ; his name is Don San Diego Mata Moros *, and he was one of the most valiant saints and knights which earth ever produced, or heaven now contains." Then they unveiled the fourth, which exhibited St. Paul falling from his horse, with all the circumstances usually set forth in the picture of his conversion, so lively represented, that one would have almost thought Christ was speaking and Paul answering the voice. "This," said Don Quixote, "was the most bitter enemy the church of God ever had, while our Lord and Saviour was on earth, and afterwards the greatest defender it will ever have: a knight-errant in his life, and a perfect saint in his death; an unwearied labourer in the vineyard of our Lord, a teacher of the gentiles, schooled by heaven, and whose professor and master was Jesus Christ himself."

There being no other images to see, Don Quixote desired the man to cover up those he had examined; and addressing himself to the bearers, "Brothers," said he, "I look upon it as a good omen to have met with these images; for, these saints and knights were of my profession, which is the exercise of arms: with this difference, however, they were saints, and fought in a divine manner, and I, who am a sinner, fight in the manner of men. They conquered heaven by the force of their arms; for, the kingdom of heaven suffers violence; whereas, I know not, hitherto, what I have conquered by the toils and troubles I have undergone: but, if my Dulcinea del Toboso should be delivered from those she now sustains, my fortune will be bettered, my judgment repaired, and, perhaps, my steps may be directed through a better path than this which I at present follow."

This declaration was closed with an exclamation of Sancho, who cried aloud, "The Lord give ear, I pray; and sin be deaf for aye." The men were equally astonished at the knight's appearance and discourse, one half of which they did not understand: never-

* Moor-killer.[1]

theless, they made an end of their meal, shouldered their images, and, taking leave of Don Quixote, pursued their journey. Sancho was, on this occasion, as much astonished at the learning of his master, as if he had never known him before that day; and imagined there was not an history or event in the whole world, that was not decyphered on his nail or nailed to his memory. "Truly, master of mine," said he, "if what has happened to us to-day may be called an adventure, it is the most sweet and delicious of all that have yet befallen us in the whole course of our peregrinations: from this, we have escaped with whole skins and fearless hearts; we have neither unsheathed our swords, battered the earth with our poor carcases; nor are we left in a starving condition: blessed be God who hath spared me to see this good luck with my own eyes!" "Thou sayest well, Sancho," replied the knight: "but, thou must take notice, that all times are not the same, nor equally fortunate; and those incidents which the vulgar call omens, tho' not founded on any natural reason, have, even by persons of sagacity, been held and deemed as fair and fortunate. One of these superstitious omen-mongers rises in the morning, goes abroad, chances to meet a friar belonging to the beatified St. Francis; and, as if he had encountered a dragon in his way, runs back to his own house with fear and consternation. Another * Foresight by accident scatters the salt upon the table, by which fear and melancholy are scattered through his heart; as if nature was obliged to foretel future misfortunes by such trivial signs and tokens: whereas, a prudent man and a good christian, will not so minutely scrutinize the purposes of heaven. Scipio chancing to fall in landing upon the coast of Afric, and perceiving that his soldiers looked upon this accident as a bad omen, he embraced the soil with seeming eagerness, saying, 'thou shalt not scape me, Afric; for, I have thee safe within my arms.' Therefore, Sancho, my meeting with those images, I consider as a most happy encounter." "I am of the same opinion," answered the squire: "but, I wish your worship would be pleased to tell me, for what reason the Spaniards, when they join battle, and invoke the same St. Diego Mata Moros, cry St. Jago, and Close, Spain! Is Spain cloven in such a manner as to want closing? or what is the meaning of that ceremony?" "Sancho," replied the knight, "thy simplicity is very great. You must know, that God has given this great knight of the red-cross, as a patron and protector to Spain, especially in those dreadful battles fought against the Moors. The Spaniards, therefore, invoke and call upon him as their defender on all such occasions; nay, many times hath he been seen overthrowing, trampling, slaying, and destroying the squadrons of the children of † Hagar: and of this truth I could convince thee by many examples recorded in the authentic histories of Spain ‡."

Sancho, changing the subject of conversation, "Signor," said he, "I was astonished at the boldness of her grace's damsel Altisidora. I'faith! she must be rarely pricked and

---

* The original word is Mendoza, the name of a great family in Spain, one of whom was remarkably superstitious.[2]
† The Moors are said to be descended from Hagar.[3]
‡ Sancho must have been very simple, indeed, to be satisfied with this explanation, which does not even hint at the main point of his question; namely, "Why do the Spanish soldiers when they charge their enemy, cry Close, Spain." A phrase of encouragement, by which the soldiers exhort one another to do their duty, and close with the foe.[4]

stabbed by him they call Cupid, who, they say, is a mischievous blind boy, and is able with those bleared eyes of his, or rather with no eyes at all, if once he takes aim, to pierce through and through with his arrows, the smallest heart that ever was seen. I have also heard it observed, that by the modesty and reserve of young women, those same amorous shafts are blunted and broken; but, in Altisidora, they seem to be rather whetted than blunted." "Sancho," replied Don Quixote, "you must know that love has no respect of persons; nor, in his progress, does he confine himself within the bounds of reason: indeed, he is of the same disposition with death; for, he assaults the lofty palaces of kings, as well as the humble cottages of swains: when he once has taken full possession of the soul, his first exploit is to expel fear and modesty; and without these did Altisidora declare her passion, which engendered—not pity, but confusion in my breast." "O monstrous and notorious cruelty!" cried Sancho, "unheard of ingratitude! I can say for myself, that the least kind word from her would have subdued and made me her bond-slave. Ah, the son of a whore! what an heart of marble, bowels of brass, and soul of plaister!— but, I cannot, for the blood of me, conceive what the damsel could see in your worship, to tame and bring her to such an humble pass: what finery, what good humour, what gentility could she observe about your person? or what beauty could she spy in that face? for, women are taken with these qualities either severally or conjunctly. Verily, verily, I have often stopped to survey your worship from the sole of your foot to the last hair upon your skull; and I protest before God! I think, you would be more apt to frighten than to captivate a fair lady; and, as I have, moreover, heard it said, that beauty is the chief and principal article that inspires love, your worship being quite destitute of that commodity, I cannot imagine what the poor creature was in love with." "Take notice, Sancho," replied Don Quixote, "there are two kinds of beauty, one of the mind and another of the body: that of the mind displays itself in the understanding, in honourable and virtuous behavior, in a liberality of disposition, and in good breeding: now all these qualifications may center in an ugly man; and when this kind of beauty, preferable to that of the body, is the object of admiration, it produces love that glows with equal impetuosity and advantage. For my own part, Sancho, I can easily see that I am not beautiful; but, I likewise know I am not deformed; and a gentleman who is not altogether monstrous, may inspire the most ardent love, provided he is in possession of those qualities of the mind which I have mentioned."

Thus discoursing together, they entered a wood, at a small distance from the highway; and, all of a sudden, without dreaming of any such lett or impediment, Don Quixote found himself intangled among some nets of green thread, which were spread and stretched from tree to tree. As he could not conceive the meaning of this phaenomenon, "I believe," said he to Sancho, "that this of the nets must be one of the newest adventures that ever were imagined or contrived. Let me die if the inchanters by whom I am persecuted, have not a mind to intangle me in them and obstruct my journey, in revenge for my rigour and indifference toward Altisidora! but, I shall give them to understand, that although these nets, instead of thread, were made of the hardest adamant, and stronger than that in which the jealous god of blacksmiths caught Mars and Venus together, I would break through them as easily as if they were of rushes and unspun cotton."

So saying, he endeavoured to proceed and destroy this obstacle, when all at once, from a tuft of trees, came forth two most beautiful shepherdesses, at least they were clad like shepherdesses, tho' their jackets and petticoats were of fine brocard—I say, their petticoats were of the richest gold tabby; their hair hung loose upon their shoulders, and, in shining, might have vied with the rays of Apollo himself; their heads were adorned with garlands of green laurel interwoven with sprigs of red amaranth; and their age seemed to be neither under fifteen, nor turned of eighteen: a sight that struck Sancho with admiration, the knight with surprize, and suspended the sun in the middle of his career. All the four, for some time remained in silent wonder; and, at length, the first who spoke was one of the two country-maidens, who, addressing herself to Don Quixote, "Forbear, sir knight," said she, "and do not break our nets, which, I assure you, were not spread for your inconvenience; but, meerly for our own pastime: and because I know you will ask for what reason they are placed, and who we are, I will satisfy your curiosity in a few words. At a village about two leagues from hence, which is inhabited by many people of fortune and fashion, it was agreed among a number of friends and relations, that they, their wives, sons, daughters, neighbours, friends and kinsfolks, should come and enjoy the fine season in this spot, which is the most agreeable situation in all this country; and here form a new pastoral Arcadia, the girls being habited like shepherdesses, and the young men like swains. We have studied two eclogues; one of the famous poet Garcilaso, and another of the most excellent Camoens, in his own Portuguese language; tho' they are not yet represented; for, we arrived only yesterday. Among these trees, we have pitched some field-tents, upon the banks of a plentiful stream which fertilizes all these meadows; and last night we spread these nets from tree to tree, in order to deceive and catch the simple little birds, which, frightened by the noise we make, may fly into the snare: if you choose to be our guest, signor, you shall be treated liberally and courteously; for, at present, neither melancholy nor disgust shall enter this place."

Here she left off speaking, and Don Quixote replied, "Assuredly, most beauteous nymph, Acteon himself could not be seized with more surprize and admiration when he all of a sudden beheld Diana bathing, than that which but now overwhelmed me at sight of such uncommon charms! I applaud the scheme of your entertainments and diversions; I thank you heartily for your courteous proffer, and if I can serve you in any shape, you may command me, with full assurance of being obeyed; for, I have chosen this profession solely because it consists in being grateful and benevolent to all mankind, especially to persons of rank such as your appearance declares you to be; and if these nets which, I suppose, occupy but a small space, were extended over the whole circumference of the globe, I would find new worlds through which I might pass, rather than by breaking the least mesh, run the risque of interrupting your diversion. That you may give some credit to this exaggeration, be pleased to take notice, that he who makes it is no other than Don Quixote de la Mancha, if peradventure such a name hath ever reached your ears."

The young lady no sooner heard these words, than turning to the other shepherdess, "O my dear companion!" cried she, "what an happy incident is this! that there knight, I assure thee, is the most valiant, enamoured, and courteous person in the whole world,

if we are not misled and deceived by the printed history of his exploits, which I have read from end to end: and I'll lay a wager that honest man who accompanies him is one Sancho Panza, his squire, whose pleasantry is above all comparison." "You are in the right," said Sancho: "I am that same pleasant fellow and loyal squire whom your ladyship hath so honourably mentioned; and that gentleman is my master, the very individual historised and aforesaid Don Quixote de la Mancha."

"Good now! my dear," said the other: "let us beseech them to stay; our fathers and brothers will be infinitely pleased with their conversation; for, I have, likewise, heard the same account of the knight's valour and the squire's pleasantry: as for Don Quixote in particular, he is said to be the most constant and loyal lover that ever was known; and that his mistress is one Dulcinea del Toboso, who bears away the palm of beauty from all the ladies in Spain." "Ay, and justly too," said the knight; "unless your unequalled beauty should invalidate her claim. Weary not yourselves, fair ladies, in persuading me to stay; for, the indispensable duties of my profession will not allow me to rest in any place whatever."

Just as he pronounced these words, they were joined by a brother of one of the two nymphs, clad likewise in the fashion of a shepherd, tho' his dress, in point of richness and gaiety, corresponded with that of the ladies, who told him that the gentleman on horseback was the valiant Don Quixote de la Mancha, and the other his squire Sancho, whose characters he already knew from his having perused their history. The gallant youth payed his compliments, and pressed Don Quixote to accompany them to the tents, in such a manner that he could not help complying. Then setting up the shout, the nets were filled with different kinds of little birds, which, deceived by the colour of the meshes, flew precipitately into the very danger they sought to avoid.

In this place they were joined by above thirty persons gayly clad like shepherds and shepherdesses, who were immediately informed of the names of Don Quixote and his squire; a circumstance which afforded them no small satisfaction, as the history had already made them acquainted with the characters of both.

Repairing to the tents, where they found tables ready furnished with elegance and abundance, they complimented the knight with the place of honour, and all the company gazed upon him with admiration. At length, when the cloth was taken away, Don Quixote raising his voice, thus harrangued them with great solemnity: "Of all the crimes which mankind commit, tho' some say pride is the greatest, I affirm that ingratitude is the most atrocious, adhering to the common supposition, that hell is crowded with the ungrateful. This crime I have, as much as in me lies, endeavoured to avoid ever since the first moment in which I could exercise my reason; and tho' I may not be able to repay in kind, the benefits which I receive, I substitute the will for the deed: when that is not sufficient, I publish them to the world; for, he that promulgates the favours he has received, would also requite them with equal generosity, if it was in his power to make such recompence. But, for the most part, people who receive benefits are inferior to those who bestow them; and, therefore, God is above all, because he is the fountain of all good things: yet there is an infinite difference between the benefits conferred by men and those bestowed by God, so as to reject all comparison; and this narrowness and insufficiency on our part, is in some measure supplied by gratitude. Now, I being grateful

for the favours you have done me, which I cannot repay in the same measure, and being hampered by the narrow limits of my ability, must offer that which is in my power to present—I say, therefore, that I will, for two natural days, in the middle of that high-road that leads to Saragossa, maintain that the ladies here present, disguised in pastoral habits, are the most fair and courteous damsels in the whole world, excepting always and only, the peerless Dulcinea del Toboso, sole mistress of my thoughts; without offence to the honourable hearers, be it spoken."

Here Sancho, who had stood listening attentively to what he said, exclaimed with great vociferation, "Is it possible now, that there can be persons in the world, who have all the presumption to say and swear that my master is a madman? pray, tell me, gentle-men and ladies, shepherds and shepherdesses, is there ever a country curate in Spain, let him be never so wise and learned, that could say what my master has just now said? or is there a knight-errant, let him be never so famed for valour, who could make such an offer as my master has made?"

Don Quixote turning to Sancho, with rage and indignation in his countenance, "Mis-creant," said he, "is it possible there should be a person upon earth who would not say thou art stark mad, and that thy soul is lined and bordered with fillets of malice and knavery? By what authority, wretch! art thou intitled to intermeddle in my affairs, and give thy opinion whether my brain be sound or crazy? Seal up thy lips, and make no re-ply; but, saddle Rozinante, if he is without his saddle, and let us go immediately and per-form my promise; for, as I have justice on my side, you may deem all those who shall contradict my assertion, as already vanquished."

So saying, he rose from his seat with great fury and demonstrations of wrath, leaving the whole company astonished, and doubting whether they should consider him as a lu-natic or person of sound intellects. However, they endeavoured to dissuade him from publishing such a declaration, saying they took his gratitude for granted; and that there was no need of new proofs to demonstrate his valour, seeing those were sufficient which they had seen recorded in the history of his atchievements.

Notwithstanding this remonstrance, the knight executed his design: he mounted Rozinante, embraced his shield, and, grasping his lance, posted himself in the middle of the king's high-way, which was not far from their verdant habitation, being followed by Sancho upon Dapple, and the whole flock of those pastoral gentry, who were curious to see the issue of his arrogant and hitherto unseen enterprize.

Having taken possession of the ground, he wounded the very vault of heaven with the loudness of the tone in which he pronounced these words: "O ye passengers and trav-ellers, knights, squires, persons on horseback or a-foot, who come or are to come this way, within the space of two days, from this present hour, know that Don Quixote de la Mancha, knight-errant, is here posted to maintain that the nymphs who inhabit these meadows and woods, excel in beauty and courtesy all the ladies upon earth, exclusive of Dulcinea del Toboso, the mistress of my soul. Let him who thinks the contrary, advance: here I am ready to receive him."

Twice did he repeat this declaration, and twice was it repeated, unheard by any knight-adventurer; but fortune, which was bent upon directing his affairs to better pur-pose, ordained that, in a very little time, he descried upon the road, a great number of

men on horseback, some of them armed with lances, riding towards him in great haste and all in a cluster. Those who were with Don Quixote no sooner perceived this troop, than they turned their backs and retired a good way from the road, knowing that some mischief would befal them, should they keep their ground: the knight alone maintained his post with an undaunted heart, and Sancho Panza shielded himself with the flanks of Rozinante.

When this troop of lancemen advanced, one of them that rode before the rest, began to hollow as loud as he could cry to Don Quixote, "Get out of the way, thou servant of the devil, or these bulls will trample thee to dust!" "So ho! caitiffs," replied the knight: "your bulls shall not avail against me, even tho' they are the fiercest that ever fed upon the banks of Xarama: confess, ye miscreants, unsight, unseen, the truth of what I have proclaimed, or meet my vengeance in the field of battle."

The herdsman had no time to reply, nor Don Quixote to retire, had he been never so willing; so that the drove of wild bulls and tame cattle, together with a multitude of drivers and other people employed to convey them to a place, where, in a few days, they were to be baited—The whole throng, I say, passed over the bellies of Don Quixote, Sancho, Rozinante and Dapple, whom they in a twinkling overthrew and rolled in the mire, in such a manner that the squire was squeezed as flat as a pancake, his master astonished, Dapple terribly bruised, and Rozinante in no very catholic condition. At length, however, all the four got upon their legs; and Don Quixote, staggering here and tumbling there, began to pursue the drove on foot, calling aloud, "Halt and wait a little, ye felonious plebeians; he is a single knight who defies you to the combat, and not of the disposition and opinion of those who say, Lay a bridge of silver for a flying enemy."

But, notwithstanding all his exclamation, the drovers did not slacken their pace, or mind his threats, more than they minded last year's weather. Don Quixote, being so tired that he could run no farther, sat down upon the side of the road, more incensed than revenged, and waited for Sancho, Rozinante, and Dapple, who soon arrived. Then the knight and squire, mounting their beasts, proceeded on their journey with more shame than satisfaction; and never dreamed of returning to take a formal leave of the feigned or counterfeit Arcadia.

## CHAPTER VII.

## In which is recounted the extraordinary incident that happened to Don Quixote, and may well pass for an adventure.

The dust and drought which Don Quixote and Sancho derived from the uncivil behaviour of the bulls, were remedied by a clear and limpid stream which they had the good fortune to find in a cool shade, and on the margin of which this down-trodden pair, the master and man, seated themselves, after Rozinante and Dapple were un-

bridled and unhaltered, and left to the freedom of their own will. Sancho immediately had recourse to the store of his wallet, from which he drew forth what he usually called his belly-timber; but, not before he had rinsed his mouth, and his master had washed his own face, in consequence of which refreshment they recovered their exhausted spirits. Nevertheless, Don Quixote forbore eating, out of pure vexation, while Sancho, who durst not touch the food that was before him, waited, out of pure good manners, until his master should begin. Seeing, however, the knight, so absorpt in his own imagination, that he forgot to lift the bread to his mouth, he, without letting one word escape his own, but trampling under foot all kind of good breeding, began to cram his paunch with the bread and cheese which constituted his provision. "Eat, friend Sancho," said Don Quixote, "and support life, which is of more importance to thee than to me, and leave me to die by the strength of imagination and the severity of my misfortunes. I, Sancho, was born to live dying, and thou to die eating; and that thou mayest be convinced of this truth, consider me recorded in history, renowned in arms, courteous in demeanor, respected by princes, courted by damsels; and, after all, when I expected palms, triumphs, crowns of laurel obtained and merited by my valiant atchievements, I have, this morning, seen myself trampled, spurned and bruised, by the feet of filthy, unclean animals! This consideration blunts my teeth, stupefies my grinders, benumbs my hands, and deprives me wholly of appetite; so that, I believe, I shall die of hunger, the most cruel of all deaths." "At that rate," answered the squire, "without suspending the action of his jaws, your worship will not approve of the proverb, which says, Let Martha die, but not for lack of pye. At least, I, for my own part, have no intention to starve myself; on the contrary, I am resolved to follow the example of the cordwainer who stretches the leather with his teeth until it is sufficient for his purpose: now, I will also employ my teeth in stretching out my life with eating, to that end which is ordained by heaven; and you must know, signor, that it is the greatest madness in nature to seek to despair like your worship. Take my advice: eat a little for refreshment, and then take a nap upon the green couch of this delightful grass, and when you awake you will see how much you'll be relieved."

The knight relished his advice, which he thought savoured more of the philosopher than of the idiot; and said to him, "Now, Sancho, if thou wouldst do that for me which I am going to mention, my relief would be more certain, and my affliction diminished: my proposal is, that while I sleep, in compliance with thy advice, thou wouldst go aside a little farther, and, exposing thy flesh to the air, bestow upon it, with the reins of Rozinante's bridle, three or four hundred stripes, of the three thousand three hundred which thou hast undertaken to endure for the disinchantment of Dulcinea; for, it is a lamentable circumstance that the poor lady should remain so long inchanted, through thy carelessness and neglect." "There is much to be said on that subject," replied Sancho: "let us both go to sleep in the mean time; and afterwards God must ordain that which will come to pass. Your worship must know that it requires great resolution in a man to scourge himself in cold blood; especially when the stripes fall upon a body which is poorly fed and supported: let my lady Dulcinea have a little patience; when she least thinks of it, she will see my body scourged into a perfect sieve; and while there is life

there is hope; my meaning is, that while I hold life, I shall never quit the desire of performing my promise."

Don Quixote, thanking him for his good will, took a little sustenance, Sancho ate voraciously, and then both laid themselves down to sleep, leaving Rozinante and Dapple, those two friends and inseparable companions, at full liberty to feed without restraint, upon the luxuriant grass with which the meadow abounded.

The day being far spent before they awoke, they remounted their cattle and pursued their journey with uncommon expedition, in order to reach an inn which they descried at a league's distance—I say an inn, because it was so called by Don Quixote, contrary to his former custom of mistaking every inn for a castle. When they arrived at this place of entertainment, they asked if they could be accommodated with lodging; and the landlord replied in the affirmative, telling them, at the same time, that his house afforded as good conveniences and entertainment as could be found in the whole city of Saragossa. They alighted accordingly, and Sancho carried his bags into an apartment, of which the innkeeper gave him the key; then he led the cattle to the stable, where he gave them their allowance; from thence he went to receive the commands of his master, who had sat down upon a bench, and thanked heaven in a particular manner, that Don Quixote had not committed his usual mistake. They retired to their chamber, and supper-time approaching, Sancho desired to know what they could have for that meal? To this interrogation mine host replied, that his taste should be fitted to a hair, and that he might bespeak what he liked best; for, as far as the birds of the air, the fowls of the land, and the fish of the sea could go, he would find the house provided. "Less than all that will serve," answered Sancho: "we shall be satisfied with a couple of chickens roasted; for, my master has a very delicate taste, and eats little; and, as for myself, I am not a very unconscionable cormorant."

The other frankly owned he had no chickens; for, the kites had destroyed the whole brood. "Well then, Mr. landlord," said the squire, "you may order a pullet to be put to the fire; but, see it be very tender." "A pullet!" cried the inn-keeper: "body o' my father! now, as I'm an honest man, I sent above half an hundred yesterday to market: but, setting aside pullets, you may have what you will." "If that be the case," said Sancho, "there will be no want of veal or kid." "At present," replied the inn-keeper, "there is really none in the house: we are just out in these articles; but, next week, we shall have enough and to spare." "To be sure, we shall be much the better for that," answered Sancho: "I'll lay a wager all these wants will be supplied with plenty of eggs and bacon." "'Fore God!" said the host, "my guest has an admirable knack at guessing: I have told him there is neither hen nor pullet in the house, and he would have me treat him with * eggs! Shift about, if you please, to some other delicacies, and think no more of poultry."

"Body o' me!" cried Sancho, "let us come to some resolution; tell me at once what is in the house, and pray, Mr. landlord, no more of your shiftings." "What I really and truly can afford," said the inn-keeper, "is a dish of cow-heel, so delicate they might be taken

---

* Why might not this inn-keeper have had eggs in his house, as he had sent no less than fifty pullets to market the very day before?

for calves feet; or, you may call them, calves feet that might pass for cow-heel. They are stewed with pease, onions, and bacon, and this blessed minute, cry, Come, eat me: come, eat me."[1] "I mark them for my own," cried Sancho, "from henceforth for ever, amen. Let no man touch the mess, for which I will pay you handsomely; for, nothing in the whole world could be more agreeable to my taste; and, provided I have cow-heel, the calves feet may go to the devil." "No man shall interfere with you," replied the landlord: "as for the other company in the house, they, out of pure gentility, bring along with them, their own cook, butler, and sumpter mule." "Nay, as for gentility," said the squire, "no man has more of that than my master; but, his profession will not admit of travelling-stores and butter-ies: lack a-day! we lay ourselves down in the middle of a green field, and fill our bellies with medlars and acorns." Such was the conversation that passed between the inn-keeper and Sancho, who would not, however, go any greater lengths in satisfying the curiosity of mine host, who was very desirous to know the office or profession of his master.

Supper being ready, Don Quixote retired to his apartment, whither the landlord brought the pot just as it was, and very decently sat down to partake of the meal. At that instant, the knight heard people talking in the next room, from which he was divided only by a partition of lath, and could plainly distinguish these words: "As you hope to live, Don Geronimo, I conjure you, as supper is not yet ready, to read another chapter of the second part of Don Quixote de la Mancha."

The knight, hearing his own name mentioned, started up immediately, and listening with great attention, heard Geronimo reply to this effect: "What pleasure can you have in reading such absurdities, Don John? No person who has seen the first part of the history of Don Quixote de la Mancha, can possibly be entertained with this which is called the second." "Nevertheless," said Don John, "it will not be amiss to read a little; for, there is no book so bad as to contain nothing that deserves regard. What displeases me most in this performance, is, in my opinion, the author's describing Don Quixote as altogether disengaged and detached from Dulcinea del Toboso——"

The knight, hearing this remark, was filled with rage and vexation, and exclaimed aloud, "If any person whatever affirms that Don Quixote de la Mancha either has forgotten or can forget Dulcinea del Toboso, I will, with equal arms, make him know and own, that his assertion is far distant from the truth; for, the peerless Dulcinea del Toboso cannot possibly be forgot; nor is Don Quixote susceptible of forgetfulness: his motto is Constancy, which he professes to maintain with gentleness and suavity of manners." "Who is he that answers?" cried the voice. "Who should it be," replied Sancho, "but Don Quixote de la Mancha, in his own person, who will make good whatever he has said, and whatever he shall say; for, A good pay-master wants no pawn."

Scarce had the squire pronounced these words, when two gentlemen, for such they appeared, entered the apartment, and one of them throwing his arms about Don Quixote's neck, "Your appearance," said he, "does not belye your name, and your name cannot but give credit to your appearance. Without all doubt, you, signor, are the true Don Quixote de la Mancha, the north star and luminary of knight-errantry, maugre and in despite of him who has thought proper to usurp your name, and annihilate your exploits; I mean, the author of this here book." Which he took from his companion and put into the hand of Don Quixote, who, without answering one word, began to turn

over the leaves, and in a very little time gave it back to the stranger, saying, "In the little I have read, I find three things worthy of reprehension in the author; first, some expressions in the prologue or preface; secondly, his using the Arragonian dialect, and writing sometimes without articles; and, thirdly, that which confirms my opinion of his ignorance, his erring and deviating from the truth in the most material circumstance of the history; for, he says the wife of my squire Sancho Panza, is called Mary Gutierrez, whereas her name is Teresa Panza: now, if he blunders in such an essential circumstance, we may justly conclude that his whole history is full of mistakes *."

"A pleasant historian, i'faith!" cried Sancho: "he must be well acquainted with our adventures, to be sure, when he calls my dame Teresa by the name of Mary Gutierrez! Take the book again, signor, and see if he has lugged me in too, under a borrowed name!" "From what you have said, friend," replied Don Geronimo, "I find you must certainly be Sancho Panza, squire to signor Don Quixote." "Even so," answered the squire; "and I am proud of the occupation." "Then, in good sooth!" said the cavalier, "this author has not treated you so handsomely as from your appearance, I conclude, you deserve: he represents you as a gormandizer, a simpleton without the least vein of humour or pleasantry; and, in short, quite different from the Sancho described in the first part of the history of your master." "The Lord in heaven forgive him!" cried Sancho: "he might have let me sleep in my corner, without remembring there was such a sinner as me upon the face of the earth: for, He † that has skill should handle the quill—and I know that St. Peter is well at Rome."

The two gentlemen invited Don Quixote to sup with them in their apartment, as they knew the inn could not afford any thing proper for his entertainment; and the knight, who was always the pink of courtesy, complied with their request; so that Sancho remaining undisputed master of the pot, Cum mero mixto imperio,[4] he seated himself at the head of the table, in company with the landlord, who vied with him in affection for the cow-heel and calves feet.

Don John, in the course of the conversation at supper, asked what news Don Quixote had concerning the lady Dulcinea del Toboso: he begged to know if she was married, brought to bed, or in a state of pregnancy; or, if still single, she, as far as modesty and decorum would permit, smiled upon the passion of her lover Don Quixote. "Dulcinea," answered the knight, "is still unmarried, and my passion more intense than ever, our correspondence stands on the old footing, and her beauty is transformed into the appearance of a base born, rustic wench."

Then he, in a very circumstantial manner, related the inchantment of his mistress, together with his adventure in the cave of Montesinos, and the means prescribed by the sage Merlin for her relief; namely, the flagellation of Sancho.

---

* I am apt to believe that this remark was intended as an ironical sarcasm on the trivial observations of hypercritics; for, we cannot suppose Cervantes did not know, by this time, that he himself had, more than once, in the first part of this history, actually called Sancho's wife by the name of Mary Gutierrez; an oversight which I have taken notice of in the proper place.[2]

† The proverb, in the original, alludes to a kind of tabor: as if one should say, He alone should attempt to play, who knows how to beat the tabor.[3]

Unspeakable was the satisfaction which the two cavaliers enjoyed in hearing Don Quixote recount the strange incidents of his history; and they were equally astonished at the folly of his adventures and the elegance with which he related them: here they esteemed him as a man of sound understanding, and there he slipped through their opinion into the sink of madness; so that they could not determine what rank he should maintain between lunacy and discretion.

Mean while, Sancho having finished his meal, left his landlord more than half seas over; and entering the chamber where his master sat, "Gentlemen," said he, "I'll be hanged if the author of that book your worships were talking of, has any mind or inclination that he and I should be mess-mates—Since he has given me the character of a glutton, as your worships have observed, I wish he may not have likewise called me a drunkard." "He has, indeed," replied Don Geronimo: "but, I do not remember the expression, tho' I know the words are very scurrilous and false above measure, as I can plainly perceive in the physiognomy of honest Sancho here present." "Take my word for it, noble gentlemen," said the squire, "the Sancho and Don Quixote of that history must be persons quite different from those recorded by Cid Hamet Benengeli, who are no other than we ourselves, here standing and sitting in your presence: my master valiant, sagacious, and enamoured; and I simple, and withal pleasant; but neither sot nor gormandizer." "I believe what you say," replied Don John: "and wish it were possible to obtain a mandate, prohibiting any person or persons from presuming to meddle with the affairs of the great Don Quixote, excepting Hamet, his original author; in the same manner as Alexander the great decreed that no painter but Apelles should draw his portrait." "Any body may draw my portrait," said the knight; "but, let no man maltreat my character; for, patience often falls to the ground, when it is overloaded with injuries." "No injury can be done to Don Quixote, but what he can easily revenge," answered Don John: "unless he choose rather to ward it off with the buckler of his patience, which, I believe, is both strong and ample."

In this and other such conversation they spent great part of the night; and although Don John would fain have persuaded Don Quixote to read a little more of the book, that they might hear him descant upon particulars, he could not accomplish his purpose; the knight assuring him he considered it as good as read, and pronounced the whole an heap of absurdities; nor did he choose that the author, who might perhaps hear it was in his hands, should have the satisfaction of thinking he had perused his performance; for, from objects of obscenity and turpitude, not only the eyes but even the imagination ought to be kept sacred. When they asked whither his course was at present directed, he told them he was bound for Saragossa, in order to signalize himself in the prize-justs which are yearly solemnized in that city.

Then Don John gave him to understand that the new history gives an account of the spurious Don Quixote's having been in that place at a course, the description of which was barren of invention, low in stile, miserably poor in devices, and rich in nothing but folly and impertinence. "For that very reason," said Don Quixote, "I will not set foot in Saragossa, and so demonstrate to the wide world, the falshood of this modern historian, and let the nations see I am not the Don Quixote whom he has described." "I applaud your resolution," replied Don Geronimo; "and there will be a tournament in Barcelona,

where Don Quixote will have an opportunity to signalize his valour." "And that I shall surely embrace," answered the knight: "at present, gentlemen, as it is high time, you will give me leave to retire to bed; and I beg you will esteem and place me among the number of your most sincere friends and humble servants." "And me also," said Sancho: "peradventure my service may be good for something." They accordingly took their leave, and retired to their apartment, leaving Don John and his companion astonished at the medley of sense and madness they had observed in his discourse: they believed, without hesitation, these to be the real Don Quixote and Sancho, and not the persons described by the Arragonian author.

Don Quixote, rising early next morning, tapped at the partition, and bade farewel to his entertainers; and Sancho paid his reckoning like a prince, advising the landlord, however, either to furnish his house better, or to brag less of his accommodations.

CHAPTER VIII.

Of what befel Don Quixote in his way to Barcelona.

The morning was cold, and seemed to promise but little less for the day on which Don Quixote departed from the inn, after having informed himself of the nearest road to Barcelona, which he could travel without touching at Saragossa; so eager he was to fix the lye upon the new historian by whom they said he was so scurvily treated.

So it happened that he met with nothing worthy of record during six days; at the end of which, having quitted the high-road, he was benighted among a thick cluster of oaks or cork trees; for, in this particular, Cid Hamet has not preserved his usual punctuality. The master and man alighting from their beasts, and accommodating themselves at the roots of two separate trees, Sancho, who had laid in a good afternoon's luncheon, entered the gates of sleep abruptly, and without hesitation; whereas the knight, who was kept awake more by fancy than by hunger, could not close an eye; but, on the contrary, rambled in his imagination through a thousand different scenes. Sometimes he conceived himself to be in the cave of Montesinos; sometimes he thought he saw Dulcinea skipping and leaping upon her ass, in that dismal state of rustic transformation; and then his ears seemed to tingle with the words of the sage Merlin, who pronounced the conditions and endeavours to be observed and exerted for the disinchantment of his mistress. He was driven almost to desperation, when he reflected on the sloth and uncharitable disposition of his squire Sancho, who, to the best of his belief, had hitherto given himself only five stripes; a number poor and inconsiderable in comparison with the infinite score unpaid: and this consideration overwhelmed him with such anxiety and chagrin, that he thus argued with his own bosom:

"If Alexander the great ventured to cut the gordian knot, on the supposition that cutting would be as effectual as untying it; and, notwithstanding this violence, became sole

master of all Asia: the same success may now attend my efforts in disinchanting Dulcinea, should I scourge Sancho against his own consent; for, if the condition of this remedy be, that Sancho shall receive three thousand three hundred stripes, what signifies it to me, whether they are bestowed by his own hand or that of some other person, seeing the essential point is in his receiving them, from what quarter soever they may come?"

Inspired with this notion, he took the reins of Rozinante's bridle, which he formed into an instrument of flagellation; and, approaching the sleeping squire, began to untruss his points; indeed, it is the general opinion, that he had but one before which kept up his breeches. But, scarce had he begun to perform this operation, when Sancho, shaking off the fetters of slumber at one start, exclaimed aloud, "What's the matter? Who the devil is that so busy untrussing me while I'm asleep?" "It is I," answered the knight, "who mean to atone for thy omissions, and remedy my own misfortunes. I come to scourge thee, Sancho, and discharge some part of the debt which thou art obligated to pay: Dulcinea pines in a state of transformation; and, while thou livest at thine heart's ease, I am dying with desire: untie these points, therefore, of thy own free will; for mine, I assure thee, is to afflict thy posteriors with two thousand stripes at least, before we quit this unfrequented place." "By no manner of means!" cried Sancho: "I advise your worship to be quiet, or by the God of Israel! the deaf shall hear us: the stripes I have obliged myself to receive, must be given with my own free will and consent, not by force or compulsion; and, at present, I have not the least inclination to discipline my own flesh: let it suffice, I give your worship my word and honour, that I will flog and fly-flap my carcase, as soon as ever I find myself disposed for such exercise." "I must not leave it to thy courtesy," replied the knight: "for, thou hast a stony heart; and, tho' a peasant, art very tender of thy flesh." He, accordingly, struggled with all his might to unbreech the squire, who, finding the affair become very serious, started up from the ground, sprung upon his master, and, closing with him in a trice, tripped up his heels, so that the knight came instantly to the ground, where he lay with his face uppermost: then the victor, clapping his right knee to the breast of the vanquished party, and gripping him fast by both wrists, hampered him in such a manner that he could scarce either breathe or move. Nevertheless, he made shift to pronounce these words: "How now, traytor! dost thou presume to rebel against thy master and natural lord, whose bread thou hast eaten?" "I neither exalt kings nor dethrone them," answered Sancho: "but, being my own master, I stand up in my own defence: if your worship will promise to be quiet, and think no more of scourging me for the present, I will forthwith free and disencumber you from these bonds; otherwise, here thou shalt die, traitor and enemy to Donna Sancha."

The knight subscribed to the conditions, swearing by the life of his inclinations, that he would not touch the nap of his garment, but leave him at full liberty to begin the flagellation when he himself should think proper. On these considerations Sancho arose, and went aside a good way, to another tree at whose root he resolved to take his lodging for the remaining part of the night. There he felt something bob against his head, and putting up his hand found two legs provided with shoes and stockings: trembling with affright, he moved with great expedition to another tree, where he met with the same salutation, which increased his terror to such a pitch that he roared aloud for assistance. His master, hearing this exclamation, ran towards the place and inquired into the cause

of his fear and confusion; when the squire gave him to understand that all these trees were loaded with human legs and feet. The knight, reaching up his hand, immediately conceived the meaning of this strange circumstance; and said to Sancho: "Thou need'st not be afraid; for, those legs and feet, which thou hast felt without seeing, certainly belong to some robbers and outlaws who are hanged upon the trees; for, when they are apprehended in this place, the officers of justice string them up by twenties and thirties; and, from this particular, I am convinced that we must now be near Barcelona." And, indeed, his conjecture was right. Soon as objects were rendered visible by the dawn, they lifted up their eyes, and saw that the clusters depending from the trees, were no other than the bodies of banditti. The morning forthwith ushered in the day; and, if they were scared by the dead, they were no less aghast when they found themselves all of a sudden surrounded by above forty living robbers, who called to them in the Catalonian language to be quiet, and stand still until their captain should arrive.

Don Quixote being a-foot, his horse unbridled, his lance leaning against a tree, and, in short, his person without any means of defence, he thought proper to cross his arms upon his breast, and hung his head, reserving himself for a better season, and more happy conjuncture. Mean while, the robbers made such dispatch in plundering Dapple, that, in the twinkling of an eye, there was not the least crumb left in the wallet and pillion; and lucky it was for Sancho that he had secured, in a concealed girdle, the duke's crowns, and the money he had brought from home: nay, notwithstanding this precaution, those honest gentlemen would have searched and rummaged him in such a manner as to have found the cash, even tho' it had been hidden between the flesh and the skin, had not they been interrupted by the seasonable arrival of their captain, who seemed to be about four and thirty years of age, of a robust make, middling stature, grave countenance, and brown complexion: he rode a strong horse, was provided with a coat of mail, and he had slung a pair of pistols with firelocks at each side of him. Seeing his squires, for so they call the gentlemen of that profession, very busy in rifling Sancho Panza, he ordered them to desist; and, as they immediately obeyed his command, the girdle happily escaped. Surprized to see a lance leaning against a tree, a shield lying on the ground, and Don Quixote armed at all points and in manifest despondence, exhibiting the most rueful and melancholy figure, that melancholy herself could have formed, he approached the knight, saying, "Be not so dejected, honest friend, you have not fallen into the hands of a cruel Osiris, but of those of Roque Guinart, who has more of compassion than cruelty in his disposition."

"My dejection," answered the knight, "does not proceed from my having fallen under thy power, O valiant Roque, whose fame the limits of this earth cannot confine; but, from the consciousness of my own neglect, in consequence of which thy soldiers found me unprepared; whereas, I am bound, by the order of chivalry which I profess, to be always alert and vigilant, and to stand, as it were, at all times centry upon myself: and give me leave to tell thee, O renowned Roque! they would not have found it such an easy task to subdue me, had I been on horseback, armed with my lance and shield; for, know I am Don Quixote de la Mancha, whose exploits are celebrated through this whole terr-aqueous globe."

Roque Guinart immediately perceived that the knight's infirmity partook more of

madness than of valour; and although he had frequently heard him named, he looked upon his atchievements as altogether fabulous, and could not believe that such a humour did ever prevail in the heart of man: he was, therefore, extremely well pleased with this encounter, that he might, with his own eyes, see immediately before him, what he had heard reported afar off. "Valiant knight," said he, "do not vex yourself, or consider your present situation in the light of a misfortune: perhaps, by stumbling in this manner, your crooked fate may be made straight; for, heaven, by strange, unforeseen windings, which mankind cannot comprehend, is wont to raise the fallen and enrich the needy."

Don Quixote's mouth was already opened to thank him for his courteous behaviour, when they heard behind them a noise like that of a whole troop of horse, tho' there was only one, upon which came, at full speed, a youth who seemed to be about the age of twenty, dressed in green damask laced with gold, long breeches, a loose coat, an hat cocked in the Walloon fashion, with strait waxed boots and spurs; armed with a gold-hilted sword and dagger, a small fusil in his hand, and a case of pistols by his side.

Roque, hearing the noise, turned about and was surprised with the sight of this hand-some figure, who accosted him in these terms: "In search of thee, courageous Roque, I came hither, hoping, by thy means, to find, if not a remedy, at least an alleviation of my misfortune: and, to keep thee no longer in suspense, as I am certain you never saw me before, know that I am Claudia Geronima, daughter of Simon Forte, who is thy intimate friend as well as the particular enemy of Clauquel Torellas thy inveterate foe, as being head of the party which thou hast always opposed. This Torellas, thou knowest, has a son called Don Vincente Torellas, at least he was, two hours ago, distinguished by that name. I will be as brief as possible in the account of my disaster, and explain the occasion of it in a few words: That youth happened to see me, and courted my good graces; I listened to his addresses. and gave him my heart, without the knowledge of my father; for, there is no woman whatsoever so retired and mewed up, but she will find a time to execute and gratify her irresistible desires. In a word, he promised to be my husband, I consented to become his wife; and this was the farthest extent of our corre-spondence. Yesterday I was informed, that forgetting this obligation, he intended to marry another woman, and that this morning he had set out to celebrate his nuptials. My brain was disturbed, and my indignation arroused to such a degree by these fatal tidings, that, taking the advantage of my father's absence, I disguised myself in this apparel, pursued a-horsebac my perfidious lover, whom, having overtaken about a league from this place, I, without staying to make complaints or hear apologies, discharged upon him this fusil and these two pistols; so that, I believe, he has more than a brace of bullets in his body; thus I opened a gate through which my honour, tho' bathed in his blood, may escape, and left him in the hands of his servants, who neither could nor presumed to exert themselves in his defence. Thence I came in quest of thee, to beg that thou wilt conduct me safely to France, where I have relations; and, at the same time, promise to defend my father from the numerous kindred of Don Vincente, who may otherwise sacrifice him to their insatiable revenge."

Roque was struck with admiration at the gallantry, gay appearance, genteel mien, and adventure of the beauteous Claudia, to whom he replied, "Come, madam, let us first see whether or not your enemy is actually dead, and then we will consider about the most

proper measures to be taken in your behalf." Here Don Quixote, who had listened with great attention to Claudia's address and Roque's reply, interposing in the conversation, exclaimed, "No man has any occasion to give himself the least trouble about the defence of this lady, which I take upon my own shoulders. Give me my horse and my arms, and stay where you are; I will go in quest of the gentleman, and dead or alive compel him to perform the promise he hath made to so much beauty." "Who doubts that!" cried Sancho: "adad! my master has an excellent hand at match-making: a few days ago, he compelled another person who likewise refused to keep his word with a young woman; and if those plaguy inchanters who persecute him so much, had not transmographied the gallant into a lacquey, that very hour, she that was a maid before, would have been a maid * no more."

Roque, whose attention was engrossed by the adventure of the beautiful Claudia, paid very little regard to what was said either by the master or the man; but, ordering his squires to restore the spoils of Dapple to Sancho and retire to the place appointed for their quarters that night, he set out with Claudia, in great haste, to reconnoitre the situation of the dead or wounded Don Vincente. When they arrived at the spot where he had been overtaken by the young lady, they found nothing but some recent blood; but, casting their eyes around, they discovered some people on the side of an hill, and conjectured they could be no other than the servants of Don Vincente carrying their master to a proper place, where he might be cured, if alive, or buried, if dead. Their supposition was just: and spurring up their horses, they soon overtook the unhappy cavalier, whom they found in the arms of his attendants, whom he entreated, with a faint and languid voice, to let him die where he was; for, the pain of his wounds would not suffer him to proceed farther. Then Claudia and Roque approached him, to the great terror of his servants, who stood aghast at sight of this famous free-booter: but, Claudia was greatly disturbed at the melancholy situation of Don Vincente; and, agitated by the conflicting passions of tenderness and resentment, took him by the hand, saying, "Hadst thou given me this of thy own accord, conformable to the mutual promise subsisting between us, thou wouldst never have been in this condition."

The wounded cavalier opened his eyes, which were almost shut for ever, and recognizing Claudia, "I plainly perceive," said he, "most beautiful and misled young lady, that I owe my death to your hand; punishment altogether unmerited and unsuited to my inclinations, which, as well as my conduct, were, in regard to your person, altogether void of offence." "What!" cried Claudia, "is it not true that you, this morning, intended to marry Leonora daughter of the rich Balvastro?" "No, surely," replied Don Vincente: "my evil genius must have alarmed you with such information, that, your jealousy being inflamed, you might deprive me of life, which, as I leave it in your arms, and your embrace, I consider as happily lost: and, that you may be convinced of my sincerity, give me your hand, and, if you please, receive me for your husband; this being the only satisfaction I can make for the offence I was supposed to have given." Accordingly, Claudia and he joined hands and hearts together, in such a manner that she fainted away upon his bloody breast, and he sunk into a mortal paroxysm.

* This rhime is substituted in lieu of Sancho's playing on the word *fuera*, in the original.[1]

Roque being confounded and perplexed, the servants ran for water which they sprinkled upon their faces, and Claudia recovered from her swoon: but, this was not the case with her unhappy lover who had already breathed his last. The young lady, perceiving her beloved husband was no more, rent the air with her groans, wounded the heavens with her lamentation, tore her locks and scattered them to the winds, and disfigured her face with her own nails, exhibiting all the marks of the most severe grief that ever took possession of an afflicted bosom. "O cruel and inconsiderate woman!" she cried: "how easily wast thou provoked to execute such dire revenge! O furious jealousy! to what fatal despair dost thou conduct all those who give thee harbour in their breasts! O my dear husband! whose unhappy fate, in being mine, hath made thy marriage bed thy grave!"

Such were the melancholy exclamations of Claudia, which brought water into the eyes of Roque, who had seldom or never shed tears before: their servants wept bitterly, the young lady swooned almost at every step, and this whole circuit seemed to be the scene of sorrow, and field of misfortune. At length, Roque Guinart ordered the servants to carry their master's body to his father's country seat, which was hard by, that it might be buried according to the old gentleman's directions; and Claudia expressed her desire of retiring to a certain monastery, the abbess of which was her aunt, where she intended to finish her life in company of a better and more eternal husband. Roque applauded her design, and offered to conduct her to the place, promising, at the same time, to defend her father from the kindred of Don Vincente, and all the world, should they conspire against his peace. She would by no means avail herself of his attendance; but, thanking him for his obliging offers, in the most courteous terms she could use, took her leave of him, shedding a torrent of tears: the servants of Don Vincente carried off the body, Roque returned to his gang, and thus ended the amour of Claudia Geronima; a catastrophe not to be wondered at, when we consider that the web of her melancholy fate was woven by the baleful and invincible force of jealousy.

Roque Guinart found his squires in the place where he had ordered them to take up their night's lodging, and in the midst of them Don Quixote upon Rozinante, exhorting them, in a long harangue, to quit that way of life so dangerous both to soul and body; but, as the greatest part of them were Gascoons,[2] a brutal and disorderly sort of people, the knight's arguments made but little impression. The chief arriving, asked Sancho Panza if the men had restored the furniture and effects they had taken from Dapple; and the squire replied in the affirmative, excepting, however, three night-caps worth as many royal cities. "What the devil does the fellow say?" cried one of the gang: "here they are, and any body may see they would not sell for three rials."

"True," said Don Quixote: "but, my squire values them at that rate, on account of the person of whom I received them in a present." Roque commanded the man to restore them instantly; then, forming his people into a line, gave orders for bringing before them all the cloaths, jewels, money, and every thing they had acquired by robbery since the last partition; then, making a short valuation, and reducing the indivisibles into cash, he shared the whole among his company, with such equity and discretion, that, in the most minute article, he neither exceeded nor fell short of distributive justice.

Having made this partition, with which every individual was perfectly well satisfied and contented, Roque turning to Don Quixote, "If we did not observe this punctuality," said he, "there would be no living among such a crew." To this declaration Sancho replied, "From what I have seen, I find justice so excellent in itself, that the practice of it is necessary even among thieves."

One of the squires, overhearing the remark, lifted up the butt end of his musket, with which, in all probability, he would have shattered Sancho's skull, had not the general commanded him to desist; while Panza, trembling in every limb, resolved never to open his lips again so long as he should sojourn among such ruffians.

About this time arrived one of the gang, who was placed centinel on the road to reconnoitre travellers, and bring intelligence; and riding up to their chief, "Signor," said he, "not far from hence, there is a large company of people travelling to Barcelona." "Have you perceived," answered Roque, "whether they are such as we seek, or such as are in quest of us?" When the squire replied that they were such as he sought; "Set out then altogether," said he, "and bring the whole company hither, without suffering one to escape."

This whole gang departed accordingly, leaving their chief alone with Don Quixote and Sancho, to wait the issue of their expedition; and, during this interval, Roque addressing himself to the knight, "This life of ours," said he, "must appear very strange to Don Quixote, exposed as it is to infinite adventures and incidents replete with danger; and, indeed, I do not wonder that it should appear in that light; for, I must own, there can be no situation so full of terror and disquiet as that in which I live, and into which I was misled by the desire of revenge, which is often powerful enough to disturb the most philosophic breast. I am naturally benevolent and compassionate; but, as I have already observed, the desire of revenging an injury which I received, hath overturned all my virtuous inclinations in such a manner, that I persevere in this career, maugre and in despite of my own understanding; and, as deep calleth unto deep,[3] and sin unto sin, different schemes of revenge are so linked together, that I undertake not only my own, but also those of other people: yet, by the blessing of God, although I find myself thus involved in a labyrinth of confusion, I have not lost the hope of being, one day, happily extricated from all my troubles."

Don Quixote was surprised to hear Roque talk so sensibly and with such moderation; for, he imagined, that among those who were in the daily practice of assaulting, robbing, and murdering their fellow creatures, there could not surely be one single person of sense and reflection. "Signor Roque," said he, "the beginning of health is the knowledge of the disease, and the patient's desire to comply with the physician's prescription. You are now in the diseased condition, sensible of your infirmity, and heaven, or rather God himself, who is the great physician, will apply those medicines which are proper for the cure of your distemper; but, these remedies are wont to operate slowly, not in a sudden miraculous manner. And sensible sinners are much more likely to recover, than delinquents of little understanding. Now, as your discourse evinces your discretion, be of good chear, and courageously wait for the perfect recovery of your conscience. If you are, in earnest, inclined to quit this road, and enter at once into that which leads to

salvation, come along with me and learn to be a knight-errant, in which capacity you will undergo such toils and disasters as will be deemed sufficient penance, and exalt you to heaven in the turning of two balls."

Roque could not help smiling at Don Quixote's advice; but, changing the conversation, he recounted the tragical adventure of Claudia Geronima, at which Sancho was exceedingly grieved; for, he had been hugely pleased with the beauty, vivacity, and demeanor of the young lady.

About this time, they were joined by the squires of the booty, who brought along with them two gentlemen on horseback, two pilgrims on foot, and a coach full of women, attended by six servants, partly mounted and partly footmen, together with two muleteers who waited upon the gentlemen. These came all in a troop surrounded by the squires, and universal silence prevailed among the victors and the vanquished; both sides expecting, with resignation, the commands of the great Roque Guinart, who, approaching the gentlemen, asked who they were, whither they were going, and what money they had.

To these interrogations one of them replied, "Signor, we are captains of the Spanish infantry, our companies are in Naples; our intention is to embark on board of four gallies, which, they say, are now in the harbour of Barcelona, ready to sail for Sicily; and our funds amount to two or three hundred crowns, with the possession of which we thought ourselves rich and happy, considering the narrow appointments of a soldier which will not permit him to heap up a great deal of wealth."

Then Roque putting the same questions to the pilgrims, they answered, that their design was to embark for Italy, in order to visit Rome, and that, between both, they could muster about sixty rials. He, likewise, desired to know the quality of those who were in the coach, the place to which they were going, and the state of their finances. In these particulars he was satisfied by one of the horsemen, who said, "The company in the coach consists of my lady Donna Guiomar de Quinones, wife to the regent of the vicariate of Naples, her little daughter, a damsel, and a duenna; I am one of the six servants who attend them, and her ladyship's cash may amount to six hundred crowns." "At that rate then," replied the mighty Roque, "here are nine hundred crowns, and sixty rials: I have sixty soldiers; see what each man's share will come to; for, I am but an indifferent arithmetician." The robbers hearing this decision, cried aloud, "Long life to Roque Guinart, and confusion to the knaves who endeavour to effect his ruin!"

The captains exhibited evident marks of affliction, my lady regent assumed a very sorrowful countenance, and the pilgrims did not at all rejoice at this confiscation of their effects. Although Roque kept them for some time in suspense, he had no mind to protract their melancholy, which was plainly perceivable a gunshot off; but, turning to the captains, "Gentlemen," said he, "be so good as to lend me sixty crowns, and my lady regent will favour me with fourscore, in order to satisfy my squadron; you know, the Abbot must not want, who for his bread doth chant: Then you may prosecute your journey without fear or molestation, by virtue of a safe conduct I will grant; in consequence of which, you will be exempted from plunder, in case you should fall in with any other of those squadrons which I have posted up and down in different divisions; for, it is not my intention to aggrieve either soldiers or ladies, especially ladies of quality."

Infinite and well turned were the compliments in which the captains acknowledged their obligation to Roque for his politeness and liberality, for such they accounted it, in leaving them possessed of their own money. My lady Donna Guiomar de Quinones would have thrown herself from the coach, in order to kiss the feet and hands of the great Roque; but, he would by no means accept such marks of submission; on the contrary, he begged pardon for the injury which he was compelled to do them, in compliance with the precise duty of his wicked profession. The lady ordered her servant to pay instantly the eighty crowns which were demanded: the captains had already disbursed three score; and the pilgrims were going to surrender their miserable pittance; when Roque desired them to desist; and, turning to his gang, "Of these crowns," said he, "two shall fall to the share of each man, and then there will be an overplus of twenty, one half of which I give to the pilgrims, and the other ten to this honest squire, that he may make a favourable report of the adventure."

After this decision, he took pen, ink, and paper, with which he was always provided, and writing a safe conduct directed to the chiefs of his squadrons, gave it to the company whom he courteously dismissed, and they proceeded on their journey, struck with admiration at his noble demeanor, gallant disposition, and strange conduct, looking upon him rather as an Alexander the great, than a notorious robber. One of the squires displeased at the booty, said, in his Catalonian dialect, "This captain of ours is fitter for Praying than Preying: if, henceforth, he has a mind to shew his generosity, let it be from his own purse, and not from what is ours by right of conquest."

The unhappy wretch did not speak so softly, but that he was overheard by Roque, who, instantly unsheathing his sword, cleft his head almost in two, saying, "Thus I chastise mutiny and presumption." All the rest of the gang were terrified at this execution, and not one of them durst open his lips, so much were they over-awed by the character of their chief.

As for Roque, he went aside and wrote a letter to a friend at Barcelona, giving him to understand how he had met with the famous Don Quixote de la Mancha, that knight-errant whose exploits were in every body's mouth; and, he assured him, that the adventurer was the most agreeable and understanding man in the whole world: he, likewise, gave him notice, that, in four days from the date of the letter, on the feast of St. John, the said knight-errant would appear on the beach of the city, armed cap-a-pee, mounted on Rozinante, and accompanied by his squire Sancho upon an ass. He, therefore, desired his correspondent to communicate this intelligence to his friends the Nearri, that they might enjoy the character of Don Quixote, and wished his enemies the Cadelli might not partake of the diversion. But that was a vain desire, because the mixture of the madness and discretion in the knight, and the pleasantries of his squire, were such as could not fail to yield entertainment to the whole world in general.

This letter was dispatched by one of his squires, who, disguising himself in the habit of a peasant, entered Barcelona, and delivered it according to the direction.

## CHAPTER IX.

Of what happened to Don Quixote on his entrance into
Barcelona, with other circumstances that partake more of truth
than of discretion.

Three days and three nights did Don Quixote remain with Roque, and, had he
stayed as many hundred years, he would not have wanted subject for inquiry and
admiration at their way of life: they lodged in one place, dined in another; sometimes
they fled from they knew not what, sometimes waited for they knew not whom. They
slept standing, and even that slumber was often interrupted; they shifted from place to
place: in a word, their whole time was spent in appointing spies, examining centinels,
and blowing matches for their musquets, tho' they had but few; for, they chiefly used
firelocks. As for Roque, he passed the night by himself, in private haunts and places con-
cealed even from the knowledge of his own gang; for, the repeated proclamations issued
by the viceroy of Barcelona, setting a price upon his head, had rendered him restless,
diffident, and fearful, so that he durst not confide in any person whatever, being appre-
hensive that even his own followers would either murder or deliver him up to justice: a
life, of all others, assuredly the most tiresome and miserable! At length, this renowned
freebooter, accompanied by Don Quixote and Sancho, and attended by six of his own
squires, set out for Barcelona, through unfrequented roads, short cuts, and private
paths, and arrived upon the Strand, after it was dark, on the eve of St. John.

Here Roque, embracing Don Quixote, and giving to Sancho the ten crowns, which,
tho' promised, had not hitherto been payed, took his leave and returned to his station,
after mutual protestations of friendship had passed between him and our hero, who re-
solved to sit on horseback, as he was, till day, which was not far off. Accordingly, they
had not tarried long in this situation, when Aurora disclosed her rosy face through the
balconies of the east, infusing vigour and seeming joy into every plant or flower, instead
of gratifying the ear, which, however, was also, that instant, regaled with the sound of
waits and kettle-drums, together with the noise of morrice bells, the clatter of horses
upon the pavement, and the repetition of "Clear the way," pronounced by the couriers
who came forth from the city. Aurora vanished before the sun, who, with a countenance
ample as a target, gradually arose from below the horizon: then Don Quixote and San-
cho, extending their view all around, perceived the sea, which they had never before be-
held, and which seemed to be infinitely vast, and abundantly more spacious than even
the lakes of Ruydera, which they had seen in La Mancha: they, likewise, beheld the gal-
lies in the road, which, when their awnings were furled, displayed a glorious sight of
pendants, flags, and streamers, that wantoned in the wind, and kissed and brushed the
surface of the deep; while they resounded with clarions, trumpets, and other sorts of
music, which filled the air for many leagues around, with sweet and martial accents.

Now they began to move and forming themselves into line of battle, exhibited the representation of a naval fight upon the tranquil bosom of the sea. At the same time, a mock skirmish was acted on the shore, by a great number of gentlemen, mounted on beautiful horses, who came forth from the city, in gay attire, with splendid liveries. The soldiers of the gallies discharged an infinite number of fire arms, which were answered from the walls and forts of the city; and to the great guns, which seemed to rend the air with their tremendous sound, the midship cannons of the gallies made a suitable reply: the joy that resounded on board, the pleasure that appeared on shore, together with the serenity of the air, which was sometimes disturbed by the smoke of the artillery, seemed to infuse and engender a sudden flow of spirits and delight in every breast. As for Sancho, he could not conceive how those great bulks could use such a number of feet in moving through the sea.

About this time, the cavaliers so richly caparisoned, crying, hollowing, and shouting, in the Moorish manner, came riding up to the place where Don Quixote sat on horseback overwhelmed with surprize and astonishment; and one of their number, who had been apprised by Roque, exclaimed in a loud voice, "Welcome to our city, thou mirrour, lanthorn, planet, and polar star of all chivalry in its utmost extent! welcome, valorous Don Quixote de la Mancha, not the false, fictitious, and apocryphal adventurer, lately in spurious history described; but, the real, legal, and loyal knight recorded by Cid Hamet Benengeli, the flower of historians."

Don Quixote answered not a word; nor did the cavaliers wait for his reply; but, with their followers, began to wheel and turn, and curvet in a circle round the knight, who, addressing himself to Sancho, "As these people know us so well," said he, "I will lay a wager they have read our history, and even that of the Arragonian, which hath been lately printed." The gentleman, who had at first accosted him, returning, renewed his address in these words: "Signor Don Quixote, be so good as to go along with us, who are all the intimate friends, and humble servants of Roque Guinart." To this entreaty the knight replied, "If courtesy ingenders courtesy, yours, signor cavalier, is the daughter, or, at least, nearly allied to that which I experienced in the gallant Roque. Conduct me whither you please to go; my will shall, in all respects, be conformable to yours, and I should be proud if you would imploy it in your service."

The gentleman answered this compliment with expressions equally polite; and all his companions surrounding the knight in a body, they, to the music of the waits and kettledrums, conducted him to the city, his entrance into which was attended with a small misfortune. That mischief, from which all mischief is produced, ordained, that two bold and impudent boys, more mischievous than mischief itself, should squeeze themselves through the crowd, and, approaching Rozinante and Dapple, clap an handful of furze under the tail of each: the poor animals, feeling the severity of this new kind of spurs, augmented the pain by pressing their tails more closely to their buttocks, so that, after a thousand plunges, they came with their riders to the ground, to the unutterable shame and indignation of Don Quixote, who, with great dispatch, delivered the posteriors of his companion from this disagreeable plumage; while Sancho performed the same kind office for his friend Dapple.

The gentlemen would have willingly chastised the boys for their presumption; but, it was not in their power to give the strangers that satisfaction; for, they had no sooner executed their purpose, than they concealed themselves among the crowd of above a thousand youngsters who followed the cavalcade: so that Don Quixote and Sancho were obliged to pocket the affront; and, remounting their beasts, proceeded with the same music and acclamation, to the house of their conductor, which was large and magnificent, and, in all respects, suitable to the rank of an opulent cavalier. Here then we shall leave him for the present; for, such is the will of Cid Hamet Benengeli.

### CHAPTER X.

## Containing the adventure of the inchanted head, with other trivial incidents which, however, must not be omitted.

D on Quixote's landlord was called Don Antonio Moreno, a wealthy gentleman of good understanding, who loved a joke in a fair and good humoured way; so that, finding our knight safely housed under his roof, he began to contrive means for extracting diversion from the madness of his guest, without prejudice to his person; for, those are no jests that give pain; nor is that pastime to be indulged which tends to the detriment of a fellow creature. His first step was to unarm Don Quixote, and in that strait shamoy doublet, which we have already painted and described, expose him to public view in a balcony that jetted out into one of the chief streets in the city, where he was surveyed by the people and the children, who gazed upon him as if he had been a monster or baboon. While he stood in this situation, the gentlemen with the rich liveries performed their courses before him, as if for his sake only, and not in order to celebrate the festival, they had provided all their finery; and Sancho was ravished with the thoughts of having so luckily found, without knowing how, or wherefore, another wedding of Camachio, another house like that of Don Diego de Miranda, and another palace equal to the duke's castle, where he had been so hospitably entertained.

Don Antonio had that day invited some friends to dinner, and all of them payed particular respect to Don Quixote, whom they treated as a renowned knight-errant; a circumstance that elevated his vanity to such a pitch, that he could scarce contain his satisfaction: while Sancho's conceits flowed so fast and humorous, that all the servants of the family, and all who heard his sallies, seemed to hang upon his lips. While he waited at table, Don Antonio accosting him, "Honest Sancho," said he, "we are informed you are such a lover of fowls and balls of forced meat, that, when you can eat no longer, you pocket what remains for the next day." "No, signor," answered Sancho; "that is not the case; and your worship must have been misinformed; I am a cleanly squire, and no such filthy glutton; for, my master, here present, knows very well, that we have often passed

eight whole days without any other sustenance than an handful of nuts or acorns. True it is, If ever the heifer is offered, the tether is at hand; my meaning is, I eat what I get, and ride the ford as I find it *. If, therefore, any person whatever hath said that I am an exceeding glutton, and foul feeder, your worship may take it for granted that he is in a mistake; and I would tell him my mind in another manner, if it was not for the respect I bear to the honourable beards of this company." "Assuredly," said Don Quixote, "Sancho's cleanliness, and moderation in eating, might be inscribed and ingraved on tables of brass, for an everlasting memorial and example to succeeding ages. True it is, when very hungry, he may seem to be a little voracious; for, he eats with precipitation, chewing with both sides of his jaws; but, cleanliness he punctually maintains; and, while a governor, learned to eat so delicately, that he took up grapes, and even the grains of a pomegranate, with a fork." "How!" cried Don Antonio, "hath Sancho been a governor?" "Yes, sure," replied the squire; "and that of an island called Barataria, which I governed according to my own will and pleasure, for the space of ten days, during which I lost my natural rest, and learned to despise all the governments upon earth: I, therefore, fled from it, as I would fly from the devil, and tumbled into a cavern, from whence, tho' I gave myself up as a dead man, I was brought up alive by a perfect miracle." Then Don Quixote gave them a circumstantial account of Sancho's government, which afforded extraordinary entertainment to the whole audience.

Dinner being ended, and the table uncovered, Don Antonio took our hero by the hand and conducted him into a private apartment, where there was no furniture, but a table that seemed to be of jasper, supported by one foot of the same substance; and upon this table was placed a bust of bronze, from the breast upwards, representing a head of one of the Roman emperors. Don Antonio, after having traversed the room with his guest, and more than once walked round the table, "Signor Don Quixote," said he, "now that I am assured no person overhears us, as no body listens, and the door is bolted, I will impart to your worship one of the rarest adventures, or, rather, one of the greatest rarities that ever was known; on condition, however, that you will deposit the secret in the most hidden recesses of your heart." "I swear to that condition," answered Don Quixote: "and, for the greater security, will put a tombstone over whatever you shall communicate; for, know, signor Don Antonio, (by this time he had learned his name) your worship is talking to one, who, tho' he has ears to hear, has never a tongue to tattle; so that you may securely transfuse the contents of your own breast into mine, and take it for granted, you have ingulphed them in the abyss of silence." "On the faith of that promise," replied Don Antonio, "I will excite your worship's admiration with what you shall see and hear; and I, myself, will enjoy some alleviation of the pain I have felt from having no person to whom I could communicate the secret, which is not to be trusted to every body's discretion." Don Quixote waited with impatience and surprise to see the result of this preamble; when his entertainer, taking him by the hand, made him feel all around the bust, the table, and the jasper foot upon which it was supported; then accosting him with great solemnity of aspect, "This bust, signor Don Quixote," said he,

* Literally, *Use the times as I find them.*[1]

"was made and contrived by one of the greatest inchanters and negromancers that ever the world produced. He was, I think, a native of Poland and disciple of the famous * Escotillo, of whose knowledge such wonders are reported. As he chanced to be in this part of the world, I took him into my house, where, in consideration of a thousand crowns which I payed, he wrought this head, in which is centered the surprizing power and virtue of answering every question communicated to its ear. The master performed certain rites, erected schemes, consulted the stars, and carefully observed the lucky and unlucky minutes, until, at length, he brought it to that perfection which we shall perceive to-morrow; for, on Fridays it is mute, and this being Friday, we must wait till another day: in the mean time, your worship may consider and prepare your questions, which, I know by experience, it will truly answer." Don Quixote was confounded and astonished at this property and virtue of the head, and, indeed, almost tempted to disbelieve Don Antonio's account; but, seeing how little time was required to make the experiment, he would not mention his incredulity; but, in very polite terms, thanked his entertainer for having entrusted him with such an important secret. They, accordingly, quitted the apartment, and Don Antonio, having locked the door, returned to the rest of the company, who were highly entertained with Sancho's recapitulation of many adventures and incidents to which his master had been exposed.

That same evening, they persuaded Don Quixote to make a progress along the streets with them, not in his armour, but in a loose coat of tawny-coloured cloth, which would have made ice itself sweat at that season; and, in the mean time, they directed their servants to amuse Sancho within doors, that he might not come forth and spoil their diversion. The knight was not mounted on Rozinante, but accommodated with an ambling mule gayly caparisoned; and, upon the back of his coat or cloak, they, without his knowledge, pinned a parchment inscribed in large letters, THIS IS DON QUIXOTE DE LA MANCHA. The procession no sooner began than this scroll attracted the eyes of the people; and, when they read it aloud, the knight was astonished to find himself known, and hear his name repeated by all the spectators. He, therefore, turning to Don Antonio, who rode by his side, "Great," said he, "is the prerogative that centers in knight-errantry, the professors of which are known and celebrated through all the corners of the earth: take notice, signor Don Antonio, how my name is repeated by the very boys who never saw me before." "It is even so, signor Don Quixote," replied Antonio: "for, as light cannot be shut up and concealed, so neither can virtue remain unknown; and, that which is acquired by the profession of arms shines with superior splendor over all other acquisitions—"

While our knight thus proceeded amidst the acclamation of the crowd, a certain Castilian happened to pass, and, reading the scroll, exclaimed aloud, "Now, the devil

---

* This was *Michael Scot*, who lived in the thirteenth century, and was such an adept in medicine, mathematics, chymistry, alchymy, and other branches of natural knowledge, that the vulgar looked upon him as a wizard or magician. But, as this philosopher died in 1291, and this conversation between Don Antonio and our knight must have happened after the year 1605, when the first part of Don Quixote was licensed, how could the disciple of *Scot* be in the house of Don Antonio? Yet, this anachronism might easily pass upon Don Quixote, as it related to matters of inchantment.[2]

take thee, Don Quixote de la Mancha! how hast thou made shift to come so far without expiring under some of those infinite drubbings which thy ribs have received? A madman surely thou art; and if the defect of thine understanding affected thyself only, and was confined within the gates of thy own madness, the misfortune would be the smaller; but, thy frenzy is of such a peculiar nature as to turn the brains of all those with whom thou hast any commerce or communication; witness these gentlemen by whom thou art now accompanied. Return to your own house, Mr. Goose-cap, mind your family concerns; look after your wife and children; and discard these vain maggots which have eaten and burrowed into your brain, and skimmed off the very cream of your understanding." "Heark ye, brother," said Don Antonio, "go about your business; and do not pretend to offer your advice to those who want none of your counsel: signor Don Quixote de la Mancha is renowned for wisdom, and we who accompany him are not so mad as you may imagine. Virtue ought to be honoured wheresoever it is found: therefore, begone with a vengeance; and seek not to meddle in those affairs with which you have no concern." "'Fore God! your worship is in the right," replied the Castilian: "advising that honest man is kicking against the pricks. Nevertheless, I am extremely sorry that the good sense which, they say, this madman displays in some things, should be unprofitably wafted through the canal of his knight-errantry: and may that vengeance, which your worship imprecated, overtake me and all my posterity, if, from this day forwards, I give advice to any person whatever, asked or unasked, even tho' I should live to the age of Methusalem." So saying, this counsellor went away, and the procession went on; but, the throng was so great, occasioned by the boys and other idle people who pressed in to read the scroll, that Don Antonio was fain to take it off, on pretence of freeing the knight from some other annoyance.

In the twilight, they returned to the house of Don Antonio, where they found a ball prepared by his lady, who was a woman of birth, beauty, good humour, and discretion; and had invited a number of her friends to come and honour her guest, and enjoy the strange peculiarities of his madness: they, accordingly, came, and after supper, at which they were entertained in a very splendid manner, the ball began about ten o'clock. Among the company were two ladies who had a turn for satire accompanied with a great deal of humour; and who, tho' persons of unblemished honour, indulged themselves with uncommon freedom of behaviour, in order to keep up the spirit of the diversion, that it might not flag. This pair of female wags persisted with incredible eagerness, in dancing with Don Quixote, until not only his body, but even his very soul seemed fainting with fatigue; and nothing could be more ludicrous than the figure of the knight, so long, so lank, so lean, so yellow, capering about in a strait shamoy doublet, with an air unspeakably aukward, and legs that were never designed for such exercise. The young ladies affected to court his good graces by stealth; and he privately treated their advances with disdain, until, finding them become more and more pressing, he pronounced aloud, "Fugite partes adversæ![3] disturb not my repose, ye unwelcome thoughts! avaunt, ladies, with your unruly desires; for, she who is queen of mine, the peerless Dulcinea del Toboso, will not consent that I should surrender or be subject to any other than her own!"

So saying, he sat down upon the floor in the middle of the hall, quite exhausted and

demolished with the violent exercise he had undergone; so that Don Antonio gave orders for his being carried forthwith to bed; and the first person who touched him in obedience to this order, was his own squire Sancho Panza, who, as he endeavoured to raise him upon his legs, could not help reprehending him in these words: "What a plague tempted your worship to fall a capering? did you suppose every valiant man was as nimble as an harlequin, or that all knights-errant must needs be masterly dancers? if that was your opinion, I say you were much deceived: for, there be men who would rather undertake to slay a giant than to cut a caper. Had it been the shoe-slapping hornpipe, I could have supplied your place; for, I slap like a jerfaulcon; but, as for your figure dances, I know not a stitch of the matter." With this address Sancho raised a laugh from the assembly, and his master from the floor, and carrying the knight to bed, covered him up very warm that he might sweat out the cold caught in dancing.

Next day, Don Antonio thought proper to try the experiment of the inchanted head, and for this purpose entered the apartment, accompanied by Don Quixote, Sancho, a couple of friends, with our hero's two waggish partners who had stayed all night with Antonio's lady. The door being fast bolted, he explained the property of the bust, after having laid injunctions on the company to keep the secret, and declared this was the day on which he intended to make the first trial of the virtue contained in the inchanted head *. Indeed, except his two friends, no other person knew the mystery; and if they had not been previously informed by Don Antonio, they would certainly have shared in the same admiration which necessarily seized the rest who were present at the execution of a scheme so artfully contrived.

The first who approached the ear of this inchanted head was Don Antonio himself, who said in a low voice, but so as to be overhead by all present, "Tell me, O head, by thy inherent virtue, what are my present thoughts?" To this interrogation the head, without moving its lips, replied in a clear and distinct voice which was heard by the whole company, "do not pretend to investigate the thoughts." Those who knew not the plot were confounded at hearing this answer, as they plainly perceived there was not a living soul under the table or in the whole apartment to utter this reply. Don Antonio addressing himself again to it, asked how many persons are here in company? and was answered in the same key. "You and your † wife, two friends of yours, and two of her companions, with a famous knight called Don Quixote de la Mancha, and his Squire Sancho Panza by name." Here was fresh amazement! here was their hair standing on end with affright: while Don Antonio stepping aside from the table, said, "This is enough to convince me that I have not been deceived by the person of whom I purchased thee, thou sage, speaking, oracular and admirable head! Let some other person go and question it at will."

As women are usually very curious and impatient, the next who approached was one of the two ladies; and her question was this: "Tell me, O head, what I shall do to be extremely beautiful?" She received for answer, "Be extremely virtuous": and replied, "I ask

---

* But in this very chapter, he has already told Don Quixote, that he knew the virtue of the head from experience.

† Antonio's wife must have been here before the others entered: for, she is not in the list of those who went in with her husband.

no more." Then her companion advanced, saying, "I want to know, sagacious head, whether or not I am fondly beloved by my husband." And she was answered; "That you will learn by observing his behaviour." The married lady retired, observing that it required no magic to solve that question, for, in effect, an husband's behaviour to his wife will always declare the state of his affection. The third person that approached the table was one of Don Antonio's friends, who asked, "What am I?" And when the voice answered, "Thou knowest best"; he replied, "That is not the purport of my question; I desire thou wilt tell me if thou knowest my name." "Yes," said the oracle: "I know thou art Don Pedro Noriz." "Then I am satisfied," answered Don Pedro; "for, that answer is sufficient to convince me, O head, that thou knowest every thing." Then he withdrew, and was succeeded by the other gentleman, who advancing to the table, "Tell me, O head," said he, "the wish of my eldest son?" "I have already owned that I cannot dive into the thoughts of men," said the voice; "nevertheless I will tell thee that the wish of thy son is to bury his father." "That is indeed his wish," replied the cavalier; "I see it with my eye; I touch it with my finger; and do not choose to ask another question." Don Antonio's lady approached, saying; "I know not how to interrogate thee, O head; but I should be glad to know if I shall long enjoy my good husband." "Yes, you will," replied the voice; "his healthy constitution and moderate way of life promise a long succession of years and a good old age, of which many men deprive themselves by their own intemperance."

Don Quixote now took his turn, and addressing himself to the bust, "Tell me then, whatsoever thou art," said he, "is my account of what befell me in the cave of Montesinos really fact, or only the illusion of a dream? will the flagellation of my squire Sancho be certainly accomplished? and will the disinchantment of Dulcinea take effect?" "With respect to the cave," replied the oracle, "much may be said: the adventure partakes both of truth and of illusion. The flagellation of Sancho will proceed slowly; but Dulcinea will be disinchanted in process of time." "And that is all I desire to know," cried the knight; "for, in the disinchantment of Dulcinea, I shall reckon all my wishes at once happily fulfilled!"

The last interrogator was Sancho, who approaching the table, "Pray, good Mr. head," said he, "shall I peradventure obtain another government? shall I ever rise above the humble station of a squire? and lastly, shall I ever see again my wife and children?" To these questions he received these answers: "If it be thy fate to return to thy own house, thou wilt govern thy family and see thy wife and children; and in ceasing to serve, thou wilt cease to be a squire." "'Fore God! an excellent response!" cried Sancho, "that I could have foretold myself: and the prophet Perogrullo could have said no more." "What answer would you have, you beast?" said Don Quixote; "is it not sufficient that the responses delivered by the head correspond with the questions you have asked?" "It shall suffice," replied the squire; "but, I wish it had explained itself a little more fully, and told me some more of my fortune."

Thus ended the questions and answers; but not the admiration of the whole company, except Antonio's two friends who had been let into the secret, which Cid Hamet Benengeli will now explain, that the world may not be kept longer in suspense, or imagine that any negromantic Talisman or extraordinary mystery was contained in this wonderful bust. He gives us therefore to understand, that Don Antonio Moreno, in imita-

Sancho Displeased by the Answers Given Him by the Enchanted Head.

tion of such another head which he had seen at Madrid, contrived by a statuary, ordered this to be made in his own house for his private amusement, and with a view to surprize the vulgar; and in this manner was the whole fabricated. The table was of wood painted and varnished like jasper, and the foot that supported it of the same materials carved into the resemblance of four eagles talons which kept it firm and steady in its position. The head formed from the medal of one of the Roman emperors, and covered with a copper colour, was hollow, as well as the table in which it was so nicely fixed, that no eye could perceive the joining: the foot was likewise hollow, and answered to the neck and breast of the bust; and the whole corresponded with another chamber below, by means of a concealed tin pipe which passed through the bust, the table and the foot. In this lower apartment communicating with that of the inchanted head, did the person who uttered the responses, fix his mouth to the pipe, so as that the voice ascended and descended in distinct and articulate sounds, and it was impossible for any person to discover the deception. The respondent was Antonio's nephew, a student of acute parts and a well cultivated understanding, who being previously informed by his uncle of the number and names of the persons whom he intended to introduce into the chamber of the inchanted head, was enabled to answer the first question with great facility and precision; and to the rest he replied by conjectures which were equally ingenious and discreet.

Cid Hamet moreover relates, that for ten or twelve days the virtue of this wonderful machine continued in full force; but, a report diffusing itself through the city, that Don Antonio had in his house an inchanted head which could answer all manner of questions, he began to be afraid that these tidings might reach the ears of the vigilant centinels of our faith; for which reason he explained the whole affair to the fathers of the inquisition, who forbad him to proceed with the deception, and gave orders that the head should be broke in pieces, lest it should give umbrage to the superstitious vulgar; but, in the opinion of Don Quixote and Sancho Panza, it passed for a head that was really inchanted and oracular; tho' it had given more satisfaction to the knight than to the squire.

The gentlemen of the city, in complaisance to Don Antonio, and for the entertainment of Don Quixote, whom they wanted to furnish with an opportunity of discovering his diverting follies, appointed a running at the ring to be performed in six days; but, this was prevented by an incident which will be explained in the sequel. Mean while, the knight was desirous of going out and viewing the city at leisure and a-foot, fearing, that should he appear on horseback, he would again be persecuted by the boys and vulgar. He, accordingly, went forth, attended by Sancho and two of Antonio's servants whom their master had chosen for that purpose; and, chancing to lift up his eyes in passing through one of the streets, he saw, inscribed over a gate in capital letters, THIS IS A PRINTING-HOUSE; a circumstance which gave him uncommon satisfaction, as hitherto he had never seen a printing press, and longed much to know something of that art: he, therefore, entered the house with all his train, and saw people casting off in one part, correcting in another, composing in a third, revising in a fourth; and, in short, the whole oeconomy of a large printing-house. Going up to one box, he asked what was doing; and, being informed by the workmen, expressed his admiration and proceeded to a second. Among others, he went up to one, and putting the same question, the workman

replied, "Signor, that there gentleman," pointing to a grave person of a very prepossessing appearance, "has translated a book from the Tuscan into the Castilian language, and I am now composing it for the press." "What is the name of the book?" said Don Quixote. "Signor," answered the author, "the book in the original is called Le Bagatelle." "And what is the signification of Le Bagatelle in our language?" resumed the knight. "Le Bagatelle," replied the author, "is, as if we should say, in Castilian, Juquetes *: and, although the title of the book be so humble, it includes and contains a great deal of excellent and substantial writing." "I am not altogether ignorant of the Tuscan language," said Don Quixote: "for, I value myself upon singing some stanzas of Ariosto; but, pray tell me, signor, and what I am going to ask is not with any intention to sound your genius; but meerly to satisfy my own curiosity, have you ever, in composing your books, met with the word Pignatta?" "Yes, frequently," replied the author. "And how do you translate it into Castilian?" resumed the knight. "How should I translate it," said the other, "but by the word Olla?" "Body o'me!" cried Don Quixote, "what progress you have made in the knowledge of the Tuscan idiom! I will lay a good wager that you translate Piace into Plaze, Piú into Mas, Su into Arriba, and Giú into Abaxo." "Certainly," said the author: "because these words of the two languages correspond with one another." "Notwithstanding all your learning," replied the knight, "I could almost swear you are hitherto unknown to the world, which is ever averse to remunerate flourishing genius, and works of merit. What talents are lost, what abilities obscured, and what virtues are undervalued in this degenerate age! yet, nevertheless, a translation from one language to another, excepting always those sovereign tongues the Greek and Latin, is, in my opinion, like the wrong side of Flemish tapestry,[5] in which, tho' we distinguish the figures, they are confused and obscured by ends and threads, without that smoothness and expression which the other side exhibits: and to translate from easy language, argues neither genius nor elocution, nor any merit superior to that of transcribing from one paper to another; but, from hence, I would not infer that translation is not a laudable exercise; for, a man may employ his time in a much worse and more unprofitable occupation. At any rate, my observation cannot affect our two famous translators doctor Christoval de Figueroa, in Pastor Fido, and Don Juan de Xaurigui in Aminta, two pieces they have so happily executed, as to render it doubtful which is the original and which the translation: but, pray, signor, is this book printed on your own account; or, have you sold the copy to a bookseller?" "I publish it on my own account," replied the author; "and expect to gain a thousand ducats, at least, upon the first impression, of which there will be two thousand copies that will fetch six rials apiece, in the turning of a straw." "That is a very clear and comfortable reckoning," answered Don Quixote: "but, you seem to be very little acquainted with the outgoings and incomings, the schemes, conspiracies, and cabals of booksellers: when you find your back burthened with two thousand copies, I give you my word, both your mind and body will be terribly fatigued; especially if the books should be harsh or a little deficient in point of spirit." "What!" said the author, "your worship thinks then, I ought to offer my performance to a bookseller, who would give me three maravedis for the copy, and insist upon it that he had

* Trifles.[4]

done me a favour into the bargain? I do not publish with a view to acquire reputation in the world, where, thank heaven, I am already well known by my works; I print for profit, without which, reputation is not worth a doit." "God send you good luck, signor," answered the knight: who advancing to another box, where he saw the corrector employed on the sheet of a book, intituled, "The Light of the Soul"; "Ay," said he, "these are the books that ought to be printed; for, although there is, already, a pretty large number of this kind in print, numerous are the sinners for whose use they are intended, and for such multitudes who are in darkness, an infinite number of lights is required." He proceeded in his inquiry, and when he asked another corrector the name of a book, on which he saw him at work; he understood it was the second part of the SAGE HIDALGO DON QUIXOTE DE LA MANCHA, written by a certain person, a native of Tordesillas. "I have heard of this performance," said the knight; "and really, in my conscience, thought it was, long before this time, burned into ashes, or pounded into dust, for the impertinence it contains; but, as we say of hogs, 'Martinmas will come in due season *.' Works of imagination are the more useful and entertaining, the nearer they approach to truth, and the more probability they contain; and, even history is valued according to its truth and authenticity."

So saying, he quitted the printing-house with some marks of displeasure; and that same day, Don Antonio proposed that he should go on board, and see the gallies in the road; a proposal which was extremely agreeable to Sancho, who had never seen the inside of a galley, in the whole course of his life; and he sent a message to inform the commodore of his intention, to visit him in the evening, with his guest the renowned Don Quixote de la Mancha, whose name and person were already well-known to this commander, and all the citizens of Barcelona. What passed during this visit, will be related in the following chapter.

## CHAPTER XI.

## Of the misfortune which befel Sancho Panza on board of the gallies, and the rare adventure of the beautiful Moor.

M anifold and profound were the self-deliberations of Don Quixote on the response of the inchanted head, without his being able to discover the deceit; and the result of all his reflections, was the promise of Dulcinea's being disinchanted, on which he reposed himself with the most implicit confidence. This was the goal of all his thoughts, and he rejoiced, in full assurance of seeing it suddenly accomplished. As for Sancho, although he abhorred the office of a governor, as we have already observed, he could not help wishing for another opportunity of issuing out orders and seeing them obeyed; a

* About Martinmas, they killed the hogs designed for bacon.⁶

misfortune which never fails to attend the exertion of power, even though founded on mock authority.

In a word, that very evening, his landlord, Don Antonio Moreno, and his two friends, went on board of the gallies with Don Quixote and Sancho; and the commodore being apprised of the visit intended by two such famous personages, no sooner perceived them coming towards the sea-side, than he ordered the awnings to be struck, and the music to play: the barge was hoisted out, covered with rich carpets, and furnished with velvet cushions, and the minute Don Quixote embarked, the cannon a-midships of the captain-galley was discharged, and the others followed her example. When the knight ascended the accommodation ladder, on the starboard side, the whole crew saluted him with three chears, a compliment usually paid to persons of the first quality; and the general, for, by this name we shall henceforth call him, who was a noble Valentian, presented his hand, and embracing Don Quixote, "This day," said he, "will I mark with a white stone, as one of the happiest I shall ever enjoy, on account of seeing the renowned signor Don Quixote de la Mancha, in whom the whole worth of knight-errantry is cyphered and concentred." No less courteous and polite was the reply of Don Quixote, who rejoiced above measure, at seeing himself treated with such respect. The whole company having ascended the poop, which was very gayly ornamented, and seated themselves upon benches, the boatswain repaired to the gangway, and making a signal with his whistle, for all the slaves to strip, was obeyed in an instant, to the no small discomposure of Sancho, who was terrified at the sight of so many naked backs; nor did his apprehension abate, when he saw the awning stretched with such incredible dispatch, that he thought all the devils in hell had assisted in the operation. Yet this was nothing but cakes and gingerbread[1] to what I am going to relate.

The squire sat upon the stentril, close by the aftermost rower on the starboard-side; who, in consequence of the previous instructions he had received, lifted up Sancho in his arms, and while the whole crew of slaves, stood up, alert with the prospect of the joke, tossed him like a tennis-ball to his fellow, who, in the same manner committed him to a third; and thus he was bandied forwards on the starboard-side, from slave to slave, and bench to bench, with such expedition, that poor Panza lost his eye-sight entirely, and firmly believed himself in the possession of the fiends: nor did they desist from this exercise, until he was reconveyed by the larboard-side, to the poop, where this miserable object lay bruised, breathless and covered with a cold sweat, and in such perturbation of spirits that he scarce knew what he had undergone.

Don Quixote seeing Sancho flying in that manner without wings, asked the general, if it was a ceremony practised upon every person at his first going on board; for, in that case, as he himself did not intend to make profession of a sea-faring life, he had no ambition to perform such an exercise; and he vowed to God, if any man should attempt to seize him, as a fit subject for flying, he would spurn his soul out of his body: in confirmation of which resolve, he started up, and laying his hand upon his sword, put himself in a posture of defence.

At that instant, the awning was furled, and the main-yard lowered with such a terrible noise, that Sancho imagined the heavens were torn from off their hinges, and tumbling down upon his head, which he forthwith shrunk between his legs in an agony of terror;

nor was all serene in the breast of Don Quixote, who, while his legs trembled under him, shrugged up his shoulders and changed colour. The crew, having hoisted the main-yard, with the same expedition and noise which were made in its descent; while they themselves, continued as silent as if they had been altogether without breath or utterance; the boatswain piped all hands to weigh anchor, and leaping into the middle of the gangway, began to ply their shoulders with his Subtle-Jack or bull's-pizzle, and the galley, by little and little, stood out to sea.

Sancho beholding such a huge body, moved by so many painted feet, for such he took the oars to be, said, within himself, "This, indeed, is really inchantment; but what my master takes for it, is no such matter. What have these miserable wretches done to be scourged in this manner? and, I wonder, how the devil, that single man, who skips up and down, piping and whistling, dares whip and flog so many people! now, on my conscience, I believe, this is hell itself, or purgatory at least!"

Don Quixote perceiving, with what attention the squire observed every circumstance, "Friend Sancho," said he, "with what facility and dispatch might you now, if you please, strip yourself from the middle upwards, and taking your place among these gentlemen, finish, at once, the disinchantment of Dulcinea; for amidst the distress of so much good company, you would hardly be sensible of bodily pain: and who knows, but the sage Merlin would reckon each of these stripes, which are bestowed with good-will, equivalent to ten of those, which, at the long run, you must receive from your own hand." The general had just opened his mouth to inquire about the nature of this flagellation and Dulcinea's disinchantment, when a mariner came and told him, that the fort of Munjuy had made signal of a rowing-bark upon the coast, to the westward. He no sooner received this intelligence, than advancing into the gangway, "Pull away, my lads," cried he, "let not this Corsair brigantine escape; for, certainly she must be a vessel belonging to Algiers, which the castle has discovered."

The other three gallies ranging along-side of the admiral to receive orders, the general directed that two of them should stand out to sea, and the other keep along shore, so as that the Algerine should not escape. The slaves, immediately, began to ply their oars, which impelled the gallies with such velocity, that they seemed to fly; while the two that put to sea, at the distance of two miles, discovered a bark, which from the view, they judged to have fourteen or fifteen banks, and their conjecture was right. This vessel no sooner descried the galleys, than she made the best of her way, in hope of being able to escape by her nimbleness; but she was baffled in this expectation; for, the admiral being one of the swiftest gallies that ever sailed, came up with her apace, and the captain of the brigantine perceiving plainly that he could not escape, desired the rowers to quit their oars and strike, that he might not, by his obstinacy, incense the officer who commanded the gallies: but fate, which conducted their affairs in another manner, ordained, that even after the admiral was within hearing, and ordered them to strike, two Toraquis, that is, a couple of drunken Turks, belonging to the brigantine, discharged two firelocks, which killed as many soldiers who chanced to be in the head of the galley: an incident, which was no sooner perceived by the general, than he swore he would not leave one person alive in the brigantine, which he ordered his people to board with all expedition; nevertheless, she, for the present, escaped under the oars, and the galley had such way,

that she shot a-head to a good distance, so that the people on board the chace, seeing themselves in danger of being destroyed, hoisted their sails and put before the wind, while the galley tacked and pursued with all her force of canvas and oars. The diligence and dexterity of the Algerines did not turn out so much to their advantage, as their presumption conduced to their prejudice; for, the admiral running along side, grappled with the brigantine, and took their whole crew prisoners. The other two galleys came up, and all four returned with the prize to the road, while a great concourse of people stood on the beach to see the contents of the ship they had taken. The general anchored close by the shore, and understanding the viceroy of the city was among the spectators, he ordered the barge to be hoisted out to fetch him on board, and commanded the yard to be lowered for the convenience for hanging the master of the brigantine, and the other Turks he had taken, to the number of thirty-six, all stout young fellows, and mostly Turkish musqueteers. When he asked, who commanded the brigantine, one of the prisoners, who was afterwards known to be a Spanish renegado, answered in Castilian; "That there young man is our master": pointing to one of the most beautiful and genteel youths that human imagination can conceive, whose age to all appearance was under twenty. "Ill-advised dog," said the general, "what induced thee to kill my soldiers, when thou sawest it was impossible to escape? Is that the respect which is due to admiral-galleys? Dost thou not know, that rashness is not valour, and that doubtful hopes ought to make men resolute, but not desperate?"

The Moor was about to reply, but, the general could not at that time hear his answer; because, he was obliged to go and receive the viceroy, who had just entered the galley, with some of his own servants, and a few other persons. "General," said this nobleman, "you have had a fine chace." "Ay, so fine," replied the other, that your Excellency shall see it presently hoisted up at the yard-arm." "For what reason?" said the viceroy. "I mean, the master of the brigantine and his crew," answered the commodore, "who have, against all law, reason, and custom of war, killed two of the best soldiers that ever served on board; so, that I have sworn, to hang all the prisoners, especially this youth who was their captain," pointing to the handsome Moor, who, by this time, waited for execution, with his hands tied, and a rope about his neck.

The viceroy, surveying this unhappy prisoner, whose beauty, genteel mein and humility, served him instead of a recommendation, was seized with the desire of saving his life, and approaching him; "Tell me, corsair," said he, "art thou a Turk, Moor, or Renegado?" To this question, the youth answered, in the Castilian tongue, "I am neither Turk, Moor, nor Renegado." "Then what art thou?" resumed the viceroy. "A christian woman," replied the captive. "A christian woman," cried the viceroy, "in such dress and situation! this is a circumstance more worthy of admiration than of credit." "Gentlemen," said the youth, "be so good as to suspend my execution, until I shall have recounted the particulars of my story; and that small delay will not much retard the accomplishment of your revenge." What heart could be so obdurate as not to relent at this address; so far, at least, as to hear the story of the afflicted youth? The general, accordingly, told him he might proceed with his relation, but, by no means, expect pardon for the crime of which he was convicted. With this permission, he began in these terms.

"I was born of that nation, more unfortunate than wise, which hath been lately over-

whelmed by a sea of trouble: in other words, my parents were Moors, and in the torrent of their misfortune, I was carried by two uncles into Barbary, notwithstanding my professing myself a christian; not one of those impostors, who are so only in appearance, but a true and faithful Roman catholic. This declaration did not avail me with those who had the charge of our miserable expulsion; nor was it believed by my uncles, who, on the contrary, supposing it no more than a lie, and expedient, by which I thought to obtain permission to remain in my native country, hurried me along with them in a forcible manner. My mother was a christian, and my father a prudent man, of the same religion: I sucked in the catholic faith when an infant at the breast, and was trained up in the ways of virtue; nor do I think, I have ever given the least marks of mahometanism, either in word or deed. In equal pace with my virtue, (for, I really think my life was virtuous) my beauty, such as it is, hath ever walked; and notwithstanding the extraordinary reserve in which I lived, concealed from public view, it was my fate to be seen by a young cavalier, called Don Gaspar Gregorio, eldest son of a gentleman who had an estate in our neighbourhood. How he became desperately enamoured of me, and how I grew fond of him to distraction, it would be tedious to relate, considering my present situation, standing as I am, with the fatal cord between my tongue and throat: I shall, therefore, only observe, that Don Gregorio resolved to accompany me in my exile, and actually mingled with those Moors who joined us in different places, without being discovered; for, he spoke the language perfectly well. Nay, in the course of our voyage, he insinuated himself into the friendship of my two uncles, with whom I travelled; for, my father, who was a man of prudence and foresight, no sooner heard the first mandate for our expulsion, than he went abroad to foreign kingdoms in quest of an asylum for his family, leaving a large quantity of pearls, valuable jewels, with some money in cruzados and doubloons of gold, concealed and interred in a certain place, to which I alone was privy; and laying strong injunctions upon me to avoid touching this treasure, in case we should be exiled before his return. I obeyed his commands in this particular, and, as I have already observed, set sail with my uncles, relations and friends, for Barbary; and the place in which we settled was Algiers, whereas we might as well have taken up our habitation in hell itself. The king hearing of my beauty, and the report of my wealth, which was partly fortunate for my designs, ordered me to be brought before him, and asked from what part of Spain I had come, and what money and jewels I had brought to Barbary. I told him the place of my nativity, and gave him to understand that the money and jewels were buried under ground; but, that I should easily recover the whole hoard, provided I could return alone for that purpose. This information I gave, that he might be more blinded by his own avarice than by my beauty: but, during the conversation a person told him that I was accompanied, in my voyage, by one of the most beautiful and genteel youths that ever was seen. I immediately understood, that this was no other than Don Gaspar Gregorio, whose beauty far exceeds the fairest that ever was extolled; and was exceedingly afflicted at the prospect of danger to which the dear youth might be exposed; for, among those barbarous Turks, a boy or handsome youth is more prized and esteemed than any woman, let her be never so beautiful.

"The king forthwith ordered his people to bring Don Gregorio into his presence, and in the mean time asked me if his person actually corresponded with this report: then I,

as if inspired by heaven, answered in the affirmative, tho' at the same time I assured him, it was no youth, but a woman like myself; and begged leave to go and dress her in her natural attire, which would shew her beauty to the best advantage, and enable her to appear in his presence with less confusion. He said I might go, in good time, and that some other day he would concert measures for my return into Spain to bring off the hidden treasure. Thus dismissed, I went and explained to Don Gaspar the risque he would run in appearing as a man, and dressing him in the habit of a Moorish woman, accompanied him that same evening to the presence of the king, who was seized with admiration at sight of her beauty, and resolved to keep her for a present to the Grand Signor. In order to avoid the danger to which this young creature might be exposed in his seraglio, from his own inordinate desires, he ordered her to be lodged, quartered and attended in the house of some Moorish ladies, whither she was immediately conveyed; and what we both felt at parting, for I cannot deny that I love him tenderly, I leave to the consideration of lovers who have experienced such a cruel separation.

"The king afterwards contrived a scheme for my returning to Spain in this brigantine, accompanied by two native Turks, the very persons who killed your soldiers, and that Spanish renegado," pointing to him who spoke first, "who I know is a christian in his heart, and is much more desirous of remaining in Spain than of returning to Barbary; the rest of the crew are Moors and Turks, whom we engaged as rowers. The two insolent and rapacious Turks, without minding the order they received, to land the renegado and me in the habit of christians, with which we were provided, on the first part of Spain they could make, resolved previously to scour the coast, with a view to take prizes, fearing that should they set us on shore before-hand, we might meet with some accident which would oblige us to discover that there was a corsair on the coast, and they of consequence run the risque of being taken by the galleys. At night we descried this road, tho' we did not perceive the four galleys, and being discovered, were taken as you see. In a word, Don Gregorio remains in the habit of a woman among the Moorish ladies, at the imminent hazard of his life, and here I stand fettered and manacled, in expectation, or rather in fear, of losing that existence of which I am already tired. This, signor, is the end of my lamentable story, which is equally true and unfortunate; and all I beg of you is, that I may die like a christian, seeing, as I have already observed, I have in no shape been guilty of the fault which hath been charged upon our unhappy nation!"

So saying, she stood silent, her lovely eyes impregnated with tears, which few of the spectators could behold unmoved; and the viceroy, whose disposition was humane and compassionate, unable to speak, advanced to the place, and with his own hands released those of the beautiful Moor.

While this christian Moor related her peregrinations, an antient pilgrim who had followed the viceroy into the galley, kept his eyes close fixed upon her countenance, and her story was no sooner finished than he threw himself at her feet, which he bathed with his tears, while in accents interrupted with a thousand sighs and groans, he exclaimed, "O, Anna Felix! my unhappy daughter! I am thy father Ricote, who have returned in search of thee to Spain, because I could not live without thee, who art dear to my affection even as my own soul."

At these words, Sancho opened his eyes, and raised his head, which he had hitherto hung in manifest despondence, reflecting upon the disgrace of his flying adventure; and, looking at the pilgrim, recognized that same Ricote whom he had encountered the very day on which he quitted his government: he likewise recollected the features of his daughter, who being by this time unbound, mingled her tears with those of her father, whom she tenderly embraced; and then the old man addressing himself to the viceroy and general, "My lords," said he, "this is my daughter, not so happy in the incidents of her life as in her name, which is Anna Felix, with the addition of Ricote, as famous for her beauty as for her father's wealth. I left my country in quest of a place where we should be received and hospitably entertained; and having found such an asylum in Germany, I returned as a pilgrim, in the company of some people of that nation, hoping to find my daughter, and fetch away the wealth which I had buried in the earth: my daughter was gone, but I recovered my hoard, which is in my possession; and now, by this strange vicissitude which you have seen, I have retrieved that treasure which is the chief object of my affection, I mean my beloved daughter. If our innocence and mutual tears can have influence enough upon your integrity and justice, to open the gates of mercy, O let it prevail in favour of us who never offended you even in thought, nor in any shape corresponded with the designs of our people, who have been justly expelled." Here Sancho interposing, "I am very well acquainted with Ricote," said he, "and know all he has said about his daughter Anna Felix to be true; but, with respect to that other trash of his comings and goings, and his good or evil designs, I neither meddle nor make." Every person present expressed admiration at this strange incident; and the general turning to the daughter, "Every tear you let fall," said he, "conspires in preventing the performance of my oath. Live, beauteous Anna Felix, the term of your life, prescribed by heaven; and let those insolent and presumptuous wretches suffer punishment for the crime they have committed."

So saying, he ordered the two Turks, who had killed his soldiers, to be hanged at the yard-arm; but, the viceroy earnestly entreating him to spare their lives, as their crime was rather the effect of madness than of preconceived design. The general granted his request, especially as he did not think it commendable to execute revenge in cold blood.

Then they began to contrive some method for extricating Don Gaspar Gregorio from the danger in which he was involved; and Ricote offered to the value of above two thousand ducats, which he had about him in pearls and jewels, to any person who could effect his deliverance. Many schemes were projected; but none of them seemed so sensible as that which was presented by the fore-mentioned Spanish renegado, who offered to return to Algiers in some small bark of about six banks, manned with christians, as he knew where, how and when he might land with safety, and was well acquainted with the house in which Don Gaspar remained. The general and the viceroy were dubious of the renegado, and scrupled to trust him with the command of christian rowers: but Anna Felix was satisfied of his integrity, and her father said he would engage to ransom them, should they chance to be taken and enslaved.

Matters being settled on this footing, the viceroy went ashore, after having laid strong injunctions on Don Antonio Moreno, who had invited the Moorish beauty and her fa-

ther to his house, to make much of his guests, and command whatever his own palace could afford for their entertainment. Such was the charity and benevolence which Anna's beauty had infused into his heart.

## CHAPTER XII.

Giving the detail of an adventure which gave Don Quixote more mortification than he had received from all the misfortunes which had hitherto befallen him.

D on Antonio's lady, as the history relates, was extremely pleased at sight of Anna Felix, whom she received with great cordiality, equally enamoured of her beauty and discretion, for, indeed, the Moor excelled in both; and here she was visited by all the people of fashion, in town as if by toll of bell. As for Don Quixote, he gave Antonio to understand, that, in his opinion, the plan they had formed for the deliverance of Don Gregorio was more dangerous than expedient, and that it would be much more effectual to set him on shore in Barbary, with his arms and horse; in which case, he would bring home the young gentleman, in despite of the whole Moorish race, as heretofore Don Gayferos had delivered his wife Melisendra. Sancho hearing this proposal, "Consider," said he, "that signor Don Gayferos delivered his wife from captivity, on the main land, and carried her off to France through the high road; but, in this case, even granting we should have the good luck to release Don Gregorio from his confinement, we shall not be able to convey him hither to Spain, because the sea is between us and Barbary." "There's a remedy for all things but death," replied the knight: "for, if there is a bark by the shore, we can go aboard, in opposition to the whole universe." "Your worship describes it as a very easy matter," said the squire: "but, between Said and Done, a long race may be run: and, for my part, I would stick to the offer of the renegado, who seems to be a very honest person, and a man of compassionate bowels." Don Antonio said, that if the renegado should fail in his undertaking, they would certainly find some means for transporting the great Don Quixote to Barbary: and, in two days, the renegado departed in a light bark with six oars on a side, manned with a crew of approved valour. In two days after her departure, the galleys, likewise, set sail for the Levant, after the general had begged and obtained the viceroy's promise to let him know the success of the scheme they had contrived for the deliverance of Don Gregorio, together with the fate of the lovely Anna Felix.

One morning, Don Quixote rode forth upon the strand, completely armed; for he often observed, arms were his ornaments, and fighting his diversion, and he never cared to appear in any other dress; and, as he pranced along, he saw coming towards him, a knight, likewise, armed cap-a-pee, having a full moon painted on his shield. This ap-

parition was no sooner within hearing, than he addressed his discourse to Don Quixote, pronouncing aloud, "Renowned cavalier, never enough applauded Don Quixote de la Mancha, I the knight of the white moon, whose unheard-of exploits may, peradventure, recal him to your remembrance, am come with hostile intent to prove the force of thine arm; to convince and compel thee to own that my mistress, whosoever she is, exceeds in beauty thy Dulcinea del Toboso, beyond all comparison: which truth, if thou wilt fairly and fully confess, thou wilt avoid thy own death, and spare me the trouble of being thy executioner; but, shouldst thou presume to engage with me in single combat, and be overcome, all the satisfaction I demand is, that thou wilt lay aside thine arms, desist from travelling in quest of adventures, and, quitting the field, retire to thine own habitation, where thou shalt continue a whole year, without drawing a sword, in comfortable peace and profitable tranquillity, which may tend to the augmentation of thy fortune, and the salvation of thy precious soul. On the other hand, if it be my fate to be vanquished, my life shall exist at thy discretion; thine shall be the spoils of all my arms and horse, and to thee shall be transferred all the fame of my atchievements: consider which of these alternatives thou wilt choose, and answer me on the spot; for, on this very day, the affair must be dispatched and determined."

Don Quixote was astonished and confounded, as well at the arrogance of the knight of the white moon, as at the cause of his defiance; and, after a short pause of recollection, replied with a solemn tone, and countenance severe, "Sir knight of the white moon, whose exploits have not, as yet, reached mine ear, I dare say you have never seen the illustrious Dulcinea; for, had you enjoyed that happiness, I know you would not have dreamed of making such a rash demand: one glimpse of her would have undeceived you perfectly, and plainly demonstrated, that there never was, or will be, beauty comparable to that which she possesses. I, therefore, without giving you the lie, but only affirming that you are egregiously mistaken, accept of your defiance on the conditions you have proposed, and will fight you forthwith before the day you have pitched upon shall be elapsed; with this exception, however, that I will, by no means, adopt the fame of your exploits; because, I know not how, where, or wherefore they were atchieved, and am content with my own such as they are: choose your ground, therefore, and I will take my share of the field; and, Let St. Peter bless what God shall bestow."

The knight of the white moon being discovered from the city, and seen talking with Don Quixote, notice was given to the viceroy, who, supposing it was some new adventure contrived by Don Antonio Moreno, or some other gentleman of the town, went down to the strand, accompanied by the said Don Antonio and a number of other cavaliers, and reached the spot just as Don Quixote wheeled about on Rozinante to measure his distance. Seeing both parties ready for returning to the encounter, he placed himself in the middle between them, and demanded the cause that induced them so suddenly to engage in single combat. The knight of the white moon answered, that it was the precedency of beauty, and briefly repeated his proposal to Don Quixote, with the mutual acceptation of the conditions proposed. Then the viceroy, taking Don Antonio aside, asked if he knew this knight of the white moon; and if this was a joke which he intended to perpetrate upon Don Quixote. Don Antonio assured him that he knew not the stranger, nor could guess whether the challenge was given in jest or earnest. He was

a little perplexed, and dubious whether or not he should allow the battle to be fought; but, as he could not conceive it to be any thing else than a preconcerted joke, he retired, saying, "Valiant knights, seeing there is no other remedy, but you must confess or die; and signor Don Quixote persists in denying what you of the white moon presume to affirm, I leave you to your fate, and God stand by the righteous."

The stranger, in very polite terms, and well selected phrase, thanked the viceroy for the permission he had granted, and his example was, in this particular, followed by Don Quixote, who, having recommended himself heartily to heaven and his Dulcinea, according to his usual practice when he engaged in any combat, turned about to take a little more ground, in imitation of his antagonist; then, without receiving a signal for engaging, either by sound of trumpet, or any other instrument, both parties wheeled about at the same instant. The knight of the white moon having the fleeter horse, coming up with his adversary, before this last had run one third of his career, lifted up his lance, purposely, that he might not wound Don Quixote, whom, however, he encountered with such an irresistible shock, that both he and Rozinante came to the ground with a very dangerous fall: the victor instantly sprung upon him, and, clapping his lance to his vizor, "Knight," said he, "you are vanquished and a dead man, unless you acknowledge the terms of the defiance." To this address the battered and astonished Don Quixote, without lifting up his beaver, replied in a languid tone and feeble voice, that seemed to issue from a tomb, "Dulcinea del Toboso is the most beautiful woman in the world, and I the most unfortunate knight on earth; and, as it is not reasonable that my weakness should discredit this truth, make use of your weapon, knight, and instantly deprive me of life, as you have already divested me of honour." "By no means," said he of the white moon: "let the fame of my lady Dulcinea's beauty flourish in full perfection; all the satisfaction I ask is, that the great Don Quixote shall retire to his own house, and there abide for the space of one year, or during the term which I shall prescribe, according to the articles agreed upon before we engaged." This whole dialogue was overheard by the viceroy, Don Antonio, and a number of other people who were present, and they were also ear-witnesses of the answer made by Don Quixote, who said, that as the victor had demanded nothing to the prejudice of Dulcinea, he would comply with his proposal like a true and punctual knight.

He of the white moon hearing this declaration, turning his horse, and, bowing courteously to the viceroy, entered the city at an half gallop, whither he was followed by Don Antonio, at the desire of the viceroy, who entreated him to make inquiry, and obtain satisfactory information concerning this romantic stranger. In the mean time, they raised up Don Quixote, and, uncovering his face, found him pale as death, and his forehead bedewed with a cold sweat, while Rozinante lay motionless from the rough treatment he had received. As for Sancho, he was so overwhelmed with sorrow and vexation, that he knew not what to say or do; this unlucky incident seemed to be a dream, and he looked upon the whole scene as a matter of inchantment. Seeing his lord and master overcome, and obliged to lay aside his arms for the space of a whole year, he imagined the splendour of his exploits was eclipsed, and all those fair hopes, produced from his late promise, dispersed in the air, as smoak is dissipated by the wind: in a word, he was

afraid that Rozinante was maimed for ever, and his master's bones dislocated, and even thought it would be a great mercy if he was not in a worse condition.

Finally, the viceroy ordered his people to bring a sedan, in which the knight was carried to the city, accompanied by that nobleman, who longed very much to know who this knight of the white moon was, by whom Don Quixote had been left in such a cruel dilemma.

## CHAPTER XIII.

Which discovers who the knight of the white moon was, and gives an account of the deliverance of Don Gregorio, with other incidents.

D on Antonio Moreno followed the knight of the white moon, who was also accompanied, and even persecuted by a number of boys, until they had housed him in one of the city inns, which was, at the same time, entered by Don Antonio, who burned with impatience to know what he was, and, without ceremony, intruded himself into the apartment to which the stranger retired, with his squire, to be unarmed. He of the white moon, perceiving how much the gentleman's curiosity was inflamed, and that he was resolved to stick close by him until it should be satisfied, "Signor," said he, "I am not ignorant that you are come hither on purpose to know who I am; and, as there is no reason why I should refuse you that satisfaction, I will, while my servant is employed in taking off my armour, explain the whole mystery, without the least reserve. You must know, then, signor, that I am called the batchelor Sampson Carrasco, a townsman of Don Quixote de la Mancha, whose madness and extravagance have given great concern to all his acquaintance, and to me in particular. Believing that his recovery would depend upon his living quietly at his own habitation, I projected a scheme for compelling him to stay at home, and, about three months ago, sallied forth upon the highway, as a knight-errant, assuming the appellation of the knight of the mirrors, fully resolved to engage and vanquish Don Quixote, without hurting him dangerously, after I should have established, as the condition of our combat, that the vanquished should be at the discretion of the victor: and, as I deemed him already conquered, my intention was to demand that he should return to his own house, from which he should not stir for the space of one year, in which time I hoped his cure might be effected. But, fate ordained things in another manner: I was conquered and overthrown, and my design entirely frustrated; he proceeded in quest of new adventures, and I returned vanquished, ashamed, and sorely bruised by the dangerous fall I had sustained in battle: nevertheless, I did not lay aside the design of returning in quest of him to overthrow him in my turn, and you have, this day, seen my intention succeed; for, he is so punctual in observing the ordinances of chivalry, that he will, doubtless, perform his promise in com-

plying with my demand. This, signor, is an account of the whole affair; nor have I omitted one circumstance; and I beg you will not discover and disclose to Don Quixote who I am, that my christian intention may take effect, and the poor gentleman retrieve his judgment, which would be altogether excellent, were he once abandoned by those mad notions of chivalry." "God forgive you, signor," cried Don Antonio, "for the injury you have done the world, in seeking to restore to his senses the most agreeable madman that ever lived! do not you perceive, signor, that the benefit resulting from the cure of Don Quixote will never counterbalance the pleasure produced by his extravagancies? But, I imagine, all the care and industry of signor batchelor will hardly be sufficient to effect the recovery of a man who is so thoroughly mad; and, if it was no breach of charity, I would say, May Don Quixote never be cured; for, in his recovery, we only lose his own diverting flights, but also those of his squire Sancho Panza; and any of these conceits are such as might convert melancholy herself into merriment and laughter: nevertheless, I shall put a seal upon my lips and say nothing, that I may see whether or not I shall judge aright, in supposing that the diligence of signor Carrasco will not answer his expectation." The batchelor answered, that all things considered, the business was already in a fair way, and, he did not doubt, would be blessed with a prosperous issue; and Don Antonio having made a tender of his services and taken his leave, Sampson ordered his arms to be fastened upon a mule, then mounting the horse on which he engaged Don Quixote, he quitted the city that same day, on his return to his own country, in which he arrived without having met with any incident worthy of being recorded in this authentic history. Don Antonio made the viceroy acquainted with all the particulars he had learned from Carrasco, which afforded no great pleasure to that nobleman, as the retirement of Don Quixote would destroy all that entertainment enjoyed by those who had the opportunity of observing his madness.

Six whole days did Don Quixote lie a-bed, pensive, melancholy, mauled, and meagre, revolving in his imagination, and meditating incessantly on the unfortunate incident of his overthrow; notwithstanding the consolations of Sancho, who, among other arguments of comfort, exhorted his worship to hold up his head, and dispel his sorrow, if possible. "Your worship," said he, "has reason to thank God, that, tho' you are overthrown, your ribs are still whole: you know that, in those matters, we must take as well as give; and where there are hooks we do not always find bacon—A fig for the physician, seeing we do not want his help in the cure of this distemper: let us return to our habitation, and leave off travelling about in quest of adventures, through lands and countries unknown: nay, if we rightly consider the case, I am the greatest loser, tho' your worship is the most roughly handled; for, tho' when I quitted the government, I, likewise, quitted all thought of governing, I did not give up the desire of being a count, which will never be fulfilled if your worship should renounce your design of being a king, and quit the exercise of chivalry; in that case all my hopes must vanish into smoke." "Peace, Sancho," said the disconsolate knight; "the term of my penance and retirement will not exceed a year, at the end of which I will return to the honourable duties of my profession, and then we shall find kingdoms to conquer and countships to bestow." "The Lord give ear, and my sin never hear!" cried Sancho: "and I have always heard it said, that righteous hope is better than unjust possession."

Their conversation was interrupted by Don Antonio, who, entering the apartment with marks of infinite satisfaction, exclaimed, "Money for my good news, signor Don Quixote: Don Gregorio, and the renegado who undertook his deliverance, are now in the road—in the road! they are, by this time, in the viceroy's palace, and will be here in an instant." The knight was a little revived by these tidings, and replied, "In truth, I was going to say, I should have been glad to hear that the scheme had not succeeded, so that I should have been obliged to cross over into Barbary, where I would, by the strength of my arm, have given liberty not only to Don Gregorio, but also to all the christian captives in Algiers—but, what am I saying, miserable caitif? am not I vanquished? am not I overthrown? am not I excluded from the exercise of arms for the space of a whole year? wherefore then promise what I cannot perform? wherefore praise my own valour, when I am fitter for handling a distaff than for wielding a sword?" "No more of that, good signor," replied the squire: "Let the hen live tho' she has the pip: To-day for thee, and to-morrow for me: as to those matters of encounters and dry bastings, they are not to be minded; for, he that falls to-day may rise to-morrow, if he does not choose to lie a-bed; I mean, if he does not choose to despair, without endeavouring to recover fresh spirits for fresh adventures. Get up, therefore, I beseech your worship, and receive Don Gregorio; for, the people are in such an uproar, that, by this time, he must be in the house."

This was really the case: Don Gregorio and the renegado having given the viceroy an account of the voyage and success of the undertaking, the young gentleman, impatient to see his dear Anna Felix, was come with his deliverer to the house of Don Antonio; and, although Don Gregorio was in woman's apparel when they delivered him from Algiers, he had exchanged it in the vessel with another captive by whom he was accompanied; but, in any dress whatsoever, his appearance was such as commanded friendship, service, and esteem; for, he was exceedingly beautiful, and seemingly not above seventeen or eighteen years of age. Ricote and his daughter went forth to receive him, the father with tears of joy, and Anna with the most modest deportment: nor did this fair couple embrace one another; for, where genuine love prevails, such freedom of behaviour is seldom indulged. The beauty of Don Gregorio and his mistress excited the admiration of all the spectators; while silence spoke for the lovers themselves, and their eyes, performing the office of the tongue, disclosed the joy of their virtuous thoughts. The renegado recounted the stratagem and means he had used for the deliverance of the youth, who, likewise, entertained the company with a detail of the dangers and distresses to which he was exposed among the women with whom he had been left; and this task he performed, not with diffused prolixity, but in elegant and concise terms, which plainly proved that his discretion far exceeded his years. Finally, Ricote liberally rewarded the rowers, and the renegado, who reunited and reincorporated himself with the church, and, from a rotten member, became fair and sound, by dint of mortification and sincere repentance.

Two days after the arrival of Don Gregorio, the viceroy consulted with Don Antonio about the means of obtaining permission for Anna Felix and her father to reside in Spain, as they were persuaded that no inconvenience could arise from such indulgence to a daughter who was so perfectly a christian, and a father so righteously disposed. Don

Antonio offered to negotiate this affair at court, whither he was pressingly called by his own occasions; observing, that by dint of interest and presents many difficulties are removed. Ricote, who was present at this conversation, said, "There is nothing to be hoped from favour or presents; neither tears, entreaties, promises, nor presents will avail with the great Don Bernardino de Velasco, count de Selaza, to whom his majesty has entrusted the charge of our expulsion; for, although he really tempers justice with mercy, as he perceives the whole body of our nation contaminated and gangrened, he applies the actual cautery instead of the mollifying ointment; so that, by his diligence, prudence, sagacity, and terrifying threats, he has sustained upon his able shoulders the weight of that vast project which he hath successfully put in execution, without suffering his Argus eyes, which are always alert, to be blinded by all our industry, stratagem, fraud, and sollicitation. He is resolved that none of our people shall remain concealed, lest, like an hidden root, they may hereafter bud and bring forth fruit which may be poisonous to Spain, already cleansed and delivered from those fears that arose from the prodigious number of the Moors: an heroic resolution of the great Philip III. who has, at the same time, displayed the most consummate wisdom, in committing the execution of the scheme to the courage and ability of Don Bernardino de Velasco." "Nevertheless," said Don Antonio, "I will, while at court, use all possible means in your behalf, and leave the determination to heaven: Don Gregorio shall go along with me, and console his parents for the grief they have suffered from his absence; Anna Felix shall stay with my wife, or be boarded in a monastery; and, I know, my lord viceroy will be pleased to lodge honest Ricote until we shall see the issue of my negotiation." The viceroy agreed to every circumstance of the proposal; but, don Gregorio, being informed of the scheme, declared he neither could nor would leave his charming Anna Felix. At length, however, he assented to the proposal, resolving to go and visit his parents, with whom he would concert measures for returning to fetch away his mistress; so that Anna Felix remained with Don Antonio's lady, and Ricote stayed in the viceroy's palace.

The hour of Antonio's departure arrived, and, in two days, was followed by that of Don Quixote, whose fall would not permit him to travel before that time. The parting of the lovers was attended with weeping, sighing, sobbing, and swooning; and Ricote offered to accommodate Don Gregorio with a thousand crowns; but, the young gentleman would take but five, which he borrowed of Don Antonio, promising to repay them at court. Thus they set out together for Madrid; and soon after, as we have already observed, Don Quixote and Sancho departed from Barcelona; the knight unarmed, in a travelling dress, and the squire trudging a-foot, because Dapple carried the armour of his master.

## CHAPTER XIV.

Treating of that which will be seen by him who reads, and known by him who hears it read.

D on Quixote, in leaving Barcelona, turned about to survey the fatal spot in which he had fallen, and thus exclaimed, "Here Troy once stood![1] here, by misfortune, not by cowardice, was I despoiled of all the glory I had acquired! Here did I feel the vicissitudes of fortune! here all my atchievements were eclipsed! and finally, here fell my fortune never more to rise!" Sancho hearing this effusion, "Signor," said he, "it is the part of a valiant man to bear with patience his sufferings in adversity, as well as to enjoy his prosperity with good humour: I judge from my own feeling; for, if I was merry when a governor, I am not melancholy now that I am a poor squire travelling a-foot: and I have often heard that she we call fortune is a drunken, fickle female, and so blind withal, that she sees not what she does, and knows not whom she is abusing, or whom exalting." "Sancho," answered the knight, "thou art very philosophical, and hast spoke with great discretion, which I know not where thou hast learned: I can tell thee, however, there is no such thing as fortune in the whole world; nor do those things which happen, whether good or evil, proceed from chance, but, solely from the particular providence of heaven; and hence comes the usual saying, that every man is the maker of his own fortune: I, at least, have been the maker of mine, tho' not with sufficient prudence, and therefore my presumptuous hopes miscarried. I ought to have considered that Rozinante's weakness could not resist the weight and magnitude of my adversary's horse: in a word I tried my fortune, did what I could, found myself vanquished and overthrown, and tho' I lost mine honour, I neither did nor can forfeit my integrity and the merit of fulfilling my promise: while I was a knight-errant valiant and intrepid, my hand and my performance gave credit to my exploits; and now that I am no more than a pedestrian squire, my word shall be confirmed by the accomplishment of my promise. Make haste then, friend Sancho, let us return to our own country, and pass the year of our probation, and during that term of confinement acquire fresh vigour and virtue to resume the never by me forgotten exercise of arms." "Signor," answered the squire, "the pastime of trudging a-foot is not quite so pleasant, as to move and instigate me to travel at a great pace: let us leave these arms of yours, hanging like a malefactor on some tree; and then I occupying the back of Dapple, with my feet no longer in the mire, we may travel just as your worship shall desire or demand; but, to think that I can make long marches a-foot, is a vain supposition." "Thou art in the right, Sancho," replied Don Quixote, "let my arms be suspended in form of a trophy; and beneath, or around them, we will engrave upon the tree, an inscription like that which appeared under the armour of Orlando:

> Let him alone these arms displace,
> Who dares Orlando's fury face."

"A most excellent device!" cried the squire, "and if it were not that we should feel the want of him in our journey, it would not be amiss to hang up Rozinante at the same time." "Nevertheless," replied Don Quixote, "neither Rozinante nor my arms will I suffer to be hung up; for, it shall never be said of me that a good service met with a bad remuneration." "Your worship talks very much to the purpose," said Sancho; "for, according to the opinion of wise men, the pannel ought not to suffer for the fault of the ass; and since your worship alone was to blame for the bad success of the last adventure, you ought to punish your self only, and not vent your indignation upon your bloody and already rusted arms, or upon the meekness of Rozinante, or lastly, upon the tenderness of my feet, in desiring them to walk at a pace which they cannot maintain."

In this conversation and other such discourse they passed that whole day, and the next four, without meeting with any incident that could interrupt their journey: on the fifth, which was an holiday, they entered a village, where they saw a number of people making merry at the gate of an inn; and when Don Quixote approached, a countryman exclaimed, "One of these gentlemen travellers, who are unacquainted with the parties, shall decide our wager." The knight assuring them he would give his opinion freely and honestly as soon as he should be informed of the matter, the peasant replied, "Worthy signor, this here is the case: One of our townsmen, who is so fat and bulky that he weighs little less than three hundred weight, has challenged one of his neighbours, a thin creature not half so heavy, to run with him one hundred yards with equal weight. The match was accordingly made; but when the challenger was asked how the weight of both should be made equal, he insisted upon the others carrying the difference in bars of iron, by which means Limberham would be upon a footing with Loggerhead."[2] "By no means," cried Sancho, interposing before his master could answer one word, "to me who have been lately a governor and a judge, as all the world knows, it belongs to resolve these doubts, and give my opinion in this dispute." "Speak then in happy time, friend Sancho," said the knight; "for, my judgment is so confounded and disturbed that I am hardly fit to throw crumbs to a cat." With this permission Sancho addressing himself to the peasants, who had assembled around him, and waited his decision with open mouths, "Brothers," said he, "the demand of Loggerhead will not hold water, and is indeed without the least shadow of justice; for if what all the world says be true, namely, that the challenged party has the choice of the weapons, it is not reasonable that the said Loggerhead should pretend to choose such arms as will encumber his adversary and secure the victory to himself; it is therefore my opinion, that Loggerhead the challenger shall scrape, shave, pare, polish, slice and take away one hundred and fifty pound weight of his own individual flesh from different parts of his body, according to his own fancy and convenience; so that leaving the other moiety, which will be sufficient to counterbalance his antagonist, the parties may run with equal advantage." "'Fore God!" cried one of the countrymen, hearing this wise decision, "the gentleman has spoken like a saint and given sentence like a canon: but, sure I am, Loggerhead will not part with an ounce, much less one hundred fifty pounds of his flesh." "The best part of the joke," replied another peasant, "is that the match cannot be run; for, Limberham will not touch a bar of iron, and Loggerhead will not pare himself; let us therefore spend the half of the money in treating these gentlemen at the tavern with some of the best wine, and

when it rains, let the shower fall upon my cloak." "Gentlemen," said Don Quixote, "I thank you for your invitation; but, I really cannot tarry a moment; for, melancholy thoughts and unlucky adventures oblige me to appear uncivil on this occasion, and to travel faster than the ordinary pace." So saying, he clapped spurs to Rozinante, and set on, leaving them astonished in consequence of having seen and observed the strange figure of the master and the sagacity of the servant, for, such they supposed Sancho to be. One of them could not help saying, "If the servant is so wise, what must the master be? I'll lay a wager if they go to study at Salamanca, they will in a trice be created Alcaldes of the court; for, it is nothing but childrens play, studying and poring, and having interest and good luck, and when a man thinks least about the matter, he finds himself with a white rod in his hand or a mitre upon his head."

That night our adventurer and his squire passed in the middle of an open field, under the spacious cope of heaven; and next day proceeding on their journey, they saw coming towards them a man on foot, with a javelin or half pike in his hand and a wallet on his back; circumstances from which they judged he was a post or courier. As he advanced he quickened his pace, and running up to Don Quixote, embraced his right thigh, for, he could reach no higher, exclaiming with marks of extraordinary satisfaction: "O my good signor Don Quixote! how will the heart of my lord duke be rejoiced when he knows your worship is returning to his castle, where he still continues with my lady dutchess!" "Friend," said the knight, "I do not recollect your features, nor do I know who you are, unless you will be pleased to tell me." "Signor Don Quixote," replied the courier, "I am my lord duke's lacquey Tosilos who refused to fight with your worship concerning the marriage of the duenna's daughter." "God in heaven protect me!" cried the knight, "is it possible that you are he whom my enemies the inchanters transformed into that same lacquey you mention, to deprive me of the glory of that combat?" "No more of that, worthy signor," replied the post; "there was no inchantment in the case, nor any sort of transformation: I was as much the lacquey Tosilos when I entered the lists, as when I left them. I thought the girl handsome, and therefore would have married her without fighting; but, the event did not answer my expectation. Your worship was no sooner gone from the castle, than my lord duke ordered me to be severely bastinado'd, for having contradicted the instructions he had given me before I entered the lists: and this is the upshot of the whole affair; the girl is by this time a nun, Donna Rodriguez is gone back to Castile, and I am now bound for Barcelona with a packet of letters from his grace to the viceroy. If your worship is inclined to take a small draught of good wine, tho' not very cool, I have here a calabash full of the best, and some slices of Tronchon cheese, which will serve as provocatives and rousers of thirst, if perchance it should be asleep." "Your invitation is accepted," cried Sancho; "truce with your compliments and skink away, honest Tosilos, maugre and in despite of all the inchanters of the Indies." "Verily, Sancho," said Don Quixote, "thou art the most insatiate glutton in the universe, and the most ignorant animal upon earth: but, as thou art not persuaded that this courier is inchanted, and no other than a counterfeit Tosilos, thou mayest tarry along with him and fill thy belly; and I will jog on at a slow pace until thou shalt overtake me." The lacquey smiled at his infatuation, unsheathed his calabash, unwalleted his cheese, and producing a small loaf, he and Sancho sat down upon the grass, where in

peace and harmony they dispatched and discussed the contents of the wallet with great perseverance and good will, and even licked the packet, because it smelled of cheese. During the repast, Tosilos said to the squire, "Doubtless, friend Sancho, thy master is bankrupt in common sense." "How bankrupt!"[3] answered Panza, "he owes no man a farthing, but pays like a prince, especially where madness is the current coin: I see the matter plain enough, and tell him my opinion freely: but, to what purpose? Now, indeed, he is going home in despair for having been vanquished by the knight of the white moon." Tosilos earnestly begged he would recount that adventure; but, Sancho declined the task, observing that it would be unmannerly to let his master wait for him; tho' at their next meeting he should have more leisure. He accordingly started up, and shaking the crumbs from his garment and beard, bad adieu to Tosilos; then driving Dapple before him, soon came up with his master, whom he found waiting for him under the shade of a tree.

## CHAPTER XV.

## Of the resolution which Don Quixote took to become a shepherd and lead a pastoral life, until the term of his confinement should be elapsed, with other incidents truly entertaining.

If Don Quixote was perplexed with cogitation before his overthrow, much more was he fatigued by his own thoughts after his late misfortune. Under the shade of a tree, as we have already observed, did he remain, and there he was stung with reflections that swarmed like flies about honey; some dwelling upon the disinchantment of Dulcinea, and others revolving plans for the life he was to lead in his compulsive retirement. When Sancho joined him, and began to expatiate upon the liberal disposition of Tosilos, "Is it possible, O Sancho," said the knight, "that thou still believest that man to be the individual lacquey? one would think thou hadst forgot that thy own eyes have seen Dulcinea converted and transformed into a country wench, and the knight of the mirrours into the batchelor Carrasco, by the wicked arts of those inchanters who persecute my virtue. But, tell me now, didst thou ask Tosilos how providence hath disposed of Altisidora? hath she bewailed my absence, or already consigned to oblivion those amorous thoughts by which she was tormented during my residence at the castle?" "My thoughts," answered Sancho, "were not such as allowed me to ask these childish questions. Body o' me! signor, is your worship at present in a condition to inquire about other peoples thoughts, especially those you call amorous?" "Sancho," said the knight, "you must consider there is a wide difference between the suggestions of love, and those of gratitude: a gentleman may very well be insensible to love; but, strictly speaking, he can never be ungrateful. Altisidora, in all appearance, loved me to distraction: she, as thou very well

knowest, made me a present of three night-caps; she bewailed my departure, loaded me with curses and reproach, and, in spite of maiden shame, complained of me in public; undoubted proofs of my being the object of her adoration; for, the indignation of lovers usually vents itself in maledictions. I had no hopes to give, nor treasures to offer; all my affections are yielded to Dulcinea; and the treasures of knights-errant are like those of the fairies, altogether phantom and illusion: all, therefore, that I can return, is a kind remembrance, without prejudice, however, to the memory of Dulcinea, who is greatly aggrieved by thy remissness in delaying to scourge and chastise that flesh which I hope will be a prey to the wolves; seeing thou seemest more inclined to reserve it for the worms, than to use it in behalf of that poor distressed lady." "Signor," answered the squire, "if the truth must be told, I cannot persuade myself that the whipping of my posteriors can have any effect in disinchanting those who are inchanted; no more than if we should anoint the shins to cure the head-ach: at least, I will venture to swear that in all the histories your worship has read concerning knight-errantry, you have never found that any person was disinchanted by such a whipping: but, be that as it may, I will lay it on when I have time, convenience and inclination to make free with my own flesh." "God grant thou mayest," said Don Quixote; "and heaven give thee grace to understand and be sensible of the obligation thou liest under, to assist my mistress, who, as thou art mine, is thine also."

With such conversation they amused themselves in travelling, until they arrived at the very spot where they had been overturned by the bulls; when Don Quixote recognizing the ground, "This is the meadow," said he, "where we met the gay shepherdesses and gallant swains, who sought to renew and react the pastoral Arcadia, a project equally original and ingenious, in imitation of which, shouldst thou approve of the scheme, we will assume the garb and employment of shepherds during the term of our retirement. I will purchase some sheep, together with all the necessary implements of a pastoral life, and taking the name of Quixotiz, while thou shalt bear that of the swain Pancino; we will stroll about through mountains, woods and meadows, singing here, lamenting there, drinking liquid chrystal from the gelid springs, the limpid rills and mighty rivers. The lofty oaks will shed upon us abundance of their delightful fruit; the trunks of hardest cork-trees will yield us seats; the willows will afford us shade; the rose, perfume; the extended meadow, carpets of a thousand dyes; the pure serenity of air will give us breath; the moon and stars will grant us light in spite of darkness; our singing will inspire delight; our lamentations, mirth; Apollo, verses; and Love himself, conceits to render us immortal and renowned, not only in the present age, but also to latest posterity." "Odds tens!" cried Sancho, "such a life will square, ay, and be the very corner-stone of my wishes:[1] the batchelor Sampson Carrasco and master Nicholas the barber, as soon as they have a glimpse of it, will wish to join us in the scheme, and turn shepherds for our company; and God grant that the curate himself may not take it in his head to enter the fold: for, he is a merry companion and a great friend to good fellowship." "Thou hast a very good notion," said the knight; "and if the batchelor shall be inclined to join our pastoral association, as he doubtless will, he may take the appellation of the shepherd Sansonino, or of the swain Carrascon: Nicholas the barber may be called Niculoso, as old Boscan called himself Nemoroso:[2] and as for the curate, I know not what title we can

confer upon him, except some derivative from his own name, such as the shepherd Curiambro. For the nymphs of whom we must be enamoured, there is plenty of names to choose; but, seeing that of my mistress will suit as well with a shepherdess as with a princess, I need not give myself the trouble to invent any other that might be more proper; as for thee, Sancho, thou mayest give thy mistress what appellation will please thy own fancy." "I have no intention," replied the squire, "to give her any other than that of Teresona, which will fit her fatness to an hair, as well as be agreeable to her own name Teresa; especially as in celebrating her in verse, I shall disclose my chaste desires, without going in search of fine bread in a neighbour's house: the curate would be in the wrong to choose a shepherdess, because he ought to set a good example to his flock; and, as for the batchelor, if he has any such inclination, let him please his own soul without let or controul."

"Good Heaven! friend Sancho," said Don Quixote, "what a life shall we lead! how will our ears be regaled with pipes and bagpipes of Zamora, Tambourines, Timbrels and Rebecks! and if these different kinds of music be reinforced with the sound of the Albogues, we shall have a full concert of all the pastoral instruments." "And pray what are the Albogues?" said Sancho, "I never saw nor heard them named before, in the whole course of my life." "Albogues," answered the knight, "are plates of brass resembling candlesticks, the hollow parts of which being clashed together produce a sound, if not ravishing or harmonious, at least not disagreeable nor unsuited to the rusticity of the bagpipe and tabor. The name of Albogues is Moorish, as are all the words in our language beginning with al; for example Almoaca, Almorcar, Alhombra, Alguazil, Alucima, Almacen, Alcanzia, and a few others; and we have only three Moorish words ending in i, namely Borcegui, Zaquicami and Maravedi; as for Alheli and Alfaqui, they are known to be Arabic, as well from their beginning with al, as from their ending in i: these observations I have made by the bye, in consequence of having mentioned Alboques which recalled them to my remembrance. But, to return to our scheme, nothing will conduce so much to the perfection of it, as my having a talent for versification, as thou very well knowest, and the batchelor's being an excellent poet. Of the curate I shall say nothing; tho' I would lay a good wager that his collars and points are truly poetical;[3] and that master Nicholas is in the same fashion I do not at all doubt; for, people of his profession are famous for making ballads and playing on the guitarre. For my own part, I will complain of absence; thou wilt extol the constancy of thy own love; the swain Carrascon will lament the disdain of his mistress; the curate Curiambro choose his own subject; and every thing proceed in such a manner as to fulfill the warmest wishes."

To this effusion Sancho replied, "Verily, signor, I am such an unlucky wretch, that I am afraid the time will never come when I shall see myself in that blessed occupation. O what delicate wooden spoons shall I make when I am a shepherd! O what crumbs and cream shall I devour! O what garlands and pastoral nick-nacks shall I contrive! and tho' these may not, perhaps, add much to my reputation for wisdom, they will not fail to convince the world of my ingenuity. My daughter Sanchica shall bring our victuals to the fold; but, 'ware mischief! the wench is buxome; and there are some shepherds more knavish than simple: I would not have her come out for wool and go home shorn. Those same amours, and unruly desires, are gratified in the open field as well as in the city-

chamber, in a shepherd's cot as well as in a royal palace. The sin will cease when the temptation is removed: The heart will not grieve for what the eye does not perceive; and, What prayers ne'er can gain, a leap from an hedge will obtain."⁴ "No more of your proverbs, Sancho," said Don Quixote; "any one of those thou hast repeated is sufficient to explain thy meaning; and I have often exhorted thee to be less prodigal of old saws, and keep them more under command; but, I see it is like preaching to the desart: and, My mother whips me, and I scourge the top." "Under correction," answered the squire, "your worship, methinks, is like the frying-pan which called to the pot, Avaunt, black-a-moor, avaunt!⁵ Even in the very act of rebuking me for uttering proverbs, your worship strings them together in pairs." "But, then, you must consider, Sancho," said Don Quixote, "that, when I use them, they are seasonably brought in, and fit the purpose as the ring fits the finger: whereas, by thee, they are not brought in, but lugged in, as it were, by the head and shoulders. If my memory fails me not, I have formally told thee, that proverbs are short sentences extracted from the experience and speculation of ancient sages; and a proverb, unseasonably introduced, is rather an absurdity than a judicious apothegm. But, let us quit the subject, and, as the day is already spent, retire from the high-way to some place where we may pass the night; for, God alone knows what will be to-morrow."

They accordingly retired to a grove, where they made a late and very indifferent supper, to the no small mortification of Sancho, who ruefully reflected upon the meagre commons of chivalry, so uncomfortably discussed among woods and mountains; tho' his imagination was also regaled with the remembrance of that abundance which he had enjoyed at the castle, as well as at the wedding of the rich Camacho, and in the houses of Don Diego de Miranda, and Don Antonio de Moreno: but, finally, considering it could not be always day, or always night, he resolved, for the present, to sleep, while his master indulged his contemplations, awake.

## CHAPTER XVI.

## Of the bristly adventure in which Don Quixote was involved.

The night was a little dark; for, although the moon was in the heavens, she was invisible to the people of our hemisphere, madam Diana having taken a trip to the Antipodes, and left our mountains obumbrated, and our vallies obscured.

Don Quixote, in compliance with nature, enjoyed his first sleep without indulging himself in a second, quite contrary to the practice of Sancho, who never desired a second, because the first always lasted from night till morning; a sure sign of little care, and an excellent constitution. As for the knight, his cares interfered so much with his repose, that he wakened his squire, to whom he said, "I am amazed, Sancho, at the indifference of thy disposition, and imagine thou art made of marble or obdurate brass, unsuscepti-

ble of sentiment or emotion. I watch whilst thou art snoring; I weep whilst thou art singing; I faint with fasting, whilst thou art overloaded and out of breath with eating! It is the province of a good servant to sympathize with his master's pain, and to share his anguish, even for the sake of decorum. Observe the serenity of the sky, and the solitude of the place, which invite us to make an intermission in our repose. I conjure thee, by thy life, to rise and go aside to some proper place, where, with good will and grateful inclination, thou mayest conveniently inflict upon thyself three or four hundred stripes, on account of Dulcinea's inchantment; and, this favour I humbly request, without any intention to try again the strength of thine arms, which I know to be heavy and robust: after the performance of that task, we will pass the remainder of the night in harmony; I, in singing the torments of absence, and thou in chanting the constancy of thy passion; and thus will we begin the pastoral life which we are to lead at our own village." "Signor," answered the squire, "I am no monk to rise and discipline my flesh in the middle of the night; nor do I think the extremity of pain is such a provocative to music: I, therefore, desire your worship will let me take out my nap, without pressing me further to scourge myself, lest I should grow desperate, and solemnly swear never to whip the nap of my garment, much less an hair of my skin." "Soul of a savage! flinty hearted squire!" cried Don Quixote: "O ill bestowed bread! O ill requited benefits, intended or conferred! By my means wast thou created governor; and through me alone dost thou now enjoy the near prospect of being a count, or something else of equal title; nor will the accomplishment of thy wishes be retarded longer than the term of one fleeting year; for, *Post tenebras spero lucem.*[1] "Your conclusion," said Sancho, "I do not understand; but, well I know, that, while I sleep, I am troubled neither with fear nor hope, nor toil nor glory; and praise be to him who invented sleep, which is the mantle that shrouds all human thoughts, the food that dispels hunger, the drink that quenches thirst, the fire that warms the cold, the cool breeze that moderates heat; in a word, the general coin that purchases every commodity; the weight and balance that makes the shepherd even with his sovereign, and the simple with the sage: there is only one bad circumstance, as I have heard, in sleep; it resembles death; inasmuch, as between a dead coarse and a sleeping man there is no apparent difference." "Truly, Sancho," said the knight, "I never heard thee talk so elegantly before, whence I perceive the truth of the proverb which thou hast often repeated, Not he with whom you was bred, but he by whom you are fed."[2] "Odds my life! sir master of mine," cried Sancho, "I am not the only person who strings proverbs: they fall from your worship's mouth in couples, faster than from mine: indeed, there is some difference; for, your worship's proverbs come at a proper time, whereas mine are always out of season; but, nevertheless, they are all proverbs."

Thus far the conversation had proceeded, when they heard a dull confused noise, intermingled with very harsh sounds, that seemed to extend through the whole valley. The knight immediately started up and unsheathed his sword; while the squire squatted down under Dapple, fencing himself on each side with his master's armour and the pannel of the ass, being as much afraid as Don Quixote was astonished; for, the noise increased every moment, as the cause of it approached the two tremblers, or rather one trembler; for, the other's valour and courage are well known. The case, in fact, was this: Some dealers were driving about six hundred hogs to a fair, and, as they travelled in the

night, the noise of their feet, together with their grunting and blowing, made such a din, as almost deafened Don Quixote and Sancho, who could not conceive the meaning of such an uproar. Mean while, the numerous grunting herd advanced, and, without shewing the least respect to the authority of Don Quixote or Sancho, ran over them in a twinkling, demolished the barricadoes of the squire, and trampled down not only the master, but also his steed Rozinante. The thronging, the grunting, and the hurry of those unclean animals, throwing every thing in confusion, and strewing the master and the man, the horse and the ass, the pannel and the armour, along the ground. Sancho, getting up as well as he could, demanded his master's sword, in order to sacrifice half a dozen of those discourteous gentlemen porkers; for, by this time, he had discovered what they were: but, the knight refused to grant his request, saying, "Let them pass, friend Sancho; this affront is the punishment of my crime, and the just chastisement of heaven inflicted upon a vanquished knight, is, that he shall be devoured by dogs, stung by wasps, and trampled upon by swine." "At that rate, then," replied the squire, "the chastisement which heaven inflicts upon squires of vanquished knights-errant, is, that they shall be bitten by fleas, devoured by lice, and assaulted by famine: if we squires were sons of the knights we serve, or even their near relations, it would be no great wonder if the punishment of their faults should overtake us to the fourth generation; but, what affinity is there between the Panzas and the Quixotes? At present, let us put things to rights again, so that we may sleep out the remainder of the night, and we shall be in better plight when God sends us a new day." "Enjoy thy repose," said Don Quixote; "thou wast born to sleep and I to watch; and, during the little of night that remains, I will give my thoughts the rein, and cool the furnace of my reflections with a short madrigal, which I have this evening, unknown to thee, composed in my own mind." "In my opinion," answered the squire, "your thoughts could not be very troublesome and unruly, if they gave you leisure to make couplets; but, however, your worship may couple as many as you please, and I will sleep as much as I can." So saying, he chose his ground, on which he huddled himself up, and enjoyed a most profound sleep, which received no interruption from the remembrance of debt, surety, or any other grievance. As for Don Quixote, he leaned against a beech or cork tree; for, Cid Hamet Benengeli has not distinguished the genus, and, to the music of his own sighs, sung the following stanzas:

I.

O cruel love! when I endure
The dreadful vengeance of thy bow,
I fly to death, the only cure
For such immensity of woe.

II.

But, when I touch the peaceful goal,
That port secure from storms of strife,
The sight revives my drooping soul,
I cannot enter for my life!

III.

Thus life exhausts my vital flame,
But death still keeps the spark alive;
O wond'rous fate! unknown to fame!
That life should kill and death revive.

Every verse he accompanied with a multitude of sighs, and a torrent of tears, as if his heart had been transpierced with grief for his overthrow and the absence of Dulcinea. In this situation he was found by the day, when Phoebus darting his rays into Sancho's eyes, the squire awoke, yawned, turned, stretched his lazy limbs, and, surveying the havock which the swine had made in his store, he bitterly cursed the whole herd; ay, and even went farther with his maledictions.

Then the two proceeded in their journey, and, towards the close of the afternoon, descried about ten men on horseback, and half that number on foot, advancing towards them; a sight which made the knight's heart throb with surprize, and the squire's with terror; for, this company was armed with lance and target, and approached in a very hostile manner. Don Quixote turning to his squire, "Sancho," said he, "if I could now exercise my arms, and my hands were not tied by a solemn promise, I would look upon that machine, which comes upon us, with contempt, as so much cake and gingerbread;[3] but, perhaps, it may be something else than we apprehend." He had scarce pronounced these words, when the horsemen coming up, and couching their lances, surrounded him in a trice; then clapping the points of their weapons to his back and breast, seemed to threaten immediate death and destruction; while one of those on foot, laying his finger on his mouth, as a signal for him to be silent, seized Rozinante's bridle, and led him out of the highway. The rest of the foot-pads drove Sancho and Dapple before them, and, while a wonderful silence prevailed, followed the knight, who attempted twice or thrice to ask whither they conducted him, and what they wanted; but, scarce had he begun to move his lips, when they threatened to shut them for ever with the points of their spears. The same menaces were practised upon Sancho, who no sooner expressed a desire to be talking, than he was pricked in the posteriors with a goad by one of his attendants; and Dapple met with the same fate, as if he too made a motion to speak, like his master.

As night approached they quickened their pace, and the terrors of the captives increased in proportion as the darkness deepened, especially as their guard pronounced from time to time, "Dispatch, ye Troglodytes! silence, ye Barbarians! now ye shall suffer, ye Anthropophagi! not a word of complaint, ye Scythians! open not your eyes, ye murderous Polyphemuses! ye carnivorous lions and beasts of prey." With these and other such appellations, they tormented the ears of the miserable master and the forlorn Sancho, who said within himself, "Draggle doits! Barbar Anns! Henry puff a Jay! City hens! and Paulfamouses! these are fine names with a vengeance! I'm afraid this is a bad wind for winnowing our corn! the mischief comes upon us altogether, like drubbing to a dog; and I wish this misventurous adventure, that threatens so dismally, may end in nothing worse!" As for Don Quixote, he was utterly astonished and confounded; nor could he, with all his reflection, comprehend the meaning of his own captivity, and those reproachful terms, from which he could only conclude, that no good, but a great

deal of mischief, was to be expected. In this state of anxious suspense he continued 'till about an hour after it was dark, when they arrived at a castle, which the knight immediately recognizing to be the duke's habitation, where he had so lately resided, "Good heaven!" cried he, "where will this adventure end? surely this is the dwelling place of politeness and hospitality; but, to those who are vanquished, good is converted into bad, and bad to worse." This cjaculation he uttered as they entered the court of the castle, which was decorated in a strange manner, that increased their admiration, and redoubled their fear, as will be seen in the following chapter.

## CHAPTER XVII.

### Of the most singular and strangest adventure that happened to Don Quixote in the whole course of this sublime history.

The horsemen alighting, with the assistance of those who were on foot, snatched up the bodies of Don Quixote and Sancho, and carried them hastily into the court of the castle, round which above an hundred flaming torches were placed, and the corridores of the court were illuminated by five hundred tapers shining with such a blaze, that, in spite of the night, which was dark, there was no want of the day. In the middle of the court appeared a monument raised about two yards from the ground, and covered with a spacious canopy of black velvet; and, upon the steps that led up to it, above an hundred tapers of virgin wax stood burning in silver candlesticks. On the tomb lay the body of a young damsel, whose beauty was such as rendered death itself beautiful: her head was raised on a cushion of brocard, and crowned with a garland of various odoriforous flowers; and in her hands, that were crossed upon her breast, appeared a bough of green victorious palm. On one side of the court was erected a theatre, on which were seated two personages, whom their crowns and sceptres declared to be either real or fictitious kings; and hard by the theatre, which was furnished with steps, two other chairs upon which Don Quixote and Sancho were seated by their captors, who still maintained their former silence, the observance of which they, likewise, recommended, by signs, to our hero and his squire; tho' these injunctions were altogether superfluous; for, their astonishment, at what they saw, had effectually tied their tongues: and, indeed, how could they help being astonished at sight of this apparatus; considering too, that, by this time, the knight had discovered the dead body on the tomb to be no other than the beauteous Altisidora? At this juncture, two noble personages, with a numerous retinue, ascended the theatre and seated themselves in magnificent chairs, hard by the figures that were crowned; then Don Quixote and Sancho, perceiving the new comers to be their former entertainers the duke and dutchess, rose up and bowed with great veneration, and their graces, rising also, returned the compliment with a slight inclination of the head. And now, an officer crossing the court, and approaching Sancho, threw

over him a robe of black buckram painted all over with flames of fire; at the same time, pulling off his cap, he put upon his head one of those pasteboard mitres which are worn by the penitents of the holy office; and, in a whisper, advised him to keep his lips fast sewed together, unless he had a-mind to be gagged or put to death without mercy. Sancho surveyed himself from head to foot, and saw his robe in flames; but, as they did not burn, he valued them not a farthing; then he took off his mitre, and, perceiving it figured with pictures of fiends, set it on his head again, saying to himself, "As the flames do not burn, and the fiends do not fly away with me, I am very well satisfied." Don Quixote, likewise, surveyed the squire, and, although his reflection was still disturbed with fear and suspense, could not help smiling at the ludicrous figure.

Sancho being thus equipped, a low yet agreeable sound of flutes seemed to issue from beneath the tomb, and being uninterrupted by any human voice, for, here silence itself kept silence, produced a very soft and pleasing melody. Then all of a sudden a beautiful youth in a Roman habit, appeared close by the cushion on which the seemingly dead body reposed, and to the sound of the harp on which he himself played, with a sweet harmonious voice he sung the two following stanzas:

I.

'Till fair Altisidora slain
By Quixote's cruelty, return;
  And all th'inchanted female train
Her hapless fate in sack-cloth mourn;
  Until duennas clad in bays
Appear in presence of her grace,
  I'll celebrate the nymph in lays
That would not shame the bard of Thrace.

II.

Nor shall thy beauty fade unsung,
When life forsakes my gelid veins;
  My clay-cold lips and frozen tongue
In death shall raise immortal strains.
  My soul when freed from cumb'rous clay,
Her flight o'er Stygian waves shall take;
  And while on Lethe's banks I stray,
My song shall charm th'oblivious lake.

Here he was interrupted by one of the two pretended kings, who said, "Enough, divine songster; it would be an infinite task to describe the death and beauties of the peerless Altisidora, not dead as the ignorant world imagines, but alive in the voice of fame and in the penance which Sancho Panza here present must undergo, in order to restore her to the light she has lost; and therefore O Rhadamanthus! who sittest with me in judgment, within the gloomy caverns of Lethe, as thou art intimately acquainted with all the determinations of the inscrutable fates, touching the revival of this damsel, relate and declare them without loss of time, that we may no longer delay that happiness which we expect from her recovery."

Scarce had Minos pronounced these words, when his fellow judge and companion Rhadamanthus stood up, saying, "So ho, ye ministers of this house, high and low, great and small, come hither one by one, and mark the face, the arms and loins of Sancho with two dozen of tweaks, one dozen of pinches, and half a dozen pricks with a pin: for, upon this execution depends the revival of Altisidora." Sancho Panza hearing this sentence, broke silence and exclaimed aloud, "I vow to God, I will sooner turn Turk, than allow my face to be marked or my flesh to be handled in any such manner. Body o'me! what has the pinching of my face to do with the resurrection of that damsel? The old woman has got a liquorish tooth, and she is still licking her fingers, forsooth. Dulcinea is in-chanted, and I must be scourged for the disinchantment of her ladyship: Altisidora is dead by the hand of God, and in order to bring her to life, I must suffer two dozen of tweaks; my body must be pinked into a sieve with large pins, and my arms pinched into all the colours of the rain-bow! such jokes may pass upon a brother-in-law; but, I am an old dog, and will not be coaxed with a crust."[1] "Then thou shalt die," cried Rhadaman-thus with an audible voice, "tame that savage heart of thine, thou tyger: humble thyself, thou proud Nimrod; suffer and be silent: we ask not impossibilities, and therefore, thou must not pretend to examine the difficulties of this affair: tweaked thou shalt be; pinked shalt thou find thyself, and pinched until thy groans declare thine anguish. So ho, I say, ye ministers, execute my command, or by the faith of an honest man, you shall see for what you were born."

In consequence of this summons, six duennas came walking through the court-yard in procession one by one, the four first with spectacles, and each with her right arm raised, about four inches of the wrist being bared according to the present fashion, that the hand may seem the larger. Sancho no sooner beheld these matrons, than he began to bellow like a bull, exclaiming, "I might have allowed myself to be handled by all the world besides, but, that duennas should touch me, I will by no means consent! they may cat-claw my face, as my master was served in this very castle: they may run me through the guts with daggers of steel: they may tear the flesh off my arms with red hot pincers: all these tortures will I bear patiently, for the service of these noble persons: but, I say again, the devil shall fly away with me, before I suffer a duenna to lay a finger on my car-case!" Then Don Quixote addressing himself to Sancho, broke silence in these terms; "Exert thy patience, my son, for the satisfaction of these noble personages, and give thanks to heaven which hath indued thy person with such virtue, that by the martyrdom of thy flesh, the inchanted are delivered from inchantment, and even the dead revived."

By this time, the duennas had surrounded Sancho, who being softened and per-suaded, seated himself in a proper posture, and held out his face and beard to the first, who treated him with a well planted twitch, and then dropped a profound curtsy. "Less courtesy, less anointing, good madam duenna," cried the squire; "for, by the Lord, your fingers smack of vinegar!" In a word, he was tweaked by all the duennas, and pinched by a great number of other persons belonging to the family: but, what he could by no means be brought to endure, was the puncture with pins, which they no sooner began to perform, than starting up in a rage, and seizing a lighted torch that stood near him, he assaulted the duennas and all the rest of his executioners, crying, "Avaunt ye minis-ters of hell! I am not made of brass, to be insensible to such torture." At this instant

Altisidora, who must have been tired with lying so long upon her back, turned herself on one side; and this motion was no sooner perceived by the spectators, than all of them exclaimed as if with one voice, "Altisidora moves, Altisidora lives!" Then Rhadamanthus desired Sancho to lay aside his indignation, seeing the intended aim was already accomplished.

Don Quixote seeing Altisidora stirring, fell upon his knees before Sancho, saying, "Now is the time, dear son of my bowels, and no longer, my squire! now is the time to inflict upon thyself some of those lashes thou art obliged to undergo for the disinchantment of Dulcinea. This I say, is the time, when thy virtue is seasoned, and of efficacy sufficient to perform the cure which we expect from thy compliance." To this apostrophe the squire replied, "This is reel upon reel, and not honey upon pancakes:[2] scourging, to be sure, is a very agreeable desert to a dish of twitches, pinches and pinprickings. There is no more to be done, but to take and tie a great stone about my neck, and toss me into a well; it will be much better for me to die at once, than to be always the wedding heifer,[3] to remedy the misfortunes of other people: either let me live in peace, or, before God! all shall out, fell or not fell."

By this time, Altisidora sat upright on the tomb, and at that instant the waits beginning to play, were accompanied by the music of flutes, and the voices of all the spectators, who acclaimed, "Live Altisidora! Altisidora live!" The duke and dutchess, together with Minos and Rhadamanthus, rising from their seats, and being joined by Don Quixote and Sancho, went to receive this young lady and help her in descending from the tomb; while they were thus employed, she assumed a languid and fainting air, and inclining her head towards the duke and dutchess and the two kings, darted a sidelong glance to Don Quixote, saying, "God forgive thee, unrelenting knight! by thy cruelty I have been doomed to remain, as I believe, above a thousand years in the other world! but, as for thee, thou most compassionate squire that this wide earth contains! I thank thee kindly for that life I now enjoy. From this day, friend Sancho, thou mayest command six of my shifts to be converted into shirts for thy own body; and if they are not quite whole, at least they are white and clean." Sancho thanked her for the present, with mitre in hand and knee on ground: and when the duke ordered his servants to take away those badges of disgrace, and restore his own cap and coat; the squire entreated his grace to let him keep the mitre and the flaming robe, and carry them to his own country, as a mark and memorial of this incredible adventure. To this supplication the dutchess replied, That he might keep these testimonials; for, he knew how much she was his friend.

The duke ordered the court to be cleared, the company to retire to their several chambers, and the knight and squire to be conducted to the apartments which they had formerly occupied.

## CHAPTER XVIII.

# Which follows the preceding, and treats of matters that must be disclosed, in order to make the history the more intelligible and distinct.

S ancho slept that night in a truckle-bed, in the apartment of Don Quixote; a circumstance which he would have waved, if possible, because he well knew his master would keep him awake with questions and replies, and he was not at all in a talkative humour; for, the pain of his past sufferings kept them still present in his fancy, depriving his tongue of its usual freedom; and he would have much rather slept alone in a hut, than in the richest chamber, thus accompanied. His apprehension was so true and his suspicion so just, that scarce had his master committed his body to the bed, when he accosted the squire in these words: "What is thy opinion, Sancho, of this night's adventure? Great and powerful is the force of amorous disdain, as thou hast seen with thy own eyes: Altisidora dead—not by shaft or sword, or warlike instrument, or mortal poison, but solely by the reflection of that rigour and disdain with which I have always treated her advances." "She might have died in good time, when and how she thought proper," cried Sancho, "and left me in quiet at my own house, seeing I never treated her either with love or disdain in the whole course of my life; for my own part, I neither know nor can I conceive, as I have formerly observed, what the health or life of such a whimsical girl as Altisidora has to do with the martyrdom of Sancho Panza: but, now at length I can clearly and distinctly perceive that this world actually abounds with inchanters and inchantments, from which I pray God may deliver me, since I cannot deliver myself: in the mean time, I humbly beseech your worship to let me sleep, without further question, if you have not a mind to see me throw myself out of the window." "Sleep then, friend Sancho," said the knight, "if thou canst enjoy the benefit of slumber, after the pinching, twitching, and pricking thou hast undergone." "No pain is comparable to that of the twitching," replied the squire; "for no other reason, but because it was inflicted by duennas, whom God in heaven confound. I again intreat your worship to leave me to my repose; for, sleep is a remedy for those miseries which we feel when awake." "Be it so," said the knight, "and the Lord make thy sleep refreshing—"

While these two are left to their repose, Cid Hamet, author of this sublime history, takes occasion to explain the motives that induced the duke and dutchess to raise the edifice of the adventure above related. He says, the batchelor Sampson Carrasco still remembring how, as knight of the mirrours, he had been vanquished and overthrown by Don Quixote, and his whole design blotted and defaced by that unlucky fall and defeat; he resolved to try his fortune once more, in hope of meeting with better success; and learning where the knight was, from the information of the page who carried the letter and present to Sancho's wife Teresa Panza; he purchased a new suit of armour, and an horse, ordered a white moon to be painted on his shield, and fastened the whole cargo

on the back of an he-mule, which was conducted by a certain ploughman, and not by his old squire Tom Cecial, lest he should be known by Sancho or Don Quixote. With this equipage he set out for the duke's castle, where he was informed of the knight's motions and route, together with his intention to assist at the tournament in Saragossa. His grace likewise gave him an account of the jokes they had executed upon our adventurer, with the contrivance of Dulcinea's disinchantment, to be effected at the expence of Sancho's posteriors. Nor did he forget to relate the trick which Sancho had practised on his master, in making him believe that Dulcinea was inchanted and transformed into a country wench; as also how my lady dutchess had persuaded the squire that Dulcinea was really and truly inchanted and transformed, and he himself the person that was mistaken and deceived: particulars which afforded abundance of mirth to the batchelor, who could not help admiring afresh the mixture of archness and simplicity in Sancho, as well as the unaccountable madness of Don Quixote. The duke begged he would return that way and communicate his success, whether he should be vanquished or victor. Sampson, having promised to comply with his request, set out in quest of our knight; and, as he did not find him in Saragossa, proceeded to Barcelona where he met with the adventure we have already related in its proper place: then he returned to the duke's castle, where he gave an account of the whole engagement and the conditions of the combat; in consequence of which, Don Quixote was already on his return, to fulfil, like a worthy knight-errant, the promise he had made to reside at his own habitation for the term of one year, during which the batchelor said he might possibly be cured of his madness. He declared this was his sole motive for disguising himself in such a manner; as it was a thousand pities that a gentleman of Don Quixote's excellent understanding should continue under the influence of such infatuation. He accordingly took his leave of the duke, and returned to his own country, in full hope that the knight was not far behind.

From this information, his grace took the opportunity to contrive this last adventure, so much was he delighted with the behaviour of Sancho and Don Quixote. He ordered a great number of his people on horseback and a-foot, to scour the country far and near, and patrole through every road by which he thought the knight could possibly return, with orders to bring him to the castle, either by fair means or foul. Accordingly, when they found him, they gave notice to his grace, who having already preconcerted what was to be done, no sooner heard of his coming than he directed that the torches and tapers should be lighted around the court, and Altisidora placed upon the tomb, together with all the apparatus already described, which was so naturally and artfully executed, that it differed very little from the real truth. Nay, Cid Hamet moreover observes, that he looked upon the jokers to be as mad as those who were joked, and the duke and dutchess to be within two fingers breadth of lunacy; seeing they placed such happiness in playing pranks upon two confirmed madmen, one of whom the new-day found sleeping at full snore, and the other watching over his disastrous thoughts, and very impatient to quit his couch; for, whether vanquished or victor, Don Quixote never took pleasure in lolling on the lazy down.

It was now that Altisidora, who in the knight's opinion had returned from death, in compliance with the humour of her lord and lady, entered his apartment, crowned with the same garland she had worn on the tomb, clad in a robe of white taffety powdered

with flowers of gold, her hair flowing loose upon her shoulders, and supporting herself upon a staff of fine polished black ebony. This apparition discomposed our hero to such a degree that he shrunk within his nest, in silent confusion, and almost covered himself wholly with the sheets, fully determined against making any return of compliment. Mean while Altisidora, sitting down upon a chair, at his bed's-head, heaved a profound sigh, and thus addressed herself to him, in a faint and tender tone: "When women of fashion, and damsels of reserve, trample upon honour, and give their tongues the liberty to break through all inconveniences, so as to divulge the secrets which their hearts conceal; their condition must be desperate indeed. I am one of those, signor Don Quixote de la Mancha; sorely hampered, vanquished and enamoured, but withal so patient and modest, that my soul broke through my silence, and I lost my life: in consequence of thy rigour, O flinty-hearted knight! more deaf than marble to my complaints, have I been dead for two days, or at least supposed to be dead by those who saw me; and if love, in pity to my fate, had not deposited a remedy in the tortures of that worthy squire, I should have remained for ever in the other world." "Love," said Sancho, "might as well have deposited the remedy in the tortures of my ass, and I should have thanked him for it heartily: but, pray, madam, tell me, so may heaven send you a kinder lover than my master, what did you see in the other world? what is going forward in hell? for, surely those who die in despair, must go to that baiting-place." "To tell you the truth," answered Altisidora, "I could not be quite dead, seeing I did not enter the infernal regions; for, had I been once fairly introduced, I could not have left the place again, whatever inclination I might have had to return. The truth is, I went no farther than the gate, where I saw about a dozen devils playing at tennis, in their drawers and doublets, having bands edged with flanders lace, and ruffles of the same at their wrists, which were naked to the length of four inches, in order to enlarge the appearance of their hands, in which they wielded rackets of fire: but, what I chiefly admired, was, that instead of balls they made use of books, which seemed to be filled with wind and flocks; a circumstance equally new and surprising! and yet there was another particular, which still increased my astonishment: for, whereas among the gamesters of this world, it is natural for the winners to be merry and for the losers to be sad; in that diabolical pastime, all the players growled and grumbled and cursed one another." "That is not to be wondered at," replied the squire; "for the devils, play or not play, win or not win, can never be content." "That must certainly be the case," answered Altisidora; "but, there was likewise another peculiarity at which I wonder, I mean at which I then wondered; namely, that after the first toss, the ball was useless, and could not be used a second time; so that they whirled them away, new and old, in a marvellous manner. On one of these, which was finely gilt and lettered, they bestowed such a violent stroke, that the guts flew out in scattered leaves. 'What book is that?' said one devil to his fellow. The other answered, that it was the second part of the history of Don Quixote de la Mancha, composed not by the original author Cid Hamet, but by an Arragonian, who calls himself a native of Tordesillas. 'Away with it!' cried the first, 'plunge it into the lowest abyss of hell, that mine eyes may never behold it again.' 'What! is it so bad?' said the second. 'So very bad,' replied the other, 'that if I myself had endeavoured to make it worse, it would not have been in my power.' They proceeded with their play, driving about the unfortunate books; and I

hearing them mention Don Quixote, whom I love and adore, endeavoured to retain the vision in my memory." "A vision it must have been, without all doubt," said Don Quixote; "for, there is no other I in the whole world; and, as for that history, it is bandied from hand to hand, without finding a resting-place; and every body has a fling at the author: nor am I, in the least, mortified to hear that I wander like a fantastic shadow through the dark abodes of hell, as well as through the enlightened mansions of this globe, as I am not the person recorded in that history, which, were it elegant, faithful, and authentic, would live for ages; but, being false and execrable as it is, there will be no great distance between its birth and burial."

Altisidora was going to proceed with her lamentations, when she was prevented by the knight, who said with great solemnity, "I have often told you, madam, that I am sorry you have placed your affection upon me, who can make no other return than that of gratitude and thanks: I was born for Dulcinea del Toboso, and the fates, if such there be, have consecrated me for her service; so that to imagine any other beauty shall ever occupy the place which she possesses in my heart, is to suppose a meer impossibility. Let this declaration, therefore, undeceive and prevail upon you to retire within the limits of virtue and decorum, seeing no man is obliged to perform impossibilities." Altisidora, in consequence of this repulse, assumed an air of indignation, and, in an affected transport of rage, exclaimed, "How now, Don stockfish! soul of a mortar! stone of a date! more positive and obstinate than a courted peasant when his arrow hath chanced to hit the mark! by the Lord! if I once fall upon you, I will tear your eyes out. Hark ye, Don beaten and cudgelled, are you such a wiseacre as to suppose I died for love of you? All you have seen, this last night, was pure fiction; for, I am not the woman to have a finger ach, much less to die, for such a camel." "O my conscience! I believe what you say," cried Sancho; "that of dying for love, is a most ridiculous affair: your lovers, indeed, may easily say they are dying; but, that they will actually give up the ghost, Judas may believe it for me."

During this conversation, the musician and poet, who had sung the two stanzas which we have already repeated, came into the apartment, and made a profound bow to Don Quixote, saying, "Sir knight, I beg you will esteem and reckon me among the number of your most humble servants; for, many days are elapsed since I have conceived the warmest affection for your person, from the fame of your character and atchievements." When Don Quixote desired to know who he was, that he might respect him according to his merit, he answered, that he was the musician and panegyrist of the preceding night. "Assuredly, your voice is extremely sweet," said the knight; "but, methinks, the verses you sung were not much to the purpose; for, what affinity is there between the stanzas of Garcilasso and the death of this young lady?" "Your worship must not wonder at that impropriety," answered the musician; "it is a common practice among the beardless poets of this age, to write what they will, and steal from whom they please to pillage, whether it be or be not to the purpose, and every absurdity that occurs in their singing or writing, they attribute to the Licentia poetica."

Don Quixote's reply was prevented by the entrance of the duke and dutchess, who came to visit him in his chamber, and a long diverting conversation ensued, in the course of which Sancho uttered so many humorous sallies and satirical jokes, that their graces admired anew the mixture of his acuteness and simplicity. As for the knight, he

humbly requested that he might be allowed to depart that very day, as it was much more proper that vanquished knights, like him, should live in hogsties, than in sumptuous palaces. They graciously complied with his request, and when the dutchess inquired if Altisidora had, as yet, acquired his good graces, "Your graces must know," said he, "that damsel's distemper wholly proceeds from idleness, which may be easily cured by continual and decent occupation: she tells me it is the fashion in hell to wear lace, and as she knows how to make it, let the work never be out of her hand, which being employed in moving the bobbins, the idea or ideas of what she loves will no longer move in her imagination; and this is the truth, the substance of my opinion, and the marrow of my advice." "Ay, and of mine too," cried Sancho; "for, never in my born days did I know a lace-maker die for love: the thoughts of girls employed at that work, run more upon the finishing of their tasks than upon the idle fancies of love; and, for myself, I can safely say, that while I am digging in the field, I never so much as dream of my duck; I mean, my wife Teresa Panza, whom I love as the apple of mine eye." "You talk like an oracle, Sancho," said the dutchess; "and I will take care, that, from this day forward, Altisidora shall be employed in some plain work, which she understands to perfection." "Your ladyship shall not need to use any such expedient," replied Altisidora; "for, the consideration of the cruelty with which I have been used by that felonious monster, will blot him effectually from my remembrance, without any other assistance; and, in the mean time, with your grace's permission, I will retire, that I may no longer have before my eyes—I will not say his rueful countenance, but his frightful and abominable aspect." "These reproaches," said the duke, "put me in mind of the old observation, that scolding among lovers is the next neighbour to forgiveness."

Altisidora, making a shew of wiping the tears from her eyes with a white handkerchief, dropped a low curtsy to her lord and lady, and withdrew; and Sancho sending after her an earnest look, "Poor damsel!" cried he, "I can bequeath, bequeath thee nothing, I say, but bad luck, seeing thou hast placed thine affection upon a soul of rush, and an heart of oak; had it lighted upon me, another sort of a cock would have crowed thy fortune."

Thus the conversation ended, Don Quixote put on his cloaths, dined with the duke and dutchess, and set out that same evening for his own habitation.

## CHAPTER XIX.

# Of what happened to Don Quixote and his squire, in their journey to their own village.

The perplexed and vanquished Don Quixote travelled along, extremely chagrined on one account, tho' greatly rejoiced on another: his melancholy was occasioned by his overthrow, and his joy produced from the consideration of that virtue inherent in

his squire, which he had seen demonstrated in the resurrection of Altisidora, tho' he had some scruples in persuading himself that the enamoured damsel was actually dead. As for Sancho, he felt no sort of pleasure; but, on the contrary, was much mortified to find Altisidora had failed in performing her promise touching the present of the shifts; and, his imagination dwelling upon this circumstance, he said to his master, "Truly, signor, I must certainly be the most unfortunate physician that ever lived upon the earth, in which there are many leeches, who, tho' they kill their patients, insist upon being payed for their trouble, which, by the bye, is no more than writing and signing a list of medicines upon a scrap of paper; for, the apothecary makes up the prescription, and so the farce is acted; whereas, I receive not a doit, tho' I cure other people's maladies at the expence of pinches, twitches, pin-pricks, lashes, and drops of blood; but, I vow to God! if any other patient is put into my hands, they shall be well anointed before I undertake the cure; for, The abbot chants, but to supply his wants: and I cannot believe that heaven hath bestowed such virtue upon me, in order that I should throw it away upon the undeserving." "Thou art in the right, friend Sancho," replied Don Quixote; "and Altisidora is much to blame in having with-held the promised shifts, altho' thy virtue is gratis data, without having put thee to the trouble of studying aught but the art of enduring personal torture; for my own part, I can say, that if thou hadst demanded payment for the disinchanting stripes, I should have allowed it to thy own satisfaction; tho' I know not how such hire might interfere with the cure; and I should not wish that the premium might impede the effect of the medicine: nevertheless, I do not think the experiment could be attended with any bad consequence. Consider, Sancho, what thou wouldst have; then proceed to the flagellation, and pay thyself fairly out of my money which is in thy own hands."

At this proposal, the squire opened his eyes and ears a full span, and resolving in his heart to scourge himself with good will, answered in these words: "Ay, now, signor, I find myself extremely well disposed to comply with your worship's desire, since my compliance will be attended with some profit; and, I own, my regard for my poor wife and children makes me seem a little selfish—Pray what will your worship please to give for every stripe?" "Were I to pay thee, Sancho," said the knight, "according to the greatness of thy deserts, and the quality of the cure, the bank of Venice and mines of Potosi would not afford a sufficient recompence: but, see how much of my money thou hast got, and set thy own price upon every lash." "The number of stripes to be given," answered the squire, "amounts to three thousand three hundred and odd: of these I have received about five, which shall stand for the odd; so that three thousand three hundred remain. Now, if we value each lash at a quarter of a rial, and I would not bate a doit tho' the whole world should desire me, the sum will be three thousand three hundred quartillos; the three thousand quartillos make fifteen hundred half rials, which are equal to seven hundred and fifty rials; and the other three hundred quartillos make one hundred and fifty half rials, which are equal to seventy-five rials, and these being added to the former seven hundred and fifty, the whole reckoning amounts to eight hundred and twenty-five rials. These I will deduct from your cash that is in my hands, and then I will return to my own house, rich and satisfied, tho' well scourged; for, We cannot catch trouts without wetting our clouts:[1] and I will say no more upon the subject." "O, blessed Sancho!

O, lovely Sancho!" cried Don Quixote; "Dulcinea and I will be bound to serve thee all the days that heaven shall permit us to live; provided she shall retrieve her lost form: and, in this hope, we cannot possibly be mistaken; her misfortune will prove fortunate, and my overthrow a most happy triumph. And now, Sancho, consider when thou wilt begin this discipline; towards the speedy performance of which, I add another hundred rials." "When!" replied the squire; "this very night without fail: if your worship will take care to choose our lodging in the open field, I will take care to open my own carcase."

At length the night arrived, after it had been impatiently expected by Don Quixote, who thought the wheels of Apollo's car had broken down, and that the day was extended to an unusual length; like those lovers whose desires ever outstrip the career of time.

In the evening, they betook themselves to the covert of some pleasant trees at a little distance from the highway, and, vacating the saddle of Rozinante and the pannel of the ass, sat down together upon the grass, and supped upon the store contained in the wallet of Sancho, who, forming a strong and flexible scourge with Dapple's halter, retired into a tuft of beeches about twenty paces from his master. The knight seeing him withdraw so brisk and resolute, "Beware, friend Sancho," said he, "of scourging thyself to pieces; perform thy discipline at leisure; let the stripes follow one another in a regular succession, and do not run so fast as to be out of breath in the middle of thy career; I mean, do not lash thyself so severely, as to destroy thy own life before the number be completed; and, that thou mayest not lose it by a card too many, or too few, I will stand aside and count the stripes upon my rosary. Mayest thou enjoy the protection of heaven which thy christian intention so richly deserves." "A good paymaster needs no bail," answered the squire: "I intend to scourge myself in such a manner as will mortify my flesh, without any hazard of my life; for, in that medium the substance of the miracle must consist." He forthwith stripped himself naked from the waist upwards, and, snatching the scourge, began to whip himself, while his master reckoned the stripes. About half a dozen or eight lashes had Sancho bestowed upon himself, when he found the joke very expensive, and the reward dog cheap; and, suspending the instrument, told the knight he had been deceived, and claimed the benefit of an appeal; for, every one of these stripes was well worth half a rial instead of a quartillo. "Proceed, friend Sancho, without dismay," replied Don Quixote, "and I will double the allowance." "At that rate," replied the squire, "to it again, by the grace of God, and let it rain lashes." But, the cunning knave no longer made application to his own shoulders, in lieu of which he began to scourge the trees, venting, between whiles, such dismal groans as seemed to tear his very soul up by the roots. The knight, from the tenderness of his own disposition, being apprehensive that he would actually put an end to his life, and of consequence defeat the purpose of his flagellation, exclaimed, "I conjure thee, by thy life, friend Sancho, to let the business rest where it now stands: the medicine seems to have a very rough operation, and it will be better to proceed leisurely; for, Zamora was not taken in one hour. Above a thousand stripes hast thou already inflicted upon thyself, if my reckoning is just, and these shall suffice for the present; for, if I may use a vulgar expression, Tho' the load must lie over the ass, he must not be overloaded." "No, no, signor," replied Sancho, "they shall never say of me, When money's paid before it's due, a broken limb will straight ensue. Pray, stand aside a little, signor, and let me lay on another thousand, if

*Vol.II . pag. 449 .*

*S. Hayman inv.et Delin.*

*G. Scotin Sculp*

Don Quixote Restraining Sancho in His Zeal to Scourge Himself.

you please: two such bouts will perform the bargain, and leave something to boot." "Since thou findest thyself in such an excellent frame and disposition," said the knight, "heaven protect thee; stick to the stuff, and I shall withdraw." Sancho, resuming his task and reckoning, had already disbarked a number of trees, with the rigorous application of his scourge, when bestowing a dreadful stroke upon an unfortunate beech, he exclaimed with great vociferation, "Here, Sampson, shalt thou die with all thine abettors." Don Quixote, hearing this dismal ejaculation, and the terrible sound of the stroke, ran up to the spot, and seizing the twisted halter that Sancho used instead of a bull's pizzle, "Fate," said he, "friend Sancho, will not permit, that, for my pleasure, thou shouldst lose that life on which the sustenance of thy wife and family must depend. Dulcinea shall wait for a more favourable conjuncture, and I will contain myself within the limits of the nearest hope, until thou shalt recover new strength to conclude this affair to the satisfaction of all parties." "Since your worship is so inclined," answered the squire, "so be it in happy time; and pray, good signor, throw your cloak about my shoulders; for, I am all in a sweat, and would not willingly catch cold, which is so often the case with new disciplinants." The knight, in compliance with his request, stripped himself of his upper garment, with which he covered up Sancho, who slept until he was wakened by the sun: then they proceeded on their journey, which, for that day, did not exceed three leagues.

They alighted at an inn; for, such it was acknowledged by Don Quixote, who did not, as usual, suppose it a castle furnished with a soffee, turrets, portcullices, and drawbridges: indeed, since his defeat, he had talked with more sanity on all subjects, as will presently appear. He was shewn into a low apartment hung with old painted serge, instead of tapestry, such as is used in country places, in one piece of which some wretched hand had drawn the rape of Helen, who was carried off from Menelaus by his presumptuous guest; and in another was represented the story of Dido and AEneas, the unhappy queen standing upon a lofty tower, making signals with a white sheet to her fugitive lover, who, in a frigate or brigantine, was flying from her coast. He observed, of these two history pieces, that Helen shewed no marks of compulsion; but, rather exhibited her satisfaction in a roguish smile: whereas, from the eyes of the beautiful Dido, tears as big as walnuts seemed to fall. Don Quixote, having considered both pictures, "These two ladies," said he, "were most unfortunate, because they did not live in this our age; and I, above all men unhappy, because I did not live in theirs. Had I encountered those gentlemen, Troy had ne'er been burnt, nor Carthage laid in ruins; for, by killing Paris only, I should have prevented such disasters." "I'll lay a wager," said Sancho, "that, in a very little time, every cook's cellar, tavern, inn, and barber's shop in the kingdom, will be ornamented with pictures containing the history of our atchievements; but, I should be glad to see them painted by a better workman than him who made these daubings." "Thou art in the right," replied Don Quixote; "he that painted these pieces is just such another as Orbaneja, a painter of Ubeda, who, being asked what he was about, answered Just as it happens: and, if he chanced to represent a cock, he wrote under it, This is a cock; that it might not be mistaken for a fox. Such a person, I suppose, is that same painter or author; for, it is the same thing, who ushered into the world the lately published history of the new Don Quixote; for, he has painted or described whatever came uppermost; or, perhaps, he resembles an old court poet called Mauleon, who pretended

to answer every question extempore; and being, one day, asked the meaning of Deum de Deo,[2] replied, De donde diere *. But, waving this subject, tell me, Sancho, if thou art resolved to take the other turn to night, and whether thou wouldst choose to go to work under an humble roof, or beneath the high canopy of heaven?" "'Fore God! signor," replied the squire, "as to what I intend to take, it matters not much, whether it be taken within doors or without: nevertheless, I should choose to go to work among trees; for, they seem to accompany and assist me wonderfully in bearing the brunt of the application." "But, it must not be so at present, friend Sancho," answered the knight; "in order to recruit your strength, the execution shall be postponed until we arrive at our own village, which we shall reach the day after to-morrow, at farthest." Sancho said he might take his own way; tho' he himself should be glad to dispatch the business now he was warm, and while the mill was a-going; "for, Delay breeds danger; and we ought still to be doing while to God we are sueing: I will give thee, is good; but, Here take it, is better: A sparrow in hand is worth an eagle on wing." "No more proverbs, Sancho, for the love of God!" cried the knight: "thou seemest to be returning to sicut erat.[4] Speak plainly and perspicuously without such intricate mazes, as I have often advised thee, and thou wilt find thyself one loaf per cent. in pocket." "I am so unlucky," answered the squire, "that I cannot give a reason without a proverb, nor a proverb that I do not think a good reason; but, I will mend if I can": And here the conversation ended for that time.

## CHAPTER XX.

## Giving an account of Don Quixote's arrival at his own habitation.

That whole day Don Quixote and Sancho tarried at the inn, waiting for night, during which the one intended to finish his whipping task in the open field, and the other hoped to see the accomplishment of that discipline on which depended the accomplishment of his desire. In the mean time, a gentleman on horseback arrived at the door, attended by three or four servants, one of whom said to him who seemed to be the master, "Signor, Don Alvaro Tarfe, your worship may pass the afternoon in this house; the lodging seems to be cool and cleanly." Don Quixote hearing this address, "Hark ye, Sancho," said he, "when I glanced over the second part of my history, I am very much mistaken if I did not perceive, as I turned over the leaves, this very name of Don Alvaro Tarfe." "Very likely," replied the squire; "first let him alight, and then we can ask questions." Accordingly the traveller having alighted, was conducted by the landlady into a room that fronted the knight's apartment, and was ornamented with the same kind of paintings which we have already described. This new come cavalier, laying aside his up-

---

* *Wherever it may hit:* An answer that has no affinity with the question, but the faint resemblance of sound.[3]

per garment, came out into the porch, which was cool and spacious, where seeing Don Quixote walking backwards and forwards for the benefit of the air, asked in a courteous manner, which way his worship was travelling. The knight told him he was going to the place of his nativity, which was a village in the neighbourhood; and in his turn expressed a desire of knowing the direction of the stranger's course. "Signor," said the cavalier, "I am travelling to Grenada, which is my native country." "And a good country it is," replied Don Quixote; "but, will your worship be so good as to tell me your name, which I believe is of more importance to me to know than I can well explain." "My name," said the stranger, "is Don Alvaro Tarfe." "Without doubt then," replied the knight, "you must be the gentleman mentioned in the second part of the history of Don Quixote de la Mancha, lately printed and published by a modern author." "The very same," answered the cavalier: "Don Quixote, the principal character of that history, was an intimate acquaintance of mine: I brought him from his own habitation; at least I persuaded him to assist at the tournament of Saragossa, whither I was going, and where I really and truly did him signal services; and particularly saved his back from being roughly handled by the hangman, for his excessive impudence and knavery." "And pray, signor Don Alvaro, is there any resemblance between me and that Don Quixote whom your worship mentions?" said the knight. "No, surely; none at all," replied the stranger. "Is that Don Quixote attended by a squire called Sancho Panza?" resumed our hero. "Yes, he is," answered the other; "and although he was reported to be a very humorous companion, I never heard him utter one merry conceit." "That I can very well believe," said Sancho, mingling in the discourse; "it is not every body that can utter conceits; and that same Sancho, whom your worship mentions, must be a very great knave, and indeed both fool and knave; for, I am the true Sancho Panza, who have as many conceits as there are drops of rain: if your worship will but try the experiment, and keep me company for a year or so, you will see them fall from me at every step; nay, they are so merry and so numerous, that very often when I myself know not what I have said, they make all the hearers burst their sides with laughing; and the true Don Quixote de la Mancha, the renowned, the valiant, the sage, the enamoured knight, the undoer of wrongs, the tutor of wards and orphans, the protector of widows, the destroyer of maids, he who owns no other mistress than the peerless Dulcinea del Toboso, is my master, this very gentleman here present: every other Don Quixote, and every other Sancho whatsoever, is no better than a dream or delusion." "Before God! I am of the same opinion," replied Don Alvaro; "for, truly, my good friend, you have uttered more pleasantry in these few sentences you have spoke, than ever I knew come from the mouth of the other Sancho Panza, tho' he was an eternal babler: he was much more of a glutton than an orator, and rather idiotical than humorous. Indeed, I am fully persuaded, that those inchanters who molest the good Don Quixote, have been pleased to persecute me with the bad Don Quixote: and yet I know not what to say; for, I can take my oath that I left him at Toledo in the nuncio's house, under the care of surgeons; and now, another Don Quixote starts up in this place, tho' of a very different character and complexion!" "I know not whether or not I am the good Don Quixote," replied the knight; "but, I will venture to say I am not the bad Don Quixote; and as a proof of what I alledge, my good signor Don Alvaro Tarfe, your worship must know, that in the whole course of my life I never was at Saragossa;

on the contrary, having been informed, that the fantastical Don Quixote had been present at the tournament of that city, I would not set foot within its walls, that I might demonstrate his imposture to the satisfaction of the whole world: I, therefore, openly repaired to Barcelona, that repository of politeness, that asylum of strangers, that hospital of the poor, that native place of gallantry, that avenging tribunal of the injured, that agreeable scene of unshaken friendship, unparalleled both in beauty and situation! and although certain adventures which there befel me did not much contribute to my satisfaction, but, on the contrary, conduced to my unspeakable disquiet; I bear my fate without repining, and count myself happy in having seen that celebrated place: finally, signor Don Alvaro Tarfe, I am the real Don Quixote de la Mancha, so well known to fame, and not that wretched impostor who has thought proper to usurp my name, and deck himself with the spoils of my reputation. I must therefor entreat your worship as you value yourself on the character of a gentleman, to make a declaration before the alcalde of the place; importing, that, before this day, you never saw me in the whole course of your life; and that I am not the Don Quixote described in the second part, nor this Sancho Panza the squire whom your worship knew in his service." "With all my heart," said Don Alvaro; "and yet I cannot help being astonished to see two Don Quixotes, and two Sanchos at the same time, so similar in name, and so unlike in character; so that I say again, and even affirm, that I have not really seen that which I thought I had seen, nor met with those incidents in which I supposed myself concerned." "Doubtless," cried Sancho, "your worship must be inchanted, like my lady Dulcinea del Toboso; and would to God your disinchantment depended upon my undergoing another tale of three thousand three hundred lashes, such as I have undertaken in her favour; I would lay them on without interest or deduction." When Don Alvaro said he did not understand what he meant by lashes, the squire answered, it was a long story, which, however, he would relate to him, should they chance to travel the same road.

Don Quixote and Don Alvaro dined together; and the alcalde of the town chancing to enter the inn, with a scrivener, our hero demanded, by a formal petition, that Don Alvaro Tarfe, the gentleman there present, should depose before his worship, that he was not acquainted with him, Don Quixote there present also, and that he the said Don Quixote was not the person described in a certain history, entitled, The second part of Don Quixote de la Mancha; composed by one Avellaneda, native of Tordesillas. In a word, the alcalde proceeded in form; the deposition was drawn up in the strongest terms, and the knight and squire were as much rejoiced, as if this certificate had been of the utmost consequence to their identity, and as if the difference between the two Quixotes and Sanchos would not have plainly appeared from their words and actions.

Many compliments and proffers of service passed between Don Alvaro and Don Quixote; and our great Manchegan gave such proofs of discretion as undeceived Don Alvaro, who persuaded himself that he was certainly enchanted, seeing he had felt, as it were, with his hand, two such contrary Don Quixotes. In the evening, they departed from the village, and travelled together about half a league, until they found the highway divided into two roads, one of which led to the habitation of Don Quixote, and Don Alvaro's journey lay through the other: yet, in that small space, the knight recounted the misfortune of his overthrow, together with Dulcinea's enchantment, and the remedy

proposed; so as to excite anew the admiration of the stranger, who, embracing Don Quixote and Sancho, took his leave, and proceeded on his own affairs, while our knight jogged on at an easy pace, and passed the night in a grove of trees, in order to give Sancho an opportunity to perform his penance, which he accomplished as before, at the expence of the beeches, and not of his own shoulders; these he defended with such care, that they felt not even the whiff of any stripe sufficient to displace a fly. The credulous knight lost not one in his reckoning of the lashes, which, including those of the preceding night, amounted to three thousand and twenty-nine: the sun seemed to rise early on purpose to behold this sacrifice, and to light our adventurer on his way, which he prosecuted, conversing with Sancho upon the mistake and deception of Don Alvaro, and his own presence of mind in obtaining such an authentic testimonial before the justice.

The whole day and night they travelled without encountring any adventure worthy of record, except that, in the dark, Sancho finished his discipline, to the unspeakable satisfaction of the knight, who waited with impatience for the day, in hope of finding his mistress Dulcinea disenchanted, upon the road: indeed, he was so much ingrossed by this notion, that he went up to every woman he met in the remaining part of his journey, to see if she was not Dulcinea del Toboso; infallibly persuaded that there could be no deceit in the promises of Merlin. While he indulged these reflections and desires, they ascended a rising ground, from whence they descried their own village, which Sancho no sooner perceived, than he fell upon his knees, saying, "Open thine eyes, beloved country! and behold the return of thy son Sancho Panza, who though not very rich in coin, is well stored with lashes: open thine arms at the same time, and receive thy son Don Quixote, who though vanquished by a stranger's hand, returns the victor of himself; and that, as he hath often told me, is the greatest conquest which can be desired: with regard to my own fate, I have money in my purse; for, though the stripes fell thick and heavy, I was rewarded like a gentleman." "Leave these fooleries," said the knight, "and let us go directly home, where we will indulge our imagination with free scope, in contriving the scheme of pastoral felicity which we intend to enjoy."

They accordingly descended the hill, and made the best of their way to their own village.

CHAPTER XXI.

Of the omens that occurred to Don Quixote when he entered the village; with other incidents which adorn and authenticate this sublime history.

Cid Hamet relates, that Don Quixote, as he entered the village, perceived two boys quarrelling in a threshing floor, and heard the one say to his antagonist; "Struggle thy fill, Periquillo, thou shalt never see it in all the days of thy life." These words no sooner reached the knight's ears, than turning to his squire, "Friend Sancho," said he, "didst not thou mark what the boy said? Thou shalt never see it in all the days of thy life." "And what signifies what the boy says?" answered the squire. "What!" replied the knight, "dost not thou perceive that these words, applied to my concerns, signify, that I shall never behold Dulcinea?" Sancho was just going to answer, when he was prevented by the sight of an hare, which being pursued by a number of greyhounds and hunters, came running through the field, and squatted down in fright under Dapple; the squire immediately saved it from the dogs, by seizing and presenting it to his master, who said, "Malum Signum, Malum Signum![1] the hare flies, the hounds pursue, and Dulcinea does not appear." "That is a strange fancy in your worship!" replied the squire: "let us, for example, suppose this hare is Dulcinea del Toboso, and these pursuing hounds the felonious inchanters who have transformed her into a country wench; she flies, I catch and deliver her to your worship, who hold and fondle her in your arms; what bad sign is that? or what ill omen can be conjured from such a circumstance?" At this juncture, the two boys who had been quarrelling came up to see the hare, and Sancho having asked the cause of their quarrel, was answered by him who said, "Thou shalt never see it in all the days of thy life," that he had taken a cage full of crickets from the other boy, which he did not intend to restore in the whole course of his life. In consequence of this information, the squire pulled out of his pocket four farthings, and gave them to the boy for the cage, which he put into the hands of Don Quixote, saying, "Behold, signor, the wreck and destruction of those omens, which I (though a fool) imagine, have no more to do with our affairs, than last year's clouds; and if I right remember, I have heard the curate of our parish observe, that no christian of common sense ought to mind such childish trifles: nay, even your worship made the same remark some time ago, and told me those christians were actually mad who put any faith in omens; and therefore we have no occasion to make a stumbling-block of this accident: but let us proceed and enter the town a God's name."

The hunters coming up, demanded the hare, which was delivered to them by our knight, who jogging on with his squire, perceived the curate and batchelor Carrasco busy at their devotion, in a little meadow that skirted the town. Now the reader must know, that Sancho Panza had, over the bundle of armour carried by Dapple, thrown, by way of sumpter-cloth, the buckram robe painted with flames of fire, which he had worn in the duke's castle, on the night of Altisidora's resurrection; and he, at the same time,

had fixed the mitre upon the head of the ass, which, thus adorned, exhibited the strangest transformation that any beast of burden in the world had ever undergone. Our adventurers were immediately recognized by the curate and batchelor, who ran to receive them with open arms, when Don Quixote alighting, embraced them with great cordiality; and the boys, who are quick-sighted as lynxes, descrying the mitre of the ass, came running in crowds to behold this new spectacle; crying to one another, "Come along, boys, and see Sancho Panza's Dapple, as fine as a May * morning, and Rozinante more lean than ever."

In a word, they entered the town, surrounded with boys, and accompanied by the curate and batchelor, who attended them to the knight's house, at the gate of which they found the niece and housekeeper already apprized of his arrival. The same intimation, neither more nor less, had been given to Sancho's spouse Teresa Panza, who came running to see her husband, half naked, with her hair hanging about her ears, and her daughter Sanchica in her hand: but, seeing he was not so gayly equipped, as she thought a governor should be, "Heyday! husband," cried she, "you come home afoot, and seem to be quite foundered, and look more like a governor of hogs than a ruler of men." "Hold your tongue, Teresa," replied the squire; "you will often find hooks where there is no bacon: let us e'en trudge home, where I will tell thee wonders: I have money in my purse, (and that's the one thing needful) earned by my own industry, without prejudice to any person whatsoever." "Do you bring home the money, good husband," said Teresa; "and let it be earned here or there, or got in what shape you please, I give myself no trouble about the matter; I am sure, in getting it, you have introduced no new fashion into the world." Sanchica embraced her father, and asked if he had brought any thing for her, who had expected him as impatiently as if he had been May-dew: then taking hold of his girdle with one hand, and leading Dapple with the other, while her mother held him by the fist, they repaired to their own house, leaving Don Quixote to the care of his niece and housekeeper, and in company with the curate and batchelor.

The knight, disregarding times and seasons, instantly retired into an apartment with his two friends, to whom he briefly related his overthrow, and the obligation under which he lay, to stay at home for the space of one year, which obligation he intended literally to observe, without failing in the least tittle, like a true knight-errant, bound by the punctuality of the order which he had the honour to profess. During this term of retirement, he proposed to turn shepherd, and enjoy the solitude of the fields, where he would give full scope to his amorous sentiments, and exercise himself in all the virtues of a pastoral life: he, at the same time, besought them (provided they had any time to spare, and were not hindered by business of more consequence) to become his companions; assuring them he would purchase a flock of sheep sufficient for a number of swains, and that the principal part of the scheme was already effected, in as much as he had invented names that would suit them with the utmost propriety. The curate expressing a desire to know these appellations, the knight said, he would call himself the shepherd Quixotiz, the batchelor should be distinguished by the name of the swain Car-

* In the original, as fine as Mingo, who was a bad poet and taudry beau, cotemporary with Cervantes.[2]

Sancho's Return to His Wife and Daughter.

rascon, the curate be denominated Curiambro, and the squire, Pancino. They were con-
founded at this new species of madness; but, lest he should once more forsake his habi-
tation to follow his new chivalries, and in hope that he might possibly be cured during
the year of his confinement, they seemingly assented to this new proposal, extolled his
madness as the very essence of discretion, and promised to be his companions in the ex-
ercise he had planned. "All the world knows that I am a celebrated poet," said Sampson
Carrasco, "and at every turn I shall compose verses, pastorals, or courtly sonnets, or
such as will best answer the purpose of entertaining us in the fields through which we
shall rove: but, there is one circumstance, gentlemen, which we must by no means ne-
glect; and that is, every man shall choose a name for the shepherdess he intends to cele-
brate, and inscribe and engrave it on every tree let it be never so hard, according to the
constant practice of enamoured swains." "A very seasonable suggestion," answered Don
Quixote: "but, altho' I am at liberty to choose a fictitious name, I shall not employ my
invention for that purpose, while there is such a person as the peerless Dulcinea del To-
boso, the glory of these banks! the ornament of these meadows! the support of beauty!
the cream of all gentility! and finally, the subject that suits all praise, how hyperbolical
soever it may be." "Very true," said the curate; "but we must put up with nymphs of an
inferior rank, who, though they will not square, may corner³ with our desires." "And
should we be at a loss," added Sampson Carrasco, "we will borrow names that abound
in printed books; such as, Phillis, Amarillis, Diana, Florida, Galatea, and Belisarda,
which, as they are publicly sold, we may purchase and appropriate to our own use. If, for
example, my mistress, or rather shepherdess, be called Ann, I will celebrate her under
the name of Anna; if her name is Frances, she shall be called Francenia; if Lucia, she shall
be known by the appellation of Lucinda: in the same manner, shall other names be
metamorphosed; and if Sancho Panza is inclined to be one of our fraternity, he may cel-
ebrate his wife Teresa Panza, under the name of Teresayna." Don Quixote could not
help smiling at this transformation; and the curate, in very high terms, applauded his
honourable and virtuous resolution, promising anew to spend in his company all the
time he could spare from his indispensable obligations. And now they took leave of the
knight, after having advised and entreated him to have a reverend care of his health, and
comfort his stomach with something good and substantial.

    The niece and housekeeper having, by accident, overheard this conversation, entered
the apartment, as soon as the curate and batchelor were gone, and the former address-
ing herself to Don Quixote, "Uncle," said she, "what is the meaning of all this! Now, that
we thought you was returned to stay at home, and lead a quiet and honourable life in
your own house, you want to reintangle yourself in new labyrinths, and turn a poor
shepherd. Thou cam'st with a crook, with a scrip thou wilt go; as the saying is;⁴ for, in
good faith, the straw is too old to make pipes of." "And does your worship think," added
the housekeeper, "that you can stay in the field, during the heats of summer and the
frosts of winter, to hear the howling of wolves? no, truly: that is the office and employ-
ment of robust clowns, tanned by the weather, and brought up to the business, even
from their christening blankets and swadling-cloaths; and weighing one evil against an-
other, you had better still be a knight-errant than a shepherd. Consider, signor, and take
my advice, which I do not give from a full stomach, but fresh and fasting, with fifty good
years over my head: stay at home in your own house, look after your estate, go fre-

quently to confession, be good to the poor, and let my conscience answer for the rest." "Hold your peace, my good children," answered Don Quixote; "I know my own duty and what I have to do; meanwhile, carry me to bed, for, methinks, I am not very well; and be assured, that whether I continue knight-errant or turn shepherd, you may depend upon my good offices and assistance, as you shall find by experience."

Comforted by this declaration, the good souls, for so they were without doubt, carried the knight to bed, where they presented him with victuals, and cherished him with all possible care.

## CHAPTER XXII.

### Giving an account of Don Quixote's last illness and death.[1]

As nothing human is eternal, but every sublunary object, especially the life of man, is always declining from its origin to its decay; and Don Quixote had no particular privilege from heaven, exempting him from the common fate, the end and period of his existence arrived, when he least expected its approach. Either in consequence of the melancholy produced by his overthrow, or by the particular dispensations of heaven, he was seized with a calenture, which detained him in bed for the space of six days, during which he was often visited by his friends, the curate, batchelor and barber, and his good squire Sancho Panza never stirred from his bed-side. These gentlemen, supposing his distemper proceeded from the chagrin inspired by his overthrow, and the disappointment of his hope, concerning the liberty and disinchantment of Dulcinea, endeavoured, by all possible means, to exhilarate his spirits. The batchelor exhorted him to chear up his heart, and forsake his couch, that they might begin their pastoral exercise, towards which he had already composed an eclogue, which would disgrace all the pastorals that ever Sannazarius wrote. He likewise gave him to understand, that he had purchased with his own money, from an herdsman of Quintanar, two famous dogs called Barcino and Butron, to defend their flock from the wolves. All these consolations, however, could not dispel the melancholy of Don Quixote; so that his friends called a physician, who having felt his pulse, made a very doubtful prognostic; saying, Happen what would, they ought to provide for the health of his soul, as that of his body was in imminent danger; and he gave it as his opinion, that the poor gentleman was overwhelmed with melancholy and vexation. The knight heard this sentence with the most heroic composure; but that was not the case with his housekeeper, niece and squire, who began to weep and wail most bitterly, as if they had already seen him deprived of life.

Don Quixote finding himself inclined to slumber, desired he might be left alone, and the company retiring, he is said to have slept six hours at a stretch; so that the housekeeper and niece began to fear he would never awake. Nevertheless, he awoke at the expiration of the aforesaid time, and exclaimed aloud, "Praised be the almighty God, for

the great benefit I have received from his bounty! his mercies know no bounds; nor are they abridged or impeded by the transgressions of man!" The niece, who listened attentively, hearing this ejaculation, more sensible and connected than any thing he had uttered since the beginning of his illness; "Uncle," said she, "what do you mean? has any thing new befallen us? what mercies and transgressions are these you mention?" "Mercies," replied the knight, "which heaven hath this instant been pleased to vouchsafe unto me, notwithstanding the heinousness of my transgressions. I now enjoy my judgment undisturbed, and cleared from those dark shadows of ignorance, in which my understanding hath been involved, by the pernicious and incessant reading of those detestable books of chivalry. I am now sensible of the falsity and folly they contain; and nothing gives me concern, but that this conviction comes too late to give me time sufficient to make amends, by reading others, which would enlighten my soul. I feel myself, cousin, at the point of death; and I would not undergo that great change, in such a manner, as to entail the imputation of madness on my memory; for, though I have acted as a madman, I should not wish to confirm the character, by my behaviour in the last moments of my life. Be so good, my dear child, as to send for my worthy friend the curate, the batchelor Sampson Carrasco, and master Nicholas the barber; for, I want to confess, and make my will."

The accidental arrival of these three saved her the trouble of sending a message to each in particular; and Don Quixote seeing them enter, "Good gentlemen," said he, "congratulate and rejoice with me, upon my being no longer Don Quixote de la Mancha, but plain Alonso Quixano, surnamed the Good, on account of the innocence of my life and conversation. I am now an enemy to Amadis de Gaul, and the whole infinite tribe of his descendants; now, are all the profane histories of knight-errantry odious to my reflection; now, I am sensible of my own madness, and the danger into which I have been precipitated by reading such absurdities, which I, from dear-bought experience, abominate and abhor." The three friends, hearing this declaration, believed he was certainly seized with some new species of madness; and, on this supposition, Sampson replied, "Now, signor Don Quixote, when we have received the news of my lady Dulcinea's being disinchanted, do you talk at this rate? when we are on the point of becoming shepherds, that we may pass away our time happily in singing, like so many princes, has your worship taken the resolution to turn hermit? no more of that, I beseech you; recollect your spirits, and leave off talking such idle stories." "Those, which I have hitherto believed, have, indeed, realized my misfortune," said the knight; "but, with the assistance of heaven, I hope my death will turn them to my advantage. Gentlemen, I feel myself hastening to the goal of life; and therefore, jesting apart, let me have the benefit of a ghostly confessor, and send for a notary to write my will; for, in such extremities, a man must not trifle with his own soul: I entreat you then to call a notary, and, in the mean time, I will confess myself to Mr. Curate." They looked at one another, surprized at this discourse, and though still dubious, resolved to comply with his desire: they considered this sudden and easy transition from madness to sanity, as a certain signal of his approaching death; for, to those expressions already rehearsed, he added a great number so rational, so christian and well-connected, as to dispel the doubts of all present; who were now firmly persuaded, that he had retrieved the right use of his intellects. The curate,

having dismissed the company, confessed the penitent; while the batchelor went in quest of the notary, with whom he in a little time returned, accompanied also by Sancho, who having received an account of his master's condition, and finding the niece and house-keeper in tears, began to pucker up his face, and open the flood-gates of his eyes.

Confession being ended, the curate came forth, saying, "The good Alonso Quixano is really dying, and, without all doubt, restored to his senses; we may now go and see the will attested." These tidings gave a terrible stab to the overcharged hearts of the two ladies and his faithful squire, whose eyes overflowed with weeping, and whose bosoms had well-nigh burst with a thousand sighs and groans; for, indeed, it must be owned, as we have somewhere observed, that whether in the character of Alonso Quixano the Good, or in the capacity of Don Quixote de la Mancha, the poor gentleman had always exhibited marks of a peaceable temper and agreeable demeanour, for which he was beloved, not only by his own family, but also by all those who had the pleasure of his acquaintance.

The notary, entering the apartment with the rest of the company, wrote the preamble of the will, in which Don Quixote disposed of his soul in all the necessary christian forms; then proceeding to the legacies, he said; "Item, Whereas Sancho Panza, whom, in my madness, I made my squire, has in his hands a certain sum of money for my use; and, as divers accounts, disbursements, and pecuniary transactions have passed between us; it is my will, that he shall not be charged or brought to account for the said money; but, if there be any overplus after he has deducted the payment of what I owe him, the said overplus, which must be a mere trifle, shall be his own, and much good may it do him: and, as, during my disorder, I contributed to his being made governor of an island, I would now, while I enjoy my perfect senses, confer upon him, were it in my power, a whole kingdom, which he richly deserves for the innocency of his heart, and the fidelity of his service." Then turning to the disconsolate squire, "Forgive me, friend," said he, "for having been the cause of thy appearing in the eye of the world, a madman, like myself; by drawing thee into my own erroneous notions, concerning the existence and adventures of knights-errant." "Lack-a-day! dear sir," cried Sancho, blubbering, "do not die—take my advice, and live many years upon the face of the earth; for, the greatest madness a man can be guilty of in this life, is to let himself die outright, without being slain by any person whatever, or destroyed by any other weapon than the hands of melancholy. Heark ye, signor, hang sloth; get up and let us take the field in shepherd's apparel, according to our agreement: who knows, but behind some bush we may find my lady Dulcinea disinchanted, and a comely sight for to see. If you take your overthrow so much to heart, lay the blame at my door, and say you was vanquished by my carelessness, in girting Rozinante; besides, your worship must have read in your books of chivalry, that it was common for one knight to unhorse another, and for him who was vanquished to-day, to be victor to-morrow." "Very true," said Sampson; "honest Sancho seems to be very well informed of these matters." "Gentlemen," replied the knight, "let us proceed fair and softly, without looking for this year's birds in last year's nests. I was mad; but now am in my right senses. I was Don Quixote de la Mancha; but now, as I have already observed, I am Alonzo Quixano the Good; and I hope, I shall, by my veracity and repentance, recover that degree of your esteem, which I formerly enjoyed. So, let Mr. Notary proceed.

"Item, I bequeath my whole estate, real and personal, to my niece Antonia Quixana here present, after deducting what shall be sufficient for the payment of my debts and legacies; and it is my will, that from the first of the money thence arising, the wages due to my housekeeper shall be paid, together with twenty ducats for a suit of mourning: and I appoint Mr. Curate, and Mr. Batchelor Sampson Carrasco, here present, my executors. Item, It is my will, that if my niece Antonia Quixana inclines to marriage, she shall not wed any man, until she is fully satisfied, from previous information, that he is an utter stranger to books of chivalry; or, if she finds he is addicted to this kind of reading, and marries him nevertheless, she shall forfeit the whole legacy, which my executors may, in that case, dispose of in pious uses. Item, I beseech the said gentlemen, my executors, if perchance they should become acquainted with a certain author, who composed and published an history, entitled, 'The Second Part of the Atchievements of Don Quixote de la Mancha'; that they will, in my name, most earnestly entreat him to forgive me for having been the innocent cause of his writing such a number of absurdities as that performance contains; for, I quit this life with some scruples of conscience arising from that consideration." The will being thus concluded, he was seized with a fainting fit, and stretched himself at full length in the bed; so that all the company were alarmed, and ran to his assistance: during three days which he lived after the will was signed and sealed, he frequently fainted, and the whole family was in confusion. Nevertheless, the niece ate her victuals, the housekeeper drank to the repose of his soul, and even Sancho cherished his little carcase; for, the prospect of succession either dispels, or moderates that affliction, which an heir ought to feel at the death of the testator.

At last, Don Quixote expired, after having received all the sacraments, and, in the strongest terms pathetically enforced, expressed his abomination against all books of chivalry; and the notary observed, that in all the books of that kind which he had perused, he had never read of any knight-errant, who died quietly in his bed, as a good christian, like Don Quixote; who, amidst the tears and lamentations of all present, gave up the ghost, or in other words, departed this life. The curate was no sooner certified of his decease, than he desired the notary to make out a testimonial, declaring, that Alonso Quixano the Good, commonly called Don Quixote de la Mancha, had taken his departure from this life, and died of a natural death. That no other author, different from Cid Hamet Benengeli, should falsely pretend to raise him from the dead, and write endless histories of his atchievements.

This was the end of the sage Hidalgo de la Mancha, whose native place Cid Hamet would not punctually describe, because he wished that all the towns and villages of that province should contend for the honour of having given him birth, as the seven cities of Greece contended for Homer. We shall here omit the lamentations of the housekeeper, niece, and squire, together with all the epitaphs, except the following, by Sampson Carrasco.

> Here lies a cavalier of fame,
>    Whose dauntless courage soar'd so high,
> That death, which can the boldest tame,
>    He scorn'd to flatter, or to fly.

A constant bugbear to the bad,
His might the world in arms defy'd,
And in his life though counted mad,
He in his perfect senses dy'd.

The sagacious Cid Hamet addressing himself to his pen, "And now, my slender quill," said he, "whether cunningly cut, or unskilfully formed, it boots not much; here from this rack, suspended by a wire, shalt thou enjoy repose, and live to future ages, if no presumptuous and wicked hand shall take thee down, in order to profane thee in compiling idle histories. But ere such insolent fingers can touch thine hallowed plume, accost, and warn them, if thou canst, in words like these:

Caitifs forbear——illustrious prince, let none
Attempt th' emprize, reserv'd for me alone *.

For me alone was Don Quixote born, and I produced for him; he to act, and I to record; in a word, we were destined for each other, maugre and in despight of that fictitious Tordesillian author, who presumed, or may presume, to write with his coarse, aukward, ostrich quill, the atchievements of my valiant knight; a burthen too heavy for his weak shoulders, and an undertaking too great for his frozen genius. Advise him, therefore, if ever thou shouldst chance to be in his company, to let the wearied and mouldering bones of Don Quixote rest in the grave, without seeking to carry him into Old Castile †, in opposition to all the prerogatives of death, or to drag him from his tomb, where he really and truly lies extended at full length, and utterly incapable of making a third sally: for, all the exploits performed by the whole tribe of knights-errant are sufficiently ridiculed by the two expeditions he has already made, so much to the satisfaction and entertainment, not only of Spain, but also of every foreign nation to which the fame of his adventures hath been conveyed. In so doing, thou wilt conform to thy christian profession of doing good to those who would do thee harm; and I shall rest satisfied and perfectly well pleased, in seeing myself the first author, who fully enjoyed the fruit of his writings, in the success of his design; for mine was no other than to inspire mankind with an abhorrence of the false and improbable stories recounted in the books of chivalry; which are already shaken by the adventures of my true and genuine Don Quixote, and in a little time will certainly sink into oblivion. Farewel."

## FINIS.

* Lines probably taken from some old ballad or romance.[2]
† The author of the Second Part, hinted, in his Preface, a design of bringing his hero into the field again, in Old Castile.[3]

## Dedication

1. "DON RICARDO WALL": Born in Ireland, Richard Wall (1694–1778) distinguished himself in the service of Spain, his adopted country: a favorite of Ferdinand VI, he was made lieutenant general in 1752 and was appointed secretary of state in 1754. Earlier, in 1748, after having represented Spain's interests in London during negotiations for the Treaty of Aix-la-Chapelle, Wall was appointed Spanish ambassador; in that capacity he remained in England until October 1752, when he was recalled. Smollett claimed to be "personally known" to Wall, and when applying for the consulship of Madrid c. 1759, he believed he could count on Wall's support (*Letters*, 111 and n. 1). Certainly, Smollett's compliments to Wall in the *Continuation* (1760) appear to be based on knowledge of the minister's character and activities. In relating the events of 1750 Smollett thus represents Wall as "a gentleman who had distinguished himself in the field as well as in the cabinet, and possessed the joint qualifications of a general and a statesman. . . . He was possessed of the most insinuating address, shrewd, penetrating, and inquisitive. While he resided in London, he spared no pains in learning the nature of those manufactures, and that commerce, by which Great Britain had been so remarkably aggrandized; and on his return to Spain, where in a little time he was placed at the helm of affairs, he turned the knowledge he had thus acquired to the advantage of his country. He not only promoted the useful arts within the kingdom of Spain, but demonstrated the infinite advantage that would accrue from an active trade, which the Spaniards had for many ages neglected; and in a few years their ships were seen to swarm in all the commercial ports of Europe" (1 [1760]:86–87; see also 232–33, 276). The tone of Smollett's final reference to Wall in the *Continuation* (4 [1762]:351), however, is noticeably less cordial, a change in attitude perhaps owing to his having by then been disappointed in his hopes for the consulship of Madrid: "this Place," he sourly remarked to John Home in December 1762, "was thought . . . far above my Pretensions" (*Letters*, 111).

## The Life of Cervantes

1. In this biographical sketch of Cervantes, Smollett was indebted for virtually every substantive detail to two sources, both unacknowledged. His principal source was John Ozell's translation of Don Gregorio Mayáns y Siscár, *Vida de Miguel de Cervantes Saavedra* (Briga-Real, 1737), the first serious attempt at a biography of Cervantes. Gregorio (1699–1781), keeper of the Royal Library at Madrid, undertook this work at the request of John, Lord Carteret, to whom it is dedicated. The year following its publication on the Continent, Gregorio's biography was included in Pedro Pineda's edition of *Don Quixote*, published in London by J. and R. Tonson (4 vols., 1738). It is clear from numerous correspondences in phrasing, however, that Smollett relied on Ozell's translation, published by the Tonsons in this same year and later included in Jarvis's translation of *Don Quixote* (1742). Smollett's other source for this biographical sketch had been overlooked not only by Gregorio and Ozell, but also—as William Windham observed as Smollett's translation was going through the press—"by all the writers which I have seen, that mention Cervantes" (*Remarks*, 30). This source was Joseph Morgan's *Complete His-*

*tory of Algiers* (1728–29). In his account of Cervantes' captivity in Algiers (see below, pp. 8–
10), Smollett identifies his source as "F. Diego de Haedo" (d. 1608), author of *Topographia e
historia general de Argel* (Valladolid, 1612), wherein may indeed be found the anecdote in ques-
tion (fols. 84–85). But Haedo was Smollett's source only insofar as Morgan had used that his-
torian as the basis of his own account (Morgan, 1:xxvii); in his narrative of Cervantes' captiv-
ity, Smollett depended on Morgan (2:563–66), often even for his phrasing.

2. "Thomas Tamayo de Vargas" and "Don Nicholas Antonio": Smollett found these scholars—
as well as the reference to *Persiles and Sigismunda*—in Gregorio (1–3, 85), who, in discussing
the uncertain circumstances of Cervantes' birth, cites as his own sources Tomás Tamayo de
Vargas (1588–1641) and Don Nicolas Antonio (1617–84), author of *Bibliotheca Hispana*
(Rome, 1672). It is now known that Cervantes was born at Alcalá de Henares, near Madrid, in
1547.

3. "He describes . . . 'Out of my country and myself I go!'": In questioning Madrid's claim to be
Cervantes' birthplace, Smollett disagrees with Gregorio (2–3), who prefers that city despite
doubts expressed by Nicolas Antonio. However, he here echoes verbatim Ozell's translation of
a passage Gregorio quoted from Cervantes' *Voyage to Parnassus* (2): *"Out of MY COUNTRY and
my self I go."*

4. "Nicholas Antonio, Biblioth. Hisp.": Nicolas Antonio makes no such assertion in his brief ar-
ticles on Cervantes in *Bibliotheca Hispana* (2:105, 310), and Gregorio merely reports the sup-
position that Cervantes "served the Duke of *Alva* in *Flanders*" (4). Smollett appears to recall
Motteux, "An Account of the Author" (1:ii): "[Cervantes] was for some time Secretary to the
Duke of *Alva*."

5. "His dedication of Galatea": Though Gregorio (4) also cites Cervantes' dedication to *Galatea*,
Smollett's anecdote concerning the ceremonial appointment of Marc Antonio Colona as com-
mander of the papal forces before the Battle of Lepanto derives from another source,
unidentified.

6. "victory of Lepanto": This famous naval battle was fought on 7 October 1571. In the preface
to part 2 of *Don Quixote* Cervantes calls it (in Smollett's words) "the most glorious occasion
that ever the past or present age beheld, or posterity can ever hope to see."

7. "In the preface to his plays": Smollett's remarks on Cervantes' reformation of the Spanish
theater are based on Gregorio's discussion of the same passage from the preface to the plays
(82–83).

8. "Lope de Vega": Lope de Vega (1562–1635), Spain's greatest playwright.

9. "In the year 1574": Smollett's sources do not mention the date or circumstances of Cervantes'
capture. Otherwise, throughout this paragraph he follows Gregorio's account of Cervantes'
captivity (4–5), quoting the same passage in *Don Quixote* (see below, p. 287) that Gregorio had
used to illustrate autobiographical elements in the story of the Captive (pt. 1, bk. 4, chaps. 12–
14). Cervantes was captured by Turks at sea in 1575 and was taken to Algiers, where he re-
mained in captivity until ransomed in 1580 (Kelly, 30–56).

10. "Hassan Aga": Following Gregorio (4), who applied to Cervantes details found in the story of
the Captive (see below, p. 287), Smollett here wrongly attributes to Hassan Aga the cruelty
of Hassan Pasha, dey of Algiers from 1577 to 1580. Below, Smollett's shift from Gregorio to
Morgan as his source results in an inconsistency in the narrative, when he correctly identifies
this "tyrant" as "Hassan Basha" (p. 9).

11. "one Saavedra, a Spanish soldier": Perhaps a vestige of an earlier state of Smollett's transla-
tion: in pt. 1, bk. 4, chap. 13, he writes "a Spanish soldier, called such-a-one de Saavedra" (See
n.1 to this chapter).

12. "F. Diego de Haedo": Smollett here cites Morgan's source as his own (see above, n.1). The following account of Cervantes' captivity is based entirely on Morgan (2:563–65).

13. "To this adventure . . . the story of the Captive": See below, p. 292.

14. "this disposition is not confined": This is the premise of Smollett's next novel, *Sir Launcelot Greaves*, whose eponymous hero is a latter-day Quixote.

15. "his Galatea": With the following account of Cervantes' *Galatea*, including the quotation of the curate's criticism of the work (see below, p. 54), compare Gregorio (6–7).

16. "in that period . . . Donna Catalina de Salazar": Though Gregorio did not speculate as to when Cervantes married, he did provide Smollett with the name of his wife (87).

17. "he composed . . . the first part of Don Quixote": With Smollett's account of Cervantes' purpose in writing *Don Quixote*, and his success in accomplishing it, compare the preface to *Roderick Random:* "But when the minds of men were debauched by the imposition of priest-craft to the most absurd pitch of credulity; the authors of romance arose, and losing sight of probability, filled their performances with the most monstrous hyperboles. If they could not equal the ancient poets in point of genius, they were resolved to excel them in fiction, and apply to the wonder rather than the judgment of their readers. Accordingly they brought negromancy to their aid, and instead of supporting the character of their heroes, by dignity of sentiment and practice, distinguished them by their bodily strength, activity and extravagance of behaviour. Although nothing could be more ludicrous and unnatural than the figures they drew, they did not want patrons and admirers, and the world actually began to be infected with the spirit of knight-errantry, when Cervantes, by an inimitable piece of ridicule, reformed the taste of mankind, representing chivalry in the right point of view, and converting romance to purposes far more useful and entertaining, by making it assume the sock, and point out the follies of ordinary life."

18. "to combat . . . knight-errantry": By insisting that Cervantes' purpose was not to discredit the ideals of chivalry, but only the improbabilities of "absurd romances," Smollett here takes issue with views expressed in the two translations he would have considered his chief competitors. In an appendix to Jarvis's preface, William Warburton asserted that *Don Quixote* "was calculated to ridicule that false system of honour and gallantry" which had been the cause of "Infinite . . . mischiefs" in society (Jarvis, 1:vii–xxiii). Motteux had anticipated this opinion: "The principal Design of [*Don Quixote*] is to ridicule by the finest Satyr in the World, the Humour of Knight-Errantry, and the Romantick Notions of Love and Honour; which at that time reign'd in the *Spanish* Nation" (1:iii).

19. "Amadis": *Amadis de Gaula* (1508), most famous of the Spanish chivalric romances of the sixteenth century.

20. "Sampson Carrasco": Following Gregorio (23–24), Smollett in this paragraph conflates two passages from *Don Quixote*, pt. 2, bk. 1, chap. 3 (below, pp. 388, 390).

21. "a conversation . . . Marques Torres": Following Gregorio (25), Smollett takes this story from the "Approbation" by Torres prefixed to part 2 of *Don Quixote* (see below, p. 374).

22. "Philip III.": For this anecdote concerning Philip III, see Gregorio (24).

23. "verses . . . Urganda the unknown": The first of the facetious commendatory verses prefixed to the original editions of *Don Quixote* purports to be by "Urganda the Unknown [La Desconocida]," the enchantress in *Amadis de Gaula*. Only Philips among previous translators attempted versions of any of the prefatory verses, though not those by "Urganda." See also below, p. 50, n. 1.

24. "Charles V.": Charles V (1500–1558), emperor of the Holy Roman Empire and, as Charles I, king of Spain.

25. "the count de Lemos": Smollett's narrative of Cervantes' relations with his patron is based on the preface to part 2 of *Don Quixote* (see especially pp. 370–71 below) and on Gregorio (66). What is new in Smollett's account is the tone of indignation that thoughts of "the barbarous indifference of . . . patrons" usually aroused in him.

26. "Laurèl de Apollo Selva 8": Gregorio quotes a passage of verse in which Lope de Vega warmly praised Cervantes' courage and genius; in a footnote (37, n. *(p)*) he identifies his source as "Laurèl de Apollo Selva 8."

27. "Composed by . . . Avellaneda": With Smollett's remarks on the spurious continuation of *Don Quixote* and its author, compare Gregorio (27–46; esp. 27–30, 36–37). Gregorio, in Ozell's translation, records the title page as follows: "*The Second Volume of the Ingenious Gentleman* Don Quixote de la Mancha, *containing his Third Sally: compos'd by the Licentiate* Alonzo Fernandez de Avellaneda, *a Native of* Tordesillas. *Inscrib'd to the* Alcalde (Bayliff) Regidores (Aldermen) *and Gentlemen of the noble Town of* Argamesilla, *the happy Country of* Don Quixote de la Mancha *Knight and Gentleman. With License; in* Tarragona *at the Printing -Office of* Philip Roberto, *Año* 1614. *In* 8vo."

28. "abused his cotemporary writers . . . critical reflexions": Gregorio (30) identifies these "reflexions" as the criticism of the irregularity of Spanish drama in the exchange between the Canon of Toledo and the curate (see below, pp.341–44). Explaining the author's motive in linking himself with Lope de Vega as targets of Cervantes' criticism, Smollett paraphrases Gregorio (36): "so covering himself with the Shield of Lopé's Reputation, he thought therewith to ward off the Blows *Cervantes* had given to himself."

29. "A Voyage to Parnassus": This paragraph summarizes Gregorio (74, 76–79).

30. "his dedication . . . to the count de Lemos": The following excerpt from the dedication paraphrases Ozell's translation of Gregorio (23).

31. "eight plays . . . to Juan Villaroel": Compare Gregorio (81).

32. "an enemy to . . . the king's company . . . murder with impunity": Compare Gregorio (65): "*Cervantes* was greatly offended at the Insolence of the Players of his Time; especially the King's Players, who were in such high Favour at Court, and had such Interest in Great Men's Families, that they wou'd sometimes commit Murder, and yet go unpunisht."

33. "In his preface to his plays": Smollett paraphrased the quoted passage from Gregorio (84), who gave his source as the preface to the plays.

34. "Preface to his novels. . . . Don Quixote": Gregorio (85) cites these same sources in his discussion of *Persiles and Sigismunda*, quoting from the dedication the following passage, which prompted Smollett's reflections on authorial pride: "*And now* [writes Cervantes to Count de Lemos] *I take my Leave with offering to your Excellency* THE TROUBLES OF PERSILES AND SIGISMUNDA: *A Book which, God willing, I shall finish in Four Months, and which will be either the worst or the best Book that was ever written in our Language: I speak of Books of Entertainment: and I'm already sorry I said the worst; for in the Opinion of my Friends, it will be the best that possibly can be.*"

35. "vie with . . . Heliodorus": With Smollett's remarks on Heliodorus's *Aethiopica*, compare Gregorio (88–89): "*Cervantes* says [in the preface to the novels] that his PERSILES and SIGISMUNDA dared to vie with HELIODORUS. . . . the fecundity of Invention marvellous. . . . The Incidents are Numerous, and vastly Various. . . . He likewise was superior to [Heliodorus] in Style . . . altho' that of *Heliodorus* is very elegant."

36. "The Loves of Theagenes and Chariclea": Heliodorus's *Aethiopica: or, The Adventures of Theagones and Chariclea* was translated into English by Thomas Underdowne, c. 1569.

37. "'Loving reader,' said he": Continuing to the end of the paragraph, this long quotation closely paraphrases Ozell's translation of the conclusion of Cervantes' preface to *Persiles and Sigismunda*, as found in Gregorio (85–86).

38. "dedication to . . . count de Lemos": With this paragraph, compare Gregorio (87).
39. "1617 . . . died the very next day": Smollett repeats Gregorio's error (87), which gives 1617 rather than 1616 as the year of the dedication to *Persiles and Sigismunda*. The error (corrected in ink in the BL copy of Gregorio [call number: 635.l.24]) is obvious in the context of the passage in Gregorio, who gives the date on which Cervantes received extreme unction as 18 April 1616, and the date of the license granted to his widow to print *Persiles* as 24 September 1616.
40. "the portrait of his person . . . his own pen": Gregorio (89–90) also concludes his biography by quoting from the preface to the novels Cervantes' own description of his physical appearance. Smollett paraphrases Ozell's translation, which reads: "'He whom thou seest here with a sharp aquiline Visage, brown chestnut-colour'd Hair; his Forehead smooth and free from Wrinkles; his Eyes brisk and chearful; his Nose somewhat Hookish or rather Hawkish, but withal well-proportion'd; his Beard silver-colour'd, which twenty Years ago was gold; his Mustachio's large; his Mouth little; his Teeth neither small nor big, and of them he has but Six, and those in bad condition and worse ranged, for they have no correspondence with one another; his Body between two Extreams, neither large nor little; his Complexion lively, rather fair than swarthy; somewhat thick in the Shoulders and not very light of Foot.'"

## Translator's Note

1. "retain the spirit . . . of the original": On Smollett's practice in this translation, see the introduction, pp. xxxv–xxxvi.
2. "it was begun . . . four years ago": Smollett here repeats verbatim his statement in the *Public Advertiser* (14 March 1754) concerning the period of composition of his translation (see the introduction, p. xl). This paragraph is omitted in the second and subsequent editions.

## Preface to the Reader

1. "This is a strong presumption . . . in a jail": Noted also in Jarvis and Motteux/Ozell.
2. "Alluding to the loss of his hand . . . Lepanto": Noted also in Jarvis and Motteux/Ozell.
3. "Non bene . . . auro": Roughly meaning, "Freedom is worth more than all the gold in the world" (from a fable of the twelfth century, *De cane et lupo:* Putnam 1:470, col. b, n. 3).
4. "Pallida mors . . . turres": "Pale death with foot impartial knocks at the poor man's cottage and at princes' palaces" (Horace *Odes* 1.4.13–14, trans. C. E. Bennett, Loeb Library, 1968).
5. "Ego autem . . . inimicos vestros": "But I say unto you, Love your enemies" (Matthew 5:44).
6. "De corde . . . malæ": "Out of the heart proceed evil thoughts" (Matthew 15:19).
7. "Donec eris . . . solus eris": "So long as you are fortunate you will count many friends; if your life becomes clouded you will be alone" (Ovid *Tristia* 1.9.5–6; trans. A. L. Wheeler, Loeb Library, 1975).

## Part 1

## Book 1

*Chapter 1*

1. "Mutton in Spain . . . beef": Compare Jarvis: "Beef being cheaper in *Spain* than mutton." Also Motteux/Ozell.

2. "*Salpicon* . . . pepper": Stevens: "Salpicón, cold beef cut in pieces [Pineda: 'Slices'], and eaten with oil and vinegar, onion and pepper."

3. "Gripes and grumblings . . . former translators": Smollett refers to the following "former translators" of the phrase *duelos y quebrantos:* (1) Stevens: "Duélo . . . *Duélos y quebrantos,* sorrows and troubles. A phrase for callops and eggs, because it is reckoned a sorry dish for poor people"; and (2) his principal source for the erudition here displayed, Ozell's note to the Motteux/Ozell translation, "Eggs and Bacon": "*Strictly,* Sorrow *for his Sops, on* Saturdays. Duelos y Quebrantos; *in* English, *Gruntings and Groanings. He that can tell what Sort of Edible the Author means by those Words,* Erit mihi magnus Apollo. Cæsar Oudin, *the famous* French *Traveller, Negotiator, Translator and Dictionary-maker, will have it to be* Eggs and Bacon, *as above. Our Translator and Dictionary-maker,* Stevens, *has it* Eggs and Collops [Shelton/Stevens], (*I suppose he means* Scotch-Collops) *but that's too good a Dish to mortify withal. Signor* Sobrino's Spanish *Dictionary says,* Duelos y Quebrantos *is* Pease-Soup. *Mr.* Jarvis *translates it an* Amlet (Aumulette in French) *which* Boyer *says is a Pancake made of Eggs* [Abel Boyer, *Royal Dictionary* (1699), s.v. 'Aumelette'], *tho' I always understood* Aumulette *to be a* Bacon-froise (*or rather* Bacon-fryze, *from its being* fry'd, *from* frit *in* French). *Some will have it to mean* Brains fry'd with Eggs [quoting Jarvis's note, who has in mind the *Diccionario* of the Spanish Royal Academy, 3 (1732), 'Duelos y quebrantos'], *which, we are told by Mr.* Jarvis, *the Church allows in poor Countries in Defect of Fish. Others* [again quoting Jarvis] *have guest it to mean some windy kind of Diet, as Peas, Herbs,* &c. *which are apt to occasion Cholicks, as if one should say,* Greens and Gripes on Saturdays. *To conclude the 'fore-cited Author* [Jarvis] *of the new Translation (if a Translator may be call'd an Author) absolutely says,* Duelos y Quebrantos *is a Cant-Phrase for some Fasting-Day-Dish in use in* la Mancha. *After all these learned Disquisitions, Who knows but the Author means a Dish of* Nichils!"
   Jarvis gave the literal meaning of the phrase as "griefs and groans." In the final paragraph of his own note Smollett gives it as "pains and breakings," preferring the alternative interpretation *("some windy kind of Diet")* offered by Jarvis and quoted by Ozell above. In his criticism of Smollett's specimen, Windham took Jarvis's part, finding Smollett's translation of this phrase particularly egregious: "But if our learned doctor had consulted the Madrid dictionary, which it is unpardonable for him not to have been provided with, as it is the only one of any authority . . . ; he would have found, *Duelos y Quebrantos llaman en la Mancha a la tortilla di huevos y sesos;* Latine, *Ex ovis cerebrisq; frixus Orbiculus;* that is, a name peculiar to La Mancha, signifying a kind of amlet made of eggs and brains of beasts" (*Remarks,* 10–11).

4. "*Podadera* . . . pruning-hook": Though Smollett was aware that Stevens, the dictionary he depended on, as well as previous translators, had correctly rendered *podadera* as "pruning-hook," he preferred to make it "hough" (*i.e.,* "hoe"), perhaps for its alliterative effect: "to saddle the horse or handle the hough." His choice again provoked Windham's criticism: "In his note, he says, that what he has translated *hough,* is in the original *podadera, or pruning-hook.* In all wine countries, the culture and dressing of the vines is the most important and essential part of their husbandry; and the head servant in husbandry is the *vigneron,* or wine-dresser: so he had done better to have translated *podadera,* according to its true meaning" (*Remarks,* 12).

5. "In the original, a lover of hunting": Original: "amigo de la caça." Jarvis has "a keen sports-man"; Motteux, "a lover of hunting."

6. "*Quixadas* . . . provision": Both Shelton and Jarvis here altered the original "Quixada" (Jaw) to "Quixana," presumably on the authority of the final chapter, where the name of Cervantes' hero is revealed as "Alonzo Quixano the Good." In a note Jarvis derives "Quixana" from "the *Spanish* word *Quixas*, which signifies *lanthorn jaws*."

7. "Siguenza . . . university": Previous translators retain the form of the original, "Ciguença." For his spelling and his note, Smollett depended on Stevens: "SIGUÉNÇA."

8. "*Hidalgo* . . . sons of nothing": "our Hidalgo" is Smollett's interpolation; the original, followed by all previous translators, has simply "èl." With his note, compare this facetious explanation of the term in *Gil Blas* (bk. 5, chap. 1; 2:194 n.), where he translated it "Squire": "Hidalgo, (in Spanish) is a gentleman literally somebody's son, in contradiction to those who are the sons of nobody." Stevens: "HIDÁLGO . . . a gentleman, a person well born; as the word implies, which is properly *Hijo dálgo*, that is, the son of something, or a son to whom his father had something to leave, that is honour and estate."

9. "the enchanted Orlando": Windham noted that the specimen (as well as the first edition) read "*the enchanter Orlando*, instead of the *enchanted*," but allowed "it may be an error of the press" (*Remarks*, 15). Smollett added the note in the second edition.

10. "Galalon . . . from Spain": Corrected from the first edition, where Smollett, ignoring notes in both Shelton/Stevens and Jarvis, has Galalon a Spaniard. The error did not escape Windham: "the doctor says in his note that [Galalon] betrayed the *Spanish* army at Roncesvalles; whereas the army which was defeated at that battle, so celebrated by the romancers and poets, for the death of Orlando and the Paladins, was the *French* army, under Charlemagne; which, on their return to France was, by the treachery of Ganellon, drawn into the narrow passes of the Pyre-nean mountains, and there in part cut off by the Moors and mountaineers. It is indeed no im-portant piece of history, but as the doctor did attempt an explanation of it, he should at least have given a true one, otherwise we may justly suspect him in other places of equal blunders" (*Remarks*, 15–16). For a later reference to the battle (in pt. 2, bk. 1, chap. 9), see below, p. 414, and n. 1.

11. "This is a joke . . . *Trapezium*": Original: "aunque tenia mas quartos que un real." Jarvis, echo-ing Motteux, translates this as "his bones stuck out like the corners of a Rial," commenting: "A ludicrous Image drawn from the irregular figure of the *Spanish* money, to express the jutting bones of a lean beast."

12. "'tantum pellis et ossa fuit'": "was all skin and bones."

13. "*Rozinante* . . . all other horses": Compare Motteux's note: "Rozin *commonly means an ordinary Horse;* Ante *is before and formerly. Thus the Word* Rozinante *may imply that he was formerly an or-dinary Horse, and also that he is now an Horse that claims the Precedence from all other ordinary Horses.*" Windham ridiculed Smollett's note on the ambiguity of the suffix *ante,* insisting with Jarvis that Rozinante's name merely "expressed his having been *Rozzino*, or a hack, before Don Quixote preferred him to be his *Corsiero*, or war-horse" (*Remarks*, 14). Modern translators, however, like Motteux and Smollett, emphasize the double meaning: see Ormsby, Watts, Put-nam.

## Chapter 2

1. "According to the ancient rules of chivalry . . . his own hand": Among the original features of Smollett's translation of *Don Quixote* are twenty-one notes on the ideals and customs of an-cient chivalry, all of which he drew from a single source, namely, the five "Mémoires" ("sur

l'ancienne Chevalerie, considérée comme un établissement politique & militaire") by M. de la Curne de Ste. Palaye, included in *Mémoires de littérature, tirés des registres de l'Académie Royale des Inscriptions et Belles-Lettres, 1744–46,* vol. 20 (Paris, 1753): 597–847 (BL call number: T.C.28.a.1). With the present note, compare Ste. Palaye, *Mémoire* 1, n. 48: "Jean Bouchet . . . représente en ces termes les conditions qu'on avoit exigées d'un homme de guerre pour l'admettre à l'état d'Écuyer. *Anciennement aulcun ne souloyt estre dict Escuyer s'il n'avoit esté trouvé en faict de souveraine presse (*bataille*); aulcun n'estoit appellé aux gaiges d'armes s'il n'avoit droictement prins prisonnier de sa main*" (20:710–11).

2. "It was common for one knight to dub another . . . .flower of chivalry": Compare Ste. Palaye, *Mémoire* 3, n. 15: "il estoit bien meilleur une fois & plus honorable de se faire créer Chevalier après la bataille, ayant tres-bien combattu & fait bien le devoir Chevalier, ainsi que le roy François I.er voulut estre fait Chevalier de la main du brave M. Bayard, après la bataille de Suisses" (20:761).

3. "He might have imitated the young knight . . . dexterity": Compare Ste. Palaye, *Mémoire* 2, n. 27. Referring to the French romance of the fourteenth century, Ste. Palaye writes: "Perceforest nous donne le portrait d'un jeune homme que le roi Alexandre venoit de faire Chevalier, & qui ensuite fuit laissé seul à l'entrée d'une forêt. . . . *il fiert le cheval des esperons: il fait un tour parmy la forest si joyeux & si désirant de jouster, que se il aydast lance recouvrer, il allast jouster au premier arbre qu'il trouvast; ainsi s'en va chevauchant parmi la forest jusques au bas Vespres.*" Perceforest continues by describing how those who were dubbed knights mounted their horses and paraded before the king: "*si bien & si gentement, que le Roy & Cassiel, le Souldan & la Chevalerie qui là estoit, dirent apertement qu'ils ne pouoient faillir à estre preux en faiz d'armes*" (20:724).

4. "hogs, (with leave be it spoken)": Original: "puercos (que sin perdon assi se llaman)." Smollett follows Jarvis in retaining this parenthesis, Jarvis rendering it literally: "hogs (for, without begging pardon, so they are called)." Ozell's comment serves to illuminate Smollett's use of his sources: "*This Parenthesis relating to* Hogs, *is left out by* Stevens, *and other Translators, but judiciously retain'd by* Jarvis, *who observes* [in his note on the passage], 'Our author here ridicules the affected delicacy of the *Spaniards* and *Italians,* who look upon it as ill manners to name the word *hog* or *swine,* as too gross an image.' *The Reader* [Ozell continues] *will find the like Excuse repeated at every mention of the Word* Hog" (Motteux/Ozell).

5. "*Sano de Castella* . . . a crafty knave": Original: "los sanos de Castilla." Compare Stevens: "Sáno . . . . *Sáno de Castilla,* in cant, a dissembling thief." The misspelling notwithstanding, Smollett is the first translator to render correctly this expression from the language of Germania, the thieves' slang of Spain. Jarvis has "The host thought he called him *Castellano* because he took him for an honest *Castilian:*"; his note, repeating the remarks of previous translators, states: "*Castellano* in *Spanish* signifies both a *governour of a castle,* and a *native of* Castile."

6. "This circumstance of the ladies disarming the knight . . . in salutation": In this note, Smollett recalls two passages from Ste. Palaye: (1) *Mémoire* 2: "Le vainqueur conduit dans le Palais, y étoit desarmé par les Dames qui le revêtoient d'habits précieux" (20:630); and (2) *Mémoire* 1: referring to the knight's divesting himself of helmet, lance, and sword "pour entrer dans une église, ou dans un autre lieu respectable, & dans les nobles maisons où il arrivoit. Nous pouvons croire que cet usage d'ôter son heaume, a donné la première origine à l'usage de se découvrir dans les lieux, & pour les personnes à qui l'on doit de la considération" (20:607).

7. "Never was knight so honoured . . . into the world": A parody of lines from the ballad quoted below, p. 83 (pt. 1, bk. 2, chap. 5).

8. "In the original, or kid to he-goat": Original: "el cabrito que el cabron." Smollett is alone among translators in preferring sheep to goats. (The note was added in the second edition.)

## Chapter 3

1. "This request was a little premature . . . demand it": With this note, compare Ste. Palaye, *Mémoire* 2, n. 11: "Comme le parrain [godfather] faisoit des présens à celui qu'il tenoit sur les fonts . . . de même aussi celui qui conféroit la Chevalerie devoit faire quelque don, accorder quelque grace à celui qui l'avoit reçûe." To illustrate this custom, Ste. Palaye quotes from the romance *Lancelot du Lac*: "*Comme c'étoit . . . la coustume alors, le nouveau Chevalier pria Galand* (qui lui avoit conféré la Chevalerie) *de lui accorder le premier don qu'il lui demandoit, & qu'en pareil cas on ne doit jamais refuser à son nouveau Chevalier, si la demande n'estoit déraisonnable, ou préjudiciable à celui à qui elle estoit faite*" (20:718).

2. "Literally the colt of Cordova . . . . sharpers": Original: "potro de Cordova." In this note Smollett conflates Stevens: "Potro, a colt. . . . *El pótro de Cordova*, a square in the city of *Cordova*, where a fountain gushes out from a horse's mouth"; and Motteux's comment: "*These are all Places noted for Rogueries and disorderly Doings.*"

3. "Here the landlord was more selfish . . . . half the number": Compare Ste. Palaye, *Mémoire* 4: "le Chevalier, conformément à l'ancien privilège des soldats Romains, étoit exempt de payer les droits de vente des denrées & des autres marchandises achetées pour son usage particulier, & même de toute espèce de péage. . . . Outre que les Chevaliers ne pouvoient être appelés en justice qu'avec les ménagemens & les égards que l'on devoit à leur dignité, s'ils obtenoient des dépens contre leurs parties, ces dépens étoient doubles de ceux que l'on adjugeoit aux Écuyers; mais aussi lorsqu'ils méritoient d'être condamnés, d'autant plus coupables qu'ils devoient aux autres l'exemple de toutes les vertus, & principalement de l'équité, ils payoient une amende une fois plus forte que celle des Écuyers. En suivant la même proportion, il fut ordonné aux Chevaliers en 1411, au siége de Dun-le-Roi, de porter huit fascines, tandis que l'on se contentoit de quatre seulement de la part des Écuyers" (20:666–67).

4. "This custom of watching armour in church . . . . the combat-proof": Compare Ste. Palaye, *Mémoire* 2: "Des jeunes austères, des nuits passées en prières (15) avec un prêtre & des parrains, dans des églises ou dans des chapelles . . . étoient les préliminaires de la céremonie par laquelle le novice alloit être ceint de l'épée de Chevalier" (20:615). In note 15, Ste. Palaye adds: "Cette pieuse coûtume, connue sous le nom *de la veille des armes*, avoit été observée dès les premiers temps pour les duels judiciaires ou épreuves du duel." That the knights invoked the aid of a patron saint in this pious practice is clear from Ste. Palaye's recalling the instance of a certain champion who, having been victorious in a duel of this kind, "rendre graces à Dieu sur le tombeau de St. Cibar où il avoit veillé la nuit précédente" (20:720). In *Sir Launcelot Greaves* (chap. 5), Smollett's quixotic hero observes these ceremonies on the eve of his being dubbed knight-errant.

5. "The slap on the shoulders . . . bold and loyal": Compare Ste. Palaye, *Mémoire* 2: "Alors le seigneur qui devoit lui conférer l'Ordre se levoit de son siége ou de son trône, & lui donnoit l'accolade ou l'accolée: c'étoit ordinairement trois coups du plat de son épée nue sur l'épaule, ou sur le col de celui qu'il faisoit Chevalier; c'étoit quelquefois un coup de la paulme de la main sur la joue. . . . En donnant l'accolade, le seigneur prononçoit ces paroles, ou d'autres semblables; *au nom de Dieu, de St. Michel & de St. George je te fais Chevalier;* auxquelles on ajoûtoit quelquefois ces mots, *soyez preux, hardi & loyal*" (20:616). Again, compare *Sir Launcelot Greaves* (chap. 5) as the ceremony of the hero's initiation into the order of knight-errantry concludes: "then we heard a loud slap which echoed through the whole chapel, and the stranger pronounce with an audible and solemn voice, 'In the name of God, St. Michael, and St. George, I dub thee knight—be faithful, bold, and fortunate.'"

## Chapter 4

1. "reproof and advice": Original: "reprehension y consejo." Compare the titles of Smollett's verse satires, *Advice* (1746) and *Reproof* (1747).

## Chapter 5

1. "The name of a good-natured enchantress . . . . was dislocated": Cervantes prefixed burlesque verses by "Urganda the Unknown" to the original edition of *Don Quixote* (see above, the "Life," p. 13, n. 23); Smollett alludes to her elsewhere in *Roderick Random* (chap. 50) and *Ferdinand Count Fathom* (chap. 23). With his comments in this note, compare Ste. Palaye, *Mémoire* 1: "J'en crois donc volontiers nos Romanciers, lorsqu'ils disent que les Demoiselles & les Dames savoient donner, même aux blessés (17), les secours ordinaires, habituels & assidus qu'une main adroite & compatissante est capable de leur procurer" (20:603). In note 17 to this passage, Ste. Palaye quotes the following passage from Perceforest: "*Atant*, dit une des héroïnes du roman de Perceforest, *beau neveu il me semble que vous avez votre bras à mal aise. Par ma foy, respondit Norgal, chere Dame il est ainsi, si vous prie que garde y veuillez prendre. Lors la Dame appella une sienne fille qui se nommoit Helaine, la quelle fist grant chere à son cousin, puis print garde à son bras, & trouva qu'il estoit hors de son lieu, & fist tant qu'elle lui remist; puis dist, mon cousin, allez vous en, car vous estes guery*" (20:702).

## Chapter 6

1. "In the original *Quirieleyson* . . . Lord have mercy": Previous translators have "Don *Kyrie-eleison*"—which, as Ozell remarks, is "*Greek for* Lord have Mercy upon us" (Motteux/Ozell).
2. "contents unknown": Original: "à carga cerrada." Smollett follows Jarvis, who first translated the phrase, commenting: "A mercantile phrase used in bills of lading." See also Stevens: "Cárga, a burden, a load. . . . *Cárga cerráda*, any thing bought or taken upon content, without examining particulars."

## Chapter 7

1. "How comes Juana . . . into Mary?": Original: "Juana Gutierrez . . . Mari Gutierrez." Smollett follows Shelton and Shelton/Stevens in preserving this inconsistency in the original, presumably because he suspected that Cervantes intended it as a trap for "hypercritics." See below, p. 671 n. (pt. 2, bk. 4, chap. 7), where he comments on Cervantes, compounding the confusion by having his hero scoff at the author of the spurious sequel to his story: "he says the wife of my squire Sancho Panza, is called Mary Gutierrez, whereas her name is Teresa Panza . . . ." Other translators silently emend the text to remove the inconsistency, Motteux preferring Joan, and Jarvis and Motteux/Ozell, Mary.

## Chapter 8

1. "Here Don Quixote . . . . battle of Pavia": In this note, except for the allusion to Davy Gam (for which see below), Smollett recalls two passages in Ste. Palaye: (1) *Mémoire* 4, n. 6: "*Nul homme, s'il n'estoit Chevalier, n'osoit combattre un Chevalier*" (20:781); and (2) *Mémoire* 1: "Chaque Écuyer étoit attentif à tous les mouvemens de son maître, pour lui donner, en cas d'accident, de nouvelles armes, parer les coups qu'on lui portoit, le relever & lui donner un

cheval frais . . . (43)" (20:608). In note 43, Ste. Palaye illustrates this custom by quoting Bran-
tôme, as follows: *"J'ai ouï dire aux anciens Capitaines, que jadis par les vieilles coûtumes des battailes,
les grands & premiers écuyers des rois de France devoient être toujours auprès d'eux, sans jamais les de-
semparer ni abandonner, & ne faire que parer aux coups qu l'on donne à leurs Maîtres, ni sans s'amuser
à autre chose que cela. Ainsi qu'on dit que fit ce brave & grand escuyer de S. Severin à la bataille de
Pavie, à l'endroit du roy François, aussi y mourut-il en la bonne grace & louenge de son Roy qui le sceut
bien dire peu après"* (20:708).

"Davy Gam, Esquire," as Shakespeare styled him in *Henry V* (4.8.109), figures prominently
in Smollett's account of the Battle of Agincourt in *Complete History,* 2 (1757): 262, 264. The
king having been stunned by the blow of a battle ax, Smollett writes: "In all probability he must
have fallen a sacrifice to the determined resolution of [the French knights], had not David Gam
the Welsh captain, and two other officers of the same nation, rushed between him and the as-
sailants, and lost their lives in his defence" (2:264).

2. "spoke . . . in bad Castilian, and worse Biscayan": Shelton had commented on this passage that
*"The* Biscainers *generally speak broken* Spanish, *as is imitated in the Original."* Smollett's prede-
cessors sought to achieve this effect by having the Biscayan speak stilted, archaic English;
Smollett comes nearer the mark by having him speak in a Somerset dialect reminiscent of
Fielding's Squire Western.

3. "The literal meaning . . . carriest to the cat": Original: "el agua quan presto veràs que al gato
llevás." With Smollett's rendering of this phrase and his note, compare Stevens: "Gáto . . . .
*Veámos quién lléva el gáto al água,* let us see who will carry the cat to the water. That is, let us see
who will have the best on't." Of Smollett's predecessors, only Shelton attempted to render the
original literally: "thou shalt see the water as soone as thou shalt carry away the Cat."

4. "This behaviour of Don Quixote . . . to demand it": Compare Ste. Palaye, *Mémoire* 4, n. 6: "La
loi étoit conforme à cet usage: elle n'accordoit point à l'Écuyer le duel ou gage de bataille con-
tre le Chevalier. Néanmoins comme les Chevaliers abusant de leurs privilèges & sûrs de l'im-
punité, auroient pû commettre des violences & des injustices au préjudice des Écuyers, notre
ancienne jurisprudence apporta des remèdes à cet inconvénient: elle soûmit dans certains cas
le Chevalier à se battre à pied contre l'Écuyer, & comme lui armé seulement de l'épée & de
l'écu" (20:781).

# Book 2

## Chapter 1

1. "Panza, in Castilian . . . spindleshanks": Original: "Pança, y de çancas." With Smollett's note,
compare Stevens: "Pánça, the paunch, the belly" and "Zánca, vid. çánça . . . a spindle shank "

## Chapter 2

1. "Of what further happened between Don Quixote and the Biscayan": Original: "De lo que
mas le avino à Don Quixote con el Vizcayno, y de Peligro en que se vio con una turba de
Yangueses." This is the wording of all the original editions, which Motteux thus rendered in
full: *"What farther befell* Don Quixote *with the* Biscayan; *and of the Danger he ran among a Par-
cel of* Janguessians." Since, however, this chapter has nothing to do either with Don Quixote's
adventures with the Biscayan (which had ended in the preceding chapter) or with the danger
to him posed by the Yanguesans (which occurs later, in bk. 3, chap. 1), Pineda in 1738 altered

the chapter heading to read: "*Del discurso que tùvo Don Quixote con su buen Escudero Sancho Pança.*" This emendation, authorized by the Spanish Academy, was first translated by Jarvis: "*Of the discourse* Don Quixote *had with his good squire* Sancho Pança."

2. "Santa Hermandad . . . safe": Smollett's note in *Gil Blas* (bk. 1, chap. 4; 1:23 n.) is similar but less concise: "The holy brotherhood in Spain, called la Santa Hermandad: was formerly, an association to suppress robbers, in times of civil commotion; and at this day, is an establishment kept up through all the kingdoms and provinces of Spain, for the same purpose." Stevens: "Hermandád . . . . *La santa hermandád*, a brotherhood formerly instituted in *Spain*, in times of great confusions, to suppress robbers, and continued to this day, by which the roads are very much secured, because the brotherhood is spread through all *Spain*, and therefore travelling is very safe."

3. "These ridiculous oaths . . . . sackcloth and hair": Ste. Palaye, *Mémoire* 3, tells the story of "Philippe le Bon duc de Bourgogne," who, at Lille in 1453, roused his fellow knights to take part in a crusade against the Turks by proclaiming at a grand banquet "le vœu du Paon ou du Faisan," which was considered "le plus authentique de tous les vœux" (20:636): "*Je voue à Dieu mon créateur tout premièrement, & à la très-glorieuse Vierge sa mère, & après aux Dames & au Faisan, &c. Le reste contenoit des promesses authentiques de porter la guerre chez les Infidèles . . . . Le vœu du Duc fut un signal auquel toute sa Cour répondit par d'autres vœux diversifiés à l'infini: . . . Tous s'imposoient des pénitences arbitraires, qu'ils juroient de continuer jusqu'à l'entier accomplissement de leur vœu. Les uns, par exemple, devoient ne point coucher dans un lit; les autres ne point manger sur nappe; ceux-ci s'abstenir de viande ou de vin certains jours de la semaine; ceux-là ne porter jamais certaine partie de leur armure, ou la porter jour & nuit, & quelques autres se vêtir d'étamine ou de haire, &c.*" (20:639–40). In *Sir Launcelot Greaves* (chap. 9) Crabshaw imitates the good duke Philip by invoking "the peacock and the ladies."

4. "Geoffroi de Rançon . . . . pulled off his horse": Compare Ste. Palaye, *Mémoire* 4, n. 16, quoting Joinville from a manuscript acquired by Louis XV in 1740: "*Quant nous feusmes à Poictiers je vis un Chevalier qui avoit nom Messire Geoffroi de Rançon, qui pour un grant oultrage que le comte de la Marche lui avoit faict, avoir juré ses Saincts qu'il ne seroit jamais roigné à guise de Chevalerie, mais porteroit greve ainsi comme les femmes portoient jusqu'à tant qu'il se verroit vangé du comte de la Marche, par luy ou par autruy: & quant Messire Geoffroy vit le comte de la Marche, sa femme & ses enfans agenoillé devant le Roy, qui lui crioient mercy, fit apporter un treteau & se fist oster sa greve & se fit rogner tout à coup en présence du Roy, du comte de la Marche & de tous ceux qui là estoient*" (20:788–89). In rendering this passage in his note, Smollett mistook the archaic term *greve* (referring to the old-fashioned manner of a woman's parting her hair on the forehead) for the singular form of *greves* (signifying boots or greaves), which he translated as "buskin." (See Randle Cotgrave, *A Dictionarie of the French and English Tongues*, ed. W. S. Woods [Columbia: University of South Carolina Press, 1968], "Greve" and "Greves.") Ste. Palaye quotes the above passage from Joinville in commenting on the following statement, which Smollett paraphrases in the concluding paragraph of his note: "Les Chevaliers . . . se rasoient le devant de la tête, soit de peur d'être saisis par les cheveux, s'ils perdoient leur casque dans le combat" (20:662).

5. "We read in Perceforest . . . . *nourriture des Heraux*": Compare Ste. Palaye, *Mémoire* 5, n. 5, citing Perceforest: "Nos Héros errant de pays en pays, par couroient sur-tout les forêts, presque sans autre équipage que celui qui étoit nécessaire à la défense de leur personne, vivoient uniquement de leur chasse: des pierres plates plantées en terre, qu'on avoit exprès placées pour eux, servoient à faire les apprêts de leurs viandes, comme à prendre leurs repas; les Chevreuils qu'ils avoient tués étoient mis sur ces tables, & recouverts d'autres pierres avec lesquelles ils

les pressoient pour en exprimer le sang, d'où cette viande est nommé dans nos Romans *Chevraux de presse, nourriture des Héraux:* du sel & quelques épices, les seules munitions dont on se chargeoit, en faisoient tout l'assaisonnement" (20:818).

6. "*Volatiles* in the original . . . more in character": Original: "la proveerè . . . de otras cosas volatiles, y de mas sustancia." Smollett added this note in the second edition. He is alone among translators in attempting to preserve the double sense of *cosas volatiles,* which can mean either things that fly (fowl) or things that are light and evanescent. For the latter sense, see the Royal Dictionary (1739), "VOLATIL." All other translators follow Shelton: "I will provide fowles and other things, that are of more substance."

## Chapter 3

1. "A sort of small fiddle . . . shepherds": Compare Stevens: "RABÉL, an instrument call'd a rebeck, a little sort of a fiddle all of a piece, with only three strings, us'd by shepherds." Smollett's usage is cited by the *OED* (rebeck *sb²*).

2. "The reader will perceive . . . . some other women": The verses Smollett criticizes are from Jarvis's translation. "The original sentiments" that Smollett renders "literally" into English prose are these: "No cuento las alabanças, / Que de tu belleza he dicho, / Que aunque verdaderas, hazen / Ser yo de algunas mal quisto."

## Chapter 4

1. "carabances": Smollett's phonetic spelling: the original was "garvanços," defined by Stevens as "a sort of pease," which is the rendering of all previous translators except Jarvis, who has "vetches." For the spelling "garavances" and Smollett's note, see below, p. 561 (pt. 2, bk. 3, chap. 6).

2. "In the original . . . natural and expressive": Original: "aunque vivays mas años que Sarna. Dezid Sarra, replicò Don Quixote. . . . Harto vive la Sarna, respondiò Pedro. . . . que por aver tanta diferencia de sarna à Sarra . . . ." For his substitution of St. Paul's/Paul for *sarna/Sarra* Smollett seems indebted to Stevens: "SÁRRA . . . . Prov. *Viéjo cómo Sárra:* As old as *Sarah.* We say, as old as *Methusalah,* or as old as St. *Paul* is. The *Spanish,* some will have to be as old as *Sarah, Abraham's* Wife . . . . But generally most people say, *Viéjo cómo la sarna,* as old as the itch, which is of great antiquity; tho it is agreed that this is only a corruption of ignorant People, saying *Sárna* for *Sárra.*"

## Chapter 5

1. "For never sure . . . from Britain came": Original: "nunca Fuera Cavallero de Damas tan bien servido, como fuera Lançarote quando de Bretaña vino." Smollett follows Shelton/Stevens and Motteux in rendering this as a quatrain; the lines are from the ballad parodied by Cervantes above, p. 35 (bk. 1, chap. 2).

2. "When a knight challenged . . . . the arms they should use": Smollett's long comment is based on Ste. Palaye, *Mémoire* 3, n. 4: "Les Chevaliers qui faisoient des emprises ou entreprises d'armes, soit courtoises, soit à outrance, c'est-à-dire meurtrières, chargeoient leurs armes de chaines [the example cited is a '*chaine d'or*'], ou d'autres marques attachées par la main des Dames . . . . [¶] Olivier de la Marche . . . explique aussi les formalités observées, en 1445, pour lever ces emprises, c'est-à-dire pour les ôter à celui qui les portoit. On lit dans le récit détaillé que cet historien nous a conservé des armes . . . à la cour de Bourgogne, que Galiot se pro-

posant d'accepter le défi d'armes fait par le seigneur de Ternant, *Il s'agenouilla devant le duc de Bourgogne, luy requérant qu'il luy donnast congé & licence de toucher à l'emprise que portoit le seigneur Ternant, & le bon Duc le fit lever & luy donna le congé. Lors demanda Galiot aux rois d'armes & béraux la coustume du pays, & dist qu'en son pays quand le requérant arrache l'emprise de son compagnon, c'est pour la vie de l'un & de l'autre; mais quand on n'y fait que toucher seulement, c'est pour Chevalerie. Sur quoy lui respondit Toison-d'or que le seigneur de Ternant avoit chargé son emprise pour Chevalerie, & que la coustume estoit de toucher à l'emprise quand on estoit présent. Lors s'avança ledict Escuyer & toucha à l'emprise du Chevalier, en soy agenouillant bien bas, & dist noble Chevalier je touche à votre emprise, & au plaisir de Dieu vous fourniray & accompliray tout ce que je sçauray que vous desirez de faire, soit à pié, soit à cheval. Et le seigneur de Ternant le mercia bien humblement, & luy dist que bien fust-il venu, & qu'en icelle journée il luy envoyerait par escript les armes qu'il desiroit à faire & accomplir.* [¶] Il falloit, pour lever ces emprises, avoir la permission du Seigneur, à la Cour duquel on se trouvoit, ainsi qu'on vient de le voir" (20:752–54).

3. "Cachopines . . . Mexico": Compare Stevens: "CACHOPÍNES, a name by which the Indians of *Mexico* call the Europeans."

4. "A SONG of Despair": In the original and all previous translations the song opens a new chapter. Original: "CAPITULO XIV. | *Donde se ponem los Versos desesperados del disunto Pastor, con otros no esperados sucessos.*" The song is entitled "Cancion de Grisostomo." Jarvis: "CHAP. VI. | *Wherein are rehearsed the despairing verses of the deceased shepherd, with other unexpected events.* | CHRYSOSTOM's SONG."

# Book 3

## Chapter 1

1. "in cuerpo": Naked. *OED* cites *Roderick Random*, chap. 10: "the drummer, who had given his only shirt to be washed, appeared *in cuerpo.*" See also *Ferdinand Count Fathom*, chap. 41: "he got up and opened the door in *cuerpo*" (p. 193).

2. "fairy blas": Original: "feo Blas," literally, "ugly Blas." Smollett was first to attempt an English equivalent for Sancho's garbled version of "Fierabras," whose balsam is mentioned above (bk. 2, chap. 2). Watts adopted Smollett's phrase.

3. "searcloth": Original: "bizmas." Compare Stevens: "BÍZMA, a sear-cloth to keep together a broken bone that is set." Below in this chapter (p. 101), see the variant spelling "cerecloth," cited by the *OED*. Previous translators have "plaisters."

4. "Tizona . . . the Moors": Smollett and Jarvis take this note verbatim from Stevens ("TIZONA").

5. "the naked rock": Original: "la peña Pobre." Only Smollett and Shelton/Stevens seem unaware that "Peña Pobre" (Poor Rock) is the name of the desolate island to which Amadis of Gaul retires after Oriana rejects him; see below, p. 169 (bk. 3, chap. 11).

## Chapter 3

1. "cakes and gingerbread": Original: "tortas y pan pintado." Compare Smollett writing at a busy time to William Huggins (20 June 1757, *Letters*, 61): "You talk of the *Pistrinum* or Cart's Tail; that is, according to the Spanish Proverb, no more than *panpintado*, Cakes and Gingerbread to what I undergo." Smollett's translation of *pan pintado* is a closer English equivalent than any previous attempt (*e.g.*, Jarvis: "tarts and cheese-cakes"), and was adopted by Putnam. For this same expression, see below, pp. 386 (pt. 2, bk. 1, chap. 2), 694 (pt. 2, bk. 4, chap. 11), and 716

(pt. 2, bk. 4, chap. 16). For a variant rendering, "custards and puff-paste," see p. 452 (pt. 2, bk. 1, chap.17).

2. "Literally, What is left in . . . his inkhorn": Original: "si se dexò algo en el tintero." Jarvis translated this expression as "if any thing be left at the bottom of the ink-horn," in a note explaining the sense of it as "leaving the work imperfect." In the preceding chapter above, Smollett renders the expression as "the most substantial circumstances are left, as it were, in the inkhorn" (p. 104); later, in bk. 4, chap. 4, he varies it to read "without leaving one syllable untold" (p. 221).

3. "Don Quixote seems in this place to have forgot . . . . a bone to pick": Owing, it would seem, to his recent friendship with William Huggins, translator of *Orlando Furioso*, Smollett in the second edition added several notes on the Orlando romances of Boiardo and Ariosto. Boiardo's *Orlando innamorato* (1483) was recast by Francesco Berni in 1541; a new edition of Berni's version was published in Florence in 1725. In November 1759 Smollett read this work in Huggins's personal copy. (See *Letters* [27 November 1759], 84.) On Smollett's friendship with Huggins, see above, p. xlv, n. 8. Smollett's quotation (with the misspellings "danari" for "denari" and "cenium" for "ceniam") is from Berni's *Orlando innamorato* (2.18.35).

## Chapter 4

1. "In the original from Ceca to Mecca . . . . Cordova": Original: "andar de ceca en meca." Compare Stevens: "CÉCA . . . a place of devotion among the Moors in the city of *Cordova*, to which they us'd to go in pilgrimage from other places. Thence the Prov. *Andár de Céca en Méca:* To go from *Ceca* to *Mecca*. That is, to saunter about to no purpose, as the Moors did upon these two pilgrimages." With Smollett's translation, compare Shelton/Stevens: "sauntering about after this manner from Post to Pillar, and from Pillar to Post."

2. "carried off . . . three or four of his grinders": In *Travels*, Letter V (Boulogne, 12 September 1763), Smollett recalls this episode as depicted in Hayman's illustration (see below, p. 120): he describes M. De Louvigny as "tall, thin, and weather-beaten, not unlike the picture of Don Quixote after he had lost his teeth" (p. 36).

3. "I have endeavoured to preserve an alliteration . . . *Diamante*": Original: "en mucho mas se ha de estimar un diente que un diamante." Smollett's predecessors sacrificed the alliteration to preserve the literal sense, as in Shelton: "a tooth is much more to be esteemed than a Diamond."

## Chapter 5

1. "to quake like quicksilver": Original: "temblar como un azogado." Smollett follows Jarvis: "trembled . . . as if he had been quick-silver"; but Shelton was more accurate: "did tremble like one infected by the savour of Quick-silver." Stevens has "AZOGÁDO . . . a man that is infected with the fumes of quicksilver." See also below, "like quicksilver," p. 530 (pt. 2, bk. 2, chap.15).

2. "Knights engaged themselves . . . by force of arms": Ste. Palaye, *Mémoire* 2, commends the following "loix de Chevalerie renfermées dans le serment" taken by a knight: "En vertu de ces loix, les veuves, les orphelins (36) & tous ceux que l'injustice faisoit gémir dans l'oppression, étoient en droit de réclamer la protection d'un Chevalier, & d'exiger pour leur défense, non seulement le secours de son bras, mais encore le sacrifice de son sang & de sa vie. Se soustraire à cette obligation, c'étoit manquer à une dette sacrée; c'étoit se deshonorer pour le reste de ses jours. Les Dames (37) avoient encore un privilège plus particulier. Sans armes pour se main-

tenir dans la possession de leurs biens, dénuées des moyens de prouver leur innocence at-
taquée, elles auroient vû souvent leur fortune & leurs terres devenir la proie d'un voisin in-
juste & puissant, ou leur réputation succomber sous les traits de la calomnie, si les Chevaliers
n'eussent toûjours été prêts à s'armer pour les défendre: c'étoit un des points capitaux de leur
institution, de ne point médire des Dames & de ne point permettre que personne osât en mé-
dire devant eux" (20:618). See also the notes to this passage (20:725–26, nn. 36–37), on which
Smollett draws below in a note to p. 654 n. † (pt. 2, bk. 4, chap. 4).

3. "according to the canon; 'Si quis . . . diabolo, &c.'": Original: "*Iuxta illud, si quis suadente
diabolo, &c.*" Jarvis translates the Latin, "*According to that*, If any one at the instigation of the
devil, *&c.*"

## Chapter 6

1. "In Castilian, Boçina signifies . . . resemblance": Original: "la boca de la bozina." See Stevens:
"Boçína, an hunter's cornet; . . . It is also the Spanish name of the northern constellation
called *ursa minor,* or the lesser bear; because the stars that form it are placed in the shape of a
cornet." Also Jarvis, who translates the phrase "the muzzle of the north-bear," commenting:
"Literally *the mouth of the hunting-horn or cornet:* so they call the *ursa minor,* from a fancied
configuration of the stars of that constellation."

2. "Cato the censer of Rome": Original: "Canton Zonzorino Romano." Smollett ignores San-
cho's blunder; he meant to say "Cato el Censorino." "Zonzorino," as Putnam notes, is a play
on *zonzo* (blockhead). Jarvis, like earlier translators, tried to retain the humor of the blunder,
commenting: "A mistake for Cato *the Censor.*"

3. "all that, when it is dry, will rub out": Original: "todo saldrà en la colada." See Stevens:
"Coláda, buck or lye for linnen. . . . *Tòdo saldrá en la coláda,* it will all out in the buck [wash-
tub]." Smollett here echoes the peculiar rendering of Shelton/Stevens: "it will rub off when it
is dry"; later, p. 557, he preserves the literal sense: "what is amiss will come out in the wash-
ing" (pt. 2, bk. 3, chap. 4).

## Chapter 7

1. "Oregano . . . bloody nose": Original: "oregano sea, y no batanes." Stevens: "Orégano, the
herb *origanum,* a sort of wild marjoram." Smollett's predecessors either ignored the literal
sense of the original or missed it altogether: Jarvis has "I pray god . . . it may not prove another
fulling-mill adventure"; Shelton, "pray God, that it be a purchase of gold, and not fulling
Mils [*sic*]."

2. "The Spaniards of old . . . the Sueldos": Original: "de devengar quinientos sueldos." Smollett
is alone in rendering this expression "the revenge of the Sueldos," but for his note he is chiefly
indebted to Jarvis's commentary: "The original is *y de devengar quinientos sueldos,* literally, *to re-
venge five hundred sueldo's.* It is a proverbial expression to signify a person's being a gentleman,
and took its rise from the following occasion. The *Spaniards* of *Old Castile* [were] obliged to
pay a yearly tribute . . . to the *Moors* . . . [of] five hundred *sueldo's* or pieces of *Spanish* coin. But
in process of time the *Spaniards,* by force of arms, delivered themselves from that gross impo-
sition; and that heroical action being performed by men of figure and fortune, they charac-
terize by this expression a man of bravery and honour, and a true lover of his country." Stevens,
who understood that *devengar* could mean either "to revenge" or "to earn, to be in the king's
pay," emphasized the ambiguity of the expression: see Stevens, "Hidálgo . . . *Hidálgo de de-
vengár quiniéntos suéldos.*" According to Juan Huarte, the expression was applied to "*a Gentle-*

*man . . . having five hundred Shillings of Pay . . . and being of a known House*" (Edward Bellamy, trans., *Examen de Ingenios: or, The Trial of the Wits* [1698], 355, n.).

3. "Literally, Never beg, when you can take": Original: "No pidas de grado lo que pueden [*sic*] tomar por fuerça," a proverbial expression that Stevens ("Grádo") translates, "Do not ask for that to be given you freely, which you can take by force." Smollett's rhyming version of this in the text is his own ("Who would beg a benison, that for the taking may have venison"), but his literal translation is a more concise rendering of Jarvis: *"Never stand begging for that which you may take by force."*

4. "In the original, A snatch from behind a bush . . . good men": Original: "Mas vale falto [*sic:* salto] de mata, que ruega de hombres buenos." Again, Smollett's rhymed version of this in the text is his own ("Better thieve than grieve"). He is also alone in rendering "salto de mata" as "A snatch from behind a bush"; all previous translators agree with Stevens ("Sálto, a leap. . . . Also an assault, a robbery"), translating *"sálto de mata"* as "A leap over a hedge, or bush." See below, p. 713, "What prayers ne'er can gain, a leap from a hedge will obtain" (pt. 2, bk. 4, chap. 15).

## Chapter 8

1. "A crime that is punished . . . the transgression": For this note Smollett, like Jarvis, was indebted to Shelton/Stevens: *"Instead of the Pillory in Spain, they carry that sort of Malefactors on an Ass and in a particular Habit, along the Streets, the Cryer going before, and proclaiming their Crime."*

2. "ear-broker": Original: "corredor de orejo." A pimp (Stevens: "Corredór").

3. "It was the custom of knights . . . . his coat of arms": Ste. Palaye, *Mémoire* 4, writing of the accoutrements of the knights: "la cotte (5) d'armes, faite d'une simple étoffe armoriée, étoit l'enseigne de leur prééminence sur tous les autres ordres de l'État & de la guerre" (20:661). He continues in note 5: "Il suffit, pour faire connoître la cotte d'armes, de rapporter comment le duc de Brabant s'en fit une à la hâte, pour aller aux ennemies à la battaille d'Azincourt, en 1415: *Alors survint le duc Antoine de Braban, qui avoit esté mandé par le roy de France, lequel y arriva moult hastivement. . . . & print une des bannières de ses trompettes, & y fit un pertuis par le milieu dont il fist cottes d'armes*" (20:780).

## Chapter 9

1. "This is an oversight . . . Segovia": Compare Jarvis: "The provisions were eaten before, and the wallet left in the inn for the reckoning; besides, the loose coat, or cloak, which the galley-slaves had taken away from *Sancho*, had been made use of as a bag for the provisions when they were first taken. *Quære*, how came *Sancho* by a fresh wallet of provisions?"

2. "A chain of dusky mountains . . . Andaluzia": Compare Jarvis: "*Sierra morena*. A great mountain (or rather chain of mountains, for so *Sierra* signifies) which divides the kingdom of *Castile* from the province of *Andaluzia*, and remarkable for being *(morena)* of a *Moorish* or swarthy colour." Also Stevens: "Sierra . . . . *Siérra Moréna*."

3. "Here Cervantes hath been caught napping . . . Passamonte": Jarvis, as well as Motteux/Ozell, comments on this slip.

4. "As it is impossible to preserve the original . . . little altered": Original: "Fili . . . . hilo." Shelton had explained Sancho's blunder as *"An allusion to the Spanish word Hilo, signifying a threed [sic]"*; Jarvis silently substituted Chloe for Phyllis in order to achieve the alliteration "Chloe . . . . clue."

5. "surrounded": Traveled around; made the circuit of (*OED:* surround *v.*, II.4).
6. "I don't chuse to steal a dog . . . his neck": Original: "no quiero perro con cencerro." Smollett, having altered the sense of this proverbial expression (which Jarvis, following Shelton, correctly translates: "I will not have a dog with a bell"), is alone in commenting on Cervantes' seeming carelessness in characterization.

## Chapter 10

1. "Queen Madasima . . . woods and desarts": An abridgment of Jarvis: "*Elisabat* is a skilful surgeon in *Amadis de Gaul*, who performs wonderful cures; and queen *Madasima* is wife to *Gantasi*, and makes a great figure in the aforesaid romance. They travel and lye together in woods and deserts, without any imputation on her honour."

## Chapter 11

1. "in the days of Hyssop": Original: "en tiempo de Guisopete." Jarvis retained the form of the original, commenting: "Meaning *Æsop*, I suppose"; Motteux/Ozell translated the phrase, "in *Æsop*'s Time," adding: "*The* Spaniards *vulgarly call* Æsop Giosopete. . . . *The* French *too, according to* Oudin, *commonly call Æsop* Isopet." Smollett's translation is unique, perhaps based on Stevens: "Isopo, the herb hyssop . . . . It is also in Spanish the name for the famous writer of fables, by us more properly call'd *Æsop*."
2. "that same Abat": Original: "aquel Abad." Jarvis, followed by Motteux/Ozell, had explained Sancho's blunder: "*Sancho*, remembering only the latter part of master *Elisabat*'s name, pleasantly calls him an Abbot."
3. "the poor rock": See above, bk. 3, chap. 1, p. 101 and n. 5.
4. "The Beautiful obscure": Jarvis, following Motteux: "The lovely obscure."
5. "the shepherd Matias Ambrosio": Original: "pastor de Matias Ambrosio." Watts noticed that a printer's error in the original editions altered the phrase "pastor de marras Ambrosio" to "pastor de Marias Ambrosio" or, as here, "pastor de Matias Ambrosio." Jarvis alone among Smollett's predecessors corrects the error: "that whileome [*marras*] shepherd, *Ambrosio.*"
6. "Lo! Sancho's ass hath disappeared again!": Jarvis: "Here *Dapple* is lost again, though he has been with *Sancho* ever since the very morning that *Gines* stole him, 'till the minute that the bill for the colts was to be given."
7. "from hell there is no retention": Original: "Quien ha infierno . . . nula es retencio." Jarvis explained Sancho's blunder: "*No redemption* [redemción], he means."
8. "Odds-niggers!": Original: "Pesia à mi," an oath that Putnam renders as "Why, damn me." Shelton has "Good God!" and Jarvis "Ods my life!" Smollett's translation is a curious variant, unrecorded in the *OED*, of the archaic expletive "odsnigs" or "God's nigs." "Nig" in this usage, if it meant anything at all, did not have the modern sense of "nigger": the earliest recorded use of "nigger" for Negro is that of Smollett's fellow Scot, Robert Burns, in 1786: "How graceles Ham leugh at his Dad, / Which made Canaan a nigger" (*Ordination,* 4); the earliest use of "nig" in the modern sense of "nigger" is 1832.
9. "Theseus": The original has "Perseus" instead of Theseus, an error corrected by both Shelton and Jarvis.
10. "cut a couple of capers": Original: "dio dos çapatetas." Smollett follows Jarvis, who comments: "*Zapatetas.* A kind of capering, striking, at the same time, the sole of the shoe, or foot, with the hand." See also below, "your shoe-slappers," p. 464 (pt. 2, bk. 2, chap. 2).

## Chapter 12

1. "Probably alluding to the epitaph of Phaeton": Jarvis: "This is plainly an allusion to that epitaph of *Phaeton*, in *Ovid*." Jarvis quotes the same passage and supplies the reference (*Metamorphoses* 2.327–28: "Here Phaëthon lies: in Phoebus' car he fared, / And though he greatly failed, more greatly dared" [trans. F. J. Miller, Loeb Library, 1916]).
2. "subterrene and sublime princess!": Original: "Alta y sobájada Señora." Smollett follows Motteux and Jarvis in rendering *sobájada* (literally, "scrubbing") as "subterrene"; Shelton has "unsavorie."

## Chapter 13

1. "Bamba or Wamba, king of the Visigoths . . . Ervige": Compare Moréri: "BAMBA ou WAMBA, Roi des Visigoths en Espagne . . . fut mis sur le thrône . . . le premier septembre 672. Julien Evêque de Tolède parle des merveilles arrivées au sacre de ce Roi [who punished those who committed depredations against the Church] . . . il fit périr une flotte de cent soixante navires Arabes, qui avoient transporté une armée d'Afrique en Espane [*sic*]. Sept ans après Ervige . . . fit donner un poison lent au Roi Bamba, qui se retira dans un monastére le 14 octobre 680, après avoir régné huit ans, un mois & 14 jours. Le premier Canon du VIII Concile de Tolède, qui fut assemblé l'an 681 pour l'élection d'Ervige, remarque que Bamba lui céda le thrône."
2. "There is no such letter . . . with Don Quixote": This note added in the second edition.
3. "Who murdered Sancho I. king of Castile . . . Zamora": Mariana (bk. 9, chap. 6, p. 145) tells of the treachery of Vellido Delphos, who murdered Sancho II (not Sancho I) at the siege of Zamora. But Smollett's source for this note was probably Shelton/Stevens: "Vellido *was a Traytor who Murder'd King* Sancho *of* Castile, *as he lay at the Siege of Zamorra*."
4. "The original *pues presente pocas vezes lo* hazia . . . . literary correspondence": Smollett at first believed that Cervantes had in fact committed the solecism to which he refers in this note added in the second edition. In the first edition, thinking to avoid the error, he altered the text to read: "she had been so sparing of her speech."

# Book 4

## Chapter 1

1. "old, rusty christians": "Christianos viejos ranciosos." Jarvis and Ozell, whom Smollett follows in this translation, explain the phrase as follows: "That is, original *Spaniards*, without mixture of *Moor* or *Jew*, for several generations, such only being qualified for titles of honour" (Jarvis); "Ranciosos *in the Original: a Metaphor taken from rusty* Bacon, *yellow and mouldy, as it were with Age. 'Tis a Farmer's Daughter speaks this*" (Motteux/Ozell).

## Chapter 2

1. "As if he had said Ape-land . . . an ape": Original: "del gran Reyno de Micomicon." Smollett was first to suggest that Cervantes here intended a play on *mico*.
2. "When a knight had once granted a boon . . . . her request": Having cited Joinville to illustrate his assertion that "nulle autre loi n'insiste avec tant de force sur la nécessité de tenir invio-

lablement sa parole *(40)*, & n'inspire tant d'horreur pour le mensonge & la fausseté" (*Mémoire* 2 [20:619]), Ste. Palaye continues in note 40: "Au récit de malheurs arrivés à l'armée Chréti- enne, & de la prison de St. Louis, il joint la description de l'état encore plus déplorable où se trouvoit réduite la Reine sa femme. Instruite de tant d'infortunes, livrée au plus affreux dés- espoir, à des agitations qui ne lui permettoient pas de fermer l'oeil, & n'attendant que le mo- ment d'accoucher, elle se voyoit encore sur le point de tomber vive au pouvoir des Infidèles. Dans cette situation . . . elle prend une dernière résolution, elle se jette aux genoux d'un *Chevalier viel & ancien, de l'aage* [*sic*] *de quatre-vingtz ans & plus*, & le conjure de lui accorder une grace; le vieillard y consent, & lui en donne sa foi. Cette grace unique, demandée avec tant d'instance, étoit de lui couper la tête avant que les Sarrazins la pussent prendre, s'ils devenoient maîtres de la ville de Damiette où elle étoit renfermée. La réponse fait encore mieux voir quelle étoit l'obligation des Chevaliers: il n'avoit pas attendu jusque-là à prendre son parti; *&* *le Chevalier,* dit Joinville, *luy respondit que très-voulentiers il le feroit, & que jà l'avoit-il eû en pen- sée d'ainsi le faire si le cas y escheoit*" (20:729).

## Chapter 3

1. "Don Hacksot or Kicksot": Original: "Don Açote, ò Don Gigote" (literally, "Sir Scourge, or Sir Stew"). The English pronunciation of *Quixote* was, and remains (see *OED*), "kwiksot" (the *o* pronounced as the *au* in "authority"). Characters in Smollett's last two novels similarly gar- ble the name: in *Sir Launcelot Greaves* (chap. 13) the hero is called "Don Quicksot"; and in *Humphry Clinker* Win Jenkins remembers Jery Melford's calling Lismahago "Dunquickset" (p. 294).
2. "This is a diverting example of the Bathos . . . art of sinking": Smollett mimics Jarvis in cit- ing Pope's *Peri Bathous: or, Martinus Scriblerus His Treatise of the Art of Sinking in Poetry* (chap. 11, sec. 3) concerning "THE third Class . . . of the *Diminishing* Figures . . . The ANTI- CLIMAX, where the second Line drops quite short of the first, than which Nothing creates greater Surprize." Jarvis had illustrated the figure by quoting Pope's first example, a couplet of Waller; Smollett instead slightly misquotes Pope's third example, a couplet from John Den- nis, "A Pindaric Ode on the King" (1691), as corrected in the second and subsequent editions: "*Nor Alps nor Pyrenæans keep it out, / —Nor* fortify'd Redoubt" (Pope and Swift's *Miscellanies* [1731], 3 ["The Last Volume"]: 57). See also Edna Leake Steeves, ed. *The Art of Sinking in Po- etry* (New York: King's Crown Press, 1952), 156–57, n. 53:19.
3. "weazond": Original: "el gaznatico." Compare Jarvis: "weason" (*OED*, weasand: gullet, wind- pipe). Previous translators have "Wind-pipe(s)."
4. "If the knight was robbed . . . this occasion?": Jarvis: "It does not appear by the story, either that *Gines* took away *Don Quixote*'s sword, or that the knight had any way exchanged his own for another."
5. "fishing for mushrooms at sea": Original: "pedir cotufas en el golfo." See Smollett's note be- low, p. 389 (pt. 2, bk. 1, chap. 3); see also p. 468 (pt. 2, bk. 2, chap. 3).
6. "without speaking a syllable . . . his intention": Original: "sin dezirle esta boca es mio." Jarvis: "without speaking a word to *Sancho*, or giving him the least warning"; in a note based on Stevens ("BÓCA"), Jarvis explained the idiom: "Literally, *without saying, this mouth is mine.*"

## Chapter 4

1. "without leaving one syllable untold": For Smollett's earlier rendering of this proverbial ex- pression, see above, p. 757, n. 2 (bk. 3, chap. 3).

2. "Literally, Sleeves are good . . . unseasonable": Jarvis rendered this proverbial expression literally, explaining it in a note. Smollett's note, however, seems closer to Jarvis's source, Stevens: "Mánga, a sleeve. . . . Prov. *Buénas son mangas después de Páscua:* Sleeves are good after *Easter.* This they say when any thing that has been long expected or desir'd comes late, or a thing out of season. For tho' the weather grows warm after *Easter,* and people may leave off cloaths, yet if a pair of sleeves be then given, they are not to be refus'd, for a good thing never comes too late."

3. "concerned about . . . potsheards": Though Jarvis rendered this as "how is your worship concerned about trifles!," his note may have suggested Smollett's more colorful version: "The original is, *como vuestra merced lastimado de essos cascos;* in which there is some ambiguity: for, *casco* signifying both *a bit of a broken pot* and *a scull,* it may be rendered, either *how is your worship troubled about these bits of a broken pot,* that is, *these trifles!* or, *how is your worship disordered in your head!* Our translators have chosen the last of these senses. But one would hardly expect *Sancho* should be so free with his master, after so late a drubbing for such sort of liberties; and therefore I have chosen the first, which agrees very well with what follows."

4. "Literally, Took the road in his hands": Original: "tomo el camino en las manos." Smollett's odd rendering of this idiom ("took his foot in his hand") is cited in the *OED* (foot, 29.a). Compare Shelton/Stevens: "took up his Heels and walk'd." The other translators have simply "went on his way" (Shelton), "went off" (Motteux), "marched off" (Jarvis and Motteux/Ozell).

## Chapter 5

1. "It will appear in the sequel . . . could not do": This note was added in the second edition.

2. "made of beans . . . boys divert themselves": Original: "como si fueran hechas de habas, como los fraylecicos que hazen los niños." Jarvis, following Shelton, was more literal: "as if they had been so many bean-cods, of which the children make little puppet-friars," commenting: "Children in *Spain* . . . make puppets resembling friars out of bean-cods by breaking as much of the upper end as discovers part of the first bean, which is to represent the bald head, and letting the broken cod hang back like a cowl."

3. "The original, which is *Curioso impertinente* . . . impertinent": Original: "curioso Impertinente." Compare Jarvis's explanation of the apparent solecism: "*Curioso Impertinente.* I have rendered this title (as all our translators have done) *verbatim;* though, in strict propriety of speech, I think the novel ought to be intitled, *The impertinently Curious,* since it is certain the subject of it is, not *Anselmo's Curious impertinence,* but his *Impertinent curiosity.*"

## Chapter 6

1. "Wherefore, Lothario observed": Smollett follows Jarvis and Shelton/Stevens in correctly assigning this passage to Lothario, Jarvis commenting, "Both *Shelton* and *Motteux* have put this sentiment in *Anselmo's* mouth."

2. "Usque ad aras": Literally, "To the very altars," that is, to the last extremity (Jones), from Plutarch, *On False Shame,* alluding to Pericles (Putnam 1:482, col. b, n. 3).

3. "Ludovico Ariosto . . . . in his absence": In the first edition Smollett, following Jarvis, merely identified "our poet" as "Ludovico Ariosto, author of Orlando Furioso." In the second edition, however, owing no doubt to his friendship with William Huggins, the translator of Ariosto, he added several references to the Orlando romances that reveal a detailed knowledge of those works (see above, for example, pt. 1, bk. 3, chap. 3, n. 3). In November 1759, he wrote Huggins that he had recently "read the orlando furioso in the Italian from one end to the other" (*Letters,* 84). The present reference is to *Orlando Furioso* (trans. Huggins, 42.60–43.49): the

contrasting stories of Rinaldo, who wisely spurns his host's offer of an enchanted cup that will reveal whether his wife has remained faithful, and the foolish judge, "Doctor" Anselmo, who consults an astrologer for that purpose.

4. "he so well feigned the necessity . . . of his absence": Jarvis rendered the passage as "he knew so well how to counterfeit a necessity for his absence, though that necessity proceeded only from his own folly." But Smollett preferred the literal translation in Jarvis's note: "The original is *supo tan bien fingir la necessidad, ò necedad de ausencia*, &c. that is, *he knew so well how to feign the necessity, or rather folly of his absence*, &c. but it being impossible to retain the gingle of *necessidad* and *necedad* in the translation, it was thought proper to give the sentence somewhat a different turn. Note, *Shelton, Motteux*, &c. have quite omitted it."

## Chapter 7

1. "*Sensato* . . . sincere": Like Jarvis ("As if we should say, *sightly, sprightly, sincere*, and *secret*"), Smollett guesses at the four qualities Cervantes had in mind and gets three wrong. According to Putnam (1:482, col. b, n. 6²), the four *s*'s were "*Sabio* (knowing); *Solo* (single-hearted); *Solicito* (diligent); *Segreto* (secret)."

## Chapter 8

1. [Chapter heading]: Original: "*Donde se dà fin à la Novela del curioso impertinente.*" Jarvis, following the reading of the first edition, also found in Pineda's text of 1738, has "*The conclusion of* The Novel of the Curious Impertinent, *with the dreadful battle betwixt* Don Quixote *and certain wine-skins.*"

2. "found the knight in a very ludicrous situation . . . night-cap": As Boucé suggests (84), Smollett in *Humphry Clinker* recalls this "ludicrous situation" of Don Quixote, Cervantes' "knight of the rueful countenance," when Lismahago is roused from his bed by a false fire alarm: "it was impossible to behold this scene without being seized with an inclination to laugh. The rueful aspect of the lieutenant in his shirt, with a quilted night-cap . . . and his long lank limbs and posteriors exposed to the wind, made a very picturesque appearance" (288).

3. "the holidays will certainly come round": Original: "Ciertos son los toros." Jarvis rendered this as "here are the bulls," commenting: "In allusion to the joy of the mob in *Spain*, when they see the bulls coming." Previous translators struggled to catch the sense of this proverbial expression: "the matter is questionlesse" (Shelton); "The day is our own" (Shelton/Stevens); "the Battel is over" (Motteux).

## Chapter 9

1. "ride with short stirrups": Original: "à cavallo à la gineta." Jarvis renders this as "on horseback *a la Gineta*," commenting: "A kind of riding with short stirrops, which the *Spaniards* took from the *Arabians* . . . and is advantageous in fight: for, being ready to strike with their sabres, they rise on their stirrops, and, following as it were the blow, give more force to it." See also Stevens ("Ginéta"). And see below, "he rode . . . with short stirrups," p. 587 (pt. 2, bk. 3, chap. 12).

2. "mask": An inadequate translation of the original: "antifazes negros." Jarvis has "black masks," commenting: "*Antifaz* is a piece of thin black silk, which the *Spaniards* wear before their faces in travelling, not for disguise, but to keep off the dust and the sun. We have nothing equivalent to it in our language, and therefore are obliged to substitute the term *masks*, though it does not convey the strict and proper idea." See also Stevens ("Antifáz").

3. "But it appears, p. 265, that he was already known . . . *homerus*": This note was added in the second edition.

## Chapter 10

1. "In the original . . . salt in thy skull": Original: "que ponga sal en la mollera." Smollett, surprisingly, missed the sense of *sal* (salt) as "wit," a commonplace metaphor in Latin and English as well as Spanish (see Stevens: "Sal"). Jarvis, following Shelton, has "as shall put wit into the noddles [of all the lying squires]." Smollett instead retained the sense of the phrase in Shelton/Stevens ("I have a good mind to make thee an Example [to all lying Squires]") and Motteux ("I have a mind . . . to make thee appear a miserable Example [etc.]").

2. "Literally, You shall see when the eggs are fried . . . . Time will discover": Original: "al freyr de los huevos lo verà." Stevens ("Huévo") comments as follows on this proverbial expression: "Prov. *Al fréir de los huévos se verá*: It will appear when you are to fry your eggs. A man stole a frying-pan, and the owner asking him what he carry'd, he said, you'll know when you go to fry the eggs." Jarvis found this same anecdote in Pineda, who took it verbatim from Stevens. Following Shelton, Jarvis rendered the proverb literally ("it will be seen in the frying of the eggs"), whereas Smollett preferred the English equivalent in Shelton/Stevens and Motteux ("the proof of the pudding, is in the eating of it").

3. "Alluding to the charity . . . monasteries": Original: "andar à la sopa." Smollett's translation ("go a sopping") echoes Jarvis, who comments: "The author means the sops in porridge, given at the doors of the monasteries." See also Stevens ("Sópa, a sop") on the phrase, *Ir a la sòpa*.

## Chapter 11

1. "*i.e.* Do not amount to 1000 . . . four figures": Original: "con tres letras de quarismo." Smollett and Shelton ("with three Arithmetical figures") translate this literally. Jarvis has "may be numbered with three figures," commenting: "*i.e.* Do not exceed *hundreds.*"

2. "The literal translation . . . . descend to their heels": Original: "porque de faldas, que no quiero dezir de mangas." For the English equivalent Smollett gives in his note ("by Hook or by Crook"), see Shelton/Stevens and Motteux. With Smollett's translation ("for, one way or another") and his explanation of the phrase, compare Stevens: "Fálda, a woman's petticoats, or that part of any garment that hangs down like them, as of a gown, cassock, &c. a skirt. . . . Prov. *Ha de salír de faldas, o de mángas:* It must come out of the sleeves, or off the skirts. When one thing must come out of another. They say so, because they wear very large sleeves and petticoats, and therefore a small quantity of stuff might be taken out: So that it may as well signify what the taylor steals, who in cutting, rather than lose his practice, says, it must come out of the sleeves, or off the skirts."

3. "Cavalier is an artificial mount . . . the enemy": With Smollett's elegant definition of "Cavallero," compare Jarvis's tortuous note: "A mount raised on some work of a fortification, to command or overlook some rising ground, which the enemy might use to overlook that part of the fortification, where the cavalier is raised to prevent their using it." See also Stevens ("Cavalléro").

## Chapter 12

1. "The stentrel or estanterol . . . the poop": Original: "el estanterol." The *OED*, which cites this passage as its only example of "stentrel," prefers Stevens's definition (also in Pineda): "Es-

TANTEROL, the mid part of the galley, where the captain stands in time of fight." Smollett, how-
ever, abridges Jarvis's pedantic note: "The *Estanterol* is the pillar near the poop, on which is
propt the awning of the poop, and it is at the end of the path of communication betwixt it and
the prow, which runs exactly along the middle of the galley, and is called in *Spanish* the *Cruxia*."
See also below, "stentril," p. 694 (pt. 2, bk. 4, chap. 11).

2. "the goleta": Original: "la Goleta" (the gullet), the fortress that commanded the channel be-
tween the sea and the lagoon of Tunis.

3. "A Dalmatian trooper": Jarvis: "A trooper of *Epirus, Dalmatia,* or some of the adjacent coun-
tries."

## Chapter 13

1. "a Spanish soldier . . . Saavedra": Jarvis's phrasing. Quoting this passage in his prefatory "Life
of Cervantes," Smollett altered the phrase to "one Saavedra, a Spanish soldier" (see above,
p. 8). In a note Jarvis mentions the common assumption that "*Cervantes* means himself in this
passage," citing Gregorio, section 12, where Smollett would have found quoted in its entirety
the identical excerpt from this chapter of *Don Quixote* that he himself quotes in his "Life" (see
above, the "Life," n. 9).

## Chapter 14

1. "*Zala* or *Sala* . . . salutation": Original: "hazer la çalà." Smollett was first to understand this as
a reference to the "salaam." Among his predecessors only Motteux has the form "*Sala*,"
defining it simply as "a Ceremony among [the Moors]."

2. "Cava or Caba . . . the year 712": Smollett was the first translator to rehearse this historic
episode in any detail. His source was Moréri: "CAVA ou CABA, fille de *Julien,* Comte de
Ceuta . . . fut violée par Rodéric Roi d'Espagne. Cette injure outra si fort Julien, qui étoit
Gouverneur pour ce Prince en Afrique, que s'étant joint à deux fils de Vitiza dernier Roi, que
Rodéric avoit aveuglé, & duquel il avoit exclus les fils de la Couronne, il appela l'an 712 les
Sarrazins en Espagne." See also below, p. 538 and n. 6 (pt. 2, bk. 2, chap. 15).

3. "claped": Swung the helm hard to windward. *OED:* clap [clape], $v^1$, IV.10.b, citing Dampier's
*Voyage* (1699): "I clapt the Helm a Starboard."

## Chapter 15

1. "Cardenio": Corrected from the first edition, in which Smollett, following the original, had
"Don Antonio," an emendation also made by all previous translators, who saw that no one by
this name is mentioned among the guests at the inn.

2. "the West Indies": Original: "las Indias." Corrected from the first edition, in which Smollett
had "the East-Indies." Curiously, Smollett, who had lived in Jamaica and was well acquainted
with the West Indies, more than once mistakenly refers to that region as the East Indies; see
*Letters,* Smollett to William Strahan (24 June 1758), 68.

3. "This is the second time . . . . Vide p. 145": This note was added in the second edition.

4. "A judge in Spanish is called *Oydor* . . . an hearer before": Original: "A todo lo qual estava tan
atento el Oydor, que ninguna vez avia sido tan Oydor como entonces." Smollett was first to
note the play on *oidor.* Stevens: "OY´DO . . . the sense of hearing"; "OYDÓR, a judge."

5. "Cervantes seems to have forgot . . . the Indies": See above, chap. 12.

## Chapter 16

1. "In the original Demi-Donzellas . . . Demireps": Original: "semidonzellas." Smollett's translation ("demi-ladies") follows Shelton/Stevens and Motteux.

2. "Alluding to the delinquents . . . these figures": Smollett was first to explain this allusion. Neither Ormsby nor Putnam comments on the passage; but Watts, also without documentation, partly confirms Smollett's note, remarking that the reference is to "criminals, who were branded with the crown on their hands."

## Chapter 17

1. "Literally, 'Lady of a crown'": Original: "Señora de un escudo." Jarvis rendered this "that would have fetched above a crown," commenting that "Señora de un escudo" meant "Literally, *Mistress of a crown-piece.*"

## Chapter 18

1. "The original would be more literally translated . . . king's pleasure": Original: "pero allà van leyes, &c. y no digo mas." Jarvis has "but, so go the laws—I say no more," commenting: "He stops in the middle of the proverb, *Alla van leyes donde quieren reys,* meaning that the powerful carry what they please; or, as we say, *might overcomes right.*" Shelton/Stevens anticipated both Jarvis and Smollett in using this English equivalent of the proverb, but Smollett's translation in his note is his own and recurs below (pt. 2, bk. 3, chap. 5) in another rendering of the same proverb (p. 560). For another version, see p. 398, "As the king minds, the law binds" (pt. 2, bk. 1, chap. 5).

2. "A bridal benediction": Original: "y à quien Dios se la dio, san Pedro se la bendiga." Evident here in Smollett's translation ("and may St. Peter bless what God bestows") and in his note are both his lively concision of phrasing and his indebtedness to his predecessors. Jarvis, echoing Shelton, translates the passage literally: "and to whom god has given it, may St. *Peter* give his blessing," commenting that this was "The form of benediction at a wedding."

## Chapter 19

1. "It were to be wished . . . satisfaction": Smollett suspects that Cervantes, not the innkeeper, has forgotten that earlier, after Sancho was tossed in a blanket, the innkeeper "had detained his bags for the reckoning" (bk. 3, chap. 3).

2. "more tricks . . . than you dream of": Original: "ay mas mal en el aldeguela que se suena." Smollett was misled by Jarvis, who alone among previous translators mistook *suena* (sound) for *sueña* (dream). Shelton/Stevens, for example, has "there are always more Tricks in a Town, than are talk'd of."

3. "the honourable lappets": A metonymy, referring to the bands hanging from the collar in the conventional dress of a magistrate or clergyman. (*OED*: lappet, *sb* 4, *and* band, *sb²* I.4.b.)

4. "Sicut erat in principio": "As it was in the beginning," from the Gloria Patri, part of the liturgy of the Mass: "Sicut erat in principio, et nunc, et semper: et in sæcula sæculorum." See also below, p. 730 and n. 4 (pt. 2, bk. 4, chap. 19).

5. "A word of equal signification with *Mentironiana* . . . a liar": Original: "Mentironiana." Motteux/Ozell retains the original word, but offers Smollett's English version in a note: "Men-

*tironiana is a fram'd Word from* Mentira, *a Lye, as if we shou'd say* Fibberiana." For *mentira,* the root cited by both Motteux/Ozell and Shelton/Stevens, Smollett substitutes *"Menteroso"* or, rather, *mentiroso,* a liar (see Stevens).

## Chapter 20

1. "In the original *mi padre! . . .* our language": Smollett's "my stars!" is his own rendering of this exclamation: Shelton and Jarvis translate it literally; Shelton/Stevens has "quoth'a"; Motteux, "my Friend."
2. "Cortadilla": Original: "Cortadillo."
3. "Written by Cervantes himself": Jarvis: "Written by *Cervantes* himself, and extant in the collection of his *Novels.*"
4. "Equivalent to . . . 'Every jack is not a good-fellow'": Original: "algo va de Pedro à Pedro." Stevens ("Pédro"), like Shelton and Jarvis, translates this expression literally: "There is some difference betwixt *Peter* and *Peter,* that is, every one that bears the like name, is not alike: Or, every like is not the same." Other translators struggled to find an English equivalent: Shelton/ Stevens has "all are not Fellows at Football"; Motteux, "there's some difference between a Hawk and a Hand-saw."

## Chapter 21

1. "the sagacious botcher . . . found his customers in thread": Original: "vendrè à ser el sastre del cantillo." Putnam observes that this form of the proverb "is meaningless": "The proverb ran: *'El sastre del Campillo, que cosia de balde y ponia el hilo'*—'The tailor of El Campillo who threaded his needle and stitched for nothing.' There were other versions, such as 'The tailor of the crossroads,' etc." (1:487, col. a, n. 2). This latter version is what Jarvis, who translates the original lamely ("I should have got nothing but my labour for my pains"), found in Stevens and repeats verbatim in his note on the passage: "Literally, *I should have been like the taylor at the street-corner.* The proverb entire is, *Ser como el sastre de la encrucixáda, que cosia de valde, y ponia el hilo de su casa.* That is, *To be like the taylor of the cross-way, who sewed for nothing, and found thread himself.*" Smollett may owe his understanding of the proverb to Jarvis or to Stevens ("Sástre"); but, free as it is, his rendering of the sense is superior to that of any of his predecessors, and his arch note on the passage is typically his own.
2. "*Buscar Gullerias . . .* to seek dainties": The original, as well as Pineda's authoritative edition of 1738, has the archaic form "gullurias" (see Alonso, *s.v.* "gulluria"); the Royal Dictionary (1734) has "gulloría," citing this passage in *Don Quixote.* Only in Stevens would Smollett have found "gulleria," which became the preferred spelling (see Cadena); in the second edition, no doubt by a printer's error, the word takes still another form, "gullirias." Smollett's rendering of the idiom ("every attempt to succeed by a contrary method is no other than a wild-goose chace") is typically free: Shelton has "they are too daintie that looke for any other"; Jarvis and the others have "all besides is meer pedantry."
3. "Lopez de Vega Carpio": Jarvis alone uses this form of the surname.

## Chapter 22

1. "Literally, Never lost the stirrups": Original: "perder los estribos." Stevens: "Estríbo, a stirrup . . . . *Hazèr a úno perdér los estríbos,* to make a man lose his stirrups; met[aphorically,] to put

him out of patience, that he loses his reason he rested on." Jarvis follows Shelton in translating the idiom literally.

2. "the suit of St. Grial": Original: "la demanda del santo Grial." Jarvis renders this "the law-suit of saint *Grial*," complaining that Cervantes ought to have written *"Graal."* But there is no error in the original; the phrase means "the quest of the Holy Grail." Shelton ("the quest of the holy *Sangriall*") and Motteux alone understood it. Stevens may be the source of the confusion: "GRIÁL . . . . a dish made of one emeraud, said to be in the treasury of *Genoa*, and carried thither from *Spain*; is said to have been called by the Spaniards, *el santo grial."*

3. "biggen": A cap or hood (*OED*, "biggin"). Original: "tocas reverendas." With Smollett's note, compare Stevens: "Tóca, a woman's coif, handkerchief, or white veil for her head, or any dress for the head."

4. "Monseigneur": Jarvis first proposed this acceptable equivalent for the original "Mosen."

5. "Messire": Jarvis: "In Spanish *Micer.* The *Noblesse* in *France*, who are below the quality of *Monseigneurs*, and above that of *Monsieurs*, are styled *Messires."*

## Chapter 25

1. "the disciplinants": Smollett follows Shelton and Jarvis in adopting this unusual English equivalent of the original "los Disciplinantes." See also *Travels*, Letter XXVII, 221, cited by the *OED*.

2. "Persons hired . . . on such occasions": Compare Jarvis: "Persons, either volunteers or hirelings, who march in procession, whipping themselves by way of public penance." See also below, p. 539 n. (pt. 2, bk. 2, chap. 15).

3. "hoc scripserunt": "[they] wrote this."

4. "Paniguado": Original: "Paniaguado."

5. "SONG": In the original, the three poems by Paniaguado (servant), Caprichoso (whimsical fellow), and Burlado (jester) are each called a "SONETO"; the second, however, has seventeen lines.

6. "The horse of Orlando Furioso . . . incomparable poem": By adding this note to the second edition, Smollett no doubt wished chiefly to puff "Ariosto's incomparable poem" for the sake of his friend William Huggins's recent translation. Baiardo, however, was the steed of Rinaldo, not of the saracen knight Ruggiero. Reviewing Huggins's translation in the *Critical Review* (3 [May 1757]: 385–98), Smollett declared Ruggier "the favourite hero of the poet" and devoted nine pages to excerpts of his battle with Mandricard. See also below, p. 569 and n. 3 (pt. 2, bk. 3, chap. 8).

7. "Forse altri canterà con miglior plettro": Ariosto, *Orlando Furioso* (30.16), trans. Huggins: "Others, perhaps, with better lyre will sing." In the second edition, by following Huggins's Italian/English edition, Smollett corrected the Italian (the first edition reads: "Fosse altro cantera con miglior plectro"). He thus became the first translator of *Don Quixote* to reproduce the original accurately. Motteux and Motteux/Ozell reprint the line as it occurs in most Spanish editions: "Por si altro cantera con miglior pletro." Shelton, Shelton/Stevens, and Jarvis omit it altogether, whereas the corrector of Jarvis (1749) offers yet another version: "Forsi altro cantarà con miglior plectro."

## Part 2

### Preface

1. "The battle of Lepanto": Except for Shelton/Stevens, which omits the preface to part 2, all previous translations explain this allusion. See also above, Smollett's "Life of Cervantes" (p. 7).
2. "There was in Sevil, a certain madman . . . . blow up a dog": Smollett recalls this anecdote in *Adventures of an Atom:* the orator Taycho "employed his emissaries to blow up the patients *à posteriori,* as the dog was blown up by the madman of Seville, recorded by Cervantes" (p. 60, and n. 668).
3. "Mingo Rebulgo": See below, p. 735 n. (bk. 4, chap. 21).

### Approbation

1. Smollett was the first to include in a translation of *Don Quixote* the important Approbation of Márquez Torres, chaplain and secretary to the archbishop of Toledo. Gregorio had quoted the Approbation in full in his *Life* of Cervantes (1737), and thus Ozell, in translating that work, produced the first English version of it (25–26); Smollett's later version was entirely new.

### The Ordinary Licence

1. [Note to heading]: Again, Smollett is the first translator to include both Gutierrez de Cetina's Licence and the following Approbation by Joseph de Valdivielso.

### Approbation

1. "'Interpone . . . curis'": "Sometimes interpose joys with your cares," from the *Disticha de Moribus,* attributed to Cato (Putnam 2: [989], col. a, n. 2).

### Book 1

#### Chapter 1

1. "Ridiculous as this scheme may seem . . . . routed and dispersed": Ste. Palaye, *Mémoire* 3: "Le Roi [Jean] demeura long-temps prisonnier . . . . tout sembloit concourir à la destruction to-tale de la Chevalerie. Une faction connue sous le nom de la Jacquerie, d'abord formée dans le Beauvoisis, s'étendit dans les Provinces & se ligua pour porter les derniers coups à cet illustre corps. [¶] Plus de cent mille paysans armés, résolus d'exterminer la noblesse, ravageoient les terres, brûloient les châteaux, faisoient main basse sur les Chevaliers, sur les Écuyers, sur tous les Gentilshommes, sans épargner les femmes ni les enfans. . . . [¶] La duchesse de Nor-mandie, femme du Regent, la duchesse d'Orléans [Smollett conflates these two duchesses] & trois cens Dames & Damoiselles étoient à Meaux avec le duc d'Orléans, & ne s'y trouvoient plus en sûreté. . . . Le danger étoit extrême; il n'y avoit point d'excès qu'on ne dût attendre de

ces bandits effrénés, que rien n'arrêtoit, & par qui rien n'étoit respecté. Le comte de Foix & le captal de Buch . . . apprirent ces funestes nouvelles à Châlons. Bien qu'ils n'eussent que soixante lances, c'est-à-dire, soixante Chevaliers, & leur suite ordinaire, sur le champ ils prennent la résolution d'aller se joindre au petit nombre de ceux qui défendoient la forteresse de Meaux. L'honneur des Dames ne permet pas au comte de Foix de réfléchir sur le danger . . . . Nos brave Chevaliers & leur suite n'avoient d'autre ressource apparente qu'une mort certaine . . . . Ils se font ouvrir les portes & marchent fièrement aux ennemis. A cet aspect la frayeur saisit les troupes de la Jacquerie; les Chevaliers se font jour à traverslseurs rangs ébranlés, leur tuent sept mille hommes & reviennent triomphans auprès des Dames" (20:643–45).

2. "to visit the Stations": Original: "andar estaciones." Jarvis explains that visiting "the station-churches" was a penitential exercise required of madmen in their lucid intervals, but Smollett's note is closer to Stevens: "ESTACIÓN . . . *Andár las estaciónes*, is to go to so many stations; that is, churches or places appointed in remembrance of the several passages of our Savior's passion, there to pray in honour of those mysteries."

## Chapter 2

1. "the tail is yet unflea'd": Original: "Aun le falta la cola por desollar." For this proverbial expression, which Smollett later renders as "the worst of which is still to come," see below, p. 555 and n. 6 (bk. 3, chap. 3).

2. "cakes and gingerbread": See above, p. 109 and n. 1 (pt. 1, bk. 3, chap. 3).

3. "Cid Hamet Bean-and-jelly? . . . . very fond of beans and jellies": Original: "Cide Hamete Berengena . . . amigos de Berengenas." In *Gil Blas* (bk. 9, chap. 4; 3:239 n.) Smollett, in part echoing Stevens, had glossed "Berengena" as "a kind of fruit growing like cucumber, and eaten like French beans, with mutton, &c." Here Sancho's "Bean-and-jelly" approximates in English the sound of the name of Cid Hamet Benengeli. Previous translators retained the form of the original, Jarvis defining *berengena* as "A sort of fruit introduced by the *Moors*, to be boiled with, or without, flesh. *Sancho* mistakes *Berengena* for *Benengeli*."

## Chapter 3

1. "*Pedir cotufas en el golfo* . . . their desires": Stevens ("COTÚFAS") explains the proverb: "To ask for *cotúfas*, that is the root we call tartuffles in the main sea. That is, to require impossibilities, as it is to expect dainties, which only the earth affords, in the midst of the ocean." With Smollett's pert rendering of the expression ("Rozinante longed for green pease in December") compare Shelton and Jarvis ("longing after the forbidden fruit"), and Shelton/Stevens and Motteux ("offering to take a little [carnal] Recreation with the Mares"). See also above, "fishing for mushrooms at sea," p. 218 and n. 5 (pt. 1, bk. 4, chap. 3); and see below, "to find troufles at the bottom of the sea," p. 468 (bk. 2, chap. 3).

2. "*Aun ay sol en las bardas* . . . . not yet too late": Jarvis, following Shelton: "There is still sunshine on the walls."

3. "Finding it impossible to translate . . . good effect": Original: "han de saber gramatica. Con la grama bien me avendria yo, dixo Sancho, pero con la tica, ni me tiro, ni me pago, porque no la entiendo." Compare Smollett's rendering of Cervantes' wordplay ("grammatical / cram . . . matted cawl") with the uninspired solution of Jarvis: "must at least understand grammar. Gramercy for that, quoth *Sancho*; it is all *Greek* to me, for I know nothing of the matter," commenting: "Literally, 'For the *grama (grass)* I could venture on it, but for the *tica*, I neither put in nor take out, for I understand it not.'" Earlier attempts to English the pun were equally

lame: Shelton has "*Grammarians.* For your Gra, I care not, but your Mare I could like"; Motteux, "Grammar . . . . give me but a *gray* Mare."

4. "The original is *De paja* . . . hay and straw": Original: "al refran de paja, y de heno, &c." With Smollett's rendering of this proverb ("so the gizzard is crammed, it matters not how"), and his note, compare Stevens: "Pája, straw . . . . Prov. *De pája o de héno, el jergón lléno:* The bed, or the tick full of hay, or straw, so it be fill'd, no matter with what. A man must fill his belly, if he has not dainties, with cold meat." See also below, "With hay or with straw we'll fill up the craw," p. 542 (bk. 3, chap. 1).

5. "Alphonsus Tostatus . . . . *discutit omne*": With this note, added in the second edition, compare Moréri: "TOSTAT (Alfonse) Espagnol, Evêque d'Avila . . . . Il avoit beaucoup de mémoire & érudition, & savoit, à ce qu'on prétend, tout ce qui se pouvoit savoir . . . . Il vint au Concile de Bâle, où il parut avec éclat, & mourut l'an 1454, âgé seulement de 40 ans, & fut enterré dans l'église d'Avila avec cette Epitaphe. [¶] *Hic stupor est mundi, qui scibile discutit omne.* [¶] Nous avons XXVII tomes de ses Ouvrages de l'impression de Venise en 1569."

6. "aliquando bonus dormitat Homerus": "at times good Homer nods" (Horace *Ars Poetica* 325).

7. "stultorum infinitus est numerus": "the number of fools is infinite" (Ecclesiastes 1:15 [Vulgate]).

8. "In Spanish, *Me pondra* . . . uneasy situation": Jarvis has: "I . . . shall be upon the rack," commenting: "Literally, *shall be stuck upon St.* Lucia's *thorn,* supposed to be a cant phrase for the *rack;* for which the *Royal Dictionary* produces no voucher but this passage."

## Chapter 4

1. "As related in the famous poem . . . the continuation": Boiardo, *Orlando innamorato* (2.5.40). Another of the notes pertaining to the Orlando romances that Smollett added in the second edition. In November 1759, having read Berni's recasting of Boiardo's poem in a copy lent to him by William Huggins, Smollett wrote his friend: "Shall I tell you a secret? Notwithstanding the Extravagancies of Boyardo, I was so transported with some parts of him that my Hair stood on End. I wish I could see him Englished by such a Hand [*i.e.,* by Huggins] as that which translated Ariosto" (*Letters,* 84).

2. "In the original, 'Black for white'": Original: "no se ponga à juzgar lo blanco por negro, y lo negro por blanco." All previous translators rendered this literally—*e.g.,* Jarvis: "let him not be judging white for black, nor black for white." Smollett instead has Sancho recall Hamlet's assurance to Guildenstern: "I know a hawk from a handsaw" (2.2.397–98).

3. "Literally *Badeas* . . . water melon": Stevens: "Badéa, a watry, spongy, unsavoury melon." Smollett alone renders this "pippins": Shelton has "young Melons"; Shelton/Stevens and Motteux, "Cucumbers"; Jarvis, "watry melons."

4. "This is the cry uttered . . . in battle": Original: "san Jago, y cierra España." With Smollett's translation and note compare Stevens ("Cerrár"): "Ciérra *españa,* the cry of the soldiers when they engage in battel, encouraging one another to close with the enemy, for it signifies *close Spain.* That is, Spaniards close with your enemy." Jarvis has "Saint Jago, and charge, Spain," commenting: "It is the cry of the *Spaniards,* when they fall on." See also below, p. 662 n. (bk. 4, chap. 6).

5. "*Baylar el agua delante* . . . resembles dancing": Original: "baylarè el agua delante." With Smollett's rendering of this proverbial expression ("I will jig it away"), and his note, compare Stevens ("Água"): "Prov. *Baylár el água delánte:* To dance with the water before one. That is, to be very nimble or quick in performing one's duty, or pleasing another. Taken from the maids watering the rooms and courts in *Spain* in hot weather against their masters come, doing it nimbly, as if they were dancing, as they carry and scatter the water before them."

6. "Alonzo de Ercilla . . . meant himself": Smollett here closely paraphrases Jarvis's note, in which he acknowledges his own debt to Gregorio (76).

### Chapter 5

1. "the proverb . . . wipe his nose and take him in": Original: "al hijo de tu vezino limpiale las narizes, y metele en tu casa." Compare Jarvis: "remember the proverb, Wipe your neighbour's son's nose, and take him into your house," commenting: "This is a literal version of the *Spanish* proverb, the meaning of which . . . is, *match your daughter with your neighbour's son*." Also Stevens ("Hɪᴊᴏ").
2. "As the king minds, the law binds": See above, p. 324 n. (pt. 1, bk. 4, chap. 18).
3. "Almohada . . . a cushion": Original: "mas almohadas de velludo, que tuvieron Moros en su linage los Almohadas de Marruecos." Smollett alone preserves the pun: previous translators substitute "cushion" for "almohadas," Jarvis, among others, explaining the jest in a note: "A sport on the word *Almohada*, which signifies a cushion, and was also the surname of a famous race of the *Arabs* in *Africk*."
4. "Alluding to the bough . . . Palm-sunday": Original: "como un palmito." Compare Jarvis, "as fine as a palm-branch," commenting: "In *Italy* and *Spain* they carry in procession, on *Palm-Sunday*, a Palm-branch, the leaves of which are platted and interwoven with great art and nicety."

### Chapter 7

1. "The original, *ventura* . . . adventures": Original: "il llama venturas." Following Jarvis, whom he had earlier wisely ignored, Smollett in the second edition altered "ventures" to "adventures" and added this note repeating Jarvis's explanation. By translating this as "adventures," however, Jarvis removed the cause of the housekeeper's bewilderment. Stevens (as well as Pineda) distinguishes *ventura*, which, "when taken absolutely, is always good luck," from *aventura*, "an adventure, us'd much in romances." The housekeeper, not well read in romances, has misheard *aventuras* as *venturas*.
2. "he that shuffles does not always cut": Original: "quien destaja no baraja." Before Ormsby ("he who binds does not wrangle"), English translators—including Smollett—misunderstood this proverbial expression. Smollett follows Jarvis and Stevens ("DᴇsᴛᴀᴊÁʀ").
3. "I have substituted this play . . . *Rata*": Meaning to say "rata por cantidad" ("quantity for quantity, or in proportion to the quantity" [Stevens: "RÁᴛᴀ"]), Sancho instead says "gata [a female cat] por cantidad." Previous translators have Sancho saying "cantity for cantity" and Don Quixote correcting him with "quantity." The humor of *gata* for *rata* is lost in all versions.

### Chapter 9

1. "singing the ballad of Ronscevalles": In a note in the first edition, corrected in the second (p. 29 n.; pt. 1, bk. 1, chap. 1), Smollett erred in crediting the French with victory at Roncesvalles. Here, he in effect conceals the error by abridging the original: "cantando aquel Romance, que dizen: mala la huvistes Franceses en essa de Roncesvalles"—literally, as in Jarvis: "singing the ballad of the defeat of the *French* in *Roncesvalles*."
2. "Like our Chevy-chase": All previous translators except Motteux draw this same analogy with the ballad of Chevy Chase.

### Chapter 10

1. "under the rich canopy of her authority": Original: "sentada en el estrado rico de su autori-dad." Only Shelton/Stevens translates "estrado," inaccurately, as "Canopy of State." Jarvis writes, "seated on the rich *Estrado* of her dignity," defining the term as "The floor raised at the upper-end of the rooms of state in *Spain*, where the ladies sit upon cushions to receive visits." Since, however, *estrado* also signifies a "court of justice" (see Stevens), Smollett's rendering of "autoridad" as "authority" seems more exact than Jarvis's "dignity"; in this he follows Shelton and Motteux.

2. "Not he with whom you was bred . . . fed": Original: "no con quien naces, sino con quien paces." Jarvis: "Not with whom thou wert bred, but with whom thou art fed." Smollett's word-ing in the first edition, "by whom you are led," signifies a sycophant, one who follows slav-ishly, as in the term "led-captain" (*OED*: led, 3). See also below, p. 714 (bk. 4, chap. 16); and see also below, p. 532: "I ask not where you was hatched, but where you was watched" (bk. 2, chap. 15).

3. "Would I had the currying that ass's hide of thine": Original: "Mas yo que te estrego burra de mi suegro." Smollett was first not only to translate this proverbial expression, but to under-stand that the wench addresses it not to the ass she rides on (as Jarvis states) but to Sancho, as depicted in Hayman's illustration. Stevens ("BÚRRA") translates the expression: "Stand still while I curry you, my father-in-law's ass. So the clowns say to their wives when they beat them."

### Chapter 12

1. "as the song goes . . . a true friend can hardly be met": Gay's *Beggar's Opera* (1728), 3.4 (Air 44): the opening of Macheath's song on false friendship. Original: "el otro que canto de amigo à amigo la chinche, &c." Jarvis rendered this truncated proverb literally: "(as the poet sings) From a friend to a friend, the bug, *&c.*," commenting, "The author here quotes either the be-ginning of some old song, or of some well-known proverb, the remainder of which ['en el ojo' (in the eye)] we cannot supply."

### Chapter 13

1. "dull as a beetle": Original: "tiene una alma como un cantaro." Smollett, following Shelton, adopts this old English expression, taking the Spanish for *beetle (maço)* in the figurative sense of "a dull fellow" (Stevens: *"beetle"*). Jarvis's more literal rendering ("has a soul as dull as a pitcher") makes little sense in English. For the sense of the original, see Stevens: "CÁNTARO, a great pitcher to carry water. . . . *álma de cantaro*, a dull heavy stupid fellow." See also below, "Mr. Wiseacre," p. 530 (bk. 2, chap. 14); and, "a simple soul," p. 604 (bk. 3, chap. 15).

2. "Literally, *a squire of wool and water* . . . appointments": Original: "algun Escudero de agua y lana." Compare Jarvis's note on this expression: "Literally, *a squire of water and wool. The Spaniards* generally have a footman only to wait upon them to mass, especially upon grand days; who step before to the font, and sprinkle their masters or mistresses with holy-water, but neither eat nor drink at their masters houses."

3. "well dammed and gristed": Original: "moliente, y corriente." Only Smollett attempted to render this idiom into English. Stevens ("MOLIÉNTE") explains: "This is properly said of a mill that is in good case to grind, the water running, or the sails going; and met[aphorically] signifies anything that is in good order, and no way defective."

4. "carrobes": Original: "algarrobas." Jarvis, following Stevens, was first to translate this as

"carobes," commenting: "A cod so called in *La Mancha*, with flat seeds in it, which green or ripe is harsh, but sweet and pleasant after it is dried."

## Chapter 14

1. "A brass statue on a steeple at Sevil ... weather-cock": Compare Jarvis, echoing Shelton/ Stevens: "A brass statue on a steeple in *Sevil*, which serves for a weather-cock."
2. "These are stone statues of bulls ... Consul II": Compare Stevens: "Guisándo, a town in the kingdom of *Castile* ... where there [are] ... two Roman figures in stone, much spoken of in Spanish writers, and call'd *los tóros de Guisándo*, the bulls of *Guisando*, being the figures of bulls erected by the Romans, with inscriptions which are now worn out; only on one of them there are still to be seen these words, *A. Quintus Cecilius Metellus Consul II.*"

## Chapter 16

1. "Est Deus in nobis": "There is a god within us" (Ovid *Fasti* 6.5).

## Chapter 17

1. "custards and puff-paste": See above, p. 109, n. 1 (pt. 1, bk. 3, chap. 3).

# Book 2

## Chapter 1

1. "must know how to swim like an herring": Original: "saber nadar, como dizen que nadava el pexe Nicolas, ò Nicolao." Jarvis, following Shelton, renders this literally: "must know how to swim like him people call *Fish Nicholas*, or *Nicholao*," commenting that Cervantes alludes to "a fabulous story in the *Theatre of the gods.*" Like Smollett, both Shelton/Stevens and Motteux preferred to simplify the expression, writing "must be able to swim like a Fish."

## Chapter 2

1. "shoe-slappers": Original: "çapateadores." Jarvis has "the shoe-dancers and caperers," commenting: "Dancers that strike the soles of their shoes with the palms of their hands in time and measure." See also above, p. 177 and n. 10 (pt. 1, bk. 3, chap. 11).
2. "Poor people ... about Zamora": Original: "al Sayagues." With Smollett's notes here and below, p. 536 n. (bk. 2, chap. 15), compare Stevens: "Sayagués, this name properly belongs to the poor country-people about *Zamóra*, in *Spain*, so call'd because they were cloth'd in sackcloth"; and "Sayágo, a territory about *Zamóra*, in the kingdom of *Léon.*"
3. "Zocodover ... cattle are sold": Smollett embellishes Stevens: "çocodovér, the name of a marketplace in the city *Toledo.*"

## Chapter 3

1. "find troufles at the bottom of the sea": See above, p. 389 n. (pt. 2, bk. 1, chap. 3).
2. "In the original there is a play upon ... the text": Original: "no ay que fiar en la descarnada, digo en la muerte, la qual tambien come cordero como carnero." Jarvis, like all previous trans-

lators, rendered this literally: "there is no trusting to madam *Skeleton* [la descarnada], I mean death, who devours lambs [cordero (sing.)] as well as sheep [carnero]."

## Chapter 4

1. "The *Patina* . . . breasts": Original: "las patenas." Compare Stevens: "Paténa, a flat piece of plate, worn formerly on people's breasts, either because it had something of devotion engraved on it, or only for ornament; now only worn by the meanest peasants."

## Chapter 5

1. "The loosened ox is well licked": Original: "el buey suelto bien se lame." Jarvis was first to translate this proverb, the sense of which he would have found in Stevens ("Buéy"): "An ox, when he is loose, licks himself at pleasure. To signify the benefit of liberty . . . . It is much us'd by batchelors against matrimony, which is called a yoke."
2. "the just will far exceed . . . the gentiles": Original: "mas justas que pecadoras." Previous translators avoided this irreverent metaphor. Jarvis, for example, has "more will hit than miss," commenting: "Literally, *more will be Just than Sinners.* It is scripture language, and, the use of it here being impertinent at least, if not prophane, it is therefore softened and qualified in the translation."

## Chapter 6

1. "skinker": Original: "escanciando el vino." See Stevens: "Escanciáno [from the verb *escanciár*], a skinker, he that fills out liquor to drink."
2. "Fouckar . . . . as rich as a Fouckar": Original: "un Fucar." Félibien was Smollett's source for this anecdote concerning the Fugger brothers, as well as for the proverbial expression "as rich as a Foucker": "On rapporte de ces riches negocians comme une chose assez singuliere & curieuse à sçavoir, que l'Empereur Charles V. au retour de Thunis, passant en Italie, & delà par la ville d'Ausbourg, fut loger chez eux; que pour luy marquer davantage leur reconnoissance & la joye de l'honneur qu'ils recevoient, un jour parmi les magnificences dont ils le régaloient, ils firent mettre sous la cheminée un fagot de canelle, qui estoit une marchandise de grand prix, & luy ayant montré une promesse d'une somme tres-considerable qu'ils avoient de luy, y mirent le feu, & en allumerent le fagot, qui rendit une odeur & une clarté d'autant plus douce & plus agreable à l'Empereur, qu'il se vit quitte d'une dette que ces affaires d'alors ne luy permettoient pas de payer facilement, & de laquelle ils luy firent present de cette maniere assez galante" (2:336–37). Félibien prefaced this anecdote by recalling the proverb Smollett quotes: "Ainsi les Fouckers firent une si grande fortune, qu'ils estoient estimez le plus opulens de toute l'Allemagne, où il y a un proverbe, qui dit d'un homme fort accommodé, qu'il est aussi riche que les Fouckers" (2:336).
3. "the infant Don Pedro": Original: "el Infante Don Pedro." Here, but nowhere else in the work, Smollett mistranslates "Infante" ("prince," a younger son of the king).

## Chapter 7

1. "A knavish trick": Original: "espilorcheria." Compare Jarvis: "A sneaking trick of a pitiful beggarly fellow." Pineda, citing this passage in *Don Quixote*, defines "*Espilochéria* [*sic*]," an Italian word, as "Cowardice, Pusillanimity." Watts and Putnam substitute *spilorceria* ("meanness"; "niggardliness").

## Chapter 8

1. "Operibus credite & non verbis": "Believe the works and not the words" (compare John 10:38).
2. "the drugoman": Jarvis has "the *Druggerman*," commenting: "*El Truxaman.* So the *Turks* call an *interpreter.*" (The forms used by Smollett and Jarvis are now obsolete [*OED:* dragoman].)

## Chapter 9

1. "In the original there is a miserable pun . . . drunkenness": Jarvis has, lamely, "not for catching the ape, but to drink," commenting: "Here, in the original, is a jingle of words *(no para tomar el mono, sino la mona)* which it is impossible to preserve in the translation. *Mono* signifies an *ape*, and *mona*, in familiar language, is used for being drunk, or drunkenness; perhaps, because men in liquor often play apish tricks."

## Chapter 10

1. "Literally, 'When choler quits the mother . . . father'": Original: "quando la colera sale de madre, no tiene la lengua padre." By ignoring his usual guides, Smollett gained a rhyme ("born/scorn") but lost the meaning: the idiom "salír de mádre" signifies a river's overflowing its banks (see Stevens, "SALÍR"). Jarvis has "when choler overflows its dam," which preserves the ambiguity of *madre*.
2. "I have ventured to deviate . . . that call them so": Original: "porque bueno seria que se matassen à cada passo los del pueblo de la Reloxa con quien se lo llama." Believing this to be unintelligible in English, Jarvis produced nonsense ("Would it not be pretty indeed, if those of the watch-making business should endeavour to knock every body's brains out, who calls them by their trade?"), requiring a ponderous explanatory note.
3. "thologister": Smollett departed from his own copy ("Theologo") to follow Jarvis ("a tologue"), the first translation based on an edition of the original (*e.g.*, Pineda, ed.) in which Sancho blunders by saying "tòlogo" instead of "teologo" (a divine).

## Chapter 11

1. "Mare magnum": Literally, the "great Sea."
2. "pinch the sign of the four nipples on my face": Original: "me hagas quatro mamonas selladas en mi rostro." Stevens: "MAMÓNA, a gripe, a pinch given on the face with all four fingers and the thumb; so called, because it resembles the womens taking their breasts to give the children suck." Smollett is the first translator since Shelton to understand the idiom in this sense (see Watts 4:333, n. 1).

## Chapter 12

1. "As it is altogether impossible, in a translation . . . set of evidences": Original: "una gentil persona, puto, y gafo, con la afiadidura de meon, ò meo, ò no sè como." Stevens: "PÚTO . . . the patient in the sin of sodomy"; "GÁFO . . . a sort of leprosy"; and Pineda: "*Meòn* . . . who pisses often," citing this passage in *Don Quixote*. Smollett's free rendering of this troublesome passage conveys the sense of the original better, and more amusingly, than the attempts of previous translators: *e.g.*, Shelton ("*To ly my* & Comtation"); Shelton/Stevens ("Gaffer *Temptation*");

Motteux ("Goodman *Tollme*, with his *Amputation* and *Cistern*"); Jarvis ("*Tolmy* . . . with his *amputation*").

2. "In allusion to the Speech that Virgil . . . *Teucrorum!*": Original: "alli avia sidò Troya para los dos." Jarvis renders this as "there had been *Troy* for them both," commenting: "*Aqui fué Troya, here stood Troy*, is a *Spanish* proverb denoting something ruined or destroyed. The meaning therefore is, that they must have inevitably perished"; also Stevens ("Tróya"). Smollett, and later Watts, detect an allusion to *Aeneid* 2.325–26: "Ilium is not, and the great glory of the Teucrians" (trans. H. R. Fairclough, Loeb Library, 1916). See also below, "Here Troy once stood," p. 707 (bk. 4, chap. 14).

## Chapter 13

1. "Don Quixote . . . made a motion to alight . . . . not without great disgrace": As Boucé has noticed (84), Smollett in *Humphry Clinker* recalls this passage in depicting Lismahgo's calamitous attempt to impress Tabitha and Liddy with his horsemanship: "Perceiving ladies at the window above, he endeavoured to dismount with the most graceful air he could assume; but the ostler neglecting to hold the stirrup when he wheeled off his right foot, and stood with his whole weight on the other, the girth unfortunately gave way, the saddle turned, down came the cavalier to the ground . . . . The greatest injury he had sustained arose from the dishonour of his descent, aggravated by the disgrace of exposing the condition of his cranium" (182).

## Chapter 14

1. "a perfect mine of history": Original: "que zahori de las Historias." Jarvis's more literal translation ("the very mine-finder of histories") required a note: "*Zahori*. A discoverer of mines . . . who has a share in the property. A child . . . supposed to see seven yards into the ground."
2. "has the repique in hand": Original: "à buen salvo està el que repica." Smollett was misled by Jarvis, the only previous translator to attempt to English this idiom: Jarvis has "as safe as the repique in hand," commenting that the phrase is an allusion "to the game of picquet, in which the repique may be safe against the greatest cards in appearance." Instead, see Stevens: "Repicár . . . . Prov. *En sálvo está el que repíca:* He is safe that rings the bell, because when it is an alarm-bell, he is in the steeple out of harms way." See also below, p. 557, "he is safe who has good cards to play" (bk. 3, chap. 4).
3. "Mr. Wiseacre": Original: "alma de cantaro." See above, p. 432, n. 1 (pt. 2, bk. 1, chap. 13).

## Chapter 15

1. "like quicksilver": See above, p. 122 and n. 1 (pt. 1, bk. 3, chap. 5).
2. "a narrow-minded pedant . . . to read Latin": Original: "aviendose criado algunos en la estrecheza de algun pupilage." Besides embellishing the original, in which there is nothing about teaching pupils to read Latin, Smollett alone, probably following Stevens ("Estrechéza, streightness, narrowness"), translates *estrecheza* as "narrow-minded" rather than "poor."
3. "not where you was hatched . . . watched": See above, p. 416 and n. 2 (pt. 2, bk. 1, chap. 10).
4. "Sayago is a district . . . cloathed": See above, p. 466 n. (pt. 2, bk. 2, chap. 2).
5. "proceed with the plummet in your hand": Original: "và con pie de plomo . . . con la sonda en la mano." Figuratively (referring to the mariner's plumb line), judging the depth of a thing accurately.
6. "Cava": See above, p. 301 n. (pt. 1, bk. 4, chap. 14).

7. "Sancho entered the hall in a fright . . . to lather his beard": Smollett recalls this episode in *Travels*, Letter V: "Captain B——, . . . with the napkin under his chin, was no bad representation of Sancho Panza in the suds, with the dishclout about his neck, when the duke's scullions insisted upon shaving him" (37).

8. "In Spain and Italy there is . . . . *Corrazini di Latta!*": Blainville (at Rome, 22 April 1707 [Holy Thursday]): "We finished this Days Work by seeing a fine and very edifying Shew; I mean the Procession of the *Battuti* or *Penitents*. Upwards of 500 People dressed in a kind of Sacks of coarse Cloth, dyed red, assembling at the Church of St. *Marcellus*, set out in regular Order to that of St. *Peter*, which is at a pretty tolerable Distance; each of those Penitents carried a lighted Flambeau in one Hand; and in the other a Whip, with which from Time to Time they gave themselves very sound Discipline . . . . There were doubtless several well-meaning Souls amongst so great a Number of Penitents who actually made their Shoulders all run down with Blood, from a Conviction that for every Drop of Blood which they lost, they had at least one Sin forgiven them: But I am perswaded not a very great Number were thoroughly of that Opinion: This is so true, that the very People who went by their Sides could discern by the Sound of the Blows they gave themselves, those amongst them who wore a Plate of Tin, from those who had a Womans Stays, or a Skin Jacket over their Shoulders beneath their Sacks; and accordingly cry'd out, such a one has a *Giuppone di Buffalo* [*giubbone*, a heavy coat]; such a one a *Busto di Donna* [a woman's corset], and such a one a *Corrazini di Latta* [*correzione di latta*, correction of a tin plate] under his Sack. Whatever was in this, the great Noise which the Strokes of the Disciplines made in falling upon the Shoulders of those Penitents, was a plain Proof that there was a great deal of Legerdemain in this Devotion" (2:328–29). (Smollett's misspellings: *"Giuppone"* and *"Busti."*) Smollett resumed this subject in *Travels*, Letter XXVII: "Amidst all the scenery of the Roman catholic religion, I have never yet seen any of the spectators affected at heart, or discover the least signs of fanaticism. The very disciplinants, who scourge themselves in the Holy-week, are generally peasants or parties hired for the purpose. Those of the confrairies, who have an ambition to distinguish themselves on such occasions, take care to secure their backs from the smart, by means of secret armour, either women's boddice, or quilted jackets" (221). See also above, pt. 1, bk. 4, chap. 25, nn. 1–2.

9. "*Su alma en Su Palma*. . . . discretion": Jarvis, following Stevens and Pineda, has "he is at his own disposal," commenting: "Literally, *his soul is in his hand.*"

## Book 3

### *Chapter 1*

1. "This is an expression proverbially applied . . . ascertained": Original: "no siendo mas verdad que por los cerros de Ubeda." Smollett's confident explanation of this proverbial expression appears to be his own invention. Both Stevens ("Úbeda") and Pineda, for instance, situate the city of Ubeda in Andalusia, "in a rich and fruitful plain." Jarvis translates the passage, "there is no more truth in it than in a story of a cock and a bull," commenting: "The original . . . cannot be rendered into any intelligible sense in *English*, nor do the dictionaries afford us any tolerable explanation of the phrase *por los cerros de Ubeda*, i.e. *by the Hills of Ubeda*. Perhaps there might be some old ballad, romance, or tale, beginning with those words." Later, when the phrase recurs (bk 3, chap. 11), Jarvis substitutes the title of the English ballad "Over the Hills and Far Away," commenting: "In the original, *By the rocks of* Ubeda. It is the beginning of an old song"; Smollett, at the same place, writes, "as foreign from the subject as an old ballad"

(p. 583). See also below, p. 658, "I know nothing of the matter" (bk. 4, chap. 5). The origin of the expression is obscure.

2. "With hay or with straw . . . the craw": See above, p. 391 n. (pt. 2, bk. 1, chap. 3).

3. "The pismire found wings . . . and so good night": This passage well illustrates a distinctive quality of Smollett's translation when compared to those of his chief rivals. Smollett's inventive rhyming and alliteration in rendering Sancho's spate of proverbs convey aurally the spirit of the original, yet he remains much closer to the literal sense of the Spanish than Motteux/Ozell, and in several instances he is more accurate than Jarvis. Consider the following, consisting of the original text with Putnam's translation followed by the versions of Motteux/Ozell and Jarvis:

Original: "de por su mal le nacieron alas à la hormiga; y aun podria ser, que se fuesse man ayna Sancho escudero al cielo, que no Sancho Governador. Tan buen pan hazen aqui como en Francia, y de noche todos los gatos son pardos: y assaz de desdichada es la persona que à las dos de la tarde no se ha desayunado, y no ay estomago que sea un palmo mayor que otro, el qual se puede llenar, como suele dezirse, de paja, ò de heno: y las avezitas de campo tienen à Dios por su Proveedor, y Despensero: y mas calientan quatro varas de paño de Cuenca, que otras quatro de limiste de Segovia, y al dexar este mundo, y meternos la tierra adentro, por tan estrecha senda va el Principe, como es jornalero; y no ocupa mas pies de tierra el cuerpo del Papa, que el del Sacristan, aunque sea mas alto el uno que el otro, que al entrar en el hoyo todos mas ajustamos, y encogemos, ò nos hazen ajustar, y encoger mal que nos pese, y à buenas noches."

Putnam: "'To her harm the ant grew wings.' It may be that Sancho the squire will go to Heaven sooner than Sancho the governor. They make as good bread here as in France, and at night all cats are gray. He is hard up who hasn't broken his fast by two in the afternoon, and there's no stomach that's bigger than another by the breadth of your palm, and you can fill it with straw or hay, as the saying goes. The little birds of the field have God for their provider, and four yards of Cuenca frieze keep you warmer than four of Segovia broadcloth. Once we have left this world and gone down under the earth, the prince travels by as narrow a path as the day laborer, and the pope's body takes up no more feet of earth than does the sacristan's, even though one is higher than the other; for, when we go to the grave, we all make ourselves as small as we can, or they do it for us whether we like it or not, and then it's good night all."

Motteux/Ozell: "the pismire had wings to do her hurt; and Sancho the squire may sooner get to heaven than Sancho the governour. There's as good bread baked here as in France, and Joan's as good as my lady in the dark. In the night all cats are gray. Unhappy's he that wants his breakfast at two in the afternoon. 'Tis always good fasting after a good breakfast. There's no man has a stomach a yard bigger than another, but let it be never so big, there will be hay and straw enough to fill it. A bellyfull's a bellyfull. The sparrow speeds as well as the sparrow-hawk. Good serge is fine, but coarse cloth is warm; and four yards of the one are as long as four yards of the other. When the hour is come we must all be pack'd off; the prince and the prick-louse go the same way at last: the road is no fairer for the one than the other. The pope's body takes up no more room than the sexton's, tho' one be taller; for when they come to the pit, all are alike, or made so in spight of our teeth, and so good-night or good-morrow, which you please."

Jarvis: "The pismire had wings to her hurt; and perhaps it may be easier for *Sancho* the squire to get to heaven, than for *Sancho* the governor. They make as good bread here as in *France*; and, In the dark all cats are gray; and, Unhappy is he, who has not breakfasted at three; and, No stomach is a span bigger than another, and may be filled, as they say, with straw or with hay; and, Of the little birds in the air god himself takes the care; and, Four yards of coarse cloth of *Cuença* are warmer than as many of fine *Segovia* serge; and, at our leaving this world, and going into the next, the prince travels in as narrow a path as the day-labourer; and the pope's body

takes up no more room than the sexton's, though the one be higher than the other; for, when we come to the grave, we must all shrink and lie close, or be made to shrink and lie close in spight of us; and so good night."

4. "In the original, And thoroughly understand *Tus*, Tus . . . a cur": Original: "y entiendo todo tus, tus." Jarvis has "I am an old dog, and understand *tus, tus*," commenting: "Words used in *Spain* to coax a dog to come to one, when one designs to beat him." For other variations, see below, p. 626, "when they throw thee some good beneficial bone, wag thy tail, and snap at the favour" (bk. 3, chap.18); and p. 719, "I am an old dog, and will not be coaxed with a crust" (bk. 4, chap. 17).

5. "A young Florentine . . . his time": Jarvis: "A young *Florentine* of exceeding great hopes, who died young, and whose loss was lamented by all the poets of his time." Motteux/Ozell, after quoting Jarvis, adds that Verino died "*at Seventeen.*"

6. "Florentibus occidit annis": "He died in his prime" (literally, "in his flourishing years"), from the Latin epitaph by Politian beginning, "Michael Verinus florentibus occidit annis" (Putnam 2:1008, col. b, n. 20).

## Chapter 2

1. "Literally, And you shall see it will be worth . . . hundred": Original: "y vereys como os vale un pan por ciento." Smollett was first to attempt an explanation of this puzzling expression. Jarvis simply renders it as "and you will find your account in it."

2. "a certain *darkness visible*": Original: "un cierto claro escuro," *escuro* being a variant of *obscuro* (Royal Dictionary). To render this oxymoron Smollett aptly recalls *Paradise Lost* 1.63, Milton's famous description of hell.

## Chapter 3

1. "*Disciplinante de Luz* . . . shame": Jarvis: "A penitent of the light, says the royal dictionary, they call in *Germany* him who is to be exposed in a publick manner, by being led through the streets, or set in the pillory."

2. "I denounce it": Original: "abernuncio." Pineda, citing this passage in *Don Quixote*, defines "*Abernuncio*" as an interjection meaning "far be it from me." This spelling is a corruption of *abrenuncio* (Royal Dictionary), which has its Latin sense of "renounce." Smollett's rendering of Sancho's blunder ("denounce") seems preferable to the attempts of his predecessors: Jarvis has "pronounce"; Shelton, "bernounce"; Motteux, "prenounce."

3. "mulish goggle eyes": Original: "ojos de machuelo espantadizo." Jarvis has "huge goggle eyes," commenting: "Literally, *your eyes of a little starting mule.*"

4. "thread by thread and skein by skein": Original: "hilo à hilo, y madexa à madexa." Jarvis, following Shelton/Stevens, has "drop after drop, and stream after stream," commenting, "Literally, thread after thread, and skein after skein."

5. "Literally, *Cacique* . . . princes": Compare Stevens: "Cacíque, so the Indians call their petty princes."

6. "the worst . . . is still to come": Jarvis has "the worst is still behind," commenting: "*Aun le falta la cola por desollar.* i.e. *The Tail still remains to be flay'd.* Which is the most troublesome and hard to be done." See above, p. 386, "the tail is yet unflea'd" (pt. 2, bk. 1, chap. 2).

7. "The other translators have interpreted *Mosqueo* . . . the passage": The "other translators" are Stevens: "Mosqueár, a flap to kill flies"; and Jarvis: "if some lashes happen only to fly-flap." With Smollett's rendering, compare Pineda: "Mosquéo . . . a Driving away of Flies; also a

Whipping by the Minister of Justice": Pineda cites this passage in *Don Quixote* as an instance
of the latter sense of the word.

## Chapter 4

1. "he is safe . . . cards to play": Original: "en salvo està el que repica." See above, p. 528 and n. 2
   (pt. 2, bk. 2, chap. 14).
2. "will come out in the washing": See above, p. 135 and n. 3 (pt.1, bk. 3, chap. 6).

## Chapter 5

1. "*Faldas* . . . signifies skirts": Original: "Condesa Tres faldas, o Tres colas." Jarvis, following
   Shelton, has "countess *Three-skirts* or *Three-tails*," commenting: "Alluding to the name *Tri-
   faldi*, as if it were *Tres-faldas.*"
2. "the law's measure . . . king's pleasure": See above, p. 324 n. (pt. 1, bk. 4, chap. 18).

## Chapter 6

1. "A kind of pea . . . Andaluzia": Original: "cada grano del grandor de un garvanço de los buenos
   de Martos." Smollett alone renders this literally, probably following Stevens: "GARAVÁNÇO, a
   sort of pease they have in *Spain*, whereof none in *England*"; and "MÁRTOS, a town in the
   province of *Andaluzia* in *Spain*." Jarvis, following Motteux, writes, "each grain would have
   been of the size of a good *Ronceval*-pea." See also above, p. 79 and n. 1 (pt. 1, bk. 2, chap. 4).
2. "This blunder is much more natural . . . . appellation": Original: "à esta su criado, digo à esta
   criada." Jarvis, without comment, has: "to this your varlet; I mean your handmaid."
3. "alguazil": Jarvis comments: "A sort of bailiff or sergeant." In *Gil Blas* (bk. 1, chap. 12, 1:69 n.)
   Smollett had defined "Alguazils" as "attendants of justice, whose office resembles that of our
   bailiffs." Compare Stevens ("ALGUAZÍL" and "*bailiff*").

## Chapter 7

1. "'Quis talia fando . . . lachrymis?'": "Who in telling such a tale, could refrain from tears" (Vir-
   gil *Aeneid* 2.6, 8, trans. H. R. Fairclough, Loeb Library 1930).

## Chapter 8

1. "taking off the hair": Original: "à quitar el bello." Motteux/Ozell, following Shelton/Stevens,
   comments: "*There are a sort of Women-Barbers in Spain, that take the Down off Women's Faces, and
   sell them Washes, and these are commonly reputed to be giv'n to Bawding.*"
2. "persons who having ceased to be principals . . . procuress": Jarvis has "most of them smell of
   the procuress, having ceased to be serviceable," commenting: "Here is a pun in the original.
   *Oliscan à* terceras, *avièndo dexàdo de sèr* primas. *Tercera* signifies a *Third* or *Go-between*, and
   *Prima* a *First* or *Principal*. That is, in plain *English*, *Bawd* after *Whore.*"
3. "Brilladoro; nor Bayarte": See above, p. 365 and n. 6 (pt. 1, bk. 4, chap. 25). In *Sir Launcelot
   Greaves* (chap. 5) the hero names his horse Bronzomarte, "hoping that he will rival in swiftness
   and spirit Bayardo, Brigliadoro, or any other steed of past or present chivalry!"
4. "Or in English, *Wooden Peg the winged*": Original: "se llama Clavileño el Aligero." With Smol-
   lett's translation, compare Motteux ("*Clavileno*, or *Wooden-Peg* the *Swift*") and Jarvis ("*Clavileno*

*the winged")*. Shelton/Stevens comments that Clavileno is *"A Name compounded of the two* Spanish *words* Clavo *a Nail or Pin, and* Leno *Wood."*

## Chapter 9

1. "Equivalent to Abington law . . . . hanged": Original: "dèn con nosotros en Peralvillo." Literally, "will make off with us to Peralvillo" (Putnam). With Smollett's note, compare Stevens, who identifies Peralvillo as "a village near *Ciudad Real*, in *Castile*": "Justícia . . . . Prov. *La justícia de Peralvíllo, que ahorcádo el hombre le haze la pesquísa: Abington* law, to hang a man first, and try him afterwards. *Peralvillo* is a place where the officers for apprehending of highway-men, called *la Santa Hermandád*, or the holy brotherhood, execute robbers they take *in flagrante*, and therefore they need no tryal." Jarvis cites Pineda as the source for his briefer note on this expression; but, except for an error ("ahor cado" for *"ahorcádo"*) not found in Smollett, Pineda merely repeats Stevens verbatim.
2. "In Spain, the Pleiades . . . nanny goats": Original: "las siete cabrillas." Beginning with Shelton/Stevens, all Smollett's predecessors explain this allusion.
3. "There is a kind of pleasantry . . . he goat": Original: "entre essas cabras algun cabron." All Smollett's predecessors except Motteux explain the double meaning of *cabron*.

## Chapter 10

1. "provided I remember my Christ-cross": Original: "tener el Christus à la memoria." Jarvis first explained this reference: "The *Cross* put at the beginning of the *A.B.C.* from thence called the *Christ-cross-row*." The *OED* (Christ-cross, 2) takes Smollett to mean the mark of the cross made by an illiterate person in "signing" his name; however, Putnam (2:1013, col. a, n. 3) concurs with Jarvis's reading.
2. "The phrase *No quiero de tu capilla* . . . tongues": Jarvis has "or a friar's hood to receive alms in," commenting that the phrase "cannot be rendered into *English*. *Cervantes* alludes to this proverb; *No quiero, mas echàdmelo en mi capilla*. i.e. 'I will not, but throw it into my hood.' It is applied to the begging friars, who refuse to take money, but suffer it to be thrown into their hood." See also Stevens ("Capílla").

## Chapter 11

1. "wind-whiffer": Original: "cernicalo" (the windhover), which Stevens defines as "a bird or hawk call'd a kestrel, or wind-whiffer."
2. "as foreign . . . as an old ballad": Original: "como por los cerros de Ubeda." See above, p. 542 n. (pt. 2, bk. 3, chap. 1).
3. "He whose father is mayor—you know": Original: "èl que tiene el padre Alcalde." Neither Smollett nor Jarvis (who vaguely supposes that Sancho "hints at some well known proverb") consulted their usual sources here. Previous translators understood the proverb as defined by Stevens: "Pádre . . . . Prov. *Quién pádre tiéne alcálde segúro va a juízio:* He whose father is judge goes safe to his trial."
4. "Instead of *saintly*": Original: "al buen callar llaman Sancho." Jarvis comments: "The proverb is, *To keep silence well is called* (santo) *holy*; but *Sancho* changes it out of archness or ignorance." See also Stevens ("Callár").

## Chapter 12

1. "with short stirrups": Original: "à la gineta." See above, p. 263 and n. 1 (pt. 1, bk. 4, chap. 9).
2. "Wast thou in deserts bred, / . . . Did serpents give thee suck": Here Altisidora's complaint to "cruel love" recalls Ægon in Pope's "Autumn": "I know thee Love! On foreign Mountains bred, / Wolves gave thee suck, and savage Tygers fed" (89–90).
3. "I was pummelled . . . the inchanted Moor": Previous translators (except Motteux) refer the reader to the beating Don Quixote suffered at the hands of the jealous carrier (pt. 1, bk. 3, chap. 2).

## Chapter 13

1. "*Barato* signifies cheap": Original: "se llamava la Insula Barataria, ò yà por el barato con que se le avia dado el Govierno." All Smollett's predecessors except Shelton define *barato*.
2. "this Robin Goodfellow": Original: "este buen hombre." Puck, the legendary, mischievous elf of Shakespeare's *A Midsummer Night's Dream;* another instance of Smollett's finding a more colorful English idiom for the plain Spanish of the original.

## Chapter 15

1. "Omnis saturatio . . . pessima": "All surfeit is bad, but that of partridges is worst." Doctor Rezio attributes to Hippocrates a proverbial saying, substituting *perdix* (partridge) for *panis* (bread) (Putnam 2:1017, col. a, n. 4).
2. "The Spanish name is *Pedro Rezio de Aguiero* [orig. *Aguero*] . . . *Tirte Afuera* . . . better understood": Smollett alone among the early translators preserved the humor of the passage by finding English equivalents for these names ("Pedro Positive de Bode-well, native of . . . Snatchaway" and Sancho's inverted version of the former "Pedro Positive de Bode-ill"). Jarvis, like his predecessors, simply reproduced the Spanish; he did, however, explain the jest: "*Rezio de Aguero* signifies *Positive of the omen;* and *Tirteafuera, take yourself away*"; "*Rezio de mal Aguero,* that is, *Doctor positive of the ill omen.*"
3. "was going to snatch himself away from his presence": Original: "hazer Tirteafuera de la sala." The verb phrase is made of the name of the doctor's hometown, which Smollett has rendered "Snatchaway" (see above, n. 2). Jarvis has "would have taken himself out of the hall," commenting: "According to the original, *would have* tirteafuera'd *it*, alluding to the doctor's . . . name. It is in some measure preserved by our cant phrase of *taking one's self away.*"
4. "The original *Ponga en pretina* . . . girdle": Smollett alone attempts to construe literally this figurative expression, which means to make someone behave. It is not found in either Stevens or Pineda, but see the Royal Dictionary: "PRETINA . . . . Poner en *pretina.*"
5. "a simple soul": Original: "una alma de cantaro." See above, p. 432, n. 1 (pt. 2, bk. 1, chap. 13).
6. "as honest as a well weighed loaf": Original: "tan bueno como el buen pan." Jarvis has, lamely, "as harmless as a piece of bread," commenting: "*Pan agradecido.* When the country-people would define an honest good natured man, they say, *He is as good as bread itself.*"
7. "She is in the original called *Perlerina* . . . play on the words": Smollett is alone in thus rendering ("Paralina . . . Paralytic") the alliteration of the play on words in the original ("Perlerina . . . Perlaticos [those afflicted with the palsy]"). Jarvis, citing *perlaticos* in a note, has "Perlerina . . . because all of that race are subject to the palsy."

## Chapter 16

1. "preserve the buckle": *OED* (buckle, *sb*, 3) quotes Johnson on this obsolete sense of the word: "The state of the hair crisped and curled by being kept long in the same state."
2. "perturbed spirit": Original: "alma en pena"—Jarvis and Motteux translate this literally as "soul in torment." Smollett's phrase recalls Hamlet addressing his father's ghost ("Rest, rest, perturbed spirit!" [1.5.183]).
3. "he will never give you an high nose . . . serve your turn": Original: "antes os la darà roma, que aguiléña." Smollett follows Jarvis, who first rendered this literally, "sooner tempt a man with a flat-nosed [*roma*] than a hawk-nosed [*aguiléña*] woman," commenting: "That is, *with a foul, than a fair object.*"
4. "dark as a dog's mouth": Original: "como boca de lobo." Jarvis, who first rendered this literally, has "dark as a wolf's mouth," commenting: "Because a wolf's mouth is black, say the dictionaries." See Stevens and Pineda ("Bóca").

## Chapter 17

1. "hachis": Hash. The earliest example in the *OED* is Smollett's *Peregrine Pickle* (1751), chap. 48: "a curious hachis of the lights, liver and blood of an hare."
2. "*Podrida* signifies rotten . . . *Pot-pourri*": In this note added to the second edition Smollett thus explains the revision "staler" for "powerfuller." He had originally been influenced, probably, by the following comment in Jarvis: "*Podrida* is usually interpreted *rotten*, as if the stewing them together was supposed to have the same effect, as to making them tender, as rottenness would have. But *Covarruvias*, in his etymologies, derives it from *poderoso*, *powerful*, because all the ingredients are substantial and nourishing. And this is confirmed by *Sancho's* adding, *the stronger they are the better.*" See Stevens: "Podrído, rotten." In *Gil Blas* (bk. 9, chap. 4; 3:239 n.) Smollett glossed the term more simply: "Olla podrida, a dish compos'd of all sorts of food."
3. "Literally, *the devil's in Cantillana* . . . Sevil": Original: "el diablo està en Cantillana." Smollett was first to gloss this expression, if not very helpfully. (The sense is that "there is disorder, or a disturbance, somewhere" [Putnam 2:1018, col. b, n. 6].) Stevens ("Cantillána") locates the town, but does not explain the expression. Jarvis alters it silently to "the devil is in the wind"; all others adopt Shelton's peculiar version, "there's rods in pisse for them."

## Chapter 18

1. "Literally, the *Aranjuez* . . . . gardens and fountains": Original: "el aranjuez de sus fuentes." Only Shelton renders this literally. Jarvis has "the fountains of her issues," but in his note Smollett follows Stevens: "Aranjuéz, a village seven leagues from *Madrid*, where the kings of *Spain* have a palace and wonderful fine gardens."
2. "he that gives . . . an egg . . . lame of a leg": Original: "quien te da el huego, no te querria ver muerta." Smollett's rendering is a rhyming paraphrase of Jarvis, who alone among previous translators literally renders the proverb as found in the Pineda edition (which has *huevo* for *huego*): "*Whoever gives thee an egg, has no mind to see thee dead.*" Three variants of the original exist: *huego* (obs. for *fuego*, fire [Stevens]); *huevo* (an egg); and *hueso* (a bone), the last being the preferred reading.
3. "I'll look upon her as an upstart": Original: "yo la pondrè como nueva." Jarvis, following Motteux, renders this as "I will make her know her distance." Smollett's translation (the reading preferred by Putnam) may have been suggested by Jarvis's comment: "Word for word, *I will*

*put her as one new.* The meaning is not obvious, and the dictionaries are of no help here. Perhaps it may be, *I will treat her as a new-comer."*

4. "like the pope's lady": Original: "como . . . una Papesa." Smollett follows Jarvis, who comments: *"Papesa. A She-pope.* Our translators have rendered this *Pope Joan* [a legendary female pope of the ninth century]. But there is more humour in making the country people so ignorant as to believe the pope had, if not a wife, a concubine, as many of the great clergy had, than in supposing they had ever heard of *Pope Joan."*

5. "throw thee some good beneficial bone . . . the favour": "te hizieren tus tus con alguna buena dadiva embasala." See above, p. 543 n. (pt. 2, bk. 3, chap. 1).

6. "There goes Mrs. ape . . . that stuff": Original: "viose el perro en bragas de cerro, y lo demas." Sanchica omits the conclusion of this rhyming proverb, "y no conoció su compañero" ("The dog saw himself in hempen breeches and did not know his companion" [Putnam 2:1019, col. b, n. 18]). Jarvis had changed the dog into a monkey ("The higher the monkey climbs, the more he exposes his bald buttocks, and so forth"); but Smollett's rendering is closer to the sense of the original and preserves the rhyming.

7. "Dubitat Augustinus": "Augustine doubts [it]," an expression used by casuists arguing points of dogma (Putnam, citing Rodríguez Marín, 2:1019, col. b, n. 19).

8. "Operibus credite & non verbis": See above, pt. 2, bk. 2, chap. 8, n. 1.

## Chapter 19

1. "Amicus Plato, sed magis amica veritas": "Plato is a friend, but a greater friend is the truth"; a proverbial rendering of a passage in Aristotle's *Nicomachean Ethics* 1.6.1 (Putnam 2:1020, col. a, n. 8).

2. "he rated the wages . . . road of interest": Original: "Puso tassa en los salarios de los criados que caminavan à rienda suelta por el camino del interesse." Jarvis dully paraphrased this as "He limited the wages of servants, which before were very extravagant," commenting, "Literally, *travelled unbridled in the road of interest."*

# Book 4

## Chapter 1

1. "soupe-meagre": Original: "gazpachos." Stevens: "Gaspácho, a sort of sops or soupe maiger." Previous translators have "porridge" or "pottage."

2. "the seven days": Original: "los diez dias." Smollett silently emends an inconsistency in the text that Jarvis pointed out: "How comes the steward to say *ten days*, when it is plain *Sancho* governed only *seven days?*" This is one of the "inadvertencies" in the narrative to which Smollett refers below, p. 654 n. (bk. 4, chap. 4).

## Chapter 2

1. "who has pilgrimized thee": Original: "quien te ha hecho Franchote." Shelton alone renders this expression literally, "who hath made such a *Franchote* of thee?" commenting: "A word of disgrace the Spaniard useth to all strangers, but chiefly to the French." Smollett's other predecessors render the word as "frenchified." His use of the verb transitively here is the only example cited by the *OED* (pilgrimize, 2).

2. "governed . . . like a perfect sagittary": Original: "como un sagitario." The simile has per-
plexed Cervantes' translators, who suggest that *sagittarius* in the Germania slang "is one who
is whipped through the streets" (Ormsby, Watts, Putnam [2:1022, col. a, n. 20])—an inept
figure, however, for an autocratic governor. Smollett's "sagittary" (a centaur) seems preferable:
*OED* cites Shakespeare, *Troilus and Cressida*, 5.5.14 ("The dreadful Sagitary / Appals our
numbers").

## Chapter 3

1. "bare as an atomy": Smollett's simile, embellishing the original "raydos" (bare) with the image
of a skeleton in an anatomy theater, is cited in *OED* ("atomy"). See also *Ferdinand Count
Fathom*, chap. 28: "like a walking atomy" (130).
2. "This was a Moorish princess . . . this day": Stevens: "GALIÁNA, the Moorish name of a
woman. There was a princess of this name at *Toledo*, for whom her father built a stately palace,
near the river *Tagus*, the ruins whereof remain, and are to this day called *The palace of* Galiana."

## Chapter 4

1. "A critic inclined to enumerate the inadvertencies . . . the bosom": For the three "inadverten-
cies" to which Smollett refers, see above, in this same book, chapters 2–3: Sancho's giving all
his provisions to the pilgrims but then feeding Dapple; chapters 1–3, and below, chapter 10:
Sancho's governing seven days, but the steward and Sancho himself declaring it to be ten (see
chap. 1, n. 2); and chapter 4: Donna Rodriguez's daughter "veiled . . . even to the bosom"
(p. 653).
2. "In the romance of Gerard de Nevers . . . now involved": Ste. Palaye, *Mémoire*, 2, n. 37: "La
Demoiselle dont Gérard de Nevers entreprit la défense, ayant vû l'empressement avec lequel
il s'y porta, *elle prit son gand senestre, si le bailla à Gérard, qui moult volentiers le prit, en lui disant:
Sire, mon corps, ma vie, mes terres & mon honneur, je mets en la garde de Dieu & de vous, auquel je
prie Dieu qu'il doint à vous telle grace octroyer que au dessus en puissiez venir & nous oster du danger
où nous sommes*" (20:726).

## Chapter 5

1. "I know nothing of the matter": Original: "como por los cerros de Ubeda." See above, p. 542
n. (pt. 2, bk. 3, chap. 1).

## Chapter 6

1. "Moor-killer": Original: "Don san Diego, mata Moros." Smollett's predecessors gloss the
Spanish epithet within the text—*e.g.*, Motteux/Ozell: "Don *Sant-Jago, Mata Moros*, or Don
St. *James the Moor-killer*."
2. "The original word is Mendoza . . . superstitious": Original: "Derramasele al otro Mendoça
la sal encima de la mesa." With Smollett's note compare Jarvis commenting on "Mendoza":
"Probably some family of that name avowed the superstition here ridiculed"; and Stevens:
"MENDÓÇA, the surname of a most noble family in *Spain*."
3. "The Moors . . . descended from Hagar": Original: "los Agarenos esquadrones." Jarvis, fol-
lowing Shelton/Stevens, has "the *Hagarene* squadrons," commenting: "They have a tradition,
that the *Moors* are descended from *Hagar*" (Genesis 16).

4. "Sancho must have been very simple . . . . close with the foe": See above, p. 394 n. (pt. 2, bk. 1, chap. 4).

## Chapter 7

1. "a dish of cow-heel . . . . Come, eat me: come, eat me": Original: "dos uñas de vaca . . . Comeme, comeme." Smollett recalls this passage in *Adventures of an Atom:* "like the cow-heel in Don Quixote, it seemed to cry, *Comenme, comenme;* Come, eat me, come, eat me" (57–58, n. 638). In *Sir Launcelot Greaves* (chap. 4) "the delicate rumps . . . seem to cry 'Come cut me— come cut me.'"

2. "I am apt to believe . . . the proper place": Smollett had earlier noticed, p. 58 n. (pt. 1, bk. 1, chap. 7), that Sancho's wife, introduced as Juana, was "suddenly metamorphosed into Mary."

3. "The proverb, in the original . . . beat the tabor": Original: "quien las sabe, las tañe." The proverb does not allude specifically to the tabor. Stevens: "TAÑÉR, to play upon some musical instrument; also to ring bells." Thus Jarvis and Putnam have "Let him who knows the instrument play on it"; Ormsby, "let him who knows how ring the bells."

4. "Cum mero mixto imperio": Literally, "mastery having been mixed with undiluted wine"—a "juridical formula," according to Putnam (2:1025, col. a, n. 18), who omits the Latin phrase altogether, preferring the following in English: "Sancho remained with the stew-pot and, invested with delegated plenary authority, seated himself at the head of the table."

## Chapter 8

1. "This rhime is substituted . . . in the original": Original: "esta fuera la hora que ya la tal Donzella no lo fuera." Jarvis has simply, "at this very hour that same maiden would not have been one."

2. "Gascoons": Original: "Gascones." ("Gascon" is the usual spelling in English.) The men of Gascony were notorious for swaggering. *OED* cites the following verses from a song in Smollett's *Reprisal* (1757, 1.3): "A peacock in pride, in grimace a baboon, / In courage a hind, in conceit a gascoon." In *Roderick Random* (1748), chap. 40, Smollett's hero chastizes a Gascon for his "insolent boasting."

3. "as deep calleth unto deep": Original: "como un abismo llama à otro, y un pecado à otro pecado." Smollett omits the latter phrase ("and one sin to another sin") and in rendering the former follows Jarvis's comment: "Literally: *One abyss calls to another.* It is a scripture phrase, borrowed from [Psalm 42:7] *Deep calleth unto deep.*"

## Chapter 10

1. "Literally, *Use the times as I find them*": Original: "y uso de los tiempos como los hallo." Though *tiempo* can mean "a term" in the sense of a period of time (see Stevens), Jarvis's translation seems preferable: "take the times as I find them."

2. "This was *Michael Scot* . . . . inchantment": Original: "del famoso Escotillo." Jarvis took this to be a reference to Michael Scot, thereby prompting Smollett's remarks on the apparent anachronism. With Smollett's note compare Moréri: "SCOT (Michel) naquit à Balwirie dans le Comte de Fife en Ecosse . . . ver l'an 1214. . . . [Il] s'appliqua à l'étude de la Médecine, dont il voulut apprendre toutes les parties, principalement la Chymie, & même l'Alchymie . . . . Il y mourut [in England] l'an 1291, âgé d'environ 77 ans. Son habileté dans la Chymie & dans les Mathématiques le fit passer pour Magicien dans l'esprit du Vulgaire." Ormsby later denied

the anachronism, proposing that Cervantes was referring to his contemporary Michael Escoto, a native of Parma, who was also suspected of being a magician.

3. "Fugite partes adversæ!": "Flee, ye adversaries!"—a formula of the Church in exorcizing evil spirits (Putnam 2:1027, col. b, n. 13).

4. "Trifles": Original: "los jugetes." Smollett's predecessors simply translate the Spanish word as *"Trifles"* in the text.

5. "a translation . . . like the wrong side of Flemish tapestry": Smollett liked this famous simile, adapting it to different contexts in the *Critical Review*, 15 (1763): 18, and in his letter to John Moore, 8 February 1767 (*Letters*, 131).

6. "About Martinmas . . . bacon": Jarvis had commented: *"Martinmas . . .* is the time for making bacon for winter." See also Stevens ("Puérco").

## *Chapter 11*

1. "cakes and gingerbread": See above, p. 109 and n. 1 (pt. 1, bk. 3, chap. 3).

## *Chapter 14*

1. "Here Troy once stood!": See above, p. 519 n. (pt. 2, bk. 2, chap. 12).

2. "Limberham . . . Loggerhead": Original: "del flaco [of the lean one] . . . del gordo [of the fat one]." The name Limberham, literally a supple-jointed person, was familiar from the character in Dryden's comedy *Limberham* (1678); it occurs earlier in Wycherley's *The Country Wife* (1675): see *OED*.

3. "'thy master is bankrupt in common sense.' 'How bankrupt!'": Original: "deve de ser un loco. Como deve, respondio Sancho, no deve nada à nadie." Compare Jarvis, who first attempted to render this pun: "ought to be reckoned a madman. Why *ought?* replied *Sancho;* he owes nothing to any body," commenting: "A *double entendre* upon the word *deve,* which is put for *must,* the sign of a mood, or for owing a debt."

## *Chapter 15*

1. "such a life will square . . . the very corner-stone of my wishes": Jarvis ("this kind of life squares and corners with me exactly") was first to render this architectural metaphor, commenting: *"Quadrado y esquinado;* alluding to the corner-stone of a building, which answers both ways." See also below, p. 737: "who, though they will not square, may corner with our desires" (chap. 21).

2. "old Boscan . . . Nemoroso": Previous translators noticed that "Boscan" derives from the Spanish *bosque* (a wood); Jarvis also noted that "Nemoroso" derives from the Latin *nemus* (a grove), commenting: "In plain *English, as if Mr.* Wood *should call himself Mr.* Grove." Smollett uncharacteristically ignores these helpful precedents.

3. "his collars and points are truly poetical": Original: "tener sus puntas y collares de Poëta." Jarvis, following Stevens ("Púnta"), was first to render this expression literally, as "he has the points and collar [*sic*] of a poet," commenting: "Formerly, in *Spain,* the men of quality wore loose coats sloped down before and unbuttoned, under which appeared the rich waistcoat, and its *collar* terminating in two *points."*

4. "What prayers ne'er can gain . . . will obtain": Original: "mas vale salto de mata, que ruego de hombres buenos." See above, p. 144 n. † (pt. 1. bk. 3, chap. 7).

5. "like the frying-pan . . . black-a-moor, avaunt!": Original: "dixo la sarten à la caldera, quitate

allà ojinegra." Compare Jarvis, following Stevens ("Sartén"), "The kettle called the pot black-arse," commenting: "Literally, *The frying-pan said to the kettle, Stand away, thou black thing.*"

## Chapter 16

1. "Post tenebras spero lucem": "After darkness I hope for light" (Job 17:12, Vulgate). Appearing on the title pages of parts 1 and 2 of the original edition of *Don Quixote*, this is the motto of Cervantes' publisher, Juan de la Cuesta (Putnam 2:1031, col. b, n. 2).
2. "Not he with whom you was bred . . . fed": See above, p. 416 and n. 2 (pt. 2, bk. 1, chap. 10).
3. "cake and gingerbread": See above, p. 109 and n. 1 (pt. 1, bk. 3, chap. 3).

## Chapter 17

1. "I am an old dog . . . coaxed with a crust": Original: "yo soy perro viejo, y no ay conmigo tus tus." See above, p. 543 n. (pt. 2, bk. 3, chap. 1).
2. "This is reel upon reel . . . pancakes": Original: "argado, sobre argado, y no miel sobre hojuelas." Jarvis, following Stevens ("Argádo"), has "Reel upon reel, and not honey upon fritters," commenting: "That is, Toil upon toil, and nothing to sweeten it."
3. "the wedding heifer": Original: "la vaca de la boda." Smollett echoes Jarvis, who explains the expression "To be slain for the use of others." Also Stevens *("Váca")*.

## Chapter 19

1. "We cannot catch trouts . . . clouts": Original: "no se toman truchas, y no digo mas." Jarvis translates this literally ("They do not take trouts—I say no more"), but in a note taken from Stevens ("Trúcha") supplies the rhyming proverb, which Smollett renders as *"No se toman truchas a bràgas enxutas.* i.e. *They do not take trouts with dry breeches."*
2. "Deum de Deo": "God from God"—from the Nicene creed, referring to the second Person of the Trinity: "Deum de Deo, lumen de lumine, Deum verum de Deo vero."
3. *"Wherever it may hit . . . sound"*: Compare Jarvis's note: *"Wherever it hits.* No affinity, but of sound, and that but small."
4. "sicut erat": See above, p. 332 and n. 4 (pt. 1, bk. 4, chap. 19).

## Chapter 21

1. "Malum Signum, Malum Signum!": "A bad sign!"—Latin phrase used by medical writers (Putnam 2:1034, col. b, n. 2).
2. "In the original, as fine as Mingo . . . Cervantes": Original: "mas galan que Mingo." Jarvis renders this literally, as "finer than Mingo," and in a note that misled Smollett comments that Mingo was "A scurvy long-winded poet of *Spain*, the author's contemporary, and probably a beau of those times." The allusion is rather to the opening lines of the fifteenth-century satire, *Mingo Revulgo:* "Mingo Revulgo! What! It's you! / What have you done with your doublet blue? / Your Sunday suit?" (Ormsby). See also the preface to part 2 above, where Smollett has Cervantes imagine "more books . . . published against me than there are letters in the couplets of Mingo Rebulgo" (p. 370).
3. "though they will not square, may corner": Original: "sino nos quadraren, no esquinen." See above, p. 711 and n. 1 (pt. 2, bk. 4, chap. 15).
4. "turn a poor shepherd. . . . as the saying is": Original: "haziendose Pastorcillo, tu que vienes

Pastorcico, tu que vas." Jarvis has simply "turning shepherd," commenting: "Literally, *making yourself, Little Shepherd that comes, Little Shepherd that goes.* An allusion, I suppose, to some *Pastorals* then well known." Rather, the lines are from a Christmas carol by Francisco de Ocaña (Putnam 2:1035, col. a, n. 15).

### Chapter 22

1. "Giving an account . . . illness and death": Original: *"De como Don Quixote cayò malo, y del Testamento que hizo, y su muerte"*; literally, as in Jarvis, *"How* Don Quixote *fell sick, made his will, and died."* Smollett alone omits reference to the making of the will in the heading to this last chapter.

2. "Lines probably . . . old ballad or romance": Original: "Tate, tate, follonzicos, de ninguno sea tocada, porque esta empresa buen Rey, para mi estava guardada." These lines, as Gregorio recognized (47, n. (*o*)), are from "an old Romance" or, rather, a ballad: the "Guerras civiles de granada" (Putnam 2:1036, col. a, n. 14).

3. "The author of the Second Part . . . Old Castile": Smollett was the first translator to note this allusion to the spurious continuation of *Don Quixote*, though the passage in question is not found in Avellaneda's preface. He was probably again indebted to Ozell's translation of Gregorio (47, n. (*q*)), who, quoting the concluding paragraph of *Don Quixote*, observes: *"The silly Continuator in his last Chapter hints as if he design'd to write some of* Don Quixote's *Rambles in* Old Castile."

# GLOSSARY

[*Note:* Reference to the *OED* after a word indicates that Smollett's usage in this translation serves in that dictionary as an illustration of its meaning.]

**alcalde** (384. 33, etc.). Magistrate, sheriff.

**atabal** (501. 21, etc.). Kettledrum used by the Moors.

**atomy** (648. 39). Skeleton (*OED:* atomy¹): see pt. 2, bk. 4, chap. 3, n. 1.

**band** (17. 31, 458. 5). Collar of a shirt (*OED:* band, *sb².* 1.4.a).

**bank** (699.36). Bench of rowers of each oar in a galley.

**beak** (279. 2). Pointed prow of a war galley.

**beam** (350. 2). Wooden roller in a weaver's loom.

**belly-timber** (408. 10). Food.

**berengena** (437. 36). Eggplant.

**biggen** (349. 37). Cap or hood: see pt. 1, bk. 4, chap. 22, n. 3.

**bored** (411. 3). To board a ship.

**botcher** (40. 24, etc.). Tailor who does repairs.

**botching** (259. 21). Repairing.

**brachman** (337. 40). Brahmin, member of the highest Hindu caste.

**breeds** (17. 31). Braids.

**brocard** (527. 10, etc.). Brocade.

**bucking** (535. 9). Washing cloth in lye to bleach it.

**buckle** (607. 6). Curl of the hair: see pt. 2, bk. 3, chap. 16, n. 1.

**buckler** (640. 15, etc.). Shield.

**budget** (385.2). Wallet.

**cabbage** (593. 36). To appropriate cloth surreptitiously (said of a tailor).

**calabash** (709. 35). Shell of a gourd, used for holding liquids.

**calenture** (124. 30 etc.). Fever.

**camblet** [camlet] (587. 9). Cloth made of Angora goat hair.

**canted** (271. 32). Tossed with a sudden jerk (*OED:* cant, *v².* 1. 4).

**capitan galley** (282. 41). Galley of the chief admiral of the Turkish fleet (*OED*).

**caption,** warrant of (328. 27). Warrant of arrest (Scotch law).

**cased** (469. 29). Skinned.

**cerecloth** (101. 7) (*OED: sb,* 2). See **searcloth.**

**chape** (17. 30). Metal plate of a scabbard.

**Christ-cross** (579. 7). Cross preceding the alphabet in school primers: see pt. 2, bk. 3, chap. 10, n. 1 (*OED*).

**clapped up** (283. 25). To settle or concoct something hastily (*OED:* clap *v¹,* IV. 13. b).

**clape** [clap] (302. 25). Swing the helm hard to windward: see pt. 1, bk. 4, chap. 14, n. 3.

**clouted** (386. 18, etc.). Patched.

**clyster** (427. 39). Enema.

**coarse** [corse](714. 29, etc.). Corpse.

**coifed** (183. 29). Covered with a coif, a woman's close-fitting cap (*OED:* coif *v,* 1).

**corse** (87. 23, etc.). Corpse. See **coarse.**

**court-hand** (173. 28). Difficult style of writing used in English law courts until abolished by statute in the reign of George II (*OED*).

**crambo** (155. 30). Rhyming.
**crupper** (85. 3, etc.). Rear of a horse.
**cuerpo,** in (98. 3). Naked: see pt. 1, bk. 3, chap. 1, n. 1.

**doit** (693. 3). Dutch coin worth half a farthing (*OED:* doit, 1).
**drugoman** [dragoman] (501. 13). Interpreter: see pt. 2, bk. 2, chap. 8, n. 2.
**draughts** (658. 26). Game of checkers.

**ear-broker** (147. 14). Pimp: see pt. 1, bk. 3, chap. 8, n. 1.
**eking** (345. 41). Adding to (*OED:* eke *v*, 1).
**eructing** (582. 30). Belching (*OED:* eruct, 1).

**flea** (43. 21, etc.). Flay.
**flummery** (433. 2). Food made of thickened oatmeal.
**fulling-hammers** (134. 26). Wooden hammers used in milling cloth.
**fusil** (676. 14). Light musket.

**galls,** cork tree (421. 19). Growths caused by insects.
**Gascoons** [Gascons] (678. 31). Natives of Gascony, a former province of southwestern France: see
    pt. 2, bk. 4, chap. 8, n. 2.
**girted** [girthed] (522. 19). Secured the girth of a saddle.
**glyster** (100. 25). See **clyster.**
**glyster-pipes** (632. 25). Tubes for administering clysters (*OED*).
**godwits** (613. 32). Marsh birds, once considered a delicious food.
**gorbellied** (384. 31–32). Potbellied.

**hachis** (613. 30). Hash: see pt. 2, bk. 3, chap. 17, n. 1.
**hansel** [handsel] (496. 7). Reward.
**hanselled** [handselled] (322. 12). Used for the first time.
**hause** [hawse] (302. 24). Bow of a ship.
**heats** (496. 39). Courses in a horse race.
**helve** (414. 1). Handle of an ax.
**hough** (28. 2). Hoe.

**inexplicable** (465. 15–16). Not capable of being disentangled.

**jack-pudding** (525. 27). Clown, buffoon.
**jolterhead** [jolt head] (390. 18). Blockhead.

**knight of the post** (527. 32). Notorious perjurer.
**knitting-sheath** (610. 17). Cylindrical sheath for holding a knitting needle steady when knitting
    (*OED:* knitting, 3).

**lappets** (331. 8). Bands hanging from the collar: see pt. 1, bk. 4, chap. 19, n. 3.
**Limberham** (708. 42). A supple-jointed person: see pt. 2, bk. 4, chap. 14, n. 2 (*OED*).
**lucifer** (169. 23, etc.). Venus, the morning star.

**matches** (682. 11). Wicks for firing muskets.
**maugre** (679. 26). In spite of (*OED*, B. 1).
**merry-andrew** (527. 33). Clown.
**minoret** [minaret] (503. 23). Tower of a mosque.
**morrice bells** [morris bells] (628. 28). Small bells worn by morris dancers.
**morrion** [morion] (30. 17, etc.). Helmet.

**mumping** (405. 19). Grimacing.

**murry-coloured** [murrey-coloured](587. 9, etc.). Purple-red, like the mulberry.

**negromancers** [necromancers] (12. 16, etc.). Magicians, conjurers.

**nervous** (622. 21). Vigorous.

**nuncio** (731. 39–40). Official papal representative in a foreign country.

**obumbrated** (713. 31). Overshadowed, darkened.

**olla podrida** (613. 38). Stew of various meats, vegetables, etc.: see pt. 2, bk. 3, chap. 17, n. 2.

**ombre** (658. 27). Card game.

**otherguise** (596. 18). Of another kind (*OED*).

**outrance,** to fight to (86. 32). To fight to the death (*OED*).

**pannel** [panel] (17. 39, etc.). Wooden saddle for an ass; also a cloth placed under the saddle of a horse to protect its back.

**pannier** (108. 9). Large basket for carrying provisions.

**pencil** (637. 7). Artist's paintbrush.

**pigsnies** (220. 42). From "pigsney," a term of endearment for a darling girl.

**pillion** (154. 23, etc.). Pad attached to the back of a saddle for carrying a second rider or luggage.

**pipkin** (637. 15). Small pot.

**placket** (622. 19). The slit at the top of a skirt or petticoat (*OED:* placket, 3).

**plantane water** [plantain water] (60. 36). Juice from plantain leaves.

**pledgit** [pledget] (277. 30). Small compress for a wound.

**points** (674. 8). Short straps to hold items of clothing in place.

**poll** (591. 8). Head.

**postern** (640. 27). Back door.

**prefer** a prayer (483. 3). To present formally.

**ravelin** (287. 27–28). Outwork of a fort.

**reachings** (111. 8). Retchings, vomiting.

**road** (682. 35, etc.). Sheltered space of water near the shore, where ships may safely anchor.

**rochets** (644. 19). Cloaks, mantles (*OED:* rochet, 1).

**romp** (536. 1). Merry, playful girl.

**rowel** (117. 8). Sharp-pointed wheel at the end of a spur.

**ruddled** (584. 7). Marked with ruddle, a red variety of ochre (*OED*, ruddle *v*).

**sabæan** (221. 36). Ancient name of Yemen in Arabia, a region famous for spices.

**sacbuts** [sackbut] (510. 31). Bass trumpet with a slide like that of a trombone.

**saggitary** (647. 4). Centaur: see pt. 2, bk. 4, chap. 2, n. 2.

**saker** (575. 21). Large falcon used in falconry (*OED:* saker[1]).

**scrip** (737. 37). Scrap of paper with writing on it.

**scut** (168. 31). Hare's tail.

**searcloth** (99. 36). Cloth used as a plaster in surgery: see pt. 1, bk. 3, chap. 1, n. 3.

**sedan** (703. 3). Sedan chair, a closed vehicle carried on poles by two persons.

**sewer** (601. 15, etc.). Chief attendant at a meal.

**shamble** (469. 27). Butcher's stall.

**skink** (709. 38). Pour out liquor (*OED:* skink *v*, 3).

**skinker** (489. 18). One who pours out liquor: see pt. 2, bk. 2, chap. 6, n. 1.

**slipslops** (568. 11). Sloppy compounds used as medicines.

**smack smooth** (576. 23–24). Perfectly smooth (*OED:* smack-smooth).

**smoak** [smoke](417. 7). To suspect a plot or design.

**smock-faced** (383. 34). Having a smooth, effeminate face.

**souse** (575. 21). With a direct and rapid course (*OED:* souse *adv.*¹, 2).

**spadille** (658. 28). Ace of spades in **ombre.**

**stentrel** (283. 15, etc.). Central gangway of a galley: see pt. 1, bk. 4, chap. 12, n. 1 (*OED*).

**stone** (653. 36). Measure of weight usually equivalent to 14 pounds avoirdupois.

**strangury** (148. 6). Disease of the urinary organs.

**straw,** in the turning of a (692. 36). Instantly (*OED:* turning *vbl. sub.*, 4. b).

**superterrenne** (181. 32). Belonging to a region above the earth (*OED:* superterrene, 2).

**surrounded** (157. 29). Traveled around: see pt. 1, bk. 3, chap. 9, n. 5.

**tens,** the (485. 20). Decades (consisting of ten small beads and one large) of the Roman Catholic rosary.

**tossle** [tassel] (227.30). Pendent ornament on the academic cap.

**tow** (622. 18). Fiber of flax or hemp for spinning.

**truck** (431. 14). To barter.

**truckle-bed** (721. 5). Trundle bed, a low bed on castors pushed beneath a standing bed when not in use (*OED;* also *Ferdinand Count Fathom,* chap. 40).

**trunk-breeches** (626. 6). Trunk hose, full breeches covering the hips and upper thighs, fashionable in the sixteenth and seventeenth centuries (*OED;* also *Ferdinand Count Fathom,* chap. 40).

**truss** (362. 37). Bundle of hay.

**tuck** (100. 36, etc.). Rapier.

**tucker** (183. 17). Frill of lace worn round the neck.

**wain** (423. 27). Wagon.

**waits** (601. 6). A band of musicians.

**waloon** [walloon](458. 4, etc.). Person speaking a French dialect from the southeastern provinces of Belgium.

**wamblings** (111. 10). Feelings of nausea in the stomach.

**weasond** (217. 7). Gullet, windpipe: see pt. 1, bk. 4, chap. 3, n. 3.

**wind-whiffer** (582. 9). Windhover: see pt. 2, bk. 3, chap. 11, n. 1.

**wine-skinker** (349. 35). See **skinker.**

**woundy** (498. 23). Very great, extreme; *adv.* **woundily** (79. 37, etc.).

# APPENDIX: HAYMAN'S DESIGNS

Francis Hayman's original designs for the twenty-eight illustrations to Smollett's translation of Don Quixote are preserved in the Department of Prints and Drawings, The British Museum (call number: 201.b.4). Five of these, selected to illustrate the differences between Hayman's drawings and the engraved prints, are reproduced here with the permission of The British Museum. To facilitate comparison, page references for the five prints based on these designs are given in brackets after the captions to the plates.

The Decay of Chivalry [frontispiece].

Maritornes and Sancho Panza Fighting in Bed [p. 107].

Dorothea Bathing Her Feet in the Stream [p. 197].

Dorothea Received by Don Quixote as the Princess Micomicona [p. 210].

Don Quixote Attacking the Wine Bags in His Sleep [p. 258].

# TEXTUAL COMMENTARY

Preliminary announcements of Smollett's translation of *Don Quixote* appeared in the *General Advertiser* for 21 November 1748 and 7 September 1749. For a variety of reasons the work did not progress as planned, and Proposals were not published, according to the *Public Advertiser*, until 14 March 1754.[1] In fact, the Proposals may have been ready as early as February 1753, when William Strahan began the following entry in his printing ledgers:[2]

| 1753 | Partners in Don Quixotte | |
|------|--------------------------|---|
| Febry | | |
| | Proposals for Do. No. 1000 | 1-3-0 |
| | Proposals Do. On Writing Paper | 0-7-6 |
| | Printing Do. 114 Sheets No. 750 | |
| | on Royal Paper @ £1:0:0 | 114-0-0 |
| | For recomposing the first 10 Sheets | |
| | and ½ to print off 250, @ 13s. | 6-16-6 |
| | Used 173 Reams, had of Mr. Johnson | 122-7-0 |
| | pd in Notes April 12. 1759 | |

Strahan's reason for recomposing and printing ten and one-half sheets after 750 copies of the entire work had been printed is a puzzle. Perhaps some of the early sheets were damaged or destroyed in the print shop or at the binders, but if so, why were the partners responsible for the cost of recomposing and printing the ten and one-half sheets? Sheets B through L exist in two settings of type, but there is no significant textual reason for recomposing the sheets and there is no clear indication that Smollett had any part in the changes, although it is possible that he may have. To the corrections made in each sheet new errors are added, and a large number of minor variations are introduced.[3]

The publication of the first edition was announced in the *Public Advertiser* for 25 February 1755. A London second edition was available by 18 August 1761.[4] A London third edition appeared in 1765 and a fourth edition in 1770. Strahan, who now owned shares in *Don Quixote*[5] and placed his name first in the imprint, printed the first two volumes of the fourth and fifth editions:

1770                    Partners in Smollet's Don Quixotte
January
            Printing Vols. 1ˢᵗ· And 2d. of Do.
                    27 Sheets No. 2000 @ £2.1            55-7-0

                                                        55-7-0
                    Paid in Notes May 7.1770

1782                    Partners in Smollet's Don Quixote 12°
Octor.
            Printing Vols. 1 and 2. 27 Sheets No. 2000 @ £2-1-0
                                                        55-7-0
                    Paid Jan. 18. 1783.

The identity of the printers for the remaining portions of the work is unknown.

## EDITORIAL PRINCIPLES

As is the case with so many eighteenth-century writings, the autograph manuscript
of *Don Quixote* has disappeared. In fact, no printer's copy for any of Smollett's works has
survived. The nature of the manuscript can only be deduced from letters, never in-
tended for publication, and from an examination of manuscript revisions the author
made in a copy of the 1766 first edition of *Travels through France and Italy* for a new edi-
tion that did not appear.[6] The revisions for the *Travels* include additions, translations of
passages in foreign languages, and corrections to the printed text. It might be argued
that Smollett, by the mid-1760s largely free from his numerous editorial tasks, had new
leisure to correct the *Travels*, but an examination of other works he saw through the press
shows much the same care, for he left uncorrected only the kinds of errors that none but
the most exacting proofreaders might have caught.[7]

The revisions to the *Travels* are written in Smollett's neat hand, which, after more
than two centuries, can be read with ease. A compositor, then, would have had no diffi-
culty reading the author's manuscript of *Don Quixote*, but in the process of setting the
type an overlay of normalization no doubt occurred. As John Smith notes in *The
Printer's Grammar* (1755), "By the Laws of Printing, indeed, a Compositor should abide
by his Copy, and not vary from it. . . . But this good law is now looked upon as obsolete,
and most Authors expect the Printer to spell, point, and digest their Copy, that it may
be intelligible and significant to the Reader; which is what a Compositor and the Cor-
rector jointly have regard to, in Works of their own language." The compositor peruses
his copy but, before beginning to compose, "should be informed, either by the Author,
or Master, after what manner our work is to be done; whether the old way, with Capi-
tals to Substantives, and Italic to Proper names and Emphatical words," and nothing "to
Italic but what is underscored in our Copy." When composing from printed copy and
"such Manuscripts as are written fair," we "employ our eyes with the same agility as we
do our hands; for we cast our eyes upon every letter we aim at, at the same moment we

move our hands to take it up; neither do we lose our time in looking at our Copy for every word we compose; but take as many words into our memory as we can retain."[8] Since *Don Quixote* and the *Travels* are printed in the new way, numerous changes must have occurred between the manuscripts and the printed books, including some normalization of spelling.

In the lengthy manuscript additions to Letter II of the *Travels*—the English translation of a Latin letter to Antoine Fizes and the professor's reply in French—Smollett followed the old practice, though somewhat inconsistently, of capitalizing nouns and some adjectives. Schooled to capitalize substantives, he continued in his habitual way.[9] But he certainly knew that his capitalization and his use of the ampersand for "and" would be brought into conformity with the rest of the book. He seems to have accepted the new style, or at least acquiesced. In the printed text of the *Travels* he corrected such small matters as a transposed letter, "muscels" (the bivalve mollusc) to "muscles," and a verb "affords" to "afford"; at the same time he allowed to stand variant spellings such as "paltry"/"paultry," "ake"/"ach," and so on. Smollett was not consistent in his spelling, although he did have a preferred spelling for some words; but the compositors, by taking as many words into their memory as they could retain, sometimes introduced their preferences. Smollett appears to have been content with the resulting inconsistencies in spelling as long as they were correct, and he did not attempt to restore his capitalization and punctuation.

The 1755 first edition of *Don Quixote*, in quarto, printed from Smollett's lost manuscript or from a fair copy made from it, has been chosen as copy-text for this edition. The copy-text is, in fact, the first edition with the corrected sheets B through L; that is, the first edition of the ten sheets have been rejected in favor of the second edition of the sheets. However, when the ten corrected and uncorrected sheets were gathered for binding into the first volume, they were chosen at random and no one copy contains all of the corrected sheets. As is indicated below, the present edition is printed from the Arizona State University Library copy, with corrected sheets not included in this copy drawn from other copies. Corrected sheets E and G appear in the Arizona State University Library copy; sheet I is from the British Library (12490.k.6); sheet K is from the Cornell University Library (PQ6329 A2+ 1755, copy 1), with sheets B and L from the same library (PQ6329 A2+ 1755, copy 2); and sheets C, D, F, and H are from McMaster University Library (D268–69).[10] The 1755 first edition copy-text has been emended with substantive revisions made by Smollett for the 1761 London second edition, the first duodecimo edition.

Compositors, paid according to the amount of type they set, in general were not interested in emendation and improvement. They normally followed their copy with some care since they knew they would be penalized for failing to do so. Hence, the normal assumption is that substantive revisions are authorial. An alert compositor or proofreader might have corrected typographical errors such as "enchanted" for "enchanter" (29.28) and "on his shield" for "in his shield" (32.11), or corrected a grammatical mistake by substituting "their spoils" for "his spoils" (59.2), or even occasionally made sense out of nonsense as when "chance" is revised to "change" (79.29). Most changes in the second edition, however, are beyond the reach of a compositor and only could have been made by someone familiar with the translation.

Smollett clearly took out time from his busy schedule of writing and publication to make a number of verbal changes and provide additional annotations for this edition. Revising and correcting were habitual with Smollett, and he liked doing both after his texts had been made public. Among his important works, only the *Travels through France and Italy* (1766) and the *Expedition of Humphry Clinker* (1771) received the care and revision they needed before reaching print. In the first editions of the *Adventures of Roderick Random* (1748) and the *Adventures of Peregrine Pickle* (1751), as well as in *Don Quixote*, appear signs of hasty composition: verbosity, run-on sentences, awkward and redundant phrases, faulty pronoun references, unintentional alliteration, and so on.[11] As in the case of the revisions for the second editions of his first two novels, Smollett seems to be primarily concerned with ridding his translation of these signs of haste in composition. Occasionally adding a noun will clear up ambiguity. Early in the narrative, when Don Quixote is visiting his horse, the reader is told that "he thought it but reasonable, that since his master had altered his condition, he should also change his name." Even in context it takes a pause to discern the reference for "his." When Smollett revises the passage to read, "his horse's name" (30.33), the "his" refers to Rozinante and the confusion disappears. Frequently, long sentences are broken up by replacing "and" and "or" with a period, thereby eliminating certain ambiguities and quickening the pace of the narrative. Awkward and redundant phrases are omitted. For example, "other such ejaculations" becomes "other ejaculations" (38.35), "eyes, as it were, into" becomes "eyes into" (119.13), and "tale is at an end" becomes "tale is ended" (132.14). It is not necessary to have Lothario "lean the side of his head on his hand" when "lean his head on his hand" (241.2) will suffice, nor does the reader need to be told that Sancho and Don Quixote "mounted in order to proceed on their journey" when "proceeded in their journey" (716.12) is clear. Numerous revisions such as these are beyond the normal powers of a compositor. The revisions, the additions to the text, and the annotations could only have been provided by Smollett.

In the present edition no attempt has been made to achieve a general consistency in spelling, punctuation, or capitalization, because in the absence of the manuscript one cannot determine whether Smollett or the compositor was responsible for their variations. Hence the spelling, punctuation, or capitalization of the 1755 first edition have been retained except when they are clearly in error, or when they obscure meaning or distract the attention of the reader.[12] All emendations to the copy-text have been made on the authority of the textual editor. Hyphenated words at a line-end have been adjusted according to the usual practice of the first edition insofar as that practice could be ascertained from other appearances or parallels. Only the following changes have been made silently: all turned letters or wrong fonts have been corrected, the long *s* has been replaced by the modern letter *s*, and "ae" and "oe" have been treated as digraphs. The display capitals that begin the first paragraph in each chapter have not been exactly reproduced. Quotations have been indicated according to modern practice, and the punctuation in relation to the quotation marks has been normalized. The length of dashes and the spaces around them have also been normalized according to modern practice.

## APPARATUS

A basic note in the list of emendations provides the page-line reference and the emended reading in the present text. Except for the silent alterations described above, every editorial change in the first edition copy-text has been recorded. Following the square bracket is the earliest source of the emendation and the history of the copy-text reading up to the point of emendation. The historical collation follows the same form, except that the square bracket is followed by the subsequent history of the substantive variants in the texts examined. The historical collation is confined to substantive variants in the first five editions, whether they are emended first-edition readings or rejected unauthoritative readings. Emendations not found in the first five editions are marked "W" and are the responsibility of the present edition, whether they originated here or with a previous editor. A wavy dash ($\sim$) is substituted for a repeated word associated with pointing, and an inferior caret ($_\wedge$) indicates pointing absent in the present text or in one of the editions from which the variant was drawn. The form of the reading both to the right and to the left of the bracket conforms to the system of silent alterations, and there is no record of any variations except for the instance recorded. When the matter in question is pointing, for example, the wavy dash to the right of the bracket signifies only the substantive form of the variant, and any variation in spelling or capitalization has been ignored. Emendations from catchwords are indicated as *cw*. A (*c*) indicates the reading in the corrected state of the form, and (*u*) the uncorrected state. A vertical stroke ( | ) indicates a line-end.

All hyphenated compounds or possible compounds appearing at line-ends in the copy-text are recorded in the word-division list. The reader should assume that any word hyphenated at a line-end in the present text, but not appearing in this list, was broken by the modern typesetter.

## COLLATION

The present edition has been printed from the copy of the 1755 first edition in the Arizona State University Library (Spec C-2269), with corrected sheets printed from copies at the British Library, Cornell University Library (PQ6329 A2+ 1755 copy 1, copy 2) and McMaster University Library (D268–69, DOO1312–13). The ASU copy was bibliographically compared with copies at the British Library (Cerv. 388, 12490.k.6), Cambridge University Library (7743.b.6), University of Chicago Library (PQ6329 A2 1755), Edinburgh University Library (Dh. 6.86–87), Harvard University, Houghton Library (*f SC6 C3375 Eg755s (A), *f SC6 C3375 Eg 755s (B)), Huntington Library (268530), University of Illinois Library (xQ863c33 OdE smo), Indiana University, Lilly Library (PQ6629 A2 1755), University of Kansas, Spenser Library (Summerfield Cerv. 25), Library Company of Philadelphia (*O Span. Cerv. 7583 F.), National Library of Scotland ([Ag}. ½. 8), Newberry Library (Case f1565 C3319), Oxford University, Bodleian Library (Fic. 27623.d.18–19), Princeton University Library ((Ex) PQ6329 A2 1755q), University of Virginia Library (PQ6329 A2 1755), and

Yale University, Beinecke Library (Im Sm79 +755). The first edition with the corrected sheets B through L was sight-collated against the University of Virginia copies of the 1761 second edition (PQ6329 A2 1761), the 1765 third edition (PR3694 H57 1765), the 1770 fourth edition (PQ6329 A2 1770), and the 1782 fifth edition (PQ6329 A2 1782).[13]

# Notes

1. For an account of the composition of the novel, see the introduction, pp. xxxiii–xlii.
2. BL Add. MS. 48803A, opening 10. Strahan seems to have made initial entries in his ledgers on the completion of his printing of a work so that the date of this entry is a fairly reliable indication of when he completed printing the Proposals. One explanation for the discrepancy in the year might be that Strahan wrote "1753" when he intended "1754." The next two entries following that for *Don Quixote*, however, are both dated "Febry 1753." Subsequent printing activities related to the same project were added to the entry, but usually with no indication of the date of completion. Hence, there is no indication when Strahan completed the initial printing of *Don Quixote* or when the ten and one-half sheets were recomposed and printed. Part of the entry in this ledger was transferred from his workbook, now in the library of the American Philosophical Society, Philadelphia. Under "Work unfinished" as of 1 January 1755 is "750. Don Quixotte 92 sheets @ 18s £82:16:0." As of 1 January, twenty-two sheets remained to be printed. For some reason, when the work was finished Strahan decided to bill the partners an extra two shillings a sheet for the printing, for a total of one pound per sheet. Since there is no mention of recomposed sheets, Strahan may have performed this work later in January or early February. See the introduction, pp. xl–xlii and nn. 49 and 54.
3. The two settings of sheets B through L were identified by examining where the signature was placed in the direction line relative to the words in the last line of the text above. The recomposed one-half sheet has not been located. Perhaps machine collation might locate it, but research libraries no longer allow collation by machines because of the severe damage they do to the books. If and when the half sheet is located it is unlikely to produce any significant variation, as an examination of the table of corrected and uncorrected sheets (see the next section) clearly indicates.
4. See above, the introduction, n. 58.
5. Entries for 4 June 1767 and 28 July 1767 in BL Add. MS. 48805, opening 28, indicate that Strahan purchased on each date a one-thirty-second share of the work from "Mr. Thos Osborne" for £9-0-0. See also BL Add. MS. 48804, opening 21, where Strahan also records that he purchased a one-thirty-second share from Osborne on 28 July 1767. For the printing of the fourth edition see BL Add. MS. 48803, opening 24, and for the fifth edition BL Add. MS. 48810, opening 23. It is unknown who printed the final two volumes of the fourth and fifth edition or who printed the second and third editions.
6. This copy of the *Travels* is in the British Library, shelf mark C.45.d.20, 21. Apart from the manuscript revisions of the *Travels* and a relatively small number of holograph letters, little survives in Smollett's hand: a one-leaf holograph note on the reign of Edward III in the Berg Collection, New York Public Library, and about a dozen signed receipts and documents. See *The Letters of Tobias Smollett*, ed. Lewis M. Knapp (Oxford: Clarendon Press, 1970), xvi–xvii.
7. Smollett was content to make small changes because the *Travels*, written at a relatively slow pace, did not require the extensive stylistic revisions of the earlier works. In the works of his

later career, revision seems to have been carried out before publication; by this time he was a more experienced writer. For discussion of the composition of the *Travels*, see the introduction by Frank Felsenstein, ed., *Travels through France and Italy* (Oxford: Oxford University Press, 1979), xxxv–xli.

8. John Smith, *The Printer's Grammar* (London, 1755), 199, 201–2, 209.

9. Bertrand H. Bronson, *Printing as an Index of Taste in Eighteenth Century England* (New York: New York Public Library, 1958), 17.

10. See the copies listed below in the bibliographical description of the first edition.

11. For Smollett's techniques of revision, see O M Brack, Jr., and James B. Davis, "Smollett's Revisions of *Roderick Random*," *Papers of the Bibliographical Society of America* 64 (1970): 295–311; and O M Brack, Jr., "Smollett's *Peregrine Pickle* Revisited," *Studies in the Novel* 27 (1995): 262–64.

12. As in earlier volumes of the Georgia Smollett, "goal," an early spelling for "jail," for example, has been changed to "gaol" (616.14, 16, 17, 21) to avoid confusion for the nonspecialist contemporary reader. See the Textual Notes to *Ferdinand Count Fathom*, p. 455.

13. I am grateful to the following for assistance with collations: Jo Alice Blondin, Gay W. Brack, Leslie A. Chilton, Jonathan Drnjevik, Ruth Drnjevik, Cheryl Gilbert, Kimber Knutson, Kristen Kreider, Lynn McClelland, Gary Walker, and Joy White.

# CORRECTED AND UNCORRECTED SHEETS

*Sheet B*

| | | |
|---|---|---|
| 27.18 | holy-days,] | ~; |
| 27n.‡.3 | which,] | ~ₐ |
| 27n.‡.5 | being,] | ~ₐ |
| 27n.‡.6 | withal;"] | ~"; |
| 27n.‡.7 | amlet,] | ~; |
| 28.3 | meagre,] | ~' |
| 28.4 | hard-featur'd] | hard-featured |
| 28.6 | though,] | ~ₐ |
| 28.10 | gentleman,] | ~ₐ |
| 28.13 | chase] | chace |
| 28.15 | firma] | Firma |
| 28.16 | much,] | ~, |
| 28.22 | beauty:"] | ~": |
| 28.29 | wounds,] | ~, |
| 28n.‡.7 | pease,porridge] | ~-~ |
| 28n.‡.8 | determined,] | ~, |
| 29.11 | Siguenza*,)] | ~*,) |
| 29.18 | entangled] | intangled |
| 29.24 | that,] | ~ₐ |
| 29.26 | back-stroke] | ~ₐ~ |
| 29.27 | Ronscval-|les] | Ronceval-|les |
| 29.30 | race,] | ~, |
| 29.35 | housekeeper] | ~-~ |
| 29n.*.1 | Siguenza] | *Siguenza* |
| 29n.†.1 | *Hildalgo,*] | ~, |
| 29n.§.1 | Galalon] | *Galalon* |

| | |
|---|---|
| 30.15 | perceived‸ that,]   ~, ~‸ |
| 30.15 | complete]   compleat |
| 30.18 | intire]   entire |
| 30.18 | is‸ that,]   ~, ~‸ |
| 30.19 | which,]   ~‸ |
| 30.25 | *rial]   †rial |
| 30.29 | qualities,]   ~‸ |
| 30.36 | Rozinante†,]   ~,† |
| 30n.*.1 | cor-|ner]   cor-|ners |
| 30n.*.3 | *Tra-|pezium*‸]   ~. |
| 31.1 | and, after]   ~‸ ~ |
| 31.5 | added to it‸]   ~ ~ ~, |
| 31.5 | and, in order]   ~‸ ~ ~ |
| 31.8 | and, at the same]   ~‸ ~ ~ ~ |
| 31.12 | wanting‸]   ~, |
| 31.14 | ‸for]   "~ |
| 31.17 | foe;]   ~, |
| 31.17 | who, coming]   ~‸ ~ |
| 31.24 | This‸ they]   ~, ~ |
| 31.26 | though,]   ~‸ |
| 31.34 | habitation]   Habitation |
| 31.36 | impatience‸]   ~, |
| 32.11 | honour*.]   ~.* |
| 32.19 | chuse]   choose |
| 32.26 | soft‸]   ~, |
| 32.28 | confessed]   confess'd |
| 32.39 | Deign,]   ~‸ |
| 33.2 | These,]   ~‸ |
| 33.2 | rhapsodies,]   ~‸ |

| | |
|---|---|
| 33.5 | fry'd] fryed |
| 33.5 | day‸] ~, |
| 33.6 | men-\|tioning:] ~; |
| 33.9 | Windmills] ~-~ |
| 33.12 | that, looking] ~‸ ~ |
| 33.13 | refreshment,] ~; |
| 33.13 | des-\|cried] de-\|cried |
| 33n.*.1 | Perceforest] Penceforest |

*Sheet C*

| | |
|---|---|
| 33.21 | represented it‸] ~ ~, |
| 33.22 | conveniencies‸ ] ~, |
| 33.28 | before-mentioned] ~ ‸ ~ |
| 34.21 | signor] signior |
| 34.27 | find,] ~‸ |
| 34.39 | ill-contrived] ill-contriv'd |
| 35.4 | ladies‸] ~, |
| 35.19 | ‸A number] "~ ~ |
| 35.25 | villainously] villanously |
| 35n.*.2 | helmet‸] ~, |
| 36.9 | Don Quixote] DON QUIXOTE |
| 36.18 | but‸ this request] ~, ~ ~ |
| 36.20 | Signor] Signior |
| 36.24 | fulfil] fulfill |
| 36.26 | knights-errant,] ~-~‸ |
| 36.30 | and, in order] ~‸ ~ ~ |
| 37.14 | but‸ that,] ~, ~‸ |
| 37.n.†.4 | *Roy*] *Roi* |
| 38.11 | thereupon,] ~‸ |

| 38.23 | inn,]    ~ₐ |
| 38.29 | carcase,]    ~, |
| 39.1 | walk,]    ~; |
| 39.12 | turn thy]    turn they |
| 39.13 | caitif]    caitiff |
| 39.14 | have acquired]    have have acquired |
| 39.16 | began,]    ~ₐ |
| 39.24 | honour]    order |
| 39.31 | tranquil-\|lity]    tranquility |
| 40.9 | before,mentioned]    ~-~ |
| 40.19 | adventurous]    adventrous |
| 40.26 | service]    serviee |
| 40.28 | fathfully]    faithfully |
| 40.29 | kind,]    ~, |
| 40.30 | Molli-\|nera;]    ~, |

*Sheet D*

| 42.5 | remembring]    remembering |
| 42.8 | fixed,]    ~ₐ |
| 42.9 | neighbourhood]    neighboured |
| 42.21 | Then turning]    then turning |
| 42.21 | place,]    ~, |
| 42.33 | tied]    tyed |
| 42.36 | replied:]    ~; |
| 42.40 | lie . . . lie]    lye . . . lye |
| 43.11 | by the bye]    by-the-bye |
| 43.18 | me;]    ~, |
| 43.19 | "Go]    ₐ~ |
| 43.26 | but, is known]    ~, ~ ~ |

| | | |
|---|---|---|
| 43.31 | pea-\|sant;] | ~, |
| 43.32 | honours] | orders |
| 43.35 | taken;] | ~: |
| 43.40 | remember͵] | ~, |
| 44.5 | increasing] | encreasing |
| 44.9 | by the bye] | by-the-bye |
| 44.17 | who͵] | ~, |
| 44.19 | village,] | ~͵ |
| 44.20 | To-\|bosa] | To-\|boso |
| 44.24 | honour] | order |
| 44.25 | To-day͵] | To͵day, |
| 44.35 | mule-drivers] | muledrivers |
| 45.2 | La] | la |
| 45.8 | produce her;] | ~ ~, |
| 45.17 | beg,] | ~͵ |
| 45.35 | again͵] | ~, |
| 45.36 | helmet͵] | ~, |
| 45.43 | that, in spite] | ~͵ ~ ~ |
| 46.1 | mummy,] | ~; |
| 46.2 | until] | untill |
| 46.11 | now͵] | ~, |
| 46.16 | story] | Story |
| 46.19 | memory͵] | ~, |
| 46.24 | therefore,] | ~͵ |
| 46.25 | exclaim,] | ~͵ |
| 46.34 | And, before] | ~͵ ~ |
| 47.4 | reply͵] | ~: |
| 47.11 | condition!͵] | ~!" |
| 47.11 | But͵] | ~, |

| | |
|---|---|
| 47.13 | wound,] ~; |
| 47.22 | indeeed] indeed |
| 47.23 | devil] Devil |
| 47.25 | Moor] moor |
| 47.26 | into captivity] in captivity |
| 47.27 | so, that,] ~, ~, |

*Sheet E*

| | |
|---|---|
| 47.41 | Abindarraez] Abindaraez |
| 47.42 | Quixada] Quixado |
| 47.42 | well,] ~, |
| 47.42 | Quixote,] ~; |
| 48.2 | together."] ~., |
| 48.7 | saying,] ~, |
| 48.9 | horse, together,] ~, ~, |
| 48.10 | lance, and armour,] ~, ~ ~, |
| 48.13 | brain:] ~; |
| 48.20 | and, drawing] ~, ~ |
| 48.21 | fatigued;] ~, |
| 48.21 | stee-|ples;] ~, |
| 50.3 | ,See] "~ |
| 50.5 | un-|derstand,] ~, |
| 50.9 | wounds;] ~, |
| 50.11 | giants,] ~, |
| 50.12 | Now,] ~, |
| 50.27 | closet,] ~, |
| 50.28 | house-keeper] housekeeper |
| 50n.*.1 | inchantress] enchantress |
| 50n.*.4 | you are] You are |
| 51.3 | books,] ~, |

| 51.9 | better,]   ~ᴧ |
|---|---|
| 51.18 | therefore,]   ~ᴧ |
| 51.19 | law-giver]   lawgiver |
| 51.25 | here,]   ~, |
| 51.27 | bonfire,]   ~ᴧ |
| 51.30 | "Proceed,"]   "~,ᴧ |
| 51.32 | then,]   ~ᴧ |
| 51.38 | she, out]   ~, ~ |
| 51.39 | be?,]   ~?" |
| 51.44 | What!]   ~, |
| 52.1 | surprizing]   surprising |
| 52.3 | sir,"]   ~,ᴧ |
| 52.6 | clergyman,]   ~; |
| 52.6 | him,]   ~ᴧ |
| 52.14 | Twelve peers]   twelve Peers |
| 52.18 | Ari- | osto;]   ~, |
| 52.20 | head,]   ~, |
| 52.20 | barber,]   ~, |
| 52.26 | energy,]   ~ᴧ |
| 52.30 | which,]   ~, |
| 52.36 | licentiate,]   ~ᴧ |
| 52.43 | art:]   ~; |
| 53.2 | perish,]   ~, |
| 53.2 | inquiry]   enquiry |
| 53.6 | castle]   Castle |
| 53.9 | house,]   ~, |
| 53.14 | there- | fore,]   ~, |
| 53.17 | found,]   ~, |
| 53.24 | Life]   life |
| 53.28 | circumstances,]   ~ᴧ |

| 53.29 | it, certainly] | $\sim_\wedge \sim$ |
| 53.41 | which, they say] | $\sim_\wedge \sim \sim$ |
| 54.5 | leave to him,] | $\sim \sim \sim_\wedge$ |
| 54.5 | God's-name,] | $\sim_\wedge$ |
| 54.9 | increase] | encrease |
| 54.12 | Production] | production |
| 54.13 | orders!] | $\sim,$ |
| 54.18 | Florence-silk."] | $\sim_\wedge\sim._\wedge$ |
| 54.20 | next,] | $\sim_\wedge$ |
| 54.20 | Nymphs] | nymphs |
| 54.22 | house-keeper;] | housekeeper, |
| 54.23 | Filida." "He] | $\sim._\wedge {}_\wedge\sim$ |
| 54.24 | courtier;] | $\sim,$ |
| 54.32 | every body:] | $\sim \sim;$ |
| 54.35 | $_\wedge$When] | "$\sim$ |
| 54.36 | "that same] | $_\wedge\sim \sim$ |
| 54.37 | mine,] | $\sim_\wedge$ |
| 54.44 | $_\wedge$These] | "$\sim$ |

*Sheet F*

| 55.8 | Ovid.] | $\sim$." |
| 55.15 | exclamation,] | $\sim;$ |
| 55.18 | tho'$_\wedge$] | $\sim,$ |
| 55.31 | doubt:] | $\sim;$ |
| 55.33 | mere] | meer |
| 55.34 | Mont-alban] | Mont-Alban |
| 55.36 | present,] | $\sim;$ |
| 56.4 | house;] | $\sim:$ |
| 56.6 | so$_\wedge$ that,] | $\sim, \sim_\wedge$ |
| 56.7 | remedy,] | $\sim_\wedge$ |

| 56.8 | friend‸ was,]   ~, ~‸ |
|---|---|
| 56.9 | that‸ upon]   ~, ~ |
| 56.10 | cease;]   ~: |
| 56.11 | all: this]   ~. This |
| 56.14 | other,]   ~‸ |
| 56.18 | answered,]   ~: |
| 56.26 | I‸ can very well]   ~, ~ ~ ~ |
| 56.30 | housekeeper]   house-keeper |
| 56.31 | knight;]   ~, |
| 56.32 | enemies;]   ~, |
| 56.32 | knows,]   ~‸ |
| 56.34 | battle‸]   ~, |
| 57.16 | countryman]   ~-~ |
| 57.25 | orders,]   ~; |
| 57.28 | mounted on an ass;]   ~ ~ ~ ~: |
| 57.29 | occurred]   occured |
| 57.37 | dawn‸]   ~, |
| 58.4 | replied,]   ~: |
| 58.5 | knights-errant,]   ~-~‸ |
| 58.6 | kingdoms‸]   ~, |
| 58.8 | until]   untill |
| 58.18 | Certainly, said the knight:]   ~: ~ ~ ~, |
| 58.19 | for‸ certain]   ~, ~ |
| 58.24 | capacity;]   ~: |
| 58.33 | per- | ceived‸]   ~, |
| 58.35 | whom‸]   ~, |
| 59.2 | his]   their |
| 59.8 | work.]   ~: |
| 59.9 | adventures;]   ~: |
| 59.9 | giants,]   ~; |

| 59.32 | war‸ are,] | ~, ~‸ |
| 59.33 | Freston‸] | ~, |
| 59.37 | rise‸] | ~, |
| 59.42 | knight‸] | ~, |
| 60.3 | meet] | met |
| 60.11 | be the case] | be case |
| 60.24 | head,] | ~‸ |
| 60.30 | it‸ the iron] | ~, ~ ~ |
| 60.36 | night,] | ~; |
| 60.39 | did‸] | ~, |
| 60.41 | road‸] | ~, |
| 61.2 | elbows‸] | ~, |
| 61.6 | licensed] | licenced |
| 61.7 | until] | untill |
| 61.9 | tittle,] | ~; |
| 61.11 | ag-|grieved‸] | ~, |
| 61.20 | Seville] | Sevile |
| 61.22 | fryars‸] | ~, |

*Sheet G*

| 61.27 | wind-mills] | ~‸~ |
| 61.27 | Sancho,] | ~; |
| 61.35 | surrender‸] | ~, |
| 62.1 | figure,] | ~‸ |
| 62.4 | princesses,] | ~‸ |
| 62.6 | pack you] | pack ye |
| 62.28 | pleasure,] | ~; |
| 62.29 | lyes] | lies |
| 62.32 | unparalelled,] | ~‸ |
| 62.35 | knight,] | ~‸ |

| 62.36 | who‸ seeing,]   ~, ~‸ |
|---|---|
| 62.38 | and‸ laying]   ~, ~ |
| 62.38 | thus‸]   ~, |
| 62.39 | zay,]   ~; |
| 62.41 | knight‸]   ~, |
| 62.43 | gentleman,]   ~! |
| 62.44 | ‸by God]   "~ ~ |
| 62.44 | Christian;]   christian: |
| 63.2 | devil,]   ~; |
| 63.3 | who‸]   ~, |
| 63.6 | mule,‸ which‸]   ~‸ (~, |
| 63.8 | upon:‸]   ~;) |
| 63.10 | present,]   ~‸ |
| 63.31 | threatened]   threatned |
| 63n.*.1 | Spanish,]   ~‸ |
| 63n.*.1 | water,]   ~; |
| 63n.*.2 | "The water . . . cat."]   ‸~ ~ . . . ~.‸ |
| 63n.†.1 | Quixote,]   ~‸ |
| 63n.†.3 | aggrieved,]   ~‸ |
| 65.22 | atchievemets]   atchievements |
| 65.24 | second-rate‸warriors]   second‸rate-warriors |
| 66.1 | inflamed me,]   ~ ~‸ |
| 66.7 | hatchet]   hachet |
| 66.22 | Portugeze]   Portugueze |
| 66.27 | book:]   ~. |
| 66.28 | laughing. ‸What]   ~, "~ |
| 66.29 | "This]   ‸~ |
| 66.29 | Dulcinea‸]   ~, |
| 66.37 | which, snatching]   ~‸ ~ |
| 67.1 | but,]   ~‸ |

| | | |
|---|---|---|
| 67.10 | rider,] | ~‸ |
| 67.11 | Rozinante] | Rozinate |
| 67.30 | depository] | repository |
| 68.17 | syllable,] | ~; |
| 68.20 | entreaties] | intreaties |
| 68.33 | Panza,] | ~‸ |
| 69.3 | bestow on me,] | ~ ~ ~‸ |

*Sheet H*

| | | |
|---|---|---|
| 69.19 | fought‸] | ~, |
| 69.21 | prison‸] | ~, |
| 69.24 | know nothing] | known othing |
| 69.28 | Quixote,] | ~; |
| 69.41 | drop of which‸] | ~ ~ ~, |
| 69n.*.2 | travelling‸] | ~, |
| 70.3 | composition‸] | ~, |
| 70.9 | see me,] | ~ ~‸ |
| 70.10 | and as sound] | and sound |
| 70.17 | knight.] | ~: |
| 70.18 | moment?] | ~. |
| 70.23 | aloud,] | ~; |
| 70.32 | punishmeut] | punishment |
| 70n.*.4 | voluntarly] | voluntary |
| 70n.*.5 | lie] | lye |
| 71.3 | devil‸] | ~, |
| 71.10 | which, far] | ~‸ ~ |
| 71.13 | cross-|ways] | cross‸|ways |
| 71.27 | matter? answered Don Quixote.] | ~, ~ ~ ~? |
| 71n.*.1 | count] | Count |

| 72.10 | them<sub>∧</sub>] ~, |
|---|---|

72.10          them<sub>∧</sub>]   ~,

72.17          but<sub>∧</sub> the hope]   ~, ~ ~

72.19          night;]   ~:

72.19          pro-|portion<sub>∧</sub>]   ~,

72.21          heaven,]   ~;

72.21          kind<sub>∧</sub>]   ~,

72.28          goat's<sub>∧</sub>flesh]   ~-~

72n.*.2        roe-buck]   roebuck

72n.*.4        called<sub>∧</sub>]   ~,

73.3           sheep-skins]   sheep-kins

73.9           attitude,]   ~;

73.13          me, thy natural]   ~<sub>∧</sub> ~ ~

73.17          Sancho;]   ~,

73.17          wor-|ship<sub>∧</sub> that,]   ~, ~<sub>∧</sub>

73.37          went<sub>∧</sub>]   ~,

73.41          antients]   ancients

73.42          iron-times<sub>∧</sub>]   ~,

73.43          people then<sub>∧</sub>]   ~ ~,

74.10          plough<sub>∧</sub>]   ~,

74.16          commanded,]   ~<sub>∧</sub>

74.17          silk,]   ~;

74.20          fashions<sub>∧</sub>]   ~,

74.21          soul<sub>∧</sub>]   ~,

74.23          justice then<sub>∧</sub>]   ~ ~,

74.25          then<sub>∧</sub> centered]   ~, ~

74.37          for<sub>∧</sub> though,]   ~, ~<sub>∧</sub>

74.41          harrangue]   harangue

75.8           goatherd]   goat-herd

75.9           after<sub>∧</sub>]   ~,

| | |
|---|---|
| 75.14 | mountains‚] ~, |
| 75.15 | informed him‚] ~ ~, |
| 75.18 | heart," replied the young man,‚] ~,‚ ~ ~ ~," |

*Sheet I*

| | |
|---|---|
| 76.23 | wont] won |
| 76.25 | mirrour] mirror |
| 77.28 | rest‚] ~, |
| 77n.*.5 | terms?] ~: |
| 77n.*.10 | these:] ~. |
| 78.5 | ‚I do not] "~ ~ ~ |
| 78.20 | rich] Rich |
| 78.22 | one.] ~, |
| 78.22 | certain that,] ~, ~‚ |
| 78.23 | Moor‚] ~, |
| 78.29 | perform every thing,] ~ ~ ~‚ |
| 78.29 | Chrysostom] Crysostom |
| 78.30 | that every thing,] ~ ~‚ |
| 78.32 | to-morrow‚] ~, |
| 78.34 | thought‚] ~, |
| 79.13 | staril."] ~": |
| 79.17 | [no] barley;] [~]~: |
| 79.20 | but‚] ~, |
| 79.20 | knew all this,] ~ ~ ~; |
| 79.25 | defunct‚] ~, |
| 79.35 | woods‚] ~, |
| 79.38 | know‚] ~, |
| 79.38 | wench is;] ~ ~: |
| 79n.*.2 | it is impossible] it impossible |
| 79n.*.2 | translation] Translation |

79n.\*.3                  apprehend]    apprehended

80.6                      built:]   ~;

80.24                     But,]   ~,

80.24                     who,]   ~,

80.41                     years,]   ~,

81.5                      farmers,]   ~,

81.7                      who,]   ~,

81.15                     sling,]   ~:

81.18                     love her,]   ~ ~;

81.32                     heaven]   Heaven

82.7                      lovers; while]   lovers. While

82.14                     goatherds,]   ~,

82.19                     path,]   ~,

82.21                     them, came]   ~, ~

82.22                     horseback,]   ~,

*Sheet K*

83.3                      per- | mit,]   ~,

83.11                     King]   king

83.12                     inchantment]   enchantment

83.14                     throne: For]   ~. ~

83.15                     raven. In]   ~: ~

83.35                     danger,]   ~,

83.39                     surprize,]   ~,

84.8                      they pray,]   ~ ~,

84.15                     toil than those,]   ~ ~ ~,

84.19                     ragged,]   ~,

84.32                     knight-errant,]   ~-~,

84.43                     rage,]   ~,

85.6                      God,]   ~,

| | | |
|---|---|---|
| 85.12 | certain$_\wedge$] | ~, |
| 85.17 | Amadis] | Armadis |
| 85.18 | but$_\wedge$ looked] | ~, ~ |
| 85.27 | that passion] | the passion |
| 85.28 | as Don] | a Don |
| 85.34 | not$_\wedge$] | ~, |
| 85.34 | mine$_\wedge$] | ~, |
| 85.38 | beauty$_\wedge$] | ~, |
| 85.38 | inpossible$_\wedge$] | impossible, |
| 86.2 | antient] | ancient |
| 86n.*.3 | strangers;] | ~: |
| 86n.†.1 | the Europeans] | Europeans |
| 87.16 | place$_\wedge$] | ~, |
| 87.23 | corse] | coarse |
| 87.26 | friendship,] | ~$_\wedge$ |
| 87.28 | abhorred] | abhored |
| 88.14 | but$_\wedge$ to think] | ~, ~ ~ |
| 88.34 | pride,] | ~$_\wedge$ |
| 89.10 | echo] | eccho |

*Sheet L*

| | | |
|---|---|---|
| 90.20 | corse] | coarse |
| 91.11 | read it$_\wedge$] | ~ ~, |
| 91.14 | objection$_\wedge$] | ~, |
| 91.19 | situation$_\wedge$] | ~, |
| 91.20 | apprehension,] | ~; |
| 91.23 | arrogance,] | ~$_\wedge$ |
| 91.27 | sudden$_\wedge$] | ~, |
| 91.34 | youth,] | ~$_\wedge$ |
| 91.35 | mountain$_\wedge$] | ~, |

| 91.36 | inhumanly]   inhumanely |
| 91.37 | corse]   coarse |
| 91.38 | Tell us,]   ~ ~ₐ |
| 91.39 | that I,]   ~ ~ₐ |
| 93.2 | ₐHeaven]   "~ |
| 93.2 | nay,]   ~ₐ |
| 93.10 | deformed?"]   ~?ₐ |
| 93.16 | divided,]   ~: |
| 93.16 | unconstrained;]   ~: |
| 93.22 | solicitation]   sollicitation |
| 94.6 | depend upon me;]   ~ ~ ~, |
| 94.6 | success;]   ~: |
| 94.8 | called,]   ~ₐ |
| 94.14 | evilₐbeing]   ~-~ |
| 94.15 | me, in his turn;]   ~ₐ ~ ~ ~, |
| 94.16 | in distress]   in my distress |
| 94.20 | wish me to lose it]   wish to see me lose it |
| 94.22 | cajole this one;]   ~ ~ ~, |
| 94.23 | but, amuse]   ~, ~ |
| 94.40 | universeₐ]   ~, |
| 95.8 | proveₐ]   ~, |
| 95.21 | during whichₐ]   ~ ~, |
| 95.22 | who,]   ~ₐ |
| 97.21 | Cordovaₐ]   ~, |
| 97.23 | fillies,]   ~ₐ |
| 97.24 | happened,]   ~ₐ |
| 97.24 | in that very valley]   in the same valley |

# LIST OF EMENDATIONS

[The following sigla appear in the textual apparatus of the Georgia Edition: 1(*a*) (the first edition uncorrected state; London, 1755), 1(*b*) (the first edition corrected state; London, 1755), 2 (the second edition; London, 1761), 3 (the third edition; London, 1765), 4 (the fourth edition; London, 1770), 5 (the fifth edition; London 1782), W (present edition).]

| | |
|---|---|
| 6.4 | comtemptuous]2    contempt'ous 1 |
| 7.38 | Lope]2    Lopè 1 |
| 8.10 | Lope]2    Lopè 1 |
| 8.20 | wantonness and]2    wantonness of 1 |
| 9.8 | screened]2    sereened 1 |
| 21.7 | creature]2    creatures 1 |
| 21.9 | my own imagination]2    his own imagination 1 |
| 27n.‡.3 | but conjectures]2    than conjectures 1 |
| 28.9 | a tittle]2    farther 1 |
| 28n.‡.7 | greens, or]2    greens, and 1 |
| 29.28 | enchanted]2    enchanter 1 |
| 29.29 | Anteus]2    Anteon 1 |
| 29n.‡ | Orlando . . . armour.]2    *om.* 1 |
| 29n.§ | betrayed . . . Spain]2    betrayed the Spanish army at Ronsevalles 1 |
| 30.22 | anew. He faced]2    anew, and faced 1 |
| 30.26 | fuit")]5    ~)" 1–4 |
| 30.33 | his horse's name]2    his name 1 |
| 30n.*.3 | *Trapezium.*]1(*a*)    ~, 1(*b*) |
| 30n.†.1 | an ordinary horse]2    an horse 1 |
| 31.4 | affirm. But]2    affirm: but 1 |
| 31.37 | errors to be amended]2    errors amended 1 |
| 32.11 | on his shield]2    in his shield 1 |
| 32.36 | Then making a sudden transition]2    Then turning his horse 1 |

35n.†    In the original . . . he-goat.]2    *om.* 1

36.13    words:]2    ~. 1

36.26    knights-errant, in imitation . . . strongly]2    knights-errant, whose genius, like mine, is strongly 1

37.35    assistance]2    friend 1

38.6    he was . . . godson]2    he was his godson 1

38.35    other ejaculations]2    other such ejaculations 1

40.14    ejaculation*. This]2    ejaculation*: this 1

40.28    faithfully]1(*a*)    fathfully 1(*b*)

42.8    squire. For this]2    squire, for which 1

42.10    chivalry. With]2    chivalry: with 1

42.16    distress. No]2    distress; and no 1

43.2    body!]2    ~: 1

44.19    self-satisfaction, pronouncing]2    self-satisfaction, and pronounced 1

44.23    remain. He who]2    remain. Who 1

44.41    be. When]2    be; and when 1

44.42    him, he pronounced]2    him, pronounced 1

45.5    author. Curious]2    author; curious 1

45.22    judge of the clue]1(*errata*)    judge the clue 1(*text*)

46.3    choler. Gathering]2    choler; but, gathering 1

46.3    lance, he reduced]2    lance, reduced 1

46.5    closed]2    shut 1

46.20    mountain: a]2    mountain. A 1

46.24    situation. Therefore]2    situation. And therefore 1

46.34    Before]2    And, before 1

47.21    groans]2    sighs 1

47.22    Indeed]2    And indeed 1(*a*); And indeeed 1(*b*)

47.39    talks!]5    ~? 1–4

48.8    (that . . . name,)]2    ˄~ . . . ~,˄ 1

48.18    (this . . . barber,)]W    ˄~ . . . ~,˄ 1–5

| | |
|---|---|
| 48.22 | blood . . . battle]2    blood of his enemies, whom he had slain in battle 1 |
| 48.34 | which last had]2    who had 1 |
| 48n.*.2 | watching]2    waking 1 |
| 50n.*.1 | name of a good-natured enchantress]2    name of an enchantress 1(*a*); name of an inchantress 1(*b*) |
| 50n.*.6 | afterwards]2    then 1 |
| 52.20 | barber,]1(*a*)    ~ₐ 1(*b*) |
| 53.21 | Godamercy]2    Don Godamercy 1 |
| 53.22 | as also an account]2    together with an account 1 |
| 54.38 | than with poetry]1(*errata*)    than poetry 1(*text*) |
| 55.35 | Mean while,]1(*cw*)    ~ₐ 1(*text*) |
| 59.2 | their spoils]1(*a*)    his spoils 1(*b*) |
| 59.4 | amaze.]2    ~? 1 |
| 60.33 | who had passed]2    who passed 1 |
| 61n.*.2 | enjoined,]W    ~ₐ 1–5 |
| 62.17 | lady]W    people 1; ladies 2–5 |
| 62.20 | the fryar mounted, as pale]2    mounted the fryar, who was pale 1 |
| 65.22 | atchievements]1(*a*)    atchievemets 1(*b*) |
| 65.29 | Jealousy]5    jealousy 1–4 |
| 66.16 | follows: the manner . . . recount. While]2    follows: While 1 |
| 66.28 | laughing,]2    ~. 1 |
| 67.30 | repository]1(*a*)    depository 1(*b*) |
| 69.8 | in bye-roads]2    on the high road 1 |
| 70n.*.4 | voluntary]1(*a*)    voluntarly 1(*b*) |
| 71.27 | matter? answered Don Quixote.] 1(*a*)    ~, ~ ~ ~? 1(*b*); ~! ~ ~ ~. 2–5 |
| 72n.† | *Volatiles . . . character.*]2    *om.* 1 |
| 74.14 | bare-headed . . . locks]2    *om.* 1 |
| 74.19 | court-ladies]2    courtiers 1 |
| 75.12 | who had made]W    who made 1–5 |

78.16            another]2    one 1

79.29            change]2    chance 1

80.1             the words]2    of words 1

82.2             for the cold . . . received]2    *om.* 1

84.24            of their desires]1(*errata*)    by their desires 1(*text*)

85.3             over his horse's crupper]1(*errata*)    by his horse's crupper 1(*text*)

85.19            summer]2    spring 1

85.36            La Mancha]2    Valencia 1

85.38            impossible]1(*b*)    inpossible 1(*a*)

86.25            black sheep-skin]2    sheep-skin, covered with black wool 1

86.26            as it afterwards appeared]1(*errata*)    as we afterwards learned
                 1(*text*)

87.17            enemy of the human]W    enemy of human 1–5

91.42            unreasonably people . . . as well as for the death]2    unreasonably I
                 am blamed for the death 1

94.16            in my distress]1(*a*)    in distress 1(*b*)

94.20            wish to see me lose it]1(*a*)    wish me to lose it 1(*b*)

98.38            it in my]2    it my 1

99.14            since]2    tho' 1

99.41            a long time]2    along time 1

101.39           befallen Rozinante]1(*errata*)    befallen to Rozinante 1(*text*)

101.40           ah's]2    ahs 1

102.21           Asturias]5    Asturies 1–4

103.17           Asturian.]W    ~, 1–2; ~! 3–5

103.19           knight-adventurer?]2    ~, 1

106.37           her; all]2    her; and all 1

108.12           search for]2    search 1

110.31           pater-noster's]W    pater-nosters 1–5

112n.*           Don Quixote . . . bone to pick.]2    *om.* 1

118.4            And truly]2    and truly 1

| | |
|---|---|
| 119.13 | eyes into]2   eyes, as it were, into 1 |
| 121.8 | worship]2   worwip 1 |
| 123.32 | done or received an injury; and]2   done, or are doing, an injury to some person and 1 |
| 123.34 | ‸replied]2   (~ 1 |
| 124.19 | licentiate]3   licientiate 1–2 |
| 126.36 | Knight]2   knight 1 |
| 126.39 | nothing]2   no 1 |
| 126.40 | your face]2   your own face 1 |
| 127.31 | Sancho's]2   Sancho' 1 |
| 132.14 | tale is ended]2   tale is at an end 1 |
| 132.21 | Quixote.]3   ~, 1–2 |
| 135.30 | islands or]2   islands and 1 |
| 136.33 | herself, the mother of all sciences; more]2   herself; more 1 |
| 137.5 | do! . . . Sancho.]W   ~, . . . ~! 1–5 |
| 140.9 | that caitiff]2   Mr. Tonsor 1 |
| 141.19 | 'behold . . . Serpent,']W   ‸~ . . . ~,‸ 1–5 |
| 143.15 | time enough to think]1(*errata*)   time to think 1(*text*) |
| 143.21 | reward: wherefore . . . deserve. True]2   reward: true 1 |
| 144.31 | every second day]2   once a day 1 |
| 146.11 | equipage.]W   ~! 1–2; ~? 3–5 |
| 146.27 | music?]W   ~‸ 1; ~, 2–5 |
| 146.42 | to pay . . . lady]2   to visit my lady 1 |
| 146.43 | Gurapas]W   Gurapa 1–5 |
| 147.11 | gallies . . . years, after]2   gallies, after 1 |
| 150.8 | sins to answer]2   sins of his own to answer 1 |
| 150.21 | one of the two . . . firelocks]2   the man . . . the fire-lock 1 |
| 151.25 | thy name]2   your name 1 |
| 151.30 | shower forth a number]2   shower such a number 1 |

153.18        had searched]1(*errata*)    have searched 1(*text*)

158.3         fall, without knowing how or wherefore." "That]2    fall." "That 1

160.29        good-will . . . satisfaction." "My]2    good-will." "My 1

161.6         your appearance and person]2    your dress and person 1

164.22        always contrived means to]2    always endeavoured to 1

167.16        whom, at least, I]2    whom I 1

171.42        waving]2    stirring 1

172.12        love and despair]2    love or despair 1

172.18        I say, be it so]2    Be it so 1

172.20        thou]2    you 1

172.22        You are pretty perfect in your]2    What will very much embellish
              your 1

172.22        knight; but, as]2    knight; as 1

174.26        flax and threshing]2    flax or threshing 1

174.27        laugh and be]2    laugh or be 1

176.21        perform so many . . . matter." "At]2    perform many more than I
              wished to see." "At 1

180.30        disclose for the eyes that stood in his head]2    disclose to ears of
              flesh and blood] 1

180.37        informed them]2    informed him 1

181.41        efforts, repeated . . . absurdities. He]2    efforts, and was guilty of
              as many blunders as before: he 1

182.33        beseech . . . station]2    beseech him to chuse that station 1

183.29        sattin . . . seemed]2    sattin, which seemed 1

184.37        affair of the utmost]2    affair that was of the utmost 1

185.4         news of his having found]2    news of having found 1

185.36        fate!]W    ~. 1–5

187.15        wondered . . . case: for]2    wondered at, if they entertain that
              opinion, for 1

187n.*        There is . . . Don Quixote.]2    *om.* 1

189.1         villainous]2    villanious 1

189.43          absence; considering . . . her pen.]2    absence; though, while I was
                present, she had been so sparing of her speech.  1

190.24          that your pretended . . . for himself]2    that he hath asked me in
                marriage for your pretended friend 1

190n.*          The original . . . correspondence.]2    *om.* 1

190n.*.2        exclaim,]5    ~ˬ 2–4

191.3           mule at]2    mule in 1

194.31          now the willing votary]2    now the votary 1

194.34          impossibility . . . comfort: a]2    the possibility of bettering their
                fate. A 1

195.12          times, barren . . . amusements, enjoy]2    times, enjoy 1

195.27          peasant, whose face, as]2    peasant, who, as 1

195.28          they could not then survey. Their approach they
                managed]2    could not perceive their approach, which was
                managed 1

201.7           creature),]W    ~)ˬ 1–5

202.17          misfortune]2    misfortue 1

203.13          whole misfortune]2    whole design 1

203.24          hear. He directed . . . town-talk. He said]2    hear: he said 1

203.40          company. It was . . . next day. When]2    company. Next day, when 1

205.9           or quit my being in this]2    or give up the ghost in this 1

205.27          she left off speaking]2    she stood silent 1

206.4           intervals which I enjoy]1(*errata*)    intervals, that I enjoy 1(*text*)

207.8           when he (Sancho) told]2    when Sancho told 1

207.17          plan they]2    plan he 1

207.23          stile]2    state 1

208.23          opinion,]2    ~. 1

211.21          at my ease]2    unmarried 1

211.25          whites]2    white 1

213.11          Meotis]2    Meotides 1

215.26          Zaramilla]2    Xaramilla 1

215.39          this giant]2    any giant 1

216.12          Dorothea.]2    ~, 1

218.44          follows.]W    ~: 1–5

219.18          please: I shall . . . went in: but]2    please: I hope my answers will
                make the end answer the beginning of your content; but 1

219.19          future.]W    ~: 1–5

219.20          revengeful? . . . knight.]W    ~, . . . ~? 1–5

220.15          invention.]W    ~: 1–5

220.38          had put it into her hand, I]2    had repeated it to the clerk, I 1

221.14          of such a letter]2    of the sender 1

223.6           death; and that]2    death: then that 1

228.16          mistress? . . . daughter.]5    ~, . . . ~? 1–4

228.22          maid? . . . Dorothea.]W    ~, . . . ~? 1–5

228.38          friend's housekeeper]2    friends the housekeeper 1

228.41          then? . . . innkeeper.]W    ~, . . . ~? 1–5

229.27          dive into the profound]2    dive to the bottom 1

229.28          he descended to the bottom]2    he had descended a great way 1

229n.*          It will appear . . . could not do.]2    *om.* 1

230.35          to himself]2    within himself 1

230.39          because . . . I expect]2    because I expect 1

231.5           taken]2    taken taken 1

232.14          The Two Friends]5    The two friends 1–4

234.37          aras; I mean, not]2    aras; but, not 1

235.23          seems to deserve]1(*errata*)    seems to desire 1(*text*)

236n.*.1        Furioso, to which . . . absence.]2    Furioso. 1

240.16          begin when he pleased]2    begin as soon as he pleased 1

241.2           lean his head]2    lean the side of his head 1

243.2           and dine . . . desired]2    and desired 1

243.12          but was . . . servants]2    but always went about the house among
                her servants 1

| | |
|---|---|
| 244.1 | Lothario] 1(*errata*)   Lotharia 1(*text*) |
| 246.14 | she then fancied]2   she fancied 1 |
| 246.14 | looked]2   once looked 1 |
| 247.3 | The dazzling rays descend amain]2   The rays descend in dazzling rain 1 |
| 248.17 | afraid?]2   ~; 1 |
| 248.17 | This]W   this 1–5 |
| 248.38 | pretended to be]2   imagined 1 |
| 250.3 | country: (And here it was where . . . him) but . . . vengeance. However]2   country. And here it was . . . him. However 1 |
| 250.21 | thing: do what you please; I hope]2   thing; and hope 1 |
| 250.24 | how foolishly he had proceeded, and]2   how ill-informed he was of the truth, and 1 |
| 252.27 | your opinion]2   my opinion 1 |
| 252.41 | ever]4   even 1–3 |
| 255.19 | having a second] 1(*cw*)   having second 1(*text*) |
| 255.23 | as well as she]2   as well she 1 |
| 255.43 | favour our]2   favour your 1 |
| 257.9 | brother? . . . book,]W   ~, . . . ~? 1–5 |
| 259.9 | saints! . . . innkeeper,]W   ~, . . . ~! 1–5 |
| 259.20 | from paying both reckonings, to]2   or either of them, from paying to 1 |
| 262.18 | that]2   thet 1 |
| 262.25 | taken? . . . Anselmo.]W   ~, . . . ~? 1–5 |
| 262.29 | This]5   These 1–4 |
| 263.29 | company? . . . Cardenio.]W   ~, . . . ~? 1–5 |
| 264.10 | lady be? . . . priest.]W   ~ ~, . . . ~? 1–5 |
| 264.17 | named? . . . curate.]W   ~, . . . ~? 1–5 |
| 267.26 | you, that . . . manner, that]2   you not only to check your indignation, but also to suppress it intirely, so, that 1 |
| 267n.* | But it appears . . . *homerus.*]2   *om.* 1 |

| | |
|---|---|
| 270.7 | happened to him, in the city,]2   happened in the city, 1 |
| 270.15 | if she]2   since she 1 |
| 270.36 | little dreaming]2   intirely ignorant 1 |
| 274.38 | baptized? . . . Lucinda.]W   ~, . . . ~? 1–5 |
| 276.26 | on earth or in heaven]2   in heaven or on earth 1 |
| 276.34 | first of all]2   chiefly 1 |
| 276.36 | his indigence]2   this indigence 1 |
| 277.5 | attain . . . degree]2   attain to the height of their wishes 1 |
| 277.21 | all other . . . apparel. In a winter . . . breath, which,]2   all the other parts of apparel; tho', in the winter, he has nothing else to skreen him from the inclemencies of the weather; nay, in the open field, he is fain to warm himself with his own breath, which, 1 |
| 278.10 | undecided, . . . reasons]2   undecided. Such are the reasons 1 |
| 278.11 | one . . . favour]2   the principal of which in favour 1 |
| 278.33 | and of falling thence]2   and then falling 1 |
| 279.7 | he]2   be 1 |
| 280.35 | But, after you have received]2   But, before you receive 1 |
| 281.8 | and, although]2   so that, although 1 |
| 281.32 | they charging . . . seize]2   after we had undertaken to seize 1 |
| 281.33 | this promise]2   the promise 1 |
| 283.2 | among them]2   among us 1 |
| 284.3 | seven]2   six 1 |
| 285.29 | Death . . . claim]2   Death sanction'd your victorious claim 1 |
| 289.5 | hand . . . signs]2   hand appeared again, making signs 1 |
| 290.8 | thou . . . Arabic]2   thou can'st not write Arabic 1 |
| 292.4 | Ala]2   Ali 1 |
| 296.30 | Juma]1(errata)   Jama 1(text) |
| 297.24 | bark . . . opposite]2   bark right opposite 1 |
| 298.10 | asked . . . voice, if]2   asked if 1 |
| 298.11 | christians.]W   ~? 1–5 |

299.6        remained . . . Moors]2    remained prisoners among us, desired the
             renegado would be so good as to dismiss the Moors 1

299.9        who loved her so much]2    whom she loved so much 1

299.24       the galleys]2    those galleys 1

299.40       course. All . . . sailed]2    course: and this method proved so
             expeditious, that we sailed 1

299.43       that they . . . should]2    as they were not slaves, they should 1

300.18       this particular]2    that particular 1

300.20       us.]W    ~? 1–5

300.22       he knew he had left]2    he thought had been left 1

300.39       have]2    have have 1

301.28       ours.]W    ~? 1–5

301.40       beard . . . nay]2    and tearing the hair of his head, which he
             scattered in handfuls upon the shore; nay 1

302.6        no other reply]2    no reply 1

302.8        Ala]2    she 1

302.23       large round vessel]2    large vessel 1

303.25       without]2    mithout 1

304.5        country]2    land 1

306.14       should have continued]2    should continue 1

306.16       Cardenio]2    Don Antonio 1

306.38       as they entered]2    alight 1

307.14       her: the beauteous . . . damsel; while]2    her; while 1

307.25       bed . . . along with him, they]2    bed, and that brought by the
             stranger, they 1

307.35       West Indies]2    East-Indies 1

307.44       virtue and prudence that appear]2    virtue that appears 1

308.23       he was]2    we were 1

308n.*       This . . . night. Vide p. 145.]2    *om.* 1

309.26       anguish . . . company; so]2    anguish; so 1

312.34       desires]2    distress 1

315.25       from my inclination]2    from inclination 1

| 316.6 | firmly]2    formerly 1 |

316.25          Retire,]W    ~∧ 1–5

317.2           landlord . . . waking]2    landlord waking 1

317.34          fifteen]2    sixteen 1

320.21          Quixote,]5    ~∧ 1–4

321.33          taken, the furniture]2    taken, by force, the furniture 1

322.16          squire]2    shaver 1

323.6           helmet.]W    ~? 1–5

323.34          gentlemen, myself, and even]2    gentlemen, and even 1

324.16          three]2    four 1

326.34          quiet]2    quite 1

328.9           squalled]2    sqalled 1

329.10          Quixote's]2    Quixot's 1

329.18          with∧]2    ~, 1

329.37          Quixote . . . well as for]2    Quixote, for 1

332.6           nonsense]2    nonesense 1

332.32          except the squire himself]2    except the master and the squire
                himself 1

335.20          Sancho . . . linnen.]2    *om.* 1

336.15          for, if I regain my liberty]2    for, if I were at liberty 1

337.3           cage, his hands . . . outstretched, leaning]2    cage, leaning 1

337.23          robber]2    rober 1

339.25          seems to fall . . . Milesian]2    seems inferior to the Milesian 1

339.37          which the hero . . . espouses]2    which our author espouses 1

342.26          Female]2    female 1

343.5           ascribed to the emperor Heraclius, who being the principal
                personage, is represented, like Godfrey]2    in which the latter had
                the principal share, ascribed to the emperor Heraclius, who, like
                Godfrey 1

343.6           carrying . . . making]2    carried . . . made 1

343.12          and say that]1(*errata*)    and that 1(*text*)

| | |
|---|---|
| 343.42 | say, and it]2    say, it 1 |
| 344.28 | delightful]2    delighful 1 |
| 345.42 | heart . . . those who]2    heart, as one may, and doth expect from those who 1 |
| 349.24 | make a man]2    make me 1 |
| 349.33 | Lancelot]2    Lançarot 1 |
| 349.42 | near]2    hard by 1 |
| 350.6 | fought in]2    fought against 1 |
| 351.34 | pebbles]3    peebles 1–2 |
| 352.11 | and silently leading]2    and leading 1 |
| 352.18 | amber and odoriferous]2    odoriferous 1 |
| 355.36 | qualifications]2    qalifications 1 |
| 359.14 | according to]2    according 1 |
| 360.2 | goatherd]2    barber 1 |
| 360.27 | frequently]2    ever 1 |
| 361.43 | disciplinants . . . and wielding]2    disciplinants wielding 1 |
| 362.8 | which he and the]2    which he was joined by the 1 |
| 362.8 | went]2    who went 1 |
| 363.41 | trouble they]W    trouble he 1–5 |
| 364.36 | Who Amadis left far behind]2    He who to Amadis turned tail 1 |
| 364.38 | Whose valour with such lustre shin'd]2    Whose gallantry did so prevail 1 |
| 365.33 | Argamasillan]2    Argamasillecian 1 |
| 365n.* | The horse . . . poem ]2    om. 1 |
| 366.30 | Forse . . . plettro]2    Fosse . . . plectro 1 |
| 366.31 | FIRST]W    FISRT 1 |
| 374.11 | treasury?]W    ~. 1, 3–5; om. 2 |
| 379.27 | graduate, having been]2    graduate, after having been 1 |
| 380.15 | the Lord]2    our Lord 1 |
| 380.23 | was obliged]2    was fain 1 |

380.29      present. The licentiate]2     present, and the licentiate 1

381.31      do I set]2     do set 1

383.24      Don Orlando]2     Don Roldan 1

384.33      Better than four cities, or the places]2     Better than the places 1

385.30      servant art]1(*errata*)     servant are 1(*text*)

385.32      So it ought to be]2     That may be 1

386.3       faithful servants]2     servants 1

386.10      won't]2     wont 1

387.14      morsel with any satisfaction, until]2     morsel, until 1

387.23      hardly]2     scarce 1

388.2       thus keeping the impulse]2     while he kept the impulse 1

388.27      careful in]1(*errata*)     careful of 1(*text*)

389.8       author]2     authors 1

389.14      exhibited]2     represented 1

390.20      Curiosity.]2     ~? 1

391.9       wittiest]2     wisest 1

391n.†      Alphonsos Tostatus . . . *discutit omne.*]2     *om.* 1

392.7       qualmishness]2     faintishness 1

392.20      of batchelor]2     of the batchelor 1

393.16      those hundred]2     these hundred 1

393.27      great many]2     many 1

393n.*      As related . . . is the continuation.]2     *om.* 1

394.31      close](*errata*)     charge 1(*text*)

397.5       two or three]3     two three 1–2

397.27      ill buckled . . . concubine.]2     ill married than well debauched. 1

397.30      high, that]2     high, as that 1

398.6       sons-in-law, and grandsons, and]2     sons and daughters‚in-law, and 1

398.7       match her]W     match me her 1–5

398.12      observe,]2     ~. 1

| | |
|---|---|
| 400.3 | money for him by]2   money by 1 |
| 401.6 | courtiers]1(*errata*)   courteous 1(*text*) |
| 401.34 | them, deserves]1(*errata*)   them‸ deserve 1(*text*) |
| 401.34 | Sanbenito]W   San benito 1–5 |
| 402.21 | attentive to]1(*errata*)   attentive in 1(*text*) |
| 402.25 | point, diminishing]2   point, like a pyramid, diminishing 1 |
| 404.18 | adventures]2   ventures 1 |
| 404n.* | The original . . . adventures.]2   *om.* 1 |
| 405.6 | you please]2   you shall please 1 |
| 405.22 | worth two]1(*errata*)   with to 1(*text*) |
| 405.38 | that island]2   the island 1 |
| 407.39 | find a compleat helmet]2   find some helmet 1 |
| 409.3 | the night . . . advanced]2   the night is dark, and so far advanced 1 |
| 409.4 | day-light]2   to-morrow morning 1 |
| 409.15 | corridores]2   piazzas 1 |
| 410.43 | Horatius]2   Horatio 1 |
| 411.5 | Cortez?]2   ~. 1 |
| 411.10 | etherial]2   eternal 1 |
| 411.34 | obelisk]2   needle 1 |
| 412.19 | an humble]2   a humble 1 |
| 412.39 | grove]2   thicket 1 |
| 413.37 | to let me search]2   to search 1 |
| 414.8 | discretion?]3   ~. 1–2 |
| 414.31 | stranger]2   country lad 1 |
| 416.39 | Toboso. Well, and]2   Toboso. And 1 |
| 416.43 | But have you . . . same princess?]2   But, have you . . . same palace or stately castle? 1 |
| 416.43 | eyes on her]2   eyes on it 1 |
| 417.5 | honourable,]2   ~. 1 |
| 417.7 | come but scurvily]2   come scurvily 1 |

417.17          fed]2    led 1

417.40          bitterly,ᴧ]2    ~,, 1

420.38          run]2    race 1

422.14          gaiety]2    good humour 1

424.19          rattle]2    pole 1

426.21          characters were introduced]2    characters introduced 1

427.23          composition, omitted them; though sometimes he
                seems]2    composition, they are here omitted, tho' sometimes the
                translator seems 1

429.30          sat down together]2    sat together 1

429.35          disdain . . . revenge." "I]2    disdain." "I 1

430.33          squire]2    squires 1

430.35          archbishopric; but . . . emperor: and I]2    archbishopric; and I 1

431.4           are not at all desirable]2    are not all so desirable 1

431.5           others]2    and others 1

431.9           pastimes]W    pastime 1–5

431.12          none]2    neither 1

431.33          squire!]5    ~? 1–4

431.35          done it!]W    ~ ~? 1–5

432.16          it. Other]2    it: other 1

432.17          full. Madness]2    full; madness 1

432.18          true, as it is] 1(cw)    true, it is 1(text)

432.31          observed]2    perceived and observed 1

432.34          them, at]2    them, hanging at 1

433.31          mystery.]W    ~: 1; ~? 2–5

433.31          But]2    but 1

434.8           mouth. In]2    mouth; and in 1

436.15          unparalleled]2    unequal 1

437.6           Sancho.]2    ~, 1

437.34          as almost to overshadow]2    as to overshadow 1

| | |
|---|---|
| 438.10 | not the grace of your countenance]2    not your countenance 1 |
| 438.14 | visage: my reason]2    visage; and my reason 1 |
| 439.4 | answered Panza]2    answered the squire 1 |
| 439.29 | ran down to]2    ran to 1 |
| 441.1 | So saying]2    And so saying 1 |
| 441.25 | for the tracts]2    for, the tract 1 |
| 442.34 | and difficulty]2    or difficulty 1 |
| 443.32 | to find]2    to meet 1 |
| 444.5 | and invincible]2    and most invincible 1 |
| 444.15 | delivering]2    liberating 1 |
| 444.18 | Signor, you will hardly believe]2    You will hardly, Sir, believe 1 |
| 444.20 | Cecial.]2    ~? 1 |
| 444.32 | arms?]3    ~. 1–2 |
| 444.34 | worship]2    honour 1 |
| 447.24 | make]2    have 1 |
| 447.25 | that I may defend]2    I defend 1 |
| 447.32 | persuaded . . . supposition]1(*errata*)    persuaded of this supposition 1(*text*) |
| 448.1 | the gifts]2    those gifts 1 |
| 448.21 | Signor]2    Sir 1 |
| 448.28 | especially as]2    especially when 1 |
| 449.19 | One so born]2    And one so born 1 |
| 449.20 | attains . . . rules only]2    attains only to the knowledge of the rules alone 1 |
| 449.23 | signor]2    sir 1 |
| 450.14 | called upon]2    called out upon 1 |
| 450.16 | summoned]2    called off 1 |
| 451.6 | was that sat]2    was sat 1 |
| 451.28 | Whither]2    Whether 1 |
| 451.41 | me?]W    ~! 1–5 |

452.6               signor]2    sir 1

452.10              then going]2    and going 1

452.11              pressing]2    praying 1

452.11              Signor]2    sir 1

452.17              signor]2    sir 1

452.17              and look after your ferrets]2    and go mind your ferrets 1

452.23              seeing]2    who saw 1

452.29              unharnessed]2    unyoked 1

452.38              Signor]2    Sir 1

454.20              worship's]2    honour's 1

454.32              cloth]2    clout 1

454.40              Harness your mules again]2    Put your mules to again 1

455.11              harnessed]2    yoked 1

455.14              tell him, it was the knight]2    tell him, the knight 1

455.15              forward]2    ever after 1

456.8               and direct]2    direct 1

456.10              But for the]2    But the 1

456.31              village]2    villa 1

457.13              reflecting on what]1(*errata*)    reflecting what 1(*text*)

458.4               breeches, and a . . . stained]2    breeches, a . . . blotted 1

458.8               and over all]2    over all 1

458.11              off exhibiting a whey]2    off a whey 1

458.12              appetite]2    appetites 1

458.13              scoured]2    rubbed 1

458.30              who, among other discourse, said]2    and, among other discourse, he said 1

458.40              make]1(*errata*)    makes 1(*text*)

459.2               name of the first]2    name of first 1

459.17              astronomer]2    astrologer 1

460.19          to the original proposition; besides] 2    to the intention and
                proposition of him who proposed it; besides 1

461.23          those] 1 (*errata*)    these 1 (*text*)

461.26          hollow] 2    cry 1

462.34          but to leave] 2    but leave 1

464.13          dancers] 2    dances 1

465.34          bestir] 1 (*errata*)    better 1 (*text*)

465.43          out!]W    ~? 1–5

465.43          wheels, or any other thing whatsover?" "O] 2    wheels?" "O 1

466.30          back; nor have I met with any man whom] 2    back; and there is
                scarce any one who 1

467.6           button] 2    buttons 1

467.21          ever. The] 2    ever: and the 1

467.22          resolved] 2    they all resolved 1

467.32          bells. As] 2    bells; and, as 1

468.7           golden] 2    dropping 1

469.3           make up] 2    makes up 1

469.35          wall; two cauldrons of oil, larger than a dyer's vat, were] 2    wall;
                two pans, as wide as cauldrons, and larger than a dyer's vat, full of
                oil, were 1

471.11          pipe. Cupid] 2    pipe; and Cupid 1

472.17          Roman cat-skin] 2    calf-skin 1

472.29          parson] 2    curate 1

473.14          life: moreover, according] 2    life; especially as, according 1

473.37          wise!]W    ~? 1–5

474.28          in adorning themselves] 2    in striving to compose themselves 1

474.30          ornamented] 2    adorned 1

474.31          they were to see] 2    they could see 1

474.34          people] 2    couple 1

475.1           interspersed] 2    interpersed 1

475.32          recovering a little]2    recollecting himself a little 1

476.20          kind . . . kindness]2    pious . . . piety 1

478.15          consent. This]2    consent; and this 1

478.18          produced. Don]2    produced, and Don 1

478.20          jars]2    cauldrons 1

478.24          same: and, as in the last]2    same; and as in the first 1

479.19          Great]2    GRFAT 1

479.21          his discretion . . . his valour]2    his valour . . . his discretion 1

479.27          his friends]2    her friends 1

480.35          remark]1(*errata*)    might remark 1(*text*)

481.25          which I propose to call]2    called 1

481.30          not forgetting those of the Piojo]2    not forgetting the Piojo 1

481.36          defluxion or]2    defluxion of 1

482.26          rope. Next]2    rope; and next 1

483.22          night]1(*errata*)    might 1(*text*)

483.27          knights-errant . . . brass! I say]2    knights-errant: I say 1

483.32          little. By]2    little; and by 1

483.44          word. When]2    word; and when 1

484.17          hungry: they]2    hungry; and they 1

484.34          which open]2    that open 1

485.30          than]1(*errata*)    when 1(*text*)

486.34          and your squire]2    your squire 1

487.5           channel,]W    ~ˬ 1–5

487.15          whom]2    which 1

487.25          in the rear of these came]2    at the head of these came 1

488.27          "My master . . . "for, as all]2    "If the truth must be told, master,"
                said Sancho, "as all 1

488.43          who, even . . . supposition, has]2    and, even . . . supposition, he
                has 1

489.12          and those two]2    and the other two 1

| | |
|---|---|
| 489.16 | many ladies]2   many other ladies 1 |
| 490.5 | her new]2   here new 1 |
| 490.19 | nor will enjoy health]2   nor ought to enjoy health 1 |
| 490.28 | more punctually than]2   as punctually as 1 |
| 490.34 | those vanities]2   these vanities 1 |
| 491.10 | coming]2   turning 1 |
| 492.35 | Egypt]2   Lybia 1 |
| 492.42 | walking fast, and switching]2   leading and switching 1 |
| 493.10 | set off]2   set on 1 |
| 493.12 | inn, which they reached]2   hermitage, which having reached 1 |
| 493.13 | twilight. The student however proposed]2   twilight, the student proposed 1 |
| 493.14 | draught at the hermitage: Sancho]2   draught. Sancho 1 |
| 493.15 | it]2   the hermitage 1 |
| 493.40 | credit]2   service 1 |
| 493.43 | them . . . baggage-waggon]2   them, and find some baggage-waggon 1 |
| 494.9 | give]2   gave 1 |
| 494.14 | before he professes]2   rather than profess 1 |
| 494.23 | than]1(*errata*)   them 1(*text*) |
| 496.39 | would]2   could 1 |
| 497.8 | twice]2   twice twice 1 |
| 497.42 | Peter is here]W   Peter here 1–5 |
| 498.28 | tail: his buttocks]2   tail, though his buttocks 1 |
| 498.31 | Peter, who answered]2   Peter, who having received the money, answered 1 |
| 498.36 | he knows]2   you know 1 |
| 498.40 | eagerness: having]2   eagerness; and having 1 |
| 500.13 | puppies . . . what]2   puppies, and of what 1 |
| 500.16 | Saturday]2   Sunday 1 |

500.28      realities; for‸ . . . mixture of both.]2    realities, for, to him the
            whole seemed real. 1

501.5       and to shew]2    and shew 1

502.13      Aljaferia. That lady]2    Aljaferia, and that 1

502.18      Melisendra? Now]2    Melisendra: now 1

504.18      had before me]2    had here before me 1

504.31      from this here Sir]2    from the inconsiderate fury of this here Sir 1

504.38      catholic and scrupulous christian]2    catholic and charitable
            christian 1

504.41      make some atonement]2    make atonement 1

506.32      "Split]2    ‿They split 1

506.37      I demand two rials]2    I demand, without the least abatement, two
            rials 1

506.40      coney]2    hare 1

507.19      dozen rials]2    half a dozen rials 1

508.32      he pretended no knowledge]2    he practised no stratagem and
            address 1

509.19      his mouth]2    and his mouth 1

510.37      and Fourthly]5    And fourthly 1–4

511.1       principal causes]2    five causes 1

513.12      nape of his neck]2    top of his head 1

513.34      laddle]2    saddle 1

514.1       God . . . oppose]2    God will not suffer me to oppose 1

514.17      public roads]2    by-places 1

514.23      that]W    then 1–5

514.43      chivalry]2    history 1

516.14      river-side]2    bank 1

516.14      bank. Don]2    bank; and Don 1

517.27      wide and extended]2    wide extended 1

518.8       it! . . . squire,]W    ~, . . . ~! 1–3; ~, . . . ~; 4–5

518.16      solstices,]2    ~; 1

| | |
|---|---|
| 521.29 | knight-errant]2    knight 1 |
| 524.34 | perceived,]2    ~ˌ 1 |
| 527.23 | respect?]5    ~! 1–4 |
| 527.32 | post?]W    ~! 1–5 |
| 528.28 | is true, for my master]2    is so true, that my master 1 |
| 528.41 | Mencia]2    Meneia 1 |
| 529.19 | all!]W    ~? 1–5 |
| 529.20 | table–methinks]W    table. Methinks 1–5 |
| 529.34 | not be quite abashed]2    not grow quite outrageous 1 |
| 530.20 | adventures?]4    ~. 1–3 |
| 534.9 | dinner]2    supper 1 |
| 535.14 | dinner]2    supper 1 |
| 535.21 | request,]2    ~. 1 |
| 535.35 | sketch]1(*errata*)    scratch 1(*text*) |
| 537.27 | Anteus]2    Anteon 1 |
| 539.27 | trays, wooden]2    trays and wooden 1 |
| 541.19 | produced by]2    produced from 1 |
| 542.23 | eaten of his]2    eaten his 1 |
| 546.13 | the servants]2    their servants 1 |
| 547.7 | ground. Perceiving himself thus suspended, that] 2    ground; then perceiving that 1 |
| 547.29 | will deprive]2    will certainly deprive 1 |
| 548.8 | idle folks than for governors]2    idle folks, who have nothing else to do, than for governors 1 |
| 548.19 | that day]2    the day 1 |
| 548.29 | day was soon]2    day soon 1 |
| 549.6 | troops]2    martial people 1 |
| 549.10 | Toboso inchanted, accompanied]2    Toboso, accompanied 1 |
| 549.10 | Frenchman]2    Francis 1 |
| 549.15 | did not see him: for]2    did not think of that: for 1 |

549.32      what had happened]2    what happened 1

550.4      but above]2    and above 1

550.14      waggon]2    waggons 1

550.17      not encounter]2   not again encounter 1

550.20      proceeded]2   poceeded 1

551.7      also in white]2   in black 1

551.10      surprize. Seated]2   surprise. And, seated 1

551.13      plaits]2   rumples 1

551.24      repeat]2   rehearse 1

553.19      pebbles]2   peebles 1

553.38      liberty the beauty]2   liberty the sleekness of my skin, the gentleness of my condition, and the beauty 1

556.4      murmuring]2   brawling 1

556.6      splendid]2   splended 1

558.34      standing; but]2   ~! But 1

559.18      drummers]W   drums 1–5

560.4      Sancho]2   And Sancho 1

560.10      three-tailed‸countess]2   three‸tailed-countess 1

561.22      duennas]2   damsels 1

562.5      white]2   black 1

562n.*.3      Varlets]W   Varlet 1–5

563.13      ever]2   every 1

563.17      may instantly favour]2   may favour 1

563.44      enamoured. Among]2   enamoured; and, among 1

564.34      fashion . . . Candaya]2   fashion at Candaya 1

564.40      them. If]2   them: and if 1

565.1      abound. When]2   abound. And when 1

565.2      Ariadne]2   Arcadia 1

565.3      balsams]2   balsam 1

565.34      stupendous]2   stupend'ous 1

566.7            swooned rather than died]2    swooned before she died 1

566.33           stupendous]2    stupend'ous 1

566.34           affected]2    effected 1

567.37           master recount]2    master ever recount 1

569.15           Reynaldo]2    Reynaldos 1

574.15           covered . . . turned]2    covered, Don Quixote adjusted himself in
                 his seat, and turned 1

574n.*.2         Real]4    real 1–3

575.17           that he could]2    that he thought he could 1

575.30           flax: his belly]2    flax, and his belly 1

577.7            what does I]W    what does me I 1–5

578.30           obeyed]1 (*errata*)    obliged 1 (*text*)

579.6            stored]2    provided 1

579.29           moonshine]2    mooonshine 1

579.31           beneficially]2    beneficently 1

579.34           tempestuous]2    tempest'ous 1

582.40           take care that it]2    take care it 1

582.43           than well chosen apothegms.]2    than a connected chain of
                 conversation. 1

583.5            throw out those that]2    throw out those only that 1

583.15           do not lean . . . saddle]2    do not throw your body over the saddle 1

584.18           threescore thousand]2    threescore 1

584.34           grinders . . . what]2    grinders: When I find one skulking in my
                 house, and cry what 1

584.36           fit to a hair]3    fit to hair 1–2

585.16           than my whole body]2    than for my whole body 1

585.18           equal all]2    all equal 1

585.31           and a strange]2    and of a strange 1

586.17           treat]2    treat of 1

586.30           related. Thus . . . consequence]2    related, and in consequence 1

586.32           sooner]2    sooned 1

587.10          Dapple]5    dapple 1–4

587.31          made; for the rest]2    made; and, for the rest 1

588.23          art: as]2    art; and as 1

588.31          imagination]2    imaginations 1

589.7           starch.]5    ~ ∧ 1–4

589.24          heard]2    could hear 1

590.10          he was there]2    he was awake 1

590.17          care and]2    care or 1

592.12          well bred]2    nobly born 1

593.16          day . . . signor]2    day, of such a month, in such a year, signor 1

594.22          loan . . . repayment]2    loan or repayment 1

594.31          cross of the rod, he]2    cross, he 1

595.32          woman? To this]2    woman? And, to this 1

595.34          deals]W    deal 1–5

596.34          as sheepishly]2    as well 1

597.11          and, being . . . lazy, dressed]2    and starting from the arms of sloth, dressed 1

597.39          Quixote. On]2    Quixote; and, on 1

599.10          starting up]2    starting from his bed 1

599.21          Seeing the unequal]2    The duke seeing the unequal 1

599.42          bed; where he was]2    bed; but, afterwards, he was 1

601.4           sumptuous]2    sumpt'ous 1

601.15          wand . . . twinkling]2    wand, it vanished in a twinkling 1

602.20          where]2    were 1

602.24          H2ark]2    Heak 1

603.3           ran]2    run 1

603.5           he. One]2    he. And one 1

603.11          recited]2    read 1

603.25          Positive . . . dungeon]2    Rezio . . . dugeon 1

603.30          luncheon]2    luncehon 1

| | | |
|---|---|---|
| 603.32 | battles with]2 | battles by 1 |
| 603.43 | presume]2 | pesume 1 |
| 604.13 | Positive]2 | Rezio 1 |
| 604.34 | and had been]2 | and been 1 |
| 605.15 | tawny. My]2 | tawny. And my 1 |
| 605.41 | take or not take]2 | Stick or not stick 1 |
| 606.2 | countryman. Scarce]2 | countryman. And scarce 1 |
| 606.10 | Paralinos]5 | Paralino's 1–4 |
| 607.15 | eagerness and]2 | eagerness of 1 |
| 607.17 | in these devout precautions, if]2 | in his occupation; and, if 1 |
| 607.26 | this disposition]2 | that disposition 1 |
| 607.30 | Quixote . . . phantome]2 | Quixote, if your worship really is Don Quixote, I am no phantom 1 |
| 607.33 | worship is]2 | worship are 1 |
| 608.2 | all disasters]2 | all the disasters 1 |
| 608.36 | tender hearted]2 | pious 1 |
| 610.7 | generous]2 | pious 1 |
| 610.22 | of the house]2 | in the house 1 |
| 611.14 | In a word, as]2 | At length, as 1 |
| 611.18 | sky lark]2 | public crier 1 |
| 611.27 | to wife]2 | to his wife 1 |
| 611.28 | a hearing]2 | the hearing 1 |
| 611.31 | give him . . . disgust]2 | give himself the least concern or uneasiness 1 |
| 611.41 | same creature Altisidora]2 | same Altisidora 1 |
| 612.2 | by the life of my soul]2 | as you hope to be saved 1 |
| 612.16 | flew]2 | burst 1 |
| 612.21 | petticoats]2 | petticoat 1 |
| 612.23 | taking. Although]2 | taking; and, although 1 |
| 613.7 | Positive]2 | Rezio 1 |

| | |
|---|---|
| 613.11 | seasons . . . affairs; and]2    seasons, and that their affairs should be solely attended to, come what will: and 1 |
| 613.16 | meals and]2    meals or 1 |
| 613.22 | was struck]W    were struck 1–5 |
| 613.38 | staler]2    powerfuller 1 |
| 613n.* | *Podrida* signifies . . . stiled *Pot-pourri.*]2    *om.* 1 |
| 614.2 | other]2    another 1 |
| 614.12 | to do]2    to doubt 1 |
| 614.15 | act any otherwise]    act otherwise 1 |
| 614.26 | worship]2    lordship 1 |
| 614.31 | round. Accordingly]2    round; and, accordingly 1 |
| 614.35 | see. Having]2    see; and having 1 |
| 615.2 | bett was‸]2    ~ ~, 1 |
| 615.7 | him out . . . most]2    him close, and in the most 1 |
| 616.14 | gaol]W    goal 1–5 |
| 616.16 | gaol]W    goal 1–5 |
| 616.17 | gaol]W    goal 1–5 |
| 616.21 | gaoler]W    goaler 1–5 |
| 617.1 | sixteen]2    seventeen 1 |
| 617.39 | sewer]2    steward 1 |
| 617.42 | other]2    steward 1 |
| 619.2 | had locked]W    has locked 1–5 |
| 619.7 | who]W    whom 1–5 |
| 619.20 | your own words]2    your words 1 |
| 619.41 | me; that . . . we shall]2    me; for, as they do not know who we are, we shall 1 |
| 620.8 | flight. ‸]2    ~.. 1 |
| 620.36 | should]2    would 1 |
| 620.37 | duke's]2    duke 1 |
| 620.38 | daughter Sanchica]2    daughter 1 |

| | |
|---|---|
| 620.41 | Thus]2    This 1 |
| 621.23 | pride]2    reputation 1 |
| 621.28 | disinchantment]2    inchantment 1 |
| 621.31 | rosary]2    string 1 |
| 622.32 | the string]2    a string 1 |
| 625.11 | but only these letters are from]2    but only, these are letters from 1 |
| 625.30 | the new-comers]2    the two new-comers 1 |
| 626.17 | may very well . . . convenience.]2    may afford to go thither, and maintain a rank. 1 |
| 626.19 | rather than to-morrow]2    before to-morrow 1 |
| 627.10 | that this is all]2    for, this is all 1 |
| 627.34 | indited by]2    signed with 1 |
| 627.35 | noddle]2    mark 1 |
| 628.6 | the air]2    and air 1 |
| 629.26 | the night before]2    the very night 1 |
| 630.1 | printed]2    imprinted 1 |
| 630.24 | intimidate]2    intimate 1 |
| 630.28 | extremities]2    extremes 1 |
| 630.31 | weights]2    weight 1 |
| 631.6 | affects]2    affect 1 |
| 631.37 | to penance]2    to do penance 1 |
| 631.37 | and as I cannot even do that, I]2    and, as every thing goes against the grain, I 1 |
| 632.1 | son-in-law]2    son‸in-law 1 |
| 632.15 | rotten]2    torn 1 |
| 632.26 | or crook]2    or by crook 1 |
| 632.39 | should be]2    should not be 1 |
| 633.34 | communicate]2    commune 1 |
| 634.26 | its acceptance]2    his acceptance 1 |
| 635.8 | ladies,]W    ~‸ 1–5 |

635.22　　　　　what nor where]2　　what 1

635.41　　　　　my coach]2　　my own coach 1

636.12　　　　　to write to me]2　　to write me 1

636.15　　　　　Sanchica]2　　Sancha 1

636.38　　　　　honour there]2　　honour 1

639.24　　　　　Sitting up . . . comprehending]2　　Hearing the alarm as he lay, he
　　　　　　　　listened attentively, in hope of comprehending 1

640.15　　　　　at that instant]2　　and that instant 1

640.33　　　　　pieces. There]2　　pieces; and there 1

644.21　　　　　already advanced]2　　already well advanced 1

644.32　　　　　smacking . . . mouthful]2　　seasoning every mouthful 1

646.31　　　　　where]2　　were 1

646.35　　　　　thy proposal]2　　your proposal 1

646.43　　　　　will not]2　　wont 1

648.10　　　　　buildings. In]2　　buildings; and, in 1

649.6　　　　　services!]3　　~? 1–2

649.23　　　　　thankfully . . . told him]2　　thankfully, and told him 1

650.2　　　　　ejaculations, he fancied he had proceeded]　　ejaculations, he had
　　　　　　　　proceeded 1

650.25　　　　　complain, but]2　　complain, replied the voice, but 1

651.33　　　　　I shall say . . . plainly.]2　　I would say no more even though I could
　　　　　　　　speak to the purpose. 1

652.16　　　　　yesterday]2　　yesterday morning 1

652.25　　　　　to the day]2　　till the day 1

653.16　　　　　his life]2　　life 1

654.26　　　　　fairly]2　　fair 1

654.28　　　　　invincible]2　　invisible 1

656.4　　　　　avail them so little]2　　happen so seldom 1

656.5　　　　　long accustomed to chop]2　　long used and accustomed to chop 1

656.14　　　　　has no]2　　had no 1

656.20　　　　　execution]2　　expected execution 1

| | |
|---|---|
| 660.26 | journey. Having]2    journey; and having 1 |
| 660.28 | certain white]2    four white 1 |
| 661.34 | for, the kingdom . . . violence; whereas]2    for, heaven may be won by force; whereas 1 |
| 662.14 | these]2    those 1 |
| 663.24 | mind . . . mind]2    soul . . . soul 1 |
| 663.32 | mind]2    soul 1 |
| 663.35 | green thread]2    green silk thread 1 |
| 663.41 | thread]2    silk thread 1 |
| 663.42 | the jealous god]2    the god 1 |
| 663.43 | were of rushes and unspun]2    were wove of rushes or unspun 1 |
| 666.40 | Let him . . . receive him."]2    *om.* 1 |
| 668.7 | Seeing, however]2    Seeing him, however 1 |
| 669.16 | he went]2    went 1 |
| 670.25 | What displeases . . . performance]2    The most distinguished part in this performance 1 |
| 671.30 | she, as far as modesty . . . smiled]2    she maintained her honour and reputation, and smiled 1 |
| 672.36 | prize-justs]2    justs 1 |
| 673.7 | discourse: they believed]2    discourse; and they believed 1 |
| 673.15 | but little less for the day]2    but little for the day 1 |
| 673.24 | whereas the knight]2    but, the knight 1 |
| 674.39 | went aside]2    going aside 1 |
| 674.39 | to take]2    to take up 1 |
| 674.40 | night. There he felt]2    night, he felt 1 |
| 675.13 | and stand . . . arrive.]2    and suffer themselves to be conducted peaceably to the captain of the band. 1 |
| 676.13 | spurs; armed]2    spurs; and armed 1 |
| 676.15 | Roque]2    Rogue 1 |
| 676.15 | the noise]2    this noise 1 |
| 677.24 | Roque approached]2    Roque alighted and approached 1 |

679.14        us?]W   ~. 1–5

679.23        by the desire]2   by a desire 1

679.27        deep . . . deep]W   Deep . . . Deep 1–5

679.27        deep, and sin . . . undertake]2   Deep, undertake 1

680.4         but, changing]2   and, changing 1

680.10        muleteers]2   Muleteers 1

680.17        four gallies]2   some gallies 1

680.19        to two]2   to about two 1

680.22        they answered,]2   was answered, 1

680.27        vicariate]2   vicarage 1

681.2         liberality . . . leaving]2   liberality, in leaving 1

681.17        looking]2   and looking 1

681.19        displeased at the booty]2   displeased at the division of the booty 1

682.26        plant or]2   plant and 1

682.29        repetition]2   repetion 1

683.1         exhibited]2   exhibiting 1

683.2         sea. At]2   sea; and, at 1

683.25        gentleman]2   gentlemen 1

683.35        That mischief]2   The mischief 1

684.4         youngsters]2   people 1

685.21        a private apartment]2   an apartment 1

685.32        ears to hear]3   ears to ear 1–2

685.39        entertainer]2   landlord 1

685n.*        *times*]2   *terms* 1

686.2         was, I think, a native]2   was a native 1

686.24        they, without his knowledge, pinned]2   they pinned 1

687.7         concerns; look]2   concerns, and look 1

687.33        that it might not flag.]2   which would otherwise have flagged. 1

688.16        fast bolted]2   just bolted 1

689.9         Noriz]W   Norroz 1; Noriez 2–5

| | |
|---|---|
| 689.15 | eye; I touch . . . Don]2   eye and touch it with my finger." As he did not choose to ask another question, Don 1 |
| 691.1 | a statuary]2   an engraver 1 |
| 691.5 | four eagles]2   eagles 1 |
| 691.6 | Roman]3   roman 1–2 |
| 692.32 | book printed]2   book to be printed 1 |
| 693.33 | accomplished. As]2   accomplished; and, as 1 |
| 694.14 | renowned]2   renowed 1 |
| 695.9 | inchantment; but what]2   inchantment; though, what 1 |
| 695.10 | matter. What]W   matter? what 1–5 |
| 695.29 | should not escape]2   could not escape 1 |
| 695.40 | Turks . . . discharged]2   Turks, discharged 1 |
| 696.25 | yard-arm]2   yards-arm 1 |
| 696.29 | captain,]2   ~. 1 |
| 698.11 | lodged,]2   ~ˬ 1 |
| 698.18 | is much]2   was much 1 |
| 698.22 | could make]2   should make 1 |
| 698.33 | few]2   not one 1 |
| 699.4 | government: he]2   government; and he 1 |
| 699.9 | beauty as for her father's wealth]2   beauty as I her father for my wealth 1 |
| 699.14 | vicissitude . . . retrieved]2   vicissitude, I have retrieved 1 |
| 699.28 | yard-arm]W   yard's arm 1–5 |
| 699.38 | The general and the viceroy]2   The general and viceroy 1 |
| 700.11 | town . . . bell.]2   town and country. 1 |
| 700.15 | bring home]2   release 1 |
| 700.16 | delivered]2   released 1 |
| 700.23 | describes it as a very]W   describes it a very 1–5 |
| 700.33 | for he often]2   for, as he often 1 |
| 701.14 | spoils of all my arms]2   spoils of my arms 1 |

| | |
|---|---|
| 701.21 | I dare say]2   I dare swear 1 |
| 702.4 | persists]2   persits 1 |
| 702.32 | turning his horse]2   turned his horse 1 |
| 702.43 | in the air]2   in air 1 |
| 703.25 | fully resolved]2   and fully resolved 1 |
| 704.12 | Panza . . . conceits are such]2   Panza; and the conceits of either are such 1 |
| 705.14 | not to be minded]2   not be minded 1 |
| 706.3 | There is nothing . . . to whom]2   Neither tears, entreaties, promises, nor presents will avail with the great Don Bernandino de Velasco, to whom 1 |
| 706.5 | Bernardino]W   Bernandino 1–5 |
| 707.10 | good humour]2   moderation 1 |
| 707.24 | knight-errant]4   ~ˆ~ 1–3 |
| 708.14 | exclaimed]2   exclaimed aloud 1 |
| 708.25 | and a judge]2   and judge 1 |
| 709.8 | wager if they go to study]2   wager they are going to study 1 |
| 709.8 | they will in a trice]2   and will in a trice 1 |
| 709.25 | mention . . . combat?" "No]2   mention?" "No 1 |
| 710.31 | Body o' me]4   Body Oˆ me 1–3 |
| 710.33 | amorous?]3   ~. 1–2 |
| 711.5 | knights-errant]3   ~ˆ~ 1–2 |
| 711.14 | knight-errantry]3   ~ˆ~ 1–2 |
| 711.24 | we will assume]2   I am resolved to assume 1 |
| 711.25 | of shepherds]2   of a shepherd 1 |
| 711.25 | our retirement]2   my retirement 1 |
| 712.15 | Albogues]2   Alboques 1 |
| 712.17 | Albogues]2   Alboques 1 |
| 712.18 | Albogues]2   Alboques 1 |
| 712.21 | Albogues]2   Alboques 1 |
| 712.24 | Borcegui]2   Borcequi 1 |

712.26        Albogues]2    Alboques 1

713.16        let us]2    let us us 1

713.24        Moreno]2    Morens 1

714.18        bestowed]2    digested 1

714.32        fed]2    led 1

714.33        strings]3    string 1–2

715.15        knights-errant]W    knight-errants 1–5

715.15        that]2    that that 1

716.12        two proceeded in their journey]2    two mounted in order to
              proceed on their journey 1

716.12        descried]2    they descried 1

717.4         end?]W    ~! 1–5

717.5         converted into bad]2    converted to bad 1

717.9         XVII]2    XVI 1

717.37        threw over him]2    threw over his head 1

719.8         damsel?]W    ~. 1–5

719.21        court-yard]2    court‸yard 1

719.24        larger.]2    ~, 1

719.25        exclaiming,]3    ~. 1–2

719.37        curtsy]W    curt'sy 1; court'sy 2–5

720.34        ‸That . . . friend.‸]W    "That . . . friend." 1–5

721.1         XVIII]2    XVII 1

721.16        she thought]2    she had thought 1

722.14        victor. Sampson]2    victor: and Sampson 1

722.16        proceeded]2    he proceeded 1

722.21        madness. He declared]2    madness; and declared 1

722.27        Quixote. He ordered]2    Quixote; and ordered 1

723.16        I should . . . heartily: but]2    I should have been as much obliged
              to him, as I think myself at present: but 1

723.27        flocks]2    rubbish 1

725.2               sumptuous]2    sumpt'ous 1

725.32              XIX]2    XVIII] 1

726.19              disinchanting]2    disinchanted 1

729.22              serge, instead of tapestry, such]2    serge, such 1

729.24              his presumptuous]2    her presumptuous 1

730.20              XX]2    XIX 1

730.33              and was ornamented]2    and ornamented 1

731.15              did him signal services]2    did him many signal services 1

731.36              than an orator]2    than of an orator 1

733.7               preceding]3    proced- l ing 1; proceeding 2

733.12              The whole]2    That whole 1

733.22              coin]2    corn 1

734.1               XXI]2    XX 1

734.28              which I]2    which, as I 1

734.30              christian]2    person 1

737.3               his new chivalries]2    his chivalries 1

737.38              good faith]2    good sooth 1

737.40              of wolves]2    of the wolves 1

737.40              wolves?]W    ~! 1–5

738.9               XXII]2    XVIII 1

738.14              approach. Either]2    approach: and either 1

741.18              assistance: during]2    assistance; and, during 1

741.28              in other words]3    other in words 1–2

# WORD-DIVISION

## I. LINE-END HYPHENATION IN THE GEORGIA EDITION

[The following compounds, hyphenated at a line-end in the Georgia Edition, are hyphenated within the line in the 1755 first edition.]

| | | | |
|---|---|---|---|
| 23.10 | back-\|bite | 127.19 | belly-\|full |
| 29.12, | | 136.35 | to-\|day |
| 73.32, | | 141.25 | palace-\|windows |
| 136.16, | | 153.29 | play-\|fellow |
| 522.10, | | 158.15, | |
| 524.1, | | 168.32, | |
| 681.28 | knight-\|errant | 666.3 | high\|-road |
| 30.15 | head-\|piece | 158.26 | cork-\|tree |
| 32.3 | back-\|door | 163.38 | country-\|girl |
| 37.3, | | 172.31 | logger-\|heads |
| 356.43 | market-place | 173.26 | school-\|master |
| 59.29 | wind-\|mills | 239.12 | fellow-\|sufferer |
| 68.7 | ill-defended | 274.5 | well-\|proportioned |
| 78.3, | | 293.14 | country-\|house |
| 257.18 | wine-\|bag | 294.22 | able-\|bodied |
| 82.20 | bitter-\|bay | 305.13 | co-\|operating |
| 101.28, | | 309.8 | first-\|born |
| 121.8, | | 326.3 | she-\|ass |
| 130.23, | | 342.37 | swaddling-\|cloaths |
| 182.27, | | 349.9, | |
| 359.25 | knights-errant | 532.19 | knight-\|errantry |
| 103.22, | | 379.8 | ginger-\|bread |
| 578.37 | to-\|morrow | 383.29 | broad-\|shouldered |
| 113.9 | Shrove\|-tide | 399.18 | back-\|bitters |

| 420.21 | country-\|wench | 509.13 | rising-\|ground |
|---|---|---|---|
| 424.8 | merry-\|andrew | 536.29 | good-\|breeding |
| 431.10 | fishing-\|rod | 539.7 | soap-\|scouring |
| 441.7 | paste-\|board | 541.11 | joint-\|stool |
| 442.35 | good-\|will | 541.21 | memorandum-\|book |
| 445.15 | jockey-\|fashion | 613.35 | goats-\|flesh |
| 458.4 | shamoy-\|leather | 615.37 | gaming-\|houses |
| 470.4 | dinner-\|time | 619.12 | bull-\|feasts |
| 470.28 | well\|-made | 634.40 | court-\|yard |
| 472.17 | cat-\|skin | 649.38 | flower-\|gardens |
| 479.10 | flesh-\|pots | 653.35 | flea-\|bitten |
| 485.20 | ostrich-\|eggs | 662.29 | red-\|cross |
| 490.25 | table-\|cloth | 683.33 | kettle-\|drum |
| 491.11 | hand-\|writing | 712.43 | city-\|chamber |
| 495.25 | arms-\|carrier | 719.20 | draw-\|bridges |
| 508.44 | by-\|standers | 734.32 | stumbling-\|block |

## 2. LINE-END HYPHENATION IN THE 1755 FIRST EDITION

[The following compounds or possible compounds are hyphenated at a line-end in the first edition. The form in which each has been given in the Georgia Edition, as listed below, represents the usual practice of the 1755 first edition insofar as it may be ascertained from other appearances or parallels.]

| 13.2 | archbishop | 59.39 | thoroughfare |
|---|---|---|---|
| 36.22, | | 79.27 | tip-top |
| 556.34, | | 87.31 | overtook |
| 626.19 | to-morrow | 93.44, | |
| 38.6 | godson | 562.13, | |
| 38.19 | sometimes | 567.7, | |
| 39.23 | base-born | 673.34 | overwhelmed |
| 54.2 | stumbling-block | 102.22 | beetle-brow'd |
| 59.23 | wind-mill | 103.34 | Self-commendation |

| | | | |
|---|---|---|---|
| 104.17 | rush-mat | 192.31 | new-married |
| 105.23 | outshone | 193.13 | overheard |
| 105.36 | high-born | 214.15 | highway |
| 106.43 | tin-box | 214.25 | saddle-bow |
| 109.16 | pack-stave | 223.14 | quicksilver |
| 110.14, | | 266.30 | handwriting |
| 114.30, | | 273.7 | to-day |
| 263.30, | | 294.16 | well-meaning |
| 271.31, | | 318.18 | re-established |
| 307.24, | | 331.39 | cupboard |
| 497.41, | | 351.9 | birthplace |
| 669.15 | innkeeper | 356.26 | market-place |
| 131.5 | goat-shepherd | 361.8 | overtaking |
| 136.28, | | 363.36 | housekeeper |
| 602.22 | right-hand | 366.26 | worm-eaten |
| 140.9 | overthrew | 397.11 | squires-errant |
| 144.32 | gunshot | 401.22 | mill-wheel |
| 146.33 | overwhelmed | 402.28 | superstructure |
| 147.12, | | 408.10 | well-lined |
| 401.12, | | 413.31 | churchyards |
| 428.4, | | 420.2 | country-wench's |
| 661.16, | | 424.6, | |
| 675.41, | | 489.38 | overtaken |
| 716.13 | horseback | 435.22 | overcame |
| 157.18 | Methinks | 437.36 | mulberry-colour |
| 171.22 | forest-trees | 439.21 | rowel-deep |
| 179.5, | | 441.13 | overthrow |
| 438.44, | | 448.12 | dung-hill |
| 439.8 | cork-tree | 455.33 | fellow-traveller |
| 181.16 | pocket-book | 485.6 | overpowered |

| | | | | |
|---|---|---|---|---|
| 497.15 | well-bestowed | | 582.18 | vain-glorious |
| 499.29 | landlord | | 612.16 | chamber-door |
| 499.35, | | | 614.42 | gaming-house |
| 525.32, | | | 619.26 | dewdrops |
| 533.42, | | | 621.13 | tale-bearing |
| 598.44, | | | 641.9 | overcome |
| 681.22 | overheard | | 641.14, | |
| 503.27, | | | 702.36 | forehead |
| 528.10 | downright | | 656.10 | country-wench |
| 508.25 | puppet-shew | | 657.15 | overnight |
| 510.28 | whale-bone | | 670.9 | travelling-stores |
| 520.37 | left-hand | | 673.34 | overwhelmed |
| 527.22 | blockhead | | 676.33 | overtaken |
| 529.11 | bowshot | | 693.23 | well-known |
| 543.39 | village-maiden | | 695.6 | bull's-pizzle |
| 546.39 | boar-spear | | 695.24 | gangway |
| 548.37 | bystanders | | 696.22, | |
| 554.3 | cross-bow | | 706.27 | viceroy |
| 564.5 | birdcages | | 703.31 | overthrown |
| 566.24 | wooden-horse | | 734.38 | sumpter-cloth |
| 577.5 | goatherd | | 740.9 | well-nigh |
| 579.7 | Christ-cross | | | |

## 3. SPECIAL CASES

[The following compounds or possible compounds are hyphenated at a line-end in both the Georgia Edition and the 1755 first edition.]

| | | | | |
|---|---|---|---|---|
| 6.1 | self- ǀ respect | | 322.36 | galley- ǀ slaves |
| 271.31 | inn- ǀ keeper | | 397.1 | round- ǀ about |

| 398.41 | towns-|man | 547.18 | hunting-|suit |
| 437.36 | fingers-|breadth | 548.37 | by-|standers |
| 469.35 | threshing-|floor | 624.7 | jer-|faulcon |
| 497.41 | inn-|keeper | 676.13 | gold-|hilted |
| 499.35 | over-|heard | 725.10 | lace-|maker |

# HISTORICAL COLLATION

| | |
|---|---|
| 6.4 | contemptuous]  contempt'ous 1 |
| 7.38 | Lope]  Lopè 1 |
| 8.10 | Lope]  Lopè 1 |
| 8.20 | wantonness and]  wantonness of 1 |
| 8.27 | If time would]  If time could 2–5 |
| 8.37 | eye₍witness]  eye-witness 2–5 |
| 9.8 | screened]  sereened 1 |
| 10n.*.3 | or Mayorca]  and Mayorca 3–5 |
| 12.17 | tho']  though 5 |
| 12.29 | to wake]  to awake 3–5 |
| 14.26 | shade]  shadow 2–5 |
| 15.8 | tho']  though 5 |
| 16.37 | shouldst]  should 2–5 |
| 17.31 | breeds]  bredes 3–5 |
| 17.37 | were obliged]  are 2–5 |
| 18.2 | so as that]  so that 5 |
| 18.3 | told him he]  told him that he 2–5 |
| 18.16 | though]  tho' 3–5 |
| 18.37 | history or tradition]  history and tradition 2–5 |
| 20.6 | into mere]  into a mere 5 |
| 20.11 | customs]  custom 2–5 |
| 20.12 | will be restored]  are restored 2–5 |
| 20.12 | whole conducted]  whole is conducted 2–5 |
| 20.16 | Whatever . . . for the press.]  *om.* 2–5 |
| 21.7 | creature]  creatures 1 |
| 21.9 | my own imagination]  his own imagination 1 |
| 21.20 | supplicate the gentle]  supplicate thee, gentle 2–5 |
| 22.2 | contemplative.]  ~? 2–5 |

22.5            may easily]    may very easily 5

22.7            and oblivion]    and in oblivion 5

24.14           though]    tho' 2–5

27.1            THE LIFE and ATCHIEVEMENTS]    THE
                ATCHIEVEMENTS 2–5

27n.‡.3         but conjectures]    than conjectures 1

28.9            a tittle]    farther 1

28.20           works.]    ~! 2–5

28n.‡.7         greens, or]    greens‸ and 1

29.28           enchanted]    enchanter 1

29.29           Anteus]    Anteon 1

29n.‡           Orlando . . . armour.]    *om.* 1

29n.§.1         betrayed . . . Spain]    betrayed the Spanish army at Ronsevalles 1

30.22           anew. He faced]    anew, and faced 1

30.26           fuit")]    ~)" 1–4

30.33           his horse's name]    his name 1

30n.*.3         *Trapezium.*]    ~‸1(*b*)

30n.†.1         an ordinary horse]    an horse 1

31.4            affirm. But]    affirm: but 1

31.37           errors to be amended]    errors amended 1

32.11           on his shield]    in his shield 1

32.36           Then making a sudden transition]    Then turning his horse 1

33.13           descried]    decried 2–5

35n.†           In the original . . . he-goat.]    *om.* 1

36.13           words:]    ~. 1

36.26           knights-errant, in imitation . . . strongly]    knights-errant, whose
                genius, like mine, is strongly 1

37.9            this castle]    the castle 2–5

37.35           assistance]    friend 1

38.6            he was . . . godson]    he was his godson 1

| | |
|---|---|
| 38.35 | other ejaculations]   other such ejaculations 1 |
| 40.14 | ejaculation*. This]   ejaculation*: this 1 |
| 40.28 | faithfully]   fathfully 1(*b*) |
| 42.8 | squire. For this]   squire, for which 1 |
| 42.10 | chivalry. With]   chivalry: with 1 |
| 42.16 | distrees. No]   distress; and no 1 |
| 43.2 | body!]   ~: 1 |
| 44.2 | these orders]   the orders 3–5 |
| 44.19 | self-satisfaction, pronouncing]   self-satisfaction, and pronounced 1 |
| 44.23 | remain. He who]   remain. Who 1; remain! he who 5 |
| 44.41 | be. When]   be; and when 1 |
| 44.42 | him, he pronounced]   him, pronounced 1 |
| 45.5 | author. Curious]   author; curious 1 |
| 45.21 | tho' it be]   tho' be it 5 |
| 45.22 | judge of the clue]   judge the clue 1–5(*text*) |
| 46.3 | choler. Gathering]   choler; but, gathering 1 |
| 46.3 | lance, he reduced]   lance, reduced 1 |
| 46.5 | closed]   shut 1 |
| 46.20 | mountain: a]   mountain. A 1 |
| 46.24 | situation. Therefore]   situation. And therefore 1 |
| 46.34 | Before]   And, before 1 |
| 47.11 | condition!]   ~: 2; ~? 3–5 |
| 47.21 | groans]   sighs 1 |
| 47.22 | Indeed]   And indeed 1(*a*); And indeeed 1(*b*) |
| 47.24 | situation. For]   situation; for 2–5 |
| 47.39 | talks!]   ~? 1–4 |
| 48.8 | (that . . . name,)]   ʌ~ . . . ~,ʌ 1 |
| 48.18 | (this . . . barber,)]   ʌ~ . . . ~,ʌ 1–5 |
| 48.22 | blood . . . battle]   blood of his enemies, whom he had slain in battle 1 |

48.34            which last had]   who had 1

48n.*.2          watching]   waking 1

50.8             brain.]   ~! 2–5

50n.*.1          name of a good-natured enchantress]   name of an enchantress
                 1(*a*); name of an inchantress 1(*b*)

50n.*.6          afterwards]   then 1

52.20            barber,]   ~ₐ 1(*b*)

53.21            Godamercy]   Don Godamercy 1

53.22            as also an account]   together with an account 1

54.38            than with poetry]   than poetry 1–5(*text*)

55.35            Mean while,]   while, 1(*cw*)

56.37            his niece]   the niece 3–5

59.2             their spoils]   his spoils 1(*b*)

59.4             amaze.]   ~? 1

60.33            who had passed]   who passed 1

61n.*.2          enjoined,]   ~ₐ 1–5

62.17            lady]   people 1; ladies 2–5

62.20            the fryar mounted, as pale]   mounted the fryar, who was pale 1

62.21            and who no sooner]   and no sooner 3–5

65.1             THE LIFE and ATCHIEVEMENTS]   THE
                 ATCHIEVEMENTS 2–5

65.22            atchievements]   atchievemets 1(*b*)

65.29            Jealousy]   jealousy 1–4

66.16            follows: the manner . . . recount. While]   follows: While 1

66.28            laughing,]   ~. 1

66.28            "What . . . purpose: "'This]   "What . . . purpose: ₐThis 2–5

67.30            repository]   depository 1(*b*)

69.6             governed an island]   governs an island 4–5

69.8             in bye-roads]   on the high road 1

69.40            vial]   phial 2–5

70.1             vial]   phial 2–5

| 70n.*.4 | voluntary] voluntarly 1(*b*) |
| 71.27 | matter? answered Don Quixote.]  ~, ~ ~ ~? 1(*b*); ~! ~ ~ ~. 2–5 |
| 72.14 | ate together] eat together 2–5 |
| 72n.† | *Volatiles . . . character.]* *om.* 1 |
| 74.14 | bare-headed . . . locks] *om.* 1 |
| 74.19 | court-ladies] courtiers 1 |
| 75.12 | who had made] who made 1–5 |
| 78.16 | another] one 1 |
| 79.29 | change] chance 1 |
| 80.1 | the words] of words 1 |
| 80.25 | an age] the age 3–5 |
| 82.2 | for the cold . . . received] *om.* 1 |
| 84.24 | of their desires] by their desires 1–5(*text*) |
| 85.3 | over his horse's crupper] by his horse's crupper 1–5(*text*) |
| 85.19 | summer] spring 1 |
| 85.36 | La Mancha] Valencia 1 |
| 85.38 | impossible] inpossible 1(*a*) |
| 86.10 | arms.]  ~! 2–5 |
| 86.25 | black sheep-skin] sheep-skin, covered with black wool 1 |
| 86.26 | as it afterwards appeared] as we afterwards learned 1–5(*text*) |
| 87.17 | enemy of the human] enemy of human 1–5 |
| 88.6 | we were informed] we are informed 3–5 |
| 91.42 | unreasonably people . . . as well as for the death] unreasonably I am blamed for the death 1 |
| 94.16 | in my distress] in distress 1(*b*) |
| 94.20 | wish to see me lose it] wish me to lose it 1(*b*) |
| 97.1 | THE LIFE and ATCHIEVEMENTS] THE ATCHIEVEMENTS 2–5 |
| 98.13 | I myself] Myself 5 |
| 98.38 | it in my] it my 1 |

| | |
|---|---|
| 99.14 | since] tho' 1 |
| 99.41 | a long time] along time 1 |
| 100.32 | the last] a last 3–5 |
| 101.39 | befallen Rozinante] befallen to Rozinante 1–2(*text*) |
| 101.40 | ah's] ahs 1 |
| 102.21 | Asturias] Asturies 1–4 |
| 103.17 | Asturian.] ~, 1–2; ~! 3–5 |
| 103.19 | knight-adventurer?] ~, 1 |
| 103.40 | authors] author 5 |
| 104.8 | would visit] should visit 5 |
| 104.36 | sleep] steep 2 |
| 106.37 | her; all] her; and all 1 |
| 108.7 | This exclamation] The exclamation 2–5 |
| 108.12 | search for] search 1 |
| 109.3 | delineate] delicate 5 |
| 109.5 | silence!] ~? 3–5 |
| 110.31 | pater-noster's] pater-nosters 1–5 |
| 112n.* | Don Quixote . . . bone to pick.] *om.* 1 |
| 118.4 | And truly] and truly 1 |
| 118.17 | knights!] ~: 2–5 |
| 119.13 | eyes into] eyes, as it were, into 1 |
| 121.7 | as to the righteous] as the righteous 2–5 |
| 121.8 | worship] worwip 1 |
| 123.32 | done or received an injury; and] done, or are doing, an injury to some person: and 1 |
| 123.34 | ˌreplied] (~ 1 |
| 124.19 | licentiate] licientiate 1–2 |
| 124.26 | convoying] conveying 4–5 |
| 124.40 | such manner] such a manner 2–5 |
| 126.9 | in getting from under] from getting under 2–5 |

| 126.36 | Knight] knight 1 |
| 126.39 | nothing] no 1 |
| 126.40 | your face] your own face 1 |
| 127.31 | Sancho's] Sancho' 1 |
| 128.26 | by their ignorance] by the ignorance 2–5 |
| 131.10 | connectedly] correctedly 5 |
| 131.26 | bounds and] bounds of 2–5 |
| 132.14 | tale is ended] tale is at an end 1 |
| 132.21 | Quixote.] ~, 1–2 |
| 134.9 | following] followed 2–5 |
| 135.18 | laughed at] laughed 2–3 |
| 135.30 | islands or] islands and 1 |
| 136.33 | herself, the mother of all sciences; more] herself; more 1 |
| 137.5 | do! . . . Sancho.] ~, . . . ~! 1–5 |
| 140.9 | that caitiff] Mr. Tonsor 1 |
| 140.9 | your worship] you worship 2 |
| 141.19 | 'behold . . . Serpent,'] ˄~ . . . ~,˄ 1–5 |
| 143.15 | time enough to think] time to think 1–5(*text*) |
| 143.21 | reward: wherefore . . . deserve. True] reward: true 1 |
| 143.38 | my residence] my own residence 5 |
| 144.15 | thy necessity] my necessity 2–5 |
| 144.31 | every second day] once a day 1 |
| 145.4 | thou art very much] thou art much 2–5 |
| 146.11 | equipage.] ~! 1–2; ~? 3–5 |
| 146.27 | music?] ~˄ 1; ~, 2–5 |
| 146.33 | having] hath 2–5 |
| 146.42 | to pay . . . lady] to visit my lady 1 |
| 146.43 | Gurapas] Gurapa 1–5 |
| 147.4 | to such good] to so good 3–5 |
| 147.11 | gallies . . . years, after] gallies, after 1 |

147.20          like other]    like the other 2–5

147.34          that there]    there 2–5

149.32          in the washing]    in washing 2–5

150.8           sins to answer]    sins of his own to answer 1

150.21          one of the two . . . firelocks]    the man . . . the fire-lock 1

150.44          around]    round 2–5

151.5           necks]    neck 2–5

151.25          thy name]    your name 1

151.30          shower forth a number]    shower such a number 1

153.18          had searched]    have searched 1–2 (*text*)

158.3           fall, without knowing how or wherefore." "That]    fall." "That 1

160.29          good-will . . . satisfaction." "My]    good-will." "My 1

161.6           your appearance and person]    your dress and person 1

164.22          always contrived means to]    always endeavoured to 1

164.40          are the feast]    are feast 2

167.16          whom, at least, I]    whom I 1

168.4           is this, that]    is, that 2–5

168.38          knight that ever professed]    knight that have professed 4; knight
                that has professed 5

170.21          need not throw]    need throw 2

170.43          family again.]    family. 2–5

171.42          waving]    stirring 1

172.12          love and despair]    love or despair 1

172.18          I say, be it so]    Be it so 1

172.20          thou]    you 1

172.22          You are pretty perfect in your]    What will very much embellish
                your 1

172.22          knight; but, as]    knight; as 1

173.12          worship hath]    worship has 3–5

174.26          flax and threshing]    flax or threshing 1

174.27          laugh and be]   laugh or be 1

175.13          possession of; for]   possession of it; for 3

176.21          perform so many . . . matter." "At]   perform many more than I
                wished to see." "At 1

177.13          hither in]   hither on 2–5

178.9           more for]   more fit for 3–5

178.14          Carpio]   Carpeio 2–5

178n.*.2        est Phaethon]   est Phaeton 2–5

179.1           attempting them.]   attempting. 2–5

179.9           them]   whom 2–5

180.30          disclose for the eyes that stood in his head]   disclose to ears of
                flesh and blood] 1

180.37          informed them]   informed him 1

181.41          efforts, repeated . . . absurdities. He]   efforts, and was guilty of as
                many blunders as before: he 1

182.33          beseech . . . station]   beseech him to chuse that station 1

183.29          sattin . . . seemed]   sattin, which seemed 1

184.33          they had charged]   they charged 2–5

184.37          affair of the utmost]   affair that was of the utmost 1

184.43          than an archbishop's]   than archbishop's 2–5

185.4           news of his having found]   news of having found 1

185.7           around]   round 2–5

185.36          fate!]   ~. 1–5

187.10          unreasonably]   unreasonable 2–5

187.15          wondered . . . case: for]   wondered at, if they entertain that
                opinion, for 1

187.39          circumstance]   circumstances 2–5

187n.*          There is . . . Don Quixote.]   *om.* 1

189.1           villainous]   villanious 1

189.43          absence; considering . . . her pen.]   absence; though, while I was
                present, she had been so sparing of her speech. 1

| | |
|---|---|
| 190.2 | hands; and how]    ~? and how 3; ~? how 4–5 |
| 190.24 | that your pretended . . . for himself]    that he hath asked me in marriage for your pretended friend 1 |
| 190n.* | The original . . . correspondence.]    *om.* 1 |
| 190n.*.2 | exclaim,]    ~∧ 2–4 |
| 191.3 | mule at]    mule in 1 |
| 194.31 | now the willing votary]    now the votary 1 |
| 194.34 | impossibility . . . comfort: a]    the possibility of bettering their fate. A 1 |
| 194.41 | *om.*]    END of the FIRST VOLUME. 2–5 |
| 195.3 | Valiant KNIGHT DON]    Valiant DON 2–5 |
| 195.12 | times, barren . . . amusements, enjoy]    times, enjoy 1 |
| 195.27 | peasant, whose face, as]    peasant, who, as 1 |
| 195.28 | they could not then survey. Their approach they managed]    could not perceive their approach, which was managed 1 |
| 199.1 | the herds and flocks]    the herds and the flocks 2–5 |
| 201.7 | creature),]    ~)∧ 1–5 |
| 202.17 | misfortune]    misfortue 1 |
| 202.31 | every night]    any night 2–5 |
| 203.13 | whole misfortune]    whole design 1 |
| 203.24 | hear. He directed . . . town-talk. He said]    hear: he said 1 |
| 203.40 | company. It was . . . next day. When]    company. Next day, when 1 |
| 205.9 | or quit my being in this]    or give up the ghost in this 1 |
| 205.27 | she left off speaking]    she stood silent 1 |
| 206.4 | intervals which I enjoy]    intervals, that I enjoy 1–5 *(text)* |
| 207.8 | when he (Sancho) told]    when Sancho told 1 |
| 207.15 | bad]    bade 2–5 |
| 207.17 | plan they]    plan he 1 |
| 207.21 | bad]    bade 2–5 |
| 207.23 | stile]    state 1 |
| 208.16 | that same lady]    the same lady 3–5 |

| | | |
|---|---|---|
| 208.23 | opinion,] | ~. 1 |
| 211.21 | at my ease] | unmarried 1 |
| 211.25 | whites] | white 1 |
| 213.11 | Meotis] | Meotides 1 |
| 215.26 | Zaramilla] | Xaramilla 1 |
| 215.39 | this giant] | any giant 1 |
| 216.12 | Dorothea.] | ~, 1 |
| 216.34 | bring him] | bring them 2–3 |
| 217.25 | which] | that 2–5 |
| 218.44 | follows.] | ~: 1–5 |
| 219.18 | please: I shall . . . went in: but] | please: I hope my answers will make the end answer the beginning of your content; but 1 |
| 219.19 | future.] | ~: 1–5 |
| 219.20 | revengeful? . . . knight.] | ~, . . . ~? 1–5 |
| 220.15 | invention.] | ~: 1–5 |
| 220.21 | Sancho] | Panza 2–5 |
| 220.38 | had put it into her hand, I] | had repeated it to the clerk, I 1 |
| 221.14 | of such a letter] | of the sender 1 |
| 221.32 | helping her to lay] | helping to lay 2–5 |
| 222.12 | bad] | bade 2–5 |
| 222.17 | knight of] | knight with 2–5 |
| 223.6 | death; and that] | death: then that 1 |
| 225.2 | words:] | ~! 2–5 |
| 227.36 | the no small] | the small 2–3 |
| 228.16 | mistress? . . . daughter.] | ~, . . . ~? 1–4 |
| 228.22 | maid? . . . Dorothea.] | ~, . . . ~? 1–5 |
| 228.30 | asked her] | asked me 5 |
| 228.38 | friend's housekeeper] | friends the housekeeper 1 |
| 228.41 | then? . . . innkeeper.] | ~, . . . ~? 1–5 |
| 229.27 | dive into the profound] | dive to the bottom 1 |

229.28        he descended to the bottom]   he had descended a great way 1

229n.*        It will appear . . . could not do.]   *om.* 1

230.1         ever existed]   never existed 2

230.35        to himself]   within himself 1

230.39        because . . . I expect]   because I expect 1

231.5         taken]   taken taken 1

232.14        The Two Friends]   The two friends 1–4

233.5         and the excuses]   and excuses 2–5

234.37        aras; I mean, not]   aras; but, not 1

235.23        seems to deserve]   seems to desire 1(*text*)

236n.*.1      Furioso, to which . . . absence.]   Furioso. 1

237.7         not all]   not at all 2

239.17        Reflect, therefore]   Reflect, there 2

240.16        begin when he pleased]   begin as soon as he pleased 1

241.2         lean his head]   lean the side of his head 1

242.2         calling]   called 2–5

242.10        thus]   this 2

243.2         and dine . . . desired]   and desired 1

243.12        but was . . . servants]   but always went about the house among her
              servants 1

243.21        thoughts were]   thoughts was 2–4

243.25        were such]   was such 2–4

243.28        and free]   and a free 2–5

244.1         Lothario]   Lotharia 1(*text*)

246.14        she then fancied]   she fancied 1

246.14        looked]   once looked 1

246.17        alone]   along 2–3

247.3         The dazzling rays descend amain]   The rays descend in dazzling
              rain 1

247.15        love]   lover 2

| | |
|---|---|
| 247.30 | thine image] thy image 5 |
| 248.16 | force] fortress 3–5 |
| 248.17 | afraid?] ~; 1 |
| 248.17 | This] this 1–5 |
| 248.38 | pretended to be] imagined 1 |
| 249.17 | gave her opportunities] gave opportunities 2–5 |
| 250.3 | country: (And here it was where . . . him) but . . . vengeance. However] country. And here it was . . . him. However 1; country: (and hear it was that . . . vengeance. However 4–5 |
| 250.21 | thing: do what you please; I hope] thing; and hope 1 |
| 250.24 | how foolishly he had proceeded, and] how ill-informed he was of the truth, and 1 |
| 252.27 | your opinion] my opinion 1 |
| 252.41 | ever] even 1–3 |
| 255.19 | having a second] having second 1(*text*) |
| 255.23 | as well as she] as well she 1 |
| 255.43 | favour our] favour your 1 |
| 257.9 | brother? . . . book,] ~, . . . ~? 1–5 |
| 257.18 | as large as a wine-bag] as a large wine bag 2–5 |
| 259.9 | saints! . . . innkeeper,] ~, . . . ~! 1–5 |
| 259.20 | from paying both reckonings, to] or either of them, from paying to 1 |
| 260.34 | to such a pitch] to a pitch 2–5 |
| 260.37 | intrigue with] intrigue without 2–5 |
| 260.39 | increasing] increased 2–5 |
| 262.15 | time, perceiving] time, he perceiving 2–5 |
| 262.18 | that] thet 1 |
| 262.25 | taken? . . . Anselmo.] ~, . . . ~? 1–5 |
| 262.29 | This] These 1–4 |
| 263.29 | company? . . . Cardenio.] ~, . . . ~? 1–5 |
| 264.10 | lady be? . . . priest.] ~ ~, . . . ~? 1–5 |

264.17          named? . . . curate.]    ~, . . . ~? 1–5

266.26          I shall]    shall I 2–5

267.26          you, that . . . manner, that]    you not only to check your
                indignation, but also to suppress it intirely, so, that 1

267.38          would be pleased]    would pleased 2

267n.*          But it appears . . . *homerus.]    *om.* 1

270.7           happened to him, in the city,]    happened in the city, 1

270.15          if she]    since she 1

270.36          little dreaming]    intirely ignorant 1

271.8           damage she]    damage he 5

271.11          as long as]    as long as long as 2

272.8           would arrive]    should arrive 5

273.18          may very possibly]    may possibly 2–5

273.26          Quixote, thou]    Quixote, that thou 2–5

273n.*          thy skull]    the skull 2–5

274.35          believe that she]    believe she 2–5

274.38          baptized? . . . Lucinda.]    ~, . . . ~? 1–5

275.34          earth, if he]    earth, if they 3–5

276.26          on earth or in heaven]    in heaven or on earth 1

276.34          first of all]    chiefly 1

276.36          his indigence]    this indigence 1

277.5           attain . . . degree]    attain to the height of their wishes 1

277.9           into gay apparel]    into apparel 5

277.21          all other . . . apparel. In a winter . . . breath, which,]    all the other
                parts of apparel; tho', in the winter, he has nothing else to skreen
                him from the inclemencies of the weather; nay, in the open field,
                he is fain to warm himself with his own breath, which, 1

278.10          undecided, . . . reasons]    undecided. Such are the reasons 1

278.11          one . . . favour]    the principal of which in favour 1

278.33          and of falling thence]    and then falling 1

279.2           soldier]    soldiers 2–5

| | |
|---|---|
| 279.7 | he] be 1 |
| 280.35 | heaven shall] heaven will 2–5 |
| 280.35 | But, after you have received] But, before you receive 1 |
| 281.8 | and, although] so that, although 1 |
| 281.32 | they charging . . . seize] after we had undertaken to seize 1 |
| 281.33 | this promise] the promise 1 |
| 283.2 | among them] among us 1 |
| 283.17 | beat him] bit him 2–5 |
| 284.3 | seven] six 1 |
| 285.29 | Death . . . claim] Death sanction'd your victorious claim 1 |
| 287.9 | plans] pains 2–5 |
| 288.5 | openings] opening 2 |
| 289.5 | hand . . . signs] hand appeared again, making signs 1 |
| 289.11 | impart] import 3–4 |
| 290.8 | thou . . . Arabic] thou can'st not write Arabic 1 |
| 291.27 | bad] bid 3–5 |
| 292.4 | Ala] Ali 1 |
| 292.37 | our lives] our own lives 4–5 |
| 295.29 | obligations] obligation 2–5 |
| 296.30 | Juma] Jama 1–5 (text) |
| 297.24 | bark . . . opposite] bark right opposite 1 |
| 298.10 | asked . . . voice, if] asked if 1 |
| 298.11 | christians.] ~? 1–5 |
| 299.6 | remained . . . Moors] remained prisoners among us, desired the renegado would be so good as to dismiss the Moors 1 |
| 299.9 | who loved her so much] whom she loved so much 1 |
| 299.24 | the galleys] those galleys 1 |
| 299.40 | course. All . . . sailed] course: and this method proved so expeditious, that we sailed 1 |
| 299.43 | that they . . . should] as they were not slaves, they should 1 |

300.18      this particular]    that particular 1

300.20      us.]    ~? 1–5

300.22      he knew he had left]    he thought had been left 1

300.39      have]    have have 1

301.4       small cape]    small creek 2–5

301.28      ours.]    ~? 1–5

301.40      beard . . . nay]    and tearing the hair of his head, which he
            scattered in handfuls upon the shore; nay 1

302.6       no other reply]    no reply 1; no better reply 5

302.8       Ala knows]    she knows 2–5

302.23      large round vessel]    large vessel 1

303.25      without]    mithout 1

304.5       country]    land 1

306.14      should have continued]    should continue 1

306.16      Cardenio]    Don Antonio 1

306.38      as they entered]    alight 1

307.14      her: the beauteous . . . damsel; while]    her; while 1

307.25      bed . . . along with him, they]    bed, and that brought by the
            stranger, they 1

307.35      West Indies]    East-Indies 1

307.44      virtue and prudence that appear]    virtue that appears 1

307.44      give]    gives 1(*errata*)

307.45      declare]    declares 1(*errata*)

308.4       sat]    set 1(*errata*)

308.23      he was]    we were 1

308n.*      This . . . night. Vide p. 145.]    *om.* 1

309.26      anguish . . . company; so]    anguish; so 1

312.34      desires]    distress 1

315.25      from my inclination]    from inclination 1

316.6       firmly]    formerly 1

316.25     Retire,]   ∼∧ 1–5

316.36     and the crown]   and crown 2–5

317.2      landlord . . . waking]   landlord waking 1

317.34     fifteen]   sixteen 1

318.16     he was engaged already]   he was engaged was already 3–5

319.20     they should]   they would 3–5

320.21     Quixote,]   ∼∧ 1–4

320.35     vengeance or]   vengeance and 3–5

321.33     taken, the furniture]   taken, by force, the furniture 1

321.43     help in]   help me in 5

322.11     greatest]   greater 4

322.16     squire]   shaver 1

323.6      helmet.]   ∼? 1–5

323.22     seconded this]   seconded his 3–5

323.34     gentlemen, myself, and even]   gentlemen, and even 1

324.16     three]   four 1

326.34     quiet]   quite 1

328.9      squalled]   sqalled 1

329.10     Quixote's]   Quixot's 1

329.18     with∧]   ∼, 1

329.37     Quixote . . . well as for]   Quixote, for 1

332.6      nonsense]   nonesense 1

332.32     except the squire himself]   except the master and the squire himself 1

335.20     Sancho . . . linnen.]   *om.* 1

336.15     for, if I regain my liberty]   for, if I were at liberty 1

337.3      cage, his hands . . . outstretched, leaning]   cage, leaning 1

337.23     robber]   rober 1

339.25     seems to fall . . . Milesian]   seems inferior to the Milesian 1

339.37     which the hero . . . espouses]   which our author espouses 1

340.43        cunning of Ulysses]   cunning Ulysses 2–3

341.5         upon the truth]   upon truth 4–5

342.26        Female]   female 1

343.5         ascribed to the emperor Heraclius, who being the principal
              personage, is represented, like Godfrey]   in which the latter had
              the principal share, ascribed to the emperor Heraclius, who, like
              Godfrey 1

343.6         carrying . . . making]   carried . . . made 1

343.12        and say that]   and that 1–5 (*text*)

343.42        say, and it]   say, it 1

344.28        delightful]   delighful 1

345.42        heart . . . those who]   heart, as one may, and doth expect from
              those who 1

349.24        make a man]   make me 1

349.33        Lancelot]   Lançarot 1

349.42        near]   hard by 1

350.6         fought in]   fought against 1

351.34        pebbles]   peebles 1–2

352.11        and silently leading]   and leading 1

352.18        amber and odoriferous]   odoriferous 1

355.36        qualifications]   qalifications 1

357.8         mother had she none]   mother she had none 3–5

358.21        a rebec]   the rebec 3–5

359.14        according to]   according 1

359.36        had not that instant]   had not at that instant 2–5

360.2         goatherd]   barber 1

360.27        frequently]   ever 1

361.43        disciplinants . . . and wielding]   disciplinants wielding 1

362.8         which he and the]   which he was joined by the 1

362.8         went]   who went 1

363.5         their return]   his return 3–5

| | |
|---|---|
| 363.41 | trouble they]   trouble he 1–5 |
| 364.36 | Who Amadis left far behind]   He who to Amadis turned tail 1 |
| 364.38 | Whose valour with such lustre shin'd]   Whose gallantry did so prevail 1 |
| 365.33 | Argamasillan]   Argamasillecian 1 |
| 365n.* | The horse . . . poem.]   *om.* 1 |
| 366.17 | Tiquiloc]   Tiquitoc 2–5 |
| 366.30 | Forse . . . plettro]   Fosse . . . plectro 1 |
| 366.31 | FIRST]   FISRT 1; END of the SECOND VOLUME. 2–5 |
| 369–75 | PREFACE . . . VALDIVIELSO.]   *om.* 2 |
| 369.22 | heaven]   haven 4–5; *om.* 2 |
| 374.11 | treasury?]   ~. 1, 3–5; *om.* 2 |
| 377.1 | THE LIFE and ATCHIEVEMENTS]   THE ATCHIEVEMENTS 2–5 |
| 377.3 | Sage Knight DON]   SAGE and VALIANT DON 2–5 |
| 379.27 | graduate, having been]   graduate, after having been 1 |
| 380.15 | the Lord]   our Lord 1 |
| 380.23 | was obliged]   was fain 1 |
| 380.29 | present. The licentiate]   present, and the licentiate 1 |
| 381.31 | do I set]   do set 1 |
| 383.24 | Don Orlando]   Don Roldan 1 |
| 384.33 | Better than four cities, or the places]   Better than the places 1 |
| 385.28 | said his master]   said the master 2–5 |
| 385.30 | servant art]   servant are 1–5(*text*) |
| 385.32 | So it ought to be]   That may be 1 |
| 386.3 | faithful servants]   servants 1 |
| 386.10 | won't]   wont 1 |
| 386.37 | any thing more?]   ~ ~ ~! 2–5 |
| 387.14 | morsel with any satisfaction, until]   morsel, until 1 |
| 387.23 | hardly]   scarce 1 |

388.2          thus keeping the impulse]   while he kept the impulse 1

388.27         careful in] (*errata*)   careful of 1

389.8          author]   authors 1

389.14         exhibited]   represented 1

390.20         Curiosity.]   ~? 1

391.9          wittiest]   wisest 1

391.22         theologicians]   theologists 2–5

391n.†         Alphonsos Tostatus . . . *discutit omne.*]   *om.* 1

392.7          qualmishness]   faintishness 1

392.20         of batchelor]   of the batchelor 1

392.32         this no]   this is no 2–5

393.16         those hundred]   these hundred 1

393.27         great many]   many 1

393n.*         As related . . . is the continuation.]   *om.* 1

394.28         a hungry]   an hungry 3–4

394.30         seasons]   reasons 4–5

394.31         close]   charge 1–5(*text*)

396.27         lovely]   lively 2–5

397.5          two or three]   two three 1–2

397.27         ill buckled . . . concubine.]   ill married than well debauched. 1

397.30         high, that]   high, as that 1

398.6          sons-in-law, and grandsons, and]   sons and daughters‸ in-law, and 1

398.7          match her]   match me her 1–5

398.12         observe,]   ~. 1

398.20         then thou wilt]   then wilt thou 3–5

399.17         an halt]   a halt 5

399.18         back-bitters]   back-biters 2–5

400.3          money for him by]   money by 1

401.6          courtiers]   courteous 1(*text*)

401.34         them, deserves]   them‸ deserve 1–5 (*text*)

401.34        Sanbenito]    San benito 1–5

402.21        attentive to]    attentive in 1(*text*)

402.25        point, diminishing]    point, like a pyramid, diminishing 1

402.30        exemplified]    examplified 2–4

402.38        your Median]    our Median 2–5

404.18        adventures]    ventures 1

404.23        into the very lowest]    into the lowest 1

404n.*        The original . . . adventures.]    *om.* 1

405.6         you please]    you shall please 1

405.22        bird in hand]    bird in the hand 2–5

405.22        worth two]    with to 1(*text*)

405.38        that island]    the island 1

406.19        these terms]    those terms 2–5

407.28        attended knights-errant]    attended the knights-errant 2–5

407.39        find a compleat helmet]    find some helmet 1

409.3         the night . . . advanced]    the night is dark, and so far advanced 1

409.4         day-light]    to-morrow morning 1

409.15        corridores]    piazzas 1

409.26        knight]    errant 3–4

410.43        Horatius]    Horatio 1

411.5         Cortez?]    ~. 1

411.10        etherial]    eternal 1

411.34        obelisk]    needle 1

412.15        beatified]    beautified 5

412.19        an humble]    a humble 1

412.39        grove]    thicket 1

413.3         thereabouts]    thereabout 3–5

413.11        by the enamoured]    by enamoured    2

413.37        to let me search]    to search 1

413.40        confusion.]    ~? 2–4; ~! 5

414.8            discretion?]    ~. 1–2

414.31           stranger]    country lad 1

416.39           Toboso. Well, and]    Toboso. And 1

416.43           But have you . . . same princess?]    But, have you . . . same palace
                 or stately castle? 1

416.43           eyes on her]    eyes on it 1

417.5            honourable,]    ~. 1

417.7            come but scurvily]    come scurvily 1

417.17           fed]    led 1

417.40           bitterly,ₐ]    ~,, 1

420.38           run]    race 1

420.42           makes]    make 2; made 3–5

421.6            at sight]    at the sight 2–5

421.22           by which we might]    by which they might 3–4

422.14           gaiety]    good humour 1

423.21           capapee]    cap-a-pie 2–5

424.19           rattle]    pole 1

425.21           you ought also to remember]    you ought to remember 5

426.21           characters were introduced]    characters introduced 1

426.33           but, when]    and, when 4

427.7            lying]    laying 4

427.19           accordingly practised]    accordingly performed 3–4

427.23           composition, omitted them; though sometimes he
                 seems]    composition, they are here omitted, tho' sometimes the
                 translator seems 1

427.30           Nisus and]    Nisus or 3–4

429.30           sat down together]    sat together 1

429.35           disdain . . . revenge." "I]    disdain." "I 1

430.33           squire]    squires 1

430.35           archbishopric; but . . . emperor: and I]    archbishopric; and I 1

431.4            are not at all desirable]    are not all so desirable 1

| 431.5 | others]    and others 1 |
|---|---|
| 431.9 | pastimes]    pastime 1–5 |
| 431.12 | none]    neither 1 |
| 431.19 | those knights-errant]    these knights-errant 2–5 |
| 431.33 | squire!]    ~? 1–4 |
| 431.35 | done it!]    ~ ~? 1–5 |
| 432.16 | it. Other]    it: other 1 |
| 432.17 | full. Madness]    full; madness 1 |
| 432.18 | true, as it is]    true, it is 1(*text*) |
| 432.31 | observed]    perceived and observed 1 |
| 432.34 | them, at]    them, hanging at 1 |
| 432.38 | How?]    ~! 2–5 |
| 433.31 | mystery.]    ~: 1; ~? 2–5 |
| 433.31 | But]    but 1 |
| 434.8 | mouth. In]    mouth; and in 1 |
| 435.30 | Casilda]    Casildea 2–5 |
| 436.15 | unparalleled]    unequal 1 |
| 437.6 | Sancho.]    ~, 1, 4–5 |
| 437.34 | as almost to overshadow]    as to overshadow 1 |
| 438.10 | not the grace of your countenance]    not your countenance 1 |
| 438.14 | visage: my reason]    visage; and my reason 1 |
| 439.4 | answered Panza]    answered the squire 1 |
| 439.29 | ran down to]    ran to 1 |
| 441.1 | So saying]    And so saying 1 |
| 441.25 | for the tracts]    for, the tract 1; for the tracks 3–5 |
| 442.34 | and difficulty]    or difficulty 1 |
| 443.32 | to find]    to meet 1 |
| 444.5 | and invincible]    and most invincible 1 |
| 444.13 | resound]    resounded 4 |
| 444.15 | delivering]    liberating 1 |

444.18     Signor, you will hardly believe]   You will hardly, Sir, believe 1

444.20     Cecial.]   ~? 1

444.29     cap-a-pee]   cap-a-pie 2–5

444.32     arms?]   ~. 1–2

444.34     worship]   honour 1

444.36     enchanters who]   enchanters that 2–5

444.38     their vanquished]   the vanquished 2–5

445.24     are going]   are a going 3–4

447.24     make]   have 1

447.25     that I may defend]   I defend 1

447.26     against those]   against these 2–5

447.32     persuaded . . . supposition]   persuaded of this supposition 1(*text*)

448.1      the gifts]   those gifts 1

448.21     Signor]   Sir 1

448.28     especially as]   especially when 1

449.3      these qualifications]   those qualifications 2–5

449.19     One so born]   And one so born 1

449.20     attains . . . rules only]   attains only to the knowledge of the rules
           alone 1

449.23     signor]   sir 1

450.14     called upon]   called out upon 1

450.16     summoned]   called off 1

451.6      was that sat]   was sat 1

451.28     Whither]   Whether 1, 4–5

451.41     me?]   ~! 1–5

452.6      signor]   sir 1

452.10     then going]   and going 1

452.11     pressing]   praying 1

452.11     Signor]   Sir 1

452.17     signor]   sir 1

| | |
|---|---|
| 452.17 | and look after your ferrets] and go mind your ferrets 1 |
| 452.23 | seeing] who saw 1 |
| 452.29 | unharnessed] unyoked 1 |
| 452.38 | Signor] Sir 1 |
| 453.17 | as far as] as fast as 3–5 |
| 454.20 | worship's] honour's 1 |
| 454.32 | cloth] clout 1 |
| 454.40 | Harness your mules again] Put your mules to again 1 |
| 455.11 | harnessed] yoked 1 |
| 455.14 | tell him, it was the knight] tell him, the knight 1 |
| 455.15 | forward] ever after 1 |
| 456.8 | and direct] direct 1 |
| 456.10 | But for the] But the 1 |
| 456.31 | village] villa 1 |
| 457.1 | THE LIFE and ATCHIEVEMENTS] THE ATCHIEVEMENTS 2–5 |
| 457.3 | Valiant KNIGHT DON] VALIANT DON 2–5 |
| 457.13 | reflecting on what] reflecting what 1–5(*text*) |
| 457.20 | hands] hand 4 |
| 458.4 | breeches, and a . . . stained] breeches, a . . . blotted 1 |
| 458.8 | and over all] over all 1 |
| 458.11 | off exhibiting a whey] off a whey 1 |
| 458.12 | appetite] appetites 1 |
| 458.13 | scoured] rubbed 1 |
| 458.30 | who, among other discourse, said] and, among other discourse, he said 1 |
| 458.40 | make] makes 1, 4(*text*) |
| 459.2 | name of the first] name of first 1 |
| 459.7 | humble] humbly 2 |
| 459.14 | so to do] to do 4 |

459.17     astronomer]   astrologer 1

460.19     to the original proposition; besides]   to the intention and proposition of him who proposed it; besides 1

461.23     those]   these 1(*text*)

461.26     hollow]   cry 1

462.34     but to leave]   but leave 1

464.13     dancers]   dances 1

465.22     undoubted]   Undoubtedly 5

465.34     bestir]   better 1(*text*)

465.43     out!]   ~? 1–5

465.43     wheels, or any other thing whatsover?" "O]   wheels?" "O 1

466.30     back; nor have I met with any man whom]   back; and there is scarce any one who 1

467.6     button]   buttons 1

467.21     ever. The]   ever: and the 1

467.22     resolved]   they all resolved 1

467.32     bells. As]   bells; and, as 1

468.7     golden]   dropping 1

468.20     advance him in life]   advance in life 2

469.3     make up]   makes up 1

469.35     wall; two cauldrons of oil, larger than a dyer's vat, were]   wall; two pans, as wide as cauldrons, and larger than a dyer's vat, full of oil, were 1

471.11     pipe. Cupid]   pipe; and Cupid 1

472.17     Roman cat-skin]   calf-skin 1

472.29     parson]   curate 1

472.43     she stuck always]   she always stuck 2–5

473.3     geese, hens, hares]   geese, hares 2–5

473.14     life: moreover, according]   life; especially as, according 1

473.37     wise!]   ~? 1–5

474.28     in adorning themselves]   in striving to compose themselves 1

474.30        ornamented]    adorned 1

474.31        they were to see]    they could see 1

474.34        people]    couple 1

475.1         interspersed]    interpersed 1

475.32        recovering a little]    recollecting himself a little 1

476.20        kind . . . kindness]    pious . . . piety 1

478.15        consent. This]    consent; and this 1

478.18        produced. Don]    produced, and Don 1

478.20        jars]    cauldrons 1

478.24        same: and, as in the last]    same; and as in the first 1

478.42        an help-mate]    a help-mate 5

479.1         played upon him]    played him 2–5

479.19        Great]    GRFAT 1

479.21        his discretion . . . his valour]    his valour . . . his discretion 1

479.27        his friends]    her friends 1

480.35        remark]    might remark 1(*text*)

481.25        which I propose to call]    called 1

481.30        not forgetting those of the Piojo]    not forgetting the Piojo 1

481.36        defluxion or]    defluxion of 1

481.42        an helping hand]    a helping hand 5

482.10        ejected]    rejected 3–5

482.26        rope. Next]    rope; and next 1

482.38        an hundred]    a hundred 5

483.22        night]    might 1(*text*)

483.27        knights-errant . . . brass! I say]    knights-errant: I say 1

483.32        little. By]    little; and by 1

483.44        word. When]    word; and when 1

484.17        hungry: they]    hungry; and they 1

484.34        which open]    that open 1

484.36        certain or]    certain and 3–5

485.30        than]    when 1; then 5 *(text)*

486.34        and your squire]    your squire 1

487.5         channel,]    ~ , 1–5

487.15        whom]    which 1

487.25        in the rear of these came]    at the head of these came 1

487.31        an heart]    a heart 5

488.27        "My master . . . "for, as all]    "If the truth must be told, master,"
              said Sancho, "as all 1

488.38        thrust]    trust 2–5

488.43        who, even . . . supposition, has]    and, even . . . supposition, he has 1

489.12        and those two]    and the other two 1

489.16        many ladies]    many other ladies 1

490.1         her eyes]    his eyes 4–5

490.5         her new]    here new 1

490.19        nor will enjoy health]    nor ought to enjoy health 1

490.28        more punctually than]    as punctually as 1

490.34        respect for]    respect to 4

490.34        those vanities]    these vanities 1

491.9         He who]    He that 4

491.10        coming]    turning 1

491.27        those adventures]    these adventures 5

491.28        the history]    his history 2–5

492.24        defect]    defects 5

492.35        Egypt]    Lybia 1

492.42        walking fast, and switching]    leading and switching 1

493.10        set off]    set on 1

493.12        inn, which they reached]    hermitage, which having reached 1

493.13        twilight. The student however proposed]    twilight, the student
              proposed 1

493.14        draught at the hermitage: Sancho]    draught. Sancho 1

493.15        it]    the hermitage 1

493.40        credit]    service 1

493.43        them . . . baggage-waggon]    them, and find some baggage-
              waggon 1

494.9         give]    gave 1

494.14        before he professes]    rather than profess 1

494.16        brought them]    brought him 4

494.23        than]    them 1(*text*)

495.15        scarce entered]    scarcely entered 4–5

495.32        an helping hand]    a helping hand 5

496.39        would]    could 1

497.8         twice]    twice twice 1

497.42        Peter is here]    Peter here 1–5

498.17        shoulders]    shoulder 5

498.28        tail: his buttocks]    tail, though his buttocks 1

498.31        Peter, who answered]    Peter, who having received the money,
              answered 1

498.36        he knows]    you know 1

498.40        eagerness: having]    eagerness; and having 1

499.36        Heark]    Hark 2–5

500.12        knew]    know 4–5

500.13        puppies . . . what]    puppies, and of what 1

500.16        Saturday]    Sunday 1

500.28        realities; for‸ . . . mixture of both.]    realities, for, to him the whole
              seemed real. 1

501.5         and to shew]    and shew 1

502.13        Aljaferia. That lady]    Aljaferia, and that 1

502.18        Melisendra? Now]    Melisendra: now 1

502.27        courts]    court 4

502.33        the thread]    your thread 3–4

502.36        own lady]    only lady 4

504.18          had before me]    had here before me 1

504.22          those dogs]    these dogs 4

504.31          from this here Sir]    from the inconsiderate fury of this here Sir 1

504.38          catholic and scrupulous christian]    catholic and charitable
                christian 1

504.41          make some atonement]    make atonement 1

506.26          this king]    the king 2–5

506.32          "Split]    ˏThey split 1

506.37          I demand two rials]    I demand, without the least abatement, two
                rials 1

506.40          coney]    hare 1

507.19          dozen rials]    half a dozen rials 1

508.32          he pretended no knowledge]    he practised no stratagem and
                address 1

509.19          his mouth]    and his mouth 1

510.37          and Fourthly]    And fourthly 1–4

511.1           principal causes]    five causes 1

511.16          his audience]    the audience 2–5

512.1           shoulders]    shoulder 2–5

513.12          nape of his neck]    top of his head 1

513.31          lag]    fag 2–5

513.34          laddle]    saddle 1

514.1           God . . . oppose]    God will not suffer me to oppose 1

514.17          public roads]    by-places 1

514.23          that]    then 1–5

514.43          chivalry]    history 1

516.14          river-side]    bank 1

516.14          bank. Don]    bank; and Don 1

517.27          wide and extended]    wide extended 1

518.8           it! . . . squire,]    ~, . . . ~! 1–3; ~, . . . ~; 4–5

518.16          solstices,]    ~; 1

| | |
|---|---|
| 519.2 | going?]    ~; 4–5 |
| 519.32 | strip]    stripe 4 |
| 519.36 | that castle]    the castle 4–5 |
| 520.34 | hawkers]    falconers 5 |
| 521.29 | knight-errant]    knight 1 |
| 524.34 | perceived,]    ~ₐ 1 |
| 527.23 | respect?]    ~! 1–4 |
| 527.32 | post?]    ~! 1–5 |
| 528.21 | apprehension]    apprehensions 4–5 |
| 528.28 | is true, for my master]    is so true, that my master 1 |
| 528.38 | story is this:]    story is: 4–5 |
| 528.41 | Mencia]    Meneia 1 |
| 529.14 | half as far]    half so far 4–5 |
| 529.16 | they say]    they said 3–5 |
| 529.19 | all!]    ~? 1–5 |
| 529.20 | table–methinks]    table. Methinks 1–5 |
| 529.34 | not be quite abashed]    not grow quite outrageous 1 |
| 530.1 | faith!]    ~; 4; ~, 5 |
| 530.2 | How!]    ~? 4–5 |
| 530.4 | she is as]    she was as 4–5 |
| 530.20 | adventures?]    ~. 1–3 |
| 530.22 | owed to the duke]    owed the duke 3–5 |
| 530.23 | with an ireful]    with ireful 3–4 |
| 534.9 | dinner]    supper 1 |
| 535.14 | dinner]    supper 1 |
| 535.21 | request,]    ~. 1 |
| 535.35 | sketch]    scratch 1(*text*) |
| 537.27 | Anteus]    Anteon 1 |
| 539.27 | trays, wooden]    trays and wooden 1 |
| 541.1 | THE LIFE and ATCHIEVEMENTS]    THE ATCHIEVEMENTS 2–5 |

541.13        as a governor]    as governor 2–5

541.19        produced by]    produced from 1

542.23        eaten of his]    eaten his 1

542.29        mayhap]    perhaps 3–4

545.12        kissed hands]    kissed his hands 2–5

545.24        place above]    place him above 3–4

546.13        the servants]    their servants 1

546.16        an hunting]    a hunting 2–5

547.7         ground. Perceiving himself thus suspended, that]    ground; then perceiving that 1

547.29        will deprive]    will certainly deprive 1

548.8         idle folks than for governors]    idle folks, who have nothing else to do, than for governors 1

548.18        babbler!]    ~; 2; ~, 3–5

548.19        that day]    the day 1

548.29        day was soon]    day soon 1

548.40        fifes]    fires 3–4

548n.*        an hundred]    a hundred 5

549.6         troops]    martial people 1

549.10        Toboso inchanted, accompanied]    Toboso, accompanied 1

549.10        Frenchman]    Francis 1

549.15        did not see him: for]    did not think of that: for 1

549.32        what had happened]    what happened 1

550.4         but above]    and above 1

550.14        waggon]    waggons 1

550.17        not encounter]    not again encounter 1

550.20        proceeded]    poceeded 1

550.26        inchanter]    inchanted 4

551.7         also in white]    in black 1

551.10        surprize. Seated]    surprise. And, seated 1

| | |
|---|---|
| 551.13 | with a delicate]   with delicate 2 |
| 551.13 | plaits]   rumples 1 |
| 551.24 | repeat]   rehearse 1 |
| 551.34 | inchanting]   inchanted 4–5 |
| 552.2 | caves]   cave 3–4 |
| 553.19 | pebbles]   peebles 1 |
| 553.30 | cheeks.]   ~, 3; ~! 4–5 |
| 553.30 | relent,]   ~? 5 |
| 553.38 | liberty the beauty]   liberty the sleekness of my skin, the gentleness of my condition, and the beauty 1 |
| 554.7 | more or less]   more nor less 4–5 |
| 555.37 | muskets was]   muskets were 4–5 |
| 555n.*.1 | of its meanings]   of his meanings 4–5 |
| 556.4 | murmuring]   brawling 1 |
| 556.6 | splendid]   splended 1 |
| 556.33 | and there]   for there 4 |
| 556.35 | an hair]   a hair 5 |
| 558.34 | standing; but]   ~! But 1 |
| 559.18 | drummers]   drums 1–5 |
| 559.19 | notes₄]   note, 2–5 |
| 560.4 | Sancho]   And Sancho 1 |
| 560.10 | three-tailed₄countess]   three₄tailed-countess 1 |
| 561.20 | om.]   THE ATCHIEVEMENTS Of the Sage and Valiant DON QUIXOTE de la Mancha. PART II. BOOK III. 2–5 |
| 561.22 | duennas]   damsels 1 |
| 561.31 | countess Trifaldi]   countess of Trifaldi 2–5 |
| 562.5 | white]   black 1 |
| 562.27 | placid]   placed 4 |
| 562n.*.3 | Varlets]   Varlet 1–5 |
| 563.13 | ever]   every 1 |

| 563.17 | may instantly favour] | may favour 1 |
|---|---|---|

563.17     may instantly favour]    may favour 1

563.44     enamoured. Among]    enamoured; and, among 1

564.34     fashion . . . Candaya]    fashion at Candaya 1

564.40     them. If]    them: and if 1

565.1      abound. When]    abound. And when 1

565.2      Ariadne]    Arcadia 1

565.3      balsams]    balsam 1

565.34     stupendous]    stupend'ous 1

566.7      swooned rather than died]    swooned before she died 1

566.9      servant of]    servant in 2–5

566.33     stupendous]    stupend'ous 1

566.34     metamorphosis]    metamorphoses 2–5

566.34     affected]    effected 1, 4–5

567.2      hands to]    hands on 2–5

567.35     Afflicted faint]    afflicted faint 2–3; afflicted duenna faint 4–5

567.37     master recount]    master ever recount 1

569.9      on the crupper]    upon the crupper 2–5

569.10     his squire]    the squire 2–5

569.15     Reynaldo]    Reynaldos 1

565.15     Montalvan]    Montalban 2–5

570.33     but for a time]    put for a time 5

574.15     covered . . . turned]    covered, Don Quixote adjusted himself in his seat, and turned 1

574.31     bestrid]    bestrode 2–5

574n.*.2   Real]    real 1–3

575.17     that he could]    that he thought he could 1

575.30     flax: his belly]    flax, and his belly 1

577.4      having been a goatherd]    have been a goatherd 3–5

577.7      what does I]    what does me I 1–5

577.16     did I see]    did see 3–5

| 577.29 | those females]   these females 5 |
| 577.37 | Heark]   Hark 2–5 |
| 577n.†.2 | an he goat]   a he-goat 5 |
| 578.30 | obeyed]   obliged 1(*text*) |
| 579.6 | stored]   provided 1 |
| 579.29 | moonshine]   mooonshine 1 |
| 579.31 | beneficially]   beneficently 1 |
| 579.34 | tempestuous]   tempest'ous 1 |
| 581.2 | your attention]   the attention 2–4; thy attention 5 |
| 581.22 | an happy]   a happy 5 |
| 582.40 | take care that it]   take care it 1 |
| 582.43 | than well chosen apothegms.]   than a connected chain of conversation. 1 |
| 583.5 | throw out those that]   throw out those only that 1 |
| 583.15 | do not lean . . . saddle]   do not throw your body over the saddle 1 |
| 584.4 | precepts]   precept 3–5 |
| 584.8 | told]   tell 2–5 |
| 584.18 | threescore thousand]   threescore 1 |
| 584.34 | grinders . . . what]   grinders: When I find one skulking in my house, and cry what 1 |
| 584.36 | fit to a hair]   fit to hair 1–2 |
| 585.16 | than my whole body]   than for my whole body 1 |
| 585.18 | equal all]   all equal 1 |
| 585.31 | and a strange]   and of a strange 1 |
| 586.15 | truth presents]   truth represents 2–5 |
| 586.17 | treat]   treat of 1, 5 |
| 586.30 | related. Thus . . . consequence]   related, and in consequence 1 |
| 586.32 | sooner]   sooned 1 |
| 586.33 | turning]   returning 4–5 |
| 587.10 | Dapple]   dapple 1–4 |

587.31          made; for the rest]    made; and, for the rest 1

588.23          art: as]    art; and as 1

588.31          imagination]    imaginations 1

589.7           starch.]    ~∧ 1–4

589.10          eaten]    eat 2–5

589.24          heard]    could hear 1

590.1           an hot . . . an heavy. . . . an harp]    a hot . . . a heavy. . . . a harp 5

590.10          he was there]    he was awake 1

590.15          sheets art]    sheets are 2–5

590.17          care and]    care or 1

590.20          an hundred]    a hundred 5

590.22          an hapless]    a hapless 5

592.12          well bred]    nobly born 1

592.21          Timbrius]    Thymbrius 2–5

593.16          day . . . signor]    day, of such a month, in such a year, signor 1

594.22          loan . . . repayment]    loan or repayment 1

594.31          cross of the rod, he]    cross, he 1

595.21          or as a sage]    or a sage 3–5

595.31          said Sancho]    says Sancho 5

595.32          woman? To this]    woman? And, to this 1

595.34          deals]    deal 1–5

596.34          as sheepishly]    as well 1

597.11          and, being . . . lazy, dressed]    and starting from the arms of sloth, dressed 1

597.39          Quixote. On]    Quixote; and, on 1

598.6           perceived]    perceiving 5

598.8           an hoarse]    a hoarse 5

599.1           an hundred]    a hundred 5

599.10          starting up]    starting from his bed 1

599.21          Seeing the unequal]    The duke seeing the unequal 1

| 599.42 | bed; where he was]   bed; but, afterwards, he was 1 |
| 601.4 | sumptuous]   sumpt'ous 1 |
| 601.15 | wand . . . twinkling]   wand, it vanished in a twinkling 1 |
| 601.19 | hand?]   ~! 2–5 |
| 602.16 | an hundred]   a hundred 5 |
| 602.20 | where]   were 1 |
| 602.24 | Heark]   Heak 1 |
| 603.3 | ran]   run 1 |
| 603.5 | he. One]   he. And one 1 |
| 603.11 | recited]   read 1 |
| 603.25 | Positive . . . dungeon]   Rezio . . . dugeon 1 |
| 603.30 | luncheon]   luncehon 1 |
| 603.32 | battles with]   battles by 1 |
| 603.43 | presume]   pesume 1 |
| 604.13 | Positive]   Rezio 1 |
| 604.14 | might not I eat]   might I not eat 5 |
| 604.34 | and had been]   and been 1 |
| 605.15 | tawny. My]   tawny. And my 1 |
| 605.41 | take or not take]   Stick or not stick 1 |
| 606.2 | countryman. Scarce]   countryman. And scarce 1 |
| 606.10 | Paralinos]   Paralino's 1–4 |
| 607.15 | eagerness and]   eagerness of 1 |
| 607.17 | in these devout precautions, if]   in his occupation; and, if 1 |
| 607.26 | this disposition]   that disposition 1 |
| 607.30 | Quixote . . . phantome]   Quixote, if your worship really is Don Quixote, I am no phantom 1 |
| 607.33 | worship is]   worship are 1 |
| 608.2 | all disasters]   all the disasters 1 |
| 608.11 | an high]   a high 5 |
| 608.36 | tender hearted]   pious 1 |

610.7        generous]   pious 1

610.22       of the house]   in the house 1

611.14       In a word, as]   At length, as 1

611.18       sky lark]   public crier 1

611.27       to wife]   to his wife 1

611.28       a hearing]   the hearing 1

611.31       give him . . . disgust]   give himself the least concern or uneasiness 1

611.41       same creature Altisidora]   same Altisidora 1

612.2        by the life of my soul]   as you hope to be saved 1

612.16       flew]   burst 1

612.21       petticoats]   petticoat 1

612.23       taking. Although]   taking; and, although 1

613.7        Positive]   Rezio 1

613.11       seasons . . . affairs; and]   seasons, and that their affairs should be
             solely attended to, come what will: and 1

613.16       meals and]   meals or 1

613.22       was struck]   were struck 1–5

613.38       staler]   powerfuller 1

613n.*       *Podrida* signifies . . . stiled *Pot-pourri.*]   *om.* 1

614.2        other]   another 1

614.12       to do]   to doubt 1

614.15       act any otherwise]   act otherwise 2–5

614.26       worship]   lordship 1

614.31       round. Accordingly]   round; and, accordingly 1

614.35       see. Having]   see; and having 1

614.42       at play in]   at play at 3–5

615.2        bett was,]   ~ ~, 1

615.7        him out . . . most]   him close, and in the most 1

615.23       excellency]   excellence 4–5

615.25       swash-buckler]   slash-buckler 2–5

| | |
|---|---|
| 616.14 | gaol] goal 1–5 |
| 616.16 | gaol] goal 1–5 |
| 616.17 | gaol] goal 1–5 |
| 616.21 | gaoler] goaler 1–5 |
| 616.27 | jail] goal 2–5 |
| 616.36 | dreamed] dreamt 2–5 |
| 617.1 | sixteen] seventeen 1 |
| 617.30 | what I say] what to say 3–5 |
| 617.39 | sewer] steward 1 |
| 617.41 | and in such an equipage] and such an equipage 3–4 |
| 617.42 | other] steward 1 |
| 619.2 | had locked] has locked 1–5 |
| 619.7 | who] whom 1–5 |
| 619.20 | your own words] your words 1 |
| 619.41 | me; that . . . we shall] me; for, as they do not know who we are, we shall 1 |
| 620.8 | flight.ᴧ] ~.. 1 |
| 620.36 | should] would 1 |
| 620.37 | duke's] duke 1 |
| 620.38 | daughter Sanchica] daughter 1 |
| 620.39 | granted that no man] granted no man 3–5 |
| 620.41 | Thus] This 1 |
| 621.23 | pride] reputation 1 |
| 621.28 | disinchantment] inchantment 1 |
| 621.31 | rosary] string 1 |
| 622.32 | the string] a string 1 |
| 625.11 | but only these letters are from] but only, these are letters from 1 |
| 625.30 | the new-comers] the two new-comers 1 |
| 626.17 | may very well . . . convenience.] may afford to go thither, and maintain a rank. 1 |

626.19      rather than to-morrow]    before to-morrow 1

627.10      that this is all]    for, this is all 1

627.34      indited by]    signed with 1

627.35      noddle]    mark 1

628.6      the air]    and air 1

628.23      end of it a gibbet]    end of the gibbet 2–4

628.34      this man]    the man 3–5

629.26      the night before]    the very night 1

630.1      printed]    imprinted 1

630.24      intimidate]    intimate 1

630.28      extremities]    extremes 1

630.31      weights]    weight 1

631.6      affects]    affect 1

631.37      to penance]    to do penance 1

631.37      an hermit]    a hermit 2–5

631.37      and as I cannot even do that, I]    and, as every thing goes against the grain, I 1

632.1      son-in-law]    son‸in-law 1

632.15      rotten]    torn 1

632.26      or crook]    or by crook 1

632.39      should be]    should not be 1

633.34      communicate]    commune 1

634.26      its acceptance]    his acceptance 1

635.8      ladies,]    ~‸ 1–5

635.10      of the other servants]    of other servants 2

635.22      what nor where]    what 1

635.41      my coach]    my own coach 1

635.44      rial, and meat]    rial, meat 4–5

636.12      to write to me]    to write me 1

636.15      Sanchica]    Sancha 1

636.38          honour there]   honour 1

639.1           THE LIFE and ATCHIEVEMENTS]   THE
                ATCHIEVEMENTS 2–5

639.24          Sitting up . . . comprehending]   Hearing the alarm as he lay, he
                listened attentively, in hope of comprehending 1

640.15          at that instant]   and that instant 1

640.23          their north star]   the north star 2–5

640.33          pieces. There]   pieces; and there 1

642.37          for the entertainment]   for entertainment 2–5

642.39          and a piece of cheese]   and half a cheese 2–5

644.21          already advanced]   already well advanced 1

644.32          smacking . . . mouthful]   seasoning every mouthful 1

644.33          tho' they ate]   tho' they are 2–4

645.27          stanch christians]   staunch christians 2–5

646.8           an hundred]   a hundred 5

646.31          where]   were 1

646.35          thy proposal]   your proposal 1

646.43          will not]   wont 1

647.11          hast spoke]   had spoke 2–3

647.35          of my Ricota]   of Ricota 2–5

648.10          buildings. In]   buildings; and, in 1

649.6           services!]   ~? 1–2; service! 4–5

649.23          thankfully . . . told him]   thankfully, and told him 1

649.25          an hole]   a hole 5

650.2           ejaculations, he fancied he had proceeded]   ejaculations, he had
                proceeded 1

650.11          that exercise]   the exercise 2–5

650.25          complain, but]   complain, replied the voice, but 1

651.4           he stands now]   he now stands 5

651.19          good deal]   great deal 3–5

651.33          I shall say . . . plainly.]   I would say no more even though I could
                speak to the purpose. 1

652.16          yesterday]   yesterday morning 1

652.25          to the day]   till the day 1

653.16          his life]   life 1

654.7           their affair]   the affair 2–5

654.26          fairly]   fair 1

654.28          invincible]   invisible 1

654.33          sprung]   sprang 2–5

654n.*.4        beauty]   beauties 3–5

655.9           replied]   applied 2–4

655.41          an husband]   a husband 5

656.4           avail them so little]   happen so seldom 1

656.5           long accustomed to chop]   long used and accustomed to chop 1

656.14          has no]   had no 1

656.20          execution]   expected execution 1

657.3           in my returning]   on my returning 5

657.22          all of a sudden]   of a sudden 4–5

660.1           CHAP. VI.]   CHAP. IV. 2–5

660.26          journey. Having]   journey; and having 1

660.28          certain white]   four white 1

661.5           himself]   themselves 2–5

661.17          this representation]   his representation 4–5

661.19          Mata Moros]   Meta Moros 4

661.34          for, the kingdom . . . violence; whereas]   for, heaven may be won
                by force; whereas 1

662.4           an history]   a history 5

662.14          these]   those 1

663.24          mind . . . mind]   soul . . . soul 1

663.32          mind]   soul 1

| | |
|---|---|
| 663.35 | green thread] green silk thread 1 |
| 663.41 | thread] silk thread 1 |
| 663.42 | the jealous god] the god 1 |
| 663.43 | were of rushes and unspun] were wove of rushes or unspun 1 |
| 664.40 | name hath] name has 4–5 |
| 664.43 | an happy] a happy 5 |
| 665.17 | in point of] in a point of 4–5 |
| 666.12 | said?] ~; 3–5 |
| 666.40 | Let him . . . receive him."] *om.* 1 |
| 667.28 | mounting] mounted 4 |
| 668.7 | Seeing, however] Seeing him, however 1 |
| 669.5 | companions] companion 4 |
| 669.16 | he went] went 1 |
| 669.32 | out in] out of 3–5 |
| 670.12 | greater] great 5 |
| 670.25 | What displeases . . . performance] The most distinguished part in this performance 1 |
| 671.30 | she, as far as modesty . . . smiled] she maintained her honour and reputation, and smiled 1 |
| 672.31 | an heap] a heap 5 |
| 672.36 | prize-justs] justs 1 |
| 672.40 | poor in] poor of 4–5 |
| 673.7 | discourse: they believed] discourse; and they believed 1 |
| 673.15 | but little less for the day] but little for the day 1 |
| 673.24 | whereas the knight] but, the knight 1 |
| 674.35 | thou] you 5 |
| 674.39 | went aside] going aside 1 |
| 674.39 | to take] to take up 1 |
| 674.40 | night. There he felt] night, he felt 1 |
| 675.13 | and stand . . . arrive.] and suffer themselves to be conducted peaceably to the captain of the band. 1 |

676.12          an hat]     a hat 2–5

676.13          spurs; armed]     spurs; and armed 1

676.15          Roque]     Rogue 1

676.15          the noise]     this noise 1

677.18          an hill]     a hill 5

677.24          Roque approached]     Roque alighted and approached 1

677.33          altogether void]     intirely void 4; entirely void 5

677n.*          This rhime]     The rhime 5

678.3           case]     cause 2

679.14          us?]     ~. 1–5

679.21          I must own]     I must know 2–5

679.23          by the desire]     by a desire 1

679.27          deep . . . deep]     Deep . . . Deep 1–5

679.27          deep, and sin . . . undertake]     Deep, undertake 1

680.4           but, changing]     and, changing 1

680.10          muleteers]     Muleteers 1

680.17          four gallies]     some gallies 1

680.19          to two]     to about two 1

680.22          they answered,]     was answered͵ 1

680.25          finances.]     ~? 2–5

680.27          vicariate]     vicarage 1

681.2           liberality . . . leaving]     liberality, in leaving 1

681.5           submission;]     ~? 2–3; ~: 4–5

681.17          looking]     and looking 1

681.19          displeased at the booty]     displeased at the division of the booty 1

681.32          cap-a-pee]     cap-a-pie 2–5

682.26          plant or]     plant and 1

682.29          repetition]     repetion 1

682.37          they resounded]     they surrounded 2; they were surrounded 3–5

683.1           exhibited]     exhibiting 1

| | |
|---|---|
| 683.2 | sea. At]    sea; and, at 1 |
| 683.6 | walls]    wall 2–5 |
| 683.25 | gentleman]    gentlemen 1 |
| 683.35 | That mischief]    The mischief 1 |
| 684.4 | youngsters]    people 1 |
| 684.29 | satisfaction: while Sancho's]    satisfaction; and Sancho's 2–5 |
| 685.1 | nuts or]    nuts and 4–5 |
| 685.21 | a private apartment]    an apartment 1 |
| 685.32 | ears to hear]    ears to ear 1–2 |
| 685.39 | entertainer]    landlord 1 |
| 685n.* | *times]    terms 1* |
| 686.2 | was, I think, a native]    was a native 1 |
| 686.19 | That same evening]    The same evening 3–5 |
| 686.24 | they, without his knowledge, pinned]    they pinned 1 |
| 687.3 | surely thou art]    thou surely art      3–5 |
| 687.7 | concerns; look]    concerns, and look 1 |
| 687.10 | Heark]    Hark 3–5 |
| 687.19 | overtake]    overtook 4 |
| 687.33 | that it might not flag.]    which would otherwise have flagged. 1 |
| 688.16 | fast bolted]    just bolted 1 |
| 689.2 | husband.]    ~? 3–5 |
| 689.9 | Noriz]    Norroz 1; Noriez 2–5 |
| 689.15 | eye; I touch . . . Don]    eye and touch it with my finger." As he did not choose to ask another question, Don 1 |
| 689.25 | truth and of illusion]    truth and illusion 3–5 |
| 691.1 | a statuary]    an engraver 1 |
| 691.5 | four eagles]    eagles 1 |
| 691.6 | Roman]    roman 1–2 |
| 691.27 | than to the squire]    than the squire 3–5 |
| 692.32 | book printed]    book to be printed 1 |

692.41          author]   other 4–5

693.33          accomplished. As]   accomplished; and, as 1

694.6           towards]   toward 5

694.14          renowned]   renowed 1

695.9           inchantment; but what]   inchantment; though, what 1

695.10          matter. What]   matter? what 1–5

695.29          so as that the Algerine]   so that the Algerine 3–5

695.29          should not escape]   could not escape 1

695.40          Turks . . . discharged]   Turks, discharged 1

696.3           of canvas and oars]   of canvas and of oars 2–5

696.7           all four returned]   all returned 3–5

696.25          yard-arm]   yards-arm 1

696.29          captain,]   ~. 1

696.35          Renegado.]   ~? 3–5

697.14          Don Gaspar Gregorio]   Don Gregorio 2–5

698.4           with less]   in less 5

698.11          lodged,]   ~ˌ 1

698.18          is much]   was much 1

698.22          could make]   should make 1

698.33          few]   not one 1

698.42          who art dear]   who are dear 4–5

699.4           government: he]   government; and he 1

699.9           beauty as for her father's wealth]   beauty as I her father for my
                wealth 1

699.14          vicissitude . . . retrieved]   vicissitude, I have retrieved 1

699.26          crime]   crimes 2–5

699.28          yard-arm]   yard's arm 1–5

699.38          The general and the viceroy]   The general and viceroy 1

700.3           heart.]   ~! 2–5

700.11          town . . . bell.]   town and country. 1

| | |
|---|---|
| 700.15 | bring home] release 1 |
| 700.16 | delivered] released 1 |
| 700.23 | describes it as a very] describes it a very 1–5 |
| 700.33 | for he often] for, as he often 1 |
| 700.36 | cap-a-pee] cap-a-pie 2–5 |
| 701.14 | spoils of all my arms] spoils of my arms 1 |
| 701.21 | I dare say] I dare swear 1 |
| 701.43 | Don Quixote.] ~ ~? 2–5 |
| 702.4 | persists] persits 1 |
| 702.32 | turning his horse] turned his horse 1 |
| 702.33 | an half gallop] a half gallop 5 |
| 702.37 | with a cold sweat] with cold sweat 4–5 |
| 702.39 | this unlucky] that unlucky 5 |
| 702.43 | in the air] in air 1 |
| 703.25 | fully resolved] and fully resolved 1 |
| 704.12 | Panza . . . conceits are such] Panza; and the conceits of either are such 1 |
| 704.41 | return] retire 4–5 |
| 705.14 | not to be minded] not be minded 1 |
| 705.23 | woman's] women's 2–5 |
| 706.3 | said,] *om.* 2–3 |
| 706.3 | There is nothing . . . to whom] Neither tears, entreaties, promises, nor presents will avail with the great Don Bernandino de Velasco, to whom 1 |
| 706.5 | Bernardino] Bernandino 1–5 |
| 706.8 | applies] applied 4–5 |
| 706.10 | hath successfully] has successfully 2–5 |
| 706.15 | of the Moors] of Moors 2–5 |
| 706.17 | Bernardino] Bernandino 2–5 |
| 707.10 | good humour] moderation 1 |
| 707.16 | those things] these things 4–5 |

| | |
|---|---|
| 707.24 | knight-errant]    ~‿~ 1–3 |
| 707.33 | marches a-foot]    marches on foot 4–5 |
| 708.13 | an holiday]    a holiday 5 |
| 708.14 | exclaimed]    exclaimed aloud 1 |
| 708.22 | insisted upon]    insisted on 2–5 |
| 708.25 | and a judge]    and judge 1 |
| 708.26 | this dispute]    every dispute 2–5 |
| 708.41 | pounds]    pound 2–4 |
| 709.8 | wager if they go to study]    wager they are going to study 1 |
| 709.8 | Salamanca]    Salamancha 2–5 |
| 709.8 | they will in a trice]    and will in a trice 1 |
| 709.25 | mention . . . combat?" "No]    mention?" "No 1 |
| 710.31 | Body o' me]    Body O‿ me 1–3 |
| 710.33 | amorous?]    ~. 1–2 |
| 711.5 | knights-errant]    ~‿~ 1–2 |
| 711.14 | knight-errantry]    ~‿~ 1–2 |
| 711.24 | we will assume]    I am resolved to assume 1 |
| 711.25 | of shepherds]    of a shepherd 1 |
| 711.25 | our retirement]    my retirement 1 |
| 712.5 | mayest]    mayst 2–5 |
| 712.7 | an hair]    a hair 5 |
| 712.15 | Albogues]    Alboques 1 |
| 712.17 | Albogues]    Alboques 1 |
| 712.18 | Albogues]    Alboques 1 |
| 712.21 | Albogues]    Alboques 1 |
| 712.24 | Borcegui]    Borcequi 1 |
| 712.26 | Albogues]    Alboques 1 |
| 713.3 | an hedge]    a hedge 5 |
| 713.16 | let us]    let us us 1 |

| | |
|---|---|
| 713.24 | Moreno] Morens 1 |
| 714.17 | an hair] a hair 5 |
| 714.18 | bestowed] digested 1 |
| 714.32 | fed] led 1 |
| 714.33 | strings] string 1–2 |
| 715.15 | knights-errant] knight-errants 1–5 |
| 715.15 | that] that that 1 |
| 716.12 | two proceeded in their journey] two mounted in order to proceed on their journey 1 |
| 716.12 | descried] they descried 1 |
| 717.4 | end?] ~! 1–5 |
| 717.5 | converted into bad] converted to bad 1 |
| 717.9 | XVII] XVI 1 |
| 717.14 | an hundred] a hundred 5 |
| 717.19 | an hundred] a hundred 5 |
| 717.37 | threw over him] threw over his head 1 |
| 719.3 | arms] arm 2–5 |
| 719.8 | damsel?] ~. 1–5 |
| 719.21 | court-yard] court‸yard 1 |
| 719.24 | larger.] ~, 1 |
| 719.25 | exclaiming,] ~. 1–2 |
| 719.37 | curtsy] curt'sy 1; court'sy 2–5 |
| 720.34 | ‸That … friend.‸] "That … friend." 1–5 |
| 721.1 | XVIII] XVII 1 |
| 721.16 | she thought] she had thought 1 |
| 721.38 | an horse] a horse 5 |
| 722.1 | an he-mule] a he-mule 5 |
| 722.14 | victor. Sampson] victor: and Sampson 1 |
| 722.16 | proceeded] he proceeded 1 |

722.21          madness. He declared]   madness; and declared 1

722.27          Quixote. He ordered]   Quixote; and ordered 1

722.29          and patrole]   and a patrole 2–5

723.16          I should . . . heartily: but]   I should have been as much obliged to
                him, as I think myself at present: but 1

723.27          flocks]   rubbish 1

725.2           sumptuous]   sumpt'ous 1

725.28          an heart]   a heart 5

725.32          XIX]   XVIII] 1

726.19          disinchanting]   disinchanted 1

729.22          serge, instead of tapestry, such]   serge, such 1

729.24          his presumptuous]   her presumptuous 1

730.20          XX]   XIX 1

730.33          and was ornamented]   and ornamented 1

731.15          did him signal services]   did him many signal services 1

731.36          than an orator]   than of an orator 1

733.7           preceding]   proced-|ing 1; proceeding 2

733.12          The whole]   That whole 1

733.22          coin]   corn 1

733.29          the best]   we best 2

734.1           XXI]   XX 1

734.13          an hare]   a hare 5

734.18          suppose this hare is Dulcinea]   suppose Dulcinea 2–5

734.28          which I]   which, as I 1

734.30          christian]   person 1

737.3           his new chivalries]   his chivalries 1

737.38          good faith]   good sooth 1

737.40          of wolves]   of the wolves 1

737.40          wolves?]   ~! 1–5

738.9           XXII]   XVIII 1

738.14          approach. Either]    approach: and either 1

741.12          an history]    a history 5

741.18          assistance: during]    assistance; and, during 1

741.26          knight-errant]    knights-errant 2–3

741.28          in other words]    other in words 1–2

# BIBLIOGRAPHICAL DESCRIPTIONS

## I. THE FIRST EDITION

THE | HISTORY and ADVENTURES | OF THE RENOWNED | DON QUI-
XOTE. | Translated from the SPANISH of | MIGUEL DE CERVANTES SAAVE-
DRA. | To which is prefixed, | Some ACCOUNT of the AUTHOR's LIFE. | By
T. SMOLLETT, M. D. | Illustrated with Twenty-eight new Copper-Plates, designed
by HAYMAN, | And engraved by the best ARTISTS. | [138 mm. rule] | IN TWO VOL-
UMES. | [138 mm. rule] | VOL. I. | [138 mm. double rule] | LONDON: | Printed
for A. MILLAR, over against Catherine-Street, in the Strand; | T. OSBORN, T. and
T. LONGMAN, C. HITCH and L. HAWES, J. HODGES, | and J. and J. RIVINGTON. |
MDCCLV.

Volume 2: Title page as in volume I except "VOL. II." substituted for "VOL I." and rules
are 135mm.

*Collation:* 4° (290 x 230 mm.) Volume 1: π⁴ a–c⁴ B–3E⁴ 3F². Pp. *1* title, *3* dedication,
*i–xx* THE | LIFE | OF | CERVANTES., *xxi* note on translation, *xxii* blank, *xxiii–*
xxviii PREFACE | TO THE | READER., *1–368, 365–372, 377–403* text, *404* blank.
Volume 2: A–3N⁴ 3O². Pp. *i* title, *iii–v* PREFACE., vi–viii APPROBATION., *1–466*
text, *467* ERRATA., *468* blank.

*Press figures:* Volume 1: *none.* Volume 2: vi-1 410-2.

*Typography:* Volume 1: Pages 369=365, 370=366, 371=367, 372=368, 373=369,
374=370, 375=371, 376=372. Headline 142 LIEE, 401 Chap. 25=15, 403 Chap.
25=15. Catchwords 23 and,] and, 33 while,] while, 48 ventures,] ventures, 267 a sec-
ond] second 392 shepherd,] shepherd, No catchword *xxi.* Volume 2: Page 376=374.
Headline 199 Chap. 15=11, 393 Chap. 9=8, 433 Chap. 16=15, 435 Chap. 16=15, 437
Chap. 17=16, 439 Chap. 17=16, 441 Chap. 18=17, 443 Chap. 18=17, 445 Chap.
18=17, 447 Chap. 19=18, 449 Chap. 19=18, 451 Chap. 19=18, 453 Chap. 20=19, 455
Chap. 20=19, 457 Chap. 21=20, 459 Chap. 21=20, 461 Chap. 22=21, 463 Chap.
22=21, 465 Chap. 22=21. Catchwords 30 court?,] court?" 70 as] it ,Gui] *Guisando
365 nor,,] nor,,. No catchword vii, viii.

*Plates:* Volume 1: frontispiece, 17, 26, 75, 92, 106, 111, 126, 159, 196, 211, 270, 281,
352. Volume 2: 54, 80, 127, 163, 186, 189, 194, 284, 296, 305, 311, 400, 449, 458.

*Copies:* (AzTeU) Arizona State University Library (Spec C-2269), (L) British Library
(12490.k.6 [copy 1], Cerv. 388 [copy 2]), (C) University of Cambridge Library
(7743.b.6), (ICU) University of Chicago Library (PQ6329 A2 1755), (NIC) Cornell
University Library (PQ6329 A2+ 1755 copy 1, copy 2), (EU) Edinburgh University

Library (Dh. 6.86–87), (MH) Harvard University, Houghton Library (*f SC6 C3375 Eg755s (A), *f SC6 C3375 Eg 755s (B)), (CSmH) Huntington Library (268530), (IU) University of Illinois Library (xQ863c33 OdE smo), (InU-Li) Indiana University, Lilly Library (PQ6629 A2 1755), (KU-S) University of Kansas, Spenser Library (Summerfield Cerv. 25), (PPL) Library Company of Philadelphia (*O Span. Cerv. 7583 F.), (CaOHM) McMaster University Library (D268–69 [copy 1], DOO1312–13 [copy 2]), (E) National Library of Scotland ([Ag}. 1/2. 8), (ICN) Newberry Library (Case f1565 C3319), (O) Oxford University, Bodleian Library (Fic. 27623.d.18–19), (NjP) Princeton University Library ((Ex) PQ6329 A2 1755q), (ViU) University of Virginia Library (PQ6329 A2 1755), (CtY) Yale University, Beinecke Library (Im Sm79 +755).

*Notes:*

| COPY | CORRECTED | UNCORRECTED |
|---|---|---|
| AzTeU | E G | B C D F H I K L |
| CaOHM copy 1 | C D F H K | B E G I L |
| CaOHM copy 2 | B E G L | C D F H I K |
| C | E G | B C D F H I K L |
| CSmH | B E G L | C D F H I K |
| CtY | E G | B C D F H I K L |
| E | E G | B C D F H I K L |
| EU | B E G L | C D F H I K |
| ICN | C D F H I K | B E G L |
| ICU | C D F G H I K | B E L |
| IU | E G L | B C D F H I K |
| InU-Li | D F H K | B C E G I L |
| KU-S | B C D F G H I K | E L |
| L copy 1 | B E G I L | C D F H K |
| L copy 2 | E G K L | B C D F H I |
| MH copy A | B L | C D E F G H I K |
| MH copy B | E G | B C D F H I K L |
| NIC copy 1 | D F G H K | B C E I L |
| NIC copy 2 | B E G L | C D F H I K |
| NjP | E G | B C D F H I K L |
| O | C D E F G H I K | B L |
| PPL | C D E F G H I K | B L |
| ViU | E G | B C D F H I K L |

## 2. THE SECOND EDITION

THE | HISTORY | AND | ADVENTURES | OF THE RENOWNED | DON QUIXOTE. | Translated from the SPANISH of | MIGUEL DE CERVANTES SAAVEDRA. | To which is prefixed, | Some Account of the AUTHOR's Life. | By T. SMOLLETT, M. D. | Illustrated with Twenty-eight new Copper-Plates, | designed

by HAYMAN, and elegantly engraved. | [70 mm. rule] | The SECOND EDITION, Corrected. | [70 mm. rule] | IN FOUR VOLUMES. | [70 mm. rule] | VOLUME I. | [70 mm. double rule] | LONDON: | Printed for T. OSBORNE, C. HITCH and L. HAWES, | A. MILLAR, H. WOODFALL, JOHN RIVINGTON, | R. BALDWIN, S. CROWDER and Co. T. LONGMAN, | H. PAYNE, T. LOWNDES, T. CASLON, and G. | KEARSLY. 1761.

Volume 2: Title page as in volume 1 except "VOLUME II." substituted for "VOL-UME I."

Volume 3: Title page as in volume 1 except "VOLUME III." substituted for "VOL-UME I." From the imprint "T. CASLON, and G. KEARSLY" are omitted.

Volume 4: Title page as in volume 1 except "VOLUME IV." substituted for "VOL-UME I."

*Collation:* 12° (178 x 100 mm.) Volume 1: $A^2$ $a^{12}$ $b^8$ B–$N^{12}$ $O^4$. Pp. *1* title, *3–4* dedication, *i*–xxix THE | LIFE | OF | CERVANTES., *xxx* blank, *xxxi* note on translation, *xxxii* blank, *xxxiii*–xl PREFACE | TO THE | READER., *1–293* text, *294* blank. Volume 2: $A^1$ B–$O^{12}$ $P^1$. Pp. *i* title, *1–314* text. Volume 3: $A^1$ B–$O^{12}$ $P^{10}$. Pp. *i* title, *1–331* text, *332* blank. Volume 4: $A^1$ B–$O^{12}$ $P^5$. Pp. *i* title, *1–322* text.

*Press figures:* Volume 1: xii-1 xv-6 13-4 36-3 71-4 292-4. Volume 2: 15-4 154-4 156-4 266-4 301-1 310-5. Volume 3: 15-4 46-4 58-1 61-4 82-7 93-3 118-1 134-6 168-7 189-2 191-6 202-3 216-2 218-7 228-3 250-4 266-6 285-2 292-4 329-1 330-6. Volume 4: 22-5 36-6 47-3 60-2 *or none* 70-1 74-1 96-3 109-6 119-2 141-3 *or none* 142-7 148-5 190-5 206-1 213-5 226-2 240-1 242-6 264-4 268-5 286-1 301-2 303-6 318-4 320-2.

*Typography:* Volume 1: Catchwords viii action₍ₐ₎] action, xii valry;] valry: xxiv judicious.] judicious—— xxvi ass₍ₐ₎] ass, xxxvii tion₍ₐ₎] tion, xxxviii perr] performance 27 distress;] distress. 113 ₍ₐ₎That] "That 122 wouldst] thou 179 In] "Suppose 185 pray₍ₐ₎] pray, 213 missary-] miscarry 217 for₍ₐ₎] for, 256 saying₍ₐ₎] saying. 258 dura-] tion. 291 por.] port. No catchword *4, xxxi,* xl. Volume 2: Catchword 164 Lo!] I. Volume 3: *none.* Volume 4: 2 maid₍ₐ₎] maid– 92 kin-] kidney 93 morning,] in 102 reaties₍ₐ₎] treaties, 275 Thus] III. 305 ment₍ₐ₎] ment, 306 time₍ₐ₎] time,. No catchword 109.

*Plates:* Volume 1: frontispiece, 26, 40, 113, 139, 159, 166, 190, 241. Volume 2: 2, 26, 114, 131, 238. Volume 3: 78, 116, 182, 231, 263, 268, 275. Volume 4: 71, 86, 99, 107, 229, 297, 309.

*Copies:* British Library (12490.bbb.26), Harvard University, Houghton Library (*SC6 C3375 Eg755sb), Library Company of Philadelphia (O. Span. Cerv. 1761), McMaster University Library (B-7764–67), Oxford University, Bodleian Library (Vet. A5. e. 2339–2342), University of Virginia (PQ6329 A2 1761), Yale University, Beinecke Library (Tinker 1930).

## 3. THE THIRD EDITION

THE | HISTORY | AND | ADVENTURES | OF THE RENOWNED | DON QUIXOTE. | Translated from the SPANISH of | MIGUEL DE CERVANTES SAAVE-DRA. | To which is prefixed, | Some Account of the AUTHOR's Life. | By T. SMOLLETT, M. D. | Illustrated with Twenty-eight new Copper-Plates, | designed by HAYMAN, and elegantly engraved. | [70 mm. rule] | The THIRD EDITION, Corrected. | [70 mm. rule] | IN FOUR VOLUMES. | [70 mm. rule] | VOLUME I. | [70 mm. double rule] | LONDON, | Printed for T. OSBORNE, C. HITCH and L. HAWES, | A. MILLAR, H. WOODFALL, JOHN RIVINGTON, | R. BALDWIN, S. CROWDER, T. LONGMAN, | T. LOWNDES, T. CASLON, J. KNOX, and | RICHARDSON and URQUHART. | MDCCLXV.

Volume 2: Title page as in volume 1 except "VOLUME II." substituted for "VOLUME I."

Volume 3: Title page as in volume 1 except "VOLUME III." substituted for "VOLUME I." Added after "S. CROWDER" is "and Co." not followed by a comma.

Volume 4: Title page as in volume 1 except "VOLUME IV." substituted for "VOLUME I."

*Collation:* 12° (173 x 100 mm.) Volume 1: $A^2$ a$^{12}$ b$^8$ B–N$^{12}$ O$^4$. Pp. *1* title, *3–4* dedication, *i–xxix* THE | LIFE | OF | CERVANTES., *xxx* blank, *xxxi* note on translation, *xxxii* blank, *xxxiii*–xl PREFACE | TO THE | READER., *1–293* text, *294* blank. Volume 2: $A^1$ B–O$^{12}$ P$^1$. Pp. *i* title, *1–314* text. Volume 3: $A^1$ a$^6$ B–O$^{12}$ P$^{10}$. Pp. *1* title, *i–vi* PREFACE., vii–xi APPROBATION., *xii* blank, *1–331* text, *332* blank. Volume 4: $A^1$ B–O$^{12}$ P$^5$. Pp. *i* title, *1–322* text.

*Press figures:* Volume 1: *none.* Volume 2: *none.* Volume 3: *none.* Volume 4: 93-2 143-2 165-2 176-2 213-2 220-2 261-2 268-2 304-2.

*Typography:* Volume 1: Catchwords xii valry;] valry: xxiv judicious.] judicious—— 27 distress;] distress. 113 ˏThat] "That 122 wouldst] thou 256 saying,] saying,. No catchword 4, xxxi, xxxvi, xxxvii, xl. Volume 2: Catchwords 164 Lo!] I. 168 sequence,] sequence:. No catchword 65, 162. Volume 3: No catchword xi. Volume 4: Catchwords 2 maid,] maid– 78 paralytic;] paralytic: 92 kin-] kidney 195 Sancho,] Sancho, 264 fatuation,] fatuation, 275 Thus] III. No catchword 109.

*Plates:* As in second edition.

*Copies:* British Library (12493.b.7), Harvard University, Houghton Library (*SC6 C3375 Eg755sc), National Library of Scotland (ABS.1.87.59), Newberry Library (Y 722 C3577), University of Toronto Library (LS C419d. Esmo 1765), University of Virginia (PR3694 H57 1765).

## 4. THE FOURTH EDITION

THE | HISTORY | AND | ADVENTURES | OF THE RENOWNED | DON QUIXOTE. | Translated from the SPANISH of | MIGUEL DE CERVANTES SAAVE-DRA. | To which is prefixed, | Some ACCOUNT of the AUTHOR's Life. | By T. SMOLLETT, M. D. | Illustrated with Twenty-eight new COPPER-PLATES, | designed by HAYMAN, and elegantly engraved. | [74 mm. rule] | The FOURTH EDITION, Corrected. | [74 mm. rule] | IN FOUR VOLUMES. | [74 mm. rule] | VOLUME I. | [74 mm. double rule] | LONDON, | Printed for W. STRAHAN, J. and F. RIVINGTON. W. JOHNSTON, | R. BALDWIN, T. LONGMAN, HAWES and Co. T. LOWNDES. | S. CROWDER, T. CASLON, W. NICOLL, RICHARDSON and | URQUHART, J. KNOX, RICHARDSON and RICHARDSON, | ROBINSON and ROBERTS, J. ALMON, and T. CADELL. | MDCCLXX.

Volume 2: Title page as in volume 1 except "VOLUME II." substituted for "VOLUME I." "RIVINGTON" and "LOWNDES" followed by a comma instead of a period.

Volume 3: Title page as in volume 1 except "VOLUME III." substituted for "VOLUME I." "RIVINGTON" and "LOWNDES" as in volume 2.

Volume 4: Title page as in volume 1 except "VOLUME IV." substituted for "VOLUME I." Hyphen absent between "COPPER" and "PLATES." "RIVINGTON" and "LOWNDES" as in volume 2.

*Collation:* 12° (170 x 104 mm.) Volume 1: $\pi^2$ $a^{12}$ $b^8$ B–N$^{12}$ O$^4$. Pp. *1* title, *3* dedication, *i*–xxix THE | LIFE | OF | CERVANTES., *xxx* blank, *xxxi* note on translation, *xxxii* blank, *xxxiii*–xl PREFACE TO THE READER., *1*–293 text, *294* blank. Volume 2: $A^2$ B–O$^{12}$ P$^2$. Pp. *i* title, *1*–314 text. Volume 3: $\pi^2$ $a^6$ B–O$^{12}$ P$^{10}$. *1* title, *i*–vi PREFACE., vii–xi APPROBATION., *xii* blank, *1*–331 text, *332* blank. Volume 4: $A^1$ B–O$^{12}$ P$^5$. *i* title, *1*–322 text.

*Press figures:* Volume 1: x-1 xxxix-6 14-5 21-* 47-9 60-5 71-6 84-3 94-4 108-† 118-7 134-4 144-7 158-1 168-* 183-7 184-3 202-5 205-1 238-7 263-5 287-7. Volume 2: 10-1 40-4 47-6 71-4 74-2 85-8 100-6 118-3 130-7 154-7 160-6 190-4 214-* 216-1 239-6 240-* 261-3 262-2 277-8 286-3 303-3 304-4. Volume 3: vii-6 98-7 134-7 165-2 194-4 232-4 250-2 277-2 309-4 310-6 325-2. Volume 4: 23-6 24-7 34-7 50-7 69-2 76-2 82-4 111-2 122-2 157-6 170-2 172-6 194-2 204-6 218-4 229-2 262-4 279-2 285-7 302-2 312-4 318-2.

*Typography:* Volume 1: Catchwords xxiv judicious.] judicious—— 10 ermine;] ermine: 19 length,] length, 27 distress;] distress. 47 major,] major, 62 company,] company) 233 ",] "My. No catchword *iv, xxxi*, xxxvi, xxxvii, 41, 67, 74, 111, 119, 129, 162. Volume 2: Page 268=168. Catchwords 23 But,] But, 83 plexed] pexed 117 broke,] broke, 153 tho,] tho' 168 sequence,] sequence: 185 som,] som,. No catchword 65. Volume 3: Catchwords 272 truth!] truth;. No catchword xi. Volume 4: Catchwords 275 Thus] III. No catchword 109.

*Plates:* As in second edition.

*Copies:* British Library (1156.g.16), University of Kansas, Spenser Library ((Cerv Y116), McMaster University Library (B-2655–58), National Library of Scotland (ABS 1.77.230), University of Virginia (PQ6329 A2 1770).

5. THE FIFTH EDITION

THE | HISTORY | AND | ADVENTURES | OF THE RENOWNED | DON QUIXOTE. | Translated from the SPANISH of | MIGUEL DE CERVANTES SAAVEDRA. | To which is prefixed, | Some ACCOUNT of the AUTHOR's Life. | By T. SMOLLETT, M. D. | Illustrated with Twenty-eight new COPPER-PLATES, | designed by HAYMAN, and elegantly engraved. | [74 mm. rule] | The FIFTH EDITION, Corrected. | [74 mm. Rule] | IN FOUR VOLUMES. | [76 mm. rule] | VOLUME I. | [75 mm. double rule] | LONDON, | Printed for W. STRAHAN, J. F. and C. RIVINGTON, T. LONGMAN, | T. CASLON, B. LAW, T. LOWNDES, W. NICOLL, RICHARDSON | and URQUHART, G. ROBINSON, T. CADELL, R. BALDWIN, W. | GOLDSMITH, J. KNOX, J. MURRAY, E. NEWBERY, J. DEBRET, | and J. Fox. | MDCCLXXXII.

Volume 2: Title page as in volume 1 except "VOLUME II." substituted for "VOLUME I."

Volume 3: Title page as in volume 1 except "VOLUME III." substituted for "VOLUME I."

Volume 4: Title page as in volume 1 except "VOLUME IV." substituted for "VOLUME I."

*Collation:* 12° (175 x 105 mm.) Volume 1: $A^2$ $a^{12}$ $b^8$ B–N$^{12}$ O$^3$. Pp. *1* title, *i*–xxix THE | LIFE | OF | CERVANTES., *xxx* blank, *xxxi* note on translation, *xxxii* blank, *xxxiii*–xl PREFACE | TO | THE | READER., *1*–293 text, *294* blank. Volume 2: $A^1$ B–O$^{12}$ P$^1$. Pp. *i* title, *1*–314 text. Volume 3: $A^1$ $a^6$ B–O$^{12}$ P$^{10}$. *1* title, *i*–vi PREFACE. vii–xi APPROBATION. *xii* blank, *1*–331 text, *332* blank. Volume 4: $A^1$ B–O$^{12}$ P$^5$. Pp. *i* title, *1*–312 text.

*Press figures:* Volume 1: ii-3 xxi-4 xxxix-3 10-7 46-7 60-6 70-3 76-3 82-6 111-5 117-6 130-7 158-1 168-8 170-4 172-8 196-3 215-1 218-1 229-4 244-8 263-2 288-3. Volume 2: 22-1 24-* 36-8 60-6 62-5 82-5 96-2 109-2 111-3 135-1 141-6 154-1 168-3 178-9 180-7 202-6 204-4 226-9 228-7 250-† 252-8 266-4 277-7 300-1 303-3. Volume 3: vii-5 24-1 48-3 61-4 70-3 84-7 94-2 117-7 143-5 167-4 178-2 180-2 207-2 213-4 231-4 250-3 264-1 285-1 301-2 311-3 314-5. Volume 4: 21-8 28-4 34-1 52-3 62-1 75-8 93-4 108-5 118-4 136-1 142-2 157-2 213-8 214-5 238-2 240-8 255-5 264-2 274-2 285-3 300-5 311-3 319-4 320-5.

*Typography:* Volume 1: Catchwords 27 distress;] distress. 106 them,] ₐhem, 156 eachₐ] each; 168 shipₐ] ship, 237 girlₐ] girl,. No catchword *iv, xxxi,* xxxvi, xxxvii, 67, 74, 119, 162. Volume 2: Catchwords 23 But,] Butₐ 100 cludedₐ] cluded, 122 These] This 123 sentence,] sentence. 164 Lo!] I. 168 sequenceₐ] sequence: 185 somₐ] som, 311 Paniₐ] Paniguado. No catchword 65. Volume 3: Pages 162=132, 164=134, 165=133. Catchwords 69 night,] nightₐ 317 fieldₐ] fields,. No catchword xi. Volume 4: Pages 264=294. Catchwords 38 butₐ] but, 120 ₐDo] "Do 190 nions,] panions, 194 cumstance,] circumstance, 216 filled] led 275 Thus] III. 285 farther] further 288 trampled] trample 300 and] hand 316 andₐ] and,. No catchword 109, 154.

*Plates:* As in second edition.

*Copies:* British Library (12491.b.14), McMaster University Library (B-1194–97), National Library of Scotland (NE.878.h.2), Oxford University, Bodleian Library (Fic. 27623e. 83–86), University of Virginia (PQ6329 A2 1782).

# INDEX

# APPENDIX TO THE INDEX

## SMOLLETT AND HIS SOURCES COMPARED

*Note:* Numbers *I* and *II* at the beginning of a series of page/note references denote the volume/part number in the first edition copy-text. Page references are to the section "Notes to the Text" (pp. 743–91); the Roman/Arabic numerals in parentheses indicate the book and chapter of the text.

*Shelton: I:* 749 n. 6 (i.1); 752 n. 1 (i.7); 753 nn. 2–3 (i.8); 755 n. 6 (ii.2); 757 nn. 3 (iii.4), 1 (iii.5); 758 n. 1 (iii.7); 759 n. 4 (iii.9); 760 nn. 6 (iii.9), 8–9 (iii.11); 763 nn. 4 (iv.4), 2 (iv.5), 1 (iv.6); 764 nn. 4 (iv.6), 3 (iv.8); 765 nn. 2 (iv.10), 1 (iv.11); 767 n. 2 (iv.18); 768 nn. 1, 4 (iv.20), 2 (iv.21), 1 (iv.22); 769 nn. 2 (iv.22), 1, 7 (iv.25)

*II:* 771 nn. 1–3 (i.3); 772 n. 3 (i.4); 774 nn. 1 (i.10), 1 (i.13); 775 n. 1 (ii.1); 777 nn. 2 (ii.11), 1 (ii.12); 781 n. 2 (iii.3); 782 n. 1 (iii.5); 784 n. 1 (iii.13); 785 nn. 3 (iii.17), 1 (iii.18); 786 n. 1 (iv.2)

*Shelton/Stevens: I:* 748 n. 3 (i.1); 749 n. 10 (i.1); 750 n. 4 (i.2); 752 n. 1 (i.7); 755 n. 1 (ii.5); 756 n. 5 (iii.1); 757 n. 1 (iii.4); 758 n. 3 (iii.6); 759 n. 1 (iii.8); 763 nn. 4 (iv.4), 1 (iv.6); 764 n. 3 (iv.8); 765 nn. 1–2 (iv.10), 2 (iv.11)); 767 nn. 1 (iv.16), 1 (iv.18), 2, 5 (iv.19); 768 nn. 1, 4 (iv.20); 769 n. 7 (iv.25)

*II:* 770 n. 1 (Preface); 771 n. 1 (i.3); 772 n. 3 (i.4); 774 n. 1 (i.10); 775 nn. 1 (i.14), 1 (ii.1); 777 n. 1 (ii.12)); 781 n. 4 (iii.3); 782 nn. 1, 4 (iii.8); 783 n. 2 (iii.9); 787 n. 3 (iv.6)

*Motteux: I:* 749 nn. 5, 11, 13 (i.1); 751 n. 2 (i.3); 752 n. 1 (i.7); 753 n. 1 (ii.2); 755 n. 1 (ii.5); 760 n. 4 (iii.11); 763 nn. 4 (iv.4), 1 (iv.6); 764 nn. 4 (iv.6), 3 (iv.8); 765 nn. 1–2 (iv.10), 2 (iv.11); 766 n. 1 (iv.14); 767 n. 1 (iv.16); 768 nn. 1, 4 (iv.20); 769 nn. 2 (iv.22), 7 (iv.25)

*II:* 771 nn. 1, 3 (i.3); 772 n. 3 (i.4); 773 n. 2 (i.9); 774 n. 1 (i.10); 775 n. 1 (ii.1); 777 n. 1 (ii.12); 781 n. 2 (iii.3); 782 nn. 1 (iii.6), 4 (iii.8); 783 n. 3 (iii.9); 784 n. 3 (iii.12); 785 nn. 2 (iii.16), 3 (iii.18)

*Motteux/Ozell: I:* 748 nn. 1, 3 (i.1); 750 n. 4 (i.2); 752 nn. 1 (i.6), 1 (i.7); 759 n. 3 (iii.9); 760 nn. 1–2 (iii.11); 761 n. 1 (iv.1); 763 n. 4 (iv.4); 767 n. 5 (iv.19); 769 n. 7 (iv.25)

*II:* 780 n. 3 (iii.1) *passage compared with Smollett;* 781 n. 5 (iii.1); 782 n. 1 (iii.8); 787 n. 1 (iv.6)

*Jarvis: I:* 748 nn. 1, 3 (i.1); 749 nn. 5–6, 11, 13 (i.1); 750 nn. 4–5 (i.2); 752 nn. 2 (i.6), 1 (i.7); 753 n. 1 (ii.2); 755 nn. 2 (ii.3), 1 (ii.4); 756 nn. 4 (iii.1), 1 (iii.3); 757 nn. 2 (iii.3), 1 (iii.5); 758 nn. 3 (iii.5), 1–2 (iii.6), 1–2 (iii.7); 759 nn. 3 (iii.7), 1 (iii.8), 1–4 (iii.9); 760 nn. 6 (iii.9), 1 (iii.10), 1–2, 4–10 (iii.11); 761 n. 1 (iv.1); 762 nn. 2–4, 6 (iv.3); 763 nn. 2–4 (iv.4), 2–3 (iv.5), 1, 3 (iv.6); 764 nn. 4 (iv.6), 1 (iv.7), 1, 3 (iv.8), 1–2 (iv.9); 765 nn. 1–3 (iv.10), 1, 3 (iv.11), 1 (iv.12); 766 nn. 3 (iv.12), 1 (iv.13); 767 nn. 1 (iv.17), 1–2 (iv.18), 2 (iv.19); 768 nn.1, 3–4 (iv.20), 1–3 (iv.21), 1 (iv.22); 769 nn. 2, 4–5 (iv.22), 1–2, 7 (iv.25)